THE SWORD OF SHANNARA

TRILOGY

THE SWORD OF SHANNARA

TRILOGY

TERRY BROOKS

BALLANTINE BOOKS
NEW YORK

A Del Rey® Book
Published by The Ballantine Publishing Group

This omnibus was originally published by The Ballantine Publishing Group
in separate volumes under the titles:

The Sword of Shannara, copyright © 1977 by Terry Brooks
Foreword copyright © 1991 by Terry Brooks
The Elfstones of Shannara, copyright © 1982 by Terry Brooks
Foreword copyright © 1991 by Terry Brooks
The Wishsong of Shannara, copyright © 1985 by Terrence D. Brooks
Foreword copyright © 1991 by Terry Brooks

Map on p. vi by the Brothers Hildebrandt. Copyright © 1977 by Random House, Inc.
All other interior art by Darrell K. Sweet. Copyright © 1985 by Random House, Inc.

Del Rey is a registered trademark and the
Del Rey colophon is a trademark of Random House, Inc.

Library of Congress Cataloging-in-Publication Data
is available upon request.

ISBN 0-345-45375-1

Text design by Holly Johnson

Manufactured in the United States of America

CONTENTS

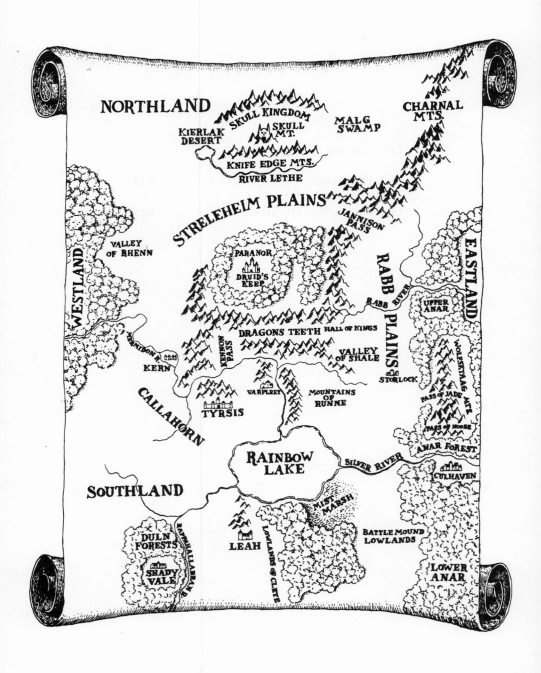

THE SWORD
OF SHANNARA

For My Parents,
Who Believed

FOREWORD

I was about fourteen when I discovered Sir Walter Scott, Arthur Conan Doyle, Robert Louis Stevenson, Alexander Dumas, and all the other eighteenth- and nineteenth- century European adventure-story writers. I was immediately hooked. What marvelous adventures! *Ivanhoe, Quentin Durward, The White Company, Sir Nigel, The Black Arrow, Treasure Island, The Count of Monte Cristo, The Three Musketeers,* and on and on. Each new tale seemed more exciting than the one before. Now here, I believed, were stories worth reading. Enough, already, of great white whales and repressed women wearing scarlet letters. Here were the kind of stories I wanted to write. And I tried, of course, but somehow they didn't work for me as they had for Dumas or Stevenson. I didn't seem to know enough. I wasn't comfortable with the time or the language or the feel of things. So I floundered about in fits and starts and eventually went away to college without ever completing anything.

But I hadn't forgotten how much I had enjoyed those stories or how profoundly they had affected me. So, four years of college and a semester of law school later, I decided to go back to them. An adventure story, something wonderfully dangerous, filled with hair-raising escapes, men and women of character and purpose, dangers that threatened from every quarter—that was what I wanted to write and that was how I would escape the mind-numbing predictability of law life. But it had to be something grand. How would D'Artagnan have handled Rupert of Hentzau from *The Prisoner of Zenda*? What if Jim Hawkins had met up with Quentin Durward? I envisioned a story that was panoramic, something vast and sweeping.

That was when I started thinking anew about J.R.R. Tolkien. I had read *The Lord of the Rings* two years earlier. What if Tolkien's magic and fairy creatures were made a part of the worlds of Walter Scott and Dumas? What if the story took place somewhere timeless and placeless, a somewhere that nevertheless hinted strongly of our own world in the future? What if our present knowledge had been lost, and science had been replaced by magic? But it couldn't be magic that was dependable or simply good or bad. And the right and wrong of things couldn't be clear-cut because life simply didn't work that way. And the central figure needed to be someone readers could identify with, a person very much like themselves, caught up in events not of his own making, a person simply trying to muddle through.

And that was how *Sword* began.

—Terry Brooks

The sun was already sinking into the deep green of the hills to the west of the valley, the red and gray-pink of its shadows touching the corners of the land, when Flick Ohmsford began his descent. The trail stretched out unevenly down the northern slope, winding through the huge boulders which studded the rugged terrain in massive clumps, disappearing into the thick forests of the lowlands to reappear in brief glimpses in small clearings and thinning spaces of woodland. Flick followed the familiar trail with his eyes as he trudged wearily along, his light pack slung loosely over one shoulder. His broad, windburned face bore a set, placid look, and only the wide gray eyes revealed the restless energy that burned beneath the calm exterior. He was a young man, though his stocky build and the grizzled brown hair and shaggy eyebrows made him look much older. He wore the loose-fitting work clothes of the Vale people and in the pack he carried were several metal implements that rolled and clanked loosely against one another.

There was a slight chill in the evening air, and Flick clutched the collar of his open wool shirt closer to his neck. His journey ahead lay through forests and rolling flatlands, the latter not yet visible to him as he passed into the forests, and the darkness of the tall oaks and somber hickories reached upward to overlap and blot out the cloudless night sky. The sun had set, leaving only the deep blue of the heavens pinpointed by thousands of friendly stars. The huge trees shut out even these, and Flick was left alone in the silent darkness as he moved slowly along the beaten path. Because he had traveled this same route a hundred times, the young man noticed immediately the unusual stillness that seemed to have captivated the entire valley this evening. The familiar buzzing and chirping of insects normally present in the quiet of the night, the cries of the birds that awoke with the setting of the sun to fly in search of food—all were missing. Flick listened intently for some sound of life, but his keen ears could detect nothing. He shook his head uneasily. The deep silence was unsettling, particularly in view of the rumors of a frightening black-winged creature sighted in the night skies north of the valley only days earlier.

He forced himself to whistle and turned his thoughts back to his day's work in the country just to the north of the Vale, where outlying families farmed and tended domestic livestock. He traveled to their homes every week, supplying various items that they required and bringing bits of news on the happenings of the Vale and occasionally the distant cities of the deep Southland. Few people knew the surrounding countryside as well as he did, and fewer still cared to travel beyond the comparative safety of their homes in the valley. Men were more inclined to remain in isolated communities these days and let the rest of the world get along as best it could. But Flick liked to travel outside the valley from time to time, and the outlying homesteads were in need of his services and were willing to pay him for the trouble. Flick's father was not one to let an opportunity pass him by where there was money to be made, and the arrangement seemed to work out well for all concerned.

A low-hanging branch brushing against his head caused Flick to start suddenly and leap to one side. In chagrin, he straightened himself and glared back at the leafy obstacle before continuing his journey at a slightly quicker pace. He was deep in the lowland forests now and only slivers of moonlight were able to find their way through the thick boughs overhead to light the winding path dimly. It was so dark that Flick was having trouble finding the trail, and as he studied the lay of the land ahead, he again found himself conscious of the heavy silence. It was as if all life had been suddenly extinguished, and he alone remained to find his way out of this forest tomb. Again he recalled the strange rumors. He felt a bit anxious in spite of himself and glanced worriedly around. But nothing stirred on the trail ahead nor moved in the trees about him, and he felt embarrassingly relieved.

Pausing momentarily in a moonlit clearing, he gazed at the fullness of the night sky before passing abruptly into the trees beyond. He walked slowly, picking his way along the winding path that had narrowed beyond the clearing and now seemed to disappear into a wall of trees and bushes ahead. He knew that it was merely an illusion, but found himself glancing about uneasily all the same. A few moments later, he was again on a wider trail and could discern bits of sky peeking through the heavy trees. He was almost to the bottom of the valley and about two miles from his home. He smiled and began whistling an old tavern song as he hurried on. He was so intent on the trail ahead and the open land beyond the forest that he failed to notice the huge black shadow that seemed to rise up suddenly, detaching itself from a great oak tree on his left and moving swiftly toward the path to intercept him. The dark figure was almost on top of the Valeman before Flick sensed its presence looming up before him like a great, black stone which threatened to crush his smaller being. With a startled cry of fear he leaped aside, his pack falling to the path with a crash of metal, and his left hand whipped out the long thin dagger at his waist. Even as he crouched to defend himself, he was stayed by a commanding arm raised above the figure before him and a strong, yet reassuring voice that spoke out quickly.

"Wait a moment, friend. I'm no enemy and have no wish to harm you. I merely seek directions and would be grateful if you could show me the proper path."

Flick relaxed his guard a bit and tried to peer into the blackness of the figure before him in an effort to discover some semblance of a human being. He could see nothing, however, and he moved to the left with cautious steps in an attempt to catch the features of the dark figure in the tree-shadowed moonlight.

"I assure you, I mean no harm," the voice continued, as if reading the Valeman's mind. "I did not mean to frighten you, but I didn't see you until you were almost upon me, and I was afraid you might pass me by without realizing I was there."

The voice stopped and the huge black figure stood silently, though Flick could feel the eyes following him as he edged about the path to put his own back to the light. Slowly the pale moonlight began to etch out the stranger's features in vague lines and blue shadows. For a long moment the two faced each other in silence, each studying the other, Flick in an effort to decide what it was he faced, the stranger in quiet anticipation.

Then suddenly the huge figure lunged with terrible swiftness, his powerful hands seizing the Valeman's wrists, and Flick was lifted abruptly off the solid earth and held high, his knife dropping from nerveless fingers as the deep voice laughed mockingly up at him.

"Well, well, my young friend! What are you going to do now, I wonder? I could cut your heart out on the spot and leave you for the wolves if I chose, couldn't I?"

Flick struggled violently to free himself, terror numbing his mind to any thought but that of escape. He had no idea what manner of creature had subdued him, but it was far more powerful than any normal man and apparently prepared to dispatch Flick quickly. Then abruptly, his captor held him out at arm's length, and the mocking voice became icy cold with displeasure.

"Enough of this, boy! We have played our little game and still you know nothing of me. I'm tired and hungry and have no wish to be delayed on the forest trail in the chill of the evening while you decide if I am man or beast. I will set you down that you may show me the path. I warn you—do not try to run from me or it will be the worse for you."

The strong voice trailed off and the tone of displeasure disappeared as the former hint of mockery returned with a short laugh.

"Besides," the figure rumbled as the fingers released their iron grip and Flick slipped to the path, "I may be a better friend than you realize."

The figure moved back a step as Flick straightened himself, rubbing his wrists carefully to restore the circulation to his numbed hands. He wanted to run, but was certain that the stranger would catch him again and this time finish him without further thought. He leaned over cautiously and picked up the fallen dagger, returning it to his belt.

Flick could see the fellow more clearly now, and a quick scrutiny of him revealed that he was definitely human, though much larger than any man Flick had ever seen. He was at least seven feet tall, but exceptionally lean, though it was difficult to be certain about this, since his tall frame was wrapped in a flowing black cloak with a loose cowl pulled close about his head. The darkened face was long and deeply lined, giving it a craggy appearance. The eyes were deep-set and almost completely hidden from view by shaggy eyebrows that knotted fiercely over a long flat nose. A short, black beard outlined a wide mouth that was just a line on the face—a line that never seemed to move. The overall appearance was frightening, all blackness and size, and Flick had to fight down the urge building within him to make a break for the forest's edge. He looked straight into the deep, hard eyes of the stranger, though not without some difficulty, and managed a weak smile.

"I thought you were a thief," he mumbled hesitantly.

"You were mistaken," was the quiet retort. Then the voice softened a bit. "You must learn to know a friend from an enemy. Sometime your life may depend upon it. Now then, let's have your name."

"Flick Ohmsford."

Flick hesitated and then continued in a slightly braver tone of voice.

"My father is Curzad Ohmsford. He manages an inn in Shady Vale a mile or two from here. You could find lodging and food there."

"Ah, Shady Vale," the stranger exclaimed suddenly. "Yes, that is where I am going." He paused as if reflecting on his own words. Flick watched him cautiously as he rubbed his craggy face with crooked fingers and looked beyond the forest's edge to the rolling grasslands of the valley. He was still looking away when he spoke again.

"You . . . have a brother."

It was not a question; it was a simple statement of fact. It was spoken so distantly and calmly, as if the tall stranger were not at all interested in any sort of a reply, that Flick almost missed hearing it. Then suddenly realizing the significance of the remark, he started and looked quickly at the other.

"How did . . . ?"

"Oh, well," the man said, "doesn't every young Valeman like yourself have a brother somewhere?"

Flick nodded dumbly, unable to comprehend what it was that the other was trying to say and wondering vaguely how much he knew about Shady Vale. The stranger was looking questioningly at him, evidently waiting to be guided to the promised food and lodging. Flick quickly turned away to find his hastily discarded pack, picked it up and slung it over his shoulder, looking back at the figure towering over him.

"The path is this way." He pointed, and the two began walking.

They passed out of the deep forest and entered rolling, gentle hills which they would follow to the hamlet of Shady Vale at the far end of the valley. Out of the woods, it was a bright night; the moon was a full white globe overhead, its glow clearly illuminating the landscape of the valley and the path which the two travelers were following. The path itself was a vague line winding over the grassy hills and distinguishable only by occasional rain-washed ruts and flat, hard patches of earth breaking through the heavy grass. The wind had gathered strength and rushed at the two men with quick gusts that whipped at their clothing as they walked, forcing

them to bow their heads slightly to shield their eyes. Neither spoke a word
as they proceeded, each concentrating on the lay of the land beyond, as
new hills and small depressions appeared with the passing of each traveled
knoll. Except for the rushing of the wind, the night remained silent. Flick
listened intently, and once he thought he heard a sharp cry far to the
north, but an instant later it was gone, and he did not hear it again. The
stranger appeared to be unconcerned with the silence. His attention seemed
to be focused on a constantly changing point on the ground some six feet
in front of them. He did not look up and he did not look at his young
guide for directions as they went. Instead, he seemed to know exactly
where the other was going and walked confidently beside him.

After a while, Flick began to have trouble keeping pace with the tall
man, who traveled the path with long, swinging strides that dwarfed Flick's
shorter ones. At times, the Valeman almost had to run to keep up. Once or
twice the other man glanced down at his smaller companion and, seeing
the difficulty he was having in trying to match strides, slowed to an easier
pace. Finally, as the southern slopes of the valley drew near, the hills began
to level off into shrub-covered grasslands that hinted at the appearance of
new forests. The terrain began to dip downward at a gentle slope, and Flick
located several familiar landmarks that bounded the outskirts of Shady Vale.
He felt a surge of relief in spite of himself. The hamlet and his own warm
home were just ahead.

The stranger did not speak a single word during the brief journey, and
Flick was reluctant to attempt any conversation. Instead, he tried to study
the giant in quick glimpses as they walked, without permitting the other
to observe what he was doing. He was understandably awed. The long,
craggy face, shaded by the sharp black beard, recalled the fearful Warlocks
described to him by stern elders before the glowing embers of a late-
evening fire when he was only a child. Most frightening were the stranger's
eyes—or rather the deep, dark caverns beneath the shaggy brows where his
eyes should be. Flick could not penetrate the heavy shadows that continued to mask that entire area of his face. The deeply lined countenance
seemed carved from stone, fixed and bowed slightly to the path before it.
As Flick pondered the inscrutable visage, he suddenly realized that the
stranger had never even mentioned his name.

The two were on the outer lip of the Vale, where the now clearly distinguishable path wound through large, crowded bushes that almost choked
off human passage. The tall stranger stopped suddenly and stood perfectly
still, head bowed, listening intently. Flick halted beside him and waited
quietly, also listening, but unable to detect anything. They remained motionless for seemingly endless minutes, and then the big man turned hurriedly to his smaller companion.

"Quickly! Hide in the bushes ahead. Go now, run!"

He half pushed, half threw Flick in front of him as he raced swiftly
toward the tall brush. Flick scurried fearfully for the sanctuary of the shrubbery, his pack slapping wildly against his back and the metal implements

clanging. The stranger turned on him and snatched the pack away, tucking it beneath the long robe.

"Silence!" he hissed. "Run now. Not a sound."

They ran quickly to the dark wall of foliage some fifty feet ahead, and the tall man hurriedly pushed Flick through the leafy branches that whipped against their faces, pulling him roughly into the middle of a large clump of brush, where they stood breathing heavily. Flick glanced at his companion and saw that he was not looking through the brush at the country around them, but instead was peering upward where the night sky was visible in small, irregular patches through the foliage. The sky seemed clear to the Valeman as he followed the other's intense gaze, and only the changeless stars winked back at him as he watched and waited. Minutes passed; once he attempted to speak, but was quickly silenced by the strong hands of the stranger, gripping his shoulders in warning. Flick remained standing, looking at the night and straining his ears for some sound of the apparent danger. But he heard nothing save their own heavy breathing and a quiet rush of wind through the weaving branches of their cover.

Then, just as Flick prepared to ease his tired limbs by sitting, the sky was suddenly blotted out by something huge and black that floated overhead and then passed from sight. A moment later it passed again, circling slowly without seeming to move, its shadow hanging ominously above the two hidden travelers as if preparing to fall upon them. A sudden feeling of terror raced through Flick's mind, trapping it in an iron web as it strained to flee the fearful madness penetrating inward. Something seemed to be reaching downward into his chest, slowly squeezing the air from his lungs, and he found himself gasping for breath. A vision passed sharply before him of a black image laced with red, of clawed hands and giant wings, of a thing so evil that its very existence threatened his frail life. For an instant the young man thought he would scream, but the hand of the stranger gripped his shoulder tightly, pulling him back from the precipice. Just as suddenly as it had appeared, the giant shadow was gone and the peaceful sky of the patched night was all that remained.

The hand on Flick's shoulder slowly relaxed its grip, and the Valeman slid heavily to the ground, his body limp as he broke out in a cold sweat. The tall stranger seated himself quietly next to his companion and a small smile crossed his face. He laid one long hand on Flick's and patted it as he would a child's.

"Come now, my young friend," he whispered, "you're alive and well, and the Vale lies just ahead."

Flick looked up at the other's calm face, his own eyes wide with fear as he shook his head slowly.

"That thing! What was that terrible thing?"

"Just a shadow," the man replied easily. "But this is neither the place nor the time to concern ourselves with such matters. We will speak of it later. Right now, I would like some food and a warm fire before I lose all patience."

He helped the Valeman to his feet and returned his pack to him. Then with a sweep of his robed arm, he indicated that he was ready to follow if the other was ready to lead. They left the cover of the brush, Flick not without misgivings as he glanced apprehensively at the night sky. It almost seemed as if the whole business had been the result of an overactive imagination. Flick pondered the matter solemnly and quickly decided that whatever the case, he had had enough for one evening: first this nameless giant and then that frightening shadow. He silently vowed that he would think twice before traveling again at night so far from the safety of the Vale.

Several minutes later, the trees and brush began to thin out and the flickering of yellow light was visible through the darkness. As they drew closer, the vague forms of buildings began to take shape as square and rectangular bulks in the gloom. The path widened into a smoother dirt road that led straight into the hamlet, and Flick smiled gratefully at the lights that shone in friendly greeting through the windows of the silent buildings. No one moved on the road ahead; if it had not been for the lights, one might well have wondered if anyone at all lived in the Vale. As it was, Flick's thoughts were far from such questions. Already he was considering how much he ought to tell his father and Shea, not wishing to worry them about strange shadows that could easily have been the product of his imagination and the gloomy night. The stranger at his side might shed some light on the subject at a later time, but so far he had not proved to be much of a conversationalist. Flick glanced involuntarily at the tall figure walking silently beside him. Again he was chilled by the blackness of the man. It seemed to reflect from his cloak and hood over his bowed head and lean hands, to shroud the entire figure in hazy gloom. Whoever he was, Flick felt certain that he would be a dangerous enemy.

They passed slowly between the buildings of the hamlet, and Flick could see torches burning through the wooden frames of the wide windows. The houses themselves were long, low structures, each containing only a ground floor beneath a slightly sloping roof, which in most instances tapered off on one side to shelter a small veranda, supported by heavy poles affixed to a long porch. The buildings were constructed of wood, with stone foundations and stone frontings on a few. Flick glanced through the curtained windows, catching glimpses of the inhabitants, the sight of familiar faces reassuring to him in the darkness outside. It had been a frightening night, and he was relieved to be home among people he knew.

The stranger remained oblivious to everything. He did not bother with more than a casual glance at the hamlet and had not spoken once since they had entered the Vale. Flick remained incredulous at the way in which the other followed him. He wasn't following Flick at all, but seemed to know exactly where the Valeman was going. When the road branched off in opposite directions amid identical rows of houses, the tall man had no difficulty in determining the correct route, though he never once looked at Flick nor even raised his head to study the road. Flick found himself trailing along while the other guided.

The two quickly reached the inn. It was a large structure consisting of a main building and lounging porch, with two long wings that extended out and back on either side. It was constructed of huge logs, cut and laced on a high stone foundation and covered with the familiar wood shingle roof, this particular roof much higher than those of the family dwellings. The central building was well lighted, and muffled voices could be heard from within, interspersed with occasional laughter and shouts. The wings of the inn were in darkness; it was there that the sleeping quarters of the guests were located. The smell of roasting meat permeated the night air, and Flick quickly led the way up the wooden steps of the long porch to the wide double doors at the center of the inn. The tall stranger followed without a word.

Flick slid back the heavy metal door latch and pulled on the handles. The big door on the right swung open to admit them into a large lounging room, filled with benches, high-backed chairs, and several long, heavy wooden tables set against the wall to the left and rear. The room was brightly lit by the tall candles on the tables and wall racks and by the huge fireplace built into the center of the wall on the left; Flick was momentarily blinded as his eyes adjusted to this new light. He squinted sharply, glancing past the fireplace and lounging furniture to the closed double doors at the back of the room and over to the long serving bar running down the length of the wall to his right. The men gathered about the bar looked up idly as the pair entered the room, their faces registering undisguised amazement at the appearance of the tall stranger. But Flick's silent companion did not seem to see them, and they quickly returned to their conversation and evening drinks, glancing back at the newcomers once or twice to see what they were going to do. The pair remained standing at the door for a few moments more as Flick looked around a second time at the faces of the small crowd to see if his father were present. The stranger motioned to the lounging chairs on the left.

"I will have a seat while you find your father. Perhaps we can have dinner together when you return."

Without further comment, he moved quietly away to a small table at the rear of the room and seated himself with his back to the men at the bar, his face slightly bowed and turned away from Flick. The Valeman watched him for a moment, then moved quickly to the double doors at the rear of the room and pushed through them to the hallway beyond. His father was probably in the kitchen, having dinner with Shea. Flick hurried down the hall past several closed doors before reaching the one that opened into the inn kitchen. As he entered, the two cooks who were working at the rear of the room greeted the young man with a cheerful good evening. His father was seated at the end of a long counter at the left. As Flick had anticipated, he was in the process of finishing his dinner. He waved a brawny hand in greeting.

"You're a bit later than usual, son," he growled pleasantly. "Come over here and have dinner while there's still something to eat."

Flick walked over wearily, lowered the traveling pack to the floor with a slight clatter, and perched himself on one of the high counter stools. His father's large frame straightened itself as he shoved back the empty plate and looked quizzically at the other, his wide forehead wrinkling.

"I met a traveler on the road coming into the valley," Flick explained hesitantly. "He wants a room and dinner. Asked us to join him."

"Well, he came to the right place for a room," the elder Ohmsford declared. "I don't see why we shouldn't join him for a bite to eat—I could easily do with another helping."

He raised his massive frame from the stool and signaled the cooks for three dinners. Flick looked about for Shea, but he was nowhere in sight. His father lumbered over to the cooks to give some special instructions on preparing the meal for the small party, and Flick turned to the basin next to the sink to wash off the dirt and grime from the road. When his father came over to him, Flick asked where his brother had gone.

"Shea has gone out on an errand for me and should return on the moment," his father replied. "By the way, what's the name of this man you brought back with you?"

"I don't know. He didn't say." Flick shrugged.

His father frowned and mumbled something about closemouthed strangers, rounding off his muffled comment with a vow to have no more mysterious types at his inn. Then motioning to his son, he led the way through the kitchen doors, his wide shoulders brushing the wall beyond as he swung to his left toward the lounging area. Flick followed quickly, his broad face wrinkled in doubt.

The stranger was still sitting quietly, his back to the men gathered at the serving bar. When he heard the rear doors swing open, he shifted about slightly to catch a glimpse of the two who entered. The stranger studied the close resemblance between father and son. Both were of medium height and heavy build, with the same broad, placid faces and grizzled brown hair. They hesitated in the doorway and Flick pointed toward the dark figure. He could see the surprise in Curzad Ohmsford's eyes as the innkeeper regarded him for a minute before approaching. The stranger stood up courteously, towering over the other two as they came up to him.

"Welcome to my inn, stranger," the elder Ohmsford greeted him, trying vainly to peer beneath the cloak hood that shadowed the other's dark face. "My name, as my boy has probably told you, is Curzad Ohmsford."

The stranger shook the extended hand with a grip that caused the stocky man to grimace and then nodded to Flick.

"Your son was kind enough to show me to this pleasant inn." He smiled with what Flick could have sworn was a mocking grin. "I hope you will join me for dinner and a glass of beer."

"Certainly," answered the innkeeper, lumbering past the other to a vacant chair where he seated himself heavily. Flick also pulled up a chair and sat down, his eyes still on the stranger, who was in the process of complimenting his father on having such a fine inn. The elder Ohmsford beamed with pleasure and nodded in satisfaction to Flick as he signaled one of the men at the serving bar for three glasses. The tall man still did not pull back the hood of the cloak shading his face. Flick wanted to peer beneath the shadows, but was afraid the stranger would notice, and one such attempt had already earned him sore wrists and a healthy respect for the big man's strength and temper. It was safer to remain in doubt.

He sat in silence as the conversation between his father and the stranger lengthened from polite comments on the mildness of the weather to a more intimate discussion of the people and happenings of the Vale. Flick noticed that his father, who never needed much encouragement any-way, was carrying the entire conversation with only casual questions inter-jected by the other man. It probably did not matter, but the Ohmsfords knew nothing about the stranger. He had not even told them his name. Now he was quite subtly drawing out information on the Vale from the unsuspecting innkeeper. The whole situation bothered Flick, but he was uncertain what he should do. He began to wish that Shea would appear and see what was happening. But his brother remained absent, and the long-awaited dinner was served and entirely consumed before one of the wide double doors at the front of the lobby swung open, and Shea ap-peared from out of the darkness.

For the first time, Flick saw the hooded stranger take more than a pass-ing interest in someone. Strong hands gripped the table as the black figure rose silently, towering over the Ohmsfords. He seemed to have forgotten they were there, as the lined brow furrowed more deeply and the craggy features radiated an intense concentration. For one frightening second, Flick believed that the stranger was somehow about to destroy Shea, but then the idea disappeared and was replaced with another. The man was searching his brother's mind.

He stared intently at Shea, his deep, shaded eyes running quickly over the young man's slim countenance and slight build. He noted the telltale Elven features immediately—the hint of slightly pointed ears beneath the tousled blond hair, the pencil-like eyebrows that ran straight up at a sharp angle from the bridge of the nose rather than across the brow, and the slimness of the nose and jaw. He saw intelligence and honesty in that face, and now as he faced Shea across the room, he saw determination in the penetrating blue eyes—determination that spread in a flush over the youthful features as the two men locked their gazes on each other. For a moment Shea hesitated in awe of the huge, dark apparition across the room. He felt unexplainably trapped but, bracing himself with sudden re-solve, he walked toward the forbidding figure.

Flick and his father watched Shea approach them, his eyes still on the tall stranger and then, as if suddenly realizing who he was, the two rose from the table. There was a moment of awkward silence as they faced one another, and then all the Ohmsfords began greeting each other at once in a sudden jumble of words that relieved the initial tension. Shea smiled at Flick, but could not take his eyes off the imposing figure before him. Shea was slightly shorter than his brother and was therefore even more in the shadow of the stranger than Flick had been, though he was less nervous about it as he faced the man. Curzad Ohmsford was talking to him about his errand, and his attention was momentarily diverted while he replied to his father's insistent questions. After a few preliminary remarks, Shea turned back to the newcomer to the Vale.

"I don't believe we have met; yet you seem to know me from somewhere, and I have the strangest feeling that I should know you."

The dark face above him nodded as the familiar mocking smile crossed it fleetingly.

"Perhaps you should know me, though it is not surprising that you do not remember. But I know who you are; indeed, I know you well."

Shea was dumbfounded at this reply and, unable to respond, stood staring at the stranger. The other raised a lean hand to his chin to stroke the small dark beard, glancing slowly around at the three men who waited for him to continue. Flick's open mouth was framing the question on the minds of all the Ohmsfords, when the stranger reached up and pulled back the cowl of his cloak to reveal clearly the dark face, now framed by long black hair, cut nearly shoulder length and shading the deep-set eyes, which still showed only as black slits in the shadows beneath the heavy brows.

"My name is Allanon," he announced quietly.

There was a long moment of stunned silence as the three listeners stared in speechless amazement. Allanon—the mysterious wanderer of the four lands, historian of the races, philosopher and teacher, and, some said, practitioner of the mystic arts. Allanon—the man who had been everywhere from the darkest havens of the Anar to the forbidden heights of the Charnal Mountains. His was a name familiar to the people of even the most isolated Southland communities. Now he stood unexpectedly before the Ohmsfords, none of whom had ventured outside their valley home more than a handful of times in their lives.

Allanon smiled warmly for the first time, but inwardly he felt pity for them. The quiet existence they had known for so many years was finished, and, in a way, it was his responsibility.

"What brings you here?" Shea asked at last.

The tall man looked sharply at him and uttered a deep, low chuckle that caught them all by surprise.

"You, Shea," he murmured. "I came looking for you."

Shea was awake early the next morning, rising from the warmth of his bed to dress hastily in the damp cold of the morning air. He had arisen so early, he discovered, that no one else in the entire inn, guest or family, was yet awake. The long building was silent as he moved quietly from his small room in the rear of the main section to the large lobby, where he quickly started a fire in the great stone hearth, his fingers almost numb with cold. The valley was always strikingly cold in the early-morning hours before the sun reached the rim of the hills, even during the warmest seasons of the year. Shady Vale was well sheltered, not only from the eyes of men, but from the fury of perverse weather conditions that drifted down from the Northland. Yet while the heavy storms of the winter and spring passed over the valley and Shady Vale, the bitter cold of early morning all year round settled into the high hills, holding until the warmth of the noonday sun filtered down to chase away the chill.

The fire crackled and snapped at the wood as Shea relaxed in one of the high, straight-backed chairs and pondered the events of the previous evening. He leaned back, folded his arms for warmth, and hunched down into the hard wood. How could Allanon have known him? He had seldom been out of the Vale and would certainly have remembered the other man if he had met him while on one of his infrequent journeys. Allanon had refused to say more on the subject after that one declaration. He had finished his dinner in silence, concluding that further talk should wait until the next morning, and he became once again the forbidding figure he had first appeared when Shea entered the inn that evening. His meal completed, he had asked to be shown to his room so that he might sleep, and then excused himself. Neither Shea nor Flick could get him to say one word further about the trip to Shady Vale and his interest in Shea. The two brothers had talked alone later that night, and Flick had related the story of his encounter with Allanon and the incident with the terrifying shadow.

Shea's thoughts drifted back to his initial question—how could Allanon have known him? Mentally he retraced the events of his life. His early years were a vague memory. He did not know where he had been born, although sometime after the Ohmsfords had adopted him, he had been told that his place of birth was a small Westland community. His father had died before he was old enough to form a lasting impression, and now he could recall almost nothing of him. For a time his mother had kept him, and he could recall bits and pieces of his years with her, playing with Elven children, surrounded by great trees and deep green solitude. He was five when she became suddenly ill and decided to return to her own people in the hamlet of Shady Vale. She must have known then that she was dying, but her first concern was for her son. The journey south was the finish for her, and she died shortly after they reached the valley.

The relatives his mother had left when she married were gone, all but the Ohmsfords, who were no more than distant cousins. Curzad Ohmsford had lost his wife less than a year earlier, and was raising his son Flick while he managed the inn. Shea became a part of their family, and the two boys had grown up as brothers, both bearing the name Ohmsford. Shea had never been told his true name, nor did he care to ask. The Ohmsfords were the only family that meant anything to him, and they had accepted him as their own. There were times that being a half-blood bothered him, but Flick had stoutly insisted that it was a distinct advantage because it gave him the instincts and character of two races to build upon.

Yet nowhere could he remember an encounter with Allanon. It was as if the event had never really occurred. Perhaps it never had. He shifted around in the chair and gazed absently into the fire. There was something about the grim wanderer that frightened him. Perhaps it was his imagination, but he could not shake off the feeling that the man could somehow read his thoughts, could see right through him whenever he chose to do so. It seemed ridiculous, but the thought had lingered with the Valeman since the meeting in the lobby of the inn. Flick had remarked on it too. And he had gone further than that, whispering in the darkness of their sleeping room to his brother, fearful that he might in some way be overheard, that he felt Allanon was dangerous.

Shea stretched himself and sighed deeply. Already it was becoming light outside. He rose to add some more wood to the fire, and heard the sound of his father's voice in the hallway, grumbling loudly about matters in general. Sighing in resignation, Shea put aside his thoughts and hastened to the kitchen to help with the morning preparations.

It was almost noon before Shea saw any sign of Allanon, who had evidently kept to his room for the duration of the morning. He appeared quite suddenly from around one corner of the inn as Shea relaxed beneath a huge shade tree at the rear of the building, absently munching on a quick luncheon he had prepared for himself. His father was occupied within, and Flick was off somewhere on an errand. The dark stranger of the previous night seemed no less forbidding in the noon sun, still a shadowed figure of tremendous height, though he appeared to have changed his cloak from black to a light gray. The lean face was slightly bowed to the path before him as he walked toward Shea and seated himself on the grass next to the Valeman, gazing absently at the hilltops to the east which appeared above the trees of the hamlet. Both men were silent for several long minutes, until at last Shea could stand it no longer.

"Why did you come to the vale, Allanon? Why were you looking for me?"

The dark face turned toward him and a slight smile played across the lean features.

"A question, my young friend, that cannot be as easily answered as you would like. Perhaps the best way in which to answer you is first to question you. Have you read anything of the history of the Northland?"

He paused.

"Do you know of the Skull Kingdom?"

Shea stiffened at the mention of the name—a name that was synonymous with all the terrible things in life, real and imagined, a name used to frighten little children who had been bad or to send shivers down the spines of grown men when stories were told before the dying coals of a late-evening fire. It was a name that hinted of ghosts and goblins, of the sly forest Gnomes of the east and the great Rock Trolls of the far north. Shea looked at the grim visage before him and nodded slowly. Again Allanon paused before continuing.

"I am a historian, Shea, among other things—perhaps the most widely traveled historian alive today, since few besides myself have entered the Northland in over five hundred years. I know much about the race of Man that none now suspect. The past has become a blurred memory, and just as well perhaps; for the history of Man has not been particularly glorious in the last two thousand years. Men today have forgotten the past; they know little of the present and less of the future. The race of Man lives almost solely in the confines of the Southland. It knows nothing at all of the Northland and its peoples, and little of the Eastland and Westland. A pity that Men have developed into such a shortsighted people, for once they were the most visionary of the races. But now they are quite content to live apart from the other races, isolated from the problems of the rest of the world. They remain content, mind you, because those problems have not as yet touched them and because a fear of the past has persuaded them not to look too closely at the future."

Shea felt slightly irritated by these sweeping accusations, and his reply was sharp.

"You make it sound like a terrible thing to want to be left alone. I know enough history—no, I know enough life—to realize that Man's only hope for survival is to remain apart from the races, to rebuild everything he has lost over the last two thousand years. Then perhaps he will be smart enough not to lose it a second time. He almost destroyed himself entirely in the Great Wars by his persistent intervention in the affairs of others and his ill-conceived rejection of an isolation policy."

Allanon's dark face turned hard.

"I am well aware of the catastrophic consequences brought about by those wars—the products of power and greed that the race of Man brought down on its own head through a combination of carelessness and remarkable shortsightedness. That was long ago—and what has changed? You think that Man can start again, do you, Shea? Well, you might be quite surprised to learn that some things never change, and the dangers of power are always present, even to a race that almost completely obliterated itself. The

Great Wars of the past may be gone—the wars of the races, of politics and nationalism, and the final ones of sheer energy, of ultimate power. But we face new dangers today, and these are more of a threat to the existence of the races than were any of the old! If you think Man is free to build a new life while the rest of the world drifts by, then you do not know anything of history!"

He paused suddenly, his grim features lined with anger. Shea stared back defiantly, though within he felt small and frightened.

"Enough of this," Allanon began again, his face softening as one strong hand reached up to grip Shea's shoulder in friendship. "The past is behind us, and it is with the future that we must concern ourselves. Let me refresh your memory for a moment on the history of the Northland and the legend of the Skull Kingdom. As you know, I'm sure, the Great Wars brought an end to an age where Man alone was the dominant race. Man was almost completely destroyed and even the geography he had known was completely altered, completely restructured. Countries, nations, and governments all ceased to exist as the last members of the human race fled south to survive. It was nearly a thousand years before Man had once again raised himself above the standard of the animals he hunted for food and established a progressive civilization. It was primitive, to be sure, but there was order and a semblance of government. Then Man began to discover there were other races besides himself inhabiting the world—creatures who had survived the Great Wars and developed their own races. In the mountains were the huge Trolls, powerful and ferocious, but quite content with what they had. In the hills and forests were the small and cunning creatures we now call Gnomes. Many a battle was fought between Men and Gnomes for the rights to land during the years following the Great Wars, and the battles hurt both races. But they fought to survive, and reason has no place in the mind of a creature fighting for its life.

"Man also discovered that there was another race—a race of men who had fled beneath the earth to survive the effects of the Great Wars. Years of living in the huge caverns beneath the earth's crust away from the sunlight altered their appearance. They became short and stocky, powerful in the arms and chest, with strong, thick legs for climbing and scrambling underground. Their sight in the dark became superior to that of other creatures, yet in the sunlight they could see little. They lived beneath the earth for many hundreds of years, until at last they began to emerge to live again on the face of the land. Their eyes were very bad at first, and they made their homes in the darkest forests of the Eastland. They developed their own language, though they later reverted to the language of Man. When Man first discovered remnants of this lost race, they called them Dwarfs, after a fictional race of the old days."

His voice trailed off and he remained silent for a few minutes staring out at the tips of the hills showing brilliant green in the sunlight. Shea considered the historian's comments. He had never seen a Troll, and only one or two Gnomes and Dwarfs, and those he did not remember very well.

"What about the Elves?" he asked finally.

Allanon looked back thoughtfully and bowed his head a little more.

"Ah, yes, I had not forgotten. A remarkable race of creatures, the Elves. Perhaps the greatest people of all, though no one has ever fully realized it. But the tale of the Elven people must wait for another time; suffice to say that they were always there in the great forests of the Westland, though the other races seldom encountered them at this stage of history.

"Now we shall see how much you know of the history of the Northland, my young friend. Today, it is a land inhabited by almost no one other than the Trolls, a barren and forbidding country where few people of any race care to travel, let alone settle. The Trolls, of course, are bred to survive there. Today, Men live in the warmth and comfort of the Southland's mild climate and green lands. They have forgotten that once the Northland, too, was settled by creatures of all the races, not only the Trolls in the mountain regions, but Men, Dwarfs, and Gnomes in the lowlands and forests. This was in the years when all the races were just beginning to rebuild a new civilization with new ideas, new laws, and many new cultures. It was a very promising future, but Men today have forgotten that those times ever existed—forgotten that they are more than a beaten race trying to live apart from those who defeated them and crippled their pride. There was no division of countries then. It was an earth reborn, where each race was being given a second chance at building a world. Of course, they did not realize the significance of the opportunity. They were too concerned with holding what they considered theirs and building their own private little worlds. Each race was certain that it was destined to be the dominant power in the years ahead—gathered together like a pack of angry rats guarding a stale, sorry piece of cheese. And Man, oh, yes, in all his glory, was groveling and snapping at the chance just like the others. Did you know that, Shea?"

The Valeman shook his head slowly, unable to believe that what he was hearing could be the truth. He had been told that Man had been a persecuted people ever since the Great Wars, fighting to keep alive his dignity and honor, to protect the little land that was his in the face of complete savagery on the part of the other races. Man had never been the oppressor in these battles; always he was the oppressed. Allanon smiled grimly, his lips curling with mocking satisfaction as he saw the effect of his words.

"You didn't realize that it was this way, I see. No matter—it will be the least of the surprises I have in store for you. Man has never been the great people he has fancied himself. In those days Men fought like the rest, although I will concede that perhaps they had a higher sense of honor and a clearer purpose to rebuild than some of the others, and they were slightly more civilized." He twisted the word meaningfully as he spoke it, lacing it with undisguised sarcasm. "But all this commentary has little to do with the main point of our discussion, which I hope to make clear to you shortly.

"It was about this same time, when the races had discovered one another and were fighting for dominance, that the Druid Council first opened the halls of Paranor in the lower Northland. History is rather vague about the origins and purposes of the Druids, though it is believed they were a group of highly knowledgeable men from all the races, skilled in many of the lost arts of the old world. They were philosophers and visionaries, students of the arts and science all at once, but more than this, they were the teachers of the races. They were the givers of power—the power of new knowledge in the ways of life. They were led by a man named Galaphile, a historian and philosopher like myself, who called the greatest men of the land together to form a council to establish peace and order. He relied on their learning to hold sway over the races, their ability to give knowledge to gain the people's confidence.

"The Druids were a very powerful force during those years and the plan of Galaphile seemed to be working as anticipated. But as time passed, it became apparent that some of the members of the Council had powers far surpassing those of the others, powers that had lain dormant and gathered strength in a few phenomenal, genius minds. It would be difficult to describe those powers to you without taking quite some time—more time than we have available to us. What is important for our purposes is to recognize that some among the Council who possessed the very greatest minds became convinced that they were destined to shape the future of the races. In the end, they broke from the Council to form their own group and for some time disappeared and were forgotten.

"About one hundred and fifty years later, there occurred a terrible civil war within the race of Man, which eventually widened into the First War of the Races, as the historians named it. Its cause was uncertain even then, and has now almost been forgotten. In simple terms, a small sector of the race of Man revolted against the teachings of the Council and formed a very powerful and highly trained army. The proclaimed purpose of the uprising was the subjugation of the rest of Man under a central rule for the betterment of the race and the furthering of its pride as a people. Eventually, almost all segments of the race rallied to the new cause and war was begun upon the other races, ostensibly to accomplish this new goal. The central figure behind the war was a man called Brona—an archaic Gnome term for 'Master.' It was said that he was the leader of the Druids of the first Council who had broken away and disappeared into the Northland. No reliable source ever reported seeing him or talking with him, and in the end it was concluded that Brona was merely a name, a fictitious character. The revolt, if you care to call it such, was finally crushed by the combined power of the Druids and the other allied races. Did you know of this, Shea?"

The Valeman nodded and smiled slightly.

"I have heard of the Druid Council, of its purposes and work—all ancient history since the Council died out long ago. I have heard of the First War of the Races, though not in the same way as you tell it. Prejudiced, I believe you would call my version. The war was a bitter lesson for Man."

Allanon waited patiently and did not speak as Shea paused to reflect on his own knowledge of the past before continuing.

"I know that the survivors of our race fled south after the war was over and have remained there ever since, rebuilding again the homes and cities lost, trying to create life rather than destroy it. You seem to think of it as an isolation born of fear. But I believe it was and still is the best way to live. Central governments have always been the greatest danger to mankind. Now there are none—small communities are the new rule of life. Some things are better left alone by everyone."

The tall man laughed, a deep mirthless chuckle that made Shea feel suddenly foolish.

"You know so little, though what you say is true enough. Truisms, my young friend, are the useless children of hindsight. Well, I don't propose to argue with you now on the fine points of social reform, let alone political activism. That will have to wait until another time. Tell me what you know of the creature called Brona. Perhaps . . . no, wait a moment. Some-one is coming."

The words were scarcely out of his mouth before the stocky figure of Flick appeared around the corner of the inn. The Valeman stopped abruptly as he saw Allanon and hesitated until Shea waved to him. He came over slowly and remained standing, his eyes on the dark face as the big man smiled slowly down at him, the familiar enigmatic twist at the corners of his mouth.

"I was just wondering where you had gone," Flick began, speaking to his brother, "and didn't mean to interrupt . . ."

"You are not interrupting anything," Shea replied quickly. But Allanon seemed to disagree.

"This conversation was for your ears alone," he declared flatly. "If your brother chooses to stay, he will have decided his own fate in the days to come. I would strongly suggest that he not remain to hear the rest of our discussion, but forget that we ever talked. Still, it is his own choice."

The brothers looked at each other, unable to believe that the tall man was serious. But his grim face indicated that he was not joking, and for a moment both men hesitated, reluctant to say anything. Finally Flick spoke.

"I have no idea what you're talking about, but Shea and I are brothers and what happens to one must happen to both. If he's in any trouble, I should share it with him—it's my own choice, I'm sure."

Shea stared at him in amazement. He had never heard Flick sound more positive about anything in his entire life. He felt proud of his brother and smiled up at him gratefully. Flick winked back quickly and sat down, not looking at Allanon. The tall traveler stroked his small, dark beard with a lean hand and smiled quite unexpectedly.

"Indeed, the choice is your own, and you have proven yourself a brother by your words. But it is deeds that make the difference. You may regret the choice in the days to come. . . ."

He trailed off, lost in thought as he studied the bowed head of Flick for several long moments before turning to Shea.

"Well, I cannot begin my story again just for your brother. He will have to follow as best he can. Now tell me what you know of Brona."

Shea thought silently for a few minutes and then shrugged.

"I really don't know much of anything about him. He was a myth, as you said, the fictional leader of the uprising in the First War of the Races. He was supposed to have been a Druid who left the Council and used his own evil power to master the minds of his followers. Historically, he was never seen, never captured, or killed in the final battle. He never existed."

"Historically accurate, I'm sure," muttered Allanon. "What do you know of him in connection with the Second War of the Races?"

Shea smiled briefly at the question.

"Well, legend has it that he was the central force behind that war also, but it turned out to be just another myth. He was supposed to be the same creature who had organized the armies of Man in the first war, except in this one he was called the Warlock Lord—the evil counterpart to the Druid Bremen. I believe Bremen was supposed to have killed him in the second war, however. But all that was only fantasy."

Flick hastened to nod his agreement, but Allanon said nothing. Shea waited for some form of confirmation, openly amused by the whole subject.

"Where is all this talk taking us anyway?" he asked after a moment.

Allanon glanced down at him sharply, cocking one dark eyebrow in wonder.

"Your patience is remarkably limited, Shea. After all, we have just covered in a matter of minutes the history of a thousand years. However, if you think you can restrain yourself for a few moments longer, I believe I can promise you that your question will be answered."

Shea nodded, feeling no little mortification at the reprimand. It was not the words themselves that hurt; it was the way Allanon said them—with that mocking smile and ill-concealed sarcasm. The Valeman regained his composure quickly, though, and shrugged his willingness to allow the historian to continue at his own pace.

"Very well," the other acknowledged. "I shall try to complete our discussion quickly. What we have spoken of up to this point has been background history to what I will tell you now—the reason why I came to find you. I recall to your memory the events of the Second War of the Races—the most recent war in the new history of Man, fought less than five hundred years ago in the Northland. Man had no part in this war; Man was the defeated race of the first, living deep in the heart of the Southland, a few small communities trying hard to survive the threat of total extinction. This was a war of the great races—the Elven people and the Dwarfs fighting against the power of the savage Rock Trolls and the cunning Gnomes.

"After the completion of the First War of the Races, the known world partitioned into the existing four lands, and the races were at peace for quite a long time. During this period, the power and influence of the Druid Council diminished greatly as the apparent need for its assistance seemed to have ceased. It is only fair to add that the Druids had grown lax in their attention to the races, and over a period of years the new members lost sight of the Council's purposes and turned away from the peoples' problems to more personal concerns, leading a more isolated existence of study and meditation. The Elven people were the most powerful race, but confined themselves to their isolated homeland deep in the west where they were content to remain in relative isolation—a mistake they were to regret deeply. The other peoples scattered and developed into smaller, less unified societies, primarily in the Eastland, though some groups did settle in parts of the Westland and Northland in the border countries.

"The Second War of the Races began when a huge army of Trolls came down out of the Charnal Mountains and seized all of the Northland, including the Druid fortress at Paranor. The Druids had been betrayed from within by several of their own people who had been won over by promises and offers from the enemy commander, who at this time was unknown. The remaining Druids, except for a very few who escaped or were away, were captured and thrown into the dungeons of the Keep and never seen again. Those who had escaped the fate of their brothers scattered about the four lands and went into hiding. The Troll army immediately moved against the Dwarf people in the Eastland with the obvious intent of crushing all resistance as quickly as possible. But the Dwarfs gathered deep within the huge forests of the Anar, which only they know well enough to survive in for any length of time, and there held firm against the advances of the Troll armies despite the aid being given by a few of the Gnome tribes who had joined the invasion force. The Dwarf King, Raybur, recorded in his own peoples' history whom he had discovered the real enemy to be—the rebel Druid, Brona."

"How could the Dwarf King believe this?" Shea interjected quickly. "If it were true, the Warlock Lord would be over five hundred years old! At any rate, I should think that some ambitious mystic must have suggested the idea to the king with the thought of reviving an old, outdated myth—perhaps to better his own position in the court or something."

"That is a possibility," Allanon conceded. "But let me continue the story. After long months of fighting, the Trolls were evidently led to believe that the Dwarfs had been beaten, so they turned their war legions to the west and began to march against the powerful Elven kingdom. But during the months the Trolls had battled the Dwarf people, the few Druids who had escaped from Paranor had been assembled by the famous mystic Bremen, an old and highly esteemed elder of the Council. He led them to the Elven kingdom in the Westland to warn the people there of this new threat and to prepare for the almost certain invasion of the Northlanders. The Elven King in that year was Jerle Shannara—the greatest of all the Elven kings, perhaps, with the exception of Eventine. Bremen warned the King of the probable assault on his lands, and the Elven ruler quickly prepared his armies before the advancing Troll hordes had reached their borders. I'm sure that you know your history well enough to remember what happened when the battle was fought, Shea, but I want you to pay attention to the particulars of what I tell you next."

Both Shea and an excited Flick nodded.

"The Druid Bremen gave to Jerle Shannara a special sword for the battle against the Trolls. Whoever held the sword was supposed to be invincible— even against the awesome power of the Warlock Lord. When the Troll legions entered the Valley of Rhenn in the borderlands of the Elven kingdom, they were attacked and trapped by the armies of the Elven people fighting from higher ground and were badly beaten in a two-day, pitched battle. The Elves were led by the Druids and Jerle Shannara, who carried the great sword given him by Bremen. They fought together against the Troll armies, who were said to have had the added might of beings from the spirit world under the domination of the Warlock Lord. But the courage of the Elven King and the power of the fabulous sword overwhelmed the spirit creatures and destroyed them. When the remainder of the Troll army attempted to escape back to the safety of the Northland across the Plains of Streleheim, it was caught between the pursuing army of Elves and an army of Dwarfs approaching from the Eastland. There was a terrible battle fought in which the Troll army was destroyed almost to the last man. During the battle, Bremen disappeared while in combat at the side of the Elven King, facing the Warlock Lord himself. It was recorded that both Druid and Warlock were lost in the fighting and neither was ever seen again. Not even the bodies were found.

"Jerle Shannara carried the famous sword given him until his death some years later. His son gave the weapon to the Druid Council at Paranor, where the blade was set in a huge block of Tre-Stone and placed in a vault in the Druid's Keep. I'm sure you are quite familiar with the legend of the sword and what it stands for, what it means to all the races. The great sword rests today at Paranor just as it has for five hundred years. Have I been sufficiently lucid in my narration, Valemen?"

Flick nodded in dumbfounded wonder, still caught up in the excitement of the history. But Shea suddenly decided that he had heard enough. Nothing that Allanon had told them of the history of the races was fact— not if he was to believe what he had been taught by his own people since he was a child. The big man had simply related to them a childhood fantasy that had been passed down through the ages from parents to small children. He had listened patiently to everything Allanon had falsely represented to be the truth about the races, humoring him out of respect for his reputation. But the entire tale of the sword was ridiculous, and Shea was through being played for a fool.

"What has all this got to do with your coming to Shady Vale?" he persisted, a faint smile betraying his disgust. "We've heard all about a battle that took place some five hundred years ago—a battle that did not even concern Man, but Trolls and Elves and Dwarfs and goodness knows what else, as you tell it. Did you say there were spirits or something? I'm sorry if I sound incredulous, but I find this whole tale a little hard to swallow. The story of the Sword of Jerle Shannara is well known to all the races, but it's only fiction, not fact—a glorified story of heroism created to stir up a sense of loyalty and duty in the races that have a part in its history. But the legend of Shannara is a tale for children that adults must outgrow as they accept the responsibilities of manhood. Why did you waste time relating this fairy tale when all I want is a simple answer to a simple question? Why are you looking for . . . me?"

Shea stopped short as he saw Allanon's dark features tighten and grow black with anger, the great brows knitting over sudden pinpoints of light in the deep shadows that hid the eyes. The tall man seemed to be fighting to contain some terrible fury within, and for a moment it appeared to Shea that he was about to be strangled by the huge hands that locked before his face as the man glared in open rage. Flick moved back hastily and tripped over his own feet in the process, fear welling up inside.

"Fool . . . you fool," rasped the giant in barely controlled fury. "You know so little . . . children! What does the race of Man know of truth— where has Man been but hiding, creeping in terror under piteous shelters in the deepest regions of the Southland like frightened rabbits? You dare to tell me that I speak of fairy tales—you, who have never known strife, safe here in your precious Vale! I came to find the bloodline of kings, but I have found a little boy who hides himself in falsehoods. You are nothing but a child!"

Flick was fervently wishing he could sink into the ground beneath his feet or perhaps simply vanish, when to his utter astonishment he saw Shea leap to his feet before the tall man, his lean features flushed in fury and his hands knotted into fists as he braced himself. The Valeman was so over-come with anger that he could not speak, and stood before his accuser, shaking with rage and humiliation. But Allanon was not impressed and his deep voice sounded again.

"Hold, Shea. Do not be a greater fool! Pay attention to what I tell you now. All that I told you has come down through the ages as legend and was so told to the race of Man. But the time for fairy tales is ended. What I have told you is not legend; it is the truth. The sword is real; it rests today at Paranor. But most important of all, the Warlock Lord is real. He lives today and the Skull Kingdom is his domain!"

Shea started, suddenly realizing that the man was not deliberately lying after all—that he did not believe this to be a fairy tale. He relaxed and sat down slowly, his gaze still riveted on the dark face. Abruptly he recalled the historian's words.

"You said king . . . you were looking for a king . . . ?"

"What is the legend of the Sword of Shannara, Shea? What does the inscription carved into the block of Tre-Stone read?"

Shea was dumbfounded, unable to recall any legend at all.

"I don't know . . . I can't remember what it said. Something about the next time . . ."

"A son!" spoke up Flick suddenly from the other side. "When the War-lock Lord appeared again in the Northland, a son of the House of Shan-nara would come forth to take up the Sword against him. That was the legend!"

Shea looked over at his brother, remembering then what the inscription was supposed to read. He looked back at Allanon, who was watching him intently.

"How does this concern me?" he asked quickly. "I'm not a son of the House of Shannara—I'm not even Elven. I'm a half-blood, not an Elf, not a king. Eventine is the heir to the House of Shannara. Are you telling me that I'm a lost son—a missing heir? I don't believe it!"

He looked quickly to Flick for support, but his brother appeared to be completely lost, staring in bewilderment at the face of Allanon. The dark man spoke quietly.

"You do have Elven blood in you, Shea, and you are not the true son of Curzad Ohmsford. That you must know. And Eventine is not directly of the blood of Shannara."

"I have always known that I was an adopted son," the Valeman admitted, "but surely I could not have come from . . . Flick, tell him!"

But his brother just stared at him in astonishment, unable to frame an answer to the question. Shea stopped speaking abruptly, shaking his head in disbelief. Allanon nodded.

"You are a son of the House of Shannara—a half son only, however, and far removed from the direct line of descent that can be traced down through the last five hundred years. I knew you as a child, Shea, before you were taken into the Ohmsford household as their own son. Your father was Elven—a very fine man. Your mother was of the race of Man. They both died when you were still very young, and you were given to Curzad Ohmsford to raise as his own son. But you are a son of Jerle Shannara, albeit a distant son and not of pure Elven blood."

Shea nodded absently at the tall man's explanation, confused and still suspicious. Flick was looking at his brother as if he had never seen him before.

"What does all this mean?" he asked Allanon eagerly.

"What I have told you is known also to the Lord of Darkness, though he does not yet know where you live or who you are. But his emissaries will find you sooner or later, and when they do, you will be destroyed."

Shea's head jerked up, and he looked at Flick fearfully, remembering the tale of the huge shadow seen near the lip of the Vale. His brother, too, felt a sudden chill, recalling that awful feeling of terror.

"But why?" asked Shea quickly. "What have I done to deserve that?"

"You must understand many things, Shea, before you can understand the answer to that question," replied Allanon, "and I have not the time to explain them all now. You must believe me when I tell you that you are descended from Jerle Shannara, that you are of Elven blood, and that the Ohmsfords are a foster family to you. You were not the only son of the House of Shannara, but you are the only son who survives today. The others were Elven, and they were easily found and destroyed. That is what prevented the Dark Lord from finding you for so long—he was unaware that there was a half son alive in the Southland. The Elven kin he knew of from the first.

"But know this, Shea. The power of the Sword is unlimited—it is the one great fear with which Brona lives, the one power he may not withstand. The legend of the Sword is a powerful amulet in the hands of the races, and Brona means to put an end to the legend. He will do this by destroying the entire house of Shannara, so that no son will come forth to draw the Sword against him."

"But I did not even know of the Sword," protested Shea. "I did not even know who I was, or anything about the Northland or about . . ."

"It does not matter!" cut in Allanon sharply. "If you are dead, there can be no doubt about you."

His voice died away in a weary murmur, and he turned to look again at the distant mountaintops beyond the fringe of tall elms. Shea lay back slowly on the soft grass, staring at the pale blue of the late-winter sky laced with small, soft wisps of white cloud that drifted from the tall hills. For a few pleasant moments the presence of Allanon and the threat of death were submerged in the sleepy warmth of the afternoon sun and the fresh smell of the lofty trees towering over him. He closed his eyes and thought of his life in the Vale, of the plans that he had made with Flick, of their hopes for the future. They would all go up in smoke if what he had been told were true. He lay quietly considering these things, and finally sat up, his arms braced behind him.

"I'm not sure what to think," he began slowly. "There are so many questions I have to ask you. I feel confused by the whole idea of being someone other than an Ohmsford—someone threatened with death at the hands of a . . . a myth. What do you suggest that I do?"

Allanon smiled warmly for the first time.

"For the moment, do nothing. There is no immediate danger to you. Think about what I have told you and we will speak further of the implications another time. I shall be glad to answer all your questions then. But do not talk about this to anyone else, not even your father. Act as if this conversation had never taken place until we have a chance to work out the problems further."

The young men looked at each other and nodded in agreement, though it would be difficult to pretend that nothing had happened. Allanon rose silently, stretching his tall frame to relieve cramped muscles. The brothers rose with him and stood quietly as he looked down at them.

"Legends and myths that did not exist in yesterday's world will exist in tomorrow's. Things of evil, ruthless and cunning, after lying dormant for centuries, will now awaken. The shadow of the Warlock Lord begins to fall across the four lands."

He trailed off abruptly.

"I did not mean to be harsh with you," he smiled gently, quite unexpectedly, "but if this is the worst thing that happens in the days to come, you should be glad indeed. You are faced with a very real threat, not a fairy tale that can be laughed away. Nothing about any of this will be fair to you. You will learn much about life that you will not like."

He paused, a tall gray shadow against the green of the distant hills, his robes gathered carefully about his gaunt frame. One great hand reached over to grip firmly Shea's lean shoulder, and for an instant bound them together as one person. Then he turned away and was gone.

3

Allanon's plan for further discussions at the inn did not work out. He left the brothers sitting in hushed conversation behind the inn and returned to his room. Shea and Flick finally went back to their chores and shortly thereafter were dispatched on an errand by their father that took them out of the Vale to the north end of the valley. It was dark by the time they returned, and they hastened to the dining room, hoping to question the historian further, but he did not appear. They ate dinner hurriedly, unable to speak to each other about the afternoon while their father was present. After eating, they waited almost an hour, but still he did not appear and eventually, long after their father had departed for the kitchen, they decided to go to Allanon's room. Flick was reluctant to go looking for the dark stranger, especially after his meeting with him on the Vale road the previous night. But Shea was so insistent that at last his brother agreed to go along, hoping that there might be safety in numbers.

When they reached his room, they found the door unlocked and the tall wanderer gone. The room looked as if no one had even used it recently. They made a hasty search of the inn and the surrounding premises, but Allanon was not to be found. At last they were forced to conclude that for some unknown reason he had departed from Shady Vale. Shea was openly angered that Allanon had left without even a parting word, yet at the same time he began to experience a growing apprehension that he was no longer under the historian's protective wing. Flick, on the other hand, was just as happy that the man was gone. As he sat with Shea in the tall, hard-backed chairs before the fire in the big lounge room of the inn, he tried to assure his brother that everything was working out for the best. He had never completely believed the historian's wild tale of the Northland wars and the Sword of Shannara, he argued, and even if some of it were true, certainly the part about Shea's lineage and the threat from Brona was completely exaggerated—a ridiculous fairy tale.

Shea listened in silence to Flick's muddled rationalization of the possibilities, offering only an occasional nod of acquiescence, his own thoughts concentrated on deciding what he should do next. He had serious doubts about the credibility of Allanon's tale. After all, what purpose did the historian have in coming to him in the first place? He had appeared conveniently, it seemed, to tell Shea about his strange background, and to warn him that he was in danger, then had disappeared without a word about his own interest in this business. How could Shea be sure that Allanon had not come on some hidden purpose of his own, hoping to use the Valeman as his cat's-paw? There were too many questions that he didn't have the answers to.

Eventually, Flick grew tired of offering advice to the silent Shea and finally ceased to speak of the matter, slumping down in his chair and gazing resignedly into the crackling fire. Shea continued to ponder the details of Allanon's story, trying to decide what he should do now. But after an hour of quiet deliberation, he threw up his hands in disgust, feeling as confused as before. Stalking out of the lounge, he headed for his own room, the faithful Flick close behind. Neither felt inclined to discuss it further. Upon reaching their small bedroom in the east wing, Shea dropped into a chair in moody silence. Flick collapsed heavily on the bed and stared disinterestedly at the ceiling.

The twin candles on the small bedside table cast a dim glow over the large room, and Flick soon found himself on the verge of drifting off to sleep. He hastily jerked awake and, stretching his hands above his head, encountered a long piece of folded paper which had partially slipped down between the mattress and headboard. Curiously, he brought it around in front of his eyes and saw that it was addressed to Shea.

"What's this?" he muttered and tossed it across to his prostrate brother.

Shea ripped open the sealed paper and hurriedly scanned it. He had scarcely begun before he let out a low whistle and leaped to his feet. Flick sat up quickly, realizing who must have left the note.

"It's from Allanon," Shea confirmed his brother's suspicion. "Listen to this, Flick:

" *'I have no time to find you and explain matters further. Something of the greatest importance has occurred, and I must leave immediately—perhaps even now I am too late. You must trust me and believe what I told you, even though I will not be able to return to the valley.*

You will not long be safe in Shady Vale, and you must be prepared to flee quickly. Should your safety be threatened, you will find shelter at Culhaven in the forests of the Anar. I will send a friend to guide you. Place your trust in Balinor.

Speak with no one of our meeting. The danger to you is extreme. In the pocket of your maroon travel cloak, I have placed a small pouch which contains three Elfstones. They will provide you with guidance and protection when nothing else can. Be cautioned—they are for Shea alone and to be used only when all else fails.

The sign of the Skull will be your warning to flee. May luck be with you, my young friend, until we meet again.' "

Shea looked excitedly at his brother, but the suspicious Flick shook his head in disbelief and frowned deeply.

"I don't trust him. Whatever is he talking about anyway—Skulls and

Elfstones? I never even heard of a place called Culhaven, and the Anar Forests are miles from here—days and days. I don't like it."

"The stones!" Shea exclaimed, and leaped for the traveling cloak which hung in the long corner closet. He rummaged through his clothes for several minutes while Flick watched anxiously, then carefully stepped back with a small leather pouch balanced gently in his right hand. He held it up and tested its weight, displaying it to his brother, and then hurried back to the bed and sat down. A moment later he had the drawstrings open and was emptying the contents of the pouch into his open palm. Three dark blue stones tumbled out, each the size of an average pebble, finely cut and glowing brightly in the faint candlelight. The brothers peered curiously at the stones, half expecting that they would immediately do something wondrous. But nothing happened. They lay motionless in Shea's palm, shimmering like small blue stars snatched from the night, so clear that it was almost possible to see through them, as if they were merely tinted glass. Finally, after Flick had summoned enough courage to touch one, Shea dropped them back into the pouch and stuffed it into his shirt pocket.

"Well, he was right about the stones," ventured Shea a moment later.

"Maybe yes, maybe no—maybe they're not Elfstones," suggested Flick suspiciously. "How do you know—ever see one? What about the rest of the letter? I never heard of anyone named Balinor and I never heard of Culhaven. We ought to forget the whole business—especially that we ever saw Allanon."

Shea nodded doubtfully, unable to answer his brother's questions.

"Why should we worry now? All we have to do is to keep our eyes open for the sign of the Skull, whatever that may be, or for Allanon's friend to appear. Maybe nothing will happen after all."

Flick continued to voice his distrust of the letter and its author for several minutes more before losing interest. Both brothers were weary and decided to call it a night. As the candles were extinguished, Shea's last act was to place the pouch carefully beneath his pillow where he could feel its small bulk pressing against the side of his face. No matter what Flick might think, he had resolved to keep the stones close at hand in the days ahead.

The next day, it began to rain. Huge, towering black clouds rolled in from the north quite suddenly and settled over the entire valley, blotting out all traces of sun and sky as they released torrents of shattering rain which swept through the tiny hamlet with unbelievable ferocity. All work in the fields came to an abrupt halt and travel to and from the valley ceased entirely—first for one, then two, and finally three complete days. The downpour was a tremendous spectacle of blinding streaks of lightning lacing the darkly clouded sky and deeply rolling thunder breaking over the valley with earthshaking blasts that followed one after the other and died into slower, more ominous distant rumblings from somewhere beyond the blackness to the north. For the entire three days it rained, and the Vale people began to grow fearful that flash floods from the hills all about them would wash down with devastating effect on their small homes and unprotected fields. The men gathered daily in the Ohmsford inn and chatted worriedly over their mugs of beer, casting apprehensive glances at the sheets of rain falling steadily beyond the dripping windows. The Ohmsford brothers watched in silence, listening to the conversation and scanning the worried faces of the anxious Valemen huddled together in small groups about the crowded lounge. At first they held out hope that the storm would pass over, but after three days there was still little sign of clearing in the weather.

Near midday on the fourth day, the rain lessened from a steady downpour to a muggy drizzle mixed with heavy fog and a sticky, humid heat that left everyone thoroughly disgruntled and uncomfortable. The crowd at the inn began to thin out as the men left to return to their jobs, and soon Shea and Flick were occupied with repairs and general cleaning chores. The storm had smashed shutters and torn the wooden shingles from the roof, scattering them all about the surrounding premises. Large leaks had developed in the roof and walls of the inn wings, and the small tool shed in the rear of the Ohmsford property had been all but flattened by a falling elm, uprooted by the force of the storm. The young men spent several days patching up leaks, repairing the roof, and replacing lost or broken shingles and shutters. It was tedious work, and time dragged by slowly.

After ten days, the rains ceased altogether, the huge clouds rolled on, and the dark sky cleared and brightened into a friendly light blue streaked with trailing white clouds. The expected floods did not come, and as the Valemen returned to their fields, the warm sun reappeared and the land of the valley began to dry from soggy mud to solid earth, spattered here and there by small puddles of murky water that sat defiantly upon an always thirsty land. Eventually even the puddles disappeared and the valley was as it had been—the fury of the passing storm only a dim memory.

Shea and Flick, in the process of rebuilding the smashed tool shed, their other repair work on the inn complete, heard snatches of conversation from Valemen and inn guests about the heavy rain. No one could ever remember a storm of such ferocity at that particular time of the year in the Vale. It was equivalent to a winter windstorm, the kind that caught unsuspecting travelers in the great mountains to the north and swept them from the passes and the cliff trails, never to be seen again. Its sudden appearance caused everyone in the hamlet to pause and reflect once again on the continuing rumors of strange happenings far to the North.

The brothers paid close attention to such talks, but they learned nothing of interest. Often they spoke quietly together about Allanon and the strange tale he had told them of Shea's heritage. A pragmatic Flick had long since dismissed the whole business as either foolishness or a bad joke. Shea listened tolerantly, though he was less willing than his brother to shrug the matter off. Yet while he was unwilling to dismiss the tale, he was at the same time unable to accept it. He felt there was too much still hidden from him, too much about Allanon that neither Flick nor he knew. Until he had all the facts, he was content to let the matter lie. He kept the pouch containing the Elfstones close to him at all times. While Flick mumbled on, usually several times a day, about his foolishness in carrying the stones and believing that anything Allanon had told them was true, Shea carefully watched all strangers passing through the Vale, eagerly perusing their belongings for any sign of a Skull marking. But as time passed, he observed nothing and eventually felt obliged to scratch the whole matter off as an experience in the fine art of gullibility.

Nothing occurred to change Shea's mind on the matter until one afternoon more than three weeks after Allanon's abrupt departure. The brothers had been out all day cutting shingles for the inn roof, and it was almost evening by the time they returned. Their father was sitting in his favorite seat at the long kitchen counter when they entered, his broad face bent over a steaming plate of food. He greeted his sons with a wave of his hand.

"A letter came for you while you were gone, Shea," he informed them, holding out a long, white folded sheet of paper. "It's marked Leah."

Shea let out an exclamation of surprise and reached eagerly for the letter. Flick groaned audibly.

"I knew it, I knew it; it was too good to be true," he muttered. "The biggest wastrel in the entire Southland has decided it's time we suffered some more. Tear up the letter, Shea."

But Shea had already opened the sealed sheet of paper and was scanning its contents, totally disregarding Flick's comments. The latter shrugged in disgust and collapsed on a stool next to his father, who had returned to his evening meal.

"He wants to know where we've been hiding," laughed Shea. "He wants us to come see him as soon as we can."

"Oh, sure," muttered Flick. "He's probably in trouble and needs someone to blame it on. Why don't we just jump off the nearest cliff? You remember what happened the last time Menion Leah invited us to visit? We were lost in the Black Oaks for days and nearly devoured by wolves! I'll never forget that little adventure. The Shades will get me before I accept another invitation from him!"

His brother laughed and clapped an arm around Flick's broad shoulders.

"You are envious because Menion is the son of kings and able to live any way he chooses."

"A kingdom the size of a puddle," was the quick retort. "And royal blood is cheap stuff these days. Look at your own . . ."

He caught himself and clamped his mouth shut quickly. Both shot hurried glances at their father, but he apparently hadn't heard and was still absorbed in eating. Flick shrugged apologetically, and Shea smiled at his brother encouragingly.

"There's a man in the inn looking for you, Shea," Curzad Ohmsford announced suddenly, looking up at him. "He mentioned that tall stranger that was here several weeks back when he asked for you. Never seen him before in the Vale. He's out in the main lounge now."

Flick stood up slowly, fear gripping at him. Shea was momentarily caught off balance by the message, but motioned hurriedly to his brother, who was about to speak. If this new stranger were an enemy, he had to find out quickly. He clutched at his shirt pocket, reassuring himself that the Elfstones were still there.

"What does the man look like?" he asked quickly, unable to think of any other way of finding out about the Skull mark.

"Can't really say, son," was the muffled reply as his father continued to chew on his dinner, face bent to the plate. "He's wrapped in a long green forest cloak. Just rode in this afternoon—beautiful horse. He was very anxious to find you. Better go see what he wants right away."

"Did you see any markings?" asked the exasperated Flick.

His father stopped chewing and looked up with a puzzled frown.

"What are you talking about? Would you be satisfied if I presented you with a chalk drawing? What's wrong with you anyway?"

"It's nothing, really," interjected Shea quickly. "Flick was just wondering if . . . if the man looked anything like Allanon . . . You remember?"

"Oh, yes," his father smiled knowingly, as Flick suppressed a swallow of relief. "No, I didn't notice any real similarity, though this man is big, too. I did see a long scar running down the right cheek—probably from a knife cut."

Shea nodded his thanks and quickly pulled Flick after him as he moved out to the hallway and started for the main lounge. They hurried to the wide double doors and halted breathlessly. Cautiously, Shea pushed one door open a crack and peered into the crowded lounge area. For a moment he saw nothing but the ordinary faces of the usual customers and average Vale travelers, but a moment later he started back, and let the door swing shut as he faced the anxious Flick.

"He's out there, near the front corner by the fireplace. I can't tell who he is or what he looks like from here; he's wrapped in the green cloak, just as Father said. We've got to get closer."

"Out there?" gasped Flick. "Have you lost your mind? He would spot you in a second if he knows who he's looking for."

"Then you go," Shea ordered firmly. "Make some pretense of putting logs on the fire and get a quick look at him. See if he bears the markings of a Skull."

Flick's eyes went wide, and he turned to escape, but Shea caught his arm and pulled him back, forcibly shoving him through the doors into the lounge and quickly ducking back out of sight. A moment later he opened one door a crack and peeped out to see what was happening. He saw Flick move uncertainly across the room to the fireplace and begin to poke the glowing embers idly, finally adding another log from the woodbox. The Valeman was taking his time, apparently trying to get in a position where he could catch a glimpse of the man wrapped in the green cloak. The stranger was seated at a table several feet away from the fireplace, his back to Flick but turned slightly toward the door behind which Shea had concealed himself.

Suddenly, just as it appeared that Flick was ready to return, the stranger moved slightly in his seat and made a quick comment and Flick went stiff. Shea saw his brother turn toward the stranger and reply, glancing hurriedly toward Shea's place of concealment. Shea slipped back farther into the shadows of the hall and let the door swing shut. Somehow, they had given themselves away. As he pondered whether to flee, Flick abruptly pushed through the double doors, his face white with fear.

"He saw you at the door. The man has the eyes of a hawk! He told me to bring you out."

Shea thought a moment and finally nodded hopelessly. After all, where could they run to that they wouldn't be found in a matter of minutes?

"Maybe he doesn't know everything," he suggested hopefully. "Maybe he thinks we know where Allanon has gone. Be careful what you tell him, Flick."

He led the way through the wide, swinging doors and across the lounge to the table where the stranger sat. They stopped just behind him and waited, but without turning, he beckoned them to seats around the table with a sweep of his hand. They reluctantly obeyed the unspoken command and the three sat in silence for a few moments looking at one another. The stranger was a big man with a broad frame, though he did not have Allanon's height. The cloak covered all of his body, and only his head was visible to them. His features were rugged and strong, pleasant to the eye except for the dark scar that ran from the outside tip of the right eyebrow down across the cheek just above the mouth. The eyes seemed curiously mild to Shea as they studied the young Valemen, a hazel color that hinted at a gentleness beneath the hard exterior. The blond hair was cut short and lay scattered loosely about the broad forehead and around the small ears. As Shea viewed the stranger, he found it hard to believe that this man could be the enemy Allanon had warned might come to the valley. Even Flick seemed relaxed in his presence.

"There is no time for games, Shea," the newcomer spoke suddenly in a mild, but weary voice. "Your caution is well advised, but I am not a bearer of the Skull mark. I am a friend of Allanon. My name is Balinor. My father is Ruhl Buckhannah, the King of Callahorn."

The brothers recognized his name instantly, but Shea was not taking any chances.

"How do I know that you are who you say you are?" he demanded quickly.

The stranger smiled.

"The same way I know you, Shea. By the three Elfstones you carry in your shirt pocket—the Elfstones given you by Allanon."

The Valeman's startled nod was barely perceptible. Only someone sent by the tall historian could have known about the stones. He leaned forward cautiously.

"What has happened to Allanon?"

"I cannot be sure," the big man replied softly. "I have not seen nor heard from him in over two weeks. When I left him, he was traveling to

Paranor. There was rumor of an attack against the Keep; he was afraid for the safety of the Sword. He sent me here to protect you. I would have reached you sooner, but I was delayed by the weather—and by those who sought to follow me to you."

He paused and looked directly at Shea, his hazel eyes suddenly hard as they bored into the young man.

"Allanon revealed to you your true identity and told you of the danger you would someday face. Whether you believed him or not is of no consequence now. The time has come—you must flee the valley immediately."

"Just pick up and leave?" exclaimed the astounded Shea. "I can't do that!"

"You can and you will if you wish to stay alive. The bearers of the Skull suspect you are in the valley. In a day, perhaps two, they will find you and that will be the end if you are still here. You must leave now. Travel quickly and lightly; stick with trails you know and the shelter of the forest when you can. If you are forced to travel in the open, travel only by day when their power is weaker. Allanon has told you where you are to go, but you must trust to your own resourcefulness to get you there."

The astonished Shea stared at the speaker for a moment and then turned to Flick who was speechless at this new turn of events. How could the man expect him just to pack up and run? It was ridiculous.

"I have to leave," the stranger rose suddenly, his great cloak wrapped tightly about his broad frame. "I would take you with me if I could, but I have been followed. Those who seek to destroy you will expect me to give you away eventually. I will serve you better as a decoy; perhaps they will follow me still farther, and I will be able to give you a chance to slip away without being noticed. I will ride south for a while, and then swing back toward Culhaven. We will meet again there. Remember what I said. Do not linger in the Vale—flee now, tonight! Do as Allanon has said and guard the Elfstones with care. They are a powerful weapon."

Shea and Flick rose with him and shook the extended hand, noticing for the first time that the exposed arm was covered with gleaming chain mail. Without further comment, Balinor moved swiftly across the room and disappeared through the front door into the night.

"Well, now what?" Flick asked as he collapsed back into his seat.

"How should I know?" replied Shea wearily. "I'm no fortune-teller. I don't have the vaguest idea if what he told us was the truth any more than what Allanon said! If he is right, and I have an uneasy suspicion that there is at least some truth in what he says, then for the sake of everyone concerned, I've got to get out of the valley. If someone is after me, we cannot be sure that others, like yourself and Father, won't be hurt if I stay."

He gazed despondently across the room, hopelessly entangled by the tales he had been told, unable to decide what his best move would be. Flick watched him silently, knowing he could not help, but sharing his brother's confusion and worry. Finally, he leaned across and put his hand on Shea's shoulder.

"I'm going with you," he announced softly.

Shea looked around at him, plainly startled.

"I can't have you doing that. Father would never understand. Besides, I may not be going anywhere."

"Remember what Allanon said—I'm in this with you," Flick insisted stubbornly. "Besides, you're my brother. I can't let you go alone."

Shea stared at him wonderingly, then nodded and smiled his thanks.

"We'll talk about it later. At any rate, I can't leave until I decide where I am going and what I will need—if I even go. I've got to leave some kind of note for Father—I can't just walk out, despite what Allanon and Balinor think."

They left the table and retired to the kitchen for dinner. The remainder of the evening was spent restlessly wandering about the lounge and kitchen area, with several side trips to the sleeping quarters, where Shea rifled through his personal belongings, absently noting what he owned and setting aside stray items. Flick followed him about silently, unwilling to leave him alone, inwardly afraid that his brother might decide to depart for Culhaven without telling him. He watched Shea push clothing and camping equipment into a leather pack, and when he asked his brother why he was packing, he was told that this was just a precaution in case he did have to flee suddenly. Shea assured him that he would not leave without telling him, but the reassurance did not make Flick any easier in his mind, and he watched Shea all the more closely.

It was pitch-black when Shea was awakened by the hand on his arm. He had been sleeping lightly, and the cold touch woke him instantly, his heart pounding. He struggled wildly, unable to see anything in the darkness, and his free hand reached out to clutch his unseen attacker. A quick hiss reached his ears, and abruptly he recognized Flick's broad features vaguely outlined in the dim light of the cloud-masked stars and a small crescent moon that shone through the curtained window. The fear eased, replaced by sudden relief at the familiar sight of his brother.

"Flick! You scared . . ."

His relief was cut short as Flick's strong hand clamped over his open mouth and the warning hush sounded again. In the gloom, Shea could see deep lines of fear in his brother's face, the pale skin drawn tightly with the cold of the night air. He started up, but the strong arms holding him grasped him tighter and drew his face near tightly clenched lips.

"Don't speak," the whisper sounded in his ears, the voice trembling with terror. "The window—quietly!"

The hands loosened their grip and gently, hastily pulled him from the bed and down along the floor until both brothers were crouched breathlessly on the hard wooden planks deep within the shadows of the room. Then Shea crawled with Flick toward the partly open window, still crouching, not daring even to breathe. When they reached the wall, Flick pulled Shea to one side of the window with hands that were now shaking.

"Shea, by the building—look!"

Frightened beyond description, he raised his head to the windowsill and carefully peered over the wooden frame into the blackness beyond. He saw the creature almost immediately—a huge, terrible black shape, stooped in a half-crouch as it crawled, dragging itself slowly through the shadows of the buildings across from the inn, its humped back covered by a cloak that rose and billowed softly as something beneath pushed and beat against it. The hideous rasping sound of its breathing was plainly audible even from that distance, and its feet emitted a curious scraping sound as it moved across the dark earth. Shea clutched the sill tightly, his eyes locked on the approaching creature, and in the instant before he ducked below the open window, he caught a clear glimpse of a silver pendant fashioned in the shape of a gleaming Skull.

Shea collapsed wordlessly next to the dark form of his brother, and they sat huddled together in the blackness. They could hear the creature moving, the scraping sound growing louder as the seconds passed, and they were certain they had heeded Balinor's warning too late. They waited, not daring to speak, even to breathe as they listened. Shea wanted to run, torn by the knowledge that the thing outside would kill him if it found him now, but afraid that if he moved he would be heard and caught on the spot. Flick sat rigid beside him, shaking in the cool of the blowing night wind that whipped the curtains about the window frame.

Suddenly they heard the sharp bark of a dog sound again and again, then shift to a hoarse growl of mingled fear and hatred. Cautiously, the brothers raised their heads above the windowsill and looked out, squinting in the dim light. The creature bearing the Skull mark was crouched against the wall of the building directly across from their window. Some ten feet away was a huge wolf dog, a hunter for one of the Valemen, its white fangs bared and gleaming as it watched the intruder. The two shapes faced each other in the night shadows, the creature breathing in the same slow, rasping wheeze, and the dog growling low and snapping the air before it, inching forward in a half-crouch. Then, with a snarl of rage, the big wolf dog sprang at the intruder, its jaws open and reaching for the blackened head. But the dog was caught suddenly in midair by a clawlike limb that whipped out from beneath the billowing cloak and jerked at the throat of the hapless animal, smashing him lifeless to the ground. It happened in an instant, and the brothers were so astonished that they almost forgot to duck down again to avoid being seen. A moment later, they heard the strange

scraping sound as the creature began to drag itself along the wall of the adjacent building—but the sound grew fainter and appeared to be moving
away from the inn.

Long moments passed as the brothers waited breathlessly in the shadows of the room, shivering uncontrollably. The night grew quiet around
them, and they strained their ears for some indication of the creature's position. Eventually Shea worked up enough courage to peer once more over
the edge of the windowsill into the darkness beyond. By the time he
ducked down again, the frightened Flick was ready to scramble for the
nearest exit, but a hurried shake of Shea's head assured him that the creature was gone. He hastened back from the window to the warmth of his
bed, but caught himself halfway under the covers as he saw Shea begin to
dress hurriedly in the darkness. He tried to speak, but Shea raised a finger
to his lips. Immediately, Flick began pulling on his own clothes. Whatever
Shea had in mind, wherever he was going, Flick was determined to follow.
When they were both dressed, Shea pulled his brother close and whispered
softly in his ear.

"Everyone in the Vale will be in danger as long as we remain. We must
get out tonight—now! Are you determined to go with me?"

Flick nodded emphatically and Shea continued.

"We'll go to the kitchen and pack some food to take with us—just
enough to get by on for a few days. I'll leave a note for Father there."

Without another word, Shea picked up his small bundle of clothing
from inside the closet and disappeared noiselessly into the pitch-black hallway that led to the kitchen. Flick hurriedly followed, groping his way from
the bedroom behind his brother. It was impossible to see anything in the
hallway, and it took them several minutes to feel their way along the walls
and around the corners to the broad kitchen door. Once inside the kitchen,
Shea lit a candle and motioned Flick over to the foodstuffs while he
scratched out a note for his father on a small sheet of paper and stuck it
under a beer mug. Flick finished his job in a few minutes and came back to
his brother, who quickly extinguished the small candle and moved to the
rear door where he stopped and turned.

"Once we're outside, don't speak at all. Just follow me closely."

Flick nodded doubtfully, more than a little concerned about what
might be waiting for them beyond the closed door—waiting to rip out
their throats as it had the wolf dog's a few minutes before. But there was no
time for hesitation now, and Shea swung open the wooden door carefully
and peered out into a brightly moonlit yard bordered by heavy clumps of
trees. A moment later, he motioned to Flick, and they stepped cautiously
from the building into the cool night air, closing the door carefully behind
them. It was brighter outside the building in the soft light of the moon
and stars, and a quick glance revealed that no one was around. There was
only an hour or two until dawn, when the hamlet would begin to awaken.
The brothers paused next to the building as they listened for any sound
that would warn of danger. Hearing nothing, Shea led the way across the

yard, and they disappeared into the shadows of an adjacent hedgerow, Flick casting a last, wistful glance back at the home he might never see again.

Shea silently picked his way through the buildings of the hamlet. The Valeman knew that the Skull Bearer was uncertain who he was or it would have caught them at the inn. But it was a good bet that the creature suspected he lived within the valley and so had come into the sleeping town of Shady Vale on an exploratory search for the missing half son of the house of Shannara. Shea ran back over the plan of travel he had hastily formed at the inn. If the enemy had discovered where he was, as Balinor had warned, then all the possible escape routes would be watched. Moreover, once they discovered he was missing, they would lose no time in tracking him down. He had to assume that there was more than one of these frightening creatures, and that they were probably watching the whole valley. Flick and he would have to seize the advantage of stealth and secrecy to get out of the valley and the country immediately surrounding it within the next day or so. That meant a forced march with very few hours' sleep. This would be tough enough, but the real problem was where they would flee. They had to have supplies within a few days, and a trip to the Anar would take weeks. The country beyond the Vale was unfamiliar to both brothers, except for a few well-traveled roads and hamlets that the Skull Bearers would certainly be watching. Given their present situation, it would be impossible to do much more than choose a general direction. But which way should they run? Which direction would the prowling creatures least expect them to go?

Shea considered the alternatives carefully, though he had already made up his mind. West of the Vale was open country except for a few villages, and if they went that way, they would be moving away from the Anar. If they traveled south, they would eventually reach the comparative safety of the larger Southland cities of Pia and Zolomach where there were friends and relatives. But this was the logical route for them to take to escape the Skull Bearers, and the creatures would be carefully watching roads south of the Vale. Moreover, the country beyond the Duln forests was broad and open, offering little cover for the fugitives and promising a long journey to the cities, during which they could be easily caught and killed. North of the Vale and beyond the Duln was a broad sweep of land encompassing the Rappahalladran River and the huge Rainbow Lake and miles of wild, unsettled land that led eventually to the kingdom of Callahorn. The Skull Bearers would have passed through it on their journey from the Northland. They would in all likelihood know it far better than the brothers and would be watching it closely if they suspected that Balinor had come to the Vale from Tyrsis.

The Anar lay northeast of the Vale, through miles and miles of the roughest, most treacherous country in all of the vast Southland. This direct route was the most dangerous one, but the one in which the enemy searchers would least expect him to run. It wound through murky forests, treacherous lowlands, hidden swamps, and any number of unknown dangers that claimed the lives of unwary travelers every year. But there was something else that lay east of the Duln forests that even the Skull Bearers could not know about—the safety of the highlands of Leah. There the brothers could seek the aid of Menion Leah, Shea's close friend and, despite Flick's fears, the one person who might be able to show them a way through the dangerous lands that led to the Anar. For Shea, this seemed the only reasonable alternative.

The brothers reached the southeast edge of town and halted breathlessly beside an old woodshed, their backs to the coarse boarding. Shea looked cautiously ahead. He had no idea where the prowling Skull creature might be by this time. Everything was still hazy in the clouded moonglow of the dying night. Somewhere off to their left, several dogs barked furiously, and scattered lights appeared in the windows of nearby houses as sleepy owners peered out curiously into the blackness. Dawn was only a little over an hour away, and Shea knew they would have to chance discovery and run for the lip of the valley and the concealment of the Duln forests. If they were still in the valley when it became light, the creature searching for them would see them climbing the slopes of the open hills, and they would be caught trying to escape.

Shea clapped Flick on the back and nodded, breaking into a slow jog as he moved away from the shelter of the Vale homes into the heavy clumps of trees and brush that dotted the valley floor. The night was silent around them except for the muffled sound of their feet padding on the long grass that was wet with early-morning dew. Leafy branches whipped at them as they ran, slapping their unprotected hands and faces in small, stinging swipes that left the dew clinging to their skin. They ran hurriedly for the gentle, brush-covered eastern slope of the Vale, dodging in and out of the heavy oaks and hickories, bounding over loose nut shells and fallen twigs that were scattered beneath the wide limbs ribbing the deep sky overhead. They reached the slope and scampered up the open grassland as quickly as their legs would carry them, not pausing to look back or even down in the darkness, but only ahead to the ground that rushed by them in sudden bounds and disappeared into the Vale behind. Slipping frequently on the damp grass, they reached the lip of the Vale, where their eyes were greeted with a clear view of the great valley walls to the east, studded with shapeless boulders and sparse shrubbery, looming like a great barrier to the world beyond.

Shea was in excellent physical condition, and his light form flew across the uneven ground, moving agilely among the clumps of brush and small boulders that blocked his path. Flick followed doggedly, the stout muscles of his legs working tirelessly to keep his heavier frame even with the fleet figure ahead. Only once did he risk a quick glance back, and his eyes recorded only a blurred image of mingled treetops that rose above the now hidden town and were outlined in the glow of the fading night stars and clouded moon. He watched Shea run ahead of him, bounding lightly over small rises and scattered rocks, apparently intent on reaching the small wooded area near the base of the eastern slope of the valley about a mile ahead. Flick's legs were beginning to tire, but his fear of the creature somewhere behind them kept him from lagging. He wondered what would happen to them now, fugitives from the only home they had known, pursued by an incredibly vicious enemy that would snuff out their lives like a small candle's flame if they were caught. Where could they go that they wouldn't be found? For the first time since Allanon had departed, Flick wished fervently that the mysterious wanderer would reappear.

The minutes passed quickly and the small woods ahead grew closer as the brothers ran on wearily, silently through the chill night. No sound reached their ears; nothing moved in the land ahead. It was as if they were the only living creatures in a vast arena, alone except for the watchful stars winking solemnly overhead in quiet contentment. The sky was growing lighter as the night came to a wistful close, and the vast audience above slowly disappeared one by one into the morning light. The brothers ran on, oblivious to everything but the need to run faster—to escape being caught in the revealing light of a sunrise only minutes away.

When the runners finally reached the wooded area, they collapsed breathlessly on the twig-covered ground beneath a stand of tall hickories, their ears and hearts pounding wildly from the strain of running. They lay motionless for several minutes, breathing heavily in the stillness. Then Shea dragged himself to his feet and looked back in the direction of the Vale. Nothing was moving either on the ground or in the air, and it appeared the brothers had gotten this far without being spotted. But they were still not out of the valley. Shea reached over and forcibly dragged Flick to his feet, pulling him along as he moved through the trees and began to ascend the steep valley slope. Flick followed wordlessly, no longer even thinking, but concentrating his ebbing willpower on putting one foot before the other.

The eastern slope was rugged and treacherous, its surface a mass of boulders, fallen trees, prickly shrubbery, and uneven ground that made the climb a long and difficult one. Shea set the pace, moving over the large obstacles as fast as he could, while Flick followed in his footsteps. The young men scrambled and clawed their way up the slope. The sky began to grow lighter and the stars disappeared altogether. Ahead of them, above the lip of the valley, the sun was sending its first faint glow into the night sky with tinges of orange and yellow that reflected vaguely the outline of the distant horizon. Shea was beginning to tire, his breath coming in short gulps, as he stumbled on. Behind him, Flick forced himself to crawl, dragging his exhausted body after his lighter brother, his hands and forearms scratched and cut by the sharp brush and rocks. The climb seemed endless. They moved at a snail's pace over the rugged terrain, the fear of discovery alone forcing their tired legs to continue moving. If they were caught here, in the open, after all this effort . . .

Suddenly, as they reached the three-quarter mark of their climb, Flick cried out sharply in warning and fell gasping against the slope. Shea whirled around fearfully, his eyes instantly catching sight of the huge black object that rose slowly from the distant Vale—climbing like a great bird into the dimness of the morning sunrise in widening spirals. The Valeman dropped flat amid the rocks and brush, motioning his fallen brother to crawl quickly from sight and praying the creature had not seen them. They lay unmoving on the mountainside as the awesome Bearer of the Skull rose higher, its circle of flight growing wider, its path carrying it closer to where the brothers lay. A sudden chilling cry burst from the creature, draining from the two young men the last faint hope that they might escape. They were gripped by the same unexplainable feeling of horror that had immobilized Flick, hidden in the brush with Allanon beneath the huge black shadow. Only this time there was no place to hide. Their terror grew rapidly into the beginning stages of hysteria as the creature soared directly toward them, and in that fleeting moment they knew they were going to die. But in the next instant, the black hunter wheeled in flight and glided north in an unaltering line, receding steadily into the horizon until it was lost from their sight.

The Valemen lay petrified, buried in the scant brush and loose rock for endless minutes, afraid the creature would come winging back to destroy them the minute they tried to move. But when the terrible, unreasoning fear had ebbed away, they climbed shakenly to their feet and in exhausted silence resumed the weary climb to the summit of the valley. It was a short distance to the lip of the rugged slope, and they hurried across the small, open field beyond to the concealment of the Duln forest. Within minutes they were lost in the great trees, and the rising morning sun in its first glow found the land that stretched back to the Vale country silent and empty.

The young men slowed their pace as they entered the Duln, and finally Flick, who still had no idea where they were going, called ahead to Shea.

"Why are we going this way?" he demanded. His own voice sounded strange after the long silence. "Where are we going anyway?"

"Where Allanon told us—to the Anar. Our best chance is to go the way the Skull Bearers least expect us to take. So we'll go east to the Black Oaks and from there travel northward and hope we can find help along the way."

"Wait a minute!" exclaimed Flick in sudden understanding. "What you mean is we're going east through Leah and hope Menion can help us. Are you completely out of your mind? Why don't we just give ourselves up to that creature? It would be quicker that way!"

Shea threw up his hands and turned wearily to face his brother.

"We do not have any other choice! Menion Leah is the only one we can turn to for help. He's familiar with the country beyond Leah. He may know a way through the Black Oaks."

"Oh, sure," nodded Flick gloomily. "Are you forgetting that he got us lost there last time? I wouldn't trust him any farther than I could throw him, and I doubt I can even lift him!"

"We have no choice," repeated Shea. "You didn't have to come on this trip, you know."

He trailed off suddenly and turned away.

"Sorry I lost my temper. But we have to do this thing my way, Flick."

He started walking again in dejected silence, and Flick followed glumly, shaking his head in disapproval. The whole idea of running away was a bad one to begin with, even though they knew that monstrous creature was prowling the valley. But the idea of going to Menion Leah was worse still. That cocky idler would lead them right into a trap if he didn't get them lost first. Menion was only interested in Menion, the great adventurer, off on another wild expedition. The whole idea of asking him for help was ridiculous.

Flick was admittedly biased. He disapproved of Menion Leah and everything he represented—he had done so from the time they met five years earlier. The only son of a family that for centuries had governed the little highland kingdom, Menion had spent his entire life involving himself in one wild escapade after another. He had never worked for a living and, as far as Flick could tell, he had never done anything worthwhile. He spent most of his time hunting or fighting, pursuits that hardworking Valemen would consider idle recreation. His attitude was equally disturbing. Nothing about his life, his family, his homeland, or his country seemed to be of very great importance to him. The highlander seemed to float through life very much the same as a cloud in an empty sky, touching nothing, leaving no trace of his passing. It was this careless approach to life that had nearly got them killed a year ago in the Black Oaks. Yet Shea was drawn to him; and in his flippant way, the highlander seemed to respond with genuine affection. But Flick had never been convinced that it was a friendship he could depend upon, and now his brother proposed to entrust their lives to the care of a man who did not know the first thing about responsibility.

He mulled the situation over in his mind, wondering what could be done to prevent the inevitable. Finally he concluded that his best chance would be to watch Menion carefully and warn Shea as tactfully as possible when he suspected they were doing the wrong thing. If he alienated his brother now, he would have no chance later of contradicting the bad advice of the Prince of Leah.

It was late afternoon when the travelers finally reached the banks of the great Rappahalladran. Shea led the way down the riverbank for about a mile until they reached a place where the far bank cut toward them and the channel began to narrow considerably. Here they stopped and gazed across at the forests beyond. The sun would be down in another hour or so, and Shea did not want to be caught on the near bank that night. He would feel safer with the water between him and any pursuers. He explained to Flick, who agreed, and they set about making a small raft, using their hand axes and hunting knives. The raft was necessarily a small one, its only purpose to carry their packs and clothing. There was no time to construct a raft large enough to carry them, and they would have to swim the river, towing their belongings. They completed the job in short order and, stripping off their packs and clothes, tied them down in the middle of the raft and slipped into the chilling waters of the Rappahalladran. The current was swift, but not dangerous at this time of the year, the spring thaws having already passed. The only problem was finding a suitable landing place along the high banks of the other shore after their swim was over. As it happened, the current swept them along for almost half a mile as they struggled to tow the cumbersome raft, and when the crossing had finally been completed, they found they were close to a narrow inlet in the far bank that offered an easy landing. They scrambled out of the cold water, shivering in the early evening air, and after dragging the raft out after them, quickly dried off and dressed again. The entire operation had taken a little over an hour, and the sun was now lost from sight beneath the tall trees, leaving only a dull reddish glow to light the afternoon sky in the minutes that remained before darkness.

The brothers were not ready to quit for the day, but Shea suggested they sleep for several hours to regain their strength and then resume their journey during the night to avoid any chance of being seen. The sheltered inlet seemed safe, so they curled up in their blankets beneath a great elm and were quickly asleep. It was not until midnight that Shea woke Flick with a light shake, and they quickly packed their gear and prepared to resume their hike through the Duln. At one point, Shea thought he heard something prowling about on the far shore and hurriedly warned Flick. They listened in silence for long minutes, but could detect nothing moving in the blackness of the massive trees and finally concluded that Shea must have been mistaken. Flick was quick to point out that nothing could be heard anyway above the sound of the surging river, and the Skull creature was probably still looking for them in the Vale. His confidence had been bolstered considerably by the mistaken belief that they had momentarily outsmarted any pursuers.

They walked until sunrise, trying to move in an easterly direction, but unable to see much from their low vantage point. Any clear view of the stars was masked by a confusing network of heavy branches and rustling leaves interlocked above them. When they finally stopped, they were still not clear of the Duln, and had no idea how much farther they had to walk before reaching the borders of Leah. Shea was relieved at the appearance of the sun rising directly before them; they were still heading in the right direction. Finding a clearing nestled in a cluster of great elms sheltered on three sides by thick brush, the young men tossed down their packs and quickly fell asleep, totally exhausted from the strenuous flight. It was late afternoon before they awoke and began preparations for the night walk. Unwilling to start a fire that might attract attention, they contented themselves with munching on dried beef and raw vegetables, completing the meal with some fruit and a little water. As they ate, Flick again brought up the question of their destination.

"Shea," he began cautiously, "I don't want to dwell on the matter, but are you sure this is the best way to go? I mean, even if Menion wants to help, we could easily get lost in the swamps and hills that lie beyond the Black Oaks and never get out."

Shea nodded slowly and then shrugged.

"It's that or go farther north where there is less cover and the country would be unfamiliar even to Menion. Do you think we have a better choice?"

"I suppose not," Flick responded unhappily. "But I keep thinking about what Allanon told us—you remember, about not telling anyone and being careful about trusting anyone. He was very definite about that."

"Let's not start that again," Shea flared up. "Allanon isn't here and the decision is mine. I don't see how we can hope to reach the Anar Forests without the help of Menion. Besides, he's always been a good friend, and he's one of the finest swordsmen I have ever seen. We'll need his experience if we're forced to stand and fight."

"Which we are certain to have to do with him along," Flick finished pointedly. "Besides, what chance do we have against something like that Skull creature? Why, it would tear us to bits!"

"Don't be so gloomy," Shea laughed, "we aren't dead yet. Don't forget—we have the protection of the Elfstones."

Flick was not particularly convinced by this argument, but felt that the whole matter was best left alone for the present. He had to admit that Menion Leah would be a good man to have around in a fight, but at the same time he was not sure whose side the unpredictable fellow would decide to take. Shea trusted Menion because of the instinctive liking he had developed for the flashy adventurer during trips to Leah with his father over the past few years. But Flick did not feel that his brother was entirely rational in his analysis of the Prince of Leah. Leah was one of the few remaining monarchies in the Southland, and Shea was an outspoken advocate of decentralized government, an opponent of absolute power. Nevertheless, he claimed friendship with the heir to a monarch's throne—facts which in Flick's opinion seemed entirely inconsistent. Either you believed in something or you didn't—you couldn't have it both ways and be honest with yourself.

The meal was finished in silence as the first shadows of evening began to appear. The sun had long since disappeared from view and its soft golden rays had changed slowly to a deep red mingling with the green boughs of the giant trees. The brothers quickly packed their few belongings and began the slow, steady march eastward, their backs to the fading daylight. The woods were unusually still, even for early evening, and the wary Valemen walked in uneasy silence through the shrouded gloom of the forest night, the moon a distant beacon that appeared only at brief intervals through the dark boughs overhead. Flick was particularly disturbed by the unnatural silence of the Duln, a silence strange to this huge forest—but uncomfortably familiar to the stocky Valeman. Occasionally, they would pause in the darkness, listening to the deep stillness; then, hearing nothing, they would quickly resume the tiring march, searching for a break in the forest ahead that would open onto the highlands beyond. Flick hated the oppressive silence and once began whistling softly to himself, but was quickly stilled by a warning motion from Shea.

Sometime during the early hours of the morning, the brothers reached the edge of the Duln and broke through into the shrub-covered grasslands that stretched beyond for miles to the highlands of Leah. The morning sun was still several hours away, so the travelers continued their journey eastward. Both felt immensely relieved to be free of the Duln, away from the stifling closeness of its monstrous trees and from the unpleasant silence. They may have been safer within the concealing shadows of the forest, but they felt considerably better equipped to deal with any danger that threatened them on the open grasslands. They even began to speak again in low voices as they walked. About an hour before daybreak, they reached a small, brush-covered vale where they stopped to eat and rest. They were already able to see the dimly lighted highlands of Leah to the east, a journey of yet another day. Shea estimated that if they started walking again at sundown they could easily reach their destination before another sunrise. Then everything would depend on Menion Leah. With this unspoken thought in mind, he quickly fell asleep.

Only minutes passed and they were awake again. It was not something moving that caused them to rise in sudden apprehension, but a deathly quiet that settled ominously over the grasslands. Immediately they sensed the unmistakable presence of another being. The feeling struck them at the same instant and both came to their feet with a start, without a word, their drawn daggers gleaming in the faint light as they looked cautiously about their small cover. Nothing moved. Shea motioned his brother to follow as he crawled up the shrub-covered slope of the little vale to where they could view the land beyond. They lay motionless in the brush, peering into the early-morning gloom, eyes straining to detect what lurked beyond. They did not question the fact that something was out there. There was no need—both had known the feeling before the window of their bedroom. Now they waited, scarcely daring to breathe, wondering if the creature had found them at last, praying they had been careful enough to conceal their movements. It seemed impossible that they could be found now after their hard struggle to escape, wrong that death should come when the safety of Leah was only a few hours away.

Then with a sudden rush of wind and leaves, the black shape of the Skull Bearer rose soundlessly from a long line of scrub trees far to their left. Its dim bulk seemed to rise and hang heavily above the earth for several long moments, as if unable to move, silhouetted against the faint light of an approaching dawn. The brothers lay flat against the edge of the rise, as silent as the brush about them, waiting for the creature to move. How it had tracked them this far—if indeed it had—they could only guess. Perhaps it was only blind luck that had brought them all together in this single, empty piece of grassland, but the fact remained that the Valemen were hunted creatures and their death had become a very real possibility. The creature hung motionless against the sky a moment longer, then slowly, sluggishly, the great wings reaching outward, it began to move toward their place of concealment. Flick gave an audible gasp of dismay and sank farther back into the surrounding brush, his face ashen in the gray light, his

hand gripping Shea's slim arm. But before reaching them, while still several hundred feet away, the creature dropped into a small grove of trees and
was momentarily lost from sight. The brothers peered desperately in the
hazy light, unable to see their pursuer.

"Now," Shea's determined voice whispered urgently in his brother's
ear, "while the creature can't see us. Make for that line of brush ahead!"

Flick did not need to be told twice. Once the black monster finished
with the trees that now occupied its attention, the next stop would be their
hiding place. The Valeman scampered fearfully from his place of concealment, half running, half crawling along the wet morning grass, his tou-
seled head jerking in quick glimpses over his shoulder, expecting the Skull
Bearer to rise any moment from the grove and spy him. Behind him ran
Shea, his lithe body bent close to the ground as he darted across the open
grassland, zigzagging his way silently behind his brother's stocky figure.
They reached the brush without mishap, and then Shea remembered they
had forgotten their packs—the packs that now lay at the bottom of the
vale they had just left. The creature could not miss seeing them and, when
it did, the chase would be over and there would be no more guessing
which way they had gone. Shea felt his stomach sink. How could they
have been so stupid? He grabbed Flick's shoulder in desperation, but his
brother had also realized their error and slumped heavily to the ground.
Shea knew he had to go back for the telltale packs, even if he were seen—
there was no other choice. But even as he rose hesitantly, the black shape
of the hunter appeared, hanging motionless in the brightening sky. The
chance was gone.

Once again they were saved by the coming of dawn. As the Skull
Bearer poised silently above the grasslands, the golden rim of the morning
sun broke from its resting place in the eastern hills and sent its first emissaries of the approaching day shooting forth to light the land and sky in
their warm glow. The sunlight broke over the dark bulk of the night creature, and seeing that its time was gone, it rose abruptly into the sky, wheeling about the land in great, widening circles. It screamed its deathlike cry
with chilling hatred, freezing for one quick moment all the gentle sounds
of morning; then turning north, it flew swiftly from sight. A moment later
it was gone, and two grateful, unbelieving Valemen were left staring mutely
into the distant, empty morning sky.

5

By late afternoon of that same day, the Valemen had reached the highland city of Leah. The stone-and-mortar walls that bounded the city
were a welcome haven to the weary travelers, even though the bright

afternoon sun made their hot, dull-gray mass appear as unfriendly as low-heated iron. The very size and bulk of the walls were repugnant to the Valemen, who preferred the freedom of the more pregnable forest lands surrounding their own home, but exhaustion quickly pushed any dislikes aside and they passed without hesitating through the west gates and into the narrow streets of the city. It was a busy hour, with people pushing and shoving their way past the small shops and markets that lined the entryway to the walled city and ran inward toward Menion's home, a stately old mansion screened by trees and hedges that bordered carefully manicured lawns and fragrant gardens. Leah appeared to be a great metropolis to the men of Shady Vale, though it was in fact comparatively small when one considered the size of the great cities of the deep Southland or even the border city of Tyrsis. Leah was a city set apart from the rest of the world, and travelers passed through its gates only infrequently. It was self-contained, existing primarily to serve the needs of its own people. The monarchy that governed the land was the oldest in the Southland. It was the only law that its subjects knew—perhaps the only one they needed. Shea had never been convinced of this, though the highland people for the most part were content with the government and the way of life it provided.

As the Valemen maneuvered their way through the crowds, Shea found himself reflecting on his improbable friendship with Menion Leah. It would have to be termed improbable, he mused, because on the surface they seemed to have so little in common. Valeman and highlander, with backgrounds so completely dissimilar as to defy any meaningful comparison. Shea, the adopted son of an innkeeper, hardheaded, pragmatic, and raised in the tradition of the workingman. Menion, the only son of the royal house of Leah and heir to the throne, born into a life filled with responsibilities he pointedly ignored, possessed of a brash self-confidence that he tried to conceal with only moderate success, and blessed with an uncanny hunter's instinct that merited grudging respect even from so severe a critic as Flick. Their political philosophies were as unlike as their backgrounds. Shea was staunchly conservative, an advocate of the old ways, while Menion was convinced that the old ways had proved ineffective in dealing with the problems of the races.

Yet for all their differences, they had formed a friendship that evidenced mutual respect. Menion found his small friend to be anachronistic in his thinking at times, but he admired his conviction and determination. The Valeman, contrary to Flick's oft-expressed opinion, was not blinded to Menion's shortcomings, but he saw in the Prince of Leah something others were inclined to overlook—a strong, compelling sense of right and wrong.

At the present time, Menion Leah was pursuing life without any particular concern for the future. He traveled a good deal, he hunted the highland forests, but for the most part he seemed to spend his time finding new ways to get into trouble. His hard-earned expertise with the long bow and as a tracker achieved no useful purpose. On the contrary, it merely served to aggravate his father, who had repeatedly but unsuccessfully attempted to interest his son and only heir in the problems of governing his kingdom. One day, Menion would be a king, but Shea doubted that his lighthearted friend ever gave the possibility more than a passing thought. This was foolish, if somewhat expected. Menion's mother had died several years ago, shortly after Shea had first visited the highlands. Menion's father was not an old man, but the death of a king did not always come with age, and many former rulers of Leah had died suddenly and unexpectedly. If something unforeseen should befall his father, Menion would become king whether he was prepared or not. There would be some lessons learned then, Shea thought and smiled in spite of himself.

The Leah ancestral home was a wide, two-story stone building nestled peacefully amid a cluster of spreading hickories and small gardens. The grounds were screened away from the surrounding city by high shrubbery. A broad park lay directly across from a small walkway fronting the home, and as the Valemen crossed wearily to the front gates, children splashed playfully through a small pond at the hub of the park's several paths. The day was still warm, and people hurried past the travelers on their way to meet friends or to reach their homes and families. In the west, the late-afternoon sky was deepening into a soft golden haze.

The tall iron gates were ajar, and the Valemen walked quickly toward the front door of the home, winding through the long stone walkway's high shrubbery and garden borders. They were still approaching the stone threshold at the front of the home, when the heavy oak door opened from within, and there, unexpectedly, was Menion Leah. Dressed in a multicolored cloak and vest of green and pale yellow, his lean, whiplike frame moved with the graceful ease of a cat. He was not a big man, though several inches taller than the Valemen, but he was broad through the shoulders and his long arms gave him a rangy look. He was on his way down a side path, but when he caught sight of the two ragged, dusty figures approaching along the main walk, he stopped short. A moment later his eyes went wide with surprise.

"Shea!" he exclaimed sharply. "What in the name of all . . . what happened to you?"

He rushed over quickly to his friend and gripped the slim hand warmly.

"Good to see you, Menion," Shea said with a smile.

The highlander stepped back a pace, and his gray eyes studied them shrewdly.

"I never expected that my letter would get results this quickly. . . ." He trailed off and studied the other's weary face. "It hasn't, has it? But don't tell me—I don't want to hear it. I'd rather assume for the sake of our friendship that you came just to visit me. And brought distrustful old Flick, too, I see. This is a surprise."

He grinned quickly past Shea at the scowling Flick, who nodded curtly.

"This wasn't my idea, you may be sure."

"I wish that our friendship alone were the reason for this visit." Shea sighed heavily. "I wish I didn't have to involve you in any of this, but I'm afraid that we're in serious trouble and you are the one person who might be able to help us."

Menion started to smile, then changed his mind quickly as he caught the mood reflected in the other's drawn face and nodded soberly.

"Nothing funny about this, is there? Well, a hot bath and some dinner are the first order of business. We can discuss what brought you here later. Come on in. My father's engaged on the border, but I'm at your disposal."

Once inside, Menion directed the servants to take charge of the Valemen, and they were led off to a welcome bath and a change of clothes. An hour later, the three friends gathered in the great hall for a dinner that would ordinarily have fed twice their number, but on this night barely satisfied them. As they ate, Shea related to Menion the strange tale behind their flight from Shady Vale. He described Flick's meeting with the mysterious wanderer Allanon and the involved story behind the Sword of Shannara. It was necessary, despite Allanon's order of secrecy, if he must ask Menion's help. He told of the coming of Balinor with his terse warning, of their narrow escape from the black Skull creature, and finally of their flight to the highlands. Shea did all the talking. Flick was unwilling to enter into the conversation, resisting the temptation he felt to elaborate on his own part in the events of the past few weeks. He chose to keep quiet because he was determined not to trust Menion. He was convinced that it would be better for the Valemen if at least one of them kept his guard up and his mouth closed.

Menion Leah listened quietly to the long tale, evincing no visible surprise until the part about Shea's background, with which he appeared immeasurably pleased. His lean brown face remained for the most part an inscrutable mask, broken only by that perpetual half smile and the small wrinkles at the corners of the sharp gray eyes. He recognized quickly enough why the Valemen had come to him. They could never expect to make it from Leah through the lowlands of Clete and from there through the Black Oaks without assistance from someone who knew the country— someone they could trust. Correction, Menion thought, smiling inwardly— someone Shea could trust. He knew that Flick would never have agreed to come to Leah unless his brother had insisted. There had never been much of a friendship between Flick and himself. Still, they were both here, both willing to seek his help, whatever the reason, and he would never be able to refuse anything to Shea, even where there was risk to his own life.

Shea finished his story and waited patiently for Menion's response. The highlander seemed lost in thought, his eyes fixed on the half-filled glass of wine at his elbow. When he spoke, his voice was distant.

"The Sword of Shannara. I haven't heard that story in years—never really believed it was true. Now out of complete obscurity it reappears with my old friend Shea Ohmsford as the heir apparent. Or are you?" His eyes snapped up suddenly. "You could be a red herring, a decoy for these

Northland creatures to chase and destroy. How can we be sure about Allanon? From the tale you've told me, he seems almost as dangerous as the things hunting you—perhaps even one of them."

Flick started noticeably at this suggestion, but Shea shook his head firmly.

"I can't bring myself to believe that. It doesn't make any sense."

"Maybe not," continued Menion slowly, inwardly musing over the prospect. "Could be I'm getting old and suspicious. Frankly, this whole story is pretty improbable. If it's true, you are fortunate to have gotten this far on your own. There are a great many tales of the Northland, of the evil that dwells in the wilderness above the Streleheim Plains—power, they say, beyond the understanding of any mortal being. . . ."

He trailed off for a moment, then sipped gingerly at his wine.

"The Sword of Shannara . . . just the possibility that the legend might be true is enough to . . ." He shook his head and grinned openly. "How can I deny myself the chance to find out? You'll need a guide to get you to the Anar, and I'm your man."

"I knew you would be." Shea reached over and gripped his hand in thanks. Flick groaned softly, but managed a feeble smile.

"Now then, let's see where we stand." Menion took charge quickly, and Flick went back to drinking wine. "What about these Elfstones? Let's have a look at them."

Shea quickly produced the small leather pouch and emptied the contents into his open palm. The three stones sparkled brightly in the torchlight, their blue glow deep and rich. Menion touched one gently and then picked it up.

"They are indeed beautiful," he acknowledged approvingly. "I don't know when I've seen their like. But how can they help us?"

"I don't know that yet," admitted the Valeman reluctantly. "I only know what Allanon told us—that the stones were only to be used in emergencies, and that they were very powerful."

"Well, I hope that he was right," snorted the other. "I would hate to discover the hard way that he was mistaken. But I suppose we'll have to live with that possibility."

He paused for a moment and watched as Shea placed the stones back in the pouch and tucked the leather container into his tunic front. When the Valeman looked up again, he was staring blankly into his wineglass.

"I do know something of the man called Balinor, Shea. He is a fine soldier—I doubt we could find his equal in the whole of the Southland. We might be better off to seek the aid of his father. You would be better protected by the soldiers of Callahorn than by the forest-dwelling Dwarfs of the Anar. I know the roads to Tyrsis, all of them safe. But almost any path to the Anar will run directly through the Black Oaks—not the safest place in the Southland, as you know."

"Allanon told us to go to the Anar," persisted Shea. "He must have had a reason, and until I find him again, I'm not taking any chances. Besides, Balinor himself advised us to follow his instructions."

Menion shrugged.

"That's unfortunate, because even if we manage to get through the Black Oaks, I really don't know much about the land beyond. I'm told that it's relatively unsettled country all the way to the Anar Forests. The inhabitants are mostly Southlanders and Dwarfs, who should not prove dangerous to us. Culhaven is a small Dwarf village on the Silver River in the lower Anar—I don't think we'll have much trouble finding it, if we get that far. First, we have to navigate the Lowlands of Clete, which will be especially bad with the spring thaws, and then the Black Oaks. That will be the most dangerous part of the trip."

"Can't we find a way around . . . ?" Shea asked hopefully.

Menion poured himself another glass of wine and passed the decanter to Flick who accepted it without blinking.

"It would take weeks. North of Leah is the Rainbow Lake. If we go that way, we have to circle the entire lake to the north through the Runne Mountains. The Black Oaks stretch south from the lake for a hundred miles. If we try to go south and come north again on the other side, it will take us at least two weeks—and that's open country all the way. No cover at all. We have to go east through the lowlands, then cut through the oaks."

Flick frowned, recalling how on their last visit to Leah, Menion had succeeded in losing them for several days in the dreaded forest, where they were menaced by wolves and ravaged by hunger. They had barely escaped with their lives.

"Old Flick remembers the Black Oaks," laughed Menion as he caught the other's dark expression. "Well, Flick, this time we shall be better prepared. It's treacherous country, but no one knows it better than I do. And we aren't likely to be followed there. Still, we'll tell no one where we're going. Simply say that we are off for an extended hunting trip. My father has his own problems anyway—he won't even miss me. He's used to having me gone, even for weeks at a time."

He paused for a moment and looked to Shea to see if he had forgotten anything. The Valeman grinned at the highlander's undisguised enthusiasm.

"Menion, I knew we could count on you. It will be good to have you along."

Flick looked openly disgusted; and Menion, catching the look, could not allow the opportunity for a little fun at the other's expense to pass.

"I think we ought to talk for a minute about what's in this for me," he declared suddenly. "I mean, what do I get out of all this if I do guide you safely to Culhaven?"

"What do you get?" exclaimed Flick without thinking. "Why should you . . ."

"It's all right," the other interrupted quickly. "I had forgotten you, old Flick, but you don't need to worry; I don't intend to take anything from your share."

"What are you talking about, sly one?" raged Flick. "I did not mean ever to take anything . . ."

"That's enough!" Shea leaned forward, his face flushed. "This cannot continue if we are to travel together. Menion, you must cease your attempts to bait my brother into anger; and you, Flick, must put aside, once and for all, your pointless suspicions of Menion. We must have some faith in one another—and we must be friends!"

Menion looked down sheepishly, and Flick was biting his lip in disgust. Shea sat back quietly as the anger drained out of him.

"Well spoken," acknowledged Menion after a moment. "Flick, here is my hand on it. Let us make a temporary truce, at least—for Shea."

Flick looked at the extended hand and then slowly accepted it.

"Words come easily for you, Menion. I hope you mean them this time."

The highlander accepted the rebuke with a smile.

"A truce, Flick."

He released the Valeman's hand and drained his wineglass. He knew he had convinced Flick of nothing.

It was growing late now, and all three were eager to complete their plans and retire for the night. They quickly decided that they would leave early the following morning. Menion arranged to have them outfitted with light camping gear, including backpacks, hunting cloaks, provisions, and weapons. He produced a map of the country east of Leah, but it was poorly detailed because the lands were so little known. The Lowlands of Clete, which spread from the highlands eastward to the Black Oaks, was a dismal, treacherous moor—yet on the map, it was no more than a blank white area with the name written in. The Black Oaks stood out prominently, a dense mass of forest land running from the Rainbow Lake southward, standing like a great wall between Leah and the Anar. Menion discussed briefly with the Valemen his knowledge of the terrain and weather conditions at this time of the year. But like the map, his information was sketchy. Most of what the travelers would find could not be accurately anticipated, and the unexpected could be most dangerous.

By midnight, the three were in bed, their preparations for the journey to the Anar complete. In the room he was sharing with Flick, Shea lay back wearily in the softness of the bedding and studied for a moment the darkness beyond his open window. The night had clouded over, the sky a mass of heavy, rolling blackness that settled ominously about the misty highlands. Gone was the heat of the day, blown east by the cooling night breezes, and throughout the sleeping city there was a peaceful solitude. In the bed next to him, Flick was already asleep, his breathing heavy and regular. Shea watched him thoughtfully. His own head was heavy and his body weary from the struggle to reach Leah, yet he remained awake. He was beginning to realize for the first time the truth about his predicament. The flight to reach Menion was only the first step in a journey that might very possibly go on for years. Even if they managed to reach the Anar safely, Shea knew that eventually they would be forced to run again. The search to find them would continue until the Warlock Lord was destroyed—or Shea was dead. Until then, there would be no going back to the Vale, to the home and father he had left, and wherever they were, their safety would last only until the winged hunters found them once again.

The truth was terrifying. In the silent darkness, Shea Ohmsford was alone with his fear, and deep within himself, he fought back against a rising knot of terror. He took a long time finally to fall asleep.

It was a dull, sunless day that followed, a day damp and chilling to human flesh and bone. Shea and his two companions found it devoid of any warmth and comfort as they journeyed eastward through the misty highlands of Leah and began a slow descent toward the cheerless climate of the lowlands beyond. There was no talking among them as they hiked in single file down the narrow footpaths which wound tediously about gray, hulking boulders and clumps of dying, formless brush. Menion led, his keen eyes carefully picking out the often obscure traces of a trail, his stride long and relaxed as he moved almost gracefully over the gradually roughening terrain. Across his lean back he carried a small pack to which he had attached a great ash bow and arrows. In addition, beneath the pack and fastened to his body by a long leather strap was the ancient sword which his father had given him when he had reached the age of manhood—the sword which was the birthright of the Prince of Leah. Its cold, gray iron glimmered faintly in the dim light; and Shea, who followed several paces back, found himself wondering if it was at all like the fabled Sword of Shannara. His Elven eyebrows lifted quizzically as he tried to peer into the endless gloom of the land ahead. Nothing seemed alive. It was a dead land for dead things, and the living were trespassers here. Not a very stimulating idea; he grinned faintly to himself as he forced his mind to turn to other matters. Flick brought up the rear, his sturdy back bearing the bulk of the provisions that would have to sustain them until they were through the Lowlands of Clete and the forbidding Black Oaks. Once they had gotten that far—if they got that far—they would be forced to buy or trade for food from the few scattered inhabitants of the country beyond, or as a last resort, seek nourishment from the land itself, a prospect that Flick did not particularly relish. Although he felt somewhat more secure in his mind now that Menion was genuinely interested in helping them on this journey, he was nevertheless still unconvinced of the highlander's ability to do so. The events of their last trip were still fresh in his mind, and he wanted no part of another hair-raising experience like that one.

The first day wore on quickly as the three traveled past the boundaries of the kingdom of Leah and by nightfall had reached the fringes of the dismal Lowlands of Clete. They found shelter for the night in a small vale under the negligible protection of a few scruffy trees and some heavy brush. The dampness of the mist had soaked their clothing completely through, and the chill of the descending night left them shivering with cold. A brief attempt was made to start a fire in an effort to gain some small warmth and dryness, but the wood in the area was so thoroughly saturated with moisture that it was impossible to get it to burn. Eventually, they gave up on the fire and settled for some cold rations while wrapped in blankets which had carefully been waterproofed at the start of the journey. Little was said because no one felt much like talking beyond mumbling curses upon the general weather conditions. There was no sound from the darkness beyond where they sat huddled within the brush; it was a penetrating stillness that prodded the mind with sudden, unexpected apprehension, forcing it to listen in a frightened effort to catch some faint, reassuring rustle of life. But there was only the silence and the blackness, and not even the wisp of a brief wind touched their chilled faces as they lay quietly in the blankets. Eventually the weariness of the day's march stole over them, and one by one they dropped uneasily off to sleep.

The second and third day were unimaginably worse than the first. It rained the entire time—a slow, chilling drizzle that soaked first the clothing, then penetrated into the skin and bone, and finally reached the very nerve centers, so that the only feeling the weary body would permit was one of thorough, discomforting wetness. The air was damp and cold in the day, dropping off to a near freeze at night. Everything around the three travelers seemed totally beaten down by this lingering coldness; what little brush and small foliage could be seen was twisted and dying, formless clumps of wood and withered leaves that silently waited to crumble and disappear altogether. No human or animal lived here—even the smallest rodent would have been swallowed up and consumed by the clutching softness of an earth seeped through with the chilling dampness of long, sunless, lifeless days and nights. Nothing moved, nothing stirred as the three walked eastward through shapeless country where there was no trail, no hint that anyone or anything had ever passed that way before, or would ever do so again. The sun never appeared during their march, no faint trace of its direct rays flickering downward to show that somewhere beyond this dead, forgotten land was a world of life. Whether it was the perpetual mist or the heavy clouds or a combination of both that so completely blotted out the sky remained an unanswered question. Their only world was that cheerless, hateful gray land through which they walked.

By the fourth day, they began to despair. Even though there had been no further sign of the winged hunters of the Warlock Lord and it appeared that any pursuit had been abandoned, the possibility offered little solace as the hours dragged by and the silence grew deeper, the land more sullen. Even Menion's great spirit began to waver and doubt wormed its stealthy way into his usually confident mind. He began to wonder if they had lost the direction, if perhaps they had even traveled in a circle. He knew the land would never tell them, that once lost in this bleak country, they were lost forever. Shea and Flick felt the fear even more deeply. They knew nothing of the lowlands and lacked the hunter's skill and instinct that Menion possessed. They relied completely on him, but sensed that something was wrong even though the highlander had purposely kept silent about his own doubts so as not to worry them. The hours passed, and the cold and the wet and the hateful deadness of the land remained unchanged. They felt their last shred of confidence in one another and in themselves begin to slip slowly, agonizingly away. Finally, as the fifth day of the journey drew to a close and still the lowland bleakness stretched on with no visible sign of the desperately sought after Black Oaks, Shea wearily called a halt to the endless march and dropped heavily to the ground, his questioning eyes on the Prince of Leah.

Menion shrugged and looked absently at the misty lowlands about them, his handsome face drawn with the chill of the air.

"I won't lie to you," he murmured. "I can't be sure that we have kept our sense of direction. We may have traveled in a circle; we may even be hopelessly lost."

Flick dropped his pack disgustedly and looked at his brother with his own special "I told you so" look. Shea glanced at him and turned hurriedly back to Menion.

"I can't believe we're completely lost! Isn't there any way we can get our bearings?"

"I'm open to suggestions." His friend smiled humorlessly, stretching as he, too, dropped his pack to the rough ground and sat down beside the brooding Flick. "What's the trouble, old Flick? Have I gotten you into it again?"

Flick glanced over at him angrily; but looking into the gray eyes, he quickly reconsidered his dislike of the man. There was genuine concern there, and even a trace of sadness at the thought that he had failed them. With rare affection, Flick reached over and placed a comforting hand on the other's shoulder, nodding silently. Suddenly, Shea leaped up and flung off his own pack, hastily rummaging through its contents.

"The stones can help us," he cried.

For a moment the other two looked blankly at him and then in sudden understanding rose expectantly to their feet. A moment later, Shea produced the small leather pouch with its precious contents. They all stared at the worn container in mute anticipation that the Elfstones would at last prove their value, that they would somehow aid them in escaping the wasteland of Clete. Eagerly Shea opened the drawstrings and carefully dropped the three small, blue stones into his upturned palm. They lay there twinkling dimly as the three watched and waited.

"Hold them up, Shea," urged Menion after a moment. "Perhaps they need the light."

The Valeman did as he was told, watching the blue stones anxiously. Nothing happened. He waited a moment longer before lowering his hand. Allanon had cautioned him against use of the Elfstones except in the gravest of emergencies. Perhaps the stones would only come to his aid in special situations. He began to despair. Whatever the case, he was faced with the hard fact that he had no idea how the stones were to be used. He looked desperately at his friends.

"Well, try something else!" exclaimed Menion heatedly.

Shea took the stones between his hands and rubbed them together sharply, then shook them and cast them like dice. Still nothing happened. Slowly he retrieved them from the damp earth and carefully wiped them clean. Their deep blue color seemed to draw him to them, and he peered closely into their clear, glasslike core as if somehow the answer might be found there.

"Maybe you should talk to them or something . . ." Flick's voice trailed off hopefully.

A mental picture of Allanon's dark face, bowed and locked in deep concentration, flashed sharply in Shea's mind. Perhaps the secret of the Elfstones could be unlocked in a different way, he thought suddenly. Holding them out in his open palm, the little Valeman closed his eyes and concentrated his thoughts on reaching into the deep blueness, searching for the power that they so desperately needed. Silently, he urged the Elfstones to help them. Long moments passed, seemingly hours. He opened his eyes and the three friends watched and waited while the stones rested in Shea's palm, their blue gleam dull in the darkness and damp of the mist.

Then, with ferocious suddenness, they flared up in a blinding blue glare that caused the travelers to reel back from the brightness, shielding their unprotected eyes. So powerful was the aura that Shea nearly dropped the small gems in astonishment. The sharp glow became steadily brighter, lighting up the dead land about them as the sun had never been able to do. The brightness intensified from the deep blue to a bright blue so dazzling that the awestruck watchers were actually hypnotized. It grew, steadied, and abruptly shot forward like a huge beacon, traveling to their left, cutting effortlessly through the mist-covered grayness to rest at last, some hundreds, perhaps thousands of yards ahead upon the great gnarled boles of the ancient Black Oaks. The light held for one brief moment, and then it was gone. The gray mist returned with its chill dampness and the three small blue stones gleamed quietly as they had before.

Menion recovered quickly, clapping Shea sharply on the back and grinning broadly. In one quick motion, he had his pack back in place and was ready to travel, his eyes already scanning the now-invisible spot through which the vision of the Black Oaks had appeared. Shea hastily returned the Elfstones to the pouch, and the Valemen strapped on their packs. Not a word was spoken as they walked rapidly in the direction the beacon had flashed, each watching eagerly for the long-expected forest. Gone was the chill of the gray darkness and slow drizzle of the past five days. Gone was the despair they had felt so strongly only minutes before. There was only the conviction that escape from these dreaded lowlands was at last at hand. They did not question, did not doubt the vision the stones had revealed to them. The Black Oaks was the most dangerous forest in the Southland, but at this particular moment, it seemed a haven of hope compared to the land of Clete.

The time seemed endless as they pushed ahead. It could have been hours or perhaps only minutes later when suddenly the graying mist grudgingly gave way to huge, moss-covered trunks which rose hulkingly into the air to be lost in the haze above. The exhausted trio halted together, their tired eyes gazing joyfully on the cheerless monsters that stood evenly, endlessly before them, their great mass an impenetrable wall of damp, scarred bark on wide, deep-rooted bases that had stood there for countless ages of man and would very likely be there until the destruction of the land itself. It was an awesome sight, even in the dim light of the misty lowlands, and the watchers felt the undeniable presence of a life force in those woods so incredibly ancient that it almost commanded a deep, grudging respect for its years. It was as if they had stepped into another age, another world, and all that stood so silently before them had the magic of an enticingly dangerous fairy tale.

"The stones were right," murmured Shea softly, a slow smile spreading over his tired, but happy face. He breathed deeply with relief and flashed a quick grin.

"The Black Oaks," pronounced Menion in admiration.

"Here we go again," sighed Flick.

They spent that night camped within the protective fringes of the Black Oaks in a small clearing, sheltered by the great trees and dense shrubbery which blotted out the dreariness of the lowlands of Clete less than fifty yards to the west. The heavy mist dissipated within the forest, and it was possible to look skyward to the magnificent canopy of interlocking boughs and leaves several hundred feet above them. Where there had been no sign of life in the deathly lowlands, within the giant oaks the mingled sounds of insect and animal life whispered through the night. It was pleasant to hear living things again, and the three weary travelers felt at ease for the first time in days. But lingering in the back of their minds was the memory of their prior journey to this deceptively peaceful haven, when they had been lost for several long days and nearly devoured by the ravenous wolves that prowled deep within its confines. Moreover, the tales of unfortunate travelers who had attempted to pass through this same forest were too numerous to be disregarded.

However, the young Southlanders felt reasonably secure at the edge of the Black Oaks and gratefully made preparations to start a fire. Wood was plentiful and dry. They stripped to the skin and hung their soggy garments on a line near the small blaze. A meal was quickly prepared—the first hot one in five days—and devoured in minutes. The floor of the forest was soft and smooth, a comfortable bed compared to the dampened earth of the lowlands. As they lay quietly on their backs gazing skyward at the gently swaying treetops, the bright light of the fire seemed to shoot upward in faint streaks of orange that gave the impression of an altar burning in some great sanctuary. The light danced and glittered against the rough bark and the soft, green moss that clung in dark patches to the massive trees. The forest insects maintained their steady hum in contentment. Occasionally one would fly into the flames of the fire and extinguish its brief life with a dazzling flash. Once or twice they heard the rustle of some small animal outside the light of the fire, watching from the protective blackness.

After a while, Menion rolled over on his side and looked curiously at Shea.

"What is the source of the power of those stones, Shea? Can they grant any wish? I'm still not sure . . ."

His voice trailed off and he shook his head vaguely. Shea continued to lie motionless on his back, staring upward for a few moments as he thought back on the events of that afternoon. He realized that none of them had spoken of the Elfstones since the mysterious vision of the Black Oaks in that awesome display of incomprehensible power. He glanced over at Flick, who was watching him closely.

"I don't think that I have that much control over them," he announced abruptly. "It was almost as if *they* made the decision . . ." He paused, and then added absently, "I don't think I can control them."

Menion nodded thoughtfully and lay back again. Flick cleared his throat.

"What's the difference? They got us out of that dismal swamp, didn't they?"

Menion glanced sharply at Flick and shrugged.

"It might be helpful to know when we can count on that kind of support, don't you think?" He breathed deeply and clasped his hands behind his head, his keen gaze shifting to the fire at his feet. Flick stirred uneasily across from him, glancing from Menion to his brother and back again. Shea said nothing, his gaze focused on some imaginary point overhead.

Long moments passed before the highlander spoke again.

"Well, at least we've made it this far," he declared cheerfully. "Now for the next leg of the trip!"

He sat up and began to sketch a quick map of the area in the dry earth. Shea and Flick sat up with him and watched quietly.

"Here we are." Menion pointed to a spot on the dirt map representing the fringe of the Black Oaks. "At least that's where I think we are," he added quickly. "To the north is the Mist Marsh and farther north of that the Rainbow Lake, out of which runs the Silver River east to the Anar Forests. Our best bet is to travel north tomorrow until we reach the edge of the Mist Marsh. Then we'll skirt the edge of the swamp," he traced a long line, "and come out on the other side of the Black Oaks. From there, we can travel due north until we run into the Silver River, and that should get us safely to the Anar."

He paused and looked over at the other two. Neither seemed to be happy with the plan.

"What's the matter?" he asked in bewilderment. "The plan is designed to get us past the Black Oaks without forcing us to go directly through them, which was the cause of all the trouble the last time we were here. Don't forget those wolves are still in there somewhere!"

Shea nodded slowly and frowned.

"It's not the general plan," he began hesitantly, "but we've heard tales of the Mist Marsh . . ."

Menion clapped his hand to his forehead in amazement.

"Oh, no! Not the old wives' tale about a Mist Wraith that lurks on the edges of the marsh waiting to devour stray travelers? Don't tell me you believe that!"

"That's fine, coming from you," Flick blazed up angrily. "I suppose you've forgotten who it was that told us how safe the Black Oaks were just before that last trip!"

"All right," soothed the lean hunter. "I'm not saying that this is a safe part of the country and that some very strange creatures don't inhabit these woods. But no one has ever seen this so-called creature of the marsh, and we have seen the wolves. Which do you choose?"

"I suppose that your plan is the best one," interjected Shea hastily. "But I would prefer it if we could cut as far east as possible while traveling through the forest to avoid as much of the Mist Marsh as possible."

"Agreed!" exclaimed Menion. "But it may prove to be a bit difficult when we haven't seen the sun in three days and can't really be sure which way is east."

"Climb a tree," Flick suggested casually.

"Climb a . . ." stuttered the other in unabashed amazement. "Why, of course! Why didn't I think of that? I'll just climb two hundred feet of slick, damp, moss-covered tree bark with my bare hands and feet!" He shook his head in mock wonderment. "Sometimes you appall me."

He glanced wearily over at Shea for understanding, but the Valeman had bounded excitedly to his brother's side.

"You brought the climbing equipment?" he demanded in astonishment; when the other nodded, he clapped him heartily on his broad back.

"Special boots and gloves and rope," he explained quickly to a bewildered Prince of Leah. "Flick is the best climber in the Vale, and if anyone can make it up one of these monsters, he can."

Menion shook his head uncomprehendingly.

"The boots and gloves are coated with a special substance just before use that makes the surface rough enough to grip even damp, mossy bark. He'll be able to climb one of these oaks tomorrow and check the position of the sun."

Flick grinned smugly and nodded.

"Yes, indeed, wonder of wonders." Menion shook his head and looked over at the stocky Valeman. "Even the slow-witted are starting to think. My friends, we may make it yet."

When they awoke the following morning, the forest was still dark, with only faint traces of daylight filtering through at the tops of the great oaks. A thin mist had drifted in off the lowlands which, when glimpsed from the edges of the forest, appeared as sunless and dismal as ever. It was cold in the woods—not the damp, penetrating chill of the lowland country, but rather the brisk, crisp cool of a forest's early morn. They ate a quick breakfast, and then Flick prepared to climb one of the towering oaks. He pulled on the heavy, flexible boots and gloves, which Shea then coated with a thick pasty substance from a small container. Menion looked on quizzically, but his curiosity changed to astonishment as the stocky Valeman grasped the base of the great tree and, with a dexterity that belied both his bulky size and the difficulty of the task, proceeded to climb rapidly toward the summit. His strong limbs carried him upward through the tangle of heavy branches and the climbing became slower and more difficult. He was briefly lost from sight upon reaching the topmost branches, then reappeared, hastening down the smooth trunk to rejoin his friends.

Quickly the climbing gear was packed and the group proceeded in a northeasterly direction. Based on Flick's report of the sun's present position, their chosen route should bring them out at a point along the east edge of the Mist Marsh. Menion believed that the forest trek could be completed in one day. It was now early morning, and they were determined to be through the Black Oaks before darkness fell. So they marched steadily, at times rapidly, in single file. The keen-eyed Menion led, picking out the best path, relying heavily on his sense of direction in the semidarkness. Shea followed close behind him, and Flick brought up the rear, glancing occasionally over his shoulder into the still forests. They stopped only three times to rest and once more for a brief lunch, each time quickly resuming their march. They spoke infrequently, but the talk was lighthearted and cheerful. The day wore quickly away, and soon the first signs of nightfall were visible. Still the forest stretched on before them with no indication of a break in the great trees. Worse than this, a heavy graying mistiness was once again seeping into view in gradually thickening amounts. But this was a new kind of mist. It lacked the inconsistency of the lowland mist; this was an almost smokelike substance that one could actually feel clinging to the body and clothes, gripping in its own peculiarly distasteful fashion. It felt strangely like the clutching of hundreds of small, clammy, chilled hands seeking to pull the body down, and the three travelers felt an unmistakable revulsion at its insistent touch. Menion indicated that the heavy, foglike substance was from the Mist Marsh, and they were very close to the end of the forest.

Eventually, the mist grew so heavy that it was impossible for the three to see more than a few feet. Menion slowed his pace to a crawl because of the increasingly poor visibility, and they remained close to each other to avoid separation. By this time, the day was so far gone that even without the mist the forest would have appeared almost black; but with the added dimness caused by the swirling wall of heavy moisture, it was nearly impossible to pick out any sort of path. It was almost as if the three were suspended in a limbo world, where only the solidity of the invisible ground on which they trod offered any evidence of reality. It finally became so difficult to see that Menion instructed the other two to bind themselves together and to him by a length of rope to prevent separation. This was quickly done and the slow march resumed. Menion knew that they had to be very near the Mist Marsh and carefully peered into the grayness ahead in an effort to catch a glimpse of a breakthrough.

Even so, when at last he did reach the edge of the marshland bordering the north fringes of the Black Oaks, he did not realize what had happened until he had already stepped knee-deep into the thick green waters. The chill, deathlike clutching of the mud beneath, coupled with his surprise, caused him to slip farther down, and only his quick warning saved Shea and Flick from a similar fate. Responding to his cry, they hauled in on the rope that bound them together and hastily pulled their comrade from the bog and certain death. The sullen, slime-covered waters of the great swamp covered only thinly the bottomless mud beneath, which lacked the rapid suction of quicksand, but accomplished the same result in a slightly longer time span. Anything or anyone caught in its grip was doomed to a slow death by suffocation in an immeasurable abyss. For untold ages its silent surface had fooled unwary creatures into attempting to cross, or to skirt, or perhaps only to test its mirrorless waters, and the decayed remains of all lay buried together somewhere beneath its placid face. The three travelers stood silently on its banks, looking at it and experiencing inwardly the horror of its dark secret. Even Menion Leah shuddered as he remembered its brief, clutching invitation to him to share the fate of so many others. For one spellbound second, the dead paraded as shadows before them and were gone.

"What happened?" exclaimed Shea suddenly, his voice breaking the silence with deafening sharpness. "We should have avoided this swamp!"

Menion looked upward and about for a few seconds and shook his head.

"We've come out too far to the west. We'll have to follow the edge of the bog around to the east until we can break free from this mist and the Black Oaks."

He paused and considered the time of day.

"I'm not spending the night in this place," Flick declared vehemently, anticipating the other's query. "I'd rather walk all night and most of tomorrow—and probably the next day!"

Their quick decision was to continue along the edge of the Mist Marsh until they reached open land to the east and then stop for the night. Shea was still concerned about being caught in open country by the Skull Bearers, but his growing dread of the swamp overshadowed even this fear, and his foremost thought was to get as far away as possible. The trio tightened the rope about their waists and in single file began to move along the uneven shoreline of the marsh, their eyes glued to the faint path ahead. Menion guided them cautiously, avoiding the tangle of treacherous roots and weeds that grew in abundance along the swamp's edge, their twisted, knotted forms seemingly alive in the eerie half-light of the rolling gray mist. At times the ground became soft mud, dangerously like that of the marsh itself, and had to be skirted. At other times huge trees blocked the path, their great trunks leaning heavily toward the dull, lifeless surface of the swamp's waters, their branches drooping sadly, motionless as they waited for the death that lay only inches below. If the Lowlands of Clete had been a dying land, then this marsh was the death that waited—an infinite, ageless death that gave no sign, no warning, no movement as it crouched, concealed within the very land it had so brutally destroyed. The chilling dampness of the lowlands was here, but coupled with it was the unexplainable feeling that the heavy, stagnant slime of the swamp waters permeated the mist as well, clutching eagerly at the weary travelers. The mist about them swirled slowly, but there was no sign of wind, no sound of a breeze rustling the tall swamp grass or dying oaks. All was still, a silence of permanent death that knew well who was master.

They had walked for perhaps an hour when Shea first sensed that something was wrong. There was no reason for the feeling; it stole over him gradually until every sense was keyed, trying to find where the trouble lay. Walking silently between the other two, he listened intently, peering first into the great oaks, then out over the swamp. Finally, he concluded with chilling certainty that they were not alone—that something else was out there in the invisible beyond, lost in the mist to their poor vision, but able to see them. For one brief moment the young Valeman was so terrified by the thought that he was unable to speak or even to gesture. He could only walk ahead, his mind frozen, waiting for the unspeakable to happen. But then, with a supreme effort he calmed his scattered thoughts and brought the other two men to an abrupt halt.

Menion looked around quizzically and started to speak, but Shea silenced him with a finger to his own lips and a gesture toward the swamp. Flick was already looking cautiously in that direction, his own sixth sense having warned him of his brother's fear. For long moments they stood motionless at the edge of the marsh, their eyes and ears concentrated on the impenetrable mist moving sluggishly above the surface of the dead water. The silence was oppressive.

"I think you were mistaken," Menion whispered finally as he relaxed his vigil. "Sometimes when you are this tired, it is easy to imagine things."

Shea shook his head negatively and looked at Flick.

"I don't know," the other conceded. "I thought I sensed something. . . ."

"A Mist Wraith?" chided Menion, grinning.

"Maybe you're right," Shea interceded quickly. "I am pretty tired and could imagine anything at this point. Let's keep moving and get out of this place."

They hastily resumed the dreary trek, but for the next few minutes remained alert for anything unusual. When nothing happened, they began to let their thoughts drift to other matters. Shea had just succeeded in convincing himself that he had been mistaken and the victim of an overactive imagination brought about by lack of sleep, when Flick cried out.

Immediately Shea felt the rope that bound them together jerk sharply and begin to drag him in the direction of the deadly swamp. He lost his balance and fell, unable to distinguish anything in the mist. For one fleeting moment he thought he glimpsed his brother's body suspended several feet in the air over the swamp, the rope still tied to his waist. In the next second, Shea felt the chill of the swamp grapple at his legs.

They might have all been lost had it not been for the quick reflexes of the Prince of Leah. At the first sharp jerk of the rope, he had instinctively grasped at the only thing near enough to keep him on his feet. It was a huge, sinking oak, its trunk embedded so far into the soft ground that its upper branches were within reach, and Menion rapidly hooked one arm about the nearest bough and with the other grasped the rope about his waist and tried to pull back. Shea, now up to his knees in the swamp mud, felt the rope go taut on Menion's end and tried to brace himself to aid. Flick was crying out sharply in the darkness above the swamp, and both Menion and Shea shouted encouragement. Suddenly, the rope between Flick and Shea went slack, and out of the gray mistiness emerged the stout, struggling form of Flick Ohmsford, still suspended above the water's surface, his waist gripped by what appeared to be a sort of greenish, weed-coated tentacle. His right hand held the long, silver dagger, which gleamed menacingly as it slashed in repeated cuts at the thing which held him. Shea yanked hard on the rope which bound them, trying to aid his brother in breaking free, and a moment later he succeeded as the tentacle whipped back into the mist, releasing the still-struggling Flick, who promptly fell into the marsh below.

Shea had barely pulled his exhausted brother from the clutches of the swamp, freed him from the rope, and helped him to his feet before several more of the greenish arms shot out of the misty darkness. They knocked the shaken Flick sprawling and one closed about the left arm of an astonished Shea before he could think to dodge. He felt himself drawn toward the swamp and drew his own dagger to strike fiercely at the slime-covered tentacle. As he fought, he caught sight of something huge out in the marsh, its bulk covered by the night and the swamp. To one side, Flick again became entangled in the grip of two more tentacles, and his stocky form was dragged relentlessly toward the water's edge. Valiantly, Shea broke free from the tentacle that held his arm, slashing through the repulsive limb with one great cut; struggling to reach his brother, he felt another tentacle grasp his leg, knocking his feet out from under him. As he fell, his head struck an oak root, and he lost consciousness.

Again they were saved by Menion, his lithe form leaping out of the darkness behind, the great sword flashing dully in a wide arc as it severed in one powerful swing the tentacle which held the unconscious Shea. A second later, the highlander was at Flick's side, cutting and chopping his way past the arms which suddenly reached for him out of the darkness, and with a series of quick, well-placed blows freed the other Valeman. For a moment the tentacles disappeared back into the mist of the swamp, and

Flick and Menion hastened to pull the unconscious Shea back from the unprotected edge of the water. But before any of them could reach the safety of the great oaks, the greenish arms again shot out of the darkness. Without hesitation, Menion and Flick placed themselves in front of their motionless friend and struck out at the encircling arms. The fight was silent, save for the labored breathing of the men as they struck again and again, chopping off bits and pieces and sometimes whole ends of the grasping tentacles. But any damage they caused did not seem to affect the monster in the swamp, which attacked with renewed fury at each stroke. Menion cursed himself for not remembering to drag the great ash bow within reach so that he might have taken a shot at whatever it was that lay beyond the mist.

"Shea!" he yelled desperately. "Shea, wake up, or for the love of heaven, we're done for!"

The silent form behind him stirred slightly.

"Get up, Shea!" pleaded Flick hoarsely, his own arms exhausted from the great strain of fighting off the tentacles.

"The stones!" yelled Menion. "Get the Elfstones!"

Shea struggled to a kneeling position, but he was knocked flat again by the force of the battle in front of him. He heard Menion shouting, and dazedly felt for his pack, realizing almost immediately that he had dropped it while helping Flick. He saw it now, several yards to the right, the tentacles waving menacingly over it. Menion seemed to realize this at the same moment and charged forward with a wild cry, his long sword cutting a path for the others. Flick was at his side, the small dagger still in his hand. With a final surge of his fading strength, Shea leaped to his feet and launched himself toward the pack containing the precious Elfstones. His slim form slipped between several of the grasping arms, and he threw himself on the pack. His hand was inside, groping for the pouch, when the first tentacle reached his unprotected legs. Kicking and struggling, he fought to keep his freedom for the few seconds he needed to find the stones. For a moment he thought he had lost them again. Then his hand closed over the small pouch, and he yanked it from his fallen pack. A sudden blow from the writhing tentacles almost caused him to drop it, and he clutched it tightly to his chest as he loosened the drawstrings with numbing slowness. Flick had been forced back so far that he stumbled against Shea's outstretched body and fell over backward, the tentacles coming down on top of them both. Now only the lean form of Menion stood between them and the giant attacker, both hands gripping tightly the great sword of Leah.

Almost without realizing it, Shea found the three blue stones in his hand, free from the pouch at last. Scrambling backward, struggling to his feet, the young Valeman let out a wild cry of triumph and held forth the faintly glowing Elfstones. The power locked within flared up immediately, flooding the darkness with dazzling blue light. Flick and Menion leaped back, shielding their eyes from the glare. The tentacles drew back hesitantly, uncertainly, and as the three men risked a second quick glance, they saw the brilliant light of the Elfstones streak outward into the mist above the swamp, cutting through its vapor with the keenness of a knife. They saw it strike with shattering impact the huge, unspeakable bulk that had attacked them as it was sinking sluggishly beneath the slime-covered waters. At that same instant the glare above the disappearing monster reached the intensity of a small sun and the water steamed with blue flames that seared upward into the shrouded sky. One moment the burning glare and the flames were there and the next they were gone. The mist and the night returned, and the three companions were alone again in the blackness of the marshland.

They quickly sheathed their weapons, picked up the fallen packs, and dropped back among the huge black oaks. The swamp remained as silent as it had been before the unexpected attack, its dull waters disturbingly placid beneath the gray haze. For several moments, no one spoke as they collapsed silently against the trunks of the great trees and breathed deeply, grateful to be alive. The whole battle had happened quickly, like the passing of a brief, horrible instant in an all-too-real nightmare. Flick was completely drenched by the swamp waters, and Shea was soaked from the waist down. Both shivered in the chill night air; after only a few seconds of rest, they began moving slowly about in an effort to ward off the numbing cold.

Realizing that they had to get free of the marshland quickly, Menion swung his tired body away from its resting place against the rough, bark-covered oak trunk and in one smooth motion swung his pack into place over his shoulders. Shea and Flick were quick to follow, though somewhat less eager. They conferred briefly to decide what direction it would be best to take now. The choice was simple: proceed through the Black Oaks and risk becoming lost and being set upon by the wandering wolf packs or follow the edge of the swamp and chance a second encounter with the Mist Wraith. Neither choice held much appeal, but the battle with the creature from the Mist Marsh was too recent to permit any of them to risk a repeat performance. So the decision was made to stick to the woods, to try to follow a course parallel to the shoreline of the swamp and hopefully gain the open country beyond within a few hours. They now had reached the point where the long hours of traveling with the keen anticipation of danger had chipped and worn away the clear reasoning of the morning. They were tired and frightened by the strange world into which they had journeyed, and the one clear thought left in their numbed minds was to break through this stifling forest that they might find a few hours of welcome sleep. With that dominating their thoughts and overriding the caution that was so desperately needed, they forgot to tie themselves together again.

The journey continued as before, with Menion in the lead, Shea a few paces back, and Flick trailing, all walking silently and steadily, their minds fixed on the reassuring thought that ahead lay the sunlit, open grasslands that would take them to the Anar. The mist seemed to have dissipated slightly, and while Menion's form was only a shadow, Shea could make him out well enough to follow. Yet at times both Shea and Flick would lose sight of the person immediately in front and would find their eyes straining wearily to keep to the path Menion was making for them. The minutes passed with agonizing slowness and the sharpness of each man's eyesight began to lessen with the increasing need for sleep. Minutes lengthened into long, endless hours and still they plodded slowly onward through the misty haze of the great Black Oaks. They found it impossible to tell how far they had traveled or how much time had passed. Soon it failed to matter at all. They became sleepwalkers in a world of half-dreams and rambling thoughts with no break in the wearing march or the never-ending, silent black trunks that came and passed in countless thousands. The only change was a gradual building of the wind from somewhere in the shrouded night, whispering its first faint cry, then growing to a numbing crescendo of sound that gripped the tired minds of the three travelers with spellbinding magic. It called to them, reminding them of the briefness of the days behind and those ahead, warning them that they were mortal creatures of no consequence in that land, crying to them to lie down in the peacefulness of sleep. They heard and fought against the tempting plea with the last of their strength, concentrating mindlessly on putting one foot before the other in an endless succession of footsteps. One minute they were all there in a ragged line; the next, Shea looked ahead and Menion was gone.

At first, he could not accept the fact, his normally keen mind hazy with lack of sleep, and he continued to walk slowly ahead, looking vainly for the shadowy form of the tall highlander. Then, abruptly he stopped as he realized with stabbing fear that they had somehow become separated. He clutched wildly for Flick and grabbed his brother's loose tunic as the fatigued Valeman stumbled into him, dead on his feet. Flick looked unthinkingly at him, not knowing, not even caring why they had stopped, his only hope that he could collapse at last and sleep. The wind in the darkness of the forest seemed to howl in wild glee, and Shea called desperately for the highland prince and heard only the echoes of his own futile cry. He called again and again, his voice rising to a near scream of desperation and fear, but nothing came back except the sound of his own voice, muffled and distorted by the wild whistling of the wind through the great oaks, whisking and wrapping about the silent trunks and limbs, and filtering out among the rustling leaves. Once he thought he heard his own name called; answering eagerly, he dragged himself and the exhausted Flick through the maze of trees toward the sound of the cry. But there was nothing. Dropping to the forest floor, he called until his voice gave out, but only the wind replied in mocking laughter to tell him that he had lost the Prince of Leah.

7

When Shea awoke the following day, it was noon. The bright sunlight streamed into his half-open eyes with burning sharpness as he lay on his back in the tall grass. At first he could remember nothing of the previous night except that he and Flick had become separated from Menion in the Black Oaks. Half awake, he raised himself on one elbow, looked about sleepily, and discovered that he was in an open field. Behind him rose the forbidding Black Oaks, and he knew that somehow, after losing Menion, he had managed to find his way through the dread forest before collapsing in exhaustion. Everything was hazy in his mind after their separation. He could not imagine how he had summoned the strength to finish the march. He could not even recall breaking free of the endless forest to find the grass-covered lowlands he now surveyed. The whole experience seemed strangely distant as he rubbed his eyes and sighed contentedly in the warm sunlight and fresh air. For the first time in days, the Anar Forests seemed to be within reach.

Suddenly, he remembered Flick, and looked anxiously about for his brother. A moment later he spotted the stocky form collapsed in sleep several yards away. Shea climbed slowly to his feet and stretched leisurely, taking time to locate his pack. He bent down and rummaged through its contents until he located the pouch containing the Elfstones, reassuring himself that they were still safely within his possession. Then picking up the pack, he trudged over to his sleeping brother and gently shook him. Flick stirred grudgingly, clearly unhappy that anyone would disturb his slumber. Shea was forced to shake him several times before he at last reluctantly opened his eyes and squinted up sourly. Upon seeing Shea, he raised himself to a sitting position and looked slowly about.

"Hey, we made it!" he exclaimed. "But I don't know how. I don't remember anything after losing Menion except walking and walking until I thought that my legs would drop off."

Shea grinned in agreement and clapped his brother on the back. He felt a measure of gratitude when he thought of all they had been through together. So many hardships and dangers, and still Flick could laugh about it. He felt a sudden, keen sense of love for Flick, a brother who, while not related by blood, was even closer for his deep friendship.

"We made it all right," he smiled, "and we'll make it the rest of the way, too, if I can get you off the ground."

"The meanness in some people is unbelievable." Flick shook his head in mock disbelief and then climbed heavily to his feet. He looked questioningly over at Shea. "Menion . . ?"

"Lost . . . I don't know where . . ."

Flick looked away, sensing his brother's bitter disappointment, but unwilling to admit to himself that they were not better off without the highland prince. He instinctively distrusted Menion, yet the highlander had saved his life back in the forest and that was not something Flick would forget easily. He thought about it a minute or so longer, then clapped his brother lightly on the shoulder.

"Don't worry about that rogue. He'll turn up—probably at the wrong time."

Shea nodded quietly, and the conversation quickly turned to the task at hand. They agreed that the best plan was to journey northward until they reached the Silver River which flowed into the Rainbow Lake, and follow it upstream to the Anar. With any luck, Menion would also follow the river and catch up to them within a few days. His skill as a woodsman should enable him to escape the Black Oaks and at some point beyond find their trail and follow it to wherever they were. Shea was reluctant to leave his friend, but was wise enough to realize that any attempt at a search for him in the Black Oaks could only result in their own entanglement. Moreover, the danger they faced if discovered by the searching Skull Bearers far outweighed any risks Menion might encounter, even in that forest. There was nothing for them to do but to continue on.

The pair walked rapidly through the green, quiet lowlands, hoping to reach the Silver River by nightfall. It was already midafternoon, and they had no way of knowing how far they might be from the river. With the sun to serve as a guide, they felt more confident of their position than they had in the misty confines of the Black Oaks, where they had been forced to depend on their own unreliable sense of direction. They talked freely, brightened by the sunlight that had been absent for so many days and by an unspoken feeling of gratitude that they were still alive following the harrowing experiences of the Mist Marsh. As they walked, small animals and high-flying birds scattered at their appearance. Once, in the fading light of the afternoon sun, Shea thought he caught sight of the small, hunched-over form of an old man some distance to the east, moving slowly away from them. But in that light and at that distance he could not be certain and an instant later found he could see no one after all. Flick had seen nothing and the incident was forgotten.

By dusk they sighted a long, ribbon-thin stream of water to the north which they quickly identified as the fabled Silver River, the source of the wondrous Rainbow Lake to the west and of a thousand firelight tales of adventure. It was said that there was a legendary King of the Silver River, whose wealth and power was beyond description, but whose only concern was in keeping the waters of the great river running free and clean for man and animal alike. He was seldom seen by travelers, the stories related, but he was always there to offer aid, should any require it, or to deal out punishment for violation of his domain. On sighting the river, Shea and Flick could only tell that it appeared very beautiful in the fading light, the sort of faint silver color that the name implied. When they finally reached its edge, the evening had become too dark to permit them to see how clear the waters really were, but upon tasting it they found it clean enough to drink.

They found a small, grass-covered clearing on the south bank of the river, beneath the spreading shelter of two broad, old maple trees that offered an ideal campsite for the night. Even the short journey of that afternoon had tired them, and they preferred not to risk moving about in the dark in this open country. They had just about exhausted their supplies, and after this evening's meal they would have to hunt for food. This was a particularly disheartening thought when they recalled that the only weapons they had between them for killing game were the short and highly ineffectual hunting knives. Menion carried the only long bow. They ate the last of their supplies in silence without the use of a cooking fire, which might have called attention to their presence. The moon was half full and the night cloudless, so that the thousands of stars in the limitless galaxy shone in dazzling white, lighting up the river and the land beyond in an eerie deep-green brightness. After their meal was completed, Shea turned to his brother.

"Have you thought about this trip, about this whole business of running away?" he queried. "I mean, what are we really doing?"

"You're a funny one to ask that!" exclaimed the other shortly.

Shea smiled and nodded.

"I suppose I am. But I have to justify it all to myself and that's not an easy task. I can understand most of what Allanon told us, about the danger to the heirs of the Sword. But what good will it do for us to hide out in the Anar? This creature Brona must be after something besides the Sword of Shannara to go to all this trouble to search for the heirs of the Elven House. What is it he wants . . . what could it be . . . ?"

Flick shrugged and tossed a pebble into the swift current of the lapping river, his own mind muddled, unable to offer any sensible answer.

"Maybe he wants to take over," he suggested vaguely. "Doesn't everyone who gets a little power, sooner or later?"

"No doubt," agreed Shea uncertainly, thinking that this special form of greed had brought the races to where they were today, following the long, bitter wars that had nearly destroyed all life. But it had been years since the last war and the appearance of separate and disassociated communities seemed to have provided a partial answer to the long quest for peace. He turned back to a watchful Flick.

"What are we going to do once we get to where we're going?"

"Allanon will tell us," his brother answered hesitantly.

"Allanon can't tell us what to do forever," replied Shea quickly. "Besides, I'm still not convinced that he has told us the truth about himself."

Flick nodded his agreement, thinking back to that first chilling encounter with the dark giant who had tossed him about like a rag doll. His behavior had always struck Flick as that of a man who was used to having his way and having it when and how he chose. He shivered involuntarily, recalling his first near-discovery by the shadowy Skull Bearer, and found himself confronted with the fact that it was Allanon who had saved him.

"I'm not sure I want to know the truth about any of this. I'm not sure I would understand," Flick murmured softly.

Shea was startled by the comment and turned back to the moonlit waters of the river.

"We may be only little people to Allanon," he acknowledged, "but from now on, I don't move without a reason!"

"Maybe so," his brother's voice drifted up to him. "But maybe . . ."

His voice trailed off ominously into the quiet sounds of the night and the river, and Shea chose not to pursue the matter. Both lay back and were quickly asleep, their tired thoughts flowing sluggishly into the bright, colorful dreams of the momentary world of sleep. In that secure, drifting dimension of fantasy, their weary minds could relax, releasing the hidden fears of tomorrow to emerge in whatever form they wished, and there, in that most distant sanctuary for the human soul, be faced privately and overcome. But even with the reassuring sounds of life all about them and the peaceful rushing of the gleaming Silver River to soothe their cares, an inescapable, gnawing specter of apprehension wormed its stealthy way into their dream world and there, in full view of the mind's eye, it perched and waited, smiling dully, hatefully—knowing well the limits of their endurance. Both sleepers tossed fitfully, unable to shake the presence of this frightening apparition entrenched deep within them, more thought than form.

Perhaps it was that same shadow of warning, radiating its special scent of fear, that locked simultaneously in the restless minds of the Valemen and caused both to waken in the same startled instant, the sleep gone from their eyes and the air filled with stark, chilling madness that gripped them tightly and began to squeeze. They recognized it instantly, and panic shone dully in their eyes as they sat motionless, listening to the soundless night. Moments passed and nothing happened. Still they remained immobile, their senses straining for the sounds they knew must come. Then they heard the dreaded flapping of the great wings and together looked to the open river to see the hulking, silent form of the Skull Bearer swoop almost gracefully from out of the lowlands across the river to the north and settle into a long glide, bearing directly toward their place of concealment. The Valemen were frozen with terror, unable even to think, let alone move, as they watched the creature begin to close the distance between them. It did not matter that it had not yet seen them, perhaps did not even know that they were there. It would know in the next few seconds, and for the brothers there was no time to run, no place to hide, no chance to escape. Shea felt the dryness of his mouth and somewhere within his scattered thoughts remembered the Elfstones, but his mind had gone numb. He sat paralyzed with his brother and waited for the end.

Miraculously, it did not come. Just when it seemed that the servant of the Warlock Lord must surely find them, a flash of light from the other bank caught its attention. Swiftly, it winged away toward the light and then there was another a bit farther down and then another—or was it mistaken? It flew swiftly now, searching eagerly, its cunning mind telling it that the search was at an end, the long hunt over at last. Yet it could not find the source of the light. Suddenly the light flashed again, only to disappear in the swiftness of a blinking eye. The maddened creature swooped toward it, knowing it was deeper in the blackness across the river, lost somewhere in the thousands of small gullies and dales of the lowlands. The mysterious light flashed again and then again, each time moving farther inland, taunting, daring the angered beast to follow. On the other bank, the petrified figures of the two Valemen remained concealed in the darkness as their frightened eyes watched the flying shadow move ever more swiftly away from them until it could no longer be seen.

They remained immobile after the departure of the Skull Bearer. Once again they had come close to death and managed to elude its fatal touch. They sat quietly and listened as the mingled sounds of insect and animal returned to the night. Minutes passed and they began to breathe more easily, their stiff poses relaxing into more comfortable slumps as they looked at each other in amazed relief, knowing the creature had gone, but unable to comprehend how it had happened. Then, before they had any chance at all to speak of the matter, the mysterious light that had flashed from across the river reappeared suddenly on a rise several hundred yards in back of them, disappeared for an instant and then flashed again, closer than before. Shea and Flick watched in wonderment as it moved toward them, weaving slightly.

Moments later the figure of an old, old man stood before them, bent with age and clothed in woodsman's garb, his hair silver in the starlight, his face framed by a long, white beard neatly trimmed and combed. The strange light in his hand appeared fiercely bright at this close distance, and there was no hint of a flame in its center. Suddenly it disappeared and in its place was a cylindrical object gripped in the old man's gnarled hand. He looked at them and smiled a greeting. Shea looked quietly at his ancient face, sensing that the strange old man deserved his respect.

"The light," Shea spoke finally, "how . . . ?"

"A toy of people long since dead and gone." The voice rolled out in a steady whisper that drifted on the cool air. "Gone like the evil creature out there . . ." The words trailed off and he pointed in the direction of the departed Skull Bearer with a thin, wrinkled arm that seemed to hang in the night like some brittle stick of dead wood. Shea looked doubtfully at him, unsure of what should be done next.

"We are traveling eastward . . ." Flick volunteered abruptly.

"To the Anar." The gentle voice cut him short, the elderly head nodding in understanding, the wrinkled eyes sharp in the soft moonlight as they looked from one brother to the other. Suddenly he moved past them to the edge of the swift river and then turned back to them and motioned for them to sit. Shea and Flick did so without hesitation, unable to doubt the old man's intentions. As they sat they felt a great weariness steal over their bodies, their eyes suddenly unable to remain open.

"Sleep, young travelers, that your journey may be shortened." The voice became stronger in their minds, more commanding. They could not resist the feeling of weariness, so pleasant and welcome, and they stretched out on the soft grassy bank in obedience. The figure before them began to change slowly into something new, and through vague, blurred eyes and half-closed eyelids, it appeared that the old man was growing younger and his clothes were not the same. Shea began to mutter slightly, trying to stay awake, to understand, but a moment later both Valemen were asleep.

As they slept they drifted cloudlike through forgotten days of sunlight and happiness in the peaceful woodland home they had left so many days ago. Once again they roamed the friendly confines of the Duln Forest and swam in the cool waters of the mighty Rappahalladran River, the fears and cares of a lifetime swept away in an instant. They moved through the wooded hills and vales of the countryside with freedom unlike anything they had ever experienced. In their sleep they touched, as if for the first time, each plant and animal, bird and insect with new understanding of its importance as a living thing, however small and insignificant. They floated and drifted like the wind, able to smell the freshness of the land, able to see the beauty of the life nature had placed there. Everything was a kaleidoscope of color and smell, with only gentle sounds reaching their tired minds—sounds of the open air and the quiet countryside. Forgotten were the long, hard days of travel through the mist-covered Lowlands of Clete, the sunless days where life was a lost soul wandering hopelessly in a dying land. Forgotten was the darkness of the Black Oaks, the madness of the endless, giant trees hiding them from the sun and sky. Gone was the memory of the Mist Wraith and the pursuing Skull Bearer, constant, relentless in its search. The young Valemen moved in a world without the fears and cares of the real world and for those hours, time dissipated into peace with the momentary beauty of a rainbow at the end of a sudden, violent storm.

They did not know how long it was that they were lost to the world of dreams nor did they know what it was that had happened to them in that time. They only knew, as they stirred into gentle wakefulness, that they were no longer at the edge of the Silver River. They knew as well that the time was new and somehow different; the feeling was exciting but very secure.

As his vision slowly returned, Shea was aware that there were people all around him, watching and waiting. He raised himself slowly up on one elbow, his hazy vision disclosing groups of small figures standing about, bending over in an anxious manner. From out of the vague background emerged a tall, commanding figure in loose-fitting clothes, leaning down to him, a broad hand on his slim shoulder.

"Flick?" he cried apprehensively, rubbing his sleep-filled eyes with one hand as he squinted to make out the features of the shrouded figure.

"You're safe now, Shea." The deep voice seemed to roll out of the shadowy figure. "This is the Anar."

Shea blinked quickly, struggling to rise as the broad hand held him gently down. His eyes began to clear, and he saw in a glimpse the half-raised figure of his brother next to him, just waking from his deep slumber. Around them were the squat, heavyset figures of men Shea instantly knew to be Dwarfs. Shea's eyes caught the strong face of the figure at his side, and at the moment they came to rest on the gleaming chain mail encasing the hand and forearm stretched out to grasp his shoulder lightly, he knew the journey to the Anar was ended. They had found Culhaven and Balinor.

Menion Leah had not found the last leg of the journey to the Anar quite so simple. When he first realized he had become separated from the two Valemen, panic set in. He was not afraid for himself, but he feared the very worst for the Ohmsfords if left alone to find their way out of the mist-shrouded Black Oaks. He, too, had called hopelessly, futilely, stumbling blindly about in the blackness until his voice was cracked. But in the end he was forced to admit to himself that the search was useless under such conditions. Exhausted, he pushed on through the woods in what he believed to be the general direction of the lowlands, consoling himself slightly with the promise that he would find the others in the daylight. He was in the forest a longer time than he had anticipated, breaking free near dawn and collapsing at the edge of the grasslands. Though he did not know it then, he had emerged at a point south of the sleeping brothers. By this time his endurance had been pushed to the limit and sleep came over him so quickly that he could not remember anything after the slow, featherlight feeling of falling as he collapsed in the tall lowland grass. It seemed to him that he slept a very long time, but in fact he awakened only several hours after Shea and Flick had begun their journey toward the Silver River. Believing that he was a considerable distance south of the point the group had been making for while in the Black Oaks, Menion quickly chose to travel north and try to cut across the trail of his companions before reaching the river. If he failed to find them by that time, he knew he would be confronted with the unpleasant probability that they were still lost in the entanglement of the woods.

Hurriedly, the highlander strapped on his light pack, shouldered the great ash bow and the sword of Leah, and began to march rapidly northward. The few hours of afternoon daylight remaining disappeared quickly as he walked, his sharp eyes searching carefully for any sign of human passage. It was almost dusk when he finally picked up the signs of someone traveling in the direction of the Silver River. He found the trail to be several hours old, and he could be reasonably certain that there was more than one person. But there was no way to tell who the travelers were, so Menion pushed on hurriedly in the half-light of dusk, hoping to catch them when they stopped for the night. He knew that the Skull Bearers would also be searching for them, but brushed his fears aside, remembering that there was no reason to connect him with the Valemen. In any event, it was a calculated risk he had to take if he expected to be of any service to his friends.

Shortly thereafter, just before the sun dropped behind the horizon completely, Menion caught sight of a figure to the east of him traveling in the opposite direction. Menion quickly called out to the other, who seemed startled by the highlander's sudden appearance and tried to move away from him. Menion quickly took up the chase, running after the frightened traveler and calling to him that he meant no harm. After several minutes he caught the man, who turned out to be a peddler selling cooking ware to outlying villages and families in these lowlands. The peddler, a bent, timid individual who had been frightened badly by the unexpected pursuit, was now thoroughly terrified by the sight of the tall, sword-bearing highlander facing him at nightfall in the middle of nowhere. Menion hastily explained that he meant no harm, but was looking for two friends from whom he had become separated while traveling through the Black Oaks. This proved to be the worst thing he could have told the little man, who was now thoroughly convinced the stranger was insane. Menion considered telling him that he was the Prince of Leah, but quickly discarded that idea. In the end, the peddler revealed to him that he had seen two travelers fitting the general description of the Valemen from a distance earlier in the afternoon. Menion could not tell if the man had told him that much for fear of his life or to humor him, but he accepted the tale and bade good evening to the little man, who was obviously delighted to be let off so easily, and made a hasty escape southward into the sheltering darkness of evening.

Menion was forced to admit to himself that it was now too dark to attempt to follow the trail of his friends, so he cast about for a likely campsite. He found a pair of large pines that appeared to be the best shelter available and he moved into them, glancing anxiously at the clear night sky. There was sufficient light to enable a prowling Northland creature to find any camped travelers with relative ease, and he inwardly prayed that his friends had sense enough to pick a carefully hidden spot to spend the night. He tossed down his own pack and weapons beneath one of the spreading pines and crawled under the shelter of its low-hanging branches. Famished from the past two days' journey, he devoured the last of his supplies, thinking as he did so that the Valemen would be faced with the same food shortage in the days ahead. Grumbling aloud at the bad luck that had separated them, he reluctantly wrapped himself in his light blanket and was quickly asleep, the great sword of Leah unsheathed at his side, gleaming dully in the moonlight.

Unaware of the events that had transpired that night while he slept soundly several miles south of the Silver River, Menion Leah rose the next day with a new plan in mind. If he could cut across country, traveling northeast, he could catch up with the Valemen much more easily. He was certain that they would be following the edge of the Silver River as it wound its way eastward into the Anar Forests, so their paths had to cross farther upriver. Abandoning the faint traces of the trail left the previous day, Menion began to journey across the lowlands in an easterly direction, thinking to himself that if he did not come across some sign of them up-river when he reached the water's edge, he could double back down-stream. He also entertained hopes of sighting some small game that would provide meat for the evening meal. He whistled and sang to himself as he walked, his lean face relaxed and cheerful at the prospect of a reunion with his lost comrades. He could even picture the stolid disbelief on old Flick's stern face at the sight of his return. He walked easily with long, loping strides that covered the ground quickly and evenly, the swinging, measured step of the experienced woodsman and hunter.

As he traveled, his thoughts drifted back to the events of the past sev-eral days, and he pondered the significance of all that had transpired. He knew little about the history of the Great Wars and the reign of the Druid Council, the mysterious appearance of the so-called Warlock Lord and his defeat by the combined might of three nations. Most disturbing of all was his almost total lack of knowledge of the legend behind the Sword of Shannara, the fabled weapon that for so many years had been a watchword symbolic of freedom through courage. Now it was the birthright of an unknown orphan, half man, half elf. The thought was so preposterous that he still found it impossible to conceive of Shea in that role. He knew in-stinctively that something was missing from the picture—something so ba-sic to the whole puzzle of the great Sword that, without knowing what it was, the three friends were so many windblown leaves.

Menion also knew that he was not a part of this adventure for the sake of friendship alone. Flick had been right about that. Even now he was un-sure exactly why he had been persuaded to undertake this journey. He knew he was less than a Prince of Leah should be. He knew that his inter-est in people had not been deep enough, and he had never really wanted to know them. He had never tried to understand the important problems of governing justly in a society where the monarch's word was the only law. Yet he felt that in his own way he was as good as any man alive. Shea be-lieved he was a man to be looked up to. Perhaps so, he thought idly, but his life to date appeared to consist of one long line of harrowing experiences and wild escapades that had served little or no constructive purpose.

The smooth, grass-covered lowlands changed to rough, barren ground, rising abruptly in small hills and dropping sharply into steep, trenchlike valleys that made travel slow and almost hazardous in places. Menion looked anxiously ahead for some indication of more level terrain, but it was im-possible to see very far, even from the top of the steep rises. He plodded on, deliberately and steadily, ignoring the roughness of the ground and silently berating his decision to come that way. His mind wandered briefly, then suddenly snapped back as he caught the sound of a human voice. He listened intently for several seconds, but could hear nothing further and dismissed it as the wind or his imagination. A moment later he heard it again, only this time it was the clear sound of a woman's voice, singing softly somewhere ahead of him, faint and low. He walked more quickly, wondering if his ears were playing tricks on him, but all the time hearing the woman's mellow voice grow louder. Soon the mesmeric sound of her singing filled the air in a gay, almost wild abandon that reached into the innermost depths of the highlander's mind, bidding him to follow, to be as free as the song itself. Almost in a trance he walked steadily on, smiling broadly at the images the happy song conjured up to him. Vaguely, he wondered what a woman would be doing in these bleak lowlands, miles from any kind of civilization, but the song seemed to dispel all his doubts in its warm assurance that it came from the heart.

At the peak of a particularly bleak rise, somewhat higher than the surrounding hillocks, Menion found her sitting beneath a small twisted tree with long, gnarled branches that reminded him of willow roots. She was a young girl, very beautiful and obviously very much at home in these lands as she sang brightly, seemingly oblivious to anyone who might be attracted by the sound of her voice. He did not conceal his approach, but moved straight to her side, smiling gently at her freshness and youth. She smiled back at him, but made no effort to rise nor to greet him, continuing the gay strains of the tune she had been singing all this time. The Prince of Leah came to a halt several feet away from her, but she quickly beckoned him to come closer and sit next to her beneath the odd-shaped tree. It was then that from somewhere deep within him a small warning nerve twinged, some sixth sense not yet entranced by her vibrant song tugged at him and demanded to know why this young girl should ask a complete stranger to sit with her. There was no reason for his hesitation other than perhaps the innate distrust the hunter has for all things out of place and time in nature; but whatever the reason, it caused the highlander to pause. In that instant the girl and the song disappeared into vapor, leaving Menion to face the strange-looking tree on the barren rise.

For one second Menion hesitated, unable to believe what had just occurred, and then hastily moved to withdraw. But the loose ground about his feet opened even as he paused, releasing a heavy cluster of thick-gnarled roots which wound themselves tightly about the young man's ankles, holding him fast. Menion stumbled over backward trying to break free. For a moment he found his predicament to be ludicrous. But try as he might, he could not work free of those clinging roots. The strangeness of the situation increased almost immediately as he glanced up to see the strange root-limbed tree, previously immobile, approaching in a slow, stretching motion, its limbs extended toward him, their tips containing small but deadly-looking needles. Thoroughly aroused now, Menion dropped his pack and bow in one motion and unsheathed the great sword, realizing that the girl and the song had been an illusion to draw him within reach of this ominous tree. He cut briefly at the roots which bound him, severing them in places, but the work was slow because they were wound so tightly about his ankles that he could not risk broad strokes. Sudden panic set in as he realized he could not get free in time, but he forced the feeling down and shouted his defiance at the plant, which by now was almost on top of him. Swinging in fury as it came within reach, he quickly severed a number of the clutching limbs and it withdrew slightly, its whole frame shuddering in pain. Menion knew that with its next approach he had to strike its nerve center if he expected to destroy it. But the strange tree had other ideas; coiling its limbs into itself, it thrust them toward the imprisoned traveler one at a time, showering him with the tiny needles that flew off the ends. Many of them missed altogether and some bounced harmlessly off his heavy tunic and boots. But others struck the exposed skin of his hands and head and embedded themselves with small stinging sensations. Menion tried to brush them off, while protecting himself from further assault, but the little needles broke off, leaving their tips embedded in his skin. He felt a kind of slow drowsiness begin to steal over him and portions of his nervous system begin to go numb. He realized at once that the needles contained some sort of drug that was designed to put the plant's victim to sleep, to render it helpless for easy disposition. Wildly, he fought the feeling seeping through his system, but soon dropped helplessly to his knees, unable to fight it, knowing that the tree had won.

But amazingly, the deadly tree appeared to hesitate and then to inch slightly backward, coiling again in attack. Slow, heavy footsteps sounded behind the fallen prince, approaching cautiously. He could not turn his head to see who it was, and a deep bass voice warned him abruptly to remain motionless. The tree coiled expectantly to strike, but an instant before it released its deadly needles, it was struck with shattering impact by a huge mace that flew over the shoulder of the fallen Menion. The strange tree was completely toppled by the blow. Obviously injured, it struggled to raise itself and fight back. Behind him, Menion heard the sharp release of a bow-string and a long black arrow embedded itself deep within the plant's thick trunk. Immediately the roots about his feet released their grip and sank into the earth and the main portion of the tree shuddered violently, limbs thrashing the air and showering needles in all directions. A moment later, it drooped slowly to the earth. With a final spasm, it lay motionless.

Still heavily drugged from the needles, Menion felt the strong hands of his rescuer grip his shoulders roughly and force him into a prone position while a broad hunting knife severed the few remaining strands binding his feet. The figure before him was a powerfully built Dwarf, dressed in the green and brown woodsman's clothing worn by most of that race. He was tall for a Dwarf, a little over five feet, and carried a small arsenal of weapons bound about his broad waist. He looked down at the drugged Menion and shook his head dubiously.

"You must be a stranger to do a dumb thing like that," he reprimanded the other in his deep bass voice. "Nobody with any sense plays around with the Sirens."

"I am from Leah . . . to the west," Menion managed to gasp out, his voice thick and strange to his own ears.

"A highlander—I might have known." The Dwarf laughed heartily to himself. "You'd have to be, I suppose. Well, don't worry, you'll be fine in a few days. That drug won't kill you if we get it treated, but you'll be out for a while."

He laughed again and turned to retrieve his mace. Menion, with his final ounce of strength, grasped him by the tunic.

"I must reach . . . the Anar . . . Culhaven," he gasped sharply. "Take me to Balinor . . ."

The Dwarf looked back at him sharply, but Menion had lapsed into unconsciousness. Muttering to himself, the Dwarf picked up his own weapons and those of the fallen highlander. Then with surprising strength, he heaved the limp form of Menion over his broad shoulders, testing the load for balance. Satisfied at last that all was in place, he began trudging steadily, muttering all the while, moving toward the forests of the Anar.

Flick Ohmsford sat quietly on a long stone bench in one of the upper levels of the lavishly beautiful Meade Gardens in the Dwarf community known as Culhaven. He had a perfect view of the amazing gardens stretching down the rocky hillside in systematic levels that tapered off about the edges in carefully laid pieces of cut stone, reminiscent of a long waterfall flowing down a gentle slope. The creation of the gardens on this once barren hillside was a truly marvelous accomplishment. Special soils had been hauled from more fertile regions to be placed on the garden site, enabling thousands of beautiful flowers and plants to flourish year round in the mild climate of the lower Anar. The color was indescribable. To compare the myriad hues of the flowers to the colors of the rainbow would have been a great injustice. Flick attempted briefly to count the various shades, a task he soon found to be impossible. He gave up quickly and turned his attention to the large clearing at the foot of the gardens where members of the Dwarf community were passing on their way to or from whatever work they were engaged in. They were a curious people, it seemed to Flick, so dedicated to hard work and a well-guarded order of life. Everything they did was always carefully planned in advance, meticulously thought out to a point where even the cautious Flick was nettled by the time spent in preparation. But the people were friendly and eager to be of service, a kindness not lost on either of the visiting Valemen, who felt more than a bit out of place in this strange land.

They had been in Culhaven for two days now, and still they had not been able to learn what had happened to them, why they were there, or how long their stay would be. Balinor had told them nothing, advising them that he knew very little himself and that all would be revealed in due time, a comment Flick found to be not only melodramatic but aggravating. There was no sign of Allanon, no word of his whereabouts. Worst of all, there was no news of the absent Menion, and the brothers had been forbidden to leave the safety of the Dwarf village for any reason. Flick glanced to the floor of the gardens again to see if his personal bodyguard was still there, and quickly spied him off to one side, his tireless gaze fixed on the Valeman. Shea had been infuriated by this treatment, but Balinor was quick to point out that someone should be with them at all times in case of an attempt on their lives by one of the roving Northland creatures. Flick had acquiesced readily, remembering all too well the close calls he had already had with the Skull Bearers. He put aside his idle thoughts at the approach of Shea on the winding garden path.

"Anything?" Flick asked anxiously as the other reached his side and sat down quietly next to him.

"Not one word," came the short reply.

Shea felt vaguely exhausted all over again, even though he had had two days to recover from the strange odyssey that had brought them from their home in Shady Vale to the Forests of Anar. Their treatment had been decent if sometimes a bit overdone, and the people seemed genuinely concerned for their welfare. But there had been no word given out as to what was to happen next. Everyone, including Balinor, seemed to be waiting for something, perhaps the arrival of the long-absent Allanon. Balinor had been unable to explain to them how they had reached the Anar. Responding to a mysterious flashing light, he had found them lying on a low river-bank just outside of Culhaven two days ago, and had brought them to the village. He knew nothing of the old man nor of how they had traveled that long distance upstream. When Shea mentioned the legends concerning a King of the Silver River, Balinor shrugged and nonchalantly agreed that anything was possible.

"No news of Menion . . . ?" Flick asked hesitantly.

"Only that the Dwarfs are still out looking for him, and it may take some time," Shea answered quietly. "I don't know what to do next."

Flick inwardly conceded that this last admission had proved to be the story of the entire outing. He glanced downward to the foot of the Meade Gardens where a small cluster of heavily armed Dwarfs were congregating around the commanding figure of Balinor, who had suddenly appeared from the woods beyond. Even from their vantage point atop the gardens, the Valemen could tell that he still wore the chain mail beneath the long hunting cloak they had come to recognize so well. He spoke earnestly with the Dwarfs for a few minutes, his face lined in thought. Shea and Flick knew very little about the Prince of Callahorn, but the people of Culhaven seemed to have the highest regard for him. Menion, too, had spoken well of Balinor. His homeland was the northernmost kingdom of the sprawling Southland. Commonly referred to as the borderlands, it served as a buffer zone fronting the southern boundaries of the Northland. The citizens of Callahorn were predominantly Men, but unlike the majority of the people of their race, they mingled freely with the other races and did not pursue a policy of isolationism. The highly regarded Border Legion was quartered in that distant country, a professional army commanded by Ruhl Buckhannah, King of Callahorn and the father of Balinor. Historically, the entire Southland had relied on Callahorn and the Legion to blunt the initial thrust of an invading army, giving the rest of the land a chance to prepare for battle. In the five hundred years since its formation, the Border Legion had never been defeated.

Balinor had begun a slow ascent to the stone bench where the Valemen sat patiently waiting. He smiled a greeting as he came up to them, aware of the discomfort they felt in not knowing what was to happen to them and of the anxiety they were experiencing for the safety of their missing friend. He sat down next to them and was silent for a few minutes before speaking.

"I know how difficult this must be for you," he began patiently. "I have every available Dwarf warrior out looking for your lost friend. If anyone can find him in this region, they will—and they won't give up, I promise you."

The brothers nodded their understanding of Balinor's efforts to help them in any way possible.

"This is a very dangerous time for these people, though I suppose Allanon did not speak of it. They are facing the threat of an invasion through the upper Anar by Gnomes. There have already been skirmishes all along the border and signs of a huge army massing somewhere above the Streleheim Plains. You may have guessed that all of this is tied in with the Warlock Lord."

"Does this mean that the Southland is in danger, too?" asked an anxious Flick.

"Undoubtedly." Balinor nodded. "That's one reason why I'm here—to arrange a coordinated defensive strategy with the Dwarf nation in case of an all-out assault."

"But where is Allanon then?" asked Shea quickly. "Is he going to get here soon enough to help us? What has the Sword of Shannara got to do with all this?"

Balinor looked at the puzzled faces and shook his head slowly.

"I must honestly confess that I cannot give you the answers to any of those questions. Allanon is a very mysterious figure, but a wise man who has been a dependable ally whenever we have needed him in the past. When I saw him last, several weeks before I spoke to you in Shady Vale, we set a date to meet in the Anar. He is already three days overdue."

He paused in quiet speculation, looking down at the gardens and beyond to the great trees of the Anar Forests, listening to the sounds of the woods and the low voices of the Dwarfs moving about in the clearing below. Then abruptly a shout went up from a cluster of Dwarfs at the foot of the gardens, joined almost immediately by the shouts and cries of others mingled in with a huge clamor swelling from the woods beyond the village of Culhaven. The men on the stone bench rose uncertainly, looking quickly about for some sign of danger. Balinor's strong hand came to rest on the pommel of his broadsword, strapped tightly at his side beneath the hunting cloak. A moment later one of the Dwarfs below came rushing up the path, shouting wildly as he ran.

"They found him, they found him!" he yelled excitedly, almost stumbling in his haste to reach them.

Shea and Flick exchanged startled looks. The runner came to a breathless stop before them, and Balinor gripped his shoulder excitedly.

"Have they found Menion Leah?" he demanded quickly.

The Dwarf nodded happily, his short, stocky frame heaving with the exertion of the dash to reach them with the good news. Without a word, Balinor bounded down the path toward the shouting, Shea and Flick behind him. They reached the clearing below in a matter of seconds and ran along the main path through the woods leading to the village of Culhaven several hundred yards beyond. Ahead of them they could hear the excited shouting of the Dwarf population congratulating whomever it was who had found the lost highlander. They reached the village and, pushing through the throngs of Dwarfs blocking the way, made straight for the center of all the excitement. A ring of guards parted to let them into a small courtyard formed by buildings on the right and left and a high stone wall in the rear. On a long wooden table lay the motionless body of Menion Leah, his face pale and seemingly lifeless. A team of Dwarf doctors bent dutifully over the inert form, apparently treating him for some injury. Shea gave a sharp cry and tried to rush forward, but Balinor's strong arm held him back as the warrior called out to one of the nearby Dwarfs.

"Pahn, what's happened here?"

The solid-looking Dwarf, dressed in armor and apparently one of the returning search party, hastened to their side.

"He'll be all right after he's treated. He was found entangled in one of the Sirens out in the middle of the Battlemound lowlands below the Silver River. Our search party didn't find him. It was Hendel, returning from the cities south of Anar."

Balinor nodded and looked about for some sign of the rescuer.

"He left for the assembly hall to make his report," the Dwarf responded to the unasked question.

Motioning the two Valemen to follow him, Balinor made his way out of the courtyard through the crowd and across the main street to the large assembly hall. Inside were the offices of the governing officials of the village and the assembly room, in which they found the Dwarf Hendel sitting on one of the long benches, eating ravenously while a scribe took down his report. Hendel looked up as they approached, glanced curiously at the Valemen and nodded briefly to Balinor, continuing to devour his meal without interruption. Balinor dismissed the scribe, and the three men

sat down across from the disinterested Dwarf, who appeared both exhausted and starved.

"What an idiot, tackling one of those Sirens with a sword," he muttered. "Got spunk though. How is he?"

"He'll be fine after he's treated," replied Balinor grinning reassuringly
at the uneasy Valemen. "How did you find him?"

"Heard him yelling." The other continued to eat without pausing. "I
had to carry him almost seven miles before I ran into Pahn and the search
party along the Silver River."

He paused and looked again at the two Valemen, who were listening
intently. The Dwarf appraised them curiously and looked back at Balinor,
eyebrows raised.

"Friends of the highlander—and of Allanon," responded the borderman, cocking his head meaningfully. Hendel merely nodded to them
curtly.

"I'd never have known who he was if he hadn't mentioned your
name," Hendel informed them shortly, indicating the tall borderman. "It
might help matters if now and then someone would tell me what was going on—before it's happened, not after."

He declined to comment further, and an amused Balinor smiled over
to the puzzled brothers, shrugging slightly to indicate the Dwarf was irascible by nature. Shea and Flick were a bit uncertain about the fellow's temperament and had purposely kept silent while the other two conversed,
though both Valemen were eager to hear the full story behind Menion's
rescue.

"What's your report on Sterne and Wayford?" Balinor asked finally, re-
ferring to the large Southland cities immediately south and west of the Anar.

Hendel ceased eating and laughed abruptly.

"The officials of those two fine communities will consider the matter
and send along a report. Typical bungling officials, elected by the disinterested people to juggle the ball until it can be passed on to some other fool.
I could tell five minutes after I opened my mouth that they thought I was
crazy. They don't see the danger until the sword is at their own throats—
then they scream for assistance from those of us who knew it all along." He
paused and resumed his meal, obviously disgusted with the whole subject.

"I should have expected that, I suppose." Balinor sounded worried.
"How can we convince them of the danger? There hasn't been a war in so
many years that no one wants to believe it could happen now."

"That's not the real problem, as you well know," interjected the irate
Hendel. "They simply don't feel they should be involved in the matter. After all, the frontiers are protected by Dwarfs, not to mention the cities of
Callahorn and the Border Legion. We've been doing it up to now—why
can't we keep doing it? Those poor fools . . ."

He trailed off slowly, finished with his statement and his meal, feeling
tired from the long trip home. He had been on the road for almost three
weeks, traveling to the cities of the Southland, and it all seemed to have
been for nothing. He felt keenly discouraged.

"I don't understand what's happened," Shea announced quietly.

"Well, that's two of us," Hendel replied sullenly. "I'm going to bed for about two weeks. See you then."

He stood up abruptly and walked out of the assembly room without even a short farewell, his broad shoulders stooped wearily. The three men watched him go without speaking, their eyes fixed on his departing silhouette until it was lost from sight. Then Shea turned questioningly to Balinor.

"It's the age-old tale of complacency, Shea." The tall warrior sighed deeply and stretched as he rose. "We may be standing on the brink of the greatest war in a thousand years, but no one wants to accept the fact. Everyone gets in the same rut—let a few take care of the gates to the city while the rest forget and go back to their homes. It becomes a habit—depending on a few to protect the rest. And then one day . . . the few are not enough, and the enemy is within the city—right through the open gates . . ."

"Is there really going to be a war?" Flick asked, almost fearfully.

"That is the question exactly," Balinor responded slowly. "The only man who can give us the answer is absent . . . and overdue."

In the excitement of finding Menion alive and well, the Valemen had temporarily forgotten Allanon, the man who was the reason for their being in the Anar in the first place. The by-now familiar questions again flashed through their minds with new persistency, but the Valemen had learned to live with them over the past few weeks and all doubts were reluctantly shoved aside once more. Balinor caught their attention as he moved toward the open door, and they quickly followed.

"You mustn't mind Hendel, you know," he reassured them as they walked. "He's gruff like that with everyone, but he's one of the finest friends you could ask for. He has fought and outwitted the Gnomes along the upper Anar for years, protecting his people and the complacent citizens of the Southland who so quickly forget the crucial role the Dwarfs play as guardians of these borders. The Gnomes would like to get their hands on him, I can tell you."

Shea and Flick said nothing, ashamed of the fact that the people of their own race could be so selfish, yet realizing that they, too, had been ignorant of the situation in the Anar before hearing of it from Balinor. They were bothered by the thought of renewed hostilities between the races, recalling their history lessons on the old race wars and the terrible hatred of those bitter years. The possibility of a third war of the races was chilling.

"Why don't you two go on back to the gardens," advised the Prince of Callahorn. "I'll have a message sent as soon as I hear of any change in Menion's condition."

The brothers reluctantly agreed, knowing they had no other choice in the matter anyway. Before turning in that night, they stopped by the room where Menion was being kept, only to be told by the Dwarf sentry that their friend was asleep and should not be disturbed.

But by the following afternoon, the highlander was awake and being

visited by the anxious Valemen. Even Flick was grudgingly relieved to see
the other alive and well, though he solemnly intoned that he had correctly
predicted their misfortune many days in advance when they first decided
to journey through the Black Oaks. Menion and Shea both laughed at
Flick's eternal pessimism, but did not argue the point. Shea explained how
Menion had been brought to Culhaven by the Dwarf Hendel, and then
went on to relate the mysterious way in which he and Flick had been
found near the Silver River. Menion was as mystified as they over their
strange journey and could offer no logical explanation. Shea carefully refrained from mentioning the legend of a King of the Silver River, knowing full well what the highlander's response would be to any speculation
that involved an old folktale.

That same day, in the early hours of the evening, word reached them
that Allanon had returned. Shea and Flick were about to leave their rooms
to visit Menion when they heard the excited shouts of Dwarfs rushing past
their open windows toward the assembly hall where some sort of meeting
was about to begin. The anxious Valemen had not taken two steps beyond
their doorway when they were surrounded by a team of four Dwarf guards
and hustled quickly through the pushing crowds, past the open doors of
the large assembly into a small adjoining room, where they were told to remain. The Dwarfs closed the door wordlessly as they exited, slid the lock
bolts into place, and assumed positions immediately outside. The room was
brightly lit and furnished with several long tables and benches, at which
the bewildered Valemen silently seated themselves. The windows to the
room were closed and even without checking, Shea knew they would be
barred like the door. From the assembly hall they could hear the deep
voice of a single speaker.

Several minutes later the door to the chamber opened and Menion,
looking flushed but otherwise quite well, was briskly ushered in by two
Dwarf guards. When they were left alone, the highlander explained that
they had come for him the same as for the Valemen. From snatches of
conversation he had heard on the way over, it appeared that the Dwarfs in
Culhaven and probably all of the Anar were preparing for war. Whatever
news Allanon had brought back with him had thrown matters into a state
of confusion in the Dwarf community. He thought he had caught a quick
glimpse of Balinor through the open doors of the assembly hall, standing
on the platform at the front of the building, but the guards had rushed him
past and he couldn't be sure.

The voices from the congregation next door rose in a thunderous roar,
and all three paused expectantly. Seconds passed as the shouting continued
to roll through the large hall, spreading to the open grounds outside where
it was taken up by the Dwarfs there. At the deafening peak of the shouting,
the door to their room suddenly burst open to admit the dark, commanding figure of Allanon.

He walked over to the Valemen quickly, shook their hands, and congratulated them on their successful journey to Culhaven. He was dressed as

he had been when Flick had first encountered him, his lean face half hidden in the long cowl, his whole appearance dark and foreboding. He greeted Menion courteously and moved to the head of the nearest table, motioning the others to be seated. He had been followed into the room by Balinor and a number of Dwarfs who were apparently leaders in the community, among them the irascible Hendel. Bringing up the rear of this procession were two slim, almost shadowy figures in curious, loose-fitting woodsman garb, who quietly took seats near Allanon at the head of the table. Shea could see them clearly from his position at the other end, and concluded after a quick observation that they were Elves from the distant Westland. Their keen features, from the sharply raised eyebrows to the strange pointed ears, marked them distinctively. Shea turned back and saw that both Flick and Menion were looking at him curiously, obviously appraising his own strong resemblance to the strangers. None of them had ever seen an Elf, and while they knew that Shea was half Elf and had heard descriptions given of the Elven people, none had ever had a chance to compare the Valeman to one.

"My friends." The deep voice of Allanon boomed out in the slight stir of voices as he rose commandingly to his full height of seven feet. The room was instantly silent as all faces turned in his direction. "My friends, I must now tell you what I have as yet told no one else. We have suffered a tragic loss."

He paused and looked at the anxious faces in turn.

"Paranor has fallen. A division of Gnome hunters under the command of the Warlock Lord has seized the Sword of Shannara!"

There was dead silence for about two seconds before the Dwarfs were on their feet, shouting in anger. Balinor rose quickly in an effort to quiet them. Shea and Flick looked at each other in disbelief. Only Menion seemed unsurprised by the announcement, his lean face carefully scrutinizing the dark figure at the head of the table.

"Paranor was taken from within," Allanon continued after some semblance of order had been restored. "There is little question as to the fate of those who guarded the fortress and the Sword. I am told that all were executed. No one knows exactly how it happened."

"Have you been there?" Shea asked suddenly, feeling almost immediately that it was a stupid question.

"I left your home in the Vale so suddenly because I received word that an attempt would be made to secure Paranor. I arrived too late to help those within and barely escaped detection myself. That is one of the reasons I am so late in reaching Culhaven."

"But if Paranor has fallen and the Sword been taken . . . ?" Flick's whispered question trailed off ominously.

"Then what can we do now?" Allanon finished harshly. "This is the problem facing us, the one we must provide an immediate answer for—the reason for this council."

Allanon suddenly left his position at the head of the long table and moved around until he was standing directly behind Shea. He placed one great hand on the slim shoulder and faced his attentive audience.

"The Sword of Shannara is useless in the hands of the Warlock Lord. It can only be raised by a son of the House of Jerle Shannara—this alone prevents the evil one from striking now. Instead, he has systematically hunted down and destroyed all members of that House, one at a time, one after another, even those I tried to protect—all whom I could find. Now they are all dead—all save one, and that one is young Shea. Shea is only half Elf, but he is a direct descendant of the King who carried the great Sword so many years before. Now he must raise it once again."

Shea would have bolted for the door if it had not been for the strong hand gripping his shoulder. He looked desperately at Flick and saw the fear in his own eyes mirrored in those of his brother's. Menion had not moved, but appeared visibly impressed by this grim declaration. What Allanon seemed to expect from Shea was more than any man had the right to ask.

"Well, I think we have shaken our young friend a bit." Allanon laughed shortly. "Do not despair, Shea. Things are not as bad as they may seem to you right now." He turned abruptly, walked back to the head of the table and faced the others.

"We must recover the Sword at all costs. There is no other choice left to us. If we fail to do this, the whole of the land will be plunged into the greatest war the races have seen since the near destruction of life two thousand years ago. The Sword is the key. Without it, we must fall back on our mortal strength, our fighting prowess—a battle with iron and muscle that can only result in uncountable thousands dying on both sides. The evil is the Warlock Lord, and he cannot be destroyed without the aid of the Sword—and the courage of a few men, not the least of whom must be those of us in this room."

Again he paused to measure the force of his words. There was absolute silence as he looked doubtfully at the silent gallery of grim faces staring back. Suddenly Menion Leah rose at the far end of the table and faced the giant speaker.

"What you are suggesting is that we go after the Sword—to Paranor."

Allanon nodded slowly, a half smile playing over his thin lips as he waited for a reaction from the startled listeners. His deep-set eyes twinkled blackly beneath the great brow, watching carefully the faces about him. Menion sat down slowly, total disbelief showing plainly on his handsome features, as Allanon continued.

"The Sword is still at Paranor; there is an excellent possibility that it will remain there. Neither Brona nor the Bearers of the Skull can personally remove the talisman—its mere physical presence is an anathema to their continued existence in the mortal world. Any form of exposure for more than several minutes would cause excruciating pain. This means that any attempt to transport the Sword north to the Skull Kingdom must be accomplished by use of the Gnomes that hold Paranor.

"Eventine and his Elven warriors were given the task of securing the

Druid stronghold and the Sword. While Paranor has been lost to us, the Elves still hold the southern stretch of the Streleheim north of the fortress, and any attempt to travel north to the Dark Lord would require breaking through their patrols. Apparently Eventine was not at Paranor when it was taken, and I have no reason to believe that he will not endeavor to regain the Sword or, at the very least, thwart any attempt to remove it. The Warlock Lord will be aware of this, and I do not think he will risk losing the weapon by having the Gnomes carry it out. Instead, he will entrench at Paranor until his army moves south.

"There is a possibility that the Warlock Lord does not expect us to attempt to regain the Sword. He may believe that the House of Shannara has been exterminated. He may expect us to concentrate on strengthening our defenses against his forthcoming assault. If we act immediately, a small party may be able to slip into the Keep undetected and retrieve the Sword. Such an undertaking would be dangerous, but if there is even the remotest chance of success, the risk is worth it."

Balinor had risen and indicated he wished to speak to those assembled. Allanon nodded and sat down.

"I do not understand the power of the Sword over the Warlock Lord—that much I freely admit," the tall warrior began. "But I do know the threat that we all face if Brona's army invades the Southland and the Anar as our reports indicate it is preparing to do. My homeland will be the first to face this threat, and if I can prevent it in any way, then I cannot do otherwise. I will go with Allanon."

The Dwarfs leaped up again at this point and enthusiastically shouted their support. Allanon stood up and raised his long arm in a plea for silence.

"These two young Elves at my side are cousins of Eventine. They will accompany me, for their stake in this matter is at least as great as your own. Balinor will go as well, and I will take one of the Dwarf chieftains—no more. This must be a small, highly skilled party of hunters if we are to succeed. Pick the best man among you and let him come with us."

He looked to the end of the table, where Shea and Flick sat watching in a mixed state of shock and confusion. Menion Leah pondered quietly, looking at no one in particular. Allanon glanced expectantly at Shea, his grim face suddenly softening as he saw the frightened eyes of the young Valeman who had come so far, through so many dangers to this apparent haven of safety, only to be told that he was expected to leave it for an even more perilous trip northward. But there had been no time to break the news to the Valeman in a gentle way. He shook his head doubtfully and waited.

"I think I had better go." The abrupt declaration came from Menion, who had again risen to his feet to face the others. "I came with Shea this far to be certain he reached the safety of Culhaven, which he has done. My duty to him is finished, but I owe it to my homeland and to my people to protect them in any way I can."

"What can you offer then?" asked Allanon abruptly, astonished that the highlander would volunteer without first speaking to his friends. Shea and Flick were clearly dumbfounded by this unexpected announcement.

"I'm the best bowman in the Southland," Menion answered smoothly. "Probably the best tracker as well."

Allanon seemed to hesitate for a moment, then looked to Balinor, who quietly shrugged. For a brief moment Menion and Allanon locked gazes, as if to judge each other's intentions. Menion smiled coldly at the grim historian.

"Why should I answer to you?" he queried shortly.

The dark figure at the other end of the table stared at him almost curiously and a deathly silence settled over the company. Even Balinor stepped back one short pace in shock. Shea knew instantly that Menion was asking for trouble and that everyone at the table except the three companions knew something about the foreboding Allanon they did not. The frightened Valeman shot a quick look at Flick, whose flushed face had gone pale at the thought of a confrontation between the two men. Desperate to avoid any trouble, Shea stood up suddenly and cleared his throat. Everyone looked in his direction, and his mind went blank.

"You have something to say?" demanded Allanon blackly. Shea nodded and his mind raced desperately, knowing what was expected. He looked again to Flick, who managed a barely perceptible nod indicating that he would go along with whatever his brother decided. Shea cleared his throat a second time.

"My special skill appears to be that I was born in the wrong family, but I had better see this matter through. Flick and I—Menion, too—will go to Paranor."

Allanon nodded his approval and even managed a slight smile, inwardly pleased with the young Valeman. Shea, more than any of the others, had to be strong. He was the last son of the house of Shannara, and the fate of so many would depend on that single, small chance of birth.

At the other end of the table, Menion Leah relaxed quietly in his seat, a barely audible sigh of relief escaping his lips as he silently congratulated himself. He had deliberately provoked Allanon, and in so doing had forced Shea to come to his rescue by agreeing to go to Paranor. It had been a desperate gamble to induce the little Valeman to make up his mind that he was going with them. The highlander had come close to what might have been a fatal confrontation with Allanon. He had been lucky. He wondered if luck would smile on all of them during the journey ahead.

Shea stood quietly in the darkness outside the assembly hall and let the night air wash over his hot face in cool waves. Flick was immediately to his right, the broad face grim in the shadowed moonlight. Menion leaned idly against a tall oak some yards off to their left. The meeting had concluded, and Allanon had asked them to wait for him. The tall wanderer was still inside making preparations with the Dwarf elders to counter the expected invasion from the upper Anar. Balinor was with them, coordinating the defense of the famed Border Legion in distant Callahorn with that of the Dwarf army of the Eastland. Shea was relieved to be out of the stuffy little room—out in the open night where he could consider more clearly his hasty decision to go with the company to Paranor. He knew—and he guessed Flick must have known as well—that they could not expect to stay out of the inevitable conflict centering around the Sword of Shannara. They could have stayed in Culhaven, living almost like prisoners, hoping that the Dwarf people would protect them from the searching Skull Bearers. They could have stayed in this strange land, apart from all who knew them, perhaps forgotten in time by everyone except the Dwarfs. But to alienate themselves that way would have been worse than any imaginable fate at the hands of the enemy. For the first time Shea realized that he must accept the fact, finally and forever, that he was no longer merely the adopted son of Curzad Ohmsford. He was a son of the Elven House of Shannara, the son of kings and the heir to the fabled Sword, and though he would have wished it otherwise, he must accept what chance had decreed for him.

He looked quietly at his brother, who stood lost in thought, staring at the darkened earth, and he felt a keen pang of sorrow at the remembrance of the other's loyalty. Flick was courageous and loved him, but he had not bargained for this unexpected turn of events that would take them into the heart of the enemy's country. Shea did not want Flick to be involved in this matter—it was not his responsibility. He knew that the stocky Valeman would never desert him so long as he felt he could help, but perhaps now Flick could be persuaded to remain behind, even to return to Shady Vale to explain to their father what had befallen them. But even as he toyed with the idea, he discarded it, knowing that Flick would never turn back. Whatever else happened, he would see this matter through.

"There was a time," Flick's quiet voice broke into his thoughts, "when I would have sworn that I would live out my life in uneventful solitude in Shady Vale. Now it appears that I will be a part of an effort to save mankind."

"Do you think I should have chosen otherwise?" Shea asked after a moment's silent thought.

"No, I don't think so." Flick shook his head. "But remember what we talked about on the trip here—about things being beyond our control, even our understanding? You see how little control we now have over what's to become of us."

He paused and looked squarely over to his brother. "I think you made the right choice, and whatever happens, I'll be with you."

Shea smiled broadly and placed a hand on the other's shoulder, thinking to himself that this was exactly what he had predicted Flick would say. It was a small gesture perhaps, but one that meant more to him than any other could have. He was aware of the sudden approach of Menion from the other side and turned to face the highlander.

"I suppose you think me some sort of fool after what happened in there tonight," Menion stated abruptly. "But this fool stands along with old Flick. Whatever happens, we'll face it together, be it mortal or spirit."

"You caused that scene in there to get Shea to agree to go, didn't you?" an irate Flick demanded. "That's the lowest trick I have ever witnessed!"

"Never mind, Flick," Shea cut him short. "Menion knew what he was doing, and he did the right thing. I would have decided to go anyway—at least I'd like to believe I would. Now we've got to forget the past, forget our differences, and stand together for our own preservation."

"As long as I stand where I can see him," retorted his brother bitterly.

The door to the conference room opened suddenly and the broad figure of Balinor was silhouetted in the torchlight from within. He surveyed the three men standing just beyond him in the darkness, then closed the door and walked over to them, smiling slightly as he approached.

"I'm glad you decided to come with us, all of you," he stated simply. "I must add, Shea, that without you, the trip would have been pointless. Without the heir of Jerle Shannara, the Sword is only so much metal."

"What can you tell us about this magic weapon?" Menion asked quickly.

"I'll leave that to Allanon," replied Balinor. "He plans to speak with you here in just a few minutes."

Menion nodded, inwardly disturbed at the prospect of encountering the tall man again that evening, but curious to hear more about the power of the Sword. Shea and Flick exchanged quick glances. At last they would learn the full story behind what was happening in the Northland.

"Why are you here, Balinor?" Flick asked cautiously, not wishing to pry into the borderman's personal affairs.

"It's a rather long story—you would not be interested," replied the other almost sharply, immediately causing Flick to believe he had overstepped his bounds. Balinor saw his chagrined look, and smiled reassuringly. "My family and I have not been on very good terms lately. My younger brother and I had a . . . disagreement, and I wanted to leave the city for a while. Allanon asked me to accompany him to the Anar. Hendel and others were old friends, so I agreed."

"Sounds like a familiar tale," commented Menion dryly. "I've had some problems like that myself from time to time."

Balinor nodded and managed a half smile, but Shea could tell from his eyes that he did not consider this a laughing matter. Whatever had caused him to leave Callahorn was more serious than anything Menion had ever encountered in Leah. Shea quickly changed the subject.

"What can you tell us about Allanon? We seem to be placing an unusual amount of trust in him, and we still know absolutely nothing about the man. Who is he?"

Balinor arched his eyebrows and smiled, amused by the question and at the same time uncertain as to how it should be answered. He walked away from them a little, thinking to himself, and then turned back abruptly and motioned vaguely toward the assembly hall.

"I really don't know much about Allanon myself," he admitted frankly. "He travels a great deal, exploring the country, recording in his notes the changes and growth of the land and its people. He's well known in all the nations—I think he has been everywhere. The extent of his knowledge of this world is extraordinary—most of it isn't in any book. He is very remarkable. . . ."

"But who is he?" Shea persisted eagerly, feeling that he must learn the true origin of the historian.

"I can't say for certain, because he has never confided completely even in me, and I am almost like a son to him," Balinor stated very quietly, so softly in fact that they all moved a bit closer to be certain they missed nothing of what was to follow. "The elders of the Dwarfs and of my own kingdom say that he is the greatest of the Druids, that almost forgotten Council that governed men over a thousand years ago. They say that he is a direct descendant of the Druid Bremen—perhaps even of Galaphile himself. I think there is more than a little truth in that statement, because he went to Paranor often and stayed for long periods, recording his findings in the great record books stored there."

He paused for a moment and his three listeners glanced at one another, wondering if the grim historian could actually be a direct descendant of the Druids, thinking in awe of the centuries of history behind the man. Shea had suspected before that Allanon was one of the ancient philosopher-teachers known as Druids, and it seemed apparent that the man possessed a greater knowledge of the races and the origins of the threat facing them than did anyone else. He turned back to Balinor, who was speaking again.

"I can't explain it, but I don't believe we could be in better company for any peril, even were we to come face-to-face with the Warlock Lord himself. Though I haven't one shred of concrete evidence nor even an example to cite you, I'm certain that Allanon's power is beyond anything we have ever seen. He would be a very, very dangerous enemy."

"Of that, I haven't the slightest doubt," Flick muttered dryly.

Only minutes later, the door of the conference room opened and Allanon stepped quietly into view. In the half-light of the moon, he was huge and forbidding, almost a replica of the dreaded Skull Bearers they feared so much, the dark cape billowing slightly as he moved toward them, his lean face hidden in the depths of the long cowl about his head. They were silent as he approached, wondering what he would tell them, what it would mean for them in the days ahead. Perhaps he knew their thoughts instinctively as he walked up to them, but their eyes could not pierce the mask of inscrutability that cloaked his grim features and sheltered the man buried within. They could only see the sudden glint of his eyes as he stopped before them and looked slowly from one face to the next. A deep silence settled ominously over the little group.

"The time has come for you to learn the full story behind the Sword of Shannara, to learn the history of the races as only I know it to be." His voice reached out and drew them commandingly to him. "It is essential that Shea should understand, and since the rest of you share the risks involved, you should also know the truth. What you will learn tonight must be kept in confidence until I tell you it no longer matters. This will be hard, but you must do it."

He motioned for them to follow him and moved away from the clearing, drawing them deeper into the darkness of the trees beyond. When they were several hundred feet into the forest, he turned into a small, almost hidden clearing. He seated himself on the worn stub of an ancient trunk and motioned the others to find a place. They did so quickly and waited in silence as the famous historian gathered his thoughts and prepared to speak.

"A very long time ago," he began finally, still considering his explanation as he spoke, "before the Great Wars, before the existence of the races as we know them today, the land was—or was thought to be—populated only by Man. Civilization had developed even before then for many thousands of years—years of hard toil and learning that brought Man to a point where he was on the verge of mastering the secrets of life itself. It was a fabulous, exciting time to live in, so expansive that much of it would be totally beyond your comprehension were I empowered to draw you the most perfect picture. But while Man worked all those years to discover the secrets of life, he never managed to escape his overpowering fascination for death. It was a constant alternative, even in the most civilized of the nations. Strangely enough, the catalyst of each new discovery was the same endless pursuit—the study of science. Not the science the races know today—not the study of animal life, plant life, the earth, and the simple arts. This was a science of machines and power, one that divided itself into infinite fields of exploration, all of which worked toward the same two ends—discovering better ways to live or quicker ways to kill."

He paused and laughed grimly to himself, cocking his head in the direction of the attentive Balinor.

"Very strange indeed, when you think about it—that Man should spend so much time working toward two such obviously different goals. Even now nothing has changed—even after all these years. . . ."

His voice trailed off for a moment and Shea risked a brief look at the others, but their eyes were fixed on the speaker.

"Sciences of physical power!" Allanon's sudden exclamation brought Shea's head around with a snap. "These were the means to all the ends of that era. Two thousand years ago the achievements of the human race were unparalleled in earth's history. Man's age-old enemy, Death, could now claim only those who had lived out their natural lifetime. Sickness was virtually eliminated and, given a bit more time, Man would even have found a way to prolong life. Some philosophers claimed that the secrets of life were forbidden to mortals. No one had ever proved otherwise. They might have done so, but their time ran out and the same elements of power that had made life free from sickness and infirmity nearly destroyed it altogether. The Great Wars began, building gradually from smaller disputes between a few peoples and spreading steadily, despite the realization of what was happening—spreading from little matters into basic hatreds: race, nationality, boundaries, creeds . . . in the end, everything. Then suddenly, so suddenly that few knew what happened, the entire world was enveloped in a series of retaliatory attacks by the different countries, all very scientifically planned and executed. In a matter of minutes, the science of thousands of years, the learning of centuries, culminated in an almost total destruction of life.

"The Great Wars." The deep voice was grim, the glint of the dark eyes watching carefully the faces of his listeners. "Very apt name. The power expended in those few minutes of battle not only succeeded in wiping out those thousands of years of human growth, but it also began a series of explosions and upheavals that completely altered the surface of the land. The initial force did most of the damage, killing every living thing over ninety percent of the face of the earth, but the aftereffects carried on the alteration and extinction, breaking the continents apart, drying up oceans, making lands and seas uninhabitable for several hundred years. It should have been the end of all life, perhaps the end of the world itself. Only a miracle prevented that end."

"I can't believe it." The words slipped out before Shea could catch himself, and Allanon looked toward him, the familiar mocking smile spreading over his lips.

"That's your history of civilized man, Shea," he murmured darkly. "But what happened thereafter concerns us more directly. Remnants of the race of Man managed to survive during the terrible period following the holocaust, living in isolated sectors of the globe, fighting the elements for survival. This was the beginning of the development of the races as they are today—Men, Dwarfs, Gnomes, Trolls, and some say the Elves— but they were always there and that's another story for another time."

Allanon had made exactly the same comment concerning the Elven people to the Ohmsford brothers in Shady Vale. Shea wanted badly to stop the narration at that point to ask about the race of Elves and about his own origin. But he knew better than to irritate the tall historian by breaking in as he had several times during their first meeting.

"A few men remembered the secrets of the sciences that had shaped their way of life prior to the destruction of the old world. Only a few remembered. Most were little more than primitive creatures, and the few could recollect only bits and pieces of knowledge. But they had kept their books of learning intact and these could tell them most of the secrets of the old sciences. They kept them hidden and secure during that first several hundred years, unable to put the words to practical use, waiting for the time when they might. They read their precious texts instead and then, as the books themselves began to crumble with age and there was no way to preserve them or copy them, those few men who possessed the books began to memorize the information. The years passed and the knowledge was passed down carefully from father to son, each generation keeping the knowledge safely within the family, guarding it from those who didn't use it wisely, who might create a world in which the Great Wars could happen a second time. In the end, even after it once again became possible to record the information in those irreplaceable books, the men who had memorized them declined to do so. They were still afraid of the consequences, afraid of one another and even themselves. So they decided, individually for the most part, to wait for the right time to offer their knowledge to the growing new races.

"The years passed in this way as the new races slowly began to develop beyond the stage of primitive life. They began to unify into communities, trying to build a new life out of the dust of the old—but as you have already been told, they did not prove equal to the task. They quarreled violently over land, petty disputes which soon turned to armed conflict between the races. It was then, when the sons of those who had first kept the secrets of the old life, the old sciences, saw that matters were steadily regressing toward the very thing that had destroyed the old world, that they decided to act. The man called Galaphile saw what was happening and realized that if nothing were done, the races would surely be at war. So he called together a select group of men, all he could find who possessed any knowledge of the old books, to a council at Paranor."

"So that was the first Druid Council," murmured Menion Leah in wonder. "A council of all the knowledgeable men of that era, pooling their learning to save the races."

"A very praiseworthy effort at explaining a desperate attempt to prevent extermination of life," laughed Allanon shortly. "The Druid Council was formed with the best intentions on the part of most, perhaps all at first. They exerted a tremendous influence over the races because they were capable of offering so much to make life considerably better for everyone. They operated strictly as a group, each man contributing his knowledge for the benefit of all. Although they succeeded in preventing an outbreak of total war, and kept peace between the races at first, they encountered unexpected problems. The knowledge that each possessed had become unavoidably altered in small ways in the telling from generation to generation, so that many of the key understandings were different than they had been.

"Complicating the situation was an understandable inability to coordinate the different materials, the knowledge of the different sciences. For many of the council members, the learning passed down to them by their ancestors lacked meaning in practical terms and much of it appeared to be so many jumbled words. So while the Druids, as they called themselves after an ancient group who sought understanding, were able to aid the races in many ways, they found themselves unable to piece together enough out of the texts they had memorized to master readily any of the important concepts of the great sciences, the concepts they felt certain would help the country to grow and prosper."

"Then the Druids wanted the old world rebuilt on their terms," spoke up Shea quickly. "They wanted to prevent the wars that had destroyed them the first time, yet re-create the benefits of all the old sciences."

Flick shook his head in bewilderment, unable to see what all this had to do with the Warlock Lord and the Sword.

"Correct," Allanon noted. "But the Druid Council, for all its vast knowledge and good intentions, overlooked a basic concept of human existence. Whenever an intelligent creature possesses an innate desire to improve its conditions, to unlock the secrets of progress, it will find the means to do so—if not by one method, then by another. The Druids secluded themselves at Paranor, away from the races of the land, while they worked alone or in small groups to master the secrets of the old sciences. Most relied on the material at hand, the knowledge of individual members related to that of the entire Council to try to rebuild and reconstruct the old means of harnessing power. But some were not content with this approach. A few felt that, instead of trying to understand the words and thoughts of the ancient recollections better, such knowledge as could be immediately grasped should be acted upon and developed in connection with new ideas, new rationalizations.

"So it was that a few members of the council, acting under the leadership of one called Brona, began to delve into the ancient mysteries without waiting for a full understanding of the old sciences. They had phenomenal minds, genius in a few instances, and they were eager to succeed, impatient to master the power that would be so useful to the races. But by a strange quirk of fate, their discoveries and their developments led them further and further from the studies of the Council. The old sciences were puzzles without answers for them, and so they deviated into other fields of thought, slowly and relentlessly intertwining themselves in a realm of study that none had ever mastered and none called science. What they began to unveil was the infinite power of the mystic—sorcery! They mastered a few of the secrets of the mystic before they were discovered by the Council and commanded to abandon their work. There was a violent disagreement and the followers of Brona left the Council in anger, determined to continue their own approach. They disappeared and were not seen again."

He paused for a moment, considering his explanation. His listeners waited impatiently.

"We know now what happened in the years that followed. During his prolonged studies, Brona uncovered the deepest secrets of sorcery and mastered them. But in the process he lost his own identity, eventually even his own soul to the powers he had sought so eagerly. Forgotten were the old sciences and their purpose in the world of man. Forgotten was the Druid Council and its goal of a better world. Forgotten was everything but the driving urge to learn more of the mystic arts, the secrets of the mind's power to reach into other worlds. Brona was obsessed with the need to extend his power—to dominate men and the world they inhabited through mastery of this terrible force. The result of this ambition was the infamous First War of the Races, when he gained domination over the weak and confused minds of the race of Man, causing that hapless people to make war on the other races, subjecting them to the will of the man who was no longer a man, who was no longer even the master of himself."

"And his followers . . . ?" asked Menion slowly.

"Victims of the same. They became servants to their leader, all slaves of the strange power of sorcery. . . ." Allanon trailed off hesitantly, as if to add something but uncertain of its effect on his listeners. Thinking better of it, he continued. "The fact that these unfortunate Druids stumbled onto the very opposite of what they were seeking is in itself a lesson to Man. Perhaps with patience, they might have pieced together the missing links to the old sciences rather than uncovering the terrible power of the spirit world that fed eagerly on their unprotected minds until they were devoured. Human minds are not equipped to face the realities of nonmaterial existence on this sphere. It is too much for any mortal to bear for long."

Again he trailed off into ominous silence. The listeners now understood the nature of the enemy they were trying to outwit. They were up against a man who was no longer a human, but the projection of some great force beyond their own comprehension, a force so powerful that Allanon feared it could affect the human mind.

"The rest you already know," Allanon began again rather sharply. "The creature called Brona, who no longer resembled anything human, was the directing force behind both of the Race Wars. The Skull Bearers are the followers of their old master Brona, those Druids once human in form, once a part of the Council at Paranor. They cannot escape their fate any more than he can. The very forms they take are an embodiment of the evil they represent. But more important for our purposes, they represent a new age for mankind, for all the people of the four lands. While the old sciences have disappeared into our history, forgotten now as completely as the years when machines were the godsend of an easy life, the enchantment of sorcery has replaced them—a more powerful, more dangerous threat to human life than any before it. Do not doubt me, my friends. We live in the age of the sorcerer and his power threatens to consume us all!"

There was a moment of silence. A deep stillness hung oppressively in the forest night as Allanon's final words seemed to echo back with ringing sharpness. Then Shea spoke softly.

"What is the secret of the Sword of Shannara?"

"In the First War of the Races," Allanon replied in almost a whisper, "the power of the Druid Brona was limited. As a result, the combined might of the other races, coupled with the knowledge of the Druid Council, defeated his army of Men and drove him into hiding. He might have ceased to be and the whole incident been written off as merely another chapter in history—another war between mortals—except that he managed to unlock the secret of perpetuating his spiritual essence long after his mortal remains should have decomposed and turned to dust. Somehow he preserved his own spirit, feeding it on the power of the mystic forces he now possessed, giving it a life apart from materiality, apart from mortality. He now was able to bridge the two worlds—the world we live in and the spirit world beyond, where he summoned the black wraiths that had for centuries lain dormant, and waited for his time to strike back. As he waited, he watched the races drift apart as he knew they must in time, and the power of the Druid Council wane as their interest in the races grew lax. As with all things evil, he waited until the balance of hatred, envy, greed—the human failings common to all the races—outweighed the goodness and kindness, and then he struck. Gaining easy control of the primitive, warlike Rock Trolls of the Charnal Mountains, he reinforced their numbers with creatures of the spirit world he now served, and his army marched on the divided races.

"As you know, they crushed the Druid Council and destroyed it—all save a few who fled to safety. One of those who escaped was an aged mystic named Bremen, who had foreseen the danger and in vain attempted to warn the others. As a Druid, he was originally a historian and in that capacity had studied the First War of the Races and learned of Brona and his followers. Intrigued by what they had attempted to do, and suspicious that perhaps the mysterious Druid had acquired powers that no one had known about nor could have hoped to combat, Bremen began his own study of the mystic arts, but with greater care and respect for the possible power he felt he might unlock. After several years of this pursuit, he became convinced that Brona was indeed still existent and that the next war upon the human race would be started and eventually decided by the powers of sorcery and black magic. You can imagine the response he received to this theory—he was practically thrown from the confines of Paranor. As a result, he began to master the mystic arts on his own and so was not present when the castle at Paranor fell to the Troll army. When he learned that the Council had been taken, he knew that if he did not act, the races would be left defenseless against the enchantment Brona had mastered, power that mortals knew nothing about. But he was faced with the problem of how to defeat a creature who could not be touched by any mortal weapon, one who had survived for over five hundred years. He went to the greatest nation of his time—the Elven people under the command of a courageous young King named Jerle Shannara—and offered his assistance. The Elven people had always respected Bremen, because they understood him better than even his fellow Druids. He had lived among them for years prior to the fall of Paranor, while studying the science of the mystic."

"There is something I don't understand." Balinor spoke up suddenly. "If Bremen was a master of the mystic arts, why could he not himself challenge the power of the Warlock Lord?"

Allanon's response was somehow evasive. "He did confront Brona in the end on the Plains of Streleheim, though it was not a battle that was visible to mortal eyes, and both disappeared. It was presumed that Bremen had defeated the Spirit King, but time has proven otherwise, and now . . ." He hesitated only an instant before quickly returning to his narrative, but the emphasis on the pause was not lost on any of his listeners.

"In any event, Bremen realized that what was needed was a talisman to serve as a shield against the possible return of one such as Brona at another time when there was no one familiar with the mystic arts to offer assistance to the peoples of the four lands. So he conceived the idea of the Sword, a weapon which would contain the power to defeat the Warlock Lord. Bremen forged the Sword of Shannara with the aid of his own mystic prowess, shaping it with more than the mere metal of our own world, giving it that special protective characteristic of all talismans against the unknown. The Sword was to draw its strength from the minds of the mortals for whom it acted as a shield—the power of the Sword was their own desire to remain free, to give up even their lives to preserve that freedom. This was the power which enabled Jerle Shannara to destroy the spirit-dominated Northland army then; it is the same power that must now be used to send the Warlock Lord back into the limbo world to which he belongs, to imprison him there for all eternity, to cut off entirely his passage back to this world. But as long as he has the Sword, then he has a chance to prevent its power from being used to destroy him forever, and that, my friends, is the one thing that must not be."

"But then why is it that only a son of the House of Shannara . . . ?" The question formed on Shea's fumbling lips, his own mind reeling confusedly.

"That is the greatest irony of all!" exclaimed Allanon before the question was even completed. "If you have followed all that I have related about the change of life following the Great Wars, the giving way of the old materialistic sciences to the science of the present age, the science of the mystic, then you will understand what I am about to explain—the strangest phenomenon of all. While the sciences of old operated on practical theories built around things that could be seen and touched and felt, the sorcery of our own time operates on an entirely different principle. Its power is potent only when it is believed, for it is power over the mind which can neither be touched nor seen through human senses. If the mind does not truly find some basis for belief in its existence, then it can have no real effect. The Warlock Lord realizes this, and the mind's fear of and belief in the unknown—the worlds, the creatures, all the occurrences that cannot be understood by men's limited senses—offer him more than enough basis upon which to practice the mystic arts. He has been relying on this premise for over five hundred years. In the same way, the Sword of Shannara cannot be an effective weapon unless the one holding it believes in his power to use it. When Bremen gave the sword to Jerle Shannara, he made the mistake of giving it directly to a king and to the house of a king—he did not give it to the people of the lands. As a result, through human misunderstanding and historical misconception, the universal belief grew that the Sword was the weapon of the Elven King alone and that only those descended of his blood could take up the Sword against the Warlock Lord. So now, unless it is held by a son of the House of Shannara, that person can never fully believe in his right to use it. The ancient tradition that only such a one can wield it will make all others doubt—and there must be no doubt, or it will not operate. Instead, it will become merely another piece of metal. Only the blood and belief of a descendant of Shannara can invoke the latent power of the great Sword."

He concluded. The silence that followed was hollow. There was nothing left to tell the four that could be told. Allanon reconsidered briefly what he had promised himself. He had not told them everything, purposely holding back the little more that would have proved the final terror for them. He inwardly felt torn between the desire to have it all out and the gnawing realization that it would destroy any chance of success; their success was of paramount importance—only he knew the full truth of that fact. So he sat in silence, bitter in his private knowledge and angered by the self-imposed limits he had set for himself—the limits that forbade a complete revelation to those who had come to depend upon him so very heavily.

"Then only Shea can use the Sword if . . ." Balinor broke the silence abruptly.

"Only Shea has the birthright. Only Shea."

It was so quiet that even the night life of the forest seemed to have stilled its incessant chatter in sober contemplation of the grim historian's reply. The future came down to each as a simple declaration of existence—succeed or be destroyed.

"Leave me now," commanded Allanon suddenly. "Sleep while you can. We leave this haven at sunrise for the halls of Paranor."

The morning came quickly for the small company, and the golden half-light of dawn found them preparing to begin their long journey with sleep-filled eyes. Balinor, Menion, and the Valemen waited for the appearance of Allanon and the cousins of Eventine. No one spoke, partly because each was still half asleep and had very little to recommend him in the way of good humor, and partly because each was inwardly thinking about the hazardous trip that lay ahead. Shea and Flick sat quietly on a small stone bench, not looking at each other as they considered the tale Allanon had related to them the previous night, wondering what possible chance they had of recovering the Sword of Shannara, using it against the Warlock Lord to destroy him, and still returning alive to their homeland. Shea, particularly, had passed the point where his chief emotion was fear; now he felt only a sense of numbness that dulled his mind into self-imposed surrender, a robotlike acceptance of the fact that he was being led to the proverbial slaughter. Yet in spite of this resigned attitude toward the journey to Paranor, somewhere in the back of his confused mind was the lingering belief that he could work out all of these seemingly insurmountable obstacles. He could feel it lurking there, waiting for a more opportune moment to arise and demand satisfaction. But for the moment he allowed himself to lapse dutifully into numbed acquiescence.

The Valemen were dressed in woodsman garb provided by the Dwarf people, including warm half-cloaks in which they now wrapped themselves to ward off the chill of the early morning. In addition, they carried the short hunting knives they had brought with them from the Vale, tucked in their leather belts. Their packs were necessarily compact, in accord with the Valemen's small size. The country they would pass through offered some of the best hunting in all the Southland, and there were several small communities friendly to Allanon and the Dwarfs. But it was also the home of the Gnome people, the longtime, bitter enemies of the Dwarfs. There was some hope the little band would be able to maintain an advantage of stealth and secrecy in their travel and avoid any confrontation with Gnome hunters. Shea had carefully packed away the Elfstones in their leather pouch, showing them to no one. Allanon had not mentioned them since he had arrived in Culhaven. Whether this was an oversight or not, Shea was not about to give up the one really potent weapon that he possessed and kept the pouch hidden within his tunic.

Menion Leah stood several yards away from the brothers, pacing idly. He wore particularly nondescript hunting clothes, loose-fitting and colored to blend with the land to make his task as tracker and huntsman as uncomplicated as possible. His shoes were soft leather, toughened by certain oils to enable him to stalk anything without being heard and still travel the toughest ground without injuring the soles of his feet. Strapped to his lean back was the great sword, sheathed now, its strong hilt glinting dully in the early light as he shifted restlessly about. Across his shoulder he carried the long ash bow and its arrows, his favorite weapon on hunting trips.

Balinor wore the familiar long hunting cloak wrapped closely about his tall, broad frame, the cowl pulled up around his head. Beneath the cloak was the chain mail which could be seen glinting sharply every so often as his arms emerged in brief gestures from beneath the shielding of the garment. He carried in his belt a long hunting knife and the most enormous sword that the Valemen had ever seen. It was so huge that it appeared to them that one sweep of its great blade would cut through a man completely. It was hidden beneath the cloak at the moment, but the brothers had seen him strap it to his side as he came out to them earlier that morning.

Their waiting finally came to an end as Allanon approached from the assembly hall, accompanied by the lithe figures of the two Elves. Without stopping, he bade them all good morning and directed them to fall into line for the trip, warning sharply that once they crossed the Silver River several miles ahead, they would be in country traveled by Gnomes and that conversation must be kept to a minimum. Their route would take them from the river directly north through the Anar Forests into the mountains that lay beyond. There was less chance that they would be detected traveling through this rough country than across the plains that lay farther west, where the terrain was admittedly more even and accessible. Secrecy was the key to their success. If the purpose of their journey became known to the Warlock Lord, they were finished. Travel would be restricted to the daylight hours while they were camouflaged by the forests and mountains, and they would resort to night travel and risk detection by the searching Skull Bearers only when they were forced to cross the plains many miles to the north.

As their representative on the expedition, the Dwarf chieftain had chosen Hendel, the closemouthed fellow who had saved Menion from the Siren. Hendel led the company out of Culhaven, since he was most familiar with this part of the country. At his side walked Menion, talking only occasionally, concentrating mostly on staying out of the sullen Dwarf's way and trying to avoid drawing attention to his presence, something the Dwarf felt was totally unnecessary. Several paces back from them were the two Elves, their slim figures like brief shadows as they moved gracefully, effortlessly, speaking with each other in quiet musical voices that Shea found reassuring. Both carried long ash bows similar to Menion's. They wore no cloaks—only the strange, close-fitting outfits they had worn at the council the night before. Shea and Flick followed them, and behind the Valemen walked the silent leader of the company, his long strides covering the ground with ease, his dark face lowered to the trail. Balinor brought up the rear. Both Shea and Flick were quick to realize that their position in the center of the company was to assure their maximum protection. Shea knew how valuable the others felt he was to the success of the mission, but he was also painfully aware that they considered him incapable of defending himself in case of any real danger.

The company reached the Silver River and crossed at a narrow spot where the winding thread of gleaming water was spanned by a sturdy wooden bridge. All talking ceased once they had passed over, and all eyes went to the dense forest about them, watching uneasily. The going was still relatively smooth; the ground was level as the path wound sharply through the great forest, leading them steadily northward. The light of the morning sun shone in long streamers through cracks in the heavy branches, occasionally cutting across their path and catching their faces as they walked, warming them briefly in the cool air of the forest. Beneath their feet, the fallen leaves and twigs were soaked with a heavy dew, making a cushion that masked the sound of their footsteps and helped to preserve the quiet of the day. All about them they could hear sounds of life, though they saw only multicolored birds and a few squirrels that scampered eagerly about their treetop domains, sometimes raining the travelers below with torrents of nuts and twigs as they leaped from branch to branch. The trees prevented the members of the company from seeing much of anything, their great girth ranging from three to ten feet in diameter, and their huge roots stretching out from the trunks like mammoth fingers, digging their way relentlessly into the earth of the forest floor. The view from every direction was masked, and the company had to content itself with relying on Hendel's familiarity with the country and the pathfinding knowledge of Menion Leah to guide them through the maze of vegetation.

The first day passed without incident, and they spent the night beneath the giant trees, somewhere north of the Silver River and Culhaven. Hendel was apparently the only one who knew exactly where they were, though Allanon conversed briefly with the taciturn Dwarf concerning their whereabouts and the route they were taking. The company ate its dinner cold, fearing that a fire might attract attention. But the general mood was light and the conversation was enjoyable. Shea took this opportunity to speak with the two Elves. They were cousins of Eventine, chosen to accompany Allanon as representatives of the Elven kingdom and to aid him in his search for the Sword of Shannara. They were brothers, the elder called Durin, a slim, quiet Westlander who gave the instant impression to Shea and the ever-present Flick that he was a man to be trusted. The younger brother was Dayel, a shy, extremely likable fellow who was several years the junior of Shea. His boyish charm was strangely appealing to the elder members of the company, particularly Balinor and Hendel, battle-hardened veterans of so many years of protecting the frontiers of their homelands, who found his youth and fresh outlook on life almost like a second chance for them to regain something that had passed them by years before. Durin informed Shea that his brother had left their Elven home several days prior to his marriage to one of the most beautiful girls in that country. Shea would not have believed Dayel old enough to marry, and found it difficult to understand why anyone would leave on the eve of his marriage. Durin assured him that it had been his brother's own choice, but Shea told Flick later that he believed that his relationship to the king had much to do with that decision. So now as the members of the company sat quietly and spoke in low tones to one another, all save the silent, aloof Hendel, Shea wondered how much the young Elf regretted his decision to leave his bride-to-be to come on this hazardous journey to Paranor. He found himself wishing inwardly that Dayel had not chosen to be a member of their party, but had remained safe within the protective confines of his own homeland.

Later that evening, Shea approached Balinor and asked him why Dayel had been allowed to come on such an expedition. The Prince of Callahorn smiled at the Valeman's concern, thinking to himself that the difference in ages between the two was hardly noticeable to him. He told Shea that in a time when the homelands of so many people were threatened, no one stopped to question why another was there to aid them—it was merely accepted. Dayel had chosen to come because his King had asked it and because he would have felt less of a man in his own mind had he declined. Balinor explained that Hendel had been waging a constant battle with the Gnomes for years to protect his homeland. The responsibility was delegated to him because he was one of the most experienced and knowledgeable bordermen in the Eastland. He had a wife and family at home that he had seen once in the past eight weeks and could not expect to see again for many more. Everyone on the journey had a great deal to lose, he concluded, perhaps even more than Shea realized. Without explaining his final remark, the tall borderman moved off to speak with Allanon on other matters. Somewhat discontented by the abrupt finish to their conversation, Shea moved back to join Flick and the Elven brothers.

"What kind of person is Eventine?" Flick was asking as Shea joined the group. "I've always heard that he is considered the greatest of the Elven kings, respected by everyone. What is he really like?"

Durin smiled broadly and Dayel laughed merrily at the question, finding it somehow amusing and unexpected.

"What can we say about our own cousin?"

"He is a great King," responded Durin seriously after a few moments. "Very young for a king, the other monarchs and leaders would say. But he has foresight, and most important of all, he gets things done before the time for doing them has passed. He holds the love and esteem of all the Elven people. They would follow him anywhere, do anything he asked, which is fortunate for all of us. The elders of our council would prefer to ignore the other lands, to try to remain isolated. Sheer foolishness, but they're afraid of another war. Only Eventine stands against them and that policy. He knows that the only way to avoid the war they all fear is to strike first and cut off the head of the army which threatens. That is one reason why this mission is so important—to see that this invasion is checked before it has time to develop into a full-scale war."

Menion had sauntered over from the other side of the small campsite and seated himself with them just in time to hear the last comment.

"What do you know of the Sword of Shannara?" he asked curiously.

"Very little actually," admitted Dayel, "although for us it's a matter of history rather than legend. The Sword has always represented a promise to the Elven people that they need never again fear the creatures from the spirit world. It was always assumed that the threat was finished with the conclusion of the Second War of the Races, so no one really concerned himself with the fact that the entire House of Shannara died out over the years, except for a few such as Shea whom no one knew about. Eventine's

family, our family, became rulers almost a hundred years ago—the
Elessedils. The Sword remained at Paranor, forgotten by nearly everyone
until now."

"What is the power of the Sword?" persisted Menion, a little too eagerly to suit Flick, who shot Shea a warning glance.

"I don't know the answer to that question," Dayel admitted and
looked to Durin who shrugged in response and shook his head. "Only Allanon seems to know that."

They all looked momentarily toward the tall figure seated in earnest
conversation with Balinor across the clearing. Then Durin turned to the
others.

"It is fortunate that we have Shea, a son of the House of Shannara. He
will be able to unlock the secret of the Sword's power once we have it in
our possession, and with that power we can strike at the Dark Lord before
he can create the war that would destroy us."

"If we get the Sword, you mean," corrected Shea quickly. Durin acknowledged this comment with a short laugh of agreement and a reassuring nod.

"There's still something about all this that doesn't set right," Menion
declared quietly, rising abruptly and moving off to find a place to sleep.
Shea watched him go and found himself in agreement with the highlander, but was unable to see what they could hope to do about their
dissatisfaction. Right now he felt that there was so little hope of their suc-
ceeding in their quest to regain the Sword that for the moment he would
concentrate on simply completing the journey to Paranor. For now, he did
not even want to think about what might happen after that.

The company was awake and back on the winding path with the
breaking of the dawn, led by a watchful Hendel. The Dwarf moved them
along at a rapid pace through the mass of great trees and heavy foliage that
had grown increasingly dense as they penetrated deeper into the Anar. The
trail was beginning to slope upward, an indication that they were approaching the mountains that ran the length of the central Anar. At some
point farther north they would be forced to cross these broad peaks in order to reach the plains to the west that lay between them and the halls of
Paranor. Tension began to mount as they moved more deeply into the domain of the Gnome people. They began to experience the unpleasant sensation that someone was constantly watching them, hidden in the denseness
of the forest, waiting for the right moment to strike. Only Hendel seemed
unconcerned as he led them, his own fears apparently eased by his familiarity with the terrain. No one spoke as they marched, all eyes searching
the silent forest about them.

About midday, the path turned sharply upward and the company began to climb. The trees now grew farther apart and the scrub foliage was
less congested. The sky became clearly visible through the trees, a deep
blue unbroken by even the faintest trace of a cloud wisp. The sun was
warm and bright, shining bravely through the scattered trees to light the

whole of the forest. Rocks began to appear in small clusters and they could see the land ahead rise in tall peaks and jutting ridges that signaled the beginning of the southern sector of the mountains in the central Anar. The air became steadily cooler as they climbed and breathing became more difficult. After several hours, the company reached the edge of a very dense forest of dead pines, clustered so closely that it was impossible to see for more than twenty or thirty feet ahead at any one place. On both sides of their path, tall, slab-rock cliffs rose hundreds of feet into the air and peaked against the blueness of the afternoon sky. The forest stretched several hundred yards in either direction, ending at the cliff walls. At the edge of the pines, Hendel called a brief halt and spoke for several minutes with Menion, pointing to the forest and then the cliffs, apparently questioning something. Allanon joined them, then motioned the remainder of the company to gather around in a close circle.

"The mountains we are about to cross into are the Wolfsktaag, a no-man's-land for both Dwarf and Gnome," Hendel explained quietly. "We chose this way because there was less chance of meeting up with a Gnome hunting patrol, something that would certainly result in a pitched battle. The Wolfsktaag Mountains are said to be inhabited by creatures from another world—a good joke, isn't it?"

"Get to the point," Allanon broke in.

"The point is," Hendel continued, seemingly oblivious of the dark historian, "we were spotted about fifteen minutes back by one or possibly two Gnome scouts. There may be more around, we can't be certain—the highlander says he saw signs of a large party. In any event, the scouts will report us and bring back help in a hurry, so we'll have to move fast."

"Worse than that!" declared Menion quickly. "Those signs said there are Gnomes ahead of us somewhere—through those trees or in them."

"Maybe so, maybe not, highlander," Hendel cut back in sharply. "These trees run like this for almost a mile and the cliffs continue on both sides, but narrow sharply beyond the forest to form the Pass of Noose, the entrance to the Wolfsktaag. That is the way we have to go. To try any other route would cost us two more days, and we would be risking an almost certain run-in with Gnomes."

"Enough debate," Allanon said fiercely. "Let's move out quickly. Once we reach the other side of the pass, we'll be in the mountains. The Gnomes will not follow us there."

"Encouraging, I'm sure," muttered Flick under his breath.

The company moved into the thickly clustered trees of the pine forest, following one another in single file, weaving among the rough, disjointed trunks. Dead needles lay in heaps over the whole of the earthen forest floor, creating a soft matting on which the passing of feet made no sound. The white-bark trees rose tall and lean, touching near their skeletal tops like some intricate spiderweb, lacing the blueness of the clear sky in fascinating designs. The party wound steadily forward through the maze of trunks and limbs behind Hendel, who chose their route quickly and without hesitation. They had not gone more than several hundred yards when Durin brought them up sharply and motioned for silence, looking questioningly about, apparently searching the air for something.

"Smoke!" he exclaimed suddenly. "They've set fire to the forest!"

"I don't smell any smoke," declared Menion, sniffing the air tentatively.

"You don't have the sharpened senses of an Elf either," Allanon stated flatly. He turned to Durin. "Can you tell where they've fired it?"

"I smell smoke, too," declared Shea absently, amazed that his own senses were as sharp as those of the Elves.

Durin cast about for a minute, trying to catch the scent of smoke from one particular direction.

"Can't tell, but it appears that they've fired it in more than one place. If they have, the forest will go up in a matter of minutes!"

Allanon hesitated for one brief second, then motioned for them to continue toward the Pass of Noose. The pace picked up considerably as they hastened to reach the other side of the firetrap in which they were encased. A blaze in those dry woods would quickly cut off any chance of escape once it spread through the treetops. The long strides of Allanon and the borderman forced Shea and Flick to run to keep from falling behind. Allanon shouted something to Balinor at one point in the race, and the broad figure dropped back into the trees and was lost from sight. Ahead of them, Menion and Hendel had disappeared, and there were only fleeting glimpses of the Elven brothers dashing smoothly between the leaning pines. Only Allanon stayed clearly in view, a few paces behind, calling to them to run faster. Thick clouds of heavy white smoke were beginning to seep between the closely bunched trunks like a heavy fog, obscuring the path ahead and making it steadily more difficult to breathe. There was still no sign of the actual fire. It had not yet grown strong enough to spread through the intertwining boughs and cut them off. The smoke was every-where in a matter of minutes, and both Shea and Flick coughed heavily with every breath, their eyes beginning to sting from the heat and irrita-tion. Suddenly Allanon called to them to halt. Reluctantly they stopped and waited for the order to continue, but Allanon appeared to be looking back for something, his lean, dark face strangely ashen in the thick white smoke. Soon the broad figure of Balinor reappeared from the forest behind them, wrapped tightly in the long hunting cloak.

"You were right, they're behind us," he informed the historian, gasp-ing out the words as he fought for breath. "They've fired the forest all along our backs. It looks like a trap to drive us into the Pass of Noose."

"Stay with them," Allanon ordered quickly, pointing to the frightened Valemen. "I've got to catch the others before they reach the pass!"

With incredible speed for a man so big, the tall leader leaped away and dashed into the trees ahead, disappearing almost immediately. Balinor mo-tioned for the Valemen to follow him, and they proceeded at a rapid pace in the same direction, fighting to see and to breathe in the choking smoke. Then, with frightening suddenness, they heard the sharp crackle of burning wood and the smoke began to billow past them in huge, blinding clouds of white heat. The fire was overtaking them. In a few minutes it would reach them and they would be burned alive! Coughing furiously, the three crashed heedlessly through the pines, desperate to escape the inferno in which they had been caught. Shea shot a quick glance skyward, and to his horror saw the flames leaping madly from the tops of the tall pines above and beyond them, burning their glowing way steadily down the long trunks.

Then abruptly, the impenetrable stone wall of the cliffs appeared through the smoke and the trees, and Balinor motioned them in that direction. Minutes later, as they groped their way along the cliff face, they saw the remainder of the company crouched in a clearing beyond the fringe of the burning trees. Ahead lay an open trail that wound upward into the rocks between the cliffs and disappeared into the Pass of Noose. The three quickly joined the others as the entire forest was enveloped in flames.

"They're trying to force us to choose between roasting in that pine forest or trying to get through the pass," shouted Allanon over the crackle of burning wood, looking anxiously toward the trail ahead. "They know we have only two ways to go, but they're facing the same choice and that's where they lose the advantage. Durin, go on ahead into the pass a little way and see if the Gnomes have set an ambush."

The Elf darted away without a sound, crouching low and keeping close to the cliff wall. They watched him until he had disappeared farther up the trail into the rocks. Shea huddled with the others, wishing that there was something he could do to help.

"The Gnomes are not fools." Allanon's voice cut into his thoughts abruptly. "Those in the pass know that they are cut off from those who fired the forest unless they can get by us first. They wouldn't risk having to retreat back through the Wolfsktaag Mountains for any reason. Either there is a large force of Gnomes in the pass ahead, which Durin should be able to tell us, or they've got something else in mind."

"Whatever it is, they'll probably try it in the section called the Knot," Hendel informed them. "At that point the trail narrows so that only one man at a time can get through the path formed by the converging cliff sides." He paused and appeared to be considering something further.

"I don't understand how they plan to stop us," Balinor cut in quickly. "These cliffs are almost vertical—no one could scale them without a long and hazardous climb. The Gnomes haven't had time to get up there since they spotted us!"

Allanon nodded thoughtfully, obviously in agreement with the borderman and unable to see what the Gnomes had in store for them. Menion Leah spoke quietly to Balinor, then abruptly left the group and moved ahead to the entrance of the pass where the cliff walls began to narrow sharply, scanning the ground intently. The heat of the burning woods had become so intense that they were forced to move farther into the mouth of the pass. Everything was still obscured by the clouds of white smoke which rolled out of the dying woods like a wall and dispersed sluggishly into the air. Long moments passed while the six awaited the return of Menion and Durin. They could still see the lean highlander studying the ground at the entrance to the pass, his tall form shadowy in the smoke-filled air. Finally, he stood up and moved back to them, joined almost immediately by the returning Elf.

"There were footprints, but no other sign of life in the pass ahead," Durin reported. "Everything is apparently undisturbed up to the narrowest point. I didn't go beyond."

"There is something else," Menion cut in quickly. "At the entrance to the pass, I found two clear sets of footprints leading in and two sets out— Gnome feet."

"They must have slipped in ahead of us and then out again by staying close to the cliff walls while we blundered up the middle," Balinor said angrily. "But if they were in there ahead of us, what . . . ?"

"We won't find out by sitting here and discussing it!" Allanon concluded in disgust. "We would only be guessing. Hendel, take the lead with the highlander and watch yourself. The rest stay in formation as before."

The stocky Dwarf moved out with Menion at his side, their sharp eyes keyed in on every boulder that lined the winding path as it narrowed into the Pass of Noose. The others followed several paces back, casting apprehensive glances at the rugged terrain surrounding them. Shea risked one quick look behind him and noticed that, while Allanon was close on his heels, Balinor was nowhere in sight. Apparently, Allanon had again left the borderman to act as a rear guard at the edge of the burning pine forest, to watch for the inevitable approach of the Gnome hunters lurking somewhere beyond. Shea knew instinctively that they were caught in a trap carefully arranged for them by the furtive Gnomes, and all that remained was to discover what form it would take.

The path ahead rose sharply for the first hundred yards or so, then tapered off gradually and narrowed to such an extent that there was only enough room for one person to pass between the cliff sides. The pass was no more than a deep niche in the face of the cliff, the sides slanting inward and almost closing far above them. Only a thin ribbon of light from the blue sky streamed downward to reach them, faintly lighting the winding, boulder-laden path ahead. Their progress slowed perceptibly as the lead men searched for traps left by the Gnomes. Shea had no idea how far Durin had gone in his scouting mission, but apparently he had not ventured into what Hendel had referred to as the Knot. He could guess where the name had originated. The narrowness of the passage left the sharp impression of being drawn through the knot of a hangman's noose to the same fate as that which awaited the condemned. He could hear Flick's labored breathing almost in his ear and experienced an unpleasant feeling of suffocation at the closeness of the rock walls. The group moved slowly onward, slightly bent to avoid the narrowed cliff sides and their razor-sharp stone projections.

Suddenly, the pace slowed further and the whole line crowded together. Behind him, Shea heard the deep voice of Allanon muttering angrily, demanding to know what had happened, asking excitedly to be let to the front. But in these close quarters it was impossible for anyone to give way. Shea peered ahead and noticed a sharp ray of light beyond the leaders. Apparently the path was widening at last. They were nearly free of the Pass of Noose. But then, just as Shea felt they had reached the safety of the other end, there were loud exclamations and the entire line came to a complete stop. Menion's voice cut through the semidarkness in surprise and anger, causing Allanon to mutter a low oath of fury and order the company to move ahead. For a moment nothing happened. Then slowly the company began to inch forward, moving into a wide clearing shadowed by the cliff sides as they parted abruptly into a sky of sunshine.

"I was afraid of this," Hendel was muttering to himself as Shea followed Dayel out of the niche. "I had hoped that the Gnomes had failed to explore this far into their taboo land. It appears, highlander, that they have us trapped."

Shea stepped out into the light on a level rock shelf where the others in the company stood talking in hushed tones of anger and frustration. Allanon emerged at almost the same moment, and together they surveyed the scene before them. The rock shelf on which they stood extended out from the opening of the Pass of Noose about fifteen feet to form a small ledge that dropped abruptly into a yawning chasm hundreds of feet deep. Even in the bright sunlight, it appeared to be bottomless. The cliff walls spread outward from their backs to form a half circle around the chasm and then slanted away brokenly, giving way to the heavy forests that began several hundred yards beyond. The chasm, a trick of nature by all appearances, bore the distinct shape of a jagged noose. There was no way around it. On the other side of the fissure dangled the remains of what had previously been some sort of rope-and-wood bridge which had served as the only means by which travelers could cross. Eight pairs of eyes scanned the sheer walls of the cliffs, seeking a means to scale their slick surfaces. But it was all too apparent that the only way to the other side was directly across the open pit before them.

"The Gnomes knew what they were doing when they destroyed the bridge!" Menion fumed to no one in particular. "They've left us trapped between them and this bottomless hole. They don't even have to come in after us. They can wait until we starve to death. How stupid . . ."

He trailed off in fury. They all knew they had been foolish in allowing themselves to be tricked into entering such a simple, but effective trap. Allanon moved to the edge of the chasm, peered intently into its depths and then scanned the terrain on the other side, searching for a means to cross.

"If it were a bit more narrow or if I had a little more running room, I might be able to jump it," volunteered Durin hopefully. Shea estimated the distance across to be easily thirty-five feet. He shook his head doubtfully. Even if Durin had been the best jumper in the world, he would have questioned such an attempt under these conditions.

"Wait a minute!" Menion cried suddenly, leaping to Allanon's side and pointing off to the north. "How about that old tree hanging off the cliff side on the left?"

Everyone looked eagerly, unable to understand what the highlander was suggesting. The tree of which he spoke grew embedded in the cliff face to the left almost a hundred and fifty yards away from them. Its gray shape hung starkly against the clear sky, its branches leafless and bare, dipping heavily downward like the tired limbs of some weary giant frozen in midstride. It was the only tree that anyone could see on the rock-strewn path that led away from the chasm and disappeared below the cliff sides into the forests beyond. Shea looked with the others but could see no help from that corner.

"If I could put an arrow into that tree with a line tied to it, someone light could go across hand over hand and secure the rope for the rest of us," the Prince of Leah suggested, gripping in his left hand the great ash bow.

"That shot is over a hundred yards," replied Allanon testily. "With the added weight of a line tied to the arrow, you would have to make the world's greatest shot just to get it there, not to mention embedding it in the tree deep enough to hold a man's weight. I don't think it can be done."

"Well, we had better come up with something or we can forget the Sword of Shannara and everything else," growled Hendel, his craggy face flushed with anger.

"I have an idea," Flick ventured suddenly, taking a step forward as he spoke. Everyone looked at the stocky Valeman as if they were just seeing him for the first time and had forgotten that he was even along.

"Well, all right, don't keep it to yourself!" exclaimed Menion impatiently. "What is it, Flick?"

"If there were an expert bowman in the group—" Flick shot Menion a venomous look "—he might be able to put an arrow with a line into the wood fragments of the bridge hanging on the other side and pull it back across to this side."

"That is an idea worth trying!" agreed Allanon quickly. "Now who . . ."

"I can handle it," Menion said quickly, glaring at Flick.

Allanon nodded shortly, and Hendel produced a stout cord which Menion Leah fastened securely about the tip of an arrow, tying the loose end to his wide leather belt. He fitted the arrow to the great ash bow and sighted. All eyes peered across the chasm to the length of rope secured at the edge on the other side. Menion followed the length of rope downward into the darkness of the pit until he spotted a piece of wood hanging about thirty feet below, still fastened to the broken bridge tie. The company watched breathlessly as he drew back the great ash bow, sighted quickly, surely, and released the arrow with a sharp snap. The arrow shot into the cavern and embedded itself in the wood, the cord dangling limply from the tip.

"Nice shooting, Menion," Durin approved at his shoulder, and the lean highlander smiled.

Carefully, the bridge was pulled back across until the severed rope ends were gathered in. Allanon looked in vain for something to secure it, but the spikes that had held it had been removed by the Gnomes. Finally, Hendel and Allanon braced themselves at the edge of the chasm and pulled the bridge rope taut while Dayel worked his way hand over hand across the yawning pit, carrying a second rope at his waist. There were a few anxious moments as the black-robed giant and the silent Dwarf held firm against the strain, but in the end Dayel stood safely on the other side. Balinor reappeared and informed them that the fire was beginning to burn itself out and the Gnome hunters would soon be making their way into the Pass of Noose. Hastily, the rope that Dayel carried was thrown back across after he had finished securing his end, and its longer length was run back into the jutting rocks at the entrance of the pass and fastened in place. The remaining members of the company proceeded to cross the chasm in the same fashion as Dayel, one by one, hand over hand in succession, until all stood safely on the far side. Then the rope was cut and dropped into the pit along with the remainder of the old bridge, to make certain that they could not be followed.

Allanon ordered the company to move out quietly to avoid warning the approaching Gnomes that they had made good their escape from the carefully laid trap. Before they left, however, the tall historian approached Flick, placed a lean, dark hand on his shoulder, and smiled grimly.

"Today, my friend, you have earned the right to be a member of this company—a right above and beyond your kinship for your brother."

He turned away abruptly and signaled Hendel to take the lead. Shea looked at Flick's flushed and happy face, and clapped his brother warmly on the back. He had indeed earned the right to stand along with the others— a right that Shea had perhaps not yet acquired.

The company journeyed another ten miles into the Wolfsktaag Mountains before Allanon called a halt. The Pass of Noose and the danger of attack by Gnomes had long since been left behind, and they were now deep within the forests. Their travel had been fast and unhindered up to this point, the paths wide and clear and the terrain level even though they were several miles high in the mountains. The air was crisp and cool, which made the march almost enjoyable, and the warm afternoon sun beamed down on the company with a glow that kept their spirits high. The forests were scattered in these mountains, cut apart by jutting ridges of slab rock and peaks which were barren and snowcapped. Although this was historically a forbidden country, even for the Dwarfs, no one could find an indication of anything out of the ordinary which might signal danger for them. All the normal sounds of the forest were there, from the resonant chirping of insects to the gay songs of a huge variety of multicolored birds of all shapes and sizes. It seemed that they had chosen a wise way in which to approach the still-distant halls of Paranor.

"We will stop for the night in several hours," the tall wanderer announced after he had gathered them about him. "But I will be leaving you in the early morning to scout ahead beyond the Wolfsktaag for signs of the Warlock Lord and his emissaries. Once we complete our journey through these mountains and through a short stretch of the Anar Forests, we still have to cross the plains beyond to the Dragon's Teeth, just below Paranor. If the creatures of the Northland or their allies have blocked off the entrance, I must know now so that we may quickly decide on a new route."

"Will you go alone?" asked Balinor.

"I think it safer for all of us if I do. I'm in little danger, and you may need everyone when you reach the central Anar Forests again. I have little doubt that the Gnome hunting parties will be watching all the passes leading out of these mountains to be certain that you do not leave them alive. Hendel can lead you through those pitfalls as well as I could, and I will try to meet you somewhere along the way before you reach the plains."

"Which way out will you be taking?" asked the taciturn Dwarf.

"The Pass of Jade offers the best protection. I'll mark the way with bits of cloth—as we've done before. Red will mean danger. Keep with the white cloth and all will be well. Now let's continue on while we still have some daylight."

They traveled steadily through the Wolfsktaag until the sun sank beneath the rim of the mountains in the west and it was no longer possible to see the path ahead clearly. It was a moonless night, though the stars cast a dim glow over the rugged landscape. The company made camp beneath a tall, jagged cliffside that rose several hundred feet above them like some great blade cutting sharply into the dark sky. On the open edges of the campsite were tall stands of pines enclosing them against the cliffside in a half circle that provided them with good protection on all sides. They ate a cold dinner for another evening, still unwilling to risk a fire which might draw attention to their presence. Hendel arranged for the posting of a continuous guard throughout the night, a practice he felt to be essential in unfriendly country. The members of the group took turns, each sitting watch for several hours while the rest of the company slept. There was little talk after the meal, and they rolled themselves into their blankets almost at once, tired from the long day of marching.

Shea volunteered to sit the first watch, eager to participate as a member of the company, still feeling that he had contributed little while all of the others were risking their lives for his benefit. Shea's attitude toward the journey to Paranor had altered considerably during the past two days. He was beginning to realize now how important it was that the Sword be obtained, how much the people of the four lands depended on it for protection against the Warlock Lord. Before, he had run away from the danger of the Skull Bearers and his heritage as a son of the house of Shannara. Now he was running toward an even greater threat, a confrontation with a power so awesome that its limits had never been defined—and with little more than the courage of seven mortal men for protection. But even with that knowledge confronting him, Shea felt deeply that to refuse to go on, to hold back what little he had to offer, would be a bitter betrayal of his kinship to both Elf and Man and a callous denial of the pride he felt in caring about the safety and freedom of all men. He knew that if he were told even now that he could not succeed, he would have to try anyway.

Allanon had turned in without a word to anyone and was asleep in a matter of seconds. Shea watched his still form during his own two-hour watch and then retired as Durin took over. It was not until Flick awoke after midnight to take his turn that the tall form of their leader stirred slightly, then rose in a single fluid motion, wrapped ominously in the great black cape, just as he had been when Flick had first encountered him on the road to Shady Vale. He stood for a moment looking at the sleeping members of the company and at Flick sitting motionless on a boulder off to one side of the clearing. Then without a word or a gesture, he turned north on the path leading away from them and disappeared in the blackness of the forest.

Allanon walked for the remainder of the night without pausing in his journey to reach the Pass of Jade, the central Anar, and beyond that, the plainlands to the west. His dark figure passed through the silent forest with the quickness of a fleeting shadow, touching the land only momentarily, then hastening on. His form seemed substanceless, passing over the lives of little beings that saw him briefly and forgot, neither changing nor yet leaving them quite the same, his indelible print fixed in their uncomprehending minds. Once more he reflected on the journey they were making to Paranor, pondering what he knew that none other could know, and he felt strangely helpless in the face of what was surely the passing of an age. The others only suspected his own role in all that had happened, in all that yet lay ahead, but he alone was forced to live with the truth behind his own destiny and theirs. He muttered half aloud at the thought, hating what was happening, but knowing that there was no other choice for him to make. His long, lean face appeared a black mask of indecision to the silent woods he passed on his lonely march, a face lined deeply with worry, but hard with an inner resolution that would sustain the soul when the heart was gone.

Daybreak found him moving through a particularly dense stretch of woods that ran for several miles over hilly terrain strewn with boulders and fallen logs. He noticed at once that this part of the forest was strangely silent, as if a special kind of death had placed its chill hand upon the earth. The trail behind was carefully marked with small strips of white cloth. He walked more slowly. There had been nothing up to this point to cause him concern, but now a sixth sense reared up within his quick mind, warning him that all was not as it should be. He reached a break in the main path that split into two branches. One, a wide, clear path that looked as if it had once been a major road, ran to the left, downward into what appeared to be a huge valley. It was difficult to tell because the forests had overgrown everything, obscuring from view the trail beyond the first several hundred yards. The second path was choked by heavy underbrush. No more than one person at a time could pass that way without cutting a wider trail. The narrow path led upward toward a high ridge which ran at an angle away from the Pass of Jade.

Suddenly the grim historian stiffened as he sensed the presence of another being, an undeniably evil life-form somewhere farther down the trail leading into the invisible valley. There was no sound of movement. Whatever it was, it preferred to lie in wait for its victims along the lower trail. Allanon quickly tore off two strips of cloth, one red and one white, tying the red cloth to the wider trail leading into the valley and the white cloth along the smaller trail leading to the ridge. When he had completed this task, he paused and listened again, but while he could still sense the presence of the creature down the valley path, he could detect no movement. Its power was no match for his own, but it would be dangerous to the men following. Checking the cloth strips one final time, he silently moved upward along the narrow ridge path and disappeared into the heavy underbrush.

Almost an hour passed before the creature that lay in wait on the path leading into the valley decided to investigate. It was highly intelligent, a possibility that Allanon had not considered, and it knew that whoever it was who had passed above had sensed its presence and purposely avoided that approach. It knew as well that this same man had powers far greater than its own, so it lay noiselessly in the forest and waited for him to go away. Now it had waited long enough. Minutes later it gazed intently at the silent fork in the main trail where the two small strips of cloth fluttered brightly in the light forest breeze. How stupid such markers were, thought the creature slyly, and with ponderous footsteps moved its great, misshapen bulk forward.

Balinor had the final watch of the evening, and as the dawn began to break sharply in dazzling golden rays over the eastern mountain horizon, the tall borderman gently awakened the remainder of the company from their peaceful slumber to the chill of the early morning. They turned out hastily, gulped down a short breakfast while attempting to warm themselves in the yet cool air of the sunny day, silently packed their gear, and prepared to begin the day's march. Someone asked about Allanon, and Flick sleepily replied that the historian had departed sometime around midnight but said nothing to him. Nobody was particularly surprised that he had left so quietly, and little more was said about the matter.

Within half an hour, the company was on the path leading northward through the forests of the Wolfsktaag, moving steadily, without conversation for the most part, in the same order as before. Hendel had relinquished his spot as point man to the talented Menion Leah, who moved with the noiseless grace of a cat through the tangled boughs and brush over the leaf-strewn floor. Hendel felt a certain respect for the Prince of Leah. In time he would be unsurpassed by any woodsman. But the Dwarf knew as well that the highlander was brash and still inexperienced, and that in these lands only the cautious and the seasoned survived. Nevertheless, practice was the only way to learn, so the Dwarf grudgingly allowed the young tracker to lead the party, contenting himself with double-checking everything that appeared on the path before them.

One particularly disturbing detail caught the Dwarf's attention almost immediately, although it completely escaped the notice of his companion. The trail failed to reveal any sign of the man who had come this way only hours earlier. Although he scanned the ground meticulously, Hendel was unable to discern even the slightest trace of a human footprint. The strips of white cloth appeared at regular intervals, just as Allanon had promised they would be. Yet there was no sign of his passage. Hendel knew the tales about the mysterious wanderer and had heard that he possessed extraordinary powers. But he had never dreamed that the man was such an accomplished tracker that he could completely hide his own trail. The Dwarf could not understand it, but decided to keep the matter to himself.

At the rear of the procession, Balinor, too, had been wondering about the enigmatic man from Paranor, the historian who knew so much that no one else had even suspected, the wanderer who seemed to have been everywhere and yet about whom so little was known. He had known Allanon off and on for many years while growing up in his father's kingdom, but could only vaguely recall him, a dark stranger who had come and gone without warning, who had always seemed so kind to him, yet had never offered to reveal his own mysterious background. The wise men of all the lands knew Allanon as a scholar and a philosopher without equal. Others knew him only as a traveler who paid his way with good advice and who possessed a kind of grim common sense with which no one could find fault. Balinor had learned from him and had come to trust in him with what could almost be described as blind faith. Yet he had never really understood the historian. He pondered that thought for a while, and then in what came as an almost casual revelation, he realized that in all the time he had spent with Allanon, he had never seen any sign of a change in his age.

The trail began to turn upward again and to narrow as the great forest trees and heavy underbrush closed in like solid walls. Menion had followed the strips of cloth dutifully and had little doubt that they were on the right path, but automatically began to double-check himself as the going became noticeably tougher than before. It was almost noon when the trail branched unexpectedly, and a surprised Menion paused.

"This is strange. A fork in the trail and no marker—I can't understand why Allanon would fail to leave a sign."

"Something must have happened to it," concluded Shea, sighing heavily. "Which route do we take?"

Hendel scanned the ground carefully. On the path leading upward toward the ridge, there were indications of someone's passage from the bent twigs and recently fallen leaves. On the lower trail, however, there were signs of footprints, though they were very faint. Instinctively he knew that something dangerous lay along one and maybe both of the trails.

"I don't like it—something's wrong here," he grumbled to no one in particular. "The signs are confused, perhaps on purpose."

"Perhaps all the talk about this being taboo land wasn't nonsense after all," suggested Flick dryly, parking himself on a fallen tree.

Balinor came forward and conferred with Hendel briefly concerning the direction of the Pass of Jade. Hendel admitted that the lower trail would be the quickest way, and it clearly appeared to be the main passage. But there was no way to tell which trail Allanon had chosen. Finally Menion threw up his hands in exasperation and demanded that a choice be made.

"We all know that Allanon would not have passed this way without leaving a sign, so the obvious conclusion is that either something happened to the signs or something happened to him. In either case, we can't sit here and expect to find the answer. He said we would meet at the Pass of Jade or beyond in the forests, so I vote we take the lower road—the quickest way!"

Hendel again voiced his confusion over the signs on the lower trail and his nagging feeling that something dangerous lay ahead, a feeling which Shea had begun to share the minute they arrived at this point without finding the strips of cloth. Balinor and the others debated heatedly for a few minutes and finally agreed with the highlander. They would follow the quickest route, but keep an especially close watch until they were out of these mysterious mountains.

The line of march re-formed with Menion leading. They started rapidly down the gently sloping lower trail which appeared to be drawing them into a valley heavily camouflaged by great trees that grew limb to limb for miles in all directions. Remarkably, the road began to widen after only a short distance, the trees and scrub brush to move back, and the geography to level off into a barely perceptible downward slope. Their fears began to dissipate as travel grew easier, and it became readily apparent that in years long since gone, the road had been a major thoroughfare for the inhabitants of this land. They walked for less than an hour's time before reaching the valley floor. It was difficult to tell where they were in relation to the mountain ranges surrounding them. The trees of the forest obscured everything from view but the path immediately ahead and the cloudless blue sky above.

After a short time of traveling across the valley floor, the party caught sight of an unusual structure that rose through the trees like a huge framework. It seemed a part of the forest about it, save for the unusual straightness of its limbs, and within moments they were close enough to see that it was a series of giant girders, covered with rust and framing square portions of the open sky. The company slowed automatically, looking cautiously about to be certain that this was not some kind of trap prepared for unwary travelers. But nothing moved, so they continued their approach, intrigued by the structure that waited silently ahead.

Suddenly the road ended and the strange framework stood completely revealed, the great metal beams decaying with age, but still straight and seemingly as sturdy as they had been in ages past. They were part of what had once been a large city built so long ago that no one recalled its existence, a city forgotten like the valley and the mountains in which it rested—a final monument to a civilization of vanished beings. The metal framework was securely set in huge foundations of something like stone, now crumbling and chipped by the weather and time. In places, remnants of what had once been walls were visible. A large number of these dying buildings were clustered together, pushing out for several hundred yards beyond the travelers and ending where the wall of the forests marked the end of man's feeble invasion into an indestructible nature. Within the structures, and through the foundation and framework, grew brush and small trees in such abundance that the city appeared to be choking to death rather than crumbling with time. The party stood in mute silence at this strange testimonial to another era, the accomplishment of people like themselves, so many years before. Shea felt an undeniable sense of futility at the sight of the grim frames, rusting their weary lives away.

"What place is this?" he asked quietly.

"The remains of some city," shrugged Hendel, turning to the young Valeman. "No one has been here for centuries, I imagine."

Balinor walked over to the nearest structure and rubbed the metal girder. Huge flecks of rust and dirt came off in a shower, leaving beneath a dull steel-gray color that told of the strength still left in the building. The others of the company followed the borderman as he walked slowly about the foundation, looking carefully at the stonelike substance. A moment later he stopped at one corner and brushed away the surface dirt and grime to reveal a single date still legible in the decaying wall. They all bent closer to read it.

"Why this city was here before the Great Wars!" Shea said in amazement. "I can't believe it—it must be the oldest structure in existence!"

"I remember what Allanon told us of the men who lived then," declared Menion in a rare moment of dreamy recollection. "That was the great age, he said, and even so, this is all it has to show us. Nothing but a few metal girders."

"How about a few minutes' rest before we leave?" suggested Shea. "I'd like to take a quick look at the other buildings."

Balinor and Hendel felt somewhat uneasy about stopping, but agreed to a short rest as long as everyone kept together. Shea wandered over to the next building, accompanied by Flick. Hendel sat down and looked warily at the huge frames, disliking every moment they spent in this metal jungle so foreign to his own forest homeland. The others followed Menion to the other side of the building on which they had just found the date, discovering a portion of a name on a fallen chunk of wall. No more than a few minutes had passed when Hendel caught himself daydreaming of Culhaven and his family and jerked into immediate watchfulness. Everyone was in view, but Shea and Flick had moved farther off to the left of the dead city, still looking curiously at the decaying remnants and searching for signs of the old civilization. In the same instant he realized that except for the low voices of his companions, the surrounding forest had gone deathly quiet. Not even the wind stirred through the peaceful valley, not a bird flew over them, not a single insect's vibrant hum was audible. His own heavy breathing was hoarse in his straining ears.

"Something's wrong." The words came out as he reached instinctively for his heavy battle mace.

At that moment, Flick caught sight of something dull-white on the ground off to one side of the building that Shea and he were examining, partially hidden by the foundation. Curiously, he approached the objects which appeared to be sticks of various sizes and shapes scattered aimlessly about. Shea failed to notice his brother's interest and moved away from the building, staring in fascination at the remains of another structure. Flick came closer, but still was unable to tell from even a few feet away what the white sticks were. It was not until he stood over them and saw them shining dully against the dark earth in the noonday sun that he realized with a sickening chill they were bones.

The jungle behind the stocky Valeman burst apart with a thunderous thrashing of limbs and brush. Forth from its place of concealment emerged a grayish, multilegged horror of monstrous size. A nightmare mutation of living flesh and machine, its crooked legs balanced a body formed half of metal plating, half of coarse-haired flesh. An insect-like head bobbed fitfully on a neck of metal. Tentacles tipped with stingers dipped slightly above two glowing eyes and savage jaws that snapped with hunger. Bred by the men of another time to serve the needs of its masters, it had survived the holocaust that had destroyed them, but in surviving and in preserving its centuries-old existence with bits of metal grafted to its decaying form, it had evolved into a misshapen freak—and worse, an eater of flesh.

It was upon its hapless victim before anyone could move. Shea was closest as the mammoth creature struck his brother with an outstretched leg, knocking him flat and pinning him helplessly to the ground, rasping as its jaws reached downward. Shea never stopped to think; he yelled fiercely and drew his short hunting knife, brandishing the insignificant weapon as he rushed to Flick's rescue. The creature had just grasped its unconscious victim when its attention was directed to the other human charging wildly to the attack. Hesitating at this unexpected assault, it released its deadly grip and took a cautious step backward, its huge bulk poised to strike a second time as its bulging green eyes fixed on the tiny man before it.

"Shea, don't . . . !" yelled Menion in terror as the Valeman struck futilely at one of the creature's twisted limbs. A rasp of fury came boiling out of the depths of the monster's great body, and it swiped at Shea with an extended leg to pin him to the ground. But Shea leaped to safety by scant inches and struck again from another point with his tiny weapon. Then, before the horrified eyes of the other travelers, the nightmare from the jungle rushed the unfortunate Valeman in a flurry of legs and hair. Just as Shea was about to seize Flick to drag him to safety, the creature bowled him over, and for a second everything disappeared in a cloud of dust.

It had all happened so fast that no one else had yet had time to act. Hendel had never seen a creature of this size and ferocity, a creature that apparently had lived in these mountains for untold years, lying in wait for its hapless victims. The Dwarf was the farthest from the scene of the battle, but moved quickly to aid the fallen Valemen. At the same moment, the others reacted as well. The instant the dust settled enough to reveal the hideous head, three bowstrings sounded in harmony and the arrows buried themselves deeply in the black, hair-covered bulk with audible thuds. The creature rasped in fury and raised its body upward, forelegs extended, searching out its new attackers.

The challenge did not go unanswered. Menion Leah discarded the ash bow and drew the great sword from its sheath, gripping it in both hands.

"Leah! Leah!" The battle cry of a thousand years burst forth as the Prince charged wildly across crumbling foundations and fallen walls to reach the monster. Balinor had drawn his own sword, the huge blade gleaming fiercely in the bright sunlight, and rushed to the aid of the highlander. Durin and Dayel fired volley after volley into the head of the giant beast as it rasped in fury, using its forelegs to brush at the arrows and knock them loose from its thick skin. Menion reached the abomination ahead of Balinor and with one great swing of his sword cut deeply into the closest leg, feeling the iron strike bone with jarring impact. As the monster reared back and knocked Menion aside, it received a powerful blow to the head; Hendel's war mace struck with stunning force. A second later, Balinor stood solidly before the huge creature, the hunting cloak thrown back and billowing out behind the flashing chain mail. With a series of quick, powerful cuts of the great sword, the Prince of Callahorn completely severed a second leg. The beast struck back savagely, trying unsuccessfully to pin one of its attackers to the earth to crush the life out of him. The three men sounded their battle cries and struck ferociously, desperately trying to drive the monster back from its fallen victims. They attacked with precision, striking at the unprotected flanks, and drawing the behemoth first to one side and then to the other. Durin and Dayel moved in closer and continued to rain arrows on the massive target. Many were deflected by the metal plating, but the relentless assault constantly distracted the maddened creature. At one point, Hendel received so severe a blow that he was knocked senseless for a few seconds and the nightmare attacker quickly moved to finish him. But a determined Balinor, mustering every ounce of strength at his command, struck so savagely and relentlessly that it could not reach the fallen Dwarf before he had been pulled to his feet by Menion.

Finally the arrows of Durin and Dayel partially blinded the creature's right eye. Bleeding profusely from its stricken eye and from a dozen other major wounds, the monster knew that it had lost the battle and would probably lose its life if it did not escape at once. Making a short feint at the closest assailant, it suddenly wheeled about with surprising dexterity and made a quick rush for the safety of its forest lair. Menion gave a brief pursuit, but the creature outdistanced him and disappeared within the great trees. The five rescuers quickly turned their attention to the two fallen Valemen, who lay crumpled and unmoving in the trampled earth. Hendel examined them, having had some experience in treating battle wounds over the years. There were numerous cuts and bruises, but apparently no broken bones. It was difficult to tell if there had been any internal damage. Both had been stung by the creature, Flick on the back of the neck and Shea on the shoulder; the ugly, deep-purple marks indicated penetration of the exposed skin. Poison! The two men remained unconscious after repeated attempts to revive them, their breathing shallow and their skin pale and beginning to turn gray.

"I can't treat them for this," Hendel declared worriedly. "We've got to get them to Allanon. He knows something about these matters; he could probably help them."

"They're dying, aren't they?" Menion asked in a barely audible whisper.

Hendel nodded faintly in the hushed silence that followed. Balinor immediately took command of the situation, ordering Durin and Menion to cut poles to make stretchers, while Hendel and he prepared hammocks to hold the Valemen in place. Dayel was placed on guard in case the creature should return unexpectedly. Fifteen minutes later the stretchers were completed, the unconscious men were securely fastened in place and covered with blankets to protect them from the cold of the approaching night, and the company was ready to march. Hendel took the lead, with the other four carrying the stretchers. The party quickly crossed through the ruins of the deathly still city and after a few minutes located a trail leading out of the hidden valley. The grim faces of the Dwarf in the lead and the bearers of the unconscious forms strapped tightly to the makeshift stretchers glanced back in futile anger at the still-visible structures rising out of the forest. A bitter feeling of helplessness welled up inside them. They had come into the valley a strong, determined company, filled with confidence in themselves and belief in the mission which had brought them together. But as they left now, their bearing was that of beaten, discouraged victims of a cruel misfortune.

They moved hurriedly out of the valley, up the gentle slopes of the enclosing mountain range, up the broad, winding path shrouded by tall, silent trees, thinking only of the wounded men they carried. The familiar sounds of the forest returned, indicating that the danger of the valley was past. None of them had time to notice now save the taciturn Dwarf, whose battle-trained mind registered the changes of his forest homeland automatically. He thought back bitterly on the choice that had brought them into the valley, wondering what had happened to Allanon and to the promised markers. Almost without considering it, he knew that the tall wanderer must have placed markers before taking the high trail, and that someone or something, perhaps the creature they had encountered, had realized what the markers were for and removed them. He shook his head at his own stupidity in failing to recognize the truth at once and stamped harder on the ground passing beneath his booted feet, grinding his wrath in bits and pieces.

They reached the lip of the valley and continued on, without pausing, through the forests that stretched ahead in an unbroken mass of great trunks and heavy limbs, tangled and woven together as if to shut out the mountain sky. The path grew narrow once more, forcing them to proceed in single file with the stretchers. The afternoon sky was rapidly changing from a deep blue to a mixed bloodred and purple that marked the close of another day. Hendel calculated that they could expect no more than another hour of sunlight. He had no idea how far they were from the Pass of Jade, but he was fairly certain that it could not be far from where they were now. All of them knew that they would not stop at nightfall, could not get any sleep that night or possibly even the next day if they expected to save the lives of the Valemen. They had to find Allanon quickly and have the injuries of the brothers treated before the poison reached their hearts. No one voiced any opinion and no one felt it necessary to discuss the matter. There was only one choice and they accepted it.

As the sun dropped behind the western mountain ridges an hour later, the arms of the four bearers had reached the limit of their endurance, stiff and strained from the uninterrupted haul out of the valley. Balinor called a brief rest and the group collapsed in a heap, breathing heavily in the early-evening quiet of the forest. With the coming of night, Hendel relinquished his position as leader of the company to Dayel, who was obviously the most exhausted from carrying Flick's stretcher. The Valemen were still unconscious, wrapped in the layered blankets for warmth, their drawn faces ashen in the fading light and covered with a thin layer of perspiration. Hendel felt their pulse and could barely discern a flicker of life in the limp arms. Menion stormed audibly about the rest area in an uncontrolled fury, swearing vengeance against everything that came to mind, his lean face flushed red with the heat of the past battle and the burning desire to find something further on which to vent his wrath.

The company resumed its forced march after a short ten minutes' rest. The sun had disappeared entirely, leaving them in blackness broken only by the pale light of the stars and a sliver of new moon. The absence of any real light made the traveling slow and hazardous over the winding and often uneven path. Hendel had taken up Dayel's position at the end of Flick's stretcher, while the slim Elf utilized his highly developed senses to locate the trail through the darkness. The Dwarf thought ruefully of the cloth strips Allanon had promised he would leave to guide them out of the Wolfsktaag. Now, more than any time previously, they were needed to mark the proper route—not for himself, but for the two Valemen, whose lives depended on speed. As he walked, his arms not yet feeling the strain of carrying the stretcher, his mind mulling over the situation facing them, he found himself gazing almost absently at two tall peaks which broke the smoothness of the night sky to his left. It was several minutes before he realized with a start that he was looking at the entrance to the Pass of Jade.

At the same moment, Dayel announced to the group that the trail split in three directions just ahead. Hendel quickly informed them that the pass would be reached by following the left path. Without pausing, they moved onward. The trail began to lead them downward out of the mountains in the direction of the twin peaks. Reassured that the end was in sight, they marched faster, their strength renewed with the hope that Allanon would be waiting. Shea and Flick were no longer lying motionless on the stretchers, but were beginning to twitch uncontrollably and even thrash violently beneath the tightened blankets. A battle was raging within the poisoned bodies between the tightening grip of death and a strong will to live. Hendel thought to himself that it was a good sign. Their bodies had not yet given up the struggle to survive. He turned to the others in the company and discovered that they were gazing intently at what appeared to be a light gleaming sharply against the black horizon between the twin peaks. Then their own ears caught the distant sounds of a heavy booming noise and a low hum of voices coming from the location of the light. Balinor ordered them to keep moving, but told Dayel to scout ahead and to keep his eyes open.

"What is it?" asked Menion curiously.

"I can't be sure from this distance," Durin answered. "It sounds like drums and men chanting or singing."

"Gnomes," declared Hendel ominously.

Another hour's travel brought them close enough to determine that the curious light was caused by the burning of hundreds of small fires, and the noises were indeed the booming of dozens of drums and the chanting of many, many men. The sounds had grown to deafening proportions, and the two peaks marking the entrance of the Pass of Jade loomed like huge pillars in front of them. Balinor felt certain that if the creatures ahead were Gnomes, they would not venture into their taboo land to post guards, so the company would be reasonably safe until they reached the pass. The sound of the drums and the chanting continued to vibrate through the heavy forest trees. Whoever was blocking the pass was there to stay for a while. Only moments later, the group had reached the edge of the Pass of Jade, just beyond reach of the firelight. Moving silently off the path into the shadows, the company held a brief conference.

"What is going on?" Balinor asked anxiously of Hendel, when they were all crouched in the protection of the forest.

"It's impossible to tell from back here, unless you're a mind reader!"

the Dwarf growled irately. "The chanting sounds like Gnomes, but the words are blurred. I had better go ahead and check it out."

"I don't think so," Durin advised quickly. "This is a job for an Elf, not a Dwarf. I can move more quickly and quietly than you, and I'll be able to sense the presence of any guards."

"Then it had better be me," Dayel suggested. "I'm smaller, lighter, and faster than any of you. Be back in a minute."

Without waiting for an answer, he faded into the forest and had disappeared before anyone could voice an objection. Durin swore silently, fearing for his young brother's life. If there were indeed Gnomes in the Pass of Jade, they would kill any stray Elf they caught prowling about in the dark. Hendel shrugged in disgust and sat back against a tree to wait for Dayel's return. Shea had begun to moan and thrash more violently, throwing aside his blankets and nearly rolling off the stretcher. Flick was behaving in the same manner, though less forcibly, groaning in low tones, his face frighteningly drawn. Menion and Durin moved quickly to wrap the blankets back around the Valemen, this time tying them securely in place with long strips of leather. The moans continued, but the company had little fear of discovery with all the noise coming from the other side of the pass. They sat back quietly waiting for Dayel, looking anxiously at the bright horizon and listening to the drums, knowing that somehow they would have to find a way past whomever was blocking the entrance. Long minutes slipped by. Then Dayel appeared suddenly out of the darkness.

"Are they Gnomes?" asked Hendel sharply.

"Hundreds of them," the Elf replied grimly. "They're spread out all across the entrance to the Pass of Jade and there are dozens of fires. It must be some sort of ceremony from the way they're beating the drums and chanting. The worst of it is that they are all facing right into the pass. No one could possibly go in or out without being seen."

He paused and looked briefly at the pain-wracked forms of the injured Valemen before turning back to face Balinor.

"I scouted the entire entrance and both sides of the peaks. There is no way out except straight through the Gnomes. They have us trapped!"

12

Dayel's bleak report brought an immediate reaction. Menion leaped to his feet, reaching for his sword and threatening to fight his way out or die in the attempt. Balinor tried to restrain him, or at least to quiet him, but there was complete bedlam for several minutes as the others joined the shouting highlander in his vow. Hendel questioned the somewhat shaken Dayel about what he had seen at the entrance to the pass, and after a few brief questions loudly ordered everyone to be silent.

"The Gnome chieftains are out there," he informed Balinor, who had finally managed to restrain Menion long enough to listen to the Dwarf. "They have all the high priests and members of surrounding villages here for a special ceremony that takes place once each month. They come at sunset and sing praises to their gods for protecting them from the evils of the taboo land, the Wolfsktaag. It will last all night, and by morning we can forget about helping our young friends."

"Wonderful people, the Gnomes!" exploded Menion. "They fear the evils of this place, but they align themselves with the Skull Kingdom! I don't know about the rest of you, but I'm not giving up because of a few half-wit Gnomes chanting useless spells!"

"No one is giving up, Menion," Balinor said quickly. "We're getting out of these mountains tonight. Right now."

"How do you propose to do that?" demanded Hendel. "Walk right through half the Gnome nation? Or perhaps we'll fly out?"

"Wait a minute!" Menion exclaimed suddenly and leaned over the unconscious Shea, searching eagerly through his clothing until he produced the small leather pouch containing the powerful Elfstones.

"The Elfstones will get us out of here," he announced to the others, grasping the pouch.

"Has he lost his mind?" asked Hendel, incredulous at the sight of the highlander eagerly waving the leather pouch.

"It won't work, Menion," declared Balinor quietly. "The only one with the power to use the stones is Shea. Besides, Allanon once told me they could only be used against things whose power lies beyond substance, dangers that confuse the mind. Those Gnomes are mortal flesh and blood, not creatures of the spirit world or the imagination."

"I don't know what you're talking about, but I do know that these stones worked against that creature from the Mist Marsh, and I saw it work . . ." Menion trailed off despondently, reflecting on what he was saying, and finally lowered the pouch and its precious contents. "What's the use? You must be right. I don't even know what I'm saying anymore."

"There has to be a way!" Durin came forward, casting about for suggestions. "All we need is a plan to draw attention away from us for about five minutes and we could slip by them."

Menion perked up at the suggestion, apparently finding some merit in the idea, but unable to think of a way to distract the attention of several thousand Gnomes. Balinor paced about for a few minutes, lost in thought while the others threw out random suggestions. Hendel suggested in bitter humor that he walk into their midst and let himself be captured. The Gnomes would be so overjoyed at getting their hands on him, the man they had tried so hard to destroy all these years, that they would forget about anything else. Menion thought little of the joke and was all for allowing him to do what he suggested.

"Enough talk!" roared the Prince of Leah finally, losing his temper altogether. "What we need now is a plan, one that will get us out of here right away, before the Valemen are completely beyond help. Now what do we do?"

"How wide is the pass?" asked Balinor absently, still pacing.

"About two hundred yards at the point the Gnomes are gathered," Dayel replied, avoiding a confrontation with Menion. He thought a minute longer, and then snapped his fingers in recollection. "The right side of the pass is completely open, but on the left side there are small trees and scrub brush growing along the cliff face. They would give us some cover."

"Not enough," interrupted Hendel. "The Pass of Jade is wide enough to march an army through, but trying to get past with the little cover offered would be suicidal. I've seen it from the other side, and any Gnome looking would spot you in a minute!"

"Then they'll have to be looking somewhere else," Balinor growled as the faint glimmer of a plan began to form in his mind. He stopped suddenly, and kneeling on the forest floor drew a crude diagram of the pass entrance, looking to Dayel and Hendel for approval. Menion had stopped complaining long enough to join them.

"From the drawing, it appears that we can stay under cover and out of the light until we reach here," Balinor explained, indicating a point of ground near the line representing the left cliff face. "The slope is gentle enough to allow us to remain above the Gnomes and within the cover of the brush. Then there is an open space for about twenty-five or thirty yards until the forests begin against the steeper cliff face beyond. That is the point of diversion, the point where the light will show us clearly to anyone looking. The Gnomes will have to be turned another way when we cross that open space."

He paused and looked at the four anxious faces, wishing fervently that he had a better plan, but knowing there was no time to come up with another if they were to preserve any chance of recovering the Sword of Shannara. Whatever else was at stake now, nothing was of such paramount importance as the life of the frail-looking Valeman who was heir to the Sword's power and the one chance left to the people of the four lands to avoid a conflict that would consume them all. Their own lives could be sold comparatively cheaply to preserve that single hope.

"It will take the best bowman in the Southland," the tall borderman announced quietly. "That man will have to be Menion Leah." The highlander looked up in surprise at the unexpected declaration, unable to hide the sense of pride he felt. "There will be only one shot," continued the Prince of Callahorn. "If it is not exactly on target, we will be lost."

"What is your plan?" interrupted Durin curiously.

"When we reach the end of our cover at the open space, Menion will locate one of the Gnome chieftains to the far side of the pass. He will have one shot with the bow to kill him, and in the confusion that follows, we can slip by."

"It won't work, my friend," growled Hendel. "The minute they see their leader struck by the arrow, they'll be all over that pass entrance. You'll be found in minutes."

Balinor shook his head and smiled faintly, but unconvincingly.

"No, we won't, because they will be after someone else. The minute the Gnome chieftain falls, one of us will show himself back in the pass. The Gnomes will be so incensed and so eager to get their hands on him, that they won't take the time to search for anyone else, and we can slip by in the confusion."

Silence greeted his appraisal of the situation, and the anxious faces looked from one person to the next, the same thought in every mind.

"It sounds just fine for everyone but the man who stays behind to show himself," broke in Menion in disbelief. "Who gets that suicidal chore?"

"It was my plan," declared Balinor. "It will be my duty to stay behind and lead the Gnomes into the Wolfsktaag, until I can circle back and join you later at the edge of the Anar."

"You must be insane if you think I'm letting you stay behind and claim all the credit," Menion declared. "If I make the shot, I stay to take the bows, and if I miss . . ."

He trailed off and smiled, shrugging casually, clapping Durin on the shoulder as the other looked on incredulously. Balinor was about to object further when Hendel stepped forward shaking his broad head in disagreement.

"The plan is fine as it goes, but we all know that the man who stays behind will have several thousand Gnomes attempting to track him down, or at best, waiting for him to come out of their taboo land. The man who stays must be a man who knows the Gnomes, their methods, how to fight and survive against them. In this case, that man is a Dwarf with a lifetime of battle knowledge behind him. It must be me.

"Besides," he added grimly, "I told you how badly they want my head. They won't pass up the chance after such an affront."

"And I've already told you," insisted Menion again, "that's my . . ."

"Hendel is right," Balinor cut in sharply. The others looked at him in amazement. Only Hendel knew that the decision the borderman had made, however distasteful, was the same one he would have made had their positions been reversed. "The choice has been made, and we will abide by it. Hendel will have the best chance to survive."

He turned to the stocky Dwarf warrior and extended a broad hand. The other gripped it tightly for a brief moment, then turned quickly from them and disappeared up the trail at a slow trot. The others watched, but he was gone in a matter of seconds. The booming of the drums and the chanting of the Gnomes rolled deeply out of the lighted sky to the west.

"Gag the Valemen so they cannot cry out," ordered Balinor, startling the other three with the sharpness of the sudden command. When Menion failed to move, but remained rooted to the spot, looking silently up the path Hendel had taken a moment before, Balinor turned to him and placed a reassuring hand on his shoulder. "Be certain, Prince of Leah, that your shot is worthy of his sacrifice for us."

The still-twisting bodies of the two Valemen were quickly secured to the makeshift stretchers and their low cries effectively muffled by tightly bound cloth gags. The four remaining men picked up their gear and the stretchers and moved out of the cover of the trees toward the mouth of the Pass of Jade. The Gnome fires blazed up before them, lighting the night sky in a brilliant aura of yellow-and-orange flame. The drums crashed out in steady rhythm, the sound deafening in the ears of the four as they drew closer. The chanting grew louder until it seemed as if the entire Gnome nation must be gathered. The overall sensation was one of eerie unreality, as if they were lost in that primitive world of half-dreams traversed by mortal and spirit alike in strange rituals that have no recognizable purpose. The walls of the towering cliffs rose jaggedly into the night sky on either side, distant but ominously huge intruders on the little scene taking place at the high entrance to the Pass of Jade. Rock walls glimmered in a shower of color—red, orange, and yellow blended into an overriding deep green that danced and flickered in the man-made firelight. The color reflected off the hardness of the rock and mirrored softly in the grim-set faces of the four stretcher bearers, touching momentarily the fear they were trying to conceal.

Finally the men stood within the corridor of the pass, just out of sight of the chanting Gnomes. The slopes rose steeply on either side, the northern incline offering little or no cover whatsoever, while the southern fairly bristled with small trees and dense scrub brush that grew so thickly it was choking on itself. Balinor silently signaled the others to make their way up the side of this slope. He took the lead himself, searching out the safest approach, moving cautiously upward toward the small trees that grew higher on the mountain. It took them quite a while to reach the safety of the trees, and Balinor motioned them slowly ahead into the mouth of the pass. As they inched forward, Menion could look through breaks in the trees and brush to catch quick glimpses of the fires burning below, still ahead of them, their bright flames almost completely masked by the hundreds of small, gnarled figures who moved rhythmically in the light, chanting in a deep, soul-searching drone to the spirits of the Wolfsktaag. His mouth felt dry as he visualized what would happen to them if they were discovered, and he thought grimly of Hendel. He was suddenly very afraid for the Dwarf. The brush and trees began to thin out, rising higher on the slope, and the four crept upward under their cover, but slower now, more hesitantly, as Balinor kept one eye fixed on the Gnomes below. Durin and Dayel walked on cat feet, their light Elven frames moving soundlessly through dry, brittle limbs and twigs, blending into the natural terrain about them. Again Menion peered worriedly at the Gnomes, closer than before, their yellowish bodies weaving to the drums, gleaming with the sweat of hours spent calling on their gods and praying to the mountains.

Then the four reached the end of their cover. Balinor pointed ahead to the yards of open space that lay between them and the dense forests of the Anar standing darkly beyond. It was a long distance, and there was nothing between the men and the floor of the pass but the scrub brush and a few sparse blades of grass, dried from the sun. Directly below were the chanting Gnomes, swaying in the fire's glow and in a perfect position to see anyone attempting to cross the brightly lighted open spaces of the southern slope. Dayel had been correct; it would have been suicide to attempt to sneak past under those conditions. Menion looked up and quickly saw that further efforts to reach higher ground with the two wounded Valemen were effectively prevented by a sheer cliff face that rose abruptly several hundred feet into the air, banking only slightly as it continued upward to its invisible peak. He turned back to look again at the open space. It appeared farther across than before. Balinor motioned the others into a tight circle.

"Menion can move to the edge of the cover," he whispered cautiously. "After he picks his target and the Gnome is hit, Hendel will focus their rage by calling attention to himself inside the pass, high on the other slope. He should be in place by this time. When the Gnomes rush him, we move across the open space as quickly as possible. Don't stop to look—keep moving."

The other three nodded and all eyes rested on Menion, who had unstrapped the great ash bow from his back and was testing its pull. He picked out a single long, black arrow, sighting it for accuracy, and hesitated for a minute, looking downward through the veiled covering of the trees to the hundreds of Gnomes on the valley floor. Suddenly he realized what was expected of him. He was to kill a man, not in battle or in fair combat, but from ambush, with stealth, and that man would never have a chance. He knew instinctively that he could not do it, that he was not the seasoned fighter that Balinor was, that he did not have the cold determination of Hendel. He was brash and even brave at times and ready to stand against anyone in open combat, but he was not a killer. He glanced back momentarily at the others, and they saw it at once in his eyes.

"You must do it!" whispered Balinor harshly, his eyes burning with fierce determination.

Durin's face was averted slightly in the half-light, grim and frozen with uncertainty. Dayel stared directly at Menion, his Elven eyes wide, frightened by the choice the highlander faced, the youthful countenance ashen and ghostlike.

"I cannot kill a man this way," Menion shook involuntarily at his own words, "even to save their lives. . . ."

He paused and Balinor continued to stare at him, waiting for something more.

"I can do the job," Menion announced suddenly after a moment's reflection and a second look to the valley below. "But it shall be done a different way."

Without further explanation he moved forward through the clump of trees and crouched silently on the fringe, almost beyond its sparse protection. His eyes scanned hurriedly the forms of the Gnomes below, finally coming to rest on a chieftain on the far side of the pass. The Gnome stood before his subjects, his wizened yellow face uplifted, his small hands extended, holding in offering a long bowl of glowing embers. He stood motionless as he led the chanting with the other Gnome chieftains, his face turned toward the entrance to the Wolfsktaag. Menion withdrew a second arrow from the quiver and laid it in front of him. Then on one knee, he inched from the safety of the small tree he had positioned himself behind, fitted the first arrow to the bow, and sighted. The other three waited grimly, breathless within the edges of the foliage, watching the bowman. For one split second everything seemed to come to a complete standstill, and then the taut bowstring was released with an audible twang and the arrow flew invisibly to its target. Almost as if a part of the same motion, Menion fitted the second arrow to the string, sighted, and fired with blinding rapidity, then dropped motionless into the cover of the closest tree.

It happened so fast that no one saw it all, but each caught glimpses of the bowman's action and the scene that followed in the midst of the unsuspecting Gnomes. The first arrow struck the long bowl in the outstretched hands of the chanting Gnome chieftain and sent it spinning in an explosion of wood splinters. Gleaming red coals flew upward in a shower of sparks. In the next instant, while the astonished Gnome and his still-mystified followers were caught momentarily frozen with uncertainty, the second arrow embedded itself painfully in the half-turned and highly vulnerable posterior of the chieftain, who gave an agonizing howl that could be heard the length and breadth of the firelit Pass of Jade. The timing was absolutely perfect. It happened so quickly that even the unfortunate victim had no time, nor inclination for that matter, to decide where the embarrassing assault had come from or who the deceitful perpetrator might have been. The Gnome chieftain leaped about in terror and pain for several wild moments as his fellow Gnomes looked on in mixed bewilderment and apprehension, emotions that quickly changed. Their ceremony had been rudely interrupted and one of their chieftains had been treacherously struck from ambush. They were humiliated and dangerously angered.

Within seconds after the arrows struck their targets, before anyone had been given a chance to collect his senses, a torch appeared far away inside the pass on the upper reaches of the northern slope, touching off a giant bonfire that blazed into the night sky as if the earth itself had erupted in answer to the cries of the vengeful Gnomes. Before the rising blaze stood the broad, immobile figure of the Dwarf Hendel, his arms raised in challenge, one great hand clutching the stone-shattering mace in menacing defiance of all who looked up at him. His laugh echoed deafeningly off the cliff walls.

"Come face me, Gnomes—worms of the earth!" he roared mockingly.

"Stand and fight—it's plain you won't be caught sitting for a while. Your foolish gods cannot save you from the powers of a Dwarf, let alone the spirits of the Wolfsktaag!"

The roar of fury that went up from the Gnomes was frightening. Almost to a man, they surged forward into the Pass of Jade to reach the mocking figure on the slope above them, determined to tear his heart out for the shame and humiliation inflicted upon them. To strike a Gnome chieftain was bad enough, but to insult their religion and their courage in the same breath was unforgivable. Some of the Gnomes recognized the Dwarf immediately and shouted his name to the others, crying out for his instant death. As the Gnomes charged blindly ahead into the pass, their ceremony forgotten, the fires burning untended, the four men on the slope leaped to their feet, clutching tightly the stretchers and their precious cargo, and raced in a low crouch across the open and unprotected southern slope, fully exposed by the glare of the blaze below, their shadows appearing as huge phantoms against the cliffside above their fleeing forms. No one paused to check the progress of the angered Gnomes; they charged madly ahead, eyes glued to the sheltering blackness of the Anar forest looming in the distance.

Miraculously, they made it to the safety of the forest. There they paused, breathing heavily in the cool shadows of the great trees, listening to the sounds in the pass. Below them, the floor of the pass entrance was deserted except for a small cluster of Gnomes, one of whom was engaged in aiding the wounded chieftain by extracting the painful arrow. Menion chuckled inwardly at the sight, a slow smile spreading over his lean face. It quickly vanished, however, as he looked into the pass where the bonfire on the northern slope still burned fiercely. The maddened Gnomes were climbing upward from all directions, an endless number of small yellowish bodies, the foremost of which had almost reached the blaze. There was no sign of Hendel, but from all appearances he was trapped somewhere on the slope. The four watched for only a minute, and then Balinor silently signaled for them to move out. The Pass of Jade was left behind.

It was dark in the heavy forests once the company had gone beyond the light of the Gnome fires. Balinor placed the Prince of Leah in the fore with instructions to move downward from the southern slope to find a trail that would take them west. It did not take long to reach such a trail, and the little band moved into the central Anar. The forests about them shut out most of the dim light of the distant stars, and the great trees framed the path ahead like black walls. The Valemen were thrashing violently on the stretchers again and moaning painfully, even through the heavy gags. The carriers were beginning to lose hope for their young friends. The poison was seeping slowly through their systems and when enough of it reached their hearts, the end would come abruptly. There was no way the four men could know how much time was left the brothers, and no way to estimate how far they might be from any sort of medical assistance. The one man who knew the central Anar was behind them, trapped in the Wolfsktaag and fighting for his life.

Suddenly, so quickly that the four had no time to get off the trail to avoid detection, a group of Gnomes appeared from out of the wall of trees on the path ahead. For a moment everyone stood motionless, each group squinting through the dim light. It took only an instant for each to realize who the other was. The four men quickly put down the cumbersome stretchers and moved forward to stand in a line across the trail. The Gnomes, numbering ten or twelve in all, clustered together for a moment and then one of them disappeared back into the trees.

"They've sent for help," Balinor whispered to the others. "If we don't get by them quickly, they will have reinforcements here to finish us off."

He had barely gotten the words out of his mouth before the remaining Gnomes let out a chilling battle cry and charged toward the four, their short, wicked-looking swords gleaming dully. The silent arrows of Menion and the Elf brothers dropped three of them in midstride before the rest swarmed over them like savage wolves. Dayel was completely bowled over by the assault and for a moment was lost from sight to the rear. Balinor stood firm as his huge blade cut two of the unfortunate Gnomes in half with one great sweep. The next several minutes were filled with sharp cries and labored breathing as the fighters battled back and forth across the narrow trail, the Gnomes seeking to get under the long reach of the men before them, the four defenders maneuvering to keep themselves between the fierce attackers and their two injured companions. In the end, the Gnomes all lay dead on the bloodied trail, their bodies small heaps in the dim light of the watching stars. Dayel had received a serious slash in the ribs that had to be bound, and Menion and Durin had received a number of small wounds. Balinor was untouched, his body protected from the Gnome swords by the lightweight chain mail beneath his shredded cloak.

The four paused only long enough to bind up Dayel's rib wound before picking up the stretchers and continuing at an even faster pace along the deserted path. They had further reason to hasten now. Gnome hunters would be quickly on their trail once they found their slain comrades. Menion tried to guess the hour from the position of the stars and by estimating their time of travel since the sun had set back in the Wolfsktaag Mountains, but could only conclude it was somewhere in the early-morning hours. The highlander felt the final signs of fatigue begin to creep through his aching arms and strained back muscles as he walked rapidly behind the broad form of Balinor, who had taken the lead. They were all close to exhaustion, their bodies worn from the day's travel and their encounters with first the monster in the Wolfsktaag and then the Gnomes. They were kept on their feet primarily because they knew what would happen to the Valemen if they stopped. Nevertheless, thirty minutes after the brief battle with the Gnome rear guard, Dayel simply collapsed in midstride from loss of blood and exhaustion. It took the others several minutes to revive him and get him back on his feet. Even then, the pace slowed noticeably.

Balinor was forced to call a second halt only minutes later to allow them all a much-needed rest. They huddled quietly at the side of the trail and listened in dismay to the growing tumult all about them. Shouting and muffled drums, still distant, had begun again since their encounter on the trail. Apparently the Gnomes were alerted sufficiently to their presence to have called out a large number of hunting parties to track them down. It sounded as if the entire Anar forest were alive with angered Gnomes, stalking the surrounding woods and hills in an effort to find the enemy that had slipped by them on the trail and killed ten or so of their number in avoiding capture. Menion glanced down wearily at the young Valemen, their faces white and covered with a heavy sheet of perspiration. He could hear them moaning through the cloth gags, see their limbs convulse as the poison seeped relentlessly through their failing systems. He looked at them and felt suddenly that he had somehow let them down when they needed him most, and that now they would pay the price for his failure. It angered him when he thought about the whole crazy idea of journeying to Paranor to retrieve a relic of another age on the offhand chance that it would save them, or save anyone for that matter, from a creature like the Warlock Lord. Yet he knew, even as he finished the thought, that it was wrong to question now something they had accepted from the first as little more than a remote possibility. He looked at Flick wearily and wondered why they couldn't have been better friends.

Durin's sudden whisper of warning sent them all scurrying off the exposed path with the cumbersome stretchers to the seclusion of the great trees, flattening themselves against the earth and waiting breathlessly. A moment later the distinct sound of heavy boots reverberated along the deserted trail and, from the direction in which they had come, a party of Gnome warriors marched out of the darkness toward their hiding place. Balinor immediately knew there were too many for them to fight and placed a restraining hand on the excited Menion to keep him from making any sudden movement. The Gnomes marched along the trail in formation, their yellow faces stony in the starlight as their wide-set eyes glanced uneasily about at the dark forest. They reached the point where the company crouched in hiding and moved on up the trail without pausing, unaware that their quarry was within a few feet. When they had disappeared from sight and there was no further sound of them, Menion turned to Balinor.

"We are finished if we don't find Allanon. We won't get another mile carrying Shea and Flick under these conditions unless we have help!"

Balinor nodded slowly, but made no comment. He knew their situation. But he knew as well that stopping now would be worse than capture or a second encounter with the Gnomes. Nor could they leave the brothers in these woods and hope they could find them after they got help—it was clearly too great a risk. He motioned the others to their feet. Without speaking, they picked up the stretchers and resumed the wearing march along the forest path, knowing now that the Gnomes were in front of them as well as behind. Menion wondered again what had befallen the gallant Hendel. It seemed impossible that even the resourceful Dwarf with all his skill in mountain fighting could have managed to evade those enraged Gnomes for any length of time. In any event, the Dwarf could not be in much worse shape than they were, wandering about the Anar with wounded men and no help in sight. If the Gnomes did find them again before they reached safety, Menion had little doubt as to the outcome.

Again Durin's sharp ears picked up the sound of approaching feet and everyone leaped to the safety of the great trees. They had barely gotten clear of the open trail and flattened themselves amidst the brush of the forest when figures appeared through the trees ahead. Even in the faint light of the stars, Durin's sharp eyes immediately picked out the leader of the small party as a giant of a man cloaked in a long black robe wound loosely about his lean body. A moment later the others saw him as well. It was Allanon. But Durin's sudden warning gesture stifled the exclamations of relief that were forming on the lips of Balinor and Menion. They squinted through the darkness and saw that the small, white-cloaked figures accompanying the historian were unmistakably Gnome.

"He's betrayed us!" whispered Menion harshly, his hand instinctively reaching for the long hunting knife at his belt.

"No, wait a minute," ordered Balinor quickly, motioning them all to lie flat as the party came closer to their hiding spot.

Allanon's tall figure approached slowly along the trail in no apparent hurry, the deep-set eyes turned straight ahead as he walked. His dark brow was furrowed in concentration. Menion knew instinctively that they would be found and tensed his muscles for the leap onto the trail where his first blow would destroy the traitor. He knew he would have no second chance. The white-garbed Gnomes followed their leader dutifully, not marching in any particular order as they shuffled along in apparent disinterest. Suddenly Allanon halted and looked around in startled realization, as if sensing their presence. Menion prepared to spring, but a heavy hand grasped his shoulder, holding him firmly against the earth.

"Balinor," called the tall wanderer evenly, moving neither forward nor to either side as he looked about expectantly.

"Release me!" demanded Menion furiously of the Prince of Callahorn.

"They have no weapons!" Balinor's voice cut through his anger, causing him to scan again the white-robed Gnomes at the tall man's side. There were no weapons visible.

Balinor stood up slowly and advanced into the clearing, his great sword gripped tightly in one hand. Menion was right behind him, noting the lean figure of Durin just within the trees, an arrow fitted to his bow in readiness. Allanon came forward with a sigh of relief and reached for Balinor's hand, stopping quickly as he saw the faint distrust mirrored in the borderman's eyes and the outright bitterness registered on the face of the highlander. He seemed baffled for a moment, and then looked back suddenly at the small figures standing motionless behind him.

"No, it's all right!" he exclaimed hastily. "These are friends. They have no weapons and no hatred toward you. They are healers, physicians."

For a moment no one moved. Then Balinor sheathed the great sword and took Allanon's extended hand in welcome. Menion followed suit, still distrustful of the Gnomes waiting up the trail.

"Now tell me what has happened," ordered Allanon, once again in command of the weary company. "Where are the others?"

Quickly Balinor recounted what had befallen them in the Wolfsktaag, their incorrect choice of the trail at the fork, the battle that had followed with the creature in the city ruins, their journey to the pass, and the plan that had gotten them past the assembled Gnomes. Upon hearing of the Valemen's injuries, Allanon immediately spoke to the Gnomes who had accompanied him, informing the suspicious Menion that they could treat the wounds his friends had incurred. Balinor continued his tale while the white-robed Gnomes hastened to the side of the injured Valemen and hovered over them in obvious concern, applying a liquid from some vials they carried. Menion looked on anxiously, wondering to himself why these Gnomes were any different from the rest. As Balinor concluded, Allanon shook his head in disgust.

"It was my fault, my miscalculation," he muttered angrily. "I was looking too far ahead in the journey and not watching closely enough for immediate dangers. If those two men die, the whole trip will have been for nothing!"

He spoke again to the scurrying Gnomes, and one of them departed at a hasty walk up the trail toward the Pass of Jade.

"I sent one of them back to see what he could learn about Hendel. If anything has happened to him, I'll be the only one to blame."

He ordered the Gnome physicians to pick up the Valemen and the whole group moved back onto the trail, heading westward, the stretcher bearers in the lead and the weary members of the company trailing behind. Dayel's rib wound had been attended to, and he was able to walk without assistance. As the company traveled along the deserted trail, Allanon explained to them why they would not encounter Gnome hunting parties in this region.

"We are approaching the land of the Stors, these Gnomes that came with me," he informed them. "They are healers, separate from the rest of the Gnome nations and all other races, dedicated to helping those in need of sanctuary or medical aid. They govern themselves, live apart from the petty bickerings of other nations—something most men could never manage to do. Everyone in this part of the world respects and honors them. Their land, which we will enter soon, is called Storlock. It is hallowed ground that no Gnome hunting party would dare to cross into unless invited. You may rest assured that invitations are at a premium this night."

He went on to explain that he had been a friend to these harmless people for many years, sharing their secrets, living with them for as long as several months at a time. The Stors could be counted on, he guaranteed Menion, to cure whatever might be wrong with the young Valemen. They were the foremost healers in the world, and it was no accident that they had come along with the historian when he had returned through the

Anar to meet the company at the Pass of Jade. Hearing of the strange events that had taken place from a frightened Gnome runner he had encountered on the trail at the edge of Storlock, who believed the spirits of the taboo land had sallied forth to consume them all, he had asked the Stors to come with him in search of his friends, fearing that they might have sustained injuries at the pass.

"I had no idea that the creature whose presence I detected in that valley in the Wolfsktaag would have the intelligence to remove the trail markers after I had passed," he admitted angrily. "I should have suspected, though, and left other signs to be certain that you bypassed that place. Worse still, I passed right through the Pass of Jade in the early afternoon without realizing that the Gnomes would be gathering that evening for the purging of the mountain spirits. It appears I have failed you badly."

"We were all at fault," Balinor declared, although Menion, listening silently from the other side, was not so willing to believe he was right. "Had we all been more alert, none of this would have happened. What matters is curing Shea and Flick and trying to do something about Hendel before the Gnome hunting parties find him."

They walked on in silence for a while, dejected men too tired to think further on the matter, concentrating only on putting one foot in front of the next until they reached the promised safety of the Stor village. The trail seemed to wind endlessly through the trees of the Anar forest, and after a while the four lost all sense of time and place, their minds dulled into sleepless exhaustion. The night slowly passed away, and finally the first tinges of the dawn's light appeared unexpectedly on the eastern horizon; still they had not reached their destination. It was an hour later when they finally saw the light of night fires burning in the Stor village, reflecting off the trees encircling the tired travelers. All at once they were in the village, surrounded by ghostlike Stors, wrapped in the same white cloaks, looking at the men with sad, unblinking expressions as they helped the exhausted travelers into the shelter of one of the low buildings.

Once within, the members of the company collapsed wordlessly on the soft beds provided, too tired to wash or even undress. All were asleep in seconds except for Menion Leah, whose high-strung temperament fought back the clutches of a soothing sleep long enough to allow his bleary eyes to search silently about the room for Allanon. Upon not finding him, he rose sluggishly from the softness of the bed and stumbled wearily to the closed wooden door, which he dimly recalled led to a second room beyond. Leaning heavily against the door, his ear pressed closely to the crack in the jamb, he listened to snatches of conversation between the historian and the Stors. In a daze of half-sleep, he heard a brief digression concerning Shea and Flick. The strange little people felt that the Valemen would recover with rest and special medication. Then abruptly a door beyond opened to admit several people, and their voices blended meaninglessly in exclamations of dismay and shock. Allanon's deep voice cut through in icy clearness.

"What have you discovered?" he demanded. "Is it as bad as we feared?"

"They caught somebody in the mountains," came the timid answer. "It was impossible to tell who it was or even what it was by the time they were finished. They tore him to pieces!"

Hendel!

Stunned, even in his exhausted condition, the highlander pushed himself upright and stumbled back to his waiting bed, unable to believe he had heard them correctly. Deep within him, a great empty space opened. Helpless tears of anger welled up, unable to reach his still-dry eyes, and hung poised there until the Prince of Leah finally dropped off into comforting sleep.

13

When Shea finally opened his eyes, it was midafternoon of the following day. He found himself resting comfortably in a long bed, tucked in with clean sheets and blankets, his hunting clothes replaced by a loose white gown tied about his neck. On the bed next to him lay the still-sleeping Flick, his broad face no longer drawn and pale, but alive once more with the color of life and peaceful in slumber. They were in a small, plaster-walled room with a ceiling supported by long wooden beams. Through the windows, the young Valeman could see the trees of the Anar and the shining blueness of the afternoon sky. He had no idea how long he had been unconscious or what had happened during that time to bring him to this unknown place. But he felt certain that the creature of the Wolfsktaag had nearly killed him, and that Flick and he owed their lives to the men of the company. His attention was quickly drawn to the opening door at one end of the small room and the appearance of an anxious Menion Leah.

"Well, old friend, I see that you've come back to the world of the living." The highlander smiled slowly as he came over to the bedside. "You gave us quite a scare there for a while, you know."

"We made it, didn't we?" Shea grinned happily at the familiar joking voice.

Menion nodded briefly and turned to the supine figure of Flick, who had stirred slightly beneath the covers and was beginning to awake. The stocky Valeman opened his eyes slowly and looked up hesitantly, seeing the grinning face of the highlander.

"I knew it was too good to be true," he groaned painfully. "Even dead, I can't escape him. It's a curse!"

"Old Flick has fully recovered as well." Menion laughed shortly. "I hope he appreciates the work it took to carry that cumbersome body of his all this way."

"The day you do any honest work, I'll be amazed," mumbled Flick, trying to clear his sleep-fogged eyes. He looked over at a smiling Shea and grinned back with a short wave of greeting.

"Where are we anyway?" asked Shea curiously, forcing himself to sit up in bed. He was still feeling weak. "How long have I been unconscious?"

Menion sat down on the edge of the bed and repeated the entire tale of their journey after escaping the creature in the valley. He told them of the march to the Pass of Jade and the encounter with the Gnomes there, the plan to get them by, and the results. He faltered a bit retelling of Hendel's sacrifice to the company. Shocked looks registered on the Valemen's faces on hearing of the gallant Dwarf's grisly death at the hands of the enraged Gnomes. Menion quickly continued with the remainder of the story, explaining how they had wandered through the Anar until discovered by Allanon and the strange people called Stors, who had treated their wounds and brought them to this place.

"This land is called Storlock," he concluded finally. "The people here are Gnomes who have dedicated their lives to healing the sick and injured. It's really amazing what they can do. They have a salve which, when applied to an open wound, closes it up and heals it over in twelve hours. I saw it work myself on an injury Dayel received."

Shea shook his head in disbelief and was about to ask for further details when the door again opened to admit Allanon. For the first time he could remember, Shea thought the dark wanderer actually seemed happy, and detected a sincere smile of relief on the grim face. The man walked quickly over to them and nodded in satisfaction.

"I am certainly pleased that you have both recovered from your wounds. I was gravely concerned about you, but it appears the Stors have done their work well. Do you feel recovered enough to get out of bed and walk around a bit, perhaps to have some food?"

Shea looked inquiringly over at Flick, and they both nodded.

"Very well, then, go along with Menion and test your strength," the historian suggested. "It is important that you feel well enough to travel again soon."

Without further word, he left by the same door, shutting it softly behind him. They watched him go, wondering how he could continue to be so coldly formal in his attitude toward them. Menion shrugged, advising them that he would find their hunting clothes which had been taken out and cleaned. He left and quickly returned with their clothing, whereupon the Valemen rose weakly from their beds and dressed while Menion told them a little more about the Stors. He explained that he had mistrusted them at first because they were Gnomes, but his fears had rapidly vanished upon watching them care for the Valemen. The others in the company had slept well into the morning before waking and were scattered now about the village, enjoying their brief respite on the journey to Paranor.

The three left the room shortly thereafter and entered another building that served as a dining hall for the village, where they were given generous portions of hot food to appease their ravenous appetites. Even with their injuries, the Valemen found themselves able to put away several helpings of the nourishing meal. After finishing, Menion led them outside where they encountered a fully recuperated Durin and Dayel, both delighted to see the Valemen back on their feet. At Menion's suggestion, the five walked to the south end of the village to see the wondrous Blue Pond that the highlander had been told about by the Stors earlier in the day. It took only a few minutes for them to reach the small pond, and they sat at its edge beneath a huge weeping willow and gazed in silence at the placid blue surface. Menion told them that the Stors made many of their salves and balms from the waters of that pond, which were said to have special healing elements that could be found nowhere else in the world. Shea tasted the water and found it different from anything he had ever encountered, but not at all displeasing to drink. The others tried it as well and murmured their approval. The Blue Pond was such a peaceful place that for a moment they all sat back and forgot their hazardous journey, thinking about their homes and the people they had left behind.

"This pond reminds me of Beleal, my home in the Westland." Durin smiled to himself as he ran a finger through the water, tracing out some image from his mind. "There, you can find the same sort of peace we have here."

"We'll be back there before you know it," Dayel promised, and then added eagerly, almost boyishly, "And I'll be married to Lynliss and we'll have many children."

"Forget it," declared Menion abruptly. "Stay single and stay happy."

"You haven't seen her, Menion," Dayel continued brightly. "She is like no one you have seen—a gentle, kind girl, as beautiful as this pond is clear."

Menion shook his head in mock despair and slapped the frail Elf on his shoulder lightly, smiling his understanding of the other's deep feeling for the Elven girl. No one spoke for a few minutes as they continued to gaze with mixed feelings at the blue waters of the Stor pond. Then Shea turned to them questioningly.

"Do you think we are doing the right thing? I mean going on this trip and all. Does it all seem worth it to you?"

"That seems funny coming from you, Shea," remarked Durin thoughtfully. "The way I see it, you have the most to lose by coming along. In fact, you are the whole purpose of this journey. Do you feel it's worth it?"

Shea considered for a moment while the others looked on silently.

"That's not really a fair question to ask him," defended Flick.

"Yes, it is," Shea cut in soberly. "They are all risking their lives for me, and I've been the only one expressing any doubts about what we're doing. But I can't answer my own question, even to myself, because I feel I still don't know exactly what's happening. I do not think that we have the whole picture before us."

"I know what you mean," Menion agreed. "Allanon hasn't told us everything about what we're doing on this trip. There's more to this business about the Sword of Shannara than we know."

"Has anybody ever seen the Sword?" Dayel asked suddenly. The others shook their heads negatively. "Maybe there is no Sword."

"Oh, I think that the Sword exists, all right," Durin declared quickly. "But once we get it, what do we do with it? What can Shea do against the power of the Warlock Lord, even with the Sword of Shannara?"

"I think we must trust to Allanon to answer that when the time comes," another voice said.

The new voice came from behind the five, and they turned around sharply, breathing an audible sigh of relief when it was Balinor who appeared. Even as he watched the Prince of Callahorn stroll over to them, Shea wondered to himself why it was that they all still felt an unspoken fear of Allanon. The borderman smiled a greeting to Shea and Flick and seated himself with the others.

"Well, it appears that our hardships in coming through the Pass of Jade were worth it after all. I'm glad to see that you're all right."

"I'm sorry about Hendel." Shea sounded awkward to himself. "I know he was a close friend."

"It was a calculated risk that the situation demanded," replied Balinor softly. "He knew what he was doing and what the chances were. He did it for all of us."

"What happens next?" asked Flick after a moment.

"We wait for Allanon to decide on our route for the last leg of the journey," replied Balinor. "Incidentally, I meant what I said about trusting him. He is a great man, a good man, though it may appear otherwise at times. He tells us what he feels we ought to know, but believe me, he does the worrying for us all. Do not be too quick to judge him."

"You know that he hasn't told us everything," Menion stated simply.

"I am certain he has told us only part of the tale." Balinor nodded. "But he is the only one who realized the threat to the four lands in the first place. We owe him a great deal, and the very least of that is a little trust."

The others nodded slowly in agreement, more for the reason that they all respected the borderman than because they felt convinced by his reassurances. This was especially true of Menion, who recognized that Balinor was a man of great courage, the kind of man whom Menion looked to as a leader. They spoke no more on the matter, but turned to a further discussion of the Stors, their history as a branch of the Gnome nations, and their long, abiding friendship with Allanon. The sun was setting when the tall historian appeared unexpectedly and joined them by the Blue Pond.

"After I am finished with you I want the Valemen back in bed for a few hours' rest. It probably wouldn't hurt the rest of you to get some sleep as well. We will leave this place some time around midnight."

"Isn't this a little sudden after the wounds Shea and Flick received?" Menion asked cautiously.

"That cannot be helped, highlander." The grim face seemed black even in the fading sunlight. "We are all running out of time. If word of our mission, or even our presence in this part of the Anar, reaches the Warlock Lord, he will try to move the Sword immediately, and without it this journey is pointless."

"Flick and I can make it," Shea declared resolutely.

"What will be the route?" Balinor asked.

"We will cross the Rabb Plains tonight, a march of about four hours. If we are lucky, we will not be caught out in the open, although I am quite sure the Skull Bearers will still be searching for both Shea and myself. We can only hope they haven't managed to trace us into the Anar. I hadn't told you before, because you had enough to concern you, but any use of the Elfstones pinpoints our position to Brona and his hunters. The mystical power of the stones can be detected by any creature of the spirit world, warning him that sorcery similar to his own is being used."

"Then, when we used the Elfstones in the Mist Marsh . . ." Flick began in horror.

"You told the Skull Bearers exactly where you were," Allanon finished with that infuriating smile. "If you hadn't lost yourselves in the mist and the Black Oaks, they might have had you right there."

Shea felt a sudden chill sweep over him as he recalled how close they had felt to death at the time, little realizing how much danger they were really in from the creatures they feared the most.

"If you knew that use of the stones would attract the spirit creatures, then why didn't you tell us?" demanded Shea angrily. "Why did you give them to us to use for protection when you knew what would happen?"

"You were cautioned, my young friend," came the slow, growling response that always indicated Allanon's temper was shortening. "Without them, you would have been at the mercy of other equally dangerous elements. Besides, they are protection enough in themselves against the winged ones."

He waved off further questions, indicating that the subject was closed, causing Shea to become even more suspicious and angered. A watchful Durin saw all the signs and placed a restraining hand on the young Valeman's shoulder, shaking his head in warning.

"If we may return to the matter at hand," Allanon continued on a more even tone, "let me explain further the chosen route for the next few days—without interruption. The journey across the Rabb Plains will put us at the foot of the Dragon's Teeth at daybreak. Those mountains offer all the protection we need from anyone searching for us. But the real problem is getting over them and down the other side to the forests surrounding Paranor. All the known passes through the Dragon's Teeth will be closely guarded by the allies of the Warlock Lord, and any attempt to scale those peaks without using one of the passes would get half of us killed. So we'll go through the mountains by a different route, one that they won't be guarding."

"Wait a minute!" exclaimed Balinor in astonishment. "You don't plan to take us through the Tomb of the Kings!"

"There is no other alternative open to us if we wish to avoid being discovered. We can enter the Hall of Kings at sunrise and be completely through the mountains and outside Paranor by sundown without the guards at the passes being any the wiser."

"But the stories say no one has ever gotten through those caverns alive!" insisted Durin, coming quickly to Balinor's aid in discounting the suggested plan. "None of us is afraid of the living, but the spirits of the dead inhabit those caves and only the dead may pass through unharmed. No living person has ever done it!"

Balinor nodded his head slowly in agreement, while the others looked on anxiously. Menion and the Valemen had never even heard of the place of which the others seemed so deathly afraid. Allanon was actually grinning strangely at Durin's last comment, his eyes dark beneath the heavy brows, his white teeth showing in menacing fashion.

"You are not entirely correct, Durin," he replied after a minute. "I have been through the Hall of Kings, and I tell you that it can be done. It is not a journey to be made without risk. The caverns are indeed inhabited by the spirits of the dead, and it is on this that Brona relies to prevent the entry of humans. But my power should be sufficient to protect us."

Menion Leah had no idea what it was about the caverns that could cause even a man like Balinor to have second thoughts, but whatever it was, he felt there was a good reason to fear it. Moreover, he was through questioning what he had called old wives' tales and foolish legends, since the encounters in the Mist Marsh and the Wolfsktaag. What really concerned him now was what sort of powers the man who proposed to lead them through the caves of the Dragon's Teeth might possess that could protect them from spirits.

"The entire journey has been a calculated risk." Allanon was speaking once again. "We all knew what the dangers were before we began it. Are you ready to turn back at this point, or do we see the matter through to the end?"

"We will follow you," Balinor declared after only a moment's hesitation. "You knew we would. The risk is worth it if we can lay our hands on the Sword."

Allanon smiled slightly, his deep-set eyes traveling over the faces of the others, meeting each gaze piercingly, coming to rest at last on Shea. The Valeman stared back unfalteringly, though his heart felt twinges of fear and uncertainty as those eyes bored into his innermost thoughts, seemingly aware of every secret doubt the Valeman had tried to conceal.

"Very well." Allanon nodded darkly. "Go now and rest."

He turned abruptly and walked back toward the Stor village. Balinor hastened after the departing figure, apparently wishing to ask something further. The others watched both until they were out of sight. Then, for the first time, Shea realized it was almost dark, the sun sinking slowly beneath the horizon and the twilight a soft white light in the deepening purple sky. For a moment no one moved, and then silently they climbed to their feet and retired to the peaceful village to sleep until the appointed hour of midnight.

It seemed to Shea that he had just fallen asleep when he felt the rough grip of a strong hand shaking him awake. A moment later, the sharp glare of a burning torch flickered through the darkened room, causing him to squint protectively while his sleep-filled eyes adjusted to this new light. Through a mist of sleep, he saw the determined face of Menion Leah, the anxious eyes telling him that the hour had come for them to depart. He rose unsteadily in the cold night air and, after a moment's hesitation, hastened to dress. Flick was already awake and half dressed, the stolid face a welcome sight in the eerie silence of midnight. Shea felt strong once again, strong enough to make the long march across the Rabb Plains to the Dragon's Teeth and beyond if necessary—anything to reach the end of the journey.

Minutes later, the three companions were making their way through the sleeping Stor village to meet the other members of the company. The darkened houses were black, squarish bulks in the dim light of a night sky which was moonless and screened by a heavy blanket of clouds that moved sluggishly toward some undetermined destination. It was a good night to travel in the open, and Shea felt reassured by the idea that any searching emissaries of the Warlock Lord would have a very difficult time spotting them. As they walked, he found that he could barely detect the tread of their light hunting boots on the damp earth. Everything seemed to be working in their favor.

When they reached the western boundary of Storlock, they found the others waiting, except for Allanon. Durin and Dayel appeared like empty forms in the blackness, their slight figures only shadows as they paced wordlessly, listening to the sounds of the night. Passing close to them at one point, Shea was struck by the distinctive Elven features, the strange pointed ears and the pencil-thin eyebrows arching upward onto the forehead. He wondered if other humans looked at him the way he now looked at the Elven brothers. Were they truly different creatures? He wondered again about the history behind the Elf people, the history that Allanon had referred to once as remarkable, but had never described further. Their history was his own; he knew now what he had always suspected. It was something he wanted to know more about, perhaps if only better to understand his own heritage and the tale of the Sword of Shannara.

He looked over to the tall, broad figure of Balinor standing like a statue to one side, his face featureless in the dark. Balinor was unquestionably the most reassuring thing about the whole expedition. There was something very durable about the borderman, a quality of indestructibility that lent itself freely to all of the members of the company and gave them courage. Even Allanon did not inspire them in quite this way, although Shea felt that he was easily the more powerful of the two. Perhaps Allanon, in his seemingly infinite awareness of all matters, knew what Balinor did for other men and had brought him along for precisely that reason.

"Quite so, Shea." The soft voice was so close to his ear that the Valeman leaped violently in surprise as the black-cloaked wanderer strolled past him and motioned the others to his side. "The journey must be made while we have the cover of the night. Stay together and keep your eyes on the men ahead. There will be no talking."

Without further greeting, the dark giant led them into the Anar Forests along a narrow trail that ran directly west out of Storlock. Shea fell into step behind Menion, his heart still in his throat from the fright he had received, his mind racing madly back over the past encounters with the strange man, wondering if what he had suspected all along were true after all. In any event, he would keep his thoughts to himself any time Allanon was close, however difficult that task might prove to be.

The company reached the western edges of the Anar Forests and the beginning of the Rabb Plains sooner than Shea had expected. Despite the blackness of the night sky, the Valemen could sense the presence of the Dragon's Teeth looming in the distance; without speaking, they looked at one another briefly, then turned back to peer anxiously into the darkness. Allanon led them across the empty plainland without pausing and without slackening the pace. The Plains were completely flat, totally free of natural obstructions and visibly lifeless. The only things growing were small scrub trees and bits of scattered brush that were bare and skeletonlike in appearance. The floor of the plain was hard-packed earth, so dry in parts that it split apart in long, jagged crevices. Nothing moved about the travelers as they marched in silence, their eyes and ears alert to anything out of the ordinary. At one point, when they were almost three hours into the Rabb Plains, Dayel brought them up with a quick gesture, indicating that he had heard something behind them, far back in the blackness. They crouched soundless and immobile for several long minutes, but nothing happened. At last Allanon shrugged and motioned them back into line, and they resumed their march.

They reached the Dragon's Teeth just before daybreak, the night sky still black and clouded as they halted at the foot of the forbidding mountains that spread upward across their path like monstrous spikes on an iron gate. Both Shea and Flick felt strong, even after the long march, and quickly indicated to the others that they were ready to continue without a rest. Allanon seemed eager to move on immediately, almost as if he were determined to keep an appointment. He took them straight into the treacherous-looking mountains along a pebble-strewn trail that wound gently upward into what appeared to be a pocket in the face of the cliffs. Flick found himself looking up at the peaks on either side of the trail as he walked, craning his stout neck at right angles to catch occasional glimpses of the jagged tips. The Dragon's Teeth seemed an appropriate name.

The mountains on either side began to fold about them as they worked their way toward the cliff pocket. Beyond that shallow pass, they could glimpse other mountains, higher than these and clearly insurmountable by anything that could not fly. Shea paused momentarily at one point, picked up a piece of the loose rock from beneath his feet, and examined it curiously as he resumed walking. To his surprise, it was smooth on its flat surfaces, almost glassy in appearance, and its color was a deep, mirroring black that reminded the Valeman of the coal he had seen burned as fuel in some of the Southland communities. Yet this appeared to be more durable than coal, as if it had been pressured and polished to reach its present state. He handed it to Flick, who glanced at it, shrugged disinterestedly, and tossed it aside.

The trail began to twist through huge clusters of fallen boulders, causing the travelers momentarily to lose all sight of the surrounding mountains. They wound about in the tangle of rock for a long time, still climbing toward the pocket, their dark leader apparently oblivious to the fact that no one had any idea where they were going. Finally they reached a clearing in the rocks where they could see enough of the high cliffs about them to tell that they were at the opening to the pocket and evidently close to the summit of the trail, which would then either have to turn downward or level off into the mountains. It was here that Balinor broke the silence with a low whistle, bringing the company to a halt. He spoke momentarily with Durin, who had fallen back with the borderman at the foot of the mountains, then quickly turned to Allanon and the others with a startled look on his face.

"Durin is certain he heard someone following us on the trail up!" he informed them tensely. "There's no question about it this time—someone is back there."

Allanon glanced up hurriedly at the night sky. His dark brow furrowed in concern, the lean face revealing that he was deeply worried by this report. He looked at Durin uncertainly.

"I'm sure there is someone back there," Durin affirmed.

"I cannot stop here to deal with this myself. I have to be in the valley ahead before the break of day," Allanon declared abruptly. "Whatever is back there must be delayed until I have finished—it is essential!"

Shea had never heard the man sound so determined about anything, and he caught the looks of consternation on both Flick's and Menion's faces as they glanced quickly at each other. Whatever it was Allanon had to do in the valley, it was critical to him that he not be interrupted until he had finished.

"I'll stay behind," Balinor volunteered, drawing his great sword. "Wait for me in the valley."

"Not alone, you won't," Menion spoke up quickly. "I'm staying, too, just in case."

Balinor smiled briefly and nodded his approval to the highlander. Allanon looked at him for a moment as if to object, then nodded curtly and motioned the others to follow him. The Elven brothers hastened up the trail behind the tall leader, but Shea and Flick hung back uncertainly until Menion motioned for them to get going. Shea waved briefly, reluctant to desert his friend, but realizing that he would be of little help in staying. He glanced back only once and saw the two men positioning themselves among the rocks on either side of the narrow trail, their swords gleaming dully in the faint starlight, their dark hunting cloaks blending with the shadows of the rocks.

Allanon led the remaining four members of the company ahead through the jumbled mass of boulders where the cliff face split apart, climbing steadily upward toward what appeared to be the rim of the mysterious valley. It was only a few short minutes before they stood quietly at its edge, gazing wonderingly at what lay before them. The valley was a barbaric wilderness of crushed rock and boulders strewn about the sides and floor, black and glistening like the rock Shea had examined on the trail; the place was completely covered with them. Nothing else was visible except for a small lake with murky waters that glistened a dull greenish-black and moved in small sluggish swirls as if possessing a life of its own. Shea was immediately struck with the strange movement of the water. There was no wind which might cause the slow rippling. He looked at the silent Allanon and was shocked to see a strange glow radiating from his dark, forbidding face. The tall wanderer seemed momentarily lost in his thoughts as he gazed downward at the lake, and the Valeman could sense a peculiar wistfulness about the man's unbroken study of the slowly churning waters.

"This is the Valley of Shale, the doorstep to the Hall of Kings and the home of the spirits of the ages." The deep voice rolled suddenly out of the depths of the great chest. "The lake is the Hadeshorn—its waters are death to mortals. Walk with me to the floor of the valley, and then I must go on alone."

Without waiting for a response, he started slowly down the slope of the valley, stepping surefootedly through the loose rock, his gaze fixed on the lake beyond. The others followed in mystified silence, sensing that this was going to be an important moment for them all, that here more than anywhere else in all the lands, Allanon was king. Without being able to explain why, Shea knew that the historian, the wanderer, the philosopher, and the mystic, the man who had brought them through countless dangers on a wild gamble that only he fully understood, the mysterious man they knew as Allanon, had at last come home. Moments later, when they stood together on the floor of the Valley of Shale, he turned to them again.

"You will wait for me here. No matter what happens next, you will not follow me. You will not move from this spot until I have finished. Where I go, there is only death."

They stood rooted in place as he moved away from them across the rocky floor toward the mysterious lake. They watched his tall, black form walk steadily ahead without variation in either speed or direction, the great cloak billowing slightly. Shea shot a quick glance at Flick, whose tense face revealed his fear of what would happen next. For a split second Shea considered getting out of there, but realized immediately what a foolhardy decision that would be. Instinctively he clutched his tunic, feeling the reassuring bulk of the small pouch that contained the Elfstones. Their presence made him feel safer, even though he doubted that they would be of

much use against anything that Allanon could not handle. He glanced anxiously at the others as they watched the diminishing figure, then turning
back, saw that Allanon had reached the edge of the Hadeshorn, where he
was apparently awaiting something. A deathly silence seemed to grip the
entire valley. The four waited, their eyes locked on the dark figure who
stood motionless at the water's edge.

Slowly, the tall wanderer raised his black-caped arms to the sky and the
amazed men saw the lake begin to stir rapidly and then churn in deep dissatisfaction. The valley shuddered heavily, as if some form of hidden,
sleeping life had been awakened. The terrified mortals looked about in
disbelief, fearing they were about to be swallowed by the rock-strewn maw
of some nightmare disguised as the valley. Allanon stood firm at the shoreline as the water began to boil fiercely at its center, a spray mist rising
toward the darkened heavens with a sharp hiss of relief at its newfound
freedom from the depths. From out of the night air came the sound of low
moaning, the cries of imprisoned souls, their sleep disturbed by the man at
the edge of the Hadeshorn. The voices, less than human and chill with
death, cut through the raw edge of sanity of the four who shivered and
watched at the valley's edge, straining their frightened minds and twisting
with unmerciful cruelty until it seemed the little courage that remained
must surely be wrested from them, leaving them stripped completely of all
defenses. Unable to move, to speak, even to think, they stood frozen in
terror as the sounds of the spirit world reached up to them and passed
through their minds, warning of the things that lay beyond this life and
their understanding.

In the midst of the chilling cries, with a low rumble that sounded
from the heart of the earth, the Hadeshorn opened at its center in the
manner of a thrashing whirlpool and from out of its murky waters rose the
shroud of an old man, bowed with age. The figure rose to full height and
appeared to stand on the waters themselves, the tall, thin body a transparent gray of ghostlike hue that shimmered like the lake beneath it. Flick
turned completely white. The appearance of this final horror only confirmed his belief that their last moments on earth were at hand. Allanon
stood motionless at the edge of the lake, his lean arms lowered now, the
black cloak wrapped closely about his statuesque figure, his face turned
toward the shade which stood before him. They appeared to be conversing, but the four onlookers could hear nothing beyond the continual,
maddening sound of the inhuman cries that rose piercingly out of the
night each time the figure from the Hadeshorn gestured. The conversation, whatever its nature, lasted no more than a few brief minutes, ending
when the wraith turned toward them suddenly, raised its tattered skeletal
arm, and pointed. Shea felt a chill slice through his unprotected body that
seemed to cut to the bones, and he knew that for a brief second he had
been touched by death. Then the shade turned away and, with a final
gesture of farewell to Allanon, sank slowly back into the dark waters of the
Hadeshorn and was gone. As he disappeared from view, the waters again

churned sluggishly, and the moans and cries reached a new pitch before dying out in a low wail of anguish. Then the lake was smooth and calm and the men were alone.

As sunrise broke on the eastern horizon, the tall, black figure on the lake's edge seemed to sway slightly and then crumple to the ground. For a second the four men watching hesitated, then dashed across the valley floor toward their fallen leader, slipping and stumbling on the loose rock. They reached him in a matter of seconds and bent cautiously over him, uncertain what they should do. Finally, Durin reached down and shook the still form gingerly, calling his name. Shea rubbed the great hands, finding the skin ice-cold to his touch and alarmingly pale. But their fears were relieved when after a few minutes Allanon stirred slightly and the deep-set eyes opened once more. He stared at them for a few seconds, and then sat up slowly as they crouched anxiously next to him.

"The strain must have been too great," he muttered to himself, rubbing his forehead. "Blacked out after I lost contact. I'll be fine in a moment."

"Who was that creature?" Flick asked quickly, afraid that it might reappear at any moment.

Allanon seemed to reflect on his question, staring into space as his dark face twisted in anguish and then relaxed softly.

"A lost soul, a being forgotten by this world and its people," he declared sadly. "He has doomed himself to an existence of half-life that may not end for all eternity."

"I don't understand," Shea said.

"It's not important right now." Allanon brushed the question aside abruptly. "That sad figure to whom I just spoke is the Shade of Bremen, the Druid who once fought against the Warlock Lord. I spoke to him of the Sword of Shannara, of our trip to Paranor, and of the destiny of this company. I could learn little from him, an indication that our fortunes are not to be decided in the very near future, but that the fate of us all will be decided in days still far away—that is, all but one."

"What do you mean?" Shea demanded hesitantly.

Allanon climbed wearily to his feet, gazed about the valley silently as if to assure himself that the encounter with the ghost of Bremen was ended, and then turned back to the anxious faces waiting on him.

"There is no easy way to say this, but you've come this far, almost to the end of the quest. You have earned the right to know. The Shade of Bremen made two prophecies on the destiny of this company when I called him up from the limbo world to which he is confined. He promised that within two dawns we would behold the Sword of Shannara. But he also foresaw that one member of our company would not reach the far side of the Dragon's Teeth. Yet he will be the first to lay hands upon the sacred blade."

"I still don't understand," Shea admitted after a moment's thought. "We've already lost Hendel. He must have been speaking of him in some way."

"No, you are wrong, my young friend." Allanon sighed softly. "Upon making the last part of the prophecy, the shade pointed to the four of you standing at the edge of the valley. One of you will not reach Paranor!"

Menion Leah crouched silently in the cover of the boulders along the path leading upward to the Valley of Shale, waiting expectantly for the mysterious being who had been trailing them into the Dragon's Teeth. Across from him, hidden in the blackness of the shadows, was the Prince of Callahorn, his great sword balanced blade downward in the rocks, one big hand resting lightly on the pommel. Menion gripped his own weapon and peered into the darkness. Nothing was moving. He could see for only about fifteen yards before an abrupt twist in the trail concealed the remainder of the pathway behind a cluster of massive boulders. They had been waiting for at least half an hour and still nothing had appeared, despite Durin's assurance that something was following. Menion wondered for a moment if perhaps the creature who had been trailing them was one of the emissaries of the Warlock Lord. A Skull Bearer could take to the air and get behind them to reach the others. The idea startled him, and he was about to signal Balinor when a sudden noise on the trail below caught his attention. He immediately flattened himself against the rocks.

The sound of someone picking his way up the twisting pathway, threading slowly among the great boulders in the dim light of the approaching dawn, was clearly audible. Whoever or whatever it was, he apparently did not suspect they were hidden above, or worse, did not care, because he was making no effort to mask his approach. Scant seconds later, a dim form appeared on the pathway just below their hiding place. Menion risked a quick glance and for one brief second the squat shape and shuffling gait of the figure approaching reminded him of Hendel. He gripped the sword of Leah in anticipation and waited. The plan of attack was simple. He would leap in front of the intruder, barring his path forward. In the same moment, Balinor would cut off his retreat.

With a lightning-quick spring, the highlander shot out of the rocks to stand face-to-face with the mysterious intruder, his sword held poised as he gave a sharp command to halt. The figure before him went into a low crouch and one powerful arm came up slightly to reveal a huge, iron-headed mace, glinting dully. One second later, as the eyes of the combatants came to rest on one another, the arms dropped in shocked recognition, and a cry of surprise burst from the lips of the Prince of Leah.

"Hendel!"

Balinor came out of the shadows to the rear of the newcomer in time to see an elated Menion leap into the air with a wild shout and charge down to embrace the smaller, stockier figure with unrestrained joy. The Prince of Callahorn sheathed the great sword in relief, smiling and shaking his head in wonder at the sight of the ecstatic highlander and the struggling, muttering Dwarf they had presumed dead. For the first time since they had escaped through the Pass of Jade from the Wolfsktaag, he felt that success was within their grasp and that the company would surely stand together at Paranor before the Sword of Shannara.

Dawn hung above the sweeping ridges and peaks of the Dragon's Teeth with a cold, gray determination that was neither cheerful nor welcome. The warmth and brightness of the rising sun was entirely screened away by low cloud banks and heavy mist that settled into the ominous heights and did not stir. The winds blew with vicious force over the barren rocks, whipping through canyons and craggy drops, across slopes and ridges, cutting into the scant vegetation and bending it close to the point of breaking, yet slipping through the mixture of clouds and mist with elusive quickness, leaving it unexplainably and strangely motionless. The sound of the wind was like the deep roar of the ocean breaking on an open beach, heavy and rolling, blanketing the empty peaks in a peculiar drone that, when one had been enveloped for a while, created its own level of silence. Birds rose and fell with the wind, their cries scattered and muffled. There were few animals at this height—isolated herds of a particularly tough breed of mountain goat and small, furry mice that inhabited the innermost recesses of the rocks. The air was more than chill; it was bitterly cold. Snow covered the upper reaches of the Dragon's Teeth, and changes in the seasons had little effect at this altitude on a temperature that seldom reached thirty degrees.

These were treacherous mountains, vast, towering and incredibly massive. On this morning they seemed shrouded with a strange expectancy, and the eight men who comprised the little company from Culhaven could not ignore the feeling of uneasiness that preoccupied their thoughts as they trudged deeper into the cold and the gray. It was more than the disturbing prophecy of Bremen or even the knowledge that they would soon attempt to pass through the forbidden Hall of Kings. Something was waiting for them, something that had patience and cunning, a life force that lay hidden in the barren, rocky terrain they were passing through, filled with vindictive hatred of them, watching as they struggled deeper into the giant mountains that shut away the ancient kingdom of Paranor. They trudged northward in a ragged line, strung out against the misty skyline, their bodies wrapped tightly in woolen cloaks for protection against the cold, their faces bent before the wind. The slopes and canyons were covered with loose rock and split by hidden crevices that made the footing extremely hazardous. More than once, a member of the little band went down in a shower of loose rock and dirt. But still the thing concealed in the land chose not to show itself, content merely to let its presence be known and to wait for the effect of that knowledge to wear away at the resistance of the eight men. The hunters would then become the hunted.

It did not take long. Doubts began to gnaw quietly, persistently at their tired minds—doubts that rose phantomlike from the fears and secrets the men concealed deep within. Locked away from one another by the cold and the roar of the rising wind, each man was cut off from his companions, and the inability to communicate only heightened the growing feeling of uneasiness. Only Hendel was immune. His taciturn, solitary nature had hardened him against self-doubt, and his harrowing escape from the mad-dened Gnomes in the Pass of Jade had drained him at least temporarily of any fear of death. He had come close to dying, so close that in the end only instinct had saved him. The Gnomes had come at him from every direction, swarming up the slope in reckless disregard, enraged to the point where only bloodshed would quiet their hatred. He had been quick, slipping back into the fringes of the Wolfsktaag, motionless in the brush, coolly letting the Gnomes overextend themselves until one had come within reach. It had taken only seconds to stun the unsuspecting hunter, to cloak his captive in his own distinctive Dwarf habit, and then yell for assis-tance. In the darkness, flushed with the excitement of the hunt, the Gnomes were unable to recognize anything except the cloak. They tore their own brother to pieces without realizing it. Hendel had stayed hidden and slipped through the pass the following day. He had survived once again.

The Valemen and the Elves did not possess Hendel's strong sense of self-reliance. The prophecy of the Shade of Bremen had left them stunned. The words seemed to repeat themselves over and over in the howl of the mountain winds. One of them was going to die. Oh, the words of the prophecy had phrased it differently than that, but the implication was un-mistakable. It was a bitter prospect to face, and none of them could really accept it. Somehow they would find a way to prove the prediction wrong.

Far in the lead, his great frame bent against the driving force of the mountain winds, Allanon was mulling over the events that had transpired in the Valley of Shale. He considered for the hundredth time his strange confrontation with the Shade of Bremen, the aged Druid doomed to wan-der in limbo until the Warlock Lord was finally destroyed. Yet it was not the appearance of the driven wraith that so disturbed him now. It was the terrible knowledge which he carried, buried deep among his blackest truths. His foot struck a projecting rock, causing him to stumble slightly, and he fought to keep his balance. A wheeling hawk screamed shrilly in the grayness and shot down out of the sky over a distant ridge. The Druid turned slightly as the thin line following struggled to keep pace. He had learned more from the Shade than the words of the prophecy. But he had not told the others, those who had trusted him, the whole truth, just as he had not told them the whole story behind the legendary Sword of Shannara. His deep-set eyes blazed with inner fury at the predicament in which he had placed himself in not telling them everything, and for a moment he even considered doing so. They had given so much of themselves, and the giving had only begun. . . . But a moment later, he wrenched the idea from his thoughts. Necessity was a higher god than truth.

The grayness of dawn passed slowly into the grayness of midday, and the march into the Dragon's Teeth wore on. The ridges and slopes appeared and faded with a dreary sameness that created the impression in the minds of the laboring travelers that no progress was being made. Ahead, a vast, towering line of peaks rose bleakly against the misty northern horizon, and it appeared that they were moving directly into a wall of impenetrable stone. Then they entered a broad canyon which wound sharply downward into a narrow, twisting path that broke between two huge cliffs and faded into the heavy mist. Allanon led them into the swirling grayness as the horizon disappeared and the wind died into stillness. The silence was abrupt and unexpected, sounding almost like a soft whisper through the towering mass of rock, speaking in hushed, cautious words in the ears of the groping travelers. Then the pass widened slightly and the mist cleared to a faint haze, revealing a high, cavernous opening in the cliff face where the winding passage ended.

The entrance to the Hall of Kings.

It was awesome, majestic, frightening. On either side of the rectangular black entryway stood two monstrous stone statues carved into the rock and rising well over a hundred feet against the dark cliff face. The stone sentries had been fashioned in the shape of armor-clad warriors, standing watchfully in the deep gloom, hands gripping the pommels of huge swords which rested blade downward at their feet. Their weathered, bearded faces were scarred by time and the wind, yet the eyes seemed almost alive, fixed carefully on the eight mortals who stood at the threshold of the ancient hall they guarded. Above the great entryway, scrolled into the rock, three words of a language centuries old and long forgotten served as a warning to those who would enter that this was the tomb of the dead. Beyond the vast opening, all was blackness and silence.

Allanon gathered them closely around him.

"Years ago, before the First War of the Races, a cult of men whose origins have been lost in time, served as priests for the gods of death. Within these caverns, they buried the monarchs of the four lands along with their families, servants, favorite possessions, and much of their wealth. The legend grew that only the dead could survive within these chambers, and only the priests were permitted to see that the dead rulers were interred. All others who entered were never seen again. In time, the cult died out, but the evil instilled in the Hall of Kings continued to exist, blindly to serve the priests whose bones had years before returned to the earth. Few men have ever passed . . ."

He caught himself, seeing in the eyes of his listeners the unasked question.

"I have been through the Hall of Kings—I alone from this age, and now you. I am a Druid, the last to walk this earth. Like Bremen, like Brona before him, I have studied the black arts, and I am a sorcerer. I do not possess the power of the Dark Lord—but I can get us safely through these caverns to the other side of the Dragon's Teeth."

"And then?" Balinor's question came softly out of the mist.

"A narrow cliff-trail men call the Dragon's Crease leads downward out of the mountains. Once there, we will be within sight of Paranor."

There was a long, awkward silence. Allanon knew what they were thinking; disregarding it, he continued.

"Beyond this entrance, there are a number of passages and chambers, a maze to one who does not know the way. Some of these are dangerous, some are not. Soon after we enter, we will reach the tunnel of the Sphinxes, giant statues like these sentries, but carved as half man, half beast. If you look into their eyes, you will be turned to stone instantly. So you must be blindfolded. In addition you will be roped to one another. You must concentrate on me, think only of me, for their will, their mental command, is strong enough to force you to tear off the blindfolds and gaze into their eyes."

The seven men looked at one another doubtfully. Already they were beginning to question the soundness of this whole approach.

"Once past the Sphinxes, there are several harmless passages leading to the Corridor of the Winds, a tunnel inhabited by invisible beings called Banshees after the legendary astral spirits. They are no more than voices, but those voices will drive mortal men insane. Your ears will be bound for protection, but again the important thing for you to do is to concentrate on me, let my mind blanket yours to prevent it from receiving the full force of those voices. You must relax; do not fight me. Do you understand?"

He counted seven barely perceptible nods.

"Once beyond the Corridor of the Winds, we will be in the Tomb of the Kings. Then there will be only one more obstacle . . ."

He stopped talking, his eyes turned warily to the cavern entrance. For a moment it seemed he might finish the sentence, but instead he motioned them toward the dark entryway. They stood uneasily between the stone giants, the graying mist clouding the high cliff walls surrounding them, the black, yawning opening before them waiting like the open maw of some great beast of prey. Allanon produced a number of wide cloth strips and gave one to each man. Utilizing a heavy length of climbing rope, the little group bound themselves to one another, the surefooted Durin taking the lead position, the Prince of Callahorn again assuming his post as rear guard. The blindfolds were securely fastened in place and hands were joined to form a chain. A moment later, the line moved cautiously through the entrance to the Hall of Kings.

There was a deep, hushed stillness in the caverns, magnified by the sudden dying of the winds and the echoing of their footfalls along the rocky passageway. The tunnel floor was strangely smooth and level, but the cold

that had settled into the aged stone from centuries of constant temperatures seeped quickly through their tensed bodies and left them chill and
shaking. No one spoke, each man trying to relax as Allanon led them carefully through a series of gently winding turns. In the middle of the groping line, Shea felt Flick's hand grip his own tightly in the blackness that
surrounded them. They had drawn closer to each other since their flight
from the Vale, bound now by ties of experiences shared more than by kinship. Whatever happened to them, Shea felt they would never lose that
closeness. Nor would he forget what Menion had done for him. He
thought about the Prince of Leah for a moment and found himself smiling. The highlander had changed so much during the past few days that he
was almost a different person. The old Menion was still in evidence, but
there was a new dimension to him that Shea found difficult to define. But
then all of them, Menion, Flick, and himself, had changed in little ways
that could not be readily detected until each man was considered as a
whole. He wondered if Allanon had seen the changes in him—Allanon,
who had always treated him somehow as less than a man, more a boy.

They came to an unsteady halt, and in the deep silence that followed
the commanding voice of the Druid leader whispered soundlessly in the
mind of each man: *Remember my warning, let your thoughts turn to me, concentrate only on me.* Then the line moved forward, the booted feet echoing
hollowly on the cavern floor. Immediately the blindfolded men could
sense the presence of something waiting ahead of them, watching silently,
patiently. The seconds flitted away as the company moved deeper into the
cavern. The men became aware of huge, still forms rising up on either
side—images carved of stone with faces that were human, but attached to
the crouched bodies of indescribable beasts. The Sphinxes. In their minds
the men could see those eyes, burning past the fading image of Allanon,
and they began to feel the strain of trying to concentrate on the giant
Druid. The insistent will of the stone monsters pushed into their brains,
weaving and tangling into their scattered thoughts, working tenaciously
toward the moment when human eyes would meet their own lifeless gaze.
Each man began to feel a rapidly growing urge to rip away the restraining
cloth which shackled his sight, to strip away the darkness and gaze freely
on the wondrous creatures staring silently down on him.

But just when it seemed that the probing whisper of the Sphinxes
must at last break through the waning resolve of the beleaguered men and
draw their thoughts completely away from the fading image of Allanon,
his iron thought cut through to them with the sharpness of a knife, soundlessly calling to them. *Think only of me.* Their minds obeyed instinctively,
wrenching free of the almost overpowering urge to gaze upward into the
watching stone faces. The strange battle wore on without respite as the line
of men, sweating and breathing harshly in the stillness, groped its way
through the tangled maze of unseen images, bound together by the rope
about their waists, the chain of tightly clenched hands, and the commanding voice of Allanon. No one lost his grip. The Druid led them steadily
down the row of Sphinxes, his own eyes locked onto the cavern floor, his

indomitable will fighting to hold the minds of his sightless charges. Then
at last the faces of the stone creatures began to fade and fall away, leaving
the mortals alone in the silence and darkness.

They kept moving, winding through a long series of twisting passages.
Then once again the line stopped, and Allanon's low voice cut through
the blackness, ordering them to remove the blindfolds. They did so hesitantly and found themselves in a narrow tunnel where the rough stone
gave off a peculiar greenish light. Their drawn faces bathed in the strange
glow, the men glanced quickly at one another to reassure themselves that
they were all present. The dark figure of the Druid passed noiselessly down
the line, testing the rope that bound their waists and warning them that
the Corridor of the Winds still lay ahead. Stuffing bits of cloth in their
ears and binding them with the loosened blindfolds to mask the sounds of
the invisible beings Allanon had named Banshees, the men joined hands
once more.

The line wound slowly through the faint green light of the narrow
tunnel, their footsteps barely perceptible to their tightly covered ears. This
section of the caverns ran for more than a mile, then faded abruptly as the
passage widened and grew into a towering corridor that was totally black.
The rock walls drew away and the ceiling rose until both had disappeared
altogether, leaving the company alone in a strange limbo of darkness
where only the smooth cavern floor offered any reassurance that the earth
had not dissolved entirely. Allanon led them into the blackness, showing
no signs of hesitancy.

Then abruptly, the sound began. Its incredible fury caught them completely unprepared, and for a moment there was panic. The initial shock
grew to an enormous roar like the sound of a thousand winds combined in
fury and biting force. But beneath this was the horrifying cry of souls
screaming in anguish, voices scraping and twisting their tortured way
through all the imaginable horrors of inhumanity in utter despair of any
hope for salvation. The roar climbed to a shriek, reaching a pitch so far beyond the comprehension of the mortals' stunned minds that their sanity
began to break apart. The terrible sounds washed over them, mirroring
their own growing despair, driving relentlessly inward and stripping away
the tattered nerve ends like layers of skin until the very bone was laid bare.

It had taken only an instant. In another instant, they would have been
lost. But for the second time the hopelessly numbed humans were saved,
this time from complete madness, as the powerful will of Allanon broke
through the crazed sound to cloak them with protective reassurance. The
screams and the roar seemed to lessen and fade into a strange buzzing as
the grim, dark face projected itself into the seven feverish minds and the
iron thoughts spoke soothingly, commandingly: *Let your minds relax—think
only of me.* The men stumbled mechanically through the heavy darkness of
the tunnel, their minds groping at the safety line of coherence and calm
that the Druid held out to them. The walls of the corridor reverberated
with the still-audible shrieks, and the massive stone of the cavern rumbled
frighteningly. One final time the voices of the Banshees rose in feverish

pitch, screeching violently in a desperate effort to break through the subconscious wall erected by the Druid's powerful mind, but the wall would
not yield and the power of the voices spent itself and faded into a deathly
whisper. A moment later, the passageway narrowed once more, and the
company was clear of the Corridor of the Winds.

Visibly shaken, their faces streaked with sweat, the men stood dumbly
as Allanon brought the line to a halt. Shaking their scattered thoughts into
some semblance of order, they removed the rope about their waists and the
cloth binding their ears. They were in a small cave, facing toward two huge
stone doors laced by iron bindings. The rock walls around them emitted
the same peculiar greenish light. Allanon waited patiently until everyone
had fully recovered, then beckoned them forward. He paused before the
stone portals. With only a slight shove from the lean hand, the massive
doors swung silently open. The Druid's deep voice was only a whisper in
the stillness.

"The Hall of Kings."

For over a thousand years, none but Allanon had entered the forbidden tomb. All that time it had remained otherwise undisturbed—a mammoth, circular cavern, the great walls smooth and polished, the ceiling
shimmering in a green glow similar to that reflected by the tunnels they
had already passed through. Along the circular wall of the giant rotunda,
standing with the same proud defiance they presumably had exhibited in
life, were stone statues of the dead rulers, each facing toward the center of
the chamber and the strange altar that rose upward in the shape of a coiled
serpent. Before each statue was piled the wealth of the dead, casks and
trunks of precious metals and jewels, furs, weapons, all the favorite possessions of the deceased. In the walls immediately behind each statue were
the sealed, rectangular openings in which rested the remains of the dead—
kings, their families, their servants. Inscriptions above the sealed crypts
gave the history of the rulers interred there, frequently in languages unfamiliar to any of the wondering members of the company. The entire
chamber was bathed in the deep green light. The metal and stone seemed
to absorb the color. Dust covered everything, a deep rock powder that had
settled over the centuries and now rose in small clouds as the footsteps of
the men disturbed its long rest. For over a thousand years, no one had violated the peace of this ancient chamber. No one had tampered with its secrets nor attempted to unlock the doors that guarded the dead and their
possessions. No one but Allanon. And now . . .

Shea shivered violently, unexplainably. He shouldn't be here; he could
feel a small, distant voice telling him he shouldn't be here. It wasn't that the
Hall of Kings was sacred or forbidden. But it was a tomb—it was a tomb
for the ancient dead. It was no place for the living. Something gripped
him, and with a start he realized it was Allanon's hand touching his shoulder. The Druid frowned darkly at him, then called softly to the others.
They huddled silently in the greenish light as he addressed them in hushed
tones.

"Through those doors at the far end of the Hall is the Assembly." He

directed their gaze to the other end of the rotunda where a second set of
huge stone doors stood closed. "A wide set of stone stairs leads downward
to a long pool fed by a spring somewhere deep beneath the mountain. At
the foot of the stairs, directly before the pool, stands the Pyre of the Dead,
where the monarchs buried here lay in state for a certain number of days,
depending on their rank and wealth, presumably so that their souls could
escape to the life beyond. We must pass through that chamber in order to
reach the passageway that will take us to the Dragon's Crease on the other
side of the mountains."

He paused and breathed deeply.

"When I traveled through these caverns before, I was able to hide myself from the eyes of the creatures put here to destroy intruders. I cannot
do this for you. There is something in the Assembly, something whose
power may prove to be greater than my own. Though it could not sense
my presence, I was conscious of it hidden beneath the deep waters of the
pool. Below the stairs, to either side of the pool, are narrow walkways
leading to the other end of the chamber and the opening to the passages
beyond. These walkways are the only way past the pool. Whatever it is that
guards the Pyre of the Dead will strike at us there. When we get into the
room, Balinor, Menion, and I will move onto the walkway to the left.
That should draw the creature out from his hiding place. When we are attacked, Hendel will take the rest of you along the right walkway through
the opening at the far end. Don't stop until you reach the Dragon's Crease.
Do you understand?"

They nodded slowly. Shea felt strangely trapped, but there was nothing
to be gained by talking about it now. Allanon straightened to his full seven-
foot height and grinned menacingly, his strong teeth gleaming. The little
Valeman felt a chill run through him that made him glad ten times over he
was not the enemy of the mystic. In one effortless motion, Balinor drew
forth his great sword, the metal blade ringing sharply as it cleared the
sheath. Hendel was already moving across the Hall, the heavy mace held
tightly in one hand. Menion started to follow, then hesitated, gazing
doubtfully on the stores of treasure heaped about the tombs. Would it hurt
to take a few? The Valemen and Elves were moving after Hendel and Balinor. Allanon stood watching the highlander, his long arms folded into the
black cloak. Menion turned and looked questioningly at the mystic.

"I wouldn't if I were you," the other warned shortly. "It's all coated
with a substance poisonous to the skin of living things. Touch it and you
will be dead in less than a minute."

Menion stared at him incredulously for a moment, shot a quick glance
back at the treasure, then shook his head resignedly. He was halfway across
the chamber when, on sudden inspiration, he whipped out two long black
arrows and walked over to an open chest of gold pieces. Carefully, he
rubbed the metal tips in the precious metal, making certain that his hands
did not touch anything but the feathered ends. Grinning with perverse satisfaction, he rejoined the others across the room. Whatever waited beyond

the stone doors was going to be given the opportunity to test its resistance to this poison that would supposedly kill any living creature. In a tight cluster, the company gathered around Allanon, their metal weapons glinting coldly. A stillness settled over the great room, broken only by the expectant breathing of the eight men huddled about the closed doors. Shea glanced back for just a moment at the Hall of Kings. The tomb seemed undisturbed save for the ragged trail of footprints in the dust leading across the chamber. A deep haze of this dust hung swirling in the greenish light, stirred by the intruders' footsteps, but settling slowly back to the ancient cavern floor. In time, all evidence of their passing would be erased as the tracks were covered over entirely.

At Allanon's touch, the stone portals swung open and the company moved noiselessly into the Assembly. They were on a high platform that ran forward into a wide alcove and then descended in a series of broad stairs. The cavern beyond was enormous, a vast, towering cave that still exhibited the full, unaltered splendor of its rough, natural creation by nature's careful hands. From the high ceiling hung jagged stalactites, stone icicles formed by water and mineral deposits over thousands of years. Beneath these sculptured stone spears lay a long, rectangular pool of deep green water, the surface smooth and glasslike. When a single drop of water fell heavily from an overhanging stone projection, the placid surface rippled outward once and was still. The wary men moved forward to the edge of the platform and looked down on the high stone altar set at the foot of the stairs before the pool, its ancient surface scarred and pocked and in places almost crumbling. The cavern was dimly lit by streaks of phosphorescence that ran brokenly through its rocky walls, giving an eerie, fluorescent glow to the ancient chamber.

Slowly the men moved down the stairway, their eyes picking out a single word inscribed in the stone surface of the altar. A few knew its meaning. *Valg*—a word taken from the ancient Gnome tongue. It meant Death. Their footsteps reverberated in muffled echoes through the vast cavern. Nothing moved. Everything was shrouded in age and silence. On reaching the foot of the long stairway, they hesitated for a second, eyes fastened on the silent pool. Impatiently, Allanon motioned Hendel and his charges to the right; then with Menion and Balinor following, he moved quickly onto the left walkway. A misstep now would prove fatal. From across the pool, Shea watched the three figures edge their way silently along the rough stone wall, keeping well to the rear of the open walkway. There was no movement in the placid waters. They were about midway now, and Shea breathed for the first time.

Then the still surface of the dark pool surged upward and from out of the depths emerged a nightmare. Serpentine in appearance, the loathsome monster seemed to fill the cavern, its slime-covered bulk raising skyward, shattering the ancient stalactites. Its shriek of fury boomed through the Assembly. The massive body twisted and flexed as it reared out of the water. Long front legs tipped with deadly hooked claws clutched the empty air, and the great jaws clashed sharply, grinding together the blackened, pointed teeth that lined the edges. The wide, staring eyes burned red amid a cluster of bumps and stunted horns that covered the misshapen head. The entire bulk of the creature was covered with a reptilian skin that dripped with scum and waste that must have been carried from the nether-world's blackest pits. The mouth oozed venom that fell into the water and rose with faint traces of steam. The monstrous thing glared at the three humans on the walkway and hissed with unbridled hatred. Jaws wide, screeching in anticipation of the kill, it attacked.

Everyone reacted instantly. Menion Leah's great ash bow sounded in staccato pings as the poisoned arrows flew with deadly accuracy, burying themselves deeply within the unprotected inner flesh of the serpent's gaping mouth. The creature reared back in pain, and Balinor quickly seized the initiative. Moving to the edge of the walkway, the giant borderman struck powerfully at the exposed forearm of the monster. But to his shock, the great sword only barely scratched the scaly hide, glancing off the heavy coating of slime. The second forearm made a quick swipe at the attacker, missing by inches as the intended victim dove to one side. On the opposite walkway, Hendel made a rush for the open passage at the far end of the pool, shoving the Valemen and the Elven brothers before him. But one of them triggered a hidden release, and a heavy stone slab collapsed in the opening, sealing off the escape route. In desperation, Hendel threw his powerful body against the stone barricade, but it refused to budge.

The serpent had been attracted by the sound of the falling stone. Turning away from its battle with Menion and Balinor, it moved eagerly toward these smaller foes. That would have been the finish if not for the quick reactions of the battle-hardened Dwarf. Forgetting the stone slab and disregarding his own safety entirely, Hendel charged at the huge monster bearing down on him and drove the heavy iron mace directly into the closest burning eye. The weapon struck with such force that it smashed the glowing orb. The serpent reared upward in excruciating pain, crashing heavily into the jagged stalactites as it whipped its bulk from side to side. Deadly rock fragments showered the entire chamber. Flick went down with a sharp blow to the head. At the edge of the pool, Hendel was buried under a cascade of crumbling stone and lay motionless. The other three fell back against the blocked entryway as the massive attacker loomed above them.

At last Allanon joined the unequal battle. Raising both arms, he extended his lean hands, and his fingers seemed to light up like small glowing balls. Streaks of blinding, blue flame shot out of the tips and struck the head of the raging creature. The force of this new attack completely stunned the unprepared serpent, who thrashed wildly above the boiling water of the pool, shrieking in pain and fury. Moving quickly ahead on the walkway, the Druid struck a second time, the blue flames flashing against the head of the enraged beast, twisting it completely around. This second strike threw the great scaled body backward against the cavern wall where, thrashing in an uncontrollable frenzy, it jarred loose the stone slab that blocked the passageway out. Shea and the Elven brothers had barely managed to drag the unconscious Flick out of the way in time to avoid being crushed by the massive body. They heard the stone slab drop forward with an audible thud and, spying the open passage, yelled wildly to the other fighters. Balinor had reattacked the writhing monster as it again came within reach, striking vainly for the head as it swung down at him, still stunned by the force of Allanon's bolts. Allanon had his eyes fixed on the serpent, and only Menion saw what the others were yelling about and waved them madly toward the opening. Dayel and Shea picked up the fallen Flick and carried him into the tunnel beyond. Durin started to follow, but then hesitated as he caught sight of the unconscious Hendel, still buried beneath the shattered stone rubble. Turning back, he rushed to the pool's edge, grasped the Dwarf's limp arm, and vainly attempted to pull him clear of the debris.

"Get out!" roared Allanon, who had suddenly spotted the Elf near the opening.

Choosing this moment of distraction, the serpent struck back. With one mighty sweep of its clawed arm it brushed Balinor aside, knocking him with crushing force against the chamber wall. Menion leaped in front of the monster, but its sudden rush bowled the Prince of Leah over, and he was knocked from sight. The serpent, still in great pain from its multiple wounds, could think only of reaching the tall figure in the black robes and crushing the life out of him. The beast had one more weapon in its arsenal, and it used it now. The venom-tipped jaws gaped wide at the sight of the intended victim, standing alone and unprotected, and great sheets of flame shot forth, completely encasing the Druid. Durin, who was in position to see everything happening on the walkway, gave an audible gasp of dismay. Shea and Dayel, standing just beyond the entrance to the tunnel leading from the Assembly, watched in mute horror as the flames covered the tall mystic. But a second later the fire died, and Allanon stood untouched before the astonished onlookers. His hands raised and the blue streaks of flame shot out of his extended fingers, striking the head of the serpent with terrific force, sending the scaled body reeling back once again. Steam rose in great clouds from the thrashing waters of the pool, mingling in a heavy mist with the dust and smoke stirred by the battle until everything was obscured from view.

Then, from out of the haze, Balinor appeared at Durin's side, his cloak torn and shredded, the shining chain mail chipped and battered, the familiar face streaked with sweat and blood. Together they pulled Hendel from beneath the rocks. With one great arm, the Prince of Callahorn lifted the silent form over his shoulder and motioned Durin ahead of him into the passage where Dayel and Shea still lingered with the unconscious Flick. The giant borderman ordered them to pick up the fallen Valeman, and without waiting to see if they obeyed, disappeared down the darkened corridor, Hendel over one shoulder, the great broad sword held tightly in his free hand. The Elven brothers quickly did as they were told, but Shea hesitated, searching worriedly for some sign of Menion. The Assembly was a shambles, the long rows of stalactites smashed, the walkways a mass of rubble, the walls cracked and shattered, and everything obscured by dust and steam from the boiling pool. To one side of the cavern, the massive form of the serpent was still visible, thrashing in agony against the broken wall, its great bulk a writhing mass of scales and blood. Neither Menion nor Allanon was in view. But a moment later both appeared from out of the thick haze, Menion limping slightly, but still clutching the ash bow and the sword of Leah, Allanon's dark form tattered and layered with dust and ash. Without speaking, the Druid waved the Valeman ahead of them, and together the three stumbled through the partially blocked opening.

What happened after was vague in everyone's mind. Numbly, the battered group hurried along the tunnel, carrying the two wounded and unconscious men. Time dragged agonizingly away, then abruptly they were outside, blinking in the bright light of the afternoon sun, standing at the edge of a dangerously steep cliff face. To their right, the Dragon's Crease wound its way downward to the open hill country below. Suddenly the whole mountain began to rumble menacingly, shaking in short tremors beneath their feet. With a sharp command, Allanon ordered them down the narrow trail. Balinor led the way, carrying the still form of Hendel, Menion Leah a couple of steps behind. Durin and Dayel followed, carrying Flick. Behind them came Shea and finally Allanon. The sinister rumbling continued somewhere deep within the mountain. Slowly the little group moved along the narrow pathway. The trail wound unevenly amid jagged overhangs and sudden drops, and the men were forced to flatten themselves against the cliff face at regular intervals to avoid losing their balance and falling to the rocks hundreds of feet below. The Dragon's Crease was well named. The continual twists and turns in the path required concentrated skill and caution to navigate successfully, and the recurring tremors made the task doubly hazardous.

They had progressed only a short distance along the treacherous pathway when a new sound became audible, a deep roar that quickly drowned out the rumblings in the mountain. Shea, last in line with Allanon, was unable to define the source of the roar until he was almost on top of its origin. Rounding a sharp cut in the side of the mountain, which brought him onto a ledge facing northward, he discovered an enormous waterfall directly across from their position on the mountainside. Tons of cascading water crashed with a deafening roar into a great river hundreds of feet below that swept between the mountain ranges and poured into a series of rapids than ran eastward to the Rabb Plains. The mighty river swept directly below the ledge on which he stood and the narrow trail ahead, its white waters churning and slapping against the confining sides of the two peaks that hemmed it in. Shea looked at it for a moment, and then hastened on down the trail at Allanon's command. The rest of the company had gone a good distance ahead of them and for a moment were lost from view in the rocks.

Shea had gone about a hundred feet past the ledge when a sudden tremor, more violent than the others, shook the mountain to its core. Without warning, the section of the trail on which he was standing broke away and slid steadily down the mountainside, carrying the hapless Valeman with it. He gave a cry of dismay, fighting to break his fall as he saw himself sliding toward a steep overhang which dropped off sharply into a long, long fall to the raging river on the valley floor. Allanon rushed forward as the Valeman slid wildly in a cloud of dust and rock toward the waiting overhang.

"Grab something!" roared the Druid. "Catch yourself!"

Shea clutched vainly, clawing at the sheer face of the cliff, and just at the edge of the drop-off caught himself on a projecting rock. He lay flat against the nearly vertical surface, not daring to try to climb back up, his arms nearly breaking from the exertion.

"Hold on, Shea!" Allanon encouraged him. "I'll get a rope. Don't move an inch!"

Allanon called down the trail for the others, but whether they could have helped, Shea never discovered. As the Druid shouted for assistance, a second tremor shook the mountain and jarred loose the unfortunate Valeman from his precarious perch, sending him sliding out beyond the overhang before he could even think to catch himself. Arms and legs flying madly, he fell headlong into the swiftly flowing waters of the river below. Allanon watched helplessly as the Valeman struck with crushing force, bobbed to the surface, and was swept away eastward toward the plains beyond, tossing and turning in the boiling river like a small cork until he was lost from sight.

15

Flick Ohmsford stood quietly at the foot of the Dragon's Teeth and stared into space. The fading rays of the late-afternoon sun crossed his stocky frame in faint glimmers, casting his shadow onto the cooling rocks of the giant mountain at his back. He listened for a moment to the sounds about him, the muffled voices of somebody from the company off to his left, the chirping cries of the birds in the forest ahead. In his own mind he heard Shea's determined voice for an instant, and he recalled his brother's great courage in the face of the countless dangers they had encountered together. Now Shea was gone, probably dead, washed out by that unknown river to the plains on the other side of the mountains they had battled so hard to cross through. He rubbed his head gently, feeling the bump and the dull pain from the blow of the rock fragment that had knocked him senseless, preventing him from being able to help when his brother had needed him the most. They had been ready to face death at the hands of the Skull Bearers, ready to perish by the swords of the roving Gnomes, and even ready to succumb to the terrors of the Hall of Kings. But for it all to be ended by a fluke of nature on a narrow cliff ledge, when they were so close to escaping, was too much for anyone to accept. Flick felt such biting hurt inside that he wanted to cry out his bitterness. But even now, he could not. His insides knotted at the anger he could not manage, and he felt instead only a great sense of waste.

Menion Leah seemed in marked contrast as he paced in furious desperation several yards away from the Valeman, his lean figure bent in what could only be described as a wounded crouch. His own thoughts burned deep with anger, the kind of futile rage that a caged beast displays when there is no hope of escape, and only its pride and its hatred of what has happened to it remain. There was nothing he could have done to help Shea, he knew. But that did little to ease the sense of guilt he felt at not having been there when the cliff ledge gave way and the Valeman was thrown to the churning waters of the rapids below. Something might have been done to prevent it had he not left Shea alone with the Druid. Yet he knew it was not Allanon's fault; he had done everything possible to protect Shea. Menion moved with long, angry strides, digging into the ground with the sharp heels of his boots. He refused to admit that the quest was ended, that they would be forced to admit defeat when the Sword of Shannara was so nearly within their grasp. He paused and considered for a moment the object of their search. It still didn't make any sense to the highlander. Even if they got the Sword, what could a man, not yet more than a grown boy, hope to do against the power of a creature like the Warlock Lord? Now they would never know, for Shea was probably dead; even if he wasn't dead, he was lost to them. Nothing seemed to make much sense anymore, and Menion Leah realized suddenly how very much that casual, relaxed friendship between them had meant. They had never spoken of it, never really openly acknowledged it, but it had been there all the same, and it had been dear to him. Now it was ended. Menion bit down on his lip in helpless anger and continued to pace.

The others in the company were gathered near the foot of the Dragon's Crease, which ended just yards behind them. Durin and Dayel spoke to each other in hushed tones, their fine Elven features wrinkled with concern, their eyes lowered, looking at each other only occasionally. Close at hand, his solid frame propped against a massive boulder, rested Hendel, who, while always closemouthed, was now moody and unapproachable. His shoulder and leg were bandaged, his stolid face scarred and bruised from the battle with the serpent. He thought briefly of his homeland, his waiting family, and for an instant wished he could see the green of Culhaven once more before the end. He knew that without the Sword of Shannara, and without Shea to wield it, his land would be overrun by the Northland armies. Hendel was not alone in his thoughts. Balinor was thinking much the same thing, his eyes on the solitary giant standing motionless in a small grove of trees some distance away from the others. He knew that they now faced an impossible decision. Either they must give up the quest and turn back in an effort to reach their homelands and perhaps locate Shea, or they must continue on to Paranor and seize the Sword of Shannara without the courageous Valeman. It was a difficult choice to make, and no one would be very pleased either way. He shook his head sadly as the memory of the bitter quarrel between his brother and himself passed momentarily through his mind. He had his own decision to make when he returned to the city of Tyrsis—and it would not be pleasant. He had not spoken to the others about it, and at the moment, his personal problems were of secondary importance.

Suddenly the Druid wheeled about and started back to them, his own mind evidently decided. They watched him approach, the black robe flowing gently as he came, the fierce dark face resolute even in this moment of bitter defeat. Menion had frozen in his tracks, his heart beating madly as he awaited the confrontation he knew must come between them, for the highlander had chosen his own course of action, and he suspected it would not be that of Allanon. Flick caught the hint of fear in the face of the Prince of Leah, but saw there, too, a strange courage as the man braced himself. All of them rose hesitantly and came together as the dark form drew closer, their tired, discouraged minds suddenly regenerated with a fierce determination not to admit defeat. They could not know what Allanon would command, but they knew they had come too far and sacrificed too much to give up now.

He stood before them, the deep eyes burning with mixed feelings, the shadowed face a granite wall of strength, worn and scarred. When he spoke, the words were frosted and sharp in the silence.

"It may be that we are beaten, but to turn back would be to dishonor ourselves in our own eyes as much as in the eyes of those who depend on us. If we are to be defeated by the evil in the Northland, by things born of the spirit world, then we must turn and face it. We cannot back away and hope for some elusive miracle to stand between us and what most surely moves even now to enslave and destroy us. If death comes, it should find us with weapons drawn and the Sword of Shannara in our hands!"

He bit off the last sentence with such icy determination that even Balinor felt a slight shiver of excitement course through him. All stood in mute admiration of the Druid's unflagging strength, and they felt a sudden pride in being with him, being a part of the little group he had chosen for this dangerous and costly quest.

"What about Shea?" Menion spoke out suddenly, perhaps a bit sharply, as the Druid's penetrating eyes turned on him. "What has become of Shea, who was the reason for this expedition in the first place?"

Allanon shook his head slowly, considering once again the Valeman's fate.

"I cannot guess any better than you. He was washed out to the plains by that mountain river. Perhaps he lives, perhaps not, but we can do nothing for him now."

"What you are proposing is that we forget him and go after the Sword—a useless piece of metal without the rightful bearer!" Menion shouted in anger, his pent-up frustration coming to the fore at last. "Well, I go no farther until I know what has happened to Shea, even if it means giving up the quest and searching until I find him. I will not desert my friend!"

"Watch yourself, highlander," warned the slow, mocking voice of the mystic. "Do not be foolish. To blame me for the loss of Shea is pointless, for I most of all would wish him no harm. What you suggest lacks any resemblance to reason."

"Enough wise words, Druid!" stormed Menion, stepping forward in absolute disregard for what might happen next, his hot temper driven to the brink by the tall wanderer's impassive acceptance of the loss of the Valeman. "We have followed you for weeks, through a hundred lands and perils without once questioning what you ordered. But this is too much for me. I am a Prince of Leah, not some beggar who does what he is told without question, caring for no one but himself! My friendship with Shea was nothing to you, but it was more to me than a hundred Swords of Shannara. Now stand aside! I will go my own way!"

"Fool, you are less a prince and more a clown to speak like this!" Allanon raged, his face tightening into a mask of anger, the great hands balling into fists and clenching before him. The others paled as the two opponents lashed verbally at each other in unbridled fury. Then sensing the physical combat that was about to ensue, they stepped between them, talking quickly, trying to calm them with reason, fearful that a split in the company now would mark the end of any chance for success. Flick alone had made no move, his own thoughts still on his brother, disgusted by the helplessness he felt at being powerless to do anything but feel inadequate. The minute Menion had spoken, he knew that the highlander had expressed his own feelings, and he would not leave here without knowing what had befallen Shea. But it always seemed that Allanon knew so much more than the rest of them, that his decisions were always the right ones. To disregard the Druid's words completely now seemed somehow wrong. He struggled within his own mind for a moment, trying to think what Shea would do in this situation, what he might suggest to the others. Then almost without realizing it, he knew the answer.

"Allanon, there is a way," he declared abruptly, shouting to be heard above the noise. They all looked over at him at once, surprised by the determined look on the stocky Valeman's face. Allanon nodded to indicate he was listening.

"You have the power to speak to the dead. We saw you do it back in the valley. Can you not tell if Shea lives? Your power is great enough to seek out the living if you can raise the dead. You can tell where he is, can't you?"

Everyone looked back at the Druid, waiting to see what he would do. Allanon sighed heavily and looked downward, his anger for Menion forgotten as he pondered the Valeman's question.

"I could do this," he responded to everyone's amazement and general relief, "but I will not. If I use my power to find out where Shea is, whether he is dead or alive, I will most certainly reveal our presence to the Warlock Lord and to the Skull Bearers. They would be alerted and waiting for us at Paranor."

"If we go to Paranor," Menion cut in darkly, whereupon Allanon wheeled on him in fury, his lagging anger revived. Again everyone leaped to separate them.

"Stop it, stop it!" Flick ordered angrily. "This is helping no one, least of all Shea. Allanon, I have asked for nothing during this entire trip. I had no right to ask; I came by my own choice. But I have the right now because Shea is my brother, perhaps not by blood or race, but by stronger bonds still. If you will not use your power to find out where he is and what has happened to him, then I will go with Menion and search until Shea is found."

"He is right, Allanon." Balinor nodded slowly, one great hand coming to rest lightly on the little Valeman's shoulder. "Whatever befalls us, these two have a right to know whether there is any chance for Shea. I know what it means if we are discovered, but I say we must take that chance."

Durin and Dayel nodded vigorously in agreement. The Druid mystic looked aside to Hendel for his opinion, but the taciturn Dwarf made no movement, staring into the other's black eyes. Allanon looked at them one by one, perhaps assessing their true feelings as he thought of the risk involved, weighing the worth of the Sword against the loss of two of the company. He stared absently at the fading sun as the twilight of early evening settled into the mountains with slow ripples of darkness blending into the red and purple of the passing day. It had been a long, hard trip, and they had nothing to show for it—only the loss of the man for whom the whole journey had been made. It seemed so wrong, and he could appreciate their reluctance to continue now. He nodded to himself in understanding, then looked back at the others and saw their eyes turn suddenly bright, believing him to be nodding his agreement to Flick's demand. Without even a small smile of acquiescence, the tall wanderer shook his head firmly.

"The choice is yours. I will do as you ask. Stand back and do not speak to me or approach me until I tell you."

The members of the company backed away while he remained quietly in place, head bent in concentration, the long arms clasped before him with the great hands buried in the long cloak. Only the distant sounds of evening were audible in the deepening gloom. Then the Druid stiffened and a white glow spread out from his tensed body, a blinding aura of light that caused the others to squint, then shield their eyes protectively. One moment the glow was everywhere and the dark form of Allanon was lost from sight, and in the next it flashed brilliantly and was gone. Allanon stood as he had before, motionless against the darkness, then slowly slumped to the ground, one lean hand pressed tightly to his forehead. The others hesitated for only a moment, then disregarded his earlier command and rushed forward, afraid that he had been injured. Allanon looked up in disapproval, angered that they had disobeyed him. Then he saw in the bent faces their deep concern. He stared in disbelief and with sudden understanding as they gathered about in silence. He was deeply touched, a strange warmth spreading through him as he realized the loyalty these six men of different races, different lands, different lives felt for him, even after all that had happened. For the first time since the loss of Shea, Allanon felt a sense of relief. He climbed shakily to his feet, leaning slightly on the strong arm of Balinor, still weak from the strain of seeking Shea. He stood quietly for a moment and then smiled faintly.

"Our young friend is indeed alive, though it's a miracle I cannot explain. I located his life force on the other side of these mountains, probably somewhere near the river that carried him out to the east plains. There were others with him, but I could not determine what their purpose was without an extensive mind probe. That would surely give our position away and weaken me to the point of uselessness."

"But he is alive, you're certain?" Flick demanded eagerly.

Allanon nodded his assurance. The entire group broke into broad smiles of relief. Menion slapped the elated Flick on his broad back and did a small dance step and leap.

"Then the problem has resolved itself," the Prince of Leah exulted. "We have to go back over the Dragon's Teeth and find him, then continue the trip to Paranor to get the Sword."

His smiling face fell abruptly and the slow burn of anger replaced it as Allanon shook his head negatively. The others stared in astonishment, certain that this was what the Druid himself would have suggested.

"Shea is in the hands of a Gnome patrol," the mystic stated pointedly. "He is being taken northward, more than likely to Paranor. We could not reach him without fighting our way back through the guarded passes of the Dragon's Teeth and trailing him over those Gnome-infested plains. We would be diverted for days, perhaps longer, and our presence would be detected in no time."

"There's no guarantee they don't already know about us," Menion shouted irately. "You said that yourself. What good will we be to Shea if he falls into the hands of the Warlock Lord? What good will the Sword do us without the bearer?"

"We cannot desert him," pleaded Flick, stepping forward once more.

The others said nothing, but stood mutely, waiting to hear Allanon's explanation. Darkness had completely enfolded the high mountain country, and the men could barely make out one another's faces in the dim light; the moon was hidden from view by the monstrous peaks that rose behind them.

"You have forgotten the prophecy," admonished Allanon patiently. "The last part promised that one of us would not see the other side of the Dragon's Teeth, but that he would be first to place hands on the Sword of Shannara. That one we now know to be Shea. Furthermore, the prophecy said that we who reached the other side of the mountains would view the Sword before the passing of two nights. It would seem that fate will bring us all together."

"That may be good enough for you, but not for me," stated Menion flatly, with Flick nodding in vigorous agreement. "How can we place our trust in some crazy promise made by a ghost? You're asking us to risk Shea's life!"

Allanon seemed to smolder in fury for a moment, fighting to control his quick temper, then calmly he looked at the two and shook his head in disappointment.

"Have you not believed in a legend from the very start?" he asked quietly. "Have you not yourself seen the foothold that the spirit world has secured in your world of flesh and blood, earth and stone? Have we not from the beginning been fighting against beings born of this other existence, beings who possess powers that surely do not belong to mortal men? You have witnessed the potency of the Elfstones. Why would you now turn your back on all that, in favor of what your common sense tells you—a reasoning process that relies on fact and stimuli accumulated in this world, your material world, unable to transpose itself to an existence where even your most basic understandings have no meaning."

They stared at him wordlessly, realizing that he was right, but unwilling to abandon their plan to find Shea. The whole journey had been premised on half dreams and old legends, not on common sense, and suddenly to decide it was time to be practical once again was indeed a ludicrous idea. Flick had given up being practical the day he had first run in fear from Shady Vale.

"I would not be concerned, my young friends," Allanon soothed, suddenly next to them, a lean hand on each shoulder, strangely comforting even now. "Shea still carries the Elfstones, and their power will give him great protection. They may also guide him toward the Sword, since they are attuned to it. With luck, we will find him when we find the Sword at Paranor. All roads now lead to the Druid's Keep, and we must be certain we are there to give what aid we can to Shea."

The other members of the company had gathered up their weapons and small packs and stood ready, their silhouettes shadowlike in the dim starlight, finely etched pencil lines against the blackness of the mountains. Flick gazed northward to the dark forest that blanketed the low country beyond the Dragon's Teeth. In its midst, rising upward like an obelisk, were the cliffs of Paranor, and there at the apex, the Druid's Keep and the Sword of Shannara. The end of the quest. Flick looked quietly for a few moments at the solitary pinnacle, then turned to Menion. The highlander nodded reluctantly.

"We'll go with you." Flick's voice was a hushed whisper in the stillness.

The swirling waters of the rushing river dashed madly against the confining walls of their mountain channel, beating and raging their way eastward, dragging with them stray debris and driftwood that had fallen into their restless grasp. They rushed down out of the mountains in heavy rapids that churned fiercely around smooth-surfaced rocks and sudden bends, winding slowly toward the calm of the quiet rivers that branched into the hilly lowlands above the Rabb Plains. It was in one of these small, quiet tributaries that the man, still bound to the splintered log by his leather belt, finally washed up on a mud riverbank, unconscious and nearly drowned. The clothes he wore were ripped and shredded, the leather boots lost, the damp face ashen and bloodied from the beating sustained when he had been swept through the series of rapids down the river that had carried him to this place. He awakened, realizing that he had at last reached land. Feebly untying himself from the beached log, he dragged himself on hands and knees farther onto the shore and into the deep grass of a low hill. As if by reflex, his battered hands felt for the small leather pouch at his waist, and to his relief it was still there, securely bound by the leather thongs. A moment later, the last of his remaining strength exhausted, he fell into a deep, welcome sleep.

He slept soundly in the warmth and quiet of the day until late afternoon, when the cooling grass whipping against his face in a building breeze caused him to stir slightly. There was something else as well, something in his now-rested mind that warned him suddenly that he was in danger. But he could barely rouse his sluggish body to a half-sitting position as a group of ten or twelve figures appeared at the crest of the hill above him, paused in astonishment as they saw his raised figure, then hastened down the hill to reach him. Instead of carefully turning his battered body to check for injuries, they flung him flat once again, gripping his helpless arms behind his back and tying them securely with leather thongs that bit into the unprotected skin. His feet were bound as well, and at last he was turned faceup where he could finally focus on his captors. His worst fears were immediately confirmed. The gnarled yellow frames, clothed in forest garb and armed with short swords, were easily recognizable after Menion's description of the incident that had taken place only days before in the Pass of Jade. He looked fearfully into the sharp Gnome eyes as they gazed with some amazement at his half-man, half-Elf features and at the remnants of his unusual Southland garb. Finally, the leader reached down and began to search him thoroughly. Shea struggled, but was slapped hard several times and at last lay motionless as the Gnome removed the small leather pouch containing the precious Elfstones.

The Gnomes gathered around curiously as the three blue stones, shining brightly in the warm sunlight, were emptied into the hand of the leader. There was a brief discussion, none of which the captive was able to follow, concerning what he was doing with the stones and where he could have found them. At last it was decided that both the captive and the stones should be taken to the main encampment at Paranor where higher authorities could be consulted. The Gnomes dragged their captive to his feet, cutting the thongs that bound his legs, and proceeded to march him northward, pushing him from time to time when he slowed from exhaustion. They were still moving northward at sunset when, on the other side of the mountain barrier known as the Dragon's Teeth, the Druid leader of a small band of determined seekers struggled within his own mind to pinpoint the missing Shea Ohmsford.

It was in the early-morning hours, wrapped with the blanket silence of darkness and hidden by the shadows of the heavy forests that so completely shut out the reassuring light of the moon and stars, that the company stood at last before the cliffs of Paranor. It was a moment that would last forever in their minds, as expectant eyes traveled upward over the steep rock walls, unbroken by trail or ledge, upward past the dwarfed height of the tall pines and oaks, which ended abruptly as the cliffs began, upward still farther to the man-made structure at its apex—the Druid's Keep. The Keep was castlelike, age-old walls of blocked stone rising to peaked turrets and spiraled towers that cut the sky in proud defiance. It was unmistakably a fortress built to withstand assault by the strongest army, the ancient home and protectorate of the all but extinguished race of men called Druids. Within the heart of this stronghold of stone and iron had long rested the memorial of Man's triumph over the forces of the spirit world, the symbol of the courage and hope of the races in times long past, forgotten over the years as generations passed away and old legends died—the wondrous Sword of Shannara.

As the seven men stood there surveying the Druid's Keep, Flick's mind traveled back over the events that had taken place since the company had departed the Dragon's Teeth at sunset. They had traveled quickly over the open grasslands separating them from the forest surrounding Paranor, reaching the seclusion of its dark perimeter without incident in only a few short hours. At that time, Allanon briefed them on what to expect next. The forest, he said, was impenetrable unless one knew how to avoid the dangerous obstacles that the Warlock Lord had created to discourage any attempt to reach the Druid's Keep. Wolves prowled the entire woodland, huge, gray beasts that could catch anything on two or four feet and tear it to pieces within seconds. Beyond the wolves, surrounding the base of the cliffs beneath the Keep, was an impregnable barrier of thorns, coated with a poison for which there was no known cure. But the resourceful Druid was prepared. They moved quickly into the black forest, not bothering to choose any approach but the direct one, their path taking them straight for the fortress. Allanon warned them to stay close to him, but the warning was quite unnecessary. Only Menion seemed eager to forge ahead of the

group, and the highlander rejoined them instantly at the first sound of
the marauding wolves. The great, gray beasts attacked within minutes after
the men entered the forest, their eyes bloodred in the darkness, their huge
jaws snapping in blind hatred. But before they could reach the alarmed
group, Allanon placed a strange whistle to his lips and blew softly. A sound
so high-pitched as to be indistinguishable to the men was emitted and the
snarling wolves scattered brokenly, wheeling about and scurrying off with
loud cries of dismay, their frightened whimpers still audible long after they
were lost from sight.

The wolves appeared twice more during the remainder of the trek
through the forest, although it was impossible to tell if it was the same pack
or a different one. Flick was inclined to believe they were different packs
after observing the effect of the strange whistle. Each time the wolves cringed
in terror, leaving the travelers untouched. The company reached the thorn
barrier without difficulty. But the bristling mass of poisonous spikes that
confronted them seemed truly impenetrable, even by the redoubtable Allanon. Once again he reminded them that this was the homeland of the
Druids, not the Warlock Lord. Leading them to the right, he skirted the
edge of the barrier until he reached a point that seemed to satisfy him.
Quickly pacing off a distance from a nearby oak that looked for all the
world to Flick like any other oak, the Druid marked a spot on the ground
before the thorny obstruction, nodding to the others that this was to be
the spot of entry. Then to their amazement, the grim mystic simply
walked up to the razor-sharp spikes and disappeared into the vegetation,
only to reappear a moment later unharmed. In hushed tones he explained
to them that at this point the barrier was fake and quite harmless, a secret
passage to the fortress. There were others as well, all indistinguishable to
any human eye unaware of what to look for. And so the company passed
through the barrier, discovering that the spikes were indeed harmless, and
stood at last before the walls of Paranor.

It seemed impossible somehow to Flick that they should be here at all.
The journey had been an endless one while they were making it, the dangers encountered by them never conquered, only evaded and ultimately
substituted, one for another. Yet here they were. All that remained was to
scale the cliffs and seize the Sword, no simple task, but nevertheless no
more difficult than the others they had faced and successfully completed.
He gazed upward to the castle battlements, studying briefly the spaced
torches that lit the ramparts, knowing that the enemy guarded those walls
and the Sword within. He wondered who the enemy was, what it was.
Not the Gnomes or the Trolls, but the real enemy—the creature that belonged in another world, but that had invaded this one in some inexplicable way to enslave the humans who inhabited it. He wondered vaguely if
he would ever know the reason behind all that had happened to them, the
reason why they stood here now, hunters for the legendary Sword of
Shannara, of which none of them save the Druid mystic knew anything.
He sensed that there was a lesson somewhere to be learned, but at the mo-

ment it eluded him. He only wanted to get the matter over with and get out of there alive.

His thoughts ended abruptly as Allanon motioned them forward along the steep walls of the cliff. Again, the Druid seemed to be searching for something. A few minutes later he halted before a smooth portion of the cliff face, touched something in the rock, and a concealed door swung open to reveal a hidden passageway. Allanon stepped inside for a moment and returned with unlit torches, giving one to each of the company and indicating that they were to follow him. They moved silently inside, halting momentarily in the small entryway as the stone door closed noiselessly behind them. Squinting in the near blackness, they saw a vague outline of stone steps leading upward into the rock, barely visible in the dim light of a lone torch flickering just ahead in the passage. They climbed carefully to that torch and each man lit his own to provide the necessary light for the ascent to the castle. Putting a single finger to his lips to indicate that he expected absolute silence, the dark figure of their leader turned and began to climb the damp stone steps, his black cloak billowing slightly as he walked, filling the entire passageway ahead with its shadow. The others followed without a word. The assault of the Druid's Keep had begun.

The staircase rose in a continual spiral, winding and twisting until at last no one knew how far they had come. The air in the passage became gradually warmer and more comfortable to breathe, and the dampness of the walls and steps diminished until it was entirely gone. Their heavy leather hunting boots scraped faintly against the stone, echoing through the deep silence of the caverns. Hundreds of steps and many minutes later, the company reached the end of the tunnel. A massive wooden door, bound with iron and fastened into the rock, blocked their passage. Allanon again proved that he knew the way well. A single touch on the binding and the door swung silently open to admit the men into a large chamber with numerous passages leading out of it, all of them well lit by burning torches. A quick look around revealed no one in sight, so Allanon brought the company around him once again.

"We are directly below the castle proper," he explained in a barely audible whisper as the others crowded close. "If we can reach the room where the Sword of Shannara rests without being seen, then we may be able to escape without a fight."

"Something's wrong," Balinor cautioned shortly. "Where are the guards?"

Allanon shook his head to indicate he couldn't answer, but the others saw the concern in his eyes. Something was amiss.

"The passage we will take runs to the main heating ducts and a back stairway that leads to the central hall. Say nothing more until we are there, but keep your eyes open!"

Without waiting for any response, he turned and moved quickly toward one of the open tunnels, and the others followed hastily. The passage led upward, twisting tightly around after a short distance until it seemed they must be cutting back on themselves. Balinor had discarded his torch and drawn his broadsword after only a few steps, then the rest of the company was quick to follow his lead. The flickering light from the torches, fastened in iron racks to the bedrock of the cavern, cast their crouched shadows against the stone walls, their reflected images moving like furtive creatures seeking to escape the light. They crept warily through those ancient tunnels—the Druid, the two Princes, the Valeman, the Elven brothers, and the Dwarf—all watching expectantly, caught up in the guarded excitement that comes with the end of a long hunt. Apart from one another, spread out along the walls of the passage, weapons held ready, eyes and ears straining for any hint of danger, they moved steadily forward, farther upward, deeper into the core of the Druid's Keep. Then the silence slowly faded, and there was a muffled sound like heavy breathing and the heat became more intense. Ahead, the passageway ended and a stone door with an iron handle came into view, its edges outlined sharply by a piercing light from the chamber just beyond. The mysterious sound increased in volume and became identifiable. It was the throbbing hum of machinery lodged in the rock beneath them, pumping with steady rhythm. Apprehensively, the members of the company approached the closed door on Allanon's silent command.

As the giant Druid opened the heavy stone barrier, the unsuspecting men were struck by a blast of hot air that surged violently through their lungs to lodge in the pits of their stomachs. Gasping for air, they momentarily hesitated, then moved reluctantly into the room. The door swung shut behind them. They knew where they were in an instant. The room was actually little more than a circular catwalk above a huge pit that dropped off into the rock for well over a hundred feet. At the bottom burned a fierce blaze, fed by some unknown source, its red-orange flames leaping into the air toward the top of the deep well. The pit cut away the greater portion of the chamber, leaving only the small walkway several feet wide with a short iron guard rail that rimmed its inner edge. From the ceiling and walls ran various heating ducts which carried the hot air to other parts of the structure. A concealed pumping system controlled the amount of heat generated by the open furnace. Because it was night, the pumping system had been shut down, and the temperature level along the catwalk was still tolerable, despite the intense heat of the pit fire below. When the bellows were in full operation, any human passing through the chamber would be fried in a matter of seconds.

Menion, Flick, and the Elven brothers paused by the railing to get a closer look at the system. Hendel hung back, uncomfortable in this confining rock structure, comparing it unfavorably to the open woodlands with which he was familiar. Allanon moved to Balinor's side and conversed with him for a few moments, glancing uneasily at the several closed doors leading into the chamber and pointing to the open spiral staircase that led to the upper halls of the castle. Finally, the two seemed to settle on something, nodding in agreement, and signaled the others to catch up. Hendel was only too glad to comply. Menion and the Elven brothers moved away

from the railing to join him. Only Flick lingered a second, strangely attracted by the fascinating blaze below. This slight delay produced an unexpected result. As he lifted his eyes with a parting glance to the other side
of the chamber, he saw the dark figure of a Skull Bearer appear out of
nowhere.

Flick froze instantly. The creature remained in a half-crouch directly
across the pit from him, its body a black mass even in the light of the
pit fires, the caped wings billowing out slightly behind it. Its legs were
crooked, the feet ending in cruel-looking claws that seemed capable of
rending the stone itself. Hunched low between the massive shoulders, the
head and face bore a vague resemblance to scarred coal. The wicked eyes
fastened on the speechless Valeman, their depths drawing him closer to
the reddish glow that burned within, an open invitation to death. With
slow, dragging steps, it began to make its way around the chamber, its
breath rasping with every labored step as it drew closer and closer to the
spellbound Flick. He wanted to cry out, run away, do anything but stay
where he was, yet the strange eyes held him motionless. He knew he was
finished.

But the others had noticed his immobile form; following his frightened gaze across the chamber, they had discovered the black Skull Bearer
creeping noiselessly around the rim of the pit. In a flash, Allanon leaped
in front of Flick, yanking him around to break the spell of the creature's
terrible eyes. Dazed, Flick stumbled backward into the waiting arms of
Menion, who had rushed to his assistance. The others stood just behind
the Druid, their weapons held ready. The creature stopped several yards
from Allanon, still in a half-crouch, hiding the hideous face from the fire's
glow with one raised wing and clawed hand. Its breath sounded in slow,
steady rasps as its cruel eyes rested on the tall figure that stood between it
and the little Valeman.

"Druid, you are a fool to oppose me." The voice hissed from somewhere deep within the creature's formless face. "You are all doomed. You
were doomed from the moment you chose to come after the Sword. The
Master knew you would come, Druid! He _knew._"

"Get away while you can, hateful one!" Allanon commanded in the
most menacing tone any of the members of the company had ever heard
him use. "You frighten no one here. We will take the Sword, and you will
not stand in our way. Step aside, lackey, and let your Master show himself!"

The words burned into the air, cutting through to the Skull Bearer like
knives. The creature hissed its fury, the rasping breath coming in quick
gasps as it took another step, crouching lower, its eyes frightful to look into
as they blazed with new hatred.

"I will destroy you, Allanon. Then no one will be left to oppose the
Master! You have been our pawn from the start, though you could not
have guessed. Now we have you within our reach, along with your most
valuable allies. And look what you have brought us, Druid—the last heir of
Shannara!"

To the shock of everyone, the clawlike hand pointed to an astonished

Flick. The creature did not seem to realize that Flick was not the heir or that Shea had been lost to them on the Dragon's Teeth. For a moment no one spoke. The fire roared in the pit below, billowing up suddenly with a gust of boiling air that singed the unprotected faces of the mortals. The claws of the black spirit creature seemed to reach toward them.

"Now, fools," the hate-filled voice rasped at them, "you shall receive the kind of death your species deserves!"

As the final words of the black creature hissed away in the flame-lit air, everything seemed to happen at once. With a dramatic sweep of one lean arm and a command so sharp it jarred them all into instant action, the giant Druid sent the tensed members of his little company charging toward the open staircase that led to the main hall of the Druid's Keep. As the six men broke in a mad dash for the winding stairway behind them, the Skull Bearer lunged for Allanon. The thudding impact of their collision could be heard even by the fleeing men, who were already starting up the staircase—save for one. Flick hesitated, torn by the desire to escape, but held spellbound by the titanic struggle between the two powerful beings locked in combat only inches from the rising flames of the great open furnace. He stood at the bottom of the staircase, hearing the disappearing footfalls of his companions as they raced for the upper hall. A moment later the footsteps were gone, leaving him the sole witness to the incredible struggle between Druid and Skull Bearer.

The black-garbed figures were immobile at the edge of the furnace, statues frozen in place with the great strain of their battle, dark faces only inches apart, the lean arms of the giant Druid holding firm the claw-tipped limbs of the deadly spirit creature. The Skull Bearer was attempting to bring his razor-sharp hands close enough to the mystic's unprotected throat to rip the life out of him and end the battle quickly. The black wings heaved with the exertion, flapping in fury to add momentum to the assault, the unmistakable rasp of its breathing cutting the heated air with ragged desperation. Then suddenly the Northland creature's wiry leg shot out, tripping the Druid so that he fell backward onto the stone floor at the edge of the pit. Like a shot, the attacker was upon him, one clawed hand sweeping downward for the kill. But the victim was too quick, rolling deftly away from the deadly talons and free from the creature's grasp. Nevertheless, Flick saw the blow catch a portion of the shoulder and heard the distinct rending of cloth as first blood was drawn. Flick gave a gasp of dismay, but a moment later the Druid was on his feet, showing no sign of injury. Twin bolts of blue flame shot out of the extended fingers of his hands, striking the rising Skull Bearer with shattering force, throwing the infuriated creature back against the railing. But while the mystic bolts had visibly hurt the serpent during the battle in the Hall of Kings, they did little more than slow the Northland creature for a few brief seconds. Roaring in fury, it counterattacked. Blazing red bolts shot from its burning eyes. Allanon brought his cloak up in a sweeping movement, and the bolts appeared to deflect into the stone walls of the chamber. For a moment, the creature hesitated, and the two opponents circled each other warily in the manner of two beasts of the forest, locked in a life-and-death struggle which only one could survive.

For the first time, Flick noticed that the temperature was rising. With the approach of dawn, the furnace tenders had risen to care for the heating needs of the awakening castle. Unaware of the battle taking place in the walkway overhead, they had activated the dormant bellows machinery at the bottom of the pit, stoking the fire to build it up to an intensity which would enable heated air to warm all the chambers of the Druid's Keep. As a result, flames were now visible above the edge of the pit and the temperature of the chamber was rising steadily. Flick felt the sweat pouring down over his face, soaking through his warm hunting outfit. But still he would not leave. He sensed that if Allanon were defeated, they would all be doomed, and he was determined to know the outcome. The Sword of Shannara would mean nothing to them if the man who had brought them to this final battleground were destroyed. With rapt fascination clouding his stocky face, Flick Ohmsford watched what might be the fate of the races and the lands being decided by the two seemingly indestructible protagonists of mortal man and Spirit Lord.

Allanon had attacked again with the flashing blue bolts, striking at the circling Skull Bearer in brief, biting blows, trying to force it into a hasty move, trying to cause it to slip, to make a single fatal mistake. The spirit creature was no fool, but an evil spawned of a hundred hunts in which it alone had been the victor and the victims all lay forgotten beyond the world of mortal men. It dodged and twisted with frightening ease, always coming back to the same tense crouch, watching and waiting for its own moment to strike. Then, in a totally unexpected move, the black wings spread wide and it circled into the air in a sweep that carried it soaring around the flames of the furnace and down again with vicious speed onto the tall figure of Allanon. The clawed hands raked downward, and for a moment Flick thought all was surely lost. Miraculously, the floored Druid escaped the deadly hands, throwing the Skull Bearer completely over him with one mighty heave of his powerful arms. The hapless creature flew wildly through the air and crashed with an audible thud into the stone wall beyond. It struggled to its feet in an instant, but the force of the blow had shaken it, slowing it down just enough, and before it could escape, the giant Druid was upon it.

The two black figures thrashed about against the wall as if inextricably joined, their limbs locked onto each other like twisted branches. When they reared to full height, Flick could see that Allanon was behind the struggling Skull Bearer, his mighty arms locked viselike about the head of the creature, the straining muscles slowly crushing the life away. The victim's wings beat madly, its hooked arms clutching vainly for something to break the hold that was destroying it. The fire-red eyes burned with the fury of the furnace pit itself, shooting forth bolts of fire that tore into the stone walls, leaving gaping, blackened holes. The combatants lurched away from the wall and rocked wildly toward the blazing pit at the center of the heated chamber until they were against the low iron railing. For a moment it appeared to the wide-eyed Valeman that both would lose their balance and plunge into the flames below. But abruptly Allanon straightened with a mighty effort, dragging his captive back from the railing a few scant feet. It was this sudden movement that brought the entangled spirit creature about, its hate-filled eyes coming to rest directly on the partially hidden Valeman. Grasping at any opportunity to divert the clinging Druid for the instant that would permit it a chance to break free of those crushing arms, the Skull Bearer struck at the unprepared Flick. Twin bolts of flame shot out of the burning eyes, shattering the stone blocks of the staircase into deadly fragments which flew in all directions like little knives. Flick acted instinctively, diving out of the staircase onto the walkway, his hands and face cut by the stone, but his life saved by his quickness. As he leaped clear, the entire entryway shuddered abruptly and collapsed in a cascade of broken stone blocks that completely shut off the passage upward, the dust billowing out of the rubble in heavy clouds.

In that same instant, as Flick lay frightened and shaken but still conscious on the stone floor of the furnace chamber, with the flames from the roaring pit rising higher to meet the clouds of dust from the blocked passage, Allanon's grip relaxed just enough to permit the crafty spirit creature to break loose. Whirling about with a cry of hatred, it struck the distracted Druid a crushing blow on the head, knocking the tall wanderer to his knees. The Northlander moved in for the kill, but somehow the dazed mystic was on his feet again, the blue bolts from the lean hands flashing fiercely as they struck the unprotected head of the attacker. Powerful fists rained resounding blows on both sides of the creature's black head, turning the battered figure about once again as the great arms wound with crushing force about its chest, pinning the wings and claw-tipped hands back against the writhing body. Holding the creature thus, the steel-eyed Druid gritted his gleaming teeth in fury and squeezed. Flick, still lying on the floor as the two combatants loomed above him several yards away, heard a horrible crunching sound as something snapped inside the Skull Bearer. Then with a lurch the two figures were again next to the low iron railing, every straining feature clearly revealed in the flames, the thunder of the burning pit matched in its power and its fury by the wail of agony from the shattered victim as the black, hooked body shuddered once. From some deep well of strength and hatred buried within, the Skull Bearer summoned one last desperate surge of power, throwing itself over the iron railing, its clutching fingers embedded in the black-cloaked attacker as it fell, dragging its hated enemy with it, and both figures were lost in the glow of the hungry flames.

The fallen Flick climbed dazedly to his feet, shock slowly spreading over his battered face. He tottered unsteadily toward the edge of the furnace pit, but the heat was so intense that he was forced back. He tried once more without success, the sweat pouring down from his forehead into his eyes and mouth, mingling slowly with tears of helpless anger. The flames from the pit soared above the low iron railing, licking hungrily at the stone and crackling with new life as if to acknowledge the addition of the two black-garbed creatures to the fuel it greedily consumed. Through the mist that coated his burning eyes, the Valeman gazed fixedly toward the bottomless pit. There was nothing beyond the red glow of the flames and the unbearable heat. Hopelessly, he called out the Druid's name over and over in futile desperation, each call sending the echoes bouncing off the stone walls and dying in the heat of the fire. But the Valeman found himself alone with the roar of the flames, and he knew at last that the Druid was gone.

He panicked then. In a mad dash, he scrambled back from the fiery pit. He reached the rubble of the stairway before he remembered that it had been blocked, and he collapsed for a moment amid the broken rock. Shaking his head to clear his muddled brain, he felt the full intensity of the fire. He knew instinctively that if he did not escape the chamber in a matter of minutes, the heat would bake him alive. He bounded up and ran to the closest stone door, pushing and pulling on it in desperation. But the door did not move, and at last he stopped, his hands bloody from the effort. He looked down the wall, his eyes finding a second door. He stumbled on to this one, but it, too, was secured from the other side. He felt his hopes dim into nothingness, certain now that he was trapped. Woodenly, he forced himself to move on to the third. It was with the last of his fading strength, as he pushed and pulled frantically on the stubborn barricade, that he touched something hidden in the rock and triggered the mechanism that permitted it to open. With a cry of relief, the battered Valeman fell through the opening into the passageway beyond, kicking the stone door shut as he lay in the semidarkness, locking himself away from the heat and the death that remained behind.

For many long minutes he lay exhausted in the darkness of the corridor, his burning body soaking up the cool of the stone floor and the soothing air. He didn't try to think, didn't care to remember, but wished only to lose himself in the peace and quiet of the tunnel rock. At last he forced himself wearily to his knees, then to his feet in a final effort, leaning dazedly against the cold stone of the passage wall as he waited for his strength to return. He realized for the first time that his clothing was torn and burned almost beyond recognition, his hands and face singed and blackened from the heat. He looked around slowly, his stocky frame straightening itself as he pushed away from the wall. The dim light of the torch on the wall ahead indicated the direction in which the winding corridor ran, and he stumbled forward until he was able to grasp the burning piece of wood from its rack. He shuffled along slowly, the torch extended to light his way. Somewhere ahead he heard shouting, and instinctively his free hand went to the handle of his short hunting knife, drawing the weapon from its sheath. After several minutes, the noise seemed to move farther away and at last die out altogether, and still the Valeman had seen nothing. The corridor wound through the rock in curious fashion, taking Flick past several doors, all of which were closed and barred, but never leading upward and never branching off into other passageways. Every so often the darkness ahead was broken by the dim light of a burning torch securely fastened to the stone, its yellow light casting his shadow against the far wall like a misshapen wraith fleeing into the darkness.

Then abruptly the passage widened and the light ahead grew stronger. Flick hesitated a moment, grasping his weapon tightly, his face streaked with lines of smoke and sweat, but grimly determined in the flickering glow. There was no sound as he inched his way forward. He knew that somewhere there had to be a stairway leading to the main hall of the Druid's Keep. So far, it had been a long and futile search, and he was becoming exhausted. He wished belatedly that he hadn't been so eager to remain behind, allowing himself to be cut off from the main party. Now he was trapped in these unfathomable corridors at the center of Paranor. Anything could have happened to the others by this time, he thought dismally, and he might never find them wandering through this maze. He edged his way a little farther around a bend in the rock, his muscles tensed, peering carefully into the light. To his surprise he found himself at the entrance to a round chamber with numerous other passages leading into it. A dozen or so torches burned cheerfully from the circular wall. He breathed a sigh of relief when he saw that the rotunda was deserted. Then he realized that he was no better off than he had been before. The other passages looked exactly like the one he had come through. There were no doors leading to other rooms, no stairways leading to the upper level, and no indication as to which way he should go. He looked around in bewilderment, desperately trying to identify one passage from another, his hope fading with each passing second and each repeated survey. At last he shook his head in confusion. Moving to one of the walls, he sat down wearily, closing his eyes as he forced himself to accept the bitter fact that he was hopelessly lost.

On Allanon's command, the remainder of the company had broken for the stairway. Durin and Dayel were closest to the stone passage and, being the fastest in the group, found themselves halfway up the steps before the others had even begun the short climb. Their lithe Elven limbs carried them up the flight of stairs in gliding, bounding leaps, barely touching the stone as they ran. Hendel, Menion, and Balinor came in a rush behind, their progress partially impeded by their heavy weapons and greater weight, and partially by each other as they tried to avoid stumbling over one another in the narrow, winding staircase. It was a wild, disorganized charge to the upper hall, each man scrambling to reach the object of the long quest and to escape the terrifying spirit creature. In their haste to accomplish both ends, the hapless Flick was not even missed.

Durin was first through the stairway entrance of the Druid's Keep, nearly stumbling into the great hall as he broke clear, the smaller form of his brother close behind. The hall was lavishly impressive, a huge, high-ceilinged corridor whose great walls were solid wood, polished until they shone with burnished magnificence in the mixed yellow light of burning torches and the reddish tinges of the dawn seeping through high, slanted windows. The panels were adorned with paintings, carved figures of stone and wood on mosaic display stands, and long, handwoven tapestries that hung in folds to the polished marble floor that ran the length of the corridor. At various intervals, there were great statues of iron and fine stone, sculptures of another age preserved through the long centuries by the shelter of this timeless refuge. They seemed to be guarding the heavy, carved wooden doors that were beautifully ornamented with handles of copper-colored brass held fast by iron studs. A few of these stood open, and in the chambers that lay beyond could be seen the same carefully designed splendor, glowing radiantly as tall, open glass windows let in the sunshine in long streams of lingering color, fresh with the new day.

The Elven brothers had little time to admire the ageless beauty of Paranor. An instant after they were through the open staircase, they were set upon by Gnome guards, who seemed to come from everywhere at once, the gnarled, yellow bodies sliding from concealment behind doors, statues, the walls themselves. Durin met the rush with his long hunting knife and withstood the assault only a moment before they were on him. Dayel came to his brother's rescue, swinging his long bow as a weapon, knocking the attackers aside until the sturdy ash broke with an audible snap. For a moment it seemed they would be torn to pieces before their stronger comrades could come to their aid, until Durin broke free and snatched a long, wicked-looking pike from an iron warrior of another age and scattered the scrambling Gnomes with sweeping cuts, knocking them away from his struggling brother. But they were reinforced in an instant and quickly reassembled for a second charge. The Elven brothers had moved back to the wall, panting with the strain and covered with slashes and the blood of their attackers. The Gnomes gathered together in a yellow group, their deadly short swords held before them, intent on breaking past Durin's swinging pike and hacking both Elves to pieces. With a wild piercing cry, they charged in for the kill.

Unfortunately for the Gnomes, they had forgotten to watch the open stairway against the possible chance that the Elves were not alone. At the instant they rushed Durin and Dayel, the other three members of the company burst through the doorway and fell upon the unprepared attackers. The Gnomes had never in their lives encountered men such as these. In the center came the huge borderman from Callahorn, his gleaming

sword cutting a path through the shorter swords with such ferocity that the
Gnomes fell over each other trying to escape. On one side they ran headlong into the bludgeoning mace of the powerful Dwarf, while on the
other they faced the quick blade of the swift, agile highlander. For a moment they stood and fought against the five madmen, then wavered slightly
as the attack pressed ahead, and finally broke and ran, all thoughts of win-
ning abandoned. Without a word, the five battered warriors charged down
the magnificent hall, leaping over the wounded and dead, their hunting
boots ringing on the polished marble. The few Gnomes who stood against
them as they came soon went down before the rush, to lie in silent, unmoving heaps. After all that they had suffered and lost, the five who remained from the little company would not be denied any longer the
victory they had sought so desperately.

Near the end of the ancient corridor, now littered with dead and
wounded Gnomes, the tapestries and paintings torn and scattered from the
sharp battle, a last desperate band of guards crowded together in tight formation before a set of tall, carved wooden doors that stood closed and
barred. Their short hunting swords held before them like a wall of spikes,
the determined Gnomes prepared to make a final stand. The attackers
made a short rush at the deadly wall, trying to break through at the center
behind the long swords of Balinor and Menion, but the battle-hardened
guards repulsed the assault after several minutes of bitter fighting. The five
withdrew in exhaustion, panting and sweating freely with the exertion,
their bodies cut and battered. Durin dropped heavily to one knee, both an
arm and a leg badly slashed by Gnome swords. Menion had been clipped
along one side of his head by a pike edge, and the blood rose to the wound
in a vivid red streak. The highlander seemed unaware of the injury. Again
the five attacked and again, after long minutes of bitter hand-to-hand
combat, they were repulsed. The number of Gnomes had diminished by
almost half, but time was running out for the men of the company. There
was no sign of Allanon, and the Gnomes would have reinforcements on
the way to protect the Sword of Shannara, if indeed it did stand within the
chamber they now so desperately sought to hold.

Then, in an amazing display of raw strength, the towering Balinor
rushed to the other side of the hall and with one mighty heave overturned
a huge stone pillar, at the top of which was affixed a metal urn. Pillar and
urn struck the stone floor with a crash that jarred everyone to the bone,
the echoes reverberating through the bloodied hall. Stone should have
shattered, but the pillar remained whole. With the aid of Hendel, the giant
borderman began to roll the rounded battering ram sideways toward the
wedge of Gnomes and the closed doors to the chamber beyond, the monstrous roller gathering speed and power with each revolution as it thundered toward the hapless guards. For an instant the wiry yellow creatures
hesitated, their short swords held ready as the crushing weight of the stone
pillar bore down on them. Then they broke, bolting for safety, their spirit
gone, the battle lost. Even so, several were not fast enough to escape the
makeshift ram and were caught beneath its great bulk as it crashed amid a

shower of stone and wood splinters into the barred doors. The doors shuddered and buckled with the blow, the wood cracking and the iron fastenings snapping like the crack of a whip, yet somehow they withstood the force of the ram. But an instant later they flew off their hinges with a resounding crash as the weight of the Prince of Callahorn struck them, and the five men rushed into the chamber beyond to claim the Sword of Shannara.

To their amazement, the room stood empty. There were tall windows and long, flowing curtains, masterful paintings that lined the walls, and even several small pieces of ornate furniture placed carefully about the large chamber. But nowhere was there any trace of the coveted Sword. In shocked disbelief, the five gazed slowly about the closed room. Durin dropped heavily to his knees, weak from loss of blood and close to passing out. Dayel came quickly to his aid, tearing up strips of cloth to bind the open wounds, then helping his brother to one of the chairs, where he collapsed in exhaustion. Menion looked from one wall to the next, searching for another exit to the room. Then Balinor, who had been pacing the floor of the chamber in slow scrutiny of its marble finish, gave a low exclamation. A portion of the floor at the very center of the room was scarred and discolored beneath a poor attempt to conceal the fact that something large and square had stood there for many years.

"The block of Tre-Stone!" exclaimed Menion quickly.

"But if it has been moved, it must have been recently," Balinor speculated, his breathing labored, his voice weary as he tried to think. "So why did the Gnomes try to keep us out . . . ?"

"Maybe they didn't know it had been moved," suggested Menion desperately.

"Perhaps a decoy . . . ?" ventured Hendel abruptly. "But why waste time with a decoy unless . . . ?"

"They wanted to keep us busy here, because the Sword was still in the castle and they hadn't gotten it out!" finished Balinor excitedly. "They haven't had time to get it out, so they tried to decoy us! But where is the Sword now—who has it?"

For a moment all three were at a loss. Had the Warlock Lord known that the company was coming all along, just as the Skull Bearer in the furnace had seemed to indicate? If their attack had caught everyone by surprise, what could have happened to the Sword since Allanon had last seen it in this chamber?

"Wait!" exclaimed Durin weakly from across the room, rising slowly to his feet. "When I came through the staircase, there was something happening on another set of stairs down the hall—men moving up those stairs."

"The tower!" shouted Hendel, racing for the open doorway. "They've got the Sword locked in the tower!"

Balinor and Menion hurried after the disappearing Dwarf, the weariness gone. The Sword of Shannara was still within reach. Durin and Dayel followed at a slower pace, the former still weak and leaning heavily on his younger brother for support, but their eyes bright with hope. A moment later, the chamber stood empty.

Flick climbed despondently to his feet after a few minutes' rest and decided that the only course of action left to him was to choose one of the passageways and follow it to the end, hoping that it would take him to a stairway leading upward to the fortress. He thought briefly of the others, somewhere in the corridors above, perhaps already in possession of the Sword. They could not know of Allanon's fall nor of his own fate, lost in these impossible tunnels. He hoped they would search for him, but realized at the same time that, if they did get the Sword, there would be no time to waste looking for him. They would have to make their escape before the Warlock Lord could send the Skull Bearers to retrieve the coveted blade. He wondered what had become of Shea, if he had been found alive, if he had been rescued. Somehow he knew that Shea would never leave Paranor while Flick was alive; but then there was no way for his brother to know that he had not perished in the furnace chamber. He had to admit that his own situation looked pretty hopeless.

At that instant there was a loud clamor from one of the tunnels, the sound of boots thudding on the stone floor, of men rushing directly toward the rotunda. In a flash, the Valeman crossed the room and hastened into concealment down a different tunnel, keeping flat against the rock in the protective shadows. He paused just within sight of the lighted rotunda and drew his short hunting knife. A few moments later a swarm of fleeing Gnome guards charged into the connecting room and disappeared down another of the passageways without pausing. The sounds of their flight were soon lost in the bends and turns of the rock. Flick had no idea what they were running from or perhaps running to, but wherever they had been was where he wanted to be. It was a good bet that they had come from the upper chambers of the Druid's Keep, and that was the place the Valeman had to reach. He moved cautiously back into the lighted chamber and crossed to the tunnel from which the Gnomes had come. Backtracking their path of flight, he entered the now-deserted corridor and disappeared into the darkness beyond. He held his knife before him, groping his way along the dimly lit walls toward the first torch rack. Freeing the burning wood from its clasp, he proceeded deeper into the passage, his eager eyes scanning the rough walls for signs of a door or an open stairway. He had gone only about a hundred yards when without warning a portion of the rock slid open almost at his elbow, and a single Gnome stepped into view.

It was disputable as to which of the two was more surprised at the appearance of the other. The Gnome guard was a straggler from the larger group fleeing the battle in the halls above, and the sight of another of the invaders here in the tunnels momentarily startled him. Although smaller than the Valeman, the Gnome was wiry and armed with a short sword. He attacked immediately. Flick dodged instinctively as the sweeping blade went wide of the mark. The Valeman leaped onto the Gnome before he could recover and wrestled him to the stone floor, trying vainly to take the sword away from his agile opponent, his own knife lost in the scuffle. Flick was not trained in hand-to-hand combat, but the Gnome was, and this gave the little yellow man a distinct advantage. He had killed before and would do so again without a second thought, while Flick sought only to disarm his attacker and escape. They rolled and fought across the floor for several long minutes before the Gnome again broke free and took a vicious cut at his adversary, barely missing the exposed head. Flick threw himself back, desperately looking for his knife. The little guard charged at him just as his groping fingers closed over the heavy wood of the torch he had dropped at the first assault. The short sword came down, glancing off Flick's shoulder and cutting into the exposed flesh of his arm painfully. At the same moment, the stunned Valeman brought the torch up with a powerful swing and felt it strike the Gnome's raised head with jarring impact. The guard sprawled forward with the force of the blow and did not move again. Flick slowly regained his footing and recovered his knife after a moment's search. His arm throbbed painfully and the blood had soaked into his hunting tunic, running down his arm and into his hand where he could clearly see it. Afraid that he was bleeding to death, he quickly tore up strips of cloth from the fallen Gnome's short cloak and bound them about the injured limb until the bleeding had stopped. Picking up the other's sword, he moved over to the still partially open rock slab to see where it led.

To his relief, he found a winding staircase beyond the doorway that spiraled upward. He slipped into the passage, closing the rock slab behind him with several pulls of his good arm. The stairs were dimly outlined by the familiar torchlight, and he proceeded to climb with slow, cautious steps. All was quiet in the passage as he moved steadily upward, the long torches in iron racks giving him enough light to pick out his footing on the rough stone. He reached a closed door at the top of the stairway and paused there to listen, his ear placed next to the cracks between the iron bindings. There was only silence beyond. Cautiously, he pushed the door open a bit and peered through into the ancient halls of Paranor. He had reached his goal. He opened the door a bit farther and stepped watchfully into the silent corridor.

Then the steel grip of a lean dark hand came down on his extended sword arm and yanked him into the open.

Hendel paused hesitantly at the bottom of the stairway that led to the tower of the Druid's Keep, peering upward into the gloom. The others stood quietly at his back, following his gaze intently. The stairway consisted of little more than a set of open stone steps, narrow and treacherous-looking, that wound upward in a spiral along the walls of the rounded turret. The entire tower was shrouded in gloomy darkness, unlighted by torches or openings in the dark stone. From their poor vantage point, the members of the company could see little beyond the first few turns in the staircase. The open stairwell dropped away from where they stood into a blackened pit. Menion crossed to the edge of the landing and peered downward, mindful of the absence of any guard rail either here or along the stairs. He dropped a small pebble into the black abyss and waited for it to hit bottom. No sound came back to him. He glanced again at the open stairs and the gloom above, then turned to the others.

"Looks like an open invitation to a trap," he declared pointedly.

"Very likely," Balinor agreed, stepping forward for a closer look. "But we have to get up there."

Menion nodded, then shrugged casually, moving toward the stairway. The others followed without a word, Hendel right at the highlander's heels, Balinor next, and the Elven brothers bringing up the rear. They moved cautiously up the narrow stone steps, alert for any sign of a trap, their shoulders close to the wall, away from the dangerous open edge of the stairwell. They wound their way steadily through the musty gloom. Menion studied each step as he went, his keen eyes searching the seams of the stone-block wall for hidden devices. From time to time, he tossed stones onto the steps ahead of them, testing for traps that might be released by any sudden weight on the steps. But nothing happened. The abyss below was a silent black hole cut into the heavy gloom of the tower air, no sound penetrating its dark serenity save the soft scraping of hunting boots ascending the worn steps. At last, the faint light of burning torches cut through the darkness far above them, the small fires flickering briskly with the gusting of an unknown source of wind from the turret peak. A small landing came into view at the summit of the staircase, and beyond, the dim shape of a huge stone door, bound with iron and standing closed. The top of the Druid's Keep.

Then Menion sprang the first hidden trap. A series of long, barbed spikes shot out of the stone wall, triggered by the pressure of Menion's foot on the stone stairway. Had Menion still been on the step, they would have cut into his unprotected legs, crippling him and forcing him over the edge of the open stairwell into the black abyss below. But Hendel had heard the click of the released spring an instant before the trap opened. With a quick pull he yanked the astonished highlander backward to the others, almost knocking them all off the narrow steps. They staggered wildly in the heavy gloom, inches from the sharpened steel spikes. Regaining their footing, the five remained flattened against the wall for several long minutes, breathing audibly in the still darkness. Then the taciturn Dwarf smashed the spikes before them with several well-placed blows of his great mace, opening the route once more. Now he led the way in alert silence, while the shaken Menion dropped back behind Balinor. Quickly Hendel found a second trap of the same type and triggered it, breaking the spikes and moving on.

They were almost to the landing now, and it appeared they would reach it without further difficulty when Dayel called out sharply. His keen Elven hearing had caught something that the others had missed, a small

click that signaled the triggering of still another trap. For a moment everyone froze in position as alert eyes searched the walls and steps. But they
found nothing, and at last Hendel ventured a single step farther on the
stairs. Surprisingly, nothing happened, and the cautious Dwarf proceeded
to the top of the stairway while the others remained in position. Once he
had safely reached the landing, the others hastened after him until at last all
five stood together at the top, looking anxiously down the winding staircase into the black pit. How they had managed to escape the third trap
they could not imagine. Balinor was of the opinion that it had failed to
function properly due to long years of neglect, but Hendel was not so
easily persuaded. He could not shake the feeling that somehow they had
overlooked the obvious.

The tower hung like a huge shadow over the open stairwell, its dark
stone chill and wet to the touch, a mass of giant blocks that had been assembled ages ago and had stubbornly withstood the ravages of time with
the endurance of the earth itself. The huge door at the landing appeared to
be immovable, its surface scarred, the iron bindings as sturdy as the day
they had been imbedded in the rock. Great iron spikes, hammered into the
stone, held the hinges and lock in place, and it appeared to the five who
stood before it that nothing less than an earthquake could force the monstrous slab of stone open even an inch. Balinor approached the formidable
barrier cautiously and ran his hands along the seams and lock, trying to
find some hidden device that might release it. Gingerly, he turned the iron
handle and pushed forward. To the astonishment of all, the stone slab slid
partially open with a shudder and a grinding of rusted iron. A moment
later, the mystery of the tower was revealed as the door swung open all the
way, striking the inner walls with a sharp crash.

In the exact center of the rounded chamber, set in the polished black
surface of the giant Tre-Stone block, blade downward so that it rose before
them like a gleaming cross of silver and gold, they beheld the legendary
Sword of Shannara. Its long blade flashed brightly in the light of the sun
streaming through the high, iron-barred windows of the tower, reflecting
sharply off the mirror finish of the square stone. None of the five had ever
seen the fabulous Sword, but they were instantly sure this was it. For a moment they remained framed in the doorway, gazing in astonishment, unable to believe that at last, after all their effort, the endless marches, the
miserable days and nights of hiding, there before them stood the ancient
talisman they had risked everything to find. The Sword of Shannara was
theirs! They had outwitted the Warlock Lord. Slowly they filed into the
stone chamber, smiles on their faces, the weariness gone, their wounds forgotten. They stood for long moments staring at it, silent, wondering,
grateful. They could not bring themselves to step forward and take the
treasure from the stone. It seemed too sacred for mortal hands. But Allanon was missing, and Shea was lost as well, and where . . .

"Where is Flick?" Dayel voiced the question suddenly. For the first
time they realized that he was missing. They glanced about the chamber,

looking blankly at one another for an explanation. Then Menion, who had turned apprehensively back to the gleaming Sword, watched the impossible happen. The great block of Tre-Stone and its precious display began to shimmer and dissolve before his astonished eyes. It took only seconds for the entire image to fade into smoke, then into a heavy haze, and at last into the air itself, until the five men stood alone in an empty room staring into space.

"A trap! The third trap!" roared Menion, recovering from the initial shock.

But behind him, he could already hear the huge rock slab swing shut on their inescapable prison, creaking and groaning sharply as the rusted hinges gave way under the monstrous weight of the stone. The highlander launched himself across the room, crashing into the door just as it closed on them, the sharp snap of its locks clicking firmly into place. He collapsed slowly to the worn stone floor, his heart beating violently in rage and frustration. The others had not moved, but stood in silent despair as they watched the slim figure at the door bury his face in his hands. The faint but unmistakable sound of muffled laughter echoed brokenly off the chill walls in long peals, mocking their foolishness and their bitter, inevitable defeat.

The cheerless cold of the Northland sky hung in thin strips of gray fog against the dull edges that formed the peaks of the solitary mountain of pitted blackness that was the castle of the Warlock Lord. Above and below the surrounding plain of the Skull Kingdom, standing like rusted sawteeth, were the blunted tips of the Razor Mountains and the Knife Edge, an impenetrable barrier to mortal life. Between them stood the dying mountain of the Spirit Lord, forgotten by nature, spurned by the seasons as it wasted slowly away. The shroud of death that claimed its tall peaks, clinging with pitiless certainty to its shattered faces, spread its evil aura across the entire land with unmistakable hatred toward the few vestiges of life and beauty that had somehow managed to survive. A doomed era waited quietly in the Northland kingdom of the Warlock Lord. Now was the hour of death, the last signs of life slowly fading back into the ground as only the shell of nature's touch, once bright and magnificent, remained.

Within the skull of the lone mountain ran hundreds of timeless caverns, their enduring rock walls sunless in the never-changing grayness of the sky beyond. They wound about with the ruthless coiling of a cornered snake, twisting violently through the core of the rock. All was silence and death in the gray mist of the spirit kingdom, a permeating somber air that marked the total extinction of hope, the complete burial of gaiety and lightness. There was movement even here, however, but it was life unlike anything known to mortal man. Its source was the single, black chamber at the peak of the mountain, a monstrous room with its north face open to the dim light of the cheerless sky beyond and the endless stretch of forbidding mountains that formed the north gate to the kingdom. In this cavernous room, its walls wet with the cold that cut knifelike through the rock, scurried the inky minions of the Warlock Lord. Their small, black forms crawled about the floor of the silent chamber, their spineless frames bent and shattered with the terrible, wrenching power their Master wielded over them. Even walking would have been redemption in their existence. They were mindless wraiths, kept only to serve the one who held them enslaved. They muttered as they hustled about, small cries and weepings that sounded of unforgettable agony. In the center of the room rose a large pedestal that held a basin of water, its murky surface placid and deathly. From time to time, one of the little crawling creatures would hasten to its edge and peer cautiously into the cold water, eyes darting furtively about, waiting, watching expectantly. A moment later, with a small whimper, it would scurry away to blend back in the shadows of the cavern. "Where is the Master, where is the Master?" the sounds would cry like whispers in the grayness as the little beings moved about uneasily. "He will come, he will come, he will come," the answer echoed back hatefully.

Then the air stirred violently as if wrenching free of the space that held it, and the mist seemed to come together in a huge black shadow that tightened slowly into material form at the edge of the basin. The mist gathered and swirled and became the Spirit Lord, a huge, cloaked figure of black that seemed to hang in the air. The sleeves rose, but there were no arms within, and the folds of the trailing robes covered nothing but the floor. "The Master, the Master," the terrified creatures' voices sounded in unison, and their bent shapes groveled obediently before him. The faceless cowl turned to them and looked down, and they could see within the blackness the tiny glints of flame that burned with satisfied hatred, flashing sparklike in a hazy green mist that hung all about the inner recesses of the shroud. Then the Warlock Lord turned from them, and they were forgotten as he gazed steadily into the waters of the strange basin, waiting for the commanded mental picture to appear. Seconds later the darkness was gone and in its place was the furnace room at Paranor where the company of Allanon again stood face-to-face with the dreaded Skull Bearer. The fiery eyes in the green mist stared first at the Valeman, then watched the battle between the two dark figures until both tumbled over the edge of the pit and were lost in the flames below. At that moment a sudden noise behind him caused the Spirit Lord to pause and turn slightly. Two of his Skull Bearers entered the room from one of the dark tunnels of the mountain to stand silently, awaiting his attention. He was not ready for them, and so returned to the waters of the basin. Again they cleared, forming a picture of the tower, where the astonished members of the company stood frozen in excited relief before the Sword of Shannara. He waited a few seconds, toying with them, enjoying his mastery of the situation as they moved closer to the Sword like mice to the baited trap of cheese. Seconds later, the trap was sprung as he dissolved his illusion before their startled eyes and watched the tower door fly shut, trapping them in the Keep for eternity. Behind him, the two winged servants could sense the chilling laugh that rolled through his substanceless frame into the cavern air.

Without turning to face them, the Warlock Lord gestured abruptly toward the open wall facing north, and the Skull Bearers moved off without hesitation. They knew without asking what was expected of them. They would fly to Paranor and destroy the captured son of Shannara, the sole heir to the hated Sword. With the last member of the House of Shannara dead and the Sword itself within their grasp, they no longer need fear a mystical power greater than their own. Even now, the precious Sword was en route from the halls of Paranor to the Northland kingdom where it would be buried and forgotten in the endless caverns of the Skull Mountain. The Warlock Lord turned slightly to watch his two servants shuffle awkwardly across the dark chamber until they reached the open wall, where they rose heavily into the gray sky and wheeled southward. To be sure, the Elf king, Eventine, would attempt to intercept the Sword, to regain it for his own people. But the attempt would fail, and Eventine would be taken—the last great leader of the free lands, the last hope of the races. With Eventine his prisoner, the Sword in his possession, the last heir to the House of Shannara dead, and the most hated enemy of all, the Druid Allanon, destroyed in the furnace at Paranor, the battle was ended before it had begun. There would be no defeat in the Third War of the Races. He had won.

A wave of his cloak sleeve and the water again turned murky, the picture of the Druid's Keep and the trapped mortals gone. Then the air rushed violently about the black spirit and his form began to dissolve back into the mist of the chamber, fading gradually until there was nothing left but the basin and the empty room. Long moments passed in silence until at last the groveling minions of the Warlock Lord were certain the Master had again gone from them, and they came forth from the shadows, their small, black shapes creeping eagerly to the basin edge where they peered curiously, crying and whimpering their misery to the placid waters.

In the high tower of Paranor, in the remote and now inaccessible room of the Druid's Keep, four silent, tired members of the little company from Culhaven paced dejectedly about their prison. Only Durin sat quietly against one wall of the tower, his wound so painful that he could no longer move about. Balinor rocked slightly on his heels as he stood close to a high, barred window of the Keep, watching the faint rays of the sun filter down in long streamers of floating dust to light the otherwise gloomy chamber with small squares of sunlight that fell carelessly across the stone slabs of the floor. They had been there for over an hour now, hopelessly imprisoned behind the mammoth, ironbound door. The Sword was lost to them and with it their hopes of any victory. At first they had waited patiently in the belief that Allanon would soon reach them, smashing through the great stone barrier that barred the way to freedom. They had even called his name, hoping he could hear them and follow their voices to the tower. Menion had reminded them that Flick was still missing, possibly wandering about the halls of Paranor searching for them. But before very long their faith faltered and at last faded entirely, as each forced himself to admit inwardly, though none would speak the words, that there would be no rescue, that the courageous Druid and the little Valeman had fallen prey to the deadly Skull Bearer, that the Warlock Lord had won.

Menion was thinking once again of Shea, wondering what had befallen his friend. The company had done all it could, but it had not even been enough to save the life of one small human being, and now no one could guess what end he had come to, left alone in the wilds of the Eastland border plains to fend for himself. Shea was gone, probably dead. Allanon had believed they would find Shea when they found the Sword, but the Sword had been lost and there was no sign of the missing heir. Now Allanon was gone as well, killed in the furnace room of the Druids' Council, his ancestral home—or if not killed, then taken prisoner, chained and shackled in some dungeon just as they were locked in this tower. They would be left to rot, or worse, and it had all been for nothing. He smiled grimly as he considered their fate, wishing he could have had at least one opportunity to confront the real enemy, to take one swift cut at the all-powerful Warlock Lord.

Suddenly a short hush of warning from the ever-alert Dayel caused the others to freeze where they were, eyes fixed on the great door, listening guardedly to the sound of faint footfalls on the stone steps beyond. Menion dropped his hand to the sword of Leah resting in the leather sheath on the floor and noiselessly pulled it free. The giant borderman at his elbow already held his drawn broadsword. All moved in short, hurried steps to encircle the entrance. Even the wounded Durin staggered to his feet, painfully limping over to stand with his companions. The footsteps reached the landing and stopped. There was a moment of ominous silence.

Then the great stone door suddenly opened, swinging ponderously inward, its iron hinges groaning only slightly as they took the full weight of the rock slab. From out of the darkness beyond appeared the frightened features of Flick Ohmsford, his eyes darting wildly as he beheld his imprisoned friends armed and ready to strike. Swords and maces lowered slowly as if the astonished men holding them were mechanical toys. The little Valeman moved reluctantly into the dim light of the tower, partially shadowed by the tall black figure following.

It was Allanon.

They stared at him wordlessly. Streaked with sweat, his dark form coated with several layers of ash and soot, he moved silently into their midst, one great hand resting gently on Flick's small shoulder. He smiled at their reaction.

"I'm all right," he assured them.

Flick was still shaking his head in disbelief at having been found by Allanon.

"I saw him fall . . ." he tried to explain to the others.

"Flick, I'm all right." Allanon patted the little Valeman's shoulder.

Balinor came a step closer, as if to convince himself that this was indeed Allanon and not another apparition.

"We thought you were . . . lost," he managed.

The familiar mocking grin appeared on the lean face.

"The blame for that lies in part at least with our young friend here. He saw me tumble into the furnace pit with the Skull Bearer and presumed me dead. What he did not realize is that the furnace is equipped with a series of iron rungs, which allow workmen to descend into the pit for the purpose of making repairs. Since Paranor has for centuries been the ancestral home of the Druids, I knew of the existence of the rungs. When I felt the evil one pull me over the railing, I reached for them and caught myself several feet below the rim. Flick, of course, could see none of this, and the roar of the fire drowned out my voice as I called out to him."

He paused to brush some of the dirt from his robe.

"Flick was fortunate enough to escape the chamber, but then he lost his way in the tunnels. The battle with the Skull Bearer left me weakened, and even though I enjoy special protection from fire, it took me quite some time to pull myself out of the pit. I went looking for Flick, lost in that maze of underground corridors, found him at last and frightened him half to death when I pulled him into the light. Then we came after the rest of you. But now we must leave—quickly."

"The Sword . . . ?" Hendel asked sharply.

"Gone—removed sometime earlier. We can speak of that later. It is dangerous for us to remain here any longer. The Gnomes will send reinforcements to secure Paranor and the Warlock Lord will dispatch others of his winged bearers to be certain you cause him no further trouble. With the Sword of Shannara still in his possession and believing you trapped in the Druid's Keep, he will quickly turn his attention to his plans for an invasion of the four lands. If he can seize Callahorn and the border countries quickly enough, the rest of the Southland will fall without a struggle."

"Then we're too late—we've lost!" exclaimed Menion bitterly.

Allanon shook his head emphatically.

"We have only been outmaneuvered, not defeated, Prince of Leah. The Warlock Lord rests easy in the belief that he has won, that we are destroyed and no longer a threat. Perhaps we can use that against him. We must not despair. Now come with me."

He led them quickly through the open doorway. A moment later, the tower chamber stood empty.

18

The little band of Gnomes marched Shea northward until sunset. The Valeman was exhausted when the march began and by the time the group finally halted for the night, he immediately collapsed and was asleep before the Gnomes had even finished binding his legs. The long trek took them from the banks of the unknown river northward into hill country west of the upper Anar Forest bordering on the Northland. Travel became considerably rougher, the terrain changing from the flat grasslands of the Rabb Plains into choppy, rolling hillocks. After a time, the band found itself doing more climbing than walking, with constant changes of direction made to avoid the bigger hills. It was beautiful country, grasslands patched with small forests of aged shade trees, their bending limbs graceful in the light spring winds. But its beauty was lost on the exhausted Valeman, who could only concentrate on putting one foot ahead of the other as his disinterested captors pushed him along without rest. By nightfall, the group was deep into the hill country, and had Shea been able to consult a map of the region, he would have discovered that they were camped directly east of Paranor. As it was, sleep came to him so fast that he could only remember dropping wearily to the grassy earth and then nothing more.

The industrious Gnomes finished tying him and then prepared a fire for their meager dinner. One Gnome was placed on sentry duty, mostly out of habit, since they felt there was little to fear this far into their own homeland, and a second was ordered to keep a close watch over the sleeping captive. The Gnome leader still did not realize who Shea was, nor did he realize the importance of the Elfstones, though he was intelligent enough to conclude that they must be worth something. His plan was to take the Valeman to Paranor where he could consult with his superiors concerning the fate of both the youth and the stones. Perhaps they would know the significance of these matters. The Gnome's only concern was doing the right thing in accordance with his orders to patrol this region, and beyond that duty, he did not care to know anything.

The fire was completed in short order, and the Gnomes ate a hastily prepared meal of bread and stripped meat. When the meal was finished, they gathered eagerly about the warm blaze and contemplated curiously the three small Elfstones which the leader had produced for inspection at his followers' urging. The wizened yellow faces bent closer to the fire and to the outstretched hand of the leader where the stones twinkled brightly in the glowing light. One eager follower tried to touch one, but a stinging blow from his superior sent him sprawling back into the shadows. The

Gnome leader touched the stones curiously and rolled them about in his open palm as the others watched in fascination. Finally, the Gnomes tired of the sport, and the stones were put back in the small leather pouch and returned to the leader's tunic. A bottle of ale was broken out to ward off the chill in the night air as well as to aid the weary Gnomes in forgetting their immediate troubles. The bottle was passed around freely, and the little yellow soldiers laughed and joked far into the night, keeping the fire blazing for warmth. Even the lone sentry wandered in, knowing that his guard duty was unnecessary. At last the ale was gone, and the weary hunters turned in, pulling up their blankets in a tight circle about the fire. The sentry even had presence of mind enough to throw a blanket over the sleeping captive, concluding that it would do no good to bring him into Paranor suffering from a fever. Moments later, the campsite was silent, all asleep save the sentry who stood drowsily in the shadows just beyond the light of the small campfire that was dying slowly into coals.

Shea slept fitfully, his slumber disturbed by recurring nightmares of his harrowing flight with Flick and Menion to reach Culhaven, and from there, the ill-fated journey to reach Paranor. He relived in his dreams the battle with the Mist Wraith, feeling its cold, slimy grip about his body, experiencing terror at the touch of the deadly swamp waters lapping about his legs. He felt desperation creeping all through him as the three again became separated in the Black Oaks, only this time he was alone in the great forest, and he knew there was no way out. He would wander until he died there. He could hear the cries of the hunting wolves closing in about him as he struggled to run, dodging madly through the endless maze of giant trees. A moment later the scene changed, and the company stood in the ruins of the city in the middle of the Wolfsktaag Mountains. They were looking curiously at the metal girders, unaware of the danger lurking silently in the jungle beyond. Only Shea knew what was about to happen, but when he tried to warn the others, he found he could not speak. Then he saw the giant creature creeping forth from its concealment to strike the unsuspecting men, and he could not move to warn them. They seemed unaware of what was about to happen, and the creature attacked, a mass of black hair and teeth. Then Shea was in the river, tossing and turning madly as he sought futilely to keep his head above the swift waters, to breathe the life-giving air. But he was being pulled down, and he knew he was suffocating. Desperately he sought to fight it, thrashing wildly as he was pulled farther and farther down.

Then suddenly he was awake and staring into the first faint tinges of light from the approaching dawn, his hands and feet cold and numb from the biting leather thongs that bound him. He looked anxiously about the clearing at the dying coals of the fire and the motionless Gnome bodies huddled in deep slumber. The hills were silent in the semidarkness, so quiet that the Valeman could hear his own breathing, rasping heavily in the stillness. To one side of the campsite was the lone figure of the sentry, his small form a dim shadow on the far edges of the clearing, near some heavy brush. His figure was so vague in the mistiness of the dying night that for several seconds Shea was not really sure he was not a part of the brush. Shea glanced about the silent camp a second time, twisting himself up on one elbow and wiping the sleep from his eyes as he peered cautiously about. Briefly, he tried to work on the thongs that bound him, hoping vaguely that he might be able to work himself loose and make a dash for freedom before the sleeping Gnomes could catch him. But after long minutes of trying to free himself, he was forced to give up the idea. The bonds were too well tied to be worked loose, and he did not have the strength to break them. For a moment he stared helplessly at the ground in front of him, convinced that he had reached Paranor, he would be turned over to the Skull Bearers and disposed of quickly.

Then he heard something. It was only a faint rustle from somewhere in the darkness beyond the clearing, but it caused him to look up alertly, listening for something further. His Elven eyes traveled quickly over the campsite and the Gnomes, but nothing seemed out of place. It took him several moments to relocate the lone guard at the edge of the brush, but the man had not moved from his position. Then a huge black shadow detached itself from the brush, and the sentry was enveloped and suddenly gone. Shea blinked in disbelief, but there was no mistake. Where the figure of the sentry had stood a moment before, there was nothing. Long moments passed as Shea waited for something further to happen. It was sunrise now. The last traces of the night faded rapidly, and the edge of the golden morning sun appeared on the tips of the distant eastern hills.

There was a soft sound off to his left, and the Valeman twisted about sharply. From behind the cover of a small grove of trees emerged one of the strangest sights that the youth had ever seen. It was a man clad all in scarlet, the like of which no one in Shady Vale had ever encountered. At first the Valeman thought it might be Menion, recalling an outlandish red hunting outfit he had once seen the highlander wearing. But it became apparent almost immediately that this stranger was not Menion, nor in any way like him. The size, the stance, the manner of approach were all different. It was impossible to make out his features in the dim light. In one hand he carried a short hunting knife and in the other was a strange pointed object. The scarlet figure crept slowly over to his side and moved in back of him before he could get a good look at his face. The hunting knife went through the leather bonds silently and easily, freeing the captive Valeman. Then the other hand came around in front of his face, and Shea's eyes went wide in shock as he saw that the man's left hand was missing and in its place a deadly looking iron pike protruded.

"Not a word," the leather-edged voice sounded in his ear. "Don't look, don't think, just move out for the trees to the left and wait there. Now move!"

Shea did not stop to ask questions, but quickly did as he was told. Even without seeing the face of the rescuer, he could guess from the rough voice and the severed limb that it would be wise to do as he was told. He scurried silently from the camp, running in a low crouch until he had reached the cover of the trees. He stopped there and turned back to wait for the other, but to his astonishment the scarlet figure was prowling noise-lessly through the midst of the sleeping Gnomes, apparently searching for something. The sun had risen into full view in the east now, and its light framed the stranger as he bent over the huddled form of the sleeping Gnome leader. One gloved hand reached cautiously into the Gnome's tu-nic, fumbled about for a moment, and came forth holding the small leather pouch with the precious Elfstones. As the hand with the pouch remained poised for an instant, the Gnome awakened, one hand coming up to seize the stranger's wrist as the other whipped a short sword around to finish the thief with one blow. But Shea's rescuer was too quick to be caught off guard. The long iron pike blocked the blow in a sharp clash of metal, and then came back in a long swipe across the Gnome's exposed throat. As the stranger rose to his feet and bounded away from the lifeless body, the entire camp came awake with the sound of the struggle. The Gnomes were on their feet in an instant, swords in hand, charging after the intruder before he could make a complete escape. The scarlet rescuer was forced to turn and fight, the short knife held in one hand as he faced a dozen attackers.

Shea was certain that this was the end for the man, and he prepared to leap from the cover of the trees to try to aid him. But the amazing stranger shrugged off the first onslaught of Gnome hunters as if they were mice, cutting through their disorganized assault and leaving two writhing on the earth with fatal wounds. Then he gave a sharp cry as the second wave of attackers moved in, and from out of the shadows on the other side of the camp charged a massive black figure bearing a huge club. Without slowing once, the black shape tore into the surprised Gnomes with indescribable fury, scattering them with great blows of the mace as if they were no more than fragile leaves. In less than a minute all the Gnomes lay motionless on the ground. Shea watched in astonishment at the edge of the trees as the huge figure approached Shea's rescuer, somewhat in the manner of a faith-ful dog seeking its master's approval. The stranger spoke softly to the giant for several moments, and then sauntered over to Shea while his companion remained to look after the Gnomes.

"I think that's about all of it," the voice rolled out as the scarlet figure came up to the Valeman, hefting the leather pouch in his good hand.

Shea took a moment to study the man's face, still uncertain as to who his benefactor might be. The way the man swaggered, there was no ques-tion in Shea's mind but that he was an arrogant fellow whose unshakable confidence in himself was probably matched only by his undeniable effi-ciency as a fighter. The tanned, worn face was clean-shaven except for a small mustache cut evenly above the upper lip. He had one of those faces that defied age; he looked neither old nor young, but somewhere in be-tween. Yet his manner was youthful, and only the leathery skin and deep eyes revealed that he would never see forty years again. The dark hair seemed flecked slightly with bits of gray, though in the misty dawn light it was difficult to be certain. The face was broad and his features prominent, particularly the wide, friendly mouth. It was a handsome, beguiling type of face, but one that Shea instinctively felt was a carefully worn mask that hid the true nature of the man. The stranger stood easily before the uncertain Valeman, smiling and waiting for some indication of his attitude toward his rescuers, apparently unsure of what it might be.

"I want to thank you," Shea quickly sputtered. "It would have been all over for me if you hadn't . . ."

"Quite all right, quite all right. Rescuing people is not exactly our business, but those devils would cut you up for sport. I'm from the Southland myself, you know. Haven't been back in quite a while, but it's my home nevertheless. You're from there, I can tell. One of the hill communities, maybe? Of course, you have Elven blood in you, too. . . ."

He trailed off abruptly, and for an instant Shea was certain that the man not only knew who he was, but what he was, and that he had stepped from the frying pan into the fire. A quick look back at the huge creature by the fallen Gnomes was necessary to reassure the youth that this was not a Skull Bearer.

"Who are you, friend, and where are you from?" the stranger demanded suddenly.

Shea gave him his name and explained that he was from Shady Vale. He told him that he had been exploring on a river to the south when his boat overturned, and he had been washed downstream and left unconscious on a bank where the band of Gnomes had found him. The fabricated tale was close enough to the truth so that the man might believe him, and Shea was not yet ready to trust strangers with the whole truth until he knew more than he knew about these two. He concluded his story by stating that the Gnomes had found him and decided to take him prisoner. The man looked at him for a long moment, an amused smile crossing his lips as he played idly with the leather pouch.

"Well, I doubt that you have told me the whole truth." He laughed shortly. "But I can't blame you. If I were in your place, I wouldn't tell me everything either. There will be time enough for the truth later. My name is Panamon Creel."

He extended his one broad hand which Shea accepted and shook heartily. The stranger had a grip like iron and the Valeman winced involuntarily at the strong handshake. The man smiled faintly and released his grip, pointing to the dark giant behind them.

"My companion, Keltset. We've been together for almost two years now and I never had a better friend, although I could have wished for a more talkative one, perhaps. Keltset is a mute."

"What is he?" asked Shea curiously, watching the great figure lumber slowly about the little clearing.

"You certainly are a stranger to this part of the world." The other laughed in amusement. "Keltset is a Rock Troll. His home was in the Charnal Mountains until his people made an outcast of him. We're both outcasts in this thankless world, but life deals a different hand to each, I suppose. We have no choice in the matter."

"A Rock Troll," Shea repeated wonderingly. "I've never seen a Rock Troll before. I thought they were all savage creatures, almost like animals. How could you . . . ?"

"Watch your tongue, friend," the stranger warned sharply. "Keltset doesn't like that kind of talk, and he is just sensitive enough to step on you for using it. Your problem is that you look at him and see a monster, a misshapen creature unlike you or me, and you wonder if he's dangerous. Then I tell you that he's a Rock Troll, and you're twice as certain he's more animal than man. Part of your limited education and lack of practical experience, I warrant. You should have traveled with me during the last few years—ha, you would have learned that even a friendly smile shows the teeth behind!"

Shea looked closely at the giant Rock Troll as Keltset bent idly over the fallen Gnomes, glancing about for anything he might have missed in his extensive search of their garments and packs. Keltset was basically man-shaped, dressed in knee-length pants and a tunic belted with a green cord. About the neck and wrists he wore protective metal collars. His really different feature was the strange, almost barklike skin that covered the entire body, coloring it something on the order of meat well done, but not yet charred. The dark face was small-featured, blunt, and nondescript, with a heavy brow and deep-set eyes. The extremities were the same as a man's except for the hands. There was no little finger on either hand—only a thumb and three stout, powerful fingers nearly as large as the Valeman's small wrists.

"He doesn't look very tame to me," Shea declared quietly.

"There you are! The perfect example of a hasty opinion totally without foundation. Just because Keltset doesn't look civilized and doesn't appear an intelligent creature on the face of things, you label him an animal. Shea, my boy, you may believe me when I say that Keltset is a sensitive man with the same feelings as you or I. Being a Troll in the Northland is every bit as normal as being an Elf in the Westland and so on! You and I are the strangers in this part of the world."

Shea looked carefully at the broad, reassuring face, the easy smile that seemed to come so naturally, and he instinctively distrusted the man. These two were more than travelers passing through this country who had seen his plight and had come to his aid out of love for their fellowman. They had stalked that Gnome encampment with skill and cunning, and when discovered, destroyed the entire Gnome patrol with ruthless efficiency. As dangerous as the Rock Troll appeared, Shea was certain that Panamon Creel was twice as deadly.

"You are most certainly better informed on the matter than I," admitted Shea, choosing his words carefully. "Being from the Southland, and having traveled little outside of its borders, I am unfamiliar with all life in this region of the world. I owe you both my life, and my thanks go to Keltset as well."

The dashing stranger smiled happily at the expression of gratitude, obviously pleased at the unexpected compliment.

"No thanks are necessary; I told you that," he replied. "Come over here and sit with me for a moment while we wait for Keltset to finish his task. We must talk more about what brought you to this part of the country. It's very dangerous in these parts, you know, especially traveling alone."

He led the way over to the nearest tree where he sat down wearily, resting his back against the slender trunk. He still held the pouch with the Elfstones in his one good hand, and Shea did not feel that he should bring that subject up just yet. Hopefully, the stranger would ask if they belonged to him, and he could recover them and be on his way to Paranor. The others in the company would be looking for him by now, either along the eastern edge of the Dragon's Teeth or farther up near Paranor.

"Why is Keltset searching those Gnomes?" the youth asked after a moment's silence.

"Well, there might be some indication of where they are from, where they were going. They might have some food, which we could use right now. Who knows, they might even have something valuable . . . ?"

He trailed off sharply and looked questioningly at Shea, one hand balancing the leather pouch with the Elfstones before the Valeman's eyes, holding it like bait before the hunted animal. Shea swallowed hard and hesitated, realizing suddenly the man had sensed all along that the stones belonged to him. He had to do something quickly, or he would give himself away.

"They belong to me. The pouch and the stones are mine."

"Are they now?" Panamon Creel grinned wolfishly at the youth. "I don't see your name on the pouch. How did you come by them?"

"They were given to me by my father," Shea lied quickly. "I've had them for years. I carry them everywhere—a sort of good-luck piece. When the Gnomes captured me, they searched me and took the pouch and the stones away. But they are mine."

The scarlet-clad rescuer smiled faintly and opened the pouch, pouring the stones into his open palm, holding the pouch with the wicked-looking pike. He hefted them and held them up to the light, admiring their brilliant blue glow. Then he turned back to Shea, raising his eyebrows quizzically.

"What you say may be true, but it may be that you stole them. They look rather valuable to be carrying around as a good-luck charm. I think I should keep them until I am satisfied that you are the true owner."

"But I have to go—I have to meet my friends," Shea sputtered desperately. "I can't stay with you until you're certain I own the stones!"

Panamon Creel rose slowly to his feet and smiled down, tucking the pouch and its contents into his tunic.

"That should pose no problem. Just tell me where I can reach you, and I'll bring the stones to you there after I've checked out your story. I'll be down in the Southland in several months or so."

Shea was absolutely beside himself with anger, and he leaped to his feet in a rage.

"Why, you're nothing but a thief, a common highwayman!" he stormed, bracing the other defiantly.

Panamon Creel erupted suddenly into a fit of uncontrollable laughter, holding his sides in mirth. He finally regained control of himself, shaking his head in disbelief as the tears rolled down his broad face. Shea looked on in astonishment, unable to see what was so humorous about the accusation. Even the huge Rock Troll had stopped momentarily and turned to look at them, his placid face dark and expressionless.

"Shea, I have to admire a man who speaks his mind," exclaimed the stranger, still chuckling in delight. "No one could accuse you of being unperceptive!"

The irate Valeman started to make a hasty retort and then caught himself quickly as the facts of the situation recalled themselves sharply in his puzzled mind. What were these two strange companions doing in this part of the Northland? Why had they bothered to rescue him in the first place? How had they even known he was a prisoner of the small band of Gnomes? He realized the truth in an instant; it had been so obvious that he had overlooked it.

"Panamon Creel, the kind rescuer!" he mocked bitterly. "No wonder you found my remark so amusing. You and your friend are exactly what I called you. You are thieves, robbers, highwaymen! It was the stones you were after all along! How low can you be . . . ?"

"Watch your tongue, youngster!" The scarlet stranger leaped in front of him, brandishing the iron pike. The broad face was distorted in sudden hate, the constant smile suddenly villainous beneath the small mustache as anger flashed sharply in the dark eyes. "What you may think of us had best be kept to yourself. I've come a long way in this world, and no one has ever given me anything! Since this is so, I let no man take anything away!"

Shea backed away guardedly, terrified that he had foolishly overstepped his bounds with the unpredictable pair. Undoubtedly, his own rescue had been almost an afterthought on their part, their primary concern having been the theft of the Elfstones from the Gnome raiders. Panamon Creel was no one to fool around with, and a reckless tongue at this stage of the game could cost the Valeman his life. The tall thief stared balefully at his frightened captive a moment longer and then stepped back slowly, the angered features relaxing and a faint hint of his former good-naturedness returning in a quick smile.

"Why should we deny it, Keltset and I?" He swaggered backward and around a few paces, wheeling abruptly on Shea again. "We are wayfarers of fortune, he and I. Men who live by their wits and by their cunning—yet we are no different than other men, save in our methods. And perhaps our disdain for hypocrisy! All men are thieves in one way or another; we are simply the old-fashioned type, the honest type who are not ashamed of what they are."

"How did you happen on this camp?" Shea asked hesitantly, fearful of aggravating the temperamental man further.

"We came across their fire last night, just after sunset," the other replied easily, all traces of hostility gone. "I came down to the edge of the clearing for a closer look and saw my little yellow friends playing with those three blue gems. I saw you as well, all trussed up for delivery. So I decided to bring Keltset down and kill two birds with one stone—ah, ha, you see, I wasn't lying when I told you that I did not like to see a fellow Southlander in the hands of those devils!"

Shea nodded, happy to be free, but unsure whether he was better off now than when he had been a prisoner of the Gnomes.

"Quit worrying, friend." Panamon Creel recognized the unspoken fear. "We don't mean you any harm. We only want the stones—they'll bring a good price, and we can use the money. You're free to go back to where you came from anytime."

He turned away abruptly and walked over to the waiting Keltset, who was standing obediently next to a small pile of arms, clothing, and assorted articles of value that he had collected from the fallen Gnomes. The huge frame of the Troll dwarfed the normally large figure of his companion; the dark, barklike skin made him appear somewhat like a gnarled tree casting its shadow over the scarlet-clad human. The two conversed briefly, Panamon speaking in low tones to his giant friend while the other replied with sign language and nods of his broad head. They turned to the pile of goods, which the man shuffled through quickly, casting most of the effects aside as useless junk. Shea watched momentarily, uncertain what he should do next. He had lost the stones, and without them he was virtually defenseless in this savage land. He had lost his companions in the Dragon's Teeth, the only ones who would stand with him, the only ones who could really help him recover the stones. He had come so far that it was unthinkable to turn back now, even if he thought he could do so safely. The others in the company depended on him, and he would never desert Flick and Menion whatever the dangers involved.

Panamon Creel cast a short glance over his shoulder to see if the Valeman had made any move to leave, and a faint trace of surprise registered on his handsome face when he saw the youth still standing where he had left him.

"What are you waiting for?"

Shea shook his head slowly, indicating that he wasn't quite sure. The tall thief watched him a moment longer, and then waved him over with a short smile.

"Come on and have a bite to eat, Shea," he invited. "The least we can do is feed you before you start back for the Southland."

Fifteen minutes later the three were seated around a small campfire, watching strips of dried beef warm enticingly in the smoking heat. The mute Keltset sat silently next to the little Valeman, the deep eyes fixed on the smoking meat, the huge hands clasped childlike as he squatted before the small fire. Shea had an uncontrollable urge to reach out and touch the strange creature, to feel the rough, barklike skin. The features of the Troll were indescribably bland even from this close distance. The Troll never moved while the meat was cooking, but sat absolutely still like some immobile rock that time and the ages had passed by without changing. Panamon Creel glanced over once and noticed Shea casting a watchful eye on the huge creature. He smiled broadly, one hand coming across to clap the startled Valeman on the shoulder.

"He won't bite—long as he gets fed! I keep telling you the same thing, but you don't listen. That's youth for you—wild and fancy-free and no time for the old folks. Keltset is just like you and me, only bigger and quieter, which is what I like in a partner in this line of work. He does his job better than any man I've ever worked with, and I've worked with quite a few, I can tell you."

"He does what you tell him, I suppose?" Shea asked shortly.

"Sure he does, sure he does," came the quick answer; then the scarlet figure bent closer to the other's pale face, the iron pike coming up sharply in emphasis. "But don't get me wrong, boy, because I don't mean to say he's any kind of animal. He can think for himself when it's needed. But I was his friend when no one else would even look his way—no one! He's the strongest living thing I've ever seen. He could crush me without half thinking about it. But do you know what? I beat him, and now he follows me!"

He paused to judge the other's reaction, eyes wide with delight at the Valeman's startled look of disbelief. He laughed merrily and slapped his knee with exaggerated humor at the reaction he had drawn.

"I beat him with friendship, not strength! I respected him as a man, treated him as an equal, and for that cheap price, I won his loyalty. Hah, surprised you!"

Still chuckling at his thin attempt at humor, the thief lifted the strips of beef from the fire and held out the stick on which they rested to the silent Troll, who removed several and began munching hungrily. Shea helped himself slowly when offered and suddenly realized that he was starving. He couldn't even remember when he had eaten last, and gnawed ravenously at the tasty beef. Panamon Creel shook his head in amusement and offered the Valeman a second piece before taking one himself. The three ate in silence for several minutes before Shea ventured a further inquiry concerning his companions.

"What made you decide to become . . . robbers?" he asked guardedly.

Panamon Creel shot a quick look at him, arching his eyebrows in surprise.

"What do you care what the reasons were? Plan on writing our life story?" He paused and caught himself suddenly, smiling quickly at his own irritability. "There's no secret to it, Shea. I've never been much at making an honest living, never very good at common work. I was a wild kid, loved adventure, loved the outdoors—hated work. Then I lost my hand in an accident, and it became even harder to find work that would make me a comfortable living, get me what I wanted. I was deep in the Southland then, living in Talhan. I got in a little trouble and then a lot more. The next thing I knew I was roaming the four lands robbing for a living. The funny thing was I found myself so good at it that I couldn't quit. And I enjoyed it—all of it! So here I am, maybe not rich, but happy in the prime of my youth—or at least, my manhood."

"Don't you ever think about going back?" Shea persisted, unable to believe the man was being honest with himself. "Don't you ever think about a home and . . . ?"

"Please, let's not be maudlin, lad!" The other roared in laughter. "Keep this up and you'll have me in tears, begging for forgiveness on my tired old knees!"

He broke into such an uncontrollable fit of raucous guffaws that even the silent Troll glanced over in quiet contemplation for a moment before returning to his meal. Shea felt a fierce flush of indignation spreading over his face and turned slowly back to his food, chewing the beef with grinding bites of anger and embarrassment. After several moments the laughter died into small chuckles, the thief shaking his head in amusement as he tried to swallow a little food. Then without further prompting, he continued his narration in a quieter tone of voice.

"Keltset has a different story than mine, I want to make that clear. I had no reason to take up this kind of life, but he had every reason. He was a mute since birth, and the Trolls don't like deformed people. Kind of a joke on them, I guess. So they made life pretty rough for him, kicked him around and beat him when they were mad at anything that they couldn't take their anger out on directly. He was the butt of every joke, but he never fought back because those people were all he had. Then he became big, so big and strong that the others were frightened of him. One night some of the young ones tried to hurt him, really hurt him so he might go away, even die. But it didn't work out quite as they expected. They pushed him too far, and he fought back and killed three of them. As a result he was driven from the village, and an outcast Troll has no home once outside his own tribe or whatever they are. So he wandered around on his own until I found him."

He smiled faintly and looked over at the massive, placid face bent intently over the last several strips of beef, eating hungrily.

"He knows what we're doing, though, and I guess he knows that it's not honest work. But he's like a child who's been so badly mistreated that he has no respect for other people because they never did him any good. Besides, we stay in this part of the country where there's only Gnomes and Dwarfs—a Troll's natural enemies. We steer away from the deep Northland and seldom get south very far. We do all right."

He returned to his piece of beef, munching absently as he stared into the dying embers of the fire, poking them with the toe of his leather boot, the sparks rising in small showers and fading into dust. Shea finished his own food without further comment, wondering what he could possibly do to regain the Elfstones, wishing that he knew where the other members of the company were now. Moments later the meal was ended, and the scarlet-clad thief rose abruptly, scattering the embers of the fire with a swift kick of his boot. The massive Rock Troll rose with him and stood quietly waiting for his friend to make the next move, his great bulk towering over Shea. The Valeman stood at last and watched Panamon Creel gather up several small trinkets and a few weapons to place in a sack which he handed to Keltset to carry. Then he turned to his small captive and nodded shortly.

"It's been interesting knowing you, Shea, and I wish you good luck. When I think of the little gems in this pouch, I shall think of you. Too bad it couldn't work out so that you could save them, but at least you saved your life—or rather, I saved it. Think of the stones as a gift for services rendered. It may make losing them easier. Now you'd better be moving along if you plan to reach the safety of the Southland in the next several days. The city of Varfleet lies just to the south and west, and you'll find help there. Just stick to the open country."

He turned to leave, motioning Keltset to follow, and had taken several long strides before he glanced back over his shoulder. The Valeman had not moved, but was looking after the departing men as if in a trance. Panamon Creel shook his head in disgust and walked a bit farther, then stopped in annoyance and wheeled about, knowing the other was still standing immobile where he had left him.

"What's the matter with you?" he demanded angrily. "Now don't tell me that you have any foolish ideas about trailing us and trying to get the gems back? That would spoil a very nice relationship because I'd have to cut your ears off—maybe worse! Now get going, get out of here!"

"You don't understand what those stones mean!" Shea shouted desperately.

"I think I do," came the quick reply. "They mean that for a while Keltset and I will be more than merely poverty-stricken thieves. It means we won't have to steal or beg for a handout for quite some time. It means money, Shea."

Desperately, Shea dashed after the two robbers, unable to think of anything but recovering the precious Elfstones. Panamon Creel watched him approach in astonishment, certain that the Valeman was crazed to the point of daring to attack them to regain possession of the three blue gems. Never had he encountered such a persistent fellow in all his days. He had spared the lad's life and graciously given him his freedom, but still it didn't seem to be enough to satisfy him. Shea came to a panting halt several yards away from the two tall figures, and the thought flashed through his mind that he had reached the end of his rope. Their patience was exhausted and now they would dispose of him without further consideration.

"I didn't tell you the truth before," he gasped finally. "I couldn't . . . I don't know it all myself. But the stones are very important—not only to me, but to everyone in all the lands. Even to you, Panamon."

The scarlet robber looked at him with a mixture of surprise and distrust, the smile gone, but the dark eyes still free of anger. He said nothing, but stood motionless waiting for the exasperated Valeman to speak further.

"You've got to believe me!" Shea exclaimed vehemently. "There's more to this than you realize."

"You certainly seem to believe so," admitted the other flatly. He looked over at the huge Keltset, who stood at his elbow, and shrugged his incredulity at Shea's strange behavior. The Rock Troll made a quick move toward Shea, and the Valeman shrank back in terror; but Panamon Creel stopped his massive companion with a raised hand.

"Look, just grant me one favor," Shea pleaded desperately, grasping at any chance to gain a little time to think. "Take me north with you to Paranor."

"You must be mad!" cried the thief, aghast at the suggestion. "What possible reason could you have for going to that black fortress? It's extremely unfriendly country. You wouldn't last five minutes! Go home, boy. Go home to the Southland and leave me in peace."

"I've got to get to Paranor," the other insisted quickly. "That was where I was going when the Gnomes captured me. I have friends there—friends who will be searching for me. I have to join them at Paranor!"

"Paranor is an evil place, a spawning ground for Northland creatures even I would be afraid to run into!" Panamon said heatedly. "Besides, if you do have friends there, you probably plan to lead Keltset and me into some sort of trap so you can get your hands on the stones. That's your plan, isn't it? Forget it right now. Take my advice and turn south while you still can!"

"You're afraid, aren't you?" Shea sputtered angrily. "You're afraid of Paranor and afraid of my friends. You haven't the courage . . ."

He trailed off sharply as the deep fires of anger kindled explosively in the scarlet thief, the broad face flushing heatedly at the accusation. For a moment Panamon Creel stood motionless, his entire frame quivering with rage as he glared at the small Valeman. Shea stood his ground, gambling everything on this final plea.

"If you won't take me with you—just to Paranor—then I'll go alone and take my chances," he promised. He watched their reaction for a moment and then continued: "All I'm asking is to be taken just to the borders of Paranor. I won't ask you to go beyond; I won't lead you into a trap."

Panamon Creel shook his head once again in disbelief, the anger gone from his eyes and a faint smile playing over his tightened lips as he turned from the Valeman to look at the giant Rock Troll. He shrugged shortly and nodded.

"Why should we be worried?" he mused mockingly. "It's your neck on the block. Come on along, Shea."

The three strange companions journeyed northward through the rough hill country until midday, when they paused for a quick meal and a few welcome minutes of rest. The terrain of the country had remained changeless during the morning's march, a consistently rugged series of elevations and depressions that made traveling extremely difficult. Even the powerful Keltset was forced to climb and scramble with the two men, unable to find sure footing or level ground that would permit him to walk upright. The land was not only humped and misshapen, but also rather barren and unfriendly in appearance. The hills were grass-covered and dotted with brush and small trees, but they conveyed a lonely and wild emptiness to the travelers that caused them to feel uneasy and moody. The grass was a tall, whiplike weed so strong that it slapped at the men's pants legs with stinging swipes. When crushed down by their heavy boots, it lay matted only seconds before springing back into place. Upon looking back in the direction from which they had come, Shea could not tell from the appearance of the land that anyone had passed that way. The scattered trees were gnarled and bent, filled with small leaves, but giving the overall impression that they were nature's stepchildren, stunted at birth and left to survive in this lonely country as best they could. There was no sign at all of any animal or bird life, and since dawn, the three men had neither seen nor heard another living creature.

Conversation was not lacking, however. In fact, there were several times when Shea wished that Panamon Creel would tire of his own voice for a few minutes. The tall thief carried on a steady conversation with his companions, with himself, and on occasion with no one in particular, for the entire morning. He talked about everything imaginable, including a good many things about which he seemed to know nothing. The one topic of conversation he scrupulously avoided was Shea. He acted as if the Valeman were merely a comrade in arms, a fellow thief with whom he could freely speak about his own wild experiences without fear of reprimand. But he meticulously avoided mentioning Shea's background, the Elfstones, or the purpose of this journey. Apparently he had concluded that the best way to handle the matter was to get the bothersome Valeman to Paranor as quickly as possible, reunite him with his friends, and without further delay continue on. Shea had no idea where the two had intended to travel before encountering him. Perhaps even they had been uncertain of their destination. He listened attentively while the thief rambled on, interjecting comments of his own when he thought it appropriate or the other seemed interested in his opinion. But for the most part, he concentrated on the journey and tried to decide the best way to go about recovering the stones. The situation was somewhat untenable no matter how he went about it; both the thieves and he knew that he was going to try to get the stones away from them. The only question remaining was the method he would try. Shea was convinced that the clever Panamon Creel would merely toy with him, give him enough rope to find out how he planned to get the stones, and then gaily haul in the noose about the Valeman's neck.

Occasionally while they walked and conversed, Shea glanced at the silent Rock Troll, wondering what sort of person lay beneath the expressionless exterior. Panamon had said the Troll was a misfit, a creature spurned by his own people, a companion to the flashy thief because the man had proved to be his friend. This could be true, as trite as the tale seemed on first appraisal, but there was something about the Troll's bearing that caused the Valeman to question that he was an exile driven out by his own people. The Troll carried himself with undeniable dignity, head erect, the massive frame ramrod straight. He never spoke, apparently because he really was mute. Yet there was an intelligence in the deep-set eyes that led Shea to believe Keltset was far more complex than his companion had indicated. Just as with Allanon, Shea felt that Panamon Creel had not told him the whole truth. But unlike the Druid, the clever thief was probably a liar, and the youth felt that he should not believe anything he had been told. He was certain that he did not know the whole story behind Keltset, whether because Panamon had lied or because the man simply didn't know it. He was equally sure that the scarlet-clad adventurer, who had in one instant saved his life and in the next calmly stolen the precious Elfstones, was more than an ordinary road agent.

They finished the midday meal quickly. As Keltset packed up their cooking implements, Panamon explained to Shea that they were not far from the Jannisson Pass at the northern borders of the hill country. Once through this pass, they would cross the Plains of Streleheim to the west to reach Paranor. There they would part ways, the thief declared pointedly, and Shea could meet with his friends or go to the Druid's Keep as he saw fit. The Valeman nodded his understanding, catching the hint of eagerness in the other's voice, knowing that they expected him to make his move to recover the stones soon. He said nothing, however, and gave no indication that he suspected they were baiting him, but picked up what little gear he still had, to continue the journey. The three men wound their way slowly through the foothills toward the low mountains that had appeared ahead. Shea was certain the distant mountains on his left were an extension of the formidable Dragon's Teeth, but this new set of mountains appeared to be a completely different range, and it was between the two chains that the Jannisson Pass must lie. They were very near the Northland now, and for the Valeman there was no turning back.

Panamon Creel had launched into another in the seemingly never-ending series of tales about his adventures. Strangely, he seldom mentioned Keltset, another indication to Shea that the thief knew less about the Rock Troll than he professed. It was beginning to appear to Shea that the giant Troll was as much a mystery to his companion as he was to the Valeman. If they had lived together as thieves for two years, as Panamon had claimed, then some of the tales certainly ought to include Keltset. Moreover, while at first it had seemed to Shea that the Troll was a doglike follower of the crimson thief, it was beginning to appear on closer observation that he traveled with the man for entirely different reasons. It was not a conclusion Shea arrived at so much by listening to Panamon as from observing the mute conduct of the Troll. Shea was mystified by his proud bearing and detached attitude. Keltset had been swift and deadly in his extermination of the Gnome hunting party, but in retrospect it seemed almost as if he had done it because it had to be done—not to please his companion or to gain possession of the stones. Shea found it difficult to surmise who Kelt-set might be, but he was certain that he was not a downtrodden, shunned misfit who had been driven from his people as a hated outcast.

It was a particularly warm day, and Shea was beginning to perspire freely. The terrain had failed to level off at all, and traversing the stubborn, winding hills was laborious and slow. Panamon Creel talked on all the while, laughing and joking with Shea as if they were old friends, companions on the road to high adventure. He told him about the four lands; he had traveled them all, seen their people, studied their ways of life. Shea thought he seemed a bit vague about the Westland, and seriously doubted that the thief had learned much about the Elven people, but decided it would be unwise to pursue the matter. He listened dutifully to the tales of the women Panamon had met in his travels, including a standard narration about a beautiful king's daughter whom he had saved and fallen in love with, only to lose her when her father stepped between them and spirited her away to distant lands. The Valeman sighed with exaggerated pity, inwardly chuckling at the tale, as the anguished thief ended by confiding that to this day he continued his search for her. Shea remarked that he hoped Panamon would find her and she might persuade him to give up this way of life. The man looked at him sharply, studying the serious face, and for a few moments he was silent as he mulled the prospect over.

They reached the Jannisson Pass about two hours later. The pass was formed by a break at the meeting of the two mountain chains, a wide, easily accessible passage leading to the broad plainland beyond. The great mountain range coming up from the south was an extension of the towering Dragon's Teeth, but the northern range was unfamiliar to Shea. He knew that the Charnal Mountains, the home of the huge Rock Trolls, lay somewhere to the north of them, and this second range could be a southerly extension. Those desolate and relatively unexplored peaks had for centuries remained a vast wilderness inhabited solely by the ferocious and warlike Troll colonies. While the Rock Trolls were the largest of that breed, there were several other types of Trolls living in that sector of the Northland. If Keltset were any example of the Rock Trolls, then Shea imagined they must be a more intelligent people than Southlanders believed. It seemed somehow strange that his own countrymen should be so misinformed about another race inhabiting the same world. Even the textbooks he had studied when he was younger had described the Troll nations as ignorant and uncivilized.

Panamon called a sudden halt at the entrance to the wide pass and walked ahead several yards, peering cautiously up into the high slopes to either side, obviously wary of what might be waiting there. After several minutes' perusal, he ordered the stolid Keltset to investigate the pass to be certain it was safe for them to proceed. Quickly the giant Troll lumbered forward and was soon lost between the hills and rocks. Panamon suggested Shea sit down to wait, smiling that unforgivably smug smile that indicated the thief thought he was incredibly clever to take this added precaution to avoid any traps that friends of Shea might have arranged for him. While he felt safe enough keeping Shea with him, being reasonably certain that Shea posed no threat by himself, he was concerned that the Valeman might have friends powerful enough to cause trouble if they found the opportunity. While waiting for his companion to return, the garrulous adventurer decided to launch into still another wild tale of his hair-raising life as a road agent. Shea found this one, like the others, incredible and obviously exaggerated. Panamon seemed to enjoy telling these stories far more than anyone could possibly enjoy listening, as if each were the very first and not the five hundredth. Shea endured the tale in stoic silence, trying to look interested as he thought about what lay ahead. They had to be quite close to the borders of Paranor now, and once they reached that point, he would be left on his own. He would have to find his friends quickly if he expected to stay alive in this region of the country. The Warlock Lord and his hunters would be searching tirelessly for any trace of him, and if they reached him before he gained the protection of Allanon and the company, his death was certain. Still, it was possible that by this time they had taken possession of the Druid's Keep and seized the precious Sword of Shannara. Perhaps the victory was already won.

Keltset appeared suddenly in the pass and signaled for them to come forward. They hastened to his side and together the three proceeded. There was little cover in the Jannisson Pass that would hide an ambush party, and it was apparent that there would be no trouble at this point. There were a few stray clumps of boulders and a few narrow hillocks, but none of these was big enough to hide more than one or two men. The pass was quite long, and it took the three travelers almost an hour to reach the other end. But it was a pleasant walk and the time passed quickly. When they reached the northern entrance, they could see plains stretching northward and beyond these still another mountain range which appeared to run toward the west. The travelers marched out of the pass onto the smooth floor of the plains which were set in a pocket, surrounded on three sides in horseshoe fashion by mountains and forests and opening out to the west. The plains were sparsely covered with a thin, pale green grass which grew in shaggy tufts over the dry earthen land. There were small bushes, all only knee-high on Shea, and these were bent and gaunt in appearance. Apparently, even in the spring, these plains were never very green, and little life existed in the lonely expanse of country beyond Paranor.

Shea knew they were nearing their destination when Panamon turned the little group westward, keeping their line of march several hundred yards north of the forest and mountain bordering to their left, careful to protect against any surprise assaults. When the Valeman asked the scarlet-clad leader where they were in relation to Paranor, the thief only smiled slyly and assured him they were getting closer all the time. Further questioning was pointless, and the youth resigned himself to being kept in the dark as to where they were until the other decided he was ready to let his

uninvited guest go on alone. Instead, Shea turned his attention to the plains
ahead, their barren vastness awesome and fascinating to the Southlander. It
was an entirely new world for him, and while he was understandably afraid
for his life, he was determined that he would miss nothing. This was the
fabulous odyssey Flick and he had always dreamed they would someday
make, and while its end might find them both dead and forgotten, the
quest a failure and the Sword lost, still he would see it all in the time remaining to him.

By midafternoon, the three were sweating and tempers were growing
short in the steady heat of the open plainlands. Keltset walked slightly
apart from the other two, his pace steady and unwavering, his rough face
expressionless, his eyes dark and unfriendly in the hot, white sunlight.
Panamon had stopped talking and was interested only in completing the
day's march and being rid of Shea, whom he had begun to regard as an unnecessary burden. Shea was tired and sore, his limited stamina greatly
sapped by the two long days of constant travel. The three were walking
right into the face of the burning sun, unprotected and unshaded on the
open plains, their eyes squinting sharply in the piercing light. It became increasingly harder to distinguish the land ahead as the sun moved closer
toward the western horizon, and after a while Shea gave up trying, relying
on Panamon's skill to get them to Paranor. The travelers were drawing
closer to the end of the mountain range northward on their right, and it
appeared that where the mountain peaks ceased the plains opened into an
endless expanse. It was so vast that Shea could see the lateral line of the
horizon where the sky dropped to the parched earth. When he asked at
last if these were the Streleheim Plains, Panamon gave no immediate answer, but after a few moments' consideration nodded shortly.

Nothing further was said about their present location or Panamon
Creel's unspoken plans for Shea. They passed out of the horseshoe valley
onto the eastern borders of the Streleheim Plains, a wide, flat expanse
extending north and west. The land immediately before them, running
parallel to the cliff face and forest land on their left, was surprisingly hilly.
It was not a change in terrain that could be distinguished by one still in
the valley, but became distinct only when one was nearly on top of it.
There were even groves of small trees and dense stretches of brush farther
on, and . . . something else, something foreign to the land. All three travelers spotted it at the same moment, and Panamon signaled a sharp halt,
peering suspiciously into the distance. Shea squinted into the strong light
of the afternoon sun, shading his eyes with one hand. He saw a series of
strange poles set in the earth, and scattered about for several hundred yards
in every direction were heaps of colored cloth and bits of shining metal or
glass. He could just barely make out the movement of a number of small,
black objects amid the cloth and debris. Finally Panamon called out loudly
to whomever might be up ahead of them. To their shock, there was a flur-
ried rushing of raven-black wings, accompanied by a frightful shrieking of
disrupted scavengers as the black objects turned suddenly into great vul-
tures rising slowly and reluctantly as they scattered into the brilliant sun-

light. Panamon and Shea stood rooted in mute astonishment as the giant Keltset moved several yards closer and peered carefully ahead. A moment later, he wheeled about and motioned sharply to his watchful comrade. The scarlet thief nodded soberly.

"There's been a battle of some sort," he announced curtly. "Those are dead men up there!"

The three moved forward toward the grisly scene of battle. Shea hung back slightly, suddenly afraid that the still, tattered forms might be his friends. The strange poles became distinct after the men had gone only several yards; they were lances and standards of battle. The bright bits of light were the blades of swords and knives, some discarded by fleeing men, others still clenched by the dead hands of their fallen owners. The cloth heaps became men, their still, blood-soaked forms sprawled in death, baking slowly in the white heat of the sun. Shea choked as the smell of death struck his nostrils for the first time and his ears caught the sound of flies buzzing busily about the human carcasses. Panamon looked back and smiled grimly. He knew that the Valeman had never before seen death at close range, and it would be a lesson he would not forget.

Shea fought the sickening feeling creeping through his stomach and forced himself to move with the other two onto the battleground. Several hundred bodies lay on the little stretch of rolling land, sprawled carelessly in death. There was no movement anywhere; they were all dead. From the random scattering of the bodies and the lack of any single concentration of men, Panamon quickly concluded in his own mind that it had been a long, bitter struggle to the death—no quarter asked and none given. He recognized the Gnome standards immediately, and the gnarled yellow bodies were easily distinguishable. But it was not until he had looked closely at several huddled forms that he realized that the opposing force had been composed of Elven warriors.

Finally Panamon halted in the middle of the slain men, uncertain what he should do next. Shea could only stare in horror at the carnage, his shocked gaze moving robotlike from one dead face to the next, from Gnome to Elf, from the raw, open wounds to the bloodied ground. At that moment, he knew what death really meant and he was afraid. There was no adventure in it, no sense of purpose or choice, nothing but a sickening disgust and shock. All those men had died for some senseless reason, died perhaps without ever knowing exactly what they had fought to accomplish. Nothing was worth such terrible slaughter—nothing.

A sudden movement by Keltset snapped his attention back to his companions, and he saw the Troll pick up a fallen standard, its pennant torn and bloodied, the pole broken in half. The insignia on the pennant was a crown seated over a spreading tree surrounded by a wreath of boughs. Keltset seemed very excited and gestured vigorously to Panamon. The other frowned sharply and hurriedly made a quick study of the faces of the nearby bodies, working his way outward from his companions in a widening circle. Keltset looked around anxiously, suddenly stopping as his deep-set eyes came to rest on Shea, apparently fascinated by something he saw in the little Valeman's face. A moment later Panamon was back at his side, an unusually worried expression clouding his broad features.

"We've got real trouble here, friend Shea," he announced solemnly, resting his hands determinedly on his hips and planting his feet. "That standard is the banner of the royal Elven house of Elessedil—the personal staff of Eventine. I can't find his body among the dead, but that doesn't make me feel any easier. If anything has happened to the Elven king, it could start a war of unbelievable proportions. The whole country will go up in smoke!"

"Eventine!" exclaimed Shea fearfully. "He was guarding the northern borders of Paranor in case . . ."

He caught himself abruptly, afraid that he had given himself away, but Panamon Creel was still talking and apparently hadn't heard.

"It doesn't make any sense—Gnomes and Elves fighting out here in the middle of nowhere. What would bring Eventine this far away from his own land? They must have been fighting for something. I can't under . . ." He paused with the thought left hanging, unspoken in the silence. Suddenly he stared at Shea.

"What did you just say? What was that about Eventine?"

"Nothing," the Valeman stammered fearfully. "I didn't say . . ."

The tall thief snatched the hapless Valeman by his tunic front, dragging him close and raising him bodily off the ground, until their faces were only inches away.

"Don't try to be clever, little man!" The flushed, angered face seemed gigantic and the fierce eyes were narrowed with suspicion. "You know something about all of this—now talk. All along I've suspected you knew a lot more than you were telling about those stones and the reason those Gnomes bothered to take you prisoner. Now your time for fooling around is over. Out with it!"

But Shea would never know what his response would have been. As he hung in midair, struggling violently in the powerful thief's ironhanded grip, a huge black shadow suddenly fell over them and then passed on in a great rustling of wings as a monstrous shape descended from the late-afternoon skies. Its giant, black bulk swooped slowly, gracefully to the battlefield only yards away from them, and in horror Shea felt the familiar chilling fear surge through him at the sight of its deathlike form. Panamon Creel, still angered, but now bewildered by the sudden appearance of this creature, lowered Shea to the earth abruptly and turned to face the strange newcomer. Shea stood on shaking legs, his blood turned to ice, his senses raw and distorted with terror, the last vestiges of his courage gone. The creature was one of the dreaded Skull Bearers of the Warlock Lord! There was no time left to run; they had found him at last.

The cruel red eyes of the creature passed quickly over the giant Troll, who had remained motionless to one side, stopped for a moment on the scarlet thief, then passed on to the little Valeman, burning into him, probing his scattered thoughts. Panamon Creel, while still bewildered at the sight of this winged monster, was nevertheless not in the least panicked. He turned fully about to face the evil being, the broad, devilish grin spreading slowly over his flushed countenance as he raised one arm and pointed in warning.

"Whatever manner of creature you might be, keep your distance," he warned sharply. "My concern is with this man alone, and not . . ."

The burning eyes fastened hatefully on him, and suddenly he was unable to continue. He stared at the black creature in shock and surprise.

"Where is the Sword, mortal?" the voice rasped menacingly. "I can sense its presence. Give it to me!"

Panamon Creel stared uncomprehendingly at the dark speaker for a long moment, then shot a sharp look at the frightened face of Shea. For the first time, he realized that for some unknown reason this terrible creature was the Valeman's enemy. It was a dangerous moment.

"It is useless to deny you have it!" The grating voice pierced the distressed mind of the thief. "I know it is here among you, and I must have it. It is useless to fight me. The battle is over for you. The last heir to the Sword has long since been taken and destroyed. You must give me the Sword!"

For once, Panamon Creel was speechless. He had no idea what the huge black creature was talking about, but he realized that there was no point in trying to tell him that. The winged monster was determined to finish them all anyway, and the time for any explanations was past. The tall thief raised his left hand and stroked the tips of his small mustache with the deadly pike. He smiled bravely, looking aside fleetingly at the motionless form of his giant companion. They both knew instinctively that this would be a battle to the death.

"Do not be foolish, mortals!" The command rang out in a sharp hiss. "I care nothing for you—only the Sword. I can destroy you easily—even in daylight."

Suddenly Shea saw a glimmer of hope. Allanon had once said that the power of the Skull Bearers faded with the light of day. Perhaps they were not invincible while the sun shone. Perhaps the two battle-hardened thieves would have a chance. But how could they expect to destroy something that was not mortal, but only the spirit of a dead soul, a wraith of deathless existence embodied in physical form? For a few moments no one moved, and then abruptly the creature took a step forward. Immediately Panamon Creel's good right hand unsheathed the broadsword at his side in a lightninglike motion and the thief crouched for the attack. The great form of Keltset moved forward a few paces at the same instant, changing from a motionless statue into an iron-muscled fighting machine, the heavy mace in one hand, the thick legs braced for the assault. The Skull Bearer hesitated and his burning eyes fastened momentarily on the face of the approaching Rock Troll, studying the huge being closely for the first time. Then the crimson eyes went wide in astonishment.

"Keltset!"

Only an instant remained to ponder how the Bearer could have known the mute giant—a split second of astonished disbelief in the creature's eyes, mirroring similar incomprehension in the eyes of Panamon Creel, and then the huge Troll attacked with blinding speed. The mace hurtled through the air, powered by Keltset's massive right arm, striking the black Skull creature directly in the chest with a sickening crunch. Panamon was already leaping forward, pike and sword blade sweeping downward toward the Bearer's chest and neck. But the deadly Northland creature was not to be so easily finished. Recovering from the blow dealt by the mace, it parried Panamon's weapons with one clawed hand, knocking the man sprawling. In the next instant the burning eyes began to smolder, and bolts of searing red light shot out at the dazed thief. He lunged quickly to one side, and the bolts caught him only a glancing blow, singeing his scarlet tunic and knocking him down again. Before the attacker could find his target for a second assault, the huge form of Keltset was upon him, bearing him heavily to the earth. Even the comparatively large size of the winged monster was dwarfed in comparison to the massive Rock Troll as the two rolled and battled over the bloodied ground. Panamon was still on his knees, shaking his dazed head, trying to regain his senses. Realizing that he had to do something, Shea rushed to the fallen thief and grabbed one arm in desperation.

"The stones!" he begged wildly. "Give me the stones, and I can help!"

The battered face turned up to him for a moment, and then the familiar look of anger crept into his eyes, and he shoved the Valeman rudely away.

"Shut up and keep out of this," he roared, climbing unsteadily to his feet. "No tricks now, friend. Just stay put!"

Retrieving his fallen sword, he rushed to the aid of his giant companion, trying vainly to strike a solid blow at the caped Skull Bearer. For long minutes the three struggled fiercely back and forth across the rolling battleground, thrashing madly over the still bodies of the fallen Gnomes and Elves. Panamon was not nearly as strong as the other two, but he was quick and extremely durable, bouncing away from the blows struck at him, dancing nimbly aside when the Northlander sent the reddish bolts flashing his way. The incredible strength of Keltset was proving to be a match for even the spirit powers of the Skull creature, and the evil being was becoming desperate. The rough Troll skin was singed and burned in a dozen places from the fire that struck it, but the giant merely shrugged the powerful jolts aside and fought on. Shea desperately wanted to help, but he was dwarfed by their power and size, and his weapons were ridiculously inadequate. If only he could get the stones . . .

At last the two mortals began to tire in the face of the repeated, inexhaustible assaults from the spirit creature. Their blows were not having any lasting effect and they began slowly to realize that human strength alone could not destroy the attacker. They were losing the battle. Suddenly the valiant Keltset stumbled and fell to one knee. Instantly the Skull creature lashed out with one clawed limb, slashing the unprotected Troll from neck to waist, knocking him backward to the earth. Panamon cried out in fury and struck wildly at the spirit creature, but his blows were parried, and in his haste he dropped his guard and left himself momentarily vulnerable. The emissary of the Warlock Lord struck viciously, one arm knocking aside the thief's piked hand as the narrowed eyes sent their fiery blasts directly into the man's chest. The deadly bolts seared the hapless Panamon Creel about the face and arms, and burned right through the chest covering with such force that he was knocked unconscious. The Skull Bearer would have finished him then had not Shea, disregarding his own fears at the other's grave peril, thrown a piece of a lance at the attacker's unprotected head, striking it full in the evil face. The clawed hands came up too late to ward off the painful blow, and they gripped the blackened visage in fury, trying angrily to recover. Panamon was still lying motionless on the ground, but the durable Keltset was back on his feet, seizing the Skull creature in an agonizing headlock, desperately trying to crush the life out of it.

There were only seconds left to act before the deadly monster was free again. Shea rushed to Panamon Creel's side, shouting at him to get up. The battered figure responded with inhuman courage, but fell back a moment later, blinded and exhausted. Shea pleaded with him, shaking him into consciousness, begging him to give him the stones. Only the stones could help now, the Valeman cried desperately! They were the only chance for survival! He glanced back at the two dark combatants, and to his horror he saw that Keltset was slowly losing his hold on the spirit creature. In seconds the evil being would be free, and they would all be finished. Then abruptly the little leather pouch was thrust into his hand by the bloodied fist of Panamon, and he had the precious stones once more.

Leaping clear of the fallen thief, the little Valeman tore open the drawstrings to the leather pouch and emptied the three blue stones into his open hand. At that moment the Skull Bearer broke free from Keltset's powerful grip and turned to finish the battle. Shea yelled wildly, holding the stones stretched forth toward the attacker, praying for their strange power to aid him now. The blinding blue glow spread outward just as the creature turned. Too late the Skull Bearer saw the heir to Shannara bring the power of the Elfstones to life. Too late he focused his burning eyes on the Valeman, the red bolts of searing fire flashing menacingly. The great blue light blocked and shattered the attack, slicing through in a powerful, blazing surge of energy to reach the crouched black figure beyond. The light struck the immobile Skull creature with a sharp crackle, holding him fast and draining the dark spirit from the mortal shell as the creature writhed in agony and screamed its loathing of the power destroying it. Keltset came to his feet in a bound, picked up a fallen lance, reared back his giant frame, the arms extended high, and with a lunge shoved the spear completely through the creature's caped back. The Northlander shuddered horribly, twisting almost completely about with one final shriek, and then slid slowly to the earth, the black body crumbling into dust as it sank. In another second it was gone, and only a small pile of black ashes remained.

Shea stood motionless, the stones extended, their piercing blue light still concentrated on the dust. Then the dust stirred in still another shudder and from its midst rose a whipish black cloud that shot upward like a thin stream of smoke and disappeared into the air. The blue light abruptly ceased and the battle was ended, the three mortals positioned like statues in the silence and emptiness of the bloodied ground.

For long seconds no one moved, still stunned by the sudden finality of the violent combat. Shea and Keltset stood staring at the small pile of black ashes as if waiting for it to come back to life. Panamon Creel lay wearily on the earth to one side, propped up on one elbow, his singed eyes trying vainly to grasp what had just transpired. Finally Keltset stepped forward gingerly and prodded the ashes of the Skull Bearer with one foot, stirring them about to see if anything had been missed. Shea watched quietly, mechanically replacing the three Elfstones in the leather pouch and dropping it back into the front of his tunic. Remembering Panamon, he turned quickly to check on the injured thief, but the durable Southlander was already struggling to a sitting position, his deep brown eyes fixed wonderingly on the Valeman. Keltset hastened over and gently raised his companion to his feet. The man was burned and cut, his face and bared chest blackened and raw in places, but nothing seemed to be broken. He stared at Keltset as well for a moment, then shrugged off the other's strong arm and tottered over to a waiting Shea.

"I was right about you after all," he growled, breathing heavily and shaking his broad head. "You did know a lot more than you were telling—especially about those stones. Why didn't you tell me the truth from the start?"

"You wouldn't listen," Shea alibied shortly. "Besides, you didn't tell me the truth about yourself—or Keltset either." He paused to glance sharply at the massive Troll. "I don't think you know very much about him."

The battered face stared at the Valeman incredulously, then the broad smile slowly spread over his handsome features. It was as if the scarlet thief suddenly saw new humor in the whole situation, but Shea thought he caught a hint of grudging respect in the dark eyes for his candid evaluation.

"You may be right. I'm beginning to think I don't know anything about him." The smile turned into a hearty laugh, and the thief looked sharply at the rough, expressionless face of the great Rock Troll. Then he looked back to Shea.

"You saved our lives, Shea, and that's a debt we can never repay. But I'll start by saying that the stones are yours to keep. I'll never argue that point again. More than that, you have my promise that should the need ever arise, my sword and my skill, such as it is, shall be in your service at a word."

He paused wearily to catch his breath, still shaken badly from the blows he had received. Shea stepped hurriedly forward to offer his aid, but the tall thief held him away, shaking his head negatively.

"I assume that we shall be great friends, Shea," he murmured seriously.

"Still, we cannot be friends when we hide things from each other. I think you owe me some sort of explanation about those stones, about that creature that nearly put an end to my illustrious career, and about this confounded sword I've never seen. In return, I shall enlighten you on a few, ah, misunderstandings concerning Keltset and myself. Do you agree?"

Shea frowned at him suspiciously, trying to read behind the battered visage into the man himself. Finally he nodded affirmatively and even managed a short smile.

"Good for you, Shea," Panamon commended heartily, clapping the Valeman on his slender shoulder. A second later, the tall thief had collapsed, weakened by loss of blood and dizzy from trying to move about too quickly. The other two rushed to his side, and despite protestations that he was quite all right, forced him to remain in a supine position while the giant Keltset cleaned his face with a wetted cloth like any mother would a small, injured child. Shea was amazed at the Troll's quick change from a nearly indestructible fighting machine to a gentle, concerned nurse. There was something very extraordinary about him, and Shea was certain that in some strange way Keltset was connected with the Warlock Lord and the quest for the Sword of Shannara. It had been no accident that the Skull Bearer had known the Rock Troll. The two had encountered each other before—and had not parted as friends.

Panamon was not unconscious, but it was clear that he was not yet in any condition to travel very far on his own legs. He tried vainly to rise several times, but the watchful Keltset gently pushed him back. The irascible thief swore vehemently and demanded to be let to his feet, all to no avail. Finally, he realized that he was getting nowhere and asked that he be taken out of the sun to rest for a while. Shea looked around the barren plainland and quickly concluded they would find no shelter there. The only shade within reasonable walking distance was to the south—the forests surrounding the Druid's Keep within the borders of Paranor. Panamon had previously indicated that he would not go anywhere near Paranor, but the decision was no longer entirely his to make. Shea pointed to the forests to the south, less than a mile's walk, and Keltset nodded his agreement. The injured man saw what Shea was suggesting and cried out furiously that he would not be carried into those forests even if it meant he would die where he lay. Shea tried to reason with him, assuring him that they would face no danger from his companions if by chance they managed to find them, but the thief seemed more disturbed by the strange rumors he had heard concerning Paranor. Shea had to laugh at this, recalling Panamon's boasts of all the past hair-raising perils he had survived. While the two men conversed, Keltset had risen slowly to his feet and was scanning the land about them, apparently in idle speculation. The two were still talking when he bent down to them and gave a sharp signal to Panamon. The thief started, the color drained from his face as he nodded shortly. Shea started to rise in apprehension, but the thief's strong hand held him down.

"Keltset has just spotted something moving in the brush to the south of us. He can't tell from here what it is; it's just on the fringes of this battlefield, about halfway between us and the forest."

Shea immediately turned ashen.

"Get your stones ready in case we need them," the other ordered quietly, an unmistakable indication that he thought it might be a second Skull Bearer lurking in the cover of the brush, waiting for sundown and a chance to catch them off guard.

"What are we going to do?" Shea asked fearfully, clutching the little pouch.

"Get him before he gets us—what other choice do we have?" Panamon declared irritably, motioning to Keltset to pick him up.

The obedient giant bent down and carefully lifted Panamon in the cradle of his two massive arms. Shea retrieved the wounded thief's fallen broadsword and followed the slowly departing form of Keltset, who proceeded southward with relaxed, easy strides. Panamon talked steadily as they walked, calling on Shea to hurry, chiding Keltset on being too rough in his duty as bearer of the wounded. Shea could not bring himself to be quite so relaxed, and was content with bringing up the rear, glancing uneasily from side to side as they moved southward, searching vainly for some sign of movement that might indicate where the danger lay. In his right hand he clutched tightly the leather pouch with the invaluable Elfstones, their only weapon against the power of the Warlock Lord. They were about a hundred yards from the scene of their battle with the Skull Bearer when Panamon called a sudden halt, complaining bitterly of an injured shoulder. Gently, Keltset lowered his burden to the ground and stood up.

"My shoulder is never going to stand such wanton disregard of its tissues and bones," growled Panamon Creel irritably, and looked meaningfully at Shea.

Instantly the Valeman knew that this was the place, and his hands shook as he loosened the strings on the pouch and withdrew the Elfstones. A moment later Keltset stood leisurely beside the still-muttering thief, the great mace held loosely in one hand. Shea glanced around hastily, his eyes coming to rest directly on the huge clump of brush immediately to the left of the other two. His heart jumped to his throat as one section of the brush moved ever so slightly.

Then Keltset made his move. With a sharp lunge he whirled about, leaped into the center of the brush, and was lost from view.

20

What followed was complete pandemonium. A terrible high-pitched shriek sounded from the bushes and the entire mass of shrubbery shook violently. Panamon struggled wildly to his knees, calling to Shea to throw him the great broadsword which the fear-struck Valeman still clutched tightly in his left hand. Shea stood frozen in place, his other hand clasping the powerful Elfstones in readiness, waiting in terror for the assault that surely would come from the unknown creature in the brush. Panamon finally fell back in hopeless exhaustion, unable to get Shea's attention and incapable of walking over to where he stood. There were a few more cries from the heavy bushes, some vague thrashing within, and then silence. A moment later the durable Keltset emerged, the heavy mace still held in one lowered hand. In the other was the squirming, twisting body of a Gnome, his neck held fast in the iron grip of the Troll. The gnarled yellow body appeared childlike next to the huge frame of its captor, the arms and legs moving all at once in different directions like snakes caught by their tails. The Gnome was one of the familiar hunters, clothed in a leather tunic, hunting boots, and sword belt. The sword was missing, and Shea correctly surmised that the struggle in the bushes involved the disarming of the little fellow. Keltset came over to Panamon, who had managed to raise himself back up to a sitting position, and dutifully held forth the struggling captive for inspection.

"Let me go, let me go, curse you!" the thrashing Gnome cried venomously. "You have no right! I have done nothing—I'm not even armed, I tell you. Let me go!"

Panamon Creel looked at the little creature humorously, shaking his head in relief. Finally, as the Gnome continued to plead, the thief burst out laughing.

"What a terrible foe, Keltset! Why, he might have destroyed us all had you not captured him. That must have been a fearful struggle! Ha, ha, I can't believe it. And we were afraid of another of those winged black monsters!"

Shea was not quite so inclined to be amused by the incident, recalling clearly the close calls the company had already had with the little yellow creatures while traveling through the Anar. They were dangerous and crafty— a foe whom he did not regard as harmless. Panamon looked over and, upon spying the serious countenance, ceased his chiding of the captive and turned his attention to Shea.

"Do not be angry, Shea. It's more habit than stupidity when I laugh at these things. I laugh at them to stay a sane man. But enough of all this. What do we do with our little friend, eh?"

The Gnome stared fearfully at the no longer laughing man, the large eyes wide as the insistent voice died away to a low whine.

"Please, let me go," he begged subserviently. "I will go away and say nothing to anyone about you. I will do whatever you say, good friends. Just let me go."

Keltset still held the hapless Gnome by the scruff of his neck about a foot off the ground in front of Shea and Panamon, and the little fellow was beginning to choke violently from the tight clasp. Seeing the prisoner's plight, Panamon at last motioned for the Rock Troll to lower his victim to the ground and release his grip. Pausing for a moment's serious contemplation of the Gnome's eager plea, the thief looked over at Shea and winked quickly, turning back to the captive sharply and snapping the pike at the end of his left arm up to the yellow throat.

"I can see no reason for permitting you to live, let alone go free, Gnome," he announced menacingly. "I think it would be best for all concerned if I just cut your throat right here and now. Then none of us would have to worry about you further."

Shea did not believe the thief was serious, but his voice sounded as if he were in deadly earnest. The terrified Gnome gulped and held forth his hands in a final desperate cry for mercy. He whined and cried so that Shea finally became almost embarrassed for him. Panamon made no move, but only sat there staring into the unfortunate fellow's horror-stricken face.

"No, no, I beg you, don't kill me," the frantic Gnome pleaded, his wide green eyes shifting from one face to the next. "Please, please let me live—I can be of use to you—I can help! I can tell you about the Sword of Shannara! I can even get it for you."

Shea started involuntarily at the unexpected mention of the Sword, and he placed a restraining hand on Panamon's wide shoulder.

"So you can tell us about the Sword, can you?" The icy voice of the thief sounded only slightly interested, and he ignored Shea completely. "What can you tell us?"

The wiry yellow frame relaxed slightly, and the eyes returned to normal size, shifting about eagerly, seizing on any chance to stay alive. Yet Shea saw something else there, something he could not quite define. It was almost a fervid cunning, revealed as the Gnome momentarily relaxed his carefully masked feelings. A second later it was gone, replaced by a look of total subjugation and helplessness.

"I can lead you to the Sword if you wish," he whispered harshly as if he were afraid someone would hear. "I can take you to where it is—if you let me live!"

Panamon moved the sharp iron tip of his piked hand back from the throat of the cringing Gnome, leaving just a small trace of blood on the yellow neck. Keltset had not moved and gave no indication that he had any interest in what was happening. Shea wanted to warn Panamon how im-

portant that Gnome might be if there was even the slightest chance of
finding the Sword of Shannara, but he realized the thief preferred to keep
the captive Gnome guessing. The Valeman could not be sure how much
Panamon Creel knew about the legend; so far, he had shown little concern
with the races generally and had not indicated he knew anything about
the history of the Sword of Shannara. The grim features of the thief relaxed briefly and a faint smile crossed his lips as he eyed the still-quivering
captive.

"Is this Sword valuable, Gnome?" he queried easily, almost slyly. "Can
I sell it for gold?"

"It is priceless to the right people," the other promised, nodding eagerly. "There are those who would pay anything, give anything to get possession of it. In the Northland . . ."

He ceased talking abruptly, afraid that he had already said too much.
Panamon smiled wolfishly and nodded to Shea.

"This Gnome says it could be worth money to us," he mocked quietly,
"and the Gnome wouldn't lie, would you, Gnome?" The yellow head
shook vehemently. "Well, then, perhaps we should let you live long enough
to prove you have something of value to barter for your worthless hide. I
wouldn't want to throw away a chance to make money simply to satisfy my
inborn desire to cut the throat of a Gnome when I get one within my
grasp. What do you think, Gnome?"

"You understand perfectly, you know my value," whined the little fellow, fawning at the knees of the smiling thief. "I can help; I can make you
rich. You can count on me."

Panamon was smiling broadly now, his big frame relaxed and his good
hand on the Gnome's small shoulder as if they were old friends. He patted
the stooped shoulder a few times, as if to put the captive at ease, and nodded reassuringly, looking from the Gnome to Keltset to Shea and back
again for several long seconds.

"Tell us what you're doing way out here by yourself, Gnome," Panamon urged a moment later. "By the way, what are you called?"

"I am Orl Fane, a warrior of the Pelle tribe of the upper Anar," he answered eagerly. "I . . . I was on a courier mission from Paranor when I
came upon this battlefield. They were all dead, all of them, and there was
nothing I could do. Then I heard you and I hid. I was afraid you were . . .
Elves."

He paused and looked fearfully at Shea, noting the youth's Elven features with dismay. Shea made no move, but waited to see what Panamon
would do. Panamon just looked understandingly at the Gnome and smiled
in friendly fashion.

"Orl Fane—of the Pelle tribe," the tall thief repeated slowly. "A great
tribe of hunters, brave men." He shook his head as if deeply regretting
something and turned again to the mystified Gnome. "Orl Fane, if we are
going to be of any service to one another, we must have mutual trust. Lies
can only hinder the purpose binding our new partnership. There was a

Pelle standard on the battlefield—the standard of your tribe in the Gnome nation. You must have been with them when they fought."

The Gnome stood speechless, a mixture of fear and doubt creeping slowly back into his shifting green eyes. Panamon continued to smile easily at him.

"Just look at yourself, Orl Fane—covered with specks of blood and a bad cut on your forehead at the hairline. Why hide the truth from us? You had to be here, isn't that right?" The persuasive voice coaxed a quick nod out of the other, and Panamon laughed almost merrily. "Of course you were here, Orl Fane. And when you were set upon by the Elf people, you fought until you were wounded, perhaps knocked unconscious, eh, and you lay here until just before we came along. That's the truth of the matter, isn't it?"

"Yes, that's the truth," the Gnome agreed eagerly now.

"No, that's not the truth!"

There was a moment of stunned silence. Panamon was still smiling, and Orl Fane was caught between emotions, a trace of doubt still in his eyes, a half-smile forming on his lips. Shea looked at both curiously, unable to follow exactly what was happening.

"Listen to me, you lying little rodent." The smile was gone from Panamon's face, the features hardened as he spoke, the voice cold and menacing once more. "You have lied from the beginning! A member of the Pelle would wear their insignia—you wear none. You weren't wounded in battle; that little scratch on your forehead is nothing! You are a scavenger—a deserter, aren't you? Aren't you?"

The thief had seized the terrified Gnome by the front of his hunting tunic and was shaking him so hard that Shea could hear his teeth rattle with the force. The wiry captive was struggling to catch his breath, gasping in disbelief at this sudden turn of events.

"Yes, yes!" The admission was throttled out of him at last, and Panamon released him with a quick thrust backward into the grip of the watchful Keltset.

"A deserter from your own people." Panamon spat the words out in distaste. "The lowest form of life that walks or crawls is a deserter. You've been scavenging this battlefield for valuables from the dead. Where are they, Orl Fane? Shea, check in those bushes where he was hiding."

As Shea moved toward the brush, the struggling Gnome let out the most frightful shriek of dismay imaginable, causing the youth to believe Keltset had twisted his neck off. But Panamon just smiled and nodded for the Valeman to proceed, certain now that the Gnome had indeed hidden something in the bushes. Shea pushed his way past the thick branches into the center of the clump, searching carefully for any sign of a cache. The ground and the limbs in the center were badly torn up from the struggle between Keltset and the Gnome, and there was nothing immediately visible. He hunted about unsuccessfully for several minutes. He was just about to give up, when his eye caught a glimpse of something half buried at the far end of the bushes beneath leaves, branches, and dirt. Using his short hunting knife and his hands, he quickly uncovered a long sack containing metal objects that rattled against one another as he worked. He called out to Panamon that he had discovered something, which immediately set off another series of whining cries from the distraught captive. When the sack was uncovered, he pulled it out of the brush into the fading afternoon sunlight and dropped it before the others. Orl Fane was in a frenzy by this time, and Keltset was forced to use both hands just to hold him.

"Whatever's in here is certainly important to our little friend." Panamon grinned at Shea and reached for the sack.

Shea moved to his side and peered over the broad shoulders as Panamon untied the leather thong binding the top and reached eagerly into the dark interior. Changing his mind suddenly, the scarlet thief removed his hand and, grabbing the other end of the sack, turned it upside down and poured the contents onto the open earth. The others stared at the cache, looking from item to item curiously.

"Junk," growled Panamon Creel after a moment's consideration. "Just junk. The Gnome is too stupid even to bother with valuable things."

Shea looked at the contents of the sack without answering. Nothing but assorted daggers, knives, and swords in the collection, some still in their leather sheaths. A few pieces of cheap jewelry sparkled in the sunlight, and there were one or two Gnome coins, practically worthless to anyone but a Gnome. It certainly appeared to be useless junk, but the whining Orl Fane had evidently considered it worth something to him. Shea shook his head in pity for the little Gnome. He had lost everything when he turned deserter, and all he had to show for it were these few worthless pieces of metal and cheap jewelry. Now it seemed certain that he would lose his life as well for having dared to lie to the volatile Panamon Creel.

"Hardly worth dying for, Gnome," Panamon growled, nodding shortly to Keltset, who raised the heavy mace to finish the hapless fellow.

"No, no, wait, wait a minute, please," the Gnome cried, his voice edged with a harsh note of desperation. It was the end for him; this was his final plea. "I didn't lie about the Sword—I swear I didn't! I can get it for you. Don't you realize what the Sword of Shannara is worth to the Dark Lord?"

Without thinking, Shea put out a hand to grasp Keltset's massive arm. The giant Troll seemed to understand. Slowly he lowered the mace and looked curiously at Shea. Panamon Creel opened his mouth angrily and then hesitated. He wanted to learn the truth behind Shea's presence in the Northland, and the secret of this Sword evidently had much to do with it. He stared momentarily at the Valeman, then turned back to Keltset and shrugged disinterestedly.

"We can always kill you later, Orl Fane, if this is another deception. Put a rope around his worthless neck and bring him along, Keltset. Shea, if you would give me a hand up and an arm to lean on, I think I can make it to the woods. Keltset will keep a close watch over our clever little deserter."

Shea helped the injured Panamon to his feet and tried to support him as he took a few careful test steps. Keltset tied Orl Fane and placed a length of rope about his neck so that he could be led. The Gnome allowed himself to be bound without complaining, though he was visibly distraught about something. Shea imagined that the fellow was still lying when he said he knew where the Sword could be found and was desperately trying to figure out how he would get free from his captors before they discovered his treachery and killed him. While Shea would not himself kill the Gnome, nor even agree to have it done, nevertheless he felt little compassion for the deceitful creature. Orl Fane was a coward, a deserter, a scavenger—a man without a people or a country. Shea was certain now that the whining, groveling attitude the Gnome had displayed earlier was a carefully studied shield for the crafty, desperate creature that lay hidden beneath. Orl Fane would cut their throats without the slightest compunction if he thought there would be no danger to himself. Shea almost wished that Keltset had ended their worries a few minutes earlier by finishing the fellow. Shea would have felt easier in his own mind.

Panamon signaled that he was ready to proceed toward the woodland, but before they had taken two steps, the whining pleas of Orl Fane had stopped them. The unhappy Gnome refused to go farther if he were not allowed to keep his sack and its treasures. He set up such a stubborn howl of protest that Panamon was again on the verge of bashing in the hateful yellow head.

"What does it matter, Panamon?" Shea finally asked in exasperation. "Let him have his trinkets if it will make him happy. We can get rid of them later after he quiets down."

Panamon shook his handsome face in dismay, finally nodding his reluctant acquiescence. He was fed up with Orl Fane already.

"Very well, I'll give in just this once," the thief agreed. Orl Fane immediately quieted down. "However, if he opens his mouth like that once more, I'll cut out his tongue. Keltset, you keep him away from that sack. I don't want him getting hold of one of those weapons long enough to cut himself free and do us in! Worthless blades probably wouldn't do a neat job of it anyway, and I'd die of blood poisoning."

Shea had to laugh in spite of himself. They were poor-looking weapons, though he rather fancied the slim broadsword with the extended arm and burning torch cut into the hilt. Even that one was rather gaudy, the cheap gold paint chipped and flecked about the hilt. Like several of the others, it rested in a worn leather sheath so it was difficult to tell what condition the blade might be in. At any rate, it could prove dangerous in the hands of the wily Orl Fane. Keltset hoisted the sack and its contents over one shoulder, and the party continued on its way toward the woodland.

It was a comparatively short hike, but by the time they reached the perimeter of the forest Shea was exhausted from supporting the weight of the injured Panamon. The little group stopped on the thief's command; as an afterthought, he sent Keltset back to cover their trail and to create a number of false trails that would confuse anyone following. Shea did not object, for although he hoped that Allanon and the others were searching for him, there was a dangerous possibility that patrolling Gnome hunters or, worse still, another Skull Bearer might come across their tracks instead.

After tying the captive Orl Fane to a tree, the Rock Troll backtracked onto the battlefield to erase any sign of their passage in this direction. Panamon collapsed wearily against a broad maple, and the tired Valeman took up a position opposite him, lying peacefully back on a small, grassy knoll, staring absently into the treetops and breathing deeply the forest air. The sun was fading rapidly now with the close of the afternoon and the faint beginnings of evening crept into the western sky in streaks of purple and deep blue. Less than an hour of sunlight remained, and the night would help to hide them from their enemies. Shea fervently wished now for the aid of the company, for the strong, wise leadership and fantastic mystical prowess of Allanon, for the courage of the others—Balinor, Hendel, Durin, Dayel, and the fiery Menion Leah. Most of all he wished Flick were with him—Flick, with his unwavering, unquestioning loyalty and trust. Panamon Creel was a good man to have on his side, but there were no real ties between them. The thief had lived too long by his wits and cunning to understand basic honesty and truth. And what about Keltset—an enigma, even to Panamon?

"Panamon, you said back there you would explain about Keltset," Shea remarked quietly. "About how the Skull Bearer knew him."

For a moment there was no answer, and Shea raised up to see if the man had heard him. Panamon was staring quietly at him.

"Skull Bearer? You seem to know a great deal more about this whole matter than I. You tell me about my giant companion, Shea."

"That wasn't the truth you told me when you saved me from those Gnomes, was it?" Shea asked him. "He wasn't a freak driven from his village by his own people. He didn't kill them for attacking him, did he?"

Panamon laughed merrily, the pike coming up to scratch the small mustache.

"Maybe it was the truth. Maybe those things did happen to him. I don't know. It always seemed to me that something of the sort must have happened to him to make him take up with someone like myself. He's no thief; I don't know what he is. But he is my friend—he is that. I didn't lie to you when I said that."

"Where did he come from?" Shea asked after a moment's silence.

"I found him north of here about two months ago. He wandered down out of the Charnal Mountains, battered, beaten, just barely alive. I don't know what happened to him; he never volunteered the information, and I didn't ask. He was entitled to keep his past hidden, just as I. I took care of him for several weeks. I knew a little sign language, and he understood it, so we could communicate. I guessed his name from his word signs. We learned a little about each other—only a little. When he was well, I asked him to come along and he agreed. We've had some good times, you know. Too bad he's not really a thief."

Shea shook his head and chuckled softly at that last remark. Panamon

Creel would probably never change. He didn't understand any other way of life and didn't want to. The only people who made any sense to him were those who told the world to hang by its thumbs and took by force what they needed for themselves. Yet friendship remained a prized commodity, even for a thief, and it was something that would not be tossed aside lightly. Even Shea was beginning to feel a strange sort of friendship for the flamboyant Panamon Creel, a friendship that was improbable because their characters and their values were complete opposites. But each had an understanding of what the other felt, though not why he felt it, and there was the experience of the battle shared against a common enemy. Perhaps that was all that anyone ever needed as a basis for friendship.

"How could the Skull creature have known him?" Shea persisted.

Panamon shrugged casually, indicating he neither knew nor cared. The watchful Valeman felt the latter was not the case, and Panamon would very much like to find out the truth behind Keltset's appearance two months earlier. His hidden past had something to do with the spirit creature's unexplained recognition of the giant Troll. There had been a trace of fear in those cruel eyes, and Shea found it difficult to imagine how anything mortal could have frightened the powerful Skull Bearer. Panamon had seen it, too, and certainly he must be asking himself the same question.

By the time Keltset rejoined them, it was sundown and the faint rays of the late-afternoon sun only barely lit the dark forest. The Troll had carefully erased all signs of their passing from the battlefield, leaving a number of confusing false trails for anyone who attempted to follow. Panamon was feeling well enough to maneuver on his own strength, but requested that Keltset help support him until they reached a suitable campsite because it was becoming dark too quickly for travel. Shea was given the task of leading the docile Orl Fane by the rope leash, a chore he did not relish, but which he accepted without complaint. Again, Panamon tried to leave the worn sack and its contents behind, but Orl Fane was not to be deprived of his treasures so easily. He immediately set up such a howl of anguish that the thief ordered him bound about the mouth until the only sound the hapless Gnome could make was a muffled groan. But when they tried to move into the forest, the desperate captive threw himself on the ground and refused to rise, even when kicked painfully by a thoroughly irate Panamon. Keltset could have carried the Gnome and supported Panamon, too, but that was more trouble than it was worth. Muttering dire threats at the whining Gnome, the thief at last had Keltset pick up the sack, and the four began their journey into the darkening woods.

When it became too dark to tell with any certainty where they were going, Panamon called a halt in a small clearing between giant oaks whose interlocking boughs formed a weblike roof for shelter. Orl Fane was tied to one of the tall oaks while the other three set about building a fire and preparing a meal. When the food was ready, Orl Fane was unfettered long enough to allow him to eat. While Panamon did not know exactly where they were, he felt safe enough to permit a fire, relatively certain that no one would be trailing them at night. He might have felt a little less secure had he known of the dangers of the impenetrable forests that surrounded the dark cliffs of Paranor. As it happened, the four men were in an adjoining forest east of the dangerous woodlands ringing Paranor. The section of woods in which they were camped was seldom traveled by the minions of the Warlock Lord, and there was little possibility that anyone would happen along to discover them. They ate in silence, a hungry and tired group after the long day's travel. Even the whines of the bothersome Orl Fane were temporarily stilled as the little Gnome ate ravenously, his crafty yellow face bent close to the warmth of the small fire as the dark green eyes shifted warily from one face to the next. Shea paid no attention, concentrating instead on what he should tell Panamon Creel about himself, the company, and most important of all, the Sword of Shannara. He had not made up his mind when dinner was completed. The captive was again bound to the nearest oak and permitted to breathe without the gag after his solemn promise that he would not begin whining and crying again. Then placing himself comfortably close to the dying fire, Panamon turned his attention to the expectant Valeman.

"The time is here, Shea, for you to tell me what you know about all this Sword business," he began briskly. "No lies, no half-truths, and leave nothing out. I promised my help, but we must have mutual trust—and not the kind I spoke of to this pitiful deserter. I have been fair and open with you. Do likewise for me."

So Shea told him everything. He didn't mean to when he started. He wasn't really sure how much he should tell, but one thing led to another and before he knew it the whole tale was out in the open. He told about the coming of Allanon, and the subsequent appearance of the Skull Bearer which forced the brothers to flee from Shady Vale. He related the events surrounding the journey to Leah and the meeting with Menion, followed by the terrible flight through the Black Oaks to Culhaven, where they joined the rest of the company. He skimmed over the details of the journey to the Dragon's Teeth, a great part of which was still hazy in his own mind. He concluded by explaining how he had fallen from the Crease into the river and been washed out onto the Rabb Plains where he was captured by the Gnome hunting party. Panamon listened without interruption, his eyes wide in astonishment at the tale. Keltset sat next to him in impenetrable silence, the rough-hewn but intelligent face gazing intently at the little Valeman during the entire narration. Orl Fane shifted about uneasily, groaning and muttering unintelligibly as he listened with the other two, his eyes darting wildly about the campsite as if expecting the Warlock Lord himself at any minute.

"That is the most fantastic tale I have ever heard," Panamon announced at last. "It's so incredible that even I find it hard to believe. But I do believe you, Shea. I believe you because I've fought that black-winged monster on the plainlands and because I've seen the strange power you have over those Elfstones, as you call them. But this business about the Sword and your being the lost heir of Shannara—I don't know. Do you believe it yourself?"

"I didn't at first," Shea admitted slowly, "but now I don't know what to think. So much has happened that I can't decide who or what to believe anymore. In any case, I've got to rejoin Allanon and the others. They may even have the Sword by this time. They may have the answer to this whole riddle of my heritage and the power of the Sword."

Orl Fane suddenly doubled up laughing, his voice high-pitched and frenzied.

"No, no, they don't have the Sword," he shrieked like a fool caught up in his own madness. "No, no, only I can show you the Sword! I can lead you to it. Only I. You can search and you can search and you can search, ha, ha, ha—go ahead. But I know where it is! I know who has it! Only I!"

"I think he's losing his mind," Panamon Creel muttered humorlessly, and ordered Keltset to regag the bothersome Gnome. "We'll find out exactly what he knows in the morning. If he knows anything about the Sword of Shannara, which I seriously doubt, he'll tell us or wish he had!"

"Do you think he might know who has it?" Shea asked soberly. "That Sword could mean so much, not only to us, but to all the peoples of the four lands. We've got to try to find out what he really knows."

"You bring tears to my eyes with that plea for the people," Panamon mocked disdainfully. "They can go hang for all I care. They've never done anything for me—except travel alone, unarmed, with fat purses, and that's been all too infrequently." He looked up at Shea's disappointed face and shrugged nonchalantly. "Still, I am curious about the Sword, so I might be willing to help you. After all, I owe you a great favor, and I'm not one to forget a favor."

Keltset finished gagging the babbling Gnome once again and rejoined them next to the small fire. Orl Fane had lapsed into a series of small, shrill laughs coupled with incoherent mumblings that even the cloth gag did not completely muffle. Shea glanced uneasily at the little captive, watching the gnarled yellow body twist about as if possessed by some devil, the dark eyes wide and rolling wildly. Panamon gallantly ignored the moans for a brief time, but at last, losing all patience, leaped to his feet and drew his dagger to cut the Gnome's tongue out. Orl Fane immediately quieted down and for a while they forgot about him.

"Why do you suppose," Panamon began after a moment, "that Northland creature believed we were hiding the Sword of Shannara? It was strange he wouldn't even argue the point. He said he could sense that we had it. How do you explain that?"

Shea thought for a moment and finally shrugged uncertainly.

"It must have been the Elfstones."

"You may be right," Panamon agreed slowly, thoughtfully, his good hand rubbing his chin. "I frankly don't understand any of this. Keltset, what do you think about it."

The giant Rock Troll regarded them solemnly for a moment and then made several brief signs with his hands. Panamon watched intently, then turned to Shea with a disgusted look.

"He thinks the Sword is very important and that the Warlock Lord is a very great danger to us all." The thief laughed humorously. "He's a great help, I must say!"

"The Sword *is* very important!" Shea repeated, his voice trailing off in the darkness, and they sat quietly, lost in thought.

It was late evening now, the night around them black beyond the faint light of the fire's reddish embers. The woods were a wall of concealment, shutting them into the little clearing, surrounding them with the sharp sounds of the insect world and the occasional cry of some faraway creature. The sky above showed through the boughs of the great trees in patches of dark blue broken by one or two distant stars. Panamon talked on quietly for a few minutes more as the coals died into ashes. Then he rose, kicking the ashes and grinding them into the earth, bidding good night to his companions with a finality that discouraged further attempts at conversation. Keltset was wrapped in a blanket and sleeping before Shea had even selected a suitable patch of forest earth. The Valeman felt incredibly weary from the strain of the long day's march and the battle with the Skull Bearer. Dropping his blanket, he lay down on his back, kicked off the hunting boots, and stared aimlessly at the blackness above him through which he could just barely discern the limbs of the trees and the shadows of the sky.

Shea thought about all that had happened to him, once again retracing mentally his long, endless journey from Shady Vale. So much of it was still a mystery. He had come so far, endured so much, and still he didn't know what it was all about. The secret of the Sword of Shannara, the Warlock Lord, his own heritage—it was no clearer now than before. The company was out there somewhere looking for him, led by the secretive, mystic Allanon, who seemed to be the only man with the answers to all the unanswered questions. Why had he not told Shea everything from the beginning? Why had he insisted on giving the company only a piece of the story at a time, always reserving that small bit, always holding back the key to their complete understanding of the unknown power locked in the elusive Sword of Shannara?

He rolled over on his side, peering through the darkness to the sleeping form of Panamon Creel just a few feet away. Beyond and to the other side of the clearing he could hear the heavy breathing of Keltset blending in with the sounds of the forest night. Orl Fane sat with his back straight against the tree to which he was bound, his eyes shining like a cat's in the dark, unmoving as they stared fixedly at Shea. The Valeman stared back for a moment, unnerved by the Gnome's gaze, but finally he forced himself to turn the other way and closed his eyes, dropping off to sleep in a matter of seconds. The last thing he remembered was clutching the small bulk of the Elfstones close to his chest within the tunic, wondering if their power would continue to protect him in the days ahead.

———————

Shea was awakened abruptly to the gray light of an early forest morning by a long string of venomous oaths of dismay and frustration from a wrathful Panamon Creel. The thief was stamping about the campsite in absolute fury, shouting and cursing all at the same time. Shea could not decide what had happened right away, and it was several minutes before he had wiped the sleep from his eyes and propped himself up on one elbow, squinting wearily in the gloom. He felt as if he had slept no more than a few minutes, his muscles sore and strained, his mind hazy. Panamon continued to storm about the small clearing as Keltset knelt silently next to one of the great oaks. Then Shea realized that Orl Fane was missing. He leaped to his feet and rushed over, suddenly afraid. In a moment his worst fears were realized; the ropes that had bound the crafty Gnome lay in pieces about the base of the huge trunk. The Gnome had escaped, and Shea had lost his one chance to find the missing Sword.

"How did he get away?" Shea demanded angrily. "I thought you tied him up, away from anything that might cut his bonds!"

Panamon Creel looked at him as if he were an idiot, disgust registered all over the flushed countenance.

"Do I look like a complete fool? Of course I tied him up away from any weapons. I even tied him to the confounded tree and had him gagged as an added precaution. Where were you? The little devil didn't cut these ropes and that gag. He chewed his way through them!"

Now it was Shea's turn to be amazed.

"I'm dead serious, I assure you," Panamon continued angrily. "The ropes were chewed through by teeth. Our little rodent friend was more resourceful than I imagined."

"Or perhaps more desperate," the Valeman added thoughtfully. "I wonder why he didn't try to kill us. He had reason enough to hate us."

"Very uncharitable of you to suggest such a thing," the other declared in mock disbelief. "I'll tell you why, though, since you asked. He was terrified that he might be caught in the act. That Gnome was a deserter—a coward of the lowest order. He didn't have the courage to do anything but run! What is it, Keltset?"

The huge Rock Troll had lumbered silently over to his comrade and made several quick gestures, pointing to the north. Panamon shook his head in disgust.

"The spineless mouse has been gone since early this morning—hours ago. Worse still, the fool fled northward, and it would not be healthy for us to chase him in that country. His own people will probably find him and dispose of him for us. They won't shelter a deserter. Bah, let him go! We're better off without him, Shea. He was probably lying about the Sword of Shannara anyway."

Shea nodded doubtfully, unconvinced that the Gnome had been lying about everything he had told them. As unbalanced as the little fellow had seemed, he had nevertheless appeared certain that he knew where the Sword could be found and who had possession of it. The whole idea that he knew such a secret was unnerving to the Valeman. Suppose he had gone after the Sword? Suppose he knew where it was?

"Forget the whole matter, Shea," Panamon interjected in resignation. "That Gnome was scared to death of us; his only thought was to escape. The story of the Sword was merely a trick to keep us from killing him until he found the opportunity to escape. Look at this! He left in such a hurry, he even forgot his precious sack."

For the first time Shea noticed the sack lying partially open at the other side of the clearing. It was strange indeed that Orl Fane should abandon his treasures after going to so much trouble to persuade his captors to bring them along. That useless sack had been so important to him, and yet there it lay forgotten, its contents still visible as small bulks beneath the cloth. Shea walked over to it curiously, staring at it with visible suspicion. He emptied the contents onto the forest earth, the swords and the daggers and the jewelry clattering together as they tumbled out in a heap. Shea stared at them, aware that the giant form of Keltset was at his side, the dark, expressionless face bent next to his. They stood together, studying the Gnome's abandoned hoard as if somehow it held a mysterious secret. Their companion watched for a few seconds, then muttered in disgust and strolled over to join them, glancing down at the weapons and jewelry.

"Let's be on our way," he advised lightly. "We've got to find your friends, Shea, and perhaps with their help we can locate this elusive Sword. What are you staring at? You've already seen that worthless junk once. It hasn't changed."

Then Shea saw it.

"It's not the same," he announced slowly. "It's gone. He's taken it."

"What's gone?" snapped Panamon irritably, kicking at the pile of junk. "What are you talking about?"

"That old sword in the leather scabbard. The one with the arm and the torch."

Panamon looked quickly at the swords in the little heap, frowning curiously. Keltset straightened abruptly and looked at Shea with those deeply intelligent eyes fixed on the little Valeman. He realized the truth as well.

"So he took one sword," Panamon growled without stopping to think. "That doesn't mean he . . ." He caught himself, his jaw dropping open in dismay, his eyes rolling back in disbelief. "Oh, no! That can't be—it can't. You mean he has . . . ?"

He couldn't finish the thought, but choked on his words. Shea shook his head in quiet despair.

"The Sword of Shannara!"

21

The same morning that found Shea and his new companions facing the awful truth about the fleeing Orl Fane and the Sword of Shannara also found Allanon and the remaining members of the company embroiled in difficulties of their own. They had escaped from the Druid's Keep under the aged mystic's sure guidance, winding downward through the maze of tunnels in the core of the mountain to the forest land below. They had encountered no initial resistance to their escape, finding only a few scattered Gnomes scurrying about the passages, remnants of the broken palace guard that had fled earlier. It was early evening by the time the little band was clear of the forbidding heights and moving northward through the forests. Allanon was certain that the Gnomes had removed the Sword of Shannara from the Keep sometime before the encounter with the Skull Bearer in the furnace room, but it was impossible to tell exactly when the removal had been accomplished. Eventine was patrolling the northern perimeter of Paranor and any attempt to move the Sword would be met with resistance from his soldiers. Perhaps the Elven king had already gained possession of the Sword. Perhaps he had even intercepted the missing Shea. Allanon was extremely worried about the little Valeman, whom he had expected to find at the Druid's Keep. There had been no mistake when he had made his mental search for the youth back at the foot of the Dragon's Teeth. Shea was in the company of others, and they were moving northward toward Paranor. Something had diverted them. Still, Shea was a resourceful fellow, and he had the power of the Elfstones to protect him from the Warlock Lord. The Druid could only hope that somehow they would find each other without further complications, and that when they did, Shea would be safe and unharmed.

Allanon had other worries, however, which demanded his immediate attention. Gnome reinforcements began to arrive in large numbers, and it did not take them long to conclude that Allanon and his little band of invaders had fled the castle and were somewhere in the dangerous Impregnable Forest surrounding Paranor. In truth, the Gnomes had no idea for whom they were searching; they only knew that the castle had been invaded, and the intruders had to be captured or destroyed. The emissaries of the Warlock Lord had not arrived, and the Skull King himself did not yet realize his prey had escaped him once again. He rested contentedly in the dark recesses of his domain, assured that the troublesome Allanon had been destroyed in the furnaces of Paranor, that the heir of Shannara and the others with him were prisoners, and that the Sword of Shannara was safely on its way to the Northland, intercepted by this time by a Skull Bearer whom he had dispatched a day earlier to be certain the precious Sword was not retaken. So the newly arrived Gnomes began to comb the forests surrounding Paranor in an effort to find the unknown intruders, believing that they would flee south and sending the majority of their hunters in that direction.

Allanon and his small band were moving steadily northward, but progress was slowed from time to time with the appearance of large Gnome search parties patrolling the woodlands. The little company would never have escaped undetected had they proceeded south, but the enemy numbers were reduced enough to the north that they managed to elude the hunting parties by hiding until they had passed and then pressing onward. It was light by the time they finally reached the fringes of the forest and could look northward over the awesome Plains of Streleheim, their pursuers momentarily behind them.

Allanon turned to them, his dark countenance worn and grim, but the eyes still bright with determination. His companions waited as he studied them one by one as if he were seeing each for the first time. Finally he spoke, the words slow and reluctant.

"We have reached the end of the road, my friends. The journey to Paranor is at an end, and it is time for the company to disband and each of us to go his own way. We have lost our chance to gain possession of the Sword—at least for the moment. Shea is still missing, and we cannot tell how long it may take to find him. But the greatest threat facing us is an invasion from the north. We must protect ourselves and the peoples of the lands south, east, and west of us from that. We have seen no sign of the Elven armies of Eventine, though they were supposed to be patrolling this region. It appears they have been withdrawn, and this would only be done if the Warlock Lord had begun to move his armies southward."

"Then the invasion has begun?" Balinor asked shortly.

Allanon nodded solemnly, and the others exchanged startled looks.

"Without the Sword we cannot defeat the Warlock Lord, so we must attempt to stop his armies. To do this, we must unite the free nations quickly. We may already be too late. Brona will use his armies to seize all of the central Southland. To do this he need only destroy the Border Legion of Callahorn. Balinor, the Legion must hold the cities of Callahorn to give the nations enough time to unite their armies and strike back at the invader. Durin and Dayel can accompany you to Tyrsis and from there travel westward to their own land. Eventine must bring his Elven armies across the Plains of Streleheim to reinforce Tyrsis. If we lose there, the Warlock Lord will have succeeded in driving a wedge between the armies, and there will be little chance of uniting them. Worse still, the entire Southland will lie open and unprotected. Men will never be able to form their armies in time. The Border Legion of Callahorn is the only chance they have."

Balinor nodded in agreement and turned to Hendel.

"What support can the Dwarfs give us?"

"The city of Varfleet is the key to the eastern sector of Callahorn." Hendel pondered the situation carefully. "My people must protect against any assault through the Anar, but we can spare enough men to help defend Varfleet as well. But you must hold the cities of Kern and Tyrsis yourself."

"The Elven armies will help you on the west," Durin promised quickly.

"Wait a minute!" exclaimed Menion incredulously. "What about Shea? You've kind of forgotten about him, haven't you?"

"Still allowing your words to precede your thinking, I see," Allanon said darkly. Menion turned scarlet with anger, but waited to see what the mystic had to say.

"I'm not abandoning the search for my brother," Flick announced quietly.

"Nor am I suggesting you should, Flick." Allanon smiled at the other's concern. "You and Menion and I shall continue to search for our young friend and for the missing Sword. I suspect that where we find one, we shall find the other. Remember the words spoken to me by the Shade of Bremen. Shea shall be the first to lay hands on the Sword of Shannara. Perhaps he has already done so."

"Then let's get on with the search," suggested Menion irritably, avoiding the eyes of the Druid.

"We shall leave now," Allanon announced, adding pointedly, "but you must see that you keep a closer guard over your tongue. A Prince of Leah should speak with wisdom and foresight, with patience and understanding—not with foolish anger."

Menion nodded grudgingly. The seven said their farewells with mixed emotions and parted. Balinor, Hendel, and the Elven brothers turned westward past the forest in which Shea and his companions had spent the night, hoping to circle the Impregnable Forest and pass down through the hill country north of the Dragon's Teeth and thereby reach Kern and Tyrsis within two days. Allanon and his two youthful companions moved eastward, searching for some sign of Shea. Allanon was convinced that the Valeman must have eventually come northward toward Paranor and perhaps was a prisoner in one of the Gnome camps in that region. Rescuing him would not be easy, but the Druid's greatest fear was that the Warlock Lord would learn of his capture and find out who he was, then have him immediately executed. If that happened, the Sword of Shannara would be worthless to them anyway, and they would have no choice but to rely on the strength of the divided armies of the three besieged lands. It was not a promising thought, and Allanon quickly turned his attention to the land ahead. Menion walked slightly in front as they traveled, his keen eyes picking out the trails and studying the footprints of all who had passed. His concern was the weather. If it rained, they would never find the trail. Even if the weather stayed favorable for them, the sudden windstorms that blew across the Streleheim would have the same effect as a rainfall, erasing all traces of anyone's passage. Flick, dutifully bringing up the rear, walked in abject silence, hoping against hope that they would find some sign of Shea, but fearful that he had seen the last of his brother.

By noonday, the barren plains were shimmering with the blistering heat of the white-hot sun, and the three travelers walked as close to the forest edge as possible to take advantage of small patches of shade from the great trees. Allanon alone seemed unperturbed by the fearful heat, his dark face calm and relaxed in the scorching sunlight, free from even the slightest trace of perspiration. Flick felt ready to collapse at any moment, and even the durable Menion Leah was beginning to feel ill. His sharp eyes were dry and blurred, and his senses were starting to play tricks on him. He was seeing things that weren't there, hearing and smelling images formed by his muddled brain in the seething flatlands ahead.

At last the two Southlanders could go no farther, and their tall leader called a brief halt, leading them into the cooling shade of the forest. In silence they ate a small, tasteless meal of bread and dried meats. Flick wanted to ask the Druid more about Shea's chances of surviving alone in that desolate land, but he couldn't bring himself to voice the questions. The answers were all too apparent. He felt strangely alone now that the others were gone. He had never felt close to Allanon, always plagued by nagging doubts about the Druid's strange powers. The mystic remained a giant shadowy figure, as mysterious and deadly as the Skull Bearers that pursued them so relentlessly. He remained a personification of the deathless spirit of Bremen that had risen from the netherworld in the Valley of Shale. He was power and wisdom of such magnitude that he didn't seem a part of Flick's mortal world; he was more a part of the Warlock Lord's domain, that black, frightful corner of the mortal mind where fear is master and reason cannot penetrate. Flick could not forget the terrible battle between the great mystic and the treacherous Skull creature which had resulted in a fiery climax in the flames of the furnace beneath the Druid's Keep. Yet Allanon had saved himself; he had survived what no other man could have survived. It was more than merely uncanny—it was terrifying. Balinor alone had seemed able to deal with the giant leader, but now he was gone, and Flick felt very alone and vulnerable.

Menion Leah felt even less certain of himself. He was not really afraid of the powerful Druid, but he was aware that the giant did not think much of him and had brought him along primarily because Shea had wanted him. Shea had believed in the Prince of Leah when even Flick had doubted the adventurer's motives. But Shea was gone now. Menion felt he had only to anger the Druid once more and the unpredictable mystic would dispose of him for good. So he ate quietly and said nothing, believing that for the moment discretion was the better part of valor.

When the silent meal was concluded, the Druid motioned them to their feet. Again they marched eastward along the fringes of the forest, their faces bathed in the withering heat of the sun, their tired eyes scanning the barren plains for the missing Shea. This time they walked for only fifteen minutes before they found signs of something out of the ordinary. Menion spotted the tracks almost immediately. A large number of Gnomes had passed that way several days earlier, booted and undoubtedly armed. They followed the tracks northward for about half a mile. Upon topping a small rise of ground, they found the remains of the Gnomes and Elves who had died in battle. The decaying bodies lay where they had fallen, still untouched and unburied, less than a hundred yards from the rise. The three walked slowly down into the graveyard of bleached bones and rotting flesh, the terrible stench rising to their nostrils in sickening waves. Flick could go no farther, and stopped where he was to watch the other two walk into the midst of the dead bodies.

Allanon wandered in silent contemplation through the fallen men, studying discarded weapons and standards, glancing only briefly at the dead. Menion discovered a fresh set of tracks almost immediately and began moving mechanically about the battlefield, his eyes fixed on the dusty earth. Flick could not tell exactly what was going on from his distant vantage point, but it appeared that the highlander retraced his own steps several times, casting about for traces of new trails, the thin hands shading his reddened eyes. Finally, he turned southward toward the forest and began strolling slowly back toward Flick, his head lowered thoughtfully. He stopped at a large clump of bushes and dropped to one knee, apparently observing something of interest. Momentarily forgetting his distaste for the battlefield and its corpses, the curious Valeman hastened forward. He had just reached the kneeling man's side when Allanon, standing in the center of the battlefield, let out a shout of astonishment. The two men paused and watched silently while the tall black figure peered downward for a moment as if to be certain, then turned and moved toward them in long strides. The mystic's dark face was flushed with excitement when he reached them, and they were relieved to see the familiar mocking smile slowly spread into a wide grin.

"Amazing! It's amazing indeed. Our young friend is more resourceful than I had imagined. Up there, I found a small pile of ashes—all that remains of one of the Skull Bearers. Nothing mortal destroyed that creature; it was the power of the Elfstones!"

"Then Shea has been here ahead of us!" exclaimed Flick hopefully.

"No other has the power to use the stones." Allanon nodded assuringly. "There are signs of a terrific battle, tracks that show Shea was not alone. But I cannot tell whether those who were with him were friends or enemies. Nor can I tell if the creature of the north was destroyed during or after the battle between Gnome and Elf. What have you found, highlander?"

"A lot of false trails left by a very intelligent Troll," Menion responded wryly. "It's impossible for me to tell much from all the footprints, but I am sure that a large Rock Troll was among the prior occupants of this field. He left his tracks all over it but none of them lead anywhere. There are indications that some sort of scuffle took place within these bushes, though. See the bent branches and newly fallen leaves? But more important, there are footprints of a small man. They could be Shea's."

"Do you think he was captured by the Troll?" Flick queried fearfully. Menion smiled at his concern and shrugged.

"If he could handle one of those Skull creatures, then I doubt he would have much trouble with an ordinary Troll."

"The Elfstones are no protection against mortal creatures," Allanon pointed out chillingly. "Is there any clear indication which way this Troll went?"

Menion shook his head negatively.

"To be certain, we would have had to find the tracks right away. These tracks are at least a day old. The Troll knew what he was doing when he left. We could search forever and never be sure which way he went."

Flick felt his heart sink at this news. If Shea had been taken by this mysterious creature, then it appeared they had reached another dead end.

"I found something else," Allanon announced after a moment. "I found a broken standard from the house of Elessedil—Eventine's personal banner. He may have been present at the battle. He may have been taken prisoner or even killed. It seems possible that the slain Gnomes were attempting to escape from Paranor with the Sword and were intercepted by the Elf King and his warriors. If so, then Eventine, Shea, and the Sword may all be in the hands of the enemy."

"I'm sure of one thing," Menion declared quickly. "Those Troll footprints and this battle in the bushes took place yesterday, while the battle between the Gnomes and Elves is several days old."

"Yes . . . yes, you're right, of course," the Druid agreed thoughtfully. "There has been a sequence of events taking place that we can't piece together from the little we know. I'm afraid we won't find all the answers here."

"What do we do now?" Flick asked anxiously.

"There are tracks leading westward across the Streleheim," Allanon mused thoughtfully, gazing in that direction as he spoke. "The tracks are blurred, but they may have been made by survivors of this battle. . . ."

He looked questioningly at the silent Menion Leah for his opinion.

"Our mysterious Troll did not go that way," Menion stated worriedly. "He would not bother with a lot of false trails if he were going to leave a clear one when he left! I don't like it."

"Do we have any choice?" Allanon persisted. "The only clear set of tracks leaving this battleground leads westward. We'll have to follow them and hope for the best."

Flick thought that such optimism was unwarranted in view of the hard facts of the situation and found the comments out of character for the grim Druid. Still, it seemed they had little choice in the matter. Perhaps whoever had made those tracks could tell them something about Shea. The little Valeman turned to Menion and nodded his willingness to follow the Druid's advice, noting the look of consternation clouding the highlander's lean features. Clearly Menion was not happy with the decision, convinced that there was another trail to be found that would tell them

more about the Troll and the slain Skull creature. Allanon beckoned to
them, and retracing their steps they began the long march back across the
Streleheim Plains to the lands west of Paranor. Flick cast one final look at
the field of slain men, their carcasses rotting slowly in the boiling heat of
the sun, shunned by man and nature in senseless death. He shook his broad
head. Perhaps this was the way it would end for them all.

The three travelers walked steadily westward for the remainder of the
day. They spoke little, lost in private thoughts, their eyes following almost
carelessly the blurred trail before them as they watched the brilliant sun
turn red in the horizon and die into evening. When it was too dark to
continue, Allanon directed them into the bordering forests where they
made camp for the night. The trio had reached a point near the north-
western sector of the dreaded Impregnable Forest and they were once again
in danger of discovery by Gnome hunting parties or prowling wolf packs.
The resolute Druid explained that, while they were in some danger of discovery, he believed the search for them would have been abandoned by
this time in favor of more urgent matters. As a necessary precaution, they
would light no fire and would keep constant watch through the night for
the wolves. Flick silently prayed that the wolf packs would not venture this
close to the plainland, but would keep to the dark interior of the woods,
closer to the Druid's Keep. They ate a brief, tasteless meal and quickly
turned in for the night. Menion offered to stand the first watch. Flick was
asleep in moments, but it seemed he had slept for only an instant when the
highlander awoke him for his turn as guard. About midnight, Allanon approached without a sound and ordered Flick to go back to sleep. The Valeman had been guarding for only about an hour, but he did as he was told
without arguing.

When Flick and Menion awoke again, it was dawn. In the faint red
and yellow slivers of sunlight which crept slowly into the shadowed forest,
they saw the giant Druid resting peacefully against a tall elm as he stared at
them. The tall, dark figure seemed almost a part of the forest, sitting there
motionlessly, the deep eyes black in the caverns beneath the great brow.
They knew that Allanon must have stood guard over them all night without sleep. It seemed impossible that he could be rested, yet he rose without
stretching, the grim face relaxed and alert. They ate a quick breakfast and
marched out of the forest onto the Streleheim once more. A moment later
they halted in shocked disbelief. All about them, the skies were clear and
faintly blue in the new light of day, the sun rising in blinding brilliance
above the mountain ranges far to the east. But to the north stood a gigantic, towering wall of darkness against the skyline, as if all the ominous
thunderclouds of the earth had been massed together and piled one on top
of the next to form a black wall of gloom. The wall rose into the air until
it was lost in the curving atmosphere of the earth's horizon, and it stretched
across all of the rugged Northland, huge, dark, and terrible—its center the
kingdom of the Warlock Lord. It seemed to foreshadow the relentless, inevitable approach of an endless night.

"What do you make of that?" Menion could barely get the question out.

For a moment Allanon said nothing, his own dark face mirroring the blackness of the northern wall as he stared in silence. The muscles of his lean jaw seemed to tighten beneath the small black beard and the eyes narrowed as if deep in concentration. Menion waited quietly, and at last the Druid seemed to realize he had spoken, turning to him in recognition.

"It is the beginning of the end. Brona has signaled the start of his conquest. That terrible darkness will follow his armies as they sweep southward, then east and west, until the whole earth is blanketed. When the sun is gone in all the lands, freedom is dead, too."

"Are we beaten?" Flick asked after a moment. "Are we really beaten? Is it hopeless for us, Allanon?"

His worried voice struck a responsive chord within the giant Druid, who turned quietly to him, gazing reassuringly into the wide, frightened eyes.

"Not yet, my young friend. Not yet."

Allanon led them westward for several hours from that point, staying close to the fringes of the forest, warning Menion and Flick to keep their eyes open for any sign of the enemy. The Skull Bearers would be flying in the day as well as by night, now that the Warlock Lord had begun his conquest, no longer afraid of the sunlight, no longer trying to conceal their presence. The Master was finished with hiding in the Northland; now, he would begin to move into the other lands, sending his faithful spirits ahead of him like great birds of prey. He would give them the power they needed to withstand the sun—the power he had harnessed in the great dark wall that shadowed his kingdom and would soon begin to shadow all of the lands beyond. The days of light were drawing to a close.

About midmorning, the three travelers turned southward on the Streleheim Plains, keeping close to the western fringes of the forests surrounding Paranor. The tracks they had been following merged at this point with others coming down from the north to continue southward toward Callahorn. The trail they left was broad and open; there had been no attempt to hide either their number or their direction. From the width of the trail and the impressions left by the footprints, Menion concluded that at least several thousand men had passed this way a few days earlier. The footprints were Gnome and Troll—obviously part of the Northland hordes of the Warlock Lord. Allanon was certain now that a giant army was massing on the plains above Callahorn to begin a sweep through the Southland that would divide the free lands and their armies. The trail had become so obscured by the intermingling of constant additional parties into the main body that it was no longer possible to tell whether a small group might have detached itself. Shea or the Sword could have been taken a different way at some point, and his friends would fail to catch it, continuing to follow the main army.

They walked southward all day with only occasional periods of rest, intent on catching the huge column of men ahead before nightfall. The trail of the invading army was so apparent that Menion merely glanced out of habit from time to time at the trampled earth. The barren Plains of Streleheim were replaced by green grasslands. To Flick, it almost seemed that they were going home again, and the familiar hills of Shady Vale might be just over the rise of the plains. The weather was warm and humid, and the terrain was considerably more friendly. They were still some distance from Callahorn, but it was clear that they were passing out of the bleakness of the Northland into the warmth and greenness of their home. The day passed quickly, and conversation between the travelers resumed. At Flick's urging, Allanon told them more about the Council of the Druids. He recounted in detail the history of Man since the Great Wars, explaining how their race had progressed to its present state of existence. Menion said little, content to listen to the Druid and keep a close watch over the surrounding countryside.

When they had begun the day's march, the sun had been bright and warm, and the sky clear. By midafternoon, the weather had changed abruptly and the brightness of the sun was replaced by low-hanging, gray rain clouds and an even more humid atmosphere that clung uncomfortably to the exposed skin. The air felt sticky and wet, and there was little doubt that a storm was approaching. They were near the southernmost boundaries of the Impregnable Forest by this time, and the jagged peaks of the Dragon's Teeth were visible in the dark horizon to the south. Still there was no sign of the massive army traveling ahead of them, and Menion was beginning to wonder how far south it might have already penetrated. They were not far now from the borders of Callahorn, which lay immediately below the Dragon's Teeth. If the Northland armies had already taken Callahorn, then the end had indeed come. The gray light of the afternoon dropped off sharply and the sky closed over in sullen darkness.

It was dusk when they first heard the ominous booming rising out of the night, echoing off the giant peaks ahead of them. Menion recognized it at once—he had heard that sound before in the forests of the Anar. It was the sound of hundreds of Gnome drums, their steady rhythm throbbing through the stillness of the humid air, filling the night with a sinister tension. The earth shook with the force of the beat, and all life had gone mute in awe and fear. Menion could tell by the intensity of the drums that there were far more than they had encountered at the Pass of Jade. If the army of the Northland could be measured by the sound of those drums, then there must be thousands. As the three moved quickly ahead, the frightening sound enveloped them entirely, booming all about them in shuddering echoes. The gray clouds of late afternoon still masked the night sky, leaving the searching men shrouded in inky darkness. Menion and Flick could no longer find the way alone, and the silent Druid led them with uncanny precision into the rough lowlands below Paranor. No one spoke, each man frozen into watchful apprehension by the deathly booming of those Gnome drums. They knew that the enemy camp was just ahead.

Then the terrain changed abruptly from the low hills and scattered brush to steep slopes dotted with boulders and treacherous rock ledges. The surefooted Allanon moved steadily ahead, his tall form unmistakable even in the near blackness, and the two Southlanders followed dutifully. Menion estimated that they must have reached the smaller mountains and foothills just above the Dragon's Teeth and that Allanon had chosen to come this way to avoid any chance encounters with members of the Northland army. It was still impossible to tell where the enemy army was encamped, but from the sound of the drums, it seemed as if they were right on top of it. The three dark shapes wound their way cautiously through the night for what must have been almost an hour, at times feeling their way blindly through the boulders and brush. Their clothes were scraped and torn, their exposed limbs scratched and bruised, but the silent Druid did not slacken the pace or pause to rest. At the end of that long hour's time, he halted abruptly and turned to them, placing a warning finger over pursed lips. Then slowly, cautiously, he led them forward into a huge mass of boulders. For several minutes, the three climbed noiselessly upward. Suddenly there were lights in the distance—dim, flickering yellow lights that came from burning fires. They crawled on hands and knees to the rim of the boulders. Upon reaching a tilted shelf of rock that sloped upward to the edge of the boulder cluster, they raised their heads slowly to the rim and peered breathlessly over.

What they saw was awesome and terrifying. As far as the eye could see, stretching miles in all directions, the fires of the Northland army burned in the night. They were like thousands of blazing yellow dots in the blackness of the plains, and moving busily about in their bright light were the dim shapes of wiry, gnarled Gnomes and bulky, thick-limbed Trolls. There were thousands of them, all armed, all waiting to descend on the kingdom of Callahorn. It was inconceivable to Menion and Flick that even the legendary Border Legion could hope to stand against such a mighty force. It was as if the entire Gnome and Troll population had been gathered on the plains below. Allanon had avoided any chance encounters with scouts or guards by approaching along the edges of the Dragon's Teeth on the western borders, and now the three were perched in a crow's nest of boulders several hundred feet up from the army encamped below. From this height, the shocked Southlanders could see the entirety of the massive force assembled to invade their poorly defended homeland. The drums of the Gnomes boomed out in steady crescendo as the men stared down, their eyes traveling from one end of the sprawled camp to the other in disbelief. For the first time, they understood fully what they were up against. Before, it had been only Allanon's words describing the invasion; now they could see the enemy and judge for themselves. Now they could feel the desperate need for the mysterious Sword of Shannara—a need for the one power that could destroy the evil being who had caused this army to materialize and march against them. But now was already too late.

For several long minutes, no one said anything as they stared down at the enemy encampment. Then Menion touched Allanon on the shoulder and started to speak, but the Druid clamped his hand quickly over the surprised highlander's mouth and pointed toward the base of the slope on which they lay concealed. Menion and Flick peered cautiously downward and to their surprise they made out the vague shapes of Gnome guards patrolling near the base of their hiding place. Neither had believed the enemy would bother to place guards this far from the actual camp, but apparently they were taking no chances. Allanon motioned for the two to move back from the edge of the boulders and they quickly complied, following his lead as he inched his way down into the tall rocks. Once they had reached the bottom of the boulder cluster, safely away from the rim of the ledge, the Druid huddled together with them in earnest council.

"We have to be very quiet," he warned in a tense whisper. "The sound of our voices would have echoed off the cliff face onto the plains from up there. Those Gnome guards would have heard us!"

Menion and Flick nodded in understanding.

"The situation is more serious than I thought," Allanon continued, his voice a hushed rasp in the gloom. "It appears the entire Northland army has bunched at this one point to strike at Callahorn. Brona intends to crush any resistance from the Southland immediately, dividing the better-prepared armies of the East and West so he can deal with them separately. The evil one already holds everything north of Callahorn. Balinor and the others must be warned!"

He paused a moment, then turned expectantly to Menion Leah.

"I can't leave now," Menion exclaimed heatedly. "I've got to help you find Shea!"

"We haven't the time to argue the priorities of the situation," Allanon declared almost menacingly, one finger coming up like a dagger at the highlander's face. "If Balinor is not warned about the situation, Callahorn will fall and the rest of the Southland will follow, including Leah. The time has come for you to start thinking about your own people. Shea is only one man, and right now there is nothing you can do for him. But there is something you can do for the thousands of Southlanders who face enslavement at the hands of the Warlock Lord if Callahorn should fall!"

Allanon's voice was so cold that Flick could feel the chills run up his spine. He could sense Menion tensing expectantly, fearfully, at his side, but the Prince of Leah kept silent in the face of this stinging reprimand. Druid and Prince faced one another in the darkness for several interminable minutes, their eyes locked in open anger. Then Menion looked away abruptly and nodded shortly. Flick breathed an audible sigh of relief.

"I'll go to Callahorn and warn Balinor," Menion muttered, his voice still muffled with fury, "but I'll be back to find you."

"Do as you wish when you have found the others," replied Allanon coldly. "However, any attempt to return through enemy lines would be foolhardy at best. Flick and I shall try to find out what has happened to Shea and the Sword. We will not desert him, highlander, I promise you."

Menion looked back at him sharply, almost in disbelief, but the Druid's eyes were clear and undisguised. He was not lying.

"Keep close to these smaller mountains until you get past the enemy picket lines," the giant wanderer advised quietly. "When you reach the Mermidon River above Kern, cross there and enter the city before dawn. I expect the Northland army will march on Kern first. There is little chance that the city can be successfully defended against a force of that size. The people should be evacuated and moved into Tyrsis before the invaders can cut off their retreat. Tyrsis is built on a plateau against the back of a mountain. Properly defended, it can withstand any assault for at least several days. That should be time enough for Durin and Dayel to reach their homeland and return with the Elven army. Hendel should be able to offer some help from the Eastland. Perhaps Callahorn can be held long enough to mobilize and combine the armies of the three lands to strike back at the Warlock Lord. It is the only chance we have without the Sword of Shannara!"

Menion nodded in understanding and turned to Flick, extending his hand in a gesture of farewell. Flick smiled faintly and clasped the hand warmly.

"Good luck to you, Menion Leah."

Allanon came forward and placed a strong hand on the highlander's lean shoulder.

"Remember, Prince of Leah, we depend on you. The people of Callahorn must be made aware of the danger they face. If they falter or hesitate, they are lost, and with them all of the Southland. Do not fail."

Menion turned abruptly and moved like a shadow into the rocks beyond. The giant Druid and the little Valeman stood silently as the lean figure flitted agilely between the rocks and then disappeared from sight. They stood for a few minutes without speaking after he was gone, and then Allanon turned to Flick.

"To us is left the task of finding out what has happened to Shea and the Sword." He spoke again in a lowered voice, sitting down heavily on a small rock. Flick moved closer to him. "I'm worried about Eventine as well. That broken standard we found back at the battlefield was his personal banner. He may have been taken prisoner, and if he has, the Elven army may hesitate to act until he has been rescued. They love him too dearly to take a chance with his life, even to save the Southland."

"You mean the Elven people don't care what happens to the people of the Southland?" Flick exclaimed incredulously. "Don't they know what will happen to them should the Southland fall to the Warlock Lord?"

"It's not quite as simple as it seems," Allanon stated, sighing deeply. "Those who follow Eventine understand the danger, but there are others who believe that the Elven people should stay out of the affairs of the other lands unless they are directly attacked or threatened. With Eventine absent, the choice will not be so clear, and discussion of what is right and proper may delay any move by the Elven army until it is too late for them to help."

Flick nodded slowly, thinking of another time at Culhaven when a bitter Hendel had reported much the same thing about the people of the Southland cities. It seemed incredible that people could be so undecided and confused in the face of such obvious danger. Yet Shea and he had been like that when they had first learned about Shea's birthright and the threat of the Skull Bearers. It was not until they had seen one crawling, searching for them . . .

"I've got to know what's happening in that camp." Allanon's voice cut into Flick's thoughts with a sharp rasp of determination. He paused in thought a moment, staring at the little Valeman.

"My young friend, Flick . . ." He smiled faintly in the darkness. "How would you like to be a Gnome for a little while?"

22

With Shea still missing somewhere north of the Dragon's Teeth and Allanon, Flick, and Menion in search of some definite sign of his whereabouts, the remaining four members of the now divided company of friends drew within sight of the great towers of the fortress city of Tyrsis. It had taken them almost two days of constant travel, their hazardous journey through the lines of the Northland army further impeded by the formidable mountain barrier cutting off the Southland kingdom of Callahorn from the land of Paranor. The first day was long, but without incident, as the four wound southward through the forests adjoining the Gnome-patrolled Impregnable Forest to reach the lowlands beyond, which formed the doorstep to the awesome Dragon's Teeth. The mountain passes were all carefully guarded by Gnome hunters, and it seemed it would prove to be impossible to get past them without a fight. But a simple ruse lured most of the guards away from the entrance to the high, winding Kennon Pass, allowing the four an opportunity to get into the mountains. The difficult task of getting out again at the southern end was accomplished only after several Gnomes were silently dispatched at a midpoint check camp and twenty more were frightened into believing the entire Border Legion of Callahorn had seized the pass and was descending on the luckless sentries with every intention of killing them all. Hendel was laughing so hard when they finally reached the safety of the forests south of the Kennon Pass that all four were forced to pause momentarily until he could recover his composure. Durin and Dayel looked doubtfully at one another, recalling the taciturn Dwarf's grim attitude during the journey to Paranor. They had never seen him laugh at anything, and somehow it seemed out of character. They shook their lean faces in disbelief and glanced questioningly at Balinor. But the giant borderman only shrugged. He was an old friend to Hendel and the Dwarf's changeable character was well known to him. It was good to hear his laughter again.

Now in the twilight of the early evening, with the sun's fading light a hazy purple and red in the vast horizon of the western plains, the four stood within sight of their destination. Their bodies were worn and sore, their normally keen minds numbed by lack of sleep and constant travel, but their spirits rose with unspoken excitement at the sight of the majestic city of Tyrsis. They paused for an instant at the edge of the forests that ran south from the Dragon's Teeth through Callahorn. To the east was the city of Varfleet, which guarded the only sizable passage through the Mountains of Runne, a small range that lay above the fabled Rainbow Lake. The sluggish Mermidon River wound its way through the forest at their backs above Tyrsis. Westward lay the smaller island city of Kern, and the source of the river was farther west in the vast emptiness of the Streleheim Plains. The river was broad at all points, forming a natural barrier against any would-be enemy and offering reliable protection for the inhabitants on the island. While the river ran full, which it did almost the year round, the waters were deep and swift, and no enemy had ever taken the island city.

Yet while both Kern, surrounded by the waters of the Mermidon, and Varfleet, nestled in the Mountains of Runne, seemed formidable and well defended, it was the ancient city of Tyrsis that harbored the Border Legion— the precision fighting machine that had for countless generations successfully guarded the borders of the Southland against invasion. It was the Border Legion that had always taken the brunt of any assault against the race of Man, offering the first line of defense against an enemy invader. Tyrsis had given birth to the Border Legion of Callahorn, and as a fortress it was without equal. The old city of Tyrsis had been destroyed in the First War of the Races, but had been rebuilt and then expanded over the years until now it was one of the largest cities in all the Southland and by far the strongest city standing in the northern regions. It had been designed as a fortress capable of withstanding any enemy attack—a bastion of towering walls and jagged ramparts set on a natural plateau against the face of an unscalable cliff. Each generation of its citizens had contributed in the construction of the city, each making it more formidable. Over seven hundred years ago, the great Outer Wall had been built on the edge of the plateau, extending the boundaries of Tyrsis as far as nature would permit on the bluff face. In the fertile plains below the fortress were the farms and croplands that fed the city, the dark earth nurtured and sustained by the life-giving waters of the great Mermidon which ran east and south. The people had their homes scattered throughout the surrounding countryside, relying on the city's walled protection only in the event of invasion. For hundreds of years following the First War of the Races, the cities of Callahorn had successfully repelled assaults by unfriendly neighbors. None of the three had ever been seized by an enemy. The famed Border Legion had never been defeated in battle. But Callahorn had never faced an army the size of that sent by the Warlock Lord. The real test of strength and courage lay ahead.

Balinor looked upon the distant towers of his city with mixed feelings. His father had been a great King and a good man, but he was growing old. For years he had commanded the Border Legion in its unceasing battle against persistent Gnome raiders from the Eastland. Several times he had been forced to wage long and costly campaigns against the great Northland Trolls, when scattered tribes had moved into his land, intent on seizing its cities and subjugating its people. Balinor was the elder son and the logical heir to the throne. He had studied hard under his father's careful guidance, and he was well liked by the people—people whose friendship could be won only through respect and understanding. He had worked beside them, fought beside them, and learned from them, so that now he could feel what they felt and look through their eyes. He loved the land enough to fight to hold it, as he was doing now, as he had been doing for a number of years. He commanded a regiment of the Border Legion, and they wore his personal insignia—a crouched leopard. They were the key unit of the entire fighting force. For Balinor, holding their respect and devotion was more important than anything. He had been gone from them for months now—gone, by his own choosing, to a self-imposed exile of travel with the mysterious Allanon and the company from Culhaven. His father had asked him not to go, pleaded with him to reconsider his decision. But he had already decided; he was not to be swayed, even by his father. His brow furrowed and a strange feeling of gloom settled into his mind as he looked down on his homeland. Unconsciously, he raised one gloved hand to his face, the cold chain mail tracing the line of the scar that ran down the exposed right cheek to his chin.

"Thinking about your brother again?" Hendel asked, although it was not so much a question as a statement of fact.

Balinor looked over at him, momentarily startled, then nodded slowly.

"You've got to stop thinking about that whole business, you know," the Dwarf stated flatly. "He could be a real threat to you if you persist in thinking of him as a brother and not as a person."

"It is not so easy to forget that his blood and mine make us more than sons born to the same father," the borderman declared gloomily. "I cannot ignore nor forget such strong ties."

Durin and Dayel looked at each other, unable to comprehend what the two were talking about. They knew that Balinor had a brother, but they had never seen him and had heard no mention of him since they had begun the long journey from Culhaven.

Balinor noticed the baffled looks on the faces of the two Elven brothers and shot a quick smile in their direction.

"It's not as bad as it might seem," he assured them calmly.

Hendel shook his head hopelessly and lapsed into silence for the next few minutes.

"My younger brother Palance and I are the only sons of Ruhl Buck-hannah, the King of Callahorn," Balinor volunteered, his eyes wandering back toward the distant city as if looking for another time. "We were very close while growing up—as close as you two. As we got older, we developed different ideas about life . . . different personalities, as all individuals must, brothers or not. I was the elder; I was next in line to the throne. Palance always realized this, of course, but it divided us as we grew older, mainly because his ideas of ruling the land were not always the same as mine. . . . It's difficult to explain, you understand."

"It's not so difficult," Hendel snorted meaningfully.

"All right, then, it's not so difficult," Balinor conceded wearily, to which Hendel responded with a knowing nod. "Palance believes Callahorn should cease to serve as a first line of defense in case of attack on the Southland people. He wants to disband the Border Legion and isolate Callahorn from the rest of the Southland. We cannot agree at all on this point. . . ."

He trailed off in bitter silence for a moment.

"Tell them the rest, Balinor." Hendel again spoke icily.

"My distrustful friend believes my brother is no longer his own master— that he says these things without meaning them. He keeps counsel with a mystic known as Stenmin, a man Allanon feels is without honor and will guide Palance to his own destruction. Stenmin has told my father and the people that my brother should rule and not I. He has turned him against me. When I left, even Palance seemed to believe that I was not fit to rule Callahorn."

"And that scar . . . ?" Durin asked quietly.

"An argument we had just before I left with Allanon," Balinor replied, shaking his head as he thought back on the matter. "I can't even remember how it started, but all at once Palance was in a rage—there was real hatred in his eyes. I turned to leave, and he grabbed a whip from the wall, striking out at me, cutting into my face with the tip. That was the reason I decided to get away from Tyrsis for a time, to give Palance a chance to regain his senses. If I had stayed after that incident, we might have . . ."

Again he trailed off ominously, and Hendel shot the Elven brothers a glance that left no doubt in their minds what would have happened if the brothers had had another altercation. Durin frowned in disbelief, wondering what sort of person would take sides against a man like Balinor. The tall borderman had repeatedly proved his courage and strength of character during their dangerous journey to Paranor, and even Allanon had relied heavily on him. Yet his brother had deliberately and vindictively turned against him. The Elf felt a deep sadness for this brave warrior, returned to a homeland where peace even in his own family was denied him.

"You must believe me when I tell you that my brother was not always like that—nor do I believe he is now a bad man," Balinor continued, more as if he were explaining it to himself than to the others. "This mystic Stenmin has some kind of hold over Palance that provokes him into these rages, turning him against me and what he knows to be right."

"There is more to him than that," Hendel interrupted sharply. "Palance is an idealistic fanatic—he seeks the throne and turns against you under pretext of upholding the interests of the people. He is choking on his own self-righteousness."

"Perhaps you are right, Hendel," Balinor conceded quietly. "But he is still my brother, and I love him."

"That's what makes him so dangerous," the Dwarf declared, standing before the tall borderman, meeting his gaze squarely. "He no longer loves you."

Balinor did not reply, but stared into the plainlands to the west and toward the city of Tyrsis. The others remained silent for a few minutes, leaving the brooding Prince to his own thoughts. Finally he turned back to them, his face relaxed and calm, looking as if the whole matter had never come up.

"Time to be moving on. We want to reach the walls of the city before nightfall."

"I'm going no farther with you, Balinor," Hendel interjected quickly. "I must return to my own land and help prepare the Dwarf armies against an invasion of the Anar."

"Well, you can rest in Tyrsis for tonight and leave tomorrow," Dayel replied quickly, knowing how tired they all were and anxious for the Dwarf's safety.

Hendel smiled patiently, then shook his head.

"No, I must travel at night in these lands. If I stay the night in Tyrsis, I lose a whole day's travel, and time is very precious to us all. The entire Southland stands or falls on how quickly we can assemble our armies into a combined fighting unit to strike back at the Warlock Lord. If Shea and the Sword of Shannara are lost to us, then our armies are all we have left. I will travel to Varfleet and rest there. Take care, my friends. Luck to you in the days ahead."

"And to you, brave Hendel." Balinor extended a great hand. Hendel clasped it warmly, then those of the Elven brothers, and disappeared into the forests with a parting wave.

Balinor and the Elven brothers waited until they could no longer see him moving through the trees and then began their walk across the plains toward Tyrsis. The sun had dropped behind the horizon, and the sky had turned from dusky red to a deep gray and blue that signaled the momentary approach of night. They were about halfway when the sky turned completely black, revealing the first of the night's stars shining in a clear, cloudless sky. As they neared the fabled city, its vast bulk sprawling and dark against the night horizon, the Prince of Callahorn described in detail to the Elven brothers the history behind the building of Tyrsis.

A series of natural defenses protected the man-made fortress. The city had been built on a high plateau which ran back against a line of small, but treacherous cliffs. The cliffs bounded the plateau entirely on the south and partially on the west and east. While they were not nearly so high or formidable in appearance as the Dragon's Teeth or the Charnal Mountains of the far Northland, they were incredibly steep. That portion of the cliffs that faced north onto the plateau rose almost straight up, and no one had ever successfully scaled it. Thus, the city was well protected from the rear, and it had never been necessary to construct any defenses to the south. The plateau on which the city was built was a little over three miles across at its widest point, dropping off sharply onto the plainlands which ran unbroken and open all the way north and west to the Mermidon River and east to the forests of Callahorn. The swift Mermidon actually formed the first line of defense against invasion, and few armies had ever gotten beyond that point to reach the plateau and the city walls. The enemy who did manage to cross the Mermidon onto the plainlands immediately found itself confronted by the steep wall of the plateau, which could be defended from above. The main route of access to this bluff was a huge iron-and-stone rampway, which was rigged to collapse by knocking out pins in the major supports.

But even if the enemy managed to reach the top of the plateau and thereby gain a foothold, the third defense waited—the defense that no army had ever broken through. Standing a scant two hundred yards from the edge of the plateau and ringing the entire city in a semicircle, the ends reaching back to the cliff sides protecting the southern approach, was the monstrous Outer Wall. Constructed from great blocks of stone welded together with mortar, the surface had been smoothed down to make scaling by hand virtually impossible. It rose nearly a hundred feet into the air, massive, towering, impregnable. At the top of the wall, ramparts had been built for the men fighting within the city, with sections cut away to allow concealed bowmen room to shoot down on the unprotected attackers. It was ancient in styling, crude and rough-hewn, but it had repelled invaders for almost a thousand years. No enemy army had penetrated into the inner city since its construction following the First War of the Races.

Just within the great Outer Wall, the Border Legion was quartered in a series of long, sloping barracks interspersed by buildings used for storage of supplies and weapons. Approximately one-third of this great fighting force was kept on duty at any given time, while the other two-thirds remained at home with their families, pursuing their secondary occupations as laborers, craftsmen, or shopkeepers in the city. The barracks were equipped to house the entire army if the need should ever arise, as indeed it had already done on more than one occasion, but at present they were only partially filled. Set back from the barracks, supply housing, and parade grounds was a second wall of stone blocks separating the soldiers' quarters from the city proper. Within this second wall, lining the neat, winding city streets, were the homes and businesses of the urban population of Tyrsis, all carefully constructed and meticulously cared for buildings. The city sprawled over most of the plateau's elevation, running from this second stone wall almost to the cliffs bordering the south approach. At this innermost point of the city, a low third wall had been built which marked the entrance to the government buildings and the royal palace of the King, complete with public forum and landscaped grounds. The tree-shaded parks surrounding the palace provided the only sylvan setting on the otherwise open and sparse flatland of the plateau. The third wall had not been built for defensive purposes, but as a line of demarcation, signifying government-owned property that had been reserved for the King's use and, in the case of the parks, for all the people. Balinor deviated from his description of the city's construction long enough to point out to the Elven brothers that the Kingdom of Callahorn was one of the few remaining enlightened monarchies in the world. While it was technically a monarchy ruled by a King, the government also consisted of a parliamentary body composed of representatives chosen by the people of Callahorn, who helped the ruler hammer out the laws that governed the land. The people took great pride in their government and in the Border Legion in which most either had served at one time or were serving now. It was a country in which they could be free men, and this was something worth fighting for.

Callahorn was a land that reflected both the past and the future. On the one hand its cities had been built primarily as fortresses to withstand the frequent assaults by warlike neighbors. The Border Legion was a carryover from earlier times when the newly formed nations were constantly at war, when an almost fanatical pride in national sovereignty resulted in a long struggle over jealously guarded land boundaries, when brotherhood between the peoples of the four lands was still only a distant possibility. The rustic, old-fashioned decor and architecture could be found nowhere else in the quickly growing cities of the deep Southland—cities where more enlightened cultures and less warlike policies were beginning to prevail. Yet it was Tyrsis, with her barbaric walls of stone and warrior men of iron, that had shielded the lower Southland and given it that chance to expand in new directions. There were signs of what was to come in this picturesque land as well, signs that told of another age and time not too far distant. There was a unity of expression in the people that spoke of tolerance and understanding of all races and peoples. In Callahorn, as in no other country in all the sheltered Southland, a man was accepted for what he was and treated accordingly.

Tyrsis was the crossroads of the four lands, and through its walls and lands passed members of all the nations, giving its people an opportunity to see and understand that the differences in face and body that distinguished the races outwardly were negligible. It was the inner person the people had learned to judge. A giant Rock Troll would not be stared at and shunned because of his grotesque appearance by the people of Callahorn; Trolls were common in that land. Gnomes, Elves, and Dwarfs of all types and species made regular passages through that country, and if they were friends, they were welcomed. Balinor smiled as he spoke of this new, growing phenomenon that had begun at last to spread to all the lands, and he felt proud that his people were among the first to turn from the old prejudices to look for common grounds of understanding and friendship.

Durin and Dayel listened in silent agreement. The Elven people knew what it was like to be alone in a world of people who couldn't see beyond their own limits.

Balinor had finished, and the three comrades swung from the tall grass of the plainland onto a broad roadway. The road wound ahead into the darkness toward the low, squat plateau looming blackly against the horizon. They were close enough now to make out the lights of the sprawling city and the movement of people on the stone ramp. The entrance through the towering Outer Wall was sharply outlined by torchlight, the giant gates standing open on oiled hinges, guarded by a number of dark-garbed sentries. From the courtyard within shone the lights of the barracks, but there was an absence of men's laughter and joking that Balinor found peculiar. The voices that were audible were hushed, even muffled, as if no one wished to be heard. The tall borderman peered ahead watchfully, suddenly concerned that something was amiss, but he could detect nothing out of the ordinary, aside from the unusual silence. He dismissed the matter from his mind.

The Elven brothers followed wordlessly as the determined Balinor mounted the causeway leading to the darkened bluff. Several people passed them as they climbed, and those who looked carefully turned to stare in open shock at the Prince of Callahorn. Balinor failed to acknowledge these strange looks, intent upon the city ahead, but the brothers missed nothing and looked at each other in silent warning. Something was seriously wrong. Moments later, as the three reached the plateau, Balinor, too, stopped in sudden concern. He peered intently toward the gates of the city, then looked about him at the shadowed faces of the people passing, who scattered quickly and wordlessly into the night upon discovering his identity. For a moment the three stood rooted in silence, watching the few remaining passersby disappear into the darkness, leaving them alone.

"What is it, Balinor?" Durin asked at last.

"I'm not certain," the Prince replied anxiously. "Look at the insignia of those guards at the gate. None of them bears the crest of the leopard—the standard of my Border Legion. Instead they wear the sign of a falcon, a mark I do not recognize. The people, too—did you notice their looks?"

The slim Elven faces nodded as one, the keen slanted eyes casting about in undisguised apprehension.

"No matter," the borderman declared shortly. "This is still my father's city, and these are my people. We'll get to the bottom of this when we reach the palace."

Again he started toward the mammoth gates of the Outer Wall, the Elves a step or two behind him. The tall Prince made no effort to hide his face as he approached the four armed guards, and their reaction was the same as that of the astonished passersby. They made no move to stop the Prince and no words passed between them, yet one hurriedly abandoned his post and disappeared quickly through the gates of the Inner Wall into the streets of the city beyond. Balinor and the Elves passed beneath the shadow of the giant gateway, which seemed to hang in the darkness above them like a monstrous stone arm. They moved past the open gates and the watchful guards into the courtyard beyond, where they could see the low, Spartanlike barracks that housed the famed Border Legion. There were few lights burning, and the barracks appeared to be nearly deserted. A few men scattered about the courtyard wore tunics bearing the insignia of the leopard, but they wore no armor and carried no weapons. One stared momentarily as the three paused in the center of the courtyard, then started in disbelief and cried out sharply to his fellow soldiers. A door burst open from one of the barracks and a grizzled veteran appeared, staring with the others at Balinor and the Elven brothers. He gave a short command, and the soldiers reluctantly turned back to whatever they had been doing, while he hastened over to the three newcomers.

"My Lord Balinor, you've come at last," the soldier exclaimed in greeting, his head bowing briefly as he came to attention before his commander.

"Captain Sheelon, it's good to see you." Balinor clasped the veteran's gnarled hand in his own. "What's going on in the city? Why do the guards wear the sign of a falcon and not that of our fighting leopard?"

"My Lord, the Border Legion has been ordered to disband! Only a handful of us still remain on duty; the rest are returned to their homes!"

They stared at the man as if he were insane. The Border Legion had been disbanded in the midst of the greatest invasion ever to threaten the Southland? Almost as one they recalled the words of Allanon telling them that the Border Legion was the only hope left to the people of the threatened lands, that the Border Legion must at least temporarily delay the awesome force assembled by the Warlock Lord. Now the army of Callahorn had been mysteriously scattered . . .

"By whose order . . . ?" Balinor asked in slow fury.

"It was your brother," the grizzled Sheelon declared quickly. "He ordered his own guardsmen to assume our duties and commanded the Legion to disband until further notice. The Lords Acton and Messaline went to the palace to beg the King to reconsider, but they did not return. There was nothing more any of us could do but obey. . . ."

"Has everyone gone mad?" the infuriated borderman demanded, clasping the soldier's tunic. "What of my father, the King? Does he not still rule this land and command the Border Legion? What does he say of this fool's play?"

Sheelon looked away, groping for the words to the answer he was afraid to speak. Balinor jerked him around violently.

"I—I do not know, my Lord," the man muttered, still trying to turn away. "We heard the King was ill, and then there was nothing more. Your brother declared himself temporary ruler in the King's absence from the throne. That was three weeks ago."

Balinor released the man in shocked silence and stared absently at the lights of the distant palace—the home he had come back to with such great hopes. He had left Callahorn because of an intolerable rift between his brother and himself, yet his going had only made matters worse. Now he must face the unpredictable Palance on terms not of his own choosing— face him and persuade him somehow of the folly of his action in disbanding the desperately needed Border Legion.

"We must go at once to the palace and speak with your brother." The eager, impatient voice of Dayel cut into his thoughts. He looked at the youthful Elf for a moment, reminded suddenly of his own brother's young age. It was going to be so hard to reason with Palance.

"Yes, you're right, of course," he agreed almost absently. "We must go to him."

"No, you mustn't go in there!" The sharp cry of Sheelon held them rooted in place. "The others who went did not come out again. There are rumors that your brother has declared you a traitor—found you to be in league with the evil Allanon, the black wanderer who serves the dark powers. It has been said that you shall be imprisoned and put to death!"

"That is ridiculous!" exclaimed the tall borderman quickly. "I am no traitor and even my brother knows this to be true. As for Allanon, he is the best friend and ally the Southland will ever find. I must go to Palance and speak with him. We may disagree, but he would not imprison his own brother. The power is not his!"

"Unless, perhaps, your father is dead, my friend," Durin cautioned from one side. "The time to be prudent is now, before we have entered the palace grounds. Hendel believes your brother to be under the influence of the mystic Stenmin, and if he is, you may be in greater danger than you realize."

Balinor paused, then nodded his agreement. Quickly he explained to Sheelon the threat to Callahorn of an impending Northland invasion, emphasizing his belief that the Border Legion would be vital to the defense of their homeland. Then he gripped the aged soldier's shoulder tightly and bent close to him.

"You will wait four hours for my return or for my personal messenger. If I have not come out or sent word in that time, you will seek out the Lords Ginnisson and Fandwick; the Border Legion is to be reassembled immediately! Then go to the people and demand an open trial of our cause from my brother. He cannot refuse this. You will also send word west and east to the Elf and Dwarf nations, informing them that we are thus held, both I and the cousins of Eventine. Can you remember all I have said to you?"

"Yes, my Lord." The soldier nodded eagerly. "It shall be done as you command. May fortune go with you, Prince of Callahorn."

He turned and disappeared back into the barracks, while an impatient and angry Balinor moved toward the inner city. Once again, Durin whispered to his younger brother, urging him to remain outside the city walls until he knew what would happen to Balinor and himself, but Dayel stubbornly refused to be left behind. Durin knew it was pointless to argue the

matter further, and at last conceded Dayel's right to go along. The slim Elf
had not yet reached his twentieth year, and for him life was just beginning.
All of the members of the little company that had come from Culhaven
had felt a special kind of affection for Dayel, the protective love that close
friends always feel for the youngest. His fresh candor and ready friendship were rare qualities in a time when most men lived lives hemmed in
by suspicion and distrust. Durin was afraid for him, for he had the most
to look ahead to and the fewest years behind. If the boy were harmed in
any way, he realized that an irreplaceable part of himself would be lost.
Durin watched his brother in silence as the lights of Tyrsis burned through
the darkness ahead.

In moments, the three crossed the courtyard and passed through the
gates of the Inner Wall to the streets of the city beyond. Once more the
guards stared in open amazement, but again they did not move to stop
the travelers from entering. Balinor seemed to grow in size as the three
proceeded down the Tyrsian Way, the main city thoroughfare, his dark
form wrapped ominously in the hunting cloak, the chain mail glinting
from exposed fists and neck. He stood taller than before, no longer the
weary traveler at his journey's end, but the Prince of Callahorn come
home. The people knew him at once, at first stopping and staring like
those at the outer gates, then gathering heart from his proud bearing and
rushing after him, eager to welcome him home. The crowd swelled from a
few dozen to several hundred as the favorite son of Callahorn strode
boldly through the city, smiling to those who followed, but hastening to
reach the palace. The shouts and cries of the people rose deafeningly,
changing from scattered voices to a single rising chant calling the tall borderman's name. A few of the crowd managed to get next to the determined man, whispering ominous warnings. But the Prince would not
listen to cautious voices any longer; shaking his head after each warning,
he continued on.

The growing crowd passed through the heart of Tyrsis, milling under
the giant archways and crosswalks that ran overhead, pushing through the
narrow portions of the Tyrsian Way past tall, white-walled buildings and
smaller single-family residences to the Bridge of Sendic which spanned
the lower levels of the people's parks. At the other end stood the gates of
the palace, darkened and closed. At the peak of the bridge's wide arch, the
Prince of Callahorn turned abruptly to face the throng still faithfully following him and threw up his hands in a command to halt. They came to
an obedient stop, their voices lowering into silence as the tall figure addressed them.

"My friends—my countrymen." The proud voice rang out in the near
darkness, its thundering echoes rolling back. "I have missed this land and
its brave citizens, but I have come home—and I will not leave again! There
is no need for fear. This land shall stand eternal! If there be trouble within
the monarchy, then it is for me to face it. You must go back now to your
homes and wait for morning to show you in a better light that all is well.
Please, go now to your homes and I shall go to mine!"

Without waiting to judge the crowd's reaction, Balinor wheeled about and proceeded on across the bridge toward the gates of the palace, the Elven brothers still close at his heels. The voice of the people rose again to call after them, but the crowd did not follow, though many might have wished to do so. Obedient to his command, they turned slowly about, some still shouting his name in defiance at the silent, darkened castle, though others mumbled grim prophecies of what awaited the tall borderman and his two friends within the walls of the imperial home. The three travelers quickly lost sight of the people as they started down the slope of the bridge's high arch in quick, determined strides. In minutes they reached the tall, metal-bound gates of the palace of the Buckhannahs. Balinor never paused, but reached for the huge iron ring fastened to the wood and brought it crashing down against the shuttered gate in thundering knocks. For a moment there was no other sound, as the men stood in the darkness without, listening with mixed feelings of anger and apprehension. Then a low voice from within called for identification. Balinor gave his name and a sharp command to those within to open the gates immediately. In an instant, the heavy bars were drawn back and the gates swung inward to admit the three. Balinor moved into the garden courtyard without a backward glance at the silent guards, his eyes on the magnificent columned building beyond. Its high windows were dark except for those on the ground floor in the left wing. Durin motioned Dayel ahead of him, taking the opportunity to peer into the shadows about them where he quickly discovered a dozen well-armed guards close at hand. All bore the insignia of the falcon.

The watchful Elf knew instantly that they were walking into a trap, just as he had silently anticipated when they had entered the city. His first inclination was to stop Balinor and warn him of what he had seen. But he instinctively knew that the borderman was far too seasoned a fighter not to know what he was getting into. Durin wished once more that his brother had stayed outside the palace walls, but it was too late now. The three crossed the garden walks to the doors of the palace. There were no guards and the doors opened without resistance to Balinor's hurried shove. The halls of the aged building glowed brightly in the torchlight, the flames catching the splendor of the colorful wall murals and paintings that decorated the Buckhannah family home. The wood trimming was old and rich, polished with care and partially covered by fine tapestries and metal plaques of family crests from generations of the famed rulers of the land. As the Elven brothers followed the tall Prince down these silent halls, they recalled darkly another time and place in the recent past—the ancient fortress of Paranor. There, too, a trap had awaited them amid the historic splendor of another age.

They turned left into another hallway, Balinor still in the lead by several strides, his big form filling the high corridor, the long hunting cloak billowing out behind him as he walked. For an instant, he reminded Durin of Allanon, huge, angered, dangerous when he moved catlike as the Prince of Callahorn did now. Durin glanced anxiously at Dayel, but the younger

Elf did not seem to notice; his face was flushed with excitement. Durin felt for the handle of his dagger, the cold metal reassuring to his hot palm. If they were to be trapped again, it would not be without a fight.

Then the giant borderman stopped suddenly before an open doorway. The Elven brothers hastened to his side, peering past his broad frame into the lighted room beyond. There was a man standing near the back of the elegantly furnished chamber—a big man, blond and bearded, his broad figure cloaked in a long purple robe with a falcon marking. He was several years younger than Balinor, but held his tall frame erect in the same manner, the hands clasped loosely behind his back. The Elves knew immediately that he was Palance Buckhannah. Balinor moved several steps into the chamber, saying nothing, his eyes riveted on his brother's face. The Elves followed the borderman, looking cautiously about. There were too many doors, too many heavy drapes that could be concealing armed guards. A moment later there was a movement in the hall behind them just out of sight. Dayel turned slightly to face the open doorway. Durin moved a little apart from the others, his long hunting knife drawn, his lean frame bent slightly in a half-crouch.

Balinor made no move, but stood silently before his brother, staring at the familiar face, amazed that the eyes were filled with a strange hatred. He had known it would be a trap, known that his brother would be prepared for them. Yet he had believed all along that they would at least be able to talk as brothers, converse with one another in a frank and reasonable manner despite their differences. But as he looked into those eyes and caught the undisguised glint of burning fury, he realized that his brother was beyond reason, perhaps beyond sanity.

"Where is my father . . . ?"

Balinor's abrupt query was cut short by a sudden swishing sound as hidden cords released a large leather and rope net that had hung unnoticed above the intruders, dropping it instantly over all three. The attached weights brought all of them crashing to the floor in staggered dismay, their weapons useless against the toughened cords. Doors flew open from all sides and the heavy drapes whipped back as several dozen armed guards rushed over to subdue the struggling captives. There was never any chance to escape the carefully prepared trap, never even a momentary opportunity to fight back. The captives were relieved of their weapons, their hands bound unceremoniously behind their backs, and their eyes blindfolded. They were lifted roughly to their feet and firmly held in place by a dozen unseen hands. There was momentary silence as someone approached and stood before them.

"You were a fool to come back, Balinor," a chilling voice sounded out of the blackness. "You knew what would happen to you if I found you again. You are thrice over a traitor and a coward for what you have done—to the people, to my father, and now even to me. What have you done with Shirl? What have you done with her? You will die for this, Balinor, I swear it! Take them below!"

The hands spun them about, shoving and dragging them down the hallway, through one door, down a long flight of stairs to a landing and another hall that wound about in a maze of twists and turns. Their feet thudded heavily on dank stones in a black, unbroken silence. Suddenly they were going down yet another set of stairs and into another passageway. They could smell the stale, chill air and feel the dampness ooze from the stone walls and floor. A set of heavy bolts was drawn slowly back with a screech of aged iron against iron, and the door they held in place ponderously opened. The hands turned them sharply, releasing them without warning as they fell dazed and battered to the stone floor, still bound and blindfolded. The door closed and the bolts slid heavily into place. The three companions listened wordlessly. They heard the sound of footsteps retreating rapidly into the distance until they had faded away altogether. They heard the sounds of clanging metal as doors were barred and shuttered, each farther away than the last, until finally there was only the sound of their own breathing in the deep silence of their prison. Balinor had come home.

23

It was nearing midnight by the time Allanon had finished disguising the reluctant Flick to his satisfaction. Using a strange lotion produced from a pouch he carried at his waist, the Druid rubbed the skin of the Valeman's face and hands until it was a dark yellow. A piece of soft coal altered the lines in the face and the appearance of the eyes. It was a makeshift job at best, but in the dark he could pass for a large, heavyset Gnome, if not closely examined. It would have been a perilous undertaking even for a seasoned hunter, and for an untrained man to attempt to pass himself off as a Gnome appeared to be suicide. But there was no alternative left. Someone had to get into that giant encampment and attempt to discover what had happened to Eventine, Shea, and the elusive Sword. It was out of the question for Allanon to go down there; he would have been recognized in an instant, even in the best disguise. So the task fell to the frightened Flick, disguised as a Gnome, under cover of darkness, to work his way down the slopes, past the watching guards, into the camp occupied by thousands of Gnomes and Trolls, and there find out if his brother or the missing Elven King were prisoners, in addition to trying to learn something of the whereabouts of the Sword. To complicate matters, the Valeman had to get clear of the enemy camp before daybreak. If he failed to do this, someone would most certainly see through his disguise in the daylight and he would be caught.

Allanon asked Flick to remove his hunting cloak and worked on the material for several minutes, altering the cut slightly and lengthening the hood covering to conceal its wearer better. When he was done, Flick covered himself and found that with the cloak pulled closely about his body, nothing was visible aside from his hands and a shadowed portion of his face. If he stayed away from any true Gnomes and kept moving until dawn, there was an outside chance that he might learn something important and still escape to tell Allanon. He checked to be certain the short hunting dagger was securely fastened to his waist. It was a poor substitute for a weapon, should he have need of one once he was within the encampment, but it gave him a little reassurance that he was not totally without protection. He stood up slowly, his short, heavyset frame wrapped in the cloak as Allanon looked him over carefully and then nodded.

The weather had become threatening during the past hour, the sky a solid bank of rolling, blackened clouds that completely blotted out the moon and stars, leaving the earth in almost complete darkness. The only visible light in any direction came from the blazing fires of the encamped enemy, the flames rushing higher with the sudden appearance of a strong north wind that howled fiercely through the Dragon's Teeth to sweep in rising gusts onto the unprotected plainlands below. A storm was on the way, and it would very likely reach them before morning. The silent Druid was hopeful that the winds and darkness would offer the disguised Valeman a little added cover from the eyes of the sleeping army.

In brief, clipped sentences, the giant mystic offered Flick a few parting words of caution. He explained the manner in which the camp would be arranged, noting the pattern in which guards would be posted about the perimeter of the main army. He told him to look for the standards of the Gnome chieftains and the Maturens, the Troll leaders, which would undoubtedly lie somewhere near the center of the fires. At all costs, he was to avoid speaking to anyone, for the tone of his voice would instantly betray him as a Southlander. Flick listened attentively, his heart pounding wildly as he waited to go, his own mind already made up that he had no chance of escaping detection; but his loyalty to his brother was too great to permit the interference of common sense when Shea's safety was threatened. Allanon closed his brief explanation by promising to see that the youth got safely past the first guard line that had been posted at the base of these slopes. He signaled for complete silence, then motioned for the other to follow.

They moved down out of the rocky shelter of the high boulders, winding their way through the darkness toward the open plain. It was so black that Flick could see almost nothing and had to be led by the hand in order to stay with the surefooted Druid. It seemed to take an interminable length of time for the two to reach an exit point from the twisting maze of boulders, but at last they were able to see once more the fires of the enemy camp burning in the darkness ahead. Flick was bruised and battered from his climb down out of the mountain heights, his limbs aching from the strain, his cloak torn in several places. The darkness of the plain seemed to stand like an unbroken wall between the fires and themselves, and Flick could neither see nor hear the guard lines he knew were there. Allanon said nothing, but crouched back in the shelter of the rocks, his head cocked slightly as he listened. The two remained motionless for long minutes, then suddenly Allanon rose, motioning Flick to remain where he was, and silently disappeared in the night.

When he was gone, the little Valeman looked about anxiously, alone and frightened because he had no idea what was happening. Leaning his heated face against the cool surface of the rock, he went over in his mind what he would do once he reached the encampment. He didn't have much of a plan to rely on. He would avoid speaking with anyone, and if possible, avoid passing close to anyone. He would stay clear of the illuminating firelight which might betray his poor disguise. The prisoners, if in the camp at all, would be held in a guarded tent near the center of the fires, so his first objective would be to find that tent. Once he found it, he would try to get a look inside to see who was there. Then, assuming he got that far, which seemed highly unlikely, he would make his way back to the slopes, where Allanon would be waiting and they would decide their next move.

Flick shook his head in frustration. He knew he would never be able to get away with this disguise—he was neither talented nor clever enough to fool anyone. But ever since losing Shea over the side of the Dragon's Crease days earlier, his attitude had completely altered and the old pessimism and hard-nosed practicality had been replaced by a strange sense of futile desperation. His familiar world had altered so drastically in the past few weeks that he no longer seemed capable of identifying with his old values and sensible practices. Time had become almost meaningless in the punishing, endless days of running and hiding, of fighting creatures that belonged to another world. The years spent living and growing in the peace and solitude of Shady Vale were distant, forgotten days of an early youth. The only constant forces in his upended life of the past weeks had been his companions, particularly his brother. Now they, too, had been scattered one by one until at last Flick stood alone, on the verge of exhaustion and mental collapse, his world a mad, impossible puzzle of nightmares and spirits that chased and haunted him to the brink of despair.

The hulking presence of Allanon had given him little comfort. The giant Druid had remained from their first meeting both an impenetrable wall of secrecy and a mystical force with powers that defied explanation. Despite the growing camaraderie of the company on the journey to Paranor and beyond, the Druid had remained aloof and secretive. Even what he had told them about his own origin and purposes did little to lighten the dark veil of mystery in which he had wrapped himself.

When the company had been together, the mystic's domination of them had not seemed so overpowering, even though he had remained the undisputed force behind their hazardous search for the Sword of Shannara. But now, with the others gone, leaving the frightened Valeman alone with this unpredictable giant, Flick found himself unable to escape that terrible

awesomeness that formed the essence of this strange man. He thought
back again on the mysterious tale of the history of the fabled Sword, and
again he remembered Allanon's refusal to tell the members of the little
company the whole story behind its power. They had risked everything for
that elusive talisman, and still no one but Allanon knew how the weapon
could be used to defeat the Warlock Lord. Why was it that Allanon knew
so much about it?

A sudden noise in the darkness behind him brought the terrified Valeman about in a flash, the short hunting knife drawn and extended in self-
defense. There was a sharp whisper and the huge form of Allanon moved
silently to Flick's side. A powerful hand gripped his shoulder, guiding him
back into the shelter of the rock-covered slope, where the two crouched
cautiously in the blackness. Allanon studied the Valeman's face for an instant as if judging his courage, reading his mind to see the nature of his
thoughts. Flick could just barely force himself to meet the penetrating
gaze, his heart pounding in mingled fear and excitement.

"The guards are disposed of—the way is clear." The deep voice
seemed to rise up out of the depths of the earth. "Go now, my young
friend, and keep your courage and your good sense close at hand."

Flick nodded shortly and rose, his cloak-shrouded form gliding quickly
and stealthily out of the cover of the boulders onto the blackness of the
empty plains. His mind ceased to reason, ceased to wonder, as his body took
command and his instincts probed the darkness for hidden danger. He
moved swiftly toward the distant firelight, running in a half-crouch, pausing
occasionally to check his position and listen for the sounds of human movement. The night was an impenetrable shroud all about him, the sky still
heavily overcast and wrapped in a huge cloud blanket that shut out even the
dim whiteness of the moon and stars. The only light came from the campfires ahead. The plainland was smooth and open, its surface a grassy blanket
that muffled the Valeman's footfalls as he raced silently forward. There were
few bushes to break the pattern, and it was left to one or two thin, twisted
trees to fill the vast emptiness. There was no sign of life anywhere in the
darkness and the only sounds were the muffled howl of the rising wind and
his own heavy breathing. The campfires that had formerly seemed a low
haze of orange light from the base of the mountains spread apart into individual fires as the Valeman drew closer, some burning brightly, their flames
well fed on new wood, while others had dimmed and nearly died into coals
as the men who tended them slept undisturbed. Flick was close enough
now to hear the faint sound of voices in the sleeping camp, but they were
not distinct enough to enable him to make out the words.

Almost half an hour passed before Flick reached the outer perimeter
of the enemy fires. He paused in a crouch just beyond the light to study
the lay of the camp ahead. The cool night wind blowing out of the north
fanned the crackling flames of the large wood fires, sending thin clouds of
smoke swirling across the open plains toward the Valeman. There was a
second ring of sentries encircling the encampment, but it was only a sec-

ondary guard line loosely set at wide intervals. The Northlanders felt there
was little need for caution this close to the campsite. The sentries were primarily Gnome hunters, although Flick could distinguish the larger bulks of
Troll men scattered about as well.

He paused momentarily to study the strange, unfamiliar features of the
Trolls. They were of different sizes, all thick-limbed and covered with a
dark, woodlike skin that appeared rough and highly protective. The sentries and the few members of the army that were not asleep, but standing idly about or crouched near the low-burning fires for warmth, had
wrapped themselves in heavy cloaks that masked most of their bodies
and faces. Flick nodded to himself in satisfaction. It would be easier for
him to slip into the camp undetected if everyone remained wrapped in
their cloaks, and judging from the increasing coolness of the wind, the
temperature would continue to drop until sunrise. It was difficult to see
much beyond the outer fires, due to the clouded darkness and the smoke
given off by the quick-burning wood.

Somehow the camp seemed smaller from this viewpoint than it had
from the heights of the Dragon's Teeth. Flick could not get the same sense
of depth from his present position, but he did not try to fool himself. Despite what it appeared to be from where he crouched, he knew that it
stretched for over a mile in all directions. Once past the inner sentry line,
he would have to pick his way through thousands of sleeping Gnomes and
Trolls, past hundreds of fires bright enough to reveal his identity, and all
the way avoid contact with the enemy soldiers who were still awake. The
first miscalculation the Valeman made would give him away. Even if he managed to avoid discovery, he still had to locate the prisoners and the Sword.
He shook his head in doubt and moved forward slowly.

The natural curiosity of the Valeman prompted him to linger near the
fringes of the firelight to study further the Gnomes and Trolls still awake,
but he resisted the impulse, reminding himself that he didn't have much
time as it was. Though he had lived all his life on the same earth with these
two foreign races, they were like species from another world to the little
Southlander. During his journey to Paranor, he had fought the cunning,
savage Gnomes several times, once hand to hand in the labyrinth passages
of the Druid's Keep. But he still knew little about them; they were simply
an enemy who had tried to kill him. He had learned nothing of the giant
Trolls, a habitually reclusive people dwelling principally in the northern
mountains and their hidden valleys. In any event, Flick knew that the army
was under the leadership of the Warlock Lord, and there was no question
as to what *his* goals were!

He waited until the wind carried the smoke from the burning fires
between the closest sentry and himself in a series of billowing gusts,
then rose and strolled in a casual manner toward the encampment. He
had carefully selected an entry point where the soldiers were all sleeping.
The smoke and the night masked his bulky form as he moved out of
the shadows and into the circle of fires nearest to him. A moment later

he stood in the midst of the soundly sleeping forms. The sentry continued to stare blankly into the darkness behind him, unaware of the hurried passage.

Flick wrapped the cloak and head covering closely about his body, making certain that only his hands were immediately visible to anyone passing by. His face was a dim shadow beneath the hood. He glanced about quickly, but there was no movement by anyone close at hand; he had made it this far unnoticed. He breathed deeply of the cool night air to steady himself, then tried to gauge his position in relation to the center of the encampment. He chose a direction which he believed would take him directly toward the hub of the burning fires, glanced about once more to reassure himself, then moved forward with steady, measured steps. Now there could be no turning back.

What he saw, what he heard, what he experienced deep within his mind that night left an indelible print in his memory that would stay with him forever. It was like a strange, somehow elusive nightmare of sights and sounds, creatures and shapes from another time and place—things that never were in and could never belong to his own world, and yet had been cast onto it like so much driftwood from an endless sea. Perhaps it was the night and the wafting smoke from the hundreds of dying fires that clouded his normal senses and created this dreamlike experience. Perhaps, too, it was the aftereffect of a tired, frightened mind that had never conceived of the existence of such creatures, nor imagined their number could be so vast.

The night passed in slow minutes and endless hours as the little Valeman wound his way through the giant encampment, shielding his face from the light of the fires as he moved steadily forward, his eyes searching, studying and always looking further. Cautiously, he picked his tortured way over thousands of sleeping bodies huddled close to the flames, often blocking his progress entirely, each another chance that he might be discovered and killed. There were times when he was certain that he had been discovered, times when his hand moved swiftly, silently to the small hunting knife, his heart dying within him as he prepared to fight for his freedom at the cost of his life. Again and again, men came toward him as if they knew he was an impostor, as if they would stop him and expose him to everyone. But each time they passed by without pausing, without speaking, and Flick would be left alone once again, a forgotten figure in a gathering of thousands.

Several times he passed close to groups of men talking and joking in low tones as they huddled around the fires, rubbing their hands and drawing from the crackling flames what little heat there was to protect them against the growing cold of the night. Twice, perhaps three times, they nodded or waved as he pushed past them, his face lowered, the cloak held close about his body, and he would make some feeble gesture in acknowledgment. Time and again he was afraid he had made a wrong move, failed to speak when he should, walked where he was not permitted—but each time the terrible moment of doubt vanished as he hurried on, and he found himself alone once more.

He wandered through the immense camp for hours without finding any clue to the whereabouts of Shea, Eventine, or the Sword of Shannara. As morning drew near, he began to despair of finding anything. He had passed countless fires, burning low and dying with the close of night, gazed on a sea of sleeping bodies, some with faces turned skyward, some with blankets all around them, all unknown. There had been tents everywhere, marked by the standards of the enemy leaders, both Gnome and Troll, but there had been no guards stationed before them to distinguish them in importance. A few he had checked closely on a chance that he might stumble onto something, but he had found nothing.

He listened to snatches of conversation between the Gnomes and Trolls who were not sleeping, trying to remain inconspicuous and at the same time come close enough to hear what was being said. But the Troll tongue was completely foreign, and what little he understood of the garbled Gnome speech consisted of useless information. It was as if no one knew anything of the two missing men and the Sword—as if they had never been brought to this camp at all. Flick began to wonder if Allanon had been completely mistaken about the trail signs they had followed these past few days.

He glanced apprehensively at the clouded night sky. He could not be certain of the time, but he knew there could be no more than several hours of darkness remaining. For a moment he panicked, abruptly realizing that he might not even have enough time to find his way back to where Allanon was concealed. But shaking off his fear, he quickly reasoned that in the confusion of breaking camp at dawn he would be able to slip quickly back through the sleepy hunters and make the short dash for the slopes of the Dragon's Teeth before the sun found him.

There was a sudden movement in the darkness off to his right, and into the firelight trudged four massive Troll warriors, all fully armed, muttering in low tones among themselves as they moved past the startled Valeman. On impulse more than reason, Flick fell in several yards behind them, curious as to where they might be going dressed in full battle array while it was still night. They were moving at right angles to the course the disguised Flick had chosen to follow into the encampment, and he stayed just behind them in the shadows as they trudged steadily through the sleeping army. Several times they passed darkened tents that Flick believed might be their destination, but they continued on without pausing.

The little Valeman noticed that the style of the encampment was changing rapidly in this particular area. There were more tents than before, some with high, lighted canopies that silhouetted men moving within. There were fewer common soldiers sleeping on the chill earth, but more sentries patrolling between the well-fed fires that lighted the open spaces between tents. Flick found it harder to remain hidden in this new light; to avoid questions and to protect against an increased risk of discovery, he moved right up behind the marching Trolls as if he were one of them. They passed numerous sentries that offered short greetings and watched as they passed, but no one attempted to question the heavily cloaked Gnome who scampered along at the rear of the small procession.

Then abruptly the Trolls turned left and automatically Flick turned with them—only to find himself almost on top of a long, low tent guarded by more armed Trolls. There was no time to turn back or avoid being seen, so when the procession came to a halt before the tent, the fearful Valeman kept right on walking, moving past them as if he were oblivious to what was taking place. The guards evidently failed to think there was anything out of the ordinary, all glancing briefly his way as he shuffled past, the cloak pulled closely about him, and in an instant he was beyond them, alone in the blackness of the shadows.

He halted sharply, sweat running down his body beneath the heavy clothing, his breathing short and labored. There had been only a second to glance through the open front of the lighted tent, between the towering Troll sentries holding the long, iron pikes—only a second to see the crouched, black-winged monster that stood within, surrounded by the lesser forms of both Trolls and Gnomes. But there was no mistaking one of those deadly creatures that had hunted them across the four lands. There was no mistaking the chill feeling of terror that ran through the Valeman's body as he stood breathlessly in the shadows to still his pounding heart.

Something vitally important was taking place inside that heavily guarded tent. Perhaps the missing men and the Sword were there, held by the servants of the Warlock Lord. It was a chilling thought, and Flick knew that he had to get a look inside. His time was up, his luck run out. The guards alone were deterrent enough to anyone trying to pass through the open flaps, and the added presence of the Skull Bearer made the idea suicidal. Flick sat back on his heels in the darkness between the tents and shook his head hopelessly. The enormity of the task utterly discouraged any hope for success, yet what other course lay open? If he returned to Allanon now, they would know nothing more than they had known previously and his arduous night of creeping about the enemy encampment would have been for nothing.

He gazed expectantly at the night sky, as if it might hold some clue to the answer to his problem. The cloud bank remained solidly in position overhead, hanging ominously between the light of the moon and stars and the blackness of the sleeping earth. The night was almost over. Flick rose and pulled the cloak closely about his chilled body once again. Fate may have decided that he should come all these torturous miles only to be killed in a foolish gamble, but Shea depended on him—perhaps Allanon and the others as well. He had to know what was in that tent. Slowly, cautiously, he began to inch his way forward.

The dawn came quickly, a sullen gray lightening of the eastern sky, heavy with mist and silence. The weather had not improved below the Strele-

heim, south of the persistent wall of darkness that marked the advance of
the Warlock Lord. Huge thunderclouds remained locked overhead like an
ominous shroud covering its earthen corpse. Near the base of the western
Dragon's Teeth, the enemy sentries had abandoned their night watch to return to the awakening encampment of the Northland army. Allanon sat
quietly in the shelter of the boulder-strewn slope, the long, black cloak
that was wrapped loosely around his lean, reedlike body offering little protection against either the chill dawn air or the faint drizzle that was rapidly
turning into a heavy downpour. He had been there all night, his eyes
watching, searching for some sign of Flick, his hopes slowly fading as the
sky lightened in the east and the enemy came to life. Still he waited, hoping against the odds that the little Valeman had somehow managed to conceal his identity, somehow managed to slip through the camp undetected
and find his missing brother, the Elven King, and the Sword, then somehow managed to work his way clear of the pickets before daylight to reach
freedom.

The encampment was breaking up, the tents disassembled and packed
as the huge army fell into columns that covered the vast plain like giant
black squares. Finally the fighting machine of the Warlock Lord began to
march southward in the direction of Kern, and the giant Druid came
down out of the rocks where he could be seen by the missing Valeman if
he were anywhere close at hand. There was no movement, no sound but
the wind blowing softly across the grasslands, and the tall dark figure stood
silently. Only the eyes betrayed the keen bitterness he felt.

At last, the Druid turned southward, choosing a course parallel to that
of the army marching ahead. Giant strides quickly ate up the distance between them as the rain began to fall in heavy sheets and the vast emptiness
of the plains was left behind.

Menion Leah reached the winding Mermidon River immediately north of
the island city of Kern only minutes before dawn. Allanon had not been
wrong when he had warned the Prince that he would have a difficult time
slipping through the enemy lines undetected. The sentry outposts extended beyond the perimeter of the sprawling plain encampment, running
west above the Mermidon from the southern edge of the Dragon's Teeth.
Everything north of that line belonged to the Warlock Lord. Enemy patrols roamed unchallenged along the southern boundaries of the towering
Dragon's Teeth, guarding the few passages that cut through these formidable peaks. Balinor, Hendel, and the Elven brothers had managed to break
the security of one of these enemy patrols in the high Kennon Pass. Menion did not have the protective shelter of the mountains in which to conceal himself from the Northlanders. Once he had left Allanon and Flick,
he was forced to proceed directly across the flat, open grasslands that stretched
south to the Mermidon. But the highlander had two things in his favor.
The night remained clouded and completely, impenetrably black, making
it nearly impossible to see more than several yards ahead. More important
than this, Menion was a tracker and hunter without equal in the Southland.

He could move through this shroudlike blackness with speed and stealth, undetected by any but the most sensitive ears.

So it happened that he moved silently from the side of his two companions, still angered that Allanon had forced him to give up the search for Shea in order that he might warn Balinor and the people of Callahorn of the impending invasion. He felt strangely uneasy about leaving Flick alone with the mysterious and unpredictable Druid. He had never completely trusted the giant mystic, knowing that the man was keeping the truth about the Sword of Shannara hidden from them, knowing that there was more to Allanon than he had chosen to tell them. They had done everything the Druid had commanded of them in blind faith, trusting him implicitly each time a crisis had arisen. Each time he had been right—but still they had failed to gain possession of the Sword, and they had lost Shea. Now on top of everything else, it appeared the Northland army would successfully invade the Southland. Only the border kingdom of Callahorn stood ready to resist the assault. Having seen the awesome size of the invader, Menion did not see how even the legendary Border Legion could hope to withstand such a mighty force. His own common sense told him that the only hope was to stall the advancing enemy long enough to unite the Elven and Dwarf armies with the Border Legion and then strike back. He felt certain the missing Sword was lost to them, and that even when they relocated Shea, there would be no further opportunity to search for the strange weapon.

He uttered a low oath as his exposed knee jammed painfully against the sharp edge of a jutting boulder, and he turned his attention to the matter at hand, all further speculation about the future put aside for the time being. Like a lean, black lizard, he skimmed noiselessly down the low slopes of the Dragon's Teeth, winding his torturous way through the maze of knife-edged boulders and rocks that covered the mountainside, the sword of Leah and the long ash bow strapped securely to his back. He reached the base of the slope without encountering anyone, and he peered into the darkness. There was no sign of life. He moved cautiously onto the grass-covered plainlands, inching forward a few yards at a time, pausing periodically to listen. He knew the sentry lines had to be posted close to this point to be effective, but it was impossible to see anyone.

At last he rose to his feet, as silent as the shadows all about him; hearing nothing, he began to walk slowly southward through the wall of darkness, his hunting knife held loosely in one hand. He walked for long minutes without incident and had just begun to relax in the belief that he had somehow slipped through the enemy lines without either of them knowing it, when he heard a small noise. He froze in midstride, trying to locate the source, and then it came again, a low cough from someone in the darkness directly in front of him. A sentry had given himself away just in time to save the highlander from stumbling into him. One cry would have brought others in an instant.

Menion dropped into a crouch on his hands and knees, the dagger clutched tightly. He began to creep forward toward the source of the cough, his movement soundless. At last his eyes were able to discern the dim outline of someone standing silently before him. From his small size, the sentry was clearly a Gnome. Menion waited a few minutes longer to be certain that the Gnome had his back turned to him, then he crept still closer until he was within several feet. In one fluid motion he rose to tower over the unsuspecting sentry, one steel-like arm gripping the fellow's throat, cutting off the cry of warning before it could escape. The butt end of the knife came down sharply on the exposed head, just back of the ear, and the unconscious Gnome crumpled to the earth. The highlander did not pause, but slipped ahead into the darkness, knowing there would be others close at hand, and eager to move beyond their range of hearing. He held the dagger ready, anticipating that there might be still another sentry line. The chill wind blew steadily and the long minutes of the night crawled on.

Finally he was at the Mermidon, just above the island city of Kern, its lights faint in the distant south. He paused at the top of a small rise which dropped off gradually and sloped downward to form the north bank of the swift river. He remained in a half-crouch, his long hunting cloak wrapped about his lean frame to protect himself from the growing chill of the dawn wind. He was surprised and relieved that he had reached the river without running into still other enemy pickets. He suspected that his earlier assumption had been correct, and that he had passed through at least one other sentry line without realizing it.

Gazing carefully around, the Prince of Leah assured himself that no one else was about, then rose and stretched wearily. He knew he had to cross the Mermidon farther downriver if he wished to avoid a chilling swim in the icy waters. Once he reached a point directly across from the island, he was certain he would find a boat or ferry service to the city. Hitching his weapons higher on his back and smiling grimly against the cold, he began to walk southward along the river rise.

He had not gone very far, perhaps no more than a thousand yards, when the rushing of the dawn wind faded for an instant, and in the sudden stillness he heard an unfamiliar murmur from somewhere ahead. Instantly he dropped to the ground, his dark form flat against the small rise. The wind rushed back into his straining ears as he listened in the blackness. The gusting breeze died a second time and again he heard the low murmur, but this time he was certain of its origin. It was the muffled sound of human voices carried out of the darkness ahead near the bank of the river. The highlander crawled hurriedly back over the rise to where the terrain again shielded him from the faint lights of the distant city. Then he rose and moved forward in a half-crouch, running parallel to the river, his passing noiseless and swift. The voices grew louder and more distinct and at last seemed to come from directly behind the grassy rise. He listened a minute longer, but found it impossible to decipher what was being said. Cautiously, he crawled on his stomach to the top of the rise where he was able to make out a group of dark figures huddled next to the Mermidon.

The first thing that caught his eye was the boat pulled up onto the riverbank and tied to a low bush. There was his transportation if he could get to it, but he discarded the idea almost instantly. Standing in a tight circle next to the moored boat were four very large, armed Trolls, their huge black bulks unmistakable even in this poor light. They were speaking with a fifth figure, smaller and slighter in build, his robes clearly marking him as a Southlander.

Menion studied them a moment with great care, trying to make out their faces, but the dim light gave him only brief glimpses of the man and he didn't appear to be anyone Menion had ever encountered previously. A small, dark beard covered the thin, shallow face of the stranger, and he had a peculiar habit of stroking the little beard in short, nervous pats while he talked.

Then the Prince of Leah saw something else. To one side of the circle of men was a large bundle covered with a heavy cloak and securely tied. Menion studied it dubiously, unable to tell what it was in the darkness. Then to his astonishment, the bundle moved slightly—enough to convince the highlander that there was something alive beneath the heavy coverings. Desperately he tried to think of a way he might move closer to the small party, but already he was too late. The four Trolls and the stranger were parting company. One of the Trolls moved over to the mysterious bundle and, in one effortless heave, threw it over his broad, bulky shoulder. The stranger was returning to the boat, loosening the fastenings and climbing in, the oars lowered to the choppy waters. There were several parting words exchanged, and Menion caught snatches of the brief conversation, including something about having the situation well in hand. The final comment as the boat moved out into the swift waters was a warning from the stranger to wait for further word from him on the Prince.

Menion inched back a bit on the damp grass of the little rise, watching the man and the small boat disappear into the misty darkness of the Mermidon. Dawn was breaking at last, but it came in the form of a dim, hazy grayness that hampered visibility almost as effectively as the night. The sky was still overcast by low-hanging cumulous clouds that threatened to drop to the earth itself should they swell further. A heavy rain would fall before much longer and already the air was coated with a damp, penetrating mist that soaked the highlander's clothing and chilled the exposed skin. The huge Northland army would be on the march toward the island city of Kern within the hour, probably reaching it by midday. There was little time remaining for him to warn its citizens of the impending assault—an onslaught of men and weapons against which the city could not hope to defend itself for long. The people had to be evacuated immediately and taken to Tyrsis or farther south for protection. Balinor had to be warned that time had run out, that the Border Legion must assemble and fight a delaying action until reinforced by the Dwarf and Elven armies.

The Prince of Leah knew there was no time to ponder further the mysterious meeting he had just accidentally witnessed, but he lingered a moment longer as the four Trolls turned from the riverbank, carrying the struggling bundle, and moved toward the rise to his right. Menion was certain that someone had been taken prisoner by the stranger in the boat and turned over to these soldiers of the Northland army. This night meeting had been prearranged by both parties and the exchange made for reasons known only to them. If they had gone to all that trouble, the prisoner must be someone very important to them—and therefore important to the Warlock Lord.

Menion watched the Trolls move away from him into the heavy morning mist, still undecided as to whether he should intervene. Allanon had given him a task to complete—a vital task that might save thousands of lives. There was no time for wild forays in enemy country just to satisfy personal curiosity, even if it meant saving . . . Shea! Suppose it was Shea they had taken prisoner? The thought flashed through the impetuous mind, and instantly the decision had been made. Shea was the key to everything—if there was any chance that he was the captive wrapped in that bundle, Menion had to try to rescue him.

He leaped to his feet and began running swiftly northward, back in the direction from which he had just come, trying to stay on a course parallel to that taken by the Trolls. In the heavy mist, it was difficult to keep his sense of direction, but Menion had no time to be concerned with that. It was going to be extremely difficult to take that prisoner away from four armed Trolls, especially when any one of them was easily a match physically for the slight highlander. There was the added danger that they might at any point pass back through the sentry lines of the Northland outposts. If he failed to stop them before then, he was finished. Any chance of rescue depended on keeping open an escape route to the Mermidon. Menion felt the first rains of the coming storm strike his face as he ran, and the thunder rumbled ominously overhead as the wind began to grow in force. Desperately he searched through the rolling clouds of mist and fog for some sign of his quarry, but there was nothing to be seen. Certain that he had been too slow and had missed them, he raced at breakneck speed across the grasslands, charging like a wild black shadow through the mist, dodging the small trees and clumps of brush, his eyes searching the empty flatlands. The rain beat against his face and ran into his eyes, blinding him, forcing him to slow down momentarily to wipe away the warm haze of mingled rain and perspiration. He shook his head in anger. They had to be somewhere close! He couldn't have lost them!

Abruptly the four Trolls appeared out of the fog behind him and off to the left. Menion had misjudged and completely overtaken and passed them. He dropped into a crouch behind a small clump of bushes and watched a moment as the four moved closer. If they stayed on their present course, they would pass almost next to a large clump of scrub brush farther ahead—still beyond their vision, but within Menion's. The highlander bounded from cover and raced back into the mist until he could no longer see the Trolls. If they had seen him make that quick dash into the fog, he was through. They would be expecting him when they reached the scrub brush. But if not, he would spring his ambush there and make a break for the river. He cut back across the plains to his left until he reached the seclusion of the brush where, panting heavily, he dropped to all fours and peered cautiously through the branches.

For a moment there was nothing but the fog and the rain, and then four bulky figures appeared out of the gray mist, moving steadily toward his place of concealment. He threw off the cumbersome hunting cloak, already soaked through by the morning rains. He would need speed to elude the massive Trolls once he managed to get the prisoner away from them, and the cloak would only slow him down. He removed the heavy hunting boots as well. At his side he placed the sword of Leah, its bright blade drawn clear of the leather sheath. Hurriedly, he fitted the loosened string to the great ash bow and withdrew two long, black arrows from their casing. The Trolls were closing quickly on his cover now, their dark forms visible through the leafy branches of the brush. They walked in pairs, one of the foremost carrying the limp form of the bound prisoner. They came carelessly toward the hidden man, obviously at ease in territory they believed entirely under the control of their own forces. Menion rose slowly to one knee, a black arrow fitted to the long bow, and waited silently.

The unsuspecting Trolls were almost on top of the scrub brush when the first arrow flew from out of nowhere with a sharp hum, striking the fleshy calf muscle of the bulky Northlander carrying the prisoner. In a roar of mingled rage and pain, the Troll dropped his burden and fell, clutching the injured leg with both hands. In that instant of shock and confusion, Menion fired the second arrow, scoring a solid hit to the exposed shoulder of the second member of the front pair, spinning the massive form entirely about so that he stumbled wildly into the two behind him.

Without pausing, the agile highlander sprang free of the scrub brush and rushed the amazed Trolls, yelling and swinging the sword of Leah. The Trolls had dropped back a step or two from the momentarily forgotten prisoner, and the quick attacker swept the limp form up onto one shoulder with his free arm before the astonished Northlanders could act. In another instant, he had swept past them, his sword cutting into the forearm of the nearest Troll, who made a vain effort to stop the fleet form. The path to the Mermidon lay open!

Two Trolls, one uninjured and the other slightly wounded, gave immediate chase, lumbering heavily across the rain-covered grasslands in determined silence. Their cumbersome armor and large frames slowed them down considerably, but they moved faster than Menion had expected, and they were refreshed and strong while he was already tiring. Even without the hunting cloak and boots, the lean highlander could not run very fast while carrying the still-bound prisoner. The rain had begun to fall in increasingly heavier sheets, windswept and stinging against his skin as he forced his aching body to run faster still. In leaps and bounds he streaked across the grasslands, twisting past small trees, dodging scrub brush and water-soaked potholes. Even in bare feet, his footing on the wet, slippery grass was unsure. Several times he stumbled and fell to his knees, only to bound immediately to his feet to run again.

There were hidden rocks and thorn-tipped plants scattered through the soft grasses, and soon his feet were cut and bleeding freely. But he didn't feel the pain and he raced onward. The vast plains alone were witness to the strange race between the huge, lumbering hunters and the shadowlike quarry as they labored southward through the driving rains and the chilling wind. They ran without hearing, without seeing, without feeling through the panoramic emptiness, and there was nothing to break the terrible silence but the rush of the gusting wind in the runners' ears. It became a lonely, fearful ordeal of survival—a trial of spirit and stamina that demanded from the youthful Prince of Leah his final, complete reserve of strength.

Time ceased to exist for the fleeing highlander as he forced his legs to move when the muscles had long since passed the normal end of endurance—and still there was no river. He no longer looked back to see if the Trolls were closing. He could sense their presence, hear their labored breathing in his mind; they must be closing the distance rapidly. He had to run faster! He had to reach the river and free Shea. . . .

In his near exhaustion, he unconsciously referred to the person wrapped in the bundle as his friend. He had known immediately upon grasping the mysterious prisoner that he was small and slight of build. There was no reason to believe it might not be the missing Valeman. The bundled captive was awake and moving awkwardly as the highlander ran, speaking in muffled phrases to which Menion replied in short, gasping assurances that they were close to safety.

The rain suddenly intensified in force until it was impossible to see more than a few feet in any direction, and the sodden plains turned quickly into a grass-tipped marsh. Then Menion fell over a water-covered root and tumbled headlong into the muddied grass, his precious burden falling in a struggling heap beside him. Bruised and exhausted, the highlander raised himself to his hands and knees, the great sword held ready, and looked back for his pursuers. To his relief, they were nowhere in sight. In the heavy rain and fog, they had momentarily lost him. But even the limited visibility would only slow them down for a few minutes and then . . . Menion shook his head sharply to clear the haze of rain and weariness from his eyes, then crawled quickly to the waterlogged heap of clothing that bound the struggling prisoner. Whoever was in that hunting cloak was in good enough shape to run beside him, and Menion's strength was nearly gone. He knew he could carry the added weight no farther.

Awkwardly, hardly aware of what he was doing, the highlander sawed at the tough bonds with his sword. It had to be Shea, his mind told him over and over, it had to be Shea. The Trolls and that stranger had gone to so much trouble not to be seen, had been so secretive . . . The bonds snapped as the sword finally severed them. It had to be Shea! The ropes unwound and the cloak flew back as the person within struggled into the open air.

An astonished Menion Leah wiped the rain from his blinking eyes and stared. He had rescued a woman!

A woman! Why would the Northlanders kidnap a woman? Menion stared through the pouring rain into the clear blue eyes that blinked back at him uncertainly. She was no ordinary woman in any case. She was strikingly beautiful—deeply browned skin covering the finely formed features of the rounded face, a slim graceful figure clothed in a silky material, and her hair . . . ! He had never seen anything like it. Even wetted and plastered against her face by the driving rain, falling shoulder length and lower in long, wistful strands, the strange color showed through the grayness of the morning in a deep reddish hue. For a moment he gazed at her in a half-conscious trance, then the throbbing pain from his cut and bleeding feet recalled him to his present situation and the grave danger still facing them.

Quickly he climbed back to his feet, wincing with the pressure on his exposed soles, the weariness flooding through him until he thought he would collapse in total exhaustion. His mind battled fiercely for several long moments as he swayed almost drunkenly, bracing himself on the great sword. The frightened face of the girl—yes, she could still be called a girl, he thought suddenly—peered up at him out of a gray haze. Then she was on her feet next to him, holding him up, talking to him in low, distant tones. He shook his head and nodded stupidly.

"It's all right now, I'm all right." The words sounded garbled as he spoke. "Run for the river—we have to reach Kern."

They began moving again through the mist and the rain, walking rapidly, at times staggering on the uncertain footing of the marshy grasslands. Menion felt his head begin to clear and his strength return as they walked, the girl next to him, her hands locked onto his arm, half holding on to him for her own support, half helping to support him. His keen eyes searched the gloom about them for some sign of the prowling Trolls, certain that they were not too far away. Then abruptly his ears picked up a new sound, the pounding, rushing throb of the Mermidon, its rain-filled waters overflowing the lowland banks as it swept southward toward Kern. The girl heard it, too, and gripped his arm tightly in encouragement.

Moments later they stood on the crest of the small rise that ran parallel with the north bank. The swift river had long since flooded its low banks and was continuing to rise. Menion had no idea where they stood in relation to Kern, but he realized that if they crossed at the wrong point, they would miss the island entirely. The girl seemed to recognize the problem; taking his arm, she began moving downstream along the low rise, peering across the river into the gloom. Menion let her lead him without question, his own eyes casting about anxiously for some sign of the pursuing Trolls. The rain had begun to slacken and the mist was beginning to clear. It would not be long before the storm would end and visibility return, leaving the two revealed to the persistent hunters. They had to chance a crossing quickly.

Menion did not know how long the young woman led him along the river's edge, but at last she halted and indicated in hurried gestures a small skiff drawn up against the grassy embankment. Quickly the highlander strapped the sword of Leah to his back, and together the two pushed off into the swift waters of the Mermidon. The river was icy and the shock of the extreme cold from the spray of the foam-tipped waves jarred Menion to the bone. He rowed fiercely across the swift current as it swept them downriver with terrific force, frequently turning them about completely as they fought to reach the other side. It was a wild, careening battle between river and man that seemed to go on endlessly, and at last everything became hazy and numb in Menion's mind.

What happened in the end was never clear to him. He was vaguely aware of hands reaching to pull him from the skiff to a grassy bank where he collapsed in a breathless stupor. He heard the girl's soft voice speaking to him, and then there was blackness and numbness all about him as he lapsed into unconsciousness. He drifted in and out of darkness and sleep, plagued by an uneasy sense of danger that prodded at his tired mind and demanded that he rise and stand ready. But his body could not respond, and finally he dropped off into a deep slumber.

When he awoke, it was still light out and the rain was falling in a slow, steady drizzle through deep, gray skies. He lay in the warmth and comfort of a bed, dry and rested, his torn feet cleaned and bandaged, and the terrible race to escape the Northlanders behind him. The slow rain beat peacefully on the paned glass windows that let in the daylight through the wood and stone walls. He glanced idly around the finely furnished chamber, realizing quickly that this was not the home of an average citizen, but of royalty. There were insignia and crests on the woodwork that Menion knew to belong to the kings of Callahorn. For a moment the highlander lay quietly and studied the room in silent leisure, allowing the sleep to disperse and his rested mind to awaken fully. He saw a dry set of clothes lying on a chair near the bed, and was just about to rise to dress when the door opened and an elderly serving woman appeared, carrying a tray of steaming food. Nodding politely and smiling, she hastened to the bed with the tray and deposited it on the highlander's lap, propping him up with pillows and urging him to eat it all while it was still hot. Strangely, she reminded Menion of his own mother, a kind, fussy woman who had died when he was twelve. The serving lady lingered until he had taken the first bite, then turned away and went out again, closing the door quietly behind her.

Menion ate slowly, savoring the excellent food, feeling the strength return to his body. It occurred to him only after he had finished almost half the meal that he had not eaten for over twenty-four hours—or perhaps it had been longer. He glanced again through the window to the rain beyond, unable to tell if it was even the same day. It might be the following day. . . .

In a flash he recalled his original purpose in coming to Kern—to warn them of the impending invasion by the Northland army. He might already be too late! He was still frozen with the thought, a fork raised halfway to his mouth, when the door opened a second time. It was the young woman he had rescued, refreshed and dry now, dressed in a flowing gown of warm, mixed colors, her long red tresses combed and shining even in the gray light of the rain-clouded day. She was easily the most stunning woman the Prince of Leah had ever encountered. Remembering suddenly the half-raised fork, he lowered it to the tray and smiled in greeting. She closed the door behind her and moved gracefully to his bedside. She was incredibly beautiful, he thought again. Why had she been kidnapped? What would Balinor know about her—what answers could he supply? She stood next to the bedside, looking down at him, studying him with those clear, deep eyes for a moment.

"You look very well, Prince of Leah," she smiled. "The rest and the food have made you whole again."

"How did you know who . . . ?"

"Your sword bears the markings of the King of Leah; that much I know. Who else but his son would carry such a weapon? But I don't know you by name."

"Menion," the highlander responded, somewhat surprised at the girl's knowledge of his little homeland, a kingdom unfamiliar to most outlanders.

The young woman stretched forth a slim bronzed hand to grasp his own in warm greeting and nodded happily.

"I am Shirl Ravenlock, and this is my home, Menion—the island city of Kern. If not for your courage, I should never have seen it again. For that I shall remain eternally grateful and your friend always. Now finish your meal while we talk."

She seated herself on the bed next to him and motioned for Menion to continue eating. Again he began to raise his fork; then remembering the invasion, he dropped it to the tray with a noisy clatter.

"You've got to get word to Tyrsis, to Balinor—the invasion from the Northland has begun! There is an army camped just above Kern waiting to . . ."

"I know, it's all right," Shirl responded quickly, raising her hand to stop him from continuing. "Even in your sleep, you spoke of the danger—you warned us before you passed out entirely. Word has been sent to Tyrsis. Palance Buckhannah rules in his brother's absence; the King is still very ill. The city of Kern is mobilizing its defenses, but for the moment there is no real danger. The rains have flooded the Mermidon and made any crossing by a large force impossible. We will be safe until help arrives."

"Balinor should have been in Tyrsis several days ago," Menion announced with alarm. "What about the Border Legion? Is it fully mobilized?"

The girl looked at him blankly, indicating that she had no idea what the situation was with regard to either the Legion or Balinor. Abruptly, Menion shoved the tray aside and climbed out of bed, an astonished Shirl rising with him, still trying to calm the excited highlander.

"Shirl, you may think that you're safe on this island, but I can guarantee that time is running out for all of us!" Menion exclaimed, reaching for his clothes. "I've seen the size of that army, and no amount of flooding is going to slow it down for long—and you can forget about any help short of a miracle."

He paused at the second button of his nightshirt, suddenly remembering the young woman with him. He pointed meaningfully to the door, but she shook her head negatively and turned away so she couldn't see him changing.

"What about your kidnapping?" Menion asked, dressing himself quickly as he studied her slim back across the room. "Do you have any idea why you would be so important to the Northlanders—other than the fact that you're a beautiful woman?"

He smiled roguishly, a little of the brashness that Flick distrusted returning. Although he could not see her face, the highlander was certain she was blushing furiously. She was silent a moment before speaking.

"I don't remember exactly what happened," the answer came at last. "I was asleep. I was awakened by a noise in the room, then someone grabbed me and I blacked out—I think I was struck or . . . No, I remember now— it was a cloth soaked in some foul liquid that prevented me from breathing. I blacked out and the next thing I remember was lying on the sand near the river—I gather it was the Mermidon. You know how I was tied in that blanket. I couldn't see anything and could hear only a little—but nothing that I could understand. Did you see anything?"

Menion shook his head and shrugged. "No, nothing much," he added, remembering that the girl was not looking at him. "One man brought you across in a boat, then turned you over to four Trolls. I couldn't see the man distinctly, but I might recognize him if I saw him again. How about answering my first question—why would anyone kidnap you? Turn around. I'm dressed now."

The young woman turned obediently and came over next to him, watching curiously as he pulled on the high hunting boots.

"I'm of royal blood, Menion," she responded quietly. Menion stopped quickly and looked up at her. He had suspected she was no ordinary citizen of Kern when she had recognized the crest of Leah on his sword. Now perhaps he would discover the reason behind her abduction from the city.

"My ancestors were kings of Kern—and for a while of all Callahorn, before the Buckhannahs came to power about one hundred years ago. I am a . . . well, I guess you could say I'm a princess—in absentia." She laughed at the foolishness of the idea, and Menion smiled back. "My father is an elder of the council that governs the internal affairs of Kern. The King is the ruler of Callahorn, but this is an enlightened monarchy, as the saying goes, and the King seldom interferes with the governmental workings of this city. His son Palance has been attracted to me for some time, and it is no secret that he plans to marry me. I . . . I believe that, to get to him, an enemy might try to harm me."

Menion nodded soberly, a sudden premonition springing into his alert mind. Palance was not in line for the throne of Callahorn unless something happened to Balinor. Why would anyone waste time trying to put pressure on the younger son unless they were certain that Balinor would not be around? Again he recalled Shirl's lack of knowledge of the arrival of the Prince of Callahorn, an event that should have taken place days ago and one that all the citizens of the land should have known about.

"Shirl, how long have I been asleep?" he asked apprehensively.

"Nearly an entire day," she answered. "You were exhausted when they pulled us from the Mermidon yesterday morning, and I thought you should sleep. You gave us your warning . . ."

"Twenty-four hours lost!" Menion exclaimed angrily. "If not for the rain, the city would have already fallen! We've got to act now, but what . . . Shirl, your father and the council! I must speak with them!" He grasped her arms with urgency when she hesitated. "Don't ask questions now, just do what I say. Where are the council chambers? Quick, take me to them!"

Without waiting for the girl to lead him, Menion took her arm and propelled her through the door to a long hallway beyond. Together they hurried through the empty home and out the front doorway onto a wide, tree-shaded lawn, running to escape the persistent drizzle of the morning rain. The walkways of the buildings beyond were partially sheltered from the rain, and they were spared a second soaking. As they proceeded toward the council hall, Shirl asked him how he happened to be in this part of the country, but Menion responded evasively, still unwilling to tell anyone about Allanon and the Sword of Shannara. He felt he could trust this girl, but Allanon's warning that none of those who journeyed to Paranor should reveal the story behind the missing Sword prevented him from confiding even in her. Instead, he explained that he had come to aid Balinor at his request upon hearing of an impending Northland invasion. She accepted his story without question, and he felt a little guilty for lying to her. Yet Allanon had never told him the complete truth, so perhaps he knew less than he imagined anyway.

They had reached the council hall, its ancient chambers housed within a tall, stone structure surrounded by weathered columns and arched windows laced with metal latticework. The guards that stood leisurely next to the entryway did not question them and they hurried inside, moving down the long, high corridors and up the winding stairways as the walls echoed with the rap of their boots on the worn stone flooring. The council met in chambers situated on the fourth floor of the great building. When at last they were outside its wooden doors, Shirl advised Menion that she would inform her father and the other members of his wish to address them. Reluctantly, the highlander agreed to wait. He stood quietly in the corridor after she had gone inside, listening to the hushed murmur of voices as the seconds ticked slowly away, and the rain continued to beat in a soft, steady rhythm on the glass of the windows that lined the silent hall.

Losing himself for a moment in the peace and solitude of the ancient building, the highlander recalled in brief flashes the faces of the divided company of friends, wondering sadly what had befallen them since Paranor. Perhaps they would never again be together as they had been during those fearful days on the road to the Druid's Keep, but he would never forget their courage and sacrifice and the pride he felt now in recalling the dangers they had faced and overcome. Even the reluctant Flick had displayed a bravery and steadfastness that Menion would not have expected from him.

And what of Shea, his oldest friend? He shook his head as he thought about his missing companion. He missed the Valeman's peculiar mixture of hardheaded practicality and antiquated beliefs. Somehow Shea could not seem to see the change in times even when the sun moved from east to west in the sky above. He did not seem to realize that the land and the people were growing, expanding once more—that the wars of the past were slowly being forgotten. Shea believed that one could turn his back on the past and build a new world with the future, never understanding that the future was inextricably tied to the past, an interwoven tapestry of events and ideas that would never be entirely severed. In his own small way, the little Valeman was a part of the passing age, his convictions a reminder of yesterday rather than a promise of tomorrow. How strange, how incredibly strange it all seemed, Menion thought suddenly, standing in the center of the hall, motionless, his gaze lost in the depths of the weathered stone wall. Shea and the Sword of Shannara—things of an age slowly dying; yet they were the hope of the hour to come. They were the key to life.

The heavy wooden doors to the council hall opened behind the highlander, and his thoughts faded with Shirl's soft voice. She seemed small and vulnerable as she waited beneath the massive beams of the high entryway, her face beautiful and anxious. No wonder Palance Buckhannah wanted this woman for his wife. Menion moved toward her, taking her warm hand in his own, and they entered the council chamber. He noted the ancient

austerity of the massive chamber as he moved into the gray light that
seemed to slide in tired streaks through the high, iron-webbed windows.
The council hall was old and proud, a cornerstone of the island city. Twenty
men were seated around a long, burnished wood table, their faces strangely
similar as they waited for the highlander to speak—all aged, wise perhaps,
and determined. The eyes betrayed the unspoken fear that lingered beneath the calm exteriors—a fear for their city and their people. They knew
what the Northland army would do when the rains ceased and the waters
of the Mermidon receded in the heat of the open sun. He stopped before
them, the girl still next to him, his footfalls dying away into the expectant
silence.

He chose his words carefully, describing the massive enemy force that
had been assembled under the leadership of the Warlock Lord. He related
in part the story of his long journey to Callahorn, speaking of Balinor and
the men of the company formed at Culhaven who were now scattered
throughout the four lands. He did not tell them about the Sword or about
Shea's mysterious origin or even about Allanon. There was no reason for
the elders of this council to know anything beyond the fact that the city of
Kern stood in danger of being overrun. As he finished, calling upon them
to save their people while there was still time, to evacuate the city immediately before all hope of retreat was cut off, he felt a strange sense of satisfaction. He had risked a great deal more than his own life to warn these
people. If he had failed to reach them, they might all have perished without ever having had a chance to flee to safety. It was important, really important, to the Prince of Leah that he had carried out his task responsibly.

The questions from the members of the council came with cries of
alarm when the highlander had finished, some angry, some frightened.
Menion answered quickly, trying to stay calm as he assured them that the
size of the Northland army was as awesome as he had described and the
threat of attack certain. Eventually the initial furor died away into a more
rational deliberation of the possibilities. A few of the elders believed that
the city should be defended until Palance Buckhannah could come up
from Tyrsis with the Border Legion, but most were of the opinion that
once the rains subsided, as they were certain to do within a few days, the
invading army would easily gain the shores of the island and the city would
stand defenseless. Menion listened silently while the council deliberated
the matter, weighing in his own mind the courses of action open to them.
Finally, the flushed, gray-haired man, whom Shirl had introduced as her
father, turned to Menion, drawing him aside in private conference as the
council continued its debate.

"Have you seen Balinor, young man? Do you know where he can be
found?"

"He should have been in Tyrsis days ago," Menion responded worriedly. "He was going there to mobilize the Border Legion in preparation
for this invasion. He was in the company of two cousins of Eventine
Elessedil."

The older man frowned and shook his head, consternation registering in his lined face.

"Prince of Leah, I must tell you that the situation is more desperate than it appears. The King of Callahorn, Ruhl Buckhannah, became seriously ill several weeks earlier and his condition does not seem to be improving. Balinor was absent from the city at the time, and so the King's younger son assumed his father's duties. While he has always been a rather unsteady personality, he has of late seemed highly erratic. One of his first acts was to disband the Border Legion, reducing it to a fraction of its former size."

"Disbanded!" Menion exclaimed in disbelief. "Why in the name . . . ?"

"He found them unnecessary," the other continued quickly, "so he replaced them with a small company of his own men. The fact of the matter is that he has always felt overshadowed by his brother, and the Border Legion was under the direct command of Balinor by the King's own order. It's highly probable that Palance felt they would remain loyal to the first-born son of the King in preference to himself, and he has no intention of returning the throne to Balinor should the King die. He has already made this quite apparent. The commanders of the Border Legion and several close associates of Balinor were seized and imprisoned—all very quietly so that the people would not be outraged by this senseless action. Our new King has taken as his only confidant and adviser a man named Stenmin, a viperous mystic and trickster whose only concern is for his own ambitions, not for the welfare of the people or even Palance Buckhannah. I do not see how we can hope to face this invasion with our own leadership so badly divided and undermined. I'm not even sure we can convince the Prince that the danger exists until the enemy is standing at the open gates!"

"Then Balinor is in grave danger," Menion said darkly. "He has gone to Tyrsis, not realizing that his father is ill and that his brother has taken command. We've got to get word to him at once!"

The council members had suddenly risen to their feet, shouting heatedly, still arguing over what should be done to save the doomed city of Kern. Shirl's father hastened to their midst, but it took several minutes for the few rational members of the distraught council to quiet the others enough to permit the discussion to continue on an orderly basis. Menion listened for a little while, then allowed his attention to drift momentarily to the high, arched windows and the solemn sky beyond. It was not as dark as before, and the rain had begun to slacken further. Unquestionably, it would end by tomorrow, and the enemy force camped beyond the flooded Mermidon would attempt a crossing. Eventual success in attaining a landing was assured, even if the vastly outnumbered soldiers stationed or living in Kern tried to defend the island. Without a large, well-organized army to protect the city, the people would be quickly slain and Kern would fall. He thought back quickly to his parting with Allanon, wondering suddenly what the resourceful Druid would do if he were there. The situation was not promising. Tyrsis was ruled by an irrational, ambitious usurper. Kern was leaderless, its councilmen divided and unsure, debating a course of action that should already have been executed. Menion felt his temper slipping. It was madness to ponder the alternatives further!

"Councilmen! Hear me!" His own voice rose in fury, reverberating back from the ancient stone walls as the voices of the elders of Kern died into whispering silence. "Not only Callahorn, but all of the Southland, my home and yours, faces certain destruction if we do not act now! By tomorrow night, Kern will be ashes and its people enslaved. Our one chance for survival is escape to Tyrsis; our one hope for victory over this mighty Northland army is the Border Legion, reassembled under Balinor. The Elven armies stand ready to fight with us. Eventine will lead them. The Dwarf people, engaged for years in fighting the Gnomes, have promised to aid us. But we must stand fast separately until all are united against this monstrous threat to our existence!"

"Your plea is well spoken, Prince of Leah," Shirl's father responded quickly as the flushed highlander paused. "But give us a solution to our immediate problem so that our people can reach Tyrsis. The enemy is camped directly across the Mermidon, and we stand virtually defenseless. We must evacuate almost forty thousand people from this island and then guide them safely to Tyrsis, which is miles to the south. Undoubtedly the enemy has already posted sentries all around our shores to prevent any attempt to cross the Mermidon before the assault on Kern. How can we overcome such obstacles?"

A fleeting smile crossed Menion's lips.

"We'll attack," he stated simply.

For a moment there was shocked silence as they all stared in utter disbelief at the deceptively passive face. The words of astonished reply were still forming on their lips as he held up one hand.

"An attack is exactly what they will not be expecting—particularly if it comes in the night. A quick strike against a flank position of their main encampment, if executed properly, will confuse them, cause them to think that it's an assault by a heavily armed force. The darkness and the confusion will hide our true size. Such an attack is certain to draw in their outlying sentry lines around the island. A small command can make a great amount of noise, set a few fires, and pin them down for at least an hour—perhaps longer. While that's going on—evacuate the city!"

One of the elders shook his head negatively.

"Even an hour would not be sufficient time, though your plan may be daring enough to catch the Northlanders off guard, young man. Even if we managed to ferry all forty thousand people from the island to the southern shore, it would still be necessary to march them southward to Tyrsis—almost fifty miles. The women and children would require days to travel that distance under normal conditions, and once the enemy finds Kern has been abandoned, they'll follow its people southward. We cannot hope to outrun them. Why should we even attempt it?"

"You will not have to outrun them," Menion declared quickly. "You won't be taking these people south by land—you will take them down the

Mermidon! Put them in small boats, rafts, anything that you now have or can build by tonight that will float. The Mermidon flows southward deep into Callahorn, within ten miles of Tyrsis. Disembark at that point, and all can easily reach the safety of the city by daybreak, long before the cumbersome Northland army can mobilize and follow!"

The council rose to its feet, shouting their approval, caught up in the fire and determination of the highlander's spirit. If there was any way that the people of Kern could be saved, even though the island city itself must fall to the enemy hordes, it must be tried. The council adjourned after a short discussion to mobilize the working people of the city. Between this time and sunset, every citizen who was able to assist would be expected to aid in the construction of large wooden rafts capable of transporting several hundred people. There were already hundreds of small boats scattered about the island which individual citizens used to navigate the river in order to reach the mainland. In addition, there were a number of larger ferries for mass transportation which could be pressed into service. Menion suggested that the council order all armed soldiers in the city to begin a vigilant patrol of the coastline, permitting no one to leave the island. All details of the planned escape would be carefully concealed from everyone but the council members for as long as possible. The highlander's greatest concern was that someone might betray them to the enemy, cutting off their escape route before they had a chance to act. Someone had seized Shirl in her own home, whisked her out of the heavily populated city, and ferried her across into the hands of the Trolls—a chore that could not have been accomplished by anyone unfamiliar with the island. Whoever he was, he remained free and hidden, perhaps still safe within the city. If he learned the exact details of the evacuation plan, he would undoubtedly attempt to warn the Northlanders. Secrecy was absolutely necessary if this dangerous venture was to be successful.

The remainder of the day passed quickly for Menion. Forgotten for the moment were Shea and his companions of the past few weeks. For the first time since Shea had come to him in the highlands, the Prince of Leah was faced with a problem that he fully understood, requiring skills he knew how to employ. The enemy was no longer the Skull King or the spirit creatures that served him. The enemy was flesh and blood—creatures that lived and died according to the same rules as other men, and their threat was one the highlander could appreciate and analyze. Time was the greatest single factor in his plan to outwit the waiting army, and so he threw himself into the most important undertaking of his life, the saving of an entire city.

Together with the members of the council, he directed the building of the giant wooden rafts which would be utilized to convey the majority of the besieged citizens of Kern down the still-flooded Mermidon to the safety of Tyrsis. The point of embarkation was to be the southwest coastline immediately below the city proper. There was a broad but well-concealed inlet from which the rafts and smaller boats would be launched under cover of darkness. Directly across the river from the inlet stood a series of low bluffs that ran to the edge of the embankment. Menion thought that a handful of men could ford the river when the main attack on the enemy encampment began later that night; once across, they could subdue the small guard post that would be keeping watch. After the sentries were dispatched, the boats and rafts would be launched, flowing downriver with the current, following the south branch of the Mermidon to Tyrsis. There was nothing to assure them that the vessels would not be spotted instantly, but it was the only possible course of action. Menion believed that if the sky remained clouded, the sentry commands were withdrawn upriver to defend against the fake assault on the main encampment, and the people of the city kept silent on the rafts, then the evacuation might be successful.

But toward late afternoon, the rain started to slacken off altogether and the clouds began to thin out, permitting small strips of blue to seep through the rolling grayness. The storm was drawing to an end, and it appeared the night sky would be cloudless and the land exposed to the revealing light of the new moon and a thousand winking stars. Menion was seated in one of the smaller rooms of the council hall when he saw these first signs of a clearing, his attention momentarily diverted from the huge map spread out on the table before him. At his side were two members of the disbanded Border Legion, Janus Senpre, a lieutenant commander of the Legion and the highest ranking officer on the island, and a grizzled veteran named Fandrez. The latter knew the country around Kern better than anyone and had been called in to advise the attack squad in its strike against the giant Northland army. Senpre, his superior, was surprisingly young for his rank, but a sharp and determined soldier with a dozen years of field duty already behind him. He was a devoted follower of Balinor, and like Menion, he was considerably upset to learn that nothing had been heard from Tyrsis concerning the Prince's arrival. Earlier that afternoon, he had selected two hundred seasoned soldiers from the disbanded Border Legion to form the strike force that would be directed against the enemy camp.

Menion had offered his aid and it had been eagerly accepted. The highlander was still cut and bruised about the feet and lower legs from his arduous flight after rescuing Shirl Ravenlock, but he refused to stay behind with the evacuation party when the feint by the small attack squad had been his idea. Flick would have written off his insistence as a foolish mixture of stubbornness and pride, but Menion Leah would not be left in comparative safety on the island while a battle was being fought across the river. It had taken him years to find something worthwhile to fight for, something more than personal satisfaction and the irresistible lure of one more adventure. He was not about to be a passive spectator while the most awesome threat in centuries decimated the race of Man.

"This point—over here by the Spinn Barr—that's the landing point to take," the slow, grating voice of Fandrez cut into his thoughts, drawing his attention back to the carefully detailed map. Janus Senpre agreed, looking at Menion to be certain he was taking careful note. The highlander nodded quickly.

"They will have sentries posted all along that grassland just above the bar," he said in reply. "If we don't dispose of them immediately, they could cut off any retreat."

"Your job will be to keep them out of there—keep the way open," the Legion commander stated.

Menion opened his mouth in objection, but was cut short.

"I appreciate your desire to come with us, Menion, but we still have to move much faster than the enemy, and your feet are in poor condition for any prolonged running. You know that as well as I. So the shore patrol is yours. Keep our path to the boats open, and you will be doing us a much greater service than by coming with us."

Menion quietly nodded his agreement, though he was keenly disappointed. He had wanted to be in the forefront of the assault. Deep in the back of his mind, he still maintained hope of finding Shea a prisoner in the enemy camp. His thoughts drifted to Allanon and Flick. Perhaps they had found the missing Valeman, as the Druid had promised they would try to do. He shook his head sadly. Shea, Shea, why did it have to happen to someone like you—someone who just wanted to be left alone? There was a madness in the scheme of life that men were forced to accept either with resigned fury or blunt indifference. There could be no final resolution—except, perhaps, in death.

The meeting ended shortly thereafter, and a despondent and bitter Menion Leah wandered aimlessly out of the council chamber still lost in thought. Almost without realizing it, he walked down the stone stairway of the huge building to the street and from there made his way back toward Shirl's home, keeping close to the covered walks and building walls. Where was it all leading? The threat of the Warlock Lord loomed before them like a towering, unscalable wall. How could they possibly hope to defeat a creature that had no soul—a creature that lived according to laws of nature completely foreign to the world into which they had been born? Why should a simple young man from an obscure hamlet be the only mortal entity with the ability to destroy such an indescribably powerful being? Menion desperately needed to understand something of what was happening to him and to his absent friends—even if it was only one small piece in a thousand comprising the puzzle of the Warlock Lord and the Sword of Shannara.

Suddenly he found himself in front of the Ravenlock home, the heavy doors standing closed, their metal latches looking cold and frosted in the graying mist that hung in wisps with the cooling of the late-afternoon air. He turned quickly from the entryway, not wishing to go in or to be with people for the moment, but preferring the solitude of the empty veranda. Slowly he moved along its stone path into the little garden at the side of the house, the leaves and flowers dripping softly with the rain of several days, the grounds beyond damp and green. He stood quietly, his own thoughts as hazy and wistful as the setting in which he paused, giving way for one brief moment to the sinking despair that seized him when he thought of how much he had lost. He had never felt alone like this before, even in the dark emptiness of the highlands of Leah when he had hunted far from his own home and friends. Something deep within hinted with dread persistence that he would never go back to what had been, that he would never go back to his friends, his home, his old life. Somewhere in the days behind, he had lost it all. He shook his head, the unwanted tears building on the edge of his lids as the dampness closed in about him and the chill of the rain slipped deep into his chest.

There were sudden footsteps on the stone behind him and a small, lithe form came to a silent halt at his elbow, the rust-red locks shadowing wide eyes that looked up at him momentarily and then strayed to the garden beyond. The two stood without speaking for a long time, the rest of the world shut away. In the sky above, heavy clouds were rolling in, covering the last faint traces of blue as the darkness of early twilight began to deepen. Rain was falling again in steady sheets on the besieged land of Callahorn, and Menion noted with absent relief that it would be a black and moonless night on the island of Kern.

It was well after midnight, the rain still falling in a soggy drizzle, the night sky still impenetrably black and ominous, when an exhausted Menion Leah stumbled heavily onto a small, crudely constructed raft moored in a peaceful inlet on the southwestern coast of the island. Two slim arms reached out to catch him as he collapsed, and he stared wonderingly into the dark eyes of Shirl Ravenlock. She had waited for him as she said she would, even though he had begged her to go with the others when the mass evacuation began. Cut and bruised, his clothing torn and his skin wet from the rain and his own blood, he let her wrap him in a cloak still somehow dry and warm and pull him against her shoulder as they crouched in the night shadows and waited.

There had been some who had returned with Menion, and a few more who boarded now, all battle weary, but fiercely proud of the courage and sacrifice they had displayed that night on the plains north of Kern. Never had the Prince of Leah seen such bravery in the face of such impossible odds. Those few men of the fabled Border Legion had so utterly disrupted the enemy camp that even now, some four hours after the initial strike, the confusion was still continuing. The enemy numbers had been unbelievable—thousands after thousands milling about, striking out at anyone within reach, inflicting injury and death upon even their own companions. They had been driven by more than mortal fear or hatred. They had been driven by the inhuman power of the Warlock Lord, his incredible fury thrusting them into battle like crazed beings with no purpose but to destroy. Yet the men of the Legion had held them at bay, repeatedly thrown back only to regroup and strike once more. Many had died. Menion did not know what had preserved his own meager life, but it bordered on a miracle.

The mooring ropes were loosened, and he felt the raft begin to drift away from the shore, the current catching it and pulling it into the center of the flooded Mermidon. Moments later they were in the main channel, moving silently downriver toward the walled city of Tyrsis, where the people of Kern had fled several hours earlier in a perfectly executed mass evacuation. Forty thousand people, huddled on giant rafts, small boats, even two-man dinghies, had slipped undetected from the besieged city as the enemy sentry posts guarding the western bank of the Mermidon hastily returned to the main encampment, where it appeared a full-scale attack by the armies of Callahorn was in progress. The beating of the rain, the rushing of the river, and the cries of the distant camp had blotted out the muffled sounds of the people on the rafts and boats, crowded and jammed together in a desperate, fearful bid for freedom. The darkness of the clouded sky had hidden them well, and their collective courage had sustained them. For the time being at least, they had eluded the Warlock Lord.

Menion dozed off for a time, aware of nothing but a gentle rocking sensation as the river bore the raft steadily southward. Strange dreams flashed through his restless mind as time drifted away in long moments of peaceful silence. Then voices reached through to him, jostling his subconscious, forcing him to wake abruptly, and his eyes were seared by a vast red glare that filled the damp air about him. Squinting sharply, he raised himself from Shirl's arms, uncertainty registering on his lean face as he saw the northern sky filled with a reddish glow that matched the brightness of the dawn's gold. Shirl was speaking softly in his ear, the words faint and poignant.

"They have burned the city, Menion. They have burned my home!"

Menion lowered his eyes and gripped the girl's slim arm with one hand. Though its people had been able to escape, the city of Kern had seen the end of its days and, with terrible grandness, was passing into ashes.

25

The hours slipped silently away in the entombed blackness of the little cell. Even after the eyes of the captives had grown used to the impenetrable dark, there remained a solitude that numbed the senses and destroyed their ability to discern the passage of time. Beyond the empty darkness of the room and their own muffled breathing, the three captives could hear nothing save the infrequent scurrying of a small rodent and the steady drip of icy water on worn stone. Finally their own ears began to lie to them, to hear sounds where there was only silence. Their own movement was meaningless, because they could expect it, identify it, and dismiss it as insignificant and hopeless. An interminable length of time lingered and faded, and still no one came.

Somewhere in the light and air above, amid the sounds of the people and the city, Palance Buckhannah was deciding their fate and indirectly the fate of the Southland. Time was running out for the land of Callahorn; the Warlock Lord moved closer with each passing hour. But here, in the silent blackness of this small prison, in a world shut away from the pulse beat of the human world, time had no meaning and tomorrow would be the same as today. Eventually they would be discovered, but would they emerge again into the sun's friendly light, or would it be a transfer from one darkness into yet another? Would they find only the terrible gloom of the Skull King, his power extended not only into Callahorn, but into the farthest reaches of all the provinces of the Southland?

Balinor and the Elven brothers had freed themselves within a short time after their captors had departed. The ropes binding them had not been secured with the intention of preventing any chance of escape once they were safely locked within that dungeon room, and the three had lost no time in working the knots loose. Huddled together in the darkness, the ropes and blindfolds cast aside, they discussed what would become of them. The dank, rotting smell of the ancient cellar almost stifled their breathing as they crouched close to one another, and the air was chill and biting even through their heavy cloaks. The floor was earthen, the walls stone and iron, the room barren and empty.

Balinor was familiar with the cellar beneath the palace but he did not recognize the room in which they had been imprisoned. The cellar was used primarily for storage, and while there had always been a number of walled rooms in which wine barrels had been placed to age, this was not one of them. Then, with chilling certainty, he realized that they had been imprisoned in the ancient dungeon constructed centuries ago beneath the cellar and later sealed off and forgotten. Palance must have discovered its existence and reopened the cells for his own use. Quite probably, he had imprisoned Balinor's friends somewhere in this maze when they had come to the palace to object to the disbanding of the Border Legion. It was a well-concealed prison, and Balinor doubted that anyone searching for them would ever find it.

The discussion was completed quickly. There was little to say. Balinor had left his instructions with Captain Sheelon. Should they fail to return, he was to seek out Ginnisson and Fandwick, two of Balinor's most dependable commanders, and order them to reassemble the Border Legion to defend against any assault by the Warlock Lord and his invading army. Sheelon had also been told to send word to the Elf and Dwarf nations, warning them of the situation and calling for their immediate support. Eventine would not permit his cousins to remain the prisoners of Callahorn for very long, and Allanon would come as soon as he heard of their misfortune. Four hours must have passed long ago, he thought, so it should only be a matter of time. But time was precious, and with Palance determined to gain the throne of Callahorn, their own lives were in grave danger. The borderman began to wish silently that he had listened to Durin's advice and avoided a confrontation with his brother until he had been certain of the outcome.

He had never imagined that matters would go this far awry. Palance had been like a wild man, his hatred so consuming that he had not even waited to hear what Balinor would say. Yet there was little mystery to this irrational behavior. It was more than personal differences between the two brothers that had prompted the youth's savage action. It was more than the illness of his father, an illness Palance somehow believed his brother was responsible for. It had something to do with Shirl Ravenlock, the alluring woman Palance had fallen in love with months before and had vowed to marry despite her own reticence toward the match. Something had happened to the young Kern girl, and Balinor had received the blame. Palance would do anything to get her back safely, if she was indeed missing, as his brother's few words immediately before they had been brought to this dungeon had indicated.

The borderman explained the situation to the Elven brothers. He felt certain Palance would come to them soon and demand information concerning the young woman. But he would not believe them when they said they knew nothing. . . .

More than twenty-four hours passed, and still no one came. There was nothing to eat. Even after their eyes gradually grew accustomed to the blackness, there was nothing to view but their own shadowy forms and the walls about them. They took turns sleeping, trying to conserve their strength for whatever lay ahead, but the abnormal silence prevented any real sleep, and they resigned themselves to a light, restless slumber that did little to refresh their bodies or their spirits. At first they attempted to find a weak spot on the hinges of the bulky iron door, but it was securely fastened in place. Without tools of any sort, they found it impossible to dig very far into the chill, iron-hard surface of the dirt flooring. The stone walls were aged, but still firm and solid, without any sign of a weak or crumbling layer in the mortar. Eventually they abandoned their attempts to escape and sat back in silence.

Finally, after endless hours of waiting in the chill darkness, they heard the distant sound of clanging metal as an ancient iron door somewhere above swung ponderously open. There were voices, muffled and soft, and then footsteps on stone as someone began to descend the worn stairs to the lower dungeon where the three were imprisoned. Quickly they rose to their feet and crowded close to the cell door, listening expectantly as the footsteps and the voices drew closer. Balinor could distinguish the voice of his brother above the rest, strangely hesitant and broken. Then the heavy latches were drawn back, the sudden grating of metal piercing to the ears of the three captives, who had become accustomed now to the deathlike silence of their prison, and they moved back from the massive cell door as

it swung slowly inward. Blazing streaks of torchlight flashed into the darkened room, forcing the prisoners to shield their weakened eyes. As they
slowly adjusted to this new light, several figures entered the room and
came to a halt just within the entryway.

The younger son of the ailing King of Callahorn stood foremost of
four figures, his broad face relaxed and his lips pursed. His eyes alone
betrayed the hatred that burned within, and there was a maddened, almost
desperate way that they moved from one captive to the next as he clenched
his hands tightly behind him. He was clearly Balinor's brother, possessing the same facial construction, the same wide mouth and prominent
nose, and the same big, rugged build. Next to him stood a man that even
the Elven brothers recognized instantly, though they had never met him.
He was the mystic Stenmin, a gaunt, slightly stooped figure, lean and sharp
in his features, and clothed in reddish robes and trappings. His eyes were
strangely shadowed, reflecting an undisguisable evil in the man who had
gained the complete confidence of the new, self-proclaimed King. His hands
moved over his body nervously, raising almost mechanically from time to
time to stroke the small, pointed black beard that shaded the angular face.
Behind him stood two armed guards, dressed in black and bearing the insignia of the falcon. Beyond them, just outside the doorway, stood two
more. All held wicked-looking pikes. For a moment no one spoke; no
one even moved as the two parties scrutinized each other in the torchlit
gloom of the little cell. Then Palance made a quick motion toward the
open door.

"I will speak with my brother alone. Take these other two out."

The guards silently complied, leading the reluctant Elven brothers
from the room. The tall Prince waited until they had left, then turned
questioningly to the scarlet-robed figure still at his side.

"I thought that perhaps you might have need of me . . . ?" The lean,
calculating face stared steadily at the impassive Balinor.

"Leave us, Stenmin. I will speak with my brother alone."

His tone of voice bordered on anger, and the mystic nodded obediently, quickly backing out of the cell. The heavy door closed with an ominous thud, leaving the two brothers alone in a silence broken only by the
hissing of the torch flame as it consumed the dry wood and flashed into
gleaming sparks. Balinor did not move, but stood waiting expectantly, his
eyes trying to probe his brother's young face, trying to reach the old feelings of love and friendship they had shared as children. But they were
missing, or at least carefully submerged in some dark corner of the heart,
and in their place was a strange, restless anger that seemed to rise as much
from dissatisfaction with the situation as from dislike of the captive brother.
An instant later the fury and the contempt were gone, replaced by a calm
detachment that Balinor found both irrational and false, as if Palance were
playing a role without any real understanding of the character.

"Why did you come back, Balinor?" The words came out slowly,
sadly. "Why did you do it?"

The tall borderman did not reply, unable to comprehend this sudden change of mood. Before, his brother had been willing to have him torn to pieces in order to learn the whereabouts of the beautiful Shirl Ravenlock, yet now he seemed to have completely dismissed the matter from his mind.

"No matter, no matter I suppose." The reply came before Balinor had recovered from his astonishment at the abrupt change. "You could have stayed away after . . . after all the . . . after your treachery. I hoped you would, you know, because we were so close as children and you are, after all, my only brother. I will be King of Callahorn . . . I should have been firstborn anyway. . . ."

He trailed off into a whisper, his mind suddenly lost in some unspoken thought. He had gone mad, Balinor thought in desperation, and could no longer be reached!

"Palance, listen to me—just listen to me. I have done nothing to you or to Shirl. I've been in Paranor since I left here weeks before, and I returned only to warn our people that the Skull King has assembled an army of such awesome proportions that it will sweep through the entire Southland unchallenged unless we stop it here! For the sake of all these people, please listen to me. . . ."

His brother's voice pierced the air in shrill command. "I will hear no more of this foolish talk of invasion! My scouts have checked the country's borders and report no enemy armies anywhere. Besides, no enemy would dare to attack Callahorn—to attack me. . . . Our people are safe here. What do I care for the rest of the Southland? What do I owe them? They have always left us to fight alone, to guard these borderlands alone. I owe them nothing!"

He took a step toward Balinor and pointed menacingly at him, the strange hatred flaming anew as the young face contorted savagely.

"You turned against me, brother, when you knew that I was to be king. You tried to poison me as you poisoned my father—you wanted me as sick and helpless as he is now . . . dying alone, forgotten, alone. You thought you had found an ally that could gain the throne for you when you left with that traitor Allanon. How I hate that man—no, not a man, but an evil thing! He must be destroyed! But *you* will remain in this cell, alone and forgotten, Balinor, until you die—the fate you had planned for me!"

He turned away suddenly, breaking his tirade off with a sharp laugh as he paced to the closed door. Balinor thought he was about to open it, when the hulking youth paused and looked back at him. Slowly he came around, the eyes sad again.

"You could have stayed away from this land and been safe," he muttered as if confused by this fact. "Stenmin said you would come back even when I assured him you would not. He was right again. He is always right. Why did you come back?"

Balinor thought quickly. He had to keep his brother's attention long enough to find out what had happened to his father and his friends.

"I . . . I discovered I had been mistaken—that I was wrong," he answered slowly. "I came home to see our father and to see you, Palance."

"Father." The word came out like an unfamiliar name as the Prince moved a step closer. "He is beyond our help, lying like one already dead in that room in the south wing. Stenmin looks after him, as I do, but nothing can be done. He does not seem to want to live. . . ."

"But what is wrong with him?" Balinor's impatience burst free, and he moved toward the other threateningly.

"Keep your distance, Balinor." Palance backed away hastily, drawing a long dagger and holding it protectively before him. Balinor hesitated a moment. It would be easy to seize the dagger, hold the Prince captive until he was released. Yet something restrained him, something deep inside that warned against such a move. Quickly he stopped, holding up his hands and backing away to the far wall.

"You must remember you are my prisoner." Palance nodded in satisfaction, his voice unsteady. "You poisoned the King and you tried to poison me. I could have you put to death. Stenmin advised me to have you executed immediately, but I am not the coward that he is. I was a commander in the Border Legion, too, before . . . But they're gone now—disbanded and sent home to their families. My reign shall be a time of peace. You don't understand that, Balinor, do you?"

The borderman shook his head negatively, desperately trying to hold his brother's attention for a few minutes longer. Palance had apparently gone mad, whether from a latent congenital defect of the mind or from the strain of whatever it was that had been happening since Balinor had left Tyrsis with Allanon; it was impossible to tell. In any event, he was no longer the brother that Balinor had grown to manhood with and had loved as he had loved no one else. It was a stranger living in the physical shell that was his brother's body—a stranger obsessed with the need to be King of Callahorn. Stenmin was behind this; Balinor knew it. The mystic had somehow twisted the mind of his maddened brother, bending it to his own uses, filling it with promises of his destiny as King. Palance had always wanted to rule Callahorn. Even when Balinor had left the city, he knew Palance felt certain he would one day be King. Stenmin had been there all the time, counseling and advising in the manner of a close friend, poisoning his mind against his brother. But Palance had been strong-willed and independent, a sane and healthy man who would not be broken easily. Yet he was changed. Hendel had been wrong about Palance, but apparently Balinor had been wrong as well. Neither could have foreseen this, and now it was too late.

"Shirl—what of Shirl?" the tall borderman asked quickly.

Again the anger faded from his brother's darting eyes and a slow smile crept over his lips, relaxing the anguished face for an instant.

"She is so beautiful . . . so beautiful." He sighed foolishly, the dagger falling harmlessly to the cell floor as the Prince opened his hands to emphasize the feeling. "You took her from me, Balinor—tried to keep her from me. But she is safe now. She was saved by a Southlander, a Prince like myself. No, I am King of Tyrsis now, and he is only a Prince. It's just a little kingdom; I had never heard of it myself. He and I will be good friends,

Balinor, the way you and I once were. But Stenmin . . . says I can trust no one. I even had to lock away Messaline and Acton. They came to me when the Border Legion was sent home, trying to persuade me to . . . well, I guess to give up my plans for peace. They didn't understand . . . why . . ."

He stopped suddenly, his lowered eyes falling on the momentarily forgotten dagger. He picked it up quickly, placing it back in its belted sheath with a sly smile at his brother, looking strikingly like a clever child that has just avoided a scolding. There was no longer any doubt in Balinor's mind that his brother was totally incapable of making rational decisions. He was suddenly struck with his earlier premonition that while he could easily seize the dagger and hold his brother prisoner, it would be a serious mistake. Now he knew why that innate sense of warning had been generated. Stenmin fully realized Palance's condition and had purposely left the brothers alone in that cell. If Balinor had attempted to disarm Palance and to escape while holding him prisoner, the evil mystic could have accomplished his obvious goal in one bold stroke by killing both brothers. Who would question him when he explained that Palance had met his death by accident while his brother was attempting to flee his prison confinement? With both brothers dead and their father incapable of governing, the mystic might be able to seize control of the government of Callahorn. Then he alone would determine the fate of the Southland.

"Palance, listen to me, I beg of you," Balinor pleaded quietly. "We were so close once. We were more than just brothers by bloodline. We were friends, companions. We trusted each other, loved each other, and we could always work our problems out by understanding each other. You can't have forgotten all that. Listen to me! Even a king must try to understand his people—even when they don't agree on the way things are to be handled. You agree with that, don't you?"

Palance nodded soberly, the eyes vacant and detached as he tried to fight the haze that blocked his thought processes. There was a glimmer of understanding, and Balinor was determined to reach the memory that lay locked somewhere deep within.

"Stenmin is using you—he is an evil man." His brother started abruptly, taking a step backward as if to avoid hearing more. "You've got to understand, Palance. I am not your enemy, nor am I the enemy of this country. I did not poison our father. I did not harm Shirl in any way. I only want to help . . ."

His plea was suddenly cut short as the ponderous cell door swung open with a sharp rasp, and the angular features of the wily Stenmin appeared. Bowing condescendingly, he entered the cell, his cruel eyes fastened intently on Balinor.

"I thought I heard you call me, my King," he smiled quickly. "You've been in here alone so long, I thought something might have happened . . ."

Palance stared at him uncomprehendingly for a moment, then shook his head negatively and turned to leave. In that instant Balinor considered leaping upon the evil mystic and crushing the life from him before the absent guards could act. But he hesitated for that single brief moment, uncertain that even this would save him or aid his brother, and so the opportunity was lost. The guards came back into the cell, leading the Elven brothers, who looked about dubiously, then rejoined their comrade on the far side of the little room. Suddenly Balinor recalled something Palance had said when he was talking about Shirl. He had mentioned a Prince from a tiny Southland kingdom—a Prince who had rescued the young girl. Menion Leah! But how could he be in Callahorn . . . ?

The guards were turning to leave now and with them the silent Palance and his evil consort, a red-clad arm guiding the mindless Prince from the room. Then abruptly, the lean figure turned to look once more on the three captives, a thin smile spreading over the pursed lips as the bowed head cocked carefully to one side.

"In the event my King should have failed to mention it, Balinor . . ." The words sounded with a slow, burning hatred. "The guards at the Outer Wall saw you speaking with a certain Captain Sheelon, formerly of the Border Legion. He was trying to speak with others about your . . . predicament, when he was seized and imprisoned. I don't believe he will have much chance to cause us any further trouble. The matter is quite ended now, and within time even you will be forgotten."

Balinor's heart sank suddenly at this final piece of news. If Sheelon had been seized and confined before he had been able to reach Ginnisson and Fandwick, then there would be no one to assemble the Border Legion and no one to appeal to the people on his behalf. His absent companions would not know of his imprisonment upon reaching Tyrsis, and even if they suspected what had happened, what hope would they have of ever finding out what had become of him? This lower level of the ancient palace was unknown to all but a very few, and its entrance was well concealed. The three despondent captives watched in bitter silence as the guards placed a small tray of bread and a jug of water just inside the open door, then moved back into the hallway, carrying with them all of the burning torches but one. The grimly smiling Stenmin held this last light as he waited for the stooped form of Palance to follow the burly guards. But Palance paused uncertainly, unable to take his eyes from his brother's proud, resigned face; the faint torchlight illuminated the broad features in reddish streaks and the long, deep-rutted scar emerged dark and cruel in the half shadow. The brothers faced each other in silence for several long moments, and then Palance started back toward Balinor with slow, measured steps, shaking off Stenmin's hand as it tried to restrain him. He came to a halt only inches away from his brother, the dazed, searching eyes still fastened on that granite-hewn countenance as if trying to absorb from it the determination mirrored there. An uncertain hand raised itself quickly, pausing for an instant, then resting firmly on Balinor's shoulder, the fingers gripping tightly.

"I want to . . . know." The words were a whisper in the near darkness. "I want to understand . . . You must help me. . . ."

Balinor nodded silently, his own great hand reaching up to take his brother's in a brief clasp of love. For a moment they remained locked together, as if the friendship and love of childhood had never faded. Then Palance turned away and moved quickly out of the cell, hastily followed by a disturbed Stenmin. The heavy door closed with the grating of iron fastenings and metal clasps, shutting in the three friends and the impenetrable darkness once more. The departing footsteps died slowly into silence. The waiting began anew, but any hope of rescue seemed irretrievably lost.

A shadowy form detached itself from the blackness of the night-shrouded trees in the deserted park beneath the high span of the Sendic Bridge and darted silently toward the palace of the Buckhannahs. In quick, surefooted leaps, the powerful, compact form cleared the low hedges and shrubs, weaving between the stately elms, a pair of watchful eyes studying the wall enclosing the royal grounds, searching carefully for any sign of the night watch. Near the iron-wrought gates above the park, where the bridge opened onto the high ground, several guards patrolled, the falcon insignia visible in the torchlight of the gate entrance. Slowly the dark form climbed the gently sloping embankment toward the moss- and ivy-covered walls above; upon gaining the higher ground, it melted instantly into the shadows of the stone.

For long moments, it remained completely invisible as it moved steadily away from the main gate and the feeble torchlight. Then the intruder was visible once more, a dark blur against the faintly moonlit west wall as strong arms clung tenaciously to the sturdy vines, pulling the bulky form silently to the rim of the stone. There the head raised itself cautiously, and the keen eyes peered down into the empty palace gardens, making certain there were no guards close at hand. With a mighty heave of the powerful shoulders, the intruder gained the lip of the wall and, springing lightly over, landed with a soft thud amid the garden flowers.

Running in a half-crouch, the mysterious figure sprinted for the shadowy cover of a huge spreading willow. Pausing breathlessly within the giant tree's protective limbs, the intruder heard the approaching sound of voices. Listening carefully for a few moments, he concluded it was nothing more than the idle conversation of several palace guards making their appointed rounds. He waited confidently, his compact frame blending so closely with the squat trunk of the tree that he was totally invisible from more than a few feet away. The guards appeared seconds later, still conversing in relaxed voices as they passed through the silent gardens and were gone. Resting furtively for a few minutes longer, the stranger studied the dark bulk that occupied the center of these tree-shaded gardens—the tall, ancient palace of the Kings of Callahorn. A few lighted windows broke the misty blackness of the massive stone structure, casting bright streamers into the deserted gardens. There were faint, distant voices within, but their owners remained anonymous.

In a quick dash, the intruder crossed to the shadows of the building, pausing briefly beneath a small, darkened window in a recessed alcove. His strong hands worked frantically at the ancient catch, pushing at it and loosening the fastening. At last, with an audible snap that seemed to penetrate the entire palace grounds, the catch broke and the window swung silently inward. Without waiting to see if the patrolling guards had heard the sounds of his forced entry, the intruder slipped hastily through the small opening. As the window closed behind him, the faint light of a clouded moon caught for just an instant the broad, determined face of the redoubtable Hendel.

Stenmin had made one serious miscalculation when he had imprisoned Balinor and the cousins of Eventine. His original plan had been a simple one. The aged Sheelon had been secured almost the moment after he left Balinor's side, preventing him from carrying out the Prince's instructions for warning his friends of his own imprisonment. With Balinor and the Elven brothers, his only companions when he had entered the city of Tyrsis, safely locked away beneath the palace, and with the Prince's close friends, Acton and Messaline, imprisoned as well, it seemed safe to assume that no one else in the city would cause any real difficulty. The word had already been spread that Balinor had come for a brief visit and gone on his way, returning to the company of the mystic Allanon, the man whom Stenmin had convinced Palance Buckhannah and most of the people of Tyrsis was an enemy and a threat to the land of Callahorn. Should any other friends of Balinor's appear and question the story of the borderman's abrupt departure, they would come first to the palace to speak with his brother, now the King, and it would be a simple matter to have them quietly disposed of. Undoubtedly this would have been exactly the situation with just about anyone except Hendel. But the taciturn Dwarf was already familiar with Stenmin's treacherous ways and suspected that he had gained an unshakable hold over the disturbed Palance. Hendel knew better than to reveal his presence before finding out what had actually happened to his missing companions.

It was a peculiar turn of events that brought him back to Tyrsis. When he left Balinor and the Elven brothers near the woodlands north of the fortress, he fully intended to travel straight to the western city of Varfleet and from there proceed back to Culhaven. Once in his own land, he would assist in mobilizing the Dwarf armies to defend the southern territories of the Anar against the expected invasion of the Warlock Lord. He traveled all night through the forests north of Varfleet and by morning entered the city, where he immediately called on old friends and, after a brief greeting, went directly to sleep. It was afternoon by the time he was awakened, and after washing and eating, he prepared to depart for his homeland. He had not yet reached the gates of the city when a ragged band of Dwarfs staggered through the streets and demanded to be taken before the council. Hendel hurried along with them, questioning one he recognized as they were escorted to the council chambers. To his dismay he learned that a massive force of Trolls and Gnomes was marching directly for the city of Varfleet from out of the Dragon's Teeth and would strike within the next day or two. The Dwarfs were part of a patrol that had spotted the huge army and tried to slip past it to warn the Southlanders. Unfortunately they were seen and most were killed in a pitched battle. Only this small handful had managed to reach the unsuspecting city.

Hendel knew that if an armed force were moving toward Varfleet, there was in all probability a second, much larger force moving against Tyrsis. He was certain that the Spirit Lord planned to destroy the cities of Callahorn quickly and thoroughly, leaving the gateway to all the Southland open and undefended. His first duty was to warn his own people, but it was a long, two-day march to Culhaven and two more days back again.

He quickly discovered that Balinor had been mistaken in his belief that his father was still the King. If Balinor were killed or imprisoned by his insanely jealous brother or the treacherous mystic Stenmin before he could secure the throne and gain command of the Border Legion, then Callahorn was doomed. Someone had to reach the borderman before it was too late. There was nobody available for the job but Hendel. Allanon was still searching the Northland for the missing Shea, accompanied by Flick and Menion Leah. He made his decision quickly, ordering one of the battered Dwarfs in the ragged patrol to leave that very night for Culhaven. Whatever else happened, word would have to be brought to the Dwarf elders that the invasion of the Southland had begun through Callahorn and that the Dwarf armies must march to the aid of Varfleet. The cities of Callahorn must not fall or the lands would be divided and the very thing Allanon feared most would come to pass. With the Southland conquered, the Dwarf armies and the Elven armies would be divided and the Warlock Lord would be assured his eventual victory over all the lands. The ragged Dwarf gave his solemn promise to Hendel that he would not fail—that they would all leave at once for the Anar.

It took Hendel many hours to get back to Tyrsis, since this time travel was slow and dangerous. The forests had been penetrated by Gnome hunters whose mission it was to prevent any communication between the cities of Callahorn. More than once Hendel was forced to hide himself until a large patrol had passed, and time and again he was compelled to go far out of his way to avoid crossing heavily guarded sentry lines. The network of sentry posts was far tighter than it had been in the Dragon's Teeth, an indication to the seasoned border fighter that the attack was close at hand. If the Northlanders planned to strike Varfleet within the next day or so, then Tyrsis would be assaulted at the same time. The smaller island city of Kern might have already fallen. It was daylight when the Dwarf succeeded in penetrating the last of the sentry lines and was approaching the plains above Tyrsis, the danger of detection by the Gnomes behind and the threat of discovery by the evil Stenmin and the misguided Palance just ahead. He had met Palance several times, but it was unlikely the prince would remember him, and he had encountered Stenmin only once. Nevertheless, it would be wise to avoid attracting anyone's attention.

He entered the waking city of Tyrsis, concealed in the midst of dozens

of traders and travelers. Once within the great Outer Wall, he wandered
for several hours through the nearly deserted barracks of the Border Legion, speaking with the soldiers there and searching for some clue concerning his friends. Finally he was able to learn that they had arrived in the
city at sunset two days ago and gone directly to the palace. They had not
been seen again, but there was good reason to believe that Balinor had visited briefly with his father and then left. Hendel knew what this meant,
and for the remainder of the daylight hours he posted himself close to the
palace grounds, watching for any sign of his missing friends.

He noticed that the palace was well guarded by soldiers wearing the
crest of a falcon, a sign he didn't recognize. There were soldiers stationed
at the main gates and throughout the city, all bearing the same insignia,
and these were apparently the only activated units in all of Tyrsis. Even if
he found Balinor alive and managed to free him, it would not be a simple
task to regain control of the city and reactivate the Border Legion. The
Dwarf heard no mention of the invasion from the north, and it appeared
the people were totally ignorant of the danger facing them. It was incredible to Hendel that even someone as disturbed and misguided as Palance
Buckhannah would refuse to prepare the city against a threat as awesome as
that posed by the Warlock Lord. If Tyrsis fell, the younger son of Ruhl
Buckhannah would have no throne left him. Hendel silently studied the
terrain composing the People's Park that stretched beneath the wide span
of the Bridge of Sendic. When it was dark, he began his assault on the
guarded palace.

Now he paused momentarily within the darkened room, closing the
window tightly behind him. He was in a small study, the walls lined with
shelves of books carefully marked and labeled. It was the personal library
of the Buckhannah family, a luxury in these times when so few books
were written and dissemination was considerably limited. The Great Wars
had nearly obliterated literature from the face of the earth, and little had
been written in the embattled, desperate years since. To have a private library and to be able to sit and read any of several hundred books at leisure
were privileges shared by very few, even in the most enlightened societies
of the four lands.

But Hendel scarcely gave the room more than a passing thought as he
moved on catlike feet for the door at the far end, his keen eyes detecting a
dim light along the crack near the floor. Cautiously the Dwarf peered into
the lighted hallway. There was no one in sight, but he suddenly realized
that he had not yet decided what his next step would be. Balinor and the
Elven brothers could be anywhere in the palace. After rapid consideration
of the alternatives, he concluded that they would be imprisoned in the cellar beneath the palace if they were alive. He would search there first. Listening for a long moment to the silence, the Dwarf took a deep breath and
stepped calmly into the hallway.

Hendel was familiar with the palace, having visited Balinor on more
than one occasion. He did not recall where specific rooms were situated,
but he knew the halls and stairways, and he had been taken to the cellar

where the wines and food were stored. At the end of the hall, he turned left at the cross passage, certain the cellar stairs were just ahead. He reached the massive door that shut out the chill of the lower passages when he heard voices in the hall behind him. Hastily he tugged at the door, but to his dismay it would not open. He pulled again with his powerful shoulders hunched down and knotted, and still the door did not move. The voices were almost on top of him now, and in desperation he moved to reach another place of concealment. At that instant his eyes fell on a safety catch close to the floor which he had missed. With the voices just beyond the corner of the hall and the footsteps of several men echoing on the polished stone flooring, the Dwarf coolly drew back this second latch, swung open the heavy door, and darted inside. The door closed behind him just as three sentries rounded the corner on their way to relieve the guards stationed at the south gate.

Hendel did not wait to find out whether he had been seen, but darted down the stone-hewn stairs into the blackness of the deserted storage cellar. Pausing at the bottom of the stairway, the Dwarf groped along the cold stone of the wall for an iron torch rack. After several long minutes he found it, wresting the torch quickly from its setting and lighting it with the aid of flint and iron.

Then, with slow, painstaking care he searched the entire cellar, room by room, corner to corner. Time passed quickly, and still he found nothing. At last he had searched everywhere without any success, and it began to appear his friends were not being held captive in that part of the palace. Reluctantly Hendel forced himself to admit that they might have been imprisoned in one of the upper rooms. It seemed strange that either Palance or his evil adviser would risk having the captives seen by people visiting. Still, Hendel considered, perhaps Balinor had indeed left the city of Tyrsis and gone in search of Allanon. But he knew that guess was wrong even before the thought was completed. Balinor was not the kind of man who would seek anyone's help with this kind of problem—he would face his brother, not run. Desperately, Hendel tried to imagine where the borderman and the brothers might have been secured, where in the ancient building prisoners could be safely concealed from everyone. The logical place was beneath the palace in the dark, windowless depths he had just . . .

Suddenly Hendel remembered that there were ancient dungeons that lay beneath even this cellar. Balinor had mentioned them in passing, remarking briefly on their history, noting that they had been abandoned and the entry sealed over. Excitedly, the Dwarf peered around the shadowed chamber, trying to recall where the ancient passage had been built. He was certain that this was where his friends had been taken—it was the one place a man could be hidden and never found. Almost no one knew of its existence outside of the royal family and their close associates. It had been sealed over and forgotten for so many years that even the eldest citizens of Tyrsis might not recall its existence.

Ignoring the small adjoining rooms and passages, the determined Hendel carefully studied the walls and flooring of the central chamber, certain that it had been here he had viewed the sealed opening. If it had indeed been reopened, it should not be difficult to find. Yet he could see it nowhere. The walls appeared solid and the molding unbroken as he probed and tapped along the base. Once again his search proved fruitless, and once again he felt that he might have been mistaken. Despondently, he collapsed against one of the wine casings resting in the center of the floor, his eyes scouring the walls desperately as he tried to remember. Time was running out for Hendel. If he did not escape before daylight, he would probably join his friends in captivity. He knew he was missing something, overlooking something that was so obvious it had managed to escape him. Cursing silently, he rose from the wine barrel and walked slowly about the large chamber, thinking, trying to recall. It was something about the walls . . . something about the walls . . .

Then he had it. The passageway was not through the walls, but through the center of the floor! Suppressing a wild shout of glee, the Dwarf rushed over to the wine casings against which he had twice that evening so casually rested. Straining his powerful muscles to almost superhuman limits, he managed to roll aside several of the unwieldy barrels so that the stone slab which covered the hidden entryway was revealed. Grasping an iron ring hinged at one end of the slab, the sweating Dwarf pulled upward with an audible groan. Slowly, the stone grating in protest, the giant slab swung upward and fell back heavily on the flooring. Hendel peered cautiously into the black hole before him, extending the feeble torchlight into the musty depths. There was an ancient stone stairway, wet and covered with a greenish moss, that disappeared into the blackness. Holding the light before him, the little man descended into the forgotten dungeon, silently praying that he was not making another mistake.

Almost immediately he felt the biting chill of the stale, imprisoned air cutting through his clothing to cling maliciously to the warm skin beneath. The musty, barely breathable atmosphere caused him to wrinkle his nose in distaste and move down the steps more quickly. Such confining, tomblike holes frightened him more than anything, and he began to question his wisdom in deciding to venture into the ancient prison. But if Balinor were truly a captive in this terrible place, the risk was worth taking. Hendel would not abandon his friends. He reached the bottom of the stairs and could see a single corridor leading directly ahead. As he moved slowly forward, trying to peer through the damp gloom that defied even the light of the slow-burning torch, he could make out iron doors cut into the solid stone of either wall at regular intervals. These ancient, rusted slabs of iron were windowless and fastened securely in place by huge metal clasps. This was a dungeon that would terrify any human being—a windowless, lightless row of cubicles where lives could be shuttered away and forgotten as surely as the dead.

For untold years the Dwarfs had lived like this following the devastating Great Wars in order to stay alive and had emerged half-blind into a nearly forgotten world of light. That terrible memory had imbedded itself in generations of Dwarfs, leaving them with an instinctive fear of unlighted, confined places that they would never completely overcome. Hendel felt it now, as nagging and hateful as the clammy chill of the earth's depths into which this ancient grave had been carved.

Forcing down the rising knot of terror that hung in his throat, the determined hunter studied the first several doors. The bolts were still rusted in place and the metal covered with layers of dust and unbroken cobwebs. As he passed slowly down the line of grim iron portals, he could see that none of them had been opened in many years. He lost count of the number of doors he checked and the dim corridor seemed to continue on endlessly into the blackness. He was tempted to call out, but the sound might carry back through the open entryway to the chambers above. Glancing apprehensively behind him, he realized that he could no longer see the opening or the stairs. The darkness looked exactly the same behind as it did ahead. Gritting his teeth and muttering softly to himself to bolster his waning confidence, he moved forward, carefully scrutinizing each door he passed for signs of recent use. Then, to his astonishment, he heard the vague whisper of human voices through the heavy silence.

Freezing into a motionless statue, he listened intently, afraid that his senses were deceiving him. Yet there they were again, faint, but clearly human. Moving ahead quickly, the Dwarf tried to follow the sound. But as suddenly as they had appeared, the voices were gone. Desperately, Hendel glanced at the doors to either side. One was rusted shut, but the other bore fresh scratches in the metal, and the dust and cobwebs had been brushed away. The latch was oiled and had been recently used! With one quick tug, the Dwarf pulled back the metal fastening and yanked open the massive door, thrusting the torch before him, the light falling sharply on three astonished, half-blinded figures who rose hesitantly to face this new intruder.

There were warm cries of recognition, a rushing together with outstretched hands, and the four friends were reunited. The rough visage of Balinor, towering above the drawn faces of the smiling Elven brothers, appeared relaxed and confident, and only the blue eyes betrayed the borderman's deep sense of relief. Once again, the resourceful Dwarf had saved their lives. But this was no time for words or feelings, and Hendel quickly motioned them back down the darkened passage toward the stairway leading up from this frightening dungeon. If daybreak found them still wandering beneath the palace, the chance of discovery and recapture would be a near certainty. They had to escape immediately into the city. In hurried steps they moved down the corridor, the dying torchlight held before them like the probing cane of a blind man seeking the way.

Then came the sudden grating of stone on stone and a heavy thudding noise as if a tomb had closed. Horrified, Hendel charged ahead, reaching the damp stone steps and stopping short. Above, the huge stone slab had been closed, the fastenings secured, and the exit to freedom barred. The

Dwarf stood helplessly beside his three friends, shaking his head in stunned disbelief. His attempt to save them had failed; he had only succeeded in becoming a captive himself. The torch in his gnarled hand was almost burned out. Soon, they would be left in total blackness, and the waiting would begin again.

Junk, nothing but junk!" roared Panamon Creel in frustration, kicking once more the pile of worthless metal blades and jewelry that lay on the ground before him. "How could I have been such a fool? I should have seen it right away!"

Shea walked silently to the north end of the clearing, his eyes staring at the faint trail in the forest earth that the crafty Orl Fane had left in his flight northward. He had been so close. He had held the precious Sword in his own hands—only to lose it through an unforgivable failure to recognize the truth. The massive form of Keltset loomed silently beside him, the great bulk bending close to the damp, leaf-strewn ground, the inscrutable face almost next to his own as the strangely gentle eyes studied and searched. Shea turned quietly back to the raging Panamon.

"It wasn't your fault—you had no reason to suspect the truth," he muttered dejectedly. "I should have listened to his raving with a little more wisdom and a little less . . . whatever. I knew the signs to look for and I forgot to keep my eyes open when it counted."

Panamon nodded and shrugged, stroking the carefully trimmed mustache with the point of his piked hand. With a last kick at the discarded implements, he called once to Keltset, and without further discussion the two began quickly to break camp, strapping together the gear and weapons that had been deposited for the night. Shea watched them for a moment, still unable to accept his failure to gain possession of the Sword. Panamon called gruffly to him to lend a hand, and he silently obeyed. He could not face the inevitable aftermath of this most recent setback. Panamon Creel had obviously been pushed as far as he would stand it, chaperoning a foolish and amazingly stupid little Valeman around in the dangerous borderlands of Paranor, searching for some people who might very well turn out to be enemies and for a Sword that only Shea knew anything about, but couldn't recognize when he had it in his own hands. The scarlet highwayman and his giant companion had nearly lost their lives once already over this mysterious Sword and undoubtedly once was more than enough. The Valeman had no choice now except to try to locate his friends. But when he did find them, he would have to confront Allanon and tell him how he had failed—failed them all. He shuddered at the prospect of facing the grim Druid, of feeling those remorseless eyes peer into his most carefully hidden thoughts for the whole truth. It was not going to be pleasant.

He recalled suddenly the strange prophecy related to them in the Valley of Shale on that dark, misted dawn over a week ago. It was the Shade of Bremen who had forewarned of the danger in the forbidding Dragon's Teeth—how one would not see Paranor, how one would not reach the other side of the mountain, yet would be first to lay hands on the Sword of Shannara. It had all been foretold, but Shea had forgotten it in the stress and excitement of the past few days.

The weary Valeman closed his eyes against the world for a few moments and wondered how on earth he could possibly be a part of this incredible puzzle that centered around a war of power with the spirit world and a legendary Sword. He felt so small and helpless that it seemed that the easiest path for him to choose now was to bury himself and pray for a quick end to life. So much depended on him, if Allanon were to be believed, and from the beginning he had been completely inadequate to the task. He had been unable to do anything for himself, depending on the strength of other men to get him this far. How much had they all sacrificed for him so that he might lay hands on the magic Sword. Yet when he had it in his grasp . . .

"I've decided. We're going after him."

Panamon Creel's deep voice cut through the quiet of the little clearing like the sharp crack of an iron blade through dry wood. Shea stared at the broad, unsmiling face in astonishment.

"You mean . . . into the Northland?"

The scarlet thief shot him one of those angry looks that dismissed the Valeman as an idiot incapable of understanding sane men.

"He made a fool out of me. I'd rather cut my own throat than let the little rat get away from me now. When I get my hands on him this time, I'll leave him for the worms to chew on."

The handsome face was emotionless, but there was undisguisable hatred in the menacing tone of voice that cut through to the bone. This was the other side of Panamon—the cold professional who had ruthlessly destroyed an entire encampment of Gnomes and later stood in battle against the incomparable power of the Skull Bearer. He wasn't doing this for Shea or even to gain possession of the Sword of Shannara. This was strictly a matter of his injured pride and desire for revenge on the unfortunate creature who had dared to bruise it. Shea glanced quickly at the motionless Keltset, but the giant Rock Troll gave no indication of either approval or disapproval; the barklike face was blank, the deep-set eyes expressionless. Panamon laughed sharply, taking a few quick strides toward the hesitant Valeman.

"Think on this, Shea. Our Gnome friend has made matters so much more simple by revealing the exact location of the Sword you have been searching so long to find. Now you don't have to search for it—we know where it is."

Shea nodded in silent agreement, still wary of the adventurer's true motives. "Do we have a chance of catching up with him?"

"That's more like it—that's the spirit we need." Panamon grinned at him, his face a mask of confidence. "Of course we can catch up with him—it's merely a matter of time. The difficulty will be if someone else catches up with him first. Keltset knows the Northland as well as anyone alive. The Gnome will not be able to hide from us. He will have to run, run, and keep running, because he has no one to turn to, not even his own people. It's impossible to know exactly how he stumbled onto the Sword, or even how he surmised its value, but I do know I was not mistaken about his being a deserter and a scavenger."

"He could have been a member of the band of Gnomes transporting the Sword to the Warlock Lord—or perhaps even a prisoner?" Shea suggested thoughtfully.

"More probably the latter," the other agreed, hesitating as if trying to recall something, staring northward into the gray mistiness of the forest morning. The sun had already cleared the horizon of the eastern edge of the world, its fresh light bright and warm, seeping slowly into the darkened corners of the forestland. But the mist of early morning had not yet cleared, leaving the three companions shrouded in a hazy mixture of sunlight and dying night. The sky to the north appeared unaccountably dark and forbidding even for early morning, causing the normally verbose Panamon to stare wordlessly at this curious blackness for several long minutes. Finally he turned back to them, his face clouded with doubt.

"Something strange is going on to the north. Keltset, let's move out now—find that Gnome before he has a chance to stumble onto a patrol of hunters. I don't want to share his final moments in this world with anyone!"

The giant Rock Troll moved into the lead in quick, easy strides, his head lowered slightly as he searched the ground before him, picking out the signs left by the fleeing Orl Fane. Panamon and Shea followed close behind in silent concentration. The trail of their quarry was readily apparent to the keen eyes of Keltset. He turned back to them and made a short signal with one hand, which Panamon translated for the curious Shea to mean that the Gnome was running hard and fast, not bothering to hide his footsteps, and had evidently decided on his eventual destination.

Shea began to speculate in his own mind where the wily little fellow would run. With the Sword in his possession, he might be able to redeem himself in the eyes of his own people by turning it over to them for presentation to the Warlock Lord. But Orl Fane had appeared highly irrational in his behavior while he was their prisoner, and Shea felt certain that the Gnome had not been faking. He had rambled on as if the victim of a madness he could only partially control, speaking in garbled sentences that had in a jumbled fashion revealed the truth concerning the whereabouts of the Sword. If Shea had thought the matter through a little more carefully, he would have seen it—he would have known that Orl Fane had the coveted talisman with him. No, the Gnome had crossed the mental barrier between sanity and madness, and his actions would not be entirely predictable. He would run from them, but to whom would he run?

"I remember now." Panamon broke into his thoughts as they continued to make their way back toward the Plains of Streleheim. "That winged creature insisted that we had possession of the Sword when it confronted us yesterday. It kept telling us that it could sense the presence of the Sword—and so it could, because Orl Fane was concealed in the brush with the weapon hidden in his sack."

Shea nodded quietly, recalling the incident bitterly. The Skull Bearer had unwittingly tipped them off that the precious Sword was in the area, but they had failed to notice this important clue in the heat and fury of their battle to survive. Panamon continued to ramble on in barely concealed fury, threatening to dispose of Orl Fane when they caught up with him in a number of extremely unpleasant ways. Then abruptly the fringes of the forest broke away, opening into the vast expanse of the Plains of Streleheim.

In astonishment, the three halted together, their disbelieving eyes fixed on the awesome spectacle that loomed directly to the north—a huge, unbroken wall of blackness, towering skyward until it vanished into the infinity of space, stretching along the horizon to encircle the entire Northland. It was as if the Skull King had bound the ancient land in the shroud of darkness that lay upon the spirit world. It was more than the blackness of a clouded night. It was a heavy mistiness that rolled and swirled in deepening shades of gray as it ran northward toward the heart of the Skull Kingdom. It was the most terrifying sight that Shea had ever witnessed. His initial fear was heightened twice over by a sudden, unexplainable certainty in his mind that this huge wall was crawling slowly southward, blanketing the entire world. It meant that the Warlock Lord was coming. . . .

"What in heaven's name is that . . . ?" Panamon trailed off into stunned silence.

Shea shook his head absently. There could be no answer to that question. This was something beyond the understanding of mortal man. The three stood looking at the massive wall for several long moments, as if waiting for something more to happen. Finally, Keltset stooped to peer carefully at the hard grassland before them, moving forward several yards at a time until he was some distance away. Then he rose and pointed directly into the center of the ominous black haze. Panamon started, his face frozen.

"The Gnome is running directly into that stuff," he muttered angrily. "If we do not catch him before he reaches it, the darkness will hide his trail completely. We will have lost him."

Several miles ahead, on the graying fringes of the blackened wall of mist and haze, the small, bent form of Orl Fane hesitated momentarily in its exhausting flight as the greenish eyes peered fearfully, uncomprehendingly into the swirling darkness. The Gnome had been moving northward since his escape from the three strangers during the early hours of the morning, running while his strength held out, then pushing forward in a shuffling trot, always with one eye straying back, waiting for the inevitable pursuit. His mind no longer functioned in a rational manner; for several weeks he had lived on instinct and luck, preying off the dead, avoiding the living. He could not force himself to think of anything beyond survival, a gut instinct to live another day among those who did not want him, would not accept him as one of their own. Even his own people had turned him away, scorning him as a creature lower than the insects that crawled the earth at their feet. It was a savage land that surrounded him—a land in which one could not survive alone for very long. Yet he was alone, and the mind that had once been sane had slowly turned inward on itself, shutting away the fears that were imbedded there until madness began to take hold and all reason began to die.

Yet the inevitable death did not come easily, as fate intervened with twisted humor and favored the outcast with a final glimmer of false hope, placing in his hands the means by which to regain the seemingly unattainable warmth of human companionship once more. While still a scavenger, still fighting a losing battle to stay alive, the desperate Gnome had learned of the presence of the legendary Sword of Shannara, its awesome secret gasped in faint warning from the rigid lips of one dying on the Streleheim Plains, the blinded eyes failing as the life thread snapped. Then the Sword was in his grasp—the key to power over mortal men in the hands of Orl Fane.

But the madness lingered, the fears and doubts wrenching ceaselessly at his failing reason as he pondered a course of action. This fatal hesitation resulted in the Gnome's capture and the loss of the coveted Sword—the lifeline back to his own kind. Reason gave way to despair and raving, and the already badly unbalanced mind collapsed. There was room now for only one burning, haunting thought—the Sword must be his or his life was over. He boasted irrationally to his unsuspecting captors that the Sword was his, that only he knew where it could be found, unwittingly betraying his last chance to keep possession. But the strangers failed to read between the lines, dismissing him too hastily as merely crazed. Then came the escape, the seizure of the Sword, and the flight northward.

He paused now, staring blankly at the mysterious wall of blackness that barred his way northward. Yes, northward, northward, he mused, smiling crookedly, the eyes widening madly. There lay safety and redemption for an outcast. Deep within, he could feel an almost uncanny desire to run back the way he had come. But the thought remained locked inescapably in his mind that his salvation lay in the Northland alone. It was there that he would find . . . the Master. The Warlock Lord. His gaze dropped mo-

mentarily to the ancient blade strapped tightly to his waist, its length dragging clumsily in the dirt behind him. The gnarled yellow hands strayed
briefly down over the carved handle, touching the engraved hand raised
high with burning torch, the gilt paint already flecking off in chips to reveal the burnished hilt beneath. He clutched the handle tightly, as if trying
to draw his own strength from its sturdy grip. Fools! Fools all, that had not
treated him with the respect he should command. For he was the bearer of
the Sword, the keeper of the greatest legend their world had ever known,
and it would be he who would . . . He shut out the thought hastily, fearful
that even the void about him could read his mind, peer into his secret
thoughts, and steal them away.

Ahead, the frightening darkness waited for him to enter. Orl Fane was
afraid of this, as he was of everything else, but there was no other way to
go. Dimly he recalled those who followed—the giant Troll, the man with
one hand, whose hatred he instinctively sensed, and the youth who was
half man, half Elf. There was something the Gnome could not explain
about the latter, something that nagged with unshakable persistence at his
already beleaguered mind.

Shaking his rounded head blankly, the little man moved forward into
the graying fringes of the dark wall, the air about him dead and silent. He
did not look back until the blackness was all about him and the silence had
disappeared in a sudden rush of wind and chilling moisture. When he did
glance back briefly, he saw to his horror that there was nothing there—
nothing but the same blackness that lay all about in heavy, impenetrable
layers. The wind began to rush violently as he moved on, and he became
aware of other creatures in the darkness. They came first as a vague awareness in his mind, then as soft cries that seemed to seep through the haze
and cling inquisitively about him. At last they appeared as living bodies,
touching softly with cringing fingers the flesh of his person. He laughed in
maddened frenzy, knowing somehow that he was no longer in a world of
living creatures, but a world of death where soulless beings wandered in
hopeless search of escape from their eternal prison. He stumbled on amidst
them, laughing, talking, even singing gaily, his mind no longer a part of his
mortal being. All about him, the creatures of the dark world followed in
cringing companionship, knowing that the maddened mortal was almost
one of them. It was all a matter of time. When the mortal life was gone,
he would be as they were—lost forever. Orl Fane would be with his own
kind at last.

Almost two hours passed, winding away with the slow, deliberate sweep of
the morning sun, and the three pursuers stood on the fringes of the wall of
mist into which their quarry had disappeared. They paused as he had done,
silently studying the forbidding blackness that marked the threshold to the
kingdom of the Warlock Lord. The haze seemed to lie upon the deadened
earth in layers, each one a little darker as the eyes peered deeper into the
unseen center, each one a little less friendly as the mind envisioned the

heart's undetermined fears. Panamon Creel paced back and forth in measured steps, his eyes never leaving the darkness as he attempted to muster enough confidence to push on. The massive Keltset, after a cursory study of the ground and a short motion to indicate that the Gnome had indeed gone northward, lapsed into statuelike immobility, the great arms folded and the eyes faint slits of life beneath the heavy brow.

There was no choice, Shea reasoned, his mind already determined, his hopes not yet dampened by the thought of temporarily losing the trail in the darkness. He had regained something of the old faith in providence, certain since they had begun this pursuit that Orl Fane would be found and the Sword regained. There was something pulling at him, reassuring him, confiding in him that he would not fail—something deep within his heart that gave him fresh courage. He waited impatiently for Panamon to give the word to proceed.

"There is a madness in what we're doing," the scarlet thief muttered as he passed by Shea once more. "I can feel death in the very air of this wall . . ."

He trailed off sharply, halting at last, waiting for Shea to speak.

"We must go on," Shea responded quickly, tonelessly.

Panamon looked slowly at his giant friend, but the Rock Troll made no movement. The other waited a moment longer, clearly disturbed that Keltset had ventured no opinion since they had undertaken this journey into the Northland. Before, when it was just the two of them, the giant had always indicated agreement when Panamon had looked to him for support, but of late the Troll was strangely noncommittal.

At last the adventurer nodded affirmatively, and the three plunged resolutely into the graying haze. The plains were level and barren, and for a while they moved forward without difficulty. Then, as the mists gradually deepened about them, their vision began to fail badly until they appeared to one another as little more than vague shadows. Panamon quickly called a momentary halt, extracted a length of rope from his pack, and suggested they tie themselves together to avoid becoming separated. When this was accomplished, they continued on. There was no sound save the occasional faint scrape of their boots on the hardened earth. The mist was not damp, but nevertheless seemed to cling to their exposed skin in a most unpleasant manner, recalling to Shea the unhealthy, fetid air of the Mist Marsh. It appeared to be moving faster the deeper they proceeded, yet they could feel no wind propelling its widening gusts. Finally it closed in from all directions and the three were left in total darkness.

They walked for what must have been hours, but their sense of time became confused in the soundless black haze that encased their fragile mortal beings. The rope held them back from the loneliness of death which permeated the mist, its strands reaching not so much to one another as to the world of sunlight and vision they had left behind them. This place into which they had dared to venture was a limbo world of half-life, where the senses were stifled and fears grew in an unfettered imagination.

One could feel the presence of death fragmenting the darkness, a touch here, a touch there, brushing softly the mortal creature it would one day claim. The unreal became almost acceptable in this strange darkness as all the restrictions of the human senses vanished into dreamlike remembrances, and the visions of the inner mind, the subconscious, pushed quickly to the fore, searching for recognition.

For a time it was almost pleasant to be able to lapse into this indulgence of the subconscious, and then it was neither enjoyable nor disagreeable, but simply deadening. For a long time this latter feeling persisted, soothing, caressing their minds into disinterest and vague boredom, leaving both bodies and minds with the sluggish drowsiness of the ancient lotus-eaters. Time disappeared entirely and the world of mist stretched on forever.

From out of the dim recesses of the world of life came the slow sensation of burning pain, coursing through Shea's deadened body with shocking abruptness. With a sudden wrenching, his mind was torn free of the listlessness which cloaked its thoughts and the searing sensation grew sharper in his breast. Still drowsy, his body strangely weightless, he groped tiredly at his tunic, his hand coming to rest at last on the source of the irritation—a small leather pouch. Then his mind snapped into alertness as he clutched tightly the precious Elfstones, and he was awake once more.

In sudden horror, he realized that he was stretched full length upon the earth, no longer walking, no longer even aware of where he had been going. Frantically he clutched the rope about his waist and pulled violently. He was rewarded by a sluggish groan from the other end; his companions were still with him. Struggling heavily, wearily to his feet once more, he realized what had happened. This frightening limbo world of eternal sleep had almost claimed them as its victims, lulling them, soothing them, dulling their senses until they had fallen and drifted closer and closer to quiet death. Only the power of the stones had saved them.

Shea felt incredibly weak but, summoning the little strength that remained, he tugged and pulled desperately on the length of rope, dragging Keltset and Panamon Creel back from the edge of the abyss of death, back to the world of the living. He shouted wildly as he yanked on the rope, then stumbled to them, kicking at the listless bodies until the pain brought them back to consciousness. Long minutes later they were roused sufficiently to be aware of what had happened; with the awakening, the spirit of life revived the will to survive, as both forced themselves to their feet. They hung on to one another with sleep-ridden limbs closely entangled, their minds fighting to remain conscious. Then they began to walk, stumbling blindly in the unbroken darkness, one foot before the other, each step an incredible struggle of mind and body. Shea was in the lead, uncertain of his direction, but relying on the instinct sparked by the powerful Elfstones to guide him.

For a long time they pushed ahead through the endless dark, fighting to remain awake and alert as the deadening mists swirled lazily about them.

The strange, sleeplike sensation of death clung to them, trying to over-power their tired minds, silently urging their exhausted bodies to accept the welcome rest that waited. But the mortals resisted with iron determi-nation, their strength a small fragment of courage and desperation that, when all else was gone, still would not quit.

At last the deep weariness began to draw back into the dark haze. Death had failed this time to stifle the will to survive. There would be other times for these three, but for the moment they would live on a little longer in the world of men. So the sluggishness passed away and the drowsiness faded—not in the normal manner of sleep, but with quiet warnings that it would come again. The three companions were suddenly the same as before, the muscles unfettered as if there had been no sleep, the mind released rather than awakened. There was no inner desire to stretch or to yawn, but only a lingering memory that the sleep of death was a slumber without sensation, without time.

For long minutes no one spoke, though all were fully revived, each still savoring in unspoken fear and quiet desperation the taste of dying they had experienced, knowing that one day its inevitable touch would claim them forever. For several brief seconds they had stood at the edge of life and gazed into the forbidden land beyond—something no mortal was permit-ted to do before the end of his natural life. To have been this close was numbing, frightening, even maddening. They should not have survived.

But then the memories were gone, all but the dim knowledge that the three had narrowly escaped dying. Regaining their composure, they con-tinued to search for an end to the confining blackness. Panamon spoke once to Shea in low tones, asking whether he knew if they were proceed-ing in the right direction. The reluctant response was a curt nod. What difference did it make if he did not know, the little Valeman wondered to himself angrily. What other direction would they take? If his instincts were wrong, then there was nothing left that could help them anyway. The Elf-stones had saved him once; he would trust them again.

He wondered how Orl Fane had fared in his attempt to pass through the strange wall of mist. Perhaps the maddened Gnome had found his own way to escape its deadening effects, but it seemed unlikely. And if the little fellow had fallen by the way, then the Sword was lost somewhere in the impenetrable blackness and they would never regain it in time. This un-pleasant prospect caused the Valeman to pause mentally for several long moments, weighing the possibilities of the Sword lying about in this haze, perhaps only yards away from them, waiting for someone to discover it once again.

Then abruptly the darkness faded into dingy gray and the wall of mist was behind them. It happened so quickly that they were caught completely by surprise. One minute they were shrouded in blackness, barely able to distinguish one another, and the next they were standing in shocked si-lence beneath the leaden gray skies of the Northland.

They took a moment to study the country into which they had emerged. It was the most dismal land Shea had ever seen—even more forbidding than the dreary lowlands of Clete and the frightening Black Oaks in the distant Southland. The terrain was barren and desolate, a gray-brown earth totally devoid of sunlight and plant life. Not even the hardiest scrub brush had survived—a mute warning that this was indeed the kingdom of the Dark Lord. The earth stretched away to the north in low, uneven hills of hardened dirt, unbroken by even a wisp of grassland. Blunted, sprawling boulders thrust upright into the dim, gray horizon, and in places the lowlands were gutted by dusty gullies where rivers had long since dried away. There was no sound of life anywhere—not even the faint hum of insects to break the haunting stillness. Nothing remained in this once living land but death. Far to the north, jutting sharply into the vacant sky, rose a low series of treacherous-looking peaks. Without being told, Shea knew that this was the home of Brona, the Warlock Lord.

"What do you propose now?" Panamon Creel demanded. "We've lost the trail entirely. We don't even know if our Gnome friend got out of that stuff alive. In fact, I don't see how he could have managed it."

"We'll have to keep looking for him," Shea replied evenly.

"While those flying creatures keep looking for us," the other pointed out quickly. "The odds are becoming a little more than I bargained for, Shea. I don't mind telling you that I'm rapidly losing interest in this chase—especially when I don't know what it is I'm fighting. We almost died back there, and I couldn't even see what was killing us!"

Shea nodded understandingly, suddenly in command of the situation. For the first time in his life, Panamon Creel was worried about staying alive, even if it meant backing away with a severely wounded pride. It was up to Shea to make sure that the journey would continue now. Keltset stood apart from the two men, the soft brown eyes fixed on the Valeman as the heavy brows knitted in understanding. Again Shea was struck with the intelligence he saw, deep-rooted and unimposing in the gentle eyes of the massive creature. He still knew nothing about the giant Troll, but there was a great deal he wanted to learn. Keltset was the key to some strange, important secret that not even Panamon Creel knew, for all his boasting of their close friendship.

"The choices are limited," the little Valeman replied at last. "We can search for Orl Fane on this side of the mist and take our chances with the Skull creatures, or we can risk another journey back . . ."

He trailed off ominously, leaving the thought unspoken as he watched Panamon turn a shade paler.

"I'm not going back through that—at least not right away," the unnerved thief declared vehemently. He shook his head emphatically, the piked hand raising quickly to ward off the very air that carried such an insane suggestion. Then, almost sheepishly, the familiar broad smile returned as the old Panamon Creel reassumed command of his wits. He was too hardened an individual, too much a professional in the game of life, to allow anything to frighten him for very long. Grimly, he fought down the memories of what he had felt while stumbling blindly through the dead world within the darkness, calling on his long experience as an adventurer and border thief to rebuild his confidence. If he was destined to die in this venture, then he would meet it with the courage and determination that had carried him through so many hard years.

"Now let's think this situation through a minute," he mused, pacing away from them and back again. The old swagger and grit were returning. "If the Gnome did not make it out of the mist barrier, then the Sword will still be in there—we can get it anytime. But if he escaped, as we did, then where . . . ?"

He paused in midsentence, his eyes studying the surrounding countryside as he tried to narrow the possibilities. Keltset stepped quickly to his side and pointed directly north to the jagged peaks that marked the borders of the Skull Kingdom.

"Yes, of course, you're right again," Panamon agreed with a faint smile. "He must have been heading there all along. It's the only place he could go."

"The Warlock Lord?" Shea asked quietly. "Is he taking the Sword directly to the Warlock Lord?"

The other nodded briefly. Shea paled slightly at the prospect of tracking the elusive Gnome right up to the doorstep of the Spirit King without even the comparatively strong mystical prowess of Allanon to aid them. If they were discovered, they would be entirely defenseless except for the Elfstones. While the stones might have prevailed over the Skull Bearers, it seemed highly doubtful that they would have any chance against a creature as awesome as Brona.

The first question was whether or not Orl Fane had even managed to get through the treacherous mist. They decided to follow the fringes of the rolling wall westward in an effort to cut across any tracks the fleeing Gnome might have left once he broke through into this region. If they discovered no trail in that direction, they would try going eastward for the same distance. If there was still no trace of Orl Fane, then they must assume that he had fallen in the killing haze, and they would be forced to reenter it in an effort to find the Sword. No one favored the latter alternative, but Shea gave them some reassurance by promising to chance using the power of the Elfstones to locate the missing talisman. Using the precious stones would undoubtedly alert the spirit world of their presence, but it was a gamble they would have to take if they expected to find anything in that impenetrable blackness.

Quickly now, the three began to hike northward, Keltset's keen eyes studying the barren ground for traces of the Gnome's footsteps. Heavy cloud banks blocked out the entire sky, enfolding the Northland in an unfriendly gray haze. Shea tried to estimate how much time had lapsed since they had entered the wall of mist, but he was unsure. It could have been a few hours or even a few days. In any event, the grayness of the land was deepening steadily, signaling the approach of nightfall and a temporary end to their search for Orl Fane.

Overhead the massing gray clouds had begun to grow darker and were rolling heavily across the hidden skies. The wind had picked up, gusting sharply through the barren hills and gullies, pushing angrily at the few clumps of boulders which barred its progress. The temperature was dropping quickly, turning so much colder that the three were forced to wrap themselves tightly in their hunting cloaks as they pushed ahead. Before long it became apparent that a storm was building, and they realized angrily that a heavy rain would wash away all traces of any footprints left by the fleeing Gnome. And if they were forced to guess whether or not he had escaped . . .

But in a rare stroke of good fortune, Keltset discovered footprints on the barren earth—footprints that came out of the wall of mist and continued northward. The Rock Troll showed Panamon Creel that the prints indicated a small person, probably a Gnome, and that whoever it was had been weaving and staggering badly, either from injury or exhaustion. Elated by this discovery and certain that they had found Orl Fane once again, they followed the faint trail northward, moving at a much faster pace than before. Forgotten was the ordeal of that morning. Forgotten was the threat of the omnipresent Warlock Lord, whose kingdom lay directly in their path. Forgotten was the exhaustion and despair they had felt since losing the precious Sword of Shannara. Orl Fane would not escape them again.

Overhead the skies continued to darken. Far to the west came the deep sound of thunder, an ominous rumble that was carried by the increasing force of the wind across the length and breadth of the Northland. It was going to be a terrific storm, almost as if nature had decided to breathe new life into this dying land by washing it clean so that it might again be fertile ground for living things. The air was bitingly cold, and although the temperature had ceased falling, the gusting wind knifed through the garments of the three travelers. Yet they scarcely felt it, their eyes scanning anxiously the northern horizon for any sign of their quarry. The trail was growing fresher; he was somewhere just ahead.

The face of the land had begun to change noticeably. The barren countryside had retained its basic feature, an iron-hard ground studded with scattered rock and boulder clumps, but it had grown steadily more hilly and rutted, making travel increasingly difficult. The cracked, dry earth was particularly difficult to maneuver because it lacked the forms of vegetation that normally offered decent footing. As the hills and vales rose higher and dipped more sharply, the three pursuers found themselves slipping and clawing their way forward.

The rising west wind had grown in force to an earsplitting howl, at times nearly sweeping the unprotected men off their feet as it rushed across the desolate hilltops in frantic bursts. The loose topsoil flew in all directions at once in the merciless grip of the wind, striking at the skin, eyes, and mouths of the three men in stinging, choking thrusts. It soon became so bad that the entire countryside was swathed in wind and dirt, as if it were a sandstorm in a desert. It became difficult to breathe, much less to see, and eventually even the keen eyes of Keltset could no longer discern the faintest trace of the trail they were following. Quite probably there was nothing left to find, so completely had the wind cut into the unprotected earth, but the three pushed on.

The rumble of distant thunder had risen to a steady crashing, interspersed by jagged flickers of lightning directly to the west and almost on top of them. The sky above had turned black, though with the blinding effect of the wind and the dust, they scarcely noticed this added hindrance to their vision. Bit by bit, a heavy haze moved closer from the western horizon—a haze that was clearly formed by sheet upon sheet of driving rain blown by the shrieking wind. Finally it became so bad that Panamon yelled wildly above the rush of the wind for a halt.

"It's no use! We've got to find shelter before that storm hits us!"

"We can't give up now!" Shea cried angrily, his words almost entirely drowned out by a sudden crash of thunder.

"Don't be a fool!" The tall thief struggled to his side, dropping to one knee as he peered through the blowing dust, his hands shielding his eyes from the stinging, blinding particles. To the right, he spotted a large hill dotted with clusters of overhanging boulders that appeared to offer some shelter against the force of the wind. Signaling the other two, he abandoned all attempts to proceed north and turned toward the rocks. Heavy drops of rain were beginning to fall, striking with chilling effect against the warm skin of the sweating men; the crashing of thunder had risen to deafening proportions. Shea continued to peer northward into the darkness, unwilling to accept Panamon's decision to give up the chase when he knew they were so very close.

They had almost reached the shelter of the rocks when he saw something moving. A dazzling flash of lightning outlined a small form near the crest of a tall hill far, far ahead, struggling madly to gain the summit in the face of the driving wind. Yelling frantically, the little Valeman grabbed Panamon's arm and pointed toward the distant hill, now almost totally invisible in the darkness. For a second the three remained frozen in place, searching the blackness as the storm descended on them in blinding sheets of rain, completely drenching them in seconds. Then the lightning flashed with shattering brightness a second time to reveal again the distant hill with its tiny challenger, still clawing wildly for footing near the crest. Then the vision was gone and the rain fell again.

"It's him! It's him!" yelled Shea in frenzied recognition. "I'm going after him!"

Without waiting for the other two, the excited Valeman plunged down the side of the wet embankment, determined that the Sword should not escape him again.

"Shea. No, Shea!" Panamon called after him in vain. "Keltset, get him!"

Lunging quickly down the hill, the giant Troll overtook the little Valeman in several leaps, picking him up effortlessly with one huge arm and carrying him back toward the waiting Panamon. Shea was yelling and kicking furiously, but he had no chance of breaking the Troll's iron grip. The storm had reached its peak already, the rain cutting away the unprotected landscape in huge chunks of earth and rock that washed down into the gullies to form small, wild rivers. Panamon led them into the rocks, ignoring Shea's repeated threats and pleas as he searched for shelter on the east slope of the hill, away from the force of the wind and rain. After a quick study, he chose a point high on the crest which was protected on three sides by large clusters of boulders that would offer good protection from the force of the storm if not from its wetness and chill. Scrambling wearily, fighting with the little strength left them against the incredible thrust of the wind, the three at last reached the meager shelter, where they collapsed in exhaustion. Panamon quickly signaled Keltset to release the struggling Shea. Angrily the Valeman confronted the tall adventurer, the rain running into his eyes and mouth in steady rivulets.

"Are you mad?" he exploded against the shriek of the wind and the deep, constant rumble of the storm. "I could have caught him! I could have had him. . . ."

"Shea, listen to me!" Panamon cut in quickly as he peered through the heavy grayness to meet the other's angry gaze. There was a sudden moment of stilled voices in the roar of the Northland storm as Shea hesitated. "He was too far ahead to be caught in this kind of a storm. We would have all been blown away or injured in mud slides. It's too treacherous in these hills to travel ten feet in a heavy rainstorm—much less several miles. Relax a bit and cool your temper. We can pick up the remains of the Gnome when this gale blows over."

For a second Shea felt compelled to argue the point, but again he paused and the anger quickly subsided as his good sense returned, and he realized that Panamon was right.

The full force of the storm was tearing away at the unprotected land, stripping away its barren face and reshaping its stark features. Slowly the hills were washing down into the water-logged gullies and the ancient Streleheim Plains began to widen gradually into the vast Northland. Huddled against the cold of the massive boulders, Shea stared out into the sheets of rain as they came and passed in endless torrents, masking out the desolation of this lifeless, dying land. It seemed as if there were no one else alive but the three of them. Perhaps if the storm continued long enough, they would all be washed away and life could begin anew, he thought disconsolately.

Although the rain did not fall directly on them within the small refuge, they could not escape the chilling dampness of their waterlogged clothing, and so their discomfort persisted. At first they sat in expectant silence, as if waiting for the storm to abate and the pursuit of Orl Fane to begin again, but gradually they grew weary of the lonely vigil and settled back to other pastimes, convinced the rain and the wind would claim the entire day.

They ate a little food, more from common sense than hunger, and then tried to sleep as best they could in the close quarters. Panamon had managed to salvage two blankets from his pack which had been sealed in watertight wrappings, and these he passed to Shea. The grateful Valeman refused, offering them to his friends, but the giant Keltset, who seemed seldom very distraught by anything, was already asleep. So Panamon and Shea wrapped themselves in the warmth of the blankets, huddled next to each other on one side of the enclosure, and stared quietly into the falling rain.

After a time they began to talk of things past, of quiet times and distant places which they felt compelled to share in this hour of vague despondency and loneliness. As usual, Panamon carried the conversation, but the stories of his travels were not the same as before. The element of improbability and wildness had been lifted, and for the first time, Shea knew the colorful thief was talking about the real Panamon Creel. It was idle, almost carefree talk that passed between the two men—a bit like the conversation of two old friends reunited after many years.

Panamon told of his youth and the hard times the people all around him had known and lived with while he grew into manhood. There were no excuses, no regrets offered, but only the simple narrative of years long past that lingered on in memories. The little Valeman told about his boyhood with his brother Flick, recalling their wild, exciting expeditions into the Duln forests. He spoke in smiles about the unpredictable Menion Leah, who in vague ways suggested Panamon Creel as a young man. Time drifted away as they talked, shutting out the storm and drawing the two strangely close to each other for the first time since they had met. As the hours passed and darkness came, Shea grew to understand the other man, to know him as he could not have known him otherwise. Perhaps the thief understood Shea a little better as well. The Valeman wanted to believe so.

At last, when night shrouded the entire land and even the pounding rain had disappeared from view, so that nothing remained but the sound of the wind and the splash of puddles and rivers, the conversation drew itself around to the sleeping Keltset. In quiet tones, the two men speculated about the giant Rock Troll's origin, trying to understand what had brought him to them, what had made him undertake this suicidal journey into the Northland. It was his home, they knew, and perhaps he planned to return to the distant Charnal Mountains. Yet had he not been driven from there—if not by his own people, then by something equally powerful and compelling? The Skull Bearer had known him on sight—but how? Even Panamon admitted that Keltset was more than a mere thief and adventurer. There was tremendous pride and courage in his bearing, a deep intelligence in his silent determination, and somewhere in his past, a terrible secret he had chosen to share with no one. Something unspeakable had happened to him, and both men could sense that it had something to do with the Warlock Lord, if only in an indirect way. There had been fear in the Skull Bearer's eyes when he had recognized the massive Troll. The two men talked a while longer until sleep came in the early-morning hours; then wrapped in the blankets for protection from the chill of the night and the rain, they drifted into slumber.

27

"You there! Hold it a minute!"

The sharp command came out of the darkness behind Flick, cutting knifelike to the bone of his already waning courage. In slow shock, the terrified Valeman turned, lacking sufficient presence of mind even to attempt to run. He had been discovered at last. It was useless to draw the short hunting knife still grasped firmly beneath the hunting cloak, but his unresponding fingers remained locked in place as his eyes sought out the dim form of the approaching enemy. His comprehension of the Gnome language was poor, but the tone of voice alone was enough to enable him to understand that brief command. Rigidly, he watched a bulky, cursing form emerge from out of the darkness of the tents.

"Don't just stand there," the voice shrilled angrily as the roundish form waddled closer. "Lend a hand where it's needed!"

Astonished, the Valeman peered closely at the squat figure as his discoverer moved toward him, the thick arms laden with trays and platters and on the verge of dropping everything with each hesitant step of the stubby legs. Almost without thinking, Flick sprang to the fellow's assistance, removing the upper layer of trays and cradling them in his own arms, his nose catching the savory smell of freshly cooked meat and vegetables seeping from beneath the covers to the warm platters.

"There now, that's a whole sight better." The stocky Gnome breathed a sigh of relief. "I might have spilled the whole mess if I'd had to go another step on my own. A whole army encamped here, and can I get anyone to help carry the chieftains' own dinners? Not one Gnome so much as offers. I have to do it all. It's maddening—but you're a good fellow to lend a hand. I'll see you're properly repaid with a good meal. Hah?"

Flick didn't know what the verbose fellow was saying for the most part, and it didn't really matter. What did matter was that he had not been discovered after all. Breathing his silent gratitude, Flick adjusted his armload of food while his new companion continued to ramble on merrily about nothing, the heavy trays balanced precariously in the stubby arms. From beneath the concealing darkness of the hunting cloak's wide hood, the wary Valeman nodded in pretended understanding of the other's conversation, his eyes still fastened intently on the shadows moving within the great tent before them.

The thought remained indelibly fixed in his mind—he had to get inside that tent; he had to know what was going on in there. But then, almost as if he had read Flick's mind, the little Gnome began to move toward the canvas housing with measured steps, the trays before him, the little yellow face half turned so that his unending monologue might be better heard by his newfound companion. There was no question about it now. They were delivering dinner to the people in that tent, to the chieftains of the two nations comprising this giant army and to the dreaded Skull Bearer.

This is madness, Flick thought suddenly; *I'll be spotted the instant they lay eyes on me.* But he needed that one quick look inside . . .

Then they were at the entrance, standing quietly before the two giant Troll guards who towered over them like trees over stalks of grass. Flick could not bring himself to look anywhere but downward, though he was conscious of the fact that, had he drawn himself up to full height to face the enemy, he would have found himself staring directly into an armored, barklike chest.

Even though he was totally dwarfed in size, Flick's self-appointed friend barked a sharp command for admittance, apparently convinced that his presence was earnestly desired by those within—or at least the food he bore was. Quickly, one of the sentries stepped into the brightly lit interior of the canopy to speak briefly to someone, then reappeared a moment later, silently beckoning the two men to enter. With a quick nod over his shoulder to the trembling Flick, the little Gnome pushed past the guards into the tent and the Valeman, scarcely daring to breathe, followed dutifully, praying for yet another miracle.

The interior of the large canvas structure was comparatively well lighted by slow-burning torches set on iron standards about a large, heavy wooden table that stood unoccupied at the center of the enclosure. There were Trolls of varying size moving busily within the great tent, some carrying rolled charts and maps from the table to a large, brassbound chest while the others prepared to sit down to a long-awaited evening meal. All wore the military trappings and insignia of Maturens—Troll commanders.

The rear section of the canvas enclosure was screened off by a heavy tapestry which even the bright torchlight could not penetrate. The air in the army headquarters was smoky and fetid, so heavy in fact that Flick found it almost difficult to breathe. Weapons and armor lay piled neatly about the room, and battered shields hung on iron standards like crude attempts at decoration. Flick could still sense the undeniable presence of the terrifying Skull Bearer, and he quickly concluded that the dark monster was behind the bleak tapestry in the other section of the tent. Such a creature did not eat—its mortal self had long since passed into dust, and the spirit that remained needed only the fire of the Warlock Lord to nourish its hunger.

Then abruptly the Valeman saw something else. At the rear of the front portion of the enclosure, close to the tapestry and half hidden by the torch smoke and moving Trolls, was a dim form seated in a tall wooden chair. Flick started involuntarily, certain for an instant that the man was the missing Shea. The eager Trolls were moving up to him now, removing the

platters of food and placing them on the heavy table, and for a moment
they blocked the Valeman's view of the figure. The Trolls conversed quietly among themselves as they stood over the two servers, their strange
tongue completely unintelligible to Flick, who was attempting to shrink
farther down into the shadowed folds of his hunting cloak in the revealing
torchlight. He should have been discovered, but the unsuspecting Troll
commanders were tired and hungry and much too concerned with the invasion plans to notice the unusual features of the rather large Gnome who
had waited on them.

The last of the trays was removed and set upon the table as the Maturens gathered wearily about it to begin the meal. The little Gnome who
had brought Flick into the quarters turned to leave, but the eager Valeman
paused a moment longer to study quickly the form at the rear.

It was not Shea. The prisoner was Elven, a man of about thirty-five,
with strong, intelligent features. More it was impossible to tell at this distance. But Flick felt certain it was Eventine, the young Elven King who
Allanon had declared could mean the difference between victory or defeat
for the Southland. It was the Westland, the great, secluded kingdom of the
Elven people, that housed the mightiest army of the free world. If the Sword
of Shannara were lost, then this man alone commanded the power to stop
the awesome might of the Warlock Lord—this man, a prisoner, whose life
could be snuffed out at a single command.

Flick felt a hand on his shoulder, and he started violently at the sudden
touch.

"C'mon now, c'mon, we must leave," the hushed voice of the little
Gnome cajoled him earnestly. "You can stare at him some other time.
He'll still be here."

Flick hesitated again, a sudden, daring plan forming as he stood there.
If he had taken time to dwell on it, the idea would have terrified him, but
there was no time and he had long since passed the point of rational deliberation. It was already too late to escape the encampment and return to
Allanon before daylight, and he had come to this dreadful place to do
an important task—one which remained uncompleted. He would not
leave yet.

"C'mon, I said, we have to . . . Hey, what're you doing . . . ?" The little Gnome yelled involuntarily as Flick grasped him harshly by one arm
and propelled him forward toward the Troll commanders, who had paused
momentarily in their eating at the sharp cry and were staring curiously at
the two small figures. Quickly Flick raised one hand and pointed questioningly at the bound prisoner. The Trolls followed his gaze mechanically.
Flick waited breathlessly as one of them gave a curt command and the others shrugged and nodded.

"You're mad, you're out of your head!" the little Gnome gasped in
amazement, trying vainly to hold his voice down to a whisper. "What do
you care whether or not the Elf gets something to eat? What does it matter if he shrivels up and dies . . . ?"

His comments were cut short. A Troll called over to them, one gnarled hand extending a plate of food. Flick hesitated momentarily, glancing quickly at his astonished companion, who was shaking his head and grumbling inaudibly at the whole proposition.

"Don't look at me!" he exclaimed shortly. "This was your idea. You feed him!"

Flick failed to pick up everything the Gnome said, but he got the gist of the exclamation, and moved quickly to take possession of the plate. At no time did he glance into anyone's face for more than an instant, and even then the shadows of the wide cowl masked his identity. He kept his cloak wrapped tightly about him as he moved cautiously toward the prisoner on the other side of the tent, inwardly cheering madly that his gamble had paid off. If he could get close enough to the bound figure of Eventine, he could let him know that Allanon was close and that some sort of attempt to rescue him would be made. Still wary, he glanced back once at the other occupants of the enclosure, but the Troll commanders had returned to their dinner and only the little Gnome chef was still staring after him. If he had tried this kind of foolish stunt anywhere but in the very teeth of the enemy forces, Flick was well aware that he would have been discovered immediately. But here, in the commanders' own headquarters, with the awesome Skull Bearer just yards away and the entire area surrounded by thousands of Northlanders, the idea of anyone even sneaking into camp, let alone into this guarded tent, was preposterous.

Quietly, Flick approached the waiting captive, his face still concealed within the dark recesses of the hood, the plate of food extended before him. Eventine was of normal height and stature for a man, although for an Elf he was big. He wore woodland garb covered by the remnants of a chain mail vest, the worn insignia of the house of Elessedil still faintly visible in the dim torchlight. His strong face was battered and cut, apparently from the battle that had ended with his capture. At first glance there appeared to be nothing distinctive about him; he was not the kind of man who would be singled out in a group. His expression was set and impassive as Flick came to a halt directly in front of him, his thoughts apparently concentrated elsewhere. Then his head moved slightly as if aware he was being studied, and the deep green eyes fastened on the small figure facing him.

When Flick saw those eyes, he froze in sudden shock. They reflected a fierce determination, a fiery strength of character and inner conviction that reminded the Valeman, rather strangely, of Allanon. They reached into him, seized his own mind in a manner of speaking, demanding his attention, his obedience. He had seen this look in no other man, not even Balinor, whom they had all felt drawn to as a natural leader. Like those of the dark Druid, the eyes of the Elven King frightened him. Looking down quickly at the plate of food in his hands, Flick paused to consider what he should do next. Mechanically, he fitted a piece of the still-warm meat to the tip of the fork. His corner of the large tent was dimly lit, and the haze of smoke aided in concealing his movements from the enemy. Only the little Gnome was watching him closely, he was certain, but a single mistake would bring them all down on him.

Slowly he raised his face until the light from the torches had fully revealed his features to the watchful captive. As their eyes met, a flicker of curiosity crossed the otherwise impassive Elven face and one eyebrow lifted sharply. Quickly Flick pursed his lips, warning silence, and looked down again at the food. Eventine was unable to feed himself, so the Valeman began to hand-feed him slowly and carefully as he planned his next step. Now the captive Elven King knew he was not a Gnome, but Flick was terrified that if he spoke to the Elf, even in a faint whisper, he would be overheard. He abruptly recalled that the Skull Bearer was just on the other side of the heavy tapestry, perhaps only inches away, and if he should possess unusual hearing powers . . . But there was no other alternative; he had to communicate somehow with the prisoner before he left. There might not be another chance. Mustering the little courage he had reserved, the Valeman leaned forward a few inches farther as he lifted the fork, carefully putting himself between Eventine and the Trolls.

"Allanon."

The word was spoken in a barely audible whisper. Eventine took the proffered bite of food and responded with a faint nod, his face stony and impassive. Flick had had enough. It was time to get out of there before his luck ran out. Taking the plate of half-finished food, he slowly turned and walked back across the enclosure to the waiting Gnome chef, whose face mirrored mingled disgust and edginess. The Troll commanders were still eating as he passed them, their conversation low and earnest. They didn't even look up. Flick handed the plate to the little Gnome as he passed him, mumbling something incoherent, then quickly hastened from the tent, exiting between the two giant Troll guards before his astonished companion could think to act. As he strolled unconcernedly away from the tent, the Gnome appeared suddenly in the open entrance, yelling and grumbling in garbled phrases that the Valeman could not begin to comprehend. Turning, the Valeman waved quickly to the little figure, a faint smile of satisfaction on his broad face, and disappeared into the darkness.

At dawn, the Northland army began its march southward toward Callahorn. Flick had been unable to work his way clear of the encampment before then; so, as a bitter and gravely concerned Allanon watched from the seclusion of the Dragon's Teeth, the subject of his misgivings was forced to continue his disguise another day. The heavy morning rains had almost persuaded the Valeman to make a dash for safety, so convinced was he that the downpour would wash out the coloring Allanon had applied to his skin to give it a yellow hue. But escape in daylight was impossible, so he wrapped himself tightly in the hunting cloak and tried to remain inconspicuous. Before long, he was thoroughly drenched. To his happy astonishment, the yellow coloring on his skin did not appear to be washing out after all. There was a certain amount of fading, but in the excitement of moving the camp, no one had time to take notice of anyone else. It was the terrible weather, in fact, that saved Flick from being unmasked. Had it been a warm, dry summer day filled with sunshine and good spirits, the army would have been more concerned with exchanging pleasantries. If the sun had been shining, there would have been no need for the heavy hunting cloaks, and Flick would have attracted the attention of everyone around him by continuing to wear his. Once it had been removed, the Northlanders would have seen through his thin disguise immediately. The bright sunlight would have revealed to anyone casting so much as a passing glance in his direction that the Valeman did not even remotely resemble a Gnome in his facial bone structure and individual features. The heavy rains and wind saved Flick from all of this and permitted him to remain isolated and concealed as the huge invasion force trudged steadily across the grasslands into the Southland kingdom of Callahorn.

The bad weather persisted throughout the remainder of that day and, as it turned out, for several days thereafter. The storm clouds sullenly locked in place between the sun and the earth in great gray and black masses that churned and rolled with ferocious discontent. The rains fell unchecked, sometimes in pounding sheets driven by the unrelenting force of the west winds, sometimes in a steady melancholy drizzle that gave false hope to the belief that the storm's end was near. The air was chill and at times almost bitter, leaving an already water-drenched army shivering and disconsolate.

Flick remained on the move throughout the day's tiring, unpleasant march, soaked through by the blowing rains, but relieved that he could move about without calling attention to himself. He made it a point to avoid walking with any particular group for very long, always staying apart, always avoiding a situation which might force him to engage in conversation with anyone. The Northland invasion force was so vast that it was an easy matter to avoid ever being with the same men twice, and his deception was further facilitated by the fact that there appeared to be no overt attempts to exercise marching discipline over the great army. Either discipline was extremely lax or so thoroughly ingrained in the individual soldier that superior officers were not needed to maintain order. Flick could not conceive of the latter and concluded that fear of the omnipresent Skull Bearers and their mysterious Master kept the individual Troll or Gnome from doing anything foolish. In any event, the little Valeman remained just another member of the Northland army, biding his time until nightfall, when he planned to make his escape back to Allanon.

By midafternoon, the army had reached the swollen banks of the upper Mermidon, directly across from the island city of Kern. Again the invasion force encamped. Its commanders realized immediately that, due to the heavy rain, the Mermidon could not be crossed without tremendous hazard; even so, it would require large rafts capable of transporting vast numbers of men in order to secure the far bank. They had no rafts, so those would have to be built. That would require several days, and by that time the storms should have diminished and the waters of the Mermidon retreated sufficiently to permit an easy crossing. Across the river in the city of Kern, the Northland force had been sighted while Menion Leah still slept in the house of Shirl Ravenlock, and the people were beginning to panic as they realized the extent of their danger. The enemy invasion force could not afford to bypass Kern and proceed to Tyrsis, the main objective. Kern would have to be taken; considering the size of the city and the extent of the reduced army defending it, this would not be difficult. Only the rising river and the fortuitous storm delayed its fall.

Flick knew nothing of these matters, his own mind preoccupied with thoughts of escape. The storm could abate in a matter of hours, leaving him defenseless in the very heart of the enemy camp. Worse still, the actual invasion of the Southland was under way, and a battle with the Border Legion of Callahorn could come at any time. Suppose he was forced into battle as a Gnome hunter against his own friends?

Flick had changed considerably since his first meeting with Allanon weeks earlier in Shady Vale, developing an inner strength and maturity and a confidence in himself he had never believed himself capable of sustaining. But the past twenty-four hours had proved a supreme test of raw courage and perseverance that even a seasoned border fighter like Hendel would have found frightening. The little Valeman, unseasoned and vulnerable, could sense that he was on the verge of cracking under the extreme pressures, of giving way completely to the terrible sense of fear and doubt gripping him with every move he made.

Shea had been the reason behind his decision to make the hazardous journey to Paranor in the beginning, but more than that, he had been the one steadying influence on a pessimistic, distrustful Flick. Now Shea had been lost to them all for many days with little indication as to whether he was dead or alive, and his faithful brother, while refusing to give up hope that they would eventually find him, had never felt more alone. Not only was he in a strange land, embroiled in a mad venture against a mysterious creature not even of the mortal world, but now he was isolated in the midst of thousands of Northlanders who would kill him without a second thought the moment they discovered who he really was. The entire situation was impossible, and he was beginning to doubt that there was any real point to anything he had done.

While the vast army encamped on the banks of the Mermidon in the shadows of the late afternoon and the gray of twilight, a disconsolate, frightened Valeman moved uneasily through the camp, trying desperately to maintain a firm grip on his fading resolve. The rain continued to fall steadily, masking faces and bodies until they were merely moving shadows, drenching men and earth alike in a cold, cheerless haze. Fires were out of the question in such weather, so the evening remained dark and impenetrable and the men remained faceless. As he moved silently about the encampment, Flick mentally noted the arrangement of the commanders' quarters, the deployment of the Gnome and Troll forces, and the setting of the sentry lines, thinking that this knowledge might be of some value to Allanon in planning a rescue of the Elven King.

He relocated without difficulty the large tent that housed the Troll Maturens and their valuable prisoner, but, like the rest of the enemy camp, it was dark and cold, shrouded in mist and rain. There was no way even to be sure that Eventine was still there; he could have been moved to another tent or removed from the camp entirely during the march southward. The two giant Troll sentries remained posted at the entrance, but there was no sign of movement within. Flick studied the silent structure for several long minutes and then slipped quietly away.

As night descended, and Troll and Gnome alike retired to a chill, water-drenched slumber that more closely resembled an uneasy doze, the Vale-man decided to make his escape. He had no idea where he might find Allanon; he could only presume the giant Druid had followed the invasion force as it moved southward to Callahorn. In the rain and darkness, it would be nearly impossible to locate him, and the best he could hope to do would be to hide out somewhere until daylight and then attempt to find him. He moved silently toward the eastern fringes of the encampment, treading carefully over the huddled forms of the half-sleeping men, winding his way through the baggage and armor, still wrapped protectively in the water-soaked hunting cloak.

He could very likely have walked through the camp without any disguise on this night. In addition to the darkness and the persistent drizzle, which had finally begun to taper off, a low rolling mist had moved across the grasslands, blanketing everything so completely that a man could see no more than a few feet in front of his nose. Without wanting to, Flick found himself thinking about Shea. Finding his brother had been the major reason behind his decision to slip into this camp disguised as a Gnome. He had learned nothing of Shea, though he had scarcely expected to. He had been fully prepared to be discovered and captured within minutes after he entered the vast encampment. Yet he was still free. If he could escape now and find Allanon, then they could find a way to help the imprisoned Elven King and . . .

Flick paused, his progress abruptly halted as he sank down into a crouch beside a canvas-covered pile of heavy baggage. Even if he did eventually find his way back to the Druid, what could they hope to do for Eventine? It would take time to reach Balinor in the walled city of Tyrsis, and they had little time remaining. What would become of Shea while they were trying to find a way to rescue Eventine—who was unquestionably more valuable to the Southland, since the loss of the Sword of Shannara, than Flick's brother? Suppose that Eventine knew something about Shea? Suppose he knew where Shea was—perhaps even where the powerful Sword had been carried?

Flick's tired mind began to rush quickly over the possibilities. He had to find Shea; nothing else was really important to him at this point. There was no one left to help him since Menion had gone ahead to warn the cities of Callahorn. Even Allanon seemed to have exhausted his vast resources without result. But Eventine might know Shea's whereabouts, and Flick alone was in a position to do something about that possibility.

Shivering in the chill night air, he brushed the rain from his eyes and peered in numbed disbelief into the mist. How could he even consider going back? He was virtually on the edge of panic and exhaustion now without taking any further risks. Yet the night was perfect—dark, misty, impenetrable. Such an opportunity might not come again in the short time left, and there was no one to take advantage of it but himself. Madness—madness! he thought desperately. If he went back there, if he tried to free Eventine alone . . . he would be killed.

Yet he decided suddenly that that was exactly what he was going to do. Shea was the only one he really cared about and the imprisoned Elven King appeared to be the only man who might have any idea what had happened to his missing brother. He had come this far alone, spending twenty-four torturous hours trying to stay hidden, trying to stay alive in a camp of enemies that had somehow overlooked him. He had even managed to get inside the Troll commanders' tent, to get close enough to the great King of the Elven people to pass him that brief message. Perhaps it had all been the result of blind chance, miraculous and fleeting, yet, could he flee now, with so little accomplished? He smiled faintly at his own dim sense of the heroic, an irresistible challenge he had always successfully ignored before, but which now ensnared him and would undoubtedly prove his undoing. Cold, exhausted, close to mental and physical collapse, he would nevertheless take this final gamble simply because circumstances had placed him here at this time and this place. He alone. How Menion Leah would smile to see this, he thought grimly, wishing at the same time that the wild highlander were here to lend a little of his reckless courage. But Menion was not here, and time was slipping quickly away. . . .

Then, almost before he realized it, he had retraced his steps through the sleeping men and the rolling fog, and was crouching breathlessly within yards of the long Maturen tent. The mist and his own sweat ran in small rivulets down his heated face and into his soaked garments as he stared in motionless silence at his objective. Doubts crowded remorselessly into his tired mind. The terrible creature that served the Warlock Lord had been there earlier, a black, soulless instrument of death that would destroy Flick without thinking. It was probably still within, waiting in sleepless watch for exactly this sort of foolish attempt to free Eventine. Worse still, the Elven King might have been removed, taken anywhere . . .

Flick forced the doubts aside and breathed deeply. Slowly he mustered his courage as he finished his study of the canvas enclosure, which was no more than a misty shadow in the unbroken darkness before him. He could not even make out the forms of the giant Troll guards. One hand reached into the damp tunic beneath his cloak and withdrew the short hunting knife, his only weapon. Mentally he pinpointed the position on the canvas of the silent tent where he imagined Eventine had been bound at the time he had fed him that previous night. Then slowly he crept forward.

Flick crouched next to the wet canvas of the great tent, the chill imprint of the weave rough against his cheek as he listened for the sounds of human life that stirred uneasily within. He must have paused for fifteen long minutes, motionless in the fog and the dark as he listened intently to the muffled sound of heavy breathing and intermittent snores emitted by the sleeping Northlanders. Briefly he contemplated attempting to sneak through the front entrance of the structure, but quickly discarded that idea as he realized that once he was inside, he would have to navigate his way in the darkness over a number of sleeping Trolls in order to reach Eventine. Instead he selected the section of the tent where he imagined the heavy tapestry formed a divider—the corner in which the Elven King had been bound to the chair. Then, with agonizing slowness, he inserted the tip of his hunting knife into the rain-soaked canvas and began to cut downward, one strand at a time, just a fraction of an inch with each pressured stroke.

He would never remember how long it took him to make the three-foot incision—only the endless sawing in the silence of the night, afraid that the slightest sound of tearing would arouse the entire tent. As the long minutes passed, he began to feel as if he were entirely alone in the giant encampment, deserted by all human life in the black shroud of the mist and the rain. No one came near him, or at least he did not see anyone pass, and the sound of human voices did not reach his straining ears. He might indeed have been alone in the world for those brief, desperate minutes. . . .

Then a long, vertical slit in the glistening canvas stared back at him in slack anticipation, inviting him to enter. Cautiously he advanced, feeling his way carefully with his hands just inside the opening. There was nothing except the canvas floor, dry, but as cold as the damp earth that braced his knees and feet. Carefully he inserted his head, peering fearfully into the deep blackness of the interior that was filled with the sounds of sleeping men. He waited for his eyes to adjust to this new darkness, trying desperately to hold his breathing to a steady, noiseless whisper, feeling horribly exposed from the rear, the bulk of his body outside the tent and vulnerable to anyone who happened to pass.

It was taking his eyes much too long to adjust and he could not risk being discovered by a chance passerby at this stage, so he risked moving a few feet farther, slipping his stocky frame through the opening and into the dark shelter of the tent. The labored breathing and the snores continued undisturbed, and there was the occasional sound of a heavy body shifting position somewhere in the darkness beyond him. But no one awoke. Flick remained crouched just inside the long slit for more endless minutes, his eyes working madly to distinguish the faint shapes of men, tables, and baggage against the blackness of the night.

It seemed to take forever, but at last he was able to discern the huddled forms of sleeping men scattered about the floor of the tent, their bodies rolled tightly in the warmth of their blankets. To his astonishment, he realized that one motionless form lay slumbering only inches in front of his balanced body. Had he attempted to crawl any farther before his eyes had adjusted to this darkness, he would have stumbled onto and undoubtedly awakened the sleeper. The old sensation of fear returned sharply, and for a moment he fought back against a rising sense of panic that commanded him to turn and run. He could feel the sweat sliding down his crouched body beneath the water-soaked clothing, tracing thin, searching paths over the heated skin as his labored breathing became more ragged. At that moment, he was aware of his every feeling, his mind pushed right to the brink of collapse—yet later, he would recall nothing of these feelings. Mercifully, they would be blocked from his memory, and all that would remain would be one sharp picture etched indelibly in his brain of the sleeping Troll Maturens and the object of his search—Eventine. Flick spotted him quickly, the lean form no longer seated upright in the wooden chair at the corner of the heavy tapestry, but lying on the canvas floor only a few feet from the poised Valeman, the dark eyes open and watching. Flick had judged his point of entry correctly, and now he moved catlike to the King's side, the hunting knife severing quickly the taut ropes that bound hands and feet.

In an instant the Elf was free, and the two shadowy figures were moving quickly to reach the vertical opening in the side of the tent. Eventine paused momentarily to pick something up from the side of one of the sleeping Trolls. Flick did not wait to see what the Elf had seized, but hastened through the slit into the misty darkness beyond. Once outside, he crouched silently next to the tent, glancing anxiously about for any sign of movement. But there was only the persistent drizzle of the rain breaking the night's deep silence. Seconds later, the canvas parted again, and the Elven King passed through and hunched down beside his rescuer. He was carrying an all-weather poncho and a broadsword. As he wrapped himself in the cloak, he paused momentarily and smiled grimly at a frightened, but elated Flick, then gripped his hand in warm, unspoken gratitude. The Valeman grinned back in satisfaction and nodded.

So Eventine Elessedil was rescued, snatched from the very teeth of the sleeping enemy. It was Flick Ohmsford's finest moment. He felt now that the worst was over, that once clear of the great Maturen tent with Eventine a free man, escape from the camp could never be denied them. He had not even thought to look beyond his entry into the Troll commanders' quarters. Now the moment to look ahead was there, but as the two paused in the shadows, the moment passed and was lost.

From out of nowhere strolled three fully armed Troll sentries, who instantly spotted the two figures crouching at the side of the Maturen tent. For an instant everyone froze; then slowly Eventine rose, standing directly in front of the tear in the canvas. To Flick's astonishment, the quick-thinking

Elven King waved the three over to them, speaking fluently in their own language. Hesitantly, the sentries approached, their long pikes lowered carelessly as they heard the familiar sound of their own tongue. Eventine stepped aside to reveal the gaping slit, nodding warningly to Flick as the unsuspecting Trolls now rushed forward. The terrified Valeman stepped away, his hand gripping the short hunting knife beneath his cloak. As the Trolls reached them, their eyes still momentarily fastened on the torn canvas, the Elven King struck out with the broadsword.

Two of the Trolls were silenced before they had a chance to defend themselves, their throats cut away. The final sentry got off a quick cry for help and slashed wildly at Eventine, cutting into the exposed flesh of the Elf's shoulder; then he, too, fell lifeless into the muddied earth. For a moment there was silence once more. Flick stood white-faced against the tent wall, staring in fright at the dead Trolls as the wounded Elven King tried vainly to stem the blood flow from his slashed shoulder. Then they heard the sharp sound of voices from close by.

"Which way?" Eventine whispered harshly, the bloodied sword still tightly clenched in his good hand.

In mute silence the little Valeman rushed to the Elf's side and pointed into the darkness behind him. The voices grew louder now, coming from more than one direction, and swiftly, wordlessly, the two fugitives fled from the Troll sleeping quarters. Stumbling between the fog-shrouded tents and baggage, unable to find their footing on the water-soaked grasslands and blinded by the darkness and the rolling mist, the two struggled to outdistance their pursuers. The voices faded to either side of them and then fell behind, only to rise sharply in alarm within seconds as the bodies of the sentries were discovered. The two dashed on as the deep, haunting sound of a Troll battle horn shattered the night sleep of the Northland army, and everywhere men awoke to the call to arms and battle.

Flick was in the lead, frantically trying to remember the quickest way back to the camp perimeter. He was running blindly now, terrified beyond reason, his one thought to gain the safety of the silent darkness beyond this hateful camp. Struggling painfully to keep up with the Valeman, his shoulder bleeding freely from the pike wound, Eventine realized what had happened to his young rescuer and called vainly after him, trying to warn him to be careful.

Too late. The words had just left his mouth when they ran headlong into a band of still-groggy Northlanders who had been abruptly awakened by the battle horn's blast. Everyone went down in a tangle of arms and legs, both parties completely caught by surprise and unable to avoid the collision. Flick felt the hunting cloak ripped from his body as he was kicked and buffeted by unseen hands and feet, and in maddened terror he fought back, slashing wildly with the hunting knife at anything that came within reach. Howls of pain and fury went up from his attackers, and for an instant the arms and legs drew back and he was free again. He leaped to his feet, only to be borne back a moment later by a renewed assault. He

caught the dull flash of a sweeping sword blade as it whisked past his unprotected head and his own knife came up to ward off the blow. For several minutes, everything became chaotic as the Valeman rolled and thrashed
his way through the clinging hands and heavy bodies, the fogbound night a
maze of wild cries and scuffling figures. He was cut and battered unmerci-
fully as he sought to fight his way clear, sometimes forced back to the
earth, but always rebounding within seconds and struggling onward, calling sharply for Eventine.

What he did not realize was that he had stumbled into a band of unarmed Northlanders who were caught completely by surprise when he
charged madly into them, wielding the hunting knife. For several minutes
they sought to pin him down and disarm him, but the terrified Valeman
struggled so violently they were unable to contain him. Eventine rushed
quickly to his aid, battling his way through the mass of attackers to reach
the youth and at last they gave way entirely, scattering for the safety of the
darkness. Quickly downing the last persistent Northlander, a rather large
Gnome who had fastened himself bodily to the struggling Flick, the Elven
King grabbed his rescuer by the tunic collar and hauled him to his feet.
The Valeman continued to struggle violently for a moment more; then
realizing who held him, he abruptly relaxed, his heart beating wildly. All
around him the sounds of the Northland battle horns blasted in deafening
tones through the camp, mingling with the rising cries of the aroused
army. Vainly he tried to listen to what the other was saying, his battered
head still ringing from the blows struck.

"... find the quickest way out. Don't run—walk steadily, but unhur-
riedly. Running will just call attention to us. Now go!"

Eventine's words died into the darkness as his strong hand gripped
Flick's shoulder and turned him about. Their eyes locked momentarily, but
the Valeman could only meet the Elven King's piercing stare for an instant,
feeling it burn right through to his frightened heart. Then they were moving toward the perimeter of the awakened encampment, side by side, their
weapons held ready. Flick was thinking rapidly but clearly now, recalling
vague landmarks within the Northland camp that indicated he was proceeding in the right direction. The fear was momentarily buried as a cold
sense of determination gripped him, fostered in part by the strong presence striding quietly at his side. It might have been Allanon himself, so unshakable was the confidence that the Elven King radiated.

Dozens of the enemy rushed past them, some coming within several
feet, but no one stopped them or spoke to them. Unmolested, the two men
passed quietly through the chaos that had engulfed the Northlanders at the
unexpected call to battle, moving steadily toward the sentry lines surrounding the encampment. The cries continued from within, although they were
dropping behind the fugitives little by little. The rains had momentarily
ceased altogether, but the heavy mist continued unbroken, shrouding the
entire grasslands from the Streleheim to the Mermidon. Flick glanced once
at his silent companion, noticing with concern that the lean figure was bent

slightly in pain, the left arm hanging limp and bleeding freely. The valiant Elf was tiring rapidly, growing steadily weaker from loss of blood, his face pale and drawn from the effort to stay on his feet. Unconsciously, Flick slowed the pace, walking closer to his companion in case he should stumble.

They reached the camp perimeter within a very short time—so quickly, in fact, that the word of what had taken place at the Maturen headquarters had not yet reached the sentries. But the battle horn had put them on the alert, and they stood close to the encampment in small groups, their weapons ready. Ironically, they believed that the danger lay from an enemy outside the camp. Their eyes were fastened dutifully away from the camp, permitting Eventine and Flick to approach undetected to the very edge of their lines. The Elven King did not hesitate, moving forward between the outposts at a steady walk, trusting to the darkness, the mist, and the confusion to prevent their discovery.

Time was running out. Within a matter of minutes the entire army would be mobilized and ready for battle, and once it was discovered that he had managed to escape, trackers would be out searching for him. He would find safety if he could reach the borders of Kern, just to the south, or alternatively, if he could reach the concealment of the Dragon's Teeth and surrounding forests to the east. It would take several hours in either case and his strength was fading. He could not pause now, even if it meant risking almost certain discovery by passing into the open unprotected.

Boldly the two strolled directly between two of the sentry parties, looking neither left nor right as they moved into the emptiness of the open grasslands beyond. They succeeded in not calling attention to themselves until they were past the perimeter of the guard lines. Suddenly several of the sentries caught sight of them at the same moment and called out. Eventine turned slightly and waved with his good arm, calling back in the Troll language, all the while maintaining a steady pace as he moved farther into the darkness. Flick followed warily, waiting expectantly as the sentries stared after them, still undecided. Then abruptly one of them called sharply and began to move after them, waving them back in excited motions. Eventine yelled to Flick to run for it, and the chase was on. As the two men raced for safety, close to twenty guards took up the pursuit, brandishing their pikes and yelling wildly.

It was an uneven contest from the beginning. Both Eventine and Flick were of lighter build and under normal circumstances could have outdistanced their pursuers. But the Elf was wounded badly and weakened from loss of blood, while the little Valeman was physically exhausted from the ordeal of the last two days. The pursuers were fresh and strong, well rested and fed. Flick knew that their only hope was to find concealment in the mist and darkness, hoping their enemies would be unable to find them. Breathing harshly, stumbling with labored strides, they pushed their failing bodies to the limits of physical endurance. Everything became a large black blur made up of rolling mist all about them and the slickness of the grasslands beneath their racing feet. They ran until they thought they could run no farther, and still there were no mountains, no forests, no place to hide.

Abruptly, from out of the darkness ahead of them, there flashed an iron-tipped pike, piercing Eventine's cloak and pinning him to the damp earth. The outer perimeter of sentries, Flick thought in horror—he had forgotten about them! A dim form shot out of the mist, hurtling itself on the fallen Elf. With the last of his waning strength, the wounded King twisted sharply to one side to avoid the sword blade that buried itself in the earth next to his head, at the same instant bringing his own weapon around and up. The rushing figure fell forward with a quick gasp, impaled on the blade.

Flick stood rooted in place, staring wildly about for other attackers. But there had only been the lone sentry. Quickly he rushed to his companion's side, wrenching the pike free and pulling the exhausted Elf to his feet with almost superhuman effort. Eventine took a few steps before collapsing to the ground once more. Fearfully, the Valeman dropped to his knees beside him, trying to shake the man awake.

"No—no, I'm finished," the hoarse reply came at last. "I can go no farther. . . ."

Behind them, the cries of the Northlanders shot out of the darkness. Their pursuers were drawing closer! Again Flick tried in vain to pull the limp form to its feet, but this time there was no response at all. Helplessly the Valeman stared into the darkness about him, the short hunting knife held ready. This was the end. In final desperation, he called wildly into the darkness and the mist.

"Allanon! Allanon!"

The call died quickly into the night. The rain had begun once more, falling in a slow drizzle onto an already oversaturated earth to form still larger puddles and mires on the quiet grasslands. Dawn was no more than an hour away, although it was impossible to tell time in such weather as this. Flick crouched silently next to the unconscious Elven King and listened to the sounds of the men closing in about him. He could tell by their voices that they were drawing nearer, though they still had not seen him. As if to further mock the futility of the situation, he realized that after risking everything to free Eventine, he had still failed to learn what had befallen the missing Shea. Sudden shouts from his left brought him about to face dim figures approaching from out of the fog. They had found him! Grimly, he rose to meet them.

An instant later the hazy darkness between them exploded in a blinding flash of fire that seemed to erupt from out of the earth, the terrific force throwing Flick to the ground, leaving him dazed and blinded. Showers of sparks and burning grass fell all about him and the thunder of a long series of explosions shook the ground violently. One instant the Northlanders were shadowy figures caught in the dazzling light and the next they disappeared altogether. Columns of crackling flame shot upward into the night like giant pillars, thrusting through the darkness and fog to reach the heavens. Squinting into the maelstrom of destruction, Flick thought it was the end of the world. For several endless minutes the wall of fire blazed skyward in unabated fury, tearing the earth into blackened chunks, scorching the night air until the heat began to burn Flick's skin. Then with a final flash of surging energy, it flared up brightly and disappeared into a hush of mingled smoke and steam, blending quickly into the mist and rain until all that remained was the intense heat of the night air, drifting slowly to rest.

Flick rose cautiously to one knee and peered into the emptiness before him, then turned sharply as he sensed rather than heard the approach of someone behind him. From out of the rolling mist and steam emerged a giant black form, cloaked in flowing robes and reaching outward as if it were the angel of death come to claim her own. Flick stared in numbed terror and then started in recognition as the awesome form passed before him. It was the dark wanderer come at last. It was Allanon.

28

Dawn had just broken with dazzling brightness against a cloudless, deep blue sky as the last band of refugees from the island city of Kern passed through the gates of the great Outer Wall and entered Tyrsis. Gone was the damp, impenetrable mist and the vast dark ceiling of storm clouds that had blanketed the land of Callahorn for so many days. The grasslands remained soggy and sprinkled with small ponds the saturated earth could not yet manage to absorb, but the persistent rains had moved on to be replaced by a fresh sky and sun that brought a new cheerfulness to the morning. The people of Kern had been arriving in scattered groups for several hours, all weary, horrified by what had happened and frightened of what lay ahead. Their home had been completely destroyed, though some did not yet realize the Northlanders had put everything to the torch following the unexpected attack on their encampment.

The evacuation of the doomed city had been a miraculous success, and, although their homes were gone, they were still alive and, for the moment, secure. The Northlanders had failed to detect the mass escape, their attention completely occupied by the courageous band of Legion soldiers that had assaulted the central camp and drawn them away from even the most distant outposts in the mistaken belief that a full-scale attack was under way. By the time they realized the strike was only a feint designed to confuse them, the island had been evacuated and its people were far down the swift Mermidon and beyond the reach of the maddened enemy.

Menion Leah was one of the last to enter the walled city, his lean frame battered and exhausted. The wounds on his feet had been reopened during the ten-mile march from the Mermidon to Tyrsis, but he had refused to be carried. It was with the last of his strength that he struggled up the wide ramp leading to the gates of the Outer Wall, supported on one side by the faithful Shirl, who had refused to leave his side even to sleep, and gripped firmly on the other by an equally weary Janus Senpre.

The youthful Legion commander had survived the fighting of that terrible night battle, escaping the besieged island on the same small raft that had carried Menion and Shirl. The ordeal they had been through had brought them closer together, and on the trip southward they had spoken frankly, though in hushed tones, about the disbanding of the Border Legion. They were in complete accord that if the city of Tyrsis were to withstand an assault by a force the size of the Northland army, the Legion would be needed. Moreover, only the missing Balinor possessed the battle knowledge and skill necessary to lead them. The Prince must be found quickly and placed in command, even though his brother would undoubtedly oppose such a move, just as he was certain to oppose the re-forming of the legendary fighting force he had so foolishly demobilized.

Neither the highlander nor the Legion commander realized at this moment how difficult their task would be, though they suspected that Balinor had been seized by his brother upon entering Tyrsis some days earlier. Nevertheless, they were resolved that Tyrsis would not be destroyed as easily as Kern. This time they would stand and fight.

A squad of black-clad palace guards met the little group just inside the gates of the city, extending warm greetings from the King and insisting that they come to him at once. When Janus Senpre remarked that he had heard the King was deathly ill and confined to his bed, the squad captain quickly, though somewhat belatedly, added that his son Palance extended the offer in his father's place. Nothing could have pleased Menion more—he was anxious to get inside the palace walls for a look around. Forgotten was the fatigue and pain, though his companions still stood close to offer their support. The squad captain signaled to the guards near the Inner Wall, and an ornate carriage was quickly brought up to convey the privileged party to the palace. Menion and Shirl climbed into the carriage, but Janus Senpre declined to accompany them, explaining that he wished first to see to the welfare of his soldiers in the vacant Legion barracks. With disarming warmth, he promised he would join them later.

As the carriage drew away to the Inner Wall, the youthful commander waved once in sharp salute to Menion, his face impassive. Then accompanied by the grizzled Fandrez and several select officers, he strode purposefully toward the Legion barracks. In the coach, Menion smiled faintly to himself and gripped Shirl's hand.

The carriage passed through the gates of the Inner Wall and moved slowly onto the crowded Tyrsian Way. The people of the walled city had risen early that day, anxious to welcome the unfortunate fugitives from their sister city, eager to offer both food and shelter to friends and strangers alike. Everyone wanted to know more about the massive invasion force that was now advancing on their own homes. Throngs of worried and frightened people lingered uncertainly in the busy streets, talking anxiously among themselves, pausing to stare curiously as the carriage escorted by the palace guards rolled slowly past them. A few pointed or waved in astonishment as they recognized the slim girl who rode within, the dark, rust-colored hair shadowing her worn and drawn face. Menion sat close to her, suddenly aware once more of the pain stabbing in quick twinges from his battered feet. He was grateful now that it was not necessary to walk any farther.

The great city seemed to rush past him in short flashes of buildings and overpasses, all crowded with men, women, and children of all ages and descriptions, all rushing somewhere in noisy waves. The highlander breathed deeply and settled back in the cushioned seat, his hand still holding Shirl's, his eyes closing momentarily as he allowed his tired mind to drift into the gray haze that clouded his thoughts. The city and its multitudes faded quickly into a faint drone of sound that soothed him, lulled him quietly toward the comfort of sleep.

He was on the verge of slipping away entirely when a gentle shaking of his shoulder brought him quickly around, and his eyes opened to view the distant palace grounds as the carriage mounted the wide avenue of the Sendic Bridge. The youth gazed appreciatively down on the sunlit parks and gardens beneath the bridge, their tree-shaded lawns dotted with color from seemingly countless carefully tended flower beds. Everything lay in peace and warmth, as if this sector of the city were somehow an unrelated part of the turbulent human existence that had created it.

At the other end of the bridge the gates to the palace swung open in reception. Menion peered ahead in disbelief. The entire entryway was lined with soldiers of the palace guard, all immaculately dressed in their black uniforms crested by the emblem of the falcon, all standing stiffly at attention. From within the enclosure, trumpets announced the arrival of the coach and its passengers. The highlander was astonished. They were being accorded the formal welcome normally reserved for only the greatest leaders of the four lands, a policy strictly observed by the few monarchies remaining in the vast Southland. The pomp and display of a full military salute clearly indicated that Palance Buckhannah was determined to ignore not only the circumstances under which they had arrived, but the inviolate tradition of centuries.

"He must be mad—absolutely mad!" the angered Southlander stormed. "What does he think this is? We're besieged by an invading army, and he turns out the troops for a dress parade!"

"Menion, be careful what you say to him. We must be patient if we are to be of any use to Balinor." Shirl gripped his shoulder and faced him for a moment, smiling quickly in warning. "Remember as well that he loves me, misguided though he may be. He was a good man once, and he is Balinor's brother still."

Impatient and impulsive as always, Menion nevertheless realized that she was right. There was nothing to be gained by showing he was angered with the foolish pageant, and he was well advised to go along with the Prince's whims until Balinor was located and freed. He sat quietly back in the coach as it entered the palace gates, passing in slow review before the rows of expressionless soldiers that formed the elite of the King's personal guard. The fanfares continued to roll from all sides, and a small squad of cavalry wheeled in precise formation about the courtyard for the benefit of the new arrivals. Then the carriage came to a gentle halt, and the big figure of the new ruler of Callahorn appeared at the coach door, the broad face smiling in nervous delight.

"Shirl—Shirl, I thought I would never see you again!" He reached into the coach and helped the slim girl from the small enclosure, holding her close to him for a moment and stepping away to view her once more. "I . . . I really thought I had lost you."

Burning quietly, an impassive Menion helped himself from the carriage, stepping down beside them, smiling faintly as Palance turned to greet him.

"Prince of Leah, you are indeed welcome in my kingdom," the big man greeted the lean highlander, reaching warmly for his hand. "You have done me . . . a very great service. Anything I have is yours—anything. We shall be great friends, you and I! Great friends! It has been . . . so long since . . ."

He trailed off sharply, looking intensely at the highlander, suddenly lost in thought. His speech was stilted and nervous, almost as if he weren't quite sure of what he was saying at any one point. If he weren't completely mad already, Menion thought quickly, he was certainly very ill.

"I'm very pleased to be in Tyrsis," he responded, "although I wish the circumstances could have been more pleasant for all concerned."

"You mean my brother, of course?" The question shot out as the other snapped awake again, his face flushed. Menion started momentarily in surprise.

"Palance, he means the invasion of the Northlanders, the burning of Kern," Shirl interposed quickly.

"Yes . . . Kern . . ." Again he trailed off, this time looking anxiously about as if someone were missing. Menion glanced about uneasily, realizing that the mystic Stenmin was strangely absent. According to Shirl and Janus Senpre, the Prince never went anywhere without his adviser. Quickly he caught Shirl's watchful eye.

"Is there something wrong, my Lord?" Menion used the formal address to catch the other's instant attention, smiling quickly in reassurance that he was a concerned friend prepared to help. The deception brought unexpected results.

"You can help me . . . and this kingdom, Menion Leah," Palance responded quickly. "My brother seeks to be King in my place. He would have me killed. My adviser Stenmin has saved me from this—but there are other enemies . . . all around! You and I must be friends. We must stand together against those who seek to take my throne—to bring harm to this lovely woman whom you have returned to me. I . . . I cannot talk with Stenmin . . . the way I would talk with a friend. But you, I could talk with you!"

Like a small child, he gazed eagerly at the amazed Menion Leah, awaiting his reply. A sudden feeling of pity for this son of Ruhl Buckhannah swept over the highlander, and he truly wished there was something he could do to help the unfortunate man. Smiling sadly, he nodded his agreement.

"I knew you would stand with me!" the other exclaimed excitedly, laughing in delight. "We are both men of royal blood, and that . . . binds us closely. You and I shall be great friends, Menion. But now . . . you must rest."

He seemed to recall suddenly that his palace corps were still standing stiffly at parade attention, waiting patiently for the Prince to give the order for dismissal. With a sharp wave of his hand, the new ruler of Callahorn led his two guests toward the Buckhannah home, nodding to the commander of his personal guard as they passed to signal that his soldiers could be dispersed for regular duty. The trio passed into the entryway of the ancient home, where a number of servants stood waiting to escort the guests to their rooms. Pausing briefly once more, the host turned to his guests, bending close to whisper.

"My brother is locked in the dungeons beneath us. You need not be afraid." He stared meaningfully at them for a moment, glancing quickly at the curious servants who waited respectfully in the background. "He has friends everywhere, you know."

Both Menion and Shirl nodded, because it was expected of them.

"He won't escape from the dungeons then?" Menion pursued the matter a bit further.

"He tried last night . . . with his friends." Palance smiled with satisfaction. "But we caught them and trapped them . . . trapped them in the dungeon forever. Stenmin is there now . . . you must meet him . . ."

Again he straightened up with the thought left unspoken, his attention given over to the servants, several of whom he beckoned to his side. He crisply directed them to escort his friends to their quarters where they could bathe themselves and don fresh clothing before joining him for breakfast. It was still only about an hour after dawn and the refugees from Kern had not eaten since the previous night. Menion needed medical treatment for his hastily bandaged wounds, and the house physician stood ready to change the dressings and apply fresh medicines. He needed rest, too, but that could wait. The small party started down one long hallway when suddenly a distracted voice called after Shirl, and the new ruler of Callahorn came after them, approaching the wondering girl with hesitant steps, finally stopping before her and quickly embracing her. Menion kept his face averted, but their words were clear.

"You must not go away from me again, Shirl." It was a command, not a request, though the words were softly spoken. "Your new home must be in Tyrsis—as my wife."

There was a long moment of silence.

"Palance, I think we . . ." Shirl's voice shook as she tried to interpose a quiet explanation.

"No—say nothing. No discussion is necessary now . . . not now," Palance interrupted quickly. "Later . . . when we are alone, when you are rested . . . there will be time. You know I love you . . . I always have. And you have loved me, I know."

Again the long moment of silence, and then Shirl was walking quickly past Menion, forcing the servants to dash ahead in order to lead the way to the guest quarters. The highlander quickly came up beside the beautiful girl, not daring to reach for her while his host stood silently watching them move down the hallway. Shirl's face was lowered, shaded by the long red hair, the slim, bronzed hands clasped tightly before her. Neither spoke as the servants led them down the wide corridor to their rooms in the west wing of the ancient home. They separated briefly while Menion allowed the persistent physician to treat his wounds and wrap them in fresh bandages. Clean clothing lay on the huge, four-posted bed, and a hot bath stood waiting, but a distraught Menion ignored them both. Quickly he slipped from his room into the empty hallway; he knocked softly, pushed open the door to Shirl's room, and entered. She rose slowly from the bed as he closed the heavy wooden door, then ran quickly to him, her arms encircling and holding him tightly to her.

They stood in silence for several minutes, just holding each other, feeling the warm life flow quickly through their bodies, knotting and winding in unbreakable ties. Softly Menion stroked the dark red tresses, gently pressing the beautiful face close against his chest. She depended on him; the thought flashed with relief through his numbed mind. When her own strength, her own courage had faltered, she had turned to him, and Menion realized that he loved her desperately.

It was very strange that it should happen now, when their world seemed destined to crumble about them and death stood waiting in the shadows. Yet Menion's turbulent life of the past several weeks had drawn him from one frightening struggle to the next, each a battle for survival that seemed senseless in mortal terms and found its logic solely in the strange legend of the mystic Sword of Shannara and the Warlock Lord. In those terrible days since Culhaven, life had raged around him like a battle, and he had surged directionless through its center. His deep friendship and love for Shea, and his now broken companionship with the members of the company that had journeyed to Paranor and beyond, had provided a faint sense of stability, an indication that something constant would remain while the rest of the world rushed away. Then unexpectedly, he had found Shirl Ravenlock, and the fast pace of events and dangers shared in those past few days, combined with a totally predictable meshing of personal needs, had drawn and bound them inextricably to one another. Menion closed his eyes and pressed her closer.

Palance had been helpful in at least one respect—he had told them that

Balinor and probably the others with him were imprisoned in the dungeons somewhere beneath the palace. Evidently one escape had already failed, and Menion was determined that he would not make any mistakes. Quietly he conversed with Shirl, trying to decide what their next step should be. If Palance insisted on keeping Shirl close to him in order to assure her protection, her movement would be severely restricted. A worse threat was the Prince's obsession with marrying her in the false belief that she truly loved him. Palance Buckhannah seemed poised on the brink of total madness, his sanity precariously balanced. It could be tipped at any moment, and if that should happen while Balinor was his prisoner . . .

Menion paused mentally, aware that time did not permit speculation of what might happen tomorrow. By then it would make little difference because the Northland invasion force would be at the gates and it would be too late for anyone to do anything. Balinor had to be freed now. Menion had a strong ally in Janus Senpre, but the palace was secured by the special black-garbed soldiers who served only the ruler, and at the moment it appeared they served Palance Buckhannah. No one seemed to know what had become of the old King; he had not been seen for weeks. Evidently he was unable to move from his sickbed, yet there was only his son's word for that—and his son relied on the word of the strange mystic Stenmin.

Shirl had once remarked that she had never seen Palance alone for more than a few moments without his adviser close at hand, yet when they arrived from Kern, Stenmin had been nowhere in sight. This was peculiar, especially since it was common knowledge that Stenmin had made himself the real power behind the unstable Prince. Shirl's father had stated in the council chambers of Kern that the evil mystic seemed to possess some strange hold over the younger son of Ruhl Buckhannah. If only Menion could discover what that power was—for he was sure that the mystic was the key to the Prince's unbalanced behavior. But there was no time left. He would have to do the best he could with what little he knew now.

When he left Shirl and returned to his own room, ready now for that hot bath and a clean change of clothing, a plan for freeing Balinor was already forming in his mind. He was still filling in the details when the bath was finished and there was a knock on the door. Slipping into a robe his host had furnished, he crossed the room and opened the door. One of the palace servants had brought him the sword of Leah. Smiling gratefully, he thanked the man and dropped the precious weapon on the bed, recalling that he had deposited it on the seat in the carriage during his ride to the palace and forgotten to remove it. His mind wandered briefly as he dressed, remembering proudly the service that battle-worn implement had seen. He had been through so much since Shea had appeared in Leah those many weeks ago—it might have been a lifetime for any man.

Pausing momentarily, he reflected sadly on his missing friend and wondered for the thousandth time if the little Valeman were still alive. He should not be in Tyrsis, he chided himself in bitter recrimination. Shea had depended on him for protection, but it appeared that his trust had been badly misplaced. Menion had repeatedly allowed himself to be governed by the wishes of Allanon, and each time his conscience had warned him that he was somehow failing his companion by following the Druid's counsel. He felt deeply angered at the thought that he had ignored his clear responsibility to the Valeman, and yet the choices that had brought him to Tyrsis had been his own. There were others besides Shea who desperately needed him. . . .

Crossing the spacious bedroom in measured steps, still lost in thought, he dropped heavily to the welcome softness of the large bed, his outstretched hand coming to rest on the cool metal of his sword. He fingered it lightly as he lay back wearily and pondered the problems facing him. Shirl's frightened face lingered in his mind, her eyes searching Menion's own. She was very important to him; he could not leave her now in order to resume the search for Shea, no matter what the consequences might be. It was a bitter choice to make, if indeed there was any real choice at all, for his duty ran beyond those two single lives to those of Balinor and his imprisoned comrades and ultimately to those of the people of Callahorn. It would be for Allanon and Flick to find and rescue the missing Valeman if he were still alive. So much depended on them all, he thought absently, his tired mind and body already drifting toward a much-needed sleep. They could only pray for success . . . pray and wait. He hovered on the brink of slumber and then softly dropped off.

A moment later his sleeping mind jerked sharply and he was instantly awake. There may have been a slight noise or perhaps only a highly keyed sixth sense, but whatever it was snapped him back from a sleep that would have ended in his death. He lay motionless on the great bed as his listening ears caught a faint scraping sound from the far wall, and through the slits of his eyelids he saw a portion of a tapestry ripple with movement. A part of the heavy stone behind the tapestry seemed to push outward and a bent, scarlet-cloaked figure slid noiselessly into view.

Menion forced himself to continue breathing in measured intervals, although his heart was beating wildly, urging him to leap from the bed and seize the mysterious intruder. The cloaked figure moved silently across the bedroom floor, the unfamiliar face glancing quickly about the room and then turning back to the highlander's sprawled form. The intruder was only several feet from the bed when a lean hand slipped beneath the scarlet cloak and emerged, gripping a long, wicked dagger.

Menion's outstretched hand rested loosely on the sword of Leah, but still he did not move. He waited a moment longer until the attacker was within about a yard of the bed, the dagger held at waist level; then with the lightning speed of a cat, he struck. The lean body whipped upward and toward the startled intruder, one hand clenching the sword still sheathed in its leather scabbard as the flat of the blade snapped sharply around at the man's unprotected face, striking it in a stinging slap. The mysterious figure reeled backward, the dagger raised defensively. The sword struck a second time, and the weapon clattered to the floor as the numbed fingers of the attacker clenched suddenly in pain. Menion did not pause, but threw himself at the scarlet figure, his own weight dragging the struggling man to the floor where he quickly pinned him, twisting one arm sharply as his fingers closed tightly about the windpipe.

"Speak up, assassin!" Menion growled menacingly.

"No, no wait, you've made a mistake . . . I'm not an enemy . . . please, I can't breathe. . . ."

The voice choked sharply and the man's breath rasped in ragged gulps as the highlander's grip remained unaltered and the cold dark eyes surveyed the face of his captive. To his knowledge, Menion had never seen the man. The face was pinched and sharp, framed by a small black beard and lined with pain. Even as he studied the teeth clenched in anger and the eyes burning with hatred, the highlander instinctively knew there had been no mistake made. Stepping quickly to one side, he jerked the intruder to his feet, one hand still firmly fastened on the scrawny neck.

"Tell me about my mistake, then. You have about a minute before I cut your tongue out and turn you over to the guards!"

He released his grip on the man's throat, his hand dropping to seize the front of the scarlet tunic. Tossing his sword on the bed, he quickly picked up the fallen dagger, holding it ready should his attacker attempt anything further.

"This was a gift, Prince of Leah . . . merely a gift from the King." The voice broke slightly as the fellow struggled to regain his composure. "The King wanted to show his gratitude, and I . . . I came through another door so as not to disturb your sleep."

He paused as if waiting for something, the sharp eyes riveted on the highlander's own. He wasn't waiting to see if his story would be believed—it was something else, almost as if he were expecting Menion to see something more. . . . The Prince of Leah jerked him sharply, snapping the lean face close to his own.

"That is unquestionably the weakest tale I have ever heard! Who are you, assassin?"

The eyes burned into his own with intense hatred.

"I am Stenmin, the King's personal adviser." He seemed to have suddenly regained his senses now. "I did not lie to you. The dagger was a present from Palance Buckhannah which I was asked to bring to you. I meant you no harm. If you do not believe me, go to the King. Ask him!"

There was a hint of confidence in the man's voice that convinced Menion that Palance would affirm his adviser's story whether it was true or not. He had in his grasp the most dangerous man in Callahorn, the evil mystic who had become the power behind the monarchy—the one man he had to eliminate if Balinor were to be rescued. Why the man had chosen to attack him when they had never met was something he did not understand, but it was clear that if he released him now or even took him before Palance in an effort to discredit him, the highlander would lose the initiative and place his own life in danger again. Roughly he threw the mystic into a nearby chair and ordered him to remain motionless. The man sat quietly, his eyes drifting aimlessly about the room, the hands moving nervously to stroke the small pointed beard. Menion eyed him absently, his mind carefully pondering the choices open to him. It took him only a moment to decide. He could no longer bide his time, waiting for the right moment to free his friends; the decision had been taken out of his hands.

"On your feet, mystic, or whatever you prefer to call yourself!" The evil face stared menacingly at him, and in fury Menion yanked the man violently up from the chair. "I ought to dispose of you without further consideration; the people of Callahorn would be much the better for it. But for the time being, I need your services. Take me to the dungeons where Balinor and the others are imprisoned—now!"

Stenmin's eyes went wide in sudden shock at the mention of Balinor.

"How could you know of him . . . a traitor to this kingdom?" the mystic exclaimed in astonishment. "The King himself has ordered his brother imprisoned until his natural death, Prince of Leah, and even I . . ."

His sentence ended in a strangled gasp as Menion grabbed him roughly by the throat and began to squeeze. Stenmin's face turned slowly purple.

"I didn't ask for excuses or explanations. Just take me to him!"

Once more he tightened his iron grip and finally the gasping captive violently nodded his acquiescence. Menion released him with a snap of his wrist and the nearly throttled man fell dizzily to one knee. Quickly the highlander slipped out of his robe and into his clothing, strapping on the sword and shoving the dagger into his belt. For an instant he thought about arousing Shirl in the next room, but quickly discarded that idea. His plan was dangerous enough; there was no reason to risk her life as well. If he succeeded in freeing his friends, there would be time enough to come back for her. He turned to his captive, drawing the dagger from his belt and holding it up for the other to see.

"The present that you were so kind to bring me will be returned to you, assassin, if you attempt to trick or betray me in any way," he warned in his most menacing tone of voice. "So don't try to be clever. When we leave this room, you will take me down the back corridors and stairs to the prison where Balinor and his companions are held. Don't try to alarm the guards—you won't be fast enough. If you doubt anything I've told you, then understand this. I was sent to this city by Allanon!"

Stenmin seemed to go suddenly white at the mention of the giant Druid and undisguised fear shot into his widening eyes. Apparently cowed into obeying his captor, the scarlet mystic moved silently toward the bedroom door and Menion fell into step directly behind him, the dagger back in his belt with one hand gripping the hilt. Time was the all-important factor now. He had to act quickly, freeing Balinor and the other imprisoned members of the company of friends and seizing the deranged Palance before the members of the palace guard were alerted. Then a quick message to Janus Senpre would bring to their aid those still loyal to Balinor, and the power of the monarchy would be restored without a battle.

Already the massive Northland army would be mobilizing on the grasslands above the island of Kern, preparing to move on Tyrsis. If the Border Legion could be reassembled and deployed quickly enough that day, there was a chance the invader might be stopped on the north shore of the Mermidon. It would be a nearly impossible task to cross that flooded river with a defensive force holding the opposite bank, and it would take the enemy several days to manage a flanking maneuver—more than enough time for the armies of Eventine to reach them. Menion knew it would all depend on the next few minutes.

The two men stepped cautiously into the hallway beyond the room. Menion quickly glanced in both directions for any sign of the black-garbed sentries, but the hall was deserted, and the highlander motioned Stenmin ahead. The mystic reluctantly led his captor toward the inner rooms of the central palace, winding his way along the corridors that ran to the rear of the ancient building, carefully avoiding the occupied rooms. Twice they passed members of the palace guard, but each time Stenmin withheld any comment or greeting, his dark face lowered in grim determination.

Through the latticework of the castle windows, Menion could see the gardens that decorated the grounds of the Buckhannah home, the sunlight falling warmly on the brightly colored flowers. It was already midmorning, and before much longer the normal gathering of visitors and business personages would begin. There had been no sign of Palance Buckhannah, and Menion was hopeful that the Prince was preoccupied with other matters.

As the two walked slowly down the hallways, the sound of voices was distinctly audible in all directions. Servants began to appear in increasing numbers, moving busily about their assigned tasks. When they passed, they pointedly ignored Stenmin and his apparent companion, a good indication that they neither liked nor trusted the mystic. None questioned their presence and at last they approached the massive doorway that led to the castle cellars. Two armed sentries were stationed before the door, and a huge metal bar now held the latches firmly in place.

"Be careful what you say," Menion cautioned in a sharp whisper as they neared the guards.

They came to a slow halt before the massive cellar door, the watchful highlander placing one hand in a leisurely manner on the hilt of the dagger as he stood close behind Stenmin. The guards glanced curiously at him for a moment, then turned their attention to the King's adviser, who had begun to address them.

"Open the door, guards. The Prince of Leah and I will inspect the wine cellar and the dungeons."

"All persons are forbidden to enter this area by order of the King, my Lord," the guard to the right stated pointedly.

"I am here by order of the King!" Stenmin shouted angrily, causing Menion to give him a warning nudge.

"Sentry, this is the King's personal counselor—not an enemy of the Kingdom," the highlander pointed out with a deceiving smile. "We are on a tour of the palace, and since it was I who rescued the King's betrothed, it was his belief that I might recognize the lady's abductors. Now if necessary, I shall disturb the King and bring him down here . . ."

He trailed off meaningfully, praying that the guards would be sufficiently forewarned of Palance's irrational behavior to think twice about calling him down. The guards hesitated momentarily, then nodded quietly, released the latches on the door and stepped aside, swinging the massive portal open to reveal the stone stairway leading downward. Stenmin again led the way without comment. Apparently he had decided to follow Menion's instructions to the letter, but the cautious highlander knew that the mystic was no fool. If Balinor were successfully freed and restored to command of the Border Legion, then his own power over the throne of Callahorn would be finished. He would undoubtedly attempt something, but the time and the place had not yet come. The heavy door closed quietly behind them and they began their descent into the torchlit cellar.

Menion saw the trapdoor in the center of the cellar floor almost immediately. The guards had not bothered to conceal it a second time with the wine barrels, but had fastened a series of iron bars and latches across the stone slab, effectively preventing anyone imprisoned below from breaking free. Although Menion could not have known, the prisoners had not been returned to their cells following the aborted escape attempt earlier that same morning. Instead, they had been left to roam in the darkness of the dungeon corridors. Two guards were stationed next to the sealed opening, their attention now focused on the two men who had just been admitted from the palace. Menion saw a plate of cheese and bread resting half-eaten on one of the wine barrels and two cups of wine placed next to a half-drained flask. They had been drinking. The highlander smiled slightly.

As the two reached the stone flooring, Menion pretended to glance about the wine cellar in great interest, beginning a jovial conversation with the silent Stenmin. The guards rose slowly and came to attention at the sight of the King's adviser, who was looking decidedly grim about something. The highlander knew they had been caught off balance by this unexpected visit and he decided to make the most of it.

"I see what you mean, my Lord." He glowered fiercely at the mystic as they drew near to the sentries. "These men have been drinking while on duty! Suppose the prisoners should have escaped while these men lay in a drunken stupor? The King must be told of this as soon as we have finished our business here."

The guards turned pale with fear at mention of the King.

"My Lord, you are mistaken," the one pleaded hastily. "We were only taking a little wine with our breakfast. We have not been lax . . ."

"The King should decide that." Menion cut him off with a wave of his hand.

"But . . . the King will not listen . . ."

Stenmin glowered in fury at the deception, but the guards misunderstood and quickly assumed he meant to have them punished. The mystic tried to say something, but Menion moved quickly in front of him, as if in an effort to restrain his advance toward the unfortunate guards, drawing the dagger and holding it close to the man's unprotected chest.

"Yes, of course they are probably lying," Menion continued without changing his tone of voice. "Still the King is a busy man and I hate to bother him with little problems. Perhaps a word of warning to them . . . ?"

He glanced back at the guards who nodded dumbly, grasping at any chance to avoid Stenmin's wrath. Like everyone else in the Kingdom, they were frightened of the power the strange mystic possessed over Palance and were more than eager to avoid angering him.

"Very good, then, you have had your warning." Menion sheathed the dagger and turned back to the still-shaken sentries. "Now open the dungeon door and bring up the prisoners."

He stood close to Stenmin, glancing at him quickly in warning. The dark face did not seem to see him anymore, the eyes staring vacantly at the stone slab that barred their entry to the dungeons beneath. The sentries had not moved, but were glancing at each other in new desperation.

"My Lord, the King has forbidden anyone to see the prisoners . . . for any reason," the one guard gulped at last. "I cannot bring them out of the dungeon."

"So you would bar the King's adviser and his personal guest." Menion did not hesitate. He had expected this. "Then we have no choice but to call the King down here . . ."

That was all it took. There was no further deliberation as the sentries raced to the stone slab, quickly sliding back the latches and bolts. Bracing themselves, the guards pulled back on the iron ring and the trapdoor swung ponderously upward and fell back heavily against the stone flooring, leaving a gaping black hole. Holding their swords ready, the sentries called down into the darkness, commanding the prisoners to come out. There were footsteps on the ancient stone stairway as Menion waited expectantly at Stenmin's side, his own sword now drawn. His free hand held the mystic's arm tightly, and in a sharp whisper he warned the lean adviser not to speak or move. Then Balinor's broad form appeared from out of the pit, closely followed by the Elven brothers and the durable Hendel, his own attempt to rescue his friends thwarted only hours earlier. They did not see Menion at first. Quickly the highlander stepped forward, still holding the silent Stenmin.

"That's it, keep them moving, keep them together. Such men must be watched carefully. They are always dangerous."

The wearied prisoners glanced over abruptly, only thinly masking their astonishment on seeing the Prince of Leah. Menion winked quickly behind the guards' backs, and the four captives turned away, only the slow smile on Dayel's young face betraying the sudden joy they were experiencing at the sight of their old friend. They were out of the pit now and standing quietly a few feet from the guards, who stood with their backs to the highlander. But before Menion could act, the heretofore passive Stenmin wrested his whiplike form free from his captor's iron grip and sprang aside to shout a quick warning to the unsuspecting sentries.

"Traitor! Guards, it's a trick . . ."

He was never able to finish. As the distracted sentries whirled about, Menion leaped catlike at the fleeing mystic, throwing him violently to the stone floor. The soldiers realized their mistake too late. The four prisoners sprang into action, closing the short space of ground separating them from their jailers and disarming them before they could recover. Within seconds the guards were subdued, quickly bound and gagged, and dragged into a corner of the cellar where they were hidden from sight. A thoroughly beaten Stenmin was yanked unceremoniously to his feet to face his new captors. Menion glanced anxiously at the closed door at the top of the cellar stairway, but no one appeared. Apparently the shout had gone unheeded. Balinor and the others came over to him with smiles of gratitude on their tired faces, clapping him on the back and shaking his hand once again.

"Menion Leah, we owe you more than we can ever hope to give back." The giant borderman gripped his hand tightly. "I did not think we would ever see you again. Where is Allanon?"

Quickly Menion explained how he had left Allanon and Flick concealed above the camp of the Northland army and come to Callahorn to warn of the impending advance against Tyrsis. Pausing momentarily to gag Stenmin in the event the evil adviser should attempt to call out another warning to the guards posted outside the cellar door, the highlander told of rescuing Shirl Ravenlock, fleeing to Kern and subsequently to the walls of Tyrsis after the island city was besieged and destroyed. His friends listened grimly until he had finished.

"Whatever else may come out of this, highlander," Hendel declared quietly, "you have proved yourself this day and we shall never forget it."

"The Border Legion must be re-formed and sent to hold the Mermidon immediately," Balinor cut in quickly. "We must get word to the lower city. Then we must find my father . . . and my brother. But I want to secure the palace and the army without a battle. Menion, can we trust Janus Senpre to come to our aid if we call for him?"

"He is loyal to you and to the King." Menion nodded affirmatively.

"You must get a message to him while we remain here," the Prince of Callahorn continued, pacing over toward the captive Stenmin. "Once he arrives with help, we should have no trouble—my brother will be left without support. But what of my father . . . ?"

Towering over the dark form of the mystic, he removed the gag from the captive's mouth and stared coldly down at him. Stenmin met his gaze briefly, his own eyes furtive and filled with hate. The mystic knew he was beaten if Palance was captured and removed as monarch of Callahorn, and he was becoming increasingly desperate as the end drew near and his plans began to break apart. Standing with the Elven brothers and Hendel as Balinor confronted the mysterious captive, Menion found himself wondering what the man had hoped to gain by encouraging Palance to take the steps he had. Certainly it was no mystery why he had supported the distraught and unstable Prince as the new King of Callahorn. His own position was assured with Balinor's brother ruling. But why had he encouraged the disbanding of the Border Legion when he knew that an invading army was threatening to overrun the little Southland kingdom and put an end to its enlightened monarchy? Why had he gone to such pains to imprison Balinor and to secrete his father in a distant wing of the palace when they could have been quietly disposed of? And why had he tried to kill Menion Leah, a man he had never met before?

"Stenmin, your rule over this land and its people and your domination of my brother are over," Balinor declared with cold determination. "Whether or not you will ever see the light of another day depends on what you do from now until the time I am again in command of the city. What have you done with my father?"

There was a long moment of silence as the mystic looked desperately around, the dark face ashen with fear.

"He . . . he is in the north wing . . . in the tower," the answer was a whisper.

"If he has been harmed, mystic . . ."

Balinor turned away sharply, leaving the terrified man momentarily forgotten. Stenmin shrank away against one wall, gazing after the tall figure of the borderman. One hand came up nervously to stroke the small, pointed beard. Menion watched him, almost in pity, and then suddenly something clicked in his mind. An image flashed sharply—a memory of a scene he had witnessed several days earlier on the banks of the Mermidon north of the island of Kern as he had lain concealed on a small hillock overlooking a windy beachhead. That same mannerism—the stroking of a small pointed beard! Now he knew exactly what Stenmin was attempting to do! His face turned to a mask of rage and he started forward, brushing past Balinor as if he wasn't even there.

"You were the man on the beach—the kidnapper!" he accused in undisguised fury. "You tried to kill me because you thought I would recognize you as the man who kidnapped Shirl—the man who turned her over to the Northlanders. You traitor! You intended to betray us all—to turn the city over to the Warlock Lord!"

Heedless of the cries of his companions, he rushed toward the now hysterical mystic, who somehow managed to evade his initial lunge and break away toward the cellar stairway. Menion was after him with a bound, the gleaming sword of his father raised to strike. Halfway up the stone steps he caught him, one hand jerking the dark form about as the man shrieked in terror. Yet the end did not come, for as the sword drew back and Menion held the maddened Stenmin tightly against the stone wall, the massive door to the ancient cellar suddenly swung open, the thrust of the pull slamming the ironbound wood back against the wall with a jarring crash. Framed in the entryway stood the broad figure of Palance Buckhannah.

29

For a moment no one moved. Even the terrified Stenmin had gone limp against the cellar wall, his dark face staring blankly at the silent form that waited statuelike at the top of the ancient stairway. The lined face of the Prince was drained of color, and the eyes reflected a curious mixture of anger and confusion. Resolutely, Menion Leah met those searching eyes, his sword arm lowering slowly, his own hatred fading with the sudden turn of events. Their lives might all be forfeited if he didn't act fast. Roughly he yanked Stenmin to his feet and threw him disdainfully toward the Prince.

"Here is your traitor, Palance—the real enemy of Callahorn. This is the man who gave Shirl Ravenlock to the Northlanders. This is the man who would give Tyrsis to the Warlock Lord. . . ."

"My Lord, you've come just in time." The mystic had recovered his wits enough to cut Menion off before any more damage could be done. He stumbled fearfully to his feet and rushed up the stairs, throwing himself at Palance's feet and pointing down at the company of friends. "I discovered them escaping—I was running to warn you! The highlander is a friend of Balinor—he came to kill you!" The words were tumbling out of the man's mouth in undisguised hatred as he groped at his benefactor's tunic and raised himself slowly to his side. "They would have killed me—and then you, my Lord. Can't you see what is happening?"

Menion fought down the urge to rush up the steps and cut the evil mystic's lying tongue out, forcing himself to remain outwardly calm, his gaze riveted on that of the stunned Palance Buckhannah.

"You have been betrayed by this man, Palance," he continued evenly. "He has poisoned your heart and your mind. He has sapped you of your will to think for yourself. He cares nothing for you; he cares nothing for this land, which he has so cheaply sold to the enemy that has already destroyed Kern." Stenmin roared in fury, but Menion continued in stony disregard. "You once said we would be friends, and friends must have trust for each other. Do not be deceived now, or your kingdom will surely be lost."

At the bottom of the stairway, Balinor and his friends watched silently, afraid that any distraction might break the strange spell Menion Leah was weaving, for Palance was still listening, his clouded mind struggling to break the wall of confusion surrounding it. Slowly he stepped forward on the landing, closing the door quietly behind him and brushing past Stenmin as if he hadn't seen him. His adviser hesitated in confusion, glancing uncertainly at the cellar door as if debating the wisdom of attempting to flee. But he was not yet prepared to accept defeat, and he whirled quickly, catching Palance by the arm and thrusting his lean face next to the man's ear.

"Are you mad? Are you as insane as some say, my King?" he whispered venomously. "Will you throw everything away now—give it all back to your brother? Was he meant to be king—or you? This is all a lie! The Prince of Leah is a friend to Allanon."

Palance turned toward him slightly, his eyes widening.

"Yes, Allanon!" Stenmin knew he had struck a nerve and was determined to pursue it. "Who do you think seized your betrothed from her home in Kern? This man who speaks of friendship was part of the kidnapping—it was all a ruse to get inside the palace and then assassinate you. You were to be killed!"

Below the stairway, Hendel took a step forward, but Balinor put out a restraining hand. Menion stood quietly, knowing that any sudden move now would only confirm Stenmin's charges. He directed a withering glance at the wily mystic, turning quickly back to Palance and shaking his head.

"He is a traitor. He belongs to the Warlock Lord."

Palance took several steps down the stairway, glancing briefly at Menion and then staring fixedly at his brother who waited patiently at the foot of the stairs. A faint smile crossed his lips as he paused confusedly.

"What do you think, brother? Am I really . . . mad? If not me, then . . . why, it must be everyone else, and I alone am . . . sane. Say something, Balinor. We should have that talk now . . . Before . . . I did want to say something . . ."

But the sentence was left unfinished as he straightened his tall frame and looked back once again at Stenmin, who had taken on the appearance of a dangerously cornered animal, crouched and waiting to attack.

"You are pathetic, Stenmin. Stand up!" The sharp command cut through the stillness and the bent figure of the mystic snapped upright. "Advise me what I should do," Palance ordered sharply. "Do I have everyone killed—will that protect me?"

In an instant Stenmin was back at his side, the sharp eyes cold with fury.

"Call your guard, my Lord. Dispose of these assassins now!"

Suddenly Palance seemed to waver, his tall frame drooping, his eyes glancing at the walls of the cellar in studied concentration of the stonework. Menion sensed that the Prince of Callahorn was again losing his grip on reality and falling back into the clouded world of madness that had impaired his once sound reason. Stenmin recognized it as well, a grim smile creeping over his dark face, his hand coming up to stroke the small pointed beard. Then abruptly, Palance spoke once more.

"No, there will be no soldiers . . . no killing. A King must be a man of judgment . . . Balinor is my brother though he wishes to be King in my

place. He and I must talk now . . . he is not to be harmed . . . not harmed."
His voice trailed off and he smiled unexpectedly at Menion. "You brought
Shirl back to me . . . I thought I had lost her, you know. Why . . . would
you do that . . . if you were an enemy . . . ?"

Stenmin screamed in fury, grasping furiously at the other's tunic, but
the Prince did not seem to realize he was even there.

"It is difficult for me . . . to think clearly, Balinor," Palance continued
in a low whisper, shaking his head slowly. "Nothing is clear anymore . . . I
don't even feel angry toward you for wanting to be King. I have always . . .
wanted to be King. I have, you know. But I have to have . . . friends . . .
someone to talk to . . ."

He turned dispassionately toward Stenmin, his eyes blank and expressionless. Something his adviser saw there caused the mystic to release his
grip on the other's arm and shrink limply back against the stone wall, his
jaw sagging in fear. Only Menion was close enough to realize what had
happened. Whatever hold the evil mystic had managed to secure over
Palance Buckhannah was gone. The man's already muddled thought processes
had been pushed beyond the brink of even basic comprehension of identi-
ties, and Stenmin was now no more than another face in a sea of indistinguishable beings that haunted the nightmare world of the maddened Prince
of Callahorn.

"Palance, listen to me," Menion called softly to him, reaching through
the web of darkness to the man beneath for just an instant. The broad figure turned slightly. "Call Shirl down from her room. Call Shirl and she will
help you."

The Prince hesitated for a moment as if trying to remember, then a
small smile crossed his haggard face and a deep calm seemed to settle
through his whole body. He remembered her soft voice, her gentle manner, her fragile beauty—memories that recalled peace and serenity, moments of deep affection that he had never found with any other human
being. If he could just be with her for a while . . .

"Shirl," he spoke her name softly and turned back to the closed cellar
door, one hand outstretched. As he brushed past Stenmin, the crouched
mystic seemed suddenly to go berserk. Shrieking with rage and frustration,
he threw himself at the other man, grappling wildly at his tunic front. Responding instantly, Menion Leah bounded quickly toward the high landing
to part the struggling men. But he was still several steps away when Stenmin's lean hand drew back momentarily, holding high a long dagger seized
from beneath his robes. The weapon raised and for one terrible second
hung poised above the men, as Balinor cried out in helpless shock. Then it
fell. Palance Buckhannah rose sharply to his full height, the dagger buried
to the hilt in his broad chest, a terrible whiteness flooding his young face.

"I give you back your brother, fool!" shrieked the maddened Stenmin,
shoving the rigid form down the stone stairway.

The stricken Prince fell heavily into Menion's outstretched arms,
knocking him back roughly against the wall, causing him momentarily to

lose his balance and the opportunity to reach the hated enemy. Stenmin had already turned to flee, pulling frantically on the massive cellar door. Balinor bounded up the stairway, desperately trying to stop the mystic's escape, the Elven brothers immediately behind him, yelling for the guards. The scarlet figure had pulled the door partially open and was just slipping to freedom when Hendel, still standing at the foot of the stairs, seized a discarded mace and hurled it wildly at the fleeing man. It struck the mystic's exposed shoulder with bone-crunching force, and a scream of pain echoed off the dank walls. Yet it wasn't enough to stop him completely, and a moment later he had disappeared through the doorway. From the hallway beyond they could hear his shrill cry that the prisoners had assassinated the King.

Balinor paused only an instant in his pursuit to glance down on the still form resting quietly in the strong arms of Menion Leah, then raced for the open cellar door. Two black-clad palace guards appeared suddenly from the hallway beyond, swords drawn, to confront the unarmed borderman. They could have been statues for all the difference their unexpected appearance made to Balinor, who bowled them over with a lightning assault, seizing a fallen sword as he disappeared from view. Durin and Dayel were only steps behind. Menion knelt alone on the stairway, gazing after them and holding the stricken Palance, cradling gently the body of the self-proclaimed King of Callahorn. Silently, Hendel climbed the stone steps to stand beside him, shaking his grizzled head sadly. The Prince was still alive, the shallow breathing harsh and the eyelids twitching sporadically. Grimly the Dwarf reached down as Menion held the limp form and slowly withdrew the deadly blade, casting the weapon away with disgust. The Dwarf bent to help the highlander raise the wounded man, and abruptly the eyes opened for an instant. Palance spoke softly, a barely perceptible murmur, and then drifted into unconsciousness once more.

"He's calling for Shirl," Menion whispered, tears in his eyes as he glanced briefly at the other. "He still loves her. He still loves her."

In the hallway beyond, Balinor and the Elven brothers were struggling to catch the fleeing Stenmin. Everything was in a state of utter confusion as guards, household servants, and visitors milled through the panic-stricken palace. Shouts of terror echoed off the ancient walls, decrying the death of the King and warning of assassins bent on killing everyone. The sounds of still another battle rose from the palace gates to add to the growing chaos. Balinor and his two companions fought their way through the knots of frightened people, who seemed to go into a state of complete hysteria at the sight of drawn weapons. A few scattered guards even attempted to bar their passage, but each time the giant borderman merely flung the unfortunate men aside without pausing and raced in pursuit of the red-cloaked figure stumbling ahead. Stenmin was still in sight when the three pursuers reached the central hallway, but he had broken through the hindering throngs and was beginning to draw away. With unbelievable fury Balinor pushed ahead, heedlessly knocking everyone in his path aside, his face grim and terrible.

Then suddenly the palace doors shuddered under the weight of dozens of battling men and burst open with a crash, directly in front of the giant borderman and his Elven friends. The confusion was complete as a huge knot of fighting men rushed wildly into the entryway and the halls beyond, shouting for Balinor and waving their drawn weapons with grand flourishes. For a moment, the Prince was uncertain who they were; then he saw that they were wearing the leopard insignia of the Border Legion. The few palace guards who remained either fled or threw down their weapons and were seized. The Legion soldiers immediately spotted Balinor and rushed over to him, grasping him and raising him to their shoulders with cheers of victory. Durin and Dayel were cut off from him, and the cheering mass of men barred their pursuit of the rapidly disappearing Stenmin. Balinor shouted and struggled furiously, desperately trying to break away, but the sheer weight of numbers prevented him from resisting the tide that suddenly surged forward, carrying him back toward the cellar.

The frustrated Elves finally broke through the mass of bodies, racing after their quarry, who had turned down a different hallway and was momentarily lost from sight. The lean Elves were very fast, however, and closed the gap between themselves and Stenmin in a matter of seconds. Rounding the corner of the hallway, they caught sight of him once again, the dark face flushed with terror, the right arm hanging limp and useless. Silently Durin cursed himself for having failed to pick up a longbow. Abruptly, the fleeing man halted and vainly tried to wrest open one of the several doors lining the left side of the passage. The latch held despite the mystic's repeated efforts to force it, and at last he turned once more and raced to open the next door down the hall. Durin and Dayel were only yards away as Stenmin succeeded in opening this one and disappeared inside, closing it with a resounding crash. The Elves were there in seconds. Finding the door secured from within, they proceeded to force the iron latch with their swords. The clasp was sturdy and it took them several endless minutes to break through. By the time they pried open the door and burst into the room with swords held ready, it was deserted.

Menion Leah stood quietly at the front gates of the Buckhannah home as Balinor conversed in low tones with the commanders of the Border Legion. Shirl was next to him, one slim arm locked in his, her young face lined with worry in the noon sunlight. Menion glanced down at her momentarily and smiled reassuringly, holding her closer to him. Beyond the great Outer Wall of the city of Tyrsis, two divisions of the reassembled Border Legion waited patiently for the command that would take them into battle against the awesome Northland army. The huge invasion force had reached the northern banks of the swollen Mermidon River, and even now was beginning to make its crossing. If the Legion could hold the southern bank, even for a few days, it might give the Elven armies a chance to mobilize and march to their aid. Time, Menion thought bitterly—all they needed was just a little more time, and so far they hadn't gotten it. The Border Legion had been reassembled as quickly as possible once the city was secured and Balinor was reinstated as commander, but by that time the advancing Northlanders had already reached the Mermidon and begun preparations for the crossing.

Balinor was now King of Callahorn, though it was anything but a cause for celebration. His brother lay in a coma, weakened and extremely close to death. The best physicians in Tyrsis had examined him with labored patience in an effort to determine the cause of his irrational behavior and after some time had concluded that he had been given a powerful drug over a long period of time to break down his resistance and reduce him, for all practical purposes, to a mindless puppet. Finally, the dosage had been increased to the point where his mind and body had been pushed beyond the point of physical and mental endurance. In the end, his madness was real.

Balinor had listened to their conclusions without comment. An hour earlier, he had found his father in a deserted room in the north tower of the Buckhannah home. The aged King had been dead for several days and a physician's report revealed that he had been systematically poisoned. Stenmin had kept everyone from that room except himself and the already unbalanced Palance, so the secret of Ruhl Buckhannah's death had been easily kept. Had the mystic succeeded in having Balinor killed, it would have been a simple matter to persuade Palance to open the gates to the armies of the Warlock Lord, and in so doing, assure the destruction of Tyrsis. He had nearly succeeded once, and he might still do so. Stenmin had managed to elude the Elven brothers and was hidden somewhere within the city.

In a very real sense, the future of the Southland rested in the hands of the Prince of Callahorn. The people of Tyrsis looked to the Buckhannah family for dependable government and strong leadership. The Border Legion functioned best as a fighting unit when Balinor was in command. Now the giant borderman was the last of his family and the man to whom everyone turned for leadership, whether openly or subconsciously. If anything were to happen to him, the Legion would lose its finest commander and the heart of its fighting strength, while the city would lose the last Buckhannah. The few who fully understood the gravity of the situation realized that Tyrsis must be held against the advancing Northland army, or the Southland would be lost and a wedge driven between the armies of the Elves and the Dwarfs. Allanon had warned them that if this should happen, the Warlock Lord had won. Tyrsis was the key to success or failure, and Balinor was the key to Tyrsis.

Janus Senpre had carried out his part in securing the city earlier that morning. After Menion left him at the gates, he sought out the Legion commanders Fandwick and Ginnisson. Secretly, they reassembled key members of the disbanded Legion and, striking quickly and quietly, seized the gates and the army barracks. Moving rapidly toward the palace, they gained strength almost without opposition until finally the entire city surrounding the Buckhannah family home and gardens was resecured. Waiting just outside the palace grounds for a signal from Menion, the three commanders and their followers heard the cries within of assassination; fearing the worst, they rushed the gates, forcing their way inside just in time to prevent Balinor from catching the fleeing Stenmin. There was almost no loss of life in the brief uprising, and the followers of Palance were either imprisoned or freed to rejoin their old units in the Legion. Already two of the five Legion divisions were reassembled, and the other three would be formed up and properly armed by sunset. But scouts from the city had reported to Balinor the progress of the Northlanders in reaching the Mermidon, and concluded that he must act immediately to prevent the crossing.

Hendel and the Elven brothers lounged restlessly off to the right on the steps of the palace, their faces reflecting mixed emotions. The Dwarf appeared as resolute as ever, his aging countenance implacable as he glanced casually over at the highlander and his beautiful charge. Durin seemed somehow older, his lean Elven features clouded by the knowledge of what lay ahead, while Dayel, though shadowed by the same uncertainty, managed a cheerful smile. Menion shifted his gaze back to Balinor and the Legion commanders. Ginnisson was heavyset with shocking red hair and powerful arms; Fandwick was aged and grizzled with a drooping white mustache and a scowl to match; Acton was a man of medium height and regular appearance, whose horsemanship was said to be matchless; Messaline was tall and broad shouldered, almost arrogant-looking as he rocked carelessly back on his heels while Balinor spoke to them; and last came Janus Senpre, recently promoted to full commander in recognition of his courageous stand at Kern and his vital role in the recapture of Tyrsis. Menion studied them carefully for long minutes as if somehow his visual appraisal could ascertain their worth. Then Balinor turned and walked over to him, motioning for Hendel and the Elves to join them.

"I'm leaving at once for the Mermidon," he informed them quietly when they were all together. Menion started to speak, but Balinor quickly cut him off. "No, Menion, I know what you are going to ask, and the answer is no. You will all remain here in the city. I would trust any one of you with my life, and since my life is of secondary importance in comparison with Tyrsis, I ask you to guard the city instead. If anything should happen to me, you will know best how to continue the battle. Janus remains with you in command of the city defenses, and I have instructed him to confer with you on all matters."

"Eventine will come," Dayel spoke quickly, trying hard to sound cheerful.

Balinor smiled and nodded in agreement.

"Allanon has never failed. He won't fail us now."

"Don't expose yourself unnecessarily," Hendel warned grimly. "This city and its people depend on you. They need you alive."

"Good-bye, old friend." Balinor gripped the Dwarf's hand tightly. "I depend on you most of all. Your experience is twice mine, and you are twice the strategist. Take care."

He turned quickly, motioning for his commanders, and entered the waiting carriage that would convey them to the city gates. Janus Senpre waved reassuringly to Menion as the palace coach drew away, the mounted escort falling into sharp formation to the rear, and the gallant procession galloped with a clashing of iron-shod hooves toward the Sendic Bridge. The four companions and Shirl Ravenlock watched until they were lost from sight and the thunder of the horses had drifted into silence. Then Hendel muttered absently about checking the palace once more for some sign of the missing Stenmin and, without waiting for a response, reentered the Buckhannah home. Durin and Dayel trailed after him, feeling strangely disconsolate. It was the first time they had been separated from Balinor for more than several hours since the long journey from Culhaven had begun many weeks earlier, and it was a disquieting experience to allow him to go on alone to the Mermidon.

Menion knew exactly how they felt, his own restless nature inwardly urging him to go after the borderman, to join him in the crucial battle against the hordes of the Warlock Lord. But he was nearly exhausted—he had not slept for almost two days. The strain of the battle above the island of Kern, the long flight down the Mermidon, and the rapid series of events which had led to the freeing of Balinor and the others had sapped even his great stamina. Almost drunkenly, he steered Shirl into the gardens at the side of the palace, dropping heavily onto a wide stone bench. The girl sat quietly next to him, watching his face as he closed his eyes and forced his mind to relax.

"I know what you must be thinking, Menion." Her soft voice drifted gently through his weariness. "You want to be with him."

The highlander smiled and nodded slowly, his thoughts hazy and jumbled.

"You must get some sleep, you know."

Again he nodded, and suddenly he thought of Shea. Where was Shea? Where had the Valeman wandered in his futile search for the elusive Sword of Shannara? Quickly he raised himself, snapping awake and turning to Shirl, almost as if he thought she might not be there. He was exhausted, but he wanted to talk—he needed to talk, because there might never be another chance. In low, somber tones he began to speak to her, telling her about himself and Shea, unfolding in bits and pieces the friendship that had so closely bound them in the years they had known each other. He spoke of the times they had spent in the highlands of Leah, drifting gradually into the full story behind the journey to Paranor and the search for the Sword. At times he rambled in vain attempts to explore in depth the rationale behind feelings they had shared and philosophies they could not. As the highlander continued, Shirl began to realize that it was not really Shea that Menion was trying to describe—it was himself. Finally she stopped him, reaching without thinking to place a slim hand over his lips.

"He was the only person you ever really got to know, wasn't he?" she asked quietly. "He was like a brother, and you feel responsible for what happened to him?"

Menion shrugged disconsolately. "I couldn't have done anything but what I did. Keeping him in Leah in the first place would have only prolonged the inevitable. But knowing all that doesn't help. I still feel a sort of . . . guilt . . ."

"If he feels as deeply for you as you do for him, then he knows in his heart the truth of what you have done, wherever he is now," she responded quickly. "No man can fault you for the courage you have shown these past five days—and I love you, Menion Leah."

Menion stared at her stupidly, the sudden declaration catching him off balance. Laughing at his confusion, the slim girl wrapped her arms around him, the reddish locks falling like a soft veil about his face as she clung to him. Menion held her close for a moment, then gripped her shoulders gently and pushed her back to study her face and eyes. She met his gaze squarely.

"I wanted to say it out loud. I wanted you to hear it, Menion. If we are going to die . . ."

She choked suddenly on the words and looked away, and the wondering Southlander saw tears slowly roll down her cheeks. He reached up and quickly brushed them away, smiling in the old way as he raised himself to his feet, drawing her up with him.

"I came a long, long way," he murmured gently. "I could have been dead a hundred times, but I survived. I've seen the evil there is in this world and in worlds that mortals only dream exist. There is nothing that can hurt us. Love supplies a kind of strength that can withstand even death. But you need a little faith. Just believe, Shirl. Believe in us."

She smiled in spite of herself.

"I believe in you, Menion Leah. Now you remember to believe in yourself."

The weary highlander smiled back at her, gripping her hands tightly. She was the most beautiful woman he had ever seen, and he loved her as much as his own life. He leaned down and kissed her warmly.

"It will be all right," he assured her quietly. "It will all work out."

They remained a few minutes longer in the solitude of the gardens, talking quietly and absently following the little paths that wound through the warm, fragrant summer flowers. But Menion was fighting to remain awake, and Shirl was quick to demand that he get some sleep while he had the opportunity. Still smiling to himself, he retired to his bedchamber in the palace, where he collapsed, still fully clothed, onto one of the wide, soft beds and immediately fell into a deep, dreamless slumber. While he slept, the hours of the afternoon drifted slowly away, the sun slipping into the western sky and finally sinking in a brilliant scarlet blaze beneath the horizon. At the coming of complete darkness, the highlander awoke, fully rested but strangely disturbed. He hastened to find Shirl, and together they walked the almost deserted corridors of the Buckhannah home, searching for Hendel and the Elven brothers. The long hallways echoed the low tapping of their boots as they hastened past statuelike sentries and darkened rooms, pausing only momentarily to observe the still, deathlike form of Palance Buckhannah, as his physicians watched over him with expressionless faces. His condition remained unchanged, his wounded body and shattered spirit struggling to survive the crushing weight of a death that was slowly, inevitably pushing down against him. When the two silent forms moved at last from his bedside, there were tears again in Shirl's dark eyes.

Convinced that his friends had gone to the city gates to await the return of the Prince of Callahorn, Menion saddled two horses and the couple rode toward the Tyrsian Way. It was a cool, cloudless night lighted by the silver shimmer of the moon and stars, and the towers of the city stood clearly outlined against the sky. As the horses swung onto the Bridge of Sendic, Menion felt the welcome coolness of a friendly night breeze blowing in soothing waves over his flushed face. It was unusually quiet along the Tyrsian Way, the streets deserted and the houses that lined the Way lighted but empty of laughter and friendly conversation. An audible hush had settled over the besieged city, a grim whispering solitude that hovered and waited for the death that came with battle. The riders rode anxiously through this eerie silence, trying to find some comfort in the beauty of the starlit sky that seemed to promise a thousand tomorrows for the races. The towering heights of the Outer Wall loomed blackly in the distance, and on the parapets burned hundreds of torches, lighting the way home to the soldiers of Tyrsis. They had been gone a long time, Menion thought to himself. But perhaps they had been more successful than anyone had dared to hope. Perhaps they had held the Mermidon against the Northland hordes. . . .

Moments later the riders were dismounting at the mammoth gates of the giant wall. The Legion barracks were alive with activity as the restless garrison worked feverishly in preparation for the battle to come. There were knots of soldiers at every turn, and it was with considerable difficulty that Menion and Shirl finally managed to reach the ramparts at the top of the broad walls, where they were greeted warmly by Janus Senpre. The youthful commander had maintained his vigilant lookout without rest since Balinor had departed, and the slim face was lined with weariness and anxiety. After a few moments, Durin and Hendel appeared out of the darkness to join them, followed somewhat later by a wandering Dayel. The little group stood in silence and stared into the darkness that ran northward to the Mermidon and the Border Legion. From far away they could hear the muffled shouts and cries of men fighting, the sounds carried tauntingly by the fresh night wind to the straining ears of those who waited.

Janus remarked absently that he had sent out half a dozen scouts in an effort to discover what was happening at the river, but none had returned— an ominous sign. He had decided several times to go himself, but a gruff Hendel had reminded him each time that he had been placed in charge of the defense of Tyrsis, and each time he had reluctantly discarded the idea. Durin had resolved in his own mind that if Balinor did not return by midnight, he was going out to search for his friend. An Elf could travel undetected through almost any opposition. But for the time being, he waited like the others in growing apprehension. Shirl spoke briefly of the unchanged condition of Palance Buckhannah, but she received only a disinterested response and quickly gave up the impossible task of trying to take their minds off the battle at the river. The little group waited one hour, then two. The sounds had grown slowly louder and more desperate, and it seemed that the fighting had moved closer to the city.

Then suddenly a vast formation of horsemen and foot soldiers appeared out of the darkness almost directly in front of the bluff, winding in staggered columns onto the wide stone rampway leading into the city. Their approach had been almost imperceptible, and their unexpected appearance from out of nowhere caused everyone atop the Outer Wall to gasp audibly. Janus Senpre sprang in alarm toward the mechanism that secured the iron fastenings to the giant gates, fearful that somehow the enemy had managed to outflank Balinor. But Hendel quietly called him back. He recognized what was happening even before the others suspected. Leaning out over the rim of the wall, the Dwarf called down sharply in his own language, and received an almost instant response. Nodding grimly to the others, Hendel pointed to the tall rider who had moved to the point of the long column. In the soft moonlight, the dust-covered face of Balinor peered upward, the grim visage confirming what they all had suspected the moment they recognized him. The Border Legion had failed to hold the Mermidon, and the army of the Warlock Lord was moving against Tyrsis.

It was nearly midnight when the five who remained together of the little band from Culhaven gathered in a small, secluded dining room in the Buckhannah family home for a brief evening meal. The long afternoon and evening battle to hold the Mermidon against the Northland army had been lost, although the cost in lives to the enemy had been terrible. For a while it appeared that the veteran soldiers of the Border Legion would succeed in preventing the floundering Northlanders from gaining the southern bank of the swift river. But there were thousands of the enemy, and where hundreds failed, thousands ultimately succeeded. Acton's horsemen had swept lightninglike along the fringes of the Legion line, shattering every attempt by the enemy to outflank the entrenched foot soldiers. Advances into the heart of the Southland ranks had resulted in the death of hundreds of Trolls and Gnomes. It was the most dreadful slaughter Balinor had ever witnessed, and eventually the Mermidon began to change color with the blood of the wounded and dying. And still they kept trying—trying as if they were mindless creatures without feeling, without understanding, without human fear. The power of the Warlock Lord had so enslaved the collective mortal mind of the giant army that even death had no meaning. Finally a large band of ferocious Rock Trolls breached the far right tip of the Legion's line of defense; although they were slain almost to a man, the diversionary tactic forced the Tyrsians to shorten their left flank. In the end, the Northlanders were across.

By this time it was almost sunset, and Balinor quickly realized that even the finest soldiers in the world would be unable to retake and hold the southern bank once darkness set in. The Legion had suffered only mild losses during the afternoon's fighting, and so he ordered the two divisions to fall back to a small rise several hundred yards south of the Mermidon and reassemble in battle formation. He kept the cavalry busy on the left and right flanks, making short rushes at the enemy to keep them off balance and to prevent an organized counterthrust. Then he waited for darkness. The hordes of the Northland army began to cross in force as twilight fell; in mingled astonishment and fear, the men of the Border Legion watched as the hundreds that had first crossed turned to thousands and still they kept coming. It was a frightening spectacle the bordermen beheld—an army of such incredible size that it completely covered the land on both sides of the Mermidon as far as the eye could see.

But its size hampered its maneuverability, and the chain of command seemed disorganized and confused. There was no concentrated effort made to dislodge the entrenched Tyrsians from the small rise. Instead the bulk of the army milled about on the banks of the southern shore after crossing, as if waiting for someone to tell them what to do next. Several squads of heavily armed Trolls made a series of rushes at the Legion command, but they were equally matched in numbers and the veteran soldiers quickly repelled them. When darkness came at last, the enemy army suddenly began to organize into columns five deep, and Balinor knew that the first sustained rush would break the Legion to pieces.

With the skill and daring that had made him the spirit behind the fabled Border Legion and the finest field commander in the Southland, the Prince of Callahorn began to execute a most difficult tactical maneuver. Without waiting for the enemy to strike, he suddenly divided his army and attacked far to the right and left of the Northland columns. Striking sharply in short feints, and taking full advantage of the darkness, in terrain every borderman knew well, the soldiers of the Legion drew in the flanks of the enemy to form a ragged half circle. Each time the circle grew tighter and each time the Tyrsians retreated a little farther. Balinor and Fandwick held the left flank while Acton and Messaline commanded the right.

The enraged enemy began to charge madly, stumbling awkwardly over the unfamiliar ground in the growing darkness, the retreating soldiers of the Legion always just a few steps out of reach. Slowly Balinor drew his flanks in and narrowed his lines, pulling the searching Northlanders in with him. Then, when the foot soldiers had completely fallen back in retreat, covered by the darkness and the battle behind them, the skilled cavalry drew their lines together in a final feint and slipped from between the jaws of the closing enemy trap and was gone. Suddenly the right and left flanks of the harried Northland army met, each believing that the other was the hated enemy that had eluded it for several hours. Without hesitating, they attacked.

How many Trolls and Gnomes were slain by their own people would never be known, but the fighting was still raging when Balinor and the two divisions of the Border Legion arrived safely at the gates of Tyrsis. The horses' hooves and soldiers' feet had been muffled to cover their retreat. With the exception of a squad of horsemen who had strayed too far west and been cut off and decimated, the Legion had escaped intact. Yet the damage done to the mammoth Northland army had not stopped its advance, and the Mermidon, the first line of defense to the city of Tyrsis, had been lost.

Now the vast encampment of the enemy sprawled on the grasslands below the city, the night fires burning as far as the eye could see through the moonlit darkness. At dawn the assault on Tyrsis would begin as the combined strength of thousands of Trolls and Gnomes, obedient to the will of the Warlock Lord, hurled itself against the towering band of stone and iron that formed the Outer Wall. One would eventually shatter.

Hendel, sitting thoughtfully across from Balinor at the small dining table, recalled again the ominous sensation he had felt earlier that day while inspecting with Janus Senpre the fortifications of the great city. Unquestionably, the Outer Wall was a formidable barrier, but there was something wrong. He had been unable to put his finger on exactly what was causing his uneasiness; but even now, in the solitude of the dining room and the warm companionship of his friends, he could not shake the nagging suspicion that something vital had been overlooked in preparing for the long siege that lay ahead.

Mentally, he retraced the lines of defense protecting the sprawling city. At the edge of the bluff, the men of Tyrsis had erected a low bulwark to prevent the enemy from gaining a foothold on the plateau. If the Northlanders could not be contained on the grasslands below the bluff, then the Border Legion would fall back into the city proper and rely on the mammoth Outer Wall to halt the enemy advance. The rear approach to Tyrsis was cut off by the sheer cliffs that rose hundreds of feet into the air directly behind the palace grounds. Balinor had assured him that the cliffs could not be scaled; they were like smooth sheets of rock, completely without the normal nooks and crannies that would permit a foothold. The defenses surrounding Tyrsis should be impenetrable, and yet Hendel remained dissatisfied.

For a moment his thoughts drifted back to his homeland—to Culhaven and to his family, whom he hadn't seen in weeks. He had never
spent much time with them, his whole life expended in the ceaseless border wars in the Anar. He missed the woodlands and the green shading that
came with the spring and summer months, and he suddenly wondered
how he had let so much time pass without a visit home. Perhaps he would
never get back. The thought swept through his mind and vanished; he had
no time for regrets.

Durin and Dayel conversed soberly with Balinor, their own thoughts
centered on the Westland. Dayel, like Hendel, was thinking of his home.
He was frightened of the battle that lay ahead, but he accepted his fear, encouraged by the presence of the others and determined that he would do
no less than they in standing firm against the army that had come to destroy them. He thought quietly of Lynliss, her shy, warm face a permanent
fixture in his mind. He would be fighting for her safety as well as his own.
Durin studied his brother, noting the sudden smile, and he knew without
asking that the youth was thinking of the Elven girl he was to marry.
Nothing was more important to Durin than the safety of Dayel; from the
beginning he had made a point of staying close to his brother to protect
him. Several times during the long journey to Paranor, they had nearly lost
their lives. Tomorrow would bring still greater danger, and once again,
Durin would be watching over his brother.

Briefly he thought of Eventine and the mighty Elven armies, wondering if they would reach Tyrsis in time. Without their great strength to
supplement the Border Legion, the hordes of the Warlock Lord would
eventually break through the city's defenses. He picked up his wineglass
and drank deeply, the liquid warm in his throat. His sharp eyes surveyed
the faces of the others and came to rest momentarily on the troubled face
of Menion Leah.

The lean highlander had devoured his dinner ravenously, having eaten
nothing for almost twenty-four hours. Finishing long before his companions, he had contented himself with a fresh glass of wine, directing continual questions to Balinor about the afternoon's battle. Now, in the quiet hours
of early morning, with dinner completed and the wine seeping through
him like a slow drowsiness, it suddenly occurred to him that the key to
everything that had happened since Culhaven, and everything that would
happen in the days remaining, was Allanon. He could not bring himself to
think anymore of Shea and the Sword, nor even of Shirl. He could only
see in the forefront of his mind the dark, forbidding figure of the mysterious Druid. Allanon held the answers to every question. He alone knew the
secret of the talisman men called the Sword of Shannara. He alone knew
the purpose behind the strange appearance of the shrouded wraith in the
Valley of Shale—the Druid Bremen, a man over five hundred years dead.
He alone, in every instance, along every step of the dangerous journey to
Paranor, had known what to expect and how to deal with it. Yet the man
himself had remained an enigma.

Now he was gone from them, and only Flick, if he were still alive, could ask him what was going to happen to them. They all depended on Allanon for survival—but what would the giant Druid do? What was left to him when the Sword of Shannara was lost? What was left when the young heir of Jerle Shannara was missing and probably dead? Menion bit his lip in anger as the hated thought slipped quickly through his mind and was banished. Shea had to be alive!

Menion cursed everything that had brought them all to this sorry end. They had allowed themselves to be backed into a corner. There was only one path still open to them. In the holocaust of tomorrow's battle, human beings would die, and few, if any, would know the reason. It was an unavoidable part of war, that men should die for unknown reasons—it had been happening for centuries. But this war was something beyond human comprehension, this war between a substanceless spirit being and mortals. How could evil such as the Warlock Lord be destroyed when it could not even be understood? Only Allanon seemed to fully appreciate the nature of the creature. But where was the Druid when they needed him most?

The candles burned low on the table before them, and the darkness of the secluded room deepened. On the wood- and tapestry-decorated walls, torches sputtered slowly in their iron racks, and the five voices dropped to low murmurs, hushed as if the night were a child in danger of being unexpectedly awakened. The city of Tyrsis slept now, and in the grasslands beyond, the Northland army. In the peace and solitude of the moonlit night, it seemed that all forms of life were at rest, and that war, with its promise of death and pain, was merely a vague, nearly forgotten memory of years past. But the five who spoke in quiet tones of better days and the friendship shared could not, even for a few moments, completely stifle the lingering realization that the horror of war was no more distant than the sunrise and as inevitable as the darkness of the Warlock Lord, reaching slowly, inexorably from out of the north to snuff out their frail lives.

30

On the morning of the third day of the search for Orl Fane, the torrential rains that had swept through the vastness of the barren Northland subsided, and the sun reappeared as a dim, fuzzy ball of white fire, burning through the misty darkness left with the passing of the Warlock Lord's black wall to the mud and rock-strewn terrain with the fury of an oven. The storm had left the topography of the land completely altered, the rains sweeping away almost every distinguishable landmark and leaving only four identical horizons of rocky hillocks and muddied valleys.

At first the appearance of the sun was a welcome sight. The heat from its rays penetrated the hateful gloom that had become permanently affixed to the barren surface of the earth to warm away the chill left by the now-vanished storm as the temperature rose steadily, and the character of the land began to alter once more. But in an hour's time, the temperature had risen thirty degrees and was continuing to rise unchecked. The rivers that washed through the winding gullies carved out by the force of the rain began to steam and mist in the heat, and the humidity soared, drenching everything in a new, even more uncomfortable wetness.

The little plant life born in the aftermath of the devastating storm withered and died in suffocation, cut off from the sun's life-giving brightness and choked by the stifling heat that permeated the graying mist. The muddied earth lay unprotected from the heat and soon baked into a cracked, hardened clay that would support no life. The rivers and lakes and puddles began to dry up quickly, and in almost no time had disappeared altogether. The exposed surface of the huge boulders that dotted the parched land quickly absorbed the burning heat like iron settled in live coals. Slowly, inexorably the land became what it had been before the rains had swept its surface—a dry, barren slab of earth, devoid of life, silent and forbidding beneath a vast, cloudless sky. The only movement came from the slow, unchanging arc of an ageless, disinterested sun as it followed its ceaseless path from east to west, turning days into years and years into centuries.

Three bent figures stepped gingerly from beneath the shelter of a rocky alcove cut in the side of one of the countless, nondescript hillocks, their cramped bodies straightening slowly, their eyes peering grimly into the unbroken wall of mist. They stood for long moments in the lifeless gloom, staring into the dying land that seemed to stretch on forever, a dismal graveyard of rocky mounds that covered the mortal remains of those who had ventured into this forbidden kingdom. There was absolute silence filtering evilly through the misty grayness, hanging its unspoken warning of death in the minds of the three living creatures. They stood in apprehensive watchfulness, staring at the wasteland surrounding them.

Shea turned to his companions. Panamon Creel was arching his back and rubbing his limbs in an effort to awaken the benumbed muscles. His dark hair was shaggy and unkempt, his broad face shaded by a three-day beard. He had a haggard look about him, but the keen eyes burned warily as he met Shea's inquisitive stare. The massive Keltset had moved noiselessly to the summit of the hill and was surveying the northern horizon.

They had huddled in the sparse shelter of their rocky alcove for almost three days while the fierce northland storm had raged unchecked through the empty lands about them. Three days lost in the pursuit of Orl Fane and the Sword of Shannara—three days during which all traces of the elusive Gnome had been thoroughly obliterated. They had crouched restlessly amid the boulders, eating because it was necessary, sleeping because there was nothing else to do. Talking had given Shea and Panamon a greater understanding of each other, though Keltset still remained a complete enigma. Shea persisted in his belief that they should have ignored the storm and pursued their quarry, but Panamon had refused to discuss the idea. No one could travel far in such a storm, and Orl Fane would be forced to seek shelter or risk being caught in a mud slide or drowned in the swift gully rivers. In any event, the thief had calmly reasoned, the Gnome would have made little progress. Keltset descended from the crest of the hill, making a quick sweeping gesture with one hand. The horizon was clear.

There was no further discussion of what should be done. It was already decided. Picking up their meager possessions, they trudged briskly down the side of the steep embankment, angling northward. For once Shea and Panamon were in complete agreement. The search for the Sword of Shannara had become more than a matter of injured pride, more than a mission to seek out a mysterious talisman. It had become a dangerous, frantic hunt for the one means, however questionable, by which they might stay alive in this savage land.

The fortress of the Warlock Lord lay amid the tall, black peaks directly north. Behind them lay the deadly wall of mist that marked the outer boundaries of the Skull Kingdom. To escape this hated land, they would have to pass one way or the other. The obvious choice was to go back through the misty darkness, but while the Elfstones might show them a passage to the Southland, using them would also reveal their presence to the spirit world. Allanon had told Shea so at Culhaven, and he in turn had told Panamon. The Sword of Shannara was the one weapon that could protect them from the Warlock Lord, and if they had it in their possession, they could be assured of at least a fighting chance. The basic plan was to regain possession of the talisman and escape back through the wall of darkness as quickly as possible. It was hardly a brilliant strategy, but under the circumstances it would have to do.

Traveling was as difficult as it had been prior to the storm. The ground was hard and coated with rubble and loose topsoil that made the footing treacherous. Scrambling and clawing their way over the rough terrain, the three were quickly covered with dirt and bruised by continual falls. Because of the unevenness of the topography, it was difficult to keep their bearings and nearly impossible to calculate their progress. Landmarks were nonexistent and the country looked almost exactly the same in every direction. The minutes wore away with agonizing slowness, and still they discovered nothing. The humidity continued to rise and the garments worn by the three men were quickly soaked through with sweat. They removed their cloaks and tied them on their backs; it would be cold again when night descended.

"This is the place we last saw him."

Panamon stood motionlessly at the summit of the broad hill they had just scaled, breathing heavily. Shea reached his side and glanced about in disbelief. All the surrounding hills looked exactly the same as this one, save for small variations in size and shape. He stared dubiously at the horizon. He wasn't even sure where they had come from.

"Keltset, what do you see?" the other man demanded.

The Rock Troll strode slowly about the hilltop, scanning the ground for any trace left by the passage of the little Gnome, but the storm appeared to have erased any signs. He moved about noiselessly for several minutes more, then turned to them and shook his head negatively. Panamon's dirt-stained face burned red in sudden anger.

"He was here. We'll walk on a bit farther."   .

They moved ahead in silence, scrambling unceremoniously down one hill and up the next. There was no further discussion. There was nothing further to be said. If Panamon were mistaken, nobody had any better idea, except to keep looking. An hour crawled by as they labored northward. Still there was nothing. Shea began to realize the hopelessness of their task. It would be impossible to search all of the land stretching east and west; if the wily Gnome had traveled just fifty yards to either side of them, they would probably never know he had gone that way. Perhaps he had been buried in a mud slide during the storm along with the Sword and they would never find him.

Shea's muscles ached from the strenuous climbing, and he considered calling a brief halt to reassess their decision to proceed in this direction. Perhaps they should try to cut across the elusive trail. Yet a glance at Panamon's dark face quickly dissuaded the Valeman from even suggesting such an action. The tall adventurer had the same look in his face Shea had seen just before he had destroyed the Gnomes days ago. He was the hunter once more. If Panamon found him, Orl Fane was a dead man. Shea shuddered involuntarily and looked away.

Several hills later, they found a piece of what they were searching for. Keltset spotted it from atop a small hillock, his sharp eyes picking out the foreign object as it lay half buried in dust at the bottom of a small ravine. Directing the other two, he slid quickly down the rock-strewn hill and rushed eagerly over to the discarded object, snatching it up and holding it out to them. It was a large strip of cloth—cloth that had once been the major portion of a tunic sleeve. They stared at it quietly for a moment, and then Shea looked at Keltset for confirmation that it was indeed Orl Fane's. The giant Troll nodded solemnly. Panamon Creel impaled the piece of cloth on the end of his pike, smiling grimly.

"So we've found him again. This time he won't get away!"

But they didn't find him that day, nor did they discover any further signs of his passing. In the heavy dust, the Gnome's footprints would have clearly shown, yet there were none. Despite Panamon's earlier opinion, Orl Fane had somehow wandered on during the storm, escaping both mud slides and drowning. The rain had washed away his tracks but, with freakish perversity, had left uncovered the torn sleeve. It could have been washed down from anywhere, so there was no way to tell which direction the Gnome had come from or gone. By nightfall, the blackness shrouding the land was so heavy that it was impossible to see more than several feet, and the search was reluctantly abandoned for the night. With Keltset standing the first watch, Panamon and Shea collapsed in near exhaustion and fell asleep almost instantly. The night air was cool, though the humidity of the day lingered on, and all three wrapped themselves once again in the half-dry hunting cloaks.

The morning returned all too swiftly in the familiar graying haze. This day was not as humid as the previous one, but it was no more cheerful; the sun was still nearly blotted out by the leaden mist that hung immovably overhead. The same eerie silence persisted and the three men stared about with a feeling of complete isolation from the living world. The vast emptiness was beginning to have a noticeable effect on both Shea and Panamon Creel. Shea had grown edgy and nervous in these past several days and the normally cheerful and talkative Panamon had lapsed into almost total silence. Keltset alone retained his usual demeanor, his face as bland and implacable as ever.

A short breakfast was consumed without interest, and the search began again. They resumed the hunt almost with distaste; their common desire was to end this wearing trek quickly. They went ahead partly out of a sense of self-preservation and partly because they had nowhere else to go. Although neither realized it, both Panamon and Shea were beginning to wonder why Keltset continued the pursuit. He was in his own country and could probably have survived alone, had he chosen to go his own way. The two men had tried unsuccessfully to decipher Keltset's reasons for continuing on with them during the three-day rain, and now, too worn to reason the matter further, they had fallen back on suspicious acceptance of his presence and a growing determination that they would know who and what he was before this journey ended. They plodded on through the dust and the haze as the morning drifted dully into noonday.

It was totally unexpected when Panamon suddenly drew up short. "Tracks!"

The tall thief let out a wild yell of delight and charged madly into the small draw to their left, leaving both Keltset and Shea staring after him in amazement. Moments later the trio knelt eagerly over a set of clearly defined footprints outlined in the heavy dust. There was no mistaking their origin; even Shea recognized that they were made by Gnome boots, worn and cracked about the heels. The trail they left was undisguised, leading generally northward, but weaving badly as if the destination of the man passing were no longer certain. It almost appeared as if Orl Fane were wandering aimlessly. They paused a moment longer and then rose hurriedly at Panamon's urgent command. The tracks were only hours old and, judging from their meandering nature, the elusive Orl Fane could be overtaken easily. Panamon could only thinly disguise the almost vicious glee that surged through his revitalized body as he saw the end of the long hunt in sight. Without speaking further, the three hitched up their cumbersome gear and moved northward in grim resolution. This was the day they would catch Orl Fane.

The trail left by the little Gnome wound in erratically confusing fashion through the dusty hills of the lower Northland. At times the three found themselves traveling almost directly eastward, and once they were turned about entirely. The afternoon wore on with tedious precision, and while Keltset indicated that the footprints were growing fresher, it appeared that they were still not gaining rapidly. If nightfall set in before they had caught up with their quarry, they might very well lose him once again. Twice before they had been on the verge of catching him, and each time an unexpected occurrence had forced them temporarily to abandon the search. They were not in the mood to have this happen a third time, and Shea had inwardly vowed that, if need be, he would track Orl Fane even in total darkness.

The giant peaks of the forbidding Skull Kingdom loomed menacingly in the distance, their black, razor tips jutting knifelike into the horizon. There was a sense of fear in the mind of the Valeman that he could not shake, a fear that had grown steadily stronger as the three men had pushed deeper into the Northland. He had begun to feel that he was undertaking much more than he had originally imagined, that somehow the search for Orl Fane and the Sword of Shannara was only a small part of a much larger scheme of events. He was not yet panicked by what he felt, but he was prodded by an urgent need to finish this insane chase and turn back to his own land.

It was midafternoon when the hilly terrain began to level off into a rolling plainland that enabled the three men to see for greater distances and to walk upright in an almost relaxed manner for the first time since they had passed through the black wall. The country ahead spread out before them with breathtaking starkness, a bleak, empty plain of brown earth and gray rock that rolled unevenly northward toward the tall peaks that bordered the Skull Kingdom and the home of the Warlock Lord. These vast flatlands diminished the farther north the eye traveled, breaking around masses of rock and mountainous ridgeland that led in stepping-stone manner to the awesome peaks beyond. The entire expanse, naked, hot, and desolate, lay masked in the same eerie, deathly silence. Nothing moved, no creature stirred, no insect hummed, no bird flew, not even the wind brushed against the layered dust. Everywhere there was the same blasted emptiness, unmarked by life, shrouded with death. The winding tracks of Orl Fane led into this vastness and disappeared far in the distance. It was as if the land had swallowed him up.

The hunters paused for several long minutes, their faces mirroring their obvious reluctance to proceed into this unfriendly land. But there was little time for weighing the merits of the matter, and they moved ahead. The twisting path was visible for a greater distance in this rolling plainland, and the three pursuers were able to track on a more direct course. They began to make up time quickly. Less than two hours later Keltset indicated that they were no more than an hour behind their quarry. Dusk was rapidly approaching, the sun dipping behind a broken horizon far to the west. The dim twilight was masked further still by the ever-present gray haze, and the terrain was beginning to take on a peculiarly fuzzy appearance.

The trio had followed the Gnome's trail into a deep draw that was formed by a series of high ridges cropped by sharp overhangs and great, jutting rock formations. The fading sunlight was lost almost entirely in the shadows of the darkened valley, and Panamon Creel, who had eagerly taken the lead sometime earlier, was forced to squint sharply to find the outline of the footprints in the heavy dust. They slowed to a halting walk as the thief bent closer to the earth. So intent was Panamon Creel on studying the tracks immediately before him that it came as a shock when the prints abruptly ended. Shea and Keltset were at his side instantly, and it was only after a careful study of the ground ahead of them that they were able to discover that someone had methodically brushed away all further traces of the little Gnome's passing.

It was in that same instant that the huge, dark forms began to detach themselves from the shadows of the draw, lumbering ponderously forward in the deepening twilight. Shea saw them first, but believed his eyes were playing tricks on him. Panamon was quicker to realize what was happening. Springing upright, the thief drew out the great broadsword and raised his pike. He might have made a rush to break through the tightening ring, but the normally predictable Keltset did a surprising thing. Springing quickly forward, he pulled the astonished thief back. Panamon stared incredulously at his silent companion, then reluctantly lowered his weapons. There were at least a dozen forms standing guardedly all around the three men, and even in the hazy twilight a terrified Shea realized that they had been discovered by a band of giant Trolls.

The company of weary Elven riders reined in their sweating mounts and gazed absently down the valley slopes into the broad length of the Rhenn. Two miles of empty valley stretched eastward before them, the high slopes to either side cresting in sharp ridges lined with thinning stretches of trees and scrub brush. The legendary pass had served for over a thousand years as the gateway from the lower Streleheim Plains to the great forests of the Westland, a natural door to the homeland of the Elves. It was in this famous pass that the awesome might of the armies of the Warlock Lord had been broken in defeat by the Elven legions and Jerle Shannara. It was here that Brona had faced and run from the aged Bremen and the mysterious power of the Sword of Shannara—run with his great armies back into the plainlands, only to be halted by advancing Dwarf armies, trapped, and destroyed. The Pass of Rhenn had seen the beginning of the downfall of the greatest threat the world had encountered since the devastating Great Wars, and the people of all the races looked upon this peaceful valley as a historic landmark. It was a natural monument of mankind's history that some had journeyed halfway around the world to see just so that they, too, might feel somehow a part of that terrible event.

Jon Lin Sandor gave the order to dismount, and the Elven riders climbed down gratefully. His concern was not with the history of the past but with the immediate future. Worriedly, he stared at the heavy black wall descending from the Northland across the Plains of Streleheim, its hazy shadow drawing daily nearer to the borders of the Westland and the home of the Elves. His sharp eyes peered far into the eastern horizon where the darkness had already permeated into the forests surrounding the ancient fortress of Paranor. He shook his head bitterly and cursed the day he had permitted himself to leave the side of his King and oldest friend. He had grown to manhood with Eventine, and when his friend became King he had stayed with him as his personal counselor and self-appointed watchdog. Together they had prepared for the invasion of the armies of Brona, the Spirit Lord they had once believed destroyed in the Second War of the Races. The mysterious wanderer Allanon had warned the Elven people, and while some had scoffed in misconceived disdain, Eventine had known better. Allanon had never been wrong; his ability to see into the future was uncanny, but unerringly accurate.

The Elven people had followed Eventine's advice and they had prepared for war, but the invasion did not come as expected. Then Paranor had fallen and with it the Sword of Shannara. Again Allanon had come to them, asking that they patrol the Plains of Streleheim above Paranor to guard against any attempt by the Gnomes holding the Druid fortress to move the Sword northward to the castle of the Warlock Lord. Again they had obeyed without question.

But the unexpected had happened, and it had happened while Jon Lin Sandor was away from the King. The Gnomes entrenched at Paranor had unexpectedly decided to break for the safety of the deep Northland, and three heavy patrols made a rush at the Elven lines. Eventine and Jon Lin had led separate commands to intercept two of these forces and would have destroyed the Gnomes easily had it not been for the planned intervention of a combined army of Gnomes and Trolls detached from the now advancing Northland army of the Warlock Lord. Jon Lin's command was nearly annihilated, and he barely escaped with his life. He had been unable to reach Eventine, and the Elven King had disappeared with his entire patrol. Jon Lin Sandor had been searching for him for nearly three days.

"We will find him, Jon Lin. He is not an easy one to kill. He will find a way to survive."

The grim Elf nodded with a barely perceptible shake of his close-cropped head, his darting eyes glancing quickly at the young face of the man standing next to him.

"It's a strange thing, but I know he's alive," the other continued soberly. "I can't really explain how I know—it's just something I can sense."

Breen Elessedil was Eventine's younger brother; he was also the next

King of the Westland Elves if his brother were dead. It was a position he was not yet ready for and quite honestly did not want. Since Eventine's disappearance he had done nothing to assume command of the languishing Elven armies or of the dismayed King's Council, but had joined immediately in the search for his brother. As a result, the Elven government was in a state of near chaos, and what had only two weeks earlier been a people united against the imminent threat of invasion from the north was now an unsure, divided cluster of separated groups, badly frightened because there was no one prepared to assume leadership of the government.

The Elven people would not panic altogether; they were far too disciplined to allow matters to fall apart totally. But Eventine had been an undeniably powerful personality, and the people had been united solidly behind him since his ascension to the throne. Young, but possessing unusual strength of character and an infallible common sense, he had always been there to advise them and they had always listened. The rumors of his disappearance had shaken the people badly.

But neither Breen Elessedil nor Jon Lin had time to worry about anything but finding the missing King. After skirting Gnome patrols and the main body of the Northland army while they searched, the haggard survivors of the decimated Elven patrols had returned briefly to the tiny outland village of Koos, where they had obtained fresh horses and supplies. Now they were on their way back to pick up the search once more.

Jon Lin Sandor believed he knew where Eventine would be found, if he were still alive. The giant Northland army had moved south toward the Kingdom of Callahorn almost a week earlier, and it would pass no farther until the famed Border Legion had been destroyed. It was probable that if Eventine were a prisoner, as both Breen and he now believed must be the case, then they would find him with the commanders of Brona's invasion force as a hostage of great bargaining value. With Eventine Elessedil defeated, cities whose leaders were lesser men would be more willing to consider surrender.

In any event, the Warlock Lord recognized the importance of Eventine to the Elven people. He was the most revered and beloved leader the Elves had known since Jerle Shannara, and they would do almost anything to have him back safely. Dead, he would serve no purpose to the Spirit King, and his execution might so enrage the Elves that they would reunite in their common desire to destroy him. But alive, Eventine was of immeasurable worth, for the Elven people would not risk injury to their favorite son. Jon Lin Sandor and Breen Elessedil harbored no false illusions that Eventine would be safely returned to them, even if the army did not intervene in the Southland invasion. They were acting on their own initiative, gambling that they could find their friend and brother before his usefulness was ended—before the Southland fell.

"That's enough. Mount up!"

Jon Lin's impatient voice cut through the momentary stillness with biting sharpness, and the lounging riders leaped to their feet hurriedly in response. He stared a final time at the distant blackness, then turned and vaulted easily onto his waiting mount, gathering the reins in one swift motion. Breen was already at his side and seconds later the small body of horsemen was moving down the valley corridor at a fast trot. It was a gray morning, the air tinged with the pungent smell of last night's rain, still lingering on the plainlands. The tall grass was wet and yielding beneath the sharp hooves of the passing horses, muffling their impact. Far to the south a trace of deep blue sky could be seen beyond the clouds. It was a cool day, and the Elves rode comfortably in the moderate temperatures.

They reached the end of the valley quickly, pulling their eager mounts to a slow trot as they entered the eastern corridor of the pass. The riders talked among themselves, though in low tones, for the borders of the Northland lay just beyond the pass gateway. The line of horsemen wound snakelike through the high ridges framing the eastern entryway, and moments later emerged onto the vast expanse of the Plains of Streleheim. Jon Lin glanced almost casually across the emptiness that stretched out before him, and then abruptly reined in his horse.

"Breen—a horseman!"

Instantly the other was at his side and together they peered at the distant rider moving rapidly toward them. The Elves stared curiously, unable to make out the features of the advancing horseman in the hazy light. For one brief instant, Breen Elessedil was convinced it was his brother returning, but a moment later his hopes faded as he realized the man was too small to be Eventine. He was certainly no horseman. As he came up to them, he was hanging on to both the reins and the saddle horn for dear life, his broad face flushed and sweating from the effort. He was no Elf; he was a Southlander.

He brought his mount to a jolting halt in front of the Elven band, pausing to catch his breath before speaking. He studied the amused faces confronting him and his face turned a shade redder.

"I met a man a few days earlier," the stranger began. Then he hesitated to be certain he had their attention. "He asked me to seek out the right arm of the Elven King."

The looks of amusement faded instantly as the Elven riders leaned forward.

"I am Jon Lin Sandor," the patrol commander acknowledged quietly.

The exhausted rider sighed gratefully and nodded. "I'm Flick Ohmsford, and I've come all the way from Callahorn to find you." With no little effort he dismounted and rubbed his aching backside. "If you'll give me a few minutes' rest, I'll take you to Eventine."

Shea marched in silence between two of his giant Troll captors, unable to shake the feeling that Keltset had betrayed them. The ambush had been cleverly sprung, but they might at least have attempted to fight their way clear. Instead, on Keltset's unexpected command, they had offered no resistance, allowing themselves to be willingly disarmed. Shea had hoped that Keltset might know one of the Trolls in the raiding party or that, being of the same race, he could reason with them and secure their release. But the giant Troll had not even tried to communicate with his captors, docilely permitting them to bind his hands without the slightest struggle. Panamon Creel and Shea had their weapons removed and their hands tied, and the three captives were marched northward into the barren flatlands. The little Valeman still had possession of the Elfstones, but they were useless against the Trolls.

He studied the broad back of Panamon, who was walking directly in front of him, wondering what the irascible thief's thoughts must be. The man had been so astonished at his companion's quick surrender that he had not spoken one word since. Obviously he could not bring himself to believe that he had so misjudged the silent giant, whose life he had saved and whose friendship he had valued. The Troll's behavior was a complete mystery to them both; but, whereas Shea was merely confused, Panamon Creel was deeply hurt. Whatever else there was between them, Keltset had been his friend—the one friend he felt he could depend on. The hardened adventurer's disbelief would quickly turn to hatred, and Shea had always known that whatever the circumstances, Panamon Creel was a dangerous man to make an enemy.

It was impossible to determine where they were being taken. The Northland night was a moonless black, and Shea was forced to turn his concentration to the task of finding his footing as the party wound its way northward through scattered boulders and high ridges strewn with loose earth and rock. The Troll tongue was completely foreign to the Valeman. Since Panamon had lapsed into brooding silence, Shea could learn nothing. If the Trolls had reason to suspect who he was, then they would be taken to the Warlock Lord. The fact that they had not bothered with the Elfstones might be an indication that his captors had seized them merely as intruders without realizing what had brought them to the Northland. The possibility offered little comfort; the Trolls would find him out quickly enough. He wondered suddenly what had become of the fleeing Orl Fane. His tracks had ended where they had been seized, so the Gnome must also be a prisoner. But where had they taken him? And what had become of the Sword of Shannara?

They marched for hours in the impenetrable darkness. Shea quickly lost all track of time, and finally became so exhausted that he collapsed and was carried like a sack of grain over the broad shoulder of one of his captors for the remainder of the journey. He awoke briefly to the flickering light of low-burning wood fires as the party entered an unfamiliar encampment, then felt himself lowered to the earth and led through the opening of a large tent. Inside his hands were checked to be certain the bonds were secure and his feet were bound. Moments later he was left alone. Panamon and Keltset had been taken elsewhere.

Briefly, he struggled with the leather thongs that held his hands and feet, but they would not loosen and finally he gave it up. He could feel himself drifting into sleep, the weariness from the long march flooding through his aching body. He tried to fight it, forcing himself to conceive a plan of escape. The harder he tried, the more difficult it became to think of anything, and everything in his tired mind grew steadily more hazy. He was asleep in five minutes.

It seemed only moments later that he was awakened by rough hands shaking him out of the deep slumber into which he had fallen. He rose dazedly as a heavyset Troll spoke something unintelligible to him and pointed to a plate of food before passing out of the tent into the sunlight beyond. Shea squinted in the darkness of the tent, absently noting the familiar grayness of the Northland morning that signaled the beginning of another day. Realizing with mild astonishment that the leather bonds had been removed, he briskly rubbed his wrists and ankles to restore the circulation and then ate quickly the meal prepared for him.

There appeared to be a great deal of excitement outside his tent, and the shouts and cries of Trolls moving hurriedly about the encampment filled the morning air. The Valeman finished his meal and had just determined to risk a glance through the closed flaps of the tent entrance, when they were abruptly whipped aside. A burly Troll guard stepped inside and motioned for Shea to come with him. With one hand tightly clenching his tunic front, where he could feel the reassuring bulk of the Elfstones, the Valeman reluctantly followed.

An escort of Trolls led the small Southlander through a large encampment consisting of various-sized tents and stone huts constructed on a wide bluff surrounded by a series of low ridges. Glancing at the distant horizon, he could tell that they were high above the barren plainlands they had crossed the previous night. The camp appeared deserted, and the voices Shea had heard earlier had faded entirely. The fires of the night before had died into ashes, and the tents and huts were all empty. A sudden chill struck the frightened captive, and it occurred to him that he was probably being led to his own execution. There was no sign of either Panamon or Keltset. Allanon, Flick, Menion Leah, and all the others were somewhere in the Southland, unaware of his predicament. He was alone, and he was going to die. He was so paralyzed with fear that he could not even attempt to flee. He moved woodenly between his captors as they wound their way through the silent camp. A low ridge, marking the boundary of the encampment, loomed directly ahead of them, and then they were past the huts and tents and standing in a broad, open clearing. Shea stared in disbelief.

Dozens of Trolls were seated in a wide semicircle facing the ridge, their heads turned toward him momentarily as he entered the clearing. At the base of the ridge sat three Trolls of varying sizes and, though Shea could not be certain, probably of varying ages as well, each holding a brightly colored staff with a black pennant. Panamon Creel had been seated within the wide circle to one side. He had a peculiarly pensive look that did not alter as he caught sight of Shea. The attention of everyone was focused on the massive form of Keltset standing motionless in the center of the expectant Trolls, his arms folded as he faced the three staff bearers. He did not turn as Shea was led into the circle and seated next to the thoughtful Panamon. There was a long moment of complete silence. It was the strangest spectacle Shea had ever witnessed. Then one of the three Trolls seated at the apex of the circle rose ceremoniously and tapped his staff lightly to the earth. The assemblage rose as one, turned sharply to face eastward, and spoke in unison several short lines in their own tongue. Then quietly they sat down again.

"Can you imagine? They were praying."

They were the first words Panamon had spoken, and Shea started in surprise. He glanced quickly at the thief, but the big man was looking at Keltset. Another of the three Trolls presiding over the strange assembly rose and spoke briefly to the attentive audience, gesturing several times toward Panamon and Shea. The little Valeman turned expectantly to his companion.

"This is a trial, Shea," the thief declared in a strangely dispassionate tone. "Not for you or me, however. We're to be taken to the Skull Mountain beyond the Knife Edge, the Kingdom of the Warlock Lord, where we'll be held for . . . whatever. I don't think they know who we are yet. It is the command of the Spirit Lord that all outlanders be brought to him, and we're being treated no differently. There's hope still."

"But a trial . . . ?" Shea began doubtfully.

"For Keltset. He has demanded the right to be tried by his own people rather than be turned over to Brona. It's an ancient custom—the request cannot be refused. He was found with us when his people were at war with our race. Any Troll found with a Man is presumed a traitor. There are no exceptions."

Shea glanced involuntarily at Keltset. The massive Troll was seated with rocklike solidity in the center of the waiting assemblage as the voice of the presiding Troll continued to drone on. They had been mistaken, the Valeman thought gratefully. Keltset had not betrayed them; he had not given them away after all. But why had he allowed them to be taken captive so easily when he knew his own life would be forfeit as well?

"What will they do to him if they decide he is a traitor?" he asked impulsively.

A slight smile appeared on the tall man's lips.

"I know what you must be thinking." There was a touch of irony in the mocking voice. "He is risking everything on this trial. If they find him guilty, he will be immediately thrown over the nearest cliff."

He paused meaningfully and for the first time looked directly at the Valeman.

"I don't understand it either."

They lapsed into silence once more as the speaker finished his lengthy statement and sat down. After a moment, a single Troll came to stand before the three presiding Trolls, whom Shea now realized must be judges, and made a brief statement. He was followed by several others, each of whom spoke briefly, responding to questions put to them by the judges. Shea could understand nothing of what was taking place, but supposed that the Trolls were members of the raiding party that had captured them the previous night. The examination seemed to drag on forever, and still Keltset had not moved a muscle.

Shea studied the impassive giant, unable to understand why he had chosen to allow matters to go this way. Both Shea and Panamon had known for some time that Keltset was no ordinary outcast, driven from his home and his people because he was unable to speak. Nor was he simply the thief and adventurer that Panamon had tried to make him. There was intelligence in those strangely gentle eyes. There was an unspoken knowledge of the Sword of Shannara, the Warlock Lord, and even Shea that had never been revealed. There was a past hidden deep within the giant's heart. He was Allanon all over again, Shea thought suddenly. Somehow both held the key to the secret of the power of the Sword of Shannara. It was a strange revelation, and the Valeman shook his head questioningly, doubtful of his own reasoning. But there was no more time to think.

The witnesses had finished, and the three judges had now called upon the accused to rise and defend himself. There was an impossibly long, agonizing moment of unbroken silence as the judges, the assembled Trolls, Panamon Creel, and Shea all waited expectantly for Keltset to rise. Still the giant Rock Troll sat motionless as if caught in an unbreakable trance. Shea was seized with an almost uncontrollable urge to shout wildly, if only to break the unbearable silence, but the sound caught in his throat. The seconds crawled by. Then without warning, Keltset rose.

He drew his massive frame erect, abruptly taking on the appearance of a creature who was somehow more than mortal. There was pride in his bearing as he faced the waiting tribunal, his eyes fixed on the three judges. Without shifting his gaze even slightly, he reached under the broad leather belt that bound his waist and drew forth a large black metal pendant and chain. For a moment he held it in his hands before the eyes of the judges, who leaned forward in obvious surprise. Shea caught a quick glimpse of a cross centered in a circle, and then the giant raised the chain ceremoniously above his head and settled it slowly about his great neck.

"By the gods that gave us life . . . I don't believe it!" Panamon gasped in startled disbelief.

The judges, too, rose in astonishment. As Keltset turned slowly about the circle of wondering Trolls, shouts of excitement broke from their mouths and they were on their feet instantly, gesturing wildly at the impassive giant in their midst. Shea stared with the rest of them, completely befuddled.

"Panamon, what's happening?!" he cried finally.

The intense roar of the aroused assemblage nearly drowned out his words, and Panamon Creel was suddenly on his feet, too, one broad hand clapping down on Shea's slim shoulder.

"I don't believe it," the thief repeated with unrestrained joy. "All these months I've never even suspected it. That's what he's been hiding from us all along, my young Valeman! That's why he allowed us to be taken without a fight. But there must be more still . . ."

"Will you tell me what's happening?" Shea demanded heatedly.

"The pendant, Shea—the cross and circle!" the other shouted wildly. "It's the Black Irix, the highest award, the greatest honor the Troll people can give to one of their own! If you see three given in your lifetime, it's unusual. To receive one, you must be the living image of everything the Troll nation cherishes and strives to attain. You must be the closest thing to a god that a mortal being can approach. Somewhere in his past, Keltset has earned this honor—and we never guessed!"

"But what about the fact that he was found with us . . . ?" The little Valeman got only part of the query out.

"Anyone who wears the Irix would never betray his own people," Panamon cut in sharply. "The honor carries with it an unbreakable trust. The wearer would never breach the laws of his people—he's presumed incapable of even contemplating such a thing. They believe that violation of such a trust would mean an eternity of punishment too horrible to imagine. No Troll would consider it."

Shea stared dazedly back at Keltset as the shouting continued unchecked. The great Troll was again facing his judges while the three vainly attempted to restore order to the unheeding assembly. It took several minutes more before the noise abated enough for anyone to be heard. The Trolls reseated themselves, anxiously waiting for Keltset to speak. There was a brief pause as a Troll interpreter appeared at the side of the silent defendant, then Keltset began to communicate in sign language. His eyes on Keltset's massive hands, the interpreter translated the explanation to the judges in the Troll language. There was a brief exchange with one of the judges, none of which Shea was able to understand, but fortunately Panamon had already begun his own translation, whispering quietly to his anxious friend.

"He told them that he comes from Norbane, one of the larger Troll cities in the far northern Charnal Mountains. His family name is Mallicos—it belongs to a very old and honored family. But they were all killed, supposedly by Dwarfs who had attempted to loot their family home. That judge on the left was asking Keltset how he had escaped; they had thought him dead as well. It must have been a pretty grisly affair for even this distant village to hear about it. But then—wait till you hear this, Shea! Keltset says the emissaries of the Warlock Lord destroyed his family! The Skull Bearers came to Norbane almost a year ago, seizing control of the government and ordering the Troll armies to accept their command. They managed to convince most of the city that Brona had come back from the dead, that he had survived for thousands of years and could not be killed by mortal hands. The Mallicos family was one of the ruling families in

Norbane, and they refused to submit, demanding that the city stand firm against the Warlock Lord. Keltset's word carried a lot of weight because he wore the Black Irix. The Warlock Lord had the entire Mallicos family decimated except for Keltset, whom he brought to his fortress in the Knife Edge. The story of the Dwarf looters was a deception to inflame the Troll citizenry to join in the Southland invasion.

"But Keltset managed to escape before they got him to the prisons, wandering southward until I found him. The Warlock Lord had ordered that his voice be burned out to prevent his communication with any living being, but he learned sign language. He waited for his chance to return to the Northland. . . ."

One of the judges suddenly interrupted and Panamon paused momentarily.

"The judge asked why he returned now. Our big friend says he learned of Brona's fear of the power of the Sword of Shannara and the legend that a son of the Elven house would appear to take up the Sword . . ."

Panamon trailed off abruptly as the interpreter turned back to Keltset. For the first time the giant Troll faced toward Shea, the strangely gentle eyes fixed intently on the little Valeman. An involuntary chill shook Shea. Then his massive companion gestured briefly to the waiting judges. Panamon hesitated, then spoke softly.

"He says they must go with him to the Skull Kingdom, and that once inside the fortress, you, Shea, will destroy the Warlock Lord!"

31

Palance Buckhannah died at dawn. Death came quietly, almost unexpectedly, as the first faint golden rays of sunlight crept searchingly into the darkness of the eastern horizon. He died without regaining consciousness. When Balinor was told, he merely nodded his head in acknowledgment and turned away. His friends stayed with him momentarily until Hendel silently motioned for them all to leave. In the hallway beyond the death room, they gathered quietly and spoke in hushed voices. Balinor was the last of the Buckhannahs. If he died in the coming battle, the family name would disappear from the earth. Only history would remember.

In the same hour, the assault on Tyrsis began. It, too, came quietly, born with the dying of the night. As the waiting soldiers of the entrenched Border Legion peered into the gray plains below the great city walls, the light from the slowly rising sun revealed the mammoth Northland army spread out all the way to the distant Mermidon, the carefully drawn formations giving a checkerboard appearance to the deep green of the grass-lands. One moment the vast army stood silent, motionless on the plains below the city, shadows etched out of the darkness by dawn into figures of flesh and blood, iron and stone, and in the next they began to advance on the Tyrsian defenders. The silence broke sharply with the sudden booming of Gnome war drums, the deep, throbbing beat ringing ominously against the stone walls of Tyrsis.

The Northlanders came slowly, steadily to the battle, the crashing of the drums matched by the thudding of booted feet marching in ragged time, metal clinking sharply against metal as weapons and armor braced for the assault. They came voicelessly, thousands and thousands of them, ar-mored figures faceless in the deep morning gloom. Great hulking ramp-ways made of timbers bound in iron creaked ponderously as they were pulled and pushed on metal-rimmed wheels through the half-light, mobile pathways to the heights of the fortified bluff.

The seconds ticked away as the massive attack force moved to within a hundred yards of the waiting Legion, and still the crashing drums main-tained their unhurried pace. The rim of the sun became sharply visible in the east and the waning night faded entirely in the western horizon. The drums abruptly ceased, and the sprawling army came to a sudden halt. For an instant there was a deep, unbroken silence that hung in frightened hesi-tation on the morning air. Then a deafening roar rose from the throats of the Northlanders; with a great surge, the massive juggernaut charged, wave upon wave rushing to grapple with the men of the Border Legion.

From beneath the closed gates of the towering Outer Wall, Balinor stared out at the awesome Northland assault, his broad face coolly impas-sive. His voice was calm and steady as he spoke briefly to his runners, send-ing one scurrying to find Acton and Fandwick on the left flank, the other to Messaline and Ginnisson on the right. His eyes returned instantly to the terrifying spectacle below the bulwarks as the wild charge drew closer. Be-hind the hastily constructed defenses, the Legion archers and spearmen waited patiently for his command. Balinor knew they could break even this massive charge from their superior defensive position, but they must first destroy the five broad rampways that were rolling slowly toward the base of the bluff. He had correctly anticipated that such devices would be used to scale the plateau and its low bulwarks, just as the enemy had fore-seen that he would destroy the city rampway. The vanguard of the North-land rush was within fifty feet of the bluff, and still the new King of Callahorn watched and waited.

Then abruptly the ground opened beneath the feet of the charging enemy and great holes appeared as the attackers fell screaming into the ring of camouflaged pits concealed all along the base of the plateau. Two of the monstrous rolling rampways tumbled unchecked into the wide openings, the wheels snapping loose and the timbers shattering in splinters. The first wave of the mighty rush hesitated and from atop the low bulwarks the Le-gion archers rose on Balinor's long-awaited signal, to fire point-blank into the ranks of the suddenly confused enemy. The dead and wounded alike fell helplessly on the plainlands and were quickly trampled under as the second wave of the sustained charge pushed through, struggling to reach the entrenched Legion.

Three of the heavy rampways had avoided the concealed pits and continued to roll unhindered toward the low bulwarks. The Legion archers quickly loosed a flurry of burning arrows onto the vulnerable wooden backs of the ramps, but dozens of nimble yellow bodies were immediately seen to scramble atop the flaming timbers to smother the fires. The Gnome archers were also in position by this time, and for several minutes a concentrated barrage of arrows cut through the ranks of both sides. The completely exposed Gnomes crawling about on the rampways were cut to pieces. Everywhere men fell screaming in pain as the deadly missiles found their human targets. The wounded men of the Border Legion were sheltered in part from further injury by the low bulwarks and could be treated for their wounds. But the fallen Northlanders lay helpless and unprotected on the open field, and hundreds were killed before they could be removed to safety.

The three remaining rampways were still rolling toward the base of the fortified bluff, though one was now burning fiercely, great clouds of billowing smoke obscuring the vision of everyone passing within a hundred yards. When the two remaining ramps were within twenty yards of the bulwarks, Balinor signaled for his final defense. Huge caldrons of oil were lifted to the rim of the Southland defenses and the contents splashed down onto the grassland below, directly in the path of the rolling rampways. Before the charging Northlanders had time to veer in either direction, torches were dropped in the midst of the spreading oil and the entire area disappeared in a mass of flames and heavy black smoke.

The sustained enemy assault broke apart as the oncoming waves of attackers hesitated in fright at the wall of flames confronting them. The foremost ranks of the enemy had been burned alive; only a few managed to flee successfully from the terrible carnage at the base of the Legion defenses. The wind was blowing the dark smoke laterally across the open plains to the west, and for several moments the center and left flank of the two great armies were visually cut off from each other and from the wounded and dying who lay helplessly in the midst of the choking fumes.

Instantly Balinor saw his chance. A sharp counterthrust now might break the assault completely and rout the Northland army. Leaping to his feet, he signaled to Janus Senpre atop the Outer Wall, who had been left in command of the city garrison. Immediately the massive ironbound gates swung ponderously outward, and the mounted regiment of the Border Legion, armed with short swords and long, hooked pikes, their leopard colors flying brightly, galloped onto the bluff, wheeling sharply left to follow the open pathway along the city wall. Within moments they had reached the left flank of the Legion defensive line where Acton and Fandwick had command of the entrenched bordermen. A portable rampway was hastily lowered from the bluff rim onto the smoke-clouded plains below, and the Legion riders, led by Acton, thundered downward and swung left in a wide circle.

Balinor's instructions called for the famed regiment to cut around the wall of smoke and launch a sustained charge on the enemy's right flank. As the Northlanders turned to meet this counterattack, Balinor would bring a regiment of foot soldiers to strike at the exposed Northland front, driving the enemy back toward the Mermidon. If the counterthrust should falter, both commands were immediately to swing back into the covering smoke and return up the waiting rampways. It was a daring gamble. The Northlanders outnumbered the Legion soldiers at least twenty to one, and if the Tyrsians should be cut off, they would be completely decimated.

Small commands of Legion foot soldiers had already descended the mobile rampway on the left flank and staged a short counterattack into the enemy ranks as a defensive measure to protect the mounted regiment's only link with the besieged city. For the moment, the enemy seemed to have disappeared entirely on the left flank, totally obscured by the smoke which was blowing in blinding clouds from the burning rampways at the center of the defensive line.

On the right defensive flank, the fighting was ferocious. Only a light, drifting haze of smoke and dust obscured the vision of the two armies at this point, and the Northland assault continued unchecked. The entrenched Legion archers had decimated the first wave of attackers, but the second wave had reached the base of the bluff and was attempting to gain the fortified heights with the aid of rough-hewn scaling ladders. Lines of Gnome archers fired hundreds of arrows into the low bulwarks in an attempt to keep the defenders pinned down long enough to allow the exposed climbers to scramble over the Tyrsian defenses. The Legion archers returned the fire while their comrades used iron-tipped pikes from the rim of the defenses to push away the enemy assault.

It was a long, bloody fight during which neither side rested. At one point, a particularly fierce band of rangy Rock Trolls breached the Legion defenses and rushed onto the open bluff. A fierce battle raged for a short time as the bulky Legion commander Ginnisson, his florid face as red as his long hair, rallied his soldiers to resist the great Trolls; in bloody hand-to-hand combat, the Legionnaires killed the small band of attackers and closed the breach.

At the summit of the high Outer Wall, four old friends stood in silence with Janus Senpre and watched the terrible spectacle unfolding below them. Hendel, Menion Leah, Durin, and Dayel had all been left inside the city, their assignment to observe the progress of the battle and to aid Balinor in coordinating the movements of the Legion. The rolling smoke clouds totally obscured the giant borderman's vision of the movements of his mounted regiment, and only those atop the towering city walls could advise him of its progress so that he could launch his own assault from the center of the defensive line at the proper moment. The King relied particularly on Hendel's judgment, for the taciturn Dwarf had been fighting nearly thirty years in the Anar border wars.

Now the grizzled hunter, the Southlander, and the Elven brothers stared anxiously at the panorama spread out on the plains beneath them. On the right defensive flank, the fighting was the heaviest, as the determined Northlanders continued to batter the entrenched Legion, struggling to scale the face of the bluff. The Border Legion was holding on, but it was taking everything it had to beat back the ferocious assault. The plains immediately below the city gates at the center of the bulwarks were obscured by the burning oil and wooden rampways, which had crumbled entirely into masses of flaming timbers. At the fringes of the smoke, the disorganized Northlanders were vainly attempting to draw up their confused battle lines to renew the shattered charge. On the left, the Legion horsemen had broken out of the cover of the rolling black smoke and were encountering their first signs of resistance.

A large squad of Gnome cavalry had been stationed on the right attack flank as a defensive measure against exactly the kind of maneuver that was under way. However, the Northlanders had anticipated some advance warning of any flanking assault and were caught completely by surprise. The poorly trained Gnome riders were quickly scattered by the Border Legion and the attack on the Northland army's exposed flank began in earnest. Fanning wide to the north, the fabled regiment lowered its hooked pikes and formed a wall three columns deep, charging into the center of the astonished enemy. Acton led his soldiers in a precision rush that cut deeply into the exposed flank and nearly routed the extreme right of the Northland army. As the little group atop the Outer Wall watched expectantly, the enemy instantly readjusted its lines to the right of center to meet this new attack; as they did so, Hendel immediately signaled down to Balinor. A second rampway was lowered from the center of the defensive lines, and the tall figure of Messaline was seen to appear at the head of a second regiment of Legion soldiers, who descended on foot onto the smoke-clouded grasslands. A rear guard remained posted at the foot of the mobile ramp as the second regiment disappeared into the dark haze. Balinor closed his defensive lines and hurriedly joined his friends atop the great wall to observe the outcome of his counterthrust.

It had been perfectly executed. Just as the surprised right flank of the massive Northland army wheeled to face the oncoming charge of the Border Legion's mounted regiment, the foot soldiers commanded by Messaline attacked from out of the smoke at the center of the defensive line. In a tightly drawn phalanx, with spears bristling through a wall of locked shields, the highly trained Legion advanced into the midst of the unprepared and confused enemy. Like cattle, the Northlanders were herded backward, scores dropping, dying and wounded every few paces. The horsemen of Acton continued to press in from the left. The entire right wing of the enemy line began to collapse, and the cries of terror grew so shrill that even the fierce assault on the right defensive flank wavered momentarily as the bewildered Northlanders stared westward in a vain effort to discover what had happened. From the summit of the Outer Wall, Menion Leah stared in amazement.

"It's unbelievable. The Legion is actually driving them back. They're beaten!"

"Not yet," breathed Hendel softly. "The real test comes in a moment."

The highlander's eyes returned to the battle. The Northlanders were still falling back before the onslaught of the attacking Legion, but there was fresh activity taking place behind the lines of the retreating enemy. The army of the Warlock Lord would not be defeated so easily; what it lacked in training, it made up for in size. Already a vast command of mounted Gnome horsemen was racing around the rear of the driven foot soldiers, called up to meet the attack of the Legion riders. The Gnomes drew up immediately north of Acton's advancing horsemen; supported by several lines of archers and slingers, they rushed to the attack. From the rear center of the enemy army, a vast body of tall figures sheathed entirely in armor had drawn into a tight, boxlike formation and had begun to advance through its own wilting army toward the Legion foot soldiers. For a moment, the men atop the Outer Wall stared speculatively, then started in astonishment as the armored warriors suddenly began to cut their way with pikes and swords through the retreating men of their own army. It was the most savage act Menion had ever witnessed.

"Rock Trolls!" Balinor exclaimed heatedly. "They'll slaughter Messaline and his whole command. Signal retreat, Janus."

Obediently, his newest commander hoisted a large red pennant on a nearby staff. Menion Leah stared curiously at the silent borderman. It seemed that the battle had been nearly won, and still he had called for a retreat. He caught the King's eye, and the borderman smiled grimly at the unspoken question in the highlander's eyes.

"Rock Trolls are trained to fight from birth—it's their way of life. In hand-to-hand combat, they are better fighters than the men of the Border Legion. They are better trained and much stronger physically. We have nothing to gain in pressing the attack. We've already hurt them badly, and we still hold the bluff. If we plan to defeat them, we must chip away at their strength a piece at a time."

Menion nodded in understanding. With a brief wave, Balinor left the battlements to return to his command below. His primary concern at the moment was protecting the path of retreat for his two regiments, and that meant a successful defense of the portable ramps, the soldiers' only link with the city. The highlander watched the broad figure disappear from view, then turned back to the wall. The carnage on the plains below was frightful. The bodies of slain and wounded men lay scattered all the way from the bluff face to the rear lines of the Northland army. It was the worst slaughter that any of the little group had ever witnessed, and they watched speechlessly as the terrible struggle continued.

In the distance, the Legion foot soldiers under Messaline's command had begun an orderly retreat back toward the city defenses, but the giant Rock Trolls had almost succeeded in forcing their way through the milling front ranks of their own army and were preparing to pursue the hated Tyrsians. While the foot soldiers were withdrawing without opposition, the mounted regiment had encountered unexpected resistance from the charging Gnome horsemen. The two forces were engaged in a fierce battle to the left of the advancing Trolls. Acton was apparently either unable or unwilling to break away from the persistent attackers, and his riders were being subjected to a withering cross fire from the double line of Gnome archers positioned directly to his north. A large mixed body of Gnome and Troll swordsmen had worked their way around behind the charging horsemen, and now Acton's command was boxed in on three sides.

Hendel began to mutter angrily to himself. For the first time, Menion became concerned. Even Janus Senpre was pacing the walkway nervously. Their worst fears were realized a moment later. The pursuing body of Trolls, fresh for the wearing chase, had rushed forward so rapidly that the retreating men of Tyrsis, tired and worn from their counterattack, had been unable to gain the safety of the bluff. Almost a hundred yards from the waiting rampway, they turned to fight. The billowing smoke from the scattered fires rolled like a black wall in front of the low bulwarks, completely obscuring Balinor's vision as he waited before the city gates, but the unexpected turn of events was clearly visible to the horrified men watching from atop the towering city wall.

"I've got to warn Balinor!" Hendel exclaimed abruptly, leaping down from his position on the parapets. "That whole command will be cut to pieces!"

Janus Senpre left with him, but Menion and the Elven brothers continued to stare helplessly, unable to tear themselves away as the giant Rock Trolls bore down on Messaline's weary men. The Legion soldiers had drawn together with shields locked and spears extended, the shafts braced against the hard earth for the rush. The Trolls, too, had gone into a phalanx formation, somewhat wider than it was long, their intention clearly to close in on the Southlanders from three sides and break their defense by sheer strength. Menion glanced hastily over the wall, but Balinor had not moved, still unaware that an entire regiment of the famed Border Legion was on the verge of annihilation. Even as the highlander shifted his glance back to the plainlands, he saw Hendel and Janus reach the tall borderman's side, gesturing wildly. It would not be in time, Menion shouted inwardly. They were going to be too late.

But suddenly a strange thing happened. Acton's entire mounted command, momentarily forgotten by the viewers on the city wall, unexpectedly broke away from the attacking Gnome horsemen with an abrupt surge and came together in perfect formation, swinging in a sharp arc directly east behind the pursuing Rock Trolls. At a full gallop, the superb horsemen cut through the Gnome riders who barred their way. Oblivious to the hail of arrows showered down from the enraged Gnome archers, they raced directly toward the Troll ranks. Pikes lowered, the regiment struck the rear lines of the Troll phalanx in a raking movement, continuing its sweep eastward across the plains. The giant warriors were caught by surprise and dozens crumpled to the ground as the pikes cut into them.

But these were the finest fighting men in the world, and they recovered instantly, closing their ranks and turning to meet this new threat. As Acton's horsemen swung westward once more, racing back at breakneck speed, raking across the rear of the Troll phalanx a second time, the Northlanders struck back viciously with hurled pikes and maces. Over a dozen riders fell lifelessly from their mounts, and an equal number slumped wounded in their saddles as the regiment charged eastward and then cut sharply south for the safety of Tyrsis.

Acton had accomplished his purpose; the timely diversion had permitted Messaline's besieged regiment to make a sudden break for the concealing smoke. It was a brilliantly executed maneuver, and atop the Outer Wall those watching shouted with unrestrained admiration.

Though pursued by the foremost ranks of the infuriated Trolls, the Legion foot soldiers had escaped into the concealing smoke, and most, with the aid of Balinor at the head of a relief squad, gained the safety of the waiting ramp. A sharp battle was fought at the foot of the bluff as the regiment struggled to withdraw the lowered bridge before the enemy could seize it. Finally, it was simply cast loose from the bulwarks and dropped onto the plain below, where it lay intact only moments before the Tyrsians set it ablaze and destroyed it.

On the left defensive flank, the embattled rear guard fought bravely to hold the other rampway, as Acton's command raced still another time within range of the maddened Gnome archers and still more died. It was a running battle all the way, and at one point the horsemen had to charge directly through the center of a thin line of swordsmen that rushed down to cut off their escape. But at last the harried riders reached the haven of the bluff, galloping up the rampway almost without slowing and swinging toward the opened gates of the city, where they were greeted by crowds of cheering soldiers and citizens. As the last of the returning cavalry gained the heights, the rear guard hastily withdrew behind their defenses and the rampway was hauled to safety.

It was midday by this time, and the heat of the noon sun settled like a humid blanket over the men of both armies. In sullen reluctance, the Northland army withdrew from the battle to regroup, dragging with it hundreds of dead and wounded. The smoke from the burning oil hung in an unmoving haze over the strangely silent grasslands as the morning wind faded quietly away. The ground before the bluff face was littered with the charred bodies of the dead, and small fires still burned persistently as the great timbers of the shattered rampways turned slowly to ashes. A foul stench began to rise from the terrible battlefield, and scavengers that flew and crawled appeared with shrill, eager cries to feast.

Across the battered land, the armies watched each other with undisguised hatred, weary and racked with pain, but eager to resume the killing that had been thrust upon them. For several long hours, the once green land lay empty beneath the cloudless blue sky as its scarred surface baked and dried in the heat of the summer sun. It began to appear to those who allowed their reason to slip in favor of wishful thinking that the assault had ended—that the destruction was finished. Thoughts turned hopefully from killing and survival to family and loved ones. The shadow of death lifted momentarily.

Then in the late hours of the waning afternoon, the Northland army attacked again. As lines of Gnome archers showered the low bulwarks and the bluff beyond with a seemingly endless barrage of arrows, large bands of mixed swordsmen, Gnome and Troll, made sharp rushes at the Southland defenses, trying vainly to discover a weak point. Portable ramps, small scaling ladders, and grappling hooks with knotted ropes—all were tried to force a breach in the Legion lines, but each time the attackers were repelled. It was a wearing, vicious assault designed to tire and discourage the men of Tyrsis. The long day died slowly into dusk, and still the pitched battle wore on. It ended in darkness and tragedy for the Border Legion. As twilight descended on the bloodied land, the weary foes launched a final hail of spears and arrows at one another across the hazy void they could scarcely see through. A stray arrow caught Acton through the throat as the Legion cavalry commander was returning from his command on the left defensive flank, knocking the great fighter from his mount into the reaching arms of his attendants, where he died moments later.

The kingdom of the Warlock Lord was the single most desolate, forbidding piece of country in the known world—a barren, lifeless ring of impassable death traps. The tender, life-giving hand of nature had long since been driven from this thankless domain of darkness, and the wilderness that remained lay wrapped in silence. Its eastern borders were mired in the gloom and fetid stench of the vast Malg Swamp, a dismal, sprawling bog that no living creature had ever successfully traversed. Beneath the shallow waters, on which floated loose patches of colorless weeds that grew and died in the span of a day, the earth had turned to mud and quicksand, and all that came within its grip were sucked quickly from sight. The Malg was said to be bottomless, and while, scattered throughout its vast expanse, small bits of solid earth and great, skeletal limbs of dying trees could still be glimpsed, even these were fading one by one.

Across the far northern stretches, extending westward from the Malg, was a rambling series of low-backed mountains appropriately named the Razors. There were no passes through these mountains and their wide, sloped backs were craggy, jutting slabs of rock, seemingly pushed upward from the bowels of the earth. An experienced and determined climber might still have found the Razors passable—one or two men had even made the attempt—had it not been for the particularly venomous species of spider that nested in vast numbers throughout the barren mountains. The bleached bones of the dead, scattered in small white patches among the darkened rocks, gave mute testimony to their unavoidable presence.

There was a break in the deadly ring where the Razors tapered off into foothills at the northwest corner of the kingdom, and for over five miles southward the country was easily passable, opening directly into the center of the circle of barriers. Here there was no natural protection against intruders, but this small gateway to the interior of the kingdom was also the obvious approach, and hence the trapdoor to the cage through which the Lord and Master waited for the unwary to step. Eyes and ears responsive only to his command guarded the narrow strip of land carefully. The ring could be locked instantly. Directly below the foothills, a vast, arid wasteland called the Kierlak Desert ran southward for nearly fifty miles. A heavy, poisonous vapor hung invisibly over the sprawling, sand-covered plains, drawn from the waters of the River Lethe, a venomous stream that wound lazily into the fiery emptiness from the south and emptied into a small lake in the interior. Even birds chancing to fly too close to the deadly haze were killed in seconds. Creatures dying in the terrible furnace of sand and poisonous air decayed in a matter of hours and turned to dust, so that nothing remained to show their passing.

But the most formidable barrier of all stretched menacingly across the southern boundary of the forbidden domain, beginning at the southeast-erly edges of the Kierlak Desert and running eastward to the marshy bor-ders of the Malg Swamp. The Knife Edge. Like great stone spears driven into the hard earth by some monstrous giant, these mountains towered thousands of feet into the sky. They had the appearance not so much of mountains as a series of awesome peaks jutting in broken lines that blocked the dim horizon like fingers stretching painfully. At their base swirled the toxic waters of the River Lethe, which had its origin in the Malg Swamp and meandered westward at the base of the great rock bar-rier to disappear into the impregnable vapors of the Kierlak Desert. Only a man driven by an unexplainable madness would have attempted to scale the Knife Edge.

There was a passage through the barrier, a small, winding canyon that opened onto a series of craggy foothills which ran for several thousand yards to the base of a single, ominously solitary mountain just within the southern boundary of the ring. The scarred surface of this mountain was chipped and worn by time and the elements, lending the southern facing a singularly menacing appearance. On even the most casual inspection, one was immediately struck by the frightening similarity the south wall bore to a human skull, stripped of flesh and life, the pate rounded and gleaming above the empty sockets of the eyes, the cheeks sunken, and the jaw a crooked line of bared teeth and bone. This was the home of the Lord and Master. This was the kingdom of Brona, the Warlock Lord. Everywhere it bore the stamp of the Skull, the indelible mark of death.

It was midday, but time seemed strangely suspended, and the vast, wasted fortress lay wrapped in a peculiar stillness. The familiar grayness screened the sun and sky, and the drab brownish terrain of rock and earth lay stripped of mortal life. Yet there was something more in the air this day, cutting through the silence and the emptiness to the flesh and blood of the men in the winding column passing through the single gateway in the massive Knife Edge. It was a pressing sense of urgency that hung poised over the blasted face of the kingdom of the Warlock Lord, as if events to come had rushed through time too quickly and, jammed together in eager anticipation, waited for their moment.

The Trolls shuffled guardedly through the twisting canyon, their comparatively huge frames dwarfed by the towering heights of the peaks so that they appeared little more than ants in the sprawling, ageless rock. They entered the kingdom of the dead the way in which little children enter an unfamiliar dark room, inwardly frightened, hesitant, but nevertheless determined to see what lay beyond. They marched unchallenged, though not unseen. They were expected. Their appearance came as no surprise, and they entered without danger of harm from the minions of the Master. Their impassive faces disguised their true intentions or they would never have passed the southern shores of the River Lethe. For in their midst was the last of a bloodline the Spirit King had thought destroyed, the last son of the Elven house of Shannara.

Shea marched directly behind the broad frame of Keltset, his hands seemingly tied at his back. Panamon Creel followed, his arms similarly bound, the gray eyes dangerous as they stared watchfully at the great rock walls on either side of the winding column. The ruse had worked perfectly. Apparent captives of the Rock Trolls, the two Southlanders had been marched to the shores of the River Lethe, the sluggish, vile stream that flanked the southernmost borders of the Skull Kingdom. The Trolls and their silent charges had boarded a wide-backed raft of rotted wood and rusted iron spikes, whose voiceless captain was a bent, hooded creature who seemed more beast than man, his face shielded in the folds of the musty black cloak, but his hooked, scale-covered hands clearly visible as they fastened tightly on the crooked leverage pole and guided the ancient craft across the tepid, poison waters. The uneasy passengers felt a growing sense of revulsion from the mere presence of their pilot and were openly relieved when, after finally permitting them to disembark on the far shore, he vanished with his ancient barge into the haze that lay across the dark river waters. The lower Northland was now entirely lost to them, the grayness so heavily disseminated through the stale, dry air that nothing beyond the river was visible. In contrast, the soaring, blackened cliffs of the Knife Edge loomed starkly before them, the great fingers of rock brushing the mist aside in the half-light of the northern midday. The party passed wordlessly through the corridor that split the vast heights, winding deeper into the forbidden domain of the Warlock Lord.

The Warlock Lord. Somehow Shea felt that he had known from the very beginning, from the day Allanon had told him of his remarkable ancestry, that it would happen this way—that circumstances would demand he face this awesome creature who was trying so desperately to destroy him. Time and events merged into a single instant, a flash of jumbled memories of the long days spent in flight, running to stay alive, running toward this frightening confrontation. Now the moment was drawing near, and he would face it virtually alone in the most savage land in the known world, his oldest, most trusted friends scattered, his only companions a band of Rock Trolls, an outcast thief and a vengeful, enigmatic giant. The latter had persuaded the tribunal to place under his command a detachment of Troll warriors, not so much because they believed that the insignificant Valeman accompanying him somehow possessed the ability to destroy the immortal Brona as because their massive kinsman was the holder of the honored Black Irix.

The three judges had also revealed the fate of Orl Fane. The Trolls had seized the little fugitive about an hour before his determined pursuers had been taken captive, and he had been marched under guard to the main encampment. The Maturen tribunal had quickly concluded that the Gnome was completely mad. He had babbled insanely to them of secrets and treasures, his wizened yellow face contorted in a hideous fixed grin. At times he had appeared to be talking to the air about him, brushing violently at his bare arms and legs as if living things had fastened there. His sole link with reality seemed to be the ancient sword that was his only possession, the sword he clung to so violently that his captors could not pry it free. They allowed him to keep the worthless piece of metal, binding his clenched yellow hands to its rusted sheath. Within the hour he was taken north to the dungeons of the Warlock Lord.

The canyon wound wickedly through the towering peaks of the Knife Edge, at times dwindling from a broad trailway to little more than a split in the rocks. The burly Trolls scrambled through the twisting passage without resting. A few had been there before, and they led the others at a steady, tiring pace. Speed was essential. If they delayed too long, the Spirit King would hear that Orl Fane and the ancient weapon he refused to release, even for the briefest moment, were safely shut away in the Warlock Lord's own dungeons.

Shea shuddered at the possibility. It might already have happened— they could be walking straight to their own execution. Each time before on the long journey from Culhaven, the Warlock Lord had seemed to know every move they had made; each time he had been waiting for them. It was madness—this terrible risk! And even if they did succeed, even if Shea finally held the Sword of Shannara within his grasp . . . why, what then? Shea laughed inwardly. Could he face the Warlock Lord without Allanon beside him, without any idea what would trigger the hidden power of the legendary talisman? No one would even know he had the Sword.

The Valeman had no idea what the others intended, but he had already determined that if by some miracle he could get his hands on the elusive weapon, he was going to run for his life. Everyone else could do as he wished. He was certain that Panamon Creel would have approved of the plan, but the two had scarcely exchanged ten words since the journey to the Skull Kingdom had begun. Shea sensed that for the first time in Panamon's life, a life composed primarily of narrow escapes and hair-raising escapades, the scarlet-clad thief was frightened. But he had gone with Keltset and Shea—gone because they were his only friends, gone because his pride would let him do no less. His most basic instinct was to survive at any cost, but he would not permit himself to be shamed even to stay alive.

Keltset's reasons for this dangerous undertaking were less apparent. Shea thought he understood why the giant Troll had quietly insisted that they must retrieve the Sword of Shannara, and it was much more than personal vengeance for the slaughter of his family. There was something about Keltset that reminded Shea of Balinor—a quiet confidence that lent strength to those less certain. Shea had felt it when Keltset indicated that they must go after Orl Fane and the Sword. Those gentle, intelligent eyes told the Valeman that he believed in him, and while Shea could not explain it in rational terms, he knew he had to go with his giant friend. If he turned away now, after the long weeks spent searching for the Sword of Shannara, he would be betraying both his friends and himself.

The cliff walls on either side fell away abruptly, and the canyon opened into a sloping valley that seemed like a wide depression in the rugged interior of the Skull Kingdom, its surface barren and dry, the earth broken by a scattering of rocky hillocks and dry riverbeds. The party halted silently, every pair of eyes involuntarily drawn to the solitary mountain in the bowl of the little valley, the southern face staring sightlessly at them from two huge, empty sockets that resembled the eyes of a skull. The blasted face waited in timeless anticipation for the coming of the Master. Standing at the mouth of the draw, Shea felt the hair on the back of his neck rise and a sudden chill surge through his small frame.

From out of the rocks to either side, a number of misshapen, lumbering creatures shuffled, their great bodies as drab as the dying land, their faces nearly featureless. Once they might have been human, but they were no longer so. They stood upright on two legs and two arms swung aimlessly at their sides, but the resemblance ended there. Their skin was the texture of chalky putty, almost rubbery in appearance, and they moved in the manner of mindless beings. Like apparitions out of some frightening nightmare, the strange creatures came all around the Trolls, staring blankly into their barklike faces as if to be certain of what manner of creatures had come to them. Keltset turned slightly and motioned to Panamon Creel.

"The Trolls call them Mutens," the adventurer whispered quietly. "Stand easy—remember that you are supposed to be a prisoner. Stay calm."

One of the misshapen beings spoke in rasping tones to the lead Trolls, gesturing briefly at the two bound men. There was a short exchange, and then one of the Trolls said something over his shoulder to Keltset, who immediately motioned for Shea and Panamon to follow him. The trio detached themselves from the main group. Accompanied by two other Trolls, they silently followed one of the lumbering Mutens as he turned and moved rather unsteadily toward the inner cliff wall to their left.

Shea glanced back once and observed the Trolls scattering idly to either side of the canyon entrance, seemingly waiting for their companions to return. The remaining Mutens had not moved. Looking ahead once more, the Valeman saw that the cliff face was split by a long fissure that ran several hundred feet up and that this gap was a passage to something beyond. The little group moved into the rock wall, their eyes trying to adjust to the sudden darkness. There was a pause as their guide took a torch from a wall rack and lit it, handing it absently to one of the Trolls before proceeding. Apparently his own eyes were accustomed to the inky darkness, for he continued to lead them.

The party passed into a dank, foul-smelling cavern that branched out into several fathomless passageways. From somewhere far away, Shea thought he detected the faint, chilling sound of screams ringing over and over as echoes against the rock walls. Panamon cursed harshly in the flickering torchlight, his broad face streaked with sweat. The silent, heedless Muten shuffled ahead into one of the passages, and the faint light from the fissure opening faded into blackness.

The lingering echo of booted feet on rock was the only sound as the men moved down the darkened corridor, their eyes wandering briefly to the windowless iron doors bolted into the face of the rock on both sides of the passageway. The screams still rang faintly in their ears, but they seemed more distant now. There were no human sounds from the cells they were passing. Finally the guide halted before one of the heavy doors, gesturing briefly and speaking in the same guttural tones to the Trolls. He turned to continue down the passage and had taken his first step when the foremost Troll brought his great iron mace crashing down on the creature's bulky head. The Muten dropped lifelessly to the cave floor. Keltset moved to loosen the ropes binding Shea and Panamon as the two remaining Trolls stood watchfully before the cell door. When his friends were freed, the massive Northlander moved catlike to the iron door and slid the latches clear of their loops. Grasping the bars, he pulled on the ancient door. With a sharp grating sound, the heavy portal swung open.

"Now we shall see," breathed Panamon harshly. Taking the light from Keltset, he stepped cautiously into the tiny room, his two companions close behind.

Orl Fane sat hunched against the far wall, his scrawny legs shackled in chains that were bolted into the rock flooring, his clothing torn and dirtied almost beyond recognition. He was clearly not the same creature they had captured several days earlier on the Plains of Streleheim. He stared at the three faces with mindless disregard, his thin, yellow face fixed in a hideous grin as he babbled meaninglessly to himself. His eyes were strangely dilated in the bright torchlight, and he glanced all about as he talked, behaving as if there were others in the little cell, creatures invisible to all eyes but his own.

The two men and the giant Troll took in his condition at a glance, their eyes traveling instantly to the bony hands that still clutched possessively the battered leather and metal scabbard that sheathed the elusive object of their long pursuit. The ancient hilt flickered back dully in the torchlight, giving them a shadowy image of the raised hand holding the burning torch. They had found it. They had found the Sword of Shannara!

For a moment no one moved as the maddened Gnome clutched the Sword closer to his emaciated frame, his eyes showing a momentary flicker of recognition as he caught sight of the sharp pike glinting at the stumped end of Panamon's slowly raising arm. The adventurer stepped forward menacingly and bent close to the Gnome's thin face.

"I've come for you, Gnome," he said harshly.

Orl Fane seemed to undergo a sudden transformation at the sound of Panamon Creel's voice, and a frightened shriek escaped his lips as he struggled to move farther back.

"Give me the Sword, you treacherous rat!" the thief demanded.

Without waiting for a response, he seized the weapon, trying to wrest it from the now thoroughly terrified Gnome's astonishingly strong grip. But even with death staring him directly in the eye, Orl Fane would not give up his precious possession. His voice rose to a scream, and in sudden fury, Panamon brought the heavy iron binding on his piked hand down across the little fellow's unprotected skull. The Gnome crumpled unconscious to the cold floor.

"All those days we chased this miserable creature!" Panamon cried. He stopped abruptly and lowered his voice to a harsh whisper. "I thought I would at least have the pleasure of watching him die, but . . . it's no longer worth it."

In disgust, he reached for the hilt of the Sword, intent on drawing it from its binding, but Keltset stepped forward and placed a restraining hand on his shoulder. Still angered, the thief stared back coldly as the Rock Troll motioned silently toward the watching Shea, then both stepped back.

The Sword of Shannara was Shea's birthright, but he hesitated. He had come so far, been through so much, all for this moment—and now he found himself afraid. He felt cold inside as he looked at the ancient weapon. For an instant, he considered refusing, knowing that a part of him could not accept the awesome responsibility that he was being asked to assume—a responsibility that had been forced on him. He recalled in a flash the terrible power of the three Elfstones. What then of the power of the Sword of Shannara? In his mind he pictured the faces of Flick and Menion and the others who had fought so hard to gain possession of the Sword for him. If he turned away now, he would have betrayed the trust they had extended him. In effect, he would be telling them that everything they had gone through for him had been pointless. He saw again the dark, enigmatic face of Allanon chastising him for his foolish ideals, his refusal to see men for what they were. He would have to answer to him as well, and Allanon would not be pleased. . . .

Woodenly he moved to the fallen Orl Fane and bent over him, his fingers closing firmly around the cold metal hilt of the weapon, feeling the raised image of the burning torch in his sweating palm. He paused. Then slowly he drew forth the Sword of Shannara.

The second day of the battle for Tyrsis bore witness to the same wholesale slaughter of the men of the Northland army as the first. The giant invasion force attacked at dawn, marching toward the face of the bluff in precision formation to the deep booming of the Gnome war drums, pausing in silence within a hundred yards; then, with an ear-shattering yell, the army rushed headlong into the terrible struggle to gain the heights. With the same utter disregard for their own lives, the attackers threw themselves in wave after wave against the outer defenses of the en-trenched Border Legion. They came without the aid of the monstrous rampways, which there had been no time to rebuild, relying instead on thousands of small scaling ladders and grappling irons. It was a ferocious, merciless, and bitter contest. Hundreds of the Northlanders died in the first few minutes.

With Acton gone, Balinor did not choose to risk the Legion mounted command a second time in counterattacking the massive enemy army. He decided instead to dig in on the bluff face and hold his position as long as possible. Burning oil and the Legion archers shredded the first waves of the assault, but this time the attackers did not break apart and run. They came in an endless, sustained charge, finally eluding both arrows and flames to reach the base of the wide plateau where scaling ladders were thrown against the bluff. Swarms of screaming Northlanders struggled up-ward and the fighting was reduced to basic hand-to-hand combat.

For nearly eight hours the valiant defenders of Tyrsis repelled an enemy twenty times its size. Scaling ladders and grappling hooks were me-thodically shattered and cut apart, Northlanders were pushed away as quickly as they gained the summit, and momentary holes in the defense lines were closed before a breach could be opened. The acts of bravery performed by individual members of the famed Legion were too numerous to recount. They fought against impossible odds without rest, without relief, knowing all the while that no quarter would be given them by the enemy, should they fail. For eight hours the enraged Northland army struggled to break through the Legion bulwarks without success. But finally a breach was opened on the defensive left flank. With a ragged shout of victory, the enemy rushed onto the bluff.

After the death of Acton, the aged Fandwick had been left in sole command of this section of the defensive lines. Calling on his diminished reserves, the Legion commander moved to block the Northland rush. An intense, fierce battle raged in the open breach for long minutes as the determined attackers battled to hold and enlarge the newly gained opening. Dozens died on both sides, including the valiant Fandwick.

Balinor rushed more reserves from the center of the line in an effort to close the breach, and he finally succeeded. But moments later a second and then a third hole opened in the left defensive flank, and the whole command began to waiver and break apart. The King of Callahorn realized his army could no longer hold the outer defenses, and passed the word to his remaining commanders to begin an orderly retreat into the city. Rallying the crumbling left flank, the giant borderman drew in his outermost defenses while holding the enemy at bay, and quickly moved the entire command into the city.

It was a bitter moment for the Southlanders, who now rushed to defend the great Outer Wall. But the Northland army did not advance to the attack. Instead, they began tearing down the defensive bulwarks and moving them inward on the bluff face, where they constructed their own defensive position, just out of range of the Legion archers. The weary soldiers of the Border Legion watched silently from atop the city walls as the sunlit afternoon turned slowly to dusk above the busy invaders. The Northland camp was moved forward to the plains below the city and the army began to light its watch fires as darkness closed in around them.

In the final moments of daylight, the enemy revealed a portion of its plan to scale the walls of Tyrsis. Great, sloping rampways from the plains to the bluff were hurriedly set in place, supported by stone and timber over the remains of the shattered walkways. Then from out of the twilight, three massive siege towers rolled into view, each one easily the height of the Outer Wall. The towers were moved to the rear of the enemy encampment within plain view of the city and anchored for the night. It was clearly a piece of psychological warfare designed to unnerve the besieged Border Legion.

From above the gates to the city, Balinor watched impassively with his Legion commanders and his companions from Culhaven. He toyed briefly with the idea of a night assault against the encamped Northlanders for the express purpose of burning the siege towers, but quickly discarded it. They would expect him to try something like that, and the city gates would undoubtedly be under careful watch the entire night. Besides, it would be no problem for the Legion to set fire to these towers as easily as they had fired the rampways, once they were moved to the attack.

Balinor shook his head and frowned. There was something very wrong about the whole Northland attack concept but he couldn't put his finger on it. Surely they must be aware that the siege towers would never enable them to breach the city's Outer Wall. They had to have something else in mind. He wondered for the hundredth time whether the Elven army would reach the beleaguered city in time. He could not believe that Eventine would fail them. It was dark now and, after ordering a double watch on all sectors of the wall, he invited the men with him to share dinner.

Concealed in a grove of trees on the summit of a low ridge several miles west of Tyrsis, a small band of horsemen surveyed the carnage of the terrible battle below them as evening settled in. They watched silently as the huge siege towers were wheeled into position at the rear of the Northland army for the morning assault on the fortress city.

"We should get a message to them," Jon Lin Sandor whispered quietly. "Balinor will want to know that our army is on its way."

Flick glanced expectantly at the bandaged figure of Eventine. The strange eyes seemed to burn as he studied the besieged city.

"I trust the army is on its way," the Elven King muttered almost inaudibly. "Breen has been gone almost three days. If he has not returned by tomorrow, I'll go myself."

His friend placed an understanding hand on the King's good shoulder.

"You are in no condition to travel, Eventine. Your brother will not fail you. Balinor is a seasoned fighter and the walls of Tyrsis have never been breached by an invader in the lifetime of the city. The Legion can defend long enough."

There was a long moment of silence. Flick looked back at the darkened city and wondered if his friends were all right. Menion must be inside those walls, too. The highlander could not know what had befallen Flick, nor what had happened to Eventine. Nor for that matter what had become of the unpredictable Allanon, who for no apparent reason at all had disappeared shortly after the Valeman's return with the Elven search party. While the Druid had been purposely vague about a great many things since his appearance in Shady Vale, he had never gone off without an explanation. Perhaps he had spoken with Eventine. . . .

"The city is encircled and guarded." Eventine's voice broke out of the growing darkness. "It would be extremely difficult to get past their lines even long enough to get a message to Balinor. But you're right, Jon Lin—he should know we have not forgotten him."

"We don't have a large enough force to break through to Tyrsis or even to strike the rear guard of the Northlanders," his friend declared thoughtfully. "But . . ."

He looked quickly at the dark bulk of the siege towers standing deserted on the plains below.

"A small gesture," finished the King meaningfully.

It was not yet midnight when Balinor was hurriedly summoned to the watchtower above the gates to the city. Moments later he stood speechless on the ramparts in the company of Hendel, Menion, Durin, and Dayel and stared down upon the chaos spreading through the half-wakened enemy camp. To the rear of the sprawling encampment, the centermost of the three giant siege towers was a burning pyre that lit the grasslands for miles. Frantic Northlanders rushed wildly over the timbers of the adjoining towers, desperately trying to prevent the flames from spreading. It was obvious that the invader had been taken completely by surprise. Balinor looked at the others and smiled wryly. Help was not so distant after all.

The morning of the third day dawned with a sullen stillness that hung shroudlike over the land of Callahorn and the armies of the North and South. Gone was the mighty crashing of the Gnome drums, the muffled thudding of booted feet marching to the battle, and the thunderous yells of attack. The sun rose fiery red in the distant east, the dark hue spreading across the fading night like blood. A deep haze clouded the dew-covered face of the land. There was a complete absence of movement, of sound. On the walls of Tyrsis, the soldiers of the Border Legion waited nervously, their eyes peering blankly into the gloom for signs of the enemy.

Balinor was in command of the center section of the Outer Wall. Ginnisson held the right and Messaline the left. Janus Senpre again commanded the city garrison and the reserves. Menion, Hendel, and the Elven brothers stood silently at Balinor's side and shivered in the cold of early morning. They had rested poorly, but they felt unusually alert and strangely calm. They had quietly accepted their situation during the past forty-eight hours. They had seen men die by the thousands, and their own lives seemed almost insignificant compared to the terrible carnage that had engulfed this ancient land—yet very precious at the same time. The grasslands beneath the city were torn and rutted, the earth discolored with blood and littered with death. There was nothing to look forward to but more of the same, and still more, until one army or the other was destroyed. Forgotten for all the defenders of Tyrsis was the moral purpose behind the word survival; war had become a mechanical reflex that served as its own excuse for the acts men performed.

The bloodred of the morning sun grew sharper, and now the shapes of men and horses came into focus as the Northland army was rediscovered, a maze of carefully drawn formations spread all across the expanse of yesterday's battlefield from the bluff defenses to beyond the charred timbers of two fallen siege towers. They did not move; they did not speak. They simply waited. Hendel recognized what was happening and whispered hurriedly to Balinor. Swiftly, the Legion Commander sent runners along the walls to his subordinates, warning them of what was expected, cautioning them to keep their soldiers calm and in place.

Menion was about to ask what was happening when suddenly there was movement on the bluff immediately below the city gates. A single armored warrior walked slowly out of the gloom, tall, erect, to stand before the giant wall. In one hand he carried a long staff with a single red pennant. With slow, deliberate movements he planted the pole in the earth, then stepped back ceremoniously, turned and strode back into his lines. Again there was a moment of complete silence. The long, low, wailing cry of a distant horn sounded mournfully across the plains—once, twice, a third time. Then silence.

"The death watch." Hendel broke the stillness with a hushed whisper. "It means we're to be given no quarter. They intend to kill us all."

The air was rent violently by the sudden crashing of Gnome war drums, and everyone began moving at once. With a rush, thousands of Gnome arrows filled the sky, sweeping downward to the ramparts of the city walls. Spears, pikes, and maces flew upward from charging Northlanders. Out of the haze of the plains below appeared the bulk of the one remaining siege tower, groaning and creaking with its own ponderous weight as hundreds of the enemy pulled and pushed the towering monster up the newly constructed rampway toward the Outer Wall. From within the city, Legion archers fired down upon the darting forms of their attackers as the balance of the men of the Border Legion hugged the stone of the defenses and waited for Balinor's order.

The giant borderman waited until the massive siege tower was within twenty-five yards of the wall. Already the enemy was attempting to scale the great barrier with grappling hooks and ladders, and the rough stone was dotted with clinging figures vainly scrambling toward the summit. Abruptly the cauldrons of oil poured downward from the ramparts, splashing over man and machine alike to saturate the bluff face immediately below. Burning torches followed, and instantly the entire front of the Northland assault force was engulfed in flames. The siege tower and the men around it simply disappeared as the black smoke billowed skyward, blotting out for the Legion defenders the carnage below them, but not the shrieks of terror and agony. The attackers attempting to scale the Outer Wall were trapped. A few managed to reach the ramparts where they were quickly dispatched, but most simply lost their hold or were overcome by the heavy smoke and dropped screaming into the fire.

Within minutes the assault was broken and the entire Northland army had again completely disappeared from view. The men on the ramparts peered watchfully into the swirling smoke, vainly trying to discover what form the next assault would take. Balinor looked at his companions and shook his head doubtfully.

"That was utter foolishness. They must have known what would happen—yet they came ahead anyway. Are they mad?"

"Perhaps they did it to confuse us . . ." muttered Hendel quietly. "Like this smoke screen we so obligingly provided them with."

"All that dying just to get a smoke screen?" Menion exclaimed incredulously.

"If so, then they have something very definite in mind—something they are certain cannot fail," declared Balinor. "Keep an eye on things here. I'm going down to the gates."

He turned away abruptly and disappeared down the winding stone stairway almost at a run. The others watched him go without comment and turned back to the wall. In front of them, thick clouds of the heavy black smoke still rose skyward as the oil on the plains continued to burn. The cries of death had ceased and there was a strange silence.

"What are they up to?" Menion voiced the question at last.

For a moment there was no response at all.

"I wish we had been able to catch Stenmin," Durin muttered at last. "I haven't felt safe even behind these walls with that madman running loose somewhere in the city."

"We almost had him," Dayel interjected quickly. "We followed him into that room, but he seemed to disappear into thin air. There must have been a secret passage."

Durin nodded in agreement and the conversation dropped off again. Menion stared into the smoke and thought about Shirl waiting for him at the palace, about Shea, Flick, his father, and his homeland—all in a rush of images that flooded his wandering mind. How was it all going to end for them?

"Shades!" Hendel jerked him around so sharply that he was momentarily startled. "I've been a fool. It was right in front of me all the time. A secret passage! In the basement of the palace, beneath the wine cellar, in the dungeons sealed off all these years—a passageway that leads through the mountains to the plain beyond. The old King spoke of it once to me, years and years ago. Stenmin must know of it!"

"A way into the city!" exclaimed Menion. "They'll catch us with our backs to them." He paused sharply. "Hendel! Shirl's back there!"

"We don't have much time." Hendel was already starting down the steps. "Menion, come with me. Dayel, find Janus Senpre and tell him to get help to us at the palace immediately. Durin, find Balinor and warn him. Hurry now, and pray we're not too late."

They were down the worn stairs in a rush, scattering across the barracks ground as if possessed. Hendel and Menion broke into a dead run, pushing their way heedlessly through clusters of soldiers toward the gates to the Tyrsian Way. Too slow, Menion's harried brain screamed at him! He nearly jerked Hendel off his feet in an effort to turn him toward a small group of saddled reserve mounts tethered to their right. Knocking an interfering attendant aside without pausing, the duo leaped into the saddles of the two nearest mounts and wheeled them toward the city. At a gallop, the horses tore through the open gateway, past the flustered guards, past swarms of reserves posted just inside the gates; with the path cleared, they raced at breakneck speed for the palace.

Everything that followed seemed to come in a rush that negated time and space. People and buildings flashed by them in a blur as the two horsemen galloped over the ancient stones of the Tyrsian Way. Precious moments were lost and then the wide arc of the Bridge of Sendic loomed in the distance, spanning the People's Park to the palace of the Buckhannahs.

A train of baggage carts scattered wildly at the foot of the bridge as the two riders tore past them without slowing, racing their mounts across the stone arch toward the open gates of the monarchial home. Dashing into the garden-ringed courtyard, Hendel and Menion drew their sweating horses up sharply and vaulted to the ground.

Everything was silent. Nothing seemed amiss. A single attendant strolled almost leisurely out of the shadows of a great willow to take the reins from the heated riders, his eyes reflecting only mild curiosity. Hendel gave the man a sharp glance and dismissed him, beckoning Menion after him as he moved hurriedly toward the front doors. Still nothing. Maybe they were in time. Maybe they were even mistaken . . .

The hallways of the ancestral manor loomed empty and silent as the two searchers paused once more in the foyer, casting quick glances at open doorways and deep alcoves, drawn tapestries and curtained windows. Menion turned to find Shirl, but his companion stopped him with a word. The red-haired daughter of kings would have to wait. Slowly now, on cat's feet, the little man led the anxious highlander down the opposite passageway toward the cellar door. At the bend in the corridor they hesitated, then flattening themselves against the polished woodwork, peered cautiously around the corner.

The massive, ironbound door to the now-familiar wine cellar stood ajar. In the open entryway, three armed men kept watch over the vacant hall. All bore the insignia of the falcon. Menion and Hendel drew back silently. For the first time, the Prince of Leah realized he was unarmed. He had left the sword of Leah hanging from the saddle pommel of his horse. Quickly he scanned the hall behind him, his eyes coming to rest at last on a set of crossed pikes fastened to the far wall. A pike was hardly the weapon he needed, but he had no other choice. Noiselessly, he retrieved one unwieldy lance and rejoined Hendel. A long look passed between them. They would have to be quick. If the cellar door were to be closed and fastened from within before they could reach it, they would have lost their chance at Stenmin and the passageway. In any event, they were only two. How many more of the enemy awaited them below?

They didn't stop to consider it further. In a sudden rush, they were out of hiding and down the hallway. The three guards barely had time to look around before their attackers were upon them. Menion shoved his lance through the man nearest the doorway and was on top of the second a moment later. The final guard dropped soundlessly before Hendel's great mace. It was over almost before it had started and the two fighters were through the cellar entryway, charging down the worn stone steps to meet the most deadly battle of their lives.

The ancient wine cellar was ablaze with torchlight. The small fires seemed to burn from every wall, cutting through the musty darkness like hazy sunlight in early morning. In the center of the vast chamber, the great stone trapdoor that led to the forgotten dungeons below was thrown open, and from out of the darkness of the pit came the distant sounds of metal striking stone. The cellar was swarming with armed men and they came at the two intruders from all directions.

Hendel and Menion met the rush with a ferocious counterassault that carried them into the very midst of their assailants. The highlander had retrieved a sword from one of the fallen guards at the top of the stairway. Standing back to back with Hendel, he began to cut away the number of his attackers. From the corner of his eye, he saw a familiar scarlet-robed figure emerging from the black pit of the dungeon; at the sight of the hated Stenmin, the Prince of Leah felt a savage rage well up inside. With renewed fury, he charged into the enemy guards, trying to cut through their ranks and reach the man who had betrayed them. An unmistakable look of fear crossed the mystic's lean features as he shrank from the terrible battle.

Back to back, the Dwarf and the highlander fought as if they had gone mad. Men lay dead and dying all about them. Both were wounded in a dozen places, but they didn't feel the pain. Twice Menion had slipped on the bloodied floor and gone down, and each time Hendel had driven off the attackers while the highlander scrambled back to his feet. Only five of the enemy were still standing, but Hendel and Menion Leah were nearly finished. They fought like mechanical creatures now, their bodies soaked in blood and sweat, their limbs leaden and nerveless. As if suddenly regaining his wits, the terrified Stenmin raced to the edge of the pit and began screaming for help. The Prince of Leah responded instantly. With a final burst of strength, he crashed into two of his attackers, knocking both sprawling. A third rushed to stop him, but the charging highlander put his sword into the man up to the hilt and left it there. Grasping a fallen lance, he pounced upon the cringing mystic and stunned him with a sweeping blow from the great weapon. As the lean frame crumpled to the stone floor, Menion Leah gripped the edges of the heavy trapdoor and heaved upward with the last of his fading strength.

It was as if the stone had been chained in open position to the cellar floor. It did not move. From far below, the sounds of metal on stone ceased, replaced by the thudding of booted feet as men raced toward the trapdoor. Only seconds remained. If they reached the stairs, Menion was a dead man. Bracing himself, the wounded man again threw all of his weight into lifting the massive piece of stone, and this time it rose. Groaning with the terrible strain, the highlander raised upward against the great trapdoor until at last it came over and fell with a great booming thud into place in the ancient floor. With numb, sweating hands he bound the chain through the sealing rings and fastened it with an iron bar. The passageway was closed. If the Northland army sought entrance here, they would have to cut their way through several feet of stone and iron.

"Menion."

The sound of his name broke the sudden silence in a cracked whisper. The highlander had fallen to his hands and knees, but his groping hand found a discarded sword and he raised his battered face. Across a floor littered with a tangled mass of fallen enemy guards, their twisted bodies either lifeless or in their final death throes, the eyes of the Prince of Leah found his friend. The Dwarf stood with his back to the wall near the bottom of the cellar stairway, the great mace still gripped tightly in one hand. There were dead bodies all about him. He had killed them all. No one had escaped. The hardened eyes met Menion's for just an instant, and it was as if they were again meeting for the first time in the lowlands beyond the Black Oaks. He was the old Hendel—taciturn, grim-faced, ever resourceful. Then the mace slipped from his hand, his eyes glazed over; with a long sigh, his body slid slowly, lifelessly to the death that had finally claimed him.

Hendel! The name raced through Menion's stunned, disbelieving mind as he struggled numbly to his feet and stood swaying unsteadily in the flickering shadows. Tears welled into his reddened eyes and ran in dark streams down his battered face. With leaden steps he picked his way over the lifeless bodies of the enemy dead, gasping now in unrestrained fury and helplessness. He was only dimly aware of Stenmin regaining consciousness somewhere behind him. He reached the Dwarf's side and knelt beside him, gently cradling the limp form next to his breast. How many times had Hendel saved his life? How many times had he saved them all, only to . . . ? He couldn't finish the thought. He could only cry. Everything seemed to break inside of him at once.

Stenmin raised himself slowly to one knee and stared blankly about the cellar at the mass of tangled corpses. His men all dead, the stone trapdoor closed and chained, and . . . Fear surged up inside his pain-wracked body. One of the intruders was still alive—the highlander! He hated that man, hated him so badly he fleetingly considered trying to kill him, but then the fear returned even stronger than before and abruptly his thoughts turned to escape. Escape so that he could live! There was only one way out—up the stairs past the kneeling man and through the open cellar door. Already he was on his feet, moving noiselessly through the carnage, half walking, half slinking toward the unguarded steps.

The highlander's back was turned to him, still holding the body of the Dwarf. Sweat beads broke out on Stenmin's forehead and the thin lips curled menacingly—yet it was fear that kept him moving. Only a few more steps. He would be free again. The city was doomed; all of them would die—all of his enemies. But he would survive. He had to fight down the sudden impulse to laugh aloud. One hand touched the stone of the ancient stairway, one foot followed; the highlander was only feet away, still unsuspecting, the outer cellar door was ajar and unguarded. Freedom! Just steps . . .

Then Menion turned. A shriek of terror escaped the mystic's lips as his eyes viewed the terrible look on the face of the Prince of Leah. Stenmin clawed his way frantically toward the open doorway, stumbling blindly in the long red robes.

He was only halfway up the steps when Menion caught him.

At the walls of Tyrsis, the impossible was happening. Upon descending from the parapets of the Outer Wall, Balinor had moved quickly to the massive city gates. The Legion guardsmen stationed before the great iron portals had snapped quickly to attention. Everything appeared to be as it should. The series of inner lock bolts, controlled mechanically from the tower gatehouse, had been run firmly into place in the crease where the gates swung outward. The cumbersome iron bar that served as an additional safeguard lay snugly in its fittings across the width of both gates. Balinor stared fixedly at the great wall, a nagging doubt persisting. Something was going to happen; he could feel it. The gates were the key to the city, the one weak link in the otherwise impenetrable stone wall that bound Tyrsis. Siege towers, grappling hooks, scaling ladders—all these were futile attempts to breach that great wall, and the Warlock Lord had to know it. The gates were the key.

His eyes drifted skyward to the tower gatehouse, a squat, windowless stone enclosure which housed the mechanism that controlled the inner locks. Two Legion soldiers stood attentively at the single door. A picked squad of men had been given the responsibility of protecting that crucial mechanism, men selected by Balinor and commanded by Captain Sheelon. On both sides of the small housing, the men of the Border Legion defended the battlements. It seemed impossible that the Northlanders expected to seize the gatehouse. Still . . .

Already the tall borderman had moved to the foot of the narrow stairway that led to the gatehouse and had begun to climb the worn stone blocks. Sudden cries from the wall diverted his attention momentarily, and he paused as the air sounded with the deep humming of a thousand bowstrings, and a rush of arrows swept the ramparts of the Outer Wall. Hurriedly Balinor gained the battlements and in three short strides reached the wall. He peered carefully down at the face of the bluff, littered with bodies and debris and dotted with small oil fires that burned hazily in the morning mist. The Northlanders had temporarily abandoned any direct assault. Instead, lines of archers five men deep were raking the defenders on the ramparts with a concentrated barrage.

The reason for this new tactic was immediately obvious. At the rim of the bluff, a detachment of heavily armored Rock Trolls pushed forward a ponderous, mobile battering ram, shielded from the top and sides by a broad canopy of sheet iron. While the Border Legion was pinned down by heavy fire from the archers, the giant Trolls would move the great ram into place before the city gates and force an entry.

The plan appeared at first glance both preposterous and unworkable. Yet if the gatehouse fell to the enemy, the inner lock bolts could be released and only the long, iron crossbar would hold the gates closed. The bar alone would not be enough to stand against the massive battering ram. Balinor ran toward the small gatehouse. The guards came silently to attention. He gave them a passing glance, his hand reaching anxiously for the door handle. Sheelon was nowhere in sight. The door swung inward, and he was a step into the closed room when he realized he had never seen either of the sentries.

The giant borderman reacted instinctively, sidestepping the noiseless rush of the guard behind him, seizing the outstretched lance that barely grazed his back and wrenching it free from the would-be assassin. His back to the wall, the King had only a moment to survey the dimly lighted room. The bodies of Sheelon and his men lay to one side, twisted in death, their stiffened corpses stripped naked of armor and clothing. From out of the shadows at the rear of the housing a group of faceless attackers rushed the borderman, daggers raised for the kill. Balinor threw the heavy lance crossways into their midst and broke for the open doorway. But the second sentry, who had remained just outside, saw him coming and quickly pulled the door shut from the other side. The trapped King had no time to force his way free. There was barely enough time to draw the great broadsword before his assailants were upon him. They bore him roughly to the floor, daggers chipping and glancing off the protective coat of chain mail that had saved his life so many times. With a mighty surge, Balinor shook himself free and regained his footing. In the faint light of the shuttered room, his attackers were only shadows, but his eyes were adjusting, and he cut at them as they moved toward him. Two of the dark forms screamed and dropped lifelessly as the great blade cut through them, but their companions had already broken past the sweeping sword and closed with the King.

For a second time, Balinor was wrestled down, but again he twisted free and the battle surged back across the little room. The din of the attack outside completely obscured the sounds of battle from within the stone housing; the borderman knew that unless he managed to get the door open, no one would come to his aid. He placed his back to the wall once more and swung the broadsword sharply as the shadowed enemies resumed the assault. Three were dead and several were wounded, but those who remained in the battle were beginning to wear him down with their repeated rushes. He had to get free quickly. Then an audible grinding of levers and gears filled the gatehouse, and he realized in horror that someone was releasing the inner lock bolts of the front gates. With a wild charge, he broke for the lock mechanism, but the determined attackers barred his path, and he was forced into a circling movement away from his objective. A moment later there was a sharp grating of metal on metal, followed by a series of hammering blows. They were jamming the release levers! In complete disregard for his own safety, the infuriated Balinor threw himself on the remaining enemies.

Then the gatehouse door burst open and the body of the traitorous sentry was thrust violently through the entryway. Gray daylight flooded the darkened room and the lean figure of Durin appeared from out of nowhere at the side of his friend. In grim silence they cut away at the few enemy attackers who remained, forcing them away from the jammed machinery, away from the open doorway and escape, and into the far corner of the small housing. There, locked together in ferocious hand-to-hand combat, they destroyed them. Without a second glance at the dead men, the bloodied King rushed back to the damaged lock mechanism, his face lined in fury as he surveyed the twisted mass of metal levers and gears. Angrily he threw his weight against the main release. It would not move. Durin turned pale as he realized what had happened.

"We don't have enough time!" Balinor exploded heatedly, wrenching violently at the jammed levers.

A great booming crash resounded through the stone housing, vibrating through the walls and shaking the two men ominously.

"The gates!" Durin exclaimed in dismay.

A second crash rocked the gatehouse, and a third. The rushing of booted feet sounded on the ramparts outside and a moment later Messaline's dark face appeared in the open doorway. He started to speak, but Balinor was already issuing commands and moving toward the battlements.

"Get this room cleared away and have our machinists try to free those gears. The gate locks are released and jammed!" Messaline looked as if he had received a mortal blow. "Fortify the gates with timbers and put your best regiment in phalanx formation fifty paces back and to either side. The Northlanders are not to break through. Put two lines of archers on the Inner Wall to bottle up the gate entrance. Reserves and the garrison command will defend the Inner Wall. All others will stay where they are at the Outer Wall. We will hold it as long as we can. If it falls, the Legion will retreat to the secondary defense and hold. If we lose that, we will regroup at the Bridge of Sendic. That will be the last line of defense. Anything else?"

Quickly Durin explained where Hendel had gone. Balinor shook his head wearily.

"We have been betrayed at every turn. Hendel will have to do what he can without our help for the moment. If the palace falls and they break through from the rear, we are finished anyway. Messaline, you'll hold the right flank of the phalanx, Ginnisson will take the left, and I'll be in the center. The enemy is not to break through! Pray that Eventine arrives before our strength fails us."

Messaline disappeared outside in a crouching run. The shattering thrusts of the massive battering ram continued to shake the great wall as Balinor and Durin faced each other across the little room. Already the gray light of day was growing dimmer as the shadow of the Warlock Lord continued to roll ominously closer to the doomed city. The giant borderman reached out slowly and gripped the slim hand of his Elven friend.

"Good-bye, my friend. This is the end for us. Time has just about run out."

"Eventine would not willingly fail us . . ." the Elf began earnestly.

"I know, I know," Balinor replied. "Nor would Allanon. He has not found the Sword or the heir of Shannara. His time has run out as well."

There was a brief silence between them, broken by the shouts of the men on the walls and the crashing of the ram against the gates of Tyrsis. Balinor wiped the blood away from a deep cut over one eye.

"Find your brother, Durin. But before you leave the Outer Wall, have the last of the oil poured onto that ram and fired. If we can't stop them altogether, we'll at least make it a hot place for them to work."

He smiled grimly and slipped quietly out of the gatehouse. Durin stared blankly after him, wondering what perverse fate had brought them to this unjust end. Balinor was the most remarkable man the Elf had ever met. Yet he had lost everything—his family, his city, his home, and now his life was to be taken from him as well. What kind of world permitted such terrible injustice, where good men were stripped of everything and soulless creatures of malice and hatred survived to glory in their pointless death? Once he had been so sure they would not fail, that somehow they would find a way to destroy the hated Warlock Lord and save the four lands. But that dream was ended.

Durin looked up dazedly as several burly Legion machinists entered the gatehouse to begin their hopeless work on the jammed lock mechanism. Quickly, the lean Elf moved out onto the ramparts. It was time to find Dayel.

The struggle to hold the Outer Wall was incredibly vicious. Despite the devastating barrage concentrated against the men of the Border Legion by the lines of Gnome archers below the bluff, the valiant defenders managed to cut away at the Trolls that manned the great battering ram before the weakened gates. The remaining cauldrons of oil were moved to the fortifications above the ram and poured on the enemy machine and its handlers as they worked. Torches followed, and instantly the entire area was consumed in a mass of flames and rolling black smoke. Metal melted and smoldered and the Trolls were burned alive after the first few minutes of the terrible heat, their armor becoming a furnace they could not escape. But new enemy soldiers quickly filled the breach and the mighty ram continued to break against the city gates in crashing, booming blows that first bent, then split the crossbar and the timbers that held the tall portals secure.

The gray sky turned black from the oily smoke that rose above the burning grasslands to cloak the city walls and their defenders in a deep, murky haze. The smell of burnt flesh choked the nose and lungs of the Legion soldiers as the charred, blackened bodies of the Troll attackers lay in heaps before the Outer Wall. Desperately the two opponents strove to break each other's strength, but the stalemate continued. For a short time, it seemed that the day might end without any further change in the fortunes of either army.

But at last the great crossbar snapped in two, the supporting timbers sagged and splintered, and the giant battering ram forced a breach in the gates of Tyrsis. In a rush, the first Northlanders poured into the parade grounds and were dropped instantly by Legion archers positioned atop the Inner Wall. Drawn up in a three-sided box opening toward the Outer Wall gates, the Legion phalanx braced for the enemy rush, spears bristling through locked shields. The ram pushed forward and the gates opened further still, and then the foremost ranks of the Northland invasion force surged through the gap and threw themselves against the spears of the Border Legion. The Legion defenses wavered slightly, but held, thrusting the attackers backward, where they milled in confusion as they were cut to pieces by the archers on the walls both above and behind them. In seconds the parade ground was blanketed with Northland dead and wounded, and the breach in the gates had momentarily been bottled up so thoroughly that the great invasion forces could not advance farther.

Durin had positioned himself next to the gatehouse on the Outer Wall, and from there he watched the Northland assault break apart on the Legion phalanx. He had discovered that his brother had gone with Janus Senpre to the palace, and reluctantly he decided to remain with Balinor for as long as possible. The enemy was attempting to regain its momentum now; on the plains below, Maturens directed the great Rock Troll commands toward the breach in the gates of the besieged city. The Northland army was calling on the backbone of its strength in a determined effort to crush the Southlanders once and for all. The Outer Wall was under attack again from all angles, as hordes of Gnomes and lesser Trolls rushed forward with ladders, ropes, and grappling hooks. The thinned ranks of the Legion defenders who remained on the battlements fought desperately to prevent a breakthrough, but their men were dying and the numbers of the Northland army seemed limitless. The battle was turning into a telling war of attrition that the men of Tyrsis could not hope to win.

Then, into the growing blackness of the sky north of the besieged city, two winged figures rose and hovered menacingly, and Durin felt his blood turn cold. Skull Bearers! Were they so certain of victory that they dared reveal themselves in daylight? The Elf felt his heart sink. He had done all he could here; it was time to join his brother. Whatever fate awaited them, they would at least face it together.

Nimbly, he turned and moved along the wall in a crouching run until he was just behind the left flank of the Legion phalanx. A steep causeway led downward to the barracks grounds that lay between the walls of the city, several hundred feet behind the Legion rear lines. A deafening roar erupted from the men engaged in battle on the walls. As Durin neared the base of the rampway, he saw the tall, armored forms of the great Rock Trolls pouring through the breach in the gates of the Outer Wall. He paused involuntarily, sensing that the next few minutes would be crucial ones for the Border Legion.

The phalanx tightened its formation and braced for the assault as the massive Trolls drew up their ranks and moved slowly toward the center of the defensive line, where Balinor held command. Ten feet separated the combatants when, to everyone's surprise, the entire Troll regiment wheeled abruptly to the left and charged directly into the Legion flank. There was a crunching sound as the two forces joined and a terrific clash of metal as spear met mace and shield struck armor. For a moment the Legion phalanx held firmly and the foremost of the giant Trolls were killed and thrown down. But the superior strength and sheer weight of the Northlanders pressed back against the smaller men of the Border Legion until at last the right end of the phalanx began to break apart.

The commanding figure of Ginnisson moved quickly into the gap, his red hair flying as he fought to hold the line. The Trolls were driven back step by step as Balinor closed on the right and Messaline from the rear. It was the most ferocious man-to-man combat Durin had been witness to in this terrible conflict, and he watched in awe as the great Rock Trolls held off the men of the Border Legion and once again pressed forward. An instant later the breach in the phalanx was forced and Ginnisson disappeared from view entirely as a rush of massive attackers overwhelmed him and raced toward the barracks and the Inner Wall.

Durin was directly in their path. There might have been time to gain the safety of the walls, but the Elf was already on one knee, the ash bow armed and drawn back. The first Troll fell at fifty paces, the second ten closer, the third at twenty-five. Legion soldiers from the wall rushed to the attack, and archers from the lesser heights of the Inner Wall tried desperately to halt the Troll offensive. Everything in front of the Elf was confusion as Troll and Legionnaire surged toward him, locked together in desperate hand-to-hand combat. Still the massive Northlanders continued to come at him, and Durin fired the last of his arrows into their midst.

He threw down the bow, and for the first time thought about escape. But there was no time left, and he barely managed to seize a discarded sword before the surging mass of fighters was upon him. He struggled wildly to keep his balance as he was forced back against the barracks wall. A giant Rock Troll loomed directly over him, a black mass of barklike skin and armor, and the Elf twisted desperately to one side as a huge mace swung downward. He felt a blinding pain in his left shoulder, followed by a strange numbness. Grimly he fought to stay conscious, his pain abruptly returning in a flood that wracked his lean frame. But he was already falling. His face lay against the earth as he breathed in shallow gasps. A terrible heaviness pushed down on him as he felt the tide of the battle move beyond him. He tried to see, but the effort of looking was too great and he slipped quietly into unconsciousness, through which pain still seemed to penetrate in great bursts.

Menion Leah bent his blood-streaked face over the body of Hendel and carefully raised the inert form in his arms. With studied, mechanical steps, he threaded his way through the bodies of their fallen enemies to reach the stairs and climbed slowly toward the open doorway, stepping carefully, but without looking, over the headless lump tangled in a loose mass of reddened robes that sprawled grotesquely across the center of the ancient stairway. Dazedly, the highlander passed through the cellar entryway and moved down the vacant palace hall, gripping the lifeless form of the Dwarf close to him. He walked aimlessly, his eyes shockingly blank, his face stricken with a terrible stunned look that screamed in silent agony for release. He reached the palace foyer and there halted as the sound of running feet echoed hollowly from the eastern corridor. Gently he laid his burden on the polished floor and stood quietly as the slim, titian-haired girl slowed in front of him, sudden tears streaming down her beautiful face.

"Oh, Menion," she whispered faintly. "What have they done?"

His eyes flickered and his mouth moved dumbly as he fought for the words that would not come. Quickly Shirl reached for him, the slim arms coming tightly around his stooped frame, her face close to his own. A moment later she felt his strong arms come around her shoulders and the terrible agony trapped deep within him broke soundlessly and flooded over her to disappear in her silence and warmth.

On the ramparts of the Inner Wall, Balinor completed a final check of the Legion defenses and paused wearily above the heavily barricaded gates. The Northlanders were already massing for a final rush. Just moments earlier, the impregnable Outer Wall had fallen and the courageous soldiers of the Border Legion had been forced back to the second line of defense. Balinor stared grimly at the enemy swarming over the heights of the towering wall and gripped the hilt of his great broadsword until his knuckles turned white beneath the chain mail. His cloak and tunic had been shredded in the terrible combat to hold the breach in the gates of the Outer Wall against the Troll assault. Balinor had held together the center of the Legion phalanx, but both wings had collapsed. Ginnisson had been killed, Messaline was severely wounded, and hundreds of Southlanders had died holding the Outer Wall until all hope was gone. Even Durin had disappeared in the fighting. Now the King of Callahorn stood alone.

He gestured sharply to the men bracing the timbers that supported the gates below, the chain mail on his arm glinting brightly in the graying light, showing where a dozen blows had chipped and nicked the protective metal. For a moment he allowed his courage to give way entirely to despair. They had failed him—all of them. Eventine and the Elven army. Allanon. The whole Southland. Tyrsis was on the brink of complete annihilation and with it the land of Callahorn, and still no one came to their aid. The Legion had fought alone to save them all—the final defense for the Southland. What purpose had it served? He caught himself quickly, roughly pushing down the doubts and despondency. There was no time to indulge himself. There were too many lives to be saved, and he was the one they depended upon.

The Northland army was drawing up its lines along the base of the Outer Wall, the familiar scaling ladders, ropes, and grappling irons held ready for the assault. Already scattered bands of the massive Rock Trolls had scaled the Inner Wall during the battle on the parade grounds and broken into the city proper. He wondered briefly what had become of the reliable Hendel and Menion Leah. Apparently they had secured the palace and prevented any rear assault, or the city would have already fallen. Now they would have to hold in the event isolated groups of the enemy breached the Inner Wall and broke for the palace.

Bits of soot from the rolling clouds of oil smoke stung his eyes, and he rubbed them until they watered freely. Everything seemed masked in a heavy gray haze as he glanced quickly at the wall fortifications. The Legion had been placed in an impossible defensive position against an enemy so vast that the loss of hundreds from their ranks was insignificant. He thought of Hendel's words after the deaths of his father and brother. The last Buckhannah. The name would die with him, die as Tyrsis and her people died. The familiar roar rose in thunderous echoes from the throats of the Northlanders, and they charged recklessly for the Legion's walled defense. The long scar on the giant borderman's cheek turned a deeper shade of purple, and he brought the broadsword up menacingly.

At almost the same moment, the first scattered remnants of the Troll advance force came together at the foot of the Bridge of Sendic and hesitated. A line of determined Legion soldiers spanned the center of the wide stone arch, barring all passage to the home of the Buckhannahs. Janus Senpre stood foremost, flanked on one side by Menion Leah, his battered frame erect as he gripped the sword of Leah with both hands, and on the other by Dayel, his youthful face drawn, but resolute. Behind the Rock Trolls, the air was thick with rolling smoke as fresh fires rose from the buildings of the city. Frightened cries sounded above the clamor of battle at the Inner Wall. In the distance, darting figures were seen scurrying across the deserted Tyrsian Way for the safety of their homes. Silently the forces faced one another, the number of Trolls growing quickly as others appeared to swell their ranks. They studied the Southlanders with the blank, experienced look of professional soldiers, confident in the knowledge that they were the best-trained fighting unit in the world. The defenders on the bridge numbered less than fifty.

The afternoon sky had gone suddenly black, and an eerie stillness settled over the two armies. From somewhere in the burning city, Menion caught the faint, clear cry of a small child. Several feet to his left, Dayel felt the cold north wind fade with a low, sighing whisper. Before them, the giant Trolls moved carefully into formation, the great maces held loosely; then as a unit, they lumbered forward. At the center of the bridge, the city's last line of defense braced for the Northland rush.

On the ridge west of the city, Flick Ohmsford and the little band of Elven horsemen watched helplessly as the destruction of Tyrsis mounted. Flanked by Eventine and Jon Lin Sandor, the Valeman felt the last trace of hope fade as the hordes of the mammoth Northland army poured unchecked through the breached gates of the Outer Wall. Clouds of dark smoke rose now from within Tyrsis, and the last remnants of the proud Border Legion had been driven from her walls. The city's defenses had been broken. He stared in horror as the grotesque figures of the Skull

Bearers hovered in full view above the advancing enemy, black wings spread wide against the darkening noon sky. The worst that Allanon had foreseen had come to pass. The Warlock Lord had won.

Then a sharp cry sounded from a rider to his left, and Eventine's flushed countenance surged into view as he spurred his mount forward, crowding the Valeman aside in his eagerness. Across the wide expanse of the empty grassland, still many miles to the west, a faint, dark line grew against the grayness of the horizon. A low rumble of pounding hooves broke out of the distance to blend with the clamor and fury of the battle behind them.

The dark line grew quickly in size and became horsemen, thousands strong, banners and lances flashing color and iron. Strident and clear, the booming wail of a war horn sounded their arrival. Cheers rose from the little band of Elves as the massive body of horsemen began to blanket the plains, sweeping at breakneck speed toward Tyrsis. Forewarned of their approach, the rear guard of the Northland army had already closed ranks and turned to face the advancing tide. It was the Elven army come at last—for the defenders of Tyrsis, for the beleaguered nations of three lands, for everything mankind had fought so hard to preserve through the ages. Come perhaps too late!

33

In a single smooth, silent motion, Shea slid the ancient blade free from its battered sheath. The metal gleamed in the faint torchlight with a deep bluish tint, the iron surface flawless as if the legendary Sword had never been carried in battle. It was unexpectedly light, a slim, balanced blade of exceptional workmanship, the handle carefully engraved with the now familiar crest of a raised hand holding forth a burning torch. Shea held the weapon guardedly, glancing quickly at Panamon Creel and Keltset, seeking their reassurance, afraid suddenly of what was going to happen. His grim-faced companions remained motionless, their expressions blank and impassive. He gripped the Sword tightly with both hands, bringing the blade around sharply until it pointed skyward. His palms were sweating freely, and he felt his body grow cold in the cell's darkness. There was a faint stirring to one side, and a feeble moan broke from the lips of Orl Fane. Moments passed, and Shea was conscious of the raised impression of the crest pressing into the palms of his clenched hands. Still nothing happened.

. . . In the gray half-light of the empty chamber at the peak of Skull Mountain, the dark waters of the stone basin were quiet and smooth. The power that was the Warlock Lord lay dormant. . . .

Abruptly the Sword of Shannara grew warm in Shea's hands, and a strange, pulsating wave of heat coursed from the dark iron into the palms of the astonished Valeman and then disappeared. Startled, he took a quick step backward and lowered the blade slightly. An instant later, the sudden warmth was replaced by a sharp tingling sensation that surged out of the weapon into his body. Though there was no pain, the abruptness of the sensation caused him to wince reflexively, and he felt his muscles tighten. Instinctively, he sought to release the talisman; to his shock, he found that he could not let go. Something touched deeply into him to forbid it, and his hands locked securely around the ancient handle.

The tingling sensation rushed through him, and now he was conscious of a return flow of energy that pulled at his life force, carrying it down through the cold metal of the Sword itself, until the weapon became a part of him. The gilt paint that coated the carved pommel began to strip away beneath the Valeman's hands, and the handle turned to polished silver, laced with reddish streaks of light that seemed to burn and twist in the bright metal like living things. Shea felt the first stirrings of something coming awake, something that was a part of him, yet foreign to everything he knew himself to be. It pulled at him, subtly but firmly, drawing him down deeper inside himself.

Several steps away, Panamon Creel and Keltset watched with growing concern as the little Valeman seemed to slip into a trance, his eyelids drooping heavily, his breathing slowing, his form turning statuelike in the dim torchlight of the cell. He held the Sword of Shannara before him in both hands, its blade raised and pointed skyward, the polished silver handle gleaming brightly. For an instant, Panamon considered taking hold of the Valeman and shaking him awake, but something restrained the thief. From out of the shadows, Orl Fane began crawling across the smooth stones toward his precious sword. Panamon hesitated a moment and then nudged him back roughly with his boot.

Shea felt himself being drawn inward, borne like a cork caught in an undertow. Everything around him began to fade from view. The walls, ceiling, and floor of the stone cell disappeared first, then the cringing whimpering figure of Orl Fane; finally even the granite forms of Panamon and Keltset vanished. The strange current seemed to wrap around him completely, and he found that he could not resist it. Slowly he was pulled into the innermost recesses of his being, until all was blackness.

. . . A momentary shudder rippled the still basin waters in the cavern depths at the crown of the solitary death's head, and the frightened, crawling beings that served the Master scampered from their places of concealment in the stone walls. The Warlock Lord stirred warily from his broken sleep. . . .

In the vortex of emotion and basic self that comprised the centermost region of his being, the bearer of the Sword of Shannara came face-to-face with himself. For a moment, there was a chaos of uncertain impressions; then the current seemed to reverse itself, carrying him off in a new direction entirely. Pictures and impressions loomed up before him. Thrust suddenly before his eyes, the world that was his birthplace and life source, from past to present, lay open and revealed to him, stripped bare of his carefully nurtured illusions, and he saw the reality of existence in all its starkness. No soft dreams colored its view of life, no wishful fantasies clothed the harshness of its self-shaped choices, no self-conceived visions of hope softened the rawness of its judgments. Amid its sprawling vastness, he saw himself displayed for the pitiful, insignificant spark of momentary life that he represented.

Shea's mind seemed to explode within him, and he was paralyzed by what he saw. He struggled wildly for his grasp of the vision of self that had always sustained him, for what had been his hold on sanity, fighting to shield himself from the awesome view of his inner nakedness and the weakness of the thing he was compelled to recognize as himself.

Then the force of the current seemed to diminish slightly. Shea forced his eyes open, avoiding for an instant the inner vision. Before him was the upright Sword, ablaze with a blinding white light that surged downward from the blade to the pommel. Beyond it, he could see Panamon and Keltset, standing motionless, their gaze fixed on him. Then the eyes of the giant Troll shifted slightly, centering on the Sword. There was a strange understanding and urgency in the gesture, and as Shea looked back to the Sword of Shannara, its light seemed to pulsate feverishly. There was a sense of impatience about its movement as it strained to advance from the blade into his body and was somehow thwarted in its efforts.

For a moment more, the Valeman struggled against this advance, then his eyes again closed and the inner vision returned. The first shock of revelation was past him now, and he made an effort to understand what was happening. He concentrated on the images of Shea Ohmsford, immersing himself completely in the thoughts, emotions, judgments, and motivations that made up this character that was both alien and familiar.

The images cleared with frightening sharpness, and abruptly he saw another side to himself, a side he had never been able to recognize—or perhaps had simply refused to accept. It revealed itself in an endless line of events, all caricatures of the memories he had believed in so strongly. Here was an accounting of every hurt he had caused to others, every petty jealousy he had felt, his deep-seated prejudices, his deliberate half-truths, his self-pity, his fears—all that was dark and hidden within himself. Here was the Shea Ohmsford who had fled the Vale, not to save and protect family and friends, but in fear of his own life, seeking any excuse for his panic— the Shea Ohmsford who had selfishly allowed Flick to share his nightmare and thereby ease the pain of it. Here was the Valeman who had sneered at and belittled the moral code of Panamon Creel, while at the same time allowing the thief to risk his own life to save Shea's. And here . . .

The images went on endlessly. Shea Ohmsford recoiled in horror from what he was seeing. He could not accept it. He could never accept it!

Yet drawing from some inner well of strength and understanding, his mind opened receptively to the images, expanding outward to embrace them, persuading him, or perhaps forcing him, to admit the reality of what he had been shown. He could not sensibly deny this other side of his character; like the limited image of the person he had always believed himself to be, this was only a part of the real Shea Ohmsford—but it was indeed a part, however difficult he found it to accept.

But he had to accept it. It was the truth.

. . . Filled with white-hot rage, the Warlock Lord came fully awake. . . .

Truth? Shea opened his eyes again to stare at the Sword of Shannara, gleaming whitely from blade to handle. A warm, pulsating feeling spread rapidly through him, bringing no new vision of self, but only a deep, inner awareness.

Abruptly, he realized that he knew the secret of the Sword. The Sword of Shannara possessed the power to reveal Truth—to force the man who held it to recognize the truth about himself; perhaps even to reveal the truth about others who might come in contact with it. For an instant, he could not bring himself to believe any of it. He hesitated in his analysis, trying desperately to follow up on this unexpected revelation—to find something more because there simply had to be more. But there was nothing else to discover. That was all there was to the Sword's vaunted magic. Beyond that, it was no more than what it appeared to be—a finely crafted weapon from another age.

The knowledge of what this meant ripped through his mind and left him stunned. No wonder Allanon had never revealed the secret of the Sword. What kind of weapon was this against the incredible power of the Warlock Lord? What possible defense could it offer against a being that could crush the life out of him with little more than a thought? With chilling certainty, Shea knew that he had been betrayed. The Sword's legendary power was a lie! He felt himself begin to panic, and he closed his eyes tightly against the chill he was feeling. The blackness about him began to churn violently until he grew dizzy with its sweep and seemed to lose consciousness altogether.

. . . In the bleak, gray emptiness of his mountain refuge, the Warlock Lord watched and listened. Slowly his rage began to subside, and the misty darkness within the hood nodded in satisfaction. The Valeman he had thought destroyed had survived. In spite of everything, he had found the Sword. But the man was pitifully weak, lacking the knowledge necessary to understand the talisman. He was already overcome with fear, and he would be vulnerable. Swiftly, noiselessly, the Master glided from the cavernous chamber. . . .

The tall figure of Allanon paused hesitantly at the crest of a barren, windswept hill, his dark eyes invisible beneath the heavy brow as they studied the stark, solitary line of mountains that rose hauntingly against the gray northern horizon. They seemed to stare back at him, their cavernous faces scarred and worn, reflecting the soul of the land that had spawned them so many years ago. A deep silence hovered expectantly over the whole of the vast wilderness that was the Northland. Even the high mountain winds had died into stillness. The Druid wrapped his black robes about him and breathed sharply. There could be no mistake; his extended mind sweep would not lie to him about this. That which he had worked so hard to achieve had finally come to pass. In the deep recesses of the Knife Edge, still far distant from where the mystic stood, Shea Ohmsford had drawn forth the Sword of Shannara.

Yet it was all wrong! Even though the Valeman might be able to withstand and accept the truth about himself and perhaps recognize the secret of the Sword, he was still not prepared to use the talisman properly against the Warlock Lord. There would be no time for him to grow into the necessary confidence while he was alone and unaided, deprived of the knowledge that only Allanon could give him. He would be filled with self-doubt and torn by fear, easy prey for Brona. Even now, the Druid could sense the awakening of the enemy. The Dark Lord was beginning the descent from his mountain refuge, fully confident that the bearer of the Sword was blind to the full power of the talisman. His attack would come quickly and savagely, and Shea would be destroyed before he could learn to survive.

Only brief minutes remained before the confrontation, and Allanon knew that he could never arrive in time to help. He had realized at last that Shea and the Sword of Shannara had somehow both gone northward. Leaving the others in Callahorn, he had rushed to the Valeman's aid. But matters had developed too quickly. Now there was only one chance for him to be of any use to Shea—if, indeed, there was any real chance at all—and he was still too far away. Clutching his robes about his spare frame, the Druid moved swiftly down the hillside, scattering the dusty surface in small clouds as he went, his features tight with determination.

Panamon Creel started forward as Shea crumpled to one knee, but Keltset's massive arm reached in front of him. The Troll was facing back toward the entrance to the caverns, listening. Panamon could hear nothing, but a sudden sensation of fear and growing horror reached down inside him, halting his motion toward the Valeman. Keltset's eyes turned, as if marking the progress of someone passing through the corridor beyond the cell, and Panamon felt his fear deepen.

Then a shadow fell over everything. The torchlight that outlined the tiny cavern room dimmed sharply. Standing at the doorway of the cell was a tall form shrouded in black robes. Instinctively, Panamon Creel knew that this was the Warlock Lord. Where a face should have been, beneath the closely drawn hood, there was nothing but darkness and a deep, green mist that moved sluggishly about twin sparks of reddish fire. The sparks turned first toward Panamon and Keltset, freezing them instantly into motionless statues, sending all the fears and terrors they had ever known rushing through their paralyzed forms. The thief struggled to cry a warning to the little Valeman, but he found that he could not speak, and he watched helplessly as the faceless cowl shifted slowly toward Shea.

The Valeman felt himself drift back into consciousness in the shadowed dampness of the little cell. Everything seemed strangely distant to him, though there was a vague warning signal sounding somewhere in the back of his clouded mind. But he responded sluggishly, and for a time there was only the musty smell of stale air and rock and the faint flickering of a single torch. Through a haze, he saw the motionless forms of Panamon and Keltset no more than five feet from him, fear mirrored in their hard features. Orl Fane crouched at the rear of the cell, twisted into a small yellow ball that whimpered and mumbled incoherently. Before him, the blade of the Sword of Shannara gleamed brightly.

Then instantly, the secret of the Sword came back to him—and with it, the helplessness of his situation. He started to lift his head, but his eyes seemed locked in front of him. Sudden fear and despair washed over him like a river of ice, and he felt himself drowning in it. He began to sweat coldly and his hands were shaking. A single thought screamed in his mind: Escape! Flee, before the fearsome creature whose forbidden kingdom he had dared invade should discover his presence and destroy him! The purpose for which he had risked everything no longer mattered; all that remained in his mind was the compelling need to flee.

He staggered erect. Every fiber of his being screamed at him to break and dash for the doorway, to throw down the Sword and run. But he could not do it. Something inside him refused to release the Sword. Desperately he fought to control his fear, his hands closing tightly about the handle of the Sword, gripping the metal until the knuckles turned white with pain. It was all that he had left, all that stood between himself and complete panic. He clung to it in desperation, his sanity held together by a talisman he knew to be useless.

MORTAL CREATURE, I AM HERE!

The words were a chilling echo in the deep silence. Shea's eyes fought to look toward the doorway. At first he found only shadows; then the shadows tightened slowly, gathering together to form the cloaked figure of the Warlock Lord. It hovered menacingly at the chamber door, an impenetrable, dark, formless robe. From within the recesses of the cowl, the green mists swirled and the sparks of flame that were its eyes flashed and grew.

MORTAL CREATURE, I AM HERE. BOW DOWN BEFORE ME!

Shea turned white with fear. Something huge and black struck at his mind, and he balanced precariously on the thin edge of total panic. A bottomless chasm seemed to open before him. It would take only one small shove . . . He forced himself to concentrate on the Sword and his own desperate need to stay alive. A crimson haze slipped over his mind, bringing with it the voices of countless doomed creatures that cried for mercy without hope. Crawling, twisted things were clinging to his arms and legs, pulling at him, drawing him downward into the chasm. His

courage turned to water. He was so small, so vulnerable. How could he resist a being as awesome as the Warlock Lord?

At the far side of the cell, Panamon Creel watched the black-robed
figure draw nearer to Shea. The Warlock Lord seemed to be a thing of no
substance, a faceless cowl, an empty robe. But he was obviously too much
for Shea to handle alone, Sword or not. With a quick warning nod to
Keltset, Panamon fought back against the sense of panic ripping at him
and attacked, the piked arm coming up in a wicked sweep. Almost casually,
the dark figure turned to him, now no longer seemingly empty, but filled
with awesome power. An arm gestured, and the thief felt something iron-
like grip his throat and hurl him back against the wall. He struggled once
more to break free, but he was held fast and Keltset with him. Helplessly,
they watched the Warlock Lord turn back toward the Valeman.

The struggle was almost over for Shea. He still held the Sword protectively before him, but the last of his resistance was breaking down before
the assault of the Dark Lord. He could no longer think rationally. He was
powerless against the emotions tearing him apart. From out of the darkness of the hood, a terrible command wrenched at him.

LAY DOWN THE SWORD, MORTAL CREATURE!

Desperately, Shea fought against the urge to obey. Everything became
hazy and he struggled to breathe. Far back in his mind, a familiar voice
seemed to be calling his name. He tried to answer, screaming inside himself for help. Then the voice of the Warlock Lord ripped at him again.

LAY DOWN THE SWORD!

The blade dipped slightly. Shea felt his mind begin to grow numb, and
the darkness moved closer to him. The Sword was of no use to him. Why
not discard it and be done? He was nothing to this awesome being. He was
only a frail, insignificant mortal.

The Sword dipped farther. Orl Fane suddenly screamed in mindless
terror and fell sobbing on the floor of the darkened cell. Panamon had
gone white. Keltset's massive form seemed pressed into the cell wall. The
tip of the Sword of Shannara hovered just inches from the stone floor, wa-
vering slowly.

Then the voice in Shea's mind called out to him again. From out of
nowhere, the words reached him in a whisper so faint that he could barely
distinguish it.

"Shea! Have courage. Trust the Sword."

Allanon!

The Druid's voice pierced the fear and doubt that tightened about the
Valeman. But it was so distant—so distant . . .

"Believe in the Sword, Shea. All else is illusion. . . ."

Allanon's words disappeared in a scream of rage from the Warlock
Lord as the creature shut the hated Druid's voice from the Valeman's mind.
But awareness came too late for Brona. Allanon had thrown a lifeline, and
Shea clung to it, pulling himself back from the edge of defeat. The fear
and doubt drew back. The Sword came up slightly.

The Warlock Lord seemed to move backward a step, and the faceless cowl turned slightly in the direction of Orl Fane. Instantly the whimpering Gnome came erect with the jerking motion of a wooden puppet. No longer his own master, the pawn of the Dark Lord surged forward, the gnarled yellow hands grasping desperately for the Sword. His fingers closed about the exposed blade and wrenched futilely at it. Then abruptly Orl Fane screamed as if in agony, jerking his hands free of the talisman. His features twisted as he dropped to the floor, and his hands groped at his eyes, covering them as if to shut out some horrible vision.

Again the Warlock Lord gestured. The trembling form struggled to its feet, and the Gnome flung himself back into the battle, shrieking his dismay. Again he seized the flashing blade. Again he screamed in anguish and dropped to his knees, releasing the talisman a second time, his eyes streaming with tears.

Shea stared down at the crumpled form. He understood what was happening. Orl Fane had seen the truth about himself, just as Shea had done upon first touching the Sword. But for the Gnome, the truth was unbearable. Yet there was something strange in all this. Why had not Brona himself attempted to wrest the Sword away? It should have been a simple effort; instead, the Warlock Lord had first tried illusion to force Shea to release the Sword, then had used the already maddened Orl Fane as his cat's-paw. Master of so much power, Brona yet seemed unable to grasp the Sword away? It should have been a simple effort; he groped for the answer, so close now—then there was the first small glimmer of understanding.

Orl Fane was on his feet once more, still hopelessly obedient to the commands of the Warlock Lord. He came at Shea in maddened desperation, his gnarled fingers groping wildly at the air before him. The Valeman tried to avoid the rush, but Orl Fane was beyond reason, his mind gone, his soul no longer his own. With a shriek of fear and frustration, he threw himself against the Sword. For an instant, the wiry form convulsed about the bright metal as the Gnome held himself wrapped about the one thing that still mattered to him in this world. For an instant, it was his at last. Then he died.

Stunned, Shea backed away, pulling the weapon free from the lifeless body. Instantly, the Warlock Lord renewed his assault, thrusting viciously at the Valeman's mind in an effort to crush all resistance. Brutal and direct, he employed no clever twists of doubt, no insinuation of uncertainty, no tricks of self-deception. There was only fear, overwhelming and devastating, hurled with the force of a sledgehammer blow. Visions swam through Shea's mind—the awesome power of the Warlock Lord pictured in a thousand horrible ways, all directed toward his extermination. He felt himself reduced down to the smallest, least significant living thing that crawled upon the earth; in another second, it seemed, the Warlock Lord would grind the helpless human into dust.

But Shea's courage held. He had almost succumbed to madness once, and this time he had to stand firm, to believe in himself and in Allanon.

Both hands gripped the Sword as he forced himself to take one small step forward into the constricting haze, into the wall of fear assailing him. He tried to believe that it was only illusion, that the fear and growing panic he felt were not his own. The wall gave slightly, and he fought harder against it. He remembered the death of Orl Fane and built upon his memory a mental picture of all the others who must die should he fail them now. He remembered the whispered words of Allanon. And he concentrated on what he believed to be the Warlock Lord's own weakness, revealed in his strange refusal to grasp the Sword. Shea forced himself to believe that the real secret of the talisman's power was a simple law that affected even a creature as awesome as Brona.

The haze thinned suddenly and the wall of fear splintered. Shea stood again before the Warlock Lord, and the red sparks flashed wildly now in the dim green mists beneath the cowl. The cloaked arms came up quickly as if to ward off some pressing danger, and the dark figure shrank from him. From the dimness of the far wall, Panamon Creel and Keltset suddenly broke free and came rushing forward, weapons drawn. Shea felt the last traces of the Warlock Lord's resistance to his advance break apart and fade. Then the Sword of Shannara came down.

An eerie, soundless shriek of terror ripped from the convulsed shroud and a long, skeletal arm jerked wildly upward. The Valeman pressed the gleaming blade hard against the writhing form, forcing it back against the nearest wall. There would be no escape, he swore softly. There would be an end to the monstrous evil of this creature. Before him, the dark robes shuddered in response as the hooked fingers clawed painfully at the damp cell air. The Warlock Lord began to crumble, and he screamed his hatred of the thing destroying him. Behind his scream, the echo of a thousand other voices cried out for a vengeance that had been too long denied them.

Shea felt the horror of the creature rush through the Sword into his mind, but with it came strength from those other voices, and he did not relent. The touch of the Sword carried with it a truth that could not be denied by all the illusion and deceit of the Warlock Lord. It was a truth he could not admit, could not accept, could not abide—yet a truth against which he had no defense. For the Warlock Lord, the truth was death.

Brona's mortal existence was only an illusion. Long ago, whatever means he had employed to extend his mortal life had failed him, and his body had died. Yet his obsessive conviction that he could not perish kept a part of him alive, and he sustained himself through the very sorcery that had driven him to madness. Denying his own death, he held his lifeless body together to achieve the immortality that had escaped him. A creature existing as a part of two worlds, his power seemed awesome. But now the Sword was forcing him to behold himself as he really was—a decayed, lifeless shell sustained only by a misconceived belief in his own reality—a sham, a fantasy created by force of will alone, as ephemeral as the physical being he had made himself appear. He was a lie that had existed and grown in the fears and doubts of mortal men, a lie that he had created to hide the truth. But now the lie was exposed.

Shea Ohmsford had been able to accept the weakness and frailty that were a part of his human nature, as it was a part of all men. But the Warlock Lord could never accept what the Sword revealed, because the truth was that the creature he had supposed himself to be had ceased to exist almost a thousand years before. All that remained of Brona was the lie; and now that, too, was taken from him by the power of the Sword.

He cried out a final time, a whimper of protest that echoed mournfully through the cell, blending with a rising shout of triumph from a chorus of other wraithlike cries. Then all sound ceased. The outstretched arm began to wither and turn to dust, falling from his shuddering form like ash as his body broke apart beneath the robes. The tiny glints of red glimmered once in the thinning green mist and disappeared. The cloak crumpled and sank emptily, falling to the floor in a pile, with the hooded cowl gradually collapsing, until only a worn tangle of cloth remained.

An instant later, Shea began to sway unsteadily. Too many emotions had chased themselves through his nerves and too much tension over too long a time were demanding their price from his overstrained body. The floor seemed to tilt beneath his feet, and he was falling slowly, slowly into darkness.

In the city of Tyrsis, the long, terrible struggle between earth-born mortal and spirit creature peaked with shocking suddenness. From deep within its rock-encrusted heart, the earth began to rumble, the tremors rippling to the scarred surface in steady, menacing shudders. On the low hills east of Tyrsis, the small band of Elven riders fought roughly to control their frightened mounts, and a haggard Flick Ohmsford stared in bewilderment as the land about him began to shake with the strange vibrations. Atop the Inner Wall, the giant, indestructible figure of Balinor repelled assault after assault as the Northland army sought vainly to breach the Southland defense, and for several minutes the tremors went entirely unnoticed in the ferocity of the battle. And on the Bridge of Sendic, the advancing Trolls halted and glanced uneasily about as the rumbling continued to build. Menion Leah started as long cracks appeared in the ancient stone, and the bridge defenders stood poised to run. The deep vibrations grew rapidly, building with frightening power into a titanic avalanche of booming shudders that swept through the earth and rock. The wind broke over the land with ferocious thrusts that bore down upon and scattered the Elven army still racing to relieve Tyrsis. From Culhaven in the Anar to the farthest reaches of the vast Westland, the great wind roared. Massive forest trees splintered and snapped, and ragged sections of mountains were torn free and crumbled into dust as the blistering force of wind and earthquake gripped the four lands. The sky had deepened into a solid black—cloudless, sunless, and empty, as if the heavens had been obliterated with the single stroke of a massive brush. Huge, jagged streaks of red lightning cut through the

darkness, spanning the sky from horizon to horizon in an impossible web
of electrical energy. It was the end of the world. It was the end of all life.
The holocaust promised since the beginning of the spoken word had finally arrived.

But a moment later it was over, dying instantly into complete and utter
stillness. The silence hung shroudlike and complete, until from out of the
impenetrable blackness the sound of wailing cries rose dismally, turning
quickly into screams of anguish. In the city of Tyrsis, the battle was forgotten. Northlander and Southlander watched in horror as the Skull Bearers
drifted skyward like formless wraiths, writhing in unspeakable agony, their
hooked limbs twisting as they screamed. They hovered momentarily in full
view of the men below, who blanched in horror but could not turn away.
Then the winged forms began to disintegrate, their dark bodies breaking
slowly into ashes and drifting earthward. Seconds later nothing remained
but the vast, empty blackness, which began to move in a huge, rushing
sweep that carried it northward, pulling in its borders as if they were the
ends of a blanket. To the south first, and then the east and west, blue sky
shot into view and the sun swept across the lands with dazzling brightness.
In awe, mortal men watched the impossible darkness fold into a single
black cloud far to the north, hover motionlessly above the horizon, and
then sink downward into the earth and disappear forever.

Time drifted away as Shea floated senselessly in a vast, black, empty void.

"I don't think he made it."

A voice reached into his mind from somewhere far, far away. His hands
and face felt the sudden chill of smooth stone against his heated skin.

"Wait a minute, his eyes are blinking. I think he's coming around!"

Panamon Creel. Shea's eyes opened and he found himself lying on the
floor in the little cell, yellowish torchlight flickering through the darkness
in a hazy glow. He was himself again. One hand still clenched the Sword
of Shannara, but the power of the talisman had left him, and the strange
bond that had briefly joined them together was gone. He stumbled awkwardly to his hands and knees, but a deep, ominous rumbling shook the
cavern and he pitched forward. Strong hands reached out to grab him as
he fell.

"Easy now, slow down a minute." Panamon's rough voice sounded almost in his ear. "Let me take a look at you. Here now, look at me." He
practically jerked the little Valeman about and their eyes locked. There was
just a trace of fear in the thief's hard stare, and then he was smiling. "He's
all right, Keltset. Now let's get out of here."

He brought Shea to his feet and started moving toward the open doorway. The massive form of Keltset lumbered several feet ahead. Shea took a
few uncertain steps and halted. Something held him back.

"I'm all right," he muttered almost inaudibly.

Then abruptly everything came back to him—the power of the Sword
coursing through his body to link them together, his inner visions of the

truth about himself, the frightening battle against the Warlock Lord, the death of Orl Fane . . . He screamed and faltered.

Panamon Creel reached down impulsively with his good arm and held the little Valeman close.

"Easy, easy, it's all over, Shea. You've done it—you've won. The Warlock Lord is destroyed. But this whole mountain is shaking apart. We've got to get out of here before the whole place comes down around our ears!"

The low rumbling had grown steadily louder, and chunks of rock were being dislodged from the cavern walls and ceiling and falling in small showers of dust and gravel. Cracks were appearing along the ancient stone as the heavy shaking continued to mount. Shea looked at Panamon and nodded.

"You'll be all right." The scarlet-clad thief rose quickly. "I'm going to get you out of this. That's a promise."

Swiftly the three men moved into the dark passageway leading from the chamber. The craggy tunnel twisted and wound through the heart of the Knife Edge, the rough walls split by jagged seams and fissures. More breaks quickly appeared as the rumbling grew stronger and the walls began to crack and fall apart. The mountain shook as if the earth were threatening to open and swallow it whole, quaking with the force of the thunderous reverberations that echoed brokenly from the core of the earth. They passed through countless small passageways and connecting chambers, moving steadily, yet unable to find an exit to safety. Several times one or more went down under a cascade of rock and dust, but each time they worked themselves free. Huge chunks of rock fell crashing before them to block the tunnel passage, but the powerful Keltset heaved the boulders aside, and the small party continued quickly on. Shea began to lose all sense of what was happening to them, a strange weariness settling into his body, pressing remorselessly down and sapping the little stamina that remained. When he thought he could no longer continue, Panamon was at his side to support him, the strong arm alternately lifting him over and shoving him through the stone rubble.

They had reached a particularly narrow section of the passageway that angled sharply to the right when a violent, wrenching quake shook the dying mountain. The entire ceiling of the corridor cracked with a grating snap and began to settle slowly downward. Panamon yelled frantically and pulled Shea down in front of him, trying to protect the Valeman with his own body. Instantly Keltset was there, the giant frame bracing as the great shoulders hunched upward against the tons of breaking rock. Dust rose in blinding clouds and for a moment everything was obscured from view. Then Panamon Creel was pulling the Valeman to his feet, hastening him past the straining form of the Rock Troll. Shea glanced up once as he crawled and scrambled through the broken stone, and the gentle eyes met his own. The ceiling dropped several inches farther, and the massive human support threw all the awesome strength of a Rock Troll against it, the

barklike body rigid with the tremendous strain. Shea hesitated, but Panamon's powerful grip closed over his shoulder, pulling him ahead, thrusting
him beyond the tunnel angle into a wider corridor. They collapsed in a
pile of loose rock and dust, gasping for air. They had just a glimpse of
Keltset, his great frame still braced against the crumbling stone. Panamon
made a sudden move to start back into the passage, but a deep rumble tore
through the core of the mountain; with a groan of sliding, shifting rock,
the tunnel behind them came apart and collapsed entirely. Tons of stone
crashed downward and the way back disappeared altogether. Shea screamed
and threw himself against the wall of rock, but Panamon pulled him back
roughly, pushing the piked hand into his face.

"He's dead! We can't help him now."

The haggard face of the Valeman stared back in shock.

"Get moving—get out of here!" The thief was livid with rage. "Do
you want him to have died for nothing? Move!"

He yanked Shea violently to his feet and thrust him toward the open
section of the tunnel. The deep rumbling continued to vibrate through
the mountain, and a series of sharp, wrenching quakes nearly threw the
two men to the cavern floor as they stumbled ahead. Shea was running
blindly now, his eyes clouded with dust and tears. It was becoming difficult
to see clearly, and he blinked and squinted in an effort to clear his fading
vision. Panamon's labored breathing was close in his ear, and he felt the
iron stub of the piked hand shoving against his back, urging him to run
faster. Shards of rock splintered from the passage walls and ceiling and
rained down on his unprotected body, cutting and bruising it, tearing
the forest clothing into tattered strips that hung from the thin, sweating
form. In his hands he clutched the gleaming Sword, useless to him now
except as proof that what had happened to him was more than an imagined madness.

Abruptly the tunnel dissolved in the gray light of the Northland sky,
and they were free of the mountain. Before them, the scattered bodies of
Troll and Muten lay broken in death. Without slowing, the two men raced
for the mouth of the winding pass that split the monstrous Knife Edge.
The hardened earth was quaking violently, long jagged cracks appearing
from the base of Skull Mountain and snaking crookedly toward the ring of
natural hazards that bound the forbidden land. A sudden, grating crash,
louder than any that had preceded it, brought the two runners about. In
speechless awe, they watched the gaunt face of the skull begin to sag and
break apart. Everything seemed to shatter at once, and the mark of the
Warlock Lord disappeared as tons of rock cascaded downward and Skull
Mountain ceased to exist. A thick cloud of yellow dust surged skyward and
a heavy booming sound burst from the bowels of the earth and echoed
through the vast emptiness of the Northland. Violent winds swept over the
remains of the dying mountain and the rumbling in the earth began to
build once more. In horror Shea saw the monstrous Knife Edge begin
to shake with the force of this new convulsion. The entire kingdom was
disintegrating!

Already Panamon was running brokenly for the pass, pulling a dazed Shea with him. But the Valeman needed no urging this time and quickly picked up the pace on his own, his form flying through the tangle of dead bodies. From some final reservoir of courage and determination, he summoned the last of his strength, and a surprised Panamon Creel suddenly found himself running to keep up. By the time they reached the mouth of the mountain pass, pieces of the towering Knife Edge were beginning to break apart and fall, snapping free with piercing cracks as the booming quakes continued to shake the land. Massive boulders fell with crushing force into the winding canyon, and a heavy avalanche of loose stone slid steadily from the heights of the ancient peaks, building in force as the seconds slipped by. Through the center of this holocaust the two Southlanders dodged and twisted—the tattered half Elf, brandishing his ancient Sword, and the one-handed thief. The force of the wind broke over their backs, thrusting them faster through the hail of stone and dust. Twists and turns in the rock walls came and disappeared, and they knew they were closing on the far end of the canyon and the open foothills beyond. Shea was suddenly aware that his eyesight was blurring once more and he stumbled uncertainly, his free hand rubbing angrily to clear his vision.

Suddenly the entire west wall of the canyon seemed to break apart and come crashing down on both men, burying them in a choking rush of broken rock and dirt. Something sharp struck his exposed head, and for a moment Shea slipped into blackness. He lay partially covered by the mass of rubble, his groping mind trying to shake itself awake. Then Panamon was digging him free, the strong arm lifting him clear of the shattered stone and holding him upright. Through a gray haze, Shea saw blood on the big man's face. Slowly Shea rose to his feet, leaning heavily on the Sword of Shannara for support.

Panamon remained on his knees. His piked hand pointed to the pass behind them. Shea glanced anxiously past him. To his dismay, he caught sight of a misshapen, lumbering creature slowly bearing down on them from out of the rising clouds of dust. A Muten! The formless, plastic face was turned toward them and the monster shuffled steadily forward. Panamon looked up at Shea and smiled grimly.

"He's been with us all the way from the other end. I thought we might lose him in the rocks, but he's persistent."

He rose slowly and drew free the long broadsword.

"Get going, Shea. I'll catch up shortly."

The startled Valeman shook his head speechlessly. He must have misunderstood.

"We can outrun him," he burst out finally. "We've almost reached the end of the pass anyway. We can fight him there—together!"

Panamon shook his head and smiled sadly.

"Not this time, I'm afraid. I've done something to my leg. I can't run anymore." He shook his head as Shea opened his mouth to speak. "I don't want to hear it, Shea. Now run—and keep running!"

Tears were streaming down the Valeman's face as he stared at the man. "I can't do that!"

A sudden rumble shook the Knife Edge, throwing Panamon and Shea to their knees again. Boulders crashed down the crumbling mountainside as the heavy convulsions continued to build from deep within the earth. The Muten lumbered mindlessly toward them, unaffected by the tremors. Panamon climbed shakenly to his feet, pulling Shea after him.

"The whole pass is coming down," he stated quietly. "We don't have time to argue. I can take care of myself—just as I did long before I met you or Keltset. Now I want you to run—get clear of this pass!"

He put one hand on the Valeman's slim shoulder and gently shoved him away. Shea took several steps backward and hesitated, bringing the Sword of Shannara up almost threateningly. Panamon Creel's broad face showed a flicker of surprise, and then the familiar devilish grin appeared and the eyes turned to fire.

"We'll meet again, Shea Ohmsford. You watch for me."

He waved the piked hand once in farewell, and turned to meet the advancing Muten. Shea stared after him momentarily. His fading eyesight must be fooling him—for an instant it seemed that the scarlet thief was not limping, after all. Then the heavy tremors rippled through the mountain pass still another time, and the Valeman broke for the safety of the foothills. Slipping and stumbling through the loose rock and earth, dodging the cascade of stone and debris that tumbled from the heights of the Knife Edge into the narrow canyon, he ran on alone.

34

The afternoon was almost gone. Sunlight slipped in long, hazy streamers through the drifting white clouds, settling with warm touches over the barren, empty Northland terrain. Here and there the light fell providently on small patches of green—the first signs of a permanent life that one day soon would flourish in this earth that had lain parched and desolate for so many years. In the distance, the blunted tips of the shattered Knife Edge broke starkly against the northern horizon, and from the devastated valley beyond, the dust still hung suspended above the ruins of the Skull Kingdom.

Shea seemed to appear out of nowhere, wandering aimlessly through the tangle of ravines and ridges that carved out the foothills immediately below the Knife Edge. Half-blind and completely exhausted, the tattered figure was barely recognizable. He came toward Allanon without seeing him, both hands gripping tightly the silver-handled sword. For just an instant, the Druid stared speechlessly at the strange spectacle of the stumbling, ragged swordsman. Then with a sharp cry of relief, he rushed forward to gather in the thin, battered frame of Shea Ohmsford, and held him close.

The Valeman was asleep for a long time, and when he came awake again, it was night. He was lying in the shelter of a rock-encrusted overhang that opened into a deep, wide-bottomed ravine. A small wood fire crackled peacefully, lending added warmth to the cloak that was wrapped tightly about him. His troubled vision had begun to clear, and he found himself staring up into a bright, starlit night sky that stretched canopylike from ridge top to ridge top above him. He smiled in spite of himself. He could imagine himself in Shady Vale once again. A moment later Allanon's dark shadow moved into the dim firelight.

"Are you feeling better?" the Druid asked in greeting and seated himself. There was something strange about Allanon. He seemed more human, less forbidding, and there was an unusual warmth in his voice.

Shea nodded. "How did you find me?"

"You found me. Don't you remember anything?"

"No, none of it—nothing after . . ." Shea paused hesitantly. "Was there anybody . . . did you see anybody else?"

Allanon studied his anxious expression for a moment, as if debating his answer, then shook his dark face.

"You were alone."

Shea felt something catch in his throat, and he lay back in the warmth of the blankets, swallowing hard. So Panamon, too, was gone. Somehow, he had not expected it to end like this.

"Are you all right?" the Druid's deep voice reached out to him in the darkness. "Would you like to eat something now? I think it would be good for you if you did."

"Yes." Shea pushed himself up into a sitting position, the cloak still wrapped protectively about him. By the fire, Allanon was pouring soup into a small bowl. The aroma reached out to him invitingly, and he breathed it in. Then suddenly he thought of the Sword of Shannara and looked for it in the darkness. He saw it almost immediately, lying next to him, the bright metal gleaming faintly. As an afterthought, he felt through the pockets of his tunic for the Elfstones. He could not find them. Panicked, he began searching desperately through his clothing for the little pouch, but the result was the same. It was gone. A sinking sensation gripped him, and he lay back weakly for a moment. Perhaps Allanon . . .

"Allanon, I can't find the Elfstones," he said quickly. "Did you . . . ?"

The Druid moved over to his side and handed him the steaming bowl of soup and a small wooden spoon. His face was an impenetrable black shadow.

"No, Shea. You must have lost them when you fled the Knife Edge." He saw the crestfallen look on the other's face and reached over to pat the slim shoulder reassuringly. "There's no point in worrying about them now. The stones have served their purpose. I want you to eat something and go back to sleep—you need to rest."

Mechanically, Shea sipped at the soup, unable to forget quite so easily the loss of the Elfstones. They had been with him from the beginning, protecting him every step of the way. Several times, they had saved his life. How could he have been so careless? He thought back for a moment, trying vainly to remember where he might have lost them, but it was useless. It could have happened anytime.

"I'm sorry about the Elfstones," he apologized quietly, feeling that he had to say something more.

Allanon shrugged and smiled faintly. He seemed weary and somehow older as he seated himself beside the Valeman.

"Maybe they'll turn up later."

Shea finished the bowl in silence, and Allanon refilled it without being asked. The warm liquid relaxed the still-weary Valeman, and a numbing drowsiness began to seep slowly through his body. He was falling asleep again. It would have been so easy to give in to the feeling, but he could not. There were still too many things bothering him, too many unanswered questions. He wanted those answers now from the one man who could give them to him. He deserved that much after everything he had been through.

He struggled to a sitting position, aware that Allanon was watching him closely from out of the darkness beyond the little fire. In the distance, the sharp cry of a night bird broke through the deep silence. Shea paused in spite of himself. Life was coming back to the Northland—after so long. He placed the bowl of soup on the ground next to him and turned to Allanon.

"Can we talk awhile?"

The Druid nodded silently.

"Why didn't you tell me the truth about the Sword?" the Valeman asked softly. "Why didn't you?"

"I told you all that you needed to know." Allanon's dark face was impassive. "The Sword itself told you the rest."

Shea stared at him incredulously.

"It was necessary for you to learn the secret of the Sword of Shannara for yourself," the Druid continued gently. "It was not something that I could explain to you—it was something that you had to experience. You had to learn to accept the truth about yourself first before the Sword could be of any use to you as a talisman against the Warlock Lord. It was a process in which I could not involve myself directly."

"Well, could you not at least have told me why the Sword would destroy Brona?" Shea persisted.

"And what would that have done to you, Shea?"

The Valeman frowned. "I don't understand."

"If I had told you everything that it was in my power to tell you about the Sword—remembering now that you would not have the benefit of hindsight, as you do now, to enlighten you—would that have helped you in practical terms? Would you have been able to continue your search for the Sword? Would you have been able to draw the Sword against Brona, knowing that it would do no more than reveal to him the truth about himself? Would you have even believed me when I said that such a simple thing would destroy a monster with the power of the Warlock Lord?"

He hunched down closer to Shea in the dim firelight.

"Or would you have given up on yourself and the quest then and there? How much truth could you have withstood?"

"I don't know," Shea answered doubtfully.

"Then I will tell you something I could not tell you before. Jerle Shannara, five hundred years earlier, knew all these things—and still he failed."

"But I thought . . ."

"That he was successful?" Allanon finished the thought. "Yet if he had been successful, would not the Warlock Lord have been destroyed? No, Shea, Jerle Shannara did not succeed. Bremen confided in the Elven King the secret of the Sword because he, too, thought that knowing how the talisman would be used might better prepare the bearer for a confrontation with Brona. It did not. Even though he had been forewarned that he would be exposed to the truth about himself, Jerle Shannara was not prepared for what he discovered. Indeed, there was probably no way that he could have adequately prepared himself beforehand. We build too many walls to be completely honest with ourselves. And I don't think that he ever really believed Bremen's warning about what would happen when he finally held the Sword. Jerle Shannara was a warrior king, and his natural instinct was to rely on the Sword as a physical weapon, even though he had been told that it would not help him in that way. When he confronted the Warlock Lord and the talisman began to work on him exactly as Bremen had warned, he panicked. His physical strength, his fighting prowess, his battle experience—all of it useless to him. It was just too much for him to accept. As a result, the Warlock Lord managed to escape him."

Shea looked unconvinced.

"It might have been different with me."

But the Druid did not seem to hear him.

"I would have been with you when you found the Sword of Shannara, and when the secret of the talisman revealed itself to you, I would have explained then its significance as a weapon against the Warlock Lord. But then I lost you in the Dragon's Teeth, and it was only later that I realized you had found the Sword and gone northward without me. I came after you, but even so, I was almost too late. I could sense your panic when you discovered the secret of the Sword, and I knew the Warlock Lord could sense it as well. But I was still too far away to reach you in time. I tried to call out to you—to project my voice into your mind. There wasn't time enough to tell you what to do; the Warlock Lord prevented that. A few words, that was all."

He paused, almost as if he had gone into a trance, his dark gaze fixed on the air between them.

"But you discovered the answer on your own, Shea—and you survived."

The Valeman looked away, reminded suddenly that, although he was alive, it seemed that everyone who had gone with him into the kingdom of the Skull was dead.

"It might have been different," he repeated woodenly.

Allanon said nothing. At his feet, the small fire was dying slowly into reddish embers as the night closed about them. Shea picked up the bowl of soup and finished it quickly, feeling the drowsiness slip through him once more. He was nodding when Allanon stirred unexpectedly in the darkness and moved next to him.

"You believe me wrong in not telling you the secret of the Sword?" he murmured softly. It was more a statement of fact than a question. "Perhaps you are right. Perhaps it would have been better for everyone if I had revealed it all to you from the first."

Shea looked up at him. The lean face was a mask of dark hollows and angular lines that seemed the wrappings of some perpetual enigma.

"No, you were right," the Valeman replied slowly. "I'm not sure I could have handled the truth."

Allanon's head tilted slightly to one side, as if considering the possibility.

"I should have had more faith in you, Shea. But I was afraid." He paused as a trace of doubt clouded the Valeman's face. "You don't believe me, but it's true. To you, to the others as well, I have always been something more than human. It was necessary, or you would never have accepted your role as I gave it to you. But a Druid is still a human being, Shea. And you have forgotten something. Before he became the Warlock Lord, Brona was a Druid. Thus to some extent, at least, the Druids must bear responsibility for what he became. We permitted him to become the Warlock Lord. Our learning gave him the opportunity; our subsequent isolation from the rest of the world allowed him to evolve. The entire human race might have been enslaved or destroyed, and the guilt would have been ours. Twice the Druids had the opportunity to destroy him—and twice they failed to do so. I was the last of my people, and if I were to fail as well, then there would be no one left to protect the races against this monstrous evil. Yes, I was afraid. One small mistake and I might have left Brona free forever."

The Druid's voice dropped to a whisper and he looked down for an instant.

"There is one more thing you should know. Bremen was more to me than simply my ancestor. He was my father."

"Your father!" Shea came fully awake for an instant. "But that's not poss . . ."

He trailed off, unable to finish. Allanon smiled faintly.

"There must have been times when you guessed that I was older than any normal man could be, surely. The Druids discovered the secret of longevity following the First War of the Races. But there is a price—a price that Brona refused to pay. There are many demands and disciplines required, Shea. It is no great gift. And for our waking time, we pile up a debt that must be paid by a special kind of sleep that restores us from our aging. There are many steps to true longevity, and some are not—pleasant. Not one is easy. Brona searched for a way different from that of the Druids, a way that would not carry the same price, the same sacrifices; in the end, he found only illusion."

The Druid seemed to retreat into himself for a long moment, then continued.

"Bremen was my father. He had a chance to end the menace of the Warlock Lord, but he made too many mistakes and Brona escaped him. His escape was my father's responsibility—and if the Warlock Lord had succeeded in his plans, my father would have earned the blame. I lived with the fear of that happening until it was an obsession. I swore not to make the mistakes he had made. I'm afraid, Shea, that I never really had much faith in you. I feared you were too weak to do what had to be done, and I hid the truth to serve my own ends. In many ways, I was unfair to you. But you were my last chance to redeem my father, to purge my own sense of guilt for what he had done, and to erase forever the responsibility of the Druids for the creation of Brona."

He hesitated and looked directly into Shea's eyes. "I was wrong, Valeman. You were a better man than I gave you credit for being."

Shea smiled and shook his head slowly.

"No, Allanon. You were the one who so often spoke to me of hindsight. Now heed your own words, historian."

In the darkness across from him, the Druid returned the smile wistfully.

"I wish . . . I wish we had more time, Shea Ohmsford. Time to learn to know each other better. But I have a debt that must be paid . . . all too soon . . ."

He trailed off almost sadly, the lean face lowering into shadow. The puzzled Valeman waited a moment, thinking that he would say something more. He did not.

"In the morning, then." Shea stretched wearily and burrowed deep into the cloak, warm and relaxed by the soup and the fire. "We've a long journey back to the Southland."

Allanon did not reply immediately.

"Your friends are close now, looking for you," he responded finally. "When they find you, will you relate to them all that I have told you?"

Shea barely heard him, his thoughts drifting to Shady Vale and the hope of going home again.

"You can do the job better than I," he murmured sleepily.

There was another long moment of silence. At last he heard Allanon moving in the darkness beyond, and when the tall man spoke again, his voice sounded strangely distant.

"I may not be able to, Shea. I'm very tired—I've exhausted myself physically. For a time now, I must . . . sleep."

"Tomorrow," Shea mumbled. "Good night."

The Druid's voice came back a whisper.

"Good-bye, my young friend. Good-bye, Shea."

But the Valeman was already sleeping.

Shea awoke with a start, the morning sunlight streaming down on him. His eyes snapped open at the sound of horses' hooves and booted feet, and he found himself surrounded by a cluster of lean, rangy figures clothed in forest green. Instinctively his hand dropped to the Sword of Shannara, and he struggled to a sitting position, squinting sharply to see their faces. They were Elves. A tall, hard-featured Elf detached himself from the group and bent down to him. Deep, penetrating green eyes locked into his own, and a firm hand came up to rest reassuringly on his shoulder.

"You're among friends, Shea Ohmsford. We are Eventine's men."

Shea climbed slowly to his feet, still grasping the Sword guardedly.

"Allanon . . . ?" he asked, looking about for the Druid.

The tall man hesitated for a moment, then shook his head.

"There is no one else here. Only you."

Stunned, Shea moved past him and pushed his way through the ring of horsemen, his eyes quickly searching the length of the wide ravine. Gray rock and dust stared back at him, an empty, deserted passage that twisted and disappeared from sight. Except for the Elven riders and himself, there was no one else. Then something the Druid had said came back to him—and he knew then that Allanon was really gone.

"Sleeping . . ." he heard himself whisper.

Woodenly, he turned back to the waiting Elves, then hesitated as tears streamed down his haggard face. But Allanon would come back to them when he was needed, he told himself angrily. Just as he had always done before. He brushed away the tears, and glanced momentarily into the bright blueness of the Northland sky. For just an instant, he seemed to hear the Druid's voice calling to him from far, far away. A faint smile crossed his lips.

"Good-bye, Allanon," he answered softly.

35

So it ended. Little more than ten days later, those who still remained of the little band that had journeyed forth from Culhaven so many weeks ago bade farewell to one another for the last time. It was a bright, clear day filled with sunshine and summer's freshness. From out of the west, a gentle breeze ruffled the emerald green carpet of the Tyrsian grasslands, and in the distance, the sluggish roar of the Mermidon floated softly through the early-morning stillness. They stood together by the roadway leading out from the walled city—Durin and Dayel, the former without the use of his left arm, which was splinted and wrapped. Dayel had found him among the wounded, and now he was healing rapidly. Balinor Buckhannah in chain mail and royal blue riding cloak, a still-pale Shea Ohmsford, the faithful Flick, and Menion Leah. They spoke in quiet tones for a time, smiling bravely, trying to appear amiable and relaxed without much success, glancing from time to time at the tethered horses that grazed contentedly behind them. At last there was an awkward silence, and hands were extended and taken, and mumbled promises to visit soon were quietly exchanged. It was a painful good-bye, and behind the smiles and the handshakes, there was sadness.

Then they rode away, each to his own home. Durin and Dayel traveled west to Beleal, where Dayel would finally be reunited with his beloved Lynliss. The Ohmsfords turned south to Shady Vale and, as Flick had repeatedly announced to his brother, a well-deserved rest. As far as Flick was concerned, their traveling days were over. Menion Leah went with them to the Vale, determined to see to it personally that nothing further befell Shea. From there, he would return for a time to the highlands to be with his father, who would be missing him by now. But very soon, he knew he must come back again to the border country and to the red-haired daughter of kings who would be waiting.

Standing silently by the empty roadway, Balinor watched after his friends until they were no more than small shadows in the distant green of the flatlands. Then slowly he mounted his waiting horse and rode back into Tyrsis.

The Sword of Shannara remained in Callahorn. It had been Shea's firm decision to leave the talisman with the border people. No one had given more to preserve the freedom of the four lands. No one had a better right to be entrusted with its care and preservation. And so the legendary Sword was implanted blade downward in a block of red marble and placed in a vault in the center of the gardens of the People's Park in Tyrsis, sheltered by the wide, protective span of the Bridge of Sendic, there to remain for all time. Carved upon the stone facing of the vault was the inscription:

> *Herein lies the heart and soul of the nations.*
> *Their right to be free men,*
> *Their desire to live in peace,*
> *Their courage to seek out truth.*
> *Herein lies the Sword of Shannara.*

Weeks later, Shea perched wearily on one of the tall wooden stools in the inn kitchen and studied blankly the plate of food on the counter in front of him. At his elbow, Flick was already starting on his second helping. It was early in the evening, and the Ohmsford brothers had spent the entire day repairing the veranda roof. The summer sun had been hot and the work had been tedious; yet, although he was tired and vaguely disgruntled, Shea found himself unable to locate his appetite. He was still picking at his food when his father appeared in the hall doorway, mumbling blackly to himself. Curzad Ohmsford came up to them without a word and tapped Shea on the shoulder

"How much longer is this nonsense going to continue?" he demanded.

Shea looked up in surprise.

"I don't know what you mean," he answered truthfully, glancing at Flick, who shrugged blankly.

"Not eating much either, I see." His father spied the dinner plate. "How do you expect to get your strength back if you don't eat properly?"

He paused for a moment, and then seemed to recall that he had gotten off the subject entirely.

"Strangers, that's what I mean. Now I suppose you'll be off again. I thought that was all done with."

Shea stared at him.

"I'm not going anywhere. What in the world are you talking about?"

Curzad Ohmsford seated himself heavily on a vacant stool and eyed his foster son closely, apparently resigned to the fact that he was not going to get a straight answer without a little unnecessary effort.

"Shea, we have never lied to each other, have we? When you came back from your visit with the Prince of Leah, I never pressed you about what went on while you were there, even though you left in the middle of the night without a word to anyone, even though you came back looking like your own ghost and very carefully avoided telling me exactly how you got that way. Now answer me," he continued quickly when Shea tried to object. "I never once asked you to tell me anything, did I?"

Shea shook his head silently. His father nodded in satisfaction.

"No, because I happen to believe that a man's business is mostly his own affair. But I cannot forget that the last time you disappeared from the Vale was right after that other stranger appeared asking for you."

"Other stranger!" the brothers exclaimed together.

Instantly all the old memories came back to them—Allanon's mysterious appearance, Balinor's warning, the Skull Bearers, the running, the fear . . . Shea slid down from his stool slowly.

"There's someone here . . . looking for me?"

His father nodded, his broad face clouding darkly as he caught the look of concern mirrored in his son's furtive glance at the doorway.

"A stranger, like before. He got in several minutes ago, looking for you. He's waiting out in the lobby. But I don't see . . ."

"Shea, what can we do?" Flick interrupted hurriedly. "We don't even have the Elfstones to protect us anymore."

"I . . . I don't know," his brother mumbled, desperately trying to think through his confusion. "We could slip out the back way . . ."

"Now wait a minute!" Curzad Ohmsford had heard enough. He gripped their shoulders tightly and turned them about to face him, staring at them in disbelief.

"I did not raise my sons to run away from trouble." He studied their worried faces a moment and shook his head. "You must learn to face your problems, not run from them. Why, here you are in your own home, among family and friends who will stand by you, and you talk about running away."

He released them and stepped back a pace.

"Now we'll all go out there together and face this man. He looks a hard sort, but he seemed friendly enough when we talked. Besides, I don't think a one-handed man is any kind of a match physically for three whole men—even with that pike."

Shea started abruptly.

"One-handed . . . ?"

"He looks like he traveled a long way to get here." The elder Ohmsford did not seem to have heard him. "He's carrying a little leather pouch that he claims belongs to you. I offered to take it, but he wouldn't give it to me. Said he wouldn't give it to anyone but you."

Now suddenly Flick understood.

"It must be something important," his father declared. "He told me you dropped it on your way home. Now how could that happen?"

Curzad Ohmsford had to wait a while longer for his answer. In a rush, his sons were past him, through the kitchen door, and halfway down the hallway to the lobby of the inn.

THE ELFSTONES
OF SHANNARA

For Barbara,
With Love

FOREWORD

I finished revision work on *The Sword of Shannara* in the fall of 1975, an undertaking that ended up consuming almost a year, and went to work several months later on a new book. I outlined the story three-quarters of the way through, but the last quarter didn't seem to want to fall into place, so I left it. Then I sat down to write. I told my editor, Lester del Rey, what I was doing. He said fine, but could he see some of it? Or at least the outline? Sometimes a second book was harder to write than the first, he cautioned. Silly old Lester, I thought, and put him off. I wanted to surprise him. The truth was I thought I would astonish him because I was certain that this book was going to be miles better than the first.

By the spring of 1977, writing nights and weekends while I practiced law, I had completed three-quarters of the book and still hadn't figured out the ending. The story seemed right enough, yet at the same time something was wrong. So at last I packed it up and sent it off to Lester. Surely he would know what to do to wrap things up.

Lester knew exactly what to do, and told me in no uncertain terms. The story would have to be scrapped, he wrote back. It had so many problems that there was no way to salvage it. I could publish it if I wanted—the success of *Sword* assured that someone would pick it up. But he advised against it. He felt so strongly that he said he would return the manuscript with specific page-by-page comments on what was wrong.

I was stunned. Two and a half years of work down the drain! I didn't know if I could accept it. Nevertheless, I waited for the comments to arrive, and when they did I read them through carefully several times. They catalogued multiple problems of plot, character, pacing, perspective, and focus, and as much as I hated to admit it, they were right on the mark.

That was the beginning of my professional education as a writer. Ruefully, I admitted that the manuscript was a mess. I would do as suggested and start over, this time submitting an outline in advance in an effort to identify potential problems before all the work was done.

I turned to a much needed and often promised story on the history of the Elves. There had been no strong female lead in *Sword*, so the new book would have one. Amberle, the Elven Chosen with a secret past and an uncertain future, came into being. As her counterpart, there was Eretria, the fiery Rover girl. Allanon would be back, and Eventine Elessedil, now in his twilight years as King of the Elves. The Free Corps Commander Stee Jans would fill the void left by Balinor. And this time the danger that threatened the people of the Four Lands would come both from without and from another time, and it would wear several faces.

After some deliberation, the title of the new book became *The Elf-stones of Shannara.*

My education as a writer continued. After submitting the outline for the story and gaining Lester's approval late in 1978, I went to work. *Elfstones* took two years to write, and when it was finished I dispatched it with an uncertain sigh of relief. It was done, but was it done right? I was no longer so certain of myself. Lester wrote back in February of 1981. The letter he sent was twenty-five pages long, single-spaced. I took a deep breath and read. The book was coming along, he advised. But . . . the other shoe dropped. Two hundred plus pages in the very middle of the book would have to be rewritten. The reason? All of the action was narrated rather too dispassionately from the viewpoint of the author. It needed to be observed and reacted to by a character in the book. SHOW—DON'T TELL! Thus spoke Lester. The focal point of narrative was to be Ander Elessedil, a character who until now was secondary to the storyline. I couldn't believe it. Twenty-five pages of changes. Over two hundred pages of rewrites. After a good bit of teeth gritting and more than a few mumbled threats, I went back to the typewriter. Four months later the story went out again. A smattering of additional changes and Lester was happy.

To this day *Elfstones* remains my favorite book if for no better reason than so much work went into seeing it completed. I think, on looking back, that Lester taught me almost everything I know about being a professional writer from that one experience. I have forgotten the title of that other book, and the manuscript has long since been lost, but I remember every mistake I made and every lesson it taught.

I should. It made me a better writer.

—Terry Brooks

The night sky brightened faintly in the east with the approach of dawn as the Chosen entered the Gardens of Life. Without, the Elven city of Arborlon lay sleeping, its people still wrapped in the warmth and solitude of their beds. But for the Chosen, the day had already begun. Their trailing white robes billowing slightly with a rush of summer wind, they passed between the sentries of the Black Watch, who stood rigid and aloof as such sentries had stood for centuries gone before the arched, wrought-iron gateway inlaid with silver scroll and ivory chips. They passed quickly, and only their soft voices and the crunch of their sandled feet on the gravel pathway disturbed the silence of the new day as they slipped into the pine-shadowed dark beyond.

The Chosen were the caretakers of the Ellcrys, the strange and wondrous tree that stood at the center of the Gardens—the tree, as the legends told, that served as protector against a primordial evil that had very nearly destroyed the Elves centuries ago, an evil that had been shut away from the earth since before the dawn of the old race of Men. In all the time that had followed, there had been Chosen to care for the Ellcrys. Theirs was a tradition handed down through generations of Elves, a tradition of service that the Elves regarded as both a coveted honor and a solemn duty.

Yet there was little evidence of solemnity in the procession that passed through the Gardens this morning. Two hundred and thirty days of the year of their service had gone by, and youthful spirits could no longer be easily subdued. The first sense of awe at the responsibility given them had long since passed, and the Chosen of the Elves were now just six young men on their way to perform a task they had performed each day since the time of their choosing, a task grown old and familiar—the greeting of the tree at the first touch of sunrise.

Only Lauren, youngest of this year's Chosen, was silent. He lagged a bit behind the others as they walked, taking no part in their idle chatter. His red head was bent in concentration, and there was a deep frown on his face. So wrapped up in his thoughts was he that he was not aware when the noise ahead ceased, nor of the steps that fell back beside him, until a hand touched his arm. Then his troubled face jerked up abruptly to find Jase regarding him.

"What's the matter, Lauren? Are you sick?" Jase asked. Because he was a few months older than the rest, Jase was the accepted leader of the Chosen.

Lauren shook his head, but the frown did not leave his face entirely. "I'm all right."

"*Something* is bothering you. You've been brooding all morning. Come to think of it, you were rather quiet last night, too." Jase's hand on his shoulder brought the younger Elf about to face him. "Come on, out with it. Nobody expects you to serve if you're not feeling well."

Lauren hesitated, then sighed and nodded. "All right. It's the Ellcrys. Yesterday, at sunset, just before we left her, I thought I saw some spotting on her leaves. It looked like wilt."

"Wilt? Are you sure? Nothing like that ever happens to the Ellcrys—at least that's what we've always been told," Jase said doubtfully.

"I could have been mistaken," Lauren admitted. "It was getting dark. I told myself then that it was probably just the way the shadows lay on the leaves. But the more I try to remember how it looked, the more I think it really was wilt."

There was a disconcerted muttering from the others, and one of them spoke. "This is Amberle's fault. I said before that something bad would come from having a girl picked as a Chosen."

"There were other girls among the Chosen, and nothing happened because of it," Lauren protested. He had always liked Amberle. She had been easy to talk to, even if she was King Eventine Elessedil's granddaughter.

"Not for five hundred years, Lauren," the other said.

"All right, that's enough," Jase interrupted. "We agreed not to talk about Amberle. You know that." He stood silently for a moment, pondering what Lauren had said. Then he shrugged. "It would be unfortunate if anything happened to the tree, especially while she was under our care. But after all, nothing lasts forever."

Lauren was shocked. "But Jase, when the tree weakens, the Forbidding will end and the Demons within will be freed . . ."

"Do you really believe those old stories, Lauren?" Jase laughed.

Lauren stared at the older Elf. "How can you be a Chosen and *not* believe?"

"I don't remember being asked what I believed when I was chosen, Lauren. Were you asked?"

Lauren shook his head. Candidates for the honor of being Chosen were never asked anything. They were simply brought before the tree—young Elves who had crossed over into manhood and womanhood in the prior year. At the dawn of the new year, they gathered to pass beneath her limbs, each pausing momentarily for acceptance. Those the tree touched upon the shoulders became the new Chosen, to serve until the year was done. Lauren could still remember the mix of ecstasy and pride he had felt at the moment a slender branch had bent to touch him and he'd heard her speak his name.

And he remembered, too, the astonishment of all when Amberle had been called . . .

"It's just a tale to frighten children," Jase was saying. "The real function of the Ellcrys is to serve as a reminder to the Elven people that they, like her, survive despite all the changes that have taken place in the history of the Four Lands. She is a symbol of our people's strength, Lauren—nothing more."

He motioned for them all to resume their walk into the Gardens and turned away. Lauren lapsed back into thought. The older Elf's casual disregard for the legend of the tree disturbed him. Of course Jase was from the city, and Lauren had observed that the people of Arborlon seemed to take the old beliefs less seriously than did those of the little northern village from which he came. But the story of the Ellcrys and the Forbidding wasn't just a story—it was the foundation of everything that was truly Elven, the most important event in the history of his people.

It had all taken place long ago, before the birth of the new world. There had been a great war between good and evil—a war that the Elves had finally won by creating the Ellcrys and a Forbidding that had banished the evil Demons into a timeless dark. And so long as the Ellcrys was kept well, so long would the evil be locked from the land.

So long as the Ellcrys was kept well . . .

He shook his head doubtfully. Maybe the wilt was but a trick of his imagination. Or a trick of the light. And if not, they would simply have to find a cure. There was always a cure.

Moments later, he stood with the others before the tree. Hesitantly, he looked up, then sighed in relief. It appeared as if the Ellcrys was unchanged. Perfectly formed, her silver-white trunk arched skyward in a symmetrically balanced network of tapered limbs clustered with broad, five-cornered leaves that were blood-red in color. At her base, strips of green moss grew in patchwork runners through the cracks and crevices of the smooth-skinned bark, like emerald streams flowing down a mountain hillside. There were no splits to mar the trunk's even lines, no branches cracked or broken. So beautiful, he thought. He looked again, but could see no signs of the sickness he had feared.

The others went to gather the tools they would use in the feeding and grooming of the tree and in the general upkeep of the Gardens. But Jase held Lauren back. "Would you like to greet her today, Lauren?" he asked.

Lauren stammered his surprised thanks. Jase was giving up his turn for the most special of tasks, obviously in an effort to cheer him.

He stepped forward under the spreading branches to lay his hands upon the smooth-skinned trunk, the others gathering about a few paces back to recite the morning greeting. He glanced upward expectantly, searching for the first beam of sunlight that would fall upon her form.

Then abruptly he drew back. The leaves directly above him were dark with patches of wilt. His heart fell. There was spotting elsewhere as well, scattered throughout the tree. It was not a trick of light and shadow. It was real.

He motioned frantically for Jase, then pointed as the other came forward. As was their custom at this time, they did not speak, but Jase gasped as he saw the extent of the damage already done. Slowly the two walked around the tree, discovering spots everywhere, some barely visible, others already darkening the leaves so badly that their blood-red color seemed drained away.

Whatever his professed beliefs concerning the tree, Jase was badly shaken, and his face reflected his dismay as he went back to confer in whispers with the others. Lauren moved to join them, but Jase quickly shook his head, motioning to the top of the tree, where the dawn's light had almost reached the uppermost branches.

Lauren knew his duty and he turned back again to the tree. Whatever else was to happen, the Chosen must greet the Ellcrys this day as they had greeted her each day since the beginning of their Order.

He placed his hands gently on the silver bark and the words of greeting were forming on his lips when a slender branch from the ancient tree dipped slightly to brush his shoulder.

—Lauren—

The young Elf jumped at the sound of his name. But no one had spoken. The sound had been in his mind, the voice little more than an image of his own face.

It was the Ellcrys!

He caught his breath, twisting his head to glimpse briefly the branch that rested on his shoulder before turning quickly back again. Confusion swept through him. Only once before had she spoken to him—on the day of his choosing. She had spoken his name then; she had spoken all their names. It had been the last time. She had never spoken to any of them after that. Never—except to Amberle, of course, and Amberle was no longer one of them.

He looked hurriedly at the others. They were staring at him, curious as to why he had stopped. Then the branch that rested upon his shoulder slipped down to wrap about him loosely, and he flinched involuntarily with its touch.

—Lauren. Call the Chosen to me—

The images appeared quickly and were gone. Hesitantly, Lauren beckoned to his comrades. They came forward, questions forming on their lips as they stared upward at the silver-limbed tree. Branches lowered to clasp each, and the voice of the Ellcrys whispered softly.

—Hear me. Remember what I tell you. Do not fail me—

A chill swept over them, and the Gardens of Life were shrouded in deep, hollow silence, as if in all the world only they were alive. Images filled their minds, flowing one after the other in rapid succession. There was horror contained in those images. Had they been able, the Chosen would have turned away, to flee and hide until the nightmare that possessed them had passed and been forgotten. But the tree held them fast, and the images continued to flow and the horror to mount, until they felt they could stand no more.

Then at last it was finished, and the Ellcrys was silent once more, her limbs lifting from their shoulders and stretching wide to catch the warmth of the morning sun.

Lauren stood frozen, tears streaming down his cheeks. Shattered, the six Chosen faced one another, and in each mind the truth whispered soundlessly.

The legend was not legend. The legend was life. Evil did indeed lie beyond a Forbidding that the Ellcrys maintained. Only she kept the Elven people safe.

And now she was dying.

Far to the west of Arborlon, beyond the Breakline, there was a stirring in the air. Something blacker than the darkness of the early dawn appeared, writhing and shuddering with the force of some blow that appeared to strike it. Momentarily, the veil of blackness held firm. Then it split wide, rent by the force from within it. Howls and shrieks of glee spilled forth from the impenetrable blackness beyond, as dozens of clawed limbs ripped and tore at the sudden breach, straining toward the light. Then red fire exploded all about and the hands fell away, twisted and burned.

The Dagda Mor appeared out of the dark, hissing with rage. His Staff of Power steamed hotly as he brushed aside the impatient ones and stepped boldly through the opening. An instant later, the dark forms of the Reaper and the Changeling followed him. Other bodies pushed forward in desperation, but the edges of the rent came together quickly, closing off the blackness and the things that lived within it. In moments, the opening had disappeared entirely and the strange trio stood alone.

The Dagda Mor looked about warily. They stood in the shadow of the Breakline, the dawn which had already shattered the peace of the Chosen little more than a faint light in the eastern sky beyond the monstrous wall of mountains. The great, towering peaks knifed into the sky, casting pillars of darkness far out into the desolation of the Hoare Flats. The Flats themselves stretched westward from the line of the mountains into emptiness— a hard, barren wasteland in which life spans were measured in minutes and hours. Nothing moved on its surface. No sound broke the stillness of the morning air.

The Dagda Mor smiled, his hooked teeth gleaming. His coming had gone unnoticed. After all these years, he was free. He was loose once more among those who had imprisoned him.

At a distance, he might have passed for one of them. He was basically manlike in appearance. He walked upright on two legs, and his arms were only slightly longer than those of a man. He carried himself stooped over, his movements hampered by a peculiar hunching motion—but the dark robes that cloaked him made it difficult to tell the cause. It was only when close that one could see clearly the massive hump that crooked his spine almost double at the shoulders. Or the great tufts of greenish hair that protruded from all parts of his body like patches of saw grass. Or the scales that coated his forearms and lower legs. Or the hands and feet that ended in claws. Or the vaguely catlike muzzle that was his face. Or the eyes, black and shining, deceptively placid on their surface, like twin pools of water that hid something evil and destructive.

Once these were seen, there was no longer any question as to the Dagda Mor's identity. What was revealed then was not man, but Demon.

And the Demon hated. He hated with an intensity that bordered on madness. Hundreds of years of imprisonment within the black hold that lay beyond the wall of the Forbidding had given his hatred more than sufficient time to fester and grow. Now it consumed him. It was everything to him. It gave him his power, and he would use that power to crush the creatures who had caused him so much misery. The Elves! All of the Elves. And even that would not be enough to satisfy him now—not now, not after centuries of being shut from this world that had once been his—shut into that formless, insentient limbo of endless dark and slow, wretched stagnation. No, the destruction of the Elves would not be enough to salve the indignity that he had suffered. The others must be destroyed as well. Men, Dwarves, Trolls, Gnomes—all those who were a part of the humanity that he so detested, the races of humanity that lived upon his world and claimed it for their own.

His vengeance would come, he thought. Just as his freedom had come. He could feel it. He had waited centuries, posted at the wall of the Forbidding, testing its strength, probing for weakness—all the time knowing that it must, one day, begin to fail. And now that day was here. The Ellcrys was dying. Ah, sweet words! He wanted to shout them aloud! She was dying! She was dying and she could no longer maintain the Forbidding!

The Staff of Power glowed redly in his hands as the hatred flowed through him. The earth beneath its tip charred to ash. With an effort he calmed himself and the Staff grew cool again.

For a time, of course, the Forbidding would still hold firm. Complete erosion would not take place overnight nor, quite possibly, for several weeks. Even the small breach that he had managed had required enormous power. But the Dagda Mor possessed enormous power, more power than any of those still trapped behind the Forbidding. He was chief among them; his word ruled them. A few had defied that word during the long years of banishment—only a few. He had broken them. He had made unpleasant examples of them. Now all obeyed him. They feared him. But they shared his hatred of what had been done to them. They, too, fed on that hatred. It had driven them into a frenzied need for revenge, and when at last they were set free again, that need would take a long, long time to be satisfied.

But for now, they must wait. For now, they must be patient. It would not be long. The Forbidding would weaken a little more each day, decaying as the Ellcrys slowly failed. Only one thing could prevent this—a rebirth.

The Dagda Mor nodded to himself. He knew well the history of the Ellcrys. Had he not been present when she had first seen life, when she had shut his brethren and himself from their world of light into their prison of dark? Had he not seen the nature of the sorcery that had defeated them—a sorcery so powerful that it could transcend even death? And he knew that this freedom could still be taken from him. If one of the Chosen were permitted to carry a seed of the tree to the source of her power, the Ellcrys might be reborn and the Forbidding invoked again. He knew this, and it was because of this knowledge that he was here now. He had by no means been certain that he could breach the wall of the Forbidding. It had been a dangerous gamble to expend so much power in the attempt, for, had he failed, he might have been left badly weakened. There were some behind the wall almost as powerful as he; they would have seized the opportunity to destroy him. But the gamble had been necessary. The Elves did not realize the extent of their danger yet. For the moment, they believed themselves safe. They did not think that any within the confines of the Forbidding possessed sufficient power to break through. They would discover their error too late. By then, he would have made certain that the Ellcrys could never be reborn nor the Forbidding restored.

It was for that reason that he had brought the other two.

He glanced about for them now. He found the Changeling immediately, his body undergoing a steady transition of colors and shapes as he practiced duplicating the life he found here—in the sky, a searching hawk and a small raven; on the earth, a groundhog, then a snake, a multilegged insect with pincers, then on to something new, almost as quickly as the eye could follow. For the Changeling could be anything. Shut away in the darkness with only his brethren to model after, he had been denied the full use of his powers. There, they had been virtually wasted. But here, in this world, the possibilities were endless. All things, whether human or animal, fish or fowl, no matter their size, shape, color or abilities—he could be any of them. He could assimilate their characteristics perfectly. Even the Dagda Mor was not certain of the Changeling's true appearance; the creature was so prone to adapt to other life forms that he spent virtually all of his time being something or someone other than what he really was.

It was an extraordinary gift, but it was possessed by a creature whose capacity for evil was very nearly as great as that of the Dagda Mor. The Changeling, too, was of Demon spawn. He was selfish and hateful. He enjoyed duplicity; he enjoyed hurting others. He had always been the enemy of the Elven people and their allies, detesting them for their pious concern for the welfare of the lesser life forms that inhabited their world. Lesser creatures meant nothing to the Changeling. They were weak, vulnerable; they were meant to be used by more powerful beings—beings such as himself. The Elves were no better than the creatures they sought to protect. They either could not or would not deceive as he did. All of them were trapped by what they were; they could be nothing else. He could be whatever he wished. He despised them all. The Changeling had no friends. He wanted none. None but the Dagda Mor, that was, for the Dagda Mor possessed the one thing he respected—power greater than his own. It was for that reason and for that reason alone that the Changeling had come to serve him.

It took the Dagda Mor several moments longer to locate the Reaper. He found it finally, not more than ten feet away, perfectly motionless, little more than a shadow in the pale light of early dawn, another bit of fading night hunched down against the gray of the Flats. Cloaked head to foot in robes the color of damp ashes, the Reaper was almost invisible, its face carefully concealed within the shadow of a broad hood. No one ever looked upon that face more than once. The Reaper permitted only its victims to see that much of it, and its victims were all dead.

If the Changeling were to be judged dangerous, then the Reaper was ten times more so. The Reaper was a killer. Killing was the sole function of its existence. It was a massive creature, heavily muscled, almost seven feet tall when it rose to its full height. Yet its size was misleading, for it was by no means ponderous. It moved with the ease and grace of the best Elven Hunter—smooth, fluid, quick, and noiseless. Once it had begun a hunt, it never gave up. Nothing it went after ever escaped. Even the Dagda Mor was wary of the Reaper, though the Reaper did not possess his power. He was wary because the Reaper served him out of whim and not out of fear or respect as did all the others. The Reaper feared nothing. It was a monster who cared nothing for life, even its own. It did not even kill because it enjoyed killing, though in truth it did enjoy killing. It killed because killing was instinctive. It killed because it found killing necessary. At times, within the darkness of the Forbidding, shut away from every form of life but its own brethren, it had been almost unmanageable. The Dagda Mor had been forced to give it lesser Demons to kill, keeping it under his control with a promise. Once they were free of the Forbidding—and they would, one day, be free—the Reaper would be given an entire world of creatures that it might prey upon. For as long as it wished, it might hunt them. In the end, it might kill them all.

The Changeling and the Reaper. The Dagda Mor had chosen well. One would be his eyes, the other his hands, eyes and hands that would go deep into the heart of the Elven people and end forever the chance that the Ellcrys might be reborn.

He glanced sharply to the east where the rim of the morning sun was rising rapidly above the crest of the Breakline. It was time to go. By tonight, they must be in Arborlon. This, too, he had planned with care. Time was precious to him; he had little to waste if he expected to catch the Elves napping. They must not know of his presence until it was too late to do anything about it.

With a quick motion to his companions, the Dagda Mor turned and slouched heavily toward the shelter of the Breakline. His black eyes lidded with pleasure as he tasted in his mind the success tonight would bring him. After tonight, the Elves would be doomed. After tonight, they would be forced to watch their beloved Ellcrys decay without even the faintest hope for any rebirth.

Indeed. Because after tonight, the Chosen would all be dead.

Several hundred yards from the mountains, deep within their concealing shadow, the Dagda Mor stopped. With both hands gripping the Staff of Power, he placed it upright, one end planted firmly in the dry, cracked earth. His head lowered slightly, and his hands tightened about the Staff. For long moments, he stood without moving. Behind him, the other two watched curiously, their dark forms huddled down, their eyes bits of yellow light.

Then abruptly, the Staff of Power began to glow faintly, a pale reddish color that silhouetted the hulking form of the Demon against the darkness. A moment later, the glow intensified sharply and began to pulsate. It ran from the Staff into the arms of the Dagda Mor, turning the greenish skin to blood. The Demon's head came up and fire shot skyward from the Staff in a thin, brilliant arc that flew into the dawn like some frightened, living thing. It was gone in seconds. The glow that lit the Staff of Power flared once and died.

The Dagda Mor stepped back a pace, the Staff lowering. The earth about him was charred and black, and the damp air smelled of burning ash. The whole of the surrounding Flats had gone deathly still. The Demon seated himself, opaque eyes lidding contentedly. He did not move again, nor did the creatures with him. Together, they waited—half an hour, one hour, two. Still they waited.

And finally, down from the vast emptiness of the Northland, swept the monstrous, winged nightmare the Demon had summoned to carry them east to Arborlon.

"Now shall we see," the Dagda Mor whispered.

3

The sun was barely above the horizon when Ander Elessedil stepped through the front door of his small house and moved up the walkway toward the iron gates that fronted the palace grounds. As second son of Eventine, King of the Elves, he could have had his rooms in the royal quarters; but years before, he had moved himself and his books to his present residence and thereby gained a privacy that he would have lacked within the palace. Or so he had thought at the time. Now he was less certain; with his older brother Arion receiving most of their father's attention, Ander would probably have found himself largely undisturbed wherever he chose to live.

He sniffed the cleanness and early warmth of the morning air and smiled briefly. A good day for a ride. Both he and his favorite horse could use the exercise.

At forty, he was no longer a young man. His lean Elven face was lined at the corners of the narrow eyes and the furrow of his sharply angled brow; but his step was quick and easy, and his face was almost boyish when he smiled—though that was seldom these days.

As he neared the gates, he saw that Went, the old groundskeeper, was already at work, tending the flower beds with a hand hoe, his thin frame bent over his work. As he heard Ander approach, Went straightened slowly, one hand going to his back.

"Good morning, Prince. Nice day, eh?"

Ander nodded. "Splendid, Went. Back still bothering you?"

"Now and then." The old man rubbed himself gingerly. "Age catching up to me, I guess. But I can still outwork the young ones they give me for help."

Ander nodded once more, knowing the old man's boast was simple truth. Went should have retired years ago, but he'd stubbornly refused to give up his duties.

As Ander made his way through the front gate, the sentries on watch nodded in greeting, and he nodded back. The guards and he had long since dispensed with formalities. Arion, as Crown Prince, might insist on being treated deferentially, but Ander's position and expectations were somewhat less.

He followed the line of the roadway as it curved left around some decorative bushes toward the stables. Then a thunder of hooves and a shout broke the morning quiet. Ander leaped aside as Arion's gray stallion plunged toward him, scattering gravel and rearing to a sudden halt.

Before the horse was fully at rest, Arion was off and facing his brother. Where Ander was short and dark, Arion was tall and fair, and his resemblance to their father at the same age was striking. That, together with the fact that he was a superb athlete and an accomplished weapons master, hunter and horseman made it inevitable that he should be Eventine's pride and joy. There was also a compelling charisma about Arion—a charisma that Ander had always felt lacking within himself.

"Where bound, little brother?" Arion asked. As usual, when speaking to the younger Prince, his tone held a slight hint of mockery and contempt. "I wouldn't bother our father, if I were you. He and I were up late working on some rather pressing matters of state. He was still sleeping when I looked in."

"I was heading for the stables," Ander replied quietly. "I had no intention of *bothering* anyone."

Arion grinned, then turned back to his horse. With a hand on the pommel, he leaped lightly into the saddle, disregarding the stirrup. Then he turned to look down at his brother. "Well, I'm off to the Sarandanon for a few days. The people in the farming communities are all stirred up—some old fairy tale of doom overtaking us all. A lot of nonsense, but I've got to settle them down. Don't get your hopes up, though. I'll be back before father leaves for the Kershalt." He grinned. "In the meantime, little brother, look after things, will you?"

He flipped the reins and was off in a rush that carried him through the gates and away. Ander swore softly to himself and turned back. He was no longer in a mood to go riding.

He should have been the one to accompany the King on the mission of state to the Kershalt. Strengthening the ties between the Trolls and the Elves was important. And while the groundwork had already been laid, it would still require diplomacy and careful negotiating. Arion was too impatient and reckless, with too little feeling for the needs and ideas of others. Ander might lack his brother's physical skills—though he was capable enough—and he might lack as well Arion's natural flair for leadership. But he possessed a gift for thorough, deliberate reasoning and the patience needed in diplomatic councils. On the few occasions when he had been called on, he'd demonstrated such abilities.

He shrugged. There was no sense in dwelling on it now, however. He had already appealed to Eventine to go on the journey and been turned down in favor of Arion. Arion would be King someday; he must have the practice at statescraft he needed while Eventine still lived to guide him. And maybe that made sense, Ander conceded.

Once, Arion and he had been close. That was when Aine was alive—Aine, the youngest of the Elessedil sons. But Aine had been killed in a hunting accident eleven years ago, and after that the bond of kinship had no longer been enough. Amberle, Aine's young daughter, had turned to Ander for support, not to Arion, and the older brother's jealousy had soon manifested itself in open contempt. Then when Amberle had forsaken her position as one of the Chosen, Arion had blamed his brother's influence, and his contempt had degenerated into thinly masked hostility. Now Ander suspected their father's mind was being poisoned against him. But there was nothing he could do about it.

Still deep in thought, he was passing through the gates down the pathway to his house when a shout brought him around.

"My Lord Prince, wait!"

Ander stared in surprise at the sight of a white-robed figure running toward him, one arm waving frantically. It was one of the Chosen, the redheaded one—Lauren, wasn't that his name? It was unusual to see any of them outside the Gardens at this hour. He waited until the young Elf reached him, stumbling to a weary halt, face and arms streaked with sweat.

"My Lord Prince, I must see the King," the Chosen gasped. "And they won't let me through, not until later. Can you take me to him now?"

Ander hesitated. "The King is still asleep . . ."

"I must see him at once!" the other insisted. "Please! This cannot wait!"

There was desperation in his eyes and on his strained, white face. His voice was cracking with his attempt to emphasize the urgency that was driving him. Ander deliberated, wondering what could be that important. "If you're in some kind of trouble, Lauren, maybe I . . ."

"It's not me, my Lord Prince. It's the Ellcrys!"

Ander's indecision vanished. He nodded and took Lauren's arm. "Come with me."

Together they hurried back through the gates toward the manor house, the sentries staring after them in surprise.

Gael, the young Elf who served as personal aide to Eventine Elessedil, shook his head firmly—yet within his dark morning robe his slim form shifted uneasily and his eyes refused to meet those of Ander. "I cannot waken the King, Prince Ander. He told me—very strongly—not to bother him for anything."

"Or anyone, Gael?" Ander asked softly. "Not even for Arion?"

"Arion has left . . ." Gael began. Then he halted and looked even more unhappy.

"Precisely. But I am here. Are you really going to tell me that I cannot see my father?"

Gael did not answer. Then, as Ander started toward the King's bedroom, the young Elf hurried past him. "I'll wake him. Please wait here."

It was several minutes before he came out again, his face still troubled, but he nodded toward Ander. "He will see you, Prince Ander. But for now, just you."

The King was still in his bed as Ander entered, finishing the small glass of wine that Gael must have poured for him. He nodded at his son, then slipped gingerly from beneath the warmth of the bedcovers, his aging body shivering for an instant in the early morning coolness of the room. Gael, who had come in with Ander, was holding out a robe, and Eventine drew it about him, belting it snugly at the waist.

Despite his eighty-two years, Eventine Elessedil was in excellent health. His body was trim and hard. He was still able to ride, still quick and sure enough to be dangerous with a sword. His mind was sharp and alert; when the situation demanded it, as the situation frequently did, he was decisive. He still possessed that uncanny sense of balance, of proportion—the capability of seeing all sides of an issue, of judging each on its merits, and of choosing almost without exception that which would work the greatest benefit to himself and to those he ruled. It was a gift without which he could not have stayed King—would not even have stayed alive. It was a gift Ander had some reason to believe he had inherited, though it seemed worthless enough, in his present circumstances.

The King crossed to the handwoven curtains that draped the far wall, drew them aside, and pushed outward several of the floor-length windows that opened into the forest beyond. Light flooded the chamber, soft and sweet, and the smell of morning dew. Behind him, Gael was moving silently about, lighting the oil lamps to chase the last of the gloom from the corners of the chamber. Eventine hesitated before a window, staring fixedly for an instant at the reflection of his face in the misted glass. The eyes mirrored there were startlingly blue, hard and penetrating, the eyes of a man who has seen too many years and too much unpleasantness. He sighed and turned to face Ander.

"All right, Ander, what's this all about? Gael said something about your bringing one of the Chosen with a message?"

"Yes, sir. He claims he has an urgent message from the Ellcrys."

"A message from the tree?" Eventine frowned. "How long has it been since she gave a message to anyone—over seven hundred years? What was the message?"

"He wouldn't tell it to me," Ander replied. "He insists on delivering the message to you."

Eventine nodded. "Then deliver it he shall. Show him in, Gael."

Gael bowed slightly and hurried out through the chamber doors, leaving them slightly ajar. A moment later a huge, shaggy dog pushed his way through and padded noiselessly to the King. It was Manx, his wolfhound, and he greeted the animal fondly, rubbing the grizzled head, stroking softly the rough coat along the back and flanks. Manx had been with him almost ten years, closer and more faithful than any man could have been.

"Getting a bit gray—like me," Eventine muttered ruefully.

The doors opened wide to admit Gael, followed by Lauren. The Chosen paused in the doorway for a moment, glancing uncertainly at Gael. The King nodded to his aide, dismissing him. Ander was about to leave as well when a slight motion from his father indicated he was to remain. Gael bowed again and left, this time closing the doors tightly behind him. When he was gone, the Chosen came forward a pace.

"My Lord, please forgive . . . they thought that I . . . I should be the one . . ." He was almost choking on the words.

"There is nothing to forgive," Eventine assured him. With a charm that Ander had always known his father could display, the King came forward quickly and put his arm about the young Elf's shoulders. "I know this must be very important to you or you would not have left your work in the Gardens. Here, sit down and tell me about it."

He glanced questioningly at Ander, then guided the Chosen to a small writing table at one side of the room, seating him in one of two chairs while he took the other. Ander followed them over, but remained standing.

"Your name is Lauren, isn't it?" Eventine asked the Chosen.

"Yes, my Lord."

"Very well, Lauren. Now tell me why you've come."

Lauren drew himself up and placed his hands on the table, folding the fingers together tightly.

"My Lord, the Ellcrys spoke to the Chosen this morning." His words were almost a whisper. "She told us . . . she told us that she is dying!"

Ander felt his blood turn cold. For an instant, the King did not respond, but sat rigidly in place, his eyes fixed on the speaker.

"There must be a mistake," he said at last.

Lauren shook his head emphatically. "There is no mistake, my Lord. She spoke to all of us. We . . . we all heard. She is dying. The Forbidding has already begun to crumble."

The King rose slowly and walked to the open window, staring wordlessly out into the forest. Manx, who had curled up at the foot of the bed, rose and followed him. Ander saw the King's hand stray down to scratch the dog's ears mechanically.

"You are certain of this, Lauren?" Eventine asked. "Very certain?"

"Yes . . . yes."

He was crying softly, almost soundlessly, at the table, his face buried in his hands. Eventine did not turn, but continued to stare fixedly into the woodlands that were his home and the home of his people.

Ander was frozen, his eyes on his father, his mind still dazed with shock. The enormity of what he had heard slowly took hold. The Ellcrys dying! The Forbidding ending. The evil that had been shut away free once more. Chaos, madness, war! In the end, the destruction of everything.

He had studied history under his tutors and again in the books of his own library. It was a history that bore the trappings of legend.

Once, long ago, in a time before the Great Wars, before the dawn of civilization in the old world, even before the emergence of the old race of Man, there had been a war between creatures of good and evil magics. The Elves had fought in that war on the side of good. It had been a long, terrible, devastating struggle. But in the end, the forces of good were victorious and the forces of evil were cast down. Yet the nature of the evil was such that it could not be totally destroyed; it could only be banished. Therefore, the Elven people and their allies pooled their magics with the life-force of the earth itself to create the Ellcrys, so that by her presence a Forbidding would be placed upon the creatures of evil. So long as the Ellcrys survived and flourished, the evil could not return upon the earth. Locked in a void of darkness, it might wail in anguish behind the wall of the Forbidding, but the earth was lost to it.

Until now! But if the Ellcrys were to die, the Forbidding must end. It had been written that this must come to pass, for no power could be so strong that it could endure forever. Yet it had seemed that the Ellcrys would, so many generations had it been there, changeless, a fixed point in a shifting maze of life. The Elven people had come to believe it would always be so. Wrongly, it seemed. Foolishly.

The King turned sharply, glanced briefly at Ander, and moved back to the table, reseating himself and taking Lauren's hands in his own to steady him. "You must tell me everything that she said to you, Lauren. Every detail. Leave nothing out."

The Chosen nodded wordlessly. His eyes were dry once more, his face calm. Eventine released his hands and sat back expectantly. Ander pulled over a high-backed chair from across the room and seated himself next to them.

"My Lord, you have heard of the form of her communication with us?" he asked cautiously.

"I was a Chosen once, Lauren," Eventine answered. Ander stared at his father in surprise. This was something he had never known. But Lauren seemed to gain a measure of confidence from the answer. He nodded, turning to Ander to explain.

"Her voice is actually not a voice of sound, but one of images that appear in our minds. There are seldom words as such; the words are our own translation of the thoughts she projects. That is how I translate when she uses my name. The images are brief and not fully drawn, and we have to interpret them as best we can."

He paused and turned back to Eventine. "I . . . the Ellcrys has never spoken to me more than once before this morning, my Lord. She had spoken to the six of us only at the time of our choosing. Until this morning, most of what we knew of her communication was based upon the writings of our Order and the teachings of the Chosen who have served before. Even now, it is very confusing."

Eventine nodded encouragingly. Lauren continued.

"My Lord, the Ellcrys spoke to us at great length this morning, something she has never done before. She called us to her and told us what was to be and what we, the Chosen, must do. The images were not entirely clear, but there can be no mistake that she is dying. Her time is short; how much time remains isn't certain. Already the erosion has begun. And as she fails, the Forbidding will fail with her. There is only one chance for her— a rebirth."

Eventine's hand shot forth, gripping Lauren's. Ander too had forgotten— shocked and confused by the Ellcrys' forecast of her death. A rebirth! It was written in the oldest histories that the Ellcrys could be reborn and the Forbidding preserved.

"Then there is still hope," he whispered.

Eventine's eyes were fixed on Lauren. "What must be done to give her this rebirth?"

Lauren shook his head. "My Lord, she has entrusted her fate to the Chosen. Only through us will she permit herself to be reborn. I do not pretend to understand her reasons, but the images were clear. She will deliver her seed to one of us—which, she did not say. No face was shown. But it was made known that only one of the Chosen who were selected by her this last time can receive that seed. No other will be considered. Whoever is selected must carry the seed to the life source of the earth—to the fountain of the Bloodfire. There the seed must be immersed within the fire by the bearer. Once returned to the site of the old tree, the seed will take root and a new tree will spring forth to replace the old."

The details of the legend were coming back to Ander now—the bearing of the Ellcrys seed, the ritual of the Bloodfire, the rebirth. It was told in the strange, formal language of the oldest histories—histories that most of the people had forgotten or never known.

"The fountain of the Bloodfire—where is it to be found?" he asked abruptly.

Lauren looked miserable. "A place was shown us, my Lord Prince, but . . . but we could not recognize it. The images were vague, almost as if she lacked the ability to describe it properly."

Eventine's voice remained calm. "Tell me what you were shown. Everything."

Lauren nodded. "There was a wilderness with mountains and swamp all around. There was a deep mist that came and went. Within the wilderness was a lone peak and beneath the peak a maze of tunnels that burrowed deep within the earth. Somewhere within the maze there was a door made of glass—glass that could not break. Behind the door was the Bloodfire."

"No names for any of the parts of this puzzle?" the King asked patiently.

"Only one, my lord. But it was a name we did not recognize. The maze in which the Bloodfire lies hidden appears to be called Safehold."

Safehold? Ander searched his memory, but the name meant nothing to him.

Eventine glanced at Ander and shook his head. He rose to his feet, walked several paces from the table, then stopped abruptly. He turned back to Lauren. "Is there nothing more that you were told? No hints—bits that might not seem to have any meaning?"

"Nothing. That was all."

The King nodded slowly to the young Elf. "Very well, Lauren. You were right in insisting I be told at once. Now, will you wait outside for a little while?"

When the door had closed behind the Chosen, Eventine walked back to his chair and lowered himself slowly. His face seemed to have aged terribly and his movements were those of an old, old man. Manx moved over in front of him, and the grizzled face stared upward sympathetically. Eventine sighed and moved his hand tiredly to the dog's head.

"Have I lived too long?" he muttered. "If the Ellcrys dies, how can I protect my people from what will happen then? I am their King; the responsibility for their protection is mine. I have always accepted that. Yet for the first time in my life, I wish it were otherwise . . ."

He trailed off reluctantly, then turned to look at Ander. "Well, we must do what we can. With Arion gone to the Sarandanon, I will need your help." Ander flushed at the unintended rebuke. "Go with Lauren and question the Chosen carefully. See if there is anything more that may be learned. Anything. I will have the old histories moved up from the vaults and examine them."

"Do you think there might be something there—or in the old world maps?" Ander asked doubtfully.

"No. You have read them more recently than I, but I can remember nothing. Still, what else can we do? If we are to have any chance at all of finding the Bloodfire, we must have more than what Lauren has been able to tell us."

He nodded in dismissal. Ander went out to join Lauren, to return with him to the tree where the other Chosen would be waiting. There he would attempt to discover something more of the mysterious Safehold. It seemed a hopeless effort. But, as his father had said, what else could they do?

4

The summer day ended with a brilliant burst of red and lavender that flooded the whole of the western skyline. For long, beautiful minutes, the sun seemed to hang at the crest of the Breakline, lighting the roof of the Westland forest and weaving shadows that draped the wooded earth with still, soft bands of darkness. The air cooled slowly, the midday heat fading now as an evening breeze rippled and sighed through the great, silent trees. Then daylight slipped into dusk, and night washed the color from the sky.

The people of the Elven city of Arborlon drifted wearily toward their homes.

Within the Gardens of Life, Ander Elessedil stared upward at the Ellcrys. Seen now against the evening light, the great tree seemed normal, deceptively unchanged. Yet before the sun had set, traces of the sickness that was destroying her had been plainly evident.

The disease was spreading rapidly. On a scattering of smaller limbs, rot had begun to eat away at the silver-white bark. Broad clusters of leaves hung limp with wilt, curling at the tips, the deep red color turned black. The Chosen had scrubbed the bark carefully with herbal salves and plucked the damaged leaves, hoping against reason that the disease could be contained, knowing all the while that it could not. Ander had seen the truth reflected in their eyes. They could not heal the Ellcrys. No one could. She was dying, and there was nothing that anyone could do to prevent it.

He sighed and turned away, not sure why he had made this last visit of the day to the Gardens. The Chosen had returned to their compound an hour earlier, tired and discouraged, silent in their sense of futility. But he had come anyway, drawn by an unreasoning hope that somehow the answers they so desperately needed could be found here. He had not found those answers, of course, and with the coming of nightfall there was little sense in staying longer.

As he passed out of the Gardens, he could feel the sentries of the Black Watch staring after him. They remained unaware of the damage to the tree, but they could sense that something was wrong. The activities of the Chosen had told them that much. Word would soon be spreading, he thought—rumors growing. Soon the people would have to be told.

But for the moment, at least, all was quiet. Lights were already going out and many windows were darkened as the people prepared for sleep. He envied them. There was little chance that he would sleep that night—he or the King.

He sighed again, wishing that there was something he could do for his father. Eventine had always been so sure of himself, had always been so supremely confident that a solution could be found to any problem. But now, in the two visits Ander had made to report his lack of progress, the old King had seemed lost somewhere within himself. He had tried half-heartedly to mask it from his son, but it was obvious that he was looking with despair on the ending of everything he had worked all his life to accomplish. Here, at last, was a challenge that was beyond all his powers. With barely a word to his son, he had sent him back to continue aiding the Chosen in any way he could.

It had proved a futile task. Ander had questioned each of them carefully, then assembled them and probed their collective memory, searching for any small piece of information that might lead to Safehold. But he had learned nothing more than what he already knew.

A search of the carefully preserved records of their Order had yielded nothing, either. He had studied histories that dated back centuries, checking and rechecking. There were repeated references to the sacred Blood-fire, the life source of their world and all its living things. But nowhere was there even the briefest mention of the mysterious place called Safehold.

Nor had the Ellcrys given them any further assistance in their search. At Ander's suggestion, the Chosen had gone back to her again. They had gone to her over and over, one by one and all together, begging her to give them something more to further their understanding of her images. But she would not speak to them. She remained silent.

As he came near the compound of the Chosen, he saw that all the lights were out. Routine had apparently taken over and they must have returned to their sleeping quarters at their usual time, shortly after finishing their evening meal. He hoped they would find some relief in sleep. Maybe they would. Sometimes hopelessness and despair were even more fatiguing than physical labor, and they had experienced little else during the long day.

He was moving quietly past their compound, following a pathway that led toward the manor house to make one final report to his father, when a dark shadow moved from under a low tree beside the path.

"My Lord Prince?"

"Lauren?" he asked. Then, as the figure moved closer, he saw that it was indeed the young Elf. "Why aren't you asleep?"

"I tried to sleep, but I couldn't. I . . . I saw you go up to the Gardens and I hoped that you'd come back this way. Prince Ander, can I speak to you?"

"You are speaking to me, Lauren," Ander reminded him. But his brief attempt at amusement did nothing to lighten the seriousness of the other's expression. "Have you remembered something?"

"Perhaps. Not about what the Ellcrys told us, but something I think you should know. Can I walk with you a ways?"

Ander nodded. They turned back along Ander's chosen path, moving slowly away from the compound.

"I feel as if I ought to be the one to solve this problem," Lauren began after a moment. "Maybe it's because the Ellcrys spoke first to me; that makes finding Safehold seem almost my personal obligation. I know that's probably giving too much importance to myself, but it's the way I feel, nevertheless. In any case, I don't want to overlook anything." He glanced at the Prince. "Do you understand what I am trying to say?"

"I think so. Have we overlooked something, then?"

"Well, something has occurred to me. I thought I should mention it to somebody."

Ander stopped and looked at the young Elf.

"I didn't want to say anything to the King." Lauren's uneasiness increased. "Or to any of the others. I'm not really sure how much of this they know . . . and we don't talk about her . . ."

He trailed off. Ander waited patiently.

"It's about Amberle. My Lord, after her choosing, she spoke with the Ellcrys many times—long conversations." The words came slowly. "It was different with her than with the rest of us. I don't know whether she ever realized that. We never really talked about it . . ."

Ander had stiffened sharply. Lauren saw his reaction and hurried on. "But maybe the Ellcrys would talk to her again. Or she might understand better. Perhaps she might learn something we could not."

There was a long moment of silence as the two faced each other. Then Ander shook his head slowly. "Amberle can't help us now, Lauren. She's gone. Even her mother doesn't know where she went. There's no possible way we could find her in time to make any difference."

The red-haired Elf nodded slowly, the last trace of hope leaving his face. "It was just an idea," he said finally, then turned back toward the compound. "Good-night, Prince Ander."

"Good-night, Lauren. Thank you for telling me, anyhow."

The Chosen nodded again before moving back up the pathway, his white robes rustling softly as he disappeared into the night. Ander stared after him for a moment, his dark face troubled. His father had asked for any hint—anything—that might offer a clue to the location of Safehold. Yet there was really no hope of finding Amberle. She might be anywhere within the Four Lands. And now was hardly the time to bring her name up to Eventine. She had been his favorite, the granddaughter whose choosing had filled him with deep pride and joy. But her betrayal of her trust had been harder for him to bear than even the death of her father Aine.

He shook his head slowly and continued on toward the manor house.

Gael was still on duty, his face drawn with fatigue and his eyes troubled. It was inevitable that he should come to know of the problem they faced, but he could be trusted to maintain secrecy. Now he started to rise, then sank back again at Ander's motion. "The King is expecting you," he said. "He's in his study, refusing to retire. If you could persuade him to sleep, even for a few hours . . ."

"I'll see what I can do," Ander promised.

Within his private study, Eventine Elessedil looked up as his son entered. His eyes studied Ander's face momentarily, reading the failure written there. Then he pushed himself back from the reading table at which he had been seated and rubbed his eyes wearily. He rose, stretched, and walked slowly to the curtained windows, peering through the folds into the darkness beyond. On the book-littered table, a tray of food had been pushed aside, hardly touched. Candles burned low, their wax dripping and puddling on the metal holders. The small study was still and somber, its oak bookcases and tapestry-covered walls a dim mix of faded colors and shadow. Scattered about in piles lay the books that Gael must have spent the day bringing up from the vaults.

The King looked back momentarily at his son. "Nothing?" Ander shook his head silently. Eventine grimaced. "Nor I—" He shrugged, pointing to the book that lay open on the table. "The last hope. It contains a single reference to the Ellcrys seed and the Bloodfire. Read it for yourself."

The book was one of more than a hundred volumes of the histories kept by the Elven Kings and their scribes from days that were lost in myth. They were worn and old, carefully bound in leather and brass, sealed in coverings that served to protect them against the ravages of time. They had survived the Great Wars and the destruction of the old race of Man. They had survived the First and Second Wars of the Races. They had survived the ages and ages of life and death that they chronicled. They contained the entirety of the known history of the Elven people. Thousands and thousands of pages, all carefully recorded through the years.

Ander bent to the open pages; the ink had turned brown with age and the script was of an ancient style. But the words were clear enough to read.

"Then shall the One Seed be delivered unto the Bearer that is Chosen. And the Seed shall be borne by the Bearer to the Chambers of the Bloodfire, there to be immersed within the Fire that it might be returned to the earth. Thereupon shall the Tree be Reborn and the Great Forbidding endure forever. Thus spake the High Wizard to his Elves, even as he did perish, that Knowledge be not lost unto his People."

Eventine nodded as Ander looked up again. "I have read through every one of those books, studying every passage that might apply. There are others—but none tells more than the one you read."

He walked back to the reading table and stood fingering the gilt-edged pages of the volume idly. "This is the oldest volume. It contains much that may be only myth. The tale of the ancient war between good and evil magics, names of heroes, everything that led up to the Forbidding. But no mention of Safehold or of the location of the Bloodfire. And nothing on the nature of the sorcery that gave life to the Ellcrys and to the power of the Forbidding."

The last omission was hardly unusual, Ander thought. His ancestors had seldom placed the secrets of their magics in writing. Such things were handed down by word of mouth so that they could not be stolen by their enemies. And some sorceries were said to be so powerful that their use was limited to but a single time and place. It might have been so with the sorcery that had created the Ellcrys.

The King lowered himself back into his chair, studied the book a moment longer, then wordlessly closed it.

"We will have to rely on the little we have learned from the Ellcrys," he said quietly. "We will have to use that to determine the possible locations of the Bloodfire and then search each of them out."

Ander nodded wordlessly. It seemed hopeless. There was only the smallest chance that they could find Safehold with nothing more than that vague description to aid them.

"I wish Arion were here," his father murmured suddenly.

Ander said nothing. There was good cause for the King to have need of Arion this time, he admitted to himself. For the leadership that would be required in directing and furthering the search, Arion was the proper choice. And his presence might give some comfort to their father. Now was no time to begrude him that.

"I think you should sleep, father," Ander suggested after a moment of silence. "You'll need rest for what lies ahead."

The King rose once more and reached out to extinguish the candles on the table. "Very well, Ander," he said, making an effort to smile at his son. "Send Gael in to me. But your day, too, has been a long one. You go on to bed as well and get whatever sleep you can."

Ander returned to his cottage. To his surprise, he did sleep. While his mind spun dully in useless circles, sheer physical fatigue took over. He awoke only once during the night, his rest broken by a nightmare of indescribable horror that left him damp with sweat. Yet within seconds of waking, he drifted back asleep, the dream forgotten. This time, he slumbered undisturbed.

It was already dawn when he came awake again, slipping hurriedly from the bedcovers to dress. A sense of renewed determination strengthened him as he breakfasted hastily and prepared to leave his house. Somewhere there was an answer to this dilemma, a means by which Safehold could be found. Perhaps it lay with the dying Ellcrys. Perhaps it lay with the Chosen. But there was an answer—there had to be an answer.

As he went down the gravel walkway, he could see the early morning sunlight seeping through the screen of the surrounding forests as the new day began. He would go first to the Chosen—they would be in the Gardens of Life by now, their day already begun—in the hope that by talking once again with them something new would be discovered. They would have been thinking about the matter, turning it over and over in their minds, and possibly one of them might have recalled something more. Or perhaps the Ellcrys would have spoken to them again this morning.

He stopped first at the manor house, where Gael was already at his post. But the young Elf raised a finger to his lips, indicating silently that the King still slept and should not be disturbed. Ander nodded and left, grateful for any rest his father might find.

Dew still glimmered on the palace lawn as he moved toward the gates. He glanced expectantly at the gardens as he passed and was surprised to see that Went was not at work. He was more surprised still to see a scattering of the old fellow's tools at the edge of the rose beds, dirt still fresh upon their metal. It was not like Went to leave a job half done. If he was having that much trouble with his back, he should be checked on. But that would have to wait. There were more pressing concerns at the moment. He glanced through the shrubbery at the flower beds a final time, then hurried on.

Minutes later he was striding past the ivy-grown walls of the Gardens of Life, following the worn pathway that led to their gates. From atop the Carolan—the towering wall of rock that rose abruptly from the eastern shore of the Rill Song, lifting Arborlon above the lands about it—he could see the vast sweep of the Westland stretched forth below: to the east and north, the towers and tree lanes of the Elven home city, wrapped close within the dense tangle of the forestland; to the south, the distant mist-gray crags of the Rock Spur and Pykon, laced with bits and pieces of blue ribbon where the Mermidon River cut apart the aged rock on its long passage eastward into Callahorn; to the west, below the Carolan and beyond the swift flow of the Rill Song, the valley of the Sarandanon, the breadbasket of the Elven nation. The homeland of the Elves, Ander thought with pride. He must find a way, he and the Chosen and his father, to save it.

Moments later he stood before the Ellcrys. There was no sign of the Chosen. The tree stood alone.

Ander stared about in disbelief. It seemed impossible that the Chosen could have all overslept, even though their routine had been so upset by the revelation of the Ellcrys. In hundreds of years, the Chosen had never failed to greet the tree at the first touch of morning light.

Ander left the Gardens hurriedly and was almost running as he came within sight of the walled compound of the Chosen. Evergreens surrounded it, flower gardens banked its stone and brick walkways, and vegetable patches ran in even rows along its backside, the black earth dotted with green stalks and sprouts. A low wall of worn rock enclosed the yard, breached on each side by white picket gates.

The house itself was shadowed and still.

Ander slowed. By now, the Chosen must surely be awake. Yet there was no sign of life. Something cold seemed to settle into the Elven Prince. He moved ahead, eyes peering into the shadowy dimness beyond the open door of the house, until at last he stood at the entrance.

"Lauren?" He spoke the young Elf's name quietly.

No answer came. He stepped through the entry into the darker shadows beyond. A flicker of movement registered at the edge of his vision, movement that came from somewhere within the surrounding evergreens. A sudden apprehension swept through him, leaving him cold all over. What was back there?

Belatedly he thought of the weapons he had left within his lodgings. He stood motionless for a time, waiting for something more. But there was no further movement, no sounds betraying the presence of another living being. Resolutely he went forward.

"Lauren . . . ?"

Then his sight adjusted to the dimmer interior, and the young Elf's name caught in his throat.

Bodies lay strewn about the main room like discarded sacks, torn and broken and lifeless. Lauren, Jase—all of the Chosen dead, ripped apart as if by maddened animals. Despair filled him. Now no Chosen remained to carry the seed of the Ellcrys in search of Safehold and the Bloodfire. Now there could be no rebirth of the tree, no salvation for the Elves. Sickened by the carnage, he nevertheless could not bring himself to move. He stood there, horror and revulsion sweeping through him, a single word shrieking in his mind:

Demons!

A moment later, he staggered outside, retching uncontrollably as he leaned up against the cottage wall and fought to still his shaking. When at last he had recovered, he went at once to give the alarm to the Black Watch, then hurried on to the city. His father would have to be told, and it was best that the news come from his son.

What had befallen the Chosen was all too clear. With the failing of the Ellcrys, the Forbidding had begun to erode. The stronger Demons were breaking loose. Nothing but a Demon could or would have done such a thing to the Chosen. In a single strike, the Demons had made certain that they would never again be imprisoned. They had destroyed all those who might aid in the rebirth of the Ellcrys and the restoration of the Forbidding that had confined them.

Back through the gates that fronted the manor house grounds he ran, down the gravel walkway that led past the gardens that old Went tended. Went was there now, digging and weeding, his leathered face lifting momentarily as the Prince went past. Ander barely saw him, said nothing to him, as he hurried on.

Went's eyes lowered in satisfaction. Hands sifting idly through the black earth, the Changeling went on with his work.

5

It was evening again when Ander Elessedil closed the door to the cottage that had housed the Order of the Chosen, latching it firmly for the final time. Silence fell about him as he paused to stare out into the growing dark. The cottage stood empty now; the bodies of the six murdered youths had long since been taken from it, and Ander had removed the last small personal possessions to return to their relatives. For these few brief moments, he was alone with his thoughts.

But his thoughts were not ones he cared to dwell on. He had supervised the removal of the mutilated bodies and then the gathering of the histories of their Order, taken now for safekeeping to the vaults beneath the Elessedil manor house. At his father's suggestion, he had gone through those records, page by page, searching for that small bit of revelation on Safehold's puzzle that they had somehow overlooked. He found nothing. He shook his head. What difference anyway, he thought bleakly. What difference now what was learned of Safehold? Without a Chosen to carry the seed, what was the need to locate the Bloodfire? Still, he had been glad to have something to do—anything to do—that would help take his mind from what he had seen when he found Lauren and the others.

He stepped away from the empty cottage, crossed the yard of the compound, and turned down the path leading to the Gardens of Life. All across the Carolan, the flicker of torches burned through the gathering darkness. There were soldiers everywhere; Black Watch ringed the Gardens and Home Guard—the King's personal corps of Elven Hunters— patrolled the streets and tree lanes of the city. The Elves were understandably frightened by what had happened. When word of the slain Chosen had spread, Eventine had acted quickly to reassure his people that they would be protected against a similar fate—though in truth, he believed them to be in no immediate danger. The thing that had killed the Chosen had not been after anyone else. The Chosen had been its sole target. Nothing else made sense. Still, it did no harm to take precautions. Such measures would do as much to stem the panic the King could sense building in his people as to safeguard the city.

The real damage, of course, had already been done. The tree was dying, and now there would be no rebirth. Once she was dead, the Forbidding would fail entirely and the evil locked within would break free. Once free, it would seek out and destroy every last Elf. And with the Ellcrys gone, what miracle of Elven magic could be found to prevent it?

Ander paused outside the wall of the Gardens. He drew a slow breath to steady himself, forcing down the feeling of helplessness that had been building inside all day, little by little, like some insidious sickness. What in the name of sanity were they to do? Even with the Chosen alive, they had not known where the Bloodfire was to be found. With the Forbidding already beginning to crumble, there had never been enough time to search it out. And now, with the Chosen dead . . .

Amberle.

Her name whispered in his mind. Amberle. Lauren's last words to him had been of her. Perhaps she could help, the red-haired Chosen had suggested. Then the idea had seemed impossible. Now anything at all seemed better than what they had. Ander's mind raced. How could he convince his father that he must consider the possibility that Amberle might help? How could he convince his father even to talk to him about the girl? He remembered the old King's bitterness and disappointment the day he had learned of Amberle's betrayal of her trust as a Chosen. Ander balanced that against the despair he had seen in his father's face this morning when he had brought him the news of the slaughtered Chosen. His decision was easily made. The King was desperate for help from some quarter. With Arion gone into the Sarandanon, Ander knew that that help must come from him. And what other help could he give but to suggest to his father that Amberle must be sought?

"Elven Prince?"

The voice came from out of nowhere, startling Ander so that he jumped away from it with a gasp. A shadow slipped from the shelter of the pines that grew close against the walls of the Gardens of Life, darker than the night about it. For an instant Ander stopped breathing altogether, freezing with indecision. Then, as he reached hurriedly for the short sword he wore belted at his waist, the shadow was upon him and a hand lay over his own, an iron grip holding back his arm.

"Peace, Ander Elessedil." The voice was soft but commanding. "I am no enemy of yours."

The shadowy form was that of a man, Ander saw now, a tall man, standing well over seven feet. Black robes were wrapped tightly about his spare, lean frame, and the hood of his traveling cloak was pulled close about his head so that nothing of his face could be seen save for narrow eyes that shone like a cat's.

"Who are you?" the Elven Prince managed finally.

The other's hands lifted and drew back the folds of the hood to reveal the face within. It was craggy and lined, shadowed by a short, black beard that framed a wide, unsmiling mouth and by hair cut shoulder-length. The cat's eyes, piercing and dark, stared out from beneath heavy brows knit fiercely above a long, flat nose. Those eyes stared into Ander's, and the Elven Prince found that he could not look away.

"Your father would know me," the big man whispered. "I am Allanon."

Ander stiffened, his face incredulous. "Allanon?" His head shook slowly. "But . . . but Allanon is dead!"

There was sarcasm in the deep voice, and the eyes glinted once more. "Do I appear to you to be dead, Elven Prince?"

"No . . . no, I can see . . ." Ander's faltered. "But it has been more than fifty years . . ."

He trailed off as the memories of his father's stories came back to him: the search for the Sword of Shannara; the rescue of Eventine from the camp of the enemy armies; the battle at Tyrsis; the defeat of the Warlock Lord at the hands of the little Valeman, Shea Ohmsford. Through it all, Allanon had been there, lending to the beleaguered peoples of the Four Lands his strength and wisdom. When it was finished and the Warlock Lord destroyed, Allanon had disappeared entirely. Shea Ohmsford, it was said, had been the last to see him. There had been rumors afterward that Allanon had come to the Four Lands at other times, in other places. But he had not come to the Westland and the Elves. None of them had ever expected to see him again. Still, where the Druid was concerned, his father had often told him, one soon learned to expect the unexpected. Wanderer, historian, philosopher and mystic, guardian of the races, the last of the ancient Druids, the wise men of the new world—Allanon was said to have been all of these.

But was this truly Allanon? The question whispered in Ander's mind.

The big man stepped close once more. "Look closely at me, Elven Prince," he commanded. "You will see that I speak the truth."

Ander stared at the dark face, stared deep into the glittering black eyes, and suddenly the doubts were gone. There was no longer any question in his mind. The man who stood before him was Allanon.

"I want you to take me to see your father." Allanon was speaking again, his voice low and guarded. "Choose a path little traveled. I wish to keep my coming a secret. Quickly now, before the sentries come."

Ander did not stop to argue. With the Druid following as closely as his own shadow, he slipped past the Gardens of Life and hurried on toward the city.

Minutes later, they crouched within a gathering of evergreens at one end of the palace grounds where a small side gate stood chained and locked. Ander drew a ring of keys from his pocket and fitted one into the lock. It turned with a sharp snick and the lock opened. In seconds, they were inside.

Ordinarily the grounds would have been guarded only by the gate watch. But earlier in the day, following the discovery of the murdered Chosen, the body of Went had been found under a bush at the edge of the south gardens, his neck broken. The manner of his death was wholly different from that of the Chosen, so as yet there was no reason to believe there was any connection. Still, this latest killing was too close to the King to suit the Home Guard. Additional security had been moved onto the grounds. Dardan and Rhoe, the King's personal guards, had taken up watch at the King's door.

Ander would not have believed it possible for anyone to reach the manor house from the exterior walls without being seen by the sentries. But somehow, with the Druid in the lead, they managed to pass without challenge. Allanon seemed little more than another of the night's shadows, moving soundlessly, always keeping Ander close beside him, until at last they reached the floor-length windows that looked in upon the King's study. There they paused momentarily while the Druid listened at the curtained window. Then Allanon gripped the iron entry latch and turned it. The window-doors swung silently open and the Druid and Elven Prince stepped inside.

From a reading table still littered with histories, Eventine Elessedil rose, staring in disbelief, first at his son and then at the man who followed him in.

"Allanon!" he whispered.

The Druid secured the window-doors, drew the curtains carefully back in place, then turned into the candlelight.

"After all these years." Eventine shook his head wonderingly and stepped out from behind the table. Then he saw clearly the big man's face and disbelief turned to astonishment. "Allanon! You haven't aged! You . . . haven't changed since . . ." He choked on the words. "How . . . ?"

"I am who I always was," the Druid cut him short. "That is enough to know, King of the Elves."

Eventine nodded wordlessly, still dazed by the other's unexpected appearance. Slowly he moved back to the reading table, and the two men took up seats across from one another. Ander stood where he was for an instant, uncertain whether to stay or go.

"Sit with us, Elven Prince." Allanon indicated a third chair.

Ander sat down quickly, grateful to be included, anxious to hear what would be said.

"You know what has happened?" The King addressed Allanon.

The Druid nodded. "That is why I have come. I sensed a breach in the Forbidding. Something imprisoned there has crossed over into this world, something whose power is very great indeed. It was the appearance of this creature . . ."

There was the faint sound of footsteps in the hallway beyond the study door, and the Druid was on his feet instantly. Then he paused, his face calm, and he looked back at the King.

"No one is to know that I am here."

Eventine did not question this. He simply nodded, rose from the chair, walked quickly to the door, and opened it. Manx sat there on his haunches, his tail wagging slowly, his grizzled muzzle raised toward his master. Eventine walked out into the hallway and found Gael approaching with a tray of tea. The King smiled and took it from him.

"I want you to go home now and get some sleep," he ordered. When Gael tried to object, he quickly shook his head. "No arguments. We have a lot to do in the morning. Go home. I'll be all right. Ask Dardan and Rhoe to keep watch until I retire. I wish to see no one."

He turned abruptly and re-entered the study, closing the door firmly behind him. Manx had wandered in, sniffed questioningly the stranger he found seated at the reading table, then, apparently satisfied, had dropped down next to the stone fireplace beside them, his muzzle resting comfortably on his paws, his brown eyes closing contentedly. Eventine sat down again.

"Was it this creature, then, that killed the Chosen?" he asked, picking up the conversation.

The Druid nodded. "I believe it to be so. I sensed the danger to the Chosen and came as quickly as I could. Not quickly enough, unfortunately, to save them."

Eventine smiled sadly. "The fault lies with me, I'm afraid. I left them unprotected, even after I was told the Forbidding had begun to fail. But perhaps it makes no difference. Even had they lived, I am not certain the Chosen would have been able to save the Ellcrys. Nothing of what she showed them of the location of the Bloodfire is recognizable. Not even the name she gave them—Safehold. Do you recognize it?"

Allanon shook his head no.

"Our records tell us nothing of Safehold—neither those of my predecessors who ruled nor those of the Chosen," the King continued. "I am faced with an impossible situation. The Ellcrys is dying. In order to save her, one of the Chosen in service to her now must carry her seed to the Bloodfire, immerse it in the flames and then return it to the earth so that a rebirth might be possible."

"I am familiar with the history," the Druid interjected.

The King flushed. The anger and frustration he had held inside was working its way to the fore.

"Then consider this. We do not know the location of the Bloodfire. We have no record of the name Safehold. And now the Chosen are all dead. We have no one to bear the Ellcrys seed. The outcome of all this seems quite inevitable. The Ellcrys will die, the Forbidding will crumble, the evil locked within will be free once more upon the land, and the Elves and very likely all of the races inhabiting the Four Lands will be faced with a war that could easily destroy us all!"

He leaned forward sharply. "I am a King; I am that and nothing more. You are a Druid, a sorcerer. If you have any help to offer, then do so. There is nothing more that I know to do."

The Druid cocked his head slightly, as if considering the problem.

"Before coming to see you, Eventine, I went into the Gardens of Life and spoke with the Ellcrys."

The King stared at him incredulously. "You spoke with . . . ?"

"Perhaps it would be more accurate to say that she spoke with me. Had she not chosen to do so, there would have been no communication between us, of course."

"But she speaks only to the Chosen," Ander interjected, then fell quickly silent as he saw his father frown in annoyance.

"My son is correct, Allanon." Eventine turned back to the Druid. "The Ellcrys speaks to no one but the Chosen—and seldom to them."

"She speaks to those who serve her," Allanon replied. "Of the Elves, only the Chosen do so. But the Druids have also served the Ellcrys, though in a different fashion. In any case, I simply offered myself to her and she chose to speak with me. What she told me suggests that you are mistaken in your view of matters in at least one respect."

Eventine waited a moment for the Druid to continue. He did not. He simply sat there, staring at the Elf questioningly.

"Very well, I will ask it then." The King forced himself to remain calm. "In what respect am I mistaken?"

"Before I tell you that," Allanon said, leaning forward, "I want you to understand something. I have come to give whatever aid I may, for the evil that is imprisoned within the Forbidding threatens all life in the Four Lands. What aid I can offer, I offer freely. But there is one condition. I must be free to act in this matter as I see fit. Even though you disapprove, Eventine Elessedil. Even then. Do you understand?"

The King hesitated, his blue eyes studying the dark face of the other man, searching for answers that clearly were not to be found there. At last, he nodded.

"I understand. You may act as you wish in this."

The Druid sat back, carefully masking any emotion as he faced Ander and the King.

"First, I believe that I can aid in discovering the location of Safehold. What I was shown of Safehold by the Ellcrys when we spoke was not familiar to me, as I have said. It was not familiar because it was drawn from her memory of the world at the time of her creation. The Great Wars altered the geography of the old world so completely that her perception of it now is quite faulty. Still, we have the name Safehold. You have told me that the histories of the Elven Kings and those of the Order of the Chosen do not record the name. But there is another place to look. At Paranor, within the Druid's Keep, there are histories devoted entirely to the sciences and mystic phenomenon of the old world. Within those books, there may be some mention of the creation of the Ellcrys and the location of the Bloodfire. This is a distinct possibility because much of the information contained in those histories was gathered at the time of the First Council of the Druids—drawn from each member as it had been handed down since the holocaust. Remember, too, that the guiding light of that council was Galaphile, and Galaphile was an Elf. He would have seen to it that something about the creation of the Ellcrys and the location of the fountain of the Bloodfire was set down."

He paused. "Tonight, when we are finished here, I will go on to Paranor. The histories are well hidden to any but the Druids, so it is necessary that I go myself. But I believe that within their pages is recorded some mention of the name Safehold. From what is written there, we may hope to discover the location of the Bloodfire."

He folded his hands on the table's edge, and his eyes fixed on those of the King.

"Now as to the Chosen, Eventine, you are mistaken entirely. They are not all dead."

For an instant, the room went deathly still. Amberle! Ander thought in astonishment. He means Amberle!

"All six were killed . . . !" Eventine began, then stopped abruptly.

"There were seven Chosen," the Druid said quietly. "Seven."

The King went rigid, his hands gripping the edges of the table until the knuckles were white. His eyes mirrored anger and disbelief.

"Amberle," he breathed the name like a curse.

The Druid nodded. "She is one of the Chosen."

"No!" The King was on his his feet, shouting. "No, Druid!"

There was a scurrying of footsteps in the hallway beyond and then a pounding on the study door. Ander realized what his father had done. His shouts had brought Dardan and Rhoe. Hurriedly, he went to the door and opened it. He was surprised to find not only the guards, but Gael as well. All peered curiously into the study, but the Elven Prince carefully blocked their view. Then his father was beside him.

"I told you to go home, Gael," Eventine reprimanded the young Elf sternly. "Do so now."

Gael bowed mechanically, his face showing the hurt he felt at the other man's words, and disappeared back down the hallway without a word. The King nodded to the Elven Hunters, reassuring them that he was all right, and they returned to their watch.

The King stood silently in the open entry a moment, then closed the door. The penetrating blue eyes swept past his son to Allanon.

"How did you find out about Amberle?"

"When the Ellcrys spoke with me, she told me that seven had been chosen to serve. One was a young girl. Her name was Amberle Elessedil."

The Druid paused, studying carefully the face of the Elven King. It was lined with bitterness. All of its color had drained away.

"It is unusual for a young woman to be selected as a Chosen," Allanon continued calmly. "There have been no more than a handful, I think—not another in the last five hundred years."

The King shook his head angrily. "Amberle's selection was an honor that meant nothing to her. She spurned that honor. She shamed her people and her family. She is no longer one of the Chosen. She is no longer a citizen of this land. She is an outcast by her own choice!"

Allanon came to his feet swiftly, his face suddenly hard.

"She is your granddaughter, and you speak as a fool would."

Eventine stiffened at the rebuke, but held his tongue. The Druid came up to him.

"Hear me. Amberle is a Chosen. It is true that she did not serve the Ellcrys as did the others. It is true that she forsook her duty as a Chosen. It is true that for reasons known only to herself she left Arborlon and the Westland, her home, despite the responsibilities that were clearly hers, that she disgraced her family and particularly you, as King, in the eyes of her people. It is true that she has made herself an outcast. It is true that she does not believe herself to be one of the Chosen any longer.

"But know this. It is not for you nor for her people to take from her what the Ellcrys has given. It is not even for her to do that. It is for the Ellcrys alone. Until the Ellcrys says differently, Amberle remains a Chosen in her service—a Chosen who may bear her seed in search of the Bloodfire, a Chosen who may give her new life."

Allanon paused. "A King may not understand all things, Eventine Elessedil, even though he be a King. Some things you must simply accept."

Eventine stared at the Druid without speaking, the anger gone now from his eyes, replaced with hurt and confusion.

"I was close to her once," he said finally. "After her father—my son Aine—died, I became her father. She was still a child, only seven. In the evenings, we would play together . . ." He stopped, unable to continue. He took a deep breath to steady himself. "There was a quality about her that I have not since found; a sweetness, an innocence, a loving. I am an old man speaking these words about his grandchild, but I do not speak blindly. I knew her."

Allanon said nothing. The King moved back to his chair and slowly seated himself once more.

"The histories record no other woman selected to serve as a Chosen since the time of Jerle Shannara. Amberle was the first—the first in more than five hundred years. It was an honor others would have given anything for." He shook his head wonderingly. "Yet Amberle walked away from it. She gave no explanation—not to me, not to her mother, not to anyone. Not one word. She just left."

He trailed off helplessly. Allanon sat down across from him again, his dark eyes intense.

"She must be brought back. She is the only hope that the Elven people have."

"Father." Ander spoke before he had time to think better of it. Impulsively he knelt next to the old man. "Father, on the night before he was killed, Lauren told me something. He told me that the Ellcrys had spoken with Amberle many times after her choosing. That had never happened before. Perhaps Amberle is our best hope."

The King looked at him blankly, as if the words he had spoken meant nothing. Then he placed his hands flat against the worn surface of the reading table and nodded once.

"I find that hope a slim one, Ander. Our people may accept her back again, if only because they have need of her. I am not altogether certain of this; what she has done by her rejection is unpardonable in their eyes. And perhaps the Ellcrys, too, may accept her—accept her both as a Chosen and as the bearer of her seed. I don't pretend to have answers to those questions. Nor do my own feelings matter in this." He turned again to Allanon. "It is Amberle herself who will stand against us, Druid. When she left this land, she left it forever. She believed strongly that it must be so; something made her believe. You do not know her, as I do. She will never return."

Allanon's expression did not change. "That remains to be seen. We must at least ask her."

"I do not know where she is." The King's voice turned suddenly bitter. "I doubt that anyone does."

The Druid carefully poured a measure of the herb tea and handed it to the King.

"I do."

Eventine stared at him wordlessly for a moment. His face clouded with conflicting emotions, and there were sudden tears in his eyes, tears that were gone as fast as they had come.

"I should have guessed," he said finally. He rose, then stepped away from the table several paces, his face partially turned into the shadows. "You are free to act in this as you will, Allanon. You already know that."

Allanon rose with him. Then, to Ander's surprise, he said, "I will require the services of your son for a brief time before I leave."

Eventine did not turn. "As you wish."

"Remember—no one is to know that I have been here."

The King nodded. "No one shall."

A moment later the Druid was through the curtained windows and gone. Ander stood looking at his father hesitantly, then moved to follow.

He knew the old man's thoughts now were of Amberle.

In the blackness of the Westland forests north of the Carolan, the Dagda Mor sat quietly, his eyes closed. When they opened again, they were bright with satisfaction. The Changeling had served him well. He rose slowly, the Staff of Power flaring sharply as his hands closed about its polished wood.

"Druid," he hissed softly. "I know of you."

He motioned to the formless shadow that was the Reaper, and the monster rose up out of the night. The Dagda Mor looked eastward. He would wait for the Druid at Paranor. But not alone. He could sense the Druid's power, and he was wary of it. The Reaper might be strong enough to stand against such power, but he had better use for the Reaper. No, other help would be necessary. He would bring a handful of the brethren through the eroding wall of the Forbidding.

Enough to snare the Druid. Enough to kill him.

Allanon was waiting for Ander when he stepped from the lighted study, and together they retraced their steps across the palace grounds and through the small side gate to the roadway beyond. Then Allanon asked to be taken to the stables. Wordlessly the two followed a back trail that took them through a small stretch of forest to the stable paddocks and from there to the stable entry. Ander dismissed the old stableman with a word of assurance, and Allanon and he stepped inside.

Oil lamps lit a double row of stalls, and the soft whicker of horses sounded in the stillness. Slowly Allanon passed down the line of stalls, eyes shifting from horse to horse as he walked to the end of the first row and started back up the second. Ander trailed after him and watched.

Finally the Druid stopped and turned back to Ander.

"That one," he pointed. "I'll need the use of him."

Ander glanced uneasily at the horse Allanon had chosen. The horse was called Artaq, a huge coal-black stallion standing fully eighteen hands high. Artaq was big enough and strong enough to carry someone of Allanon's size, and he could withstand a great deal of punishment. He was a hunting horse, built for stamina rather than for speed. Yet Ander knew him to be capable of great speed over short distances. His head was narrow and rather small, particularly when viewed in comparison to his great, barrel-chested body. He had eyes that were set rather wide and colored a startling azure. There was intelligence in those eyes; Artaq was not a horse that could be mastered by just any man.

Indeed, that was exactly the problem. Artaq was strong-willed and thoroughly unpredictable. He enjoyed playing games with his riders, games that usually ended with the riders being thrown. More than a few had been injured in those falls. If the man riding Artaq was not strong enough and quick enough to prevent it, Artaq would find a way to shake him off within seconds after he was mounted. Few men bothered to chance this. Even the King seldom rode him anymore, though once he had been a favorite.

"There are others . . ." Ander suggested hesitantly, but Allanon was already shaking his head no.

"This horse will do. What is his name?"

"Artaq," the Elven Prince replied.

Allanon studied the horse carefully for a time, then lifted the stall latch and stepped inside. Ander moved over to watch. The Druid stood quietly before the big black, then lifted his hand in invitation. To Ander's surprise, Artaq came over. Allanon stroked the satin neck slowly, gently, and he bent forward to whisper in the horse's ear. Then he fitted a halter to the black and led him from his stall down the walkway to where the tack was stored. Ander shook his head and followed after. The Druid selected a saddle and bridle and strapped them snugly in place after removing the halter. With a final word of encouragement, he swung up upon the horse's back.

Ander held his breath. Slowly Allanon walked the black down one row of stalls and back along the other. Artaq was obedient and responsive; there would be no games played with this man. Allanon brought him back to where Ander stood waiting and stepped down.

"While I am gone, Elven Prince," he said, his black eyes fixed on Ander, "I entrust to you the care of your father. Be certain that no harm comes to him." He paused. "I depend on you in this."

Ander nodded, pleased that Allanon would show this kind of confidence in him. The Druid studied him a moment longer, then turned away. With the Elven Prince following once more, he walked Artaq to the rear of the stable and pushed ajar the wide double doors.

"Goodbye then, Ander Elessedil," he offered and remounted. Easing Artaq through the open doors, he rode swiftly away into the darkness.

Ander watched after him until he was out of sight.

For the remainder of that night and for the better part of the three days that followed, Allanon rode Artaq eastward toward Paranor. His journey took him through the deep forests of the Westland to the mouth of the historic Valley of Rhenn and from there onto the sprawling emptiness of the Streleheim Plains. He traveled steadily, pausing only to rest, feed, and water Artaq, carefully keeping within covered areas of the land where possible, steering wide of caravan routes and well-traveled roadways. As yet, no one but the Elven King and his son knew that he had returned to the Four Lands. No one but they knew of the Druid histories at Paranor or of the seventh Chosen. If the evil that had broken through the Forbidding were to discover any of this, his quest would be seriously threatened. Secrecy was his greatest ally, and he intended that it might remain so.

At sunset on the second day of travel, he arrived at Paranor. He was certain that he had not been followed.

While still some distance from the ancient fortress, he left Artaq in a small grove of spruce where there was good grass and water and proceeded the rest of the way on foot. It was not as it had been in the time of the Warlock Lord. The packs of wolves that had prowled the surrounding forests were no more. The barrier of poison thorns that had walled away the Keep was gone. The woodlands were quiet and peaceful in the early evening dusk, filled with the pleasant sounds of nightfall.

Within minutes, he stood at the foot of the Druid's Keep. The aged castle sat atop a great mass of rock, rising above the forest trees as if it had been thrust from out of the bowels of the earth by some giant's hand. It was a breathtaking vision from a child's fairy tale, a dazzling maze of towers and walls, spires and parapets, their weathered white stones etched starkly against the deep blue of the night sky.

Allanon paused. The history of Paranor was the history of the Druids, the history of his forebears. It began a thousand years after the Great Wars all but annihilated the race of Man and changed forever the face of the old world. It began after years of desolation and savagery as the survivors of the holocaust struggled to subsist in a lethal new world where man was no longer the dominant species. It began after the one race of Man became reborn into the new races of Men, Dwarves, Gnomes and Trolls—after the Elves reappeared. It began at Paranor, where the First Council of the Druids came together in a desperate effort to save the new world from total anarchy. Galaphile called them here—Galaphile, who was the greatest of the Druids. Here the histories of the old world, written and spoken, were set down in the Druid records, to be preserved for all the generations of man yet to come. Here the mysteries of the old sciences were explored, the fragments patched together, the secrets of a few restored to knowledge. For hundreds of years, the Druids lived and worked at Paranor, the wise men of the new world seeking to rebuild what had been lost.

But their efforts failed. One among them fell victim to ambition and ill-advised impatience, tampering with power so great and so evil that in the end it consumed him entirely. His name was Brona. In the First War of the Races, he led an army of Men against the other races, seeking to gain mastery over the Four Lands. The Druids crushed this insurrection and drove him into hiding. They believed him dead. But five hundred years later, he returned—Brona no longer, but the Warlock Lord. He trapped the unsuspecting Druids within their Keep and slaughtered them to a man—all save one. That one was Bremen, Allanon's father. Bremen forged an enchanted Sword and gave it to the Elven King, Jerle Shannara, a talisman that the Warlock Lord could not stand against. It won for the Elves and their allies the Second War of the Races and drove the Warlock Lord again from the world of men.

When Bremen died, Allanon became the last of the Druids. He sealed the Keep forever. Paranor became history to the races, a monument of another time, a time of great men and still greater deeds.

The Druid shook his head. All that was past now; his concern must be only with the present.

He began to skirt the stone base of the castle, his eyes studying the deep crevices and jagged outcroppings. Finally he stopped, his hands reaching to the rock and touching. A portion of the stone swung inward, revealing a cleverly concealed passageway. The Druid slipped quickly through the narrow opening, and the stone sealed itself behind him.

There was total blackness within. Allanon's hands searched until they found a cluster of wall torches set in iron brackets hammered into the rock. Lifting one free, he worked with the flint and stone he carried in a pouch at his waist until a spark ignited the pitch that coated the torch head. Holding the burning brand before him, he allowed his eyes a moment to adjust. A passage stretched away before him, the faint outline of rough-hewn steps cut into the rock floor disappearing upward into darkness. He began to climb. The smell of dust and stale air filled his nostrils, and he wrinkled his nose in distaste. The caverns were cold, their chill sealed in permanently by tons of rock. The Druid pulled his heavy cloak about him. Hundreds of steps passed beneath his feet, and still the tunnel twisted through the black.

It ended finally at a massive wooden door. Allanon paused and bent close, his eyes studying the heavy iron bindings. After a moment, his fingers touched a combination of metal studs, and the door swung open. He stepped through.

He stood in the furnace of the Keep. It was a round, cavernous chamber that consisted wholly of a narrow walkway encircling a great dark pit. A low iron railing rimmed the pit at its edge. About the walkway, a succession of wooden and ironbound doors were set into the chamber wall, all closed and barred.

The Druid moved to the railing and, holding the torch before him, peered downward into the pit. The faint illumination of the fire danced off blackened walls crusted over with ash and rust. The furnace was cold now, the machinery that once pumped heat to the towers and halls of the castle locked and silent. But far below, beyond the pale glimmer of the torchlight, beneath massive iron dampers, the natural fires of the earth still burned. Even now, their stirrings could be felt.

He remembered another time. More than fifty years ago, he had come to Paranor and the Druid's Keep with the little company of friends from the Dwarf village of Culhaven: the Ohmsfords, Shea and Flick; Balinor Buckhannah, Prince of Callahorn; Menion, Prince of Leah; Durin and Dayel Elessedil; and the valiant Dwarf Hendel. He had come in search of the legendary Sword of Shannara, for the Warlock Lord had returned to the Four Lands, and only the power of the Sword could vanquish him. Allanon had come with his little band into the Keep and very nearly had not come out again. In this very room, he had battled to the death with one of the Skull Bearers. The Warlock Lord had known he was coming. It had been a trap.

His eyes lifted sharply, and he listened to the deep silence. A trap. The word disturbed him; it triggered some instinct, a sixth sense of warning. There was something wrong. Something . . .

He stood there for a moment, indecisive. Then he shook his head. He was being foolish. It was the memory, nothing more.

Carrying the torch before him, he moved along the walkway until he reached a tight spiral stairway that led upward. Without a backward glance to the pit or the furnace chamber, he climbed the stairs quickly and entered the upper halls of the Druid's Keep.

All was as it had been fifty years earlier. Starlight filtered through high windows in thin ribbons of silver, touching softly the heavy wooden panels and polished timbers that framed up the towering corridor. Paintings and tapestries hung the length of the hall, their rich colors muted into grays and deep blues by the nightfall. Statues of stone and iron stood silent watch before massive wooden doors with handles of brass. Dust lay over everything, a thick soft carpet, and long streamers of cobweb fell from ceiling to marble floor.

Allanon moved down the hallway slowly, the torchlight burning through the haze of musty air that hung motionless through the Keep. All was silence, deep and penetrating. His footfalls echoed eerily as he walked, and small puffs of dust rose in the air behind him, stirred by the passing of his feet. Doors came and went to either side, all closed, their metal fittings glinting fire as the torchlight struck the mirrored surface. The hall he traveled intersected another, and he turned right. He walked almost to its end, stopping finally before a smallish door of white oak and iron. A huge lock secured this door. The Druid fumbled for a moment at the pouch about his waist, finally producing a large metal key. He placed the key in the lock and turned it twice. The mechanism creaked in protest, its workings rusty with disuse, but the heavy bolt drew back. The iron handle slipped free of its catch. Allanon stepped inside and closed the door behind him.

The room he had entered was small and windowless. It had once been a study. Shelves of fraying, cloth-bound books lined its four walls, the colors of the bindings long since faded, the pages dried almost to dust. Against the far wall were placed two small reading tables with chairs constructed of reed and cane, stiff and solitary, like sentries at attention. Closer to the doorway were two more comfortable-looking armchairs formed of thickly padded leather. An aged, handwoven rug lay loosely across wooden plank flooring hammered down with iron nails. The fabric of the rug was laced with heraldic designs and bits of gold leaf.

The Druid glanced about the room perfunctorily and moved to the wall on his left. Reaching behind the books at the end of the third shelf down, he located two large iron studs. When he touched these, a section of the bookcase swung silently ajar. He pushed the shelving out a bit to allow himself room to pass through, then pulled the casing closed behind him.

He stood within a vault constructed entirely of massive granite blocks cut to interlock with one another and then tightly sealed with mortar. Except for a single long wooden table and half a dozen high-backed chairs, the chamber was bare. There were no windows and no door save the one through which he had entered. The air here was stale with age, but breathable. Not surprisingly, given the chamber's tight construction, there was an almost total absence of dust.

Using the torch he carried, Allanon lit torches bracketed in the wall to either side of the entry and two squat candles that rested on the table. Once that was done, he moved to the wall to the right of the door and began running his hands lightly over the smooth stone. After a moment, he placed the tips of his fingers and thumbs firmly in place against the granite, bridging both palms out, and lowered his head in concentration. At first nothing happened, but then suddenly a deep blue glow began to spread outward from his fingers and ran through the stone like veins through flesh. An instant later the wall erupted in soundless blue fire; then both wall and fire were gone.

Allanon stepped back. Where the granite wall had been stood row upon row of massive, leather-bound books elaborately engraved with gold. It was for this that the Druid had come to Paranor—for these were the histories of the Druids, the whole of the knowledge of the old and new world salvaged from the holocaust of the Great Wars, recorded from the time of the First Council of the Druids to the present.

Allanon reached up and carefully removed one of the heavy tomes. It was in good condition, the leather soft and pliable, the edges of the pages sharp, the binding solid. They had weathered the ages well. Five centuries earlier, after the death of Bremen, after he had come to the realization that he was the last of the Druids, he had constructed this vault to protect these histories so that they might be preserved for the generations of men and women who would one day live upon this earth and would have need of the knowledge the books contained. From time to time he returned to the Keep, dutifully recording what he had learned in his travels about the Four Lands, setting down the secrets of the ages that might otherwise be lost. Much of what was recorded here dealt with the secrets of sorcery, with power that no one, be he Druid or ordinary man, could hope to comprehend fully—much less put to practical use. The Druids had thought to keep those secrets safe from men who might use them foolishly. Yet the Druids were gone now, save for Allanon, and one day he, too, would be gone. Who then would inherit the secrets of power? It was a matter of no small concern to Allanon—a dilemma for which, as yet, he had found no agreeable solution.

He leafed quickly through the book he held and placed it back again, selecting another. He glanced at this second book, then moved to the long table and seated himself. Slowly, he began to read.

For nearly three hours, he did not stir, other than to turn the pages of the history, his face bent close to the carefully inscribed writing.

At the end of the first hour, he discovered the location of Safehold. But he continued to read. He was looking for something more.

At last his eyes lifted and he leaned back wearily. For a time he just sat there in the high-backed chair, staring fixedly at the rows of books that comprised the Druid histories. He had found all that he had been looking for and wished that he had not.

He thought back to his meeting with Eventine Elessedil two days earlier. He had told the Elven King that he had gone first to the Gardens of Life and that the Ellcrys had spoken with him. But he had not told the King all that she had revealed. In part, he had not done so because much of what she had shown had been confusing and unclear, her memories of a time and a life long gone altered beyond anyone's recognition. But there had been one thing that she had shown him that he had understood all too well. Yet it had been so incredible that he felt he could not accept it without first checking the Druid histories. This he had done. Now he knew it to be true and knew it must be kept hidden—from Eventine, from everyone. He experienced a sense of despair. It was as it had been fifty years ago with young Shea Ohmsford; the truth must be left to reveal itself through an inexorable passage of events. It was not for him to decide the time and the place of its revelation. It was not for him to tamper with the natural order of things.

Yet he questioned this decision. Alone with the ghosts of his ancestors, the last of his kind, he questioned this decision. He had chosen to conceal the truth from Shea Ohmsford—indeed, from all who had comprised the little company of adventurers from Culhaven, all who had risked their lives in search of the Sword of Shannara because he had convinced them that they must—but most especially from Shea. In the end, he had come to believe that he had been wrong to do so. Was he wrong now, as well? This time, should he not be candid from the beginning?

Still lost in thought, he closed the book in front of him, rose from the table, and carried the heavy volume back to the niche from which he had taken it. He made a quick circular motion of one hand before the bank of histories, and the granite wall was restored. He stared absently at it for a moment, then turned away. Retrieving the torch he had brought with him into the Keep, he extinguished the vault's remaining lights and triggered the release on the concealed door.

Within the Druid study once more, he paused long enough to close the open section of shelving so that all was as it had been. He looked about the little room almost sadly. The castle of the Druids had become a tomb. It had the smell and taste of death in it. Once it had been a place of learning, of vision. But no more. There was no longer a place for the living within these walls.

He frowned his displeasure. His attitude had soured considerably since reading the pages of the Druid history. He was anxious to be gone from Paranor. It was a place of ill-fortune—and he, in chief, must bear that ill-fortune to others.

Silently he walked to the study door, pulled it open, and stepped through into the main hallway.

Not twenty feet beyond stood the humped form of the Dagda Mor.

Allanon froze. The Demon waited alone, his hard gaze fixed upon the Druid, the Staff of Power cradled loosely in his arms. The harsh sound of his breathing cut sharply through the deep silence, but he did not speak a word. He simply stood there, studying carefully the man he had come to destroy.

The Druid stepped away from the study door, moving cautiously to the center of the corridor, his eyes sweeping the hazy blackness about him. Almost immediately he saw that there were others—vague, wraithlike forms that crept from out of the shadows on four limbs, their eyes slits of green fire. There were many, and they were all around him. They edged steadily closer, circling slightly from side to side in the manner of wolves gathered about some cornered prey. A low mewling sound came from their faceless heads, a horrible catlike whining that seemed to find pleasure in the anticipation of what was to come. A few slipped into the pale fringes of his torchlight. They were grotesque creatures, their bodies a sinuous mass of gray hair, their limbs bent and vaguely human, their multiple fingers grown to claws. Faces lifted toward the Druid, faces that turned him cold. They were the faces of women, their features twisted with savagery, their mouths become the jaws of monstrous cats.

He knew them now, though they had not walked the earth for thousands of years. They had been shut behind the wall of the Forbidding since

the dawn of Man, but their legend was written in the history of the old
world. They were creatures who lived on human flesh. Born of madness,
their bloodlust drove them beyond reason, beyond sanity.

They were Furies.

Allanon watched them circle, creeping about the edges of his torchlight, savoring the prospect of his death. It was a death that seemed assured. There were too many for the Druid; he knew that already. His
power was not great enough to stop them all. They would attack as one,
lunging at him from all sides, tearing and ripping him until nothing
remained.

He glanced quickly to the Dagda Mor. The Demon remained where
he was, beyond the circle of his minions, his dark gaze fixed on the Druid.
It was obvious he felt no need to bring his own power to bear; the Furies
would be enough. The Druid was trapped and hopelessly outnumbered.
He would struggle, of course; but in the end, he would die.

The mewling of the Furies rose sharply, a dry wailing that reverberated the length of the Keep, echoing hollow and shrill through the castle
of stone. Clawed fingers raked the marble floor like the scraping of shattered bone, and the whole of Paranor seemed to freeze in horror.

Then, without warning, Allanon simply disappeared.

It happened so abruptly that for an instant the bewildered Furies
ceased all movement and stared in disbelief at the spot where the Druid
had stood just one moment earlier, their cries dying into stillness. The
torch still hung suspended in the haze of darkness, a beacon of fire that
held them spellbound. Then it dropped to the floor of the hall in a shower
of sparks. The flame disintegrated and the corridor was plunged into
blackness.

The illusion lasted only seconds, but it was long enough to permit Allanon to escape the circle of death that had ensnared him. Instantly, he was
through the Furies and racing toward a pair of massive oaken doors that
stood closed and barred at the near end of the hall. The Dagda Mor
shrieked in anger, and the Staff of Power came up. Red fire blazed the
length of the corridor, scattering the maddened Furies as it arced toward
the fleeing Druid. But Allanon was too quick. With a sweep, his cloak
came up, deflecting the attack. The Staff's fire shot past him and burst
apart the double doors, tearing them from their iron bindings and leaving
them shattered. The Druid leaped through the entryway into the room beyond and was lost in the darkness.

Already the Furies were after him, bounding down the hallway like
animals, their cries thick with hunger. The fleetest among them surged
through the gaping doorway and caught the Druid as he struggled to free
the clasp that secured a floor-length window leading to the battlements.
Allanon turned to face them, his tall form crouching. He seized the two
closest to him as they leaped for his throat and threw them into the
rest. His hands came up and blue fire scattered from his fingers, turning
the floor between them into a wall of flame. Still the Furies came after

him. The nearest hurtled recklessly into the flames and perished. When the fire vanished a moment later, the windows stood open, and the Druid was gone.

A thousand feet above the canopy of the surrounding forestland, his back pressed against the towering wall of the Druid's Keep, Allanon edged his way along a narrow stone ledge that dropped away into blackness. With each step he took, the wind threatened to tear him loose. He worked his way quickly to a slender stone catwalk that bridged to an adjoining tower. The catwalk was less than three feet wide; below there was only emptiness. The Druid did not hesitate. This was his only chance to escape. He started across.

Behind him he heard the screams of rage and frustration that burst from the throats of the Furies as they followed him through the open windows. They came after him in a rush, more sure than he on the smooth castle stone, their clawed limbs gripping tightly as they raced to catch him. At the windows, the Dagda Mor raised the Staff of Power once more, and the killing fire streaked toward the fleeing Druid. But Allanon had seen that he would not cross before the Furies reached him. Dropping to one knee, he brought both arms up in a wide circle, and a shield of blue fire materialized in front of him. The flame from the Demon's staff shattered harmlessly against it. Yet the force of the attack threw the Druid backward, and he tumbled down upon the narrow bridge. In the next instant, the foremost of his pursuers were upon him.

This time Allanon was not quick enough. Clawed fingers ripped through the fabric of his cloak and tore into his flesh. Searing pain wracked his shoulders and chest. With a tremendous heave, he threw back the Furies that held him, and they fell from the narrow arch, screaming. Staggering to his feet, he lurched toward the waiting tower. Again the Furies came at him, stumbling over one another in their eagerness to reach their prey, howling their frustration; their strange, half-woman faces twisted with hate. Again the Druid threw them back, his body shredded further, his clothing soaked with blood.

Then at last he reached the far end of the bridge, his body sagging against the wall of the tower. He turned, hands raising. Blue fire erupted downward into the stone walk, shattering it apart. With a shudder, the whole of the arch collapsed. Shrieking with horror, the Furies tumbled down into the night and disappeared.

Fire from the Staff of Power flared all about him, yet the Druid managed to evade it, dodging quickly around the circle of the tower wall until he was beyond the Demon's sight. There he found a small iron door, closed and locked. With a single powerful shove of one shoulder, he burst through the door and was gone.

7

It was midmorning. In the Village of the Healers, the tiny Gnome community of Storlock, the thunderstorm was finally ending. It had been spectacular while it had lasted—masses of rolling black clouds streaked with wicked flashes of lightning and punctuated by long, booming claps of thunder—torrential rains that hammered the forestland with the force of winter sleet—winds that uprooted whole trees and stripped roofs from the low stone and plaster buildings that comprised the village. The storm had blown out of the Rabb Plains at dawn, and now it was drifting eastward toward the dark ridge of the Wolfsktaag, leaving the woodlands of the central Anar sodden and muddied with its passing.

Wil Ohmsford stood alone on the porch of the Stor rest center, the major treatment facility for the community, and watched absently as the rain slowed to a thin trickle. The clouds still screened away the sunlight, leaving the day wrapped in somber tones of gray, and a fine mist had formed in the mix of cool storm air and warm earth. The eaves and walls of the center were wet and shiny, and droplets of moisture clung to the leaves of the vines that grew about them, glistening with green freshness. Bits of wood littered the ground, forming small dams against the rivers of surface water that flowed everywhere.

The Valeman yawned and stretched wearily. He had been up all night, working with children afflicted by a particularly nasty fever that dried away the fluids of the body and sent temperatures soaring. He could have asked to have been relieved earlier, of course, but he would not have felt comfortable doing that. He was still a student among the Stors, and he was very conscious of the fact that he must continue to prove himself if he were to one day become a Healer. So he had stayed with the children, all yesterday, all night, until at last the fever had broken.

Now he was too tired to sleep, too keyed up from his night's work. Besides, he knew he should spend some time with Flick. He grinned in spite of his exhaustion. Old Uncle Flick would very likely drag him bodily from his bed if he failed to visit for at least a few minutes before trundling off to sleep.

He swung down off the porch, the muddied earth sucking at his boots as he plodded through the damp, head lowered. He was not very big, an inch or two taller than Flick perhaps, and his build was slight. He had his grandfather's halfling Elven features—the slim nose and jaw, the slightly pointed ears hidden beneath locks of blondish hair, the narrow eyebrows that angled up sharply from the bridge of his nose. Distinctive features, they had marked Shea Ohmsford and now they marked his grandson as well.

The sound of running footsteps brought him about. It was one of the Servers, Gnome aides to the Stors. He came up to Wil, wizened yellow face streaked with rain, forest cloak wrapped close to ward off the weather.

"Sir, your uncle has been asking for you all night," he panted, slowing. "He insisted I ask after you . . ."

Wil nodded understandingly and reached out to clasp the Gnome's shoulder. "I am on my way to see him now. Thank you."

The Server turned and darted back through the mist to whatever shelter he had been forced from. Wil watched him disappear from view, then started back up the roadway.

A smile creased his face. Poor Uncle Flick. He would not be here at all if Shea had not taken ill. Flick cared little for the Eastland, a country he could live without quite nicely, as he was fond of reminding Wil. He particularly disliked Gnomes, though the Stors were decent enough folk. Too many Gnomes had tried to do away with him in the past, particularly during the search for the Sword of Shannara. That was not something he could forget easily; such memories lingered on and could not be put aside simply for the sake of being fair-minded about Gnomes.

In any case, Flick really didn't care to be here at all and wouldn't have been, except that Shea had not been able to come as he had promised Wil he would and Flick had felt duty-bound to come in his place. Viewed in that perspective, the whole thing was Shea's fault—as Flick had announced to Wil ten seconds after his arrival. After all, if Shea hadn't made his ill-advised promise to visit Wil, then Flick would be back in the Vale instead of sitting around in Storlock where he did not want to be in the first place. But Flick was Shea's brother and therefore Wil's uncle—Flick refused to think of himself as anyone's granduncle—and since Shea could not come, someone had to make the trip in his stead. The only other someone was Flick.

The little guest cottage where Flick was staying came into view, and Wil turned reluctantly toward it. He was tired and he did not feel like an argument, but there would probably be one, because he had spent very little time with Flick during the few days his uncle had been in Storlock and none at all in the past thirty-six hours. His work was demanding, but he knew that his uncle viewed that as a lame excuse.

He was still mulling the matter over when Flick appeared abruptly on the porch of the cottage, gray-bearded face lapsing into stony disapproval. Resigned to the inevitable, Wil mounted the steps and brushed the water from his cloak.

Flick studied him wordlessly for a moment, then shook his head.

"You look exhausted," he declared bluntly. "Why aren't you in bed?"

Wil stared at him. "I'm not in bed because you sent word that you wanted to see me."

"Not right away, I didn't!"

"Well," Wil shrugged helplessly. "I guess I thought I should come to see you now. After all, I haven't been able to give you much time so far."

"True enough," his uncle grunted, a hint of satisfaction in his voice at eliciting this admission. "Still, you pick an odd time to mend the error of your ways. I know you were up all night. I checked. I just wanted to see if you were all right."

"I'm fine." Wil managed a brief smile.

"You don't look fine. And it's this weather as much as anything." Flick rubbed his elbows gingerly. "Confounded rain hasn't stopped since I got here. It doesn't bother just old people like me, you know. Bother's everyone— even would-be Healers." He shook his head. "You would be better off back in the Vale."

Wil nodded absently.

It had been a long time since Shady Vale. For almost two years now he had been living and working in the village of the Stors, learning the art of Healing from the recognized masters of the craft, preparing himself for the time when he might return to the Southland as a Healer, to lend the benefit of his skills to his own people. Unfortunately the whole business of becoming a Healer had proven a source of constant irritation to Flick, though Wil's grandfather had come to accept it well enough. When the fever had taken Wil's parents, a very young Wil Ohmsford had bravely re- solved that, when he grew older, he would become a Healer. He had told his grandfather and Flick, in a child's way and with a child's determination, that he wished to save others from sickness and pain. That was fine, they agreed, thinking it a child's whim. But his ambition had stayed with him. And when, on reaching manhood, he had announced that it was his inten- tion to study, not with the Healers of the Southland, whom he knew to be only adequate in their skills, but with the very best Healers in the Four Lands—with the Stors—their attitude had undergone an abrupt change. Good old Uncle Flick had long ago made up his mind about Gnomes and the Eastland. Even his grandfather had balked. No Southlander had ever studied with the Stors. How could Wil, who did not even speak the lan- guage, expect to be taken into their community?

But Wil had gone despite their reservations—only to be taken before the Stor council upon his arrival and told politely but firmly that no one who was not of the village of Storlock had ever been permitted to study with them. He might stay as long as he wished, but he could not become one of them. Wil did not give up. He decided that he must first learn their language, and he spent almost two months doing so. Then he appeared again before the council and again attempted to persuade them, this time speaking to them in their own tongue. He was not successful this time ei- ther. Every week for nearly a month after that, he went before the council to plead his cause. He told them everything about himself and his family, everything that had led to his decision to become a Healer—everything that he thought might convince them that he should be allowed to study with them. Something must have worked, because finally, without a word of explanation, he was told that he would be permitted to remain and that they would teach him what they knew. In time, if he proved diligent and capable, he would become a Healer.

He smiled fondly at the memories. How pleased he had been—and his grandfather and Flick, when they had learned of his acceptance, though the latter would never admit it any more than he would admit to the real reason for his disapproval of the whole venture. What really distressed Flick was the distance separating him from Wil. He missed the hunting, fishing, and exploring that they had shared while Wil was growing up. He missed having Wil there in the Vale with him. Flick's wife had died a long time ago, and they had never had any children of their own. Wil had been his son. Flick had always believed that Wil would stay on in the Vale and manage the inn with Shea and him. Now Wil was gone, settled in Storlock, far from the Vale and his old life, and Wil knew that his uncle simply could not accept the way things had worked out.

"Are you listening to me?" Flick asked suddenly, a frown creasing his bearded face.

"I'm listening," Wil assured him. He placed a hand gently on his uncle's shoulder. "Be patient, Uncle Flick. I'll be back some day. But there is so much to learn yet."

"Well, it's you I'm concerned about, not me," Flick pointed out quickly, his stocky form straightening. "Your grandfather and I can manage just fine without you, but I'm not so sure you can manage without us. Look at you. You push yourself too hard, Wil. You have this stubborn streak in you that seems to have blinded you to the fact that you cannot do everything that you might like to do. You are a normal human being like the rest of us. What do I have to do to get you to see that?"

It appeared that he wanted to say more, but with an effort he stopped himself. "This isn't the time for it." He sighed. His hand came to rest on Wil's. "Why don't you go to bed? We can talk when you . . ."

His gray eyes shifted suddenly, and his voice trailed off. Wil turned to follow his gaze. There was movement in the mist—a shadow, dark and solitary. They stared at it curiously, watching it slowly materialize. It became a horse and rider, each blacker than the other. The rider sat bent forward in the saddle, as if quite weary from the ride, dark clothing soaked by the rain and plastered against his tall frame.

A sudden apprehension stole through Wil. This was no Stor that came; indeed, this looked to be no man the like of which he had ever seen.

"It cannot be . . ." he heard Flick mutter.

His uncle did not finish the thought. He brushed past Wil and stepped to the edge of the porch, bracing himself with an outstretched arm against the rain-slicked railing. Wil moved to stand with him. The horseman was coming directly toward them. So strong was the sense of foreboding that the rider's approach engendered within him that the Valeman gave momentary consideration to fleeing. Yet he could not flee. He could only wait, eyes fixed on the spectral form.

The rider drew to a halt before the Valemen. His head was lowered, his face hidden within the folds of a dark cowl.

"Hello, Flick."

The rider's voice was a deep, low whisper. Wil saw his uncle start.

"Allanon!"

The big man slipped from the back of his horse, but one arm remained hooked about the animal's neck, as if he could not stand alone. Wil came forward a pace and stopped. Something was clearly wrong.

Allanon's gaze shifted slowly to meet his own. "Wil Ohmsford?" The Valeman nodded, surprised. "Go quickly and ask the Stors to come . . ." he began, then sagged downward, barely catching himself in time to keep from collapsing.

Wil came down the porch steps instantly, moving to the Druid's aid, but stopped as the big man's hand came up in warning.

"Do as I say, Valeman—go!"

Then Wil saw clearly what the rain had hidden from him before. Allanon's clothes were deeply stained with blood. Without another word the Valeman bounded back up the roadway toward the center, the weariness and discomfort slipping from him like a dream lost in waking.

8

The Stors took Allanon to the rest center, and although both Wil and Flick sought to accompany the injured Druid, they were told gently but firmly that their assistance was not needed. Enigmatic and silent, Stors and Druid disappeared into the corridors of the center, and the Valemen were left standing in the rain. Since it was apparent that for the moment nothing further would be learned of the Druid's coming, Wil Ohmsford bade his uncle good-night and went off to bed.

Later that same day, during the early evening hours, Allanon sent word that he wanted to see both Valemen. Wil received the news with mixed emotions. On the one hand, he was curious to discover what had befallen the Druid. Stories of Allanon were familiar territory; his grandfather and Flick had told them all a dozen times over. Yet never in those tales had there been mention of injuries like those the big man had suffered in coming to Storlock. Not even the Skull Bearer that had attacked him in the furnace room at Paranor during the search for the Sword of Shannara had done this kind of damage, and Wil wanted to know what manner of creature walked the Four Lands that was more dangerous than the winged servants of the Warlock Lord. On the other hand, he was disturbed by the Druid's presence in Storlock. It might have been coincidence that Allanon came at a time when he found both Flick and Wil in the village. It might have been by chance that he stumbled upon them rather than the Stors. But Wil did not believe it for a moment. Allanon had come to them deliberately. Why had he done that? And why had he summoned them to this meeting? Wil could understand Allanon's wish to confer with Flick; after all, they had met before and shared common adventures. By why Wil? The Druid didn't even know the youngest Ohmsford. Why would Allanon be interested in meeting with him?

Nevertheless, he left his quarters and dutifully trooped off through the growing darkness across the village square toward the guest house where he knew Flick would be waiting. Much as he mistrusted the purpose behind this meeting, he was determined to go anyway. He was not one to back away from trouble—and besides, he could be wrong in his suspicions. Perhaps the Druid merely wanted to thank him for his help.

He found Flick waiting on the porch of the guest cottage, wrapped tightly in his heavy travel cloak, mumbling irritably about the weather. The elder Ohmsford came down the porch steps to join him, and they struck off together down the roadway toward the Stor rest center.

"What do you think he wants, Uncle Flick?" Wil asked after a moment, pulling his own cloak closer about him to ward off the evening chill.

"Hard to say," Flick grunted. "I'll tell you one thing. Every time he appears, it means trouble."

"His coming to Storlock has something to do with us, doesn't it?" Wil ventured, watching his uncle's face.

Flick shook his head uncertainly. "He's come here for a purpose sure enough. And he's called us over to say something more than hello and how are you. Whatever it is he has to say, it won't be anything we want to hear. I know that much. It never has been before and I see no reason to expect anything different this time around." He stopped abruptly and faced his nephew. "You watch yourself in there with him, Wil. He is not to be trusted."

"I'll be careful, Uncle Flick, but I don't think there is much to worry about," Wil replied. "We both know something of Allanon, don't we? Besides, you'll be there to keep an eye on things."

"I fully intend to." Flick turned and they continued walking. "Just remember what I said."

Moments later they mounted the porch steps of the rest center and stepped inside. The center was a long, low building constructed of stone and mortar walls and a clay-tiled roof. A large, comfortably furnished lobby opened on either side into hallways that disappeared into the wings of the center, where numerous small rooms provided for the care of the sick and injured. As they entered, one of the white-robed Stors in attendance came up to greet them. He beckoned wordlessly, then led them down a long, empty hallway. At its end was a single closed door. The Stor knocked once, turned, and left. Wil glanced uneasily at Flick, but the elder Ohmsford was staring fixedly at the closed door. Together they waited.

Then the door swung open and Allanon stood before them. He looked for all the world as if he had not been injured at all. No wounds were visible. The black robes that cloaked his tall frame were clean of blood. His face was somewhat drawn, but showed no sign of any pain. His penetrating gaze settled on the Valemen for a moment, then one hand motioned toward a small table with four chairs set about it.

"Why don't we sit there while we talk?" He made the suggestion seem almost an order.

They entered and seated themselves on the chairs. The room was windowless and bare of furnishings, except for the table and chairs and a large bed. Wil glanced about briefly, then turned his attention to the Druid. Allanon had been described to him by both Flick and Shea on dozens of occasions, and he looked now exactly as he had been described. But how could that be, Wil wondered, when the descriptions were of a man they had not seen since before the time of his birth?

"Well, here we are," Flick said finally, when it appeared that no one was ever going to say anything.

Allanon smiled faintly. "It seems so."

"You look well enough for a man who was half-dead just a few hours earlier."

"The Stors are very adept at their art, as you of all people should know," the Druid replied rather too pleasantly. "But I'm afraid I do not feel half so well as I should. How are you, Flick?"

"Older and wiser, I hope," the Valeman declared meaningfully.

Allanon did not respond. His gaze shifted abruptly to Wil. For a moment he said nothing further, his dark face inscrutable as he studied the younger Ohmsford. Wil sat quietly and did not turn away, though the Druid's eyes made him uneasy. Then slowly Allanon leaned forward in his chair, his great hands settling on the tabletop and folding together.

"I need your help, Wil Ohmsford," he stated quietly. Both Valemen stared at him. "I need you to come with me into the Westland."

"I knew it," muttered Flick, shaking his head.

Allanon smiled ruefully. "It is comforting to know, Flick, that some things in this life never change. You are certainly proof of that. Would it matter at all if I were to tell you that Wil's help is needed not for me, but for the Elven people and in particular, a young Elven girl?"

"No, it would not," the Valeman replied without a moment's hesitation. "He's not going and that's the end of it."

"Wait a minute, Uncle Flick," Wil interjected quickly. "It may well be that I'm not going, but I would like to be the one who makes that decision. At least, we can hear something more about what it is that I'm needed to do."

Flick ignored the reprimand. "Believe me, you do not want to hear another word. This is exactly how the trouble begins. This is exactly how it began for your grandfather fifty years ago." He looked quickly at Allanon. "Isn't that true? Isn't this exactly how things started when you came to Shady Vale and told us all about the Sword?"

Allanon nodded. "It is."

"There—you see!" Flick declared triumphantly. "Exactly the same. I'll wager this journey you've got planned for him is dangerous, too, isn't it?"

Again the Druid nodded.

"Well, then." The Valeman sat back, satisfaction etched into his bearded face. "I should think that settles the matter. You're asking too much. He's not going."

Allanon's dark eyes glittered. "He must go."

Flick looked startled. "He must?"

The Druid nodded. "You will see why, Flick, once I have explained what has happened in the Four Lands these past few days. Listen closely to me, Valemen."

He edged his chair closer to the table and leaned forward. "A long time ago, a very long time ago, before the Great Wars and the evolution of the new races, even before the development of Man as a civilized species, there was a terrible war fought between creatures that, for the most part, no longer exist. Some of these creatures were good and caring; they revered the land and sought to protect and preserve it against misuse and waste. For them, all life was sacred. But there were others who were evil and selfish; their ways were destructive and harmful. They took from the land and from its life without need or purpose. All were creatures whose physical characteristics and capabilities differed in the main from your own— that is to say, their appearance was different from yours, and they were capable of behavior no longer innate to the men of this world. In particular, they possessed to varying degrees powers of magic—at least, we would call it magic or sorcery or the mystic. Such power was common at that time, though some among these creatures possessed the power to a greater extent than others; thus their capacity for good or evil was enhanced proportionately. All of these creatures, both good and evil, existed together in the world and, because Man had not yet developed beyond a primitive life form existing within a narrow geographical space, the world was theirs alone. It had been so for centuries. But their existence together had never been harmonious. They lived in continuing conflict, for they worked at cross-purposes—the good to preserve, the evil to destroy. From time to time the balance of power between the conflicting sides would shift, as first the good and then the evil would dominate the drift of things.

"The struggle between them intensified through the years until finally, after centuries had passed without resolution of the conflict, the leaders in each camp banded together all who supported them, and the war began. This was not a war the like of which we have seen since. This was not a war on the order of the Great Wars, for the Great Wars employed power of such awesome proportion that the men who wielded it lost control entirely and were engulfed in the resulting cataclysm. Rather it was a war in which power and strength were skillfully employed at each turn—in which the creatures involved stood toe to toe in battle and lived and died on the skill they wielded. This was like the Wars of the Races, which have dominated the history of the new world; in the Race Wars, the Warlock Lord perverted the thinking of those who served him, turning them against one another so that in the end he might enslave and rule them all. But in this war, there was never any deceit or illusion that swayed those who fought it. Good and evil were polarized from the beginning; no one stood aside in neutrality for there were no neutral corners to be found. This was a war fought to determine forever the character and mode of evolution of life on the earth across which it was waged. It was a war that would decide whether the land would be forever preserved or forever desecrated. Each camp had resolved once and for all to achieve total victory over the other. For the creatures of evil, if they were defeated, it meant banishment; for the creatures of good, if they lost, it meant annihilation.

"So the war was fought—a terrible, monstrous war that I will not even attempt to describe, for there would be no point in doing so. For our purposes here it is only important that you know that the evil ones were defeated. Their power was broken and they were driven back and finally trapped. Those who had defeated them used their powers to create a Forbidding, a wall of imprisonment behind which the evil was to be placed. Their prison was not of this world nor any world, but a black hole of emptiness and isolation where nothing but the evil would be permitted to exist. Into this hole the evil was banished, sealed away behind the wall of the Forbidding for all time.

"The strength behind the Forbidding was a marvelous tree called an Ellcrys. The creatures of good created the Ellcrys out of the earth's life source, which they called the Bloodfire, and out of their own power. They gave her life so that, by her presence in the world, the Forbidding might endure long after they themselves were gone, long after the world they had struggled so long and desperately to preserve had altered and evolved beyond any recognition. Her life span was not to be measured by any standard that they possessed. But so long as she lived, the Forbidding continued, and so long as the Forbidding continued, the evil would remain shut within its prison."

He settled back in his chair, easing his tall frame gingerly away from the table to relieve cramped muscles, his arms slipping down into his lap. His dark eyes stayed locked on those of the Valemen.

"It was believed that the Ellcrys would live forever—not by those who gave her life, for they knew that all things must eventually pass away—but by those who followed them, by all who nurtured and loved and honored this wondrous tree that was their protector for countless centuries. For them, the Ellcrys became a symbol of permanency; she survived the destruction of the old world in the holocaust of the Great Wars, she survived the Race Wars and the power of the Warlock Lord, and she survived after every other living thing that had existed with her had passed away—everything but the earth herself, and even the earth had changed while the Ellcrys had remained constant."

He paused. "So the legend grew. The Ellcrys would live forever. It was eternal. That belief never faltered." His face lifted slightly. "Until now. Now the belief is shattered. The Ellcrys is dying. The Forbidding begins to erode. The evil ones imprisoned within begin to break free once more and come back into this world that was once theirs."

"And these creatures caused your injuries?" Wil surmised.

Allanon nodded. "Some already walk the Four Lands. Though I thought to keep my presence secret, they have discovered me. They found me at Paranor within the Druid's Keep and very nearly finished me."

Flick looked alarmed. "Are they still searching for you?"

"They are—but I have reason to believe that they won't be so quick to find me this time."

"That doesn't reassure me much," the Valeman grumbled, glancing toward the doorway of the little room a bit apprehensively.

Allanon let the remark pass. "You may remember, Flick, that I once told to Shea and to you the history of the races. I told you how all of the races evolved from the old race of Man following the destruction wrought by the Great Wars—all of the races but one. The Elves. I told you that the Elves were always there. Do you remember?"

Flick grunted. "I remember. That was something else you never explained."

"I said that theirs was another story for another time. That time is now—in part, at least, though I don't propose to digress on the history of the Elven people at any great length. But some things you should know. We have spoken only in the abstract of the creatures that fought this war of good and evil that culminated in the creation of the Ellcrys. We must give them identity. All were creatures that became part of the old legends of faerie when men emerged from the darkness of barbarism and began to populate and build upon the world. They were creatures of magics, as I have said, both great and small. There were diverse species—some all good, some all bad, some whose individual peoples divided and went in opposite ways. They had names that you will recognize—Faeries, Sprites, Goblins, Wraiths, and the like. The new races, though human in ancestry, were named from four of the more numerous and best recorded of these creatures of supposed legend—Dwarves, Gnomes, Trolls and Elves. Except, of course, that the Elves are different. They are different because they are not simply a legend reborn—they are the legend survived. The Elven people are the descendants of the faerie creatures that existed in the old world."

"Now wait a minute," Flick cut in quickly. "You mean to say that the Elven people are the same Elven people that all the old legends tell about—that there really were Elves in the old world?"

"Certainly there were Elves in the old world—just as there were Trolls and Dwarves and all the other creatures that gave birth to the legends. The only difference is that all of the others have been gone from the world for centuries, while the Elves have remained. They have altered, of course; they have evolved considerably. They were forced to adapt."

Flick looked as if he didn't understand one word of what he was hearing.

"There were Elves in the old world?" he repeated incredulously. "That is just not possible."

"Of course it's possible," the Druid replied calmly.

"Well, how did they survive the Great Wars?"

"How did Man survive the Great Wars?"

"But the old histories tell us of Man—they do not mention a single word about Elves!" the Valeman snapped. "Elves were a fairy tale people. If there really were Elves in the old world, where were they?"

"Right where they had always been—Man just couldn't see them."

"Now you're telling me Elves were invisible?" Flick threw up his hands. "I don't believe any of this!"

"You didn't believe any of what I told you about Shea and the Sword of Shannara either, if I remember correctly," Allanon pointed out, the faintest hint of laughter on his lips.

"I don't see what any of this has to do with why the Elves need my help," Wil interjected, heading off another outburst from Flick.

The Druid nodded. "I'll try to explain if Flick will just be patient with me for a moment longer. The history of the Elves is important to this discussion for one reason only. The Elves were the ones who conceived the idea of the Ellcrys and who brought her into being. It was the Elves who gave her life and afterwards cared for her down through the ages. Her protection and well-being are entrusted to an order of Elven youth called Chosen. For a single year, the Chosen stand in service to the tree, their task to see to it that she is properly looked after. At the end of that year, they are replaced. It has been so since the tree's creation. One year of service only. The Chosen are revered and honored among the Elven people; only a few are ever selected to serve and those who do so are guaranteed a position of high esteem in the Elven culture.

"All of which brings us to the present. As I have told you, the Ellcrys is dying. A few days earlier, she made this known to the Chosen. She was able to do this because she is a sentient being and possesses the ability to communicate. She revealed to them that her death was inevitable and close. She revealed as well what the Elven legends had foretold, what the first Elves had known, but what generations of Elves thereafter had virtually forgotten—that although the Ellcrys must die in the manner of other living creatures, unlike them she could be reborn. Yet her rebirth must depend heavily on the efforts of the Chosen. One among them would be required to bear her seed in search of the earth's life source—the Bloodfire. Only one of the Chosen presently in her service could do this. She told them where the Bloodfire might be found and bade them make preparations to seek it out."

He paused. "But before this could be done, some of the evil ones locked within the Forbidding broke free, finding the wall sufficiently weakened as the strength of the Ellcrys began to fail. One slipped into the Elven city of Arborlon, where the Ellcrys stands, and killed the Chosen it found there, believing that with their deaths any chance for a rebirth would be ended. I arrived too late to prevent this from happening. But I spoke with the Ellcrys and discovered through her that one of the Chosen still remains alive—a young girl who was not within the city when the others were killed. Her name is Amberle. I left Arborlon in search of her."

He leaned forward once more. "But the evil ones have learned of her also. They sought once already to prevent me from reaching her and very nearly succeeded. They will certainly try again if they have the chance to do so. But they do not know where she can be found nor, for the moment at least, do they know where I am. If I am quick enough, I should be able to reach her and return her safely to Arborlon before they discover me again."

"Then I should think that you are wasting valuable time conversing with us," Flick declared firmly. "You should be on your way to the girl."

The Druid ignored him, though his face darkened slightly. "Even though I return Amberle to Arborlon, there are problems still that must be dealt with. As the last of the Chosen, it will fall to her to bear the Ellcrys' seed in quest of the Bloodfire. No one, myself included, knows exactly where the Fire can be found. Once, the Ellcrys knew. But the world she remembers is gone now. She gave the Elves a name—Safehold. It is a name that means nothing to them, a name from the old world. When I left Arborlon, I traveled first to Paranor to search the Druid histories compiled by the Council after the Great Wars—histories which record the mysteries of the old world. Reading through those histories, I was able to discover the country within which Safehold lies. Still, the exact location of the Bloodfire must be discovered by those who seek it."

And suddenly Wil Ohmsford realized why it was that Allanon wanted him to go into the Westland.

He realized it and still he could not believe it.

"Amberle cannot undertake this search alone," Allanon continued. "The country into which she must go is dangerous—much too dangerous for a young Elven girl to travel by herself. It will be a difficult journey at best. Those who have crossed through the Forbidding will continue to seek her out; if they find her, she will have no protection against them. She must not be harmed in any way. She is the last hope of her people. If the Ellcrys is not reborn, the Forbidding will eventually fail altogether and the evil locked within it will be loose once more upon the earth. There will be war with the Elves that they cannot, in all probability, win. If they are destroyed, the evil will move into the other Lands as well. It will grow stronger as it comes, as is the nature of beings such as these. In the end, the races will be devoured."

"But you will be there to help her . . ." Wil began, searching for a way out of the trap he felt closing about him.

"I cannot be there to help her," Allanon cut in quickly.

There was a long silence. Allanon spread his hands on the table.

"There is good reason for this, Wil Ohmsford. I have told you that the evil already begins to break through the wall of the Forbidding. The

Ellcrys will grow steadily weaker; as she does so, the creatures she imprisons will grow bolder. They will continue to push against the wall of the Forbidding. They will continue to break through. Eventually, they will tear down the wall entirely. When this happens, they will converge upon the Elven nation and attempt to destroy it. This may very well happen long before the Bloodfire is found. There is also a possibility that the Bloodfire may never be found or that it may be found too late. In either case, the Elven people must be prepared to stand and fight. But some of the creatures within the Forbidding are very powerful; at least one possesses sorcery very nearly as great as my own. The Elves will have no defense against such power. Their own magic is lost. The Druids who once aided them are gone. There is only me. If I leave them and go with Amberle, they will be defenseless. I cannot do that. I must give them whatever aid I can.

"Yet someone must go with Amberle—someone who possesses power enough to resist the evil that will pursue her, someone who can be trusted to do everything humanly possible to protect her. That someone is you."

"What are you talking about?" Flick exclaimed in exasperation. "What possible help can Wil be against creatures such as these—creatures that very nearly succeeded in doing you in? You don't mean for him to use the Sword of Shannara?"

Allanon shook his head. "The power of the Sword works only against illusion. The evil we face is very real, very tangible. The Sword would have no power against it."

Flick almost came to his feet. "What then?"

The Druid's eyes were dark and filled with insight and Wil Ohmsford felt his heart sink.

"The Elfstones."

Flick was aghast. "The Elfstones! But Shea has the Elfstones!"

Wil put his hand quickly on the other's arm. "No, Uncle Flick, I have them." He groped within his tunic and then withdrew a small leather pouch. "Grandfather gave them to me when I left Shady Vale to come to Storlock. He told me that he no longer had need of them and that he thought they should belong to me." His voice was shaking. "It's strange; I only took them to please him—not because I ever thought that I would use them. I've never even tried."

"It would do you no good, Wil." Flick turned back hurriedly to Allanon. "He knows. No one but Shea could ever use the Elfstones. They are useless to anyone else."

Allanon's expression did not change. "That is not entirely true, Flick. They can only be used by one to whom they are freely given. I gave them to Shea to use when I warned him to flee the Vale to Culhaven. They remained his until he gave them to Wil. Now they belong to Wil. Their power is his to invoke, just as it was once Shea's."

Flick looked desperate. "You can give them back," he insisted, turning once more to Wil, seeing the confusion in his eyes. "Or you can give them to someone else—anyone else. You don't have to keep them. You don't have to become involved in any of this madness!"

Allanon shook his head. "Flick, he is already involved."

"But what of my plans to become a Healer?" Wil interjected suddenly. "What of the time and work I have put into that? Becoming a Healer is all that I have ever wanted to do, and I am finally on my way to doing it. Am I expected just to give it all up?"

"If you refuse your aid in this matter, how can you then become a Healer?" The Druid's voice turned hard. "A Healer must give whatever help he can, whenever he can, in any way that he can. It is not something he can pick and choose. If you refuse to go and all that I have foreseen comes to pass—as I am certain that it then will—how will you live with yourself, knowing that you never even tried to prevent it?"

Wil flushed. "But when will I be able to return again?"

"I don't know. It may be a long time."

"And even if I come with you, can you be certain that the power of the Elfstones will be strong enough to protect this girl?"

Allanon's face closed in about itself, dark, secretive.

"I cannot. Such power as the Elfstones possess draws its strength from the holder. Shea never tested their limits; you may have to."

"Can you give me no assurances, then?" The Valeman's voice had dropped to a whisper.

"None." The Druid's gaze never left him. "Still, you must come."

Wil slumped back in his chair, stunned. "It seems I have no choice."

"Of course you have a choice!" Flick snapped angrily. "Will you give up everything for no other reason than this—that Allanon says you must? Will you go with him for that alone?"

Wil's eyes lifted. "Didn't you, Uncle Flick—grandfather and you—to search out the Sword of Shannara?"

Flick hesitated uncertainly; then he reached over and took his nephew's hands in his own, clasping them tightly.

"You are too quick in this, Wil. I warned you of Allanon. Now you listen to me. I see more in this than you. There is something hidden behind the Druid's words. I can feel it." His voice tightened, and the lines in his gray-bearded face creased even more deeply. "I am afraid for you. It is because I am afraid that I speak to you as I do. You are like my own son; I don't want to lose you."

"I know," Will whispered. "I know."

Flick straightened. "Then don't go. Let Allanon find another."

The Druid shook his head. "I cannot, Flick. There is no other. There is only Wil." His eyes again sought those of the young Valeman. "You must come."

"Let me go instead," Flick offered suddenly, a hint of desperation in his voice. "Wil can give the Elfstones to me, and I can watch over the Elven girl. Allanon, we have traveled together before . . ."

But the Druid was already shaking his head no. "Flick, you cannot come," he said gently. "Your heart is greater than your strength, Valeman. The journey that lies ahead will be long and hard and must be made by a younger man." He paused. "Our travels together are over, Flick."

There was a long silence, and then the Druid turned again to Wil Ohmsford, waiting. The Valeman looked at his uncle. They stared at each other wordlessly for a moment, Flick's gray eyes uncertain, Wil's now steady. Flick saw that the decision had been made. Almost imperceptibly, he nodded.

"You must do what you feel is right," he mumbled, reluctance sounding in his every word.

Wil turned to Allanon. "I will come with you."

Early the next morning, Allanon came to Wil Ohmsford and told him that they were leaving Storlock at once. Dark and grim-visaged, the Druid appeared at the door of the Valeman's cottage without a word of forewarning and while Wil gave thought to arguing against such an abrupt departure, something in the big man's face and voice convinced him that he should not. Last evening, when they had parted company, there had been no urgency in the Druid's behavior; now there clearly was. Whatever it was that had persuaded Allanon to make this decision, it was compelling. Wordlessly the Valeman packed his few belongings and latched the door of the cottage behind him as he followed the Druid out.

It was raining once more as a new storm approached from out of the northwest, and the dawn skies were heavy and leaden. Allanon led the Valeman up the muddied roadway, his tall form wrapped in the black robe, his cowled head bent slightly against a steadily rising wind. A handful of white-robed Stors waited to receive them on the steps of the rest center with a small kit for Wil and provisions for the journey. Artaq was saddled and shaking his head with impatience, and Allanon mounted the black at once, a gingerness in his movements suggesting that his wounds were not yet fully healed. A wiry gray gelding named Spitter was given to Wil, and he had one foot in the stirrup when Flick came dashing up, bearded face dripping and flushed. Hastily his uncle pulled him back into the shelter of the rest center's covered porch.

"They just told me," he panted, wiping the rain from his eyes. "I'm surprised they bothered!" He glanced angrily toward Allanon. "Is it necessary that you leave so quickly?"

Will nodded slowly. "I think something may have made it necessary."

Frustration and concern showed in Flick's eyes. "It is not too late to rethink your decision in all this," he whispered harshly and would have said more, but Wil was already shaking his head. "Very well. I'll tell your grandfather what has happened, though I am certain he won't like it any better than I do. Be careful, Wil. Remember what I said about all of us having our limitations."

Wil nodded. They said their goodbyes quickly and gruffly, almost as if they were afraid to express what they were really feeling, their faces fixed and drawn as they exchanged uneasy glances and hurriedly embraced. Then Allanon and he were riding away. Flick, the Stors, and the village became dark shadows that faded into the mist and gray of the Eastland forests and disappeared from view.

The Druid and the Valeman rode west out of Storlock to the edge of the Rabb Plains, then turned south. Allanon paused long enough to tell Wil that the first leg of their journey would take them below the Silver River to a small village on the western edge of the lower Anar called Havenstead. It was at Havenstead that they would find Amberle. The Druid did not volunteer anything further on the matter, and Wil did not ask. Rain washed over them in sheets as the storm worsened; keeping within the fringe of the forestland, they bent their heads over their horses' necks and rode without speaking.

As they traveled, Wil's thoughts drifted back to the events of the previous evening. Even now, he was not sure exactly why he had decided to go with the Druid. And that disturbed him. Surely he should be able to explain why he had agreed to such an improbable journey—to himself, at least, if to no one else. Yet he could not. There had been sufficient time to think about his reasons for making the decision, and indeed he had thought about little else. Hindsight should have lent clarity to his actions; it did not. Rather, he felt a lingering sense of confusion. Everything seemed to jumble together in his mind—all the disparate, incomplete reasoning, all the emotions that intertwined and colored. They would not sort themselves out for him; they would not arrange themselves in a neat, orderly fashion. They merely shuffled about like stray sheep and he chased after them hopelessly.

He wanted to believe that he had chosen to go because he was needed. If all that Allanon had told him were true—and he felt it was, despite Flick's obvious doubts—then he could be of great service to the Elven people and particularly to the girl Amberle. But who was he fooling? He had no idea at all whether he could use the Elfstones that his grandfather had entrusted to him. Suppose their power was beyond him. Suppose Allanon was wrong in thinking that the Elfstones could be passed down to him. Suppose anything at all. The fact was that he had made a rather impulsive decision, and now he must live with it. On the other hand, the impulsiveness of the decision did not necessarily detract from its merit. If he possessed aid to offer the Elves, he must extend that aid. He must at least try to help them. Besides, his grandfather would have gone; he knew that as surely as he knew anything. Shea Ohmsford would have gone, had Allanon asked him, just as he had gone on his quest for the Sword of Shannara. Wil could do no less.

He took a deep breath. Yes, he had made the right decision in going, and he believed that he had made that decision for the right reasons, though they seemed jumbled and out of order to him now. What bothered him most, he realized suddenly, had nothing to do with the decision itself or the reasons for that decision. It had to do with Allanon. Wil would have liked to believe that the decision to go with the Druid had been his own. Yet the more he considered the matter, the more certain he became that the decision had not really been his at all. It had been Allanon's. Oh, he had spoken the words as if they were his own, spoken them bravely and despite his uncle's warnings. Yet he knew that the Druid had been able to foresee exactly what it would take to persuade Wil to speak those words, and he had directed the conversation accordingly. Somehow he had known what the younger Valeman's reactions would be, what Flick's would be, how the two would interact, and how his own comments would influence them. He had known all this and used that knowledge accordingly. Shea Ohmsford had once told Wil that Allanon possessed the ability to see into the minds of other men, to know their thoughts. Wil understood now exactly what his grandfather had been talking about.

Thus he had committed himself. It was not something that could be undone, even if he should choose to do so, and he did not. But from here forward, he would be on his guard against such clever manipulation by the Druid. In so far as it was possible for him to do so, he would look beyond the words and actions of the big man to the reasons that lay behind them, the better to see where it was that he was being led. Wil Ohmsford was nobody's fool. He had been looking after himself for several years, and he was not about to quit doing so now. He must be wary of the Druid. He would trust him, but not blindly and not without proper consideration. Perhaps he could be of service to the Elves and to the girl Amberle; he did not reject that possibility simply because of what he felt about the manner in which his cooperation in all this had been secured. But he would be careful to choose his own manner of giving aid. He would be careful to decide for himself whose interests he might best look after. He would accept nothing as he found it.

His face lifted guardedly, and he peered through the rain at the dark form riding ahead of him—Allanon, last of the Druids, a being who came from another age, whose powers dwarfed anything known to this current world. And Wil must both trust him and yet not trust him. He felt a moment of deep consternation. What had he gotten himself into? Perhaps Flick had been right after all. Perhaps he would have done well to have given a little more thought to his decision. But it was too late for that now. Too late, as well, for thoughts such as these. He shook his head. There was little point in dwelling on it further. He would be well advised to turn his thoughts in another direction.

He spent the remainder of the day trying unsuccessfully to do so.

The rain turned to drizzle as the day lengthened, then at last died away entirely in the cold gray of early evening. Thunderclouds continued to blanket the skies as nightfall turned from gray to black, and the air filled with mist that wandered at the forest's edge like a child lost. Allanon turned into the shelter of the great trees, and they made camp in a small clearing several hundred yards from the borders of the Rabb. Behind them, rising above the roof of the forest, was the dark wall of the Wolfsktaag, little more than a deeper shade of black against the night. Despite the damp, they managed to salvage enough dry wood and kindling to make a small fire, and the flames lent some warmth to the evening chill. Travel cloaks were hung on lines stretched overhead, and the horses were tethered close by.

They consumed a sparse meal of cold beef, fruit, and nuts that they had packed before leaving Storlock, exchanging only a few perfunctory words as they ate. The Druid sat in brooding silence, preoccupied with his own thoughts, as he had been ever since they had left the village, and seemingly disinterested in carrying on any sort of conversation. But Wil had determined to learn something more of what lay ahead and he had no intention of waiting any longer to begin talking about it. When they had finished their meal, he eased himself a bit closer to the fire, making sure the movement caught Allanon's attention.

"Can we talk a bit?" he asked carefully, bearing in mind his grandfather's many tales of the big man's uncertain temperament.

The Druid stared at him expressionlessly for a moment, then nodded.

"Can you tell me something more about the history of the Elven people?" Wil decided the conversation should begin there.

Allanon smiled faintly. "Very well. What would you like to know, Wil Ohmsford?"

The Valeman hesitated. "Last night you told us that even though the histories of the old world make no mention of the Elven people other than in fairy tales and in folklore, they were a real people nevertheless, just as men were. You said they were there, but humans couldn't see them. I didn't understand that."

"You didn't?" The big man seemed amused. "Well, then you shall have an explanation. Simply put, the Elves have always been creatures of the forest—but more so in the times before the Great Wars. In those days, as I've told you before, they were creatures of magic. They possessed the ability to blend in quite naturally with their surroundings, much as if they were a bush or plant that you might pass by a thousand times and never notice. Humans couldn't see them because they did not know how to look for them."

"But they weren't invisible?"

"Hardly."

"Just difficult to see?"

"Yes, yes." There was a touch of annoyance in the Druid's answer.

"But why don't we have trouble seeing them now?"

Allanon straightened himself. "You're not listening. In the old world, the Elves were creatures of magic, as were all the creatures of faerie. They are creatures of magic no longer. They are men, just as you are a man. Their magic is lost to them."

"How did this happen?" Wil settled his elbows against his knees and propped his chin in his hands, somewhat in the manner of a curious child.

"That is not so easy to explain," the Druid advised him. "But I can see that you will not be satisfied until I've tried, so I will attempt to do so."

He leaned forward slightly. "After the creation of the Ellcrys, after the banishment of the creatures of evil magic from the earth, the Elves and their faerie brethren drifted apart once more. It was natural enough that this should happen since they had united in the first place only for the purpose of defeating their common enemy and, once that was accomplished, there was little left to keep them together. Beyond their general concern in preserving the earth as a homeland, they had almost nothing in common. Each species of creature had its own way of life, its own habits, its own interests. Elves, Dwarves, Sprites, Gnomes, Trolls, Witches, and all the rest, were as different from each other as the beasts of the forest from the fish in the sea.

"Humankind had not yet begun to emerge from its early, primitive existence, and would not do so for hundreds of years to come. The faerie creatures paid the humans little attention, and indeed there seemed little reason to do so. After all, at this stage in time humans were simply a higher form of animal life, possessing greater innate intelligence than other animals, but lesser instincts. The Elves and their brethren did not foresee the influence that humans would eventually have upon the development on the earth."

The Druid paused. "It was something they could have foreseen, had they paid closer attention to the differences between themselves and humankind. Two differences were of particular importance. The Elves and their brethren did not procreate rapidly; humans did. The Elves, for example, were one of the more populous faerie people, yet their longer life spans resulted in fewer births. Many of the other faerie creatures gave birth only once every several hundred years. But humans had frequent multiple births within the family unit, and their population grew quickly. In the beginning, the creatures of magic far outnumbered the humans. Within a thousand years' time, that situation reversed itself dramatically. Thereafter the human population expanded steadily, while the faerie population began to diminish—but I'll get to that in a moment.

"The second difference between the Elves and their brethren and humankind had to do with the ability to adapt, or lack thereof. The Elves were creatures of the forestland; they seldom left the shelter of their woods. It was the same with most of the others. Each resided within a particular geographic area, a carefully bounded terrain. It had always been so. Some lived within the forests, some within the rivers and seas, some within the mountains, some within the plainlands. They had adapted their way of life to the terrain that served as their homeland; they could not and would not live anywhere else. But humans were more adaptable; they lived everywhere. The forests, the rivers, the mountains, the plains—they claimed it all. Thus their expansion as their population grew came naturally, easily. They adapted to any change in environment. The Elves and their brethren resisted all change."

Allanon paused, then smiled faintly. "There was a time, Wil Ohmsford, when life in the old world was much as life is now—when humans lived and worked and played much as the races do in this world. Does that surprise you?"

Wil nodded. "A little, I guess."

The Druid shook his head. "There was such a time. It was then that the Elves should have come forward and joined with humans to shape their world. But they did not—neither they nor their brethren. They chose instead to remain hidden within their forestland, observers only, still believing that their own existence would not be affected by the development of humankind. They saw no threat to themselves; the humans possessed no magic and their ways were not destructive—not then. So the Elves kept to their policy of isolation, foolishly thinking it could always be so. It was their undoing. The human population continued to expand and to develop. As time wore on, they learned of the Elves and their brethren. But because the faerie creatures chose concealment as their way of life, they earned the distrust of humans. They were deemed creatures of ill-fortune, creatures who spied and connived against others, creatures who performed acts of mischief and whose favorite pastime was to discover new ways of making the lives of hard-working humans more difficult. There was some truth to the charges, since a few of the faerie creatures did indeed delight in tormenting humans with small acts of enchantment, but by and large the reputation was undeserved. In any case, the Elves and their brethren chose to ignore it all. The attitude of humankind toward them did not concern them. Their sole concern was with the preservation and protection of the land and the living things within it, and this they could accomplish very well, despite the ill feelings humans bore them.

"Then even this state of affairs began to change. Humans continued to populate the earth with increasing rapidity, growing, expanding, now building cities and fortresses, now sailing the seas in search of new lands, now pushing back the wilderness about them. They began, for the first time, seriously to affect the character of the land, changing whole regions for habitation and consumption needs. The Elves were forced to move deeper and deeper into the forestlands that were their homes, as the human population cut away the trees and brush. All of the faerie creatures found their homelands being encroached upon by this expansion until finally, for some, there were no homes at all."

"But didn't they resist this intrusion?" Wil interrupted suddenly.

"It was far too late for that," Allanon replied, his smile bitter. "By this time, many of the faerie creatures had become extinct, some by failure to reproduce sufficient young, some by their failure to adapt to a changing environment. Those who remained were no longer able to unite as they once had done; it had been hundreds of years since their war with the faerie creatures of evil magic, and they had scattered far and wide about the earth and long since lost contact with one another. Worst of all, they no longer had their own magic. When the evil magic had flourished upon the earth, there had been need for good magic to withstand it. But once that evil had been banished, the need for the good magic was past. The faerie creatures ceased using most of it. As time passed, much of it was forgotten altogether. Human beings used no magic of any consequence, so the Elves and their brethren saw no need for the very powerful magics that had once been employed to defeat their evil counterparts. By the time they recognized the need for it again, it was lost to them—all but a small part of it. Thus their resistance to the expansion of the human population into their homelands was weakened badly. At first they fought very hard, using all the power they still possessed to stop what was happening. It availed them nothing. There were too many humans and too few of them. Their magic was ineffective. It won them small victories, brief respites, nothing more. They were simply overwhelmed in the end, driven from their homes to find new ones or to perish—driven out, in the final analysis, by sciences and technologies against which they had no real defense."

"And the Elves—what of them?" Wil asked quietly.

"They learned to survive. Their population dwindled, but they did not become extinct as did so many of the others. They remained within their forestland, moving steadily deeper, hidden now completely from the humans who had come to occupy almost the whole of the earth. They watched in horror the destruction that was being performed on their world. They watched it being stripped of its resources and its animal life. They watched as its ecological balance was utterly and irreversibly disrupted. They watched the humans war between themselves incessantly as the separate governments struggled to achieve domination over one another. They watched and they waited and they prepared—for they saw how it all must end."

"The Great Wars." The Valeman anticipated the Druid.

"The Great Wars." Allanon nodded. "The Elves foresaw that such horrors would come. They used what magic they still possessed in an effort to preserve themselves and a few carefully chosen treasures of their past— among these, the Ellcrys—from the holocaust that followed. It was a remarkable effort, and it allowed them to survive. Most of the other faerie creatures were destroyed. A small number of humans survived, though it was not through their foresight that they did so. They survived because there were so many of them in so many different parts of the earth that the holocaust simply missed a few of them. But everything that the humans had built was destroyed. All of their vast, sprawling civilization was erased. The old world was reduced to a barren, desolate wilderness.

"For hundreds of years after, all life was caught up in a savage struggle to stay alive. The few creatures that remained alive in this new world were forced to adapt to the primitive environment about them, an environment in which nature had been altered beyond recognition. Humankind was changed forever. From out of the old race of humans emerged four new and distinct races: Men, Dwarves, Gnomes, and Trolls. It was believed, and is still believed by most, that the Elves were a fifth race born of the holocaust. For the new races, it was the beginning of life. Most of the history of the old world was quickly forgotten; most of the old ways vanished. The Elves kept much of their history and their tradition. Only their magic was lost to them—but this time it was lost for good. Their need to adapt resulted in changes that would not otherwise have occurred, changes that brought them closer culturally and physiologically to the new races. Reborn humans and surviving Elves assimilated together in their new world until finally, inexorably, they became much the same.

"And when at last, almost a thousand years after the Great Wars had ended, the new races began to emerge from the primitive lives they had endured while struggling to survive the aftereffects of the holocaust, the Elves stood with them. No longer would they hide in their forestland as impartial observers to the development of a world. This time they would be a part of that development, working openly with the new races to be certain that men did not travel a second time that roadway which had almost ended with the destruction of all life. Thus did the Elves, through the Druid Galaphile, convene the First Council at Paranor. Thus did the Elves seek to turn the races from an ill-advised search for the old sciences of energy and power, counselling instead a more cautious approach to life's mysteries. Thus did they seek to regain the small magics they had lost, believing these arts would help them best in their efforts to preserve their new world and its life."

"Yet the Elves have no magic," Wil reminded the big man. "Only the Druids did."

"The Druids and a handful of others scattered through the land," Allanon corrected. He seemed to lose himself momentarily. When he spoke again, his voice was distant. "The Druids learned early of the dangers inherent in the search for the lost magic. A Druid named Brona taught them well. His need to explore the limits of the magic destroyed him, created in his physical shell the creature we know as the Warlock Lord. When the Druids realized what hunger for the magic had done to him, they forbade further exploration. The magic they had found was not altogether good, nor altogether bad; it was simply powerful—too powerful for mortal men to master. For a time, it was left alone. Then Brona caught and killed all of the Druids at Paranor, signalling the start of the Second War of the Races, and suddenly there was only Bremen left to teach the magic. Then, when he was gone, there was only me . . ."

He trailed off momentarily, dark eyes narrowing as he stared down into the little fire at their feet. Then he looked back suddenly at Wil.

"What else would you know, Valeman?"

The tone of his voice was sharp, almost angry. Its abruptness caught Wil by surprise, but he kept his gaze steady, forcing his eyes to meet the Druid's.

"What else would you have me know?" he replied quietly.

Allanon said nothing, waiting. There was a long, uncomfortable silence as the two men faced each other. At last the Valeman looked away again, poking idly at the embers of their fire with the toe of one boot.

"These creatures that were shut within the place beyond the Forbidding—what of them?" he asked finally. "How have they survived for so many years? Why have they not perished?"

Allanon's dark expression did not change. "Call them Demons, for that is what they have become. They were sent to a non-place, a dark emptiness beyond any living world. Within that darkness, there was no passing of time to bring age and death. The Elves failed to realize this, I suppose, or perhaps thought it of little importance, since their only concern was to remove the evil from their own world. In any case, the Demons did not die; rather, they multiplied. The evil that lived within them fed upon itself and grew stronger. It bred new life. For evil left to itself, Valeman, does not simply perish; it thrives. Evil contained is not evil destroyed. It nourishes itself, grows within its confinement, swells and rages until it works loose, and then . . . then it runs free."

"And its magic?" Wil followed quickly. "Has its magic grown also?"

Some of the harshness faded from the other's visage, and he nodded. "Fed in the same way, and practiced, for the evil ones warred with each other in their prison, driven nearly mad with need to release their hatred of what had been done to them."

Now it was the Valeman's turn to be silent. His face lowered into shadow; his arms wrapped protectively about his knees as he drew his legs up tightly to his chest. In the east, there sounded the faint, distant thunder of the departing storm as it faded into the broken wall of the Wolfsktaag.

A touch of impatience revealed itself in Allanon's dark face as he watched the young man. He leaned forward once more.

"Are all of your questions answered now, Wil Ohmsford?"

The Valeman blinked. "No." His head lifted sharply. "No, I have one more."

Allanon frowned. "Indeed. Let's have it, then."

He was clearly displeased. Wil hesitated, weighing inwardly the advisability of proceeding any further with this. He decided that he must. He chose his words carefully.

"Everything that I've heard suggests that these Demons are more than a match for the Elves. It seems from your own encounter with them that they are a match even for you." There was anger now in the big man's face, but Wil pushed ahead quickly. "If I accompany the Elven girl Amberle in search of the Bloodfire, as you have asked me, they will surely come after us. Suppose we are found. What chance do I stand against them, Allanon? Even with the Elfstones, what chance do I have? You would not answer me before. Answer me now."

"Well." The Druid rocked back slightly, the lean, dark visage suddenly expressionless in the firelight, creased in shadow. "I thought this was all leading up to something."

"Please give me an answer to my question," Wil persisted quietly.

Allanon cocked his head reflectively. "I don't know the answer."

"You don't know?" the Valeman repeated the words incredulously.

The Druid blinked. "In the first place, I hope to keep them from finding you. If they cannot find you, they cannot harm you. At the moment, they know nothing of you at all. I intend that it should stay that way."

"But if they do find me—then what?"

"Then you have the Elfstones." He hesitated. "Understand this, Wil. The Elfstones are a magic from the old world—a magic that existed when the Elves first defeated these creatures. The power of the Stones is measured by the strength of the man or woman who wields them. There are three Elfstones—one each for the heart, mind, and body of the user. All three must unite as one; when this is done properly, the power released can be very great."

He looked at the Valeman sharply. "Do you understand, then, why I cannot answer your question? You will determine the strength of your defense against your enemies; it must come from within you, not from the Stones themselves. I cannot measure that in you. Only you can do that. I can only tell you that I judge you to be as good a man as your grandfather—and I've met no better man, Wil Ohmsford."

The Valeman stared wordlessly at the Druid for a moment, then looked down at the fire.

"Nor have I," he whispered.

Allanon smiled faintly. "Your grandfather's chances seemed very poor when he went in quest of the Sword of Shannara. He would admit to that. The Warlock Lord knew of him from the beginning; the Skull Bearers actually came into the Vale in search of him. He was hunted every step of the way. Yet he survived—and he did so despite his own considerable doubts."

He reached over and put his hand on Wil's shoulder, the cavernous eyes glinting in the firelight. "I like your chances in this. I believe in you. Now you must start believing in yourself."

He took his hand away and rose. "We've talked enough this night. You need to sleep. We've a long ride ahead of us tomorrow." He wrapped his black robes tightly about him. "I'll keep watch."

He started to move away from the Valeman.

"I can keep watch," Wil offered quickly, remembering the Druid's injuries.

"You can sleep," Allanon grunted, and the night shadows swallowed him up.

Wil stared after him for a second, then shook his head. Spreading his blankets next to the fire, he rolled himself into them and stretched wearily. He would not sleep, the Valeman told himself. Not yet. Not until he had taken time to consider carefully all that had been said this evening, until he had decided how much of it he should believe, until he was convinced that he knew what he was doing in all this. Not until then.

He let his eyes close for just a moment. Immediately he was asleep.

10

They resumed their journey at daybreak. Although the forestland still glistened damply with yesterday's rain, the skies were clear and blue and filled with sunlight as the pair rode southward along the fringes of the Anar. The drab emptiness of the Rabb brightened into rolling grasslands, and the enticing smell of fruit-bearing trees was carried past them on a gentle morning breeze.

Late that afternoon they arrived at the legendary Silver River and came upon a company of Dwarf Sappers engaged in the construction of a footbridge at a heavily forested narrows. Leaving Wil concealed in a copse of fir with the horses, the Druid went down to the river's edge to confer with the Dwarves. He was gone for a time and, when he returned, seemed preoccupied with something. It was not until they had remounted and were riding downriver away from the Dwarves that he volunteered to Wil that he had given warning of the danger to the Elves and requested that the Dwarves send aid as quickly as possible. One among the Sappers had recognized the Druid and had promised that help would be sent. Still, marshalling any sizable force would take time . . .

Allanon left the matter there. Minutes later they forded the Silver River at a shallows where a broad sandbar split the clear waters apart and rock shallows slowed the current enough to permit horse and rider safe passage. From there they rode south at a leisurely pace, watching the shadows they cast lengthen as the day wore on. It was nearly sunset when Allanon reined in Artaq at the crest of a tree-lined rise and dismounted. Wil followed him down, leading Spitter forward several paces to where the Druid waited. They tethered the horses in a small grove of hickory and together walked ahead to where an outcropping of rock split apart the wall of trees. With Allanon in the lead, they moved up into the rocks and peered out.

Below them lay a broad, horseshoe-shaped valley, its slopes and floor heavily forested, but open at its western end to grasslands that had been tilled and planted with farm crops. A village sat at the juncture between forest and field, and a narrow stream ran from the woodlands through the cluster of homes north across the top of the farmland, its waters irrigating the soil in dozens of neatly inscribed ditches. Men and women moved busily about the little community, tiny figures to the two who looked down on them from the valley rim. Far to the south, the grasslands ended in a rock-strewn lowland that stretched unbroken to the horizon and disappeared.

"Havenstead," Allanon announced, indicating the village and the farmlands. His finger lifted slightly and pointed into the lowland. "Out there, is the Battlemound."

Wil nodded. "What do we do now?"

The Druid seated himself comfortably. "We wait until it gets dark. The fewer people who see us, the better. The Stors would say nothing in any case, but these villagers are free with their talk. Secrecy is still our greatest ally, and I don't intend to lose it unnecessarily. We'll go in quickly and quietly and leave the same way." He glanced up at the sun, already beginning to drop rapidly into the western horizon. "We only have about an hour."

They sat together without talking until the rim of the sun was barely visible above the tree line, and the dusk had begun to slip her gray shadow over the length of the valley. Finally, Allanon rose. They walked back to where they had tied the horses, remounted and started out once more. The Druid led them eastward for a time, skirting the valley rim until they had reached a heavily forested section of the slope that concealed a narrow draw. There they started down. They wound their way slowly through the trees, watching the woodlands darken steadily into night, allowing the horses to pick their way through the brush. Wil quickly lost all sense of direction, but Allanon seemed to know exactly where he was going and did not slow as he guided them forward.

After a time, they reached the valley floor, and travel grew easier. A clear, moonlit sky peeked down on them through breaks in the forest roof, and night birds called out sharply at their passing. The air was sweet and heavy with the smell of the woods, and Wil grew drowsy.

Finally, scattered bits of yellow light began to flicker into view ahead of them, slipping through the screen of the forest, and the faint sounds of voices reached out through the stillness. Allanon dismounted, motioning for Wil to do likewise, and they walked the horses forward afoot. The forest thinned out noticeably, clear of heavy brush and deadwood, and ahead of them they could see a low stone wall with a wooden gate. A line of tall evergreens bordered the wall and screened away most of what lay beyond, though it was clear to Wil that they were at the eastern edge of the farming village and the yellow lights were the flames of oil lamps.

Upon reaching the wall, they tied the horses to an iron post. Allanon put a single finger across his lips. Silently, they passed through the little wooden gate.

What they found on the other side brought Wil up short. A sweeping, terraced garden spread out before them, its tiers of multicolored flowers dazzling even in the pale moonlight. A stone walkway, glistening with flecks of silver, wound downward out of the gardens to a gathering of wooden benches and from there to a small cottage constructed of timber and stone. The cottage was a single story with a loft and was fronted by the familiar open-air porch. Flower boxes hung below latticed windows, and thick, low bushes bordered the roughened walls. Crimson yews and blue spruce grew at the immediate front of the home. A second walkway ran from the porch beneath the arch of a magnificent white birch and disappeared through a hedgerow to a roadway beyond. In the distance, glimmerings of light from other cottages broke the night.

Wil stared at it all in wonderment. Everywhere there were touches of color and life—all with the look of something drawn from a child's storybook. Everything was perfectly ordered.

He glanced questioningly at Allanon. The mocking smile flashed briefly, and the Druid motioned for him to come. They followed the pathway through the gardens to the benches, then moved on toward the cottage. Light shone brightly through the curtained windows of the little house, and from within came the low, gentle sound of voices—no, Wil corrected himself, children's voices! He was mildly surprised at his discovery and very nearly missed seeing the fat, striped house cat that lay sprawled across the first step of the porch. He caught himself just in time to keep from stepping on the sleeping animal. The cat raised its bewhiskered face and stared up at him insolently. Another cat, this one coal black, scooted off the porch hurriedly and slipped down into the bushes without a sound. Druid and Valeman climbed the porch steps and moved to the front door. From within, the children's voices rose sharply in laughter.

Allanon knocked firmly and the voices went still. Footsteps came to the other side of the door and stopped.

"Who is it?" a voice asked softly, and the patterned curtains that screened a glass port parted slightly.

The Druid leaned forward, allowing the light from within to fall across his dark countenance.

"I am Allanon," he answered.

There was a long silence, then the sound of a latch drawn back. The door opened and an Elven girl stepped through. She was small, even for an Elf, her body slender and brown with sun. Chestnut hair fell all the way to her waist, shadowing a child's face at once both innocent and knowing. Her eyes flashed briefly to Wil—eyes that were green and deep with life—then settled once more on the Druid.

"Allanon has been gone from the Four Lands for more than fifty years." Her voice was steady, but there was fear in her eyes. "Who are you?"

"I am Allanon," he repeated. He let a moment of silence pass. "Who else could have found you here, Amberle? Who else would know that you are one of the Chosen?"

The Elven girl stared up at him speechlessly. When she tried to speak, the words would not come. Her hands came together tightly; with a visible effort, she composed herself.

"The children will be frightened if they are left alone. They must be put to bed. Wait here, please."

Already there was a scurrying of small feet at the other side of the door and the faint whisper of excited voices. Amberle turned and disappeared back into the cottage. They could hear her voice, low and soothing, as she ushered the children up wooden stairs to the loft overhead. Allanon moved to a wide-backed bench at the other end of the porch and seated himself. Wil remained where he was, standing just to one side of the door, listening to the sounds of the Elven girl and the children from within, thinking as he did so: she is only a child herself, for goodness' sake!

A moment later she was back, stepping lightly onto the porch, closing the cottage door carefully behind her. She glanced at Wil, who smiled at her awkwardly.

"This young man is Wil Ohmsford." Allanon's voice floated out of the dark. "He studies at Storlock to become a Healer."

"Hello . . ." Wil began, but she was already walking past him to the big man.

"Why have you come here, Druid—if Druid you are?" she demanded, a mixture of anger and uncertainty in her voice. "Has my grandfather sent you?"

Allanon rose. "Can we sit in the gardens while we talk?"

The girl hesitated, then nodded. She led them from the porch back along the stone walkway to the benches. There she seated herself. The Druid sat across from her, Wil a little off to one side. The Valeman recognized that his rôle in this confrontation was that of a spectator and nothing more.

"Why are you here?" Amberle repeated, her voice a bit less unsettled than a moment earlier.

Allanon folded his robes about him. "To begin with, no one has sent me. I am here of my own choice. I am here to ask you to return with me to Arborlon." He paused. "I will be brief. The Ellcrys is dying, Amberle. The Forbidding begins to crumble; the evil within breaks free—Demons all. Soon they will flood the Westland. Only you can prevent this. You are the last of the Chosen."

"The last . . ." she whispered, but the words caught in her throat.

"They are all dead. The Demons have found and killed them. The Demons search now for you."

Her face froze in horror. "No! What trick is this, Druid? What trick . . ." She did not finish this either, but stopped as tears formed in her eyes and streaked her child's face. She brushed them away swiftly. "Are they really all dead? All of them?"

The Druid nodded. "You must come with me to Arborlon."

She shook her head quickly. "No. I am no longer one of the Chosen. You know that."

"I know that you would wish it so."

The green eyes flared angrily. "What I would wish is of no matter in this. I no longer serve; that is all behind me. I am no longer one of the Chosen."

"The Ellcrys selected you as one of the Chosen," Allanon replied calmly. "She must decide whether you remain one. She must decide whether you shall carry her seed in search of the Bloodfire, so that she may be reborn and the Forbidding restored. She must decide—not you, not I."

"I will not go back with you," Amberle stated quietly.

"You must."

"I will not. I will never go back. This is my home now; these are my people. I have made this choice."

The Druid shook his head slowly. "Your home is wherever you make it. Your people are whomever you wish them to be. But your responsibilities are sometimes given you without choice, without consent. It is so in this, Elven girl. You are the last of the Chosen; you are the last real hope of the Elves. You cannot run away from it; you cannot hide from it. You most certainly cannot change it."

Amberle rose, paced away a step, and turned. "You do not understand."

Allanon watched her. "I understand better than you think."

"If you did, you would not ask me to return. When I left Arborlon, I knew that I would never go back again. In the eyes of my mother, my grandfather, and my people, I had disgraced myself. I did something that could not be forgiven—I rejected the gift of being a Chosen. Even should I wish it, and I do not, this cannot be undone. The Elves are a people whose sense of tradition and honor runs deep. They can never accept what has happened. If it were made known to them that they would all perish from the earth unless I alone chose to save them, still they would not have me back. I am outcast from them, and that will not change."

The Druid rose and faced her, tall and black as he towered over her small form. His eyes were frightening as they fixed on hers.

"Your words are foolish ones, Elven girl. Your arguments are hollow and you speak them without conviction. They do not become you. I know you to be stronger than what you have shown."

Stung by the reprimand, Amberle went taut.

"What do you know of me, Druid? You know nothing!" She stepped close to him, green eyes filled with anger. "I am a teacher of children. Some of them you saw this night. They come in groups of half-a-dozen or eight and stay with me one season. They are given into my care by their parents. They are entrusted to me. While they are with me, I give to them my knowledge of living things. I teach them to love and to respect the world into which they were born—the land and sea and sky and all that lives upon and within it. I teach them to understand that world. I teach them to give life back in exchange for the life they were given; I teach them to grow and nurture that life. We begin simply, as with this garden. We finish with the complexity that surrounds human life. There is love in what I do. I am a simple person with a simple gift—a gift I can share with others. A Chosen shares nothing with others. I was never a Chosen—never! That was something I was called upon to be that I did not wish to be nor was suited to be. All that, I have left behind me. I have made this village and its people my life. This is who I am. This is where I belong."

"Perhaps." The Druid's voice was calm and steady and it brushed aside her anger. "Yet will you turn your back on the Elves for no better reason than this? Without you, they will surely perish. They will stand and fight as they did in the old world when the evil first threatened. But this time they lack the magic to make them strong. They will be destroyed."

"These children have been given into my keeping . . ." the girl began hurriedly, but Allanon's hand rose abruptly.

"What do you think will happen once the Elves are destroyed? Do you think the evil ones will be content to stay within the borders of the Westland? What of your children then, Elven girl?"

Amberle stared at him wordlessly for a moment, then dropped slowly back down onto the bench. Tears ran again from her eyes, and she closed them tightly.

"Why was I chosen?" she asked softly, her words barely more than a whisper. "There was no reason for it. I did not seek it—and there were so many others who did." Her hands clenched in her lap. "It was a mockery, Druid—a joke. Do you see that? No woman had been chosen in over five hundred years. Only men. But then I was chosen—an impossible, cruel mistake. A mistake."

The Druid stared at the gardens, his face expressionless once more.

"There was no mistake," he responded, though Wil believed he was speaking almost to himself. The Druid looked back at her, turning quietly. "What frightens you, Amberle? You are afraid, aren't you?"

She did not look up, did not open her eyes. Her head nodded once.

Allanon reseated himself. His voice was gentle now. "Fear is part of life, but it should be faced openly, never hidden. What is it that frightens you?"

There was a long silence. Wil leaned forward quietly on his seat several benches away.

Finally Amberle spoke, her words whispered. "She does."

The Druid frowned. "The Ellcrys?"

But this time Amberle did not answer him. Her hands lifted to her stricken face and wiped away the tears. Her green eyes opened, and she came to her feet once more.

"If I were to agree to travel with you to Arborlon, if I were to agree to face my grandfather and my people, if I were to go before the Ellcrys one final time—if I were to do all this, all that you have asked, what then if she will not give to me her seed?"

Allanon straightened. "Then you may return to Havenstead, and I will trouble you no more."

She paused. "I will think about it."

"There is no time to think about it," Allanon insisted. "You must decide now, tonight. The Demons search for you."

"I will think about it," she repeated. Her eyes settled on Wil. "What is your part in all of this, Healer?" Wil started to reply, but her quick smile stopped him. "Never mind. Somehow I sense that we are alike in this. You know no more than I."

Less, Wil wanted to tell her, but she had already turned away.

"I have no place for you in my home." She spoke to Allanon again. "You may sleep here, if you like. Tomorrow we'll talk about this further."

She started toward the cottage, chestnut hair trailing sail-like down her back.

"Amberle!" the big man called after her.

"Tomorrow," she replied and did not slow.

Then she was gone, disappearing silently through the cottage door, leaving Druid and Valeman staring after her in the dark.

The creature came for Wil through the sluggish haze of his sleep, a formless creation of his dreams that rose up hauntingly out of the depths of his subconscious. It was a thing of terror, a thing that lurked in the dark recesses of his mind where he hid his deepest fears. It came for him with stealth and cunning, slipping easily past the obstacles with which he sought to block it, its motion fluid and quick as it pressed in about him. He could not see it as it came; he never would. It lacked substance or identity; it lacked reason. There was only the overwhelming sense of terror it created by its being. He ran from it, of course— ran swiftly through the landscapes of his imagination, ran and ran until it seemed he must surely have left it behind. But he had not. It was there at once, closing swiftly, surely. He lunged from it in desperation, screaming soundlessly for help, anyone's help. But there was no one. He was alone with this thing and he could not escape it. Yet he must, for if it were to reach him, if it were to touch him, he knew with certainty that he would die. So he ran in fear, blindly, feeling the breath of the thing hot upon his neck . . .

He came awake with a start, lurching upward from beneath the blankets to a sitting position. The night air was cold on his face and body. Sweat ran from beneath his arms, and from within his head he could hear the sound of his heart pounding wildly.

Allanon's dark form crouched next to him, strong hands holding fast to Wil's shoulders. The Druid's voice was a harsh whisper.

"Quick, Valeman. They have found us."

Wil Ohmsford did not need to ask who it was that had found them. It was his dream become reality. He came to his feet with a bound, grabbing up his blanket and hurrying after the Druid, who was already moving toward the little cottage. As if by intuition, Amberle appeared at the edge of the porch, white night dress blowing eerily about her slender form, giving her a ghostly appearance. Allanon went to her at once.

"I told you to dress," he whispered angrily.

She looked unconvinced. "You would not seek to trick me, Druid? This would not be some game you are playing to help me make up my mind to come back with you to Arborlon?"

Allanon's face went black. "Another few minutes of standing around and you will have your answer! Now dress!"

She stood her ground. "Very well. But I cannot leave the children. They must be taken to a place of safety."

"There is not time enough for that," the Druid urged. "Besides, they will be safer here than stumbling about in the dark."

"They will not understand being left like this."

"Remain and they will share your fate!" Allanon's patience was gone. "Wake the oldest. Tell him that you must go away for a time, that you have no choice. Tell him that when it is light out, to take the others to a neighbor's home. Now do as I say—hurry!"

This time she did not argue, but turned and disappeared back inside the cottage. Wil straightened his clothing and rolled his blanket tight. Together, Druid and Valeman saddled the horses and brought them around to the front of the darkened home to wait for the Elven girl. She was with them almost immediately, dressed in boots, slacks, belted tunic and a long blue riding cloak.

Allanon brought the girl and the Valeman close before Artaq, whispering softly to the animal, stroking the satin neck. Then he handed the reins to Wil. "Get on."

Wil did as he was told, scrambling aboard the big black. Artaq shook his head and whickered. Allanon continued to whisper gently, then took Amberle by the waist and swung her up behind the Valeman as if she were no more than a feather's weight. Then he mounted Spitter.

"Quiet, now," he cautioned. "Not a word."

They turned onto the roadway that ran in front of the little cottage and followed it eastward through the sleeping village. Only the sound of their horses' hooves thudding softly on the earthen trail broke the deep stillness. In minutes, the buildings of the village were behind them, and they were at the forest's edge. Before them stretched the tilled fields, the waters of the irrigation ditches sparkling with moonlight as they crisscrossed through neatly planted rows of grain and corn already grown and ripening. In the distance, on either side, the wooded slopes of the valley fell away into the grasslands.

Allanon dismounted wordlessly. He stood motionless for a time, listening to the silence of the night, his dark face anxious. Finally he stepped close to Artaq, motioning for Wil and Amberle to bend close.

"They are all around us." He breathed the words. Wil went cold. The Druid looked at him as if to measure his worth. "Have you ridden in hunt before?" Wil nodded. "Good. You and Amberle will stay with Artaq. If you are pressed, give him his head. He will see you safely through this. We will ride north along the edge of the village to where the valley drops into the grasslands. Once there, we will break through their circle. Do not stop for anything, do you understand? If we become separated, do not turn back. Ride north until you reach the Silver River. If I do not come at once, cross and ride west to Arborlon."

"What will you . . . ?" Wil asked hurriedly.

"Do not concern yourself with what I might be doing," the Druid cut him short. "Just do as you are told."

Wil nodded reluctantly. He did not like the sound of this at all. When Allanon turned away, he glanced back at Amberle.

"Hold tight," he whispered and tried a quick smile. She did not smile back. There was undisguised fear in her eyes.

Allanon remounted. Slowly, cautiously they made their way along the forest's edge, skirting the western borders of the village of Havenstead. Silence hung deep and penetrating across the whole of the valley. Like shadows, they slipped through the darkness of the trees, their eyes searching the night for movement. Ahead of them, the north slope of the valley began to loom up darkly through breaks in the forest.

Then Allanon reined in sharply, motioning for them to be still. He pointed wordlessly toward the fields on their left. Wil and Amberle followed the line of his arm. At first, there was nothing to be seen, only row upon row of stalks shaded dark gray in the moonlight. But a moment later their eyes picked out the quick movement of something vaguely like an animal as it crept from one of the irrigation ditches and disappeared into the stalks of the field.

They waited for a time, frozen against the trees, then started forward once more. They had only gone a short distance when, from out of the woodlands behind them, a deep, searing howl rose. Amberle tightened her grip about Wil's waist and put her head against his back.

"Demon-wolves." Allanon spoke the name quietly. "They've found our trail."

He kicked Spitter's flanks firmly and urged the horse into a slow trot. Artaq snorted anxiously and followed. The howl was picked up by others, and there was the sudden sound of bodies plunging through the trees.

"Ride!" Allanon shouted.

The horses lunged forward, veering sharply left from the cover of the woodlands. At a gallop, they raced along the edge of the fields, following the line of the irrigation ditch toward the break that led to the grasslands. The howling rose all about them, fierce and hungry. Huge, leaping shadows sprang above the stalks of grain and corn in the darkness on their left, crashing wildly toward them. Wil bent low over Artaq's neck and urged the big horse on. Before them, the pass leading from the valley came into view.

Half-a-dozen bristling, dark forms broke from the woods ahead of them, things that were wolflike, but much larger, and with faces that appeared grotesquely human as they lifted in the moonlight, long teeth snapping. Allanon turned Spitter directly toward them, blue fire sparking on the fingers of one hand as it raised menacingly. An instant later the fire lanced out, burning into the pack, scattering it wildly. Spitter surged through its midst, his call shrill with terror.

Artaq was already past both Druid and Demon-wolves, his sleek body leveled out as he raced for the open plains. Several dark bodies lunged from out of the fields before them, jaws snapping at the horse's legs. Artaq did not slow. He caught one beast with his shoulder and knocked him spinning. The others were quickly left behind. Wil bent lower, pulling Amberle down with him against Artaq's back, loosening slightly his grip on the reins. To their right, more Demon-wolves bolted from the trees, their howls filling the night air. Streaks of blue fire cut through them, and the howls turned to shrieks of pain. Artaq ran on.

Then a single huge Demon-wolf appeared at the forest's edge ahead of them, running parallel to the woodland stream that fed the irrigation ditches. It lunged forward to intercept them, moving with astonishing speed, bounding through the long grass, its movements fluid and soundless. Wil felt something cold and hard tighten in his chest. The beast was narrowing the gap between them too quickly; they would not escape it. He did the only thing he could think to do. He shouted wildly to Artaq and gave him his head. The big black responded. From somewhere deep within, he found new strength. His stride lengthened. The beast was almost upon them, a massive, dark terror that seemed to rise up suddenly out of the night beside them. Wil closed his eyes and yelled one final time. Artaq screamed in response. Gathering himself, the stallion hurdled the woodland stream that lay across his path. Gaining the far bank, he raced from the woodlands and fields of Havenstead into the open plains beyond.

For an instant after, Wil's eyes remained closed, locked tight with fear. He simply clung to Artaq's neck, feeling the comforting movement of the great horse beneath him as they fled into the night. When he finally lifted his head once more and risked a quick look behind him, past Amberle's huddled form, he found that they were alone. Fire and smoke rose out of the darkness from within the valley, and the air was filled with frenzied yowling. There was no sign of the Demon-wolves. There was no sign of Allanon.

Almost without thinking, Wil reined in Artaq sharply and wheeled him about. Allanon had been firm in his instructions. Under no circumstances was he to turn back. Amberle was his first consideration. She had been given into his safekeeping; she was to be protected at all costs. He glanced quickly at her child's face as it rose out of the shadow of his back, green eyes questioning. He knew what he should do. Yet he knew that the Druid was still back there, probably in trouble. How could he simply leave him and go on?

His indecision lasted only a moment. From out of the valley behind them galloped a terrified Spitter, wiry gray body extended in full stride. Bent low over his back, black robes billowing out wildly, his dark figure silhouetted against a horizon colored red with fire, was the Druid. Close behind ran the Demon-wolves, their shaggy forms leaping madly through the tall grass, howling their hatred of the humans who had escaped them.

Wil turned Artaq north instantly and put his heels to him. The big black snorted and leaped ahead. The Valeman did not give him his head this time, but held him carefully in check. Their chase might be a long one, and the black's great strength was not without its limits. Artaq did not fight him, but followed his lead, running easily. Wil bent forward, feeling Amberle's grip about his waist tighten, her face burying itself against his back once more.

A mile further on, Spitter drew abreast, his heaving body streaked with sweat and dirt, his nostrils flaring. Already, he was growing tired. Wil glanced anxiously at Allanon, but the Druid did not look over; his dark gaze was fixed on the land ahead as he urged his horse on with small movements of his hands.

The chase through the grasslands of the Silver River country wore on with grim determination. The maddened howling of the Demon-wolves died quickly, changing to the sound of ragged breathing punctuated by snarls of frustration. For the fleeing horsemen, there was only the muffled whistle of the wind and the steady pounding of their horses' hooves. Through vales that cut between gently sloping hills and over broad, empty rises they ran, hunter and hunted—past groves of fruit trees, past solitary oaks and willows, past small winding streams of water, all through the silence and dark of the plains. Time slipped away without meaning. They had run nearly a dozen miles. Still the distance between them and their pursuers remained unchanged.

At last the Silver River slipped into view, a broad ribbon of moonlit water shining out of the dark through breaks in the low hills that bounded her near bank. Wil saw the river first and shouted. Artaq jumped ahead instantly at the sound of his voice, moving in front of Spitter once more. Belatedly, Wil sought to hold him back, but the big black would not be curbed this time. He was still running easily, smoothly, and he quickly left the tiring Spitter behind.

The gap between Artaq and those who came after widened further. Wil was still trying to rein in the black when he caught sight of the crouching, dark forms that appeared abruptly from out of the night ahead of him— forms that were bent and twisted and covered with bristling gray hair. Demons! Wil felt his stomach tighten. It was a trap. They had been waiting here, waiting in case any managed to escape from the Demon-wolves at Havenstead. Now they were spread out all along the banks of the Silver River, closing as the horsemen approached.

Artaq saw them and veered sharply left toward a small rise. Fifty yards further back, Spitter followed his lead. Further back still, but closing now on the tiring animal, ran the Demon-wolves, howling once more. Artaq gained the summit of the rise at full gallop and broke downward for the Silver River. The Demons in front of him moved quickly to bar his passage. Wil could see them clearly now, catlike beasts with the faces of women, twisted and grotesque. They bounded toward the big black, mewling hideously, muzzles lifting to reveal their long, sharp teeth.

At the last second, Artaq wheeled sharply and circled back toward the rise, leaving the cat things screeching with frustration. In that moment, Spitter topped the rise, stumbled wearily and went down. Allanon tumbled to the ground in a tangle of robes, rolled over several times, and sprang back to his feet. Demon-wolves came at him from all sides, but the blue fire spread from his fingers in a broad, cutting sweep that scattered them like leaves in a strong wind. Artaq wheeled left again, Wil and Amberle clinging desperately to his back to keep from being thrown. Screaming his hatred of the cat-things that sought to trap him, he ran at them once more, parallel now to the riverbank, moving so swiftly that he was on top of them before they had time to realize what he was about. Several of the beasts reached for him, clawed limbs ripping, but he was past them almost at once, clearing their grasping talons with a mighty leap and racing away into the night. Behind him, an arc of blue fire lanced into the nearest pursuers, burning them to ash. Wil glanced back once and saw Allanon still standing atop the rise, Demon-wolves and cat things alike closing about him from every direction. Too many! Wil heard the words scream through his brain. Fire sprang from the Druid's hands, and he disappeared in a haze of smoke and dark, leaping forms.

Then some sixth sense triggered within the Valeman, warning of new danger. His gaze shifted hurriedly from the battle atop the rise. From out of nowhere appeared half-a-dozen more of the Demon-wolves, racing toward Artaq in great, silent bounds. Wil felt a quick moment of panic. He and Amberle were trapped between the beasts and the river. Ahead of them a dense stretch of wood blocked their passage. Behind them were the Demons they had just fled. There was nowhere for them to go.

Artaq did not hesitate. He veered toward the Silver River. The wolves came after, soundless, fluid, black terror. Wil was sure that this time they would not escape. Allanon was no longer there to help them; they were all alone.

The Silver River drew closer. There were no shallows in view—only an open expanse of water too broad, too deep and too swift for them to cross; if they were to try, Wil realized, they would most certainly be swept away. Yet Artaq did not slow. Whatever the danger might be to them, the big black had made his choice. He was going into the river.

The Demon-wolves sensed it as well. Less than a dozen yards back, they threw themselves forward in a determined effort to catch Wil and the Elven girl. Amberle screamed in warning. Frantically Wil fumbled in his tunic for the leather pouch that contained the Elfstones, not knowing if he could even use them, only knowing that he must do something. He was too late. As his hand closed about the stones, they reached the edge of the Silver River. Artaq gathered himself and sprang clear of the riverbank, Wil and Amberle clinging to his back. In that same instant, white light burst all about them, freezing their motion as if they had been captured in a painting. The wolves disappeared. The Silver River vanished. Everything was gone. They were alone, rising upward in a slow, steady climb into the light.

12

Before time became time recorded, he was there. Before men and women, before nations and governments, before all the history of humankind, he was there. Even before the world of faerie split in war between good and evil, fixing unalterably the character of life thereafter, he was there. He was there in that time when the world was a sacred Eden and all living things existed together in peace and harmony. He was young then, a faerie creature himself while the faerie creatures of the earth were just being born. He lived within gardens that had been given over into his keeping, entrusted with the responsibility of seeing that they and all the living things that dwelt within were cared for and preserved, sheltered and renewed. He had no name, for names were not needed. He was who he was, and his life was just beginning.

He had not understood what he was to become. His future was a vague and distant promise whispered in the corridors of his dreams, and he could not have foreseen its reality. He could not have foreseen that his life was not to be finite in the manner of other living things, but was to extend down through centuries of lives celebrated in birth and forgotten in death until his own became cloaked in the trappings of immortality. He could not have foreseen that all who had been born into the world with him and all who were thereafter to be born, whether faerie or human, would fade and be lost while he alone would continue on. Nor would he have wanted to, for he was still young enough to be filled with the conviction that his world would always be as it was then. Had he known that he would live to see it all changed beyond any possible recognition, he would not have wished to survive. He would have wished to die and become one again with the earth that had bred him.

It would have been an irreparable loss, for he was to become the last remnant of that fabled time that was the world in its inception, the last remnant of peace and harmony, of beauty and light that was the Eden of life. It had been decreed in the twilight of the beginning, changing forever the course of his existence, changing forever the purpose of his life. He was to become for a world fallen from grace a small reminder of what had been lost. He was to become as well the promise that all that had once been might one day come again.

In the beginning, he had not comprehended this. There was only shock and dismay at discovering that the world was changing, its beauty fading, its light dying—that all that had been so filled with peace and harmony was to be lost. Soon his gardens were all that remained. Of all who had come into the world with him, not one was left behind. He was alone.

He despaired for a time, consumed with grief and self-pity. Then the changes that had altered the land about him began to encroach upon his own small world, threatening to change it as well. He remembered then his responsibilities, and he began the long and difficult struggle to preserve the gardens that were his home, determined that this last bit of the first world would survive, though all else had been lost. The years slipped away, and his struggle wore on. He found himself aging only slightly. He found within himself power that he had not known he possessed. After a time, he began to realize the purpose for his solitary existence—that a new trust had been given him, a trust he must not abandon. With realization came acceptance, and with acceptance came understanding.

For centuries he labored in anonymity, his existence little more than a myth that became part of the folklore of the nations building about him, a fantasy told with wry smiles and smug indulgence. It was not until after the cataclysm men called the Great Wars, the final destruction of the old world and the emergence of the new races, that the myth began to gain acceptance as truth. For it was then that he chose for the first time ever to go out from the gardens into the land beyond. His reasons were carefully drawn. There was magic in the world again, and his was the highest and best magic—the magic of life. The land without was new and fresh once more, and he saw in that rebirth an opportunity to recapture all that he had known when he was young. Through him, the past and future might at last be joined. It would not come easily or quickly; still, it would come. But he could no longer remain secluded and hidden within his gardens. He must go out from them. Contained within his small sanctuary was the seed of all that the world so desperately needed to regain; it was the trust he had first been given. He saw that it was not enough that it be preserved. He saw that it must be built upon—more, that it must be made visible and accessible. He must see that this was done.

Thus he went out from the gardens that had been his home for so many centuries, traveling into the country that lay about it—a country of sweet grasslands and gently rolling hills, of shaded woodland glens and quiet ponds, all bound together by a river that was the lifestream of the land. He would not travel far from the gardens, however, for they were his first concern and their need for his protection demanded that he stay close. Still, it did not prove necessary to journey farther than he did. The country he found pleased him. He planted the seed of the first world within its heart, marking it as his own, giving to it a special radiance that made it easily recognizable, giving to its inhabitants and to its travelers, whomsoever should require it, his blessing and protection from harm. In time, the new races came to understand what he had done; they spoke of him and of his land with awe and with respect. They began to tell his story throughout the Four Lands. The story grew with each new telling until at last they had made of him a legend.

They named him after the country he had made his own. They called him the King of the Silver River.

He came to Wil and Amberle in the guise of an old man, appearing from out of the light, wizened and bent with age, his robes hanging about his thin frame as if he were made of brittle sticks. His hair fell about his shoulders in thick, white locks. His ancient face was wrinkled and brown with sun; his deep blue eyes were the color of seawater. He smiled in greeting, and Wil and Amberle smiled in response, sensing that there was no harm in this man. They still clung tightly to Artaq's broad back, the black extended in full stride, unmoving in the light that held them all frozen. Neither Valeman nor Elven girl understood what had happened, yet there was no fear in them, only a deep, comforting drowsiness that immobilized them with the strength of iron chains.

The old man stopped before them, blurred and indistinct in the haze of the light. His hand touched Artaq's sleek face and the black nickered softly. The old man looked at Amberle then, and there were tears in his eyes.

"Child, that you were mine," he whispered. He stepped closer, reaching up to take her hand in his own. "No harm shall come to you in this land. Be at peace. We are joined in purpose and shall be one with the earth."

Wil struggled to speak and could not. The old man stepped back again, and one hand raised in farewell.

"Rest, now. Sleep." He began to fade, slipping back into the light. "Sleep, children of life."

Wil's eyes grew heavy. It was a pleasant, welcome sensation and he did not fight it. He was conscious of Amberle's small form slumped heavily against his own, her hands locked loosely about his waist. The light seemed to draw back from them, fading into darkness. His eyes closed, and he drifted into slumber.

He began to dream. He was standing in the midst of a garden filled with incredible beauty and serenity, dazzling in its color and fragrance, so wondrous that all else that he had known in life or had imagined possible paled in comparison. There were streams shimmering silver as they flowed from out of springs hidden with the earth and spilled into quiet ponds. There were trees canopied overhead, filtering sunlight that speckled with touches of golden warmth. There were soft, sweet grasses that carpeted the lanes and walkways in emerald silk. All manner of birds flew, fish swam, and animals walked through these gardens—passed in harmony and contentment and in peace. The Valeman was filled with a sense of deep, abiding tranquillity, fulfillment, and a happiness so intense that he cried.

Yet when he turned to share what he was feeling with Amberle, he found her gone.

13

When Wil Ohmsford awoke once more, it was dawn. He lay in a grassy vale beneath the sheltering limbs of twin maples, the morning sun filtering down through masses of broad green leaves in long streamers of brightness that made him blink. Close by, there was the faint sound of water lapping against a shore. For an instant, he believed himself still within the wondrous gardens of his dream. So real had they seemed to him that, almost without thinking about it he pushed himself up on one elbow and looked about hurriedly for them. But the gardens were gone.

Amberle lay next to him, still sleeping. He hesitated, then reached over and shook her shoulder gently. She stirred restlessly and her eyes opened. She looked at him in surprise.

"How are you?" he asked.

"I'm fine." She brushed the sleep from her eyes. "Where are we?"

Wil shook his head. "I don't know."

The Elven girl sat up slowly and looked about the small vale.

"Where is Allanon?"

"I don't know that either." Wil stretched his legs tentatively, surprised to find them loose and uncramped. "He's gone. They're all gone—Allanon, those creatures . . ." He paused, hearing movement in the brush at the far end of the hollow. A familiar black face poked through the leaves, nickering softly. Wil smiled. "Well, at least we still have Artaq with us."

The black cropped lazily at the grass, shook himself clear of the brush, and trotted over to nuzzle Wil. Wil stroked the sleek head for a moment, rubbing at the horse's ears. Amberle watched quietly.

"Did you see the old man?" Wil asked her.

She nodded solemnly. "That old man was the King of the Silver River."

Wil looked at her. "I thought as much. My grandfather saw him once, years ago. I don't think I was ever really sure whether he was real or not until now, though. Funny." Artaq moved off several paces and began feeding. Wil shook his head. "He saved our lives back there. The Demonwolves almost had us . . ." He caught the look that crept into the Elven girl's eyes and stopped. "Anyway, I guess we're safe now."

"It was like a dream, wasn't it?" she said softly. "We were floating in the light, riding Artaq with nothing beneath us but the light. Then he came up to us, walking, came out of nowhere and said something . . ." She trailed off, as if the memory of it confused her. "Did you see it?"

The Valeman nodded.

"And then he disappeared," she continued, speaking more to herself than to him, as if trying to recall all that had happened. "He disappeared and the light disappeared and . . . and then . . ." She looked at him curiously.

"The gardens?" he suggested. "Did you see the gardens?"

"No." She hesitated. "No, there were no gardens, just a darkness and a . . . a sensation I can't describe. I . . . a sort of reaching, I think." She looked at him for help, but he just stared back at her in confusion. "You were standing there with me," she went on. "You were standing there, but you couldn't see me. I called to you, but you didn't seem to hear me. It was so strange."

Wil hunched forward. "I remember the old man and the light, just as you've described them. I remember that. When they disappeared, I remember falling asleep . . . or at least, I think I fell asleep. Anyway, you were there with me on Artaq. I could feel your arms about my waist. The next thing I knew, I was standing in these gardens—I'd never seen anything like them; they were so peaceful and beautiful and quiet. But when I looked around for you, you weren't there. You were gone."

They looked at each other wordlessly for a moment.

"I suppose we had better worry about where we are now," Wil said finally.

He climbed to his feet and looked about again. Belatedly, he thought about helping Amberle up, but by then she was already standing next to him, brushing leaves and grass from her hair. He hesitated a moment, then led the way through the brush surrounding them toward the sound of the water.

Moments later, they stood at the edge of a lake so vast that its shoreline circled in either direction to the horizon and disappeared. Waves crested in sudden flashes of silver foam, the waters deep and clear blue in the morning sun. Groves of trees bordered its grass-covered banks, willow and elm and ash, leaves rippling softly in a light southerly wind that carried with it the scent of honeysuckle and azaleas. In the cloudless blue sky that canopied above the lake arced a brilliant, shimmering band of colors that seemed to rise from one end of the horizon and disappear into the other.

Wil glanced upward to fix the sun's location, then turned to Amberle, shaking his head in disbelief.

"Do you know where we are? We're somewhere on the north shore of the Rainbow Lake. The old man carried us all the way down the Silver River and across the lake to wherever it is we are now. We're miles from where we started."

The Elven girl nodded almost absently. "I think you're right."

"I know I'm right." Wil paced away excitedly and stopped at the water's edge. "I just don't know how he managed it."

Amberle sat down on the grass, gazing out over the lake.

"The legend says he helps those who need it when they travel in his land—that he keeps them safe from harm." She paused, her mind clearly elsewhere. "He said something to me . . . I wish I could remember . . ."

Wil was not listening. "We should get moving. Arborlon's a long way off. But if we travel in a northwest direction, we should be able to find the Mermidon, then follow it all the way to the Westland. That's a lot of open country, but we won't be so easy to find now. There's no trail to follow this time."

He missed entirely the look of annoyance that crossed Amberle's face, his mind preoccupied with the journey ahead.

"It should only take us about four days—maybe five, since we only have one horse between us. If we get lucky, we might find another one somewhere along the way, but I suppose that's asking a bit much. It would help if we had some weapons, too; we don't even have a hunting bow. That means eating fruit and wild vegetables, I guess. Of course we might . . ."

He trailed off, suddenly aware that Amberle was shaking her head in disapproval. The Elven girl crossed her legs before her and sat back.

"What's the matter?" he asked, dropping down next to her.

"You are, for one thing."

"What do you mean, I am?"

"You seem to have fixed in your mind everything that happens from here on. Don't you think you ought to hear my thoughts on the matter?"

Wil stared at her, somewhat taken aback. "Well sure, I . . ."

"I haven't noticed you asking for them," she continued, ignoring him. "Do you not think it necessary to ask?"

The Valeman reddened. "I'm sorry. I was just . . ."

"You were just making decisions that you have no right to make." She paused and regarded him coolly. "I don't even know what you're doing here. The only reason I've come this far with you is that I really didn't have any choice in the matter. It's time to find out a few things. Why did Allanon bring you along in the first place, Wil Ohmsford? Who are you?"

Wil told her, starting with the story of Shea Ohmsford and the quest for the Sword of Shannara and ending with Allanon's visit to Storlock to seek his aid in tracking the Bloodfire. He told her everything, deciding that it was pointless to hold anything back, sensing that if he were not completely honest with this girl, she would have nothing further to do with him.

When he finished, Amberle stared at him wordlessly for a moment, then shook her head slowly.

"I don't know whether to believe you or not. I should, I suppose. I really don't have any reason not to. It's just that so much has happened that I'm not really very certain of anything right now." She hesitated. "I've heard stories of the Elfstones. They were an old magic, said to have all been lost long before the Great Wars. Yet you claim Allanon gave three to your grandfather and he in turn gave them to you. If that much of what you've told me were true . . ." She trailed off, her eyes fixed on his. "Would you show them to me?" she asked.

The Valeman hesitated, then reached into his tunic. He realized that she was testing him, but then he guessed that she had a right to do that. After all, she had only his word for everything he had told her, and she was being asked to place her safety in his hands. He pulled out the worn leather pouch, loosened the drawstrings and dropped the stones in his hand. Perfectly formed, their color a deep, brilliant blue, they flashed sharply in the morning sunlight.

Amberle bent close, regarding them solemnly. Then she looked back at Wil again.

"How do you know these are Elfstones?"

"I have my grandfather's word on it. And Allanon's."

She did not look impressed. "Do you know how to use them?"

He shook his head. "I've never tried."

"Then you don't really know whether they're any good to you or not, do you?" She laughed softly. "You won't know until you need them. That's not very comforting, is it?"

"No, not very," he agreed.

"Yet here you are anyway."

He shrugged. "It seemed like the right thing to do." He dropped the Elfstones back in the pouch and tucked the pouch into his tunic. "I guess I'll have to wait and see how it works out to know whether or not I was mistaken."

She studied him carefully for a moment, saying nothing. He waited.

"We have much in common, Wil Ohmsford," she said finally. She crossed her arms about her knees, drawing them up. "Well, you've told me who you are—I think you're entitled to the same courtesy. My family name is Elessedil. Eventine Elessedil is my grandfather. In a sense, we're both involved in this because of who our grandfathers are."

Wil nodded. "That's true, I suppose."

The wind caught her chestnut hair and blew it across her face like a veil. She brushed the strands away and looked out across the lake again.

"You know that I do not want to go back to Arborlon," she said.

"I know."

"But that's where you think I ought to go, isn't it?"

He eased back on his elbows, watching the rainbow's arc above him.

"That's where I think you have to go," he replied. "Obviously you cannot go back to Havenstead; the Demons will be looking for you there. Pretty soon, they'll be looking for you here as well. You have to keep moving. If Allanon escaped . . ." He paused, distracted by the implications of that statement. "If Allanon escaped, he will expect us to go on to Arborlon, and that's where we'll find him." He looked over at her. "If you've got any better ideas, I'm ready to listen."

For a long time, she didn't say anything. She just kept staring out over the Rainbow Lake, watching the graceful movement of the water, letting the wind blow freely across her face. When she finally spoke again, it was just a whisper.

"I'm afraid."

Then she looked at him, seemed about to say something more, and thought better of it. She smiled—the first genuine smile he had seen from her.

"Well, we're a pair of fools, aren't we? You with your Elfstones that may or may not be what you think and me about to do the one thing I swore I'd never do." She rose, walked away a few paces, then turned as he came to his feet behind her. "I want you to know this. I think that going to Arborlon is pointless. I think that Allanon is wrong about me. Neither the Ellcrys nor the Elven people will accept me back again because, despite what the Druid may think, I am no longer one of the Chosen."

She paused. "Still, doing anything else wouldn't make much sense, would it?"

"Not to me, it wouldn't," he agreed.

She nodded. "Then I guess it's settled." Her child's face regarded him soberly. "I just hope this isn't a mistake."

Wil sighed. "If it is, we'll probably know soon enough." He forced a thin smile. "Let's collect Artaq and find out."

They spent the remainder of that day and all of the next traveling north and west through the grasslands of Callahorn. The weather was warm, dry, and pleasant, and the time passed quickly. Dark thunderclouds appeared to the north around noon of the first day, hanging ominously over the craggy expanse of the Dragon's Teeth, but by sunset they had blown east into the Rabb and were gone. The Valeman and the Elven girl alternated between riding Artaq and walking, doubling up when they rode, then both traveling afoot for a time in order to rest the big black. Artaq looked fresh even after several hours of being ridden, but Wil was not about to risk tiring the horse. They saw nothing of the Demons that they had lost at the Silver River, but the creatures were certainly still out there and looking for them. If they were unlucky enough to be found again, Wil wanted Artaq ready to run.

Bereft of any weapons at all, save for a small hunting knife Wil carried tucked in his belt, they were forced to eat fruits and vegetables that grew wild on the grasslands. Wil found the fare ample, if somewhat less than satisfying, but Amberle seemed not to mind at all. If anything, she seemed quite pleased with their meals. She showed the Valeman a talent for discovering food where he would not have guessed food existed, pulling from the most unlikely places edible plants and roots that she readily identified and described in quite thorough detail. Wil listened attentively and asked questions from time to time, finding this the one topic of conversation she seemed willing to pursue. Initially, he had tried to draw her out on other subjects, but had met with little success. So they talked of plants and roots and the rest of the time traveled in silence.

They slept that first night in a grove of cottonwood near a small spring that provided them with clean drinking water. By midafternoon of the second day, they reached the Mermidon and began following it north. Up until that point, they had seen no one, but thereafter passed half-a-dozen travelers, some afoot, some on horseback, one riding in a small wooden cart drawn by oxen. All exchanged with them a word of friendship and a wave before continuing on their way.

At sunset they made camp along the Mermidon, west and south of the city of Tyrsis, finding shelter in a grove of white pine and willow. Using a willow branch, a length of twine, and a hook from his clothing, Wil fashioned a crude fishing pole. Within half-an-hour he had landed a pair of striped bass. He was still cleaning the fish by the river's edge when a caravan of wagons swung into view from the south and wound its way down toward the far bank. Gaily painted houses on wheels, with peaked roofs of cedar shingles, hand-carved wooden doors, and windows studded with brass, the wagons flashed brightly in the setting sun. Teams of finely groomed horses pulled the wagons, their traces laced with bits of silver. Several riders kept pace, their graceful forms cloaked in silk and trailing streamers of color from their throats and from the bridles of their mounts. In spite of himself, Wil stopped what he was doing and watched the strange procession approach the river, wagon axles groaning, leather harness creaking, voices calling and whistling encouragement. Almost directly across from where the Valeman sat, the caravan swung into a loose circle and lurched to a halt. Men, women and children climbed from the wagons and began unhitching the teams and setting up camp.

Amberle appeared from the trees behind Wil and joined him. The Valeman glanced over at her briefly, then followed her gaze back across the river to the gathering on the far bank.

"Rovers," he announced thoughtfully.

She nodded. "I've seen them before. The Elves don't have much use for them."

"No one has." He went back to cleaning the fish. "They'll steal anything that isn't nailed down—or if it is, find a way to talk you out of it. They have their own rules and they don't pay any attention to anyone else's."

Amberle touched his arm, and he looked up to watch a tall man, dressed all in black save for a cloak and sash of forest green, accompany two older women in long, multicolored skirts and blouses as they carried water buckets down to the water's edge. As the women stooped to fill the buckets, the tall man removed a wide-brimmed hat and, with a flourish, bowed low to Wil and Amberle, his darkly tanned face flashing a broad smile through a shading of black beard. Wil raised one arm and waved back cordially.

"I'm just as glad that they're on that side of the river," he muttered to Amberle as they rose to return to their camp.

They enjoyed a savory meal of fish, fruit, vegetables and spring water, then settled back next to the campfire and gazed out through breaks in the forest to the glimmer of the Rover fires as they blazed up from out of the darkness across the river. They were quiet for a time, lost in their own thoughts. Then Wil looked over at the Elven girl.

"How is it that you know so much about growing things—the gardens at your cottage in Havenstead, the roots and plants you found for us during our journey? Did someone teach you all that?"

A look of surprise crossed her face. "For being part Elf, you certainly don't know very much about us, do you?"

Wil shrugged. "Not really. The Elven blood is all on my father's side, and he died when I was very young. I don't think that my grandfather has ever gone into the Westland—at least he never speaks about it. In any case, I guess I've just never thought that much about being part Elf."

"It is something that you should have thought about," she said quietly. Her green eyes found his. "We first need to understand who we were before we can understand who we are."

The words were spoken not as a criticism of the Valeman, but almost in self-reproach. Wil found himself suddenly wishing that he knew more about this girl, that he could find a way to persuade her to confide even a small piece of herself in him, rather than keeping it all so tightly locked away.

"Maybe you could help me gain at least a part of that understanding," he offered after a moment's thought.

There was instant doubt in her eyes, almost as if she believed that he was playing some game with her. She hesitated a long time before answering him.

"Very well, maybe I can." She squared herself around so that she was seated facing him. "You must first understand that the Elven people believe that preservation of the land and all that lives and grows upon it, plant and animal alike, is a moral responsibility. They have always held this belief foremost in their conduct as creatures of the earth. In the old world, they devoted the whole of their lives to caring for the woodlands and forests in which they lived, cultivating its various forms of vegetation, sheltering the animals that it harbored. Of course, they had little else to concern them in those days, for they were an isolated and reclusive people. All that has changed now, but they still maintain a belief in their moral responsibility for their world. Every Elf is expected to spend a portion of his life giving back to the land something of what he has taken out of it. By that I mean that every Elf is expected to devote a part of his life to working with the land—to repairing damage it may have suffered through misuse or neglect, to caring for its animals and other wildlife, to caring for its trees and smaller plants where the need to do so is found."

"Is that a part of what you were doing in Havenstead?"

She nodded. "In a way. The Chosen are exempt from this service. When I ceased to be one of the Chosen and no longer felt welcome in my homeland, I decided that I should do service to the land. Most of the work done by the Elves is carried out in the Westland because that is the Elven homeland. But we believe that the care of the land is not simply an Elven responsibility, but the responsibility of all men. To some extent the Dwarves share our concern, but the other races have never been much persuaded. So some of the Elves go out from the Westland to other communities, trying to teach the people living there something of their responsibility for the care and preservation of their land. This is what I was trying to do at Havenstead."

"And you were working with the children of the village," Wil surmised.

"Primarily the children, for the children are more receptive to what I teach and have the time to learn. I was taught of the earth when I was a child; it is the Elven way. I was more adept than most at translating the lesson into use—one of the reasons, I guess, that I was selected to be a Chosen. The skills of the Chosen in the preservation and care of the earth and its life forms are of the highest order; the Ellcrys has some sense of this. She has this ability . . ."

Amberle seemed to catch herself in the middle of a thought she did not wish to express. She stopped abruptly, shrugging.

"Anyway, I was very good at teaching the children of Havenstead, and the people of the village were very kind to me. Havenstead was my home, and I did not want to leave."

She shifted her gaze abruptly to the fire between them. Wil said nothing, leaning forward to add several pieces of stray wood to the flames. After a moment's silence, Amberle looked up at him again.

"Well, now you know something of the Elven feeling for the land. It's a part of your heritage, so you should try to understand it."

"I think I do understand it," the Valeman replied, reflecting. "At least in part. I have not been trained in the Elven manner, but I have been trained by the Stors as a Healer. Their concern for human life is much the same as the Elven concern for the land. A Healer must do whatever is in his power to do to preserve the lives and health of the men, women, and children whom he treats. This is the commitment I made when I chose to become a Healer."

The Elven girl looked at him curiously. "Somehow that makes it seem even stranger that you were persuaded by Allanon to look after me. You are a Healer, dedicated to preserving life. What will you do if you are placed in a situation where, in order to protect me, you must harm others, perhaps even cause them to die?"

Wil stared at her wordlessly. He had never even considered the possibility that such a thing might happen. Thinking on it now, he experienced an unpleasant feeling of doubt.

"I don't know what I'll do," he admitted uncomfortably.

They were silent for a moment, staring across the fire at each other, unable to break through the awkwardness of the moment. Then Amberle rose abruptly, came over to the Valeman, and sat next to him, impulsively clasping his hand in her own. Her winsome face looked out at him through the shadow of her hair.

"That wasn't a fair question to put to you, Wil Ohmsford. I'm sorry I asked it. You came on this journey because you believed that you might help me. It is wrong of me to doubt that you would do so."

"It was a fair question," Wil replied firmly. "I just don't have an answer to it."

"Nor should you," she insisted. "I, of all people, should know that some decisions cannot be made in advance of the time that will demand them. We cannot always anticipate the way in which things will happen and therefore cannot anticipate what we will do. We must accept that. Again, I am sorry. You might as well ask me what decision I will make if the Ellcrys tells me that I am still one of the Chosen."

Wil smiled faintly. "Be careful. I am tempted to ask exactly that."

She released his hand instantly and rose. "Do not. You would not like the answer I would give you." She shook her head sadly. "You think my choice in this is a simple one, one that you could make easily. You are wrong."

She walked back to the other side of the fire and reached down for her travel cloak, shaking it out upon the ground. As she prepared to roll herself in it to sleep, she turned back to him one final time.

"Believe me, Valeman, should our decisions become necessary, yours will be the easier of the two."

She lowered her head to the folds of the cloak and was asleep in moments. Wil Ohmsford stared thoughtfully into the fire. Although he could not begin to explain why, he found that he believed her.

14

When they awoke the following morning, Artaq was missing. At first they thought that he might have wandered off during the night, but a quick check of the woods in which they were camped and the open grasslands beyond failed to turn up any sign of the big black. It was at this point that an unpleasant suspicion began to form in the back of Wil's mind. Hurriedly, he examined the area in which Artaq had been left to graze, moving from there along the perimeter of their campsite, dropping to his knees from time to time as he went to smell the earth or touch it with his fingers. Amberle watched him curiously. After a few minutes of this, the Valeman seemed to find something. Eyes still fixed on the ground before him, he began walking southward through the small stand of timber and into the grasslands—one hundred feet, two. He began to angle toward the river. Wordlessly, the Elven girl trailed after. Moments later, they both stood at the edge of the Mermidon, staring out across a series of shallows several hundred yards downstream from their camp.

"Rovers." Wil spat the word out like a bitter pill. "They crossed here during the night and stole him."

Amberle looked surprised. "Are you sure?"

"I'm sure." Wil nodded. "I found their tracks. Besides, no one else could have managed it. Artaq would have called out if it were anyone but an expert horse handler, and the Rovers are the best. Look, they're already gone."

He pointed across the river to the spot on the empty grasslands the caravan had occupied the previous night. They stared at it silently for a moment.

"What do we do now?" Amberle asked finally.

Wil was so mad he could barely speak. "First we go back and pack our things. Then we cross the river and have a look at their campsite."

They returned to their own camp, hastily put together the few items they had carried with them, and returned to the river. They crossed at the shallows without difficulty. Minutes later they stood at the now-deserted Rover camp. Once more Wil began studying the ground, moving more quickly this time as he paced the area from end to end. Finally he walked back to where Amberle stood waiting.

"My Uncle Flick taught me to read signs when I hunted the woods about my home in Shady Vale," he informed her conversationally, his mood considerably improved. "We used to fish and trap the Duln Forests for weeks at a time when I was little. Always thought I might again have need of what I learned some day."

She nodded impatiently. "What did you find?"

"They've gone west, probably just before daybreak."

"Is that all? Isn't there some indication of whether or not Artaq is with them?"

"Oh, he's with them, all right. Back at the shallows, there are signs of a horse going into the river from the other side and coming out again over here. One horse, several men. No mistake, they've got him. But we're going to get him back again."

She looked at him doubtfully. "You mean you're going after them?"

"Of course I'm going after them!" He was getting angry all over again. "We're both going after them."

"Just you and me, Valeman?" She shook her head. "On foot?"

"We can catch up to them by nightfall. Those wagons are slow."

"That assumes that we can find them, doesn't it?"

"There's no trick to that. At one time, I could track a deer through wilderness timber where there hadn't been rain for weeks. I think I can manage to track an entire caravan of wagons across open grasslands."

"I don't like the sound of this at all," she announced quietly. "Even if we do find them and they do have Artaq, what are we supposed to do about it?"

"We'll worry about that when we catch up to them," he replied evenly.

The Elven girl did not back away. "I think that we should worry about it right now. That's an entire camp of armed men you're talking about chasing after. I don't like what's happened any better than you do, but that's hardly sufficient excuse for failing to exercise sound judgment."

With an effort, Wil held his temper. "I am not about to lose that horse. In the first place, if it weren't for Artaq, the Demons would have had us, back at Havenstead. He deserves a better fate than spending the rest of his years in the service of those thieves. In the second place, he is the only horse we had and the only horse we are likely to get. Without him, we will be forced to walk the rest of the way to Arborlon. That will take more than a week, and most of that week will be spent crossing these open grasslands. That increases rather substantially the chances of our being discovered by those things still searching for us. And I don't like the sound of that. We need Artaq."

"You seem to have made up your mind on this," she said expressionlessly.

He nodded. "I have. Besides, the Rovers are traveling toward the Westland anyway; at least we'll be headed in the right direction."

For a moment she didn't say anything; she merely looked at him. Then finally she nodded.

"All right, we'll go after them. I want Artaq back too. But let's think this through a bit further before we catch up to them. We had better have some sort of plan worked out by then, Valeman."

He grinned disarmingly. "We will."

They walked all day through the open grasslands, following the trail of the Rover caravan. It was hot and dry, and the sun beat down on them from out of a cloudless blue sky. They found little shade along the way to relieve them from the heat. What water they carried was soon gone, and they did not run across even a small stream to replenish their supply. By late afternoon, all they could taste in their mouths was the dust of the plains and their thirst. Leg muscles ached and their feet blistered. They spoke to each other only infrequently, conserving their strength, concentrating on putting one foot in front of the other, watching the sun sink slowly into the horizon ahead of them until all that remained of the day was a dull orange glow above the sweep of the land.

A short time later, it began to darken, the day to disappear into dusk, the dusk into night. Still they walked on, no longer able to find the marks of the wagon wheels in the plains grass, relying now on their sense of direction to keep them moving in a straight line westward. Moon and stars brightened in the night sky, casting down upon the open grasslands their faint light to guide the Valeman and the Elven girl as they moved steadily forward. Dirt and sweat cooled and dried on their bodies, and they felt their clothing stiffen uncomfortably. Neither suggested stopping to the other. Stopping meant admitting they would not catch up to the caravan that night, that they would be forced to go on like this for another day. They kept walking, silent, determined, the girl as much so as the man now, a fact that surprised him and caused him to feel genuine admiration for her spirit.

Then they saw light in the distance ahead, a fire burning through the dark like a beacon, and they realized that they had found the Rovers. Wordlessly, they trudged to within shouting distance of the firelight, watching the peaked roofs of the wagon homes gradually take shape in the night until finally the entire caravan stood revealed, wound into a loose circle as it had been on the banks of the Mermidon.

Wil took hold of Amberle's arm and gently pulled her down into a crouch.

"We're going in," he whispered, his eyes never leaving the Rover camp.

She looked at him in disbelief. "That's your plan?"

"I know something of these people. Just go along with whatever I say, and we'll be fine.

Without waiting for her response, he stood up and began walking toward the caravan. The Elven girl stared after him for a moment, then rose to her feet and followed after. As they drew closer to the circled wagons, the faces of the men, women, and children passing within the firelight grew visible. Laughter and bits of conversation became audible and distinct. The Rovers had just finished their evening meal and were visiting casually with one another. From somewhere within the camp came the soft thrum of a stringed instrument.

Twenty yards from the perimeter of the circle, Wil called out. It surprised Amberle so that she jumped. Within the camp, everyone instantly stopped what was being done, and all heads turned in their direction. There was a sudden scrambling of feet as a handful of men appeared at the gap between the wagons nearest the approaching pair. Wordlessly, the men peered out into the night, the firelight behind them now, leaving them shadowed and faceless. Wil did not slow. He kept walking directly toward them, Amberle a step or two behind. The entire caravan had gone suddenly still.

"Good evening," Wil said cheerfully as he reached the gathering of Rovers who blocked their passage into the camp.

The men said nothing. In the glimmer of the firelight, the Valeman caught a glimpse of metal blades.

"We saw your fire and we thought you might give us something to drink," he continued, still smiling. "We've been walking since daybreak without water and we're about worn out."

Someone pushed his way through the knot of silent men, a tall man in a cloak of forest green and a broad-brimmed hat—the man they had seen at the river.

"Ah, our young travelers from last evening," he announced quietly and not in greeting.

"Hello again," Wil responded pleasantly. "I'm afraid we've had some very bad luck. We lost our horse during the night—he must have wandered off while we were sleeping. We've been walking all day without water and we could use something cool to drink."

"Indeed." The big man smiled without warmth. He was tall, well over six feet, lean and rawboned, his dark face shaded with a black beard and mustache that gave his smile an almost menacing appearance. Eyes that looked blacker than the night about them peered out from beneath a lined and weathered brow that sloped into a nose hooked slightly at the bridge.

The hand that came up to beckon to the men behind him was ringed on each finger.

"Have water brought," he ordered, his eyes still on the Valeman. His expression did not change. "Who are you, young friend, and what is your destination?"

"My name is Wil Ohmsford," the Valeman replied. "This is my sister, Amberle. We're on our way to Arborlon."

"Arborlon." The tall man repeated the name thoughtfully. "Well, you're Elves, of course—in part, at least. Any fool can see that. But now, you say that you lost your horse. Would you not have been wiser to stay along the Mermidon in your travels, rather than coming straight west as you did?"

Wil smiled some more. "Oh, yes, we thought about that; but you see, it's important that we reach Arborlon as soon as possible, and walking would take much too long. Of course, we saw you camped across the river from us last night and we saw, too, that you seemed to have a number of very fine horses. We thought that if we could manage to catch up with you by nightfall, we might trade something of value for one of your horses."

"Something of value?" The big man shrugged. "Possibly. We would have to see what it is that you propose to trade, of course."

Wil nodded. "Of course."

An old woman appeared, carrying a pitcher of water and a single wooden cup. She handed these to Wil, who accepted them wordlessly. With the Rovers looking on, he poured some of the water into the cup. He did not offer it to Amberle, who looked at him in surprise as he ignored her completely and drank the water down. Then he poured a second cup and drank it as well. When he was finished, he handed her the empty cup and pitcher without comment.

"You know something of the Way," the tall man remarked, interest showing in his dark eyes. "You know also that we're Rovers, then."

"I have treated Rovers before," Wil said. "I'm a Healer."

A quick murmur went through the assemblage, which had grown considerably since the conversation had begun and now consisted of almost the entire camp, some thirty men, women, and children, all dressed colorfully in bright silks with woven ribbons and scarves.

"A Healer? This is unexpected." The tall man stepped forward, removed his hat with a flourish, and bowed low. Straightening once more, he extended his hand in greeting. "My name is Cephelo. I am Leader of this Family."

Wil accepted the hand and shook it firmly. Cephelo smiled.

"Well, you mustn't stand out here while the night grows cold about you. Come with me. Your sister is welcome, too. You both look as if you could do with a bath and something to eat."

He led the way through the crowd of Rovers into the circle of the wagons. An immense fire burned at the center of the camp, a tripod and iron kettle suspended above it. The glow of the fire reflected off the gaily painted wagons, mixing the rainbow of colors with shadows of the night. Wooden benches sat beneath the wagons, intricately carved and polished, their broad seats cushioned by feather pillows. Brass-handled windows stood open to the light, laced with curtains and strings of beads. On a long table to one side lay an assortment of wicked-looking pikes, swords, and knives, all carefully arranged. Two small boys were diligently oiling the metal blades.

They reached the cooking fire and Cephelo turned abruptly.

"Well now, which shall it be first—a meal or a bath?"

Wil did not even glance at Amberle. "A bath, I think—my sister, as well, if you can spare the water."

"We can spare it." Cephelo nodded, then turned. "Eretria!"

There was a whisper of silk, and Wil found himself face to face with the most stunning girl he had ever seen. She was small and delicate, in the manner of Amberle, but without the childlike innocence that marked the Elven girl. Thick, black hair tumbled in ringlets to her shoulders, framing eyes that were dark and secretive. Her face was beautiful, her features perfectly formed and immediately unforgettable. She was wearing high leather boots, dressed in pants and tunic of scarlet silk that failed to hide anything of the woman beneath. Bands of silver flashed on her wrists and neck.

Wil looked at her in astonishment and could not look away.

"My daughter." Cephelo sounded bored. He motioned toward Amberle. "Take the Elven girl and let her bathe herself."

Eretria smiled wickedly. "It would be much more interesting to bathe him," she offered, nodding toward Wil.

"Just do as you're told," her father ordered sharply.

Eretria kept her eyes on the Valeman. "Come along, girl," she invited. She turned and was gone. Amberle followed after, looking none too happy.

Cephelo led Wil to the far side of the encampment where a series of blankets hung across a small area between two of the wagons. Within stood a tub of water. Stepping behind the blankets, Wil stripped off his clothing and laid it neatly on the ground beside him. He was well aware that the Rover was watching everything he removed, looking to see if he possessed anything of value, and he was careful to see to it that the pouch containing the Elfstones did not fall loose from its pocket within his tunic. He began to pour water over himself with a ladle, washing away the dirt and sweat of the day's travel.

"It is not often that we encounter a Healer who will treat Rovers," Cephelo said after a moment. "We usually must care for our own."

"I was trained by the Stors," Wil answered him. "Their help is given freely."

"The Stors?" Cephelo was surprised all over again. "But the Stors are all Gnomes."

The Valeman nodded. "I was an exception."

"You appear an exception in many ways," the tall man declared. He seated himself on a nearby bench and watched the Valeman towel dry and begin rinsing his clothes. "We have work for you that will enable you to pay for your food and rest, Healer. There are some among us who have need of your skills."

"I will be happy to do what I can," Wil replied.

"Good." The other man nodded in satisfaction. "I'll find you some dry clothing to use."

He rose and walked away. Instantly Wil slipped the Elfstones from his tunic pocket into his boot, then quickly resumed washing out his clothing. Cephelo was back almost at once, carrying Rover silks for Wil to wear. The Valeman accepted the clothes and dressed himself. Despite the uncomfortable knot at the toe of his right boot, he pulled it on firmly, then the left boot. Cephelo summoned the old woman who had brought the water earlier to take Wil's damp clothing. The Valeman handed the clothes over without comment, knowing they would be thoroughly searched and nothing found for the effort.

Then they returned to the fire at the center of the encampment, where Amberle joined them, washed clean and dressed in clothing similar to Wil's. Each was given a plate of steaming food and a cup of wine. They sat next to the fire and ate silently while the Rovers settled about them, watching curiously. Cephelo took up a position across from them, sitting cross-legged on a wide, gold-tasseled cushion, his dark face expressionless. There was no sign of Eretria.

When the meal was finished, the Rover Leader assembled the members of his Family who needed Wil's attention. Without comment, the Valeman examined them one by one, treating a series of infections, internal disorders, skin irritations, and minor fevers. Although she was not asked to do so, Amberle worked next to him, providing bandages and hot water, aiding in the application of simple herb medicines and salves. It took the better part of an hour for Wil to complete his work. When he was finished, Cephelo stepped up to him.

"You have done your work well, Healer." He smiled a bit too pleasantly. "Now we must see what we can do for you in return. Walk with me a bit—this way."

He put one long arm about the Valeman's shoulders and steered him away from the fire, leaving Amberle by herself to clean up after their work. They walked toward the far side of the Rover camp.

"You say that you lost your horse last night near where we camped on the Mermidon." Cephelo's voice was thoughtful. "What did this animal look like?"

Wil's face remained expressionless. He knew the game that was being played.

"A stallion, all black."

"Well, now." Cephelo appeared even more thoughtful. "We found a horse such as you have described, a very fine animal, just this morning, quite early. It wandered into our camp from out of the grasslands as we were getting our teams hitched for the day's travel. Perhaps this was your horse, Healer."

"Perhaps," Wil agreed.

"Of course, we didn't know whose animal he was." Cephelo smiled. "So we brought him along with our own. Why don't we take a look at him?"

They passed through the ring of wagons into the plains beyond. Fifty feet from the camp, the Rover horses were tethered in a line. Two dark forms materialized from out of the night, Rovers armed with pikes and bows. A word from Cephelo sent them back into hiding. The tall man led Wil down the tether line to its furthest end. There stood Artaq.

Wil nodded. "That's the horse."

"Does he bear your mark, Healer?" the other man asked, almost as if the question embarrassed him. Wil shook his head. "Ah, that is most unfortunate, for now we can't be certain that he really is your horse, can we? After all, there are a fair number of black stallions in the Four Lands, and how are we to tell them apart if their owners do not mark them? This presents quite a problem, Healer. I wish to give this horse to you, but there is a great risk to me in doing so. I mean, suppose I give him to you, as I wish to do, but then another man comes to me and tells me that he has lost a black stallion as well, and we then discover that I have mistakenly given his horse to you. Why then, I would be responsible for that man's loss."

"Yes, that's true, I guess." Wil nodded with just the right touch of doubt, carefully avoiding any argument with the big man's ridiculous supposition. It was, after all, just a part of the game.

"I believe you, of course." Cephelo's bearded face turned solemn. "Certainly a Healer is to be trusted, if anyone is to be trusted in this world." He grinned at his own humor. "However, there is still some risk to me if I choose to hand this animal over to you—I must accept that fact, being a practical man in an often hard business. And then there is the matter of feed and care given to this animal. We groomed him and tended him as we do our own; we fed him with meal we carry for our own. You will understand if I tell you that I feel we are owed something for all this."

"Indeed." Wil nodded.

"Well, then." Cephelo rubbed his hands in satisfaction. "We are in agreement. All that requires settling is the price. You spoke earlier of trading something of value for a horse. Perhaps now we can make a fair exchange—whatever you carry with you in satisfaction of your debt to us. And in the bargain, I would say nothing of finding this horse to any other who might claim the loss of a black stallion."

He winked knowingly. Wil walked up to Artaq and stroked his sleek forehead, letting the horse nuzzle up against his chest.

"I'm afraid I don't have anything of value, after all," he said finally. "I brought nothing with me in my journey that could possibly repay you for what you've done."

Cephelo's jaw dropped. "Nothing?"

"Nothing at all."

"But you said you brought something of value . . ."

"Oh, yes." Wil nodded quickly. "I meant that I could offer you my services as a Healer—I thought that might have some value."

"But you've given those services in payment of food and shelter and clothes for yourself and your sister."

"Yes, true." The Valeman looked less than happy with the thought. He took a deep breath. "Perhaps I could suggest something?" A look of renewed interest appeared in the other's face. "Well, it seems that we are both traveling to the Westland. If you would allow us to accompany you, we might find some opportunity to repay you yet—possibly you might have need of my skill another time."

"That seems unlikely." Cephelo pondered the thought. He shook his head. "You've nothing of value to give for the horse—nothing at all?"

"No, nothing."

"That seems a poor way to travel," the Rover muttered, rubbing his bearded chin. The Valeman said nothing, waiting. "Well, I suppose it will do no harm to have you travel with us as far as the forestland. That's only a few days travel, though, and if you've done nothing for us by then, we may have to keep the horse for our trouble. You understand that."

Wil nodded wordlessly.

"One thing more." Cephelo stepped close, his face no longer pleasant. "I trust that you would not be so foolish as to try to steal that horse from us, Healer. You know us well enough to realize what would happen to you if you were to try such a thing."

The Valeman took a deep breath and nodded once more. He knew.

"Good." The big man stepped back. "See to it that it doesn't slip your mind." He was clearly unhappy at the way in which matters had worked out, but he shrugged his indifference. "Enough of business. Come to my home and drink with me."

He led the way back through the caravan circle, clapping his hands sharply as he entered, calling to those within to gather and to join with wine and music in celebrating the good fortune of the day and in welcoming the young Healer who had shown them such kindness. Wil was seated next to the Leader on a cushioned bench set before the big man's wagon home as the men and women and children of the Rover camp crowded about eagerly. Wine was drawn from a great vat and cups were passed about to everyone. Cephelo came to his feet and offered a flowery toast to the good health of his Family. Cups were raised high in answer and quickly drained. Will drank his with the rest. He looked about hurriedly for Amberle and found her seated near the perimeter of the circle of faces surrounding him. She did not look at all pleased. He wished he could take time to explain all that had happened, but that would have to wait until they had a moment alone. For now, she would simply have to bear with him.

Cups were refilled now, another toast was proposed, and they all drank again. Cephelo called loudly for the music. Stringed instruments and cymbals were brought forth, and their owners began to play. The music was at once wild, haunting, and free as it rose into the night. The laughter of the Rovers rose with it, careless and gay. More wine was poured and quickly consumed, followed by shouts of encouragement for the musicians. Wil felt himself growing light-headed. The wine was strong, too strong for one not used to drinking it as the Rovers did. He must be careful, he thought to himself, raising his cup once more as a new toast was proposed, yet sipping this time rather than draining the amber liquid. In the toe of his right boot, he felt the reassuring bulk of the Elfstones pressed against his foot.

The musicians played faster, and now the Rovers were on their feet and dancing, half-a-dozen or eight, forming a circle with arms interlocked as they wheeled about the fire. More rose quickly to join the procession, and those still seated began to clap wildly. Wil joined them, setting his cup on the bench beside him. When he reached down for it a moment later, it was full again. Caught up in the spirit of the music, he drank it down without thinking. The dancers broke apart, pairing off now, spinning and leaping before the flames. Someone was singing, a wistful cry that blended eerily with the music and the dance.

Then suddenly Eretria was there before him, dark and beautiful, her slender form clad all in scarlet silk. Her smile was dazzling as she reached down for his hands and brought him to his feet. She pulled him into the midst of the dancers, broke from him for an instant, and twirled away in a flash of ribbons and trailing black hair. Then she was before him once more, slim arms holding him as they danced. The fragrance of her hair and body mingled with the warmth of the wine coursing through his blood. He felt her press close against him, feather light and soft, speaking words that he could not seem to hear clearly. The movement of the dance dizzied him; everything about him began to blend in a maze of colors that whirled against the backdrop of the night. The music and the clapping roared louder, and the shouts and whistles of the Rovers. He felt himself begin to leave the ground, still holding Eretria close.

And then she was gone as well, and he began to fall.

15

He came awake with the worst headache of his life. It was the sensation of being shaken like a slender branch in a high wind that brought him around, and it took him several long minutes to realize that he was stretched out in the back of one of the Rover wagons. He lay on a straw-filled pallet in a wooden frame bed against the rear wall of the mobile house, staring upward at a strange assortment of tapestries, silks and laces, and metal and wooden implements, all swaying with the motion of the wagon as it bounced and rolled across the grasslands. A shaft of bright sunlight slipped through a partly cracked window, and he knew he had slept the night.

Amberle appeared next to him, a look of reproof in her sea-green eyes.

"I don't need to ask how you're feeling this morning, do I?" she declared, her words barely audible above the rumble of the wheels. "I hope it was worth it, Valeman."

"It wasn't." He sat up slowly, feeling his head throb violently with the movement. "Where are we?"

"In Cephelo's wagon. Since last night, if you can remember that far back. I told them that you were still recovering from a fever and that you might be sick from more than the wine. So they put me in here with you to look after you until I was sure you were feeling better. Drink this."

She handed him a cup with some dark liquid in it. Wil eyed the unpleasant-looking concoction suspiciously.

"Drink it," she repeated firmly. "It's an herbal remedy for excessive use of wine. There are some things you don't need to be a Healer to know."

He drank it down without arguing. It was then that he noticed that his boots were gone.

"My boots! What happened to . . . ?"

"Be quiet!" she warned, motioning quickly toward the front of the wagon where a small wooden door stood closed. Wordlessly, she reached beneath the bed and produced the items in question, then pulled from the sash about her waist the small leather pouch containing the Elfstones.

The Valeman sat back with a look of relief.

"The party proved to be a bit too much for you," she continued, a trace of sarcasm in her voice. "After you passed out, Cephelo had you carried to his wagon to sleep. He was about to have that old woman strip you when I convinced him that if the fever had come back, it would be contagious and that, in any case, you would be offended if your clothes were taken without your permission. Apparently he didn't consider the matter all that important because he ordered the old woman out. After he was gone, as well, I searched you and found the Elfstones."

He nodded approvingly. "You've kept your wits about you."

"Good thing one of us did." She brushed aside his compliment with an arch of her eyebrows. She glanced again toward the closed door. "Cephelo left the old woman in the next compartment to keep an eye on us. I don't think he was entirely persuaded that he knows everything he should about you."

Wil leaned forward, resting his chin on his hands. "That wouldn't surprise me."

"Then why are we still here—other than the fact that you drank too much wine last night?" she wanted to know. "For that matter, why are we here in the first place?"

He reached for the Elfstones and she gave them to him. He put the leather pouch back into his right boot and pulled both boots on firmly. Then he motioned for her to lean close.

"Because we have to find a way to get Artaq back from these people and we can't do that if we don't stay with them," he whispered loud enough for her to hear him over the creaking of the wagon. "And there's another reason. The Demons that chased us from Havenstead will be looking for just two people—not an entire caravan. Perhaps traveling with the Rovers will throw them off. Besides, we're still traveling west, which is where we want to go, and we're traveling faster than we could on foot."

"Fine. But this is dangerous as well, Valeman," she pointed out. "What do you plan to do when we reach the Westland forests and Cephelo still refuses to give you Artaq?"

He shrugged. "I'll worry about that when it's time."

"We've been over this ground before." She shook her head in disgust. "At least you might try confiding in me a bit more than you have so far. It is not very reassuring to have to rely on you and not have the faintest idea what you're about."

"You're right," he agreed. "I'm sorry about last night. I should have told you more before we entered the camp, but, to tell you the truth, I hadn't made up my mind what we were going to do until just after we found it."

"I believe that." She frowned.

"Look, I'll try to explain some of it now," he offered. "Rovers travel in Families—you already know that much. The term 'Family' is somewhat misleading though because its members are not always blood-related. Rovers frequently trade or even sell wives and children to other camps. It is a kind of communal property situation. Each Family has one Leader—a father figure who makes all the decisions. Women are considered subservient to men; that is what is called the Way. For the Rovers, that is the natural order of things. They believe quite firmly that women are to serve and obey the men who protect and provide for them. It is a tradition among them that those entering their camp should observe this custom in order to be made welcome. That's why I took the water first. That's why I left you to clean up after we treated the sick. I wanted to convince them that I understood and honored their beliefs. If they believed that, there was a chance they would give Artaq back to us."

"It doesn't seem to have worked out that way," Amberle remarked.

"No, not yet," he admitted. "But they have let us come along with them; ordinarily they would not even consider such a thing. Rovers have little use for outsiders."

"They have let us come along because Cephelo is curious about you and wants to find out more than he has been told." She paused. "Eretria has more than a passing interest in you as well. She made that quite apparent."

He grinned in spite of himself. "And I suppose you think I enjoyed all that dancing and drinking last night?"

"If you really want to know—yes, that is exactly what I think."

She said it without the faintest trace of a smile. Wil sat back, his head throbbing with the movement.

"All right, I admit that I overdid it. But there was a good reason for what I did, despite what you may think. It was necessary for them to believe that I wasn't smarter than they were. If they believed that I was, we would both be dead. So I let myself drink and dance and behave as any other outsider would under the same circumstances—just to keep them from becoming suspicious." He shrugged. "I cannot help what Eretria thinks about me."

"I am not asking you to." She grew suddenly angry. "I don't care what Eretria thinks about you. I only care that you don't give us both away by being foolish!"

She saw the look of surprise that crept into his eyes and she flushed darkly.

"Just be careful, will you?" she added quickly, took the empty cup from his hands, and turned away, moving to the far end of the wagon. Wil stared after her curiously.

A moment later she was back, calm and collected once more.

"There is something else you should know about. Early this morning the caravan met with an old line trapper traveling east. He had just passed through the Tirfing—the lake country fronting the Westland forests below the Mermidon. He warned Cephelo not to go in. He said there was a Devil there."

Wil frowned. "A Devil?"

"He called it a Devil—it is a name the Rovers use for something not human, something evil." She paused meaningfully. "It may be that this Devil is one of the Demons that has broken through the Forbidding."

"What did Cephelo say about this Devil?"

Amberle smiled faintly. "He is not afraid of Devils. He intends to go into the Tirfing anyway—his mind is made up on that. I think he has business that requires that he pass that way. The rest of the Family is not too happy about his decision."

Wil nodded. "I would be inclined to go along with them."

The Elven girl gave him a long, careful look. "I would not be inclined to go along with anyone in this camp, if I were you. Keep that in mind if you are offered any more wine."

She wheeled without a word and moved back once again to the far end of the wagon, hiding her movements from the Valeman. Wil started up after her irritably, but the pain in his head made him reconsider quickly. He sat back carefully, resting his throbbing head against a piece of woven reed backing lining the wagon wall. One thing was certain, he thought glumly. She need not worry about him drinking any more of that wine.

The caravan traveled steadily westward until midday, then halted long enough for the Rovers to partake of a quick lunch. By this time, Wil was feeling much improved and was able to eat some of the dried meats and vegetables that comprised the meal. Cephelo spoke to him briefly, inquiring politely as to his health, then moved away, his mind clearly on other matters. There were vague mutterings among the Rovers of the rumored Devil, and it was apparent to the Valeman that the Family was more than a little concerned with the old trapper's report. Rovers were a superstitious lot anyway, and Cephelo's decision to ignore a warning such as this one was not popular.

The remainder of the afternoon passed quickly. Wil took a turn at driving Cephelo's wagon while the old woman napped in the back. Amberle rode beside him as he guided the four-horse team forward in the caravan line through the broad expanse of the grasslands, humming and singing softly to herself but saying very little to him. The Valeman left her alone, concentrating on the task at hand, staring out thoughtfully into the emptiness of the plains. Several times Cephelo rode a big sorrel past them, his forest-green cloak billowing out behind him, his dark face covered with a sheen of sweat from the heat of the day. Once Wil caught a quick glimpse of Artaq as the Rover relief horses were driven past the wagons toward a watering hole somewhere ahead of the caravan. He was not being ridden, and it appeared that as yet Cephelo had not decided how he would use the big black—which meant, hopefully, that he had not decided if he intended to keep him.

A little more than an hour before sunset, they entered the Tirfing, a land of small lakes and surrounding woodlands spread out beneath the rim of the grasslands. Far to the west, beneath the red ball of the setting sun, lay the dark mass of the Westland forests. The Rover wagons wound their way down out of the plains into the wooded stretches of the Tirfing along a rutted earthen trail worn by the passing of countless other travelers before them. The heat of the open grasslands dissipated quickly as they entered the sheltering trees, shadows lengthening across the trail before them with the onset of dusk. Through breaks in the woodlands, they began to glimpse bits and pieces of the lakes that dotted the country about them.

It was dark when Cephelo finally brought them to a halt in a large clearing, ringed by oaks and overlooking a small lake several hundred feet to the north. The wagons swung into the familiar circle, rumbling and creaking to a weary halt. Wil was so stiff that he could barely move. While the Rover men worked to unhitch the teams and the women began preparations for the evening meal, the Valeman climbed down gingerly from the hard board seat and tried walking off the stiffness. Amberle chose to walk another way, and he did not bother to follow her. He limped through the caravan circle to the fringes of the surrounding trees, pausing there to stretch himself painfully and allow the blood to circulate through cramped limbs.

Moments later he heard footsteps and turned to find Eretria approaching, her slim form another shadow in the evening dusk. She was dressed in high boots and leather riding clothes, a red silk scarf about her waist and another at her throat. Black hair tumbled down about her shoulders, loose and windblown. She smiled as she came up to him, her dark eyes twinkling mischievously.

"Do not stray too far, Wil Ohmsford," she advised. "A Devil might find you and then what would you do?"

"Let him have me." Wil grimaced, rubbing his backside. "Anyway, I do not plan on doing much straying until after I've been fed."

He eased himself down into the tall grass, placing his back against one of the oaks. Eretria watched him wordlessly for a moment, then sat down beside him.

"Where have you been all day?" the Valeman asked conversationally.

"Watching you," she replied, then smiled wickedly as she saw the look that appeared on his face. "You didn't see me, of course. You weren't supposed to."

He hesitated uncomfortably. "Why were you watching me?"

"Cephelo wanted you watched." She arched her eyebrows. "He doesn't trust you—or the Elven girl you claim is your sister."

She was staring at him boldly now, as if daring him to contradict her. Wil felt a quick moment of panic.

"Amberle is my sister," he stated as assertively as he could.

Eretria shook her head. "She is no more your sister than I am Cephelo's daughter. She does not look at you as a sister would; her eyes say that she is something else. Still, it makes little difference to me. If you wish that she be your sister, then so shall she be. Just don't let Cephelo catch you playing this little game."

Now it was Wil's turn to stare. "Wait a minute," he said after a moment's pause. "What do you mean she is no more my sister than you are Cephelo's daughter? He said you were his daughter, didn't he?"

"What Cephelo says and what is true are not necessarily the same—in fact, very seldom the same." She leaned forward. "Cephelo has no children. He bought me when I was five from my father. My father was poor and could offer me nothing. He had other daughters, so one would not be missed. Now I belong to Cephelo. But I am not his daughter."

She said it so matter-of-factly that for a moment Wil could think of nothing to say in response. She saw his confusion and laughed merrily.

"We are Rovers, Wil—you know our ways. Besides, it could have been much worse for me. I could have been given to a much lesser man. Cephelo is a Leader; he has respect and position. As his daughter, I benefit from this. I have more freedom in my life than most women. And I have learned much, Healer. It has made me more than a match for most."

"I would not want to be the one to test that," he admitted. "But why are you telling me this?"

She pursed her lips teasingly. "Because I like you—why else?"

"That is what I am wondering." He ignored the look.

She straightened abruptly, her face petulant.

"Are you married to this Elven girl? Is she promised to you?"

His surprise was evident. "No."

"Good. I thought not." The petulance disappeared. She paused, her smile wicked once more. "Cephelo does not plan to return your horse to you."

Wil considered the statement carefully. "You know this?"

"I know how he is. He will not return your horse. He will let you go on your way if you do not cause him any trouble or try to take back the horse, but he will never give it back to you willingly."

The Valeman's face was expressionless. "I'll ask again—why are you telling me this?"

"Because I can help you."

"And why should you do that?"

"Because you, in turn, can help me."

Wil frowned. "How?"

Eretria crossed her legs before her and placed her hands on her knees, rocking back. Her dark eyes danced with amusement.

"I would guess, Wil Ohmsford, that you are much more than what you have told us—that you are most certainly more than a simple Healer traveling the grasslands of Callahorn with your sister. I would guess that this Elven girl has been given into your care and that you accompany her as an escort, perhaps a protector." One brown hand came up hurriedly. "Do not bother to deny this, Healer—a lie from your lips would be wasted on me, for I am the daughter of the world's foremost liar and know the art far better than you."

She smiled and put one hand on his arm. "I like you, Wil—there is no lie in that. I want you to have your horse back again. Obviously it is important that you get him back or you would not have come after us. Alone, you will not be successful. But I could help you."

Wil looked doubtful. "Why would you do that?" he asked finally.

"If I help you regain your horse, then I want you to take me with you when you go."

"What!" The exclamation was spoken before he could think better of it.

"Take me with you," she repeated firmly.

"I cannot do that!"

"You can if you wish your horse back."

He shook his head helplessly. "Why would you want to leave? You just finished telling me that . . ."

She cut him short. "All that is in the past. Cephelo has decided that it is time that I married. In Rover tradition, he will select my husband and for a price, turn me over to him. My life has been good, but I have no intention of being sold a second time."

"Couldn't you just leave on your own? You seem capable of that."

"I am capable of a great deal more, should it come to that, Healer. That is why you have need of me. If you take back your horse—something I doubt you can do without my help—the Rovers will come after you. Since you will be pursued in any event, it will cause you no further burden to take me as well as the horse—especially since I know enough of Rovers to give you the guidance you will need to elude them."

She shrugged. "As for leaving on my own, I have given thought to that. If there were no other choice, I would do so rather than be sold again. But where would I go? A Rover is welcome nowhere and, like it or not, a Rover is what I am. Alone, I would be little better than an outcast among the races, and my life would not be a pleasant one. But with you I could find acceptance; you are a Healer and you have respect. I could even travel with you. I could aid you in the mending of the ill. You would find that I . . ."

"Eretria," Wil cut in gently. "There is no point in discussing it. I cannot take you with me. I can take no one with me but Amberle."

Her face darkened. "Do not be so quick to spurn me, Healer."

"This has nothing to do with spurning you," he responded, at the same time trying to decide how much he could tell her. Not very much, he quickly realized. "Listen. It would not be safe for you to travel anywhere with me right now. When I leave, Cephelo will not be the only one looking for me. There will be others, much more dangerous than he. They search for me now. If I took you along, you would be in great danger. I cannot allow that."

"The Elven girl travels with you," she insisted.

"Amberle travels with me because she must."

"Words. I do not believe them. You will take me with you, Wil Ohmsford. You will take me with you because you must."

He shook his head. "I cannot."

She rose abruptly, her beautiful dark face angry and set. "You will change your mind, Healer. The time will come when you will have no other choice."

She turned and stalked away. A dozen yards from him, she paused and glanced back suddenly, her black eyes fixing on his. From out of the shadow of her face flashed that wondrous, dazzling smile.

"I am for you, Wil Ohmsford," she called.

She held his gaze a moment longer, then turned and continued walking back toward the Rover caravan. The Valeman stared after her in mild amazement.

Dinner was set out and eaten, and it was shortly thereafter that the deep, booming cough broke through the peaceful sounds of the night and froze them into stillness. It came from the south end of the lake on which the Rovers were encamped—once, twice and then was gone. All heads turned as one, faces startled and expectant. Moments later the cough sounded again, rumbling out of the darkness like the huffing roar of some monstrous bull calling in challenge. The Rovers scrambled hurriedly for their weapons, then rushed to the perimeter of the circle of wagons and peered out into the night. But the sound died, and this time it did not repeat. Cephelo and more than a dozen of his men stood waiting for a time, anticipating something further. When nothing happened, he gruffly ordered everyone back to the fire and the evening wine. Joking loudly about Devils and things that prowled the night, he boasted that none of these would dare to come into a Rover camp without first seeking permission. Cups of wine were refilled and distributed, and everyone drank heartily. Yet glances continued to stray in the direction of the sound.

Half-an-hour later it came again, closer than before, sudden and heavy in the night. Startled Rovers sprang to their feet, snatching up their weapons a second time and racing for the edge of the camp. Wil went with them this time, Amberle only a step behind as he reached a gap between two of the Rover wagons and stared out guardedly. There was nothing to be seen. Nothing moved. Hesitantly, Cephelo stalked to the very edge of the woods surrounding the small clearing, both hands securely grasping the handle of a heavy broadsword. He stood for a time, his tall form black against the trees, poised to defend himself. There was only silence. Finally he turned and walked back again, his face set. There was no further joking. The horses, which were tethered on a line along a small inlet from the lake, were brought close in to the caravan in order that they could be better watched. Guards were placed all about the perimeter of the clearing and warned to keep their eyes open. Everyone else was taken back inside the circle of the wagons where they settled themselves within the comforting light of the fire. The wine was passed about, though fewer drank this time. Conversation resumed, but it was low and guarded and the word "Devil" was mentioned frequently. The men kept the women and children close, and everyone looked thoroughly disquieted.

Wil walked Amberle several paces back from the anxious group, his head lowered.

"I want you to stay close," he said quietly. "Do not leave me for any reason."

"I won't," she promised. Her eyes were intense as they found his and then glanced away quickly. "Do you think . . . ?"

Cephelo cut short her thought, calling suddenly for music, clapping his hands and encouraging those about him to do likewise. The Valeman and the Elven girl joined in obediently. A few weak cheers greeted Cephelo as he moved about the fire.

Wil glanced about uneasily. "If there is anything out there, and if whatever it is attacks this camp, then you and I are getting out. We will try to reach Artaq, then make a run for it. Are you willing to risk it?"

She nodded. "Very."

Cymbals shivered their silver cry, and the stringed instruments hummed softly. Hands began to clap, steady and confident.

Then the cough broke almost on top of them, booming out of the darkness with frightening suddenness, heavy and terrible. Shouts sounded from the guards—shouts filled with terror, shouts that cried, "Devil, Devil!" Those gathered about the fire scattered, the men rushing for their weapons, the women and children fleeing in confusion. A scream rose above the clamor, high and quick, dying almost immediately into stillness. Beyond the circle of the wagons, something huge and dark moved in the night.

"Demon!" Wil whispered the name almost without thinking.

An instant later the creature appeared through a gap between two of the wagons, pushing aside the wooden homes as if they were made of paper. It was unquestionably a Demon—but much bigger than anything the Valeman and the Elven girl had encountered fleeing Havenstead. It stood on two legs, more than fifteen feet tall, its massive body bent and heavy and covered with mottled brown and gray hide that hung from it in thick folds. A crest of scales ran from its neck the length of its back and down either leg. Its face was blasted and empty, a mass of teeth curving out from jaws that opened wide to emit its deep, booming cough. From two great, clawed hands dangled the broken body of a Rover guard.

It flung the dead man aside and came forward. Cephelo and a dozen more Rovers met it with pikes and swords. A few thrusts penetrated the thick hide, but most were turned aside. The creature was slow and ponderous, but incredibly strong. It shambled forward through the wall of defenders, swatting them aside effortlessly. Cephelo threw himself directly into the Demon's path, leaping up to thrust his broadsword deep into the creature's gaping mouth. The monstrous thing barely slowed, jaws snapping the sword into splinters, clawed hands reaching for the Rover Leader. Cephelo was too quick, but another Rover went down, tripping over his own feet in his haste to escape. The Demon's foot dropped on the struggling man like a rock.

Wil was already moving Amberle toward the far side of the encampment, intent on reaching the tethered horses, when he saw Cephelo go down as well. The defenders were attempting to entangle the Demon's legs when one massive arm caught the big man a glancing blow and sent him tumbling head over heels. Hesitating in a gap between the wagons, Wil watched the other Rovers spring to Cephelo's defense, two grabbing the inert form and pulling it to safety while the others feinted and jabbed at the monster to draw its attention. The Demon swung about, pikes and swords hacking at its armored body, and reached for the nearest Rover wagon. It seized the heavy carrier and, with a single lunge, threw it over. The wagon fell with a crash, splitting apart, metal ornaments and silk rolls spilling into the firelight. The defenders cried out in fury and resumed their hopeless attack.

Amberle was pulling urgently on Wil Ohmsford's arm, but still the

Valeman hesitated. He could not bring himself to believe that something so huge and so slow had managed to track them all the way from Havenstead. No, this creature had escaped through the wall of the Forbidding on its own, wandered down into the Tirfing, and simply stumbled on their caravan. It had come alone, blindly, stupidly—but a thing of such destruction that it was clear already that the Rovers were no match for it. Despite their efforts to turn or stop it, the Demon would surely destroy the entire caravan.

But the Rovers would not run. The garish wagons, the cumbersome wheeled houses—these were their homes. Everything they owned was in them. No, the Rovers would not run. They would stand and fight; and if they did so, they would die. The Demon was a thing of another age; its power was greater than that of flesh and blood and bone. It would take power as great as its own to stop it. Only he possessed that power. But this was not his fight. These people had stolen from him; he owed them nothing. His first and only responsibility was for Amberle. He should take her and go quickly. Yet if he did, what would become of the Rovers—not only the men, but the women and children as well? Had they harmed him? Without his help, they stood no chance at all against the Demon.

His indecision was complete when he remembered that his grandfather had once told him that when he had used the Elfstones in his flight from the Warlock Lord, he had inadvertently told his enemy exactly where he could be found. It might well be the same now. Some of these Demons were creatures capable of using magic; Allanon had told him this was so. If he were to use the Elfstones, he might lead them right to him.

He looked quickly to Amberle. What she saw in his eyes told her at once what he intended to do. Wordlessly she released his arm. He pulled off his right boot and reached into it for the Elfstones. At least he must try, he told himself. At least he must do that much. He could not let these people die. He opened the pouch and poured the three blue Stones into his open palm. Closing his fist over them tightly, he started back into the camp.

"Stay here," he told the Elven girl.

"No, wait . . ." she called after him, but he was already running.

The Demon had turned away from the wagons and was driving the Rovers before it as it advanced toward the center of the encampment. Cephelo was back on his feet, swaying unsteadily as he leaned against a wagon at one side and yelled encouragement to the defenders. Wil closed the distance between himself and the combatants until no more than twenty yards separated them. Raising his fist above his head, he willed forth the power of the Elfstones.

Nothing happened.

He experienced a sinking sensation in the pit of his stomach. The one thing he had feared most had come to pass—he could not control the power of the Elfstones. Allanon had been wrong. Only his grandfather could invoke their power, not he. They were not his to command. They would not obey him.

Yet they must! He tried again, concentrating on the feel of the Stones in his hand, calling down to the magic that lay buried somewhere within them. Still nothing. Yet this time he sensed something he had missed before—a barrier of some sort that blocked his efforts, a barrier somewhere within himself.

The shouts of the Rovers broke sharply through his thoughts, and he saw that the Demon was coming directly toward him. The defenders were behind the creature now, stabbing and thrusting with their weapons at its legs and flanks, trying to turn it from the Valeman. One massive arm swung out, knocking two men sprawling, and scattering the rest. The booming cough rolled out of its throat. Cephelo began hobbling frantically toward the battle, supporting himself with a broken pike, his dark clothing torn and covered with dust and blood. Wil saw them all as if they had been frozen in a single instant of still life, struggling as he did so to free the power that lay locked within the Elfstones. It did not occur to him to run; he simply stood there in the center of the Rover camp, a solitary figure with one arm raised to the night sky.

Then Eretria appeared from out of nowhere, darting forward, her slender form a shadow of sudden movement that flashed between the Demon and the Valeman, one brown hand hurtling a fiery torch into the monster's face. The creature caught the burning stick of wood in its jaws, snapping at it reflexively—yet slowing as it did, as if somehow bothered by the fire and smoke. Taking advantage of its momentary hesitation, Eretria caught hold of Wil and began pulling him backward until both lost their footing, stumbled and went down. The Rover defenders rallied at once, snatching up brands from the fire and throwing them at the Demon in an effort to confuse it. But the monster had already started forward again. Wil scrambled back to his feet hurriedly, pulling Eretria up with him. At that same moment Amberle reached his side, a long pike held firmly in both small hands as she prepared to defend them all. Wordlessly the Valeman grabbed her arm, pushed both women behind him, and turned to face the advancing Demon.

The creature was almost on top of them. Wil Ohmsford held forth the hand that gripped the Elfstones. There was no hesitation, no confusion within him now. Driving inward, he smashed aside the barrier that stood between himself and the power of the Stones, smashed it aside through strength of will born of desperation and need, without yet understanding what it was. As he did so, he sensed something change within himself that he could not explain and did not feel was altogether good. There was no time to give it thought. Reaching down within the heart of the Elfstones, he brought them to life at last. Brilliant blue light flared up from his clenched hand, gathered itself, then burst forward to strike the Demon. The monstrous thing roared as the power of the Stones burned through it. Still it came on, its clawed hands grasping. Wil did not give ground. He took himself further into the Stones, feeling their power intensify. Everything about him grew hazy with their glow, and again the Elfstones lashed out at the Demon. This time the creature could not withstand the Elven magic. Its massive form erupted in flames and became a pillar of blinding light. For an instant it burned deep blue in the night, then exploded into ash and was gone.

Wil Ohmsford brought his arm down slowly. Where the Demon had stood, there was only charred earth and a wisp of black smoke rising into the night. The whole of the surrounding woodlands had gone deathly still, and only the crackling of the Rover fire disturbed the silence. The Valeman looked about uncertainly. Not a single Rover moved; they just stood there, the men with their weapons still poised to do battle, the women and children huddled close to one another, all with disbelief and fear reflected in their faces. Wil felt a moment of panic. Would they turn on him, knowing now that he had deceived them? He looked back quickly at Amberle, but she, too, stood frozen, her deep green eyes filled with wonder.

Then Cephelo hobbled forward, casting aside the broken pike as he came up to the Valeman, his dark bearded face streaked with blood and soot.

"Who are you?" he asked softly. "Tell me who you are."

The Valeman hesitated. "I am who I said I was," he said finally.

"No." Cephelo shook his head. "No, you are surely no simple Healer. You are more than that." His voice was hard and insistent. "I was right about you all along, wasn't I?"

Wil did not know how to respond.

"Tell me who you are," Cephelo repeated, his voice low and dangerous.

"I have already told you who I am."

"You have told me nothing!" The Rover Leader's face flushed with anger. "I think you knew of this Devil. I think that he came here because of you. I think that all of this was because of you!"

Wil shook his head. "The creature found you by chance; it was chance that I was with you when he did."

"Healer, you are lying to me!"

Wil felt his temper slip. "Who has lied to whom, Cephelo. This was your game we played—you made all the rules!"

The big man took a quick step forward. "There are rules you might yet be taught."

"I do not think so," the Valeman replied evenly.

He brought the fist that held the Elfstones up slightly. Cephelo did not miss the gesture. He stepped back slowly. The smile that followed was painfully forced.

"You said you carried nothing of value, Healer. Did you forget these?"

Wil shook his head. "The Stones have no value to anyone but me. They would be worthless to you."

"Indeed." The Rover did not bother to conceal the sneer in his voice. "Are you a sorcerer, then? A Devil yourself? Why not tell me who you are?"

Wil hesitated. He was getting nowhere this way. He had to put an end to this whole conversation. Amberle stepped up beside him, one small hand reaching out to take his arm, touching it lightly. It was reassuring to have her there.

"Cephelo, you must return my horse to me," he said quietly. The Rover's face went black. "Amberle and I must go at once. There are more Devils than this one I destroyed—that much I will tell you. They track both the Elven girl and me. Because I used the Stones, they will know now where we can be found. We must go—and you must leave here, as well."

Cephelo stared wordlessly at him for several long moments, obviously trying to determine if what he was being told was the truth. In the end, caution overruled mistrust. He nodded curtly.

"Take your horse and go. I want no more of either of you."

He wheeled and walked away, calling loudly to his people to strike camp. Clearly he wished to be gone from the Tirfing as well. Wil watched him for a moment, then dropped the Elfstones into their leather pouch and tucked the pouch back within his tunic. Taking Amberle by the arm, he began moving toward the horses. Then he remembered Eretria. He looked for her and found her in the shadow of the wagons, her dark eyes watching him.

"Goodbye, Wil Ohmsford," she said quietly.

He smiled faintly. She knew that she had lost her chance to go with him. For an instant, he hesitated. She had saved his life; he owed her something for that. Would it be so wrong for him to help her now? Yet he knew that he could not. His sole concern now must be for Amberle. He could not distract himself from that, even for this Rover girl he found so enchanting. The debt he owed her must be paid another time.

"Goodbye, Eretria," he replied.

A touch of that dazzling smile broke through the shadow of her face.

"We will meet again," she called, then whirled and was gone.

Five minutes later, Wil and Amberle rode Artaq north out of the Rover camp and disappeared into the night.

17

With little more than an hour remaining before dawn, they arrived at the south bank of the Mermidon several miles downstream from where the river emerged from the forests of the Westland into Callahorn. They had ridden Artaq for most of the night, maintaining a steady pace as they journeyed north through the open, more easily traveled grasslands, seeking to put as much distance as possible between themselves and the Tirfing. They had rested only once, a brief stop for water and relief from rapidly cramping muscles, then remounted and gone on. By the time they reached the river's edge, both horse and riders were close to exhaustion. The Valeman could discern no readily accessible point for crossing, the Mermidon being both wide and deep for as far as the eye could see in both directions, and it quickly became apparent that they either would have to swim the river or follow its banks until a shallows was found. Having no wish to attempt either while it was still dark, Wil decided that the best thing for them to do was to rest until daylight. Turning Artaq into a grove of cottonwood, he unsaddled and tethered the big black, then spread blankets for both Amberle and himself. Screened by the trees, all three fell quickly asleep.

It was almost noon when Wil awoke once more, feeling the warmth of the summer day filter through the cottonwoods from out of yet another clear, sunlit sky. The Valeman touched Amberle gently, and she came awake. They rose, washed, ate a brief meal, and resumed their journey toward Arborlon.

They rode Artaq upstream for several miles, almost to the edge of the Westland forests, but found no shallows that would afford them a safe crossing. Rather than waste further time retracing their steps downstream, they decided they would chance swimming the river. Strapping their few possessions about Artaq's neck, they tied themselves to his saddle with a length of rope, led the big black down to the water's edge, and plunged in. The water was chill, and the shock of the sudden immersion numbed them. They thrashed wildly for a few minutes, fighting the cold and the pull of the current, then settled into a steady kick, hands gripping the safety rope tightly. Artaq swam strongly. Even though the river swept them downstream for nearly half-a-mile, they reached the far bank unharmed.

From there they rode north at a leisurely pace, walking Artaq frequently to rest him. Wil believed that they had traveled far enough from the Tirfing to confuse any immediate pursuit, and he saw no reason to tire the black further. The previous night's run had taken a lot out of the gallant horse, and he needed a chance to regain his strength. If he were not given that chance now, he would be useless to them later—and Wil was not about to discount the possibility that they might have great need for him before Arborlon was reached. Besides, even at this slower pace, they would reach the Valley of Rhenn by the following morning. That was soon enough, he reasoned. They would be safe until then.

Amberle might have had a different opinion, but she kept it to herself. Free of the Rovers, her spirits were noticeably improved. She sang and hummed once more as they walked, pausing frequently to observe small flowers and plants, bits and pieces of tiny life that would have gone unnoticed by the Valeman in the vast carpet of the grasslands. She had little to say to Wil, although she answered pleasantly when he spoke to her and smiled patiently at his questions about the growing things she was drawn to. But for the most part, she stayed reserved and distant in her attitude toward him, refusing to engage in general conversation, walled away in that private world she had chosen for herself since the time they had begun this journey north from the banks of the Rainbow Lake.

As the day wore on, Wil found himself thinking of Eretria, wondering if she would leave Cephelo and the caravan as she had threatened and if he would indeed see her again one day. There was an excitement to the Rover girl that he found fascinating. She reminded him of a brief vision created by the Sirens that grew on the Battlemound—mesmeric and alluring, stirring within the mind wild and beautiful thoughts. He smiled at the comparison. It was foolish, really. She was flesh and blood, no vision. Still, if he were to probe the surface of her, would he find that she, like the Siren, was a thing of deception? There was something to her that suggested this, and it bothered him more than a little. He had not forgotten how she had risked her own life to save his; he would hate to discover that there had been any deception in that.

By nightfall, they were angling west, following the line of the forest-land as it wound northward toward the vast expanse of the Streleheim. As darkness closed about them, Wil turned Artaq into the woods, trailing a small stream through the trees for several hundred feet until it pooled below a rapids, providing them with suitable drinking water. There they made camp, bedding down Artaq in a patch of thick grass, feeding and watering him before turning to their own needs. A cooking fire would call attention to their presence, so they settled for fruits and vegetables provided by Amberle. Once again, these were unfamiliar foods to the Valeman, but he enjoyed them nonetheless. He sensed that, given enough time, he might even become used to the strange fare. He was almost finished with the last of the peculiar, elongated, orange fruits when the Elven girl turned to him suddenly, a quizzical look on her face.

"Do you mind if I ask you something?" she wanted to know.

He grinned. "How do I know if I mind, if I don't know what it is you plan to ask?"

"Well, you needn't answer if you don't wish to—but this has been bothering me ever since we left the Rover camp."

"In that case, ask."

The small clearing in which they sat was very dark, the pale light of the moon and stars screened by the tangle of tree limbs that interlocked above them, and she moved close to him so that she could see his face clearly.

"Will you be honest with me?" Her eyes fixed on his.

"I will."

"When you used the Elfstones, did you . . . ?" She hesitated, as if not sure of the word she wanted. "Did you . . . hurt yourself?"

He stared at her, a sudden premonition stirring at the back of his mind, undefined still, but there nevertheless.

"That is a curious question."

"I know." She nodded, and a faint smile escaped before her face grew serious once more. "I cannot explain it, really—it was a feeling I had when I watched you. At first you could not seem to control the Elfstones. You held them up and nothing happened, although it was clear enough that you were trying to use their power to stop the Demon. Then, when they did at last come alive, there was a change in you—a change that showed in your face . . . almost like pain."

The Valeman was nodding slowly. He remembered now, and the memory was not pleasant. After it had happened, he had blocked it from his mind—blocked it without thinking, almost as a reflex action. Even now, he did not know why. It was not until this moment, when she recalled it to him, that he remembered what he had felt.

There was concern mirrored in the Elven girl's eyes as he stared into them now. "If you do not wish . . ." she began quickly.

"No." His voice was quiet, firm. He shook his head slowly. "No. I do not know if I understand it myself, though—but it would help to talk about it, I think."

He took a deep breath, choosing his words carefully. "There was a block somewhere within me. I do not know what it was or what caused it, but it was there and it would not let me use the Stones. I could not seem to pass around it or go through it." He shook his head again. "Then the Demon was almost on top of me, and you and Eretria were both there, and all of us were going to die, and I somehow smashed the block— smashed it apart and reached down into the Stones . . ."

He paused. "There was no pain, but a sense of something unpleasant happening within me, something . . . I don't know how to describe it. A sense of having done something wrong—yet there was nothing wrong in what I did."

"The wrong may have been to yourself," she murmured after a moment's consideration. "Perhaps the Elven magic is harmful to you in some way."

"Perhaps," he agreed. "Yet my grandfather never spoke of this. Can it be that the magic did not affect him, yet does affect me? Why would it be different with me?"

She shook her head doubtfully. "Elven magic causes different reactions in different people. It has always been so. It is a magic born of the spirit, and the spirit is never a constant."

"But my grandfather and I are so much alike—even more so than my father and I were." Wil pondered. "Kindred spirits, you might say—and not so diverse as to cause this . . . this difference in our use of the Stones. Surely he would have felt this as well—and he would have told me."

Amberle's hand reached for his arm, holding it firmly.

"I do not think you should use the Elfstones again."

He smiled. "Even to protect you?"

He said it lightly, but she did not return the smile. There was nothing humorous in this to her.

"I would not be the cause of any injury to you, Healer," she announced quietly. "It was not my choice that brought you on this journey, and I feel badly that you are here at all. But since you are here, I will speak my mind. Elven magic is nothing to be toyed with; it can prove to be more dangerous than the evil it was created to protect against. Our histories have left us with that warning, if little else. The magic may act against not only the body, but the spirit as well. Wounds of the body may be treated. But what of wounds to the spirit? How will you treat them, Healer?"

She bent close. "No one is worth such injury—no one. Especially me."

Wil stared at her silently for a moment, startled to see tears glistening at the corners of her eyes. He reached out his hand to cover hers.

"We shall be careful for each other," he promised. He tried a quick smile. "Maybe we won't have need of the Stones again."

The look she gave him in response suggested that she did not believe a word of it.

It was midnight when the howl of the Demon-wolves rose out of the stillness of the grasslands, shrill, hungry, and filled with hatred. Wil and Amberle came awake at once, the contentment of their sleep twisted with fear. For an instant they did not move, their bodies pushed upright from beneath the blankets, their eyes wide and staring as they sought each other out in the dark. The cry died, echoed in the silence that followed, then rose again, piercing and high. This time neither Valeman nor Elven girl hesitated. Without a word, both were on their feet, pulling on their boots, slipping their riding cloaks about their shoulders. In seconds they had saddled Artaq, mounted, and were riding north once more.

They moved ahead at a steady trot, keeping to the open plains where the way was clear and lit by moon and stars, following the line of the forestland. Cool night air rushed over them as they rode, damp with moisture gathering into morning dew, filled with the smells of the dark. Behind them, the howling continued, far back still, somewhere above the line of the Mermidon. The Demon-wolves were searching. The trail they followed was a day old; they did not realize yet how close they actually were to their prey.

Artaq ran smoothly, his great body working effortlessly as he raced across the grasslands, little more than another shadow slipping through the summer night. He had gotten most of the rest he needed for this run and he would not be winded quickly. Wil rated him carefully, keeping the pace steady, not letting the black overextend himself. It was early still; the chase had just begun. Their pursuers would discover soon enough the truth of matters. The Valeman was angry with himself; he had not believed they could be found again so quickly. The Elfstones must have revealed their presence in the Tirfing. The Demon-wolves had come for the Valeman and the Elven girl immediately, tracked them north, and now flushed them from the Westland forests. Once they found the campsite their quarry had abandoned, the wolves would come after them with a vengeance. The Demons would run them until they were caught.

They rode on for better than an hour without sighting the valley, the howling trailing after them as they fled. It was answered now by cries that rose out of the grasslands below the Dragon's Teeth and the plains to the north. Wil felt his heart sink. The wolves had them ringed. Only the Westland had been left open to them. He wondered suddenly if that way, too, might be closed. He remembered how it had been at the Silver River. The Valley of Rhenn might be a trap as well. Perhaps they were purposely being driven into the valley and it was there that the Demons planned to finish them. Yet what other choice was left them but to take that chance?

Moments later the howls behind them rose in a frenzy. The Demon-wolves had found their camp.

Wil put Artaq into a full gallop. The Demons would come quickly now, certain that their prey was close ahead, knowing that they could be caught. Cries north and east of them sounded in answer to those behind, shrill and ragged as the hunters began to run. Artaq was sweating, his head extended forward, his ears laid back. The grasslands thinned into barren scrub; they had crossed into the Streleheim. The Valley of Rhenn could not be far. Wil stretched himself low over Artaq's straining neck and urged the gallant horse onward.

It was during the third hour of the chase, when the grasslands of Callahorn had been left far behind and the earth beneath Artaq's pounding hooves had gone hard and cracked, when the howls of the Demon-wolves had drawn so near that it seemed the huge gray forms must spring into view at any moment, when wind and dust had blinded them and sweat from fear had streaked their bodies beneath their tangled clothes, that Valeman and Elven girl at last caught sight of the broken ridges that formed the mouth of the Valley of Rhenn. They rose out of the flatlands below the Elven forests, rock and scrub black against the night sky. The riders turned toward the pass without slowing. Artaq's flanks were heaving, his nostrils flaring; sweat and lather coated his sleek black body. He stretched out further, racing through the darkness, the two hunched forms on his back holding on desperately.

In seconds, the pass was before them, craggy ridges looming up on either side. Down into the narrow slot of the valley thundered the black. Wil peered frantically through tear-filled eyes as the wind ripped across his face, searching for the Demons that he had feared would be waiting to trap them. Astonishingly, he found none. They were alone in the valley. He felt a quick sense of exhilaration. They were going to escape! Their pursuers were too far back to catch them before they were safely into the Westland forests, into the country of the Elven. By then there would be help . . .

The incomplete thought hung suspended in his mind, repeating itself over and over in cadence with the sound of Artaq's pounding hooves as the black raced along the floor of the valley. Wil went cold. What was he thinking? There would be no help for them. No one even knew they were coming—no one but Allanon, and the Druid was gone. Help? What help did he expect? Already the Demons had gone into the very heart of the city of Arborlon to destroy the Chosen. What did he think would stop them from trailing one incredibly foolish Valeman and an unarmed Elven girl into forestland miles from anything? All he had succeeded in doing in gaining the Valley of Rhenn was to take Artaq out of the open grasslands, where he could run, into the confinement of the woods, where he could not. There was nothing there that would prevent the wolves from coming after them—creatures that were quicker and more agile than they, better able to penetrate the maze of trees and brush, better able to pursue than they would be able to flee. He wanted to scream what he was feeling. Stupid! His shortsightedness had taken away their one slim chance of escape. He had been so concerned with what they had been running from that he had forgotten to consider what they had been running into. They were not going to escape at all. They would be caught; they would be killed. It was his fault. He had done this to them.

He must do something.

His mind raced, searching desperately. He had only one weapon left. The Elfstones.

Then Amberle screamed. The Valeman jerked about, following the Elven girl's rigid arm as it pointed skyward.

Through the mouth of the valley flew a monstrous black creature with leathered wings that spanned the line of the ridges and a head hooked and bent like some twisted limb. Shrieking, it swept out of the Streleheim into the crease of the valley and came for them. Wil had never seen anything so huge. He yelled frantically to Artaq, but the black had nothing left to give—he was running now on spirit alone. A hundred yards away loomed the draw that marked the far pass. Beyond lay woods that would hide them from this nightmare, woods into which a thing of such size could not possibly go. All they needed was a few seconds more.

The creature dove for them. It seemed to fall toward them like some massive rock, plummeting downward out of the night. Wil Ohmsford saw it come and glimpsed momentarily the rider it bore, a thing vaguely manlike, yet humped and misshapen, its eyes red against the black of its face. The eyes seemed to transfix him, and he felt his courage melt.

For an instant he thought they were finished. But then, with a final lunge, Artaq gained the far pass, broke clear of the high ridges, and plunged into the darkness of the trees.

Down a narrow rutted earthen trail the big horse thundered, barely slowing as his sleek body dodged and twisted through the tangle of trunks and heavy brush. Wil and Amberle hung on desperately, limbs and vines whipping across them, threatening to unseat them at every turn. Wil tried to slow the black, but Artaq had taken the bit between his teeth. The Valeman had lost control of him entirely. He was running his own race now.

In seconds the riders lost all sense of direction, confused by the forest dark that had closed about them and by the winding trail. Although he could no longer hear the howl of the Demon-wolves nor the shriek of that flying monster, Wil was terrified that they might inadvertently become turned about and end up traveling back toward the very creatures from whom they sought to escape. He sawed angrily on the reins in an effort to free the bit, but Artaq held on firmly.

The Valeman had just about given up hope of ever stopping the black when the big horse abruptly slowed and then stopped altogether. Standing in the middle of the forest trail, sides heaving, nostrils flaring, he lowered his finely shaped head and nickered softly. A long moment of silence followed. Wil and Amberle glanced at one another questioningly.

Then a tall, black form appeared right in front of them, slipping from the forest night without a sound. It happened so quickly that Wil did not even have time to think to reach for the Elfstones. The dark figure stepped forward, one hand touching gently Artaq's sweating neck, slowly stroking the satin skin. From out of the shadow of a hooded cloak, his face lifted to the light.

It was Allanon.

"Are you all right?" he asked softly, reaching up to take Amberle from the saddle and lower her carefully to the ground.

The Elven girl nodded wordlessly, astonishment filling her sea-green eyes—astonishment, and a touch of anger. The Druid frowned, then turned to aid Wil, but the Valeman was already scrambling down from Artaq's back.

"We thought you dead!" he burst out in disbelief.

"It seems that someone is forever declaring me dead before the fact," the mystic remarked somewhat petulantly. "As you can see, I am quite . . ."

"Allanon, we have got to get out of here." Wil was already glancing anxiously over his shoulder. His words tripped over one another in his haste to get them out. "The Demon-wolves chased us north all the way from the Mermidon, and there's a black, flying thing that . . ."

"Wil, slow down."

". . . almost caught us in the valley, bigger than anything I've ever . . ."

"Wil!"

Wil Ohmsford went silent. Allanon shook his head reprovingly.

"Would you please let me get a word in edgewise?" The Valeman flushed and nodded. "Thank you. First of all, you are quite safe now. The Demons no longer pursue you. The one who leads them can sense my presence. He is wary of me and has turned back."

The Valeman looked doubtful. "Are you sure?"

"Very sure. No one has followed you. Now come over here with me, both of you, and sit down."

He led them to a fallen log that lay next to the trail, and the Valeman and Elven girl seated themselves wearily. Allanon remained standing.

"We must go on to Arborlon tonight," he advised them. "But we can spare a few moments to rest before we leave."

"How did you get here?" Wil asked him.

"I might ask you the same question." The big man hunched down on one knee, drawing the black robes close about him. "Do you understand what happened to you at the river?"

The Valeman nodded. "I think so."

"It was the King of the Silver River," Amberle interjected quietly. "We saw him; he spoke to us."

"It was to Amberle that he spoke," Wil corrected. "But what happened to you? Did he help you as well?"

Allanon shook his head. "I am afraid I did not even see him—only the light which enveloped and took you away. He is a reclusive and mysterious being, and he shows himself to very few. This time, he chose to appear to you. His reasons must remain his own, I suppose. In any case, his appearance caused considerable confusion among the Demons, and I took advantage of that confusion to make my own escape."

He paused. "Amberle, you said that he spoke with you. Do you recall what it was that he said?"

The Elven girl looked uneasy. "No, not exactly. It was like a dream. He said something about . . . joining."

For an instant there was a flicker of understanding in the Druid's dark eyes. But neither Wil nor Amberle saw it, and it disappeared at once.

"No matter." The mystic brushed the incident aside casually. "He helped you when you needed help, and for that we are in his debt."

"His debt, to be sure—but certainly not yours." Amberle did not bother to disguise her anger. "Where have you been, Druid?"

Allanon seemed surprised. "Looking for you. Unfortunately, when he helped you, the King of the Silver River caused us to become separated. I knew you were safe, of course, but I did not know where you had been taken nor how to go about finding you again. I might have used magic, but that seemed unnecessarily risky. The one who leads these Demons who have broken through the Forbidding has power as great as my own—perhaps greater. Using magic might have led him to us both. So I chose instead to continue on toward Arborlon, searching for you as I went, believing that you would remember and follow accordingly the instructions I had given you. Because I was forced to go afoot—your gray, Wil, was lost in the battle—I was certain that you were ahead of me the entire time. It was not until you used the Elfstones that I realized I was mistaken."

He shrugged. "By then I was almost to Arborlon. I started back at once, traveling south through the forestland, thinking that you would seek sanctuary by entering the woods below the Mermidon. Again, I was mistaken. When I heard the howling of the Demon-wolves, I realized that you were trying to reach the Valley of Rhenn. That brought me here."

"It appears that you have been mistaken much of the time," Amberle snapped.

Allanon said nothing, his eyes meeting hers.

"I think you were mistaken in coming to me in the first place," she continued, her voice accusing now.

"It was necessary that I come."

"That remains to be seen. What worries me at the moment is that the Demons have been one step ahead of you from the beginning. How many times now have they almost had me?"

Allanon rose. "Too many times. It will not happen again."

Amberle rose with him, her face flushing darkly. "I no longer feel particularly reassured by your promises. I want this journey finished. I want to go home again—to Havenstead, not to Arborlon."

The Druid's face was expressionless. "Understand—I do what I am able to do for you."

"Perhaps. Perhaps you only do what suits you."

The Druid stiffened. "That is unfair, Elven girl. You know less about this than you suppose."

"I know one thing. I know that neither you nor your choice for my protector have proven very capable. I would be much happier if I had never seen either one of you."

She was so angry she was almost in tears. She stared at them furiously, daring them to contradict her. When they did not, she turned away and started walking down the darkened trail.

"You said we must go on to Arborlon tonight, Druid," she called out. "I want this finished!"

Wil Ohmsford stared after her, resentment and confusion showing in his face. For a moment he seriously considered just sitting there and letting the Elven girl go her own way. She obviously had little enough use for him. Then he felt Allanon's hand on his shoulder.

"Do not be too quick to judge her," the Druid said softly.

The hand withdrew, and Allanon moved over to gather up Artaq's reins. He looked back at Wil inquiringly. The Valeman shook his head and rose. After all, he had come this far. There was nothing to be gained by not going on.

The Druid had already started after the slender figure of the Elven girl as she disappeared up the pathway into the trees. Grudgingly, Wil followed.

18

It was evening of the following day. Shadows lengthened across the forested city of Arborlon and gray dusk deepened steadily into night. Eventine Elessedil sat alone in the seclusion of his study, pouring over Gael's list of matters that would require his attention in the morning. Fatigue lined his face, and his eyes squinted wearily in the light of the oil lamp that sat atop the wooden desk he occupied. The room was still, closing the aged King of the Elves away in the silence of his thoughts.

He glanced over briefly at Manx, who lay sprawled across the room against a bookcase, sleeping soundly. The wolfhound's graying flanks rose and fell rhythmically, his breath exhaling through his nose with a curious nasal whine. Eventine smiled. Old dog, he thought, sleep comes easily to you, deep and dreamless and troublefree. He shook his head. He would give much to enjoy just a single night's undisturbed sleep. There had been little rest for him. Nightmares crowded his slumber—nightmares that were distortions of the unpleasant realities of his waking hours, carried with him into sleep. They teased and tormented him; they stole wickedly through his slumber, disruptive and hateful. Each night they returned, prodding at his subconscious, fragmenting his sleep so that time and again he shook himself awake, until at last dawn brought an end to the struggle.

He rubbed his eyes, then his face, closing off the light with his hands. He would have to sleep soon because sleep in some form was necessary. But he knew that he would find little rest.

When he took his hands away again, he found himself staring at Allanon. For an instant he did not believe that he was seeing the Druid; this was only a trick of his mind, brought on by his weariness. But when he squinted sharply and the image did not disappear, he came to his feet with a start.

"Allanon! I thought I was seeing things!"

The Druid came forward and they locked hands. There was the barest flicker of uncertainty in the Elven King's eyes.

"Did you find her?"

Allanon nodded. "She is here."

Eventine did not know how to respond. The two men stared at each other wordlessly. Against the bookcase, Manx raised his head and yawned.

"I did not think she would ever come back," the King said finally. He hesitated. "Where have you taken her?"

"Where she can be protected," Allanon responded. He released the King's hand. "We do not have much time. I want you to summon your sons and the most trusted of your advisors—those to whom you have confided the truth of the danger that threatens the Elves. Be certain of your choice. Have them gather in one hour in the chambers of the Elven High Council. Tell them that I would speak with them. Tell no one else. See to it that your guard keeps watch without. One hour. I will meet you then."

He turned and started back toward the open windows he had come through.

"Amberle . . . ?" Eventine called after him.

"One hour," the Druid repeated, then slipped through the curtains and was gone.

The allotted hour passed, and those summoned by the Elven King assembled in the High Council. The council room was a cavernous, hexagonal chamber built of oak and stone with its cathedral ceiling peaked starlike overhead at a joinder of massive beams. A set of huge wooden doors opened into the room, lighted by low-hanging oil lamps suspended at the ends of black iron chains. Against a facing wall was settled the dais of the King, a riser of steps leading to a great, hand-carved oaken throne flanked by a line of standards from which hung flags bearing the insignia of the houses of the Elven Kings. Gallery seats bordered the remaining walls, each set a dozen rows deep, all overlooking a broad expanse of polished stone flooring encircled like an arena by a low iron railing. At the exact center of the room stood a wide oval table with twenty-one chairs where sat the members of the Elven High Council.

Only six of these chairs were occupied this night. At one of them sat Ander Elessedil. He spoke little to the five seated with him, his eyes straying restlessly to the closed double doors at the far end of the chamber. Thoughts of Amberle crowded together in his mind. Although the girl had not been mentioned by his father when he had come to him with the news of Allanon's return, he was certain nevertheless that the Druid had succeeded in bringing her back to Arborlon; if not, this Council would not have been convened in such haste. He was equally certain that Allanon intended to bring her before the Council and ask that they entrust to her the search for the Bloodfire. He was not certain what the Council would say in response. If the King chose to speak first on the Druid's request and to lend it his support, then the others would probably acquiesce to his wishes—though this was by no means a foregone conclusion, given the strong feelings the Elves bore about Amberle. In any case, he did not believe that his father would do that. He would listen first to the advice of the men he had gathered about him. Then he would decide.

Ander glanced briefly at his father, then looked away again. What would his own advice be, he wondered suddenly? He would be asked to speak, yet how could he trust himself to be objective where Amberle was concerned? Conflicting emotions colored his reason with their intensity. Love and disappointment intermingled. His hands locked before him on the table in response to what he was feeling. Perhaps it would be best if he said nothing. Perhaps it would be best if he simply deferred to the judgment of the others.

His gaze shifted momentarily to their faces. Other than Dardan and Rhoe, who kept watch outside the chamber doors, no one else had been told of this meeting. There were others his father might have called—good men. But he had chosen these. It was a balanced choice, Ander thought to himself as he considered the character of each. But what sort of judgment would they exercise when they heard what was being asked?

He found that he was not sure.

Arion Elessedil sat on his father's right, the place at the Council table reserved for the Crown Prince of the realm. It was Arion to whom the King would look first, just as he always did whenever an important decision was required. Arion was his father's strength, and the old man loved him fiercely. Just his presence lent Eventine a sense of reassurance that Ander knew he could not provide, however he might try. But Arion lacked compassion and at times exhibited a stubbornness that obscured his good sense. It was difficult to predict what he might do where Amberle was concerned. Once he had been fond of the girl, the only child of his beloved brother Aine. But all that was long since past. His feelings had changed with the death of his brother—changed further with Amberle's betrayal of her trust as a Chosen. There was great bitterness within the Crown Prince, much of it caused by the obvious hurt that this girl had brought to the King. It was impossible to tell how deep that bitterness ran. Deep, Ander thought and was troubled by what that might mean.

The King's First Minister, Emer Chios, occupied the chair next to Arion. As First Minister, it was Chios who presided over the Council in the King's absence. An articulate, persuasive man, he could be depended upon to express his feelings candidly. Although Eventine and his First Minister were not always in agreement on matters that came before the Council, they nevertheless had great respect for each other's opinions. Eventine would listen closely to what his First Minister had to say.

Kael Pindanon, Commander of the Elven Army, was the King's oldest and closest friend. Though ten years younger than the King, Pindanon looked at least that much older, his face seemed like dry wood, his gnarled frame rawhide tough, scarred and knotted from a lifetime of combat. White hair flowed down below his shoulders, and a great, drooping mustache arced about the thin line of his mouth. Iron hard and fixed of purpose, Pindanon was the most predictable of Eventine's advisors. The old soldier was completely devoted to the King; he always advised with the King's best interests foremost in mind. It would be so with Amberle.

The last man at the table was not a member of the High Council. He was younger even than Ander, a slim, dark-haired Elf with an alert air and anxious brown eyes. He sat next to Pindanon, his chair drawn back slightly from the oval table, not speaking to the others but watching them in silence. Twin daggers were strapped about his waist and a broadsword hung in its scabbard from the back of his chair. He wore no insignia of office save for a small medallion that bore the crest of the Elessedils and dangled from a silver chain about his neck. His name was Crispin. He was Captain of the Home Guard, the elite corps of Elven Hunters whose sole duty was the protection of the King. His presence at this Council was something of a mystery; he was not a man from whom Ander would have expected his father to seek advice. But then, his father did not always do what Ander expected.

He paused in his evaluation. With different backgrounds and different personalities, the men his father had gathered were alike only in their absolute loyalty to the old King. Perhaps because of that loyalty, they were men to whom Eventine felt he might safely entrust the decision, however difficult, that must be made concerning Amberle. Perhaps, too, they were here because they were the ones whose counsel he would seek when it came time to defend the Elven homeland.

And that time was near. The inevitability of a terrible struggle between Elves and Demons confronted them at every turn. Each day the Ellcrys weakened further, decay and wilt spreading inexorably through her branches, stripping her of beauty and life, weakening the power that maintained the Forbidding. Each day new reports were received of strange and frightening creatures, things born of nightmares and dark fantasies, prowling the borders of the Westland. Elven soldiers patrolled from the Valley of Rhenn to the Sarandanon, from the Matted Brakes to the Kershalt, and still the number of these creatures grew. It was certain that more would follow, until at last enough had broken free to unite and attack the Elves in force.

Ander rested his elbows on the table and folded his hands together against his forehead, shading his eyes against the light. The Ellcrys was failing so quickly that he wondered whether enough time remained to reach the Bloodfire, even if Allanon had succeeded in his quest. Time! It all came down to that.

The massive doors at the far end of the chamber swung open and six heads turned as one. Allanon strode through, tall and forbidding in his black robes. With him came two smaller figures, cloaked and hooded, their faces hidden.

Amberle! Ander thought at once. One of them must be Amberle!

But who was the second?

All three moved wordlessly to the opposite end of the wide oval table. There the Druid seated his companions, then raised his dark face toward the King.

"My Lord Eventine." He bowed slightly.

"Allanon," the King replied. "You are welcome."

"All are assembled?"

"All," Eventine assured him, then named them one by one. "Please say what you have come to say."

Allanon came forward several paces until he stood midway between the Elves and the two cloaked figures.

"Very well. I would say this once only, so I ask that you listen and heed. The Elven nation stands in grave peril. The Ellcrys is dying. She fails quickly now, more quickly with the passing of each day. As she fails, the wall of the Forbidding weakens. Already the Demons your forefathers imprisoned within begin to break loose once more into your world. Soon all will be free and, once free, they will seek your annihilation."

The Druid came forward a pace. "Do not disbelieve this, Elven Lords. You do not yet appreciate, as I do, the extent of the hatred that drives them. I have seen but a handful of these creatures, a handful that have crossed already through the Forbidding, but even those few conveyed to me the whole of the hatred that has consumed them all. That hatred is awesome. It gives them power—more power than they possessed when they were first shut from the earth. I do not think that you will be able to stand against it."

"You do not know the Elven army!" Pindanon's face was dark.

"Commander." Eventine spoke softly. The old soldier turned at once. "Let us hear him out."

Pindanon sat back, frustration lining his jaw.

"The Ellcrys is the key to your preservation," Allanon continued, ignoring Pindanon. "When the Ellcrys dies, the Forbidding will be lost. The magic that created it will be lost. One thing can prevent that, and one thing only. In accordance with the Elven legend and the laws of magic that gave her life, the Ellcrys must undergo a rebirth. That can be accomplished in only one way. You know it well. A Chosen in service to the tree must carry her seed to the source of all life, the earth's Bloodfire. There the seed must be wholly immersed in the Fire, then returned to the earth where the mother tree roots. Then will there be new life for the Ellcrys. Then will the wall of the Forbidding be restored and the Demons shut once more from the earth.

"Men of Arborlon. Two weeks earlier, having discovered that the Ellcrys was dying, I came to Eventine Elessedil to offer what aid I could. I came too slowly. The Forbidding had begun to weaken already, permitting a few of the Demons imprisoned within to escape. Before I could act to prevent it, they had slain the Chosen, killing them as they slept, killing all they found.

"Nevertheless, I told the King that I would seek to aid the Elves in two ways. First, I would travel to Paranor to the castle of the Druids and there search the histories of my predecessors in an effort to learn the secret of the word 'Safehold.' I have done this. I have discovered where the Bloodfire can be found."

He paused, studying the faces of the men who listened. "I told the King as well that I would seek out one who might bear the seed of the Ellcrys in quest of the Bloodfire, for I believed that such a person existed. I have done this also. I have brought that person with me to Arborlon."

Ander tensed expectantly as a murmur of disbelief rose out of the men assembled. Allanon turned and beckoned to the smaller of the two cloaked figures.

"Come forward."

Hesitantly, the dark form rose, then walked to stand beside the Druid.

"Lower your hood."

Again there was hesitation. The Elves leaned forward impatiently—all but Eventine, who sat rigidly in his chair, hands gripping the carved wooden arms.

"Lower your hood," Allanon repeated gently.

This time the cloaked figure obeyed. Slim brown hands reached from beneath the folds of the robe and pulled back the concealing hood. Amberle's sea-green eyes, frozen with uncertainty, met those of her grandfather. There was an instant of stunned silence.

Then Arion sprang to his feet, livid with rage. "No! No, Druid! Take her out here! Take her back to wherever it was you found her!"

Ander rose halfway out of his chair, shock reflected in his face at his brother's words, but his father caught his arm and brought him back to his seat. Quick, angry comments were exchanged, but the words were lost in a jumbled mix of voices that drowned one another out.

Eventine's hand went up sharply, and the room was still again.

"We will hear Allanon out," he repeated firmly, and Arion slipped back into his chair.

The Druid nodded. "I would ask you all to remember this. Only a Chosen in service may bear the seed of the Ellcrys. When the year began, there were seven. Six are dead. Amberle Elessedil is your last hope."

Arion leaped up. "She is no hope! She is no longer a Chosen!" The Elven Prince's voice was hard and bitter. Kael Pindanon nodded in agreement, distaste showing on his seamed face.

Allanon came forward a step. "You would question whether she is still a Chosen?" The faint, mocking smile passed quickly across his lips. "Know then that she questions this as well. But I have told her, and I have told her grandfather, and now I tell you, that no feelings in this, neither yours nor hers, will determine the truth of what she is. Your feelings are not of any consequence. King's grandchild or outcast from her people—what matter, Elven Prince? Your concern should be with the survival of your people— your people and the peoples of all the Lands, for this danger threatens them as well. If Amberle can be of service to you and to them, then what has gone before must be forgotten."

Arion stood his ground. "I will not forget. I will never forget."

"What is it that you ask of us?" Emer Chios interrupted quickly, and Arion sat down once more.

Allanon turned to face the First Minister. "Just this. Neither you nor I nor Amberle herself has the right to determine whether she is still a Chosen. Only the Ellcrys has that right, for it was the Ellcrys who determined that she should be a Chosen in the first place. Therefore we must know the tree's feelings. Let Amberle go before the Ellcrys; let the Ellcrys decide whether to accept or reject her. If she is accepted as a Chosen, she will be given a seed and she will go in search of the Bloodfire."

"And if she is rejected?"

"Then we had best hope that Commander Pindanon's faith in the Elven army is well placed."

Arion rose once more, ignoring the warning glance his father gave him.

"You ask too much of us, Druid. You ask that we place our trust in one who has already proven untrustworthy."

Allanon's voice was steady. "I ask that you place your trust in the Ellcrys, much as you have done for countless centuries. Let the decision be hers."

Arion shook his head. "No, I sense a game being played here, Druid. The tree speaks to no one; she will not speak to this girl." His angry gaze shifted to Amberle. "If the girl would have us trust her, let her tell us why she left Arborlon in the first place. Let her tell us why she disgraced herself and her family."

Allanon seemed to consider the request for a moment, then finally looked down at the Elven girl beside him. Amberle's face was white.

"I did not mean to bring disgrace to anyone," she replied quietly. "I did what I felt I had to do."

"You disgraced us!" Arion exploded. "You are my brother's child, and I loved my brother very much. I would like to understand what you did, but I do not. What you did brought shame to your family—to all of us. It brought shame to the memory of your father. No Chosen has ever rejected the honor of serving. None! But you, you discarded the honor as if it meant nothing!"

Amberle was rigid. "I was not meant to be a Chosen, Arion. It was a mistake. I tried to serve as did the others, but I could not. I know it was expected of me, but I . . . could not do it."

"Could not do it?" Arion came forward threateningly. "Why? I want to know why. This is your chance to explain—now do so!"

"I cannot!" she answered in a tight whisper. "I cannot. I could not make you understand, not if I wished, not if . . ." She looked imploringly at Allanon. "Why did you bring me back, Druid? This is senseless. They do not wish me here. I do not want to be here. I am frightened, do you understand? Let me return home."

"You are home," the Druid answered gently, a sadness in his voice that had not been there before. He looked over at Arion. "Your questions are pointless, Elven Prince. Give thought to the purpose for those questions. Give thought to their source. Hurt gives way to bitterness, bitterness to anger. Travel too far that road and the way is lost."

He paused, dark eyes fixing those of the Elven Council. "I do not pretend to understand what caused this girl to leave her people. I do not pretend to understand what caused her to choose a life different from that which was offered her in Arborlon. It is not my place to judge her, nor is it yours. What has gone before is done. She has shown courage and resolve in making the journey back to Arborlon. The Demons have learned of her; they have hunted her. They hunt her still. She has endured hardship and risked danger in returning. Should that have been for nothing?"

At the mention of danger to Amberle, alarm flickered briefly in Eventine's eyes. Ander saw it; it was there and then quickly gone.

"You might have taken this girl before the Ellcrys without consulting us," Emer Chios pointed out suddenly. "Why didn't you?"

"Amberle did not wish to return to Arborlon," Allanon responded. "She came because I persuaded her that it was necessary, that she must help her people if she could. Still, she should not be forced to come in secrecy and stealth, but openly. If she is to go before the Ellcrys, it should be with your approval."

His arm slipped about her slender shoulders. She glanced up at him, surprise reflected in her child's face.

"You must make your choice." The Druid's face was impassive. "Which of you will stand beside her, Elven Lords?"

The chamber grew still. Elves and Druid stared wordlessly at one another, eyes locked. All but forgotten by now, the second cloaked form shifted nervously at the far end of the table. The seconds slipped away. No one rose.

Then suddenly Ander Elessedil found Allanon looking directly at him. Something unspoken passed between them, an understanding almost. In that instant Ander knew what he must do.

Slowly he came to his feet.

"Ander!" he heard his brother protest.

He glanced quickly at Arion's dark face, saw the warning mirrored in the other's hard eyes, then looked away again. Wordlessly, he moved around the table until he stood before Amberle. She stared up at him, frightened, like a wild thing poised to flee. Gently he took hold of her shoulders and bent to kiss her forehead. There were tears in her eyes as she hugged him back.

Emer Chios rose. "I do not see that there should be any difficulty in making this decision, my Lords," he adressed them. "Whatever options we may have, we should certainly take advantage of them."

He stepped over to join Ander.

Crispin glanced briefly at Eventine. The King sat rigid, his face expressionless as he met his Captain's eyes. Crispin stood up and crossed to stand beside Ander.

The Council had divided evenly. Three stood with Amberle; three remained seated at the table. Eventine looked at Arion. The Crown Prince of the Elves met his father's gaze squarely, then turned his bitter eyes on Ander.

"I am not the fool that my brother is. I say no."

The King looked at Pindanon. The old soldier's face was hard.

"My trust is in the Elven Army, not this child." Then he seemed to hesitate. "She is your flesh and blood. My vote will be as yours, my King. Cast it well."

All eyes fixed now on Eventine. For an instant he did not seem to have heard. He sat staring at the table before him, a look of sadness and resignation on his face. His hands slid slowly across the polished wooden surface, then locked tightly.

He came to his feet.

"It is decided then. Amberle shall go before the Ellcrys. This Council is adjourned."

Arion Elessedil rose, cast a withering glance at Ander, and stalked from the High Council without a word.

Within the concealing shadow of his cowl, Wil Ohmsford saw the pain and disbelief mirrored in Ander Elessedil's eyes as he stared after his brother. A breach had been opened between these two that would not quickly be closed again. Then the Elven Prince's gaze shifted suddenly to meet his own, and he looked away self-consciously.

Allanon was speaking again, advising those who remained that Amberle would rest a day or two before going to the Ellcrys and that after she had done so they would meet once more. Wil rose, keeping his robes drawn close about him, for Allanon had warned that he was not to reveal himself. The chamber began to empty, and he moved over to stand with Amberle. He saw Ander Elessedil cast a glance back at them, hesitate, then follow the others out. Allanon had drawn Eventine aside and was speaking to him, their words hushed and secretive. There appeared to be some argument between them. Then, with a reluctant nod, the Elven King departed as well. Wil and Amberle were left alone with the Druid.

Allanon beckoned. "Follow me."

Quickly he led them from the council room, ushering them back down the outer hallway until they stood once more in the cool dark of the entry beyond. The Druid paused, listened, and then turned to them.

"Amberle." He waited until her eyes were fixed on his. "I want you to go to the Ellcrys tonight."

Surprise and confusion registered on the Elven girl's face.

"Why?" she asked in disbelief, then quickly shook her head. "No. No, this is too quick! I want time to prepare myself before I do this. Besides, you just finished telling my father and the others that it would be a day or two before I went to her!"

Allanon nodded patiently. "A small but necessary deception. As for preparation, what preparation will you make? This is not a test of skill or endurance; no amount of preparation will help you. Either you are still a Chosen in service to the tree or you are not."

"I am tired, Druid!" She was angry now. "I am tired and I need to sleep! I cannot do this thing now!"

"You must." He paused. "I know that you are tired; I know that you need sleep. But that will have to wait. You must first go to the tree—and you must do so now."

She went rigid at his words, a trapped look springing into her eyes. Then she began to cry, uncontrollably. It was as if everything that had happened—the unexpected appearance of the Druid at her cottage, the news that the Ellcrys was dying and the Chosen slain, the realization that she must return to Arborlon, the harrowing flight north from Havenstead, the confrontation with the Council and her grandfather, and now this— had caught up with her all at once and overwhelmed her completely. All of her defenses seemed to give way. She stood before them, small and vulnerable, sobbing, choking on words that would not come. When Allanon reached for her, she pulled quickly away, stepping apart from them both for several long minutes. Wil Ohmsford stared after her helplessly.

She stopped crying finally, her face still turned away from them. When she spoke, her voice was barely a whisper.

"Is it truly necessary, Allanon—truly necessary—that I go to her tonight?"

The Druid nodded. "Yes, Elven girl."

There was a long silence. "Then I will do so."

Quiet and composed once more, she rejoined them. Without a word, Allanon led them out into the streets of the city.

19

Pale silver moonlight spilled down out of the heavens and washed the summer night. Sweet smells and comforting hums rose out of the dark in slow, dizzying waves that floated and danced in the warm breezes and brushed the hedgerows and stands, the flower banks, and the bushes of the Gardens of Life. Dappled shadows layered the Gardens' colors in oddly knit patterns of black and white. Tiny life forms that awoke with darkness skittered and flew with sudden, invisible bursts that left no trace of their passing.

In the midst of it all, solitary and ignored atop the small hillock that overlooked the homeland of the Elves, the wondrous tree they called the Ellcrys continued its slow, inevitable march toward death. The long journey had begun to take its toll. The perfect beauty that had marked the Ellcrys in health was gone, the perfect symmetry of her form marred and broken. Silver bark peeled away from trunk and limbs, black and rotting, hanging in strips like tattered skin. Blood-red leaves curled tight with wilt, a scattering of those that had already fallen dotting the earth beneath, dried and withered husks, rustling with the wind. Like some weathered scarecrow set upon a pole above the fields, she stood stark and skeletal against the night horizon.

Allanon, Wil Ohmsford, and Amberle stared up at her wordlessly from the base of the rise, cowled faces lifted against the screen of moonlight. For a long time they were still, motionless save for the ripple of cloth garments in the light breezes, silent. When Amberle finally spoke, her whisper filled the quiet with deep, sudden poignancy.

"Oh, Allanon, she looks so sad."

The Druid did not respond, his tall spare frame rigid beneath the robes, his face hidden within the shadow of the cowl. The smell of lilacs wafted past them, lingered momentarily, and was gone. After a moment, Amberle glanced over at the big man, arms folding tightly into her robe.

"Is she in pain?"

The movement of the Druid's head was barely perceptible. "Some."

"She is dying?"

"Her life is ending. Her time is almost gone."

There was a long pause. "Can you do nothing for her?"

"What can be done for her must be done by you." Allanon's deep voice was a gentle murmur.

Amberle's sigh was audible, a shiver of acceptance that passed through her slender body. The seconds slipped away. Wil shuffled his feet wearily, waiting for the Elven girl to come to terms with herself. This was not easy for her. She had not expected even to be here tonight; neither of them had. They had expected that, with the adjournment of the Council, they would be allowed at long last to sleep. There had been no sleep since before their flight into the Valley of Rhenn and their unexpected reunion with Allanon. They were exhausted.

"She is sleeping," Amberle whispered suddenly.

"She will wake for you," the Druid responded.

She does not want this, Wil thought. She has never wanted this. She is not simply unwilling, she is frightened. She said so that first night in the little garden behind her home. Yet she has never said why.

Wil looked toward the summit of the rise. What was it about the Ellcrys that frightened her so?

"I am ready."

She said it simply, her voice calm. Allanon was silent for a moment, then nodded, the cowl bending slightly with his response.

"Then go. We will wait for you here."

She did not move at once, but stood quietly for a moment as if seeking something more from the Druid. But there was nothing more offered. Gathering her robes about her, she started forward, moving up the gentle slope, face lifted toward the still, ragged tree that waited at the top.

She did not look back.

She completed the climb in only moments and stood alone before the Ellcrys. She stood, not yet within reach of the tree, but just beyond, her small form withdrawn into the concealing folds of the dark robe, her arms clenched tightly against her sides. From atop the rise, the Westland lay open to the sweep of the horizon, and she felt small and unprotected. The night breeze blew across her face, laced with the scents of the garden, and she breathed it deeply, steadying herself.

I need only a moment, she told herself. Just one moment.

But she was so afraid!

She still did not understand why this was, not even now, after all this time. She should be able to understand it; she should be able to control it. Yet she could not. That made it all the worse. The fear was unreasoning, senseless, blind. It was always there, lurking in the back of her mind like some beast of prey, slipping from its place of hiding whenever she gave thought to the Ellcrys. She fought against it, struggled determinedly, but it swept through her nonetheless, irrepressible, dark. She had been able to suppress it in Havenstead, for in Havenstead the cause was distant and past. But now, returned once more to Arborlon, standing less than a dozen feet away, remembering the touch of the Ellcrys . . .

She shuddered at the memory. It was the touch she really feared. Yet why should that be? No harm came from it, no injury. It served only to allow the Ellcrys to communicate her thoughts through images. But there was this sense of something more that had always come with the touch, ever since that first time the Ellcrys had spoken with her. Something.

Her thoughts scattered at the sound of an owl's soft hoot. She was aware that she had been standing there for several minutes and that the two men waiting below must be watching her. She did not want that.

Quickly, she began to walk around to the far side of the tree.

Druid and Valeman watched silently as the dark figure of the Elven girl circled the Ellcrys and disappeared from view. They remained standing a moment longer; but when she did not reappear, Allanon seated himself wordlessly on the grass. Wil paused, then sat down next to him.

"What will you do if the Ellcrys decides that she is no longer one of the Chosen?"

The Druid did not turn his head. "That will not happen."

The Valeman hesitated a moment before speaking again.

"You know something about her that you have not told either of us, don't you?"

Allanon's voice was cold. "No. Not in the sense that you mean."

"But in some sense."

"What must concern you, Valeman, is seeing that nothing happens to her after you leave Arborlon."

The way he said it left Wil with the very distinct impression that this particular subject was closed. The Valeman shifted his weight uncomfortably.

"Can you tell me something else, then?" he asked a moment later. "Can you tell me why she is so afraid of the Ellcrys?"

"No."

Wil flushed heatedly within his cowl. "Why not?"

"Because I am not sure that I understand it myself. Nor do I think that she does. In any case, when she is ready for you to know about it, she will tell you herself."

"I doubt it." Wil slouched forward, arms resting loosely on his knees. "She does not seem to think much of me."

Allanon did not respond. They sat in silence for a time, glancing periodically toward the summit of the rise and the solitary tree. There was no sign of Amberle. Wil glanced over at the Druid.

"Is she safe up there alone?"

The mystic nodded. Wil waited for him to explain why she was safe, but he did not offer an explanation. The Valeman shrugged. Being this close to her, he must have some means of seeing to it that she was protected, he decided.

At least he hoped so.

For a long time Amberle did not move. She could not. Her fear had paralyzed her. She stood rigid and chilled not five feet from the nearest branches, staring hypnotically at the Ellcrys. Within her, the fear ran like liquid ice, numbing even her thoughts. She lost all sense of time, of place, of everything but her inability to take those last few steps forward.

When at last she did take them, it seemed that it was someone else who took them for her. She remembered only the distance between herself and the Ellcrys closing and then disappearing altogether. She was beneath the canopy of the tree, lost in shadow. The night breeze died into stillness, and the cold within her turned to heat.

Wordlessly, she dropped to her knees amid the clutter of dead leaves and broken twigs that blanketed the ground, her hands folding tightly in her lap. She waited.

Moments later, a ragged branch dipped downward and wrapped gently about her shoulders.

—Amberle—

The Elven girl began to cry.

There had been silence between them for quite some time when Wil suddenly recalled something odd that Allanon had said earlier. He had determined that he would ask nothing further of the Druid following their last exchange, but his curiosity got the better of him.

"Allanon?"

The Druid looked at him.

"Something is bothering me." He took a moment to arrange his words. "When you told Amberle that we must come here tonight, she reminded you that you had informed the Elvens at the High Council that she would be given a day or two to rest. You answered her by saying that what you told them was a necessary deception. What did you mean by that?"

Moonlight revealed the familiar mocking smile as it slanted across the mystic's lean face.

"I was wondering when you would get around to that question, Wil Ohmsford." He laughed softly. "Your inquisitiveness is all-encompassing."

Wil grinned ruefully. "Do I get an answer to my question?"

Allanon nodded. "An answer that will not please you. The deception was necessary because there is a spy within the Elven camp."

The Valeman went cold. "How do you know that?"

"Logic. When I arrived at Paranor, the Demons were waiting for me. Waiting for me, Valeman—I was not followed. That suggests rather strongly that they knew in advance that I would be coming there. How did they know that? For that matter, how did they know about me in the first place? Only Eventine knew that I had returned to the Four Lands. Only Eventine knew of my plans to travel to Paranor; I told him in confidence that I would go there to study the Druid histories in an effort to discover the location of Safehold. Eventine was cautioned to say nothing and would have done exactly that."

He paused. "That leaves only one possibility. Someone listened in on our conversation—someone who had reason to betray us to the Demons."

Wil looked doubtful. "But how could that have happened? You said yourself that no one even knew that you had returned to the Four Lands before you spoke to Eventine."

"That puzzles me, also," the Druid admitted. "The spy must be someone with easy access to the King, someone who would know everything that he is about. One of his household staff, perhaps."

He shrugged. "In any case, it was fortunate that I did not mention to the King where Amberle could be found or the Demons would almost certainly have reached her before I did." He paused, black eyes fixing on the Valeman. "They would have reached you, as well, I imagine."

Wil felt his skin crawl. The suggestion was a thoroughly disconcerting one, even now. For the first time since he had met Allanon, he was grateful that the Druid was so closemouthed about what he knew.

"If all this is so, then why did you tell the Elves at the High Council so much?" he asked. "If there is a spy, isn't there a rather good possibility that he may discover everything that was said at that meeting?"

The Druid leaned forward. "A very good possibility. In fact, I intend to make certain that he does. That is the reason for the deception. You see, the Demons already know that we are here, and they know why we are here. They know who I am; they know who Amberle is. They do not yet know who you are. All this they have discovered from my conversation with Eventine and from what they have seen in pursuing us from Havenstead. We have told the Elves at the High Council nothing new—except for one small item. We have told them that Amberle will rest for several days before she goes to the Ellcrys. So, for the next several days, at least, the Demons will expect us to do nothing. That deception, I hope, will give us a small but very useful advantage."

"What kind of advantage?" Wil frowned. "What do you have in mind, Allanon?"

The Druid pursed his lips. "As to that, Wil, I am afraid that I will have to ask you to be patient for a bit longer. But I promise that you will have your answer before the night is done. Fair enough?"

There was nothing particularly fair about any of this, Wil thought glumly. Still, there was no point in pressing the matter. When Allanon had made up his mind, Wil knew that that was the end of it.

"One thing more." The Druid put a cautionary hand on his shoulder. "Say nothing of this to Amberle. She is frightened enough as it is, and there is no reason that she should be frightened further. Let this remain a secret between you and me."

The Valeman nodded. That much, at least, they could agree upon.

Only minutes later, Amberle appeared suddenly from beneath the shadow of the tree. She stood for a moment silhouetted against the night sky, hesitated, then started toward them. She walked slowly, carefully, as if uncertain of her movements, hands held clasped together against her breast. Her cowl was lowered, her long, chestnut hair fanning out behind her in the breeze. As she neared them, they could see plainly her stricken face. It was pale and drawn and streaked with tears, and fear reflected brightly in her eyes.

She came up to them and stopped. Her slender form was trembling.

"Allanon . . . ?" she cried softly, choking on his name.

The Druid saw that she was on the verge of collapsing. He reached for her at once, took her in his arms and held her close against him. She allowed herself to be held this time, crying soundlessly. For a long time he held her, all the while saying nothing. Wil watched uncomfortably and felt generally useless.

After a time, the crying stopped. Allanon released the Elven girl and stepped back. Her face remained lowered for a moment, then lifted to his.

"You were right," she whispered.

Clasped hands came away from the folds of her robe and slowly opened. Nestled in her palms, like a perfectly formed silver-white stone, was the seed of the Ellcrys.

20

Moments later, Allanon led them from the Gardens. Cowls drawn close about their faces and cloaks laced tight, they slipped through the gates and past the sentries of the Black Watch and started back toward the city. The Druid did not offer any explanation as to where he was taking them, and they did not ask. They walked in silence, Allanon a step or two ahead, Wil and Amberle following. Both were exhausted. The Valeman glanced often at the Elven girl, more worried about her than he cared to admit even to himself, but she gave little indication of her emotional state, and he caught only an occasional glimpse of her face within the covering of the hood. Once he asked quietly if she was all right, and she nodded back to him without speaking.

A short time afterward, they found themselves approaching the manor house of the Elessedils. Beckoning wordlessly, Allanon led them onto the grounds surrounding the darkened home, directing them through a screen of pine that bordered the south lawn, then along a series of hedgerows to a small alcove and a pair of floor-length glass windows draped in heavy shadow. Standing before the doors, Allanon tapped softly on the glass. There was a moment's wait, then the curtains covering the window moved slightly. A latch within was released, and the doors swung open. Quickly Allanon motioned them through, glanced furtively about, and followed, closing the doors behind him.

They stood for a few seconds in darkness, listening to the faint sound of footfalls as someone moved slowly about the room. Then a light was struck to a candle's wick. Wil found that they were in a small study, burnished oak from walls and shelving gleaming in the candle's dim flame, soft tracings of color from leather-bound books and tapestries visible through the heavy shadows. At the far side of the little room, an aged wolfhound raised his grizzled head from a small earthen-colored rug on which he lay and thumped his tail in greeting.

Eventine Elessedil placed the candle on a small worktable and turned to face them.

"Is everything arranged?" Allanon's deep voice broke the stillness.

The old King nodded.

"And your household?" The Druid was already moving across the room to the single door that led into the rest of the home. He opened it, looked through briefly, then closed it again.

"Everyone sleeps but Dardan and Rhoe, and they stand watch at my bedroom door, believing me asleep as well. There is no one here but old Manx."

The wolfhound glanced over at the mention of his name, then lowered his head between his paws and closed his eyes.

Allanon walked back across the room. "Then we can begin."

He motioned Wil and Amberle to take chairs about the worktable, drawing a third chair over for himself. The Valeman sat down wearily. Amberle started forward, then stopped, her eyes on her grandfather. Eventine looked back at her, hesitated, then moved quickly to embrace her. The Elven girl went rigid for a moment, then her arms went about him.

"I love you, grandfather," she whispered. "I missed you."

The old King did not speak, but nodded into her shoulder, one hand coming up to stroke her hair. Then he took her head gently in his hands and tilted it back so that she was facing him.

"What has happened is behind us, Amberle. Forgotten. There will be no more harsh words between us. This is your home. I want you here with me, with your family."

The Elven girl shook her head sadly. "I have spoken with the Ellcrys, grandfather. She has told me that I am her Chosen. She has given to me her seed."

The old man's face went pale, and his eyes dropped. "I am sorry, Amberle. I know that you wish it could be otherwise. Believe me, I wish it could be otherwise, too."

"I know you do," she replied, but there was despair in her eyes.

She separated from him and seated herself at the table with Allanon and Wil. The King remained standing for a moment, his eyes staring over at his granddaughter. There was a lost and frightened look to him that suggested a child strayed. Slowly he recovered himself, then moved to sit with the others.

Allanon leaned forward, hands folding carefully atop the table.

"Eventine and I agreed at the close of the High Council that we would meet in secret later this night. What is said here shall remain between the four of us and no other. Time slips away from us, and we must act quickly if we are to save the Elven people. The Ellcrys is failing. Soon the Demons contained within the Forbidding will break through into the Four Lands. Eventine and I shall be there to meet them when they do. But you, Amberle, and you also, Wil, must go in search of the Bloodfire."

He turned to the Elven girl. "I would go with you if I could. I would go with you if there were any possible way to do so, but there is not. One of the Demons that has already broken through the Forbidding, as well as some still locked within possess powers that your grandfather and the Elven people cannot stand against without my help. It will be my task to shield the Elves from those powers. Sorcery to withstand sorcery. It must be so.

"But in my place, I send Wil Ohmsford, and I have not chosen lightly to entrust your care and safety to him. It was his grandfather who went with me in search of the Sword of Shannara, who found it, and who then stood alone against the Warlock Lord and saw him destroyed. His great-uncle Flick once saved your grandfather's life. Wil has the strength of character that marked both men; he has their sense of honor. You have seen that he holds the Elfstones that I once gave to his grandfather. He will protect you as I would. He will stand with you, Amberle—he will not fail you."

There was a long moment of silence. The Valeman felt embarrassed by the Druid's words—embarrassed and uneasy. He was not so sure of himself. He glanced quickly at Amberle and found her staring back at him.

"You are a Chosen in service to the Ellcrys," Allanon continued, drawing the Elven girl's eyes back to meet his own. "Though we all might wish it were otherwise, the matter has been settled as we agreed that it should be. You are the last of the Chosen, and therefore the last hope of your people. You alone can restore the Forbidding. A terrible responsibility, Amberle, but it belongs to you. If you fail, Demon and Elf will do battle until one or both have been utterly destroyed. The Ellcrys has given you her seed, and so you must take it in quest of the Bloodfire. That will not be easily done. The Bloodfire lies within a place called Safehold, and Safehold is a part of the old world. That world is gone, forever changed. Down through the ages, the place called Safehold has been all but forgotten. Even the Ellcrys no longer recognizes the path that leads there. If not for the Druid histories, Safehold might have been irretrievably lost to us. Yet the histories are a link between past and present. I have read them and know where Safehold lies."

He paused. "It lies within the Wilderun."

No one said a word. There was no need. Even Wil Ohmsford, a Southlander and a Valeman who until now had never set foot in the Westland, had heard of the Wilderun. Buried within the forests that lay south of the Elven homeland, it was a treacherous and forbidding stretch of wilderness virtually encircled by mountains and swamp. Fewer than half-a-dozen hamlets could be found there, and those were peopled by thieves, cutthroats, and outlaws of every conceivable sort. Even they seldom strayed far from their villages or the few well-worn trails that crisscrossed the region, for in the timber beyond, the rumors said, were creatures no man would care to encounter.

Wil took a deep breath. "You wouldn't happen to know where within the Wilderun we are to find the Bloodfire?"

Allanon shook his head. "I cannot be sure. Even the Druid histories refer in part to the geography of the old world, and the landmarks that existed then are gone. You will have to rely on the Elfstones."

"I thought as much." The Valeman sagged back in his chair. "Use of the Elfstones will tell the Demons where we can be found."

"Unfortunately true. You will have to exercise great discretion, Wil. I will relate to you what the Ellcrys told the Chosen about Safehold before they were slain—what she later told also to me. This may help you in your search. The Bloodfire lies within a wilderness with mountains and swamp all around—obviously the Wilderun, as the Druid histories record. Now here is the rest of what she said. There is a deep mist that comes and goes. Within the wilderness can be found a lone peak; beneath the peak is a maze of tunnels that burrow deep within the earth. Somewhere within the maze is a door made of glass that will not break. Behind the door you will find the Bloodfire."

He cocked his head reflectively. "As you can see, the general description of the Wilderun remains surprisingly accurate, even after the passage of so many years and the cataclysmic changes wrought in the geography of the earth by the Great Wars. Perhaps the balance of the description remains accurate as well. Perhaps the Bloodfire may still be found beneath a lone peak, within a maze of tunnels." He shrugged. "I would give you more help if I had it to give, but I do not. You must do the best you can with that."

Wil managed a faint, if somewhat forced, smile of encouragement. He did not dare look over at Amberle.

"How do we reach the Wilderun?" he asked.

The Druid glanced questioningly at Eventine, but the Elven King appeared preoccupied. At last, distracted by the silence, he looked over at Allanon and nodded absently.

"Everything has been arranged."

The Druid seemed to hesitate, then turned to Amberle. "Your grandfather has selected Captain Crispin, who commands the Home Guard, to be your guide and protector on this journey. Crispin is a very resourceful and courageous soldier; he will serve you well. He has been instructed to choose half-a-dozen Elven Hunters as your escort. Six is a small number, but a small number may be best in this case. It will attract far less attention than a large command and it should enable you to travel more swiftly.

"The plan that the King and I have settled on is this. You will be taken from the city in secret; the means have been left to Captain Crispin. Only Crispin will be aware of your mission. He and the Elven Hunters under his command will go with you as far as you need them. All will have been instructed that no harm is to befall you, that they are to do whatever is necessary to protect you."

"Allanon."

It was Eventine who spoke, glancing over suddenly, a worried look on his face. His penetrating blue eyes found those of the Druid.

"There is something I have not yet told you. I did not speak of this before because we had only those few moments at the close of the Council. But I think something should be said now. There is reason for concern in this venture beyond the obvious danger of being tracked by the Demons who have pursued you this far."

He leaned forward, arms crossing loosely on the table to support his weight. His face, caught in the dim light of the candle, seemed very old.

"You know how the Chosen died—perhaps Wil and Amberle do not." His gaze shifted. "They were torn apart, mangled almost beyond recognition."

Horror reflected in the faces of the Elven girl and the Valeman. The King put his hand gently on his granddaughter's shoulder.

"I do not tell you this to frighten you more, Amberle, nor you, Wil, but because of this." He looked back at Allanon. "Since you have been gone from Arborlon, there have been more deaths like those of the Chosen. A great many deaths. Whatever it was that killed them has been roaming the surrounding country, systematically destroying everything and everyone it encounters, man or beast, young or old. Over fifty Elves have died—all in the same manner, all by being ripped apart. Three nights ago, an entire Elven patrol was waylaid and destroyed. Six armed men. A week earlier, an army compound at the north edge of the city was invaded and twenty men were killed while they slept. There has been an increasing number of Demons sighted in the Westland since the Ellcrys began to fail and more than a few unpleasant pitched fights as well—but nothing on this order, nothing as deliberate and premeditated. This creature knows what it is about; it kills with purpose. We have tried without success to track it. We cannot find it. We have not even seen it. No one has. But it is out there—and it hunts us."

He paused. "It was sent once, Allanon, for the purpose of destroying the Chosen. It did so—all but one. It may be that it will be sent again."

Amberle had gone white. Allanon rubbed his bearded chin thoughtfully.

"Yes, there was such a Demon in the old days," he mused. "A Demon that killed out of instinctive need. They called it a Reaper."

"I don't care what they called it," Wil spoke up suddenly. "What I want to know is how to avoid it."

"Secrecy," the Druid offered. "However vicious and cunning this Demon, it will have no more reason than its brethren to suspect that you have left Arborlon. If it believes that you are still here—if they all believe that you are still here—they will not be looking for you elsewhere. Perhaps we can give them that impression."

He turned to Eventine. "The time will come very soon now when the Ellcrys can no longer maintain the wall of the Forbidding with sufficient strength to contain the remainder of the Demons still imprisoned within. When that time comes, the Demons will concentrate their strength at the wall's weakest point and break free. We cannot wait for that to happen. We must find the place where they will attempt their crossover and do what we can to prevent it. Even if we fail, we can fight a delaying action which will slow them in their march on Arborlon. They will try to march here, for they will seek to destroy the Ellcrys. They must. They cannot tolerate her. Remember that while she was strong, she was anathema to them. But as she weakens, she becomes less so. Once they have broken through her wall, they will move quickly to destroy her. We must do what we can to prevent that. We must give Amberle time to reach the Bloodfire and return again. We must keep the Demons from Arborlon until then.

"So." He let the word hang for a moment in the silence of the little room. "We shall deceive the Demons who are already through the Forbidding by acting as if preparations to seek the Bloodfire are yet to be completed. We shall make it appear as if you have not left. The Demons know that it was I who brought Amberle here; they will expect me to be with her when she leaves. We can make use of that. We can focus their attention on me. By the time they realize that they have been misled, you should be well beyond their reach."

Unless their spy is more resourceful than you anticipate, Wil wanted to say; but he decided not to.

"It all sounds very promising," he said instead. "That seems to settle everything except the matter of when we should leave."

The Druid leaned back in his chair. "You will leave at dawn."

Wil stared at him in disbelief. "At dawn? Tomorrow?"

Amberle sprang to her feet. "That is impossible, Druid! We are exhausted! We have not slept in almost two days—we have to have more than a few hours' rest before setting out again!"

Allanon held up his hands. "Peace, Elven girl. I understand this as well as you. But consider. The Demons know that you have come here for the purpose of carrying the seed of the Ellcrys to the Bloodfire. They know that you will attempt to leave the city, and they will be watching closely. But they will not be watching as closely now as they will in a day or two. Do you know why? Because they will expect you to rest first. That is exactly why you must leave at once. Surprise offers you your best chance to slip past them."

Understanding flickered in Wil's eyes. This was the advantage that the Druid had hoped his deception at the High Council might yield them.

"There will be sufficient rest for you after you are gone from the city," Allanon promised. "Two days of travel will enable you to reach the Elven outpost in Drey Wood; you can catch up on your lost sleep there. But delay in Arborlon is dangerous. The quicker you are gone from here, the better your chances."

Wil hated to admit it, but there was logic in the Druid's argument. He glanced quickly at Amberle. She stared down at him silently for a moment, frustrated and angry, then turned back to Allanon.

"I want to see my mother before I leave."

The Druid shook his head. "That is not a good idea, Amberle."

Her jaw tightened. "You seem to think that you have the final say in whatever I wish to do, Druid. You don't. I want to see my mother."

"The Demons know who you are. If they know also of your mother, they will expect you to go to her. They will be waiting for just that. It is dangerous."

"Just being here is dangerous. Surely you can find a way for me to spend five minutes with my mother." Her eyes dropped. "Do not be so foolish as to suggest that I should see her when I return."

There was an unpleasant moment of silence. Allanon's dark face turned suddenly expressionless, as if he were afraid he might reveal something he wished to remain hidden. Wil did not miss the change, and it puzzled him.

"As you wish," the Druid agreed. He rose. "Now you must sleep while you can. We must go."

Eventine stood up with him, turning to face his granddaughter.

"I am sorry that Arion spoke so harshly at the Council," he apologized, looking as if he had something more to say, but could not. He shook his head. "I think that in time he will come to understand as I did . . ."

He trailed off awkwardly, then put his arms around Amberle and kissed her cheeks.

"If I were not so old . . ." he began emotionally, but the girl put her fingers to his mouth to stop him. She shook her head.

"You are not so old that you do not see that you are needed here more than you are needed to go with me." She smiled, and there were tears in her eyes as she kissed him back.

Feeling a bit self-conscious, Wil stepped away from the table and moved quietly over to the sleeping Manx. The aged wolfhound heard his approach. One eye stared up at him questioningly. On impulse, Wil reached down to pet the dog, but Manx gave a low, barely audible growl of warning. Wil drew back.

Unfriendly beast, the Valeman thought to himself.

He returned to the others. Eventine shook hands with him and wished him well. Then with Amberle beside him, Wil followed Allanon back through the floor-length windows into the night.

21

The Druid took them to a small cottage nestled on a forested slope at the northern edge of the city amid a cluster of similarly structured homes. There was nothing to set this particular cottage apart from any of the others, and this suggested to Wil the principal reason for its selection. Though unoccupied when they entered, it was fully furnished and had been lived in recently. Allanon did not offer to explain what had become of the owners. He entered the cottage as if it were his own, moved through the darkness of a living room to light several oil lamps, then carefully drew closed all the curtains that decorated the cottage windows. Having checked once through the remaining rooms while Wil and Amberle sat waiting at a small table graced with freshly cut flowers and embroidered mats, he returned momentarily with bread, cheese, fruit, and a pitcher of water. They ate in silence, Wil consuming a full meal despite the late hour, Amberle eating almost nothing. When dinner was finished, Allanon led the Elven girl to a small bedroom at the rear of the home. A single shuttered window stood latched and barred behind drawn curtains. The Druid checked the fastenings thoroughly, then nodded. Wordlessly, Amberle moved to the feather bed. She was so tired that she did not even bother to undress, but simply kicked off her boots and fell wearily across the covers. She was asleep almost immediately. Allanon paused long enough to place a light blanket over the exhausted girl, then stepped from the room, closing the door noiselessly behind him.

Alone in the living room, Wil Ohmsford stared through the curtained windows into the darkness beyond, where the lights of the city proper winked back at him like fireflies in the forest shadows. He glanced about restlessly as the Druid reappeared.

"We have to talk, Allanon."

The big man did not look surprised.

"Still more questions, Wil Ohmsford?"

"Not exactly." The Valeman looked uncomfortable.

"I see. Well then, why don't we sit down?"

Wil nodded, and they moved over to take chairs across from one another at the little table where they had eaten their meal. Once seated, the Valeman seemed uncertain as to how to proceed. Allanon regarded him expressionlessly, waiting.

"Something happened to me when I tried to use the Elfstones on that Demon in the Tirfing—something that I do not understand," Wil began finally, avoiding the other's dark eyes. "I had almost decided against saying anything to you about it because I did not want you to think that I was looking for an excuse not to make the journey into the Wilderun."

"That would have been foolish." Allanon spoke quietly. "Tell me what it is that happened."

The Valeman did not seem to hear him. "The only reason I decided to speak about it was that I grew concerned for Amberle's safety if I remained quiet. If I am to be her protector, then I cannot afford to play games with my pride."

"Tell me what happened," the Druid repeated.

Wil looked up uneasily. "I will explain it in the best way I can. As I said, when the Demon came at me and I tried to use the Elfstones, something inside of me resisted. It was like some sort of blockage, like a wall that had imposed itself between me and the Elfstones so that I could not call upon them for aid. I held them out before me and tried to reach down into them, to call forth their power, but nothing happened. In that instant, I was certain that you had been wrong in your belief that I could use the Stones as my grandfather had done. I thought that I was going to die. But then, just before the Demon reached me, the wall within me seemed to break apart, and the power of the Stones flared out and destroyed the creature."

He paused. "Since then, I have thought carefully about what happened. At first I decided that I simply had not understood how to use the Elfstones, that it was my inexperience or confusion that caused the resistance. But I no longer believe that. It was something different. It was something about me."

The Druid stared back at him wordlessly for several minutes. One hand toyed idly with the small black beard, pulling at it, twisting it. Finally the hand moved away.

"You will remember that I told you that the Elfstones were an old magic, a magic from the days before Man, a magic that belonged to the age when the faerie people ruled the earth and magic was commonplace. There were many different Elfstones then, and they served many different purposes. Their colors identified their uses. The blue Elfstones, such as those that you hold, were the seeking Stones. Possession of the blue Elfstones enabled the holder to find that which was hidden from him merely by willing that it be so—for example, the Bloodfire for which you will search. Other Elfstones exhibited other characteristics. All possessed the common characteristic of offering the holder protection against other magics and things created of magic and sorcery. But the extent of that protection—indeed, the extent of the power of the Stones—was dependent entirely on the strength of character of the holder. The Stones were grouped in sets of three; there was a reason for this. Each Stone represented a part of the holder: one Stone for the heart, one Stone for the body, one Stone for the mind. For the magic to be given life, the three would have to act in concert—three individual strengths joining as one. The success of the holder in employing the Elfstones was a measure of his ability to unite those strengths."

He spread his hands upon the table. "The Elfstones have another characteristic, Wil—one basic to their use. The Elfstones are an Elven magic; they were created by Elven wizards for the Elves only. They have been passed from generation to generation, family to family, hand to hand—but always by Elves to Elves, for none other could ever use the Stones."

A look of disbelief crossed the Valeman's face. "Are you trying to tell me that I cannot use the Elfstones because I am not an Elf?" he exclaimed.

Allanon shook his head. "It is not as simple as that." He leaned forward, choosing his words carefully. "You are partially an Elf, Wil. It is so with your grandfather as well. But he is half Elf, having been born the child of an Elf and a Man. You are something quite different. Neither your mother nor your grandmother was an Elf; both were of the race of Man.

All that is Elf in you is that part inherited from your father by way of your grandfather."

"I do not see what difference any of that makes," Wil persisted. "Why should I have difficulty using the Elfstones when my grandfather did not? There is at least some of his Elven blood in me."

"It is not your Elven blood that would cause you difficulty," the Druid replied quickly. "It is your Man blood. You have the physical characteristics of your grandfather—that part of you marks your Elven heritage unmistakably. But that is only a small part of the whole; the greater part of you is Man. Much of the Elf has been bred out of you."

He paused. "Understand, when you attempt to use the Elfstones, only that small part of you that is Elf can link you to their power. The balance of your heart and mind and body resists the intrusion of the magic. It forms a block against it. The three strengths are weakened, for the strength of each is diminished to that which is solely due to your Elf blood. That may be what you have experienced in your use of the Stones—a rejection by that considerable part of you that is Man of the Elven magic."

Wil shook his head in confusion. "But what of my grandfather? He did not experience this rejection."

"No, he did not," Allanon agreed. "But your grandfather was half Elf. The Elf half dominated and gave him command over the power of the Elfstones. The resistance that he experienced was barely measurable. For you, it is a different matter entirely. Your link with the power of the Elfstones is more tenuous."

Wil stared at him. "Allanon, you knew this when you came to me in Storlock. You had to know. Yet you said nothing. Not one word. Not one."

The Druid's expression did not change. "What was I to say, Valeman? I could not determine the extent of the difficulty that you might encounter in using the Elfstones. Any use of the Stones depends greatly on the character of the holder. I believed you strong enough to overcome any resistance within yourself. I still believe that. Telling you then of the problem would have caused you considerable doubt—doubt that might have resulted in your death in the Tirfing."

The Valeman rose wordlessly, a stunned look on his face. He walked away from the table several paces, then turned back again.

"This could happen again, couldn't it?" he asked quietly. "Every time I try to use the Elfstones."

The Druid nodded. Wil studied the dark face silently for a moment, the implications of this admission whirling through his mind like blown leaves.

"Every time," he repeated. The leaves froze sharply. "Then there could come a time when the resistance within me might prove too great. There could come a time when I would call upon the power of the Elfstones and they would not respond."

Allanon took a long time to answer. "Yes, that is possible."

Wil sat down again, the disbelief in his face changing now to horror.

"How can you entrust Amberle's protection to me, knowing that?"

The Druid's hand came down on the table like a hammer. "Because there is no one else!" His dark face flushed with anger, but his voice remained calm. "I suggested to you once before that you should start believing in yourself. I will suggest it one time more. We are not always properly equipped to face the difficulties life places in our path. It is so now. I wish that my power was such that your aid were not necessary in this matter; I wish that I could give you something more with which to protect the Elven girl and yourself. I wish much that cannot be. I brought you to Arborlon because I knew that I alone could not hope to save the Elves from the danger that threatens them. We are both inadequate in this, Wil Ohmsford. But we must do the best we can with what we are. The Druids are gone; the Elven magics of the old world are lost. There is only you and me. There are only the Elfstones that you hold and the magic that I wield. That is all, but that must do."

Wil held his gaze steady. "I am not afraid for me; I am afraid for Amberle. If I should fail her . . ."

"You must not fail her, Valeman." The Druid's voice was hard, insistent. "You must not! You are all that she has."

Wil straightened. "I may not be enough."

"Not enough?" The words were laced with sarcasm. Allanon shook his head. "Your grandfather once believed as you did, not so many years ago. He could not understand how I thought it possible that he might possess the means of destroying a being as awesome as the Warlock Lord. After all, he was only one insignificant little Valeman."

There was a long silence. Valeman and Druid stared wordlessly at one another in the stillness, the flicker of the oil lamp flame dancing across their faces. Then Allanon's black form rose, slowly and deliberately.

"Believe in yourself. You have already used the Elfstones once; you have experienced and overcome the resistance within you and summoned the magic. You can do so again. You *will* do so. You are a son of the house of Shannara; yours is a legacy of strength and courage stronger than the doubt and fear that makes you question your Elven blood."

He leaned down. "Give me your hand."

The Valeman obeyed. Allanon clasped it tightly in his own.

"Here is my hand and thus my bond. Here is my oath to you. You shall succeed in this quest, Wil Ohmsford. You shall find the Bloodfire and bring safely home again the last of the Chosen, she who shall restore the Ellcrys." His voice was low and commanding. "I believe that, and so must you."

The hard, dark eyes penetrated deep into the Valeman's own, and Wil felt himself laid bare. Yet he would not look away. When he spoke, his words were almost a whisper.

"I will try."

The Druid nodded. He was wise enough to leave it at that.

Eventine Elessedil remained in the small study for a long time after the other three had departed. He sat in silence at the fringe of the circle of light cast by the solitary flame of the oil lamp, a rumpled figure formed of shadows and gathered robes. Collapsed in the familiar embrace of his favorite chair, a leather-bound furnishing worn with age and shaped with use, the King of the Elves stared unseeing at the bookcases, paintings, and woven tapestries that lined the wall across from him, thinking of what had been and what was yet to be.

Midnight came and went.

Finally the King rose. Gathering his scattered thoughts and half-drawn plans as he went, he extinguished the oil lamp and moved wearily through the study door into the hallway beyond. There was nothing more to be done this night, nothing more that he could expect to accomplish. By dawn, Amberle would be on her way toward the Wilderun. His concern must no longer be with her; it must be with his people.

Down the length of the darkened hallway the old King passed, anxious now for the rest that sleep would bring him.

All the while, the eyes of the Changeling watched him go.

In the deep blackness of the forest south of the city of Arborlon, the Dagda Mor rose up from the stone on which he had been seated. Cruel red eyes reflected the Demon's sense of exhilaration. This time there would be no mistake, he thought. This time he would make certain that they were all destroyed.

His humped form slouched forward. First he would see to the Elven girl.

One clawed hand beckoned, and from out of the shadows stepped the Reaper.

Dawn broke misted and iron-gray across Arborlon, and the sky was filled with rolling black clouds. By the time Wil and Amberle had dressed and eaten, the rains had begun, a spattering of drops that turned quickly to a steady downpour, thrumming against the cottage roof and windows. Thunder rolled in the distance, long booming peals that shook the forestland.

"You will not be so easily found in this," Allanon observed with satisfaction and took them out into the storm.

Wrapped in long, hooded traveling cloaks that covered woolen tunics and breeches and high leather boots, they trailed after the Druid as he led them through sheets of driving rain down wooded pathways that skirted the westernmost edge of the city along the broad bluff of the Carolan. Barely able to find their way through the dawn gloom, Valeman and Elven girl followed closely. Fragmented images of cottages, and fence lines, and gardens slipped into view and away again, appearing miragelike through the haze of the storm, then melting back into it once more. A sharp, chill wind blew rain into their faces through the folds of their cowls, and they bent their heads against its force. Boots sloshed wetly through puddles and gullies of surface water that formed before them as they passed along the rutted forest trail.

At the far side of the city, Allanon abruptly departed from the pathway and led them toward a solitary stable that sat back against a hillside to their left. Double wooden doors stood slightly ajar, and they stepped quickly inside out of the weather. Cracks in shuttered windows and ruined walls filled the interior of the structure with gray, hazy light. Rows of stalls and a high loft stood empty, layered in shadows and dust. The air had a stale, pungent smell. They paused momentarily to brush the water from their cloaks, then moved toward a solitary door at the rear of the stable. Almost immediately they were flanked by two heavily armed Elven Hunters, who appeared soundlessly from out of the gloom to either side. Allanon took no notice of them. He walked directly to the door without turning. Tapping softly, he placed one hand on the rusted iron handle and looked back at Amberle.

"Five minutes. That is all the time we can spare."

He pushed the door open. Valeman and Elven girl stared in. A small tack room lay beyond. Crispin waited there and with him an Elven woman, cloaked and hooded. The woman slipped the hood to her shoulders, and Wil was startled to find that her face, though older, mirrored Amberle's. Allanon had kept his promise; it was the Elven girl's mother. Amberle went to her at once, held her, and kissed her. Crispin stepped from the room and closed the door softly behind him.

"You were not followed." The Druid made it a statement of fact.

The Captain of the Home Guard shook his head. He was dressed as were the other Elven Hunters, clothed in gray and brown colored garments that were loose and comfortable and blended well with the forestland. Beneath a cloak draped across his shoulders, he wore a brace of long knives belted at his waist. Across his back were strapped an ash bow and short sword. Rain had dampened his light brown hair, giving him a decidedly boyish look, and only the hard brown eyes suggested the boy in him was long since gone. He nodded briefly to Wil in greeting, then stepped over to speak with the Elves. One turned and disappeared wordlessly back out into the rain, the other into the loft. They moved on cat's feet, silent, fluid.

The minutes slipped away. Wil stood silently beside Allanon, listening to the drumming of the rain against the stable roof, feeling the dampness of the air work through him. At last the Druid stepped back to the tack room door and tapped softly once more. A moment later it opened, and

Amberle and her mother reappeared. Both had been crying. Allanon reached for the Elven girl's hand and held it in his own.

"It is time to go now. Crispin will see you safely out of Arborlon. Your mother will remain here with me until you are gone." He paused. "Keep faith in yourself, Amberle. Be brave."

Amberle nodded silently. Then she turned back to her mother and embraced her. As she did so, Allanon drew Wil aside.

"I wish you good fortune, Wil Ohmsford." His voice was barely audible. "Remember that I depend on you most of all."

He gripped Wil's hand and stepped back. Wil stared at him a moment, then turned as he felt Crispin's hand on his shoulder.

"Stay close," the Elf advised, and started toward the double doors.

Valeman and Elven girl moved after him wordlessly. He stopped them as he reached the doors, whistling sharply to signal the other Elven Hunters. The call was answered almost immediately. Crispin slipped through the doors into the rain. Tightening their cloaks about them, Wil and Amberle followed.

They hastened quickly down the rise to the pathway, backtracked in the direction from which they had come for some fifty feet or so, then turned down a new trail that ran east toward the Carolan. In a matter of seconds, three Elven Hunters had fallen in behind them like shadows slipped from the forest. Wil glanced back once at the solitary barn, but it had faded already into the mist and the rain.

The trail narrowed sharply now, and the woods closed in about them. Slipping through dark, glistening trunks and sagging boughs heavy with rain, the six cloaked figures followed the rutted pathway as it began to slope downward. The path ended at a long, rambling flight of wooden stairs that wound down out of the Carolan through the tangle of the forest. Far below and barely visible through clouds of thinning mist lay the gray ribbon of the Rill Song. To the east, meadowland and forest mixed in patchwork fashion across the sweep of the land.

Crispin motioned them forward. It was a long and somewhat arduous descent, for the steps were rain-slicked and narrow, and the footing was uncertain. A guide rope, frayed and rough, hung loosely from posts fastened to the stairs, and Wil and Amberle gripped it cautiously as they went. Hundreds of steps later the stairway ended, and they started along a new pathway that disappeared into a short stretch of pine. Somewhere ahead they could hear the sullen rush of the river, rain-swollen and sluggish, its roar blending with the deep howl of the wind coming down off the heights.

When the forest broke in front of them several hundred yards further on, they found themselves at a heavily wooded cove that opened through a wall of great, drooping willows and cedar into the main channel of the Rill Song. Within the shelter of the cove, anchored beside a creaking, badly rotted dock, rode a solitary barge, its deck laden with canvas-covered crates and stores.

Crispin signalled for them to halt. The Elven Hunters behind him faded into the trees like ghosts. Crispin glanced about, then whistled sharply. A response sounded almost at once from aboard the barge, then another from the head of the cove. Nodding to Wil and Amberle to follow, the Captain of the Home Guard left the cover of the forest. Bent against the force of the wind, the three moved quickly onto the dock, boots thudding hollowly, then aboard the waiting barge. An Elven Hunter appeared suddenly from beneath the canvas, pulling back a section hastily, to reveal an opening between the stacked crates. Crispin motioned for the Valeman and the Elven girl to enter. They did so, and the canvas dropped silently behind them.

Inside, it was sheltered and dry. The darkness confused them at first, and they stood uncertainly, feeling the rocking of the boat beneath them. But a faint sliver of light filtered through where the canvas dropped to the deck, and slowly their eyes adjusted. They discovered that a space had been cleared to form a small cabin within the center of the crates. Foodstuffs and blankets lay neatly stacked against the far wall, and there were weapons bundled carefully in leather casings in one corner. Stripping their cloaks away, they stretched them out to dry next to the stores and sat down to wait.

Moments later they felt the barge lurch free of the old dock and begin to move with the current. Their journey to the Wilderun was under way.

They spent all of that day and the next concealed within their little cabin, forbidden by Crispin to make even the briefest appearance on deck. The rain continued to fall in a steady drizzle, and the land and the sky remained gray and shadowed. Occasional glances through the flaps of the canvas covering showed to them the land through which they traveled, a mix of forestland and rolling hills for the most part, although, at one point during their journey, a series of high bluffs and ragged cliff sides hemmed in the Rill Song for several hours as she churned her way sluggishly southward. Through it all, mist and rain masked everything in shimmering gray half-light and gave the impression of some vaguely remembered dream. The river, swollen with the rains, roiling with limbs and debris, rocked and buffeted the barge.

Sleep was impossible. They took what rest they could get, brief naps that left them disoriented when they awoke and always tired still. Muscles and joints ached and stiffened, and the constant rolling motion of the boat took away what little appetite they might have been able to muster.

Time seemed to drag endlessly. They spent it alone with each other, save for the few occasions when Crispin or one of the other Elven Hunters came in out of the weather. When the Elves ate or slept was anybody's guess, for it appeared that most of their time was spent navigating the river and keeping close watch over their passengers. There was always at least one Elf on guard directly outside the entry to their little cabin. They came to know the names after a time, some when one ducked into the cabin momentarily, some by conversations that took place without. A few they could put faces to, such as Dilph, the small, dark Elf with the friendly eyes and the iron grip, and Katsin, the big, rawboned Hunter who never spoke at all. Kian, Rin, Cormac and Ped remained little more than voices, though they came to recognize Kian's quick, deep oaths of irritation and Ped's cheerful whistling. They saw more of Crispin than any of the others, for the Elven Captain made regular visits to inquire of their needs and to inform them of their progress. But he never stayed for more than a few minutes, always excusing himself politely but firmly, to return to the Elves under his command.

In the end, it was the talks with each other that made the confinement, the dreariness, and the loneliness of the journey bearable. The talks began out of mutual need, Wil thought, but cautiously and awkwardly, for they still regarded each other with a strong sense of uncertainty. The Valeman was never sure why the Elven girl chose to discard the shell into which she had withdrawn for much of their journey north from Havenstead, but her attitude seemed to undergo a surprising transformation. Before, she had been reluctant to discuss much of anything with Wil. Now she was eager to converse with him, drawing out by her questions stories of his early years in Shady Vale, the years when his parents had been alive, then later when he had lived with his grandfather and Flick. She wanted to know of his life with the Stors and the work that he would be doing when he left their village again and returned to the Southland as a Healer. Her interest in him was genuine and pervasive, and it whispered of need. Nor did they speak only of him. They spoke of her as well, of her childhood as the granddaughter of the King of the Elves, of growing up the only child of Eventine's lost son. She told Wil of the Elven way of life, of their strong belief in giving back to the land that nourished and sheltered them something of themselves, something of their lives. She exchanged with him ideas on the ways in which the races might better serve the needs of one another and of the land. Each argued gently and persuasively for understanding, compassion, and love, discovering as they did so, with some surprise, that their beliefs were very much the same, that their values were values shared.

Carefully, by cautious degrees, they bound themselves, each to the other. Deliberately, they avoided saying anything of the journey on which they had been sent, of the danger that threatened the Elven people and of their own responsibility for putting an end to that danger, or of the ancient and mysterious tree they called the Ellcrys. There would be time enough later for that; this time could be better used. It was an agreement arrived at not by words spoken, but by simple understanding. They would speak openly of the past and the future; they would say nothing of the present.

The talks gave them comfort. Without, the rains fell unceasingly, the gray haze of the storm washed the land, and the Rill Song rumbled in discontent on its passage south. Shut within their dark concealment, buffeted by winds and water, lacking sleep and appetite, they might easily have given way to apprehension and doubt. But the talks gave them comfort, born of feelings shared, of companionship, and of understanding. It gave them a sense of security in each other's presence, muting at least in part the unpleasant sensation that the whole of their world was passing away and that, with that passing, their lives would be forever changed. It gave them hope. Whatever was to befall them in the days to come, they would face it together. Neither would be forced to stand alone.

Sometime during those gray, rain-filled hours, a strange thing happened to Wil Ohmsford. For the first time since that night in Storlock when he had agreed to travel to the Westland with Allanon, he found himself caring, deeply and compellingly, about what was to become of Amberle Elessedil.

It was late afternoon on the second day of their journey when they arrived at Drey Wood. The heavy rains had diminished to a slow drizzle, and the air had gone sharply chill with the approach of nightfall. Gray dusk shrouded the forestland. From out of the west, a new bank of threatening black clouds had begun to roll toward them.

Drey Wood was a stretch of dense forest covering a series of low rises which ran eastward from the left bank of the Rill Song to a line of high, craggy bluffs. Elms, black oaks, and shag-bark hickories towered over a choked tangle of scrub and deadwood, and the forest smelled of rot. A dozen yards inland from the riverbank, there was nothing but blackness, deep and impenetrable. Rain falling into the trees in a steady patter was the only sound that broke the stillness.

The Elven Hunters guided the unwieldly barge into a shallow bay where a docking slip jutted outward from the bank, waves breaking against its pilings and washing over its wooden slats. On shore, just within the fringe of the woods, stood a weathered, empty cabin, its single door and windows closed and shuttered. Easing the barge against the pilings, the Elves fastened the mooring lines and stepped off.

Crispin brought Wil and Amberle out from their cabin, carefully admonishing them to keep their hooded cloaks securely in place. Stretching gratefully, they joined him on the docking slip. The Rill Song splashed up at them, and they hastened ashore.

Dilph moved to the cabin, opened its door, peered momentarily about, and withdrew. He shook his head at Crispin. The Elf Captain frowned and glanced about guardedly.

"Is something wrong?" Wil asked.

Crispin looked away. "Just being cautious. The main post is half-a-mile inland, built into the trees at the top of a rise to permit an overview of the surrounding country. I thought that the Hunters stationed there would have seen us coming, but the weather might have prevented that."

"What about this cabin?" the Valeman wanted to know.

"One of several watches the post keeps. Usually there is someone on duty." He shrugged. "With the weather this bad, though, the commander of the post may have pulled in all one-man sentries. He was not told that we would be coming and had no reason to expect us."

He glanced back at the forest. "Excuse me for a moment, please."

He signalled the other Elves to join him, and they huddled quickly, their voices low and furtive.

Amberle stepped close to Wil. "Do you believe him?" she whispered.

"I'm not sure."

"I am. I think something is wrong."

The Valeman did not reply. Already the conference was ending. Katsin had moved back to the dock to stand close to the moored barge. Cormac and Ped had taken up positions at the edge of the forest. Crispin was talking now to Dilph, and Wil edged closer to hear what was being said.

"Take Rin and Kian and scout to the outpost." The Elf Captain glanced over his shoulder at the Valeman. "If all is well, come back for us."

Wil made a quick decision and stepped forward. "I'm going, too."

Crispin frowned. "I don't see any reason for that."

Wil stood his ground. "I think I can give you one. Protecting Amberle is my responsibility as well as yours; that is why Allanon sent me with her. Exercising that responsibility is a matter of judgment, Captain, and in this instance I think I should scout ahead with Dilph."

Crispin thought it over for a moment, then nodded. "As long as you do exactly as Dilph tells you."

Wil turned back to Amberle. "Will you be all right?"

She nodded, then watched wordlessly as he followed the Elven Hunters into the darkness of the trees and disappeared from view.

Like ghosts, the four slipped through the sodden curtain of the woods, their steps soundless. Mist trailed about them in streamers thick with dampness, and rain fell softly. Rows of dark trunks and masses of scrub and thicket passed away as the forest wound on over steep rises and ridge lines. The minutes slipped by, and Wil Ohmsford felt himself grow increasingly uneasy.

Then Kian and Rin split off to either side, disappearing into the trees, and Wil found himself alone with Dilph. An empty clearing appeared suddenly from out of the gloom, and Dilph dropped to a crouch, motioning Wil down behind him. The Elf pointed upward into the trees.

"There," he whispered.

High in the interwoven branches of two great oaks sat the Elven outpost. Rain and mist shrouded the buildings and their connecting passageways. Neither oil lamp nor torchlight burned from within. Nothing moved. Nothing sounded. It was as if the post were deserted.

But that should not be.

Dilph eased forward slightly, peering left through the gloom until he caught sight of Rin, then right until he found Kian. Both knelt within the cover of the trees some thirty yards to either side, watching the silent post. Dilph whistled softly to catch their attention. When he had it, he signalled for Kian to go in for a closer look. Rin he sent left to scout the perimeter of the clearing.

Wil watched Kian sprint to the base of the oaks which supported the post, find the concealed footings in one massive trunk, and begin to climb. Then, with Dilph leading, Wil started right, staying just within the fringe of the clearing, eyes searching the forest for some sign of the missing Elves. The woodland was sodden and murky, and it was difficult to see much of anything through the tangle of scrub.

The Valeman glanced back to the post. Kian had almost reached the lowest building, a small command hut set just below the main living quarters. Rin was nowhere to be seen. Wil was still looking for the Elf when he took a step forward and tripped, sprawling facedown across the broken, lifeless body of an Elven Hunter. He sprang back to his feet in horror, eyes sweeping the gloom about him. To his left lay two more bodies, limbs twisted, bones shattered and crushed.

"Dilph!" he whispered harshly.

At once the Elf was beside him. Pausing only an instant to survey the grisly scene, Dilph stepped to the edge of the clearing and whistled sharply. Rin appeared from out of the forest, a startled look on his face. At the rail of the platform surrounding the command hut, Kian looked down. Frantically, Dilph motioned them back.

But almost immediately, Kian disappeared. Something seemed to reach out and snatch him from view, so suddenly that it appeared to an astonished Wil as if he had simply evaporated. Then Kian's scream sounded, short and strangled. His body flew out of the trees, sailing like a fallen limb into the rain, tumbling lifelessly to the ground below.

"Run!" Dilph cried to Wil and bolted into the trees.

The Valeman froze for a single, terrible instant. Kian was dead. Almost certainly, the entire Elven outpost of Drey Wood was dead as well. All of his thoughts scattered, save one—if he did not get to Amberle in time, she would be dead as well. Then he ran, darting like some stricken deer through the tangle of the forest, leaping and twisting through scrub and deadwood, desperate to reach the barge and the unsuspecting Elven girl whose life he guarded. Somewhere off to his right he could hear Dilph, fleeing as he did, and further back Rin. He knew instinctively that something pursued them. He could not see it, could not hear it, but he could sense it, terrible and black and pitiless. Rain streaked his face and ran into his eyes, clouding his vision as he sought to avoid fallen logs and thorny brush. Once he went down, but he was up again almost immediately, never slowing, his lean form straining to put further distance between himself and his unseen pursuer. His chest heaved with the effort, and his legs ached. There had been few times in his life when he had been afraid, but he was afraid now. He was terrified.

Rin's scream sounded sharply through the stillness. The thing had him. Wil gritted his teeth in fury. Perhaps the Elves at the barge would be warned now. Perhaps they would cast off at once, so that, even if he too were caught, at least Amberle would escape.

Branches and leaves tore at him like clutching hands. He looked for Dilph, but the Elf was no longer in view. Alone, he ran on.

Dusk began to slip rapidly over Drey Wood, turning gray afternoon to night. The drizzle which had fallen at a steady rate for most of the day changed abruptly to a heavy downpour, the wind gusting sharply as a new mass of black stormclouds rolled across the sky. Thunder rumbled in the distance, deep and ominous. On the banks of the Rill Song, the Elven Hunters and their charge pulled rain-soaked cloaks closer about their chilled bodies.

Then the scream sounded from somewhere within the wood, high and short, almost lost in the heavy rush of the wind. For an instant no one moved, staring wordlessly at the dark wall of trees. Then Crispin was barking orders, sending Amberle back to the barge and into hiding once more, calling Ped and Cormac to him. Weapons drawn, the three Elven Hunters backed to the end of the dock, scanning the hazy tangle of the forest. Aboard the barge, Katsin loosened the mooring lines and stood ready to cast off.

Amberle huddled for a few moments within the dark of the cabin, listening to the sound of the wind and the rain without. Then abruptly she rose, pushed aside the canvas flap, and stepped back out into the weather. Whatever the consequences, she could not stay hidden in that cabin without knowing what was going on out here. She edged her way along the stacked crates until she was able to gain the dock. Katsin had looped the lines that moored the barge several turns about a piling; with the loose ends gripped firmly, he stood braced to release them on command. He gave Amberle a sharp look when he saw her, but the girl ignored it. At the edge of the bank, several feet from the dock, the remaining Elven Hunters faced the wood, sword blades glistening dully with rain.

Abruptly a disheveled figure broke from the trees not twenty yards downriver, stumbled, and pitched forward. When he scrambled up again, they saw that it was Dilph.

"Get away!" he cried in warning, his voice ragged. "Quick, get away!"

He started toward them, lost his footing once more and went down.

Crispin was already moving. A sharp command sent Ped and Cormac to the barge as he raced for the fallen Dilph. Barely slowing, he snatched the other man up in his arms, flung him over one shoulder and streaked back toward the waiting boat.

Amberle peered through the mist and rain into the forest. Where was Wil Ohmsford?

"Drop the lines!" Crispin was shouting.

Katsin did as he was told, then hurriedly shoved Amberle aboard the barge where Ped and Cormac already waited. A second later Crispin had Dilph aboard as well, and the heavy craft began to drift.

Then suddenly Wil appeared, thrusting clear of the forest and racing for the dock. Amberle saw him, started to cry out, and then went cold. In the shadow of the trees behind the fleeing Valeman, something huge followed in pursuit.

"Look out!" she screamed in warning.

Spurred by her cry, the Valeman gained the dock in a single bound, sprinted its length without slowing, and sprang to reach the drifting barge, barely catching its deck with an outstretched foot. He would have tumbled into the river but for the Elven Hunters, who reached out and pulled him to safety.

The barge swung into the main channel of the Rill Song and began to pick up speed. Katsin seized the tiller, bringing the cumbersome boat about. As Wil stumbled back against the crates and sank down in exhaustion, Amberle quickly removed her own cloak and wrapped it tightly about him. Close at hand, Crispin bent over Dilph. Wind and the roar of the river scattered Dilph's words.

". . . Dead, all of them—smashed, broken like twigs . . . like the patrol in Arborlon, like . . . the Chosen." His mouth opened and he choked for breath. "Kian, too . . . and Rin, both dead . . . the Demon caught them . . . it was waiting for us. . . ."

Amberle didn't hear the rest. Her eyes were locked on Wil's. With terrible certainty, each had realized the truth.

It was waiting for them. The Demon.

Allanon had given it a name. He had called it the Reaper.

It was midnight when Crispin took the barge ashore again. Immediately below Drey Wood, the Rill Song swung westward on its twisting journey to the Innisbore. When the Elves finally guided the barge into a narrow, heavily wooded inlet that broke south from the main channel, they found themselves at the northernmost edge of the Matted Brakes, miles from where they had intended to leave the river. The rains had diminished once more to a soft drizzle that hung in the chill air like fine mist. Heavy clouds obscured moon and stars, and the night was so black that even Elven eyes could see no further than a dozen paces. The wind had died away into stillness, and a deep haze had settled over the whole of the land.

The Elven Hunters grounded the barge on a low sand bar at the head of the inlet, pulled her nearly clear of the river and made her fast. Moving safely and quietly, they scouted the land about them for several hundred yards in all directions, determined that nothing threatened them, then reported back to Crispin. The Elf Captain decided that it would be pointless to attempt further travel until morning. Wil and Amberle were told to remain in their cabin. Wrapped in warm blankets to ward off the cold, free for the first time in two days from the river's discomforting pitch and roll, they fell asleep at once. The Elves ringed the barge and its sleeping passengers, standing watch in shifts. Crispin posted himself beside the cabin entry and settled in for the night.

At dawn, the little company rose, packed what provisions and weapons they could carry, then freed the barge from its moorings and let the river carry it away. It disappeared swiftly, twisting in the pull of the current. As soon as it was gone, they struck out across the Matted Brakes.

The Brakes were lowlands choked with scrub and brush and dotted with stagnant lakes, bramble runs, and sink holes. They split apart the vast Westland forests from the banks of the Rill Song to the wall of the Rock Spur, a maze of wilderness through which few travelers dared to journey. Those who did risked losing themselves hopelessly in a tangle of thicket and clustered bogs shrouded in mist and darkness. Worse, they risked an encounter with any number of unpleasant denizens of the Brakes, creatures that were vicious, cunning, and indiscriminate in their choice of prey. Not much of anything lived within these lowlands, but what did live there understood well that all creatures were either hunter or hunted and that only the former could survive.

"If there were another alternative, we would not come this way," Crispin advised Wil, dropping back momentarily to share his thoughts with the Valeman. "If all had gone as planned, we would have taken horses from the outpost south along the western edge of the Brakes to the Mermidon, then ridden west into the Rock Spur. But Drey Wood has changed all that. Now we have to be concerned as much with what may follow as with what may lie ahead. The one virtue to the lowlands is that they will hide any trace of our passing."

Wil shook his head doubtfully. "A thing like the Reaper won't give up easily."

"No, it will keep hunting us," the Elf agreed. "But it won't catch us like that a second time. It was waiting for us at Drey Wood because it knew we were coming. I don't know how it knew, but it did." He glanced at the Valeman, but Wil said nothing. "In any case, it won't know where we are now. If it expects to find us again, it will have to track us. That might have been done easily enough if we had stayed within the forestland, but it will be very difficult here. It will have to determine first where we left the River; that alone could take days. Then it will have to follow us into the Brakes. But the Brakes swallow you up without a trace; this marsh hides tracks ten seconds after you've made them. And we've got Katsin, who was born in this country and has crossed the Brakes before. The Demon, however powerful it may be, is in strange country. It will have to hunt by instinct alone. That gives us a very definite edge."

Wil Ohmsford did not agree. Allanon had thought that the Demons would not track him when he fled Paranor. But they did. The Valeman had thought they would not find him again once Amberle and he were carried to the far shores of the Rainbow Lake by the King of the Silver River. But again they did. Why should it be any different this time? The Demons were creatures of another age; their powers were the powers of another age. Allanon had said that himself. He had said as well that the one who led them was a sorcerer. Would it be so difficult for them to track a handful of Elven Hunters, a young girl, and a Valeman?

Still, there was nothing to be done about it, the Valeman knew. If the Reaper could track them in the Brakes, it would track them anywhere. Crispin had made the right decision. The Elven Hunters possessed considerable skill; perhaps that would be enough to see them safely through.

The Valeman was far more concerned about another unpleasant possibility, and since their encounter with the Reaper at Drey Wood he had been able to think of little else. The Reaper had known that they were coming to that Elven outpost. It had to have known, because it had lain in wait for them. Crispin was right about that. But there was only one way it could have known—it must have been told by the spy concealed within the Elven camp, the spy that Allanon had worked so carefully to deceive. And if the Demons knew of their plan to travel south to the Elven outpost at Drey Wood, then how much more about this journey did they know? It was altogether possible, the Valeman realized, that they knew everything.

It was a chilling possibility, one that he would have preferred not to consider further, but which seemed more and more plausible as he weighed the facts. Allanon had been certain that there was a spy within the Elven camp. Somehow the spy had managed to overhear their conversation in Eventine's study. He could not conceive of how that could have been accomplished, but he was certain that it had. Drey Wood had been mentioned; that would account for the Reaper. But the Wilderun had also been mentioned. That meant that the Demons knew exactly where they were going after Drey Wood; and if the Demons knew that, then regardless of the route the little company chose to follow or the deceptions they chose to employ to elude would-be pursuers, chances were excellent that when the company arrived at the Wilderun there would be Demons waiting for them.

The thought lingered with Wil Ohmsford all that day as the little company slogged through the marshy tangle of the Brakes. Thorny brush and saw grass cut them at every passing, mist turned their clothing damp and chill, and mud and foul-smelling water seeped through their boots and filled their nostrils with its stench. They walked separate and apart from each other, speaking little, eyes peering guardedly through rain and swirling haze as the land passed away about them in a changeless wash of gray. By nightfall, they were exhausted. They made their camp in a sparse outcropping of brush that grew up against a low rise. There was too much risk in a fire, so they wrapped themselves in blankets that were damp with the lowland's chill and ate their food cold.

The Elven Hunters finished quickly and prepared to stand watch in shifts. Wil had just completed his own small meal of dried meat and fruit, washed down with a little water, when Amberle came over and huddled down beside him, her child's face peering out at him from within the folds of the blanket she had pulled up about her head. Stray locks of chestnut hair fell loosely over her eyes.

"How are you holding up?" he inquired.

"I'm fine." She had the look of a lost waif. "I need to talk."

"I'm listening."

"I have been thinking about something all day."

He nodded wordlessly.

"The Reaper was waiting for us at Drey Wood," she said quietly. She hesitated. "You realize what that means?"

He said nothing. He knew what was coming next. It was as if she had read his mind.

"That means that it knew we were coming." She spoke the words he was thinking. "How could that have happened?"

He shook his head. "It just did."

That was the wrong answer, and he knew it. Her face flushed.

"Just as the Demons found us at Havenstead? Just as they found Allanon at Paranor? Just as they seem to find us everywhere we go?" Her voice stayed low, but there was anger in it now. "What kind of a fool do you think I am, Wil?"

It was the first time that she had ever used his given name, and it startled him so that for a moment he simply stared at her. There was hurt and suspicion in her eyes, and he saw that he must either tell her what Allanon had directed him to keep secret or lie to her. It was an easy decision to make. He told her about the spy. When he had finished, she shook her head reprovingly.

"You should have told me before now."

"Allanon asked me not to," he tried to explain. "He thought that you already had enough to worry about."

"The Druid does not know me as well as he thinks. Anyway, you should have told me."

He no longer felt like arguing the point. He nodded in agreement.

"I know. I just didn't."

They were silent for a moment. One of the Elves on watch appeared, wraithlike, out of the mist, then disappeared into it again. Amberle stared after him, then glanced over at Wil. Her voice floated out of the folds of her hood, her face masked in shadow.

"I'm not angry. Really, I'm not."

He smiled faintly. "Good. This marsh is dismal enough as it is."

"I would have been angry if you had not told me the truth just now."

"That was why I told you."

She let the matter drop. "If this spy overheard what was said in my grandfather's study that night before we left Arborlon, then the Demons know where we are going, don't they?"

"I imagine so," he replied.

"That means they know about Safehold as well; they know everything the Ellcrys told the Chosen, because Allanon repeated it to us. They have as much chance of finding the Bloodfire as we do."

"Maybe not."

"Maybe not?"

"We have the Elfstones," he pointed out, wondering as he did so if it made any difference that they did. After all, he did not really know if he could use the Stones again. The thought depressed him.

"Who could have gotten close enough to hear what we were saying?" She frowned and looked at him.

He shook his head wordlessly. He had been wondering that, too.

"I hope that my grandfather is all right," she murmured after a minute.

"I would guess that he is better off than we are." Wil sighed. "At least he has someplace warm to sleep."

He hunched his knees up to his chest, trying to find an extra bit of warmth. Amberle moved with him, shivering with the cold. He let her settle close against him, bundled in her coverings.

"I wish this were finished," she whispered distantly, almost as if she were saying it to herself.

The Valeman grimaced. "I wish it had never begun."

She turned her head to look at him. "As long as we are wishing, I wish you would be honest with me after this. No more secrets."

"No more secrets," he promised.

They were quiet after that. A few moments later, Amberle's head slipped down against his shoulder and she was asleep. The Valeman did not disturb her. He left her that way and stared out into the dark, thinking of better times.

For the next two days, the little company trudged through the gloom of the Matted Brakes. It rained most of the time, a steady drizzle interspersed with heavy showers that drenched further an already sodden earth and left the travelers cold and miserable. Mist hung overhead and swirled thick across ridge tops and still, marshy lakes. The sun remained screened by banks of stormclouds, and only a faint lightening of the sky for several hours near midday gave any indication of its passing. At night, there was only the impenetrable dark.

Travel was slow and arduous. In single file, they worked their way across the tangle of the Brakes, through bramble thickets that sword blades could barely hack apart, past bogs that bubbled wetly and sucked from sight everything that came within their grasp, and around lakes of green slime and evil smells. Deadwood littered the ground, mingling with pools of surface water and twisting roots. The vegetation had a gray cast to it that muted its green and left the whole of the land looking sick and wintry. What lived within the Brakes stayed hidden, though faint sounds skittered and lurched in the stillness, and shadows slipped like wraiths through the rain and the gloom.

Then, shortly before noon on the third day, they arrived at a massive body of stagnant water, choked with roots and deadwood that protruded like the earth's broken bones from amid a covering of lily pads rippling gently with the rainfall. The shores of the lake were massed thick with bramble runs and scrub as far as the eye could see. Mist rolled across the surface of the water in a deep haze, and there was no sign of the far shore.

It was apparent immediately that any attempt at circling the lake would require several hours of backtracking to escape the heavy brush. There was only one other alternative open to them, and they took it. Katsin led them, as he had for most of their journey through the Brakes, with the other four Elven Hunters split in pairs so that two walked before Wil and Amberle and two followed. Cutting through the scrub that blocked their passage, they stepped onto a narrow bridge of earth and roots that jutted out from the shoreline and disappeared into the mist. If they were lucky, the bridge would span to the far shore.

They proceeded cautiously, picking their way along the uneven course, carefully staying back from the mire that lay to either side. The mist closed about them almost at once, and the land behind faded into it. The minutes slipped away. Rain blew sharply into their faces, caught on a sudden gust of wind. Then the mist cleared unexpectedly, and they saw that their bridge dropped away into the lake not a dozen yards ahead. Beyond lay a huge mound of earth encrusted with rock and vegetation. The far shore of the lake was nowhere to be seen. They had reached a dead end.

Crispin started forward for a closer look at what lay beyond the mound of earth, but Katsin's hand came up sharply in warning. He glanced back quickly at the others of the little company, placing a finger to his lips. Then he pointed to the mound, his hand moving to a long ridge that curved downward into the lake. At its tip, steam rose in small jets from two ragged holes that protruded from just above the water line.

Breathing holes!

Wordlessly, Crispin motioned them back. Whatever it was that lay sleeping out there, he had no intention of disturbing it.

But he was too late. The creature had sensed them. Its bulk heaved up suddenly out of the lake, showering them with stagnant water. It huffed loudly as yellow eyes snapped open from beneath the covering of lily pads and vines. Writhing feelers flared from its mud-covered body, and a broad, flat snout swung toward them, jaws gaping wide in hunger. It hung suspended above the lake for an instant, then sank quietly beneath the water and was gone.

Wil Ohmsford had only a glimpse of the monstrous thing. Then he was fleeing through the mist behind Ped and Cormac, pulling Amberle with him, struggling to keep his footing on the rutted path. He heard Katsin, Dilph and Crispin coming up quickly behind him and risked a quick glance back to see if the creature had followed them. In the same moment that he looked back, his foot caught and he went down, dragging Amberle with him.

The fall saved both their lives. Out of the mist rose the creature, massive jaws sweeping across the narrow bridge before them like a fisherman's net. Cries of terror sounded from Ped and Cormac as the thing caught them up and pulled them into the lake. The huge bulk settled downward into the water and disappeared.

Wil froze in horror, staring fixedly into the mist where the monstrous thing had gone. Then Crispin leaped forward, catching Amberle up over his shoulder and sprinting for the safety of the shore. Katsin snatched up Wil before the Valeman could think to act on his own and followed. Dilph raced after them, short sword drawn. In seconds, they were stumbling back through the wall of scrub and bramble. Far back from the water's edge, they collapsed in the muddied earth, their breathing heavy in the stillness as they listened for the sounds of any pursuit. There were none. The creature was gone.

But now they were only five.

24

Nightfall drifted down across the Westland in gossamer sheets of gray dusk, and the chill of evening settled into the forestland. The clouds which had masked the summer sky for nearly seven days began to break apart so that thin strips of blue glimmered brightly in the fading sunlight. In the west, the horizon turned scarlet and purple, the glow falling softly across the rain-drenched woodlands.

From beneath the smudge of haze that shrouded the Matted Brakes appeared the five who remained of the little company from Arborlon, surfacing like lost souls out of the netherworld. Haggard and worn, their hands and faces covered with welts and bruises, their clothing soiled and torn and hanging damply from their bodies, they had the look of beggars. Only their weapons suggested that they were something more. Trudging wearily through the last row of thicket, past the last clump of bramble, they scrambled up a small rise of loose rock and scrub and came to a ragged halt before the twin towers of the Pykon.

It was an awesome, spectacular sight. Straddling the broad channel of the Mermidon as the river wound its way eastward toward the grasslands of Callahorn, the Pykon formed a natural gateway into the sprawling, humpbacked mountain range the Elves had named the Rock Spur. The Pykon stood solitary and aloof, twin pinnacles of rock towering into the skyline like massive sentinels set guard over the land below. Ridge lines and crevices scarred the surface in a maze of creases and splits that shadowed the stone cliffs like the lines on an oldster's seamed face. A pine forest grew at the north base of the peaks, thinning as the slope grew steeper, until all that remained was scrub and wildflowers that spotted the dark rock with brilliant dabs of color. Higher up, pockets of snow and ice glistened dazzling white.

Crispin held a hurried conference. In their meanderings through the tangle of the Brakes, they had drifted further eastward than he had intended, coming out here rather than at the edge of the Rock Spur. It might seem logical that they should skirt the Pykon, then travel upriver along the Mermidon until it intersected the Rock Spur. But the entire journey would have to be made on foot, and it would take them at least two days more to get that far. Worse, they would risk leaving a trail that could be followed. The Elf Captain thought that he had a better alternative. Nestled deep within the Pykon, bridging a massive split in the near peak, was an Elven fortress that had stood abandoned since the Second War of the Races. Crispin had been there once years ago, and if he could find it again, there were passages leading from that ancient stronghold downward through the mountain rock to the Mermidon where it split apart the twin peaks. There were docks on the river and a boat as well, perhaps; or if not, there would be wood enough to construct one. From there, the Mermidon flowed eastward for several miles, but then doubled back on itself to where the Rock Spur bordered on the impenetrable mire of the Shroudslip. If they were to utilize the river as their means of travel, the journey could be completed in half the time it would take them if they went on foot—a day, perhaps less than a day. There was another reason for going this way, the Elf Captain added. The river would hide all trace of their passing.

This last argument decided them. None of them had forgotten the encounter with the Reaper at Drey Wood. The Demon would still be searching for them, and anything they might do to thwart that hunt must be tried. It was quickly agreed that it would be best to follow Crispin's advice.

Without wasting any further time, they began the climb onto the Pykon. They passed quickly through the scattered pines that grew at the base of the near peak, reaching the lower slopes as the afternoon sun dipped down behind the forest horizon and night descended. A half-moon began to brighten in the east and clusters of stars winked into view against the deep blue of the sky, lighting the way for the five as they hiked upward onto the rock. It was a still, peaceful night, filled with sweet smells carried from the forest on a gentle south wind. A pathway was found, broad, well-trodden, twisting its way through clumps of boulders and past craggy drops, winding steadily upward into the shadow of the mountain. Behind them, the forestland began to drop away, revealing the dark vista of the Brakes as they spread northward below them toward the thin line of the Rill Song.

It was nearing midnight when the Elven fortress at last came into view. The great stronghold sat back within a deep crevice, a twisting maze of parapets, towers, and bulwarks rising up darkly against the moonlit stone of the cliffs. A long, winding stairway ran up the slope to a gaping entry in the castle's outer wall. Ironbound wooden doors, weathered and split with age, their hinges rusted fast, stood open against the night. Watchtowers perched like squat beasts of prey atop massive stone-block walls, their narrow windows black and vacant. Spikes protruded from the crest of the parapets; high within the cluster of peaked turrets, chains that had once carried the standards of the Elven Kings clanged sharply against iron poles. From somewhere above the fortress, deep within the mountain's crags, sounded the piercing cry of a night bird, its shriek rising until it matched the shrill pitch of the wind, hanging momentarily, then fading into echo.

The five who remained of the little company from Arborlon climbed the steps to the entrance of the abandoned fortress and stepped cautiously through. A high, tightly enclosed walkway ran back to a second wall. Weeds and scrub had grown through the stone block that formed the walk. The five started forward, boots echoing hollowly in the stillness of the passage. Bats flew from chinks and cracks, their leathery wings flapping wildly. Small rodents scurried across the broken stone in flashes of sudden movement. Cobwebs hung like sheets of thin, fine linen, clinging in streamers to the company's clothing as they passed.

At the end of the walkway, an entry opened into a huge courtyard littered with debris and filled with the whine of the wind. To either side of an encircling battlement, a broad stairway wound upward toward a balcony that fronted the main tower of the ancient fortress, a monstrous walled citadel that rose hundreds of feet into the night sky, its rugged stone curving back into the shadow of the mountain. Windows marked the rising floors of the tower, overlooking the tangled blackness of the Matted Brakes. At the center of the balcony, a deep alcove sheltered a single wooden door. Below, leading directly from the courtyard into the tower, was a second door. Both stood closed.

Wil glanced about uneasily at the walls and battlements that loomed over him, dark and sinister and crumbling with age. The wind howled in his ears and blew dirt in his eyes, and he tightened the cowl of his cloak about his face for protection. He did not like this place. It frightened him. It was a haven for the ghosts of dead men, a haven in which the living were intruders. He looked at Amberle and saw the same uneasiness reflected in her face.

Crispin had dispatched Dilph to explore the balcony. With Katsin in tow, the Elf Captain moved now to the tower entry before him. He worked the latch unsuccessfully, then put his weight against the door. It held firm. Katsin tried with no better luck. The door was blocked solidly. Wil watched their struggles to free it with growing apprehension. The fortress shut them in like a prison, and he was anxious to be free of it.

Dilph reappeared from the balcony, his words nearly lost in the shriek of the wind. The upper door was open. Crispin nodded. Gathering up

several loose sticks of wood that could serve as torches once they had
gained access to the tower, he led the company up the balcony stairs and
into the shelter of the alcove. The door stood ajar. Stepping just inside, the
Elf Captain used tinder to catch fire to one of the brands he carried, lit a
second to give to Dilph, then motioned them all inside, pushing the door
closed against the wind.

They found themselves in a small anteroom that branched off into
a series of darkened hallways. A stairwell cut into the far wall, winding
out of the stone-block floor and upward into the gloom. Dust hung
heavily in the wind-stirred air, and the rock of the tower was permeated
with the smell of musty dampness. Holding out his torch, Crispin paced
across the room and back again, tested the heavy iron latch that secured
the anteroom door, then turned back to the others. They would rest
here until dawn. Katsin and Dilph would stand watch in the courtyard
while Wil and Amberle slept. Crispin would go in search of the passageway that would take them through the mountain to the banks of the
Mermidon.

Dilph handed his torch to Wil. With Katsin following, he slipped out
into the night. Crispin bolted the door behind them, cautioned Wil and
Amberle to keep the latch down, and then disappeared into the darkness of
one of the hallways. The Valeman and the Elven girl watched until the
light from his torch had faded into the gloom. Then Wil moved over to
the entry, set his torch into an iron rack fixed in the stone and hunched
down with his back against the door. Amberle wrapped herself in her
blanket and lay down next to him. Through chinks in the fastenings that
held the door, the howl of the wind sounded its eerie call down the tunnel-
like halls of the tower.

It was a long time before either of them fell asleep.

Wil was never certain that he did sleep. He seemed to doze more than
sleep, a light drifting rest that left him groping uncertainly between wakefulness and slumber. Almost at once, he began to dream, moving through
the tangle of half-sleep that hung like a fog across his subconscious. Darkness and mist enfolded him in a forest of imaginings, and he wandered lost.
Yet he had been here before, it seemed. It was familiar to him, this darkness and the haze that drifted through it, the mass of jumbled landscapes
through which he passed. It was a dream, yet not a dream, that he had had
before . . .

Then he felt the terrible presence of the creature as it crouched somewhere in the dark about him and abruptly he remembered. Havenstead—
he had dreamed this dream at Havenstead. The creature had come for him
and he had fled, but fled in vain, for there had been no escape. He had
come awake finally. But could he do so now? Panic surged through him.
It was out there, the thing, the monster. It was coming for him again.
He could not run from it, could not escape it unless he could wake. But he
could not find the way out of the dark and this mist.

He heard himself scream as it reached for him.

Instantly, he was awake. In the pocket of his tunic, the Elfstones burned like fire against his body. Lurching up wildly from his blanket, he peered into the smoky haze of the torchlight as it flickered redly from the tower's stone walls. Amberle crouched beside him, sleep clouding her vision, her face pale and frightened. Wil touched the small bulk of the Elfstones uncertainly. Had it been his scream that had wakened them, he wondered? But the Elven girl was not looking at him. She was looking fixedly at the door.

"Out there," she whispered.

Hurriedly, the Valeman rose, drawing the girl up with him. He listened but heard nothing.

"It might have been the wind," he said finally, his voice hushed and filled with doubt. He put his hand on her arm. "I had better have a look. Lock the door after me. Do not open it unless you hear my voice."

He rose, pulled back the heavy bar, and slipped out into the night. Wind whistled sharply through the door as it closed behind him. Amberle pushed the latch securely in place and waited.

Wil crouched for a moment in the shadow of the alcove, staring out into the dark beyond. Moonlight fell across the length of the deserted balcony and across walls and battlements that rose all about. Cautiously, he crossed to the parapet and peered downward into the courtyard. It was empty. There was no sign of Katsin or Dilph. He hesitated, uncertain as to what he should do next. A moment later he started along the length of the balcony. At the top of the stairway, he stopped again to scan the courtyard. Still nothing. He started down.

Tumbleweeds and dust balls blew randomly across the debris-littered court, scattering wildly with each new gust of wind. Wil slipped down the stairs soundlessly. He was almost to the bottom when he saw Katsin. At least he saw what was left of Katsin, his body twisted grotesquely as it slumped against the tower wall beneath the balcony. A few feet beyond lay Dilph, barely visible under what remained of the heavy tower door that earlier had been solidly blocked.

Wil felt himself go cold. The Reaper! It had found them. And it was inside the tower.

In the next instant he was scrambling back up the stairs toward the balcony entry, praying that he was not already too late.

Alone in the tower anteroom, Amberle thought she heard a noise rise out of the gloom of the stairwell behind her, a noise that came from somewhere deep within the structure. Uneasily she glanced about, then listened. She was still listening when a pounding on the tower door startled her so that she jumped away in surprise, crying out.

"Amberle! Open the door!"

It was Wil's voice, so muffled by the wind that it was barely recognizable.

Hurriedly she threw back the heavy latch. The Valeman darted inside, shoving the door closed behind him. He was white with fear.

"They're dead—both of them!" He kept his voice low with an effort. "The Reaper got them. It's here, in the tower!"

Amberle started to say something, but Wil quickly put his hand to her mouth, silencing her. A noise—he had heard a noise—there, on the stairwell. It was the Reaper. He knew it with a certainty that defied argument. It was coming for them. Once it found its way up to this room, it would have them. The Valeman felt a moment of utter panic. How could this have happened? How could the Demon have found them so quickly? What was he supposed to do now?

Holding the torch before him like a shield, he moved away from the door, away from the stairwell. Amberle seemed frozen to him, stumbling back mechanically as he did. They could not stay here, he told himself numbly. He glanced at the passageways about him. Which one had Crispin gone into? He was not certain. He chose the one he believed the Elf Captain had gone down, and raced into its darkness, holding tightly to Amberle.

Several hundred feet further on, they stumbled to a halt. The passageway ended, branching into three new corridors. Again the Valeman panicked. Which should he take? He brought the torch close to the tower floor. The passing of a single pair of Elven boots had stirred the dust collected over the years, leaving a clear and easily recognizable trail, one that he could follow to Crispin—one that the Reaper could follow to them. He choked down his fear and rushed quickly on.

Together, Valeman and Elven girl fled down the dark corridors of the fortress, into halls thick with must and cobwebs, through chambers filled with rotting tapestries and crumbling pieces of furniture, and along balconies and parapets that dropped away into pits of blackness. Silence filled the ancient citadel, deep and pervasive within its bowels so that even the sound of the wind faded and there was only the pounding of their boots on the stone flooring as they ran. Twice they lost their way entirely, racing down a wrong corridor before finding that the trail had disappeared and that they had missed a turn in their haste. Several times they found more than one set of prints where Crispin had doubled back on himself in trying to find the right path. Each time precious seconds were used to discover where he had actually gone. Always there was the feeling that at any moment the Reaper would appear from out of the gloom behind them, and their last chance for escape would be gone.

Then a flicker of torchlight cut through the darkness in the corridor ahead of them. They stumbled toward it, watching with relief as Crispin's lean form materialized out of the shadows. The Elf Captain was returning from his search for the passage that led through the mountain. He came up to them at a dead run, sword blade glinting dully in the red firelight.

"What has happened?" he asked, seeing at once the fear in their eyes.

Quickly the Valeman told him. Crispin's face went ashen.

"Dilph and Katsin, too! What will it take to stop this thing?" Staring down at the sword he held, he hesitated, then beckoned for them to follow. "This way. There may yet be a chance for us."

Together they raced back down the passage through which Crispin had come, turning left into another corridor, passing through a massive hall that had once been an armory, hastening down a flight of stairs into an empty rotunda, then into yet another passage. At the end of this final corridor was an iron door, fixed to the rock of the mountain by bolts and crossbars. Crispin drew back the bars and pulled open the heavy door. Wind roared in their faces, bursting through the opening and thrusting them backward violently. Motioning for Wil and Amberle to follow, the Elf Captain discarded his torch, lowered his head resolutely, and pushed through the opening into the darkness beyond.

They found themselves staring out across a deep gorge where the mountain split apart from crest to base. Bridging the two halves was a slender catwalk that led from the small rocky niche in which they stood to a single tower set into the far cliff. Wind howled across the drop of the chasm, shrieking in fury as it buffeted the narrow iron span. Only a thin sliver of moonlight penetrated the deep crevice, its white band falling across a small section of the catwalk near its far end.

Crispin pulled the Valeman and the Elven girl close.

"We have to cross!" he shouted above the roar of the wind.

"Hold tight to the railing! Don't look down!"

"I'm not sure I can do this!" Amberle shouted back, looking anxiously out at the catwalk. Wil felt her small hands grip his arm tightly.

"You have to!" Crispin's response left no room for argument. "This is the only way out!"

The wind howled in their ears. Amberle glanced momentarily at the closed door behind her, then looked back again at Crispin. Wordlessly, she nodded.

"Stay close now!" the Elf warned.

In a line, they started onto the catwalk, the Elf Captain leading, Amberle behind him, Wil trailing. They moved slowly, carefully, hands gripping the railing to either side, heads bent low. The wind ripped across their bodies in fierce gusts, tearing at their clothing and shaking the slender iron walk until it seemed certain that it must collapse and fall into the gorge. As they passed from the shelter of the cliff face, the freezing air of the mountain's upper slopes blew down across them. Hands and feet went quickly numb, and the iron of the bridge felt like ice. Step by step, they made their way across, moving at last from the shadow of the cliffs into the slender band of moonlight that marked the final leg of their crossing. Moments later they gained the platform that fronted the solitary tower. The structure rose up before them against the cliff face, its narrow windows recessed and dark, its stone walls trailing moisture frozen to ice. A single door, now closed, marked the entrance into the keep.

Crispin guided Amberle from the walk and placed her against the tower entry. When Wil had scrambled up beside them, the Elf reached into a wooden box built against the tower wall and withdrew a pair of heavy mallets. He handed one to the Valeman and pointed out toward the bridge. His voice was muffled by the wind's shriek.

"There are six pins that hold the supports of the catwalk—three on each side! Knock out those pins and the walk will collapse! It was constructed that way to prevent pursuit by enemies in case the fortress was ever overrun. Take the three on the right!"

Wil hastened onto the platform. Three horizontally fixed pins driven through eyelets secured the struts on each side of the catwalk to the platform on which he stood. Taking the mallet firmly in hand, he began to hammer at the first. Rust and dirt had congealed about it, and it moved very slowly from its seating. When at last it came free, it tumbled soundlessly into the gorge. He went quickly to the next, the wind deafening him to the sound of the blows he struck, the cold numbing his unprotected hands. The second pin edged clear of its seating and fell.

Something heavy shook the bridge. Wil and Crispin looked up together, mallets poised. In the deep shadows at the far end of the walk, something moved.

"Hurry!" the Elf Captain called.

Wil hammered frantically at the final pin, raining blows on its rounded head, desperately trying to knock it free. It was rusted in place. He struck it with both hands, and at last it inched a fraction of the way out.

On the bridge, just beyond the band of moonlight, a shadow darker than the night about it edged into view. Crispin came to his feet with a bound. Two of the pins on his side were free, the third driven halfway through.

But time had run out. The Reaper appeared, stepping forward into the light—huge, cloaked, faceless. Crispin brought up the ash bow and sent his arrows winging at the thing so quickly that Wil could barely follow the archer's movements. All were brushed aside effortlessly. Wil felt his stomach tighten. Desperately he hammered at the pin before him, sending it several inches further through the eyelet. But there it froze.

Then abruptly he remembered the Elfstones. The Elfstones! He must use them now! Determination surged through him. He bounded up, reached into his tunic and pulled free the leather pouch that held them. In seconds, he held the Stones in his hand, gripped so tightly that they cut him. The Reaper was moving toward them, still crouched low upon the catwalk, huge and shadowy. It was not twenty feet away. The Valeman brought up the fist that held the Stones and, with every bit of willpower he could muster, he called up the fire that would destroy this monster.

The Elfstones flared sharply, the blue fire spreading. But then something seemed to lock within Wil. In the next instant the power died.

Terror gripped the Valeman. He tried desperately. Nothing happened. Amberle rushed to his side, calling frantically to him—but her words were lost in the shriek of the wind. Wil staggered back, stunned. He had failed! The power of the Elfstones was no longer his to command!

An instant later, Crispin was on the bridge. He never hesitated. Dropping the bow, he drew his sword and started toward the Demon. The creature seemed to hesitate slightly. It had not expected a direct confrontation. Wind buffeted the catwalk, causing metal supports to creak in protest as the structure swayed unsteadily.

"The pins!" Crispin called back sharply.

In a daze, Wil thrust the Elfstones back into his tunic, retrieved his mallet, and resumed striking futilely at the frozen pin. Still it would not move. From the shadows behind him, Amberle darted forward. Picking up the mallet that Crispin had discarded, she began to hammer wildly at the other pin.

On the catwalk, Crispin closed with the Reaper. Feinting and lunging, the Captain of the Home Guard sought to catch the Demon off balance, hoping that it might slip and tumble from the walk. But the Reaper stayed low upon the slender bridge, warding off the Elf's thrusts with one massive arm, waiting patiently for its chance. Crispin was a skilled swordsman, yet he could not penetrate the creature's defenses. The Reaper edged forward, and the Elf was forced to give ground.

Rage and frustration swept through Wil Ohmsford. Gripping his mallet in both hands, he pounded the rusted pin with every ounce of strength left in him, and at last the pin flew from its seating into the chasm. But as it did, the bridge buckled slightly and Crispin was thrown off balance. As he stumbled back, the Reaper lunged. Claws fastened about the Elf's tunic. As Wil and Amberle watched in horror, the Reaper lifted Crispin clear of the catwalk. The Elf Captain's sword flashed downward toward the Demon's throat, the blade splintering as it struck. The Reaper shrugged off the blow as if it were nothing. Holding Crispin above its shrouded head, it threw the Elf from the catwalk into the void beyond. Crispin fell soundlessly and was gone.

Again, the Reaper started forward.

Then a sudden burst of wind caught the already weakened catwalk with a powerful thrust that snapped the final pin in its seating. Separating from the platform, the narrow span fell away from the cliff face, carrying with it the clinging form of the Reaper. Slowly it dropped, falling with a groan of iron toward the far cliff, metal snapping, breaking, twisting. It swung through the narrow band of moonlight back into the shadows, crashing against the mountainside. Yet it did not break free entirely, but continued to hang from its ruined supports, swinging precariously with the motion of the wind. In the darkness of the cliffs, it was barely visible. The Reaper was nowhere to be seen.

Amberle's voice rose above the pitch of the wind, a thin frightened wail, calling to Wil. Wind howled past the Valeman in frenzied bursts, chilling him to the bone, filling his ears with its whine. He could not understand what the girl was saying. He did not care. His fist still clutched his mallet uselessly. His mind whirled. Crispin and the Elven Hunters were gone. The power of the Elfstones was lost. Amberle and he were alone.

She was crying into his shoulder, pleading with him to come away. He turned to her now and pulled her close against him. For an instant he seemed to hear Allanon's voice telling him that it was he most of all whom the Druid would depend upon. He stood at the edge of the chasm a moment longer, holding the Elven girl, staring helplessly into the blackness below. Then he turned away. With Amberle clutched tightly against him, he disappeared into the shelter of the tower.

It took them the remainder of the night to find their way out again. With only the single torch that Crispin had left fastened in an iron wall bracket at the tower entry to guide them, they followed a seemingly endless succession of passages and stairways that wound steadily downward through the mountain's rock. Completely exhausted by the ordeal of the past few days, they stumbled mindlessly along the corridors of the ancient keep, eyes fixed on the blackness ahead, hands clasped. They did not speak; they had nothing to say. The shock of all that had happened had left them numb with fright. They wanted only one thing now—to escape this mountain.

Their sense of time slipped quickly away from them until it no longer had meaning. It might have been minutes or hours or even days that they had been shut within the rock; they no longer knew. They had no idea where the passageways were taking them. They were trusting blindly to luck and to instinct, following the tunnels and corridors with a desperate, unvoiced insistence that somehow they would eventually break free. Muscles ached and cramped, and their vision blurred with fatigue. The single torch they carried burned down until it was little more than a stump. Still the passageway burrowed on.

But at last it ended. A massive iron door sealed with double locks and a crossbar stood before them. Wil was reaching for the locks when Amberle seized his arm, her voice weary and strained.

"Wil, what if there are Demons waiting for us out there as well? What if the Reaper wasn't alone?"

The Valeman stared at her wordlessly. He hadn't considered that possibility until now. He hadn't allowed himself to consider it. He thought back to all that had befallen them since Drey Wood. Always, the Demons seemed to find them. There was a sense of inevitability about it. Even if the Reaper were finally gone, there were other Demons. And the spy at Arborlon had heard everything.

"Wil?" Amberle's face was anxious as she waited for him to respond.

He made his decision. "We have to chance it. There is nowhere else for us to go."

Gently he removed her hand from his arm and positioned her behind him. Then cautiously he released the locks, lifted clear the crossbar and swung open the door. Hazy daylight slipped through the opening. Beyond, the murky waters of the Mermidon lapped softly at the walls of a deep grotto that housed the hidden docks of the Elves. Nothing moved. Valeman and Elf girl exchanged quick glances. Wordlessly, Wil dropped the torch to the tunnel floor where it died.

The docks and boats moored to them were rotted and useless. Valeman and Elf girl made their way along a narrow ledge within the grotto until they had emerged onto the forested riverbank that lay at the base of the Pykon. There was no one there. They were alone.

Dawn was just breaking, a chill, frosted morning half-light that had crystallized the dew of nightfall on the trees and brush and left the land white with a covering of false snow. They stared at it wonderingly, seeing their own breath cloud the air before their faces, feeling the chill seep into their damp bodies beneath the covering of their clothes. The river churned noisily between the mountain peaks, flowing eastward through the forestland, its broad surface shrouded in a heavy blanket of fog. The Pykon rose into this fog, massive, dark spires that shadowed the land.

Wil glanced about uncertainly. Within the darkness of the cave, the boats of the Elves lay in ruins. There was nothing here that could help them. Then he caught sight of a small skiff pulled up on the riverbank and partially concealed within the brush just a dozen yards away. Taking hold of Amberle's hand, he led the way along the heavily overgrown bank until they had reached the skiff. It was a fishing boat in good condition, secured by lines, obviously left by someone who from time to time must have enjoyed the fishing close to the deep grotto waters. The Valeman released the lines, placed Amberle within the skiff, and pushed off into the river. Their need for the boat was much greater than that of the absent fisherman.

They drifted eastward with the river's flow as dawn lengthened into morning and the day began to warm. Wrapping herself in her cloak, Amberle was asleep almost at once. Wil would have slept as well had sleep been possible. But sleep would not come to him, his weariness so great that it actually inhibited sleep. His mind filled with thoughts of what had befallen them. Fitting a small oar that lay within the skiff into a stern oarlock, he propped himself at the rear of the little boat and guided it along the river's channel, watching numbly as the sun rose from behind the mountains and the haze of early morning burned away. Bit by bit, the frost melted away in the forest about him. The peaks of the Pykon disappeared as the river carried them on, and the damp green of the forestland rose up in their stead. The sky was free once more from rain clouds and darkness, turned a brilliant blue and laced with thin white streamers that floated lazily through the morning sunshine.

Toward noon, the Mermidon began to swing back on itself, curving slowly south until at last it swung westward toward the dark line of the Rock Spur. The day had warmed, and the dampness and chill of dawn had seeped from their bodies and clothing. Across the span of the Mermidon flew birds in brilliant bursts of sound and color. The smell of wildflowers filled the air.

Amberle stretched and came awake, her sleepy eyes settling quickly on the Valeman.

"Have you slept?" she asked drowsily.

He shook his head. "I couldn't."

She pushed herself into a sitting position. "Then sleep now. I will steer the boat while you do. You have to get some rest."

"No, it's okay. I am not tired."

"Wil, you are exhausted." There was concern in her voice. "You have to sleep."

He stared at her wordlessly for a moment, his eyes haunted.

"Do you know what happened to me back there?" he asked finally.

She shook her head slowly. "No. And I don't think you do, either."

"I know, all right. I know exactly what happened. I tried to use the Elfstones and could not. I no longer command their power. I have lost it."

"You don't know that. You had trouble with the Stones before when you tried to use them in the Tirfing. Perhaps this time you tried too hard. Perhaps you did not give yourself enough of a chance."

"I gave myself every chance," he declared softly. "I used everything I had within me to call up the power of the Elfstones. But nothing happened. Nothing. Allanon told me this might happen. It is because of my Elf blood mixing with my human blood. Only the Elf blood commands the Stones, and mine is thin indeed, it seems. There is a block within me, Amberle. I overcame it once, but I can no longer do so."

She moved over to sit close to him, her hand resting lightly on his arm.

"Then we will get by without the Stones."

He smiled faintly at the suggestion. "The Elfstones are the only weapon we have. If the Demons find us again, we are finished. We have nothing with which to protect ourselves."

"Then the Demons must not find us."

"They have found us every time, Amberle, despite every precaution we have taken; they have found us wherever we have gone. They will find us this time as well. You know that."

"I know that you are the one who insisted that we not turn back after our flight from Havenstead," she responded. "I know that you are the one who has never once suggested giving up. I know that you are the one Allanon chose as my protector. Would you desert me?"

Wil flushed. "No. Not ever."

"Nor I you. We began this journey together and we shall end it to-gether. We shall depend on each other, you and I. We shall see each other through. I think maybe that will be enough." She paused, a quick smile crossing her face. "You realize, of course, that you should be giving this talk to me, not I to you. I was the one without faith in my heritage, with-out belief in the words the Druid spoke. You have always believed."

"If the Stones had not failed me . . ." Wil began glumly.

Amberle's hand came up quickly against his lips, silencing him. "Do not be so certain that they have failed you. Think a moment on what you tried to do with them. You sought to use them as a weapon of destruction. Is this possible for you, Wil? Remember, you are a Healer. It is your code of life to preserve, not destroy. Elven magic is but an extension of the one who wields it. Perhaps you were not meant to use the Elfstones in the way in which you tried to make them act when you faced the Reaper."

The Valeman thought it over. Allanon had told him that the three Stones acted to mesh heart, mind, and body into the power that formed the magic. If any one were lacking . . .

"No." He shook his head emphatically. "The distinction is too finely drawn. My grandfather believed in the preservation of life as strongly as I and yet he used the Elfstones to destroy. And he did so without the diffi-culty that I have experienced."

"Well then, there is another possibility," she continued. "Allanon warned you of the resistance caused by the mix of human blood with Elven. You have experienced it once already. Perhaps this has caused you to create your own block—a block within your mind that convinces you subcon-sciously that the power of the Elfstones is lost, when in fact it is not. Perhaps the block you experienced at the catwalk was one of your own making."

Wil stared at her wordlessly. Was that possible? He shook his head. "I don't know. I cannot be sure. It happened so fast."

"Then hear me." She moved close, so that her face was next to his. "Do not be so quick to accept as truth what is only conjecture. You have used the Elfstones once. You have called upon their power and made it your own. I do not think that such a gift is so easily lost. Perhaps it is just misplaced. Take time to look for it before you decide that it is no longer yours."

He looked at her with amazement. "You have more confidence in me than I do. That seems very strange. You thought me worthless on our journey north from Havenstead. You remember that?"

She drew back slightly. "I was wrong to think that. I said things that I should not have said. I was afraid . . ."

For an instant it appeared as if she would say more; but, as on the other occasions when she had seemed ready to explain her fear, she let the matter drop. Wil was wise enough to do likewise.

"Well, you were right about one thing," he offered, trying to keep the tone of his voice light. "I should be giving this talk to you, not you to me."

There was a wistful look in her eyes. "Then remember to do so when you see that I need it. Now will you sleep?"

He nodded. "I think I might—for a little while, at least."

He eased forward, letting the Elf girl slip her arm about the small rudder. Lowering himself into the bottom of the boat, he made a pillow of his cloak and laid his head down wearily. Thoughts of the Elfstones played teasingly within his mind. He closed his eyes, enfolding such thoughts in blackness. Believe in yourself, Allanon had told him. Did he have that belief? Was that belief enough?

The thoughts scattered, drifting. He slept.

He was awake by midafternoon. Cramped and sore, he eased himself up from the hard bottom of the skiff and moved back to take the rudder from Amberle. He was hungry and thirsty, but there was nothing to eat or drink. They had lost everything in their flight through the Pykon.

A short time later, the channel began to narrow, and the limbs of the trees on either bank closed above them like a canopy. Shadows lengthened across the spread of the river; in the west the sun dropped low above the wall of the Rock Spur, its golden light turning red with the coming of dusk. A stretch of rapids bounced the skiff wildly along the channel, but Wil kept their little boat free of the rocks and straight on her course until they were clear. When the river again began to swing south on its long journey back toward the grasslands of Callahorn, the Valeman brought the skiff ashore and they disembarked.

They spent the night at the base of a massive old willow several hundred yards back from the river's edge. Concealing the skiff in the brush beside the riverbank, they gathered fruit and vegetables for an evening meal and set out in search of drinking water. There was none to be found, however, and they were forced to make do with the food. They ate, conversed briefly and fell asleep.

Morning dawned bright and pleasant, and Valeman and Elven girl began the hike westward to the Rock Spur. They walked briskly, enjoying the warmth of the early morning, consuming as they went the remainder of the fruit they had gathered the previous evening. The hours passed quickly, and the stiffness they had experienced on first awakening disappeared as they wound their way steadily ahead. By midmorning, they had discovered a small stream where rapids emptied down into a pond and the water was suitable for drinking. They drank their fill; but, having no containers, they could take nothing with them.

As the day wore on, the mountains of the Rock Spur loomed closer above the wall of the forest in a massive, humped line of peaks that stretched away across the whole of the western horizon. Only to the far south, where lay the vast impenetrable mire of the Shroudslip, were the mountains absent, and there the skyline was filled with thick, gray mist that rose out of the swamp like heavy smoke. For the first time since they had escaped the Pykon, Wil began to worry about where they were going.

Their decision to follow the Mermidon down to the forests bordering the mountains had seemed obvious enough. But now that they were there, he found himself wondering how they were ever going to manage a crossing of these monstrous peaks. Neither of them was familiar with this range; neither knew if there were passes that would take them safely through. Without the Elven Hunters to guide them, how were they to keep from becoming hopelessly lost?

By sunset, they were right up against the Rock Spur, staring upward thousands of feet at a maze of peaks that loomed one above the next and offered no sign of passage nor hint of break. Valeman and Elven girl climbed out of the forest until they had reached the lower slopes of the nearest mountain. Broad, grassy pastures there were covered with brilliant bluebells and red centauries. The sun was almost gone, and they looked for a campsite. They quickly found a stream that emptied down out of the rocks; at a small pool within a grove of pine, they settled in for the night. Another meal of fresh fruit and vegetables was consumed, but Wil found himself hungry for meat and bread and ate what they had without much interest. A new moon and a spectacular display of stars filled the sky. Bidding each other good-night, they rolled themselves into their traveling cloaks and closed their eyes.

Wil was still wondering how they were going to get through the mountains when sleep came to him.

When he awoke, a boy was sitting there, looking at him. It was dawn, and the sun was rising out of the distant forestland in a hazy, golden burst of light that scattered night in fleeting bits of gray. On the broad, open slopes of the mountain which rose above them, the wildflowers were just opening and the dew glistened damply on the grass.

Wil blinked in surprise. At first he thought that his eyes were playing tricks on him, and he waited expectantly for the boy to disappear back into his imagination. But the boy remained where he was, seated on the grass, legs crossed before him, silently contemplating Wil. This was no illusion, the Valeman decided and pushed himself up on one elbow.

"Good morning," he said.

"Good morning," the boy replied solemnly.

Wil brushed the sleep from his eyes and took a moment to study the boy. He was an Elf, rather small, his tousled, sand-colored hair falling down about a rather ordinary face that displayed a light sprinkling of freckles. Leather pants and tunic fitted close on his small frame, and a number of assorted pouches and bags hung about his neck and from his waist. He was very young, certainly much younger than either Wil or Amberle.

"I didn't want to wake you," the boy announced.

Wil nodded. "You were very quiet."

"I know. I can walk through a stretch of dry pine without making a single sound."

"You can?"

"Yes. And I can hunt to a fox lair without starting him. I did that once."

"That's very good."

The boy looked at him curiously. "What are you doing out here?"

Wil grinned in spite of himself. "I was just wondering the same thing about you. Do you live here?"

The boy shook his head. "No. I live to the south, below the Irrybis. In the Wing Hove."

Wil did not have the faintest idea what a Wing Hove might be. Behind him, he heard Amberle stir awake.

"She is very pretty," the boy ventured quietly. "Are you married?"

"Uh, no—just traveling together," the Valeman managed, a bit taken back. "How did you get here?"

"I flew," the boy answered. "I'm a Wing Rider."

Wil stared at him speechlessly. The boy glanced past him to Amberle, who was just sitting up, still wrapped in her cloak.

"Good morning, lady," he greeted.

"Good morning," Amberle replied. Amusement mixed with puzzlement in her green eyes. "What is your name?"

"Perk."

"My name is Amberle." The Elven girl smiled. "This is Wil."

The boy got to his feet and came over to grip Wil's hand in greeting. The Valeman was surprised to find the youngster's palm heavily calloused. The boy seemed conscious of the fact and drew his hand back quickly. He did not offer it to Amberle, but simply nodded.

"Would you like some breakfast?" he asked.

Wil shrugged. "What do you have in mind, Perk?"

"Milk, nuts, cheese, and bread. That is all I have with me."

"That will do nicely." The Valeman grinned, glancing back quickly at Amberle. He had no idea what Perk was doing here, but the food sounded delicious. "We would be very happy to share breakfast with you."

They seated themselves in a circle. From one of the pouches he carried, the young Elf produced the promised nuts, cheese, and bread together with three small cups. The cups he filled with milk he carried in a second pouch. Valeman and Elven girl consumed the small meal ravenously.

"Where did you get the milk?" Amberle asked after a moment.

"Goats," the boy mumbled, his mouth full. "A goatherd keeps a small flock in a meadow several miles north. I milked one earlier this morning."

Amberle glanced questioningly at Wil, who shrugged.

"He tells me that he is a Wing Rider. He flies."

"I'm not really a Wing Rider—not yet," the boy interrupted. "I'm too young. But one day I will be."

There was an awkward moment of silence as the three stared wordlessly at one another.

"You didn't say what you were doing out here," Perk said finally. "Are you running away from something?"

"Why do you ask that, Perk?" Amberle wanted to know immediately.

"Because you look like you are running away from something. Your clothes are torn and dirty. You carry no weapons and no food and no blankets. You build no fire. And you look like something has frightened you."

"Perk, you are a bright boy," Wil responded quickly, deciding at once how he was going to handle this. "Will you promise to keep it secret if I tell you something?"

The boy nodded, anticipation showing in his face. "I promise."

"Good." Wil leaned forward confidentially. "This lady—Amberle—is very special. She is a Princess, a granddaughter of Eventine Elessedil, the King of the Elves."

"King of the Land Elves," Perk corrected. When Wil hesitated, confused by the distinction, the boy edged forward anxiously. "Do you go in quest of treasure? Or is the lady enchanted? Is she bewitched?"

"Yes. No." The Valeman stopped. What had he gotten himself into? "We go in search of a . . . a talisman, Perk. Only the lady can wield it. There is a very great evil that threatens the Elven people. Only the talisman can protect against that evil, and we must find it quickly. Would you be willing to help us?"

Perk's eyes were wide with excitement. "An adventure? A real adventure?"

"Wil, I don't know about this . . ." Amberle interrupted, frowning.

"Trust me, please." Wil held up his hands placatingly. He turned back to Perk. "This is a very dangerous business, Perk. The things that hunt us have already killed a number of Elves. This will not be a game. You must do exactly as I ask, and when I tell you that it is finished, you must leave us at once. Agreed?"

The boy nodded quickly. "What do you want me to do?"

The Valeman pointed toward the Rock Spur. "I want you to show me a way through those mountains. Do you know one?"

"Of course." Perk sounded very indignant. "Where is it that you are going?"

Wil hesitated. He was not certain that he wanted the boy to have that information.

"Does that matter?" he asked finally.

"Certainly it matters," Perk replied at once. "How can I show you how to get to where you want to go if I don't know where it is that you are going?"

"That sounds very sensible," Amberle offered, giving Wil a knowing glance that suggested that he should have foreseen all this. "I think you had better tell him, Wil."

The Valeman nodded. "All right. We are going into the Wilderun."

"The Wilderun?" Perk shook his head solemnly, some of the enthusiasm fading from his eyes. "The Wilderun is forbidden to me. It is very dangerous."

"We know," Amberle agreed. "But we have no choice. We have to go there. Can you help us?"

"I can help you," the boy declared firmly. "But you cannot go through the mountains. That would take days."

"Well, if we don't go through the mountains, then how do we get there?" Wil demanded. "Is there another way?"

Perk grinned. "Sure. We can fly."

Wil looked over at Amberle for help.

"Perk, we cannot . . . really fly," she said gently.

"We can fly," he insisted. "I told you, I'm a Wing Rider—almost a Wing Rider, anyway."

Some imagination, thought Wil. "Look, Perk, you have to have wings to fly and we don't have wings."

"Wings?" The boy looked confused. Then he grinned. "Oh, you thought . . . Oh, I see. No, no, not us. We have Genewen. Here, come with me."

He rose quickly and moved out of the shelter of the pine grove. Mystified, Wil and Amberle trailed after, exchanging confused glances as they went. When they were all beyond the trees and standing on the open slope, Perk reached into a leather pouch tied about his neck and produced a small, silver whistle. Putting the whistle to his lips, the boy blew into it. There was no sound. Wil looked at Amberle a second time and shook his head slowly. This was not working out the way he had intended it. Perk slipped the silver whistle back into its pouch and turned to scan the skyline. Mechanically, the Valeman and the Elven girl looked with him.

Suddenly a great, golden-hued form soared out of the Rock Spur, shimmering brightly in the warm morning sunlight as it dipped downward through the mountains and came toward them. Wil and Amberle started wildly. It was the biggest bird they had ever seen in their lives, a huge creature with a wing span of fully thirty feet, a sleek, crested head the color of fire tinged with flecks of black, a great hooked beak, and powerful talons that extended forward as it approached. For just an instant, both were reminded of the winged black thing that had very nearly caught them in their flight through the Valley of Rhenn, but then they realized that this was not the same creature. It dropped to the meadow not a dozen feet in front of them, wings folding close against its golden, feathered body, crested head arching upward as it came to roost. Its piercing cry split the morning stillness, and it dipped its head sharply toward Perk. The boy gave a quick, odd call in reply, then turned again to his astonished companions.

"This is Genewen," he announced brightly. Then he grinned. "You see? I told you we could fly."

Seeing Genewen made Wil and Amberle more willing to accept the story that Perk then proceeded to tell them.

Before the time of Jerle Shannara and the advent of the Second War of the Races, a small community of Elves migrated south from their traditional homeland—for reasons which had long since been forgotten—

to settle below the Irrybis along a rugged, uncharted stretch of mountainous forestland that bordered a vast body of water known to the races as the Blue Divide. These Elves were Perk's ancestors. Over the years, they became hunters and fishermen, their small villages built back upon a string of shoreline cliffs that abutted the Blue Divide west of the Myrian. The Elves quickly discovered that they were sharing the cliffs with a rookery of massive hunting birds that nested within caves opening out over the waters of the Divide. They called the birds Rocs after a legendary bird from the old world. The Rocs and the Elves kept a respectable distance from one another at first, but in time it became apparent to the Elves that the giant birds would be useful to the men if they could be trained to serve as carriers. The Elves were resourceful and determined, and they set out to accomplish this end. After numerous failures, they managed to discover a means of communication with the birds, which in turn led to harnessing several of the young and finally to mastery of the entire rookery. The birds became carriers of the Elves, who were now able to expand their hunting and fishing grounds. The birds became protectors as well, trained to do battle against the enemies of the community. The Elves, in their turn, kept the Rocs safe from creatures that sought to invade their rookery or to encroach upon their feeding grounds. They learned to care for the great birds, to treat them for sickness and injury, to heal them, and to keep them well. With the passage of the years, the bond between the two grew stronger. The community they shared they called the Wing Hove. It was small and isolated in a wilderness only sparsely settled by men and rarely traveled. All contact between the Wing Hove and the larger Elven communities that lay north of the Wilderun had long since ceased. The Elves in the Wing Hove had formed their own government and, although they recognized the sovereignty of the Elven Kings at Arborlon over the majority of the Westland Elves, they considered themselves a separate people. Thus they came to refer to themselves as Sky Elves and to the rest of the Westland Elves as Land Elves.

Perk was the son and grandson of Wing Riders. Wing Riders were the men who trained and rode the giant Rocs, the men who directed the search for food and the defense of the Wing Hove. There were other designations given to the men and women of the Wing Hove, but Wing Rider was the most coveted. Only the Wing Rider was given command over the Roc. Only he was given the power of flight, to ride the skylanes from one corner of the land to the other. The Wing Rider was a man who commanded the honor and trust of his people, who would spend his life in their service, and who would be recognized forever as a symbol of their way of life.

Perk was in the second year of his training to become a Wing Rider. The choice of one who would become a Wing Rider was made at an early age, and the training then continued until the boy reached manhood. Often the choice was virtually predetermined, as in the case of Perk, where both his father and his grandfather were Wing Riders, and it was expected that he should follow in their footsteps. Genewen was his grandfather's mount, but his grandfather was too old to fly in regular service for the Wing Hove; when Perk reached manhood, Genewen would become his. The Rocs lived to be very old, their lives spanning four and sometimes five Elven generations. Thus a Roc would serve several masters during its lifetime. Genewen had seen service first as the carrier of Perk's grandfather, but if her health remained good, she would one day serve Perk's son or grandson as well.

For the moment, however, she served Perk as he trained under the supervision of his grandfather to become a Wing Rider. It was a training exercise that had brought the Elven boy into the Rock Spur and to his meeting with Wil and Amberle. His development as a Wing Rider required that he make longer and longer flights from the Wing Hove. For each flight, he was given certain tasks to accomplish and rules to follow. On this particular outing, he was required to stay away from the Wing Hove for a period of seven days, carrying with him only a small ration of bread and cheese and a container of water. He was to find additional food and drink on his own. He was to explore and be able to describe accurately on his return certain portions of the mountainous country surrounding the Wilderun. The Wilderun itself was forbidden to him, as it was to all who were still in training. He might set down upon the land that bounded the Wilderun, but not within. He was to avoid all contact with its denizens.

The instructions seemed explicit enough, and Perk did not question them. But then on the morning of his second day out, while flying south along the eastern edge of the Rock Spur, he caught sight of Wil and Amberle, two bundled forms asleep in a pine grove below him. After winging downward for a closer look, he found himself faced with an immediate dilemma. Who were these travelers, Elves like himself, a young man and a younger girl, clearly from another part of the land? What were they doing in this rugged country, so poorly equipped? A moment's thought was all that it took, and the decision was made. He had been ordered to avoid any contact with the denizens of the Wilderun, but no directions had been given him regarding his contact with anyone else—an oversight on the part of his grandfather, perhaps, but a fact nevertheless. Despite the maturity and caution instilled in Perk by the intense demands of his training, he was still a boy with a boy's spirit of adventure. His grandfather had left the door cracked before him, and it was natural enough that he should want to push it open the rest of the way. After all, although he was an obedient boy, he was also a curious one. Sometimes the former must be permitted to give way to the latter.

Fortunately for Wil and Amberle, this proved to be one such time.

Perk finished his story, then patiently answered questions for a moment or two. But his eagerness to begin his new adventure finally got the better of him. With an unmistakable look of anticipation, he asked his new companions if they were ready yet to depart. Genewen, although not used to carrying more than one rider, could easily do so. She would have them across the mountains of the Rock Spur before they knew it.

Wil and Amberle looked doubtfully at the giant bird. Had there been another way, they would have taken it gladly. Even the thought of flying made their stomachs feel queasy. But there was no alternative, and there the boy stood, hands on hips, waiting for matters to get under way. With a shrug of his shoulders to Amberle, Wil announced that they were ready. After all, if a mere boy could do this, certainly they could also.

With Perk in the lead, they moved over to Genewen. The giant bird was equipped with a leather harness that was bound tightly about her body. Perk showed them foot loops that would allow them to climb the harness to the center of the Roc's feathered back. He held Genewen steady while they did so, then fitted their boots to toe straps, directed their hands to knotted grips, and, as an added precaution, bound them to the harness with safety lines. That way, he informed them, if the wind should blow them loose, they still would not fall. Such assurances gave small comfort to the Valeman and the Elven girl, who were scared enough as it was. Perk then gave each a small section of a brownish root which he told them to chew and swallow. This root, he explained, would ease the discomfort of flying. They ate it hurriedly.

When both were secure, the Elven boy removed a long, leather-bound crop from beneath the harness straps and slapped Genewen smartly. With a piercing cry, the Roc spread her great wings and rose sharply into the morning air. Petrified, Wil and Amberle watched the ground drop away beneath them. The trees of the pine grove shrank as Genewen circled high above the meadowland, catching the wind currents and arcing swiftly west toward the peaks of the mountain range. For the Valeman and the Elven girl, the sensation was indescribable. At first there was a feeling somewhere between sickness and exhilaration, and only the juice of the strange root kept their stomachs from turning over entirely. Then the sickness lessened, and the feeling of exhilaration began to heighten, sweeping through them as they watched the horizons of the land below broaden and stretch wide, a spectacular panorama of forestland, swamp, mountains, and rivers. It was an incredible sight. Before them the black peaks of the Rock Spur rose up like jagged teeth out of the earth, and the thin, blue ribbon of the Mermidon wound its way down out of the rock; to the north was the dark smudge of the Matted Breaks, set deep within the green of the Westland forests; to the east, and now far distant, lay the twin towers of the Pykon; to the south, the haze of the Shroudslip settled against the threshold of the Irrybis. It was all there, the whole of the land, spread out below them as if contained in some hidden valley upon whose crest they stood, all sharply revealed by a rising morning sun that burned down out of a cloudless, brilliant blue sky.

Genewen rose to a height of several hundred feet, winging her way steadily into the Rock Spur, weaving through its maze of peaks, slipping deftly through breaks and splits, dipping downward into valleys, then rising again to clear each new ridge line. Wil and Amberle clung to the harness with grips of iron, yet the ride was smooth; the great bird responded to the motions of the small boy who guided her, his hands and legs nudging and coaxing with a series of movements familiar to the Roc. The wind whipped across them in short bursts, yet was light and warm on this summer's day, blowing softly out of the south. Perk glanced quickly over his shoulder at his new companions, a fierce grin splitting his freckled face. The smiles they returned were less than enthusiastic.

They flew on for nearly an hour, winging deep within the mountains until the forestland had disappeared from view entirely. From time to time, they could see the haze of the Shroudslip appear through breaks in the peaks to the south, gray and friendless; then even that was gone. The mountains closed in about them, massive towers of rock that rose up across the sunlight and left them in shadow. Wil found himself thinking momentarily of what it would have been like for Amberle and him, had they attempted to cross this forbidding range afoot. It was unlikely that they could have done it, particularly without the aid of the slain Elven Hunters. He wondered if Demons still tracked them. Undoubtedly they did, he decided, but he took some small measure of satisfaction in the knowledge that even the Reaper, had it managed somehow to survive the collapse of the catwalk in the Pykon, would find it impossible to follow their trail this time.

A short while later, Perk guided Genewen down to a high, treeless bluff, covered with long grass and wildflowers, which overlooked a mountain lake. The Roc settled smoothly back upon the earth and her riders disembarked, Perk springing nimbly from the giant bird's back, Wil and Amberle stiff and awkward in their movements, their faces filled with relief.

They rested on the bluff for half-an-hour, then climbed back upon Genewen and were off once again, winging westward through the massive peaks. Twice more during the morning they landed, resting themselves and Genewen, and then continued on. Each time Perk offered to share food and drink with his companions, and each time they quickly declined. All they would agree to accept was another piece of the strange root. Perk offered it to them without comment. It had been like this for him, too, when he had first flown.

By late morning, they had reached the eastern edge of the Wilderun. From atop Genewen, they could see the whole of the valley clearly, a tangled mass of forest ringed by the mountains of the Rock Spur and Irrybis and the broad, misty sweep of the Shroudslip. It was a forbidding stretch of woodland, heavily overgrown, a jumble of depressions and ridges, spotted with bogs and a scattering of solitary peaks that broke out of the trees like grasping arms. There was no sign of habitation, no villages nor isolated dwellings, no planted fields nor grazing stock. The whole of the valley was wilderness, dark and friendless. Wil and Amberle stared down into it apprehensively.

Moments later, Perk guided Genewen back into the shadow of the mountains and the Wilderun disappeared behind the peaks. They flew on without stopping until shortly after midday, when Perk turned Genewen south again. In a slow, gradual arc, the Roc slipped through a narrow break in the peaks. Ahead of them, the Wilderun again came into view. They flew toward it, dropping along a rugged slide that fell away at its lower end into the bowl of the valley. At the edge of the slide, Genewen banked right, winging downward toward a broad slope that sat back against the base of the peak and overlooked the Wilderun. Scattered clumps of trees dotted the slope, and Perk brought Genewen to rest behind a covering of fir.

Wil and Amberle climbed gingerly from the Roc's back, rubbing muscles that had grown stiff and cramped with the long ride. After a quick command to Genewen, Perk followed them down, his face flushed and excited.

"You see? We did it!" He was grinning from ear to ear.

"We did, indeed." Wil smiled ruefully, massaging his backside.

"What do we do next?" the boy wanted to know immediately.

Wil straightened himself, grimacing. "You don't do anything, Perk. This is as far as you go."

"But I want to help," Perk insisted.

Amberle stepped forward and put her arm about the boy. "You did help, Perk. We would not have gotten this far without you."

"But I want to go . . ."

"No, Perk," Amberle interrupted quickly. "What we must do now is far too dangerous for you to become involved in. Wil and I must go down into the Wilderun. You have said yourself that the Wilderun is forbidden to you. So you must leave us now. Remember, you promised Wil that you would do so when we asked."

The boy nodded glumly. "I am not afraid," he muttered.

"I know." The Elven girl smiled. "I don't think much of anything would frighten you."

Perk brightened a bit with this compliment, a quick smile lighting his face.

"There is one thing more you can do for us." Wil put a hand on his shoulder. "We don't know very much about the Wilderun. Can you tell us anything about what we might find down there?"

"Monsters," the boy answered without hesitation.

"Monsters?"

"All kinds. Witches, too, my grandfather says."

The Valeman could not decide whether to believe that or not. After all, the grandfather was trying to keep the boy out of the Wilderun and that was the kind of warning one would expect him to give.

"Have you ever heard of a place called Safehold?" he asked impulsively.

Perk shook his head no.

"I didn't think so." Wil sighed. "Monsters and witches, huh? Are there any roads?"

The boy nodded. "I will show you."

He led them out of the fir trees to a small rise where they could look down upon the valley.

"See that?" he asked, indicating a mass of fallen trees at the base of the slope. Wil and Amberle peered downward until they saw where he was pointing. "There is a road beyond those trees that leads to the village of Grimpen Ward. All roads in the Wilderun lead to Grimpen Ward. You cannot see anything of it from here, but it's down there, several miles into the forest. My grandfather tells me that it is a bad place, that the people are thieves and cutthroats. Maybe, though, you could find someone there to guide you."

"Maybe we can." Wil smiled his thanks. At least the thieves and cutthroats were preferable to the monsters and witches, he thought to himself. Still, it wouldn't hurt to be careful. Even if all the thieves and cutthroats and witches and monsters were imaginary, there were Demons searching for them, perhaps even waiting for them, who were not.

Perk was deep in thought. After a moment, he looked up. "What will you do when you find this Safehold?" he asked.

Wil hesitated. "Well, Perk, when we find Safehold, we find the talisman I told you about. Then we can return to Arborlon."

The boy's face lighted. "Then there is something more that I can do," he announced eagerly.

He reached into the small pouch that hung about his neck and withdrew the silver whistle, handing it to the Valeman.

"Perk, what . . . ?" Wil began as the whistle was thrust into his palm.

"I have five days more before I must return to the Wing Hove," the boy interrupted quickly. "Each day I will fly once across the valley at noon. If you need me, signal with that whistle and I will come. The sound cannot be heard by humans—only by the Rocs. If you can find the talisman within the five days that I have left, then Genewen and I will carry you north again to your homeland."

"Perk, I don't think so . . ." Amberle started to object, shaking her head slowly.

"Wait a minute," Wil interjected. "If Genewen could fly us north again, we would save days. We would avoid all of the country we had to travel through to get here. Amberle, we have to get back as quickly as we can—you know that."

He turned quickly to Perk. "Could Genewen make such a trip? Could you?"

The boy nodded confidently.

"But he has said already that the Wilderun is forbidden to him," Amberle pointed out. "How can he land within it, then?"

Perk thought it out. "Well, if I set Genewen down just long enough to pick you up—that would only take a moment."

"I do not like this idea one bit," Amberle declared, frowning at Wil. "It is entirely too dangerous for Perk—and it is a violation of the trust that he has been given."

"I want to help," the boy insisted. "Besides, you told me how important this was."

He sounded so determined that for a moment Amberle could not think of a further argument. Wil took this opportunity to step in again.

"Look, why don't we compromise? I'll make a promise. If there is any danger to Perk, I'll not summon him under any circumstances. Fair enough?"

"But Wil . . ." the boy began.

"And Perk will agree that at the end of five days he will return to the Wing Hove as he has promised his grandfather, whether or not I have summoned him," the Valeman finished, cutting short the objections Perk was about to raise.

Amberle thought it over for a moment, then nodded reluctantly. "All right. But I will hold you to your promise, Wil."

The Valeman's eyes met hers. "Then it is agreed." He turned back to the boy. "We have to be going now, Perk. We owe you a lot."

He took the Elf's rough hand and gripped it firmly in his own.

"Goodbye," Amberle said, bending down to kiss him lightly on the cheek.

Perk flushed, his eyes lowering. "Goodbye, Amberle. Good luck."

With a final wave of farewell, the Valeman and the Elven girl turned and started down the long slope toward the forest wilderness. Perk watched them until they were out of sight.

26

In the late afternoon hours of the second day following the departure of Wil and Amberle with the Elven Hunters who served as their escort from the city of Arborlon, Eventine Elessedil sat alone in the study of his home, maps and charts spread out on the worktable in front of him, his head bent close in concentration. Outside, the rain continued to fall in steady, gray sheets, just as it had fallen for two days past, drenching the whole of the Elven forests. Already dusk was beginning to creep forth, its shadow falling long and dark through the curtained, floor-length windows at the far side of the room.

Manx layed curled at his master's feet, grizzled head resting comfortably on his forepaws, his breathing deep and even.

The old King lifted his head from his work, rubbing eyes reddened with fatigue. He stared across the room absently, then pushed his chair back from the table. Allanon should have been here by now, he thought anxiously. There was still much to be done, much that could not be done without the aid of the Druid. Eventine had no idea where the big man had gone this time; he had departed early that morning and had not been seen since.

The King stared out into the rain. For three days now he had worked with the Druid and the members of his Council preparing a defense for the Elven homeland—a defense that he knew would be necessary. Time was slipping away from him. The Ellcrys continued to fail, the Forbidding to weaken. With the passage of each day, the King expected to learn that both had crumbled, that the imprisoned Demons had broken free, and that the invasion of the Westland had begun. The Elven army was mobilized and stood ready: pikemen, swordsmen, archers and lancers; foot soldiers and cavalry; Home Guard and Black Watch; regular army and reserve; Elven fighting men from one end of the land to the other. The call had gone out, and all who were able had come to serve, leaving homes and families and pouring into the city to be outfitted with arms and equipment. Yet the King knew that even the iron will of the Elven army would not be enough to withstand an assault of the entire Demon horde, once it had broken free and welded itself into a cohesive unit. He knew this because Allanon had said that it would be so, and Eventine knew better than to question the Druid when he made a pronouncement as dire as this one. The Demons were physically stronger than the Elves; their numbers were greater. They were savage, maddened creatures driven by a hatred that had begun with the day of their banishment from the earth and had focused in whole upon the people responsible for that banishment. For centuries, there had been nothing else. Now that hatred would be given vent. Eventine harbored no illusions. If the Elves did not receive help from some quarter, the Demons would destroy them all.

It was no good depending solely on Amberle and the seed of the Ellcrys. However painful the thought, Eventine knew he must accept the fact that he might never see his granddaughter again. Even before her return to Arborlon, the King had dispatched messengers to the other races, requesting that they stand with the Elves against this evil that threatened his land—an evil that would ultimately consume them all. The messengers had been gone more than a week; as yet, none had returned. It was still too early, of course, to expect an answer from any of the other races, for even Callahorn was several days' ride. Even so, it was doubtful that many would come to stand with them.

Certainly the Dwarves would come, just as they had always come. The Dwarves and the Elves had stood together against every foe the free peoples of the Four Lands had faced since the time of the First Council of the Druids. Yet the Dwarves must come all the way from the deep forests of the Anar. And they must come afoot, for they were not horsemen. Eventine shook his head. They would come as quickly as they could—yet perhaps not quickly enough to save the Elves.

There was Callahorn, of course, but not the Callahorn of old, not the Callahorn of Balinor. Had Balinor still lived, or the Buckhannahs still ruled, the Border Legion would have marched at once. But Balinor was dead, the last of the Buckhannahs, and Callahorn's present ruler, a distant cousin who had ascended the throne more by accident than by acclaim, was an indecisive and overly cautious man who might find it convenient to forget that the Elves had come to the aid of Callahorn when last they called. In any case, the combined councils of Tyrsis and Varfleet and of Kern, rebuilt since its destruction fifty years earlier, wielded more power now than the King. They would be slow to act, even if Eventine's messenger were successful in conveying the urgency of the situation, for they lacked a strong leader to unite them in their thinking. They would debate, and while they debated the Border Legion would sit idle.

Ironically, it was their mistrust of their fellow Southlanders—and more particularly, their mistrust of the Federation—that would be likely to delay action on the part of the men of Callahorn. Following the destruction of the Warlock Lord and the defeat of his armies, the major cities of the deep Southland belatedly realized the extent of the threat that the Dark Lord had posed; acting in a haste born of fear, they had formed an alliance with one another, an alliance that began as a loose-knit organization of territories sharing common borders and common fears and quickly grew into the highly structured Federation. The Federation was the first cohesive form of government that the race of Man had known in more than a thousand years. Its professed goal was the final unification of the Southland and the race of Man under a single ruling government. That government, of course, was to be the Federation. To that end, they had begun a concerted effort to unite the remaining cities and provinces. In the four decades since its formation, the Federation had come to dominate almost the whole of the Southland. Of the major Southland cities, only those of Callahorn had resisted the suggested unification. The decision to do so had resulted in no small amount of friction between the two governments—especially as the Federation continued its steady advance northward toward Callahorn's borders.

Eventine folded his arms across his chest, frowning. He had dispatched a messenger to the Federation, yet he had little hope that there would be help forthcoming. The Federation had shown scant interest in the affairs of the other races, and it was doubtful that they would see a Demon invasion of the Westland as being of legitimate concern. In fact, it was doubtful that they would even believe that such an invasion was possible. The Men of the deep Southland knew little of the sorcery that had troubled the other lands since the time of the First Council of the Druids; theirs had been a closed, introverted existence, and in their new expansion they had not yet encountered many of the unpleasant realities that lay beyond their own limited experience.

Again the King shook his head. No, the cities of the Federation would not come. Just as had been the case when they were warned of the coming of the Warlock Lord, they would not believe.

No messenger had been sent to the Gnomes. It would have been pointless to do so. The Gnomes were a tribal race. They did not answer to a single ruler or governing council. Their chieftains and their seers were their leaders, and there were different chieftains and seers for each tribe, all constantly feuding with one another. Bitter and disgruntled since their defeat at Tyrsis, the Gnomes had not mixed in the affairs of the other races in the fifty years that had since passed. It was hardly reasonable to expect that they should choose to do so now.

There remained the Trolls. The Trolls, too, were a tribal race, yet since the conclusion of the aborted Third War of the Races, the Trolls had begun unifying within the vast stretches of the Northland, tribes banding together within certain territories under council leadership. The closest and one of the largest of these communities lay within the Kershalt Territory, at the northern borders of the Elven homeland. The Kershalt was occupied principally by Rock Trolls, though some of the lesser tribes inhabited portions of this region as well. Traditionally, Elves and Trolls had been enemies; in the last two Race Wars, they had fought bitterly against one another. But with the fall of the Warlock Lord, the enmity between the two races had lessened appreciably, and for the past fifty years they had lived in comparatively peaceful coexistence. Relations between Arborlon and the Kershalt had been particularly good. Trade had opened up and plans had been made to exchange delegations. There was a chance then that the Kershalt Trolls might agree to aid them.

The old King checked his thoughts and smiled wanly. A slim chance, he conceded. But he knew he could not afford to pass over any chance. The Elves would have need of whomever they could find to stand with them if they were to survive.

He stood up slowly, stretched, then glanced down again at the array of maps spread out on the worktable. Each depicted a different sector of the Westland, chartings of all the known country that comprised the Elven homeland and the territories surrounding it. Eventine had studied them until he thought it possible to trace their configurations in his sleep. Out of one of those sectors the Demons would come; and there the Elven defenses must be settled. But out of which? Where would the Forbidding crumble first? Where would the invasion begin?

The King let his eyes wander from one map to the next. Allanon had promised that he would discover where the break would come, and it was for that vital piece of information that the Elven army waited. Until then . . .

He sighed and walked to the window-doors that opened onto the manor house grounds. As he stared out through the growing dusk he caught sight of Ander coming up the walkway, head bent against the rain, arms laden with the troop registers and supply listings that he had been instructed to collect. The frown that creased the old King's face softened. Ander had been invaluable these past few days. To his youngest son had fallen the tedious, if necessary, task of information gathering—thankless work at best and work that Arion would certainly have disdained. Yet Ander had undertaken the job without a single word of complaint. The King shook his head. Strange, but even though Arion was Crown Prince of the Elves and the closer of his sons, there were times these past few days when he saw more of himself in Ander.

He let his gaze shift then to the leaden evening skies and wondered suddenly if Ander ever felt the same.

Fatigue lined Ander Elessedil's face as he pushed through the manor house doors, shed his rain-soaked cloak, and turned down the darkened hallway that led to his father's study, the troop registers and supply listings cradled protectively in his arms. His day had been a difficult one and it had not been helped any by his brother's continuing refusal to have anything to do with him. It had been like that since he had taken Amberle's part at the High Council. What had always been a rather broad gulf between them had widened into a chasm that he could not begin to bridge. Today's encounter with his brother had illustrated just how wide that chasm had grown. Sent by his father to collect the information he now carried, he had gone to Arion for assistance because Arion had been given responsibility for mobilizing and outfitting the Elven army. Though Arion could have shortened his work by hours, he had refused even to meet with him, sending a junior supply officer in his stead and keeping himself conveniently absent the entire day. It had angered Ander so much that he had very nearly chosen to force a confrontation. But that might have involved their father, and the old King did not need any additional problems to occupy his time. So Ander had kept silent. For as long as the Demon hordes threatened the homeland, personal difficulties must be set aside.

He shook his head. Such reasoning did not make him feel any better, however, about the way things were working out between Arion and him.

He reached the study door, nudged it open with his boot, entered, and nudged it closed again. He managed an encouraging smile for his father, who crossed to relieve him of the charts and listings. Then he sank down wearily into an empty chair.

"That's everything," he said. "Inventoried, recorded, and placed in order."

Eventine set the material his son had brought him on the table with the maps and turned back. "You look tired."

Ander rose and stretched. "I am . . ."

In a rush of wind and rain, the window-doors flew open. Father and son whirled as maps and charts scattered to the floor and oil lamps flickered. Allanon stood framed in the entry, black robes glistening wetly in the dusk, trailing water onto the study floor. The angular features were strained, the thin line of his mouth hard. Both hands held firm a slim wooden staff, its surface the color of silver.

For an instant Ander's eyes met those of the Druid, and the Elven Prince felt his blood turn to ice. There was something terrible in the Druid's expression, glimmerings of fierce determination, power, and death.

The Druid wheeled and shoved closed the window-doors, fastening once again the latch he had somehow managed to loosen from without. When he turned back again, Ander saw clearly the silver staff and his face went deathly pale.

"Allanon, what have you done!" the words slipped out before he could think better of them.

His father saw it as well and cried out in a horrified whisper. "The Ellcrys! Druid, you have cut a branch from the living tree!"

"No, Eventine," the tall man replied softly. "Not cut. Not harmed her who is the life of this land. Never that."

"But the staff . . ." the King began, his hands reaching out as if to touch a thing that would burn.

"Not cut," the other repeated. "Look closely now."

He held forth the staff and turned it slowly so that it could be inspected. Ander and his father bent close. Each end of the staff was smooth and rounded. Nowhere was it splintered or knicked by a blade. Even the boles that roughened its length were healed and free of markings.

Eventine looked bewildered. "Then how . . . ?"

"The staff was given to me, King of the Elves—given by her, given that it might be carried against the enemies who threaten her people and their land." The Druid's voice was so cold that it seemed to freeze the very air of the small room. "Here, then, is magic that will give strength to the Elven army, power to withstand the evil that lives within the Demon hordes. This staff shall be our talisman—the right hand of the Ellcrys, carried forth when the armies meet to do battle."

He stepped forward, the staff still clenched before him, his dark eyes hard within the shadow of his brow.

"Early this morning I went to her, alone, seeking to find a weapon with which we might stand against our enemy. She gave me audience, speaking with the images that are her words, asking why I had come. I told her that the Elves had no magic save my own with which to counter the power of the Demons; I told her that I feared that this alone might not be enough, that I might fail. I told her that I sought something of what she is with which to do battle against the Demons, for she is an anathema to them.

"Then she reached down within herself and stripped away this staff which I hold, this limb of her body. Weakened, knowing that she dies, she yet managed to give to me a part of herself with which to aid the Elven people. I did not touch her, did nothing but stand in awe of her strength of will. Feel this wood, King of the Elves—touch it!"

He thrust the staff into Eventine's hands, and they closed about it. The King's eyes widened in shock. The Druid took the staff from him then and passed it wordlessly to Ander. The Elven Prince started. The wood of the staff was warm, as if the blood of life flowed within.

"It lives!" the Druid breathed reverently. "Apart and separate from her, yet still filled with her life! It is the weapon that I sought. It is the talisman that will protect the Elves against the black sorcery of the Demon hordes. As long as they bear the staff, the power that lives within the Ellcrys shall watch over them and work to keep them safe."

He took the staff from Ander's hands and once more their eyes met. The Elven Prince felt something unspoken pass between them, something he could not quite comprehend—just as it had been that night in the High Council when he had gone to stand with Amberle.

The Druid's eyes shifted to the King. "Now hear me." His voice was low and quick. "The rains will end this night. Does the army stand ready?"

Eventine nodded.

"Then we march at dawn. We must move quickly now."

"But where are we marching to?" the King asked immediately. "Have you discovered where the break will come?"

The Druid's black eyes glistened. "I have. The Ellcrys told me. She senses the Demons massing at a single point within the Forbidding, senses herself weakening where they gather. She knows that it is there that the Forbidding will fail first. The rent has been made once already by the ones who crossed through to slay the Chosen. The breach was closed, but the wound was not healed. There the Forbidding will break. It weakens already, straining with the force that pushes against it. The Demons are summoned to that place by the one who commands them, and who wields the power of sorcery so near my own. He is called the Dagda Mor. With his aid, the breach will be forced once again, and this time it will not be closed.

"But we will be waiting for them." His hand tightened on the staff. "We will be waiting. We will catch them while they stand newly crossed and still disorganized. We will close off their passage to Arborlon for as long as we are able. We will give Amberle the time she needs to find the Bloodfire and return."

Wordlessly he beckoned Ander and his father forward. Then he reached down and pulled from the floor one of the fallen maps, setting it squarely on the worktable.

"The break will come here," he said softly.

His finger pointed to the broad expanse of the Hoare Flats.

27

That same afternoon, when the daylight had nearly gone and the rain had turned to fine mist, the Legion Free Corps rode into Arborlon. The people of the city who saw them pass paused in the middle of their endeavors and turned to one another with guarded whispers. From high atop the tree lanes to the forest roadways below, hushed voices spoke as one. There was no mistaking the Free Corps.

Ander Elessedil was still closeted in the manor house study with his father and Allanon—kept there, oddly enough, at the Druid's insistence that he familiarize himself with Westland maps of the Sarandanon and proposed defensive plans—when Gael brought word of their arrival.

"My Lord, a cavalry command of the Border Legion has ridden in from Callahorn," the young aid announced, appearing abruptly at the study door. "Our patrols picked them up an hour east of the city and escorted them in. They should be here in a few minutes."

"The Legion!" A broad smile spread across the old King's weary face. "I hadn't dared to hope. What command, Gael? How many are they?"

"No word, my Lord. A messenger from the patrol brought the news, but there were no details."

"No matter." Eventine was on his feet and moving toward the door. "Any help is welcome, whoever . . ."

"Elven King!" Allanon's deep voice brought Ander's father about sharply. "We have important work to do here, work that should not be interrupted. Perhaps your son might go in your place—if only to give greeting to the Bordermen."

Ander stared at Allanon in surprise and turned eagerly to his father. The King hesitated, then seeing the look in his son's eyes, he nodded.

"Very well, Ander. Extend my compliments to the Legion Commander and advise him that I will meet with him personally later this evening. See that quarters are provided."

Pleased with having been given a responsibility of some importance for a change, Ander hurried from the manor house, an escort of Elven Hunters in tow. The surprise he had experienced at Allanon's unexpected suggestion turned quickly to curiosity. It occurred to him that this was not the first time that Allanon had gone out of his way to include him when the Druid need not have done so. There was that first meeting when he had told Eventine of Amberle and the Bloodfire. There was his admonition to Ander upon leaving for Paranor to assume responsibility for his father's protection. There was that sense of alliance that had brought him to his feet in the High Council to stand with Amberle when no one else would do so. There was this afternoon's meeting when Allanon had given the Ellcrys staff to his father. Arion should have been present for these meetings, not he. Why was Arion never there?

He had just passed through the gates fronting the manor house grounds, still pondering the matter, when the foremost ranks of the Border cavalry crested the roadway leading in and the entire command wound slowly into view. Ander slowed, frowning. He recognized these riders. Long gray cloaks bordered in crimson billowed from their shoulders and wide-brimmed hats with a single crimson feather sat cocked upon their heads. Long bows and broadswords jutted from their saddle harness, and short swords were strapped across their backs. Each rider held a lance from which fluttered a small crimson and gray pennant, and the horses wore light armor of leather with metal fastenings. Escorted by the handful of Elven Hunters who had picked them up while on patrol east of the city, they rode through the rain-soaked streets of Arborlon in their precise, measured lines and glanced neither left nor right at the crowds who gathered to stare after them.

"The Free Corps," Ander murmured to himself. "They have sent us the Free Corps."

There were few who had not heard of the Free Corps, the most famous and the most controversial command ever attached to the Border Legion of Callahorn. It drew its name from the promise it gave to those who joined its ranks—that its soldiers might leave behind without fear of question or need for explanation all that had come before in their lives. For most, there was much to be left. They came from different lands, different histories, and different lives, but they came for similar reasons. There were thieves among them, killers and cheats, soldiers broken from other armies, men of low blood and high, men with honor and men without, some searching, some fleeing, some drifting—but all seeking to escape what they were, to forget what they had been, and to start anew. The Free Corps gave them that chance. No soldier of the Free Corps was ever asked about his past; his life began with the day he joined. What had come before was finished; only the present mattered and what a man might make of himself for the time that he served.

For most, that time was short. The Free Corps was the Legion's shock unit; as such, it was considered expendable. Its soldiers were the first into battle and the first to die. In every engagement fought since the inception of the Corps some thirty years earlier, its casualty rate had been the highest. While the past had been left behind by the soldiers of the Free Corps, the future was an even more uncertain prospect. Still, it was a fair exchange, most thought. After all, there was a price for everything, and this price was not so unreasonable. If anything, it was a source of pride for the soldiers who paid it; it gave them a sense of importance, an identity that set them apart from any other fighting man in the Four Lands. It was a tradition of the Free Corps that its soldiers should die in battle. It was not important to the men of the Corps that they should die; death was the reality of their existence, and they viewed it as an old acquaintance with whom they had brushed shoulders on more than one occasion. No, it was not important that they should die; it was important only that they should die well.

They had proven it often enough before, Ander knew. Now it appeared they had been sent to Arborlon to prove it once again.

The Legion command drew to a halt before the iron gates, and a tall, gray-cloaked rider in the forefront dismounted. Catching sight of Ander, he passed the reins of his horse to another and strode forward. On reaching the Elven Prince and his guard, he removed the wide-brimmed hat he wore and inclined his head slightly.

"I am Stee Jans, Commander of the Legion Free Corps."

For an instant Ander did not respond, so startled was he by the other's appearance. Stee Jans was a big man, seeming to tower over Ander. His weathered, yet still-youthful face was crisscrossed with dozens of scars, some of which ran through the light red beard that shaded his jaw, leaving streaks of white. A tangle of rust-colored hair fell to his shoulders, braided and tied. Part of one ear was missing and a single gold ring dangled from the other. Hazel eyes fixed those of the Elven Prince, so hard that they seemed chiseled from stone.

Ander found himself staring and quickly recovered. "I am Ander Elessedil—Eventine is my father." He extended his hand in greeting. Stee Jans' grip was iron hard, the brown hands calloused and knotted. Ander broke the handshake quickly and glanced down the long lines of gray riders, searching in vain for other units of the Legion. "The King has asked me to extend his compliments and to see that you are quartered. How soon can we expect the other commands?"

A faint smile crossed the big man's scarred visage. "There are no other commands, my Lord. Only the soldiers of the Free Corps."

"Only the . . . ?" Ander hesitated in confusion. "How many of you are there, Commander?"

"Six hundred."

"Six hundred!" Ander failed to hide his dismay. "But what of the Border Legion? How soon will it be sent?"

Stee Jans paused. "My Lord, I believe that I should be direct with you. The Legion may not be sent at all. The Council of the Cities has not yet made a decision. Like most councils, it finds it easier to talk about making a decision than to make it. Your ambassador spoke well, I am told, but there are many voices of caution on the Council, some of opposition. The King defers to the Council; the Council looks south. The Federation is a threat that the Council can see; your Demons are little more than a Westland myth."

"A myth!" Ander was appalled.

"You are fortunate to have even the Free Corps," the big man continued calmly. "You would not have that if it were not for the Council's need to soothe its collective conscience. A token force, at least, must be sent to the aid of their Elven allies, they argued. The Free Corps was the logical choice—just as it always is whenever there is an obvious sacrifice to be made."

It was a simple statement of fact, made without rancor or bitterness. The big man's eyes stayed flat and expressionless. Ander flushed.

"I would not have thought that the men of Callahorn would be so stupid!" he snapped, a sense of anger rushing through him.

Stee Jans studied him a moment, as if measuring him. "I understand that when Callahorn was under attack from the armies of the Warlock Lord, the Borderlands sent a request to the Elves for assistance. But Eventine was made prisoner by the Dark Lord, and in his absence the High

Council of the Elves found itself unable to act." He paused. "It is much the same with Callahorn now. The Borderlands have no leader; they have had no leader since Balinor."

Ander eyed the other critically, his anger subsiding. "You are an outspoken man, Commander."

"I am an honest man, my Lord. It helps me to see things more clearly."

"What you have told me might not sit so well with some in Callahorn."

The Borderman shrugged. "Perhaps that is why I am here."

Ander smiled slowly. He liked Stee Jans—even without knowing any more about him than he did at this moment. "Commander, I did not mean to seem angry. It has nothing to do with you. Please understand that. And the Free Corps is most welcome. Now let me see you to your quarters."

Stee Jans shook his head. "No quarters are necessary; I sleep with my soldiers. My Lord, the Elven army marches in the morning, I am told."

Ander nodded. "Then the Free Corps will march as well. We need only rest the night. Please tell this to the King."

"I will tell him," Ander promised.

The Legion Commander saluted, then turned and walked back to his horse. Remounting, he nodded briefly to the riders of the Elven patrol who escorted his command, and the long gray columns swung left once more down the muddied road.

Ander stared after him with mingled admiration and disbelief. Six hundred men! Thinking of the thousands of Demons that would come against them, he found himself wondering what possible difference six hundred Southlanders would make.

28

At dawn, the Elves marched forth from Arborlon, to the wail of pipes and the roll of drums, voices raised in song, banners flying in splashes of vivid color against a sky still leaden and clouded. Eventine Elessedil rode at their head, gray hair flowing down chain mail forged of blue iron, his right hand holding firmly the silver-white staff of the Ellcrys. Allanon was at his side, a spectral shadow, tall and black atop a still taller and blacker Artaq, and it was as if Death had ridden from the pits of the earth to stand watch over the Elves. Behind rode the King's sons: Arion, cloaked in white and bearing the Elven standard of battle, a war eagle on a field of crimson; Ander, cloaked in green and carrying the banner of the house of the Elessedils, a crown wreathed in boughs set over a spreading oak. Dardan, Rhoe, and three dozen hardened Elven Hunters came next, the Elessedil guard; then the gray and crimson of the Legion Free

Corps, six hundred strong. Pindanon rode alone at the forefront of his command, a gaunt, bent figure atop his warhorse, his battle-scarred armor lashed about his spare frame as if to hold his bones in place. The army followed him, massive and forbidding, six columns wide and thousands strong. They numbered three companies of cavalry, battle lances hoisted out of their midst in a forest of iron-tipped shafts, four companies of foot soldiers with pikes and body shields, and two companies of archers bearing the great Elven long bows—all clad in the traditional manner of the Elven warrior, lightly armored with chain-mail vests and leather guards to assure mobility and quickness.

It was an awesome procession. Trappings and weapons creaked and jingled in the early morning stillness, flashed in dull glimmerings through the new light, and cast the Elves in half-human forms that whispered of death. Booted feet and iron-shod hooves thudded and splashed along the muddied earth as the columns of men and horses wound from the parade grounds north of the city to the bluff of the Carolan and prepared to turn onto the Elfitch, the hooked rampway that led down from the heights of Arborlon to the forestlands beneath. The people of the city had come to watch. Atop the Carolan, on walls and fences, in fields and gardens, lining the way at every step, they bade farewell with cheers of encouragement and hope and with silences born of emotions that had no voice. Before the gates to the Gardens of Life, the Black Watch stood assembled, present to a man, their lances raised in salute. At the bluff's edge were gathered in review the Elven Hunters of the Home Guard and the man who would command them in their King's absence—Emer Chios, First Minister of the High Council, now the designated defender of the city of Arborlon.

Down out of the Carolan the Elven army wound, following the spiral of the stone-block ramp as it dropped along the forested cliffs through seven walled gates that marked its levels of descent. At its lower end, the army swung south toward the narrows. A solitary bridge spanned the Rill Song, the lone passage west from the city, its iron struts nearly awash with the swollen waters of the river. Like a metal-backed snake, the army moved onto the bridge, crossed, and passed into the silent woods beyond. The glitter of weapons and armor twinkled into darkness, banners slipped from view, and the strains of song, the wail of pipes, and the roll of drums faded into echoes quickly lost in the leafy canopy of the trees. By the time the morning sun had broken through the clouds of the departing storm to rise above the crest of the Carolan and light the forestland below, the last remnants of this grand procession had disappeared from view.

For five days the army journeyed west from Arborlon, winding its way through the deep forests of the homeland toward the Sarandanon. The rains had moved east into Callahorn, and the sun shone down out of cloudless blue skies to warm the woodland shadows. Travel was measured, the cavalry forced to slow its place to match that of the soldiers afoot. Evi-

dence of the danger threatening the Elves became steadily more apparent
as the army passed westward through the outlying provinces. Tales filtered
back from Elven families on their way eastward to the home city with their
possessions bundled in carts and on the backs of oxen and horse. Their
homes and their villages were abandoned behind them. Terrifying creatures roamed the land west, their frightened voices warned—dark and brutal monsters that killed without reason and disappeared as quickly as they
had come. Cottages had been stripped and homes violated, the Elves
within left torn and broken. Such incidents were scattered, but that merely
served to convince the fleeing villagers that there was no longer any place
west of Arborlon that was safe. As the army marched past, the villagers sent
up cheers and shouts of encouragement, but their faces remained clouded
with doubt.

The march west wore on until, late in the afternoon of the fifth day,
the army passed out of the forestland into the valley of the Sarandanon.
The valley lay sandwiched between woodlands on the south and east, the
Kensrowe Mountains on the north, and the broad expanse of the Innisbore
on the west. A flat, fertile stretch of farmland dotted with small clumps of
trees and pockets of spring water, the Sarandanon was the breadbasket of
the Elven nation. Corn, wheat, and other seed crops were sown and har-
vested seasonally by the families who lived within the valley, then bartered
or sold to the remainder of the homeland. Mild temperatures and a balanced rainfall provided an ideal climate for farming, and for generations
the Sarandanon had served as the principal source of food for the Elven
people.

The Elven army encamped that night at the eastern end of the valley; at
dawn on the following day, it began the journey across. A broad, earthen
road wound through the heart of the Sarandanon past fence lines and clusters of small dwellings and sheds, and the army followed it west. In the
fields, the families of the valley toiled with quiet determination. Few Elves
here had yet gone east. Everything that had meaning in their lives lay rooted
in the land they farmed, and they would not be frightened off easily.

By midafternoon, the army had reached the western end of the valley.
In the distance, beyond the Innisbore, the humped ridge of the Breakline
rose up against the horizon, curving north above the Kensrowe into the
wilderness of the Kershalt Territory. The sun already lay atop the crest of
the mountains, brilliant golden light spilling down out of the rock. In the
growing darkness of the eastern sky, the moon's whiteness glimmered
faintly.

The army swung north. Between the Innisbore and the Kensrowe,
Baen Draw opened down out of the rugged hill country below the Break-
line into the valley of the Sarandanon. It was there that the army of the
Elves made its camp.

At dusk, Allanon came down out of the Kensrowe as silently and unexpectedly as he had gone into them hours before, his tall form moving into

the Elven camp like one of night's shadows, dark and solitary as he passed through the maze of cooking fires that dotted the grasslands. He went directly to the tent of the Elven King, oblivious to the soldiers who stared after him, his head lowered within the darkness of his cowl. The Elven Hunters who stood watch before Eventine's quarters stepped aside wordlessly at his approach and let him enter without challenge.

Within, he found the King at a small, makeshift table of planks laid crosswise atop logs, his evening meal spread out before him. Dardan and Rhoe stood silently at the rear of the tent. At a glance from the Druid, Eventine dismissed them. When they were gone, Allanon moved to the table and seated himself.

"Is all in readiness?" he asked quietly.

Eventine nodded.

"And the plan of defense?"

In the light of the oil lamps, the King could see that the Druid's dark face was streaked with sweat. He stared uncertainly at the mystic, then pushed aside his dinner and laid a map of the Elven homeland upon the table.

"At dawn, we march to the Breakline." He traced the route with his finger. "We will secure the passes of Halys Cut and Worl Run and hold them against the Demons for as long as we are able. If the passes are forced, we will fall back to the Sarandanon. Baen Draw will be our second line of defense. Once through the Breakline, the Demons will have three ways to go. If they turn south out of the passes, they must circle below the Innisbore through the forests, then come north again. If they turn north first, they must make their way through the rugged hill country above the Kensrowe and come south. Either route will delay their advance on Arborlon by at least several days. Their only other choice will be to come through the Draw—and through the Elven army."

Allanon's dark gaze fixed on the King. "They will choose the Draw."

"We should be able to hold it for several days," the King continued. "Longer, perhaps, if they do not think to flank us."

"Two days, no more." The Druid's voice was flat, unemotional.

Eventine stiffened. "Very well, two days. But if the Draw is taken, the Sarandanon will be lost. Arborlon will be our last defense."

"So be it." Allanon leaned forward, hands knotting together before him. "We need to speak now of something else, something that I have kept from you." His voice was soft, almost a whisper. "The Demons are no longer with us—those who have crossed already through the Forbidding, the Dagda Mor and his followers. They neither watch us nor follow after us. If they did, I would sense it, and I have sensed nothing from the time that we left Arborlon."

The Elven King stared back at him wordlessly.

"I thought it strange that they should take so little interest in us." The Druid smiled faintly. "This afternoon I went up into the mountains so that I might be alone to discover where it was that they had gone. It is within my power to search out those who are hidden from my eyes. I have that power, but it must be used sparingly, for in using it I reveal to others with powers similar to my own—such as the Dagda Mor—both my own presence and the presence of any whom I seek. I could not risk using it to follow Wil Ohmsford and your granddaughter on their journey south; if I did I might tell the Demons where they could be found. Yet to search out the Dagda Mor himself—that, I felt, was a risk that should be taken.

"I did seek him then, searching the whole of the surrounding land to discover where he had concealed himself. But he was not concealed. I found him beyond the wall of the Breakline, within the Hoare Flats, he and those who follow him. Still, I could tell little of what they were about; their thoughts were closed to me. I could but sense their presence. The evil that pervades them is so strong that even brushing against it momentarily caused me great pain, and I was forced to withdraw at once."

The Druid straightened. "It is certain that the Demons gather within the Flats in anticipation of the collapse of the Forbidding. It is certain that they work to hasten that collapse. They do this openly and without concern for what the plans of the Elves may be. That suggests to me that they already know those plans."

Eventine paled. "The spy within my house—the spy who warned the Demons that you would be at Paranor."

"That would explain why it is the Demons show such an obvious lack of interest in our movements," Allanon agreed. "If they already know that we intend to stop them at the Breakline, they have little need to follow after us to see what we are about. They have only to await our coming."

The implication of that statement was not lost on Eventine. "Then the Breakline may be a trap."

The Druid nodded. "The question is, what kind of trap do the Demons set? There are not enough of them yet to withstand an army of this size. They have need of those still imprisoned within the Forbidding. If we are quick enough . . ."

He left the sentence unfinished and rose. "One thing more, Eventine. Be cautious. The spy is still with us. He may be within this camp, among those you trust. If the opportunity presents itself, he may seek your death."

He turned and moved back toward the entry, the shadow of his dark form rising up against the tent wall like some giant in the flickering light of the oil lamps. The King stared after him wordlessly for a moment, then lurched sharply to his feet.

"Allanon!"

The Druid looked back.

"If the Demons know why we march to the Breakline—if they know that—then they may also know that Amberle carries the Ellcrys seed into the Wilderun."

There was an unpleasant silence. The two men faced each other. Then, without replying, the Druid turned and disappeared through the tent flap into the night.

At that same moment, Ander was picking his way through the crowded Elven encampment in search of the Legion Free Corps and Stee Jans. Ostensibly his mission was to inquire into the needs of the Legion soldiers, but underlying this was his personal interest in their Commander. He had not spoken again with Jans since the Free Corps had arrived in Arborlon and he was admittedly curious to know more about the enigmatic Southlander. With nothing else immediate to occupy his time, he had decided to take this opportunity to seek him out and talk further with him.

He found the Free Corps camp at the southern edge of the Kensrowe, their watch already posted, their horses tethered and fed. No one challenged him as he wandered into their midst. When he could not immediately locate the Free Corps Commander's quarters, he stopped a number of soldiers to ask if they knew where Jans could be found and was directed finally to a Legion Captain.

"Him?" The Captain was a burly fellow with a heavy beard and a laugh that rang deep and hollow. "Who knows? He's not in his tent, I can tell you that much. He left almost as soon as we pitched camp. Went out into the hills."

"Scouting?" Ander was incredulous.

The Captain shrugged. "He's like that. Wants to know everything about a place where he might die." He laughed roughly. "Never leaves that kind of checking to another—likes to do it himself."

Ander nodded uncomfortably. "I suppose that's why he's still alive."

"Still alive? Why, that one will never die. You know what they call him? The Iron Man. Iron Man—that's him. That's the Commander."

"He looks hard enough," Ander agreed, his curiosity peaked.

The Captain motioned him closer, and for a moment each forgot whom he was addressing. "You know about Rybeck?" the Borderman asked.

Ander shook his head, and a glint of satisfaction leaped into the other's hard eyes. "You listen then. Ten years ago a band of Gnome raiders was burning and killing the people at the eastern edge of the borderlands. Vicious little rats, and a bunch of them at that. The Legion tried everything to trap them, but nothing worked. Finally the King sent the Free Corps after them—with orders to track them down and destroy them, even if it took the rest of the year. I remember that hunt; I was with the Corps even then."

He squatted down next to a cooking fire, and Ander hunched down beside him. Others began drifting in to listen.

"Five weeks the hunt went on, and the Corps tracked those Gnomes all the way east into the Upper Anar. Then one day, when we were getting close, a patrol of our men, only twenty-three of them, stumbled into a rear guard of several hundred raiders. The patrol could have fallen back, but it didn't. These were Free Corps soldiers and they chose to fight. One man was sent back for reinforcements and the rest made their stand in this little village called Rybeck—just a bunch of nothing buildings. For three hours those twenty-two soldiers held out against the raiders—threw back every assault they mounted. A lieutenant, three junior officers and eighteen soldiers. One of those junior officers was just a kid. Just seven months with the Corps—but already a corporal. No one knew much about him. Like most, he didn't say much about his past."

The Captain leaned forward. "After the first two hours, that boy was the only officer still alive. He rallied the half-dozen soldiers left into a small stone cottage. Refused surrender, refused quarter. When the relief force broke through finally, there were dead Gnomes all over the place." The man's hand tightened into a fist before Ander's face. "More than a hundred of them. All of our men were gone, all but two, and one of them died later that day. That left just one. The boy corporal."

He paused and chuckled softly. "That boy was Stee Jans. That's why they call him the Iron Man. And Rybeck?" He shook his head solemnly. "Rybeck shows how a soldier of the Free Corps should fight and die."

The soldiers gathered about him murmured their assent. Ander paused a moment, then rose. The Captain stood up with him, straightening himself as he seemed to remember again who it was that he was conversing with.

"Anyway, my Lord, the Commander's not here right now." He paused. "Can I do something for you?"

Ander shook his head. "I came to ask if there was anything you need."

"A bit to drink," someone cried, but the Captain waved him off with a quick oath.

"We'll be fine, my Lord," he responded. "We have what we need."

Ander nodded slowly. Hard men, these Free Corps soldiers. They had made the long journey to Arborlon and then, with but a single night's rest, a forced march to the Sarandanon. He doubted that there really was much that they needed.

"Then I'll say good-night, Captain," he said.

He turned and walked back toward the Elven camp, mulling over in his mind the tale of the Legion Commander they called the Iron Man.

29

The following morning the army of the Elves and their Legion allies marched north out of the Sarandanon. With the dawn still a faint silver glow above the eastern forestline, the soldiers wound through Baen Draw and turned into the hills that lay beyond. Armor and harness jangled and creaked, boots and hooves thudded in rough cadence, and men and horses huffed clouds of white vapor in the frosty morning air. No one spoke or whistled or sang. A sense of anticipation and wariness pervaded the ranks. On this morning, Elven Hunter and Borderman knew they were marching into battle.

Up into the hills they circled, hills barren and rugged, their slopes sparse with short grass and scrub, rutted and eroded by wind and rain. Ahead, still far distant, the dark mass of the Breakline stood silhouetted against the dying night. Slowly, as the sun brightened the skyline, the mountains etched themselves out of the blackness, a maze of peaks and crags, drops and slides. The day began to warm. The morning hours slipped away and the army swung west, columns of riders and men afoot winding through gullies and over ridges, stretching out across the land. To the south, the waters of the Innisbore sparkled in flashes of blue, and above the choppy surface flew a sprinkling of white-backed gulls, their wings tipped with black, their cries shrill and haunting.

By noon, the army had reached the Breakline, and Eventine signalled a halt. The mountains loomed up against the horizon, a dark and massive wall of rock. Cliffs and spires rose thousands of feet into the sky, massed close as if some giant had gathered them within his hands and squeezed until the stone had broken and split from the pressure. Still and silent, barren and cold, they were filled with emptiness, darkness, and death.

Two passes split the Breakline, slender threads that tied the land of the Elves to the Hoare Flats. South lay Halys Cut. North lay Worl Run. If the Demons were to break through the Forbidding within the Flats as Allanon had foreseen, then, to reach the city of Arborlon, they would be forced to come east through one or both of these passes. It was there that the Elven army would try to stop them.

"We part company here," Eventine announced when he had assembled his officers. Ander edged his mount closer to the small circle of men to hear clearly what was being said. "The army will divide. Half will march north with Prince Arion and Commander Pindanon to secure Worl Run. The other half will march south with me to Halys Cut. Commander Jans?" The bronzed face of the Free Corps Commander pushed into view. "I would like the Free Corps to march south. Pindanon, give the order."

The ring of horsemen broke apart as the word was passed down the line. Ander glanced briefly at Arion, who met his gaze coldly and turned away.

"Ander, I want you to ride with me," his father called over to him.

Kael Pindanon came galloping back to the King. All was in readiness. The two old comrades bade farewell to each other, hands clasping tightly. Ander looked one time more for his brother, but Arion was already moving to the head of his column.

Allanon appeared, dark face impassive. "His anger is misplaced," the Druid said quietly, then nudged Artaq past.

Pindanon's voice rang out. Banners and lances lifted in salute as the army of the Elves split apart. Shouts and cheers broke the morning stillness, echoing through the crags and rifts of the mountain rock. For long moments the air was filled with sound, reckless and fierce. Then Pindanon's command swept north, winding into the hills in a broad cloud of dust until it was lost from view.

The soldiers of the King turned south. For several hours they worked their way along the fringe of the Breakline, following the steady rise and fall of the lowland hills. Overhead, the sun passed west across the ridge of the mountains, and shadows began to lengthen in dark swatches. The still, sultry air of midday cooled in a southerly breeze that swept out of the distant forests. Gradually the hills broadened into grasslands. At their edge, straddled by a series of narrow, ragged peaks, the dark mouth of Halys Cut opened into the rock.

Eventine brought his army to a halt and held a brief conference with his officers. Below the eastern entrance to the pass lay several miles of open plains that ran south to the forestline. If the Demons were to find a way to cross the Breakline below Halys Cut, they could slip north through the forestland and trap the Elven army within the pass. A rear guard would be necessary to protect against that possibility. A cavalry unit could best handle the assignment; the cavalry would be of little use in any case within the narrow confines of the pass.

Ander saw his father's gaze fall briefly on Stee Jans, then move away. Elven cavalry units would form that guard, the King announced.

The order was given. The Elven cavalry detached itself from the main body of the army and began to deploy across the length of the grasslands. At a signal from Eventine, the remainder of the army turned into Halys Cut. Through the broad, shadowed gap the Elves marched, rugged cliffs towering up about them. The floor of the pass began to climb almost immediately, and the soldiers trudged upward into the rock. Quickly the air cooled, and the sound of shod hooves and booted feet striking against stone echoed eerily. As the trail continued to rise, the footing grew less sure. Loose rock littered the pathway, and cracks split its surface. Men and horses stumbled and slid with each step, and the pace slowed.

Then abruptly it stopped. Before them a huge chasm opened, a massive fissure that dropped away into black emptiness, splitting the length of the pass ahead for hundreds of yards. To the left, the trail sloped down along the mountainside, broad and even as it ran to a defile at the far end of the chasm. To the right, a narrow ledge skirted the fissure, a thin, crumbling pathway that would barely permit the passage of a single rider. All about, sheer cliff walls seemed to bend inward as they rose until all that remained of the sky was a thin, ragged blue line.

The army swung left along the broader path, staying well back of the black mouth of the chasm. When it had gained the defile, it found itself entering a canyon bright with afternoon sunlight and grown green with scrub and saw grass. Clusters of boulders dotted the canyon floor, and a thin stream trickled down out of the cliff walls and pooled in a small, brush-grown hollow. Jackrabbits bounded through the brush at the army's approach, and a scattering of birds drinking at the water's edge took sudden flight.

The Elves crossed to the far end of the canyon. There the pass opened down a broad, winding gorge into the vast emptiness of the Hoare Flats. Eventine's hand came up sharply, signalling a halt. His eyes swept the length of the gorge, past a maze of jumbled rock pockets and drops angling down through hulking cliffs and long, rugged slides. Wordlessly, he nodded. It was here that the army would make its stand.

Dusk crept into the Breakline, shadowed gray light chasing toward a sunset that lit the sky above the Hoare Flats in a blaze of scarlet and gold. Behind the wall of the mountains, the moon's silver disk rose above the forestland and one by one the stars winked into view. Within Halys Cut, the silence began to deepen.

Ander Elessedil stood alone on a small knoll midway down the gorge that ran to the Flats, arms cradling protectively the silver-white staff of the Ellcrys. Wordlessly he surveyed the lines of Elven Hunters and Free Corps soldiers, reconstructing in his mind for the twentieth time in the past half hour the strategy his father had devised for the defense of the pass. A broad rise straddled the pass several hundred yards from its mouth, a flat shelf of rock that overlooked a rugged slide strewn thick with loose stone and scrub. It was here that the army would make its initial stand. Archers would line the front of the rise, shooting into the Demons as they came out of the Flats through the mouth of Halys Cut to scramble up the slide. When the Demons were too close for the long bows to be effective, the archers would be replaced by a phalanx of lancers and pikemen who would bear the brunt of the assault. A second phalanx would be held in reserve to reinforce the first. The defenders would hold the rise for as long as they were able, then fall back several hundred yards to a similar position. If the gorge were lost, they would fall back to the mouth of the canyon. If that, too, were lost, the canyon itself would be defended—and so on, until the army was forced entirely from Halys Cut. It was a good plan. Ander was satisfied on thinking it through that the pass would not be easily taken. The defensive positions had been well chosen; when the attack came, it would find the Elves ready.

He lifted his gaze and stared out toward the Flats. Nothing moved. The land lay silent and empty. There was still no sign of the Demons.

Yet they would come. His hands moved slowly over the smooth wood of the Ellcrys staff, tracing the grain of the skin. His father had left the staff in his care momentarily while he had descended the slide to make his own inspection of the Elven defenses. Ander breathed the night air deeply. Would the staff truly protect the Elves? Would it lend its magic to those who were mortal men now, no longer the creatures of faerie that their forefathers had been? He looked down at it, gripping it tightly within his hands, and tried to find his own strength in its firmness. Allanon had said that the power of the Ellcrys over the Demons was carried within this staff and that it would weaken the evil and make it vulnerable to Elven weapons. Yet doubt clouded Ander's mind. The Demons were an incomprehensible evil, born of a world long since gone, a world that none but they had ever seen nor could begin to imagine.

He caught himself. None but Allanon, he corrected himself. And Allanon was himself perhaps a part of that dark, forgotten world.

His father appeared suddenly from the darkness, slipping from the shadows to stand beside him. Wordlessly, Ander passed back the Ellcrys staff. Fatigue and worry lined the old man's face, reflected in his eyes, and Ander forced himself to look away.

"Is everything all right?" he asked after a moment.

The King nodded distantly. "All of the defensive positions are established."

They were silent again. Ander tried to think of something more that he could say. There was an uneasiness in him that would not settle, one that gave rise to a need to be close to his father. He wanted Eventine to understand this. Yet it was difficult, somehow, to speak with his father of such things. Neither of them had ever been very good at expressing feelings to the other.

His mood darkened. It was that way with Arion as well—particularly with Arion. There was a distance between them that he had never really understood, a distance that might have been shortened had either of them been able to talk about it. But neither had tried. It was worse now, of course. Arion was angered by what had taken place at the High Council, by Ander's refusal to reject Amberle as the rightful bearer of the Ellcrys seed, and by his refusal to demand of her, as Arion thought proper, an accounting of her actions; now he would not talk with his brother at all. There was such bitterness in Arion! Still, it was bitterness that Ander understood. When Amberle had left Arborlon those many months ago, abandoning without explanation her responsibilities as one of the Chosen, both brothers had experienced that bitterness—he as much as Arion because he, too, had loved the child. For too long a time he had let the bitterness blind him to everything that she had once meant to him. Yet seeing her again had allowed him to rediscover something of his old feeling for her. He would have liked to explain that to Arion; he needed to explain it. But somehow he could not seem to find a way to do so.

He started sharply as he realized that Allanon was standing beside him. The Druid had materialized from nowhere, without even the faintest whisper of those black, concealing robes. The cowled face studied him momentarily, then looked past him to his father.

"You do not sleep?"

Eventine seemed distracted. "No. Not yet."

"You must rest, Elven King."

"Soon. Allanon, do you think that Amberle is still alive?"

Ander caught his breath and glanced fleetingly at the Druid. Allanon was quiet a moment before answering.

"She is alive."

When he said nothing more, Eventine looked over. "How can you know that?"

"I cannot know; it is what I think."

"Then why is it that you think she is alive?"

The Druid's head lifted slightly, deep-set eyes studying the sky. "Because Wil Ohmsford has not yet used the Elfstones. If Amberle's life were threatened, the Valeman would use the Stones."

Ander frowned. Elfstones? Wil Ohmsford? What was all this about? Then he remembered the second cloaked figure at the High Council, the one whom Allanon had brought into the chamber with Amberle, and who had never shown himself. That would be Wil Ohmsford.

He turned quickly to Allanon, questions forming on his lips, then caught himself and turned away again. Perhaps this was not something he should be asking about, he thought. After all, nothing had been said before. If Allanon had wanted him to know more, he would have told him. But then why had the Druid said anything at all?

Confused, he stared out across the Flats as the sun slipped beneath the horizon, the colors of the sunset fading slowly into the night.

"There are watch fires laid across the mouth of the pass," his father murmured after a moment. "I must order them lighted."

He walked down into the gorge, and Ander was left alone with Allanon. The two stood wordlessly, motionless statues in the growing dark, looking after the stooped figure of the old King as he wound his way down along the broken rock. The minutes slipped away. Ander thought himself forgotten when the Druid's voice floated up suddenly out of the silence.

"Would you know something more of Wil Ohmsford, Elven Prince?"

Ander stared at the big man in astonishment, then managed a startled nod.

"Then so you shall." Allanon never even glanced at him. "Listen."

Quietly he told Ander of Wil Ohmsford—of his heritage and of his mission to the Elves. Memories came back then to the Elven Prince of his father's stories of the Valemen, Shea and Flick Ohmsford, and of their search for the legendary Sword of Shannara. And now Shea's grandson, heir to the power of a magic that no Elf had wielded since the destruction of the old world, had been made Amberle's protector.

When the Druid finished, Ander was silent for a moment. He stared down into the shadows where his father had disappeared, thinking. Then he glanced once more at the Druid.

"Why have you told me this, Allanon?"

"It is something you should know."

Ander shook his head slowly. "No—I mean, why me?"

Then at last the Druid turned to look at him, hawk face barely visible within the shadows of the cowl. "For many reasons, Ander," he said softly and paused. "Perhaps because when no one else would come forward to stand with Amberle that night in the High Council, you did. Perhaps because of that."

His black eyes remained fixed on Ander for a moment, and then he turned away again. "You should rest now. You should sleep."

Ander nodded, his mind elsewhere. Had the Druid really answered his question? He glanced briefly at Allanon, then looked away again, puzzled. Moments later, when he glanced back once more, the Druid was gone.

30

Dawn broke, and a deep, gray mist covered the whole of the Hoare Flats. Thick, still, and impenetrable, it lay stretched across the earth like a death shroud. Night drew away from the mist as the pale, silver light of sunrise crept down out of the Breakline; when the night had gone, the mist came awake. With a sluggish heave, it began to churn against the wall of the mountains like some foul soup stirred within its kettle. Faster and faster it swirled, surging up against the cliffs until it seemed the rock must be swallowed and lost.

High within the shadowed closure of Halys Cut, flanked by his father and Allanon and ringed by the Home Guard, Ander Elessedil stared downward. Below, the army of the Elves prepared to defend against the Demon hordes. Row upon row of archers, lancers, and pikemen bridged the gorge that opened onto the Flats, their weapons held ready, their eyes riveted on the mist as it boiled before the mouth of the pass. Out of this mist must come the Demons, yet nothing could be seen of them. As the minutes slipped by and still the attack did not come, the soldiers began to grow restless. Ander could sense their uneasiness, like his own, turning slowly to fear.

"Stand fast; do not be frightened!" Allanon's voice rang out suddenly, and all eyes turned toward the black-cloaked Druid. "It is but mist, though Demon-wrought! Courage, now! The Forbidding gives way; the Demons are about to cross over!"

Still the mist churned wildly at the entrance to the Cut, as if shut away by some invisible barrier that would not let it advance further. Silence hung across the land, deep and pervasive. Ander's hands were trembling as he gripped the staff from which the banner of the House of the Elessedils hung limply, and he fought silently to still them.

Then abruptly the cries began, distant and haunting, as if drifting out of the bowels of the earth. Within the mist, streaks of red fire lanced upward to the still-darkened morning sky, and the roiling haze seemed to heave. The cries grew louder, turning suddenly to screams that were shrill and savage, filled with madness. They rose steadily, building into a single, unending shriek that emptied out of the Flats into the narrow defile of Halys Cut.

"It comes," Allanon whispered harshly.

The soldiers of the Elven army dropped to their knees, the sound breaking over them like a wave. Arrows were notched quickly in bow strings; spears and pikes were braced against the earth. Across the mouth of the pass, the mist erupted in red fire that turned the whole of the sky and earth crimson with its reflection. The shrieks and screams rose to a deafening pitch, and suddenly the air itself seemed to explode in a thunderous clap that burst out of the wilderness to the wall of the Breakline and shook the rock to its core. Ander cried out in dismay, and the force of the thunder threw them all to the earth. Hurriedly, they scrambled back to their feet, eyes searching. The air had gone silent. The mist hung gray and still once more.

"Allanon?" he questioned softly.

"It is finished—the Forbidding is broken," the Druid breathed.

In the next instant the screams welled up anew from out of the emptiness of the Flats, a maddened roar of exultation, and the Demon hordes, freed at last from their centuries-old prison, spilled through the mouth of Halys Cut. Down the length of the gorge they came, a wave of struggling, dark bodies. The Demons were of all shapes and sizes, bent and twisted by the blackness that had encased them. There were teeth and claws and razor-sharp spines, hair and scales and bristled fur; they slouched and crawled, burrowed and flew, leaped and slithered; all were things of legend and nightmare. Every creature from the oldest tales of horror was there: were-creatures, half-human, half-animal, fleet gray shadows that the eye could barely follow; massive, shambling Ogres with hideously distorted features; Gremlins that flitted about as if blown on the wind; Imps and Goblins, black with muck and slime; serpent forms that hissed their venom and twisted in frenzy; Furies and Demon-wolves; Ghouls and other things that ate of human flesh and drank of human blood; Harpies and bat-things that blackened the sky as they lifted their unwieldy bodies from the mass of their brethren. Surging through the mist, they ripped and tore at one another in their eagerness to break free.

Elven long bows hummed, and a rush of black arrows cut apart the foremost Demons. The rest barely slowed, scrambling quickly over the bodies of those who had fallen. Elven archers shot again and yet again, and still the Demons came at them, screaming their rage and frustration. Less than fifty yards separated the two forces, and now the archers fell back and to either flank as the forward phalanx of lancers and pikemen moved to the crest of the rise, bracing their weapons in readiness. The Demons surged forward, a mass of twisting bodies as they bounded up the broken rock of the gorge to where the Elves waited.

With a muffled crunch, the tide broke against the wall of the phalanx, claws and teeth ripping. The front ranks of the Elven line wavered slightly, but held. Demons hung impaled on spears, their shrieks filling the narrow gorge. With a heave, the Elven Hunters threw them back onto their own, watching in horror as the shattered forms were swallowed in the mass that came after. Again the Demons surged up against the Elves, and this time several knots broke through, only to perish instantly as the rear phalanx moved quickly to plug the gaps in the forward lines. But now the Elves were dying also, buried under the black mass of their attackers, dragged forcibly from their ranks and torn apart. And still the Demons continued to pour out of the mist, thousands strong, spreading out across the floor of the gorge and up its walls. Arrows cut them down in steady numbers; but where one fell, three more appeared to take its place. The Elven flanks were beginning to buckle under the rush of attackers, and the entire line was in danger of being overrun.

Eventine gave the order to fall back. The Elves disengaged hurriedly, retreating to their second line of defense, a broken shelf of rock lying just below the passage that led back into the canyon. Again the long bows sang out, and a hail of arrows flew into the surging mass below. Lancers and pikemen formed their ranks, bracing for the assault. It came almost at once, the wave of struggling dark forms clawing their way over scrub and stone to tear at the hedge of Elven spears. Hundreds died in the rush, pierced through by arrow and lance, trampled beneath the feet of their brethren. Yet still they came, surging forth from the mist into the deep funnel of the gorge, against the lines of Elven defenders. The Elves threw them back—once, twice, a third time. Halys Cut filled with dark bodies, crushed and bleeding, screaming in pain and hatred.

At the mouth of the canyon, Ander watched silently the ebb and flow of the battle. The Elves were losing ground. As Allanon had promised, the Ellcrys staff weakened the Demons who came at the Elves so that they died under the thrust and cut of Elven iron. Yet this was not going to be enough to stop the hordes pouring forth—not even with the gallantry of the soldiers, the defensive positions chosen, or all the careful planning. There were simply too many Demons and not enough of the Elves.

He glanced hurriedly at his father, but the King did not see him. Eventine's hands were fastened on the gnarled length of the Ellcrys staff and the whole of his concentration was fixed on the struggle below. The entire Elven defensive line was beginning to buckle dangerously. Using weapons stripped from Elven dead, rocks and makeshift wooden clubs, teeth and claws and brute strength, the Demons fought to breach the thinning ranks of lancers and pikemen that yet barred their passage forward. The Legion Free Corps, held in reserve until now, threw itself into the center of the Elven line, battle cry ringing out. Still the Demons came on.

"We cannot hold," Eventine muttered and prepared to give the command to withdraw.

"Stay close," Allanon whispered suddenly to Ander.

At that same moment, the Demons broke through the left flank and came streaming up the gorge toward the knot of men who stood before the canyon mouth. The Home Guard stepped in front of the King and Ander protectively, Dardan and Rhoe a pace or two to either side. Short swords slipped from their leather scabbards, the metal glinting. Hurriedly, Ander jammed the Elessedil standard into the rocky earth and drew his own weapon. Sweat ran down his body beneath the chain-mail armor, and his mouth went dry with fear.

Now Allanon moved forward, black robes flying as his arms lifted.

Blue fire shattered the half-light, bursting from the Druid's fingers, and the ground about the attackers exploded. Smoke billowed out of the rock, then dispersed across a scattering of lifeless dark bodies. But not all had fallen. For an instant the survivors hesitated. Behind them, the breach had closed again; there could be no turning back. Shrieking in fury, they came on, ripping into the Home Guard. The struggle was desperate. Demons fell dying under the swords of Elven Hunters, yet a handful broke through and hurtled themselves at the King. A lean, black Goblin sprang at Ander, claws ripping for his throat. Frantically the Elven Prince brought up the short sword, warding off the attack. Again the creature lunged at him, but one of the Home Guard came quickly between them, pinning the Demon to the earth with a single thrust.

Ander stumbled back in horror, watching the battle surge closer. The left flank had collapsed anew and again Allanon stepped forward to meet the rush. Blue fire lanced into the attackers, and screams filled the air. A knot of Demons had breached the right flank as well and came charging down off the slope in a desperate effort to aid those of the brethren trapped behind the Elven defensive line. Ander froze. There were not enough Home Guard to stop them all.

Then shockingly, impossibly, Eventine went down, felled by a club thrown from the mass of attackers. The blow caught the old King on the temple, and he toppled instantly to the earth, the Ellcrys staff falling from his hand. A roar rose out of the throats of the Demons, and they pressed forward with renewed fury. Half-a-dozen from the band that had come down off the slope closed about the fallen King to finish him.

But Ander was already springing to his father's side, his own fear forgotten, his face contorted with fury. With a howl of rage, he charged into the foremost attackers, black Goblins like the one that had nearly finished him moments earlier, and two lay dying before the others realized what had happened. As if gone mad, Ander tore into the rest, thrusting them back from the fallen King.

For an instant, everything was in chaos. On the ridge, the Elven line of defense had been forced backward almost to the mouth of the canyon. Demons surged forward in droves, hacking at the Elves who barred their way, shrieking with glee at the sight of the fallen Eventine. Ander struggled to keep the Demons from his father. In his fury, he tripped over one he had slain and went down. Instantly, they were on him. Claws ripped into him, tearing at his armor, and, for one terrible moment, he believed himself a dead man. But Dardan and Rhoe fought their way to his side, scattered his attackers, and pulled him to safety. Dazed, he stumbled back to where his father lay and knelt down beside the old man, disbelief and shock flooding into his face. His hands groped to find a pulse. It was there, faint and slow. His father was still alive, but fallen, lost to the Elves, lost to Ander—the King, the only one who could save them from what was happening . . .

Then Allanon was beside him. Snatching from the earth the fallen Ellcrys staff, he brought Ander to his feet with a yank and thrust the talisman into his hands.

"Grieve later, Elven Prince." He placed his dark face close to Ander's. "For now, you must command. Quickly—withdraw the Elves into the canyon."

Ander started to object, then stopped. What he saw in the Druid's eyes convinced him that this was neither the time nor the place for argument. Wordlessly he obeyed. He ordered his father carried from the fighting. Then rallying the Home Guard about him at the canyon entrance, he sent runners to the center and both flanks of the Elven defensive line and ordered them to pull back. With Allanon at his shoulder, he placed himself squarely at the head of the gorge where the Elves and the Bordermen might see him and watched the battle sweep toward him.

Back surged the lancers and pikemen of the Elven phalanx and the gray soldiers of the Free Corps, clogging the canyon mouth. Stee Jans appeared, red hair flying, a huge broadsword in his hands. Then Allanon's arms rose high above his head, black robes spreading wide, and the blue fire spurted from his fingers.

"Now!" he commanded Ander. "Back into the canyon!"

Ander lifted the Ellcrys staff and called out. The last of the Elves and Free Corps disengaged from the struggle and sprinted back through the pass connecting gorge and canyon. Shrieks of rage broke from the Demons, who surged forward after them.

Allanon stood alone at the head of the pass. In a rush, the Demons came for him, scrambling up the gorge, a wave of black bodies. The Druid seemed to gather himself, his lean form straightening against the shadow of the rock walls. Again his hands lifted and the blue fire burst forth. All across the canyon entrance it burned, rising up like a wall before the enraged Demons, barring their passage. Howling and screaming, they backed away.

Within the canyon, Allanon turned to Ander.

"The fire will last only a few moments." The Druid's face was drawn and streaked with sweat and dirt. "Then they will be on us again."

"Allanon, how can we stand against such odds . . . ?" Ander began hopelessly.

"We cannot—not here, not now." The Druid gripped his arm. "The passes of the Breakline are lost. We must escape quickly."

Ander was already shouting orders. His command sent the army of the Elves streaming back across the canyon floor, cavalry reserves riding ahead with wounded that could sit a horse; pikemen, lancers, and archers followed, carrying those who could not. The Home Guard bore the unconscious King. Allanon and Ander trailed. They had gone just beyond the brush-sheltered pool that lay at the canyon's center when the flame barring the far entrance flared and went out.

In midflight, the Elves looked back. For an instant the entrance lay open, but then the Demons poured through, choking the narrow passage as they fought to gain the canyon beyond. Howling, they swept after the fleeing Elves. They were too late. The main body of the army had already gained the defile that led into the split and had scrambled through. A rear guard of Free Corps under Stee Jans set their lines as Allanon, Ander, and the remnants of the Home Guard crossed the last hundred yards of canyon floor. At the mouth of the defile, they turned momentarily to watch the approach of the Demon hordes.

It was an awesome, frightening spectacle. Like a dark wave, the Demons filled the canyon, spreading out across its grass-covered floor from wall to wall, their struggling black bodies heaving and tossing like rats driven before the waters of some great flood. The earth grew dark with leaping, twisting, writhing forms, and the air above was dotted with those that flew. Druid and Elves stared back in disbelief. It was as if their numbers were endless.

Then abruptly the wave seemed to part where it broke from the gorge and a monstrous, scaled form lurched into view. Dark green and brutish, it dwarfed its brethren as it reared upward within the canyon pass and shoved its way through, scattering those about it like twigs. The Elves cried out in horror. It was a Dragon, its serpentine body spine-covered and slick with its own secretions. Six ponderous, gnarled legs, clawed and tufted with dark hair, supported its sagging bulk. Its head arched searchingly into the air, horned and crusted, a distorted lump out of which burned a single, lidless green eye. As the scent of Elven blood touched its nostrils, its snout split wide to reveal rows of jagged teeth and its tail thrashed frenziedly behind it, filling the air with shattered bodies. The Demons gave way hurriedly, and the monster shambled forward, shaking the rock with the weight of its passing.

At the far end of the canyon, Allanon watched the Dragon's approach for an instant more before turning to Ander.

"Move back beyond the split. Quickly now."

Ander was pale. "But the Dragon . . ."

". . . is too much for you." The Druid's voice was cold. "Do as I tell you. Leave the Dragon to me."

Ander stepped back to give the command, and the army of the Elves withdrew to the far end of the split. With Stee Jans beside him, Ander turned to watch. Allanon stood alone, staring down into the canyon. The Dragon had passed through the center of the canyon and was lurching up the slope toward the defile. Already it had caught sight of the Druid, that solitary black figure that did not run like the others, and it hungered to reach him so that it might crush out his life. Massive legs churned, tearing apart the rock and earth beneath. Behind and to either side, the Demons followed, shrieking with anticipation, scrambling to stay clear of their monstrous brother.

Allanon held his ground, black robes drawn close about him, until the Dragon was less than a hundred yards from the defile. Then the robes flew wide and the lean arms lifted, hands extending toward the monster. Blue fire lanced from his fingers, striking the Dragon's head and throat, and the

smell of charred flesh filled the air. Yet the creature did not slow, but
shrugged aside the attack as if it were little more than bothersome, its huge
form surging forward. Again the fire struck, singeing forelegs and chest,
leaving trailers of smoke that rose from the Dragon's body. Its hiss of anger
was sharp and cold, but it came on.

Allanon slipped back into the defile, moving quickly to the far end.
Again he turned. The Dragon reared into view, pushing forward into the
narrow passage. Allanon struck, blue fire searing in sharp, sudden bursts.
The Dragon's hiss was venomous as it snapped the air before it, frustrated
that it could not yet reach the taunting creature ahead. The walls of the
defile hindered its movements as it blundered forward awkwardly. Behind
it, the cries of the Demon brethren urged it on.

Slowly Allanon backed away from the mouth of the defile toward the
split. The passage was clogged with smoke and dust, and the brutish form
of the Dragon was obscured by the haze. Then suddenly it surged into
view, its snout gaping hungrily. With both hands locked before him, Allanon sent a bolt of fire into the monster's eye. When the fire struck, the
creature's entire head was enveloped. This time the Dragon cried out, a
terrible howl that spoke of pain and rage. Its body rose high within the defile, slamming against the stone walls until the cliffs shuddered with the
force of the blows. Boulders tumbled down about the monster as it heaved
and thrashed with pain.

A moment later the south wall cracked wide and the entire cliff face
began to slide slowly into the defile. Sensing the danger it was in, the
Dragon lurched forward, desperate to get clear of the pass. Half-blinded by
the pain and dust, it broke from the defile as tons of rock crashed down
behind it, burying the Demons who tried to follow. Blue fire struck it instantly, but without effect. The Dragon was ready this time, its lumpish
head bobbing guardedly to avoid the fire. Before it crouched the dark figure of the Druid. Hissing in fury, the monster shambled toward its enemy,
massive jaws snapping. Allanon wheeled and darted back, moving not to
the broader trail that lay right, but sprinting onto the narrow ledge that
curved left above the split. Maddened beyond reason, heedless of what
lay ahead, the Dragon came after him. In a rush it thundered onto the
ledge, snout reaching for the human fleeing before it, massive legs driving
it forward.

But suddenly the ledge was no longer there. Broken rock gave way beneath the weight of the monstrous creature. With a desperate effort, the
Dragon lunged toward the Druid. Allanon sprang back as massive jaws
swept barely a foot short of his head. Then with a final, terrible hiss, the
Dragon slipped away from the crumbling ledge into the black pit of the
chasm, disappearing in an avalanche of earth and stone, screaming its hatred. Down into the emptiness it fell and was gone.

Ander Elessedil stood at the far end of the split and watched as Allanon
made his way back along the remains of the ledge. After a moment, his
gaze shifted. A quick glance at the defile showed it blocked by tons of

rock. A slow, bitter smile creased his bloodied face. The Demons would follow them no further through Halys Cut. The Elves had gained a brief respite, a chance to regroup so that they might make their stand elsewhere.

He turned. Behind him, within the mouth of the pass, the soldiers of the Elven army stared out of the shadows in silence, weariness and uncertainty clouding their faces. The Elven Prince could read what was reflected there. So many Demons had come through the Forbidding—so many more than any of them had believed possible. They had failed utterly to stop them here. How would they stop them at the Sarandanon?

Wordlessly, he looked away again. He did not have the answer. He wondered if anyone did.

It was a dispirited army that came down out of Halys Cut, shamed by the defeat that had been inflicted upon it and shocked by the number of its dead and wounded. For the dead, lost in the flight back through the pass, there could be no proper return of the body to the earth which had given it life. For the wounded, there could be no relief from the excruciating pain of injuries inflamed by the poison of Demon claws and teeth; their moans and cries lingered unbearably in the midday stillness. For the rest, those who marched south along the wall of the Breakline, there could be no comfort taken in what had passed that day, nor little in what most certainly lay ahead. As the noon sun beat down upon them, mouths went dry with thirst and thoughts turned black with bitterness.

Ander Elessedil led them, no leader in his own mind, little more than a victim of capricious circumstance, and his thoughts were dark. He wanted this to be ended, his father restored to consciousness, and his brother returned. He held in his hands the gnarled length of the Ellcrys staff and thought himself a fool. None of this was meant to be. Still, he knew he must play the role that had been forced upon him a while longer, at least until the army reached Baen Draw. Mercifully, it would be ended then.

His gaze shifted to Allanon. The Druid rode silently beside him, dark and enigmatic within his concealing robes, his thoughts locked carefully away from Ander. Only once during the march back had he spoken.

"I understand now why they let us come this far," he had said, his voice rather quiet in its suddenness. "They wanted us within these mountains."

"Wanted us?" Ander had questioned.

"Wanted us, Elven Prince," Allanon had replied coldly. "With so many, they knew there was nothing we could do to stop them. They let us trap ourselves."

A rider appeared on the horizon, a solitary horseman, his mount driven almost to exhaustion as it galloped wildly across the grasslands toward the approaching Elves. Lifting the Ellcrys staff, Ander signalled a halt. With Allanon beside him, he rode forward to meet the horseman. Disheveled and dust-streaked, the rider jolted to a stop before them. Ander knew this man, a messenger in his brother's service.

"Flyn," he spoke the Elf's name in greeting.

The messenger hesitated, then glanced quickly past him to the column of soldiers. "I am to report to the King . . ." he began.

"Give your message to the Prince," Allanon snapped.

"My Lord," Flyn saluted, his face white. Suddenly there were tears in his eyes. "My Lord . . ." he began again, but his voice broke and he could not continue.

Ander dismounted and beckoned Flyn down with him. Wordlessly he put an arm about the distraught messenger and led him forward several paces to where they might speak alone. There he faced the Elf squarely.

"Slowly now—give me your message."

Flyn nodded, his face tightening. "My Lord, I am instructed to tell the King that Prince Arion has fallen. My Lord . . . he is dead."

Ander shook his head slowly. "Dead?" It seemed as if someone else were speaking. "How can he be dead? He *can't* be dead!"

"We were attacked at dawn, my lord." Flyn was crying openly. "The Demons . . . there were so many. They forced us from the pass. We were overrun. The battle standard fell . . . and when Prince Arion tried to recover it, the Demons caught him . . ."

Ander quickly put his hand up to check the Elf's words. He did not want to hear the rest. It was a nightmare that could not be happening. His eyes flashed quickly to Allanon, and he found the Druid's dark face turned toward his own. Allanon knew.

"Do we have my brother's body?" Ander forced himself to ask the question.

"Yes, my Lord."

"I want it brought to me."

Flyn nodded silently. "My Lord, there is something more." Ander turned back now, waiting. "My Lord, Worl Run is lost, but Commander Pindanon believes that it can be retaken. He requests additional cavalry to make a sweep back across the grasslands that border the pass so that . . ."

"No!" Ander cut him short, his voice suddenly urgent. With an effort he composed himself. "No, Flyn. Tell Commander Pindanon that he is to withdraw at once. He is to return to Sarandanon."

The Elf swallowed hard, glancing hurriedly at Allanon. "Forgive me, my Lord, but I was instructed to speak with the King on this. The Commander will ask . . ."

Ander understood. "Tell the Commander that my father has been wounded." Flyn paled further, and Ander took a deep breath. "Tell Kael Pindanon that I command the army of the Elves and that he is to withdraw at once. Take a fresh horse, Flyn, and go quickly. Safe journey, messenger!"

Flyn saluted and hurried off. Ander stood alone, staring out across the empty grasslands, a strange numbness stealing through him as he realized that there no longer remained any chance to bridge that gulf that had always separated Arion and him. Arion was lost to him forever.

His back to Allanon, he let himself cry.

Dusk slipped silently across the valley of the Sarandanon, its shadow lengthening to Baen Draw and the army of the Elves. Within his tent, Eventine Elessedil lay sleeping, unconscious still, his breathing shallow and uneven. Ander sat alone at his bedside, staring down at him wordlessly, wishing that he would come awake again. Until the King woke, it would be impossible to judge how serious his injury might be. He was an old man, and Ander was frightened for him.

Impulsively, he reached for his father's hand and took it gently in his own. The hand was limp. The old man did not stir. Ander held the hand for a moment, then released it again and leaned back wearily.

"Father," he whispered, almost to himself.

He stood up and moved away from the bed, distracted. How could it have happened—his father fallen, grievously injured; his brother killed; himself become leader of the Elves—how could it have happened? It was a madness that he could not bring himself to accept. Certainly the possibility had always been there that his father and his brother would be gone and that he alone of the Elessedils would be left to rule. But it had been an absurd possibility. No one had believed it would truly happen, least of all he. He was ill-prepared for this, he thought gloomily. What had he ever been to his father and his brother but a pair of hands to act in their behalf? It had been their destiny to rule the Elven people, their wish, their expectation—never his. Yet now . . .

He shook his head wearily. Now he must rule, at least for a time. And he must lead this army that his father had led before him. He must defend the Sarandanon and find a way to stop the Demon advance. Halys Cut had shown the Elves how difficult this would be. They knew as well as he that if the rock slide brought about by the battle between Allanon and the Dragon had not blocked Halys Cut, the Demons might have caught and annihilated them all. His first task, then, was to give the Elves reason to believe that this would not happen to them here at Baen Draw, despite the loss of both the King and his firstborn son. In short, he must give them hope.

He sat down again next to his father. Kael Pindanon could help him; he was a veteran of many wars, an experienced soldier. But would he? He knew that Pindanon was angry with him because of his order to the Commander to withdraw from the passes of the Breakline. Pindanon had not returned yet, remaining behind with a rearguard of Elven cavalry to slow the Demon advance on the Sarandanon. But forewarning of his displeasure had already reached Ander's ears through comments voiced by a handful of his officers. When he rode in, he would confront Ander directly. Then things would really come to a head. Ander already knew he would ask that command of the army be given to him. Ander shook his head once more. It would be easy enough to do that, to turn command of the army over to Pindanon and let the old warrior assume responsibility for the defense of the Elven homeland. Perhaps that was what he should do. Yet something inside of him resisted so simplistic a resolution to the dilemma; there was need for caution in shedding too quickly duties that were clearly his.

"What would you do?" he asked softly of his father, knowing there would be no answer, yet needing one.

The minutes slipped past, and the dusk deepened.

Finally Dardan appeared through the tent flap. "Commander Pindanon has returned," he announced. "He asks to speak with you."

Ander nodded and wondered momentarily where Allanon had gone. He had seen nothing of the Druid since their return. Still, this meeting with Pindanon was his problem. He started to his feet, then remembered the Ellcrys staff which lay on the floor next to his father's bed. Lifting it in both hands, he hesitated a moment, staring down at the old man beside him.

"Rest well," he whispered finally, then turned and stepped from the room.

In the adjoining chamber, he found Pindanon waiting. Dust and blood covered the Commander's armor, and his white-bearded face was flushed with anger as he advanced on the Elven Prince.

"Why did you order me to withdraw, Ander?" he snapped.

Ander held his ground. "Lower your voice, Commander. The King lies within."

There was a moment's silence as Pindanon glared at him. Then, more quietly, the Elven Commander asked, "How is he?"

"He sleeps," Ander replied coldly. "Now what is your question?"

Pindanon straightened. "Why was I ordered to withdraw? I could have retaken Worl Run. We could have held the Breakline as your father intended that we should!"

"My father intended that the Breakline be held for as long as it was possible to do so," Ander responded, his eyes locked on Pindanon's. "With my father injured, my brother dead, and Halys Cut lost, it was no longer possible. We were driven from Halys Cut, just as you were driven from Worl Run." Pindanon bristled, but Ander ignored him. "In order to retake Worl Run, I would have had to make a forced march north with an army that had just been routed, knowing that they would immediately be thrown back into battle. If our combined forces were then defeated, they would face an exhausting march back to the Sarandanon with little chance to rest before undertaking a defense of this valley. Worst of all, any battle fought within the passes of the Breakline would be fought without the use of Elven cavalry. If we are to withstand the Demon advance, we will need the whole of our strength to do so. That, Commander, is why you were ordered to withdraw."

Pindanon shook his head slowly. "You are not a trained soldier, my

Lord Prince. You had no right to make a decision as crucial as this one without first consulting with the Commander of the Army. Had it not been for my loyalty to your father . . ."

Ander's head came up sharply. "Don't finish that sentence, Commander."

His gaze shifted momentarily as the outer tent flaps parted to admit Allanon and Stee Jans. Allanon's appearance was not unexpected, but Ander was somewhat surprised to find the Free Corps Commander there as well. The Borderman nodded courteously, but said nothing.

Ander turned back to Pindanon. "In any case, the matter is done. We had better concern ourselves with what lies ahead. How much time do we have before the Demons reach us?"

"A day, possibly two," Pindanon offered abruptly. "They must rest, regroup."

Allanon's black eyes lifted. "Dawn tomorrow."

There was instant silence. "You are certain?" Ander asked quietly.

"They are driven beyond the need for sleep. Dawn tomorrow."

Pindanon spat upon the earthen floor.

"Then we must decide now how we will stop them once they are here," Ander declared, hands running lightly over the Ellcrys staff.

"Simple enough," Pindanon snapped impatiently. "Defend Baen Draw. Cordon it off. Stop them at the narrows before they reach the valley."

Ander took a deep breath. "That was tried at Halys Cut. It failed. The Demons forced the Elven phalanx by sheer strength of numbers. There is no reason to believe that it would be any different this time."

"There is every reason," Pindanon insisted. "Our strength is not divided here as it was in the Breakline. Nor will the Demons be fresh and rested, if they march straight from the Flats. Cavalry may be used in support where it could not at the Cut. Oh, much is changed, I promise you. The result will be different this time."

Ander glanced momentarily at Allanon, but the Druid said nothing. Pindanon came a step closer.

"Ander, give me command in your father's stead. Let me set the defense as I know he would set it. The Elves can hold the draw against those creatures, whatever their strength. Your father and I know . . ."

"Commander." The Elven Prince spoke softly, firmly. "I saw what the Demons are capable of doing at Halys Cut. I saw what they did to a defensive line that my father felt certain would hold them. This is a different sort of enemy we fight. It hates the Elves beyond understanding; it is driven by that hatred—so much so that dying means nothing. Can we say the same, we to whom life is so precious? I think not. We need something more than standard tactics if we are to survive this encounter."

Out of the corner of his eye, he caught Allanon's brief nod.

Pindanon bristled. "You lack faith, my Lord Prince. Your father would not be so quick . . ."

Ander cut him short. "My father is not here. But if he were, he would speak to you as I have spoken. I seek suggestions, Commander—not an argument."

Pindanon flushed darkly, then turned suddenly toward Allanon. "What has this one to say? Has he no thoughts to offer on how these Demons are to be stopped?"

Allanon's dark face was expressionless. "You cannot stop them, Commander. You can only slow them."

"Slow them?"

"Slow them so that the bearer of the Ellcrys seed may gain time enough to find the Bloodfire and return."

"That again!" Pindanon snorted. "Our destiny in the hands of that girl! Druid, I do not believe in old world legends. If the Westland is to be saved, it must be saved through the courage of her men-at-arms—through the skill and experience of her soldiers. Demons may die as other things of flesh and blood."

"Such as Elves," the Druid replied darkly.

There was a long silence. Pindanon turned away from the others, hands clasping angrily behind his back. After a moment, he wheeled back on them.

"Do we stand at Baen Draw or not, Prince Ander? I hear no suggestions but my own."

Ander hesitated, wishing Allanon would say something. But it was Stee Jans who stepped forward, his rough voice breaking the silence.

"My Lord, may I speak?"

Ander had almost forgotten that the Legion Commander was there. He glanced at the big man and nodded.

"My Lord, the Free Corps has faced similar odds on more than one occasion while in the service of the Borderlands. It is a matter of pride with us that while our enemies have frequently been stronger than we, still we have survived and they have not. We have learned some hard lessons, my Lord. I offer one of them to you now. It is this—never settle a stationary defensive line where superior numbers will overrun you. We have learned to split our defensive front with a series of mobile lines that shift with the flow of battle. These lines attack and retreat in sequence, pulling the enemy first one way, then the other, striking always on the flanks as the enemy turns to repel each new assault, withdrawing beyond the enemy's reach when the strike is done."

Pindanon snorted. "Then you neither gain nor even hold ground, Commander."

Stee Jans turned to him. "When the enemy has been pulled far enough out in his efforts to catch you, when his lines have thinned and split, then you close ranks to either side and collapse on him. Like so."

He placed his hands in a V and brought them together with a clap. There was a startled silence.

"I don't know," Pindanon muttered doubtfully.

"How would you defend Baen Draw?" Ander pressed.

"I would use a variation of what I have just described to you," Stee Jans replied. "Long bows on the slopes of the Kensrowe over the mouth of the Draw to harry the advance. Foot soldiers at its head, as if you meant to hold it as you tried to hold Halys Cut. When the Demons attack, stand for a time, then give way. Let them break through. Give them a rabbit to chase, a cavalry command to draw them on. When their lines are strung out, their flanks exposed, close on them from both sides, quickly, before they can fall back or be reinforced. Use lances to keep them from you. The Demons lack our weapons. If you stay beyond their reach, they cannot harm you. When you have destroyed their front ranks, let the rabbit pull through a second rush. Take them another way; keep them off balance. Concentrate on their flanks."

He finished. The Elves stared at the Borderman. Pindanon frowned.

"Who would be the rabbit in this?"

Stee Jans smiled crookedly. "Who else, Commander?"

Pindanon shrugged. Ander looked over at him questioningly.

"It might work," the old warrior admitted grudgingly. "If the rabbit is any good, that is."

"The rabbit knows a few tricks," Stee Jans replied. "That is why it is still alive after so many chases."

Ander glanced quickly at Allanon. The Druid nodded.

"Then we have our plan for the defense of the Sarandanon," the Elven Prince announced. His hand clasped Pindanon's, then that of the Iron Man. "Let us make certain now that it succeeds."

Later that night, when all was in readiness for the morrow's battle and he was alone, Ander Elessedil paused to reflect on how fortunate it was that Stee Jans had been present at his meeting with Pindanon. It was only then that it occurred to him that it might not have been good fortune at all, but a foresight peculiar to the enigmatic dark wanderer they knew as Allanon.

32

They buried Arion Elessedil at first light of dawn. His brother, Pindanon, and four dozen of the Home Guard interred him in the traditional manner of the Elves, at the birth of the new day, at the time of beginning. They bore him in silence to an oak-shaded bluff below Baen Draw that looked west over the blue expanse of the Innisbore and east across the green valley of the Sarandanon. There the firstborn of Eventine Elessedil was laid to rest, his body returned to the earth that had given it life, his spirit set free once more.

They left no marker to the Crown Prince. Allanon had warned that there were some among the Demons who would search out such testaments and prey upon the dead. There were no songs, no words of praise, no flowers—nothing to show that Arion Elessedil had ever been. There remained nothing of Eventine's firstborn but memories.

Ander saw the tears in the eyes of those who gathered with him and felt that memories might be enough.

Less than an hour later, the Demons attacked the Elves at Baen Draw. Down out of the northern hills they streamed, their screams and howls shattering the stillness of the dawn. They came as they had come at Halys Cut, a mass of twisted dark bodies surging forward like the unleashed waters of a flood.

At the lower end of the Draw, the Elven phalanx waited, rows of lancers and pikemen standing shoulder to shoulder with weapons braced. As the foremost Demons clawed their way toward them, Elven long bows hummed along the slopes of the Kensrowe and the air was filled with feathered arrows. Demons convulsed and fell, buried beneath those who came after. Wave after wave of dark shafts ripped through their ranks, and hundreds died in the rush.

But at last the phalanx was reached and the Demons flung themselves against it, shrieking with pain as the iron-tipped shafts pierced their bodies and held them transfixed. The attack faltered and was thrown back. Again it came, a sudden surge forward of malformed bodies, teeth and claws ripping, and again it was thrown back. The ground before the Elven defensive wall grew littered with dead and dying. Still the horde of Demons pressed ahead, endless in number, and at last the Elven line wavered and broke, its center seeming to fall away. Into the breach surged the Demons, bounding and leaping and scrambling from the draw.

Instantly they were set upon by a body of horsemen, gray-cloaked riders with crimson trim, their leader a tall, scar-faced man on a giant blue roan. The riders swept across the head of the Demon rush, lances scything. Then they were gone, turning back into the valley, gray cloaks flying, lean forms bent low over their mounts as they galloped away. The Demons gave chase in a frenzy. Moments later, the riders came about, charging back into their pursuers, lances lowered, scattering bodies as again they struck and swung quickly away. The Demons howled their frustration and scrambled after them.

Then suddenly the gray-cloaked riders wheeled in a solid line that barred the Demons' path forward, and the arm of the scar-faced man lifted. No longer massed protectively, but strung out along the grasslands for hundreds of yards beyond the mouth of Baen Draw, the Demons who had breached the Elven defensive line stared about wildly, seeing now what had been done to them. To either side, lines of Elven cavalry burst into view, hemming them in like cattle. Behind them, the breach had been closed by a tall, black robed figure, standing atop the lower slopes of the Kensrowe, with fire spurting from his outstretched hands to scatter the Demons who milled uncertainly within the Draw. Desperately, those trapped without sought to break the lines about them. But the Elves converged quickly, sword and lance cutting apart the black forms that reached up for them. In moments, the whole of the Demon advance had been destroyed. Through the length of the Baen Draw, the Elven cry of victory echoed.

It did not end there. For the remainder of the morning and into early afternoon, the battle raged on. Time and again, the Demons massed for a rush on the Elven phalanx that barred passage through Baen Draw. Time and again, they broke through, battling their way past Elven archers and Druid fire, past lancers and pikemen, only to find themselves face to face with the gray riders of the Legion Free Corps. Teased and harassed, they gave chase. Heedless of what lay ahead, they allowed themselves to be drawn on, sometimes toward the shoreline of the Innisbore, sometimes toward the slopes of the Kensrowe, or into the valley of the Sarandanon. Then, when it appeared that they had caught the elusive horsemen, they found themselves encircled by Elven cavalry, their own ranks thinned and unprotected, their thrust having carried them far from those brethren who battled still within the Draw. Raging, they threw themselves at their enemy, but there was no escape. The Elves swept back, and again their lines closed across Baen Draw.

For a time the Demons sought to gain the slopes of the Kensrowe, thinking to put an end to the hated long bows. But, carefully placed, their ranks deep and sheltered within the rocks, the Elven archers cut to pieces those who tried to reach them. In their midst stood the black-robed giant, sorcerous fire lancing from his hands, his awesome power sheltering the Elves who struggled below. All forms of Demons tried to reach him— Demons that burrowed within the earth, Demons that flew, Demons that scaled cliff walls like flies. All failed; all died.

In one attack, the Demons smashed through the Elven phalanx where it bordered the shoreline of the Innisbore, turning it back across the Draw as hundreds of attackers swarmed over the sandswept hills toward the open valley beyond. For a moment it appeared that the Elven defensive line was finally broken. But, with a valiant effort, the cavalry converged east of this new advance and rode into it in a charge that drove the Demons back into the waters of the Innisbore. Again the evil ones could not mass, but were strung out along the beachhead, their backs to the lake. The attack faltered and broke apart, shattered on the lances of the Elves. The breach closed one time more.

Thousands of Demons died that afternoon in senseless, mindless, savage rushes through Baen Draw. They attacked ceaselessly, surging forward on their race to the cliffs with the blind determination of lemmings, oblivious to the destruction that waited. Elves and Bordermen died with them, caught up in their frenzy to break through to the Sarandanon. Yet the rout that had occurred at Halys Cut was not repeated this day; time and again the Demons were thrown back, the forefront of their assault destroyed before it had an opportunity to gain reinforcement from the masses that came after.

Finally, in midafternoon, the Demons launched their final attack. Massing within Baen Draw, they surged against the Elven phalanx, bore it backward by sheer force of numbers, and snapped it apart. Into the seams they poured, and suddenly there was no time for carefully wrought tactics, or for skill and finesse. The Elves and the Legion struck back, their horsemen charging into the midst of the onslaught. Sword and spear cut deep into the tangle of twisted dark forms below. Horses and riders screamed and went down. The lines of fighters surged back and forth desperately. But at last the Demons broke, snarling and clawing as they fled back into the Draw, shrieks of anger rising from their midst. This time they did not turn. They continued on, trampling through their own dead and dying, hobbling and crawling and scrambling into the hills beyond, until Baen Draw stood empty.

The Elves stared after the retreating forms in weary disbelief, watching as the last of them disappeared into the curve of the hills, the sound of their passing fading slowly into silence. Then the Elves looked about them and saw clearly the enormity of the struggle that had taken place. Thousands of tangled dark bodies lay scattered across the grasslands, spreading east out of Baen Draw from Kensrowe to Innisbore, still and lifeless and broken. The Draw itself was massed thick with them. The Elves were appalled. It was as if life had meant nothing to the Demons, as if death were somehow preferable. Eyes began to search out the faces of friends and comrades. Hands stretched out to one another, clasping tightly, and the Elves were filled with relief, grateful that they had somehow survived through such terrible destruction.

At the head of the Draw, Ander Elessedil found Kael Pindanon and impulsively hugged the veteran soldier to him. Cries of elation began to rise from the throats of their countrymen as the realization set in that the day was theirs. Stee Jans rode in at the head of the Free Corps and the Bordermen joined the Elves, lances raising in salute. Down the length of the Sarandanon, the roar of victory swelled and echoed.

Only Allanon stood apart. Alone now on the slopes of the Kensrowe, his dark face turned north toward the hills into which the Demons had so abruptly fled, he found himself wondering why it was that they had been willing to give their lives so cheaply and, perhaps more important still, why it was that through all that slaughter there had been no sign of the one they called the Dagda Mor.

The afternoon faded into dusk and the night slipped silently away. At the mouth of Baen Draw, the army of the Westland waited for the Demons to attack. But the Demons did not come. Nor did they come at dawn, though Elves and Bordermen stood ready once more. The morning hours began to creep past, and a growing uneasiness pervaded the ranks of the defenders.

At midday, Ander went looking for Allanon, hoping that the Druid could give some explanation for what was happening. Alone, he climbed the slopes of the Kensrowe to where Allanon kept a solitary vigil within the shelter of an outcropping of rock, half hidden in shadow as he gazed out across the Sarandanon. The Elven Prince had not spoken with Allanon since yesterday when the Druid had come up into these mountains; no one had. Caught up in the jubilation of the Elven victory over the Demons, he had given little thought to the Druid's going. After all, Allanon came and went all the time, seldom with any explanation. But now, as he approached the Druid, he found himself wondering nevertheless why Allanon had chosen this time to be alone.

He was given his answer the moment the Druid turned to face him. Allanon's face, once so dark, was ashen. Harsh lines creased the skin, giving it a slack and weary caste, and there was a brooding look to the piercing black eyes. Ander drew up short, staring.

The stare brought a faint smile to Allanon's lips. "Does something trouble you, Elven Prince?"

Ander started. "No, I . . . it's just that . . . Allanon, you look . . ."

The Druid shrugged. "There is a price for the ways in which we use ourselves. That is one of nature's laws, though we often choose to disregard it. Even a Druid is subject to its dictates." He paused. "Do you understand what I am saying?"

Ander looked uncertain. "The magic does this to you?"

Allanon nodded. "The magic takes life from the user—it drains strength and being. Something of what is lost can be recovered, but recovery is slow. And there is pain . . ."

The sentence died away, unfinished. Ander felt a sudden chill.

"Allanon, have you lost the magic?"

The cowled head lifted. "The magic is not lost while the user lives. But there are limits that cannot be exceeded, and the limits shorten with the passing of the years. We all grow old, Elven Prince."

"Even you?" Ander asked quietly.

The black eyes were veiled. Allanon changed the subject abruptly. "What brings you to me?"

Ander took a moment to recover his thoughts. "I came to ask why the Demons do not attack."

The Druid looked away. "Because they are not yet ready." He was silent a moment, then his gaze shifted back again. "Do not be misled; they will come. They but delay, and there is a purpose behind that delay. The one who leads them, the one who is called the Dagda Mor, does nothing without reason." He bent forward slightly. "Give thought to this. The Dagda Mor was not among those who attacked us yesterday."

Ander frowned worriedly. "Where was he then?"

Allanon shook his head. "The question we should be asking is where is he now?" He watched Ander for a moment, then drew the black robes close about him. "I have been thinking that it would be wise to send trackers north above the Kensrowe and south below the Innisbore to be certain that the Demons do not intend to flank us."

There was a long silence. "Are there Demons enough to do that?" Ander asked finally, thinking of the thousands that had come against them already at Baen Draw.

Allanon's laugh was brittle. "Demons enough." The Druid turned away. "Leave me alone now, Elven Prince."

Ander went back down out of the Kensrowe, riddled with doubt. On his return, trackers were dispatched, and the waiting resumed. Morning passed into afternoon and afternoon into evening. A heavy bank of clouds rolled across the darkening sky, and shadows lengthened quickly into night.

Still the Demons did not come.

It was nearing midnight when the attack finally came. It was sudden, so sudden that the sentries standing watch had barely enough time to give the alarm before the first of the Demons were upon them. They came through Baen Draw in a massive rush, waves of black, corded bodies surging down out of the darkened northern hills into the light of the watch fires. One by one the fires winked out, smothered by the Demons as they swept through the Draw and onto the slopes of the Kensrowe. With the watch fires gone and the night sky screened by the clouds that had swept east out of the Breakline, the whole of Baen Draw was plunged into blackness. It was a blackness that the Demons knew well, to which they had grown accustomed during the time of their imprisonment within the Forbidding, a darkness that would be made to serve them. For, while the Elves and the Southlanders could now see little, the Demons saw as if it were brightest day. Shrieking in frenzied anticipation, they attacked.

At the head of the Draw, rallying about Ander Elessedil and the gleaming white staff of the Ellcrys, an Elven phalanx met the rush. The impact threw the soldiers backward, yet they held their lines. Hundreds of dark bodies crushed up against them, teeth and claws ripping. The Elves fought back determinedly, lances and pikes thrusting blindly into the mass of Demons that pushed forward, and screams of pain tore through the night. But the Demons kept coming, surging into the Elves, struggling to break apart their defense. For a few desperate minutes, the Elves withstood the savage rush, holding back the masses that hurtled against them. But the darkness confused and hindered them. In the end, they were overwhelmed. The phalanx began to give, falling back raggedly, splitting apart. Seconds later, the Demons broke through.

That would have been the finish if not for Allanon. Gaining the lower slopes of the Kensrowe, where the Elven archers fought a losing battle in the darkness to keep back the onrushing Demons, the Druid seized a handful of glittering dust from a small pouch tied at his waist and tossed the dust high into the air. Instantly the dust spread out across the night sky above the struggling Elves, filling the darkness with a brilliant white glow that lit the land beneath with the brightness of moonlight.

Gone was the blackness and the Demons' concealment. From behind the broken phalanx, a rallying cry went up. Into the main breach, where the largest mass of Demons thrust forward, rode Stee Jans and the men of the

Legion Free Corps. Like an iron wedge, they split the forefront of the assault. Less than four hundred now, they hammered into the horde before them and bore it back toward the mouth of Baen Draw. To their aid galloped the Elven cavalry, Kael Pindanon leading, head bare, white hair flying. All along the shattered defensive line, the lances of the horsemen tore into the advancing Demons and drove them back.

On the slopes of the Kensrowe, the Demons had broken through the ranks of archers and were pouring down into the Sarandanon. Allanon stood virtually alone in their path, blue fire lancing from his hands. They came at him from everywhere, howling in frenzy as the fire burned them to ash. The Druid did not give way. When they grew too many for him, he turned the whole of the grasslands about him for hundreds of feet in either direction into an inferno of death, a wall of blue fire that ringed the maddened Demons and destroyed any that tried to breach it.

A hundred yards back from the mouth of Baen Draw, the Elves and the Free Corps fought desperately to keep the main body of Demons from breaking through into the Sarandanon. It was a terrible, frightening battle and the smell of death filled the summer night. At its height, Kael Pindanon went down, his horse stumbling beneath him. The old warrior was shaken and came to his feet unsteadily, fumbling for his broadsword. Instantly, the Demons were upon him, howling. Elven Hunters fought to reach their beleaguered Commander, slashing and cutting their way through the Demons that rose before them. But the Demons were too quick. Clawed hands reached for Pindanon, warding off the blows struck at them, and the old soldier was pulled to his death.

At the same moment, a handful of Demons broke from the crush of fighters about them and hurtled toward Ander Elessedil. Through the ring of Home Guard that battled about him the Demons came, bounding like cats, to lunge for the Elven Prince. In desperation he brought up the Ellcrys staff like a shield and his attackers shrank from it, howling with rage. But Ander was all alone now, surrounded by twisted black forms, and they snapped and tore at him, waiting for a chance to break through the guard of his talisman. Elven Hunters fought desperately to reach the Prince, yet the Demons blocked their way, tearing apart those who came too close, parrying wildly the cut and slash of lance and sword. Their brethren surged to their aid, seeing that they had within their grasp the bearer of the hated talisman. Clawed hands reached out, grasping.

Then through the tangle of fighters hurtled a giant, scar-faced Borderman, gray-cloaked body streaked with dirt and blood. Up against the Demons he went, cutting through corded black bodies with great sweeps of his broadsword until at last he stood next to Ander. Shrieks of rage rose from the Demons, and they threw themselves at him. But Stee Jans held his ground like some immovable rock, keeping Ander's attackers from him as he called to his Bordermen. They came instantly, riding to his aid, gathering about him in a circle of iron. Then he was back atop his roan, sword lifted. The gray riders charged forward, their battle cry ringing out through the night.

For an instant, Ander did not realize what was happening. Then, through the hazy glow of false moonlight, he caught sight of the men of the Free Corps, Stee Jans at their head, red hair flying, one hand gripping the great broadsword, the other the Free Corps standard of battle. Alone, a handful against hundreds, the Free Corps was attacking! At once the Elven Prince seized the reins of a riderless horse, mounted, then spurred the animal ahead, crying out to his countrymen. As the Elves rallied to him from every quarter, he rode into the ranks of the Demons, forward to the side of the Legion Free Corps. In a wave, the Elves and the Bordermen swept down into Baen Draw, driving the Demons before them. Like men gone berserk, they battered their way ahead, horsemen and foot soldiers, with lance and pike and sword, shouting as one the battle cries of their homelands.

For an instant, the Demons stood their ground, shrieking with rage and hate, tearing at the madmen who thrust so recklessly into their midst. But the big man with the broadsword and the Free Corps battle standard had given fresh courage to the Elves, courage that bore them forward to face death without fear, to forget everything but their determination to destroy utterly those twisted black forms that stood before them. The Demons wavered and fell back, slowly at first, then in headlong flight, for the fury generated within the army of the Elves was much greater now than their own. Into the hills north they fled once more, scrambling down from the slopes of the Kensrowe through the rocks and crags of the Draw, flying into the concealing shadows of the night.

In moments, Baen Draw had been cleared, and the Sarandanon was again in the hands of the Elves.

Ander Elessedil sat within his tent, stripped to the waist, as Elven Hunters worked on the wounds the Demons had inflicted upon him during the battle. He sat in silence, his body aching with fatigue and the pain of his injuries. Messengers came and went, reporting on the progress of the army as it prepared to entrench once more across the mouth of Baen Draw. Home Guard ringed the tent, the iron of their weapons glinting in the light of the watch fires.

The Elven Prince had finished with the bandaging and was pulling on his armor when the tent flaps parted suddenly and Stee Jans appeared out of the night, his giant form streaked with dirt and ash and blood. Those within the tent immediately fell silent. With a single word, Ander bade them all leave. The tent emptied, and Ander moved forward to stand before the Borderman. Wordlessly, he clasped the big man's hand in his own.

"You saved all of us tonight, Commander," he said quietly. "There is a debt owed you that will be difficult to repay."

Stee Jans studied him a moment, then shook his head slowly. "My Lord, there is nothing owed to me. I am a soldier. Anything I did this night was no more than I should have done."

Ander smiled wearily. "You will never convince me of that. Still, I respect and admire you far too much to argue the matter. I will simply thank you." He released the big man's hand and stepped back. "Kael Pindanon is dead, and I must find a new field commander. I want you."

The Borderman was quiet a moment. "My Lord, I am not an Elf nor even of this country."

"I have no Elf nor countryman better suited to command this army than you," Ander replied at once. "And it was your plan that enabled us to hold Baen Draw."

Stee Jans did not drop his gaze. "There are some who would question this decision."

"There are some who would question any decision." Ander shook his head. "I am not my father nor my brother nor the leader they thought to have. But be that as it may, the decision is mine to make and I have made it. I want you as field commander. Do you accept?"

The Borderman thought for a long time before he spoke again. "I do."

Ander felt a bit of the weariness slip from him. "Then let us begin . . ."

A sudden movement in the shadows by the entry brought them both about with a start. Allanon stood there, his iron face grim.

"The trackers sent north and south within the valley have returned." The Druid spoke softly, the words almost a hiss as they left his mouth. "Those who went south along the Innisbore found nothing. But those who went north encountered an army of Demons so massive as to dwarf that which battles us within Baen Draw. It comes south along the eastern wall of the Kensrowe. Already it will have entered the Sarandanon."

Ander Elessedil stared silently at the big man, hope fading within his eyes.

"This was their plan from the beginning, Elven Prince—to engage you here at Baen Draw with the lesser force while the greater skirted the Kensrowe north, to come down into the Sarandanon from behind, thereby trapping the army of the Elves between the two. Had you not sent those trackers . . ."

He trailed off meaningfully. Ander started to speak and stopped, choking on the words. Suddenly there were tears in his eyes, tears of rage and frustration.

"All the men who have died here—here and at Halys Cut . . . my brother, Pindanon—all dead that the Sarandanon might be held . . . is there nothing we can do?"

"The army that comes down out of the north contains Demons whose powers far exceed anything you have yet encountered." Allanon's head shook slowly. "Too much power, I am afraid, for you to withstand—too much. If you try to hold the Sarandanon longer, if you attempt to stand here at Baen Draw or even to fall back to some other line of defense within the valley, you shall most certainly be destroyed."

Ander's youthful face was bleak. "Then the Sarandanon is lost."

Allanon nodded slowly. The Elven Prince hesitated, glancing back momentarily toward the rear compartment of the tent where the King still lay unconscious, unknowing, locked in dreamless sleep, far from the pain and the reality that confronted his anguished son. Lost! The Breakline, the Sarandanon, his family, his army—everything! Within, he felt himself breaking apart. Allanon's hand gripped his shoulder. Without turning, he nodded.

"We shall leave at once."

Head bowed, he walked from the tent to give the order.

Wil Ohmsford found the Wilderun as bleak and forbidding as the stories had foretold. Though the afternoon sky had been brilliant with sunlight when he and Amberle had left the Rock Spur, the Wilderun was a tangle of shadows and murky darkness, screened away from the world about it by trees and scrub that was twisted and interwoven until there seemed to be neither beginning nor end to its maze. Trunks thick with mold grew gnarled and bent, the limbs coiling out like spider's legs, choked with vines and brush, heavy with spiny leaves that shimmered in streaks of incandescent silver. Deadwood and scrub littered the valley floor, decaying slowly in the dark ground, giving it an unpleasantly soft, spongy feel. Damp with must and rot, the Wilderun had the look of something misshapen and grotesque. It was as if nature had stunted the land and the life that grew within it, then bent it down within itself, so that it might ever be made to breathe, eat, and drink the stench that rose out of its own slow death.

Down the crooked forest road the Valeman walked, the Elven girl close beside him, peering into the darkness about them with cautious, worried eyes, hearing distantly the sounds of the life that prowled and hunted within. The road was like a tunnel, walled about by forest, lighted only by faint streamers of sunlight that somehow slipped past the tangle overhead to touch faintly the dank earth below. There were no birds within this forest; Wil had noticed that at once. Birds would not live within such blackness, Wil had thought to himself—not while they might fly in sunlight. There were none of the usual small forest animals, nor even such common insects as brightly-colored butterflies. What lived here were things best left to blackness, night, and shadow: bats, leathered and reeking of disease; snakes and scaled hunters that nested and fed on vermin that lived within fetid ponds and marsh; cat-things, sleek and quick as they stalked the treeways on silent pads. A time or two their shadows crossed the roadway, and Valeman and Elven girl paused guardedly. Yet as quickly as they had come, they were gone again, lost in the blackness, leaving the humans on the empty path to stare anxiously at the forest and to hurry on.

Once, when they had gone deep into the gloom, the pair heard something massive move, pushing through trees as if it were pushing through fragile twigs, its breath huffing loudly in the stillness that fell across the forest with its passing. Lumbering invisibly through the gloom, it either did not see or did not care to bother with the two small creatures who stood frozen upon the trail. Slowly, deliberately, it moved off. In the silence that followed, Valeman and Elven girl fled quickly away.

They encountered only a handful of travelers as they walked the forest, all but one afoot and that one slouched atop a horse so thin and worn as to appear more an apparition than flesh and blood. Cloaked and hooded, the travelers passed them by singly and in pairs, offering no greeting. Yet within the shadow of their cowls, their heads turned and their eyes blinked with the cold interest of cats, staring after the intruders as if to measure their purpose. Chilled by those looks, the Southlander and the girl found themselves glancing back over their shoulders long after the cloaked forms had disappeared from view.

It was nearing sunset when they passed at last from the gloom of the wilderness forest into the town of Grimpen Ward. A less inviting community would have been hard to imagine. Set down within a hollow, Grimpen Ward was a ramshackle cluster of wooden plank buildings so closely jammed together as to be nearly indistinguishable, one from the other. They were a seedy lot, these shops and stalls, inns and taverns. The garish paint that colored them was chipped and faded. Many stood shuttered, bars drawn, locks fastened. Poorly lettered signs hung from swaying posts and over doors, a patchwork maze of promises and prices beneath proprietors' names. Through windows and entryways, lamps of oil and pitch burned, casting their harsh yellow light into the shadows without as dusk closed down about the hollow.

It was in the taverns and inns of Grimpen Ward that her denizens were gathered, at rough-hewn tables and bars formed of boards set atop barrels, about glasses and tankards of ale and wine, their voices loud and rough, their laughter shrill. They drifted from one building to the next, hard-eyed men and women of all races, some dressed gaily, some ragged, bold in the glare of the lamplight, or furtive as they stole through alleyways, many stumbling, lurching, and reeking of drink. Money clinked and changed hands quickly, often in stealth or in violence. Here a lumpish figure slumped down within a doorway, asleep in drunken stupor, his clothes stripped from his body, his purse gone. There a tattered form lay still and twisted within a darkened passage, the lifeblood seeping from the wound at his throat. All about, dogs prowled, ragged and hungry, slinking through the shadows like wraiths.

Thieves and cutthroats, harlots and cheats, traders in life and death and false pleasure. Wil Ohmsford felt the hair on the back of his neck rise. Perk's grandfather had been right about Grimpen Ward.

Holding tight to Amberle's hand, he followed the rutted line of the road as it wound through the tangle of buildings. What were they to do now? Certainly they could not go back into the forest—not at night. He was reluctant to remain in Grimpen Ward, but what other choice did they have? They were both tired and hungry. It had been days since they had slept in a bed or eaten a hot meal. Still, there seemed to be little chance that they would get either here. Neither of them had any money to buy or anything of value to trade for a night's food and lodging. Everything had been lost in their flight out of the Pykon. The Valeman had thought to find someone within the town who might be persuaded to let them work for a meal and a bed, but what he saw about him suggested that no one of that disposition lived in Grimpen Ward.

A drunken Gnome lurched up against him and fumbled for his cloak. Wil shoved the fellow away hurriedly. The Gnome tumbled into the street and lay laughing foolishly at the sky. The Valeman stared down at him a moment, then clasped Amberle's arm and hurried on.

There were other problems facing them as well. Once they left Grimpen Ward, how were they to find their way from there? How were they to keep from becoming quickly lost within the wilderness beyond? They desperately needed someone to guide them, but whom in Grimpen Ward could they trust? If they were forced to continue on without any idea of where they were going, then it would become necessary for Wil to use the Elfstones—or at least attempt to use them—before they had found the tunnels of Safehold and the Bloodfire and long before they were ready to flee. The moment he did that, he would bring the Demons down on them. Yet without the use of the Stones or the aid of a guide, they would have no chance at all of finding Safehold—not if they had all year to do so instead of only days.

Wil paused helplessly, staring at the lighted doors and windows of the buildings of the town, the shadowy figures who milled within, and the backdrop of the wilderness and the night sky. It was an impossible dilemma, and he had no idea at all how he was going to resolve it.

"Wil," Amberle tugged anxiously at his arm. "Let's get off this street."

The Valeman glanced at her quickly and nodded. First things first. They must find a place to sleep for the night; they must have something to eat. The rest would have to wait.

With Amberle's hand in his, he started back up the roadway, studying the inns and taverns at either side. They walked about fifty feet further before the Valeman caught sight of a small, two-story lodging house set back from the other buildings within a grove of scrub pine. Lights burned through the windows of the first floor, while the second story stood dark. The loud voices and raucous laughter were missing here, or at least diminished, and the crowd was small.

Wil moved over to the courtyard fronting the inn and peered through the streaked glass of the windows opening on the main room. Everything appeared quiet. He glanced up. The sign on the gatepost indicated it was the Candle Light Inn. He hesitated a moment longer, then made up his mind. With a reassuring nod to Amberle, who looked more than a little doubtful, he led her through the gate and moved up the walk through the pine. The inn doors stood open to the summer night.

"Put your cowl about your face," he whispered suddenly, and when she stared over at him blankly, quickly did so for her. He gave her a smile which belied his own sense of uncertainty, then took her hand firmly in his and stepped through the entry.

The room within was cramped and thick with smoke from oil lamps and pipes. A short bar stood at the front, and a knot of rough-looking men and women clustered about it, talking among themselves and drinking ale. Various tables ringed by chairs and backless stools filled the back, a few occupied by cloaked figures who hunched over drinks and spoke in low voices. Several doors led from this room to other parts of the building, and a stairway ran up the left wall and disappeared into darkness. The floor was splintered and worn, and cobwebs hung from the corners of the ceiling. Next to the doorway, an aged hound chewed contentedly on a meat bone.

Wil guided Amberle to the back of the room where a small table stood empty save for a fat, low-burning candle, and they seated themselves. A few heads lifted or turned as they passed, then just as quickly looked away again.

"What are we doing here?" Amberle asked anxiously, finding it difficult to keep the tone of her voice low enough that they would not be overheard.

Wil shook his head. "Just be patient."

A few moments later a lumpish, unfriendly-looking woman of uncertain age trudged over to them, a towel thrown loosely across one arm. As she came up to them, Wil noticed that she was limping badly. He thought he recognized that limp, and the germ of an idea began to form.

"Something to drink?" she wanted to know.

Wil smiled pleasantly. "Two glasses of ale."

The woman walked away without comment. Wil watched her go.

"I do not like ale," Amberle protested. "What are you doing?"

"Being sociable. Did you notice the way that woman limped?"

The Elven girl stared at him. "What has that got to do with anything?"

Wil smiled. "Everything. Watch and see."

They sat in silence for a moment, then the woman was back again, carrying with her the glasses of ale. She placed them on the table and stood back, her beefy hand passing through a string of tangled, graying hair.

"That all?"

"Do you have any dinner?" Wil wanted to know, taking a sip of the ale. Amberle ignored her glass entirely.

"Stew, bread, cheese, maybe some cakes—fresh today."

"Mmmm. Hot day for baking."

"Real hot. Waste of effort, too. No one's eating."

Wil shook his head sympathetically. "Shouldn't let that kind of effort go to waste."

"Most would rather drink," the heavy woman offered with a snort. "Me, too, I guess, if I had the time."

Wil grinned. "I suppose. Do you run the inn alone?"

"Me and my boys." She warmed a bit, folding her arms across her chest. "Husband run off. Boys help me when they're not drinking or gambling—which is seldom. I could do it myself if it weren't for this leg. Cramps up all the time. Hurts like there's no quitting."

"Have you tried heat on it?"

"Sure. Helps some."

"Herb mixes?"

She spit. "Worthless."

"Quite a problem. How long has it been that way?"

"Aw, years, I guess. I lost count; doesn't do any good thinking about it."

"Well." Wil looked thoughtful. "The food sounds good. I think we will try it—a plate for each of us."

The proprietress of the Candle Light Inn nodded and moved away again. Amberle leaned forward quickly.

"How do you plan to pay for all this? We don't have any money."

"I know that," the Valeman replied, glancing about. "I don't think we are going to need any."

Amberle looked as if she were going to hit him. "You promised you would not do this again. You promised you would tell me first what it was you were planning to do before you did it—remember? The last time you tried something like this was with the Rovers, and it nearly cost us our lives. These people look a lot more dangerous than the Rovers."

"I know, I know, but I just thought of it. We have to have a meal and a bed, and this looks like our best chance for both."

The Elven girl's face tightened within the shadow of the cowl. "I do not like this place, Wil Ohmsford—this inn, this town, these people, any of it. We could do without the meal and the bed."

Wil shook his head. "We could, but we won't. Shhh, she's coming back."

The woman had returned with their dinner. She set the steaming plates before them and was about to leave when Wil spoke.

"Stay a moment," he asked. The proprietress turned back to them. "I have been thinking about your leg. Maybe I can help."

She stared at him suspiciously. "What do you mean?"

He shrugged. "Well, I think I can stop the pain."

The look of suspicion grew more pronounced. "Why would you want to do that for me?" She scowled.

Wil smiled. "Business. Money."

"I don't have much money."

"Then how about a trade? For the price of the ale, this meal, and a night's lodging, I'll stop the pain. Fair enough?"

"Fair enough." Her lumpish body dropped heavily into the chair next to him. "But can you do it?"

"Bring out a cup of hot tea and a clean cloth and we will see."

The woman came to her feet at once and lumbered off to the kitchen. Wil watched her go, smiling faintly. Amberle shook her head.

"I hope you know what you are doing."

"So do I. Eat your dinner now in case I don't."

They had finished most of their meal by the time she returned with the tea and cloth. Wil glanced past her to the patrons gathered about the bar. A few heads were beginning to turn. Whatever happened next, he thought, he did not want to call further attention to himself. He looked up at the woman and smiled.

"This should be done in private. Do you have somewhere we might go?"

The woman shrugged and led them through one of the closed doors into a small room containing a single table with a candle and six stools. She lit the candle and closed the door. The three seated themselves.

"What happens now?" the woman asked.

The Valeman took a single dried leaf from a pouch about his waist and crumbled it into dust, dropping the dust into the tea. He stirred the mixture about, then handed it back to the woman.

"Drink it down. It will make you a bit sleepy, nothing more."

The woman studied it a moment, then drank it. When the cup was empty, Wil took it from her, dropped in another kind of leaf and poured a small measure of ale from his glass, which he had carried in with him. These he stirred slowly, watching the leaf dissolve away to nothing. Across the table from him, Amberle shook her head.

"Put your leg up on this stool," Wil ordered, shoving a vacant stool in front of the woman, who dutifully placed her leg on it. "Now pull up your skirt."

The proprietress gave him a questioning look, as if wondering what his intentions might be for her, then hiked her skirt up to her thigh. Her leg was corded, veined, and covered with dark splotches. Wil dipped the cloth into the mixture in the cup and began rubbing it into the leg.

"Tingles a bit." The woman giggled.

Wil smiled encouragingly. When the mixture was gone from the cup, he reached into the pouch once more and this time produced a long, silver needle with a rounded head. The woman leaned forward with a start.

"You're not going to stick that in me, are you?"

Wil nodded calmly. "You won't feel it; just a touch." He passed it slowly through the flame of the candle that burned at the center of their table. "Now hold very still," he ordered.

Slowly, carefully, he inserted the needle into the woman's leg, just above the knee joint, until only the rounded head was showing. He left it there a moment, then withdrew it. The woman grimaced slightly, shut her eyes, then opened them again. Wil sat back.

"All done," he announced, hoping that indeed it was. "Stand up and walk about."

The perplexed woman stared at him a moment, then pulled down her skirt indignantly and rose to her feet. Gingerly, she stepped away from the table, testing the feel of the bad leg. Then abruptly she wheeled about, a broad grin creasing her rough face.

"It's gone! The pain's gone! First time in months!" She was laughing excitedly. "I don't believe it. How'd you do that?"

"Magic." Wil grinned with satisfaction, then immediately wished he hadn't said that. Amberle shot him an angry glance.

"Magic, huh?" The woman took a few more steps, shaking her head. "Well, if you say so. It sure feels like magic. No pain at all."

"Well, it wasn't really magic . . ." Wil began anew, but the woman was already moving toward the door.

"I feel so good, I'm going to give everyone a free glass." She opened the door and stepped through. "Can't wait to see their faces when they hear about this!"

"No, wait . . ." Wil called after her, but the door closed and she was gone. "Confound it," he muttered, wishing belatedly that he had made her promise to keep quiet about this.

Amberle folded her hands calmly and looked at him. "How *did* you do that?"

He shrugged. "I'm a Healer, remember? The Stors taught me a few things about aches and pains." He leaned forward conspiratorially. "The trouble is, the treatment doesn't last."

"Doesn't last!" Amberle was horrified.

Wil put a finger to his lips. "The treatment is only temporary. By morning the pain will be back, so we had better be gone."

"Wil, you lied to that woman," the Elven girl cried. "You told her you could cure her."

"No, that was not what I said. I said that I could stop the pain. I did not say for how long. A night's relief for her, a night's sleep and a meal for us. A fair trade."

Amberle stared at him accusingly and did not reply.

Wil sighed. "If it is any comfort to you, the pain will not be as bad as it was before. But her condition is not one that any Healer could cure; it has to do with the life she leads, her age, her weight—a lot of other things over which I have no control. I have done as much as I can for her. Will you please be reasonable?"

"Could you give her something for when the pain returns?"

The Valeman reached over and gripped her hands. "You are a truly gentle person, do you know that? Yes, I could give her something for the pain. But we will leave it for her to find after we are gone, if you don't mind."

A sudden clamor from the other room brought him to his feet, and he moved to the door, slipping it open just a crack. Before, the inn had been all but empty. Now it was nearly filled as people drifted in off the roadway, attracted by the promise of free drinks and the antics of the proprietress, who was gleefully demonstrating her newfound cure.

"Time to be going," Wil muttered and hurriedly led Amberle from the room.

They had not taken a dozen steps when the woman called out shrilly and came rushing over to stop them. Heads shook and fingers pointed at Wil. Too many for the Valeman's comfort.

"A glass of ale, you two?" the heavy woman offered. Her hand clapped Wil on the shoulder and nearly knocked him off his feet. He managed a weak grin.

"I think we should get some sleep. We have a long journey and we are really very tired."

The woman snorted. "Stay up and celebrate. You don't have to pay. Drink all you want."

Wil shook his head. "I think we better get some sleep."

"Sleep? With all this noise?" The woman shrugged. "Take room number ten, top of the stairs and down the hall. Sits at the back of the inn. Might be a little more quiet for you." She paused. "We're even now, right? I don't owe you anything more?"

"Nothing," Wil assured her, anxious to be gone.

The proprietress grinned broadly. "Well, you sold out cheap, you know that? I would have paid you ten times what you asked for what you done. Why, a couple hours without the pain is worth the ale and the meal and the bed! You got to be clever if you expect to get anywhere in this country. Remember that bit of advice, little Elf. It's free."

She laughed roughly and turned back to the bar. The free drinks were over. With a crowd of this size, there was money to be made. The woman scurried along the serving board, snatching the coins up eagerly.

Wil grabbed Amberle's arm and guided her away from the table to the stairway and up the steps. The stares of the patrons followed after them.

"And you were worried about her," the Valeman muttered as they reached the upper hallway and turned down it.

Amberle smiled and said nothing.

34

They had been asleep several hours when they heard the noises at the door of their room. Wil came awake first, sitting upright in the bed with a start, peering through the deep night blackness. He could hear sounds without—a shuffling of feet, whispered voices, heavy breathing. Not Demons, he told himself quickly, but the chill within him would not subside. The latch on the door jiggled as hands worked quietly to free it.

Amberle was awake as well, sitting next to him, her face white within the shadow of her long chestnut hair. Wil put a finger to his lips.

"Wait here."

Silently he slipped from the bed and moved to the door. The latch continued to rattle, but the Valeman had thrown the bolt above it, so the room was secure. He bent toward the doorway and listened. The voices without were low and muffled.

". . . careful, fool . . . just lift it . . ."

"I am lifting it! Step out of the light!"

". . . waste of time; just break it in . . . there's enough of us."

". . . not if he uses magic."

"The gold is worth the risk . . . break it!"

The voices argued on, whispers laced with the slur of ale, mixed with grunts and ragged breathing. There were at least half-a-dozen men out there, the Valeman decided—thieves and cutthroats, most probably, undoubtedly led to them by the idle tongue of someone who had heard the tale of their miraculous cure of the proprietress of the inn and who could not resist a few embellishments in a retelling of the story. He backed away hurriedly, groping for the bed. Amberle's hand gripped his arm.

"We have to get out of here," he whispered.

Wordlessly, she moved off the bed into the dark. They had slept in their clothes and it took them only moments to pull on the travel cloaks and boots. Wil hastened to the window at the rear of the room and pushed it open. Immediately below, a veranda roof sloped downward from the wall. From its edge, there was a drop of a dozen feet to the ground. Wil turned back to find Amberle again and brought her to the window.

"Out you go," he whispered and took her arm.

In that same instant, there came a loud oath from the hall, and a heavy body crashed into the door, splintering boards and metal fastenings. The would-be thieves had lost their patience. Wil all but shoved the Elven girl through the open window, glancing back hurriedly to see if the intruders had broken through completely. They had not. The door still held. But then the door was struck again. This time the bolt gave way. Into the room surged a knot of cloaked figures, stumbling over one another, cursing and yelling.

Wil did not wait to see what might happen next. Scrambling through the window, he leaped hurriedly onto the veranda roof.

"Jump!" he yelled to Amberle, who crouched in front of him.

The Elven girl slipped over the edge of the roof and dropped to the earth below. In a moment's time, Wil was beside her. Above them, leaning through the open window, the cloaked figures shouted in anger. Wil pulled Amberle back within the shadows of the building, then looked about hurriedly.

"Which way?" he muttered, suddenly confused.

Wordlessly Amberle took his hand and sprinted to the end of the wall, then broke for the building next to the inn. The shouts of their pursuers rose sharply, followed by the sound of booted feet on the veranda roof. Valeman and Elven girl ran silently through the darkness of the buildings, slipping down passageways, through alleys, and along walls until at last they were back to the edge of the main roadway.

Still the shouts pursued them. Grimpen Ward seemed to come suddenly awake, lights flaring in darkened buildings all about them, voices raising in anger. Amberle started out onto the roadway, but Wil pulled her hastily back. Less than a hundred feet away, in front of the Candle Light

Inn, several dark forms fanned out onto the road, searching carefully the shadows about them.

"We have to go back," the Valeman whispered.

They retraced their steps, following the wall of the building until they reached its end. A series of sheds and stalls stood clustered together against the dark backdrop of the forest. Wil hesitated. If they tried to escape into the forest, they would become hopelessly lost. They had to work their way back around the buildings to where the main roadway wound south out of Grimpen Ward. Once beyond the town, they would probably not be pursued further.

Cautiously they moved along the rear of the building. Walls and fences hemmed them in on all sides and barrels of trash cluttered the path forward. But the shouts had quieted now, and the buildings ahead were still dark. A few minutes more and they might be clear of their pursuit.

They turned down a narrow alley that ran through a row of stables behind a feed store. Horses whickered softly at their scent, stamping impatiently within their stalls. A small paddock stretched out before them beyond a line of sheds.

Wil started along the paddock fence with Amberle at his side. They had taken no more than a dozen steps when a sharp cry went up behind them. From out of the shadows of the feed store, a dark form appeared, arms waving, voice raised in alarm. Answering cries sounded from the buildings beyond. Startled by the suddenness of their discovery, Valeman and Elven girl stumbled over one another in their haste to flee, lost their footing, and went down.

Instantly their pursuer was on top of them. Arms flailed and fists pummeled wildly. Wil grappled with the man, a wiry fellow reeking of ale, as Amberle rolled clear. His hands fastened on his attacker's cloak; with a sudden heave, Wil threw the man sideways into the paddock. There was a sharp whack as the man's head struck the fence boards, and he collapsed in a heap.

Wil scrambled back to his feet. Lights came on in the rooms above the feed store and in the surrounding buildings. In the darkness behind them, torchlight flickered through the night. Cries of pursuit sounded from everywhere. The Valeman seized Amberle's hand and they raced together along the ring of the paddock to the line of sheds. There they turned back toward the main roadway, following a narrow alley that ran between two shuttered buildings. Shadows darkened the passage and the two ran blindly, Wil leading. Ahead, the earthen line of the roadway slipped into view.

"Wil!" Amberle cried out in warning.

Too late. The Valeman's eyes were not as sharp as the Elven girl's, and he stumbled headlong into a pile of loose boards strewn across the alley passage. Down he tumbled, crashing into the side of the building. Pain exploded in his head; for an instant, he lost consciousness completely. Then somehow he was back on his feet, weaving forward dizzily, Amberle's voice a faint buzzing sound in his ears. His hand reached for his forehead and came away wet with blood.

Abruptly the Elven girl was next to him, her arms wrapping tightly about his waist. He sagged against her weakly, forcing himself to stagger ahead toward the distant light of the street. He felt himself blacking out again and fought against it. He had to keep moving; he had to keep awake. Amberle was talking to him, her voice urgent, but he could not make out the words. He felt like a fool. How could he have let something this stupid happen now?

They staggered clear of the alley and turned into the shadows of a porch. Down its length they stumbled, the Elven girl fighting to keep the Valeman on his feet. Blood ran down into Wil's eyes, blinding him further, and he muttered in anger.

Suddenly he heard Amberle gasp in surprise. Through the haze that blurred his vision, he watched a tangle of shadows appear out of the dark. Voices sounded, low and rough, and there was a hiss of warning. Then Amberle was gone, and he felt himself being lifted. Strong hands bore him quickly through the dark. There was a swirl of color before his clouded eyes, mingled with a rush of torchlight. Then he was being lifted again, this time through a narrow opening of canvas flaps. An oil lamp flickered beside him. Voices sounded, whispers of caution, and he felt a damp cloth wipe his face clean of blood. Hands worked busily to wrap him in blankets and to place a pillow beneath his head.

Slowly he opened his eyes. He lay within a gaily colored wagon, its walls decorated with tapestries, beads, and bright silks. The Valeman started. He knew this wagon.

Then a face bent close, dark and sensuous, framed in ringlets of thick black hair. The smile that greeted him was dazzling.

"I told you we would meet again, Wil Ohmsford."

It was Eretria.

35

For five days the army of the Elves and the Legion Free Corps fought their way back across the Westland to Arborlon. Across the broad valley of the Sarandanon, through woodlands dense and tangled, and down forest roads and rutted trails they fell back slowly, steadily eastward, pursued at every turn by the Demon hordes. They marched in daylight and at night, without rest, often without food, for the creatures that tracked them neither slept nor ate. Unburdened by human needs, freed of human limitations, the Demons came after them, purposeful, unrelenting, driven by their own peculiar form of madness. Like dogs at hunt, they harried the withdrawing army, nipping and slashing at its flanks, rushing it now and then in full assault, striving to turn it from its course, to cripple it, to destroy it. The attack was incessant, and the Elves and their allies, already weary from their stand at Baen Draw, grew quickly exhausted. With exhaustion came despair and then fear.

Ander Elessedil fell victim to that fear. It began for the Elven Prince with his own sense of failure. The dead, the defeats of the few days past, and all that the Elves had hoped to accomplish and had not done haunted him. Yet even this was not the worst. For as his battered army struggled eastward and his countrymen continued to die all about him, Ander began to realize that none of them might survive the long march back—that all of them might die. Out of this stark realization was born the fear that became his own private devil—faceless, insidious, lurking just within the shadow of his determination. Leader of the Elves, it asked slyly, what will you do to save them? Are you so helpless, then? So many have been lost— yet what if all those who remain be lost? It teased and tormented him, threatening to turn weary resolve into total despair. Even Allanon's presence did not help, for the black-robed Druid stayed distant and aloof as he rode at Ander's side, veiled in his own world of dark secrets. So Ander fought his fear alone within the silence of his mind, the whole of his strength directed toward its defeat, as slowly, grimly he led his failing soldiers back toward Arborlon.

In the end, it was Stee Jans who saved them all. It was in this darkest time of seeming failure and desperation that the giant Borderman displayed the tenacity, endurance, and courage that had created the legend of the Iron Man. Assembling a rear guard of Elves and Free Corps, he began a defense of the main column of his army as it bore its dead and wounded eastward under cover of night. In a series of lunges and feints, the Legion Commander struck out at his pursuers, drawing them after him, first one way, then another, utilizing the same tactics that he had so successfully employed at Baen Draw. Time and again the Demons came at him, sweeping first through the valley of the Sarandanon, then into the forestland beyond. Time and again they sought to trap the fleet, gray-cloaked Legion riders and the swift Elven horse, always to close an instant too late, finding only an empty grassland, a blind draw, a hollow dark with shadow, or a scrub-choked trail that turned back upon itself. With a deftness that baffled and maddened the Demons, Stee Jans and the riders following him played a deadly cat-and-mouse game that seemed to place them everywhere at once, yet always away from where the main body of the army moved back toward the safety of Arborlon.

Demon anger and frustration mounted; as night became day and day night again, the pursuit grew frenzied. These Demons were different from the lean, black creatures that had swarmed out of the hill country north of Baen Draw to seize the Sarandanon. These were Demons that had gone east above the Kensrowe, more dangerous than their lesser brethren, with powers that no ordinary human could withstand. Some were monstrous in size, corded with muscle and scaled with armor—creatures of mindless destruction. Others were small and fluid and killed with just a touch. Some were slow and ponderous, some quicksilver as they slipped through the forest shadows like wraiths. Some were multilimbed; others had no limbs at all. Some breathed fire as the Dragons of old, and some were eaters of human flesh. Where they passed, the land of the Elves was left blackened and scarred, ravaged so that nothing might live upon it. Yet the Elves themselves remained just beyond their reach.

The chase wore on. Elven Hunter and Free Corps soldier fought side by side in a desperate attempt to slow the Demon advance, watching their numbers dwindle steadily as their pursuers swept after them. Without Stee Jans to lead them, they would have been annihilated. Even with him, hundreds fell wounded and dead along the way, lost in the terrible struggle to prevent the long retreat from turning into a complete rout. Through it all, the Legion Commander's tactics remained the same. The strength of the Demons made it imperative that the Elven army not be forced to stand again this side of Arborlon. So the rear guard continued to strike quickly and slip away, always to swing back for yet another strike and then another—and each time a few more riders were lost.

At last, on the afternoon of the fifth day, the tattered and exhausted army came again to the shores of the Rill Song. With a ragged shout, it crossed back into Arborlon. Then it discovered the price that had been paid. A third of the Elves who had marched west to Sarandanon were dead. Hundreds more lay injured. Of the six hundred soldiers of the Legion Free Corps who had followed after them, less than one in every three remained alive.

And still the Demons advanced.

Dusk fell over the city of Arborlon. The day had gone cool at its end, a bank of heavy stormclouds moving eastward out of the flats to screen away moon and stars and fill the night air with the smell of rain. Lamps began to light within the homes of the city as families and friends gathered together for their evening meal. On the streets and in the treeways, units of the Home Guard began their nightly patrol, slipping through pooled shadows in uneasy silence. Atop the Carolon, on the Elfitch and along the eastern bank of the Rill Song, the soldiers of the Elven army stood ready, staring past rows of iron stanchions filled with burning pitch to the blackness of the forest beyond. Within the trees, nothing moved.

In the chambers of the Elven High Council, Ander Elessedil came face to face for the first time since his return from the Sarandanon with the King's Ministers, the army commanders, and the few outlanders who had arrived to aid the Elves in their fight against the Demons. He passed through the heavy wooden doors at the end of the council room, carrying the silver Ellcrys staff in his right hand. Dust, sweat and blood covered the Elven Prince; while he had permitted himself a few brief hours of sleep, he had not yet taken time to wash, perferring to come as quickly as possible before the Council. Beside him walked Allanon, tall and black and forbidding, his shadow rising up against the walls of the chamber as he entered, and Stee Jans, his weapons still strapped about him, his hazel eyes cold with death.

From their high-backed chairs about the council table, the seats of the gallery, and the risers at the edge of the Dais of the Kings, those gathered came at once to their feet. A rush of whispers and mutterings filled the hall, and questions began to rise up in shouts as each man sought to be heard. At the head of the table, Emer Chios brought his open hand down upon the wooden surface with a crash and the room went silent again.

"Be seated," the First Minister directed.

Grumbling, the men assembled did as they were told. Ander waited a moment, then came forward a step. He knew the rules of the High Council. When the King lay disabled, the First Minister presided. Emer Chios was a powerful and respected man, the more so in this situation. Ander had come before the Council with a very specific purpose in mind, and he would need the support of Chios if he were to achieve that purpose. He was tired and he was anxious, but it was necessary that he take time to go about matters in the proper way.

"My Lord First Minister," he addressed the Minister. "I would speak to the Council."

Emer Chios nodded. "Do so then, my Lord Prince."

Slowly, haltingly, for he was not the speaker that his father was or his brother had been, Ander told of all that had befallen the Elven army since its departure to the Sarandanon. He described the injury to the King and the death of Arion. He told them of the battles and defeats at the Breakline, of the withdrawal and gallant stand at Baen Draw, and finally of the retreat back through the Sarandanon and the Westland forests to Arborlon. He told them of the courage of the Legion Free Corps, of the leadership of Stee Jans when Pindanon had fallen. Graphically, he described the nature of the enemy they had faced—its size, its shape, its frenzy, and its power. The Demons, he warned them, now approached Arborlon, there to exterminate the last of the Elven people, to lay waste to the city, and to take back again the land they had lost centuries ago. What lay ahead was a battle in which one or the other, Elf or Demon, must surely be destroyed.

As he spoke, he studied the faces of his listeners, seeking in their eyes and expressions something of how they judged his actions since the loss of both their King and his heir-apparent. He accepted now that his father might die, and that he might then be King; he knew that the High Council and the Elven people must come to accept it as well. Acceptance had been difficult for Ander because, before the battle at Halys Cut, the possibility of such a thing happening had always seemed so remote and because he had not wanted to believe that he would lose both his father and his brother. But his father now lay within his bed at the manor house, unchanged since his fall. All the while that the Elves had fought at Baen Draw and on the long march home again, Ander Elessedil had waited for his father to wake, refusing to believe that he would not. But the King had not regained consciousness, and now it seemed that perhaps he would not do so ever. The Elven Prince understood that, accepted it, and thus looked past it to what must then be.

"Elven Lords," he finished, his voice worn and empty. "I am my father's son and I know what is expected of a Prince of the Elves. The Elven army has come out of the Sarandanon and now must stand here. I intend to stand with it. I intend to lead it. I would not have it so if there were any way that this moment could be undone, if all that had happened within these past few weeks might be wiped from the record of our lives. But that cannot be. Were my father here, you would rally to him to a man—I know that. I stand then in my father's place and ask that you rally to me, for I am the last of his blood. These men who stand with me have given me their support. I seek yours as well. Pledge me that support, Elven Lords."

Wordlessly, he waited. He need not have asked for their support, he knew, but merely assumed it. His was the power of the Elessedil rule, and there were few who would dare to challenge that. He could have asked Allanon to speak for him; the Druid's voice alone might have silenced any opposition. Yet Ander wanted no one to intercede for him in this, nor did he wish to take anything for granted. The support of the High Council and of the outlanders who had come to give them aid, should be won over by what they might see in him—not by fear or any claim of right that did not ground itself squarely on whatever strength of character he had shown in his command of the Elven army since the moment that his father had fallen.

Emer Chios came to his feet. His dark eyes swept briefly over the faces of those assembled. Then he turned to Ander.

"My Lord Prince," his deep voice rumbled. "All who gather in this Council know that I follow no man blindly, even though he be of royal blood and the child of Kings. I have said often and publicly that I trust the judgment of my people better than the judgment of any one man, though he be King of all the known world."

He looked about him slowly. "Yet I am Eventine Elessedil's faithful Minister and his great admirer. He is a King, Elven Lords, as a King was meant to be. I wish that he were here to lead us in this most dangerous time. But he is not. His son offers himself in his place. I know Ander Elessedil—I think I know him as well as any. I have listened to him; I have judged him by his words and by his acts and by what he has shown himself to be. I say now that in the absence of the King there is no man to whom I would more willingly entrust the safety of my homeland and my life than he."

He paused, then carefully placed his right hand over his heart—the Elven pledge of loyalty. There was a moment's silence. Then others rose with him from the table, a few at first, then all, hands placed across their hearts as they faced the Prince. The commanders of the Elven army stepped forward as well—Ehlron Tay, dour-faced and bluff, who, after the death of Pindanon, ranked highest in command; Kobold, the tall, immaculately dressed Captain of the Black Watch; and Kerrin, commanding the Home Guard. In moments, all of the Elves who had assembled within the High Council stood facing their Prince, hands lifted in salute.

At Ander Elessedil's side, a dark figure leaned close.

"Now they follow you, Elven Prince," Allanon spoke softly.

Ander nodded. He could almost regret that it was so.

They talked then of the defense of Arborlon.

Preparations for that defense had begun almost immediately following the departure of the Elven army to the Sarandanon two weeks earlier. Emer Chios, as ruler of the home city in the King's absence, had convened the High Council, together with the commanders of the Elven army who had not accompanied the King, for the purpose of deciding what steps should be taken to protect Arborlon in the event the Demons broke out of the Sarandanon. A series of carefully drawn defensive measures had been settled upon. The First Minister reviewed them now with Ander.

There were but two approaches to the city—from the east, along the trails that ran through the Valley of Rhenn and the forests beyond, and from the west, out of the Sarandanon. North and south of Arborlon stood mountains that offered no passage, tall peaks that shut away the lowland woods and ringed the Carolan in a wall of rock. Allanon had warned that the break in the Forbidding would come in the Hoare Flats. That meant the Demons must come east through the Sarandanon, and unless they turned north or south to bypass the mountains sheltering Arborlon—a march that would consume at least several days' additional time—the attack on the Elven home city would come from the west.

Yet it was here that the Elven defenses were strongest. Two natural barriers would immediately confront the Demons. First was the Rill Song, somewhat narrow where it arced eastward below the Carolan, but deep and difficult to navigate in the best weather. Second was the bluff itself, a sheer cliff that rose more than four hundred feet to its summit, its stone face split by a web of deep crevices and choked with scrub and heavy brush. A single bridge spanned the Rill Song below the Carolan at a point where the channel narrowed. There were no shallows for miles in either direction. The Elfitch provided the primary access route to the Carolan, although a series of smaller stairways wound upward through wooded sections of the cliff further south.

The defense of Arborlon depended then upon the river and the bluff. It had been decided that the bridge spanning the Rill Song would be destroyed immediately upon the return of the Elven army. This had been done as planned, Chios pointed out, and the last link between Arborlon and the Sarandanon had been severed. On the east bank, the Elves had anchored hundreds of pitch-burning stanchions to give light in the event a night crossing should be attempted and they had constructed a stone and earthen redoubt almost at the edge of the Rill Song that ran for several hundred yards along the riverbank at the base of the bluff and arced backward into the cliff face at either side of the Elfitch. The east bank extended back from the river about two hundred feet to the cliffs, and most of this ground was wooded and grown thick with scrub. Here the Elves had set dozens of traps and pitfalls to ensnare any Demons who sought to flank the redoubt.

But it was the Elfitch that provided the major defense to Arborlon. All of the smaller stairways leading to the great tableland of the Carolan had been destroyed. All that remained was the Elfitch—seven stone-block ramps and ironbound gates that ran upward from the base of the bluff to the heights. Battlements ringed each gate to close off passage to the gates and ramps above it. Each ramp and gate was set back slightly from the ones below and, as the Elfitch rose toward the heights, it spiralled upward in a series of evenly measured turns that permitted each successive gate and ramp to offer some measure of protection through the use of long bows and darts to the gates and ramps beneath. In times of peace, the gates to the seven ramps stood open, the battlements were left undefended but for a token watch, and the ancient stone grew thick with flowering vines. But now, with the retreat of the Elven army from the Sarandanon, the ramparts bristled with Elven pikes and lances and the gates stood locked and barred.

No defenses had been constructed atop the Carolan. The plateau ran back to the deep forest in a broad, rolling plain spotted with woods, isolated cottages and the solitary closure of the Gardens of Life. East, within the fringe of the forest trees, stood Arborlon. If the Demons were successful in reaching the Carolan, the choices left to the defending Elves were few. If enough of them remained, they might stand upon the plain in an attempt to sweep the invaders over the cliff edge. Failing that, they would be forced to fall back to the Valley of Rhenn, there to fight one final battle or face being driven from the Westland altogether.

Chios paused in his report. "Of course if they bypass the mountains and come in from the east . . ." he began.

Allanon cut him short. "They will not. Time becomes important to them now. They will come from the west."

Ander glanced questioningly at Stee Jans, but the Free Corps Commander merely shrugged. Ander turned back to Emer Chios. "What other news, First Minister?"

"Mixed news, I'm afraid, regarding our request to the other lands for aid. Callahorn has sent us another two hundred and fifty horse—Old Guard, the Legion's regular army. There is a vague promise of some additional aid to come, though no indication as to how soon we might expect it. Our messenger reports that the members of the Council of the Cities have not yet been able to resolve their differences over what the extent of

Callahorn's involvement in this 'Elven War' should be and the King has chosen not to intervene. It appears that sending the Old Guard command was basically another compromise solution. The matter is still under debate, but we have heard nothing more."

As Stee Jans had warned, Ander thought darkly.

"The Federation has sent a message as well, my Lord Prince." Chios' smile was bitter. "A message that is brief and to the point, I might add. It is the policy of the Federation that it not become involved in the affairs of other lands and other races. If a threat to others touches upon the sovereignty of its own states, the Federation will act. As matters stand now, that does not appear to be the case. Therefore, until the situation changes, no aid will be forthcoming." He shrugged. "Not altogether unexpected."

"And the Kershalt?" Ander asked quickly. "What of the Trolls?"

Chios shook his head. "Nothing. I took the liberty of dispatching another messenger."

Ander nodded his approval. "And the Dwarves?"

"We're here," a rough voice answered. "Some of us, at least."

A bearded, thickset Dwarf made his way forward through the men gathered about the Council table. Quick blue eyes blinked through a face that was weathered and browned by the sun, and a pair of gnarled hands fastened on the table's edge.

"Druid." The Dwarf nodded briefly to Allanon, then turned to Ander. "My name is Browork, Elder and citizen of Culhaven. I've brought one hundred Sappers to the service of the Elessedils. You can thank the Druid for that. He found us some weeks ago at work on a bridge crossing the Silver River and warned us of the danger. Allanon is known to the Dwarves, so there were no questions asked. We sent word to Culhaven and came on ahead—ten days' march and a hard march at that. But we're here."

He extended his hand and Ander shook it warmly.

"What of the others, Browork?" Allanon asked.

The Dwarf nodded rather impatiently. "On their way by now, I presume. You should have an army of several thousand by week's end." He gave Allanon a disapproving frown. "In the meantime you've got us, Druid, and mighty lucky you are to have us. No one but the Sappers could have rigged that ramp."

"The Elfitch," Chios explained quickly to a puzzled Ander. "Browork and his Sappers have been working with us on our defenses. In the process of studying the Elfitch, he saw that it was possible to rig the fifth ramp to collapse."

"Child's play." Browork dismissed the accomplishment with a wave of his hand. "We undercut the stone block, removed the secondary supports, then split the primary with iron wedges fixed to chains. The chains we concealed in the brush beneath the ramp, ran them to the heights, and lined them to a system of pulleys. If the Demons reach the fifth ramp, just draw in the chains, slip the wedges and the whole ramp from the fifth gate down falls away. Simple."

"Simple if you have the engineering skill of a Dwarf Sapper, I think." Ander smiled. "Well done, Browork. We have need of you."

"There are others here that you need as well." Allanon put his hand on Ander's shoulder and pointed to the far end of the Council table.

The Elven Prince turned. A lone Elf dressed all in leather stepped forward and placed his hand across his heart in the pledge of loyalty.

"Dayn, my Lord Prince," the Elf said quietly. "I am a Wing Rider."

"A Wing Rider?" Ander stared at the Elf in surprise. He had heard stories from his father of the people who called themselves the Sky Elves—stories almost forgotten by most, for no Wing Rider had come to Arborlon in the last hundred years. "How many of you are there?" he asked finally.

"Five," Dayn replied. "There would be more but for the fear of a Demon attack on the Wing Hove, our own home city. My father has sent those of us who are here. We are all of one family. My father is called Herrol." He paused and glanced at Allanon. "There was a time when the Druid and he were friends."

"We are still friends, Wing Rider," Allanon said quietly.

Dayn acknowledged the Druid's commitment with a nod, then returned his gaze to Ander.

"My father's sense of kinship with the Land Elves is stronger than that of most of his countrymen, my Lord Prince, for most have long since broken all ties with the old ways and the old rule. And my father knows that Allanon stands with the Elessedils—and that has meaning. Thus he sends us. He would be here himself but for the absence of his Roc Genewen, who trains with my brother's son so that he may one day be a Wing Rider as was his father. Still, those of us who are here may be of some use. We can fly the whole of the Westland skies, if need be. We can seek out the Demons who threaten and tell you of their movements. We can spy out strengths and weaknesses. That much, at least, we can offer."

"That much we accept with gratitude, Dayn." Ander returned the Wing Rider's salute. "Be welcome."

Dayn bowed and stepped back. Ander glanced at Chios. "Are there any others come to stand with us, First Minister?"

Chios shook his head slowly. "No, my Lord Prince. These are all."

Ander nodded. "Then these will be enough."

He motioned for all who were gathered to seat themselves with him at the council table, and a general discussion ensued on such matters as soldier placement, weapons distribution, battle tactics, and the taking of additional defensive measures. Reports were heard from Ehlron Tay on the Elven Hunters of the regular army, from Kerrin on the Home Guard and from Kobold of the Black Watch. Browork gave his assessment of the overall structural efficiency of the Elven defenses, and Stee Jans was consulted on strategies that might be implemented to offset the superior strength of the Demon hordes. Even Dayn spoke briefly on the fighting capabilities of the Rocs and their uses in aerial combat.

Time slipped past rapidly, and the night drifted away. Ander grew light-headed with fatigue, and his thoughts began to wander. It was in the middle of one of these wanderings that a tremendous crash jerked him upright as the doors of the High Council flew open and a disheveled Gael appeared, flanked by the chamber guards. Breathless, the little Elf rushed forward and dropped to his knee before Ander.

"My Lord!" he gasped, his face flushed with excitement. "My Lord, the King is awake!"

Ander stared. "Awake?"

Then he was on his feet and sprinting from the chamber.

While he slept, it felt to Eventine Elessedil as if he were floating through a blackness layered with gossamer threads that wrapped his body in a seamless blanket. One by one, he felt the threads enfold him, mold about him, join with him. Time and space were nothing; there was only the blackness and the weave of the threads. It was a warm, pleasant sensation at first, much like the feel to an infant of a mother's close embrace, filled with comfort and love. But then the embrace seemed to tighten, and he began to suffocate. Desperately he struggled to break free and found that he could not. He began to sink downward through the blackness, spinning slowly, his blanket a shroud and he no longer a creature of life, but one of death. Terrified, he thrashed within his silken prison, tearing and ripping at its fabric until, with a sudden rending, it flew apart and was gone.

His eyes opened. Light blinded him momentarily, harsh and flickering. He blinked in its glare, disoriented and confused, fighting to gain some sense of where he was and what he was doing. Then the outlines of a room began to gather form, and he recognized the smell of oil lamps and the feel of cotton sheets and woolen blankets wrapped close about his body. All that had happened in the moments before he slept came back again in a rush, images that ran mad and disjointed across his mind: the Breakline; Halys Cut and the Demons attacking from out of the deep mist; lines of Elven archers, lancers and pikemen spread out below him; cries of pain and death; dark forms hurtling toward him through a wall of blue fire; Allanon, Ander, the glint of weapons, then a sudden blow . . .

He twitched violently beneath the covers, and sweat bathed his body. The room sharpened abruptly before his eyes—it was his sleeping room in the manor house in Arborlon—and there was a figure moving toward him.

"My Lord?" Gael's frightened voice sounded in his ear and the youthful face bent down close to his own. "My Lord, are you awake?"

"What has happened?" he muttered, his own voice thick and barely recognizable.

"You were wounded, my Lord—at Halys Cut. A blow struck here." The Elf pointed to the King's left temple. "You have been unconscious ever since. My Lord, we were so worried . . ."

"How long . . . have I slept?" he interrupted. His hand reached to touch his head and the pain lanced downward through his neck.

"Seven days, my Lord."

"Seven days!"

Gael started to back away. "I will bring your son, my Lord."

His mind whirled. "My son?"

"Prince Ander, my Lord." His aide dashed toward the sleeping room door. "He meets now with the High Council. Lie back—I will bring him at once."

Eventine watched him wrench open the door, heard him talk briefly with someone beyond, then watched the door close again, leaving him in silence. He tried to raise himself, but the effort was too much and he fell back weakly. Ander? Had Gael said that Ander was meeting with the High Council? Where was Arion? Doubt clouded his thoughts, and the questions came in a flurry. What was he doing here in Arborlon? What had befallen the army of the Elves? What had become of their defense of the Sarandanon?

Again he tried to raise himself and again fell back. A wave of nausea swept through him. He felt suddenly old, as if the number of his years was a sickness that had wasted him. His jaw tightened. Oh, that he might have back again five minutes of his youth to give him strength enough to rise from this bed! Anger and determination fired him, and he inched himself upward against his pillows until he lay propped against them, breathing raggedly.

Across the room, Manx raised his grizzled head. The King opened his mouth to call out to the old wolfhound. But suddenly the dog's eyes met his, and the words died in his throat. There was hate in those eyes—hate so cold that it cut through Eventine like a winter frost. He blinked in disbelief, fighting the sense of repulsion that welled up within him. Manx? What was he thinking!

He forced himself to look away, to stare elsewhere in the sleeping room, at walls and their hangings, at furniture, and at the drapes drawn tight across the windows. Desperately, he tried to compose himself and could not. I am alone, he thought suddenly, unreasonably, and was filled with fear. Alone! He glanced back again at Manx. The wolfhound's eyes fixed him, veiled now, hiding what had been so evident before. Or had he imagined it? He watched as the old dog rose, turned about, and lay down again. Why does he not come to me? the King asked himself. Why does he not come?

He slipped back against the pillows. What am I saying? The words whispered in his mind, and he saw the madness that threatened to slip across him. Seeing hatred in the eyes of an animal that had been faithful to him for years? Seeing in Manx an enemy that might do him harm? What was wrong with him?

Voices sounded in the outer corridor. Then the sleeping room door opened and closed again, and Ander crossed the room to reach down and hold him close. The King hugged his son to him, then broke the clasp, searching Ander's shadowed face as the Prince seated himself on the edge of the bed.

"Tell me what has happened," Eventine ordered softly. Then he saw something flicker in his son's eyes, and he felt a sudden chill pass through him. He forced the question from his lips. "Where is Arion?"

Ander opened his mouth to speak, then stared at the old man wordlessly. Eventine's face froze.

"Is he dead?"

Ander's voice was a whisper. "At Worl Run."

He seemed to search for something more to say, then gave up, shaking his head slowly. Eventine's eyes filled with tears and his hands shook as he grasped his son's arms.

"Arion is dead?" he spoke the words as if they were a lie.

Ander nodded, then looked away. "Kael Pindanon, too."

There was a moment of stunned silence. The King's hands fell away.

"And the Sarandanon?"

"Lost."

They stared at each other wordlessly, father and son, as if some frightening secret had been shared that should never have been told. Then Ander reached down and clasped his father to him. For long moments, they held each other in silence. When at last the King spoke, his voice was flat and distant.

"Tell me about Arion. Everything. Leave nothing out."

Ander told him. Quietly, he related how his brother had died, how they had brought him out of the Breakline to the Sarandanon, and how they had buried him at Baen Draw. Then he spoke of all that had befallen the army of the Elves from that first day of battle at Halys Cut through the long march back to Arborlon. Eventine listened and said nothing. When Ander had finished, he stared blankly at the flicker of the oil lamps for a moment. Then his eyes shifted to his son.

"I want you to return to the High Council, Ander. Do what must be done." He paused, his voice breaking. "Go on. I will be all right."

Ander looked at him uncertainly. "I can ask Gael to come in."

The King shook his head. "No. Not now. I just want to . . ." He stopped, choking back what he was about to say, one hand gripping his son's arm tightly. "I am . . . very proud of you, Ander. I know how difficult . . ."

Ander nodded, his throat tightening. He placed his father's hands within his own. "Gael will be outside in the hall when you need him."

He rose and started toward the door. His hand was on the latch when Eventine called out after him, his voice strangely anxious.

"Take Manx out with you."

Ander stopped, looked at the old wolfhound, whistled him to his side, and led him out. The door closed softly behind him.

Alone again, this time truly alone, the King of the Elves lay back upon the cushion of his pillows and let the enormity of all that had happened wash over him. In a little more than seven days, the finest army in the Four Lands had been driven like a herd of cattle before wolves from its own country—driven from the Breakline, from the Sarandanon, and all the way back to its home city, there to stand or fall. Somewhere deep within him there was a terrible sense of failure. He had let this happen. He was responsible.

"Arion," he whispered suddenly, remembering.

Then the tears welled up in his eyes and he began to cry.

"Eretria!" Wil exclaimed softly, surprise and wariness in his voice. Disregarding the pain from his injury, he pushed himself up on one elbow for a closer look. "What are you doing here?"

"Saving you, it would appear." She laughed, her dark eyes mischievous.

Sudden movement caught his eye, and he stared past her into the shadows. Two Rover women busied themselves at a sideboard near the rear of the wagon, rinsing cloths red with his blood in a basin of water. Instinctively, he reached up to his head and found that a bandage had been placed across the wound. He touched it gingerly and winced.

"I wouldn't do that." Eretria brushed his hand aside. "It is the only part of you that is clean."

The Valeman glanced about quickly. "What have you done with Amberle?"

"Your sister?" she mocked. "She is safe enough."

"You will excuse me if I am a bit skeptical about that." He started to rise from the bed.

"Stay, Healer." She forced him down again. Her voice lowered so that the women behind her could not hear. "Do you fear I might seek revenge because of your ill-conceived decision to leave me behind at the Tirfing? Do you think so little of me?" She laughed and tossed her head. "Perhaps now though, if you were given the chance, you would reconsider that decision. Is that possible?"

"Not in the least. Now what about Amberle?"

"Had I intended harm to you, Wil Ohmsford—or to her—I would have left the both of you to the cutthroats who chased you through Grimpen Ward. The Elven girl is well. I will have her brought after we have talked."

She turned to the women at the sideboard. "Go. Leave us."

The women stopped what they were doing and disappeared through a flap at the other end of the wagon. When they had gone, Eretria turned back to the Valeman, her head cocked to one side.

"Well, what shall I do with you now, Wil Ohmsford?"

He took a deep breath. "How did you find me, Eretria?"

She grinned. "Easily enough. Word of your great healing power spread the length and breadth of Grimpen Ward within ten minutes of the time it took you to cure that fat woman innkeeper. Did you think that such a noisy performance would go unnoticed? How do you think it was that you were found by those cutthroats?"

"You knew of that, too, then?"

"Healer, you are a fool." She said it kindly, her hand reaching up to touch his cheek. "Rovers are the first to know anything that happens in the places where they travel. If it were not so, they would not long survive—a lesson you apparently have yet to learn. Once word spread of your wondrous act of healing, it was obvious to anyone with half a brain that there would be some who would soon decide that one with your talent must surely be a man of wealth. Greed and drink mix well, Healer. You are lucky to be alive."

"I suppose so," he acknowledged, chagrined. "I should have been a bit more careful."

"A bit. Fortunately for you, I realized who you were and prevailed upon Cephelo to let me find you, once the cry went up from the inn. Otherwise, you might be food for the dogs."

"A pleasant thought." Wil grimaced. He glanced at her quickly. "Cephelo knows that I am here?"

"He knows." She smiled and the mischievousness returned to her eyes. "Does that frighten you?"

"Let's just say that it concerns me," Wil admitted. "Why should he do anything for me after what happened back in the Tirfing?"

Eretria leaned close and put her slim, dark arms about his neck. "Because his daughter is persuasive, Healer—persuasive enough that at times she may influence even so difficult a man as Cephelo." She shrugged. "Besides, he has had time to rethink what happened at the Tirfing. I have convinced him, I think, that it was none of your doing—that in fact you saved the lives of the Family."

Wil shook his head doubtfully. "I don't trust him."

"Nor should you," she agreed. "But for tonight, at least, he should cause you no concern. He will wait until morning to have you answer to him. By then, at any rate, your pursuers will have worn themselves out chasing shadows and have gone back again to the taverns for fresh ale and a more tangible source of gain."

She rose then, slipped away in a flash of blue silk, and returned a moment later with a damp cloth and a fresh basin of water which she placed on the floor next to the bed.

"We must clean you up, Healer. You reek of sweat and dirt, and your clothes are ruined." She paused. "Take them off and I'll wash you."

Wil shook his head. "I will wash myself. Can you lend me some clothes?"

She nodded, but made no move to go. The Valeman flushed.

"I would like to do this by myself, if you don't mind."

The dazzling smile broke across her face. "Oh, but I do mind."

He shook his head. "You really are incorrigible."

"You are for me, Wil Ohmsford. I told you that before."

The smile faded, replaced by a look so sensuous and compelling as to cause Wil to forget momentarily what it was that he was about. When she started to lean toward him, he forced himself to sit up quickly on the bed. Dizziness washed over him, but he kept himself upright.

"Will you bring me the clothes?"

For an instant her eyes went dark with anger. Then she rose, crossed to a cupboard, removed some clothing, and brought it to him.

"You may have these." She tossed them in his lap.

She started past him, then dipped suddenly and kissed him quickly on the mouth. "Wash and dress yourself then." She sniffed, slipping away.

She opened a door at the end of the wagon and disappeared into the night, closing the door behind her securely and latching it from without. Wil grinned in spite of himself. Whatever her intentions, she was not about to let him run off. Quickly he stripped away his old clothing, washed, and put on the clothes Eretria had supplied. They fit well, though they were the clothes of a Rover and he felt more than a little strange wearing them.

He had just finished dressing when the door opened again and Eretria appeared with Amberle. The Elven girl was dressed in Rover pants and tunic, with a sash and headband to hold back her waist-length hair. Her face was freshly scrubbed and a bit startled. She glanced at Wil's head and there was immediate concern in her green eyes.

"Are you all right?" she asked quickly.

"I have seen to his needs." Eretria brushed her question aside smoothly. She pointed to the bed opposite Wil's. "You can sleep there. Be certain that you do not try to leave the wagon tonight."

She gave Wil a knowing smile, then turned away and moved to the door. She was halfway through when she glanced back suddenly.

"Good-night, brother Wil. Good-night, sister Amberle. Sleep well."

With a grin, she slipped through the door. The latch fastened behind her with a click.

The Valeman and the Elven girl slept that night within the Rover wagon. It was dawn when they awoke, the new light seeping through cracks in the shuttered windows to light the dusky gloom. Wil lay silent for a time, gathering his thoughts, waiting for the sleep to clear from his eyes. After a moment, he reached within his tunic for the small leather pouch containing the Elfstones, checked to be certain that they were still there, then replaced the pouch. It did not hurt to be careful, he thought. He was halfway out of the bed when Amberle ordered him back in again, scrambling up from the other bed to reach him. Carefully she examined the injury to his head and readjusted the bandage. When she had finished, Wil pushed himself up beside her and surprised her with a quick kiss on one cheek. She flushed slightly and smiled, her child's face beaming.

A short time later the door latch released and Eretria stepped through, carrying a tray of bread, honey, milk, and fruit. Brown limbs slipped from beneath a diaphanous white gown that swirled about the Rover girl like smoke. The dazzling smile flashed at the Valeman.

"Well rested, Wil Ohmsford?" She deposited the tray on his lap and winked. "Cephelo will speak with you now."

She left without saying a word to Amberle. Wil glanced at the Elven girl when Eretria had gone and shrugged helplessly. Amberle's smile was forced.

Minutes later, Cephelo appeared. He entered without knocking, his tall, lean frame stooping slightly as it passed through the entry. Dressed in black and wrapped in the cloak of forest green, he appeared just as he had when they had first observed him on the banks of the Mermidon. The wide-brimmed hat was cocked jauntily on his head, and he removed it with a flourish as he entered, a broad grin splitting his swarthy face.

"Ah, the Elflings, the Healer and his sister. We meet again." He bowed. "Still looking for your horse?"

Wil smiled. "Not this time."

The Rover looked down the length of his hooked nose at them. "No? Have you lost your way then? Arborlon, as I remember, lies north."

"We have been to Arborlon and left again," the Valeman replied, setting aside the tray.

"Come to Grimpen Ward."

"Both of us, it seems."

"Indeed." The tall man seated himself opposite the two. "In my case, business takes me many places that I might not otherwise care to go. But what of yourself, Healer? What brings you to Grimpen Ward? Surely not the prospect of applying your art to the denizens of so shabby a village as this one."

Wil hesitated a moment before responding. He was going to have to be very careful what he told Cephelo. He knew the man well enough by now to appreciate the fact that if the Rover were to discover anything that he might turn to his own advantage, he would be quick to do so.

"We have business of our own," he replied carelessly.

The Rover pursed his lips. "You do not seem to be doing very well in its pursuit, Healer. Your throat would be cut by now if not for me."

Wil wanted to laugh aloud. The old fox! He was not about to admit that Eretria had anything to do with saving them.

"We seem to be in your debt once again," he offered.

Cephelo shrugged. "I was hasty in my judgment of you at the Tirfing; I let my concern for my people override my common sense. I blamed you for what happened when I should have thanked you for aiding. That has bothered me. Saving you now eases my sense of guilt."

"I am gratified to learn that you feel this way." Wil did not believe one word of it. "This has been a difficult time for my sister and me."

"Difficult?" Cephelo's dark face mirrored sudden concern. "Perhaps there is something more that I can do to aid you—something to be of service. If you would tell me what it is, exactly, that brings you to this most dangerous part of the country . . . ?"

Here it comes, Wil thought. Out of the corner of his eye, he watched Amberle frown in warning.

"I wish that it were within your power to help." Wil did his best to sound sincere. "But I am afraid that it is not. What I need most is the guidance of someone familiar with the history of this valley, its marks, and its legends."

Cephelo clapped his hands lightly. "Well, then, perhaps I can be of assistance after all. I have traveled the Wilderun many times." He lifted a long finger to the side of his head. "I know something of its secrets."

Perhaps, Wil thought. Perhaps not. He wants to know what we are doing here.

The Valeman shrugged. "I do not feel that we should impose further on your hospitality by involving you in our affairs. My sister and I can manage."

The Rover's face was expressionless. "Why not tell me what it is that brings you here—let me judge if the imposition is so great."

Amberle's hand closed tightly on Wil's arm, but he ignored it, keeping his eyes locked on Cephelo's. He knew that he was going to have to tell the Rover something.

"There is a sickness within the house of the Elessedils, rulers of the Elves." He lowered his voice. "The King's granddaughter is very ill. The medicine she needs is an extract from a root that can only be found here, within the Wilderun. I alone know that—I and my sister. We have come here in search of that root, for if we can find it and carry it to the Elven ruler, the reward will be great."

He felt Amberle's grip loosen abruptly. He did not dare to look at her face. Cephelo was silent for a moment before replying.

"Do you know where within the Wilderun this root can be found?"

The Valeman nodded. "There are books, ancient books of healing from the old world, that speak of the root and the name of its location. But it is a name long since forgotten, long since erased from the maps that serve the races now. I doubt that the name would mean anything to you."

The Rover leaned forward. "Tell it to me anyway."

"Safehold," Wil declared, watching the other's dark face. "The name is Safehold."

Cephelo thought a moment, then shook his head. "You were right—the name means nothing. Still . . ." He paused deliberately, rocking back slightly as if deep in thought. "There is one who might know the name, one familiar with the old names of this valley. I could lead you to him, I suppose. Ah, but Healer, the Wilderun is very dangerous country—you know that yourself since you most certainly crossed through some small part of its forests to reach Grimpen Ward. The risk to my people and myself if we were to aid you in such a perilous search would be great." He shrugged apologetically. "Besides, we have other commitments, other places to which we must travel, other business to which we must attend. Time is a precious thing to such as we. Surely you can appreciate that."

"What is it that you are saying?" The Valeman demanded quietly.

"That without me, you will fail in your quest. That you need me; that I in turn wish to offer my help. But such help as you seek cannot be given without, ah . . . adequate recompense."

Wil nodded slowly. "What recompense, Cephelo?"

The Rover's eyes glittered. "The Stones you carry. The ones that hold the power."

The Valeman shook his head. "They would be useless to you."

"Would they? Is their secret so dark?" Cephelo's eyes narrowed. "Do not suppose me a fool. You are no simple Healer. That much was obvious almost from the moment we first met. Still, it matters not to me who you are—only what you have. You have the power of the Stones and I wish it."

"Their magic is Elven." Wil forced himself to remain calm, hoping desperately that he had not lost control of the situation. "Only one of Elven blood can wield their power."

"You lie badly, Healer." The big man's voice was ugly.

"He speaks the truth," Amberle interjected quickly, her face frightened. "If not for the Stones, he would not have even attempted this search. You have no right to ask him to give them up to you."

"I have the right to ask whatever I choose," Cephelo snapped, brushing her words aside with a wave of his hand. "In any case, I believe neither of you."

"Believe what you wish." Wil's voice was steady. "I will not give you the Stones."

The two men stared wordlessly at each other for a moment, the Rover's face hard and threatening. Yet there was fear there as well—fear generated by Cephelo's vivid memory of the power locked within the Elfstones, power that Wil Ohmsford had mastered. With great effort, he forced himself to smile.

"What will you give me then, Healer? Am I expected to do this service for nothing? Am I expected to risk lives and property without any form of recompense at all? There must be something of value that you can give me—something that has worth equal to that of the Stones you so stubbornly refuse to yield. What then? What will you give me?"

Wil tried desperately to come up with something, but there was absolutely nothing else he carried that was worth more than a few pennies. Yet just when he had decided that the situation was hopeless, Cephelo snapped his fingers sharply.

"I will make a bargain with you, Healer. You say that the Elven King will reward you if you bring to him the medicine that will cure his granddaughter. Very well. I will do what I can to help you learn something of this place you call Safehold. I will take you to one who might know the name. I will do that and nothing more. In exchange for this, you must give me half of whatever reward you receive from the Elven King. Half. Is it agreed?"

Wil thought it over a moment. A curious bargain, he decided. Rovers seldom, if ever, gave anything away without first getting something in return. What was Cephelo about?

"Are you saying that you will help me learn the location of Safehold . . ."

"If I can."

". . . but you will not come with me to find it?"

Cephelo shrugged. "I have no wish to risk my life unnecessarily. Finding the medicine and conveying it to the Elven King's granddaughter is your problem. My part of the bargain is merely to help you on your way." He paused. "Do not, however, presume that once gone you are therefore free of me. Any attempt to cheat me of what you owe would end very badly for you."

The Valeman frowned. "How will you know whether or not I am successful if you do not come with me?"

Cephelo laughed. "Healer, I am a Rover—I will know! I will know all that happens to you, believe me."

His smile was so wolfish that for an instant Wil was certain that there was another meaning to his words. Something was wrong; he could sense it. Yet they needed help from somewhere in finding their way through the Wilderun—help that would permit him to forgo any use of the Elfstones. If Cephelo were to give them that help, it might mean the difference between success and failure in finding the Bloodfire before the Demons found them.

"Is it agreed?" Cephelo asked again.

Wil shook his head. He would test the Rover. "One half is too much. I will give you a third."

"A third!" Cephelo's face darkened momentarily, then relaxed. "Very well. I am a reasonable man. A third."

That had been entirely too easy, Wil thought. He glanced at Amberle, seeing in her eyes the same mistrust that flickered in his own. But the Elven girl said nothing. She was leaving the decision to him.

"Come, come, Elfling," Cephelo pressed. "Do not be all day about it."

The Valeman nodded. "All right. It is agreed."

"Good." The Rover stood up immediately. "We will leave at once since our business here is ended. But you are to remain within the wagon for a time. It would not do to have you seen again in Grimpen Ward. Once we are into the deep forest, you may come out."

He smiled broadly, dipped the wide-brimmed hat in parting and passed back through the entry. The door closed softly behind him and locked. Wil and Amberle sat staring at each other.

"I don't trust him," Amberle whispered.

Wil nodded. "Not at all."

Moments later, the wagon lurched forward and began to roll and their journey into the Wilderun was under way once more.

The old man hummed softly to himself as he sat in the cane-backed rocker and stared out into the darkening forest. Far to the west beyond the wall of trees that locked tightly about the clearing in which he sat, beyond the valley of the Wilderun and the mountains that ringed it, the sun slipped beneath the earth's horizon and the day's light faded into dusk. It was the old man's favorite time of day, the midday heat cooling into evening shadow, the sunset coloring the far skyline crimson and purple, then deepening into blue night. From atop the ridge line, where the woodland trees broke apart enough to permit glimpses of sky, moon, and stars through a screen of limbs and trunks, the air smelled clean for a time, freed of the damp and mustiness that clung to it through the swelter of the day, and the leaves of the forest whispered in a soft, slow nighttime wind. It was as if, for those few moments, the Wilderun were like any other country, and a man might look upon it as an old and intimate friend.

The old man looked often upon the valley that way, more now than at any other time of the day or night perhaps, but always with that same sense of deep and abiding loyalty. Few others could ever feel as he, but few others knew the valley as he had come to know it. Oh, it was treacherous—hard and filled with dangers to snare and destroy a man. There were creatures within the Wilderun the like of which could be found in no other place this side of a midnight campfire legend, told with hushed whispers and frightened looks. There was death here, death that came with the passing of every hour, harsh, cruel, and certain. It was a land of hunter and hunted, each living creature a bit of both, and the old man had seen the best and worst of each in the sixty years that he had made the valley his home.

He drummed his fingers on the rocker's arms and thought back dreamily. It was sixty years since he had first come to the Wilderun—a long time, yet barely gone. This had been his home for all those years, and it was a home that a man could respect—not simply another place with houses and people all crowded close, safe, secure, and senselessly dull, but a place of solitude and depth, of challenge and heart, a place to which only a few would ever come because only those few would ever belong. A few like himself, he thought, and now only he remained of those who had once come into the valley. All the rest were gone, claimed by the wilderness, buried somewhere deep within her earth. Of course there were those fools that huddled like frightened dogs within the ragged shacks of Grimpen Ward, cheating and robbing each other and any other fool that might venture into their midst. But the valley was not theirs and never would be, for they had no understanding of what the valley was about nor any wish to learn. They might as well be locked within the closet of some castle for all it meant to any claim that they were its lords and ladies.

Crazy, they called him—those fools in Grimpen Ward. Crazy to live in this wilderness, an old man alone. He grinned crookedly at the thought. Madness peculiar to its owner, perhaps; but he would choose his own over theirs.

"Drifter," he called gruffly, and the monstrous black dog that stretched at his feet came awake and rose, a giant animal that had the look of both wolf and bear, its massive body bristling with hair, its muzzle yawning wide.

"Hey, you." The old man grunted, and the dog came over, dropping its great head onto its master's lap, waiting for its ears to be scratched.

The old man obliged. Somewhere in the growing dark, a scream sounded, quick and piercing, to linger in the sudden stillness as a fading echo, then die. Drifter looked up quickly. The old man nodded. Swamp cat. A big one. Something had crossed its path and paid the price.

His gaze wandered idly, picking out familiar shapes and forms in the half-light. Behind him sat the hut in which he lived, a small but solid structure, built of logs and shingles caulked with mortar. A shed and well sat just back of the hut, and a fenced closure that held his mule, and a workbench and lumber. He liked to whittle and carve, liked it well enough that much of his day was spent shaping and honing the wood he took from the great trees about the clearing into odds and ends that it pleased him to look upon. Worthless, he supposed, to everyone but himself, but then he didn't care much about anyone else, so that was all right. He saw little enough of people and little enough was more than enough, and he didn't look to give them reasons to seek him out. Drifter was all the company he needed. And those worthless cats that wandered about looking for new places to sleep and table scraps, as if they were no better than common scavengers. And the mule, a dumb but dependable creature.

He stretched and rose. The sun was down and the night sky was laced with stars and moonlight. It was time to fix something to eat for himself and the dog. He looked momentarily toward the tripod and kettle which sat atop a small cooking fire several yards in front of him. Yesterday's soup, and precious little of that—enough, maybe, for one more meal.

He moved toward the fire, shaking his head. He was a smallish man, old and bent, his stick-thin frame clothed in a ragged shirt and half-pants. White hair ringed his bald head in a thin fringe of snow that ran down the length of a roundish jaw to a beard spotted with soot and bits of sawdust. Brown, wrinkled skin covered his tough old body like leather, and his eyes were barely visible through lids that pouched and drooped. He walked with a sort of hunching motion, as if he had just come awake and, finding his muscles cramped with sleep, was attempting to work out the stiffness.

He halted beside the kettle and stared down into it, trying to decide what he might do to improve the appeal of its contents. It was at that moment that he heard the approach of the horses and wagon, distant still, lost in the dark somewhere up the trail from his hut, winding uncertainly toward him. He turned and stared into the night, waiting. At his side, Drifter growled in an unfriendly manner, and the old man gave him a warning cuff. The minutes slipped away, and the sounds drew closer. Finally a line of shadows emerged from the dusk, winding down over the crest of the rise fronting the clearing—a single wagon with horses in trace and half-a-dozen riders in tow. The old man's mood soured the moment he saw the wagon. He knew it well enough, knew it to be Rover, knew it to belong to that rogue Cephelo. He spat to one side with distaste and thought seriously about loosing Drifter on the bunch of them.

The riders and wagon halted just inside the fringes of the clearing. Cephelo's dark form dismounted and came forward. When he reached the old man, the Rover's wide-brimmed hat swept down in greeting.

"Well met, Hebel. Good evening to you."

The old man snorted. "Cephelo. What do you want?"

Cephelo looked shocked. "Hebel, Hebel, this is no greeting for two who have done as much for one another as we. This is no greeting for men who have shared the hardships and misfortunes of humankind. Hello, now."

The Rover took the old man's hand and shook it firmly. Hebel neither resisted nor aided the effort.

"Ah, you look well." Cephelo smiled disarmingly. "The high country is good for the aches and pains of age, I imagine."

"Aches and pains of age, is it?" Hebel spat and wrinkled his nose. "What are you selling, Cephelo—some cure-all for the infirm?"

Cephelo glanced back at those who had come with him and shrugged apologetically. "You are most unkind, Hebel, most unkind."

The old man followed his gaze. "What have you done with the rest of your pack? Have they taken up with some other thief?"

This time the Rover's face darkened slightly. "I have sent them on ahead. They follow the main roadway east to await my coming in the Tirfing. I am here with these few on a matter of some importance. Might we talk a bit?"

"You're here, aren't you?" Hebel pointed out. "Talk all you want."

"And share your fire?"

Hebel shrugged. "I don't have the food to feed you all—wouldn't if I did. Maybe you brought something with you, huh?"

Cephelo gave an exaggerated sigh. "We did. Tonight you shall share our dinner."

He called back to the others. The riders dismounted and began caring for the horses. An old woman had been driving the wagon in the company of a young couple. She climbed down now, removed provisions and cookware from the rear of the wagon, and shuffled wordlessly to the cooking fire. The two who sat with her hesitated momentarily, then came forward at Cephelo's invitation. They were joined by a slim, dark-haired girl who had been one of the riders.

Hebel turned away wordlessly and reseated himself in the rocker. There was something peculiar about the two who had come down off the wagon seat, but he could not quite put his finger on what it was. They looked like Rovers and yet at the same time they didn't. He watched them approach with Cephelo and the dark-haired girl. All four seated themselves on the grass about the old man—the dark-haired girl slipping suggestively close to the young man and giving him a bold wink.

"My daughter, Eretria." Cephelo shot the girl an irritated look as he introduced her. "These two are Elves."

"I'm not blind," Hebel snapped, recognizing now why they appeared to be something more than Rovers. "What are they doing with you?"

"We have undertaken a quest," the Rover announced.

Hebel leaned forward. "A quest? With you?" He glanced at the young man, his aged face wrinkling. "You seem like a bright sort. What made you decide to take up with him?"

"He requires a guide through this miserable country," Cephelo answered for him—rather too quickly, Hebel thought. "Why is it, Hebel, that you insist on making this forsaken wilderness your home? One day I'll pass by and find your bones, old man, and all because you were too stubborn to take your worthless hide to safer regions."

"Much you'd care," Hebel grunted. "For a man such as myself, this land is as safe as any other. I know it, know what walks and breathes and hunts it, know how to keep my distance and when to show my teeth. I'll outlive you, Rover—mark my words on that." He pushed back in the rocker, watching Drifter's dark shadow settle in behind him. "What do you want with me?"

Cephelo shrugged. "A bit of talk, just as I've said."

Hebel laughed hoarsely. "A bit of talk? Come now, Cephelo—what do you want? Don't waste my time—there isn't that much of it left."

"For myself, nothing. For these young Elflings, something of the knowledge stored in that balding old pate. It has taken me a great deal of effort to reach you up here, but there are causes that merit special . . ."

Hebel had heard enough. "What are you cooking over there?" He allowed himself to be distracted by the smell of the food simmering in the cooking kettle. "What's in there?"

"How should I know?" Cephelo snapped, irritated by the old man's seeming inattention.

"Beef, I think. Beef and vegetables." Hebel rubbed his weathered hands. "I think we should eat before we talk. Got some of that Rover ale with you, Cephelo?"

So they ate plates of stew, day-old bread, dried fruit, and nuts, with glasses of ale to wash it all down. Not much was said while they ate, though a considerable number of glances were exchanged, and those glances told Hebel a good deal more about the situation than whatever words his visitors might have spoken. The Elves, he decided, were there because they had run out of choices in the matter. They cared nothing more for Cephelo and his band than he did. Cephelo, of course, was there because there was something in all of this for him, but what that might be would undoubtedly be kept carefully concealed. It was the dark-haired girl, the Rover's daughter, who puzzled him most. The way she looked at that Elf lad told him something of what she was about, yet there was more to her than that, more than she was willing to let on. The old man grew increasingly curious as to what it might be.

At last the food was gone and the ale was drunk. Hebel produced a long pipe, struck flint and tinder to its contents, and puffed a broad wreath of smoke into the night air. Cephelo tried again.

"This young Elf and his sister need your help. They have already come a long way, but they won't be able to go any further if you don't give them that help. I told them, of course, that you would."

The old man snorted. He knew this game. "Don't like Elves. They think they're too good for this country, for people like me." He lifted one eyebrow. "Don't like Rovers either, as you well know. Like them even less than Elves."

Eretria smirked. "There seems to be a lot you don't like."

"Shut your mouth!" Cephelo snapped, his face darkening. Eretria went still and Hebel saw the anger in her eyes.

He chuckled softly. "I don't blame you, girl." He looked at Cephelo. "What will you give me if I help the Elflings, Rover? An even trade now, if you want what I know."

Cephelo glowered. "Do not try my patience too severely, Hebel."

"Ha! Will you cut my throat? See what words you find then! Now speak again—what will you give me?"

"Clothes, bedding, leather, silk—I don't care." The Rover brushed aside the question stiffly.

"I got all that." Hebel spat.

Cephelo controlled himself only with a monumental effort. "Well, what is it that you want, then? Speak up, old man!"

From behind the rocker, Drifter growled in warning. Hebel reached back and gave the dog a cuff.

"Knives," he announced. "Half-a-dozen good blades. An axe head and wedges. Two dozen arrows, ash wood and feathered. And a cutting stone."

The big man nodded, looking less than pleased. "Done, thief. Now give me something back for all that."

Hebel shrugged. "What is it you want to know?"

Cephelo pointed at the young man. "The Elfling is a Healer. He looks for a root that produces a rare medicine. His books of healing say that it can be found here, within the Wilderun, in a place called Safehold."

There was a long moment of silence as the Rover and the old man stared at each other and the others waited.

"Well?" Cephelo demanded finally.

"Well what?" the old man snapped.

"Safehold! Where is it?"

Hebel grinned crookedly. "Right where it's always been, I imagine." He saw the surprise in the other's face. "I know the name, Rover. An old name, forgotten by everyone but me, I'd guess. Tombs of some sort—catacombs beneath a mountain."

"That's it!" The young man came to his feet, his face flushed. Then he saw that everyone was staring at him and he sat down again quickly. "At least that is the way that the books described it," he added lamely.

"Did they now?" Hebel rocked back, puffing. "Did they speak as well of the Hollows?"

The young man shook his head and glanced at the Elf girl, who shook her head as well. It was Cephelo who leaned forward sharply, his eyes narrowing.

"You mean that Safehold lies within the Hollows, old man?"

There was an edge to Cephelo's voice that did not escape Hebel. Cephelo was frightened.

Hebel chuckled. "Within the Hollows. Do you still seek Safehold, Rover?"

The young man hunched forward. "Where can the Hollows be found?"

"South, a day's walk," the old man answered. It was time to put an end to this foolishness. "Deep and dark they are, Elfling—a pit in which anything that drops falls from sight and is lost forever. Death, Elfling. Nothing that goes into the Hollows comes out again. Those who live there choose to keep it so."

The young man shook his head. "I do not understand."

Eretria muttered something under her breath, her eyes darting quickly to the face of the young Elf. She knew, Hebel saw. His voice dropped to a whisper.

"The Witch Sisters, Elfling. Morag and Mallenroh. The Hollows belong to them and to the things they make to serve them—things of Witch power."

"But where within the Hollows lies Safehold?" the other persisted. "You spoke of a mountain . . . ?"

"Spire's Reach—a solitary peak that rises up out of the Hollows like an arm stretched forth from death's grave. There lies Safehold." The old man paused, shrugging. "Or so it was once. I have not been to the Hollows myself in many, many years." He shook his head. "No one goes there anymore."

The young man nodded slowly. "Tell me something of these Witch Sisters."

Hebel's eyes narrowed. "Morag and Mallenroh—the last of their kind.

Once, Elfling, there were many such as they—now there are but two. Some say they were the handmaidens of the Warlock Lord. Some say they were here long before even he. Power to match that of the Druids, some say." He spread his hands. "The truth is hidden with them—seek it if you wish. The loss of another Elf, more or less, means nothing to me."

He laughed sharply, choking a bit until he lifted his cup and drank down a swallow or two of ale. His thin frame bent forward as he sought the young man's eyes.

"Sisters, they are, Morag and Mallenroh. Blood sisters. But there is a great hate between them, a hate from some wrong suffered long ago—real or imagined I could not say, nor anyone else I'd guess. But they war within the Hollows, Elfling—Morag holds the east, Mallenroh the west, each trying to destroy the other, each trying to seize for herself her sister's land and power. And at the center of the Hollows, just between the two, stands Spire's Reach—and there, Safehold."

"Have you seen Safehold?"

"I? Not I. The Hollows belong to the Sisters; the valley is room enough for me." Hebel rocked back, remembering. "Once, so many years ago that I no longer care to count, I hunted along the rim of the Hollows. Foolish it was, but I was still of a mind to know the whole of the land that I had chosen for my home, and the stories were but stories. For days I hunted within the shadow of the Hollows, seeing nothing. Then one night as I slept, alone but for the dimming embers of my campfire, she came to me—Mallenroh, tall and like some creature from a dream, gray hair long and woven with nightshade, her face the face of Mistress Death. She came to me, told me she felt the need to speak to one of human blood, one such as I. All the rest of the night she talked and told me of herself and her sister Morag and of the war they fought to own the Hollows."

He was lost in the memory now, his voice distant and soft. "In the morning she was gone, almost as if she had never been. I never saw her again, of course, not from that moment to this. I might have thought it all imagined, not real at all, except that she took some part of me with her— some bit of life I'd suppose you'd say."

He shook his head slowly. "Most of what she told me scattered like the fragments of some dream. But I remember her words of Safehold, Elfling. Catacombs beneath the arm of Spire's Reach, she said. A place from another age where some strange magic had once been done. So old it was that even the Sisters did not know its meaning. She told me that, did Mallenroh. I remember . . . that much, at least."

He was silent then, thinking back on what had been. Even after all these years, the memory of her was as clear as the faces of those who sat about him. Mallenroh! Strange, he thought, that he should remember her so well.

The young man was speaking quietly, his hand touching the edge of the rocker.

"You remember enough, Hebel."

The old man looked at the Elf in surprise, not understanding. Then he saw in the other's eyes what he intended. He meant to go there, Hebel realized. He meant to go into the Hollows. Impulsively he leaned down.

"Do not go," he whispered, his head shaking slowly. "Do not go."

The young man smiled faintly. "I must, if Cephelo is to have his reward."

The Rover said nothing, his dark face inscrutable. Eretria glanced sharply at him, then turned back to the young man.

"Healer, do not do this," she begged. "Listen to what the old man has said. The Hollows are no place for you. Seek your medicine elsewhere."

The Elf shook his head. "There is nowhere else. Let it alone, Eretria."

For an instant, the Rover girl's entire body seemed to go taut, her dark face flushing with emotions that struggled to break free. Yet she held them carefully in check, rising to her feet and staring down at him coldly.

"You are a fool," she announced and stalked away into the dark.

Hebel watched the young man, saw his eyes follow after Eretria as she went from them. The Elven girl did not look, her strange green eyes introspective and all but lost in the shadow of her long hair as it fell forward about her child's face.

"Is this root so important?" the old man asked wonderingly, not just to the young man, but to the girl as well. "Can it not be found another place?"

"Let them be." Cephelo spoke up suddenly, his dark eyes slipping from face to face. "The decision is theirs to make and they have made it."

Hebel frowned. "So quick to send them to their deaths, Rover? What then of this reward of which the Elfling speaks?"

Cephelo laughed. "Rewards are given and taken away by the whims of fortune, old man. Where one is lost, another is gained. The Elfling must do what he chooses, he and his sister. We have no right to pass judgment."

"We have to go." The Elven girl spoke softly, for the first time since they had been seated, looking deep into the old man's eyes.

"Well, then." Cephelo rose. "Enough said of the matter. The evening is not yet done and there is good Rover ale to be drunk. Share it with me, friends. We shall talk of the times that have been, rather than guess at what might yet be. Hebel, you shall hear what those fools that people Grimpen Ward have done of late—madness the like of which only men such as you and I can truly appreciate."

He called sharply to the old woman, who scurried to his side with a flask of ale. Several more of the Rovers drifted over to join them, and Cephelo poured freely from the flask into the cups of all. Laughing and joking, he began a series of wild-eyed stories of places he had probably never been and people he had certainly never met. Bold and easy was the Rover, his talk filling the night with the laughter of his people and the clink of their glasses raised in salute. Hebel listened with distrust. Cephelo had been too quick to disparage his warning to the Elflings and to disclaim interest in the supposed reward that would come, it seemed, only if the young Elf found the medicine he sought and returned again. Too quick by far, he thought—for the Rover knew as well as he that no one had ever returned from the Hollows.

He rocked slowly in his cane-backed chair, one hand dropping idly to find Drifter's shaggy head. What more warning could he give this Elf, he wondered? What could he say that he had not already said to discourage his foolishness? Perhaps nothing; the lad seemed determined that he must go.

He wondered then if the Elfling would meet Mallenroh as he had done so many years ago; thinking that he might, he envied him.

It was a short time later when Wil Ohmsford rose from the company of revelers and walked to the well that sat just back of the old man's hut. Amberle already slept, wrapped in blankets close to the fire, exhausted, it seemed, from the day's journey and the events leading up to it. He also was experiencing an unusual drowsiness, though he had drunk little of the Rover ale. The cold water might help, he thought, and a good night's sleep after. He had just taken a long drink from a metal cup hooked to the well-bucket's chain when Eretria stepped from the shadows to stand before him.

"I do not understand you, Healer," she said bluntly.

He replaced the cup within the bucket and seated himself on the stone wall of the well. This was Eretria's first appearance since she had called him a fool in front of the others.

"I went to a considerable amount of trouble to save your life back in Grimpen Ward," she continued. "It was not easy persuading Cephelo that he should allow me to help you—not easy at all. Now it seems that my efforts were wasted. I might as well have let those cutthroats have you, you and this Elven girl you pretend is your sister. Despite the warnings you have been given, you insist on going into the Hollows. I want to know why. Has Cephelo anything to do with this? I don't know what bargain you struck with him, but nothing he promised—even if he were of a mind to deliver, which I doubt he is—would be worth the risk that you take."

"Cephelo has nothing to do with it," Wil replied quietly.

"If he has threatened you in any way, I would stand with you against him," the girl declared firmly. "I would help you."

"I know that. But Cephelo has no part in the decision."

"Then why? Why must you do this?"

The Valeman looked down. "The medicine that is needed for . . ."

"Don't lie to me!" Eretria dropped next to him on the well wall, her dark face angry. "Cephelo may believe that nonsense about roots and medicines, but he reads only the truth of your words, Healer, and not the truth of your eyes. You may disguise the first, but never the second. This girl is not your sister; she is your charge, a responsibility that you clearly hold dear. It is not roots and medicines you seek, but something more. What is it then that lies within the Hollows?"

Wil looked up slowly to meet her gaze and hold it. For a long moment he stared at her without replying. She reached out impulsively, her hands grasping his.

"I would never betray you. Never."

He smiled faintly. "Perhaps that is the one thing about you of which I am certain, Eretria. I will tell you this. There is a danger that threatens this land—that threatens all the Lands. The thing that will protect against it can be found only in Safehold. Amberle and I have been sent to find it."

The Rover girl's eyes were filled with fire. "Then let me go with you. Take me with you now as you should have taken me before."

Wil sighed. "How can I do that? You have just finished telling me that I am a fool for insisting on going into the Hollows. Now you would have me treat you as a fool as well. No. Your place is with your people—at least for now. Better that you continue east, far from the Westland and what may come."

"Healer, I am to be sold by that devil who masquerades as my father the moment we reach the larger Southland cities!" Her voice was hard, brittle. "Am I to see myself as better off with that fate than any that you might encounter? Take me with you!"

"Eretria . . ."

"Hear me out! I know something of this country, for the Rovers have traveled it since the time of my birth. I may know something that could help you. If not, at least I will be no hindrance to you. I can take care of myself—better than your Elven girl. I ask nothing of you, Healer, that you would not ask of me were our positions reversed. You must let me come!"

"Eretria, even if I were to agree to this, Cephelo would never let you go."

"Cephelo would not know until it was too late to do anything about it." Her voice was quick and excited. "Take me with you, Healer. Say yes to me."

He almost did. She was so wonderfully beautiful that it would have been hard to refuse her anything under normal circumstances. But now, seated next to him, her eyes bright with anticipation, there was a desperation in her words that moved him. She was frightened of Cephelo and what he would do with her. She would not beg, the Valeman knew, but she would come as close to that as possible if it would persuade him to help her get free.

But the Hollows were death, the old man had said. No one went into the Hollows. It would be difficult enough looking after Amberle; and despite what Eretria had said about taking care of herself, Wil knew that, if she were permitted to come with them, he would worry for her just as he worried for the Elven girl.

He shook his head slowly. "I can't, Eretria. I can't."

There was a long moment of silence as she stared at him, disbelief and anger shading her eyes, the excitement and expectation fading. Slowly she rose.

"Though I have saved your life, you will not save mine. Very well."

She stepped back from him, tears streaking her face. "Twice you have spurned me, Wil Ohmsford. You will not get the chance to do so again."

She wheeled and started away, only to stop again a dozen paces on.

"There will come a time, Healer, I promise you, when you will wish that you had not been so quick to refuse me aid."

Then she was gone, lost in the night shadows as the Valeman stared after her. He remained where he was for a time, wishing desperately that things might be different than they were, wishing that there were some sensible way that he might give to her the help she needed.

Then at last he rose, the drowsiness growing, and stumbled off to sleep.

38

D awn broke gray and sullen over the Wilderun, draping the forestland in shadows that spread like bloodstains across the dark earth. Clouds masked the morning sky, hanging still and deep over the valley, and an expectant hush filled the air, warning of the approach of a summer storm. Atop the ridge line, Cephelo and his small band began their descent out of the hills, following the trail that would take them back down to the main roadway and a continuation of their journey toward the Hollows. The Rovers went from Hebel's camp as they had come, like shadows strayed, the horsemen leading the single wagon that bore Wil and Amberle, hands raised in brief farewell to the old man who stood wordlessly before the little hut and watched them depart. Slowly they passed into the gloom of the forest, massive trees wrapping close about them until all but the faintest streamers of light were shut away and there was nothing but the roadway, narrow and rutted and dark, burrowing down into the depths of the valley.

By midmorning they had reached the main road again and turned east. Mist began to gather on the valley floor, sifting through the trees as the day grew hot and the cool of the night turned to steam. Wil and Amberle rode in silence with the old woman, thinking of what lay ahead. There had been no further conversations with Hebel, for they had slept soundly that night and with their awakening, Cephelo had made certain that the old man had kept his distance from them. Now they found themselves wondering what more he might have told them had he been given the chance. As they pondered this, Cephelo rode back to speak with them, yet the smile and the conversation seemed forced and lacking any real purpose. He appeared several times more during the course of the morning and each time it was the same. It was almost as if he were looking for something, yet neither Valeman nor Elven girl had the slightest idea what it was that he might be seeking. Eretria stayed away from them entirely, and while Amberle was mystified as to the Rover girl's sudden change in behavior, Wil understood it all too well.

It was nearing midday when Cephelo signalled a halt at a narrow crossroads somewhere deep within the forest. In the distance, thunder rumbled ominously and the wind blew in sudden gusts that shook the trees and scattered leaves and dust. Cephelo rode back to the wagon and stopped beside Wil.

"This is where we part company, Healer," he announced. He pointed to the crossroads. "Your way lies south, down the smaller road. The path is clear—simply stay on it. You should reach the rim of the Hollows before nightfall."

Wil started to speak, and the Rover quickly held up his hand. "Before you say anything, let me advise you not to ask that I go with you. That was not our bargain, and I have other obligations that I intend to satisfy."

"I was about to ask you if we might have some provisions to take with us," Wil informed him coolly.

The Rover shrugged. "Enough for a day or two, no more."

He nodded to the old woman, who stepped back through the door of the wagon. Wil watched the Rover shift uneasily in his saddle. Something was bothering Cephelo.

"How will I find you to pay you your share of the reward?" he asked suddenly.

"Reward? Oh, yes." Cephelo seemed to have forgotten it momentarily. "Well, as I said before, I will know when you have been paid. I will seek you out, Healer."

The Valeman nodded, rose and stepped down from the wagon, then turned back to help Amberle. He glanced at her briefly as he lifted her down. She did not feel any easier about the Rover's behavior than he did. He turned back to Cephelo.

"Could you give us a horse? One would . . ."

Cephelo cut him short. "There are no horses to be spared. Now I think you should be going. There is a storm coming."

The old woman reappeared and handed Wil a small sack. The Valeman slung it over one shoulder and thanked her. Then he glanced up at the Rover once more.

"A safe journey, Cephelo."

The big man nodded. "And a quick one to you, Healer. Farewell."

Wil took Amberle's arm and led her through the gathering of horsemen to the crossroads. Eretria sat astride her bay, black hair blowing wildly as the wind swirled past her. When the Valeman reached her side, he stopped momentarily and extended his hand.

"Goodbye, Eretria."

She nodded, her dark face expressionless, cold and beautiful. Then without a word, she rode back to join Cephelo. The Valeman stared after her a moment, but she did not look at him again. He turned to the pathway leading south. Dirt blew into his eyes, and he shielded them with his hand, squinting into the gloom. With Amberle beside him, he started ahead.

Hebel spent the morning at his workbench behind the little hut, hunched over a carving of a swamp cat. As he worked, his mind drifted back to the events of the previous night, to the Elflings and their strange quest, and the warning he had given them which they had ignored. He could not understand it. Why had they refused to heed him? Certainly he had made it clear enough that it was death to go into the Hollows. And certainly he had made it clear as well that the domain of the Witch Sisters could not be violated. What was it then that could prompt this brother and sister to go there for nothing more than some obscure root medicine?

Then it occurred to him that perhaps there was something more. He thought about that for a moment and the more he thought about it the more plausible it seemed. After all, they would not be so foolish as to entrust a rogue like Cephelo with the truth; no, not that young man—he was too quick for that. Safehold lay within the depths of Spire's Reach; what sort of root would grow deep within a mountain where no sunlight could ever reach to nourish its growth? But magic had once been done within Safehold, the Witch Sister had whispered to him—magic from another age, lost and forgotten. Did the Elflings hope to discover it again?

Overhead, the sky darkened further as the storm rolled out of the far country, the howl of the wind in the trees rising to a higher pitch. The old man paused in his work and looked up momentarily. This would be a big one, he thought idly. Another bad sign for those Elflings who would be caught in the open, for the storm would overtake them before they reached the Hollows. He shook his head. He would go after them if he thought it would do any good, but their minds were obviously made up. Still, it was too bad. Whatever they hoped to find within Safehold, be it root medicine or magic, they would have been better off to have forgotten it entirely. They would never live to use it.

At his feet, Drifter lifted his shaggy head and sniffed the wind. Then abruptly the dog growled, low, deep, and angry. Hebel stared down at him curiously and glanced about. Shadows fell across the clearing from the forest trees, but nothing moved.

Drifter growled again and the hackles on the back of his neck rose. Hebel looked around guardedly. There was something out there, something hidden back in the gloom. He stood up, reaching for the broad axe. Cautiously, he started toward the trees, Drifter crouched beside him, still growling.

But then he stopped. He did not understand why he stopped except that suddenly he felt something cold slip into his body, chilling him so badly that he could barely stand. At his feet, Drifter lay on his belly and cried as if he had been struck, his great body cringing. The old man caught a glimpse of something moving—a shadow, massive and cloaked, there one moment and then gone. A fear passed through him, so terrible that he could not find the will to thrust it from him. It gripped him cruelly and held him fast as he stared helplessly at the dark forest and wished with everything that was left him that he might turn and flee. The axe fell from his hands and tumbled to the earth, useless.

Then the feeling slipped from him, gone as quickly as it had come. All about him the wind howled, and a spattering of rain struck his leathery face. Drawing a deep breath, he reached down for the axe and, with Drifter close against him, backed slowly away until he felt his legs brush up against the workbench. He paused then, one hand gripping the neck of the big dog to keep himself from shaking. With frightening certainty he knew that, in sixty years of struggling to survive the dangers of the valley, never before had he come so close to dying.

Wil and Amberle had walked for less than an hour when the storm overtook them. A sprinkling of heavy drops that slipped teasingly through the dense canopy of trees turned quickly to a downpour. Sheets of rain swept across the pathway, driven by a west wind, and thunder boomed and reverberated through the sodden forest. Ahead, the gloom of the narrow trail darkened further with the rainfall, and water-laden tree limbs began to droop about them in damp trailers. They were soaked in minutes, bereft of the travel cloaks which they had failed to recover from the Rovers along with the rest of their clothing. The light garments they had been fitted with in their stead clung to their bodies. There was nothing to be done that would ease their discomfort, however, so they simply put their heads down and walked on.

For several hours the rain continued to fall at a steady pace, save for occasional brief lulls that gave false promise of an end to the storm. Through it all, the Valeman and the Elven girl trudged on, water dripping from their bodies and their clothing, mud caking on their boots, their eyes fixed on the rutted path ahead. When at last the rain did slow and the storm moved eastward, mist began to seep out of the forest to mix with the deep gloom. Trees and brush shone dark and shiny through the haze, and water dripped noisily in the sudden stillness. Overhead, the sky stayed clouded and dark; to the east thunder rumbled, distant and lingering. The mist began to deepen, and the pace of the travelers slowed.

It was then that the pathway began to slope downward, a slight dropping off that at first was barely perceptible, but gradually increased. Valeman and Elven girl slipped and skidded in the muddied earth as they followed it down, peering hopefully into the gloom ahead, yet finding nothing more than the dark tunnel of the road and the closure of the trees. The stillness had grown even more pronounced. Even the faint sounds of insects singing at the passing of the storm had faded into silence.

Then suddenly, so suddenly that it was as if someone had removed a veil from before their eyes, the trees of the woods split apart, the slope dropped away, and the great, dark bowl of the Hollows lay spread before them. Valeman and Elven girl stopped where they were in the center of the muddied trail and stared down into the awesome expanse. They knew at once that they had found the Hollows; this massive pit of black forest could be nothing else. It was as if they had come upon some monstrous dead lake, still and lifeless, its dark surface grown thick with vegetation so that what lay beneath its waters could only be guessed at. From its shadowed center rose Spire's Reach, a solitary column of rock thrusting up into the gloom, barren and pitted. The Hollows were bleak like an open grave that whispered of death.

The Valeman and the Elven girl stood silently upon the rim, fighting a sense of revulsion that grew with each passing moment that they gazed down into the soundless gloom. Nothing that either had ever encountered had looked so desolate.

"We have to go down there," Wil ventured finally, hating the idea.

She nodded. "I know."

He cast about hopefully for a way to proceed. Ahead, the trail appeared to stop altogether. Yet when the Valeman walked forward a bit, he saw that it did not end after all, but split to either side to wend downward into the shadows below. He hesitated a moment, studying the two paths, trying to decide which would provide the easier descent, then chose the one that ran left. He held out his arm to Amberle and she gripped it firmly. Leading the way, he started down, feeling his boots slide as the damp earth and rock gave way in clumps. Amberle stayed close, leaning heavily on him for support. Cautiously they moved ahead.

Then abruptly Wil lost his footing and went down. Amberle fell with him, tripping forward across his legs, tumbling headlong from the muddied path to disappear with a sharp cry into the wooded darkness. Frantically, Wil scrambled after her, pushing his way through heavy brush that ripped his clothing and cut his face. He might not have found the Elven girl at all but for the bright silk of her Rover clothing, a splash of red against the dark. She lay lodged against a clump of scrub, the breath knocked from her body, her face smeared with mud. Her eyes flickered uncertainly as he touched her.

"Wil?"

He eased her into a sitting position, cradling her in his arms. "Are you all right? Are you hurt?"

"No, I don't think so." She smiled. "You're pretty clumsy, you know that?"

He nodded, grinning with relief. "Let's get you up."

He put his arm about her waist and lifted her clear of the scrub, her small frame feather-light as he set her back on her feet. Instantly she cried out and dropped back to the earth, reaching for her ankle.

"It's twisted!"

Wil felt along the ankle, checking the bones. "Nothing broken, just a bad sprain." He sat down beside her. "We can take a few moments to rest, then go on. I can help you down the slope; I can even carry you if it becomes necessary."

She shook her head. "Wil, I am so sorry. I should have been more careful."

"You? I was the one who fell." He grinned, trying to appear cheerful. "Well, maybe one of the old man's Witch Sisters will come along to help us out."

"That is not funny." Amberle frowned. She looked about uneasily. "Maybe we should wait until morning to climb down any further. My ankle might feel better by then. Besides, even if we made it down before dark, we would have to spend the night there, and I don't much care to do that."

Wil nodded. "Nor I. Nor do I think we should try to find our way about at night. Daylight will be soon enough."

"Maybe we should go back up to the rim." She looked at him hopefully.

The Valeman smiled. "Do you really believe the old man's story? Do you think there are Witches living down there?"

She stared at him darkly. "Don't you?"

He hesitated and then shrugged. "I don't know. Maybe. Yes, I guess so. There is very little I don't believe anymore." He sat forward slowly, arms coming up about his knees. "If there are Witches, I hope they are frightened of Elfstones, because that is just about all the protection we have left. Of course, if I have to use the Stones in order to make them afraid, we may be in a lot of trouble."

"I don't think so," she responded quietly.

"You still think I can use them, don't you—even after what happened on the Pykon?"

"Yes. But you shouldn't."

He looked at her. "You said something like that once before, remember? After the Tirfing, when we camped above the Mermidon. You were worried for me. You said that I should not use the Stones again, even if it meant saving you."

"I remember."

"Then later, when we fled the Pykon, I told you that I could no longer use the Stones, that their power was lost to me, that my Elven blood was not strong enough. You told me that I should not be so quick to judge myself—that you had confidence in me."

"I remember that, too."

"Well look at what we have been saying. I think I should use the Stones, but don't think I can. You think I can, but don't think I should. Funny, isn't it?" He shook his head. "And we still don't know which of us is right, do we? Here we are, almost to Safehold, and I still haven't found out . . ."

He stopped suddenly, realizing what it was that he was saying.

"Well, it's not important," he finished, looking away. "Better that we never find out. Better that they be given back to my grandfather."

They were silent for a moment. Almost without thinking, Wil reached into the Rover tunic and lifted out the pouch that held the Elfstones. He fingered it idly and was about to return it again when he noticed something odd about its feel. Frowning, he opened the drawstrings and dumped the contents into his open palm. He found himself staring at three ordinary pebbles.

"Wil!" Amberle exclaimed in horror.

The Valeman stared at the pebbles in stunned silence, his mind racing.

"Cephelo," he whispered finally. "Cephelo. Somehow he switched these for the Stones. Last night, probably, while we slept. It had to be then; they were in the pouch that morning in Grimpen Ward—I checked." He rose slowly, still talking. "But this morning, I forgot. I was so tired last night—and you fell asleep almost at once. He must have drugged the ale to be certain I would not awake. No wonder he was so anxious to be rid of us. No wonder he made light of Hebel's warning about the Hollows. He would be happy if we never came back. The reward meant nothing to him. It was the Elfstones that he wanted all along."

He started up the trail, his face livid. Then abruptly he remembered Amberle. Turning quickly back, he lifted the Elven girl in his arms, held her close against him, and scrambled back to the rim of the Hollows. For a moment he looked about, then walked to a clump of high bushes several yards back. Stepping beneath the shelter of their boughs, he set the Elven girl down.

"I have to go back for the Elfstones," he declared quietly. "If I leave you here, will you be all right?"

"Wil, you don't need the Stones."

He shook his head. "If we have to test that theory, I would prefer that it be done with the Stones in my possession. You heard what the old man said about the Hollows. The Stones are all that I have to protect you."

Amberle's face was white. "Cephelo will kill you."

"Maybe. Maybe he has gotten so far up the trail by this time that I won't even get close to him. But Amberle, I have to try. If I don't find him by dawn, I'll turn back, I promise. With or without the Elfstones, I will be with you to go into the Hollows."

She started to say something more, but then stopped. Tears ran down her cheeks. Her hands lifted to touch his face.

"I care for you," she whispered. "I really do."

He looked at her in astonishment. "Amberle!"

"Go on," she urged him, her voice breaking. "Cephelo will have stopped for the night and you may catch him if you hurry. But be careful, Wil Ohmsford—do not give your life foolishly. Come back for me."

She reached up to kiss him. "Go. Quickly."

He stared at her wordlessly for one instant more, then sprang to his feet. Without looking back, he ran from her and in seconds had disappeared into the forest gloom.

39

At dawn of the same day that found Wil and Amberle faced with the disappearance of the Elfstones, the Demons attacked Arborlon. With a frightening shriek that shattered the morning stillness and reverberated through the lowland forests, they burst from the cover of the trees, a massive wave of humped and twisted bodies that stretched the length of the Carolan. In a frenzy that cast aside reason and thought, the creatures of the dark swept out of the gloom that was still thick within the shadowed woods and threw themselves into the waters of the Rill Song. Like a huge stain spreading over the water, they filled the river, large and small, swift and slow, leaping, crawling, shambling bodies surging and heaving through the swift current. Some swam the river's waters, thrusting and kicking to gain the far bank. Those light and fleet flew above, hopped upon, or skimmed over the river's surface. Others so huge that they might walk upon the river's bottom, lunged awkwardly ahead, snouts and muzzles stretched high, bobbing and dipping. Many rode crude boats and rafts, poling mindlessly into the river and grasping tightly at whomever or whatever came within reach, thus to be pulled to safety or carried to the bottom with that which had failed to give them aid. Madness gripped the Demon horde, born of frustration with and hatred for the enemy that waited a scant few hundred yards away. This time, certainly, they would see that enemy destroyed.

But the Elves did not panic. Though the number, size, and ferocity of the Demons who came at them might have broken the spirit of a less determined defender, the Elves stood their ground. This was to be their final battle. It was their home city that they defended, the heart of the land that had been theirs for as long as the races had existed. All else had been lost now, from the Rill Song west. But the Elves were determined that they would not lose Arborlon. Better that they fight and die here, the last man, woman and child of them, than that they be driven entirely from their homeland, outcasts in foreign lands, hunted like animals by their pursuers.

Atop the battlements of the Elfitch, Ander Elessedil watched the Demon tide sweep forward. Allanon stood beside him. Neither man spoke. After a moment, Ander's eyes lifted. High overhead a small dot appeared out of the clear blue of the dawn skies, growing in size as it circled downward until it took shape. It was Dayn and his Roc Dancer. Downward they flew, gliding along the cliffs of the Carolan to settle finally on the open rampway above Ander and the Druid. Dismounting, Dayn came hurriedly to where the Elven Prince waited.

"How many?" Ander asked at once.

Dayn shook his head. "Even the woods and the mist can't hide them all. The ones we see before us are only a handful."

Ander nodded. So many, he thought darkly. But Allanon had said it would be so. He refrained from looking at the Druid. "Do they seek to flank us, Dayn?"

The Wing Rider shook his head. "They come directly against the Carolan—all of them." He glanced down momentarily at the attacking Demons as they struggled and thrashed in the waters of the Rill Song, then turned and started back toward the battlements. "I'll rest Dancer a few minutes more, then fly back for another look. Good luck, my Lord Prince."

Ander barely heard him. "We must hold here," he murmured, almost to himself.

Already the struggle was under way. At the river's edge, row upon row of Elven long bows hummed, and black shafts flew into the mass of heaving bodies that filled the waters of the Rill Song. Arrows bounced like harmless twigs from those armored with scales and leather hides, yet some found their mark, and the screams of their victims rose above the cries of attack. Dark forms twisted and sank into the boiling waters, lost in the wave of bodies that came after. Fire-tipped arrows thudded into the boats, rafts, and logs, but most were quickly extinguished and the craft churned ahead. Again and again the archers shot into the advancing horde as it streamed out of the forest and into the river, but the Demons came on, blackening the whole of the west bank and the river as they struggled to gain the Elven defensive wall.

Then a cry sounded from atop the Carolan, and cheers rang out. In the predawn gloom, Elves turned hurriedly to look, disbelief and joy reflecting in their faces as a tall, gray-haired rider came into view. Down the length of the Elfitch the cry passed on from mouth to mouth. All along the front line of the Rill Song, behind the barricades and walls, it rose into the morning until it became a defening roar.

"Eventine! Eventine rides to join us!"

In an instant's time the Elves were transformed, filled with new hope, new faith, new life. For here was the King who had ruled them almost sixty years—for many the whole of their lives. Here was the King who had stood against and finally triumphed over the Warlock Lord. Here was the King who had seen them through every crisis the homeland had faced. Wounded at Halys Cut, seemingly lost, he was returned again. With his return surely no evil, however monstrous, could prevail against them.

Eventine!

Yet something was wrong; Ander knew it the instant his father dismounted and turned to face him. This was not the Eventine of old, as his people believed. He saw in the King's eyes a distance separating the Elven ruler from all that was happening about him. It was as if he had withdrawn into himself, not out of fear or uncertainty, for he could master those, but out of deep, abiding sadness that seemed to have broken his spirit. He looked strong enough, the mask of his face reflecting determination and iron will, and he acknowledged those about him with the old, familiar words of encouragement. Yet the eyes betrayed the loss he felt, the despondency that had stripped him of his heart. His son read it there and saw that Allanon read it, too. It was only the shell of the King riding forth that morning to be with his people. Perhaps it was the deaths of Arion and Pindanon that had done this; it might have been the injury he had suffered at Halys Cut, the defeat of his army there, or the terrible devastation of his homeland; but more probably it was all of these and something more—the thought of failing, the knowledge that if the Elves lost this battle they would allow an evil into the Four Lands that no one could stop and which would fall upon all the races and devour them. The responsibility for this must lie with the Elves, yet with no man more than with Eventine, for he was their King.

Ander embraced his father warmly, masking the sadness that he felt. Then he stepped back and held forth the Ellcrys staff.

"This belongs to you, my Lord."

Eventine seemed to hesitate momentarily, then slowly shook his head. "No, Ander. It belongs to you now. You must carry it for me."

Ander stared at his father wordlessly. He saw in the old man's eyes what he had missed before. His father knew. He knew that he was not well, knew that something within him was changed. The pretense he made to others was not to be made to his son.

Ander withdrew the staff. "Then stand with me on the wall, my Lord," he asked softly.

His father nodded, and together they climbed the battlements.

Even as they did so, the foremost of the Demon horde gained the east bank of the Rill Song. Out of the river they surged, heaving up with savage cries to throw themselves against the lances and pikes that bristled from behind the Elven bulwarks. In moments there were Demons emerging from the river's dark waters along the entire length of the defensive line, horned and clawed, a jumble of limbs and jaws ripping and tearing at the defenders that barred their path. At its center, Stee Jans and the last of his Free Corps anchored the defense, the giant red-haired Borderman standing at the forefront of his men, broadsword raised. On the flanks, Ehlron Tay and Kerrin of the Home Guard called out to their soldiers: Hold, Elven Hunters, stand!

But finally they could stand no longer. Outflanked and outnumbered, they saw their line begin to crumble. Huge Demons thrust through the defenders and breached the low walls to open holes to those who followed. The waters of the Rill Song were dark with Demon lifeblood and twisted bodies; but, for every one that fell, still another three came on, a savage rush that no lesser force could hope to stop. Atop the gates of the second level of the Elfitch, Ander gave the order to fall back. Quickly the Elves and their allies abandoned the crumbling river wall and slipped into the

forest behind following carefully memorized paths to the safety of the
ramp. Almost before the Demons realized what was happening, the defenders were within its walls and the gates were shut behind them.

Instantly the Demons were in pursuit. Pouring through the forest at
the base of the heights, they ran afoul of the hundreds of snares and pitfalls
the Elves had laid for them. For a few moments, the entire rush stalled. But
as their numbers increased upon the riverbank, they overran those caught
within the traps and came onto the ramp of the Elfitch. Massing quickly,
they attacked. Up the walls of the first gate they charged, swarming atop
one another until they were pouring over the defenses of the lower level.
The Elves were driven back; almost before the gates to the second level
could be closed, the first had fallen. Without slowing, the Demons came
on, scrambling up the ramp to the second gate. They swarmed along the
walls and even up the rugged face of the cliff, clinging to the rock like insects. Bodies clawed, leaped, and bounded up the slope of the ramp and
the bluff face, shrieking with hunger. The Elves were appalled. The river
had not stopped the Demons. The defenses at the bank had been overrun
in minutes. Now the first level of the Elfitch had been lost and even the
cliff wall did not seem to slow them. It was beginning to look as if all their
defenses would prove useless.

Demon bodies thudded against the gates of the second ramp, clawing
upward. Spears and pikes thrust down, impaling the attackers. The gates
sagged on their hinges with the weight of the rush. Yet this time the defenders held, iron and sinew bracing the gates and repelling the attack.
Cries of pain and death filled the air, and the Demon force built into a
mass of writhing forms, surging mindlessly against the walls of the ramp.
Out of their midst came a handful of Furies, lithe gray forms bounding
atop the stone walls, cat-women's faces twisted with hate. Elven defenders
fell back from them, shredded by their claws, crying out in fear. Then Allanon's blue fire burst amid the Furies, scattering them wildly. The Elves
counterattacked, throwing the cat-things from the walls until the last had
disappeared into the dark mass below.

The Druid and the Elessedils moved upward to the third gate. From
there they watched as the Demon attack gathered force. Still the Elven defenders held, archers from the higher levels lending support to the lancers
and pikemen below. Demons clung to the cliff face all about the ramp of
the Elfitch, working their way upward toward the heights in a slow, arduous climb. From atop the bluff, the Dwarf Sappers used long bows and
boulders to knock the black forms loose. One after another the Demons
fell, screaming and twisting to the rocks below.

Then suddenly a monstrous Demon rose out of the attackers that
came at the gates of the second ramp, a scaled creature that stood upon its
hind legs like a human but had the body and head of a lizard. Hissing in
fury, it threw its bulk against the gates, snapping the crossbars and loosening the hinges. In desperation the Elves sought to thrust it back, but the
monstrous thing merely shrugged aside the blows, Elven weapons snapping
apart on its armored body. A second time it threw itself against the gates

and this time they split apart, shattering backward into the Elves. The defenders fell back at once, fleeing up the Elfitch to the third level where the next set of gates stood open to receive them. The lizard thing and its brethren followed after, pouring onto the rampway.

For an instant it did not appear that the Elves would succeed in closing the gates to the third ramp before the Demons breached it. Then Stee Jans appeared at the entrance to the ramp, a huge spear gripped in his hands. Flanked by the veteran soldiers of the Free Corps and by Kerrin and a handful of Home Guard, he stepped in front of the advancing Demons. Dropping forward in a crouch, the lizard Demon reached for him. But the Borderman was too quick. Sidestepping the monster's lunge, he thrust the great spear upward through the back of the gaping jaws. Hissing and choking, the lizard reared back on its hind legs, the shaft driven through its head. Clawed hands ripped at the Legion Commander, but the men of the Free Corps and the Elves rallied about him, warding off the blows. In seconds, they were back within the safety of the battlements, the gates closing behind them. For an instant the lizard Demon stood within the center of the ramphead, trying to pull free the killing shaft. Then its life was gone, and it fell backward into the midst of its brethren, sweeping them from the ramp as it tumbled over the wall and dropped to the forest below.

Snarling, the Demons renewed their attack. But their momentum had been lost. Strung out along the length of the Elfitch, they could not seem to muster a sustained rush. The biggest among them had been slain; lacking another to take his place, they milled uncertainly within the walls of the ramp below. Heartened by the courage of the Free Corps and their own Home Guard, the Elven defenders beat them back. Arrows and spears cut into their midst, and hundreds of black forms collapsed upon the ramp. Still the Demons scrambled forward, but confused now and vulnerable.

Ander recognized his opportunity. He gave the signal to counterattack. At Kerrin's order, the gates to the third ramp were thrown wide and the Elves rushed forth. Into the mass of Demons they charged, driving them back down the Elfitch, back through the shattered gates of the second ramp. Sweeping clear the ramp, the defenders battled downward to the edge of the lower gates before the Demons finally rallied. Back they came, reinforced by the thousands that still poured out of the Rill Song to the base of the cliff. The Elves held a moment only, then retreated to the gates of the second level, bracing them anew with timbers and iron, and there they stood.

So it went for the remainder of the day and into the evening. Back and forth along the rampway the battle raged, from the base of the bluff to the gates of the third level, Elves and Demons hacking and tearing at one another in a struggle where no quarter was asked and none given. Twice the Demons retook the second set of gates and pushed up against the third. Twice they were driven back, once all the way to the base of the bluff. Thousands died, though the dead numbered highest among Demons, for they fought without regard for life, spending themselves willingly on the defenders' carefully drawn formations. Yet Elves were lost as well, injured and dead, and their numbers began to dwindle steadily while the numbers of the Demons never seemed to grow less.

Then abruptly, without warning, the Demons gave up the attack. Back down the length of the Elfitch they went, not in flight nor in haste, but slowly, reluctantly, snarling and rasping as they faded back into the forests. Black forms huddled down in the shadowed gloom of night, crouched motionless and silent as if waiting for something to happen. Behind the gates and walls of the Elfitch and from the rim of the Carolan, the exhausted defenders peered down into the dark. They did not question what had happened, but were merely grateful for it. For one more day, at least, the city of Arborlon was safe.

That same night, scarcely two hours after the Demons had withdrawn into the wooded blackness below the Carolan, a messenger came to Eventine and Ander as they met with the Elven Ministers in the High Council. In an excited voice, he announced that an army of Rock Trolls had arrived from the Kershalt. Hurriedly, the King and his son emerged from the council building, the others trailing after, to find the entire courtyard filled with row upon row of massive, barklike forms, armored with leather and iron. Broadswords and spears glimmered in the smoky light of torches ringing the assemblage, and a sea of deep-set eyes fixed on the Elves' astonished faces.

Their Commander stepped forward, a huge Troll with a great, two-edged axe strapped across his back. With a quick glance at the other Elves, he placed himself before the King.

"I am Amantar, Maturen of this army," he informed them, speaking in the rough Troll dialect. "We are fifteen hundred strong, King Eventine. We come to stand with the Elves."

Eventine was speechless. They had all but given up on the Trolls, believing that the Northlanders had chosen not to become involved in this conflict. Now, to find them suddenly here, just when it appeared that no more help would be coming . . .

Amantar saw the old King's surprise. "King Eventine, you must know that much thought was given to your request for aid," he growled softly. "Always before, Trolls and Elves have fought against one another; we have been enemies. That cannot be forgotten all at once. Yet for everyone, there is a time to begin anew. That time has come for Elf and Troll. We know of the Demons. There have been encounters with a scattering of them already. There have been injuries; there have been deaths. The Rock Trolls understand the danger that the Demons pose. The Demons are as great an evil as the Warlock Lord and the creatures of the Skull mark. Such evil threatens all. Therefore it is seen that Elf and Troll must put aside their differences and stand together against this common enemy. We have come, my countrymen and I, to stand with you."

It was an eloquent statement. Amantar finished and, in a carefully measured gesture, dropped to one knee, signifying in the manner of the Rock Trolls his pledge of service. Behind him, his men followed him down, silent as they knelt before Eventine.

Ander saw the tears that appeared suddenly in the old man's eyes. For that one moment, Eventine came all the way back from the place to which he had withdrawn, and there was hope and fierce pride in his face. Slowly he placed his right hand on his heart, returning the Trolls' pledge in the Elven way. Amantar rose, and the two clasped hands.

Ander found himself wanting to cheer.

Allanon walked the narrow paths of the Gardens of Life beneath a clouded night sky through which moon and stars slipped like hunted things. Solitary, noiseless, his tall form passed through the cooling, fragrant blackness of the flowered tiers and sculpted hedges, head bent to the walk before him, arms gathered within the folds of the long, dark robe. His hard face was lost within the shadow of the cowl, lean features etched with lines of worry and bitter resolve. For this night he went to a meeting with death.

He walked to the foot of the rise ringed by the soldiers of the Black Watch. Impatient, he lifted his hand and slipped through them with the swiftness of a passing thought, and they did not see. Slowly he climbed to the top of the rise, not wishing to look at that which he had come to see, eyes lowered and fixed upon the grassy slope he trod.

When at last he was atop the rise, his head lifted. Before him stood the Ellcrys, the once slender and graceful limbs withered and bent like the drying bones of some dead thing. Gone was the fragrance and the color, so that no more than a shadow remained of what had once been so incredibly beautiful. Blood-red leaves lay scattered upon the ground like wads of crumpled parchment. The tree stood bare, nailed against the night sky in a tangle of sticks and peeling bark.

Allanon went cold. Even he had not been prepared for this, not for what he saw, nor for what he felt in seeing. Sorrow welled up within him at the inevitability of what was happening. He was powerless to prevent this, for even the Druids lacked the gift of life eternal. All things must one day pass from the earth, and it was her time.

His hand lifted to touch her withered limbs, then dropped again. He did not want to feel her pain. Yet he knew that he must have the measure of her, and he brought his hand up again, slowly, gently clasping. Just an instant he lingered, willing a sense of comfort and hope to flow from his mind into her own, then withdrew. Another day or two, perhaps three. No more. Then she would be gone.

His tall form straightened, hands falling limply to his sides as his dark eyes fixed upon the dying tree. So little time.

As he turned away he wondered if that little time would be time enough to bring Amberle back again.

40

Wil Ohmsford raced back through the forest of the Wilderun, following the dark rut of the pathway as it tunneled ahead through mist and gloom. Trailing limbs and vines heavy with dampness brushed and slapped at him as he ran, and water splattered from puddles dotting the rain-soaked trail, leaving him streaked with mud. But the Valeman felt none of it, his mind crowded with emotions that spun and twisted, to leave him dazed with despair at the loss of the Elfstones, anger against Cephelo, fear for Amberle, and wonderment at the words she had spoken to him.

I care for you, she had said and meant it. I care for you. So strange to hear her say such a thing to him. Once he would never have believed it possible. She had resented and mistrusted him; she had made that clear enough. And he had not really liked this Elven girl. But the long journey they had begun in the village of Havenstead had taught them much about each other, and the dangers and hardships they had faced and overcome had brought them close. Their lives in that brief span of time had become inextricably bound together. It was not really so unexpected then that out of that binding should come some form of affection. The words throbbed in his head, repeating themselves. I care for you. She did, he knew, and wondered suddenly how much he in turn now cared for her.

He lost his footing and went down, tumbling forward into the muck and the damp. Angrily he scrambled up, brushed the mud and water away as best he could, and ran on. The afternoon was waning far too rapidly; he would be fortunate just to regain the main roadway before nightfall set in. When that happened, he would have to find his way in total blackness, alone in an unfamiliar land, weaponless save for a hunting knife. Stupid! That was the kindest description he could render for what he had done, letting Cephelo fool him into thinking that he could have the Rover's aid for nothing more than a vague promise. Clever Wil Ohmsford, he chided himself, anger burning through him. And Allanon had thought that you were the one to whom he might safely entrust Amberle!

Already his muscles were beginning to cramp with the strain of running. Despair washed through him for a moment as he thought of all that Amberle and he had endured to reach this point, only to face losing everything for want of a bit more caution. Seven Elven Hunters had given their lives so that he and Amberle might reach the Wilderun. Countless more would have already died defending the Westland against the Demons, for surely the Forbidding had given way by now. All for nothing, then? All to no end but this? Shame and then determination rushed through him, car-

rying away the despair. He would never give up—never! He would retrieve the stolen Elfstones. He would return to Amberle. He would see her
safely to Spire's Reach, to the Bloodfire, and back once more to Arborlon.
He would do all this because he knew that he must, because to do anything less would be to fail—not just Allanon and the Elves, but himself as
well. He was not about to do that.

Even as the thought passed from his mind, a shadow appeared on the
trail ahead, materializing out of the gloom like some wraith, tall and silent
as it awaited his approach. The Valeman drew up short, frightened so badly
that he very nearly bolted from the pathway into the forest. Breathing
raggedly, he stared at the shadow, realizing suddenly that what he was looking at was a horse and rider. The horse shifted on the trail and stamped.
Wil walked forward cautiously, wariness turning to disbelief and finally to
astonishment.

It was Eretria.

"Surprised?" Her voice was cool and measured.

"Very," he admitted.

"I have come to save you one last time, Wil Ohmsford. This time, I
think, you will hear better what I have to say."

Wil came up to her and stopped. "Cephelo has the Stones."

"I know that. He drugged your wine, then took them from you last
night while you slept."

"And you did nothing to warn me?"

"Warn you?" She shook her head slowly. "I would have warned you,
Healer. I would have helped you. But you would not help me—remember?
All that I asked of you was that you take me with you when you left. Had
you done that, I would have told you of Cephelo's plans for the Elfstones
and would have seen to it that you kept them safe. But you spurned me,
Healer. You left me. You thought yourself able to manage well enough
without me. Very well, I decided, I will see how well the Healer does
without me."

She bent down to examine him, her eyes appraising. "It does not appear that you are doing too well."

Wil nodded slowly, his mind racing. This was no time to say something foolish. "Amberle is hurt. She fell and twisted her leg and cannot
walk alone. I had to leave her at the rim of the Hollows."

"You seem very good at leaving women in distress," Eretria snapped.

He held his temper. "I guess it must appear that way. But sometimes
we cannot always do what we want when it comes to helping others."

"So you have said. I guess that you must believe it. Have you left the
Elven girl, then?"

"Only until I get the Stones back again."

"Which you won't without me."

"Which I will, with or without you."

The Rover girl stared down at him for a moment, and her face
softened.

"I guess you believe that, too, don't you?"

Wil put his hand on the horse's flank. "Are you here to help me, Eretria?"

She regarded him wordlessly for a moment, then nodded. "If you, in turn, will help me. This time you must, you know." When he did not respond, she continued speaking. "A trade, Wil Ohmsford. I will help you get back the Stones if you will agree to take me with you when you have them back again."

"How will you get the Stones back?" he asked carefully.

She smiled for the first time, that familiar, dazzlingly beautiful smile that took his breath away. "How will I do it? Healer, I am the child of Rovers and the daughter of a thief—bought and paid for. He stole them from you; I will steal them from him. I know the trade better than he. All we need do is find him."

"Won't he be wondering about you by now?"

She shook her head. "When we parted company with you, I told him that I wished to ride ahead to join the caravan. He agreed that I could, for the paths of the Wilderun are well known to the Rovers, and I would be clear of the valley by nightfall. As you know, Healer, he wants to be certain that he keeps me safe. Damaged goods bring a poor price. In any case, I rode but a mile beyond Whistle Ridge, then took a second trail that cuts south and joins this one several hundred yards further back. I thought to catch up to you by nightfall, either at the Hollows or coming back this way, should you discover sooner the loss of the Stones. So you see, Cephelo will not realize what I have done until he reaches the main caravan. The wagon slows him, so he will not do that until sometime tomorrow. Tonight, he will camp on the road leading out of the valley."

"Then we have tonight to get back the Stones," Wil finished.

"Time enough," she replied. "But not if we continue to stand here and talk about it. Besides, you don't want to leave the Elven girl alone at the Hollows for very long, do you?"

The mention of Amberle jarred him. "No. Let's be off."

"One moment." She backed the horse away from him. "First your word. Once I have helped you, then you will help me. You will take me with you when we have the Stones back. You will let me stay with you after that until I am a safe distance from Cephelo—and I will decide when that is the case. Promise me, Healer."

There was very little else that he could do short of taking her horse from her, and he was not at all sure that he could do that.

"Very well. I promise."

She nodded. "Good. To see that you keep that promise, I will keep the Stones once I have taken them back again until we are both safely out of this valley. Climb up behind me."

Wil mounted the horse without comment. There was no way that he was about to let her keep the Elfstones, once she had retrieved them from Cephelo, but it was pointless to argue about it here. He settled himself behind the girl, and she turned to look at him.

"You do not deserve what I am doing for you—you know that. But I like you; I like your chances in life—especially with me to aid you. Put your hands about my waist."

Wil hesitated, then did as he was told. Eretria leaned back into him.

"Much better," she purred seductively. "I prefer you this way to the way you are when the Elven girl is about. Now hold tight."

With a sudden yell, she put her boots into the flanks of the horse. The startled beast reared up with a scream and shot back along the pathway. Down the wilderness trail they rode, bent low across the horse's neck, limbs whipping against them as they flew through the dark. Eretria seemed to have the eyes of a cat, guiding their mount with a sure and practiced hand past fallen logs and deadwood, over gullies and ruts formed by the sudden rain, down one muddied slope and up the next. Wil hung on desperately, wondering if the girl had lost her mind. At this pace, they were certain to take a fall.

Amazingly, they did not. Scant seconds later, Eretria wheeled their horse from the trail through a narrow gap in the trees that was all but completely grown over. With a surge, the animal sprang into the brush, then broke free along a second trail—one that Wil had missed completely in his trek south to the Hollows—and galloped ahead into the misty gloom. On they rode, Rover girl and Valeman, barely slowing for the obstacles that barred their path forward, racing ahead into the growing dark. What little light there was had begun to fade as dusk approached. The sun, lost somewhere beyond the canopy of the forest, sank downward toward the rim of the mountains. Shadows deepened and the air cooled and still Eretria did not slow.

When at last they did stop, they were back once more on the main roadway. Eretria reined the horse in sharply, patted the animal's sweating flanks and glanced back at Wil with an impish grin.

"That was just to let you know that I can hold my own with anyone. I need no looking after from you."

The Valeman felt his stomach begin to settle. "You have made your point, Eretria. Why are we stopping here?"

"Just to check," she replied and dismounted. Her eyes scanned the trail for a few moments, and then she frowned. "That's odd. There are no wagon tracks."

Wil followed her down. "Are you sure?" He studied the roadway, finding no sign of wheel marks. "Maybe the rain washed them out."

"The wagon was heavy enough that the rain should not have washed away all traces of its passing." She shook her head slowly. "Besides, the rain would have been nearly ended by the time it reached this point. I don't understand it, Healer."

The light was growing steadily dimmer. Wil glanced about apprehensively. "Would Cephelo have stopped to wait out the storm?"

"Maybe." She looked doubtful. "We had better backtrack a bit. Climb on."

They remounted and began riding west, glancing from time to time at the muddied earth for some sign of the Rover wagon. There was nothing. Eretria urged their mount into a slow trot. Ahead, mist curled out of the forest on either side, thin, wispy trailers that slipped like feelers through the gloom. Night sounds came from deep within the trees as the creatures of the valley awoke and began to hunt.

Then a new sound rose from somewhere ahead, faint at first, lingering like an echo in the midst of the sharper, quicker sounds, then stronger and more insistent. It grew into a howl, high-pitched and eerie, as if such pain had been inflicted upon some tortured soul that the limits of endurance had been passed and all that was left before death was that final, terrible cry of anguish.

Wil gripped Eretria's shoulder in alarm. "What is that?"

She glanced back. "Whistle Ridge—just ahead." She grinned nervously. "The wind makes that sound sometimes."

It grew worse, a harsher, more biting cry, and the land began to rise through the forest in a rocky slope that took them above the mist, the trees parting to reveal small patches of blue night sky. The horse had begun to respond to the sounds, huffing nervously, dancing and shifting as Eretria sought to calm it. They moved more slowly now, edging ahead through the dusk until they were atop the ridge line. Beyond, the roadway straightened once more and disappeared into the gloom.

Wil saw something then, a shadow moving toward them, materializing out of the howl of the wind and the night. Eretria saw it as well and reined in sharply. The shadow came closer. It was a horse, a big sorrel, riderless, its reins trailing in the earth. It came slowly up to them and rubbed noses with their own mount. Both Valeman and Rover girl recognized it at once. It was Cephelo's.

Eretria dismounted, handing the reins of her own horse to Wil. Wordlessly, she examined the sorrel, walking quickly about it, patting its flanks and neck to keep it calm. There were no marks on the animal, but it was sweating heavily. When she glanced again at Wil, Eretria's dark face was uncertain.

"Something has happened. His horse would not stray."

The Valeman nodded. He was beginning to get a very bad feeling about this.

Eretria climbed atop Cephelo's horse and took up the reins. "We will go on a bit further," she decided, but there was doubt in her voice.

Side by side, they rode along the ridge line, the wind whistling its eerie cry through the high rock and the trees of the forest. Overhead, the stars winked into view, pale white light shining down into the dark of the Wilderun.

Then something else appeared through the gloom, another shadow, this one black and squarish and motionless upon the trail. Valeman and Rover girl slowed, easing their horses ahead cautiously, uneasiness reflecting in their eyes. Gradually the shadow began to take shape. It was Cephelo's wagon, the garish colors caught in the starlight. They rode closer, and uneasiness then turned to horror. The team of horses that had pulled the wagon were dead, twisted and broken, still locked in their leather and silver-studded traces. Several more of the animals lay close by and, with them, their riders, scattered on the trail like straw men, torn and crumpled, bright clothing stained with blood that seeped through the fabric to mix with the muddied earth.

Quickly Wil looked about, peering into the shadows of the forest, searching for some sign of the thing that had done this. Nothing moved. He glanced at Eretria. She sat rigid on her mount, the color draining from her face as she stared fixedly at the bodies on the trail. Her hands dropped slowly to her lap, and the reins slipped free. Wil dismounted, scooped up the fallen reins, and tried to hand them back to the frightened girl. When Eretria did not move to take them, he gripped her hands, placed the reins of both horses between her fingers, and forced them closed. She glanced down at him wordlessly.

"Wait here," he ordered.

He walked toward the wagon, studying the twisted forms about him as he went. All lay dead, even the old woman who had driven the wagon, bodies broken like deadwood. The Valeman felt his skin crawl. He knew what had done this. One by one, he checked them until at last he found Cephelo. The big man was dead as well, his tall form stretched full length upon the ground, forest-green cloak shredded, angular features frozen with a look of horror. So ruined was his body that it was nearly impossible to recognize.

Wil bent down. Slowly he felt through the dead Rover's clothing, searching for the Elfstones. He found nothing. Fear knotted his stomach. He had to find the Stones. Then he noticed Cephelo's hands. The right hand clutched at the earth in a gesture that spoke of unbearable agony. The left was flung wide and closed into a fist. The Valeman took a deep breath and reached for the left. One by one he pried open the rigid fingers. Blue light winked from between them, and relief flooded through him. Embedded in the flesh of the palm lay the Elfstones. Cephelo had sought to use them as he had seen Wil do in the Tirfing, but the Stones had not responded to the Rover and he had died still clutching them.

The Valeman pulled them free of the dead man's grip, wiped them on his tunic, and dropped them back into their leather pouch. Then he rose, listening to the shriek of the wind whistling through the ridge. Dizziness washed over him as the smell of death filled his nostrils. Only one thing could have done this. He remembered the Elven dead at the camp at Drey Wood and in the fortress of the Pykon. Only one thing. The Reaper. But how had it found them again? How had it trailed them all the way from the Pykon to the Wilderun?

He steadied himself and hastened back to Eretria. She still sat astride Cephelo's horse, dark eyes bright with fear.

"Did you find him?" she asked in a whisper. "Cephelo?"

Wil nodded. "He's dead. They're all dead." He paused. "I took back the Stones."

She did not seem to hear him. "What kind of thing could do this, Healer? Some animal, maybe? Or the Witch Sisters, or . . . ?"

"No." He shook his head quickly. "No, Eretria, I know what did this. The thing that did this tracked Amberle and me all the way south from Arborlon. I thought that we had lost it on the other side of the Rock Spur, but somehow it has found us again."

Her voice shook. "Is it a Devil?"

"A special kind of Devil." He glanced back at the dead upon the trail. "They call it a Reaper." He thought a moment. "It must have believed we were traveling with Cephelo. Perhaps the rain confused it. It followed after him and caught him here . . ."

"Poor Cephelo," she murmured. "He played one game too many." She paused and glanced back at him sharply. "Healer, this thing knows now that you did not come east with Cephelo. Where will it go next?"

Valeman and Rover girl stared wordlessly at each other. Both knew the answer.

At the rim of the Hollows, Amberle crouched within the shelter of the bushes where Wil had hidden her and listened to the sounds of the night. Darkness lay over the Wilderun like a shroud, deep and impenetrable, and the Elven girl sat locked within it, unable to see beyond the covering brush, hearing the creatures that prowled the gloom. Knowing that it would be dawn before Wil could return to her, she tried for a time to sleep. But sleep would not come; her ankle pained her and her mind crowded with thoughts of the Valeman and his quest, of her grandfather, of the dangers all about her. At last she gave it up. With her knees pulled up against her body, she hunched forward, determined that she would become as nearly as she could a part of the forest about her, still, motionless, and unseen.

For a time she succeeded. None of the forest creatures ventured near her, staying back within the deep woods, back from the rim of the Hollows. The Hollows themselves lay wrapped in a silence so profound that the Elven girl could hear it as clearly as she heard the sounds of the night. Once or twice something flew past her shelter, the quick flap of wings breaking the stillness briefly, then fading once more. Time slipped away, and she began to nod sleepily.

Then the chill swept through her suddenly, as if the warmth had been sapped from the air about her. She came awake and rubbed her arms briskly. The chill left and the heat of the summer night slipped back across her. Uncertain now, she glanced about her shelter. Everything was as it had been before; in the darkness nothing moved, nothing sounded. She took a deep breath and closed her eyes again. The chill came back. She waited this time before moving, keeping her eyes tightly shut, trying to trace the source of the chill. She discovered that it came from somewhere within herself. She did not understand. Cold, bitter cold, within her, pushing through her, numbing like the touch of . . . death.

Her eyes snapped wide. Instantly she understood. She was being warned—how she did not know—that something was going to kill her. Had she been anyone but who she was, she might have ignored the feeling as being nothing more than the workings of her imagination. But she was highly sentient; such feelings had come over her before and she knew better than to dismiss them. The warning was real. It was only the source that confused her.

She hunched forward in momentary indecision. Something was coming for her, something monstrous, something that would destroy her. She could not hide from it; she could not stand against it. She could only run.

Ignoring the pain in her ankle, she slipped from beneath the bushes, crouched down beyond them, and stared into the forest gloom. The thing that stalked her was close; she could sense its presence clearly now as it moved soundlessly through the night. She thought suddenly of Wil, and she wished desperately that he were there to help her. But Wil was not there. She must save herself and she must do so quickly.

There was only one place for her to go, one place that her stalker might not follow—the Hollows. She hobbled to their edge and stared down into the depthless black. Fear gripped her. The Hollows were as frightening to her as the thing behind. She steadied herself, green eyes sweeping across the black to the tower of Spire's Reach. It was there that she must go. It was there that Wil would look for her.

She found a pathway leading down and started along it, easing carefully into the shadows. In moments, she was enveloped by the blackness; the light of the stars and moon were lost above the trees. Her child's face tightened with determination, and she felt her way forward. She kept as still in her movements as she was able, and there was only the slight scraping of her boots on earth and rock to betray her passage. Below, there was only silence.

At last she was on the floor of the Hollows. She paused then, sitting back against a tree trunk, rubbing gingerly the injured ankle. It was badly swollen by now, aggravated by her decision to walk upon it. Sweat bathed her face as she stared upward into the gloom and listened. She heard nothing. No matter, she told herself. Whatever it was that sought her, it was up there still, searching. She had to get deeper into the Hollows. Her eyes had begun to adjust to the blackness; she could discern vaguely the shapes of trees and clumps of brush about her. It was time to go on.

She pushed herself up and hobbled ahead into the dark, trying to keep her weight off her injured ankle. Moving from one tree to the next, she rested a moment at each, listening anxiously to the deep silence. The pain was growing worse, a steady throb that seemed to intensify with each step forward. The muscles of her good leg had stiffened and cramped with the constant hobbling; already she was beginning to tire.

Finally she had to stop. Breathing heavily, she lowered herself to the

ground beside a thicket and leaned back against the cooling earth. Carefully, she composed herself and tried to trace anew the source of the warning. For a moment nothing happened. Then the chill swept back across
her, penetrating, biting. She caught her breath. The thing that sought her
was within the Hollows.

She hauled herself back to her feet and went on, limping blindly
through the gloom. At one point it occurred to her that she might be traveling in a circle, but she pushed the thought quickly from her mind. She
fell constantly. Several times she went down so hard that she nearly blacked
out. Each time she came to her knees gasping for breath, rose, and forced
herself to go forward. The minutes slipped by until she lost all track of
time. About her, the silence and the dark deepened.

At last she could go no further. She fell to her knees, the sound of her
breathing harsh in her ears. Crying with frustration, she began to crawl.
Rock and deadwood scraped at her hands and knees as she worked her way
through the brush, her ankle throbbing with pain. She would not give up,
she swore silently. The thing would not have her. She turned her thoughts
to Wil. She saw in her mind the look that had crossed his face when she
told him that she cared for him. She should not have said it, she knew. But
she had wanted to tell him so badly at that moment; she had needed to tell
him. It surprised her how much she had needed to tell him. And the wonder in his eyes . . .

She collapsed on her face, weeping. Wil! She whispered his name like
a talisman to ward off the evil that stalked her through the blackness. Then
she lifted herself and crawled on. Her mind wandered, and she seemed to
sense the presence of other creatures about her, moving with her through
the night, quick and all but soundless. Little people, she thought. But the
thing, where was the thing? How close to her was it?

She crawled and crawled until her strength was gone entirely; then she
lay down upon the forest earth. She was finished, she knew. She had nothing left to draw upon. Her eyes closed and she waited to die. A moment
later, she slept.

She was still sleeping when the crooked wooden fingers of a dozen
gnarled hands lifted her up and bore her away.

The Valeman and the Rover girl rode down the rock-strewn trail and
off Whistle Ridge, the wind whistling past their ears. Into the
blackness of the lower forest they flew, Rover silks whipping about
their bodies as they bent low across their horses' necks and peered blindly

into the gloom. The trees quickly closed about them and the night sky disappeared. With reckless disregard for their lives, they rode on, trusting to the surefootedness of their mounts and to luck.

There was no discussion of this; they had no time for discussion. The instant that Wil realized that the Reaper would backtrack until it found the trail Amberle and he had taken south to the Hollows after parting company with the Rovers, his mind went blank to every thought but one—Amberle would be at the end of that trail, alone, injured, and unprotected. If he did not reach her before the Reaper did, she would die, and it would be his fault because it had been his decision to leave her. An image of the torn and broken bodies of the Rovers on the trail flashed in his mind. At that moment he forgot everything but his need to get to Amberle. Scrambling back atop his horse, he wheeled the animal about and galloped away.

Eretria gave chase immediately. She might have done otherwise. With Cephelo dead, she had no further need for the Valeman's protection. She no longer belonged to anyone; she was her own person at last. She might have turned her horse about and ridden safely from the valley and the terrible thing that had killed Cephelo and the others. But Eretria did not even stop to consider this. She thought only of Wil, riding off without her, leaving her behind once more. Pride, stubbornness, and the strange attraction she felt for the Valeman flared within her. She could not permit him to do this to her again. Without hesitating, she went after him.

So began their race to save Amberle. Wil Ohmsford, riding as if he were a man possessed, quickly lost all track of where he was. Gloom and mist slipped about him as he came down off the ridge line into the deep forest, and he could barely make out the dark shapes of the trees at either side as he whipped past them. Yet he did not slow; he could not. He heard the sound of another horse following and realized that Eretria had come after him. He muttered a quick oath; did he not have enough to worry about already? But there was no time to concern himself with the Rover girl. He dismissed her from his thoughts and concentrated his efforts on finding the cutoff leading south.

Even so, he rode right past it. If Eretria had not called out to him, he might have kept riding east all the way to the mountains. Wheeling about in surprise, he charged back again. But now Eretria had taken the lead, spurring her mount forward into the darkness. More familiar than he with the trail, she galloped ahead, calling for him to follow. Surprised all over again, he gave chase.

It was a harrowing ride. The darkness was so thorough that even the sharp eyes of the Rover girl could barely pick out the pathway as it twisted through the forest night. Several times the horses almost went down, barely springing clear of gullies and fallen logs that lay across the narrow trail. But these were Rover horses, trained by the finest riders in the Four Lands, and they responded with a quickness and agility that brought a fierce cry from the lips of the Rover girl and left the Valeman breathless.

Then suddenly they were back upon the roadway that Amberle and

Wil had followed south to the Hollows, with branches and vines slapping against them and muddied water splashing up from the deep puddles that had collected upon the trail. Without slowing, they turned south. The minutes slipped by.

At last they broke from the forest onto the rim of the Hollows, its black circle spread out before them like some bottomless pit in the earth. Reining in their horses sharply, they sprang to the ground, staring about at the forest gloom. Silence hung across the Hollows, deep and pervasive. Wil hesitated only a second, then began searching for the bushes in which he had hidden Amberle. He found them almost at once and pushed his way to their center. There was no one there. For an instant, he panicked. He groped about for some sign of what might have happened to the Elven girl, but there was nothing to be found. His panic increased. Where was she? He rose, backing from the bushes. Perhaps these were the wrong ones, he thought suddenly, and began to look about for others. He stopped almost at once. There were no others like them close enough to be seen. No, it was here that he had hidden her.

Eretria hurried up to him. "Where is she?"

"I don't know," he whispered, his lean face sweating. "I can't find her."

He regained control of himself with an effort. Reason it through, he told himself. Either she fled or the Reaper took her. If she fled, where would she go? He looked at once to the Hollows. There, he decided—to Spire's Reach or as close to it as she could get. What if she had been taken, what then? But she had not been taken, he realized, because there was no sign of a struggle. She would have fought back; she would have left him some sign. If she had fled, on the other hand, she would have been careful to leave nothing behind to show her pursuer that she had been there at all.

He took a deep breath. She must have fled. But then a new thought struck him. He was assuming in all of this that Amberle had fled from the Reaper. What if it had not been the Reaper, but something that had come out of the Hollows? His jaw locked in frustration. There was no way to tell. In this blackness, he could not hope to find a trail. Either he would have to wait until morning, when it might be too late to help Amberle, or . . .

Or he would have to use the Elfstones.

He was reaching for the pouch when Eretria's hand gripped his arm sharply, causing him to jump in surprise.

"Healer!" she whispered. "Someone is coming!"

He felt his stomach knot sharply. For an instant he simply stood there, his gaze following the girl's as it turned north up the trail they had just traveled. On its shadowed rut, something moved. Fear welled up within the Valeman. His hand fumbled within his tunic and lifted free the Elfstones. At his side, Eretria snatched from her boot a wicked-looking dagger. Together they faced the approaching shadow.

"Just hold on now!" A familiar voice called out to them.

Wil looked at Eretria and she at him. Slowly they lowered Elfstones and dagger. The voice belonged to Hebel. Eretria muttered something under her breath and moved to retrieve the horses, which had strayed back into the forest.

Down the trail trudged Hebel, the shaggy form of Drifter close at his heels. He wore leather woodsman's garb and carried a sack strapped across his back, a long bow and arrows over one shoulder, and a hunting knife at his waist. He moved with a peculiar hunching motion, leaning heavily on a gnarled walking stick. As he came up to them, they could see that he was spattered from head to foot with mud.

"You nearly ran me down, you know!" he snapped. "Look at me! If I'd been foolish enough to stand any further out on the trail than I did when I hailed you back there, I'd be covered with hoof prints as well as mud! What do you think you are doing, riding about the forest like that? It's black as six feet under out there and you ride about like it was broad daylight. Why didn't you stop when I called out to you, for cat's sake?"

"Well . . . because we didn't hear you," Wil answered in bewilderment.

"That's because you weren't listening like you should have been!" Hebel was not about to forgive them. He lurched right up to the Valeman. "Took me all day to get here—all day. Without a horse, I might point out. What took you so confounded long then? The way you were riding a minute ago, you could have been here and gone again half-a-dozen times!"

He caught sight of Eretria as she reappeared with the horses. "What are you doing here? Where is the Elfling girl? That thing didn't get her, did it?"

Wil started. "You know about the Reaper?"

"Reaper? If that's what it's called, yes, I know about it. It came to my camp earlier today—just after you'd left. Looking for you, it appears now, though at the time I wasn't sure. Never really saw the thing—just caught a glimpse. I think if I'd seen it close up, I'd be dead now."

"I think so, too," the Valeman agreed. "Cephelo and the others are. It caught up with them on Whistle Ridge."

Hebel nodded soberly. "Cephelo was bound to come to that end sooner or later." He glanced at Eretria. "Sorry, girl, but that's the truth of it." Then he turned back to Wil. "Now where's the little Elfling?"

"I don't know," Wil answered him. "I had to go back . . ." He hesitated. "I had to go back for something I left behind with Cephelo. Amberle had injured her ankle, so I hid her in some bushes. I went back a different way than I had come or I would probably be dead as well. I found Eretria, or she found me, I guess; and after we saw what had happened to Cephelo, we came back here as fast as we could. But now Amberle is gone, and I can't be sure what has happened to her. I can't even be sure whether the Reaper has been here yet or is still tracking us."

"It's come and gone," Hebel told him. "Drifter and I have been tracking it while it's been tracking you. Lost the trail at the fork because the Reaper went east to Whistle Ridge while Drifter and I came south after you. But then the trail started up again further south. Thing must have cut through the wilderness. If it could do that, it's dangerous, Elfling."

"Ask Cephelo how dangerous it is," Eretria muttered, glancing about at the forest shadows. "Healer, can we get out of here now?"

"Not until we find out what happened to Amberle," Wil insisted.

Hebel tapped his arm. "Show me where you left the girl."

Wil walked to the clump of bushes, with Eretria, the old man, and the dog trailing after, and pointed to the opening leading in. Hebel bent down, peered inside, and whistled Drifter to him. He spoke quietly to the dog, and the animal came forward, sniffed about, then moved over to the rim of the Hollows as the others watched.

"He has the scent, Drifter has." Hebel grunted with satisfaction. Drifter stopped and growled softly. "She is down in the Hollows, Elfling. The Reaper is down there, too. Probably still tracking her. I'd have guessed as much."

"Then we have to find her right away." Wil started forward.

Hebel caught his arm. "No need to rush, Elfling. That's the Hollows we're talking about, remember? Nothing down there but the Witch Sisters and the things that serve them. Anything else sets one foot in the Hollows gets snatched right up—I know that from what Mallenroh told me sixty years ago." He shook his head. "By now, the girl and the thing tracking her are keeping company with one of the Sisters—that or they're dead."

Wil went white. "Would the Witches kill them, Hebel?"

The old man seemed to think it over. "Oh, not the girl, I'd guess—not right away. The thing they would. And don't think they couldn't, Elfling."

"I don't know what to think anymore," Wil replied slowly. He gazed down into the blackness of the Hollows. "I do know this much—I am going down there and I am going to find Amberle. Right now."

He started to say something to Eretria, but the Rover girl cut him short. "Don't waste your breath, Healer. I'm going with you."

The way she said it left little room for argument. He glanced at Hebel.

"I'm coming, too, Elfling," the old man announced.

"But you said yourself that no one should go into the Hollows," Wil pointed out. "I don't understand why you're even here."

Hebel shrugged. "Because it doesn't matter where I am anymore, Elfling, and hasn't for a long time. I'm an old man; I've done in this life the things I've wanted to do, been where I wanted to go, seen what I've wanted to see. Nothing left for me now—nothing except for maybe this one thing. I want to see what's down there in those Hollows."

He shook his head ruefully. "Thought about it for sixty years, off and on. Always told myself that one day I'd find out—like thinking about a deep pool; you always wonder what's at the bottom." He rubbed his bearded chin. "Well, a sane man wouldn't waste his time with a thing like that, and I was a sane man when I was younger, though I guess some thought different. Now I'm tired of being sane, tired of just thinking about going down there instead of doing it. You made me decide. When you first told me what you intended, I thought to persuade you otherwise—just as I'd persuaded myself. I was certain that you would lose interest quick enough when you heard what I had to say. I was wrong. I saw that whatever it was that you were looking for was important enough that being afraid didn't matter to you. So why should it matter so much to me, I thought? Then after that Reaper thing passed me by and left me knowing how close I'd come to dying, I realized it didn't. All that really mattered was finding out about those Hollows. So I came after you. I decided that we should go looking together."

Wil understood. "Let's hope that we both find what we are looking for."

"Well, maybe I can be of some help to you." The old man shrugged. "This is Mallenroh's end of the Hollows. She might remember me, Elfling." For an instant his thoughts wandered, then he glanced at Wil. "Drifter can track for as long as it's needed." He whistled. "Take us down, dog. Go, boy."

Drifter disappeared over the rim of the Hollows. Eretria stripped saddles and bridles from the horses and slapped them sharply to send them galloping back through the forest. Then she joined Wil and the old man. In a line, they started down into the Hollows.

"Won't have to rely on Drifter very long," Hebel declared firmly. "Mallenroh—she'll find us quick enough."

If that were so, Wil found himself thinking, then he hoped that she would find Amberle as well.

Amberle came awake in the darkness of the Hollows forest. It was the slight swaying, jostling motion of being carried that awoke her, and for an instant she panicked. Gnarled fingers held her fast, locked tightly about her arms and legs, her body, even her neck and head—fingers so rough they felt as if they were made of wood. Her first reaction was to want to break free, but she resisted it with a desperate effort and forced herself to remain still. Whatever had her did not yet know she was awake. If she were to have any advantage at all, it lay in this. For the moment, at least, she must continue to feign sleep and learn what she could.

She had no idea how long she had slept. It might have been minutes or hours or even longer. She thought, though, that it was still the same night. Logic told her it must be. She thought, too, that whatever it was that had her, it was not the thing that had pursued her into the Hollows. Had that thing found her, it would simply have killed her. This, therefore, must be something else. The old man, Hebel, had told Wil and her that the Hollows were the private domain of the Witch Sisters. Perhaps it was one of them that had her.

She felt somewhat better, having reasoned that much through, and she relaxed a bit, trying to make out something of the terrain through which she was moving. It was difficult to do this; the trees shut away even the smallest trace of stars and moon, leaving everything shrouded in deepest

night. Were it not for the familiar woodland smells, she might not have
known there was a forest about. The silence was intense. The few sounds
were distant and brief, cries that came from the wilderness beyond the
Hollows.

Yet there was another sound, she corrected herself, a sort of skittering
noise like the chafing of limbs in a breeze—except that there was no
breeze, and the sound came from beneath her, not from above. Whatever it
was that carried her was making the noise.

The minutes slipped by. She thought briefly of Wil, trying to imagine
what he might do in her place. That made her smile in spite of herself.
Who could tell what wild stunt Wil might try in such a situation? Then
she wondered if she would ever see him again.

Her muscles were beginning to cramp, and she decided to see if she
could do something to ease the discomfort without giving herself away.
Experimentally she stretched her legs, pretending to stir in her sleep, testing the fingers that held her. They moved with her, but did not release. So
much for that.

The sound of running water reached her, growing stronger with each
passing second. She could smell it now, fresh and scented with wildflowers—
a stream that twisted and churned in the quiet of the forest. Then it was
beneath her, and the rustle of the sticks and the night sounds faded in its
rush. Footsteps echoed hollowly on wooden planks, and she knew she had
been carried over a bridge. The gurgle of the stream faded slightly. Chains
clanked and rumbled as if being gathered in, and there was a dull thud.
Something had closed behind, a door—a very heavy door. An iron bar and
locks snapped into place. She heard them clearly. Night air washed about
her as before, but it carried with it the unmistakable smell of stone and
mortar. Fear welled up within her once more. She was inside a walled area,
a courtyard perhaps, being taken, she now believed, to some sort of confinement, and if she did not break free at once, she would not break free at
all. Yet the fingers that constrained her showed not the slightest hint of
loosening, and there were many of them. It would take a tremendous effort to wrench free, and she did not believe that she had that kind of
strength left in her. Besides, she thought dismally, even if she were to break
free, where would she go?

Ahead, another door opened, creaking slightly. Still no light came to
her; there was nothing but blackness all about.

"Pretty thing," a voice said suddenly, and the Elven girl started with
surprise.

She was carried ahead. Behind her, the door closed and the smells of
the forest disappeared. She was inside—but inside of what? Twisting and
turning, her captors carried her along passageways that smelled damp and
musty; yet there was another odor, a kind of incense, a perfume. The Elven girl breathed it deeply and it left her head in a momentary spin.

Then at last there was a light, suddenly, unexpectedly, glimmering just
ahead from within a tall archway. Amberle blinked at the unfamiliar brightness, her eyes still accustomed to the dark. She was carried through the

archway and down a winding stairs. The light blinked above her, fell behind momentarily, then followed after, weaving and bobbing against the dark.

Her forward motion stopped. She felt herself being lowered onto a thick, woven matting, and the wooden fingers slipped free. She raised herself up on her elbows and squinted toward the light. It hung there before her for just an instant, then retreated slowly behind a wall of iron bars. A door swung shut and the light was gone.

But just before it disappeared, the Elven girl caught a glimpse of her captors, their slender forms outlined clearly in the white glow. They appeared to be made out of sticks.

On the floor of the Hollows, Wil called a halt. It was so black that he could barely see his hand in front of his face; he could not see Hebel or Eretria at all, nor they him. If they attempted to proceed under these conditions, they would soon become separated and hopelessly lost. He waited a few moments for his vision to sharpen. It did, but only slightly. The Hollows remained a dim, barely perceptible mass of shadows.

It was Hebel who came up with a plan to resolve their difficulty. Whistling Drifter to him, he produced a length of rope from the sack he carried, and bound one end to the dog; the rest he fastened about his waist and to the waists of the Valeman and the Rover girl. Thus tied, they could follow after one another without risk of separation. The old man tested the line, then spoke softly to Drifter. The big dog started ahead.

It seemed to Wil as if they walked the Hollows for hours, stumbling through an endless maze of trees and brush, nearly blind in the impenetrable blackness, trusting to the instincts of the dog that led them. They did not talk to one another at all, moving through the forest as silently as they could, all too conscious of the fact that somewhere within that same forest the Reaper prowled. Wil had never felt quite so helpless as he did then. It was bad enough that he could see almost nothing; it was worse knowing that the Reaper was down there with him. He thought constantly of Amberle. If he were frightened, what must it be like for her? His fear made him ashamed. He had no right to be afraid, not when she was the one who was alone and unprotected, and he was the one who had left her that way.

Yet the fear stayed with him. To ward it off, he clutched the pouch with the Elfstones in one hand, grasping it firmly, as if having it there might somehow protect him against whatever hid within the forest night. Yet deep within, the feeling persisted that the Elfstones would not protect him, that their power was lost to him and he could not get it back again. It made no difference what Amberle had told him or what he had told himself. The feeling lacked reason or purpose; it was simply there—haunting, malignant, terrifying. The power of the Elfstones was no longer his.

He was still trying to shake the feeling when the rope before him went suddenly slack. He almost stumbled over Hebel, who had come to a complete stop. Eretria bumped up against him, and the three stood bunched together, peering ahead into the gloom.

"Drifter's found something," the old man whispered to Wil.

Dropping to his knees, he worked his way forward to where Drifter was sniffing the ground, Wil and Eretria following close behind. He patted the dog soothingly and felt along the earth for a time, then rose.

"Mallenroh." He spoke her name softly. "She's got the Elfling girl."

"Are you sure?" Wil whispered back.

The old man nodded. "Has to be. That Reaper thing's somewhere else now. Drifter doesn't smell it anymore."

Wil did not understand how Hebel could be certain of all this, especially when it was so impossibly black, but there was no point in arguing the matter.

"What do we do now?" he asked anxiously.

"Keep going." Hebel grunted. "Drifter—go, boy."

The dog started ahead once more, the three humans trailing after. The minutes slipped away, and gradually the forest began to lighten. At first Wil thought his eyes were playing tricks on him, but finally he realized that night was fading and a new day had begun. Trees and brush began to take shape about him, the dimness sharpening slowly as the sun slipped its faint glow through the forest roof. Ahead, the shaggy black form of Drifter became visible for the first time since they had descended from the Hollows rim, head lowered to the trail as he sniffed his way along the damp earth.

Then abruptly the big head lifted and the dog stopped. The humans stopped with him, startled looks on their faces. Before them stood the strangest creature that any of them had ever seen. It was a man made of sticks—two arms, two legs and a body all of sticks, gnarled roots curling out from the ends of the arms and legs to form fingers and toes. It had no head. It faced them—or at least they thought it faced them since the roots that formed its fingers and toes appeared to point in their direction. Its slender body swayed slightly as if it were a sapling caught in a sudden wind. Then it turned and walked back into the forest.

Hebel glanced quickly at the other two. "I told you. That's Mallenroh's work."

Beckoning hurriedly to them, he started after the creature. Wil and Eretria looked doubtfully at each other, then followed. Wordlessly, the little procession trudged ahead into the gloom, weaving and twisting through the maze of the forest. After a time, other stick men like the first began to appear about them, headless, gnarled things, noiseless but for the slight skittering sound they made as they walked. Almost before the humans knew it, there were dozens of the creatures ringing them, trailing like ghosts through the shadows.

"I told you," Hebel kept whispering back to the Valeman and the Rover girl, his leathered face intense.

Then abruptly the forest thinned. Before them stood a solitary tower, its dark turret rising up into the trees that grew about it. It sat atop a small knoll, a nearly windowless keep, its stone aged, worn, and grown thick with vines and moss. The knoll had become an island, encircled by a stream that flowed from somewhere back in the forest, wending its way down in a series of drops and turns before meandering off into the trees to their left. A low wall ringed the tower, built close to the bank of the stream; where it faced them, a drawbridge stood open and empty, chains hanging limply from small watch houses at either side, a heavy wooden bridgehead spanning the waters beneath. All about the rise and the tower grew massive oaks, ancient trees whose boughs interwove and shut away the morning sky, leaving the isle, like the rest of the Hollows, draped in deepest shadow.

The stick man they had followed stopped. It turned about slightly, as if its headless form would ascertain whether or not they were there. Then it began walking toward the drawbridge. Hebel limped after it without hesitating, Drifter at his side. Wil and Eretria hung back a moment, less certain than the old man that they ought to go further. The tower was a forbidding structure; they knew that they should not set foot within its walls, knew that they had already gone much farther than they should. But the Valeman sensed somehow that it was here he would find Amberle. He looked back at Eretria, and they started forward.

Down to the edge of the stream the little band went, following the silent stick man, its brethren all about them. Except for the sounds of their movements and the flow of the stream, the forest lay wrapped in silence. The stick man stepped onto the bridgehead and walked across, fading from sight in the shadow of the gate. The men, the girl, and the dog passed over the bridge behind it, Wil and Eretria casting apprehensive glances at the massive black tower beyond.

Then they were beneath the gate. The stick man reappeared before them, standing now just beyond the shadowed arch. In a line, they moved forward, watching as it started once more toward the tower. They had barely walked clear of the gateway when they heard the sudden sound of chains creaking and groaning. Behind them, the drawbridge lifted and sealed against the wall.

Now there was no turning back. In a knot, they walked to the tower. The stick man was waiting, standing within a high alcove that sheltered a pair of broad, ironbound wooden doors. One door stood open. The stick man stepped through and was gone. Wil stared upward at the massive stone face of the tower, then reached into his tunic and brought forth the pouch that contained the Elfstones. With the others, he stepped through the doorway into blackness.

For an instant no one moved, standing just within the entry, peering blindly into the gloom. Then the door swung shut behind them, locks snapping into place. Light flared from within a glass-enclosed lamp that hung suspended from above, its glow white and soft, neither from burning oil nor pitch, but something that gave off no flame as it burned. All about stood the stick men, their gnarled shadows cast upon stone walls, swaying gently in the light.

From the gloom behind them, a woman appeared, cloaked all in black and trailing long streamers of crimson nightshade.

"Mallenroh," Hebel whispered, and Wil Ohmsford felt the air about him turn to ice.

42

The second day of the battle for Arborlon belonged to Ander Elessedil. It was a day of blood and pain, of death and great courage. All during the night the Demon hordes had continued to ferry their brethren across the waters of the Rill Song, singly and in groups, until, for the first time since their break from the Forbidding, the whole of their army was gathered to strike, massed at the base of the Carolan from cliff face to riverbank, stretched north and south as far as the eye could see, awesome and terrible and endless in number. At dawn, they attacked the city. Up against the walls of the Elfitch they rushed, wave upon wave, maddened and howling with hate. Up against the heights they surged, scrambling onto the sheer rock, clawing their way through a hail of arrows. Onward they came, like a wave that would sweep across the defenders who waited and leave them buried.

It was Ander Elessedil who made the difference. It was as if on that day he became at last the King his father had been, the King who had led the Elves against the armies of the Warlock Lord those fifty years past. Gone was the weariness and the disillusion. Gone was the doubt that had haunted him since Halys Cut. He believed again in himself and in the determination of those who fought with him. It was an historic moment, and the Elven Prince became its focal point. Gathered about him were the armies of four races, battle standards flying in the morning wind. Here were the silver war eagles and spreading oak of the Elves, the gray and crimson slash of the Free Corps, and the black horses of the Old Guard; there flew the forest greens of the Dwarf Sappers split by the twist of the Silver River, and the hammer and twin blue mountains of the Rock Trolls of the Kershalt. Never before had they flown as one. In the history of the Four Lands the races had never before been united in a common cause, to form a common defense, and to serve a common good. Troll and Dwarf, Elf and Man—the humans of the new world stood together against an evil from ancient times. For that single, wondrous day, Ander Elessedil became the spark that gave them all life.

He was everywhere at once, from the rim of the bluff to the gates of the Elfitch, sometimes on horseback, sometimes afoot, always where the fighting was the heaviest. Chain mail gleaming, Ellcrys staff held high, he stood foremost among the defenders of the city against the Demons who rushed to slay him. Wherever he went, the cry went up and the defenders rallied. Always outnumbered, always pressed, still the Elven Prince and his comrades-at-arms threw back their attackers. Ander Elessedil was something more than human that day, fighting with such ferocity that it seemed as if nothing could stand against him. Time after time, the Demons sought to pull him down, recognizing quickly that this single man was the heart of the Elven defense. Time after time, it seemed as if they would succeed, ringing Ander in a swarm of raging black bodies. But each time he fought his way free. Each time, the Demons were driven back.

It was a day of heroes, for all of the defenders of Arborlon were inspired by the courage of the Elven Prince. Eventine Elessedil stood with his son and fought bravely, his very presence lending heart to the Elves about him. Allanon was there as well, his cloaked form standing head and shoulders above the armored men about him as the blue fire arced from his fingers into the midst of the raging Demons. Twice the Demons broke through the gates of the third ramp, and twice the Rock Trolls under the command of Amantar drove them back again. Stee Jans and the men of the Free Corps broke a third assault, counterattacking with such savagery that they swept the Demons all the way back to the second ramp and for a time threatened to retake its gates. Elven cavalry and Dwarf Sappers repulsed sally after sally along the rim of the Carolan, throwing back scores of Demons who managed to scale the cliff face and threaten to flank the defenders on the Elfitch.

But it was Ander who led them, Ander who gave them renewed strength when it seemed that they could stand no longer, Ander who rallied them at every point. When the day at last was ended and darkness began to fall, the Demons were forced to withdraw once more, slipping back into the forests below the heights, shrieking with rage and frustration. For yet a second day, the defenders of Arborlon had held. It was Ander Elessedil's finest hour.

Then the fortunes of the defenders of the city took a turn for the worse. With the coming of night, the Demons attacked again, waiting only until the sunlight was gone, then rising up out of the forests to sweep over the Elven defense. One by one, they extinguished the torches that had been lit along the lower Elfitch, battling their way forward to the gates of the third ramp. Desperately, the defenders braced for the assault, massive Rock Trolls blocking the gates while Elves and Legion soldiers fought from atop the walls. But the rush was too strong; the gates buckled and snapped apart. Into the breach surged the Demons, clawing their way forward.

On the heights as well, the Demons began to break through. Dozens of black forms slipped between the lines of cavalry patrolling the bluff and scattered wildly toward the city. Of these, more than a hundred converged on the Gardens of Life, aware that within its gates stood the thing that for so many centuries had held them imprisoned. There they came face to face with the soldiers of the Black Watch who stood ready to fulfill the purpose of their order and to defend to the last man the ancient tree that was their trust. Maddened beyond reason, the Demons attacked. Up against the lowered pikes of the Black Watch they charged and were cut to pieces.

At the southern end of the Carolan, another band of Demons managed to tunnel beneath a line of Dwarf traps set along a dismantled secondary stairway leading up from the Rill Song and thus gain the heights. Skirting the Black Watch and the Gardens of Life, they slipped east away from the Carolan, crawling through the shadows behind the line of torches set against its rim and broke for the city. Half-a-dozen Elven wounded, en route to their homes from the battle, were caught in the open and killed. More might have perished but for a patrol of Dwarf Sappers, who had agreed to aid the Elves in keeping watch along the perimeter of the city. Realizing that the Demons had broken through the defenders of the bluff, they followed the cries of the dying and fell upon their slayers. When the struggle was ended, only three Dwarves were still standing. All the Demons lay dead.

By dawn, the heights had been cleared and the Demons thrown back once more. But the third ramp of the Elfitch had been lost and the fourth was threatened. At the base of the bluff, the Demons massed anew. Cries rang out through the morning stillness as they charged up the ramp, solidly massed, the foremost among them bearing a massive wooden battering ram. Into the gates they carried the ram, smashing the wooden barrier apart, then pouring through. Trolls and Elves formed quickly into a tight phalanx, a wall of iron spears and lances that cut deep into the writhing black forms. But the Demons came on, surging up against the harried defenders until they had forced them back within the fortress of the fifth ramp.

It was a desperate moment. Four of the seven levels of the Elfitch had been lost. The Demons were halfway to the summit of the bluffs. Ander rallied the defenders, flanked by Amantar and Kerrin and surrounded by Home Guard. The Demons charged, hammering against the gates of the ramp. But just when it seemed that they must break through, Allanon appeared on the walls, arms lifting. Blue flame raced the length of the ramp below, splitting wide the Demon rush, turning the battering ram to ash. Momentarily stunned, the Demons fell back.

All through the morning the Demons sought to breach the Elven defense of the fifth ramp. At midday, they finally succeeded. A pair of monstrous Ogres pushed to the forefront of their brethren and threw themselves against the gates—once, twice. Wood and iron shattered into fragments and the gates broke apart. The Ogres burst through onto the ramp beyond, scattering the defenders. A handful of Rock Trolls tried to stop them, but the Ogres shoved the Trolls aside as if they were made of paper. Again Ander rallied his soldiers, urging them forward. But Demons were pouring through the ruined gates now, sweeping over the defenders.

Then Eventine Elessedil's horse was killed beneath him as he rode back toward the safety of the gates above, and the old King tumbled to the rampway. The Demons saw him fall. With a howl, they surged forward. They would have had him but for Stee Jans. With a scattering of Legion Free Corps, the Borderman sprang into their path, swords cutting. Behind them, Eventine staggered to his knees, dazed and bloodied, but alive. Quickly Kerrin brought the Home Guard to the King's rescue, and they carried him from the battle.

The soldiers of the Free Corps held for a moment longer, then they too were swept aside. The Demons pushed forward, thrusting past the Elves who tried to bar their way. Leading the assault were the Ogres who had forced the gates, crushing all who came within reach. Ander Elessedil leaped to stop them, Ellcrys staff raised high as he called to the defenders of the city to stand with him. But the rush was too strong. Amantar and Stee Jans were fighting for their lives at the walls of the ramp, unable to reach the Elven Prince. For one terrifying moment, he stood virtually alone before the Demon rush.

But only for a moment. Atop the gates of the sixth court, Allanon whistled Dayn down from the edge of the Carolan. Without a word, he snatched Dancer's reins from the surprised Wing Rider and vaulted atop the giant Roc. In the next instant he was winging downward, black robes billowing out like sails. Dancer screamed once, then dropped into the midst of the Demons who threatened Ander, claws and beak tearing. Shrieking, the black forms scattered. Blue fire spurted from the Druid's fingers, and the ramp before him erupted in flame. Then pulling an astonished Ander up beside him, the Druid called out to Dancer and the Roc lifted back into the air; below, the last of the defenders fell back, pouring through the gates of the sixth ramp to safety.

For a few seconds longer, the Druid fire burned, then sputtered and died. Enraged, the Demons charged after the fleeing defenders. But by now the Dwarf Sappers on the heights had been alerted. Winches and pulleys began to turn as the chains wrapped about the supports of the ramp were drawn tight. Browork's carefully concealed trap was about to be sprung. Out from beneath the Elfitch flew the already weakened supports, cracking and snapping as the chains twisted them free. With a shudder, the ramphead below the sixth level sank downward and fell apart. The Demons caught upon it disappeared in a cloud of rubble. Shrieks and cries filled the air, and the whole of the lower ramp was lost from view.

When the dust cleared again, the Elfitch was a pile of crushed stone and shattered wooden beams from the gates of the sixth ramp downward to the fourth. Demon bodies lay scattered on the cliff face, lodged within the rubble, broken and lifeless. Those who had survived fell back toward the base of the bluff, dodging boulders and debris that tumbled down about them, disappearing finally into the woodlands below.

The Demons did not come again that day against the city of Arborlon.

———

Suffering from yet another head wound as well as from a number of smaller cuts and scrapes, Eventine Elessedil was carried from the battle atop the Elfitch to the seclusion of his manor house. Faithful Gael was there to care for him, to wash and dress his wounds, and to help him to his bed. Then, with Dardan and Rhoe to watch over him, the King of the Elves was left to sleep.

But Eventine did not sleep. He could not. He lay within his bed, propped up against the feathered pillows, staring disconsolately into the darkened corners of the room, despair washing through him. For all the help that the Legion, the Dwarves, and the Rock Trolls had given the Elves, the battle was still being lost. All of their defenses had failed. Another day, perhaps two, and the sixth and seventh gates of the Elfitch would fall and the Demons would be atop the Carolan. That would be the end. Hopelessly outnumbered, the defenders would be swiftly overrun and destroyed. The Westland would be lost and the Elves scattered to the four winds.

The implications behind what he was thinking burned through him. If the Demons won here, it would mean that Eventine Elessedil had failed. Not just his own people, but the peoples of all the Lands—for the Demons would not stop with the Westland, now that they were free of the Forbidding. And what of his ancestors who had imprisoned the Demons so many centuries ago, at a time so remote that he could barely envision its being? He would have failed them as well. They had created the Forbidding, but they had entrusted its care to those who followed after them, depending on those who came after to keep it strong. Yet the Forbidding had been forgotten over the centuries in the upheaval of the old world and the rebirth of the races, forgotten by them all. Even the Chosen had come to think of it as little more than a distant part of their history, a legend that belonged to another age, to the past or to the future—yet never really to the present.

His throat tightened. If Arborlon fell, if the Westland were lost, it would be his failure. His! His penetrating blue eyes turned hard with anger. For eighty-two years he had lived upon this earth; for more than fifty of them, he had been the leader of his people. He had accomplished much in that time—and now it would all be lost. He thought of Arion, his firstborn, the child who should have lived to carry on what he had worked so hard to achieve, and of Kael Pindanon, his old comrade-at-arms, his loyal follower. He thought of the Elves who had been lost defending the Sarandanon and Arborlon. All of them dead, and for nothing.

He eased himself down within the coverings of the bed, mulling over the choices that were left, the tactics that might yet be employed, the resources that might be called upon when the Demons came again. His mind filled with them, and deep within he felt a sense of hopelessness. They were not enough; they would never be enough.

Groping for answers to the questions he posed himself, he suddenly remembered Amberle. It startled him to think of her, and he sat upright in the bed. In the confusion of the past few days he had forgotten his grand-daughter, she who was the last of the Chosen, who Allanon had told him was the only real hope for his people. What, he wondered sadly, had become of Amberle?

He lay down again and stared through the shadow of the drapes to the growing darkness beyond. Allanon had said that Amberle was alive, by now deep within the lower Westland; but Eventine did not believe that the Druid really knew. The thought depressed him. If she were dead, he did not want to know, he decided suddenly. It would be better that way, not knowing. Yet that was a lie. He needed to know, desperately. Bitterness welled up within him. Everything was slipping away from him—his family, his people, his country, everything he loved, everything that had given meaning to his life. There was a basic unfairness to it all that he could not understand. No, it was more than that. The basic unfairness of it all was something he could not accept. If he did, he knew that it would finish him.

He closed his eyes against the light. Where was Amberle? He must know, he insisted stubbornly. He must find a way to reach her, to help her if his help were needed. He must find a way to bring her back to him. He took a deep breath, then another. Still thinking of Amberle, he drifted off to sleep.

It was dark when he awoke. At first he was not certain what it was that brought him awake, his mind still drugged with sleep, his thoughts scattered. A sound, he thought, a cry. He raised himself up against the gathering of pillows and stared into the darkness of the room. Pale, white moonlight seeped through the fabric of the drawn curtains, illuminating faintly the lines of the bolted double windows. Uncertain, he waited.

Then he heard another sound, a muted grunt, quick and surprised, fading almost instantly into silence. It had come from outside his room, from the hall where Dardan and Rhoe stood watch. He sat up slowly, peering into the gloom, straining to hear something more. But there was only the silence, deep and ominous. Eventine slid to the edge of the bed and dropped one leg cautiously to the floor.

The door to his bedchamber swung slowly open, light from the oil lamps of the hallway beyond spilling into the room. The Elven King froze. Through the opening came Manx, heavy body hunched forward in a low crouch, grizzled head swinging to where his master sat upon the bed. The wolfhound's eyes glittered like a cat's, and his dark muzzle was streaked with blood. But it was his forelegs and paws that startled the King most; they seemed in the half-light to have become the corded limbs and claws of a Demon.

Manx passed from the light of the oil lamps into shadow, and Eventine blinked in surprise. In that instant he was certain that what he had seen was something left over from a dream, that he had imagined that Manx was not Manx, but something else. The wolfhound moved toward him slowly, and the King could see that his tail was wagging in a friendly manner. He exhaled in relief. It was just Manx, he told himself.

"Manx, good boy . . ." he started to say and stopped as he caught sight of the reddened tracks that the dog had left on the floor behind him.

Then Manx was springing for his throat, quick and silent, jaws gaping wide, clawed hands reaching. But Eventine was quicker. Snatching the coverings from the bed before him, he caught Manx within their folds. Twisting the coverings about the struggling dog, the King slammed the animal down hard upon the bed and sprang for the open door. In an instant he was through, yanking the door shut behind him, hearing the latch snap into place.

Sweat ran down his body. What was happening? In a daze, he stumbled back from the door, nearly tripping over the lifeless body of Rhoe, who lay sprawled half-a-dozen feet away, his throat ripped open. Eventine's mind whirled. Manx? Why would Manx . . . ? He caught himself sharply. But it was not Manx. Whatever it was that had come at him within his sleeping chamber was not Manx, just something that looked like Manx. Numb, he started down the hallway, searching for Dardan. He found him near the front entry, a lance driven through his heart.

Then the door to his bed chamber burst open, and the thing that looked like Manx, yet surely was not, bounded into view. Frantic, Eventine sprang for the entry doors, wrenching at the handles. They were jammed, the locks sealed. The old King turned, watching as the beast in the hall stalked slowly toward him, reddened jaws gaping. Fear surged through Eventine, fear so terrible that for an instant it threatened to overwhelm him completely. He was trapped within his own house. There was no one to help him, no one that he might turn to. He was alone.

Down the length of the hall the monster came, the sound of its breathing a slow rasp in the silence. A Demon, Eventine thought in horror, a Demon pretending to be Manx, faithful old Manx. He remembered then awakening after the fall of the Sarandanon to find Manx and thinking suddenly, irrationally that it was not Manx at all, but something else. An illusion, he had thought—but he had been wrong. Manx was gone, dead he guessed for many days, even weeks . . .

Then the awful truth dawned on him. His meetings with Allanon, the plans they had worked so hard to keep secret, the care they had taken to protect Amberle—Manx had been there. Or the Demon that looked like Manx. There was a spy within the Elven camp, Allanon had warned—a spy that all the while had been as close to them as they had been to each other. The old King thought of the times that he had stroked that grizzled head, and it made his skin crawl.

The Demon was less than a dozen feet from him now, inching along the floor, jaws open, clawed forelegs bent. Eventine knew in that instant that he was a dead man. Then something happened within him, something so sudden that the Elven King was blinded to everything else. Rage swept through him—rage at the deception that had been done him, rage at the deaths that had occurred because of that deception, and most of all, rage at the helplessness he felt now, trapped as he was within his own house.

His body went taut. Next to the fallen Dardan lay the short sword that had been the Elven Hunter's favorite weapon. Keeping his eyes fixed upon those of the Demon, Eventine inched away from the doors. If he could manage to reach that sword . . .

The Demon came at him suddenly, bounding across the space that separated them, launching itself at the Elven King's head. Eventine brought his arms up to protect his face and fell backward, kicking violently. Teeth and claws ripped into his forearms, but his feet caught the underside of the creature and sent it tumbling past him into the darkened recesses of the entry. Quickly he rolled back to his feet, throwing himself over Dardan and grasping the fallen sword. Then he was up again, turning to face his attacker.

Astonishment flooded his face. From the darkened corner where it had tumbled, the Demon slouched, no longer Manx, but something different now. It was changing even as it stalked toward him, changing from Manx into a lean, black thing, corded with muscle, its body sleek and hairless. It came at him on four legs that ended in clawed hands, and its mouth split wide with gleaming teeth. It circled the King, lifting itself from time to time on its hind legs, feinting with its hands like a boxer, hissing with hate. A Changeling, Eventine thought and forced down a new wave of fear. A Demon that could be anything it wanted to be.

The Changeling lunged at him suddenly, claws ripping at his shoulder and side, leaving him torn and bloodied. He swung at the thing with the sword—too late. It was past him and gone before he could reach it. Back the Demon circled, slowly, like a cat watching its cornered prey. I must be quicker this time, the old King told himself. The Demon lunged again, feinted at his chest, and slipped beneath the arc of his sword, tearing at the muscles of his left leg. Pain shot through the leg, and he dropped to his knees, struggling to remain upright. For an instant his vision blurred, then cleared once more as he forced himself to rise.

Before him the Changeling crouched, waiting. When he stayed on his feet, it began to circle once more. Blood streamed down Eventine's body, and he felt himself weakening. He was losing this battle as well, he thought frantically, and it would end in his death if he did not find a way to take the offensive against this monster. Weaving and bobbing, the Demon stalked him. The King tried to corner it, but it stepped nimbly away from him, far too quick for the wounded old man. Eventine stopped his pursuit; it was gaining him nothing. He watched as the Demon continued to circle, hissing.

Then, in a desperate gamble, the Elven King pretended to stumble and fall, staggering heavily to his knees. Pain shot through him as he did so, but the deception worked. Thinking the old man finished, the Changeling lunged. But this time Eventine was waiting. He caught the monster in the chest, the sword biting deep through bone and muscle. Shrieking in pain, the Demon clawed and bit at the Elven King, then twisted free. Blood ran from the slash, a greenish-red ichor that stained the sleek, black body.

They crouched face to face, Elven King and Demon, both wounded, each waiting for the other to drop his guard. Once more, the Demon began to circle, blood trailing after it along the floor. Eventine Elessedil braced, turning to follow the Demon's movement. He was covered with blood, and his strength was ebbing from him. Pain wracked his torn body. He knew that he could only last a few minutes more.

Abruptly the Changeling sprang at his throat. It happened so quickly that the King did not have time to do much more than tumble backward, arms raised before his face, sword held high. The Demon landed on top of him, bearing him to the floor, teeth and claws ripping. Eventine screamed in pain as the claws tore into his chest and the jaws closed about his forearm.

Then the doors to the manor house burst apart, locks splintering, hinges ripped from their fastenings. Shouts rang through the darkened entryway as it filled with armed men. In a haze of anguish, Eventine cried out. Someone had heard! Someone had come!

From atop the fallen King, the Changeling rose up, shrieking. In that instant it left its throat exposed. Eventine's sword swept up, glittering. Back flew the Demon, head nearly severed from its body, its voice lost in a sudden gasp. As it fell, the King's rescuers closed in about it, swords thrusting deep into its body.

The Changeling shuddered with the impact of the blows and died.

Eventine Elessedil staggered to his feet, sword still clutched within his hand, blue eyes hard and fixed. A numbing sensation spread through his body as he turned to find Ander reaching out for him. Then the King of the Elves tumbled downward, and the night closed in.

43

Like Mistress Death she came for the humans, taller even than Allanon, gray hair long and woven thick with nightshade, black robes trailing from her slender form, a whisper of silk in the deep silence of the Tower. She was beautiful, her face delicate and finely wrought, her skin so pale that she seemed almost ethereal. There was an ageless look to her, a timelessness, as if she were a thing that had always been and would forever be. The stick men fell back from her as she approached, the clicking of their wooden legs a faint rustle in the gloom. She passed them without a glance, her strange violet eyes never leaving the three who stood transfixed in her presence. Her hands stretched forth, small and fragile, their fingers curving as if to draw them close.

"Mallenroh!" Hebel whispered her name a second time, his voice expectant.

She stopped, her perfect features devoid of expression as she looked down upon the old man. Then she turned to Eretria and finally to Wil. The Valeman had gone so cold that he was shaking.

"I am Mallenroh," she said, her voice soft and distant. "Why are you here?"

No one spoke, their eyes riveted on her. She waited a moment, then her pale hand passed before them.

"The Hollows are forbidden. No human is allowed. The Hollows are my home and within them I hold the power of life and death over all living things. To those who please me, I grant life. To those who do not, death. It has always been so. It will always be."

She looked at each of them in turn, carefully this time, violet eyes reaching out to hold their own. Finally her gaze rested on Hebel.

"Who are you, old man? Why have you come to the Hollows?"

Hebel swallowed. "I was looking for . . . for you, I guess." His words stumbled over one another. "I brought you something, Mallenroh."

Her hand stretched forth. "What have you brought me?"

Hebel removed the sack he carried, lifted its flap and fumbled through its contents, searching. A moment later he withdrew a polished wooden figure, a statue carved from a piece of oak. It was Mallenroh, captured so perfectly that it seemed as if she had stepped from the carving into life. She took the wooden figure from the old man and examined it, her slender fingers running slowly over its polished surface.

"A pretty thing," she said finally.

"It is you," Hebel told her quickly.

She looked back at him, and Wil did not like what he saw. The smile she gave the old man was faint and cold.

"I know you," she said, then paused as her eyes studied anew his leathered face. "Long ago it was, upon the rim of the Hollows, when you were still young. A night I gave you . . ."

"I remembered," Hebel whispered, pointing quickly to the wooden figure. "I remembered . . . what you were like."

At Hebel's feet, Drifter crouched against the stone floor of the tower and whined. But the old man never heard him. He had lost himself completely in the Witch's eyes. She shook her gray head slowly.

"It was a whim, foolish one," she whispered.

Holding the statue, she stepped past him to where Eretria stood. The Rover girl's eyes were wide and frightened as the Witch came up to her.

"What have you brought me?" Mallenroh's question teased through the silence.

Eretria was speechless. Desperately she looked at Wil, then back again to Mallenroh. The Witch's hand passed once before her eyes in a gesture that was both soothing and commanding.

"Pretty thing," Mallenroh smiled. "Have you brought yourself?"

Eretria's slender body shook. "I . . . no, I . . ."

"Do you care for this one?" Mallenroh pointed suddenly to Wil. She turned to face the Valeman. "He cares for someone else, I think. An Elven girl, perhaps? Is this so?"

Wil nodded slowly. Her strange eyes held his own, and her words reached out to him, bold and insistent.

"It is you who holds the magic."

"Magic?" Wil stammered in reply.

Her hands slipped back within the black robes. "Show it to me."

So compelling was her voice that before Wil Ohmsford knew what he had done, he had opened the hand that held the leather pouch. She nodded to him faintly.

"Show it to me," she repeated.

Unable to help himself, the Valeman emptied the Elfstones from the pouch into his outstretched hand. Cupped within his palm, they glittered and flared. Mallenroh drew in her breath sharply, and one hand lifted toward them.

"Elfstones," she said softly. "Blue for the Seeker." Her eyes found Wil's. "Shall they be your gift to me?"

Wil tried to speak, but the cold within him tightened and no words came from his lips. His hand locked before him, and he could not draw it back again. Mallenroh's eyes looked deep into his own; what he saw there terrified him. She wanted him to know what she could do to him.

The Witch stepped back. "Wisp," she called.

From the shadows sidled a small, furry-looking creature, like a Gnome in appearance, with the face of a wizened old man. Scurrying to Mallenroh's side, the creature peered up at the cold face anxiously.

"Yes, Lady. Wisp serves only you."

"There are gifts . . ." She smiled faintly, her voice trailing into silence.

Wordlessly, she handed Wisp the wooden statue of herself, then moved back to stand again before Hebel. Wisp hastened after, crouching down within the folds of her cloak.

"Old man," she addressed Hebel, her pale face bending close to his own. "What would you have me do with you?"

Hebel seemed to have recovered his senses. His eyes were no longer distant as they glanced quickly at the Witch and then away again. "Me? I don't know."

Her smile was hard. "Perhaps you should stay here within the Hollows."

"It doesn't matter," he insisted, as if he sensed somehow that the Witch would do with him as she pleased anyway. Then he looked up. "But the Elflings, Mallenroh. Help them. You could . . ."

"Help them?" she cut him short.

The old man nodded. "If you want me to stay, I will. There's nothing else for me. But let them go. Give them the help they need."

She laughed softly. "Perhaps there is something that you can do to help them, old man."

"But I have done all that I can . . ."

"Perhaps not. If I told you there was something more that you might do, you would be willing to do it, wouldn't you?"

Her eyes fixed the old man. Wil saw that the Witch was toying with him.

Hebel looked uncertain. "I don't know."

"Of course you know," she said softly. "Look at me." His head lifted. "They are your friends. You want to help them, don't you?"

The Valeman was frantic. Something was terribly wrong, but he could neither move nor speak to warn Hebel. He caught a glimpse of Eretria's frightened face. She, too, sensed the danger.

Hebel sensed it as well. But he sensed, too, that he could not escape it. His eyes met those of the Witch. "I want to help them."

Mallenroh nodded. "Then so you shall, old man."

She reached to touch his face. Hebel saw in the Witch's eyes what was to become of him. Drifter rose, teeth suddenly barred, but Hebel's hand caught the back of the big dog's neck and held him fast. The time for resistance was over. The Witch's fingers stroked the old man's bearded cheek gently, and his whole body seemed to go suddenly rigid. No! Wil tried to scream, but it was already too late. Mallenroh's cloak enfolded both Hebel and Drifter, and they were lost from sight. The cloak remained wrapped about them for a moment, then slipped free. Mallenroh stood alone. In one hand she held a perfectly sculpted wooden carving of the old man and the dog.

"In this way shall you help them best." She smiled coldly.

She handed the wooden figures to Wisp, who gathered them in. Then she turned to Eretria.

"Now what shall I do with you, pretty one?" she whispered.

Her hand lifted, and a single finger pointed. Eretria was forced to her knees, head bowed. The fingers curled back, and Eretria's hands stretched out to the Witch in a gesture of submission. Tears streaked her face. Mallenroh watched without comment for a moment, then looked abruptly at Wil.

"Would you see her become a wooden statue as well?" Her voice had an edge to it that cut through the Valeman like a knife. Still he could not speak. "Or the Elven girl, perhaps? You know, of course, that I have her."

She did not wait for the response she knew he could not give. She stepped forward, her tall figure bending down until her face was close before his own.

"I wish the Elfstones, and you shall give them to me. You shall give them, Elfling, for I know that if they are taken from you by force, they are useless." Her violet eyes burned into him. "I would have their magic, do you understand? I know their worth far better than you. I am older than this world and its races, older than the Druids who played at Paranor with magics long since mastered by my sister and me. It is so with the Elfstones. Though I am not of Elven blood, yet my blood is the blood of all the races, and so I may command their power. Still, even I cannot break the

law that calls their power into being. The Elfstones must be given freely.
And so they shall."

Her hand came close before his face, nearly touching it. "I have a sister, Elfling—Morag, she has named herself. For centuries we have lived
within these Hollows, called the Witch Sisters, the last of our Coven.
Once, long ago, she wronged me greatly, and I have never forgiven. I
would have been rid of her except that our powers match so evenly that
neither one nor the other of us may prevail. Ah, but the Elfstones are a
magic that my sister does not possess, a magic that will enable me to put an
end to her. Morag—odious Morag! Sweet, to see her made to serve me as
these men of sticks! Sweet, to still that hateful voice! Oh, I have waited
long to be rid of her, Elfling! Long!"

Her voice rose as she spoke until the words rang against the stones of
the tower, echoing through the deep stillness. The beautiful, cold face
moved back from the Valeman, the slender arms folding within the black
robes. Wil Ohmsford could feel the sweat running down his body.

"The Elfstones shall be your gift to me," she whispered. "My gift to
you shall be your life and the lives of the women. Accept my gift. Remember the old man. Think of him before you choose."

She stopped as the door to the tower slipped open to admit a handful
of the stick men. They came to her in a scuttling of wooden legs, clustering about her. She bent low about them for a moment, then straightened,
glancing coldly at Wil.

"You have brought a Demon into the Hollows," she cried. "A Demon—
after all these years! It must be found and destroyed. Wisp—his gift!"

The furry creature hastened forward and took from the helpless Valeman the pouch and the Elfstones. The wizened face glanced up at him,
then withdrew behind the folds of Mallenroh's cloak. The Witch lifted her
hand, and Wil felt himself grow suddenly weak.

"Remember what you have seen, Elfling." Her voice seemed distant
now. "I hold the power of life and death. Choose wisely."

She moved past him and disappeared through the open door. His
strength began to fail, his vision to blur. At his side, Eretria collapsed on
the tower floor.

Then he was also falling. The last thing he remembered was the feel of
wooden fingers closing tight about his body.

44

"Wil."

The sound of his name hung like an echo strayed in the black haze which enveloped him. The voice seemed to come from a great distance, floating downward through the dark to probe him in his sleep. He stirred sluggishly, feeling as if he were weighted and bound. With a great effort, he reached up from within himself, searching.

"Wil, are you all right?"

The voice belonged to Amberle. He blinked, forcing himself awake.

"Wil?"

She was cradling his head in her lap, her face bent close to his own, her long chestnut hair trailing down about him like a veil.

"Amberle?" he asked sleepily, pushing himself upright. Then he reached for her wordlessly and held her close against him.

"I thought I had lost you," he managed.

"And I you." She laughed softly, her arms tight about his neck. "You have been sleeping for hours, ever since they brought you here."

The Valeman nodded into her shoulder, aware suddenly of the pungent smell of incense in the air. He realized it was the incense that was making him feel so groggy. Gently he released the Elven girl and looked about. They were enclosed by a windowless cell, black but for a single light that shone from within a glass container suspended from a ceiling chain, another of the lights that burned neither oil nor pitch and gave off no smoke. One wall of the cell was composed entirely of iron bars fastened vertically into the stone of the floor and ceiling. A single door opened through the bars, fastened in place by hinges on one side and a massive key lock on the other. Within the cell had been placed a pitcher of water, an iron basin, towels, blankets, and three straw-filled sleeping mats. On one of the mats lay Eretria, her breathing deep and even. Beyond the wall of iron bars was a passageway that ran to a set of stairs, then disappeared into blackness.

Amberle followed his gaze to the Rover girl. "I think she is all right—just sleeping. Until now, I have not been able to wake either of you."

"Mallenroh," he whispered, remembering. "Has she harmed you?"

Amberle shook her head. "She has barely spoken to me. In fact, I did not even know who it was that had taken me prisoner at first. The stick men brought me here, and I slept for a time. Then she came to me. She told me that there were others searching for me, that they would be brought to her as I had been brought. Then she left." Sea-green eyes sought his own. "She frightens me, Wil—she is beautiful, but so cold."

"She is a monster. How did she find you in the first place?"

Amberle paled. "Something chased me down into the Hollows. I never saw it, but I could feel it—something evil, searching for me." She paused. "I ran for as long as I was able, then I crawled. Finally I just collapsed. The stick men must have found me and brought me to her. Wil, was it Mallenroh I sensed?"

The Valeman shook his head. "No. It was the Reaper."

She stared at him wordlessly for a moment, then looked away. "And now it is here in the Hollows, isn't it?"

He nodded. "The Witch knows about it, though. She has gone to look for it." He smiled grimly. "Maybe they will destroy each other."

She did not smile back. "How did you manage to find me?"

He told her then everything that had happened since he had left her concealed in the bushes on the rim of the Hollows—the encounter with Eretria, the deaths of Cephelo and the Rovers, the recovery of the Elfstones, the flight back through the Wilderun, the meeting with Hebel and Drifter, the journey down into the Hollows, the discovery of the stick man, and the confrontation with Mallenroh. He finished by telling her what the Witch had done to Hebel.

"That poor old man," she whispered, and there were tears in her eyes. "He meant no harm to her. Why did she do that to him?"

"She doesn't care a whit about any of us," the Valeman replied. "All that interests her are the Elfstones. She means to have them, Amberle. Hebel was just a convenient example for the rest of us—particularly me."

"But you won't give them to her, will you?"

He looked at her uncertainly. "If it means saving our lives, I will. We have to get out of here."

The Elven girl shook her head slowly. "I don't think that she will let us go, Wil—not even if you give her what she wants. Not after what you have told me about Hebel."

He was silent a moment. "I know. But maybe we can bargain with her. She would agree to anything to get the Stones . . ." He stopped abruptly, listening. "Shhh. Someone is coming."

They peered wordlessly through the bars of their cell into the darkness of the corridor beyond. There was a slight shuffling sound upon the stairs. Then a figure appeared within the fringe of their single light. It was Wisp.

"Something to eat," he announced brightly, holding forth a tray with pieces of bread and fruit on it. Shuffling to the cell, he slipped the tray through a narrow slot in the bars at the base of the door.

"Good food," he told them, turning to leave.

"Wisp!" Wil called after him. The furry creature turned, staring at the Valeman quizzically. "Can you stay and talk with us?" Wil asked.

The wizened face broke into a grin. "Wisp will talk with you."

Wil glanced at Amberle. "The ankle—can you walk?"

She nodded. "It's much better," she answered him.

He took her hand and led her to the tray of food. Wordlessly, they seated themselves. Wisp hunched down on the lowest step of the darkened stairway, his head cocking. Wil helped himself to a piece of the bread, chewed and nodded in appreciation.

"Very good, Wisp."

The little fellow grinned. "Very good."

Wil smiled. "How long have you been here, Wisp?"

"A long time. Wisp serves the Lady."

"Did the Lady make you—as she made those stick men?"

The furry creature laughed. "Stick men—clack, clack. Wisp serves the Lady—but not made of wood." His eyes brightened. "Elf, like you."

Wil was surprised. "But you are so small. And what about the hair?" He pointed to his own arms and legs, then to Wisp. "Did she do that?"

The Elf nodded happily. "Cute, she says. Makes Wisp cute. Roll and jump and play with stick men. Cute." He stopped and glanced past them to where Eretria slept. "Pretty thing." He pointed. "Prettiest of all."

"What do you know about Morag?" the Valeman pressed, ignoring Wisp's obvious interest in the Rover girl.

Wisp's face screwed itself up into a grimace. "Evil Morag. Very bad. A long time she lives within the Hollows, she and the Lady. Sisters. Morag in the east, the Lady in the west. Stick men for both, but just Wisp for the Lady."

"Do they ever go out of the Hollows—Morag and the Lady?"

Wisp shook his head solemnly. "Never."

"Why not?"

"No magic beyond the Hollows." Wisp grinned cunningly.

That told Wil something he had not suspected. The power of the Witch Sisters had its limits; it did not extend beyond the Hollows. That explained why no one had ever encountered them anywhere else within the Westland. He began to see a glimmer of hope. If he could find a way to get clear of the Hollows . . .

"Why does the Lady hate Morag so?" Amberle was asking.

Wisp thought a minute. "Long ago, there was a man. Beautiful, the Lady says. The Lady wanted him. Morag wanted him. Each tried to take the man. The man . . ." He clenched his hands, fingers joining, then wrenched them apart. "No more. Gone." He shook his head. "Morag killed the man. Evil Morag."

Evil Mallenroh, Wil thought. In any case, it was clear enough how the Witch Sisters felt about each other. He decided to find out what else Wisp knew about the Hollows.

"Do you ever go out of the tower, Wisp?" he asked.

The wizened face broke into a proud grin. "Wisp serves the Lady."

Wil took that answer as a yes. "Have you ever gone to Spire's Reach?" he asked.

"Safehold," Wisp replied at once.

There was a hushed silence. Amberle gripped Wil's arm and glanced at him quickly. The Valeman was so stunned by the abruptness of the response that he was left momentarily speechless. Collecting himself, he hunched forward, crooking his finger conspiratorially. Wisp inched a bit closer, head cocked.

"Tunnels and tunnels that wind and twist," Wil said. "Easy to get lost in those tunnels, Wisp."

The furry Elf shook his head. "Not Wisp."

"No?" he challenged. "What of the door made of glass that will not break?"

Wisp thought a moment, then clapped his hands excitedly. "No, no, just pretend glass. Wisp knows pretend glass. Wisp serves the Lady."

Wil was trying to decipher that answer when Wisp pointed past them. "Look. Pretty thing, hello, hello."

The Valeman and the Elven girl turned around. Eretria was sitting up on the straw mat, awake at last, her black tresses falling down about her face as she rubbed the back of her neck. Slowly she looked up at them, started to speak, then caught Wil's warning finger as it passed before his lips. She glanced past him to where Wisp crouched half-a-dozen feet from the bars of their cell, grinning broadly.

"Pretty thing, hello," Wisp repeated, one hand lifting tentatively.

"Hello," she replied uncertainly. Then, seeing Wil's quick nod of encouragement, she flashed her most dazzling smile. "Hello, Wisp."

"Talk with you, pretty thing." Wisp had forgotten all about Wil and Amberle.

Eretria rose unsteadily, her eyes blinking with sleep, and came over to sit with her companions. She scanned quickly the stairs and the passageway beyond.

"What game are we playing now, Healer?" she whispered out of the corner of her mouth. There was fear in her dark eyes, but she kept her voice even.

The Valeman did not look away from Wisp. "Just trying to learn something that will get us out of here."

She nodded approvingly, then wrinkled her nose. "What is that smell?"

"Incense. I can't be sure, but I think that it acts like a drug when you breathe it in. I think that is what is making us feel so weak."

Eretria turned back to Wisp. "What does the incense do, Wisp?"

The furry Elf reflected, then shrugged. "Nice smell. No worries."

"Indeed," the Rover girl muttered, glancing at Wil. She gave Wisp another broad smile. "Can you open the door, Wisp?" she asked, pointing at the bars.

Wisp smiled back. "Wisp serves the Lady, pretty one. You stay."

Eretria did not change her expression. "Is the Lady here now, in the tower?"

"She looks for the Demon," Wisp answered. "Very bad. Breaks all her stick men apart." His wizened face grimaced. "She will hurt the Demon." He rubbed two fingers together. "Make him go away." Then he brightened. "Wisp could show you wooden statues. Little man and dog. In the box, pretty things like you."

He pointed to Eretria, who went pale and shook her head quickly. "I don't think so, Wisp. Just talk with me."

Wisp nodded agreeably. "Just talk."

Listening to their conversation, Wil had a sudden thought. He sat forward, gripping the bars of their cell.

"Wisp, what did the Lady do with the Elfstones?"

Wisp glanced at him. "In the box, safe in the box."

"What box, Wisp? Where does the Lady keep this box?"

Wisp pointed disinterestedly toward the darkened passageway behind him, all the while keeping his eyes fixed on Eretria. "Talk, pretty thing," he pleaded.

Wil glanced at Amberle and shrugged. He was not having much success coaxing anything more out of Wisp. The little fellow was only interested in talking with Eretria.

The Rover girl crossed her legs before her and rocked back. "Would you show me the pretty stones, Wisp? Could I see them?"

Wisp glanced about furtively. "Wisp serves the Lady. Faithful Wisp." He paused, considering. "Show you wooden figures, pretty one."

Eretria shook her head. "Just talk, Wisp. Why do you have to stay here in the Hollows? Why don't you leave?"

"Wisp serves the Lady." Wisp repeated his favorite response anxiously, and his face grew troubled. "Never leaves the Hollows. Cannot leave."

From somewhere high within the tower, a bell rang once and was still. Wisp rose hurriedly.

"Lady calls," he told them, starting up the stairs.

"Wisp!" Wil called after him. The little fellow stopped. "Will the Lady let us leave if I give her the Elfstones?"

Wisp did not seem to understand. "Leave?"

"Go out of the Hollows?" Will pressed.

Wisp shook his head quickly. "Never leave. Never. Wooden figures." He waved to Eretria. "Pretty thing for Wisp. Take good care of pretty thing. Talk some more. Talk later."

He turned and darted up the stairs into the gloom. Wordlessly, the prisoners watched him go. Above them, the bell sounded a second time, its echo reverberating into silence.

Wil spoke first. "Wisp could be wrong. Mallenroh wants the Elfstones badly. I think she would let us leave the Hollows if I agreed to give them to her."

They huddled down before the door of their cell, eyes drifting uneasily to the darkness of the stairway beyond.

"Wisp is not wrong." Amberle shook her head slowly. "Hebel told us that no one goes into the Hollows. And he said that no one ever comes out, either."

"The Elven girl is right," Eretria agreed. "The Witch will never let us go. She will make wooden figures of us all."

"Well, then, we had better come up with another plan." Wil gripped the bars of the cell, testing their strength.

Eretria rose, peering guardedly into the gloom of the stairway. "I have another plan, Healer," she said softly.

She reached down into her right boot, separated the folds of leather along the inner side, and extracted a narrow metal rod with a curious hook at one end. Then she reached into her left boot and pulled forth the dagger she had displayed to Wil when they had been surprised by Hebel on the rim of the Hollows. She held up the dagger with a quick grin, then slipped it back into the boot.

"How did Mallenroh miss that?" Wil asked her in surprise.

The Rover girl shrugged. "She did not bother to have the stick men search me. She was too busy making us feel helpless."

She moved to the cell door and began examining the lock.

"What are you doing?" Wil came over to her.

"I am getting us out of here," she declared, peering carefully into the keyhole. She glanced back at him momentarily and indicated the metal rod. "Picklock. No Rover would be without one. Too many ill-advised citizens spend their time trying to keep us locked up. I guess they don't trust us." She winked at Amberle, who frowned.

"Some of those people probably have good reason not to trust you," Amberle suggested.

"Probably." Eretria blew dust from the lock. "We all deceive one another at times—don't we, *sister* Amberle?"

"Wait a minute." Wil dropped down beside her, ignoring the exchange. "Once you succeed in picking that lock, Eretria, what do we do then?"

The Rover girl looked at him as if he were a fool. "We run, Healer—just as fast and as far as we can away from this place."

The Valeman shook his head. "We can't do that. We have to stay."

"We have to stay?" she repeated in disbelief.

"For a while, at least." Will glanced momentarily at Amberle, then made his decision. "Eretria, I think this might be a good time to put aside a few of those deceptions you mentioned. Listen carefully."

He motioned for Amberle to join them, and the three hunched down together in the gloom. Quickly Wil explained to the Rover girl the truth of who Amberle was, who he was, why they had come into the Wilderun and what it was that they were really seeking. He left nothing out in his narration, for it was necessary now that Eretria appreciate the importance of their search for the Bloodfire. They were in grave danger in this tower, but the danger to them would not lessen, even if they were to get clear of it. If anything were to happen to him, he wanted to be certain that the Rover girl would do what she could to see that Amberle escaped the Hollows.

He finished, and Eretria stared at him wordlessly. She turned to Amberle.

"Is all this true, Elven girl? I trust you better, I think."

Amberle nodded. "It is all true."

"And you are determined to stay until you find this Bloodfire?"

Amberle nodded again.

The Rover girl shook her head doubtfully. "Can I see this seed you carry?"

Amberle withdrew the Ellcrys seed, carefully wrapped in white canvas, from within her tunic. She unwrapped it and held it forth, silver-white and perfectly formed. Eretria stared at it. Then the doubt faded from her eyes, and she turned again to Wil.

"I go where you go, Wil Ohmsford. If you say we must stay, then the matter is settled. Still, we have to get out of this cell."

"All right," Wil agreed. "Then we find Wisp."

"Wisp?"

"We need him. He knows where Mallenroh has hidden the Elfstones and all about Safehold, its tunnels, and its secrets. He knows the Hollows. If we have Wisp to guide us, then we have a chance to do what we came here to do and still escape."

Eretria nodded. "First we have to escape from here. It will take me awhile to figure out this lock. Be as quiet as you can. Watch the stairs."

Carefully she inserted the hooked metal rod into the keyhole and began to work it about.

Wil and Amberle moved to the far end of the iron bars where they could watch more closely the darkened passageway leading down the flight of stairs from the tower. The minutes slipped away, and still Eretria did not open the cell door. Faint scrapings cut through the deep silence as the hooked rod moved about within the lock, the Rover girl muttering as time and again the latch mechanism slipped free. Amberle crouched close against Wil, and her hand rested loosely on his knee.

"What will you do if she fails?" the Elven girl whispered after a time.

Wil kept his eyes on the passageway. "She won't."

Amberle nodded. "But if she does—what then?"

He shook his head.

"I do not want you to give Mallenroh the Elfstones," Amberle announced quietly.

"We have been over that. I have to get you out of here."

"Once she has the Stones, she will destroy us."

"Not if I handle it right."

"Listen to me!" Her voice was angry. "Mallenroh has no regard for human life. Humans serve no purpose in her eyes beyond the uses she may put them to. Hebel did not understand that when he met her that first time on the rim of the Hollows sixty years ago. All he could see was the beauty and the magic with which she cloaked herself, the dreams she spun with her words, the impressions she left by her passing—all fabrication. He did not see the evil that lay beneath—not until it was too late."

"I am not Hebel."

She took a deep breath. "No. But I worry that your concern for me and what I have come here to do is beginning to color your judgment.

You have such determination, Wil. You think that you can overcome any obstacle, however formidable. I envy you your determination—it is something that I sadly lack."

She took his hands in her own. "I just want you to understand that I depend on you. Call it what you wish—I need your strength, your conviction, your determination. But neither that nor what you feel for me must be allowed to distort your judgment. If it does, we are both lost."

"Determination is just about all I have to work with," he responded, eyes shifting momentarily to find hers. "Nor do I agree with you that you lack that same determination."

"But I do, Wil. Allanon knew that when he chose you to be my protector. He knew, I think, how important your own determination would be to our survival. And without it, Wil, we would have been dead long ago." She paused, her voice softening further until she could barely be heard. "But you are wrong when you say that I do not lack that same determination. I do. I always have."

"I do not believe that."

She caught his sudden glance down. "You do not know me as well as you think, Wil."

He studied her face. "What do you mean?"

"I mean that there are things about me . . ." She stopped. "I mean that I am not as strong as I would like to be—not as courageous, not even as dependable as you. Remember, Wil, when we began the journey from Havenstead? You did not think much of me then. I want you to know that I did not think much of me either."

"Amberle, you were frightened. That does not . . ."

"Oh, I was frightened all right," she interrupted quickly. "I am still frightened. My being frightened is the reason for everything that has happened."

By the cell door, Eretria muttered angrily and sat back, eyeing the still tightly locked barrier. She glanced once at the Valeman and went back to work.

"What are you trying to tell me, Amberle?" Wil asked quietly.

Amberle shook her head slowly. "I suppose I am trying to work up enough courage to tell you the one thing that I have been unable to bring myself to tell you since we began this journey." She stared back into the gloomy interior of their little cell. "I suppose I want to tell you now because I do not know if I will have another chance."

"Then tell me," he encouraged.

Her child's face lifted. "The reason that I left Arborlon and did not continue as a Chosen in service to the Ellcrys was that I became so frightened of her that I could no longer bear even to be around her. That sounds foolish, I know, but hear me out, please. I have never told this to anyone. I think that my mother understood, but no one else ever has. I cannot blame them for that. I might have explained myself, but I chose not to. I felt that I could not tell anyone."

She paused. "It was difficult for me once I had been chosen by her. I knew well enough the uniqueness of my selection. I knew that I was the first woman to be chosen in five hundred years, the first woman since the time of the Second War of the Races. I accepted that, though there were many who questioned it and questioned it openly. But I was the grand-daughter of Eventine Elessedil; it was not then altogether strange that I should be chosen, I thought. And my family—especially my grandfather—were so proud.

"But the uniqueness of my selection went beyond the fact that I was a woman, I discovered. From the first day of my service, it was different for me from what it was for my companion Chosen. The Ellcrys, it was well known, seldom spoke to anyone. It was virtually unheard of for her to converse with her Chosen after the time of their selection, save in very rare instances. Even then, a conversation with her might take place once during the entire time of a Chosen's service. But from the first day for-ward, she spoke to me—not once or twice, but every day; not in passing, not in brief, but at length and with purpose. Always, I was alone; the oth-ers were never there. She would tell me when to come, and I would do so, of course. I was honored beyond belief; I was special to her, more special than anyone had ever been, and I took great pride in that."

She shook her head at the memory. "It was wonderful at first. She told me things that no one else knew, secrets of the land and the life upon it that had been lost to the races for centuries—lost or forgotten. She told me of the Great Wars, of the Race Wars, of the birth of the Four Lands and their peoples, of all that had been since the beginning of the new world. She told me something of what the old world had been like, though her memory failed her as she went back in time. Some of what she told me, I did not understand. But I understood much. I understood what she told me of growing things, of planting and nurturing. That was her gift to me, the ability to make things grow. It was a beautiful gift. And the talks were magical—just being able to hear about all those wonderful things.

"That was at first. That was when I had just begun my service and the talks were so new and exciting that I accepted what was happening with-out question. But soon something very unpleasant began to take place. This will sound odd, Wil, but I began to lose myself in her. I began to lose all sense of who I was. I wasn't *me* anymore; I was an extension of her. I still do not know if that was intentional on her part or merely the natural result of our close relationship. At the time, I believed it intentional. I grew frightened of what was happening to me—frightened and then an-gry. Was I expected as a Chosen to forgo my own personality, my own identity, in order to satisfy her needs? I was being toyed with, I felt; I was being used. It was wrong.

"The rest of the Chosen began to see a change in me. They began to suspect, I think, that there was something different about my relationship with the Ellcrys. I felt them avoiding me; I felt them watching. All the while, I was losing myself in her—a little more of me gone with every day. I was determined to stop it. I began avoiding her as the other Chosen avoided me. I refused to go to her when she asked; I sent another in my stead. When she asked me what was wrong, I would not tell her. I was frightened of her; I was ashamed of myself; I was angry at the whole situation."

Her mouth tightened. "At last I decided that the real problem was that I was never meant to be a Chosen. I did not seem able to cope with the responsibility, to understand what was expected of me. She had done something for me that she had done for no other Chosen—a wondrous, marvelous thing—and I could not accept it. It was wrong that I should feel this way; none of the others would have reacted as I had. My selection as a Chosen had been a mistake.

"So, I left, Wil, barely a month after my choosing. I told my mother and my grandfather that I was leaving, that I could no longer continue to serve. I did not tell them why. I could not bring myself to do that. Failing as a Chosen was bad enough. But to fail because she had made demands on me that anyone else would have been pleased to meet—no. I could admit to myself what had happened between the Ellcrys and me, but I could not admit it to anyone else. My mother seemed to understand. My grandfather did not. There were harsh words exchanged that left us both bitter. I went out of Arborlon disgraced in my own eyes as well as in the eyes of my family and my people, determined that I would not come back again. I swore an Elven vow of outland service; I would make my home in one of the other lands and teach what I knew of the care and preservation of the earth and her life. I traveled until I found Havenstead. That became my home."

There were tears in her eyes. "But I was wrong. I can say that now—I must say it. I walked away from a responsibility that was mine. I walked away from my fears and my frustrations. I disappointed everyone and in the end, I left my companion Chosen to die without me."

"You judge yourself too harshly," Wil admonished her.

"Do I?" Her mouth twisted. "I am afraid that I do not judge myself harshly enough. If I had remained in Arborlon, perhaps the Ellcrys would have spoken sooner of her dying. I was the one to whom she had spoken before—not the others. They did not even realize what had taken place. She might have spoken to me, soon enough that the Bloodfire could have been found and the seed planted before the Forbidding began to crumble and the Demons to break through. Don't you see, Wil? If that is so, then all the Elven dead must be on my conscience."

"It is equally possible," the Valeman pointed out, "that had you not gone out from Arborlon, but remained as you suggest, the warning from the Ellcrys would have come no sooner than it did. Then you would lie dead with the others and be of no use whatsoever to the Elves still living."

"You are asking me to justify my actions through the convenience of hindsight."

He shook his head. "I am asking you not to use hindsight to second-guess what is past. Perhaps it was intended that matters should work out the way they have. You cannot know." His voice hardened. "Now listen to me a minute. Suppose that the Ellcrys had decided to select another of your companion Chosen as the one to whom she would speak. Would that Chosen have reacted any differently from how you did to the experience? Would another have been immune to the emotions that affected you? I do not think so, Amberle. I know you. Maybe I know you better than anyone, after what we have been through. You have strength of character, you have conviction and, despite what you say, you have determination."

He took her chin in his hand and held it. "I do not know anyone—anyone, Amberle—who would have weathered this journey and all its perils any better than you have. I think that it is time for me to tell you what you are so fond of telling me. Believe in yourself. Stop doubting. Stop second-guessing. Just believe. Put a little trust in yourself. Amberle, you merit that trust."

She was crying openly, silently. "I do care for you."

"And I for you." He kissed her forehead, no longer doubting. "Very much."

She lowered her head against his shoulder, and he held her. When she looked up at him again, the tears were gone.

"I want you to promise me something," she told him.

"All right."

"I want you to promise me that you will make certain that I see this quest through to its conclusion—that I do not falter, that I do not stray, that I do not fail to do what I came to do. Be my strength and my conscience. Promise me."

He smiled gently. "I promise."

"I am still afraid," she confessed softly.

At the door to their cell, Eretria stood up. "Healer!"

Wil scrambled to his feet, Amberle with him, and together they hurried over to join the Rover girl. Her black eyes danced. Wordlessly she slipped the metal rod from the keyhole and returned it to her boot. Then with a wink at the Valeman, she grasped the iron bars to the cell door and pulled. The door swung silently open.

Wil Ohmsford gave her a triumphant grin. Now if they could only find Wisp.

45

They found him almost immediately. They had left the cell, moved to the bottom of the stairway, and were peering upward tentatively into the gloom of the passageway when they heard the sound of approaching footfalls. Quickly, Wil motioned Eretria to one side of the passage opening, while drawing Amberle back against the other. Flattened against the stone, they waited expectantly as the footsteps drew closer, a light, familiar scuttling sound that Wil recognized at once.

Seconds later, Wisp's wizened face poked out of the darkness of the passage.

"Pretty one, hello, hello. Talk with Wisp? . . ."

Wil's hand latched firmly onto his neck. Wisp gasped in fright, struggling madly to break free as the Valeman lifted him clear of the floor.

"Keep still!" Wil whispered in warning, yanking the little fellow about so that he could see who had him.

Wisp's eyes went wide. "No, no, cannot leave!"

"Be quiet!" Wil shook him until he was still. "One more word, and I will snap your neck, Wisp."

Wisp nodded frantically, his wiry form squirming in the Valeman's grip. Wil dropped to one knee, lowering his captive to the floor again, still holding tightly to his neck. Wisp's eyes were like saucers.

"Now listen carefully, Wisp," the Valeman said. "I want the Elfstones back again, and you are going to show me what the Witch has done with them. Do you understand?"

Wisp shook his head violently. "Wisp serves the Lady! Cannot leave!"

"In a box, you said." Wil ignored him. "Take me to where she keeps that box."

"Wisp serves the Lady! Wisp serves the Lady!" the little fellow repeated in desperation. "You stay! Go back!"

Wil was momentarily at a loss. Then Eretria stepped forward, her dark face just inches from Wisp's. The dagger flashed from her boot and fastened against the little fellow's throat.

"Listen, you little furball!" she said. "If you do not take us to the Elfstones at once, I will cut your throat from one ear to the other. You won't serve anybody then."

Wisp grimaced horribly. "Don't hurt Wisp, pretty one. Like you, pretty one. Care for you. Don't hurt Wisp."

"Where are the Elfstones?" she asked, moving the dagger blade tighter against the Elf's throat.

Abruptly the tower bell sounded—once, twice, three times, then a fourth. Wisp let out a frightened moan and thrashed violently against Wil's grip. The Valeman shook him angrily.

"What's happening, Wisp? What is it?"

Wisp slumped down helplessly. "Morag comes," he whimpered.

"Morag?" Wil felt a sudden sense of desperation. What brought Morag to her sister's keep? He glanced quickly at the others, but the confusion in his eyes was mirrored in theirs.

"Wisp serves the Lady," Wisp muttered and began to cry.

Wil looked about hurriedly. "We need something to bind his hands."

Eretria loosened the long sash about her waist and used it to tie Wisp's hands behind his back. Wil picked up the loose ends and wrapped them about one hand.

"Listen to me, Wisp." He jerked the moaning Elf's chin upright until their eyes met. "Listen to me!" Wisp listened. "I want you to take us to where the Lady keeps the Elfstones. If you try to run or if you try to give any warning, you know what will happen to you, don't you?"

He waited patiently until Wisp nodded. "Then do not be foolish enough to try. Just take us to the Elfstones."

Wisp started to say something, but Eretria brought the dagger up at once. Meekly, the little fellow nodded one time more.

"Good for you, Wisp." Wil released his chin. "Now let's go."

In a line, they started up the stairway, Wisp leading, Wil just a step behind, holding firmly onto the sash that bound Wisp's arms, Eretria and Amberle trailing. Into the blackness they went, eyes peering blindly, hands groping to find the stone walls of the passage. For several moments they were in total blackness. Then a new light glimmered ahead, and the faint outline of the stairs reappeared from the dark. A globe similar to the one that had illuminated their cell came into view, and they passed beneath it. Ahead, others flickered through the gloom.

The climb wore on, the stairway spiralling upward through the tower. From time to time they passed black, empty passageways tunneling through the stone and isolated doors, closed and latched, but Wisp did not slow. The bells had gone still after the first sounding; the entire tower lay wrapped in silence. The musky smell of incense burned more strongly as they climbed, filling the stairwell with its pungent odor. It made the Valeman and the women groggy, and they tried not to breathe it. Wil began to grow suspicious as the minutes slipped away. Perhaps Wisp was smarter than he appeared.

But then they reached a landing and Wisp stopped. He pointed down a dimly lighted corridor that ran a short distance into the tower and ended at a massive, ironbound door. From beyond the door came the sound of voices.

Wil bent down hurriedly. "What is it, Wisp?"

The wizened face was furtive and beaded with sweat. "Morag," Wisp whispered, then shook his head quickly. "Very bad. Very bad."

Wil straightened. "Morag is not our concern. Where are the Elfstones?"

Wisp again pointed to the door. Wil hesitated, staring at him uncertainly. Was Wisp telling him the truth? Then Eretria knelt down next to the little fellow, her voice gentle this time, the dagger no longer in view.

"Wisp, are you certain?"

Wisp nodded. "Not lie, pretty one. Don't hurt Wisp."

"I do not want to hurt you," she assured him, her eyes holding his. "But you serve the Lady, not us. Are we to believe what you say?"

"Wisp serves the Lady," Wisp agreed rather weakly, then shook his head. "Wisp does not lie. Pretty stones there, across great hall, in small room at top of stairs, in box with pretty flowers, red and gold."

Eretria stared at him a moment longer, then glanced at Wil and nodded. She believed him, she was saying. Wil nodded back.

"Is there any other way to get to the box?" Wil pressed the little Elf.

Wisp shook his head. "One door." He pointed down the corridor.

Wil looked at him silently for a moment, then motioned for the others to follow. Quietly, he crept down the short passageway until he stood before the door. Beyond, voices rose, shrill and angry. Whatever was taking place in there, Wil wanted no part of it. He took a deep breath, then slowly, carefully released the latch that held the door before him and pulled. The door slipped open just a crack. The Valeman peered through.

Beyond was the hall where Mallenroh had seized them, massive and shadowed, illuminated faintly by a handful of the strange, smokeless lights that hung like spiders from an invisible ceiling. Immediately past the door, a landing swept downward in a series of half-circle steps to the floor of the hall. There hundreds of the stick men jammed tightly together, encircling two willowy black figures that faced each other at less than a dozen paces and shrieked as if they were cats at bay.

Wil Ohmsford stared. The Witch Sisters, Morag and Mallenroh, last of their Coven, bitter enemies through a centuries-old conflict forgotten by everyone but themselves, were identical twins. Black robes flung back from their tall figures, woven gray hair trailing nightshade, flawless white skin, ghostlike in the dark—they were mirror images. Both were exquisitely formed, both lithe and delicate. But at this moment their beauty was marred by the hatred that contorted their features and hardened their violet eyes. Their words reached out to the Valeman, softer now as the shrieking subsided, yet harsh and biting.

"My power is as strong as your own, Sister, and I fear nothing that you might do. You cannot even keep me from this dreary refuge of yours. We are as rock to stone, and neither one nor the other may prevail." The speaker shook her head mockingly. "But you would change all that, Sister. You would seek to arm yourself with magic that does not belong to you. In so doing, you would bring an end to our shared dominion over these Hollows. Foolish, Sister. You can have no secrets from me. I know as soon as you what it is that you intend." She paused. "And I know of the Elfstones."

"You know nothing," shrieked the other, whom Wil now saw to be Mallenroh. "Go from my home, Sister. Go while still you may or I will find a way to make you wish that you had."

Morag laughed. "Be still, foolish one. You cannot frighten me. I will leave when I have what I came to get."

"The Elfstones are mine!" Mallenroh snapped. "I have them and will hold on to them. The gift was meant for me."

"Sister, no gift shall be yours if I do not wish it. Such power as the Elfstones offer must belong to her who is best suited to wield it. That one is me. It has always been me."

"You have never been better suited to anything, Sister." Mallenroh spat. "I have permitted you to share this valley with me because you were the last of my sisters, and I felt some pity for one as ugly and purposeless as yourself. Think on it, Sister. I have always had my share of pretty things; but you, you have had nothing but the company of your voiceless stick men." Her voice became a hiss. "Remember the human you tried to take from me, the beautiful one that was mine, the one you wanted so badly? Remember, Sister? Why even that pretty one was lost to you, wasn't he? So careless you were that you let him be destroyed."

Morag stiffened. "It was you who destroyed him, Sister."

"I?" Mallenroh laughed. "One touch from you and he withered with horror."

Morag's face was frozen with rage. "Give me the Elfstones."

"I will give you nothing!"

Crouched motionlessly behind the massive wooden door, Wil Ohmsford felt a hand on his shoulder and he jumped in surprise. Eretria peered past him through the crack. "What is happening?"

"Stay back," he whispered, and his own eyes returned at once to the confrontation taking place within the hall.

Morag had come forward and now stood directly in front of Mallenroh.

"Give me the Elfstones. You must give them to me."

"Go back to the hole out of which you crawled, lizard." Mallenroh sneered. "Go back to your empty nest."

"Snake! You would feed on your own kind!"

Mallenroh screamed. "Ugly thing! Leave now!"

Morag's hand whipped from beneath her robe and struck Mallenroh a stinging blow across the face. The sound reverberated through the stillness. Mallenroh staggered back in surprise. The wooden limbs of the stick men rattled as they shifted anxiously about the cavernous hall, moving away from the two antagonists.

Then Mallenroh's laughter rose sharply, unexpectedly. "You are pitiful, Sister. You cannot hurt me. Go home. Wait for me to come to you. Wait for me to give you the death you merit. You are not worth having as a slave."

Morag came forward and struck her again, a quick, sudden blow that brought a shriek of rage from Mallenroh. "Give me the Elfstones!" Morag's voice had a desperate edge to it. "I will have them, Sister! I will have them! Give them to me!"

She came at Mallenroh, hands closing about her sister's throat. Mallenroh lurched back again, her beautiful face twisting with rage. Down upon the floor of the tower the Witch Sisters tumbled, scratching and clawing at each other like cats. Then Mallenroh broke free and scrambled back to her feet. One hand stretched forth. Instantly a massive root broke forth from the stone at her feet to wrap tightly about Morag's writhing form. Upward it swept toward the darkness, carrying the struggling Morag with it and growing huge and towering as it reached beyond the glow of the lamps. Morag screamed. Abruptly the darkness blazed with a brilliant flash, and green fire burned the length of the root, turning it to ash. It crumpled lifelessly, smoke billowing out from its remains in thick clouds. Then Morag reappeared, floating downward through the haze like some wraith, to stand again upon the tower floor.

Mallenroh shrieked with frustration, and the green fire swept now from her fingers, engulfing her sister. Morag struck back. For an instant, both were consumed by the fire, their cries filling the hall. Then the fire was gone, and the Sisters stood face to face once more, tall black forms circling slightly away from each other.

"I shall be free of you this time," Mallenroh whispered, her voice filled with cold fury, and she leaped at her sister.

Morag met the rush and threw Mallenroh back. Again the green fire lanced from her fingers. Mallenroh's cry rose high and terrible, and she disappeared in a wall of smoke. An instant later she emerged a dozen feet to the right, fire bursting from her hands. Back and forth the Sisters darted, attacking each other in a frenzied whirl. Sparks from the green fire showered into the hapless stick men; in moments, dozens of them were aflame.

Once more the Sisters closed, grappling wildly, fire lancing from their fingers. Black robes flew wide as they swept together, and the fire burst like a massive pillar out of the stone floor beneath them. A terrible shriek came from both throats as hands locked and their tall forms straightened with the force of their struggle. Flame spattered like water thrown to the far corners of the hall, sparking and burning into the milling stick men. Heat exploded from the pillar of fire with such intensity that it swept through the crack in the door behind which crouched the Valeman and his companions and singed their faces.

Then the tower itself began to shudder, stone and wood shaking free in chips and splinters that cascaded downward through the smoke and gloom. Wil watched the pillar of fire rise from the Witch Sisters to lick hungrily at the great wooden beams that were the tower's support. Everywhere the stick men were burning, spreading the flames across the length and breadth of the hall.

Wil came hurriedly to his feet. If they remained where they were any longer, the flames would trap them. Worse, the entire tower might collapse and bury them. They would have to break out now. It would be dangerous, but less so than staying where they were.

He thrust Wisp before the crack in the door. "Where is the room with the box, Wisp?" Wisp was moaning and sobbing. Wil shook him angrily. "Show me the room!"

Wisp pointed through the door. Far to their right, nearly all the way across the hall, was a narrow, spiralling stairway that ran upward to a landing and a solitary door.

Wil looked quickly at Amberle. Her injured ankle would slow her. "Can you make it?" he asked. She nodded wordlessly. He looked at Eretria, and she nodded as well. He took a deep breath. "Then let's go."

With the struggling Wisp tucked under one arm, he pulled wide the wooden door and darted through. Heat from the flames came at him like a wall, searing his face, burning down his throat. He lowered his head, followed the tower wall to the right, and bounded down the half-circle steps. Stick men milled about him in confusion, but he knocked them aside, clearing the way for his companions. Down to the tower floor they went, skirting the scattered fires, pushing and shoving toward the distant stairs.

Then abruptly the pillar of fire thrust upward in an explosion that threw them all flat. Dazed, they scrambled back to their knees, watching as the struggle between the Witch Sisters intensified. The fire suddenly began to change from mystic green to crackling yellow, a true and natural flame. The Sisters screamed. The fire leaped and streaked along their slender limbs, down the tangle of their long gray hair. It was burning them.

"Sister!" cried one in a wail of recognition and fear.

There was a crackle of burning flesh; with astonishing quickness, the conflagration curled about the Witch Sisters like a shroud and they were consumed. One minute they were standing there, locked in furious battle; the next they were gone. Immune to each other's power, they were unable to survive a joining of the two. All that remained was a shrinking lump of ash and blackened flesh.

Wil heard Amberle gasp in horror. Then the stick men were falling, collapsing like rag dolls, arms and legs separating from bodies, fingers and toes wilting, until nothing was left of them but a vast pile of smoldering deadwood. The magic that had made them and kept them had died with the Witch Sisters. In the burning hall, nothing remained alive but the three outlanders and Wisp.

Their time was growing short. Choking as smoke billowed over him, Wil sprang back to his feet. Holding fast to Wisp, he pushed ahead through the flames and the smoke, kicking aside what remained of the stick men as he went, calling wildly to Amberle and Eretria to follow him. Wisp was crying and muttering, but Wil had little patience with that and ignored him, struggling onto the stairway at the far side of the room and stumbling upward. At the landing, he groped for the latch that held the door closed, praying that it would open. It did. Eyes watering, throat raw and burning, he pushed his way inside.

The roar of the fire followed him, drowning out Wisp's frantic cries. The room was a maze of dark silks and nightshade that trailed along walls and down iron trelliswork. Anxiously the Valeman peered through the dark, finding at last what he sought. On a table at the far side of the chamber, nestled amid clusters of ornaments and jars of incense and perfume, sat a large, intricately carved wooden box, its lid adorned with flowers painted red and gold. The Elfstones! A fierce joy swept through him. Wisp was screaming madly, but Wil did not hear him, dizzied by the heat and the smoke, preoccupied with regaining the Stones. He was vaguely aware of Eretria and Amberle entering the room behind him as he stumbled forward toward the box. He was reaching for the lid when Eretria cried out in warning and knocked him quickly aside.

"How many times must I save you, Healer?" she shouted to make herself heard above the roar of the fire. Snatching an iron latch bar from its hook against one wall, she edged to one side of the box and extended the bar gingerly to flip open the lid. A blur of green shot from within the box, wrapping tightly about the bar. Quickly the Rover girl hammered the bar against the stone floor, leaving the thing still curled about it, a lifeless husk.

Wil stared in horror. It was a viper.

"He was trying to warn you!" Eretria pointed to Wisp. The little fellow had collapsed in tears.

Wil was shaken so badly that for an instant he could neither move nor speak. One bite from that viper . . . Eretria prodded the wooden box with her dagger, pushing it clear of the table. It fell to the chamber floor, and a cluster of precious stones and jewelry tumbled free. In their midst lay the leather pouch. The Rover girl snatched it up, held it a moment as if deciding what should be done with it, then handed it to Wil. He took it wordlessly, loosened the drawstrings, and peered inside.

A faint smile touched his lips. The Elfstones were his once more.

A new shudder swept through the tower; in the hall beyond, one of the massive support timbers gave way, crashing downward in a shower of flames. Wil stuffed the Elfstones into his tunic and started for the door, pulling Wisp and Eretria after him. They had to get out at once.

But a sudden hammering from within a massive wooden wardrobe cabinet brought him about—a hammering that was mixed with muffled cries and the deep snarl of some animal. Wil glanced quickly at Eretria. Something was trapped within that cabinet. The Valeman hesitated only a moment. Whatever it was, it deserved a chance to get clear of the tower. He hastened to the cabinet and flipped clear the restraining latch. The doors flew back and a massive, dark form hurtled into Wil, flinging him back. Shouts rang through the smoke-filled chamber as Wil sought to ward off his attacker. Then the creature was yanked roughly aside and a familiar face came into view.

"Hebel!" Wil exclaimed, in astonishment.

"Back, Drifter!" The old man cuffed the dog sharply, extending a hand down. "What's happening here, anyway? What am I doing in that closet, for cat's sake?"

Wil came to his feet unsteadily. "Hebel! The Witch, Mallenroh—she changed you to wood! Don't you remember?" He grinned in relief. "We thought you lost! I don't see how you . . ."

Amberle took hold of his arm. "It was the magic, Wil. When Mallenroh died, so did the magic. That was why the stick men collapsed—the magic was gone. It must have happened that way with Hebel and the dog as well."

A fresh wave of smoke poured through the open doorway, and Eretria called out anxiously.

"We have to get out of here." Wil started for the door once more, still cradling the terrified Wisp beneath his arm. "Bring Amberle," he called back to Hebel.

On the landing, they stopped in dismay. The entire hall was in flames. Burning stick men littered the floor. The timbers that spanned the arched ceiling sagged and cracked, the fire burning them through. Even the stone walls had begun to shimmer redly with the heat. At the front of the hall, the entry doors stood closed and barred. Hesitantly, Wil started down the stairs, searching through the flames and smoke for a path that would take them to those doors.

Then suddenly the doors flew open with a crash, hammered back against the stone by something breaking through from without. At the bottom of the narrow stairway, Wil Ohmsford and the others stopped in surprise, peering through the wall of fire. Daylight streamed through the shattered opening, and Wil thought for just an instant that he saw something shadowy move into the hall. Uncertain, he stared past the flames, trying to decide what it was that he had seen. Had he imagined that shadow . . .

A few steps back, Drifter dropped hurriedly in a crouch, snarling and whining.

And then he knew. The Reaper! He had forgotten about the Reaper.

"Wisp!" he cried frantically, shaking the Elf so hard the wizened face whipped back and forth in front of him. "How do we get out of here? Listen to me! Show me another way out!"

"Wisp . . . out . . . over there." One arm pointed weakly.

Wil saw it—a door, to their left, perhaps twenty yards through the fire. He never hesitated. Calling to his companions to follow, he stumbled through the flames and the smoke for the door. He could almost feel the Reaper breathing over his shoulder. Somewhere back in the hall, it was coming for them.

They reached the door. Choking and gagging, Wil found the handle and twisted. This door, too, was unlocked. Pushing the others before him, he followed them through, slamming the door closed with a heave and throwing the latch bar tight.

Then they ran—down a stairwell that spiralled deep beneath the tower, through gloom lit dimly by the smokeless lights, into musty dampness that cooled their heated bodies, stumbling and lurching, footfalls echoing through the stillness. Only twice did the Valeman turn to speak as he led the others from the ruined tower, once to speak the name of their pursuer, once to warn that the Reaper had found them at last. Then no one spoke again. They simply ran.

At the bottom of the stairs, a passageway opened ahead, tunneling through the light of a scattering of the lamps and twisting from view. Down the corridor they went, Wil carrying the hunched form of Wisp, who moaned and whimpered at every step; Hebel—with Drifter beside him—and Eretria were lending support to Amberle, who still hobbled weakly upon her damaged ankle. The passageway twisted and turned through the earth, angling first one way, then another, filled with insects that skittered and dust that flew, as they ran past.

Time and again Wil glanced back through the shadows. Had something moved? Had something sounded? Tears blurred his vision, and he brushed at them angrily. Where was the Reaper? It had tracked them all the way from Arborlon to this tunnel. It was here, close; he could sense it. It was here, hunting.

Ahead, the passageway ended and a second stairwell curled upward, dark and empty. At its foot, the Valeman paused until the others were next to him, then led the way quickly onto the stairs. For long minutes they wound upward through the gloom, watching the curve of the steps slip teasingly ahead, listening for the sounds of the thing that pursued them. But they heard nothing save their own movements. Silence wrapped the passage and those who climbed it.

The stairwell ended at a trapdoor, a latchbolt thrown tight into its stone seating. Wil wrenched the bolt free, placed his shoulder against the door, and heaved upward. With a muffled thud, the trapdoor toppled back; clouded, dull sunlight spilled down into the passage. Quickly the humans and the dog stumbled from the earth.

They stood again within the Hollows, misted, gray, and still. Behind them the island keep of Mallenroh, shrouded in smoke that rose high into the trees and curled down about the moat and wall, crumbled slowly into ruin.

The forest all about lay empty. The Reaper was nowhere to be seen.

Wil glanced about uncertainly. Mist and gloom masked everything but the bright flicker of the fires that still burned within the tower of Mallenroh. Nothing else was distinguishable. The Valeman had no idea at all where they should go from there.

"Hebel, where is Spire's Reach?" he asked hurriedly.

The old man shook his head. "Can't be certain, Elfling. Can't see anything."

Wil hesitated, then knelt quickly on the forest earth and brought the cringing form of Wisp out from under his arm. Wisp had buried his face in his hands, and his furry body was curled tightly into a ball. Try as he might, the Valeman could not get the little Elf to unfold. Finally he gave up, holding Wisp by his shoulders and shaking him urgently.

"Wisp, listen to me. Wisp, you have to talk to me. Look at me, Wisp."

The little fellow peeked reluctantly through his fingers. His body shook.

"Wisp, where is Spire's Reach?" Wil asked quickly. "You have to take us to Spire's Reach."

Wisp did not respond, staring out through his parted fingers like a fascinated child for a moment, then locking his hands tight.

"Wisp!" Wil shook him again. "Wisp, answer me!"

"Wisp serves the Lady!" the Elf exclaimed suddenly. "Serves the Lady! Serves the Lady! Serves the . . ."

Wil shook him so hard his teeth rattled. "Stop it! She's dead, Wisp! The Lady is dead! You don't serve her anymore!"

Wisp went still and slowly the hands fell away from his face. He began to cry, great wracking sobs that shook his small frame. "Don't hurt Wisp," he pleaded. "Good Wisp. Don't hurt."

Then he collapsed in a ball, crying and rolling on the ground like a wounded animal. Wil stared down at him helplessly.

"Well done, Healer." Eretria sighed and stepped forward. "You've frightened him half to death. He should be of great use now." She gripped the Valeman's arm and lifted him out of the way. "Let me handle this."

Wil moved over beside Amberle and they watched in silence as the Rover girl knelt beside Wisp and cradled the sobbing Elf in her arms. Whispering softly, she held him close against her and stroked the furry head. Long moments passed and finally Wisp stopped crying. His head lifted slightly.

"Pretty thing?"

"It's all right, Wisp."

"Pretty thing take care of Wisp?"

"I'll take care of you." She gave Wil a stern look. "No one will hurt you."

"Not hurt Wisp?" The wizened face lifted to find her own. "Promise?"

Eretria gave him a reassuring smile. "I promise. But you have to help us, Wisp. Will you do that? Will you help us?"

The little fellow nodded eagerly. "Help you, pretty thing. Good Wisp."

"Good Wisp, indeed," Eretria agreed. Then she bent close to him. "But we have to hurry, Wisp. The Demon—the one that followed us into the Hollows—it still hunts for us. If it finds us, it will hurt us, Wisp."

Wisp shook his head. "Not let it hurt Wisp, pretty one."

"No, it won't hurt you, Wisp—not if we hurry." She stroked his cheek. "But we have to find this mountain—Healer, what is it called?"

"Spire's Reach," Wil offered.

She nodded. "Spire's Reach. Can you show us how to get there, Wisp? Can you take us there?"

Wisp glanced uncertainly at Wil, then past him to the burning tower. His eyes remained fixed on the tower for a moment, then shifted back to Eretria.

"I will take you, pretty one."

Eretria rose and took the little fellow's hand. "Don't worry, now. I'll take care of you, Wisp."

As they moved past Wil, the Rover girl winked. "I told you that you needed me, Healer."

They melted into the gloom of the forest. Wisp led, slipping eel-like through the mist and the tangle of the woods, Eretria's hand gripped firmly in his own. Hebel followed with Drifter, then Wil with Amberle, his arm about her waist to lend support as she limped along gamely beside him. But almost immediately, the others began to widen the distance between them; in trying to catch up, Amberle stumbled and went down. Wil did not hesitate. He simply picked up the Elven girl and went on, cradling her in his arms. To his surprise, Amberle did not protest. He had expected that she would, so fiercely self-reliant had she been throughout their journey. But she was quiet now, her head resting on his shoulder, her arms draped loosely about his neck. Not a single word passed between them.

Wil pondered her behavior momentarily, then his mind was racing on to other matters. Already he was working on a plan for their escape—not just from the Hollows, but from the Reaper as well. For it did them no good to escape from the Hollows, if they did not escape from the Reaper as well. Certainly the Hollows were dangerous, but it was the Reaper that really frightened Wil—a relentless hunter that nothing seemed able to stop, a creature that defied the laws of reason and probability and simply pushed aside the obstacles that hindered its search for the fragile woman-child the Valeman carried. He knew he must not let it find her. Even the Elfstones, could he find a way to unlock their awesome power, might not be enough to stop this creature. They must escape it, and they must escape it quickly.

He thought that he had the means to do so. It was the fifth day of their descent into the Wilderun—the last day that Perk would fly Genewen across the valley before winging home. The Valeman dropped one hand from Amberle momentarily to feel the outline of the small object that nestled in his tunic pocket—the silver whistle that Perk had given him to summon Genewen. It was their sole link to the youthful Wing Rider, and Wil had guarded it carefully. He knew that he had promised Amberle that he would not call upon the boy if their situation were not desperate, but surely it could not be more desperate than this. If they were forced to hike back through the Hollows, back through the Wilderun, and back through the whole of the lower Westland in order to reach the safety of Arborlon, they would never make it. The Reaper would find their trail and catch them. It would be foolish to believe otherwise. They must find another way back, and the only other way he knew was to fly Genewen. The Reaper would still come after them, just as it had come after them before, but by then they would be safely beyond its reach.

Maybe, he cautioned himself. Maybe. They still needed time to escape, and what time remained was slipping rapidly away from them. There had not been much to begin with, and most of that had already been used up. The Reaper hunted them. Even though they had outmaneuvered it in the ruins of the Witch Sister's tower, still it would find them again quickly enough. If they were to escape, they must reach Safehold, locate the Bloodfire, immerse the Ellcrys seed, gain the high slopes of Spire's Reach, signal Perk, who could be anywhere over the Wilderun, board Genewen, if the great Roc could carry them all, and fly to safety—all before the Reaper caught up to them. That was asking a lot, Wil knew.

The forest brushed and tore at him as he followed after Eretria's slim form, branches and vines slapping at his face. He cradled Amberle close, the strain of carrying her already beginning to wear at his arms. All about, the forest lay deep and still.

He wondered momentarily about Arborlon and the Elves. By now, the Demons must have broken through the Forbidding and flooded the Westland, and the Elven people must be engaged in the defense of their homeland. The terrible conflict that Eventine had sought to avoid must have come to pass. And what of the Ellcrys? Had Allanon found a way to protect the dying tree? Had the Druid's power been strong enough to withstand the onslaught of the Demons? Only a rebirth of the Ellcrys could save the Elves, Allanon had said. Yet how much time remained before even that would come too late? Pointless questions, Wil Ohmsford chided himself. Questions that he could not answer, for it was not possible for him to know what was happening beyond the Hollows. Yet he found himself wishing that it were possible for Allanon to reach out to him, tell him something of what was happening in the homeland of the Elves, and let him know that there was still time—if Wil could just find a way to get back again.

Despair washed through him then, sudden, frightening in its certainty—as if he knew that even if he were to succeed here in what he sought to accomplish, still it would be too late for those who awaited his return. And if that were so . . .

Wil Ohmsford did not let the thought finish itself. That way lay madness.

The terrain began to rise, gently at first, then sharply. They were upon the slopes of Spire's Reach. Rock slides and clumps of boulders materialized through the tangle of the woods, and a narrow trail curled upward into the mist. They pushed ahead. Gradually the mist began to fade, and the roof of the forest fell away below them. Large stretches of gray sky appeared through breaks in the trees, and the gloom of the lower forest began to dissipate in small streamers of sunlight. Slowly, carefully, the climbers worked their way up the slopes, catching brief glimpses through the thinning trees of the Hollows spread out beneath them in a sea of tangled limbs.

Then abruptly the trees opened before them and they stood upon a bluff that faced out across the Hollows to the higher walls of the Wilderun. Clusters of scrub and deadwood rose out of deep swatches of saw grass and ran back to the cliff face and a massive cavern that opened down into Spire's Reach like a great dark throat.

Wisp led the little company to the entrance to the cavern, skirting the maze of heavy brush, then stopped just outside and turned quickly to Eretria.

"Safehold, pretty thing—there." He pointed into the cavern. "Tunnels and tunnels that wind and twist. Safehold. Good Wisp."

The Rover girl smiled reassuringly and glanced back to Wil. "Now what?"

Wil came forward and peered unsuccessfully into the darkness. He set Amberle upon her feet momentarily and turned to find Wisp. The little fellow moved at once behind Eretria, hiding his face within the folds of her pants.

"Wisp?" Wil called him gently, but Wisp would have nothing to do with the Valeman. Wil sighed. There was no time for this foolishness.

"Eretria, ask him about a door made of glass that will not break."

The Rover girl bent down so that Wisp was facing her again.

"Wisp, it's all right. I won't let anyone hurt you. Look at me, Wisp." The little fellow raised his head and smiled uncertainly. Eretria stroked his cheek. "Wisp, can you show us a door made of glass that will not break? Do you know of such a door?"

Wisp cocked his head. "Play games, pretty thing? Play games with Wisp?"

Eretria was at a loss. She glanced quickly at Wil, who shrugged and nodded.

"Sure, we can play a game, Wisp." Eretria smiled. "Can you show us this door?"

Wisp's wizened face crinkled with glee. "Wisp can show."

He bounded up, dashed into the mouth of the cavern, then back out again to grab Eretria's hand and pull her after him. Wil shook his head hopelessly. Wisp was more than a little crazed, whether from all that had happened to him during his confinement within the Hollows or from the shock he had suffered at losing his Lady, and they were risking a great deal in believing that he could show them the chamber of the Bloodfire. Still, they had little choice. He glanced again at the blackness of the cavern.

"I'd hate to become lost in there," Hebel muttered next to him.

Eretria seemed to be of the same opinion. "Wisp, we can't see anything." She pulled him to a stop. "We have to make torches."

Wisp froze. "No torches, pretty thing. No fire. Fire burns—destroys. Hurts Wisp. Fire burns the tower of the Lady. The Lady . . . Wisp serves . . ."

He broke down suddenly, tears flooding his eyes, his small arms wrapping tight about the Rover girl's legs. "Not hurt Wisp, pretty thing!"

"No, no, Wisp," she assured him, picking him up and holding him close to her. "No one will hurt you. But we need light, Wisp. We cannot see in this cavern without light."

Wisp raised his tear-streaked face. "Light, pretty thing? Oh, light—there is light. Come. Over here is light."

Mumbling half to himself, he led them to the mouth of the cavern once more. Then moving to the near wall, he reached into a small niche in the rock and extracted a pair of the strange lamps. As he thrust them into the cavern, the glass-enclosed interiors came alive with the same smokeless light that had burned throughout the Witch Sister's tower.

"Light." Wisp smiled eagerly, handing the lamps to Eretria.

She took them, keeping one for herself and handing the second to Wil. The Valeman turned back to Hebel.

"You don't have to come any further with us if you don't want to," he pointed out.

"Don't be stupid," the old man snorted. "What if you get lost in there? You'll need Drifter and me to get you out again, won't you? Besides, I want a look at this Safehold place."

Wil could see that there was little to be gained by arguing the matter further. He nodded to Eretria. The Rover girl took a firm grip on Wisp's hand; holding the lamp she carried before them both, she started into the cave. Wil lifted Amberle in his arms and followed. Hebel and Drifter brought up the rear.

They moved ahead cautiously. Gradually their eyes began to adjust, and they could see that the cavern ran well back into the core of Spire's Reach, its roof and walls far beyond the glow of the lamps. The floor of the cavern was uneven, but free of obstructions, and they walked deep into the blackness. At last Wisp brought them to the rear wall of the cavern. Before them were a series of openings, little more than narrow clefts in the rock, one very much like another, splitting the cavern wall and disappearing from view.

Wisp had no problem deciding which opening he wanted. Without any hesitation at all, he chose one and led the way through. He took them into a labyrinth of cuts and turns, twisting and winding along a maze of tunnels that sloped steadily downward. The others were soon hopelessly lost. Still Wisp led them on.

Then suddenly they stood before a stairway, and the character of the tunnels underwent an abrupt change. Gone were the naturally-formed rock walls, roof, and floor. The stairs and surrounding passageway were formed of stone blocks, rough-hewn and massive, but unquestionably fashioned by hand. Patches of dampness glistened on the walls and roof of the passage, and trailers of water ran upon the steps. There were sounds in the darkness below. Small bodies scattered with a scratching of tiny feet and squeaks of annoyance. Flashes of sudden movement revealed the sleek, dark forms of rats.

Wisp led them down the stairs into the darkness. For hundreds of feet the stairs wore on, bending and turning at odd angles, leveling off once or twice in small rampways, then twisting deep into the mountain. All about them, just beyond the glow of the smokeless lamps, the rats scurried through the dark, their cries faint and unpleasant in the stillness. The air grew pungent with the smell of musty dampness and decay. Still they descended, watching the steps wind away before them.

Finally the steps ended. They stood within a great hall, its high arched ceiling braced with massive columns. Broken stone benches filled the chamber, arranged in widening rows about a low, circular platform. Strange markings were carved in the stone of the columns and walls, and iron stanchions and standards rusted upon the platform. Once this chamber had been a council room or meeting hall, or perhaps even a place of offerings and strange rites, Wil thought. Once another people had gathered here. He stared about momentarily, and then Wisp was leading them through the rows of benches and past the platform to a massive stone door that stood ajar at the far end of the hall. Beyond, another set of stairs led downward.

They descended this new stairway. Wil was growing more than a little concerned. They had come a long way into the mountain, and only Wisp had any idea at all where they were. If the Reaper caught them here . . .

The steps ended. They moved into another passageway. From somewhere ahead, Wil thought he heard the sound of water splashing, as if a brook were tumbling down through the stone. Wisp hurried forward eagerly, pulling at Eretria's hand, casting anxious glances over one shoulder as if to be certain that she still followed him.

Then they were through the passage and standing in a great cavern. Gone were the stone-block walls that had formed the tunnels that had led them here. This cavern was nature's work, its walls pocked and split, its roof a mass of jagged stalactites, its floor cratered and littered with broken rock. In the darkness beyond the circle of light cast by their lamps, they could hear water rushing.

Wisp led them across the cavern, stepping nimbly through the rock, muttering as he went. Against the far wall lay stacked a mass of boulders that looked to be the result of a rock slide. Down through their midst, a narrow band of water tumbled and gathered in a pool that spread outward in a series of tiny streams, bubbling and twisting and finally disappearing into the gloom.

"Here," Wisp announced brightly, pointing to the waterfall.

Wil lowered Amberle to her feet and stared at the little fellow blankly.

"Here," Wisp repeated. "Door made of glass that will not break. Funny game for Wisp."

"Wil, he means the waterfall." Amberle spoke up suddenly. "Look closely—where the water spreads out between those rocks above the pool."

Wil did look, seeing now what the Elven girl had seen. Where the water spilled down into the pool, it fell in a thin, even sheet between twin columns of rock, causing it to look very much as if it were a door made of glass. He moved forward several paces, watching the light cast from his lamp reflect back from the water's surface.

"But it is not glass!" Eretria snapped. "It's just water!"

"But would the Ellcrys remember that?" Amberle countered quickly, speaking still to the Valeman. "It has been so long for her. Much of what she once knew has become forgotten in the passing of time. On much she is confused. Perhaps she remembers this waterfall only for what it appeared to be—a door made of glass that will not break."

Eretria looked down at Wisp. "This is the door, Wisp? You're sure?"

Wisp nodded eagerly. "Funny game, pretty thing. Play funny game with Wisp again."

"If this is the door, then there should be a chamber beyond . . ." Wil started forward.

"Wisp can show!" Wisp darted ahead of him, pulling Eretria as he went. "Look, look, pretty thing! Come!"

He drew the Rover girl with him until they stood just to the right of the waterfall beside the pool into which it spilled. The wizened face glanced back briefly, and the little fellow released her hand.

"Look, pretty thing."

An instant later he had stepped into the waterfall and disappeared. The Rover girl stared after him. Almost immediately he was back again, his fur plastered down against his body, his face beaming.

"Look," he beckoned and seized the girl's hand once more, pulling her after him.

In a knot, the little company passed through the waterfall, still holding the smokeless lamps before them, shielding their eyes as they slipped within the rocks. An alcove lay behind the fall, with a narrow passage beyond. Dripping, they followed it back, Wisp leading them on, until they had walked to its end, where yet another cavern lay, this one much smaller and unexpectedly dry, free of the musty dampness that filled the other, its floor sloping up into the gloom in a series of broad shelves. Wil took a deep breath. If the waterfall were the door made of glass that would not break to which the Ellcrys had directed them, then it was here, in this chamber, that they would find the Bloodfire. He walked wordlessly to the rear of the cavern and back again. There were no other tunnels leading in, no other passages. Rock walls, floor, and cavern roof reflected dully in the glow of his lamp as he held it up and looked carefully about.

The chamber was empty.

At the mouth of the cavern that opened down into Spire's Reach, a shadow passed from the tangle of brush that clogged the bluff and disappeared soundlessly into Safehold. In the wake of its passing, the forest had gone suddenly still.

A rush of wild imaginings crowded Wil Ohmsford's mind as he stood within that empty cavern and stared helplessly about. There was no Blood-fire. After all they had endured to reach Safehold, there was no Bloodfire. It was lost, perhaps gone from the earth for centuries, gone with the old world. It was a fiction, a vain hope conceived by the Ellcrys in her dying, a magic that had disappeared with the passing of the land of faerie. Or if there was a Bloodfire, it was not here. It lay somewhere else within the Wilderun, somewhere other than these caverns, and they would never find it. It lay beyond their reach. It lay hidden . . .

"Wil!"

Amberle's call broke the stillness, sudden and quick. He turned to find her standing apart from him, one hand groping before her as if she were blind and sought to see.

"Wil, it is here! The Bloodfire is here! I can feel it!"

Her voice trembled with excitement. The others stared at her, watching as she hobbled forward through the cavern gloom, watching the mesmerizing play of her fingers as they stretched forth like feelers into the dark.

Eretria moved quickly over to Wil, still grasping Wisp's hand as the lit-tle Elf cowered behind her.

"Healer, what does she . . . ?"

His hand came up to silence her. He shook his head slowly and he did not speak. His eyes remained fixed on the Elven girl. She had moved now to one of the higher levels of the cavern, a small shelf that stood almost in the exact center of the chamber. Painfully, she limped for-ward, stepping onto the shelf. At its far edge, a large boulder sat. Amberle hobbled to the boulder and stopped, hands reaching down to stroke its surface.

"Here." She breathed the word.

Wil started forward at once, bounding onto the shelf. Instantly the El-ven girl turned back to face him.

"No! Come no closer, Wil!"

The Valeman stopped. Something in the tone of her voice forced him to stop. They faced each other wordlessly in the gloom of the cavern for an instant, and in the Elven girl's eyes there was a look of desperation and fear. Her eyes stayed locked on his a moment longer, and then she turned away. Placing her slim body against the boulder, she shoved. As if it were made of paper, the boulder rolled back.

White fire exploded from the earth. Upward toward the roof of the cavern it lifted, the flame glistening like liquid ice. It burned white and brilliant as it rose, yet gave off no heat. Then slowly it began to turn the color of blood.

Wil Ohmsford staggered back in shock, unaware momentarily that in the rush of Fire Amberle had disappeared altogether. Then behind him he heard Wisp scream in horror.

"Burn! Wisp will burn! Hurt Wisp!" His voice became a shriek. His wizened face contorted as the fire flooded the cavern with red light. "The Lady, the Lady, the Lady—burns, she burns! Wisp . . . serves the . . . burns!"

His mind snapped. Wrenching free of Eretria, he ran from the chamber, screaming one long wail of anguish. Hebel grabbed for him and missed.

"Wisp, come back!" Eretria cried. "Wisp!"

But it was too late. They heard him pass through the waterfall and he was gone. In the crimson glare of the Bloodfire, the three who remained faced one another wordlessly.

In the next instant Wil Ohmsford realized that he could no longer see Amberle. He hesitated, thinking that somehow his eyes were deceiving him, that the Fire was hiding her in its mix of shadows and crimson light, that she must still be standing there on that shelf of rock where she had stood a moment earlier. Yet if that were so, why was it that he couldn't see her?

He was starting toward the Bloodfire to find out when the scream sounded—high and terrible as it lingered in stillness.

"Wisp!" Eretria whispered in horror.

She was already moving toward the passageway when Wil caught up with her and pulled her quickly back toward the Fire. Hebel backed away with them, one hand gripping Drifter's neck as the big dog growled in warning.

Then they heard something pass through the waterfall. Not Wisp, Wil knew; this was something else, something much bigger than Wisp. The sound of its passing told him that much. And if it was not Wisp then . . .

The hackles on the back of Drifter's neck bristled up in fear and the big dog dropped to a crouch, snarling.

"Behind me." Wil motioned Eretria and Hebel back.

Already he was reaching into his tunic, pulling free the pouch that held the Elfstones. Backing to the edge of the rock shelf where the Bloodfire burned, his eyes fixed on the chamber entry, he yanked open the leather drawstrings, his fingers groping frantically.

It was the Reaper.

Its shadow moved in the chamber entry, as soundless as the passing of the moon. The Reaper walked like a man, though it was much larger than any ordinary man, a massive, dark thing, larger even than Allanon. Robes and a cowl the color of damp ashes were all that could be seen of it. As it slipped from the passage, the Fire's crimson light fell across it like blood.

Eretria's frightened hiss cut through the silence. From a gathering of great hooked claws dangled the broken form of Wisp.

Instantly the curved dagger appeared in the Rover girl's hand. From within the black shadow of its cowl, the Reaper stared out at her, faceless, implacable. Wil felt himself go impossibly cold, colder even than when he had first seen Mallenroh. He felt total evil in the Demon's presence. He thought suddenly of its victims, of the Elven watch at Drey Wood, of Crispin, Dilph, and Katsin at the Pykon, of Cephelo and the Rovers at Whistle Ridge—all of them destroyed by this monster. And now it had come for him.

He began to shake, the fear within him so strong that it was like a living thing. He could not take his eyes from the Demon, could not bring himself to look away, though every fiber of his body begged him to do so. At his side, Eretria's face was gray with terror, her dark eyes darting to find the Valeman's. Hebel retreated a step further, and Drifter's snarl became a frightened whine.

When the Reaper stepped clear of the chamber wall, the motion was smooth and noiseless. Wil Ohmsford braced himself. The hand that held the Elfstones came up. The Reaper stopped, its faceless hood lifting slightly. But it was not the Valeman that caused it to hesitate. It was the crimson Fire that burned beyond. There was something about the Fire that disturbed the Reaper. Silently the Demon studied the blood-red flames as they licked at the smooth surface of the rock shelf and rose to the chamber ceiling. The Fire did not appear to threaten. It simply burned, cool, smokeless, and steady, leaving no mark. The Reaper waited a moment longer, watching. Then it started forward.

The dreams came back to Wil Ohmsford in that instant, the dreams that had plagued his sleep at Havenstead and again at the fortress in the Pykon, the dreams of the thing that hunted him through mist and night, the thing from which he could not escape. The dreams came to him now as they had come to him in his sleep, and all of the feelings that had swept through him then were reborn, yet stronger and more terrifying. It was the Reaper that had pursued him, its face never seen as it stalked him from one imagined dream world to the next, always just a step away—the Reaper, now come out of nightmare into reality. But this time there was nowhere to flee, nowhere to hide, no waking out of sleep. This time there was no escape.

Allanon! Help me!

He retreated deep within himself and found the Druid's words floating in a sea of unreasoned fear. Believe in yourself. Believe. Have confidence. I depend on you most of all. I depend on you.

He gathered the words to him. Hand steady, he called upon the magic of the Elfstones with everything that he could muster. Down into the Stones he plunged, feeling himself drop through layers of deep blue light. His vision seemed to cloud as he fell, and the scarlet glow of the Bloodfire seemed to fade to gray. He was close now, close. He could feel the fire of the Elfstone's power.

Yet nothing happened.

He panicked then, and for an instant the fear overwhelmed him so completely that he almost broke and ran. It was only the realization that there was nowhere left to run to that made him stand fast. The barrier was still there, still within him—just as it had been within him following the encounter with the Demon in the Tirfing—as it would always be within him because he was not a true master of the Elfstones, not their rightful holder, nothing but a foolish Valeman who had presumed that he could be something more than what he was.

"Healer!" Eretria cried desperately.

Again the Valeman tried and again he failed. The power of the Elfstones would not be called forth. He could not reach it, could not command it. Sweat bathed his face, and he clenched the Elfstones so tightly that the edges cut into his palm. Why would the power not come?

Then Eretria stepped away from him, feinting suddenly with the dagger, calling the Demon after her. The Reaper turned, the faceless cowl following her as she moved slowly down the rock shelf, as if she thought to escape back through the chamber entry. Wil recognized at once what she was doing; she was giving him time—a few precious seconds more to bring the power of the Elfstones to life. He wanted to call out to her, to tell her to come back and to warn her that he could no longer use the magic. But somehow he could not speak. Tears ran from the corners of his eyes as he strained to break the barrier that locked him from the Stones. She was going to die, he thought frantically. The Reaper was going to kill her while he stood there and watched it happen.

Lazily, the Reaper tossed aside what remained of Wisp. From beneath its robes, hooked claws stretched out into the crimson light of the Bloodfire and stretched out toward the Rover girl.

Eretria!

What happened next was to be etched in his mind as if carved into rock. In a few seconds of frozen time, past and present were gathered into one; as had once happened to his grandfather, Wil Ohmsford came face to face with himself.

He seemed to hear Amberle speaking to him, her voice lifting from out of the red glow cast by the Bloodfire on the chamber rock, steady, calm, and filled with hope. She spoke to him as she had spoken to him that morning after they had fled the Pykon, when the Mermidon was carrying them safely south, far from the horror of the night gone past. She told him, as she had told him then, that despite all that had happened the power of the Elfstones was not lost, that it was still his and that he might use it.

But the power *was* lost. She had seen what had happened on the fortress catwalk. He had wanted desperately to destroy the Demon after what he had seen it do to the gallant Crispin! Yet he had stood there, the Elfstones clutched uselessly in his hand, unable to do anything. If the wind had not caused the catwalk to collapse, the Reaper would have had them. Surely she must see that the power was lost.

Her sigh came back, a whisper in his mind. It was not lost. He was trying too hard. He was trying so hard that he was shutting himself away from the Elfstones, something that would not be happening but for his inability to understand the nature of the power he sought to master. He must try to understand. He must remember that Elven magic was but an extension of the user . . .

Her voice faded and Allanon's replaced it. Heart and mind and body— one Stone for each. A joining of the three would give life to the Elfstones. But Wil must create that joining. Maybe it would not be as effortless for him as it had been for his grandfather because he was a person different from his grandfather. He was two generations removed from Shea Ohmsford's Elven blood, and what had come to his grandfather with but a thought might not come so easily to him. Much within him resisted the magic.

Yes, yes! Wil cried to himself. The Man blood resisted. It was the Man blood that kept him from the power of the Elfstones. It was the Man blood, the non-Elven part of him that rejected the magic.

Allanon's laugh was low and mocking. If that were so, then how was it that he had been able to use the Elstones once before . . . ?

The Druid's voice faded as well.

And then Wil Ohmsford saw the deception he had worked upon himself since that moment within the Tirfing when he had called forth the power of the Elfstones and felt the awesome magic flood through him like liquid fire. He had let the lie grow out of doubt that the power of the Elfstones was ever truly his to wield, and he had unwittingly reinforced it with Allanon's startling revelation that only Elven blood gave mastery over the Stones. How quick he had been to conclude that his Man blood was the reason for his failure to use again the very same power that he had used within the Tirfing—even though his mix of Man blood and Elven blood was no different now than it had been then.

He had deceived himself completely! Perhaps not knowingly, perhaps not willingly, but he had deceived himself nevertheless, and in doing so had lost the power of the Elfstones. How had it happened? Amberle had touched upon the truth when twice during their travels she had cautioned that in his use of the Stones within the Tirfing it seemed as if he had done something to himself. He had made light of the caution, trying to brush aside her concern—even while admitting to her that she was right. He *had* done something to himself when he had used the Elfstones. Yet he could not trace it. He had thought that what he had done was physical in nature, but he found nothing wrong. Amberle had suggested that it might be something more, that Elven magic could affect the spirit as well. But he hadn't wanted to believe that. When he found nothing immediately wrong, he had been quick to dismiss the entire matter, to block it from his mind completely because after all he could not afford to spend time worrying about himself when he had Amberle to look out for. That had been a very large mistake. He should have seen then as he saw now that Amberle had been right, that his use of the Elfstones had most certainly done something to his spirit, something so damaging that, until he came to grips with it, the power of the Stones would be lost to him.

For what had happened to Wil Ohmsford was that he had become afraid.

He could admit it now. He must admit it. This was a fear he had not been able to recognize until now, easily confused, cleverly concealed. All these weeks it had been there, and he had not recognized it for what it was. For this was not a fear of the thing that haunted him in his dreams or of the Demon that had hunted Amberle and him south from Arborlon. It was fear of the very thing that he had relied upon to protect them, of the Elfstones and of the effect that the use of their awesome, unpredictable power might have upon him.

Understanding flooded through him. It was not the mix of his Man blood with his Elven blood that was shutting him from the power of the Stones. It was his fear of the magic.

It had been his own doing. So determined had he been to succeed in the task that Allanon had given him and that nothing would prevent him from carrying it out that he had buried his fear at the instant of its birth in a well of determination. He had refused to admit it might exist, but had hidden it, even from himself. Eventually it had begun to affect his use of the Elfstones. There could be no joining of himself, of heart and mind and body, with the power of the Stones while such fear lay unrecognized within him. He had let himself believe that he was experiencing a rejection of the Elven magic by his Man blood. With that, he had made the deception complete, and any further use of the Stones had become impossible.

Until now. Now he understood the nature of the barrier that shut him from the power of the Elstones. It was the fear that had blocked him from the Stones—and he might deal with that.

He reached down within himself, a quick and deliberate act, joining as one heart, mind, and body, willingness and thought and strength, in a single, unbreakable purpose. It did not happen easily. The fear was still there. It rose up before him like a wall, warning him back, eroding his purpose. It was strong, so strong that for an instant Wil thought that he could not go on.

There was danger in his use of the Elfstones, a danger that he could neither see nor touch, define nor understand. It was there, real and tangible, and it could damage body and spirit irreparably. It could destroy him. Worse, it could let him live. There were things more terrible than dying . . .

He fought against it. He thought of his grandfather. When Shea

Ohmsford had used the Sword of Shannara, there had been danger that the Valeman had sensed yet not understood. He had told Wil that. But there had been need for the magic of the Sword, and the choice his grandfather had made had been a necessary one. So it was now with Wil. There was need greater than his own. There was a trust that had been given him, and there were lives that only he could preserve.

He thrust himself deep into the blue light of the Elfstones, and the fear shattered before him. Man blood gave way to Elven, and the power of the Stones surged up within him.

Past and present split apart, and the seconds were gone.

Eretria!

The Reaper was moving, springing soundlessly through the Bloodfire's crimson glow toward the Rover girl. Wil brought up the Elfstones and their fire exploded from his hands into the Demon, driving the creature back into the cavern wall.

There was no sound as the Reaper struck—only a terrible silence as its robes collapsed against the rock. In the next instant it was on its feet again, lunging for the Valeman. Wil would not have believed that anything so huge could be that quick. Almost before he could act, the Reaper was before him, claws ripping downward. Again the blue fire burst from the Elfstones, hammering into the Demon, hurtling it backward like a rag doll. Again there was no sound. Wil felt the fire within his body this time, coursing through him as if it were his lifeblood, and the feeling was as it had been in the Tirfing. Something had been done to him—something not altogether pleasant.

But there was no time to think on it. The Reaper's ash-gray form darted like a shadow through the half-light in a soundless rush. Fire burst from the Valeman's outstretched hand, but this time the Reaper was too quick. Dodging the attack, it came on. Again Wil tried to stop it, and again he failed. He stumbled back, frantically trying to bring the Elven magic to bear, but his concentration was broken, and the fire had begun to scatter. The Reaper darted through it, looming up before him. At the last possible moment, Wil managed to gather the fire before him like a shield. Then the Reaper was upon him, knocking him violently back. Down he went, head slamming against the stone of the chamber floor. For an instant he thought he would black out. Claws tore at the blue fire, struggling to reach him. But the Valeman fought the dizziness and the pain, and the Elfstones' magic stayed alive. The Reaper sprang back in frustration and circled silently away.

Dazed, Wil scrambled to his feet. His body ached from the force of the Reaper's attack, and there were spots dancing before his eyes. With an effort, he kept himself erect. Things were not working out as he had expected. He had thought when he had broken through to the Elven magic that the worst was over, that at last he possessed mastery of a weapon against which the Reaper could not stand, that however powerful and dangerous the Demon, it would be no match for the Stones. Now he was no longer certain.

Then he remembered Eretria. Where was Eretria? Within him the Elven fire twisted like an imprisoned creature. For one terrible moment he was afraid that he had lost control of it completely. In that moment, the Reaper attacked him again. It came out of the shadows, silent and swift, bounding into the glare of the Bloodfire and into the Valeman. Almost of its own volition, the Elven magic flared up between the combatants in a blinding explosion that threw both from the narrow shelf. The unprepared Valeman was flung back into the cavern wall, ribs and the elbow of his free arm cracking like deadwood as he smashed against the rock. Searing pain lanced through him, and the arm went quickly numb.

Somehow he struggled up again, bracing himself against the wall. Fighting the pain and the nausea that washed through him, he cried out for Eretria. The Rover girl darted from the shadows, reaching him barely a step ahead of the Reaper. With a noiseless lunge the monster came for them, too quickly this time for the dazed Valeman to act. It would have had them but for Drifter. Forgotten by all, the huge dog tore free of Hebel's grip and hurtled into the Demon. The monster tumbled back, a blur of bristling hair and teeth ripping into the ash-colored robes. For an instant both disappeared into the shadows at the front of the cavern. Drifter's snarl was deep and terrible. Then the Reaper heaved upward, flinging the gallant dog from him, swatting it as one might swat a fly. Drifter flew through the air and smashed into the cavern wall, collapsing with a startled whimper into silence.

Yet even those few seconds gave Wil the time he needed to recover. His arm rose instantly, and the blue fire thrust out. It caught the Reaper a glancing blow, but again the creature twisted free, circling swiftly away through the cavern half-light until the pillar of the Bloodfire screened it from view.

The Valeman waited, eyes sweeping the chamber. There was no sign of the Demon. Frantically he searched the shadows, knowing that it would come again. He could not find it. Eretria crouched sobbing beside him, one hand still clutching the dagger, her face streaked with dirt and sweat. Hebel bent close to Drifter, whispering urgently. The seconds slipped away. Still nothing moved.

Then Wil glanced up. The Reaper was on the cavern roof.

He saw it just as it dropped toward him, gray robes flying wide. Frantically he shoved Eretria aside and brought up the Elfstones. Like a cat, the Demon landed before them, massive and soundless. Eretria screamed and stumbled back in horror. Slowly, slowly, the black hole of the cowl widened, freezing Wil Ohmsford with its empty stare. The Valeman could not move. The blackness held him, faceless and deep.

Then the Reaper lunged, and for just an instant Wil felt himself swallowed by the thing. He would have died then but for the power of the Elfstones. Seeking stones, Allanon had called them, and the warning cried out in his mind—seek the Reaper's face! Quicker than thought, the magic acted, blinding him to the terrible monster, to his fear and pain, and to everything but a primitive instinct for survival. He heard himself scream, and the blue fire exploded from him. It tore through the Reaper's faceless cowl, gripped the Demon like a vice about its invisible head and held it fast. Twisting desperately, the monster sought to break free. Wil Ohmsford's hands locked before him, and the Elven magic swept from his shattered body into the Reaper, lifting it, thrusting it back against the cavern wall. There the Reaper hung, impaled upon the blue fire, writhing in fury as it burned. An instant later the fire swept downward through the Demon's robes and exploded in a flare of blinding light.

When the fire died, all that remained of the Reaper was a charred outline of its twisted robes burned deep into the cavern rock.

48

The Bloodfire enfolded Amberle Elessedil with the gentle touch of a mother's hands. All about her the flames rose, a crimson wall that shut away the whole of the world beyond, yet did no harm to the wondering girl. How strange, she thought, that the Fire did not burn. Yet when she had pushed away the rock and the Fire had burst forth about her, somehow she had known that it would be so. The Fire had consumed her, but there had been no pain; there had been no heat nor smoke nor even smell. There had been only the color, deep hazy scarlet, and a sense of being wrapped in something familiar and comforting.

A drowsiness crept through her and the pain and fear of the past few days seemed to drain slowly away. Her eyes wandered curiously through the flames, trying to catch a glimpse of the cavern that housed the Fire and the companions who had come with her. But there was nothing; there was only the Fire. She thought to step through it momentarily, to reach beyond its haze, yet something within her dissuaded her from doing so. She should remain here, she sensed. She should do what she had come here to do.

What she had come here to do—she repeated the words and sighed. Such a long journey it had been; such a terrible ordeal. But now it was ended. She had found the Bloodfire. Curious how that had happened, she thought suddenly. She had been standing there within that darkened, empty cavern, as dispirited as her companions that there was no Bloodfire to be found beyond the door made of glass that would not break, that all of their efforts had been for nothing, when suddenly . . . suddenly she had sensed the Fire's presence. She hesitated in describing it so, but there was no better way. The sensing was similar to what she had experienced upon the rim of the Hollows when she had hidden within that clump of bushes to await Wil's return, similar to what had warned her of the Reaper's approach. It was a feeling that came from deep inside, telling her that the Bloodfire was there within that cavern and that she must find it. She had groped her way forward then, trusting to her instincts, not understanding what it was that made her do so. Even when she had found the Fire beneath that cavern shelf and warned Wil back from her, even when she had pushed aside the rock to free the Fire, she had not understood what it was that was guiding her.

The thought disturbed her. She still did not understand. Something had touched her. She needed to know what it was. She closed her eyes and sought it out.

Understanding came slowly.

At first she thought it must be the Bloodfire, for it was the Fire to which she had been drawn. Yet the Fire was not a sentient thing; it was an impersonal force, old and vital and life-giving, yet without thought. It was not the Fire. Then she thought that if it were not the Fire, it must be the seed she carried, that tiny bit of life given her by the Ellcrys. The Ellcrys was sentient; her seed could be sentient as well. The seed could have warned her of the Reaper and the Fire. . . . But that, too, was wrong. The Ellcrys seed would possess no life until bathed in the flames of the Bloodfire. It lay dormant now; the Fire was needed to awaken it. It was not the seed.

But if it was not the Bloodfire and it was not the seed, what was left?

Then she saw it. It was she. Something within her had warned of the Reaper. Something within her had warned of the Bloodfire. The warnings had come from within her because they belonged to her. It was the only answer that made any sense. Her eyes opened in surprise, then quickly closed again. Why were the warnings hers? Memories flooded through her of the strange influence the Ellcrys had exercised over her, of the way the tree had begun to make her over until she had felt no longer so much herself as an extension of the tree. Had the tree done this to her? Had she been affected even more than she believed?

She was frightened momentarily by the possibility, just as she was always frightened when she thought of the way the Ellcrys had stolen her away from herself. With an effort, she forced down her fear. There was no reason to be frightened now. That was all behind her. The journey to find the Bloodfire was done. Her promises were kept. All that remained was to give life back to the Ellcrys.

Her hand slipped down within her tunic and closed about the seed that was the source of that life. It felt warm and alive, as if anticipating an end to its dormancy. She was about to withdraw her hand when the fears came back again, sudden and intense. She hesitated, feeling her strength of will begin to ebb. Was there more to this ritual than she imagined? Where was Wil? He had promised to see her through this. He had promised to make certain that she did not falter. Where was he? She needed the Valeman; she needed him to come to her.

But Wil Ohmsford would not come. He was beyond the Fire's wall, and she knew that he could not reach her. She must do this by herself. It was the task she had been given; it was the responsibility she had accepted. She took a deep breath. A moment's time to place the Ellcrys seed in the flames of the Bloodfire and the task would be finished. It was what she had come all this way to do; now she should do it. Yet the fear persisted. It filled her like a sickness and she hated it, because she did not understand it. Why was it that she was so frightened?

In her hand, the seed began to pulsate softly.

She glanced down. Even this seed frightened her, even so small a part of the tree as this. Memories came and fled again. In the beginning they had been close, the Ellcrys and she. There had been no fear, only love. There had been joy and sharing. What had changed that? Why had she begun to feel that she was losing herself in the tree? Such a frightening thing that had been! Even now it haunted her. What right had the Ellcrys to do that to her? What right had the Ellcrys to use her so? What right . . . ?

Shame filled her. Such questions served no purpose. The Ellcrys was dying and she needed help, not recrimination. The Elven people needed help. The Elven girl opened her eyes and blinked into the Bloodfire's crimson glow. There was no time to indulge her bitterness or to explore her fear. There was only time to do what she had come to do—to bathe the seed she held in the Fire.

She started. The Fire! Why had the seed not already been affected by the fire? Could the flames not reach it within her tunic? Had they not already touched it? What difference whether she took the seed out?

More questions. Pointless questions. Again she started to withdraw the seed and again the fear held her back. Tears filled her eyes. Oh, that there might be someone else to do this thing! She was not a Chosen! She was not suited! She was not . . . she was not . . .

With a cry, she wrenched the seed from her tunic and held it forth into the Bloodfire's scarlet flame. It flared within her hand, alive with the Fire's touch. From deep within the Elven girl the feeling came again, the feeling that had warned her of the Reaper's coming, the feeling that had called her to the Bloodfire, flooding through her now in a dazzling sweep of images that wracked her with such intense emotions that she dropped weakly to her knees.

Slowly she brought the Ellcrys seed to her breast, feeling the life within it stir. Tears ran down her cheeks.

It was she. It was she.

Now at last, she understood. She held the seed close against her and drew the Bloodfire in.

49

Huddled against the cavern wall, Wil Ohmsford and Eretria watched the Fire's crimson glow wink into darkness. It happened suddenly, a final spurt of flame and then the Bloodfire was gone. All that remained to light the chamber gloom were the discarded lamps they had carried in, their soft white glimmer faint and small.

Valeman and Rover girl blinked in the sudden night, peering blindly through the shadows. Slowly their vision sharpened, and they saw movement from atop the shelf where the Bloodfire had burned. Guardedly Wil brought up the hand that held the Elfstones, and the Elven magic rose in a flicker of blue fire.

"Wil . . ."

It was Amberle! She emerged from the gloom like a lost child, her voice a thin, desperate whisper. Ignoring the pain that wracked his body, the Valeman started toward her, Eretria a step behind. They reached her as she stumbled from the shelf, caught her in their arms and held her.

"Wil," she murmured softly, sobbing.

Her head lifted and the long chestnut hair fell back from her face. Her eyes burned crimson with the Bloodfire.

"Shades!" Eretria gasped and stepped back from the Elven girl.

Wil caught Amberle up in his arms; despite the pain that lanced through his injured arm, he cradled her against him. She was feather-light, as if the bones had withered within her and all that remained was a shell of flesh. She was crying still, her head buried in his shoulder.

"Oh, Wil, I was wrong, I was wrong. It was never her. It was me. It was always me."

The words came in a rush, as if she could not speak them fast enough. The Valeman stroked her pale cheek.

"It's all right, Amberle," he whispered back to her. "It's over."

She looked up at him again, the blood-red eyes fixed and terrible.

"I didn't understand. She knew . . . all along. She knew, and she tried . . . and she tried to tell me, to let me see . . . but I didn't understand, I was frightened . . ."

"Don't talk." The Valeman gripped her tightly, a sudden, unreasoning fear slipping through him. They had to get free of this blackness. They had to get back to the light. He turned quickly to Eretria. "Pick up the lamps."

The Rover girl didn't argue. She retrieved the smokeless lights and hurried back to him. "I have them, Healer."

"Then let us hurry from this . . ." he began and caught himself. The

Ellcrys. The seed. Had the Elven girl . . . ? "Amberle," he whispered gently. "Has the seed been placed within the Fire? Amberle?"

"It . . . is done," she said so softly he barely caught her words.

How much had this cost her, he wondered bitterly? What had happened to her within the Fire . . . ? But no, there was no time for this. They must hurry. They must climb from these catacombs back to the slopes of Spire's Reach and then return to Arborlon. There Amberle could be made well again. There she would be all right.

"Hebel!" he called out.

"Here, Elfling." The old man's voice was thin and harsh. He appeared out of the shadows, cradling Drifter in his arms. "Leg's broke. Maybe something more." There were tears in Hebel's eyes. "I can't leave him."

"Healer!" Eretria's dark face was suddenly close before his own. "How are we to find our way back without the dog?"

He stared at her as if he had forgotten she existed, and she flushed with shame, thinking him angry for her reaction to the Elven girl.

"The Elfstones," he muttered finally and did not stop to question whether he could use them. "The Elfstones will show us the way."

He shifted Amberle slightly in his arms, grimacing as the pain from his shattered body rose up in waves.

Eretria caught his arm. "You cannot carry the Elven girl and use the Stones as well. Give the girl to me."

He shook his head. "I can manage," he insisted. He wanted Amberle to stay close to him.

"Don't be so stubborn," she pleaded softly. Her jaw tightened, and it was with difficulty that she spoke. "I know how you feel about her, Healer. I know. But this is too much for you. Please, let me help. Give her to me to carry."

Their eyes met momentarily in the half-light, and Wil saw the tears that glistened on her cheeks. That admission had hurt her. Slowly he nodded.

"You are right. I cannot do this alone."

He gave Amberle to the Rover girl, who cradled her as if she were a baby. Amberle's head slipped down against Eretria's shoulder and she slept.

"Stay close," Wil admonished, taking one of the smokeless lamps and turning away.

They went back through the waterfall and through the cavern that housed it, picking their way carefully across the rock-strewn floor. Blood and sweat mingled freely on Wil Ohmsford's body, and the pain grew worse. By the time they had reached the passageway leading up into the maze, the Valeman could barely walk. Yet there was no time to rest. They had to reach Perk quickly, for it was his final day. They had to get free of Safehold, back to the surface of the Hollows, to the slopes of Spire's Reach, before the sun set or the little Wing Rider would be gone. That would be the finish for them. Without Perk and Genewen to carry them to Arborlon, they would never get clear of the Wilderun.

Staggering to a halt before the passage entry, Wil fumbled through the compartments of the pouch he carried at his waist. Within were the herbs and roots that aided him in his healing. After a moment's search, he brought forth a dark purple root, its six-inch length coiled tight. He held it before him, hesitating. If he ate it, its juice would kill the pain. He would be able to go on until they reached the slopes of the mountain above. But the root had other effects. It would make him drowsy and eventually render him unconscious. Worse, it would cause him to become increasingly less coherent. If it took effect too quickly, before they succeeded in finding their way clear of the catacombs . . .

Eretria was watching him wordlessly. He glanced up at her and the frail body she carried. Then he bit into the root and began to chew. It was a chance he had to take.

They stumbled ahead in the dark. When the maze began to open up before them, the Valeman brought up the hand that held the Elfstones and called forth the magic within. It came quickly this time, flooding through him like a sudden rush of heat, whirling through his limbs and exploding outward into the dark. Like a beacon, it curled before them through the catacombs, leading them on. They followed, shadows in the passage gloom. Onward they trudged, the crippled Valeman willing forth the blue fire to give them direction, the Rover girl close beside him, holding the sleeping Elf girl gently, and the old man cradling the giant dog. The minutes slipped slowly away.

Pain from the wounds suffered in the battle with the Reaper faded into numbness, and Wil Ohmsford felt himself drift through the darkness like a thing filled with air. Slowly the juice of the root worked through him, sapping his strength until his body felt as if it were made of damp clay, sapping his reason until it was all that he could do to remember that he must go on. All the while the Elven magic stirred his blood, and, as it did so, he felt himself changing in that same unexplainable way. He was no longer the same, he knew. He would never be the same. The magic burned him through and left an invisible, permanent scar upon his body and his consciousness. Helpless to prevent it, he let it happen, wondering as he did what effect it would have upon his life.

Yet it did not matter, he told himself. Nothing mattered but seeing that Amberle was made safe.

The little company pushed ahead in the wake of the brilliant blue fire, and the tunnels and corridors and stairways disappeared into the blackness behind them.

When they finally staggered from the cavern mouth of Safehold, into the air and light of the valley, they had spent themselves. The Rover girl had carried Amberle the entire way, and her strength was gone. The Valeman was barely conscious, numbed through by the pain-killing root, drifting in and out of coherence as if wandering directionless through a deep mist. Even Hebel was exhausted. Together they stood upon the open bluff high on the slopes of Spire's Reach and blinked in the mix of fading sunlight and lengthening shadow, their eyes following its sweep across the expanse of the Hollows westward to where the sun set slowly into the forest, a brilliant blaze of golden fire.

Wil felt his hopes fall away from him.

"The sun . . . Eretria!"

She came to him and together they laid Amberle upon the ground, dropping wearily to their knees as they finished. The Elven girl slept still, her soft breathing the only sign of life she had shown during the whole of their journey up from the catacombs. She stirred slightly now, as if she might wake, yet her eyes remained closed.

"Eretria . . . here," Wil called to her, his hand fumbling within his tunic. His eyes were lidded and his words slurred. His tongue felt thick and useless. Struggling to hold himself upright, he produced the tiny silver whistle and passed it to the girl. "Here . . . use it . . . quickly."

"Healer, what am I . . . ?" she began, but he seized her hand angrily.

"Use it!" he gasped and fell back weakly. Too late, he was thinking. Too late. The day is finished. Perk is gone.

He was losing consciousness rapidly now—just a few minutes more and he would be asleep. His hand still clutched the Elfstones, and he felt their edges bite against the palm. A few minutes more. Then what would protect them?

He watched Eretria rise and place the whistle to her lips. Then she turned to him, her dark eyes questioning.

"There is no sound!"

He nodded. "Blow . . . again."

She did, then turned a second time.

"Watch . . ." He pointed toward the sky.

She turned away. Hebel had laid Drifter upon a bed of saw grass, and the big dog was licking his hand. Wil took a deep breath and glanced down at Amberle. So pale, as if the life had been drained from her. A sense of desperation gripped him. He had to do something to help her; he couldn't leave her like this. He needed Perk badly! If only they had been a little quicker, a little swifter in their flight! If only he had not been hindered by his injuries! Now the day was gone!

Shadows fell about them, and the pinnacle of the mountain was cloaked in dusk's gray light. The sun had slipped into the west, a small crest of gold glimmering against the distant treeline as it died.

Perk, don't be gone, he cried soundlessly. Help us.

"Wil."

His head jerked sharply about. Amberle was staring up at him through blood-red eyes. Her hand found his.

"It's all right . . . Amberle," he managed, swallowing against the dryness that coated his throat. "We're . . . out."

"Wil, listen to me," she whispered. Her words were clear now, no longer vague or hurried, only faint. He tried to answer her, but her fingers came up to seal his lips, and her head shook slowly. "No, listen to me. Don't speak. Just listen."

He nodded, bending down as she moved her body close.

"I was wrong about her, Wil—about the Ellcrys. She was not trying to use me; there were no games being played. The fear . . . that was unintentional, caused by my failure to understand what it was that she was doing. Wil, she was trying to make me see, to let me know why it was that I was there, why it was that I was so special. You see, she knew that I was to be the one. She knew. Her time was gone, and she saw . . ."

She stopped then, biting her lip against the emotions welling up within her. Tears began rolling down her cheeks.

"Amberle . . ." he started to say, but she shook her head.

"Listen to me. I made a choice back there. It is my choice and there is no one but me to answer for it. Do you understand? No one. I made it because I had to. I made it for a lot of reasons, for reasons that I cannot . . ." She faltered, her head shaking. "For the Chosen, Wil. For Crispin and Dilph and the other Elven Hunters. For the soldiers at Drey Wood. For poor little Wisp. All of them are dead, Wil, and I can't let it be for nothing. You see, you and I have to . . . forget what we . . ."

The words would not come for her, and she began to sob.

"Wil, I need you, I need you so much . . ."

Fear rushed through him. He was losing her. He could feel it, deep down within him. He struggled to free himself from the numbness that weighted him.

Then Eretria called out to them, her voice sharp with excitement. They turned, eyes lifting to follow the line of her outstretched arm as it pointed skyward. Far to the west, through a haze of dying sunlight, a great golden bird soared downward toward the bluff face.

"Perk!" Wil cried softly. "Perk!"

Amberle's arm went about him and held him close.

Then he was being carried and through a fog of half-sleep he heard Perk's voice speaking to him.

"It was the smoke from that burning tower, Wil. Genewen and I circled all day. I knew you were down here. I knew it. Even when the day was almost gone and it was time to return to the Wing Hove, I couldn't leave. I knew the lady would need me. Wil, she looks so pale."

The Valeman felt himself being hoisted onto Genewen's back, and Eretria's slim brown arms began fastening the harness straps tightly about him.

"Amberle," he whispered.

"She's here, Healer," the Rover girl responded quietly. "We are all safe now."

Wil let himself sag back against her, drifting slowly toward unconsciousness as the night about him deepened.

"Elfling," a voice called gently, and his eyes opened to find Hebel's weathered face looking up. "Goodbye, Elfling. I'll go no further with you now. The wilderness is my home. I've taken my search as far as I care to. And Drifter, he's going to be fine. The Rover girl helped me splint the leg, and he's going to be just fine. He's a tough one, that dog."

The old man bent close. "You and the Elfling girl—I wish you luck."

Wil swallowed hard. "We . . . owe you, Hebel."

"Me?" The old man laughed gently. "Not me, Elfling. Not a thing. Luck, now."

He stepped away and was gone. Then Amberle appeared, her slim form hunching down in front of him, and Perk was back, quickly checking harness straps and lines. A moment later the boy's strange call sounded; with a sudden lurch, Genewen lifted slowly into the sky, her great wings spanning outward across the dark bowl of the Hollows. Upward rose the giant Roc, the forests of the Wilderun falling away below. In the distance, the wall of the Rock Spur came into view.

Wil Ohmsford's arms tightened around Amberle. A moment later, he was asleep.

50

Night lay over Arborlon. In the solitude of the Gardens of Life, Allanon walked alone to the top of the small rise where the Ellcrys stood, his black robes wrapped close to ward off the evening chill, the silver staff she had entrusted to his care cradled within his arms. He had come to be with her, to comfort her in whatever way he might, to give to her what companionship he could. These were to be her final hours; the burden that had been given her so many years ago was about to be lifted.

He paused momentarily, staring up at her. It would have seemed curious had someone come upon them, he thought—the Druid and the Ellcrys, stark black silhouettes framed against a moonlit summer sky, the man standing wordlessly before the withered, barren tree as if lost in some private reverie, his dark face an impassive mask that told nothing of what feelings might lie beneath. But no one would come. He had decreed that the tree and he should spend this night alone and that no one should be witness to her dying but he.

He stepped forward then, her name whispered in his mind. Her limbs reached for him at once, frightened and urgent, and his thoughts went quickly to comfort her. Do not despair, he soothed. This very afternoon, while the battle to save Arborlon was at its most furious, while the Elves fought so gallantly to stem the Demon advance, something unexpected happened, something that should give us hope. Far, far to the south in the dark of the wilderness forests where the Chosen has gone, her protector brought to life the magic of the Elfstones. The moment that he did so, I knew. I reached out to him then and I touched his thoughts with my own—quickly, for but a moment's time, because the Dagda Mor could sense what I did. Still, that moment was enough. Gentle Lady, the Blood-fire has been found! The rebirth can still come to pass!

Tinged with expectancy, the thoughts rushed from him. Yet nothing came back. Weakened almost to the point of senselessness, the Ellcrys had not heard or understood. She was conscious only of his presence, he realized then, conscious only of the fact that in her final moments she was not alone. What he might say to her now would have no meaning; she was blind to everything but her desperate, hopeless struggle to fulfill her trust—to live, and by living to protect the Elven people.

A sadness filled him. He had come to her too late.

He went quiet then, for there was nothing more that he could do, except to stay with her. Time slipped away, agonizingly slow in its passing. Now and again her random thoughts reached him, filtered down like scattered bits of color in his mind, some lost in the history of what had been, some cloaked in wishes and dreams of what might yet be, all hopelessly tangled and fragmented by her dying. Patiently he caught those thoughts as they slipped from her and he let her know that he was there, that he had heard, that he was listening. Patiently he shared with her the trappings of the death that sought to cloak her. He felt the chill of those trappings, for they spoke all too eloquently of his own mortality. All must pass the way that she was passing, they whispered. Even a Druid.

It caused him to ponder momentarily the inevitability of his own death. Even though he slept to prolong his life, to lengthen it far beyond the lives of ordinary men, still one day he, too, must die. And like the tree, he was the last of his kind. There were no Druids to follow him. When he was gone, who then would preserve the secrets handed down since the time of the First Council at Paranor? Who then would wield the magic that only he had mastered? Who then would be guardian of the races?

His dark face lifted. Was there yet time, he wondered suddenly, to find that guardian?

Night sped away with soundless steps, and dawn's pale light broke across the darkness of the eastern sky. Within the vast Westland forests, life began to stir. Allanon felt something change in the Ellcrys' touch. He was losing her. He stared fixedly at the tree, hands gripping tightly the silver staff as if by clasping it so he might hold fast to the life that drained from her. The morning sky brightened; as it did, the images came less frequently. The pain that washed into him lessened, and a curious detachment replaced it. Bit by bit, the detachment widened the distance between them. In the east, a crest of sunlight edged above the horizon, and the night stars faded way.

Then the images ceased altogether. Allanon stiffened. In his hands, the silver staff had gone cold. It was over.

Gently he laid the staff beneath the tree. Then he turned and walked from the Gardens and did not look back.

Ander Elessedil stood silently by his father's bed and stared down at the old man. Torn and battered, the King's frail body lay wrapped in bandages and blankets, and only the shallow rise and fall of his chest gave evidence of life. He slept now, a fitful, restless sleep, hovering in the gray zone between life and death.

A rush of feelings swept through the Elven Prince, scattering like leaves in a strong wind. It was Gael who had wakened him, frightened and unsure. The young aide had come back to the manor house, restless, unable to sleep, thinking to do some work in preparation for the coming day. But the doors were jammed, he told Ander—the sentries gone. Did the King sleep unguarded? Should something be done? Instantly Ander had come to his feet, dashing from his cottage and calling out to the gate watch. In a rush they had broken through the front entry, frantic, hearing the old King's cries from within. There they had witnessed the finish of the death struggle between his father and that monster—the Demon that had masqueraded as Manx. His father had regained consciousness for just a short time as they carried him, bleeding and broken, to his bed chamber, to whisper in horror of the battle that had been fought and the betrayal he had suffered. Then consciousness had left him, and he had slept.

How could his father have survived? Where had he found the strength? Ander shook his head. Only the few who had found him could begin to appreciate what it must have taken. The others, the Ministers and the commanders, the guards and the retainers, had come later. They had not seen the old King sprawled in that blood-smeared entry, torn and shredded. They had not seen what had been done to him.

There was speculation, of course—speculation that bred rumors. The King was dead, they whispered. The city was lost. Ander's jaw tightened. He had silenced them quickly enough. It would take more than a single Demon to kill Eventine Elessedil!

He knelt suddenly beside his father and touched the limp hand. He would have cried had there been tears left to cry. How terribly fate had treated the old King. His firstborn and his closest friend were dead. His beloved granddaughter was lost. His country was overrun by an enemy he could not defeat. He himself had been betrayed in the end by an animal that he had trusted. Everything had been stripped from him. What was it that kept him alive after all that he had suffered? Surely death would come as a welcome relief.

He clasped the hand gently. Eventine Elessedil, King of the Elves—there would never be another such King. He was the last. And what would be left to remember him by other than a land destroyed and a people driven into exile? Ander was not bitter for himself, he knew. He was bitter for his father, who had spent his entire life working for that land and those people. There was nothing owed to Ander Elessedil perhaps. But what of that old man whose heart was wedded to this land that would be ravaged and this people that would be destroyed? Was not something owed him? He loved the Westland and the Elves more than the life he was about to give up, and that he should be forced to see it all taken away . . . it was so terribly unjust!

Ander bent down impulsively and kissed his father's cheek. Then he straightened and turned away. Through the curtained windows, he could see the sky brightening with the new day. He had to find Allanon, he thought suddenly. The Druid did not yet know. Then he must return to the Carolan, to stand with his people where his father would have stood had he been able. No matter the bitterness. No matter the regrets. What was needed now was the same courage and strength that his father had shown in his last battle, a courage and strength that would sustain the Elves in theirs. Whatever was to happen this day, he must be his father's son.

Tightening his armor as he went, Ander Elessedil walked quickly from the darkened room.

On the threshold of the entry to the manor house he paused momentarily and peered toward the brightening eastern sky. Dark circles shadowed his eyes, and his face was haggard and drawn. The dawn air chilled him, and he drew his heavy cloak close. Behind him the manor house windows blazed with light, and grim-faced Elven Hunters prowled the hallways like hunting dogs.

"Useless now . . ." he murmured to himself.

He set off toward the front gates, moving alone down the gravel walk, his mind clouded by his need for sleep. How long had he slumbered before Gael had come to him? One hour? Two? He could no longer remember. When he tried, it was the face of his father that appeared, blood-spattered and terrible, piercing blue eyes fixed upon his own.

Betrayed, those eyes cried out. Betrayed!

He passed through the wrought-iron gates into the street beyond, failing to notice the giant figure that emerged from the shadows where the war horses were tethered.

"Prince Ander?"

He started at the sound of his name, stopped, and turned. The dark figure approached silently, the new light glinting from chain-mail armor. It was the Free Corps Commander, Stee Jans.

"Commander." He nodded wearily.

The big man nodded in reply, the scarred face impassive. "A bad night, I am told."

"Then you have heard?"

Stee Jans glanced toward the manor house. "A Demon found its way into the King's house. His guard was slain, and he himself struck down when he slew the creature. You can scarcely expect to keep such news a secret, my Lord."

"No—nor have we tried." Ander sighed. "The Demon was a

Changeling. It made itself appear as my father's wolfhound, an animal he had had with him for many years. None of us know how long it has been there, playing this game, but tonight it decided the game was finished. It killed the guards, bolted the doors leading out, and attacked the King. A monster, Commander—I saw what was left of it. I don't know how my father managed . . ."

He trailed off hopelessly and shook his head. The Borderman's eyes shifted back to him.

"So the King still lives."

Ander nodded slowly. "But I don't know what it is that keeps him alive."

They were silent then, their eyes glancing back toward the lighted manor house and the armed figures that patrolled its shadowed grounds.

"Perhaps he waits for the rest of us, my Lord," Stee Jans said quietly.

Their eyes met. "What do you mean?" Ander asked him.

"I mean that time draws short for all of us."

Ander took a deep breath. "How much longer do we have?"

"Today."

The hard face remained expressionless, as if the Borderman spoke of nothing more significant than what the weather might be that day.

Ander straightened. "You seem resigned to this, Commander."

"I am an honest man, my Lord. I told you that when we met. Would you wish to hear something other than the truth?"

"No." Ander shook his head firmly. "Is there no chance that we can hold longer?"

Stee Jans shrugged. "There is always a chance. Measure it as you would measure the King's chances of surviving beyond this day. That is the chance we all have."

The Elven Prince nodded slowly. "I accept that, Commander." He extended his hand. "The Elves have been fortunate to have you and the Free Corps soldiers to stand with them. I wish that we could find a better way to thank you."

The Iron Man gripped the other's hand. "I wish that we could offer you the opportunity. Good fortune, Prince Ander."

He saluted and was gone. Ander stared after him for a moment, then turned and started back up the street.

Moments later Allanon found him as he was preparing to ride to the Carolan. The Druid rode out of the predawn gloom aboard Artaq, black shadows slipping from the forest mist. Ander stood wordlessly as the big man reined Artaq to a halt and stared down at him.

"I know what has happened," the deep voice rumbled softly. "I am sorry, Ander Elessedil."

Ander nodded. "Allanon, where is the staff?"

"Gone." The Druid stared past him toward the manor house. "The Ellcrys is dead."

Ander felt the strength drain from him. "Then that's the end, isn't it? Without the magic of the Ellcrys to aid us, we are finished."

Allanon's eyes were hard. "Perhaps not."

Ander stared at him in disbelief, but the Druid was already turning Artaq back up the roadway.

"I will wait for you at the gates to the Gardens of Life, Elven Prince," he called back. "Follow quickly, now. There is still hope for us."

Then he put his heels into the black and they disappeared from view.

D aybreak was an hour gone when the Demons attacked. They swarmed up the face of the Carolan, scrambling over the rubble of the shattered Elfitch to converge on the walls and gates of the sixth ramp. No longer weakened by the power of the Ellcrys or held back by the anathema of the Forbidding, the Demons shrugged aside the arrows and spears that showered down on them and came on. Wave upon wave of black bodies surged upward from the forests. In moments the cliffs were thick with them. Crude grappling hooks forged of captured weapons and trailing heavy vines were flung atop the walls and gates to catch upon the massive stone blocks. Hand over hand, the Demons began to climb.

The defenders stood ready—Kerrin and the Home Guard atop the gates, Stee Jans and the Free Corps upon the left wall, Amantar and the Rock Trolls upon the right. As their attackers climbed toward them, the defenders hacked and cut the scaling ropes. Back the Demons fell, screaming. Elven long bows hummed, and a hail of black arrows cut into the attackers. But still the Demons came, throwing up new hooks, new vines. Heavy wooden beams, hewn from whole trees and notched with steps, were flung against the gates, and the Demons scrambled up. Clubs and rocks flew out of the black mass below, cutting into the defenders as they tried to withstand the assault. Again and again the Demons were beaten back. But in the end they gained the walls, and the Elves and their allies found themselves locked in fierce hand-to-hand combat.

To either side of the Elfitch, the Demons spread wide along the cliff face, clawing their way determinedly toward the rim of the Carolan. There waited the Elven horse, Legion Old Guard, Dwarf Sappers and scattered units of the other companies of defenders. Ehlron Tay was in command. Leading one charge after another into the swarms of attackers that appeared above the bluff rim, he thrust them back, sweeping them from the Carolan. But the defenders' lines were thin and the bluff was long and dotted with bits of sheltering forest which hid the Demons' approach. Isolated groups began to break through, and the Elven flanks began to buckle.

On the Elfitch, the Demons breached the gates of the sixth ramp. Breaking through the defenders' ranks, they shattered the bolts and crossbars that secured the gates and flung them wide. Into the gap they poured, clawing their way upward through the bodies of their dead. Amantar still held the right wall, but Stee Jans and his decimated Bordermen were being forced steadily back. At the center of the Elven defense, Kerrin rallied the Home Guard and counterattacked the Demon rush, desperately trying to throw it back. Into the howling mass the Elven Hunters charged, hammering the Demons aside, slowing the assault. For an instant it appeared that the Home Guard would recapture the gates. But then a handful of Furies launched themselves from the walls onto the attacking Elves, claws and teeth ripping. Kerrin went down, dying. The counterattack stalled, then fell back, broken.

Slowly the defenders retreated up the Elfitch through the open gates of the seventh and last ramp, keeping their lines tightly formed as the enemy tried to break through. With Amantar and Stee Jan holding the center, the defenders slipped back within the walls, and the gates slammed shut. Below, the Demons massed once more.

Three hundred yards east of the ramphead, Ander Elessedil stared out over the battlefield and felt his hopes begin to fade. At his back, the soldiers of the Black Watch ringed the Gardens of Life. He glanced quickly to Kobold, who stood at their head, then to Allanon. The Druid was at his side, seated on Artaq, dark face impassive as he watched the tide of battle shift back and forth.

"Allanon, we must do something," he whispered finally.

The Druid did not turn. "Not yet. Wait."

All along the rim of the Carolan, the Demons continued to scramble to the top of the cliffs, battling to turn the Elven flanks. To the south, they had gained a toehold on the bluff and were swelling their ranks, turning back the assaults of Elven horse that sought to dislodge them. To the north, the Dwarf Sappers still held their ground against repeated attacks, the resourceful Browork rallying horse and foot soldiers in a succession of strikes that time and time again threw the Demons from the heights. Ehlron Tay rode south, leading a reserve company of horse to regain the lower bluff. They charged into the Demons, lances lowered. There was a frightful clash of bodies, screams and cries rising up, and the battle raged so heatedly that, from a distance, it was impossible to tell friend from foe. But when at last the struggle broke off, it was the Elves who were in retreat. The left flank of the defense curled up quickly now, and the Demons surged forward, howling with glee.

Then the gates of the seventh ramp splintered and broke, and the Demons poured through. The defenders were flung back, and it appeared that they would be overrun completely. But the Trolls led a sudden, savage counterattack that swept the Demons back through the broken gates, and for an instant the walls were regained. Then the Demons rallied, the largest, most brutal moving to the fore, and the hordes broke through again. This time even the Rock Trolls could not stem the advance. Dragging their wounded with them, the defenders abandoned the gates and moved back up the ramp toward the bluff rim.

By now the Demons had gained the north end of the Carolan as well as the south, thrusting back the determined Dwarves, and the flanks folded in toward the center point. Slowly, surely, the Gardens of Life became an island on the battlefield as the Demons surged toward it. Ehlron Tay went down, ripped from his horse. Torn and battered, he was pulled to safety by his soldiers and carried from the bluff. Browork had suffered half-a-dozen wounds, and the Demons were all about him. The Old Guard had lost a third of its strength. Two of the Wing Riders were down and the three who remained, including Dayn, had flown back to the Gardens of Life to stand with Allanon. Everywhere, the Elves and their allies were in retreat.

The defenders on the Elfitch had been forced back to the ramphead by their attackers. Stee Jans held the center position in the defense, surrounded by his Free Corps soldiers. Elves and Trolls held the flanks. It was clear to all that they could not hold long. The scar-faced Borderman recognized the danger of their position at a glance. Below, the Demons massed for another assault. To either side along the bluff rim, the defenders' lines had collapsed and were pinching in upon the ramphead. In moments, all would be caught in a vice from which none would escape. They had to fall back at once, to re-form their lines at the perimeter of the Gardens of Life where they might consolidate their strength and gain the support of the Black Watch. But they needed time to do that, and someone must give them that time.

Red hair flying, the Free Corps Commander snatched the crimson and gray battle standard of his company and jammed it between the ramp stones. Here the Free Corps would make its stand. Rallying his Bordermen to him, he formed a narrow phalanx at the center of the ramphead. Then he ordered the Elves and Trolls to fall back. No one questioned the order; Stee Jans had been given command of the army. Quickly they abandoned the Elfitch, moving back toward the ranks of Black Watch that ringed the Gardens of Life. In moments, the remnants of the Free Corps stood alone.

"What is he doing!" Ander screamed to Allanon, horrified. But the Druid did not answer.

The Demons attacked. Up the ramp they charged, howling with rage. Incredibly, the Free Corps withstood the assault and thrust it back. All the while the Elven defenders continued to slip free of the noose that had threatened to snare them. Again the Demons came up the Elfitch, and again the Free Corps thrust them back. No more than two dozen Bordermen remained alive. At their head stood the tall figure of Stee Jans. Regrouping before the Gardens of Life, the defenders who had fled the Elfitch looked back, watching the tiny knot of men who still held against the Demon rush. A silence settled over their ranks. They knew how this must end.

Now the whole of the Carolan lay open. Stee Jans wrenched free the battle standard, lifted the gray and crimson pennant high above his head, and the Free Corps battle cry rang out. Then slowly, deliberately, the little band began to move back across the Carolan, back toward the Elven defenders who ringed the Gardens of Life. Not a single Borderman broke formation. Not a single Borderman ran.

Ander's breath escaped from his lips with a sharp hiss. It was a hopeless retreat. At his elbow, Browork's battered face shoved into view.

"It's too far, Bordermen!" he muttered, almost to himself.

A wave of Demons edged over the lip of the ramphead, snarling. North and south along the Carolan, they began to mass.

"Run!" Ander whispered. "Run, Stee Jans!"

But there was no time left to run. Shrieks filled the morning air, shattering the momentary stillness, and the whole of the Demon army swept forward.

Then Allanon was moving. A quick word to Dayn and Dancer's reins were in his hands. A moment later he had swung astride the giant Roc and was lifting skyward. Ander Elessedil and those who stood with him stared after the Druid in astonishment. High above the Gardens Allanon flew, black robes billowing out, lean arms raised. On the Carolan, the converging Demons slowed abruptly and stared skyward. Then a monstrous clap of thunder burst across the grasslands as if the earth had split apart in anger, and blue fire spurted from the Druid's fingers. In an arc that reached from one end of the Demon advance to the other, the fire swept the foremost ranks of the attackers and burned them to ash. Howls and shrieks rose from the Demons as a wall of flame lifted before them, forcing them back from the encircled Free Corps.

A roar of excitement went up from the Elves. A narrow corridor had opened through the ring of fire to the Gardens and the embattled army of the Elves. Back through this corridor came the Bordermen—quickly now, for their trap might close again at any moment. All about them the Demons raged, but the fire held them at bay. Run! Ander cried silently. There is still a chance! Back raced the Bordermen, and the distance between them narrowed. A handful of Furies gave chase, maddened beyond reason, hurtling through the flames. But Allanon saw them. One dark hand raised, clenching. Druid fire lanced into the cat-things and they disappeared in a brilliant explosion, a pillar of fire rising skyward to mark their end. High overhead, Dancer screamed his battle cry.

And then Stee Jans and his Free Corps soldiers broke clear of the fire and were back once more within the safety of the Elven lines. Shouts and cheers welcomed them, and the battle standards of the Four Lands lifted in the morning air.

On the Carolan, the Druid fire burned lower now, but still the Demons did not try to cross. With the Furies so easily destroyed, none cared to face Allanon alone. Milling behind the wall of flames, they snarled and raged at the lone black flyer. And they waited.

The Druid glided past, eyes searching. He knew what must happen now. A challenge had been issued, and one among the Demons must answer it. Only the Dagda Mor was strong enough to do so—and answer he would, Allanon believed, because he had no other choice. The Dagda Mor could sense the magic of the Elfstones as well as Allanon. He, too, would know that Wil Ohmsford had used the Stones, that the quest for the Bloodfire had been successful, and that the thing he feared most might yet come to pass—a rebirth of the hated Ellcrys and a restoration of the Forbidding. It was a dangerous moment for the Demon Lord. His Changeling was dead. His Reaper had failed. His army had stalled. If he were stopped now, even though all that remained of the Westland was his, he had lost. The Ellcrys was the key to the Demons' survival. The mother tree must be destroyed and the earth in which she rooted razed so that nothing could ever again grow there. Then the seed could be hunted at leisure and the last Chosen found. Then the Demons could be assured that they would not again be banished from the land. Yet none of this would come to pass if Allanon were not first destroyed. The Dagda Mor knew that, and now he would have to act . . .

A frightful shriek rose from the Demons. From beneath the rim of the Carolan, a massive black shadow lifted into the clear morning sky. Allanon turned. It was the winged creature that had nearly caught Wil Ohmsford and Amberle in the Valley of Rhenn on their flight north from Havenstead. The Druid saw the thing clearly now, a monstrous bat, sleek and leathery, its blunt snout split wide to reveal gleaming fangs, its legs crooked and taloned. He had heard rumors of such bats living deep in the mountains of the far Northland, but even he had never seen one until now. It hovered above the Demon hordes, its cry a high, grating squeal that froze the black mass beneath it into sudden stillness.

Allanon tensed. Seated astride the creature's hooked neck was the Dagda Mor. The challenge had been accepted.

The Druid swung Dancer about sharply. Downward flew the bat, the Demon's humped form bent close. In one hand, the Staff of Power began to gleam redly. Allanon waited, holding Dancer steady beneath him. The bat squealed in anticipation. Out from the Demon's Staff of Power the red fire lanced, but just an instant too late. Dancer banked sharply, guided by the Druid's touch, then swung abruptly left. As the winged monster swooped down, taloned feet reaching and missing, Demon fire exploding into the Carolan, Allanon wheeled Dancer about. The bat was ponderous and slow in its flight; as it rose, the Druid flew beneath it and struck back. Blue fire burned the monster's wings and body, searing its leathered skin, and it cried out shrilly.

But it flew back, and again the Dagda Mor brought down the Staff of Power. Demon fire knifed across the morning sky, sweeping in front of the Druid and his mount. A wall of flame hung in the air before them, and this time there was no chance to turn. Dancer never hesitated. With a scream, the giant Roc looped upward, carrying Allanon clear of the fire, then straightened and swept downward across the Carolan. From the Gardens of Life, cheers rose from the throats of the Elves and their allies.

Again the Demon attacked, his massive carrier dropping swiftly. Again Dancer was too quick. Back across the bluff the giant Roc flew. Demon fire burst from the Staff of Power, lancing past the Roc, burning the grasslands to ash. Dancer swung right, then left, changing directions so quickly that the Dagda Mor could not bring the fire to bear. All the while Allanon fought back, Druid fire ripping into the monstrous bat, burning it over and over again until smoke trailed from its ruined body in small swirls as it flew.

The battle wore on, a terrifying duel that carried Druid and Demon back and forth above the scarred surface of the Carolan, twisting and turning, each trying to outmaneuver the other. For a time they fought evenly, and neither could gain an advantage over the other. The bat was ponderous and easily struck, but it was also strong and seemed unaffected by its injuries. Dancer was simply too quick; the fire never touched him. But as the minutes slipped by and still the struggle did not end, the Roc began to tire. For three days, he had flown in battle, and his strength was ebbing fast. Each time he swept back above the bluff, the Demon fire burned closer. Silence fell over the ranks of the defenders. Through each mind the same thought passed. Sooner or later, the Roc would falter or the Druid would guess wrong. Then the Demon Lord would have them.

Moments later, their fears were realized. Fire lanced across Dancer's path of flight as the Roc banked suddenly left, shattering the great bird's wing. Instantly Dancer faltered and began to spiral downward toward the Carolan. A cry of horror went up from the Elves. Again the Staff of Power flared, and again the fire burned into the broken Roc. Down swept the bat, taloned feet flexed. Desperately Allanon turned as the monstrous thing dropped toward him, and his arms stretched skyward, hands clenched. The bat was almost on top of him when blue fire burst from the Druid's fingers. The bat's entire head seemed to explode and disappear. But its momentum carried it into the stricken Dancer. Thirty feet above the Carolan, the bat and the Roc collided, slamming into each other with terrifying force. Locked together, they dropped earthward, carrying their riders with them. Downward they plummeted and struck the ground with crushing force. Dancer shuddered once and lay still. The bat never moved.

In that instant it appeared to all as if the battle were lost. Dancer and the bat were dead. Allanon lay stretched upon the ground, still and burned. And the Dagda Mor was in motion. One leg was smashed, but the Demon pulled himself free of the stricken bat and started toward the Druid. Allanon stirred, head lifting weakly. Slowly the Dagda Mor dragged himself forward until he stood not ten feet from the fallen Druid. Face twisting with hate, the Demon braced. In his hands, the Staff of Power began to glow.

"Allanon!" Ander Elessedil heard himself cry out, and the echo reverberated in the sudden stillness.

Perhaps the Druid heard. Somehow he was on his feet, sidestepping the bolt of fire that lanced past him, moving so swiftly that he was on top of the Dagda Mor before the Staff of Power could be brought to bear a second time. The Demon tried to swing the Staff about, and then Allanon's hands were locked on its gnarled length. Demon fire flared within the Staff, and pain swept through the Druid. But his own magic rose in defense, and blue fire mingled with the red. Back and forth the Druid and the Demon wrestled, bodies straining, each trying to wrench the Staff free from the other's hands.

Then Allanon reached deep within some final well of strength, some last inner reserve, and the blue fire exploded from him. It burst from his hands and swept the length of the Staff of Power, smothering the Demon fire, coursing into the body of the Dagda Mor. The Demon's eyes went wide with horror, and he screamed once, high and terrible. Allanon heaved upward, throwing back the humped form, forcing the Demon slowly to his knees. Again the Demon screamed, the hatred spilling out of him. Desperately he fought against the fire that engulfed his body, struggling to break the Druid's hold. But Allanon's hands closed over his own like iron locks, fastening them tightly to the failing Staff. The Dagda Mor shuddered wildly and sagged, his cry dying into a whisper, and the terrible eyes went blank.

The Druid fire swept through him unhindered then, cloaking him in a shroud of blue light until his body exploded into ash and was gone.

A silence fell over the Carolan. Allanon stood alone, the Staff of Power still clutched within his hands. He stared down wordlessly at the ruined bit of wood, charred and smoking. Then he snapped it apart and threw the pieces to the ground.

Turning back toward the Gardens of Life, he whistled Artaq to him. Alone, the black trotted out from the Elven lines. Allanon knew he had only moments left. His strength was gone, and he was still on his feet only through sheer force of will. Before him the wall of fire that had held back the Demons was dying. Already they massed along its perimeter, eyes fixed hungrily upon him, waiting to see what would happen next. The destruction of the Dagda Mor meant nothing to them. Their hatred of the Elves was what mattered. The Druid returned their stares, his smile slow and mocking. All that held them back now was their fear of him. The moment they lost that, they would attack.

Artaq nudged his shoulder and whickered softly. His eyes never leaving the Demons, Allanon edged carefully back until he could grip the horse's mane and harness. Then painfully he pulled himself into the saddle, nearly blacking out with the effort. Grasping the reins, he turned Artaq about. Seemingly unhurried, he started back toward the Elven defensive lines.

It was an agonizingly slow escape. He kept Artaq at a deliberate walk; a faster gait would have been too much for him. Foot by foot, the Gardens of Life drew closer. Out of the corner of his eye he could see movement in the lines of the encircling Demons. A few among them were already darting challengingly past the dying flames, shrieking at his back. Others quickly began to follow their lead. He gripped the saddle harness with both hands and did not turn. Soon now, he thought, soon.

Then suddenly the entire mass broke, howling and screaming. From all sides the Demons came after him. He knew at once that he was still too far from the Gardens of Life to escape them at this pace. He had no choice. He put his boots into Artaq's flanks, and the black leaped forward. Across the Carolan the big horse raced, powerful body leveled out and straining. Dizziness washed over the Druid, and he felt his grip loosening. He was going to fall.

Yet somehow he did not. Somehow he managed to hold on until finally the Elven lines were before him. With a lunge, Artaq was through, carrying him past the outstretched hands of Elf and Troll and Dwarf to the Gardens' iron gates, there at last to thunder to a halt.

Even then Allanon did not fall. Iron determination kept him astride the black. His face streaked with sweat, he turned to look back across the bluff as the Demon hordes converged upon the Gardens. At its walls, the defenders braced.

At least they have a chance now, he thought. At least I have given them that.

Then a flurry of shouts rose all about him and hands pointed skyward. Dayn was beside him, disbelief reflecting in his cry.

"Genewen! It's Genewen!"

The Druid's eyes lifted. Far to the south, nearly lost in the glare of the noonday sun, a great golden bird was winging its way downward toward Arborlon.

52

Wil Ohmsford stared downward in horror. The sun was a dazzling burst of white light that made him squint. Within him, the fever still burned. He felt weak and light-headed, and sweat bathed his body, drying in the rush of the wind. Genewen bore him high above the green, wooded landscape of the Westland, her wings stretched wide as she glided smoothly in the currents of the wind. Leather straps bound Wil to the Roc, and his shattered arm was splinted and wrapped. In front of him sat Perk, the small body swaying easily with Genewen's movements, his hands and voice guiding her flight. Huddled close against the little Wing Rider, nearly lost within a covering of heavy robes, was Amberle. The arms about his waist belonged to Eretria. He turned, and the Rover girl's dark eyes met his. The look she gave him was stricken.

Below lay the Elven city of Arborlon. Bodies littered the Carolan, fires burned across its bluff, and the Elfitch lay in ruins. Horsemen and lancers, pikemen and bowmen, ringed the Gardens of Life like an iron wall. All about them a wave of twisted black bodies swarmed, thousands strong, and it seemed as if at any moment the defenders might all be swept away.

The Demons, he whispered soundlessly. The Demons!

He was conscious suddenly of movement from Amberle. The Elven girl had straightened slightly, still bent close to Perk, and she was speaking to the boy. One small hand gripped the Wing Rider's shoulder. He nodded. Then Genewen began to descend, dropping swiftly toward the Carolan and the Gardens of Life. The Gardens stood like an island, sculpted hedgerows and flower beds carefully ordered and serene, awash in a sea of scarred grasslands and shrieking black Demons. Wil watched the glitter of weapons in the sunlight as the defenders fought back against the hordes that came against them. Already the black creatures were breaking through. A scattered few were within the walls.

On the small rise at the Gardens' center, the lifeless husk that had once been the Ellcrys stood forgotten.

Genewen cried out suddenly, a piercing shriek that cut through the din of the battle taking place below. For an instant all eyes were turned upon the giant Roc. Downward she plunged, like a falling piece of sunlight. Scattered cries of recognition rose from among the Elves. A Wing Rider, they cried and searched futilely for others.

Then Genewen was within the Gardens, dropping slowly to the foot of the small rise. Great wings folded in and the scarlet head dipped sharply. Perk scrambled down, working swiftly to release the harness straps that secured the others. He freed Amberle first, and she slid limply from Genewen's back, crumpling to her knees as her feet touched the ground. Wil struggled to reach her, but the fever had weakened him and the straps would not loosen.

Beyond the hedgerows and flowered tiers, the sounds of battle drew closer.

"Amberle!" he called.

She was on her feet again, standing not a dozen paces from him, her child's face lifting. For an instant the terrible blood-red eyes fixed upon his, and it seemed as if she would speak. Then, wordlessly, she turned and started up the rise.

"Amberle!" Wil screamed and thrashed against the straps that bound him. Genewen lurched sharply, crying out, and Perk fought to steady her.

"Be still, Healer!" Eretria tried to caution him, but he was beyond being cautioned. All he could see was Amberle moving away from him. He was losing her. He could sense it.

Genewen started to rise then, frightened by the Valeman's struggles. Perk grasped her harness and pulled himself up, vainly trying to bring her under control. Then Eretria's knife was out, severing the straps that secured both Wil and her. An instant later they were falling, tumbling headlong into a line of bushes. Pain shot through the Valeman's injured body as he struggled back to his feet. Eretria called out to him, but he ignored her, stumbling after the retreating figure of the Elven girl. Already she was halfway up the rise, moving slowly toward the tree.

Howls rose from close at hand. Abruptly half-a-dozen Demons broke from the hedgerows. Perk had Genewen grounded again and had just dismounted and gone after Wil. Instantly the Demons came at him. But the Valeman had seen them. His fist swung about, the Elfstones gripped within it. Blue fire exploded into the Demons and they disappeared.

"Get away!" he called back to Perk. "Fly, Wing Rider!"

Eretria stumbled to his side. Other Demons began to emerge from the sheltering hedgerows, shrieking as they came. A scattering of Black Watch burst through to intercept them, pikes lowered. But the Demons fought their way past the Elves and came at Wil. The Valeman turned to face them, and again the Elfstones flared. Perk was back atop Genewen, but instead of flying to safety, the little Wing Rider had turned the giant Roc toward the closest attackers, driving them back. Yet there were dozens more, converging from everywhere, and even the fire of the Elfstones was not enough to stop them all.

Then a single piercing cry rose above those of the Demons and seemed to hang in the heat of the summer noon. Wil turned. Atop the rise stood Amberle, arms stretched forth to clasp the trunk of the Ellcrys. At her touch the tree appeared to shimmer like the waters of a stream caught in a blaze of sunlight, then disintegrate in a shower of silver dust that fell about the Elven girl like snow. She stood alone then, arms lifting, frail body straightening.

And she began to change.

"Amberle!" Wil screamed one final time, falling stricken to his knees.

The Elven girl's body began to loose its shape, the human form melting, clothing shredding and falling from her; her legs fused and tendrils from her feet slipped downward into the earth; slowly, her upraised arms lengthened and split.

"Oh, Wil!" Eretria whispered as she sank down beside him.

Amberle was gone. In her place stood the Ellcrys, perfectly formed, silver bark and crimson leaves gleaming in the sunlight, born anew into the world of the Elves.

A wail of anguish rose from the Demons. The Forbidding was restored. All across the Carolan they cried out as it began to draw them back again. Frantically they stumbled away, fighting to escape the blackness that closed inexorably about them. But there was no escape. One by one they faded from the light, hundreds and then thousands, large and small, black forms writhing, until finally the last had vanished.

Silence fell over the defenders of Arborlon as they stared wordlessly about. It was as if the Demons had never been.

In the Gardens of Life, Wil Ohmsford wept.

53

The Elves found him there moments later. At Ander Elessedil's command, they carried him to Arborlon. Too stunned by the loss of Amberle to argue, his body wracked with fever, he let them take him. He was carried to the manor house of the Elessedils, down its hallways and corridors, silent and shadowed, to a room where he was bedded. Elven Healers washed and dressed his wounds and bound his shattered arm. They gave him a bitter liquid to drink that made him drowsy, and they wrapped him carefully in linen and blankets. Then they left him, closing the door quietly as they went. In seconds, he was asleep.

As he slept, he dreamed that he wandered through a deep, impenetrable darkness, hopelessly lost. Somewhere within the same darkness was Amberle, but he could not find her; when he called, her response was faint and distant. Gradually he became aware of another presence, cold and evil and strangely familiar—a thing that he had encountered before. Terrified, he began to run, faster and faster, fighting his way through webs of black silence. But the thing pursued him; though it made no sound, he could sense it nevertheless, always just a step behind. At last its fingers touched him, and he cried out in fear. Then abruptly the darkness disappeared. There were gardens all about him, beautiful and rich with color, and the thing was gone. Relief flooded through him; he was safe again. But in the next instant the ground beneath his feet buckled and he was lifted into the air. Suddenly he could see that a black wave beyond the gardens was sweeping slowly inward, closing about him, rising like an ocean in which he would surely drown. Desperately he turned to find Amberle, and he saw her now, darting like some voiceless wraith through the garden's center—just a glimpse and then she was gone. Over and over he called for her, but there was no answer. Then the black wave washed over him, and he began to sink . . .

Amberle!

He awoke with a start, his body damp with sweat. On a small table set against the far wall, a single candle burned. Shadows wrapped the room, and nightfall lay over the city.

"Wil Ohmsford."

He turned at the sound of his name, searching. A tall, cowled figure sat at his bedside, black and faceless against the faint glow of the candle's flame.

The Valeman blinked slowly in recognition.

Allanon.

Then everything came back to him in a rush. Bitterness stirred within him, bitterness so tangible that he could taste it. When at last he was able to speak, his voice was a low hiss.

"You knew, Allanon. You knew all the time."

There was no reply. Tears stung the Valeman's eyes. He thought back to that first night in Storlock, when he had met the Druid. He had known then that he could not afford to trust Allanon, that he must not trust him. Flick had warned him; Allanon was a man of secrets, and he hid those secrets well.

But this—how could he have hidden this!

"Why didn't you tell me?" The words were a whisper. "You could have told me."

There was a movement within the shadows of the cowl. "It would not have helped you to know, Valeman."

"It would not have helped you—isn't that what you mean? You used me! You let me think that if I could protect Amberle from the Demons, if she could be brought safely back to Arborlon, then everything would be all right. You knew that was what I believed and you knew it wasn't so!"

The Druid was silent. Wil shook his head in disbelief. "Couldn't you at least have told her?"

"No, Valeman. She would not have believed me. She would not have let herself. It would have been too much to ask of her. Think back to what happened when I spoke with her at Havenstead. She did not even want to believe that she was still a Chosen. Her selection as a Chosen had been a mistake, she insisted. No, she would not have believed me. Not then. She needed time to learn the truth about herself and to understand that truth. It was not something that I could have explained to her; it was something that she had to discover for herself."

The Valeman's voice shook. "Words, Allanon—you are so practiced in their use. You can persuade so easily. You persuaded me once, didn't you? But I will not be persuaded this time; I know what you did."

"Then you must know also what I did not do," Allanon replied quietly. He bent forward. "The final decision was hers, Valeman—not mine. I was never there to make that decision, only to see to it that she was given the opportunity to make it herself. I did that and nothing more."

"Nothing more? You made certain that she made the decision the way you wanted it made. I wouldn't call that nothing."

"I made certain she understood what the consequences of the decision would be, whichever way she chose to make it. That is somewhat different . . ."

"Consequences!" Wil's head jerked up from the pillow and his sudden laugh was laced with irony. "What do you know about consequences, Allanon?" His voice broke. "Do you know what she meant to me? Do you know?"

Tears streamed down his face. Slowly he lay back again, feeling strangely ashamed. All of the bitterness drained out of him, and he ached with the emptiness that was left. He looked away from Allanon self-consciously, and they both stayed silent. In the darkness of the sleeping room, the lone candle's glow touched them softly.

It was a long time before the Valeman looked back again. "Well, it's finished now. She's gone." He swallowed hard. "Would you at least explain why?"

The Druid said nothing for a moment, hunched down within the concealing shadows of his robe. When he finally spoke, his voice was almost a whisper.

"Listen then, Valeman. She is a marvelous creature—this tree, this Ellcrys—a living bit of magic formed by the bonding of human life with earth-fire. Before the Great Wars, she was made. The Elven wizards conceived her when the Demons were finally brought to bay and there was a need to prevent them from again threatening the land of faerie. The Elves, you remember, were not a violent people. Preservation of life was their purpose and their work. Even with creatures as destructive and evil as the Demons, they would not consider deliberate annihilation of a species. Banishment from the land appeared the most acceptable alternative, but they knew it would have to be a banishment of such power that the Demons thousands of years hence would still be subject to its laws. And the banishment would have to be to a place where no harm would come to others. So the Elven wizards used their most powerful magics, the ones that called for the greatest sacrifice of all, the willing gift of life. It was this gift that enabled the Ellcrys to come into being and the Forbidding to be created."

He was quiet a moment. "You must understand the Elven way of life, the nature of the code that governs that way of life, to appreciate what the Ellcrys truly represents and why, therefore, Amberle chose to become her. The Elves believe that they owe a debt to the land, for the land is the creator of and the provider for all life. The Elves believe that when one takes from the land, one must give something back in return. This belief is traditional; it is ritual. Their lives are given them; therefore they must give life back again. They accomplish this, Valeman, through a life marked by service to the land, endeavoring each in his own way to see to it that the land is preserved. The Ellcrys is but an expansion of that dedication. She is the embodiment of the belief that the land and the Elves are mutually dependent. The Ellcrys is a joining of the land with Elven life, a joining conceived to protect against an evil that would see both destroyed. Amberle understood that in the end. She saw that the only way in which the West-land and her people could be saved was through her sacrifice, her willing-ness to become the Ellcrys. She saw that the seed she bore could be given life only through a giving up of her own."

He paused and bent forward slowly, his dark figure casting its shadow over the listening Valeman. "You realize that the first Ellcrys was a woman also; it is not by chance that we refer to the tree as a lady. The Ellcrys must always be a woman, for only a woman can reproduce others of her kind. The wizards foresaw this need for procreation, though they were not able to foresee how often it might be necessary. They chose a woman, a young girl who, I would imagine, was very much like Amberle, and they trans-formed her. Then they established the order of the Chosen so that she might be cared for and when the time came might have the means to select her successor. But it was men, not women, that she selected as her Chosen down through the years, all but a handful. The histories do not record why—even she no longer knew. The selections had been made from habit for a very long time; she chose women only when the need was there. Per-haps it had something to do with her creation in the time of the Elven wizards. Perhaps they promised her young men to serve her—perhaps she requested it. Perhaps the choice of young men to serve was more accept-able to the Elves. I don't know.

"In any case, when she chose Amberle, the Ellcrys suspected that she might be dying. She could not be certain, of course, because she was the first of her kind, and no one had ever known when her death might come or what signs might foretell it. Indeed, many believed that she could not die. And the physical characteristics of that part of her that had been human had long since evolved into something far different, so there was no help there. There had been other times in her life when she had thought she might be dying, when she had thought she was in such dan-ger that she must choose the one who would succeed her. Each time she selected a woman—a handful of times only. The last was five hun-dred years ago. I don't know what prompted it, so don't ask. It isn't really important.

"When Amberle was made a Chosen, the first woman in five hun-dred years, there was no small amount of surprise among the Elves. But the selection of Amberle had far greater significance than anyone real-ized because the Ellcrys in making her choice was looking upon the girl as a possible successor. And more than that really. She was looking upon Amberle as a mother would her unborn child. An odd characterizat-ion you might argue, but consider the circumstances. If the tree were to die, she would then produce a seed, and that seed and Amberle would become one, a new Ellcrys born in part at least from the old. The selec-tion of Amberle was made with that foreknowledge, and it necessarily en-tailed much of the feeling that a mother would bear for an unborn child. Physically the woman that had been the Ellcrys had changed, but emo-tionally she retained much of what she had been. Something of this the tree sensed in the Elven girl. That was why they were so close in the beginning."

He reflected a moment. "Unfortunately it was this closeness that eventually caused problems. When I first came to Arborlon, awakened by the erosion of the Forbidding and the threatened crossover of the Demons, I went to the Gardens of Life to speak with the Ellcrys. She told me that after her selection of Amberle as a Chosen, she attempted to strengthen the ties that bound the Elven girl to her. She did this because she felt the sickness within her growing. Her life, she realized, was coming to an end; the seed that was beginning even then to form within her was to be passed to Amberle. In her dying, she responded to the girl with that same mothering instinct. She wanted to prepare her for what was to come, to see something of the beauty and grace and peace that she had enjoyed in her life. She wanted Amberle to be able to appreciate what it meant to become one with the land, to see its evolution through the years, to experience its changes—in short, I suppose, to understand a little of the growing up that a mother knows and a child does not."

Wil nodded slowly. He was thinking of the dream that Amberle and he had shared after the King of the Silver River had rescued them from the Demons. In that dream they had searched for each other—he within a beautiful garden, so breathtaking that it had made him want to cry; she in darkness, calling out as he stood there but would not answer. Neither had understood that the dream was a prophecy. Neither had understood that the King of the Silver River had given them a glimpse of what was destined to be.

The Druid continued. "The Ellcrys was well intentioned, but overzealous. She frightened Amberle with her visions and her constant motherings and her stealing away of Amberle's identity. The Elven girl was not yet ready for the transition that the Ellcrys was so anxious for her to make. She became frightened and angry, and she left Arborlon. The Ellcrys did not understand; she kept waiting for Amberle to come back. When the sickness grew irreversible and the seed was completely formed, she called the Chosen to her."

"But not Amberle?" Wil was listening closely now.

"No, not Amberle. She thought Amberle would come on her own, you see. She did not want to send for her because, when she had done that before, it had only driven the girl further away. She was certain that once Amberle knew that she was dying, the girl would come. Unfortunately there was less time remaining to her than she thought. The Forbidding began to erode, and she could not maintain it. A handful of the Demons broke through and the Chosen were slain—all but Amberle. When I appeared, the Ellcrys was desperate. She told me that Amberle must be found, so I went to seek her out."

A hint of renewed bitterness darkened the Valeman's face.

"Then you knew at Havenstead that the Ellcrys still considered Amberle a Chosen."

"I knew."

"And you knew that she would give Amberle the seed to bear."

"I will save you the trouble of asking further questions. I knew everything. The Druid histories at Paranor revealed to me the truth of how the Ellcrys had come into being—the truth of how she must come into being again."

There was a brief hesitation. "Understand something, Valeman. I cared for this girl also. I had no desire to deceive her, if you wish to characterize my omissions as deceptions. But it was necessary that Amberle discover the truth about herself another way than through me. I gave her a path to follow; I did not give her a map that would explain its twists and turns. Such choices as might be necessary I thought were hers. Neither you, I, nor anyone else had the right to make those choices for her. Only she had that right."

Wil Ohmsford's eyes lowered. "Perhaps so. And perhaps it would have been better if she had known from the beginning where that path you set her upon would end." He shook his head slowly. "Odd. I thought that hearing the truth about everything that has happened would help somehow. But it doesn't. It doesn't help at all."

There was a long silence. Then Wil looked up again. "In any case, I do not have the right to blame you for what has happened. You did what you had to do—I know that. I know that the choices were really Amberle's. I know. But to lose her like this—it's so hard . . ." He trailed off.

The Druid nodded. "I am sorry, Valeman."

He started to rise, and Wil asked suddenly, "Why did you wake me now, Allanon? To tell me this?"

The big man straightened, black and faceless. "To tell you this, and to tell you goodbye, Wil Ohmsford."

Wil stared up at him. "Goodbye?"

"Until another day, Valeman."

"But . . . where are you going?"

There was no response. Wil felt himself grow sleepy again; the Druid was letting him drift back into the slumber from which he had been awakened. Stubbornly he fought against it. There were things yet to be said, and he meant to say them. Allanon could not leave him like this, disappearing into the night as unexpectedly as he had come, cloaked and hooded like some thief who feared that even the slightest glimpse of his face might give him away . . .

A sudden suspicion crossed his mind in that instant. Weakly he stretched forth his hand and caught the front of the Druid's robe.

"Allanon."

Silence filled the little sleeping room.

"Allanon—let me see your face."

For a moment he thought the Druid had not heard him. Allanon stood motionlessly at his bedside, staring down from the shadows of his robe. The Valeman waited. Then slowly the Druid's big hands reached up and pulled back the hood.

"Allanon!" Wil Ohmsford whispered.

The Druid's hair and beard, once coal black, were shot through with streaks of gray. Allanon had aged!

"The price one pays for use of the magic." Allanon's smile was slow and mocking. "This time I fear that I used too much; it drained more from me than I wished to give." He shrugged. "There is only so much life allotted to each of us, Valeman—only so much and no more."

"Allanon," Wil cried softly. "Allanon, I'm sorry. Don't go yet."

Allanon replaced the hood, and his hand stretched down to grasp Wil's. "It is time for me to go. We both need to rest. Sleep well, Wil Ohmsford. Try not to think ill of me; I believe that Amberle would not. Be comforted in this: You are a Healer, and a Healer must preserve life. You have done so here—for the Elves, for the Westland. And though Amberle may seem lost to you, remember that she may be found always within the land. Touch it, and she will be with you."

He stepped away into the dark and pinched out the candle's flame.

"Don't go," Wil called out sleepily.

"Goodbye, Wil." The deep voice drifted out of a fog. "Tell Flick that he was right about me. He will like that."

"Allanon," The Valeman mumbled softly and then he was asleep.

Through the dimly lit corridors of the Elessedil home the Druid stole, as silent as the shadows of the night. Home Guard patrolled these corridors, Elven Hunters who had fought and survived in the battle of the Elfitch, hard men and not easily moved. Yet they stepped aside for Allanon; something in the Druid's glance suggested that they should.

Moments later he stood within the bedchamber of the Elven King, the door closing softly behind him. Candlelight illuminated the room with a dim, hazy glow that seeped through the gloom into shadowed corners and hidden nooks with a blind man's touch. Windows stood closed and drapes drawn, masking the room in silence. On a wide double bed at the far end of the chamber lay Eventine, swathed in bandages and linen sheets. At his side Ander dozed fitfully in a high-backed wicker chair.

Wordlessly Allanon came forward and stopped at the foot of the bed. The old King slept, his breathing ragged and slow, his skin the color of new parchment. The end of his life was near. It was the passing of an age, the Druid thought. They would all be gone now, all those who had stood against the Warlock Lord, all those who had aided in the quest for the elusive Sword of Shannara—all but the Ohmsfords, Shea and Flick.

A grim, ironic smile passed slowly across his lips. And himself, of course. He was still there. He was always there.

Beneath the linen coverings, Eventine stirred. It will happen now, Allanon told himself. For the first time that night, a touch of bitterness showed in his hard face.

Silently he moved back within the concealing shadows at the rear of the room and waited.

Ander Elessedil came awake with a start. Eyes blurred with sleep, he peered guardedly about the empty bedchamber, searching for ghosts that were not there. A frightening sense of aloneness swept through him. So many of those who should have been there were not—Arion, Pindanon, Crispin, Ehlron Tay, Kerrin. All dead.

He slumped back in the wicker chair, weariness numbing him until he could feel nothing but the ache of joints and muscles. How long had he slept, he wondered? He didn't know. Gael would be back soon, bringing food and drink, and together they would keep this vigil, watching over the stricken King. Waiting.

Memories haunted him, memories of his father and what had been, spectral images of the past, of times and places and events that would never be again. They were bittersweet, a reminder both of the happiness shared and its transience. On balance, he would have preferred that the memories leave him in peace this night.

He thought suddenly of his father and Amberle, of the special affection they had felt for each other, the closeness that had been lost and found again—gone now, all of it. It was difficult even now to comprehend the transformation that Amberle had undergone. He had to keep reminding himself that it was real, that it was not imagined. He could still see the little Wing Rider, Perk, telling him what he had witnessed, his child's face awestruck and frightened all at once, so determined and so concerned that he should not be doubted.

His head tilted back and his eyes closed. Few knew the truth yet. He was still undecided as to whether or not it should remain that way.

"Ander."

He jerked upright, and his father's penetrating blue eyes met his own. He was so surprised that, for an instant, he simply stared down at the old man.

"Ander—what has happened?"

The Elven King's voice was a thin, harsh whisper in the stillness. Quickly Ander knelt down beside him.

"It is over," he replied softly. "We have won. The Demons are locked once more within the Forbidding. The Ellcrys . . ."

He could not finish. He did not have the words. His father's hand slipped from beneath the coverings to find his own.

"Amberle?"

Ander took a deep breath, and there were tears in his eyes. He forced himself to meet his father's gaze.

"Safe," he whispered. "Resting now."

There was a long pause. A trace of a smile slipped across his father's face. Then his eyes closed. A moment later he was dead.

Allanon stood within the shadows several minutes more before stepping forward.

"Ander," he called softly.

The Elven Prince rose, releasing his father's hand. "He's gone, Allanon."

"And you are King. Be the King he would have wanted you to be."

Ander turned, his eyes searching. "Did you know, Allanon? I have wondered often since Baen Draw. Did you know that all this would happen, that I would be King?"

The Druid's features seemed to close in about him momentarily, and his dark face lost all expression. "I could not have prevented from happening that which happened, Elven Prince," he replied slowly. "I could only try to prepare you for what was to be."

"Then you knew?"

Allanon nodded. "I knew. I am a Druid."

Ander took a deep breath. "I will do the best that I can, Allanon."

"Then you will do well, Ander Elessedil."

He watched the Elven Prince move back to the dead King, saw him cover his father as he would a sleeping child, then kneel once more at the bedside.

Allanon turned and slipped noiselessly from the room, from the manor house, from the city, and from the land. No one saw him go.

It was dawn when Wil Ohmsford was shaken gently awake, silver-gray light seeping through curtained windows to chase the fading dark. His eyes blinked slowly open and he found himself staring up at Perk.

"Wil?" The little Wing Rider's face was a mask of seriousness.

"Hello, Perk."

"How are you feeling?"

"A little better, I think."

"That's good." Perk tried a quick smile. "I was really worried."

Wil smiled back. "Me, too."

Perk sat down on the edge of the bed. "I'm sorry to wake you, but I didn't want to leave without saying goodbye."

"You're leaving?"

The youth nodded. "I should have left last night, but I had to rest Genewen. She was pretty tired after that long flight. But I have to leave now. I should have been back at the Wing Hove two days ago. They will probably be searching for me." He paused. "But they'll understand when I explain what happened. They won't be mad."

"I hope not. I wouldn't want that."

"My Uncle Dayn said he would explain it to them, too. Did you know that my Uncle Dayn was here, Wil? My grandfather sent him. Uncle Dayn said I acted like a true Wing Rider. He said what Genewen and I did was very important."

Wil pushed himself up slightly against his pillows. "So it was, Perk. Very important."

"I couldn't just leave you. I knew you might need me."

"We needed you very much."

"And I didn't think my grandfather would mind if I disobeyed just this once."

"I don't think he will mind."

Perk looked down at his hands. "Wil, I'm sorry about the Lady Amberle. I really am."

Wil nodded slowly. "I know, Perk."

"She really was enchanted, wasn't she? She was enchanted and the enchantment turned her into the tree." He looked up quickly. "That was what she wanted, wasn't it? To turn into the tree so the Demons would disappear? That was the way it was supposed to be?"

The Valeman swallowed hard. "Yes."

"I was really scared, you know," Perk said quietly. "I wasn't sure whether that was supposed to happen or not. It was so sudden. She never said anything about it to me before it happened, so when it did happen it scared me."

"I don't think she wanted to scare you."

"No, I don't think so either."

"She just didn't have time enough to explain."

Perk shrugged. "Oh, I know that. It was just so sudden."

They were quiet a moment, and then the little Wing Rider rose. "I just wanted to say goodbye, Wil. Would you come visit me sometime? Or I could come to see you—but that wouldn't be until I'm older. My family won't let me fly out of the Westland."

"I will come visit you," Wil promised. "Soon."

Perk gave a sort of half-wave and walked to the door. His hand was on the latch when he paused and glanced back at the Valeman.

"I really liked her, Wil—a whole lot."

"I liked her, too, Perk."

The little Wing Rider smiled briefly and disappeared through the door.

54

They went home then, all those who had come to Arborlon to stand with the Elves, all but two.

The Wing Riders went first, at the dawn of the day that began the reign of Ander Elessedil as the new King of the Land Elves—three who remained of the five who had flown north together and the boy called Perk. They left quietly, with barely a word to anyone but the young King, and were gone before the sun fully crested the eastern forests, their golden-hued Rocs chasing after the disappearing night like the first rays of the morning sun.

At midday the Rock Trolls departed, Amantar at their head, as fierce and proud as when they had come, weapons raised in salute as the Elven people gathered along the streets and in the tree-lanes to cheer their passing. For the first time in more than a thousand years, Troll and Elf parted not as enemies, but as friends.

The Dwarves stayed several days longer, lending to the Elves the benefit of their vast engineering expertise by assisting in the drafting of plans for the rebuilding of the shattered Elfitch. A most difficult task lay ahead in that rebuilding, for not only was it necessary to replace the demolished fifth rampway, but most of the remainder of the structure was in need of shoring up as well. It was the kind of challenge that the redoubtable Browork relished; with the aid of those Sappers yet able to work, he traced for the Elves the steps by which the task might best be accomplished. When finally he did take leave of Ander and the Elven people, he did so with the promise that another company of Dwarf Sappers—one in better condition to serve than his own—would be sent at once to give whatever aid was necessary.

"We know that we can depend upon the Dwarves." Ander gripped Browork's rough hand in parting.

"Always," the crusty Dwarf agreed with a nod. "See that you remember that when we have need of you."

Finally it was the turn of the men of Callahorn to depart—the handful of Legion Free Corps and Old Guard who had survived the ferocious struggle to hold the Elfitch. Not a dozen of the former remained and of those not six would fight again. The command had virtually ceased to exist, the bodies of its soldiers scattered between the passes of the Breakline and Arborlon. Yet once more the tall, scar-faced Borderman called Stee Jans had survived where so many others had not.

He came to Ander Elessedil early on the morning of the sixth day following their victory over the Demon hordes, riding out on his great blue roan to where the Elven King stood at the edge of the Carolan and reviewed with his engineers the plans drafted by the Dwarf Sappers. Excusing himself hurriedly, Ander walked quickly to where the Free Corps Commander had dismounted and stood waiting. Ignoring the nod of respect the big man gave him, Ander seized the other's hand and gripped it firmly.

"You are well again, Commander?" he greeted him, smiling.

"Well enough, my Lord." Stee Jans smiled back. "I came to thank you and to say goodbye. The Legion rides again for Callahorn."

Ander shook his head slowly. "It is not for you to thank me. It is for me—and for the Elven people—to thank you. No one gave more to us and to this land than the men of the Free Corps. And you, Stee Jans— what would we have done without you?"

The Borderman was quiet for a moment before speaking. "My Lord, I think we found in the people and the land a cause worth fighting for. All that we gave, we gave freely. And you did not lose this fight—that is what matters."

"How could we lose with you to aid us?" Ander gripped his hand anew. He paused. "What will you do now?"

Stee Jans shrugged. "The Free Corps is gone. Perhaps they'll rebuild. Perhaps not. If not, perhaps there will be a new Legion command. I will ask for one, in any case."

Ander nodded slowly. "Ask me, Stee Jans—ask me and the command is yours. I would be honored to have you. And the Elven people would be honored. You are one of us. Will you consider it?"

The Borderman smiled, turned, and swung back into the saddle. "I am already considering it, King Ander Elessedil." He saluted smartly. "Until we meet again, my Lord—strength to you and to the Elves."

He reined the big roan about, gray cloak flying, and rode east across the Carolan. Ander watched him go, waving after him. Until we meet again, Borderman, he replied without speaking.

Thus they went home, all those who had come to Arborlon to stand with the Elves, all the brave ones, all but two.

One was the Valeman, Wil Ohmsford.

Sunshine lay across the Carolan in a blanket of warmth and hazy brightness as the noonday neared and Wil Ohmsford approached the gates leading into the Gardens of Life. Down the gravel pathway the Valeman walked, his stride measured and even, and there was no sign of hesitation in his coming. Yet when he stood at last before the gates, he was not sure that he could go further.

It had taken him a week to come this far. The first three days following his collapse in these same Gardens had been spent in his chambers in the Elessedil manor house, asleep most of the time. Two more had been spent in the seclusion of the grounds surrounding the ancient home, wrestling with the jumble of emotions that seethed within him as memories of Amberle came and went. The last two days he had spent studiously avoiding the very thing he had now come to do.

He stood for a long time at the Gardens' entrance, staring upward at the arch of silver scroll and inlaid ivory, at the ivy-grown walls, and the pines and hedgerows leading in. Heads turned toward him questioningly as the people of the city came and went, passing into and out of the gates before which he stood. They were there for the same reason that had brought him and were wondering as they saw him if he were perhaps even more awed and self-conscious than they. Sentries of the Black Watch stood rigid and aloof to either side, eyes shifting momentarily to watch the motionless figure of the Valeman, then looking quickly away again. Still Wil Ohmsford did not go forward.

Yet he knew he must. He had thought it through quite carefully. He must see her one time more. One final time. There could be no peace within him until it was done.

Almost before he realized it, he was through the gates, following the curve of the pathway that would take him to the tree.

He felt oddly relieved as he went, as if in making the decision to go to her he was doing something not only necessary, but right. A bit of the determination that had seen him through so much these past few weeks returned to him now—determination that had been drained from him when he had lost the Elven girl, so complete was his belief that he had failed her. He thought he understood that feeling better now. It was not so much a sense of failure that he had experienced as a sense of his own limitations. You cannot do everything you might wish that you could do, Uncle Flick had told him once. And so, while he had been able to save Amberle from the Demons, he had not been able to save her from becoming the Ellcrys. Yet saving her from that, he knew, was not something that had ever been within his power. It had only been within hers. Her choice, as she had told him—as Allanon, too, had told him. No amount of anger, bitterness, or self-remorse would change that or bring him the peace he needed. He must reconcile what had happened another way. He thought he knew that way now. This visit to her was the first step.

Then he passed through an opening in a tall row of evergreens and she was before him. The Ellcrys rose up against the clear blue of the noonday sky, tall silver trunk and scarlet leaves rippling in the golden sunlight, a thing of such exquisite beauty that in the instant he saw her tears came to his eyes.

"Amberle . . ." he whispered.

Gathered at the foot of the small rise upon which she stood were Elven families from the city, their eyes fixed upon the tree, their voices lowered and hushed. Wil Ohmsford hesitated, then moved forward to join them.

"You see, the sickness is gone," a mother was saying to a little girl. "She is well again."

And her land and her people are safe, the Valeman added silently. Because of Amberle—because she had sacrificed herself for both. He took a deep breath, gazing upward at the tree. It was something she had wanted to do, something she had had to do—not just because it was needed but because in the end she had come to believe it to be the purpose for her existence. The Elven ethic, the creed that had governed her life—something of the self must be given back to the land. Even when she had banished herself from Arborlon, she had not forgotten the creed. It had been reflected in her work with the children of Havenstead. It had been a part of the reason that she had returned with him to discover the truth of her destiny.

Something of the self must be given back to the land.

In the end, she had given back everything.

He smiled sadly. But she had not lost everything. In becoming the Ellcrys, she had gained an entire world.

"Will she keep the Demons from us, Mommy?" the little girl was asking.

"Far, far away from us." Her mother smiled.

"And protect us always?"

"Yes—and protect us always."

The little girl's eyes flitted from her mother's face to the tree. "She is so pretty." Her small voice was filled with wonderment.

Amberle.

Wil gazed upon her for an instant longer, then turned and walked slowly from the Gardens.

He had just passed back through the gates leading in when he spied Eretria. She stood a little to one side on the pathway leading up from the city, her dark eyes shifting quickly to meet his own. The bright Rover silks were gone, replaced by ordinary Elven garb. Yet there could never be anything ordinary about Eretria. She was as stunningly beautiful now as she had been the first time Wil had laid eyes on her. Her long black hair shimmered in the sunlight as it curled down about her shoulders, and that dazzling smile broke over her dusky face as she caught sight of him.

Wordlessly, he walked over to greet her, permitting himself a small grin in reply.

"You look like a whole man again," she said lightly.

He nodded. "You can take whatever credit is due for that. You're the one who got me back on my feet."

Her smile broadened at the compliment. Every day for the past week she had come to him—feeding him, dressing his wounds, giving him company when she had sensed he needed it, giving him peace when she had seen that he needed to be alone. His recovery, both physical and emotional, was due in no small part to her efforts.

"I was told that you had gone out." She glanced briefly toward the Gardens. "It didn't require much imagination to know where you had gone. So I thought I would follow and wait for you." She looked back at him, the smile winsome. "Are all the ghosts laid to rest at last, Healer?"

Wil saw the concern in her eyes. She understood better than any what the loss of Amberle had done to him. They had talked about it constantly in the time they had spent together during his recovery. Ghosts, she had called them—all those purposeless feelings of guilt that had haunted him.

"I think maybe they're resting now," he answered. "Coming here helped, and in a little more time, maybe . . ."

He trailed off, shrugged and smiled. "Amberle believed that something was owed to the land for the life it gave her. She told me once that her belief was a part of her Elven heritage. My heritage, too, I think she was suggesting. You see, she always thought of me more as a Healer than as a protector. And a Healer is what I should be. A Healer gives something to the land through the care he provides to the people who look after her. That will be my gift, Eretria."

She nodded solemnly. "So you will go back now to Storlock?"

"Home first, to Shady Vale—then to Storlock."

"Soon?"

"I think so. I think I should go now." He cleared his throat uneasily. "Did you know that Allanon left me the black—the stallion Artaq? A gift. I suppose he felt it might help make up for losing Amberle."

Her dark face glanced away. "I suppose. Can we walk back now?"

Without waiting for his answer, she began to retrace her steps along the pathway. He hesitated in confusion a moment, then hurried after her. Together, they walked in silence.

"Have you decided to keep the Elfstones?" she asked after several minutes had passed.

He had told her once, when his depression had been deepest, that he intended to give them up. The Elven magic had done something to him, he knew. Just as surely as magic had aged Allanon, it had affected him as well—though as yet he could not tell how. Such power frightened him still. Yet the responsibility for that power remained his; he could not simply pass it carelessly to another.

"I'll keep them," he answered her. "But I'll never use them again. Never."

"No," she said quietly. "A Healer would have no use for the Stones."

They walked past the Gardens' walls and turned down the pathway toward Arborlon. Neither spoke. Wil could sense the distance separating them, a widening gulf caused by her certainty that he would be leaving her once again. She wanted to go with him, of course. She had always wanted to go with him. But she would not ask—not this time, not again. Her pride would not let her. He mulled the matter over in his mind.

"Where will you go now?" he asked her a moment later.

She shrugged casually. "Oh, I don't know. Callahorn, maybe. This Rover girl can go where she chooses, be what she wants." She paused. "Maybe I'll come to see you. You seem to require a great deal of looking after."

There it was. She said it lightly, jokingly almost, but there was no mistaking the intent. I am for you, Wil Ohmsford, she had told him that night in the Tirfing. She was saying it again. He glanced over at her dark face, thinking fleetingly of all that she had done for him, all that she had risked for him. If he left her now, she would have no one. She had no home, no family, no people. Before, when she had wanted to go with him, there had been a reason to refuse her. What was his reason now?

"It was just a thought," she added, brushing the matter off quickly.

"A nice thought," he said quietly. "But I was thinking that maybe you'd like to come back with me now."

The words were spoken almost before he realized what he had decided. There was a long, long silence, and they kept walking along the pathway, neither one looking at the other, almost as if nothing at all had been said.

"Maybe I would," she replied finally. "If you mean it."

"I mean it."

Then he saw her smile—that wondrous, dazzling smile. She stopped and turned toward him.

"It is reassuring to see, Wil Ohmsford, that you have come to your senses at last."

Her hand reached for his and clasped it tightly.

Riding back along the Carolan toward the city, his mind still occupied by thoughts of the rebuilding of the Elfitch, Ander Elessedil caught sight of the Valeman and the Rover girl as they walked back from the Gardens of Life. Reining in his horse for a moment, he watched the two who had not yet gone home, saw them stop, then saw the girl take the Valeman's hand in her own.

A slow smile creased his face as he swung his horse wide of where they stood. It looked very much as if Wil Ohmsford, too, would be going home now. But not alone.

THE WISHSONG
OF SHANNARA

For
Lester del Rey
Expert

FOREWORD

Wishsong was a surprisingly easy book to write in the sense that I came up with the storyline almost immediately. The end of *The Elfstones of Shannara* dictated that we discover in the next book the consequences of Wil Ohmsford's decision to use the Elfstones even though he lacked the necessary Elven blood. Those consequences would be felt by his children—a sister and brother this time—who would be the central characters. The Elven magic was constantly evolving and it would manifest itself differently in Brin and Jair. It would give one of Wil Ohmsford's children the ability to change the physical characteristics of living things through a wishsong. But which child? Then it occurred to me that perhaps the magic would be evident in both, but function differently in each. They wouldn't necessarily be comfortable with its presence, either, or even understand all of its ramifications. And surely the wishsong's magic wouldn't be all good. It would simply *be*, power that charted its own course, affecting the user in unexpected ways.

The second element of the storyline was born out of a desire to write a sort of Magnificent Seven adventure—a tale about a small band of life-weary professionals traveling into enemy country where they would be forced to make a desperate last stand against impossible odds. Some thought on the subject led to the creation of Garet Jax, the Weapons Master, a kind of natural force, a complex man searching for something without knowing quite what it was. Slanter came later, the suggestion of Lester (evolving from a minor character in the outline to a major character in the book). There would be a journey that would include Brin and Jair, but their reasons for going might not be the same as those of the Weapons Master and the others. Perhaps they shouldn't even be traveling together. Perhaps there ought to be more than one journey involved, much as there had been in the second half of *The Sword of Shannara*. And what part was Allanon to play in all of this? Surely the Druid would still be around, solitary and enigmatic as always, the catalyst for whatever happened. And wouldn't he be searching by now for his successor? After all, his life was drawing to a close. For that matter, what was to become of Allanon when this third *Shannara* book ended?

I wrote *Wishsong* in about a year and a half, which was very fast. It was approved by Lester with minimal changes. I saw light at the end of the tunnel where my professional writer's education was concerned. Some of the lessons of the last book had stayed with me, it appeared.

One year after publication of *Wishsong* I gave up the practice of law and started writing full-time. For better or worse, I had a new career.

—Terry Brooks

A change of seasons was upon the Four Lands as late summer faded slowly into autumn. Gone were the long, still days of midyear where sweltering heat slowed the pace of life and there was a sense of having time enough for anything. Though summer's warmth lingered, the days had begun to shorten, the humid air to dry, and the memory of life's immediacy to reawaken. The signs of transition were all about. In the forests of Shady Vale, the leaves had already begun to turn.

Brin Ohmsford paused by the flowerbeds that bordered the front walkway of her home, losing herself momentarily in the crimson foliage of the old maple that shaded the yard beyond. It was a massive thing, its trunk broad and gnarled. Brin smiled. That old tree was the source of many childhood memories for her. Impulsively, she stepped off the walkway and moved over to the aged tree.

She was a tall girl—taller than her parents or her brother Jair, nearly as tall as Rone Leah—and although there was a delicate look to her slim body, she was as fit as any of them. Jair would argue the point of course, but that was only because Jair found it hard enough as it was to accept his role as the youngest. A girl, after all, was just a girl.

Her fingers touched the roughened trunk of the maple softly, caressing, and she stared upward into the tangle of limbs overhead. Long, black hair fell away from her face and there was no mistaking whose child she was. Twenty years ago, Eretria had looked exactly as her daughter looked now, from dusky skin and black eyes to soft, delicate features. All that Brin lacked was her mother's fire. Jair had gotten that. Brin had her father's temperament, cool, self-assured, and disciplined. In comparing his children one time—a time occasioned by one of Jair's more reprehensible misadventures—Wil Ohmsford had remarked rather ruefully that the difference between the two was that Jair was apt to do anything, while Brin was also apt to do it, but only after thinking it through first. Brin still wasn't sure who had come out on the short end of that reprimand.

Her hands slipped back to her sides. She remembered the time she had used the wishsong on the old tree. She had still been a child, experimenting with the Elven magic. It had been midsummer and she had used the wishsong to turn the tree's summer green to autumn crimson; in her child's mind, it seemed perfectly all right to do so, since red was a far prettier color than green. Her father had been furious; it had taken almost three years for the tree to come back again after the shock to its system. That had been the last time either she or Jair had used the magic when their parents were about.

"Brin, come help me with the rest of the packing, please."

It was her mother calling. She gave the old maple a final pat and turned toward the house.

Her father had never fully trusted the Elven magic. A little more than twenty years earlier he had used the Elfstones given him by the Druid Allanon in his efforts to protect the Elven Chosen Amberle Elessedil in her quest for the Bloodfire. Use of the Elven magic had changed him; he had known it even then, though not known how. It was only after Brin was born, and later Jair, that it became apparent what had been done. It was not Wil Ohmsford who would manifest the change the magic had wrought; it was his children. They were the ones who would carry within them the visible effects of the magic—they, and perhaps generations of Ohmsfords to come, although there was no way of ascertaining yet that they would carry within them the magic of the wishsong.

Brin had named it the wishsong. Wish for it, sing for it, and it was yours. That was how it had seemed to her when she had first discovered that she possessed the power. She learned early that she could affect the behavior of living things with her song. She could change that old maple's leaves. She could soothe an angry dog. She could bring a wild bird to light on her wrist. She could make herself a part of any living thing—or make it a part of her. She wasn't sure how she did it; it simply happened. She would sing, the music and the words coming as they always did, unplanned, unrehearsed—as if it were the most natural thing in the world. She was always aware of what she was singing, yet at the same time heedless, her mind caught up in feelings of indescribable sensation. They would sweep through her, drawing her in, making her somehow new again, and the wish would come to pass.

It was the gift of the Elven magic—or its curse. The latter was how her father had viewed it when he had discovered she possessed it. Brin knew that, deep inside, he was frightened of what the Elfstones could do and what he had felt them do to him. After Brin had caused the family dog to chase its tail until it nearly dropped and had wilted an entire garden of vegetables, her father had been quick to reassert his decision that the Elfstones would never be used again by anyone. He had hidden them, telling no one where they could be found, and hidden they had remained ever since. At least, that was what her father thought. She was not altogether certain. One time, not too many months earlier, when there was mention of the hidden Elfstones, Brin had caught Jair smiling rather smugly. He would not admit to anything, of course, but she knew how difficult it was to keep anything hidden from her brother, and she suspected he had found the hiding place.

Rone Leah met her at the front door, tall and rangy, rust brown hair loose about his shoulders and tied back with a broad headband. Mischievous gray eyes narrowed appraisingly. "How about lending a hand, huh? I'm doing all the work and I'm not even a member of the family, for cat's sake!"

"As much time as you spend here, you ought to be," she chided. "What's left to be done?"

"Just these cases to be carried out—that should finish it." A gathering of leather trunks and smaller bags stood stacked in the entry. Rone picked up the largest. "I think your mother wants you in the bedroom."

He disappeared down the walkway and Brin moved through her home toward the back bedrooms. Her parents were getting ready to depart on their annual fall pilgrimage to the outlying communities south of Shady Vale, a journey that would keep them gone from their home for better than two weeks. Few Healers possessed the skills of Wil Ohmsford, and not one could be found within five hundred miles of the Vale. So twice a year, in the spring and fall, her father traveled down to the outlying villages, lending his services where they were needed. Eretria always accompanied him, a skilled aide to her husband by now, trained nearly as thoroughly as he in the care of the sick and injured. It was a journey they need not have made—would not, in fact, had they been less conscientious than they were. Others would not have gone. But Brin's parents were governed by a strong sense of duty. Healing was the profession to which both had dedicated their lives, and they did not take their commitment to it lightly.

While they were gone on these trips of mercy, Brin was left to watch over Jair. On this occasion, Rone Leah had traveled down from the highlands to watch over them both.

Brin's mother looked up from the last of her packing and smiled as Brin entered the bedroom. Long black hair fell loosely about her shoulders, and she brushed it back from a face that looked barely older than Brin's.

"Have you seen your brother? We're almost ready to leave."

Brin shook her head. "I thought he was with father. Can I help you with anything?"

Eretria nodded, took Brin by the shoulders, and pulled her down next to her on the bed. "I want you to promise me something, Brin. I don't want you to use the wishsong while your father and I are gone—you or your brother."

Brin smiled. "I hardly use it at all anymore." Her dark eyes searched her mother's dusky face.

"I know. But Jair does, even if he thinks I don't know about it. In any case, while we are gone, your father and I don't want either of you using it even a single time. Do you understand?"

Brin hesitated. Her father understood that the Elven magic was a part of his children, but he did not accept that it was either a good or necessary part. You are intelligent, talented people just as you are, he would tell them. You have no need of tricks and artifices to advance yourselves. Be who and what you can without the song. Eretria had echoed that advice, although she seemed to recognize more readily than he that they were likely to ignore it when discretion suggested that they could.

In Jair's case, unfortunately, discretion seldom entered into the picture.

Jair was both impulsive and distressingly headstrong; when it came to use of the wishsong, he was inclined to do exactly as he pleased—as long as he could safely get away with it.

Still, the Elven magic worked differently with Jair . . .

"Brin?"

Her thoughts scattered. "Mother, I don't see what difference it makes if Jair wants to play around with the wishsong. It's just a toy."

Eretria shook her head. "Even a toy can be dangerous if used unwisely. Besides, you ought to know enough of the Elven magic by now to appreciate the fact that it is never harmless. Now listen to me. You and your brother are both grown beyond the age when you need your mother and father looking over your shoulder. But a little advice is still necessary now and then. I don't want you using the magic while we're gone. It draws attention where it's not needed. Promise me that you won't use it—and that you will keep Jair from using it as well."

Brin nodded slowly. "It's because of the rumors of the black walkers, isn't it?" She had heard the stories. They talked about it all the time down at the inn these days. Black walkers—soundless, faceless things born of the dark magic, appearing out of nowhere. Some said it was the Warlock Lord and his minions come back again. "Is that what this is all about?"

"Yes." Her mother smiled at Brin's perceptiveness. "Now promise me."

Brin smiled back. "I promise."

Nevertheless, she thought it all a lot of nonsense.

The packing and loading took another thirty minutes, and then her parents were ready to depart. Jair reappeared, back from the inn where he had gone to secure a special sweet as a parting gift for his mother who was fond of such things, and good-byes were exchanged.

"Remember your promise, Brin," her mother whispered as she kissed her on the cheek and hugged her close.

Then the elder Ohmsfords were aboard the wagon in which they would make their journey and moving slowly up the dusty roadway.

Brin watched them until they were out of sight.

Brin, Jair, and Rone Leah went hiking that afternoon in the forests of the Vale, and it was late in the day when at last they turned homeward. By then, the sun had begun to dip beneath the rim of the Vale and the forest shadows of midday to lengthen slowly into evening. It was an hour's walk to the hamlet, but both Ohmsfords and the highlander had come this way so often before that they could have navigated the forest trails even in blackest night. They proceeded at a leisurely pace, enjoying the close of what had been an altogether beautiful autumn day.

"Let's fish tomorrow," Rone suggested. He grinned at Brin. "With weather like this, it won't matter if we catch anything or not."

The oldest of the three, he led the way through the trees, the worn and battered scabbard bearing the Sword of Leah strapped crosswise to his back, a vague outline beneath his hunting cloak. Once carried by the heir-apparent to the throne of Leah, it had long since outlived that purpose and been replaced. But Rone had always admired the old blade, borne years earlier by his great-grandfather Menion Leah when he had gone in search of the Sword of Shannara. Since Rone admired the weapon so, his father had given it to him, a small symbol of his standing as a Prince of Leah— even if he were its youngest prince.

Brin looked over at him and frowned. "You seem to be forgetting something. Tomorrow is the day we set aside for the house repairs we promised father we would make while he was away. What about that?"

He shrugged cheerfully. "Another day for the repairs—they'll keep."

"I think we should do some exploring along the rim of the Vale," Jair Ohmsford interjected. He was lean and wiry and had his father's face with its Elven features—narrow eyes, slanted eyebrows, and ears pointed slightly beneath a thatch of unruly blond hair. "I think we should see if we can find any sign of the Mord Wraiths."

Rone laughed. "Now what do you know about the walkers, tiger?" It was his pet name for Jair.

"As much as you, I'd guess. We hear the same stories in the Vale that you hear in the highlands," the Valeman replied. "Black walkers, Mord Wraiths—things that steal out of the dark. They talk about it down at the inn all the time."

Brin glanced at her brother reprovingly. "That's all they are, too—just stories."

Jair looked at Rone. "What do you think?"

To Brin's surprise, the highlander shrugged. "Maybe. Maybe not."

She was suddenly angry. "Rone, there have been stories like this ever since the Warlock Lord was destroyed, and none of them has ever contained a word of truth. Why would it be any different this time?"

"I don't know that it would. I just believe in being careful. Remember, they didn't believe the stories of the Skull Bearers in Shea Ohmsford's time either—until it was too late."

"That's why I think we ought to have a look around," Jair repeated.

"For what purpose exactly?" Brin pressed, her voice hardening. "On the chance that we might find something as dangerous as these things are supposed to be? What would you do then—call on the wishsong?"

Jair flushed. "If I had to, I would. I could use the magic . . ."

She cut him short. "The magic is nothing to play around with, Jair. How many times do I have to tell you that?"

"I just said that . . ."

"I know what you said. You think that the wishsong can do anything for you and you're sadly mistaken. You had better pay attention to what father says about not using the magic. Someday, it's going to get you into a lot of trouble."

Her brother stared at her. "What are you so angry about?"

She was angry, she realized, and it was serving no purpose. "I'm sorry," she apologized. "I made mother a promise that neither of us would use the wishsong while she and father were away on this trip. I suppose that's why it upsets me to hear you talking about tracking Mord Wraiths."

Now there was a hint of anger in Jair's blue eyes. "Who gave you the right to make a promise like that for me, Brin?"

"No one, I suppose, but mother . . ."

"Mother doesn't understand . . ."

"Hold on, for cat's sake!" Rone Leah held up his hands imploringly. "Arguments like this make me glad that I'm staying down at the inn and not up at the house with you two. Now let's forget all this and get back to the original subject. Do we go fishing tomorrow or not?"

"We go fishing," Jair voted.

"We go fishing," Brin agreed. "After we finish at least some of the repairs."

They walked in silence for a time, Brin still brooding over what she viewed as Jair's increasing infatuation with the uses of the wishsong. Her mother was right; Jair practiced using the magic whenever he got the chance. He saw less danger in its use than Brin did because it worked differently for him. For Brin, the wishsong altered appearance and behavior in fact, but for Jair it was only an illusion. When he used the magic, things only seemed to happen. That gave him greater latitude in its use and encouraged experimentation. He did it in secret, but he did it nevertheless. Even Brin wasn't entirely sure what he had learned to do with it.

Afternoon faded altogether and evening settled in. A full moon hung above the eastern horizon like a white beacon, and stars began to wink into view. With the coming of night, the air began to cool rapidly, and the smells of the forest turned crisp and heavy with the fragrance of drying leaves. All about rose the hum of insects and night birds.

"I think we should fish the Rappahalladran," Jair announced suddenly.

No one said anything for a moment. "I don't know," Rone answered finally. "We could fish the ponds in the Vale just as well."

Brin glanced over at the highlander quizzically. He sounded worried.

"Not for brook trout," Jair insisted. "Besides, I want to camp out in the Duln for a night or two."

"We could do that in the Vale."

"The Vale is practically the same as the backyard," Jair pointed out, growing a bit irritated. "At least the Duln has a few places we haven't explored before. What are you frightened about?"

"I'm not frightened of anything," the highlander replied defensively. "I just think . . . Look, why don't we talk about this later. Let me tell you what happened to me on the way out here. I almost managed to get myself lost. There was this wolf-dog . . ."

Brin dropped back a pace as they talked, letting them walk on ahead. She was still puzzled by Rone's unexpected reluctance to make even a short camping trip into the Duln—a trip they had all made dozens of times before. Was there something beyond the Vale of which they need be frightened? She frowned, remembering the concern voiced by her mother.

Now it was Rone as well. The highlander had not been as quick as she to discount as rumors those stories of the Mord Wraiths. In fact, he had been unusually restrained. Normally, Rone would have laughed such stories off as so much nonsense, just as she had done. Why hadn't he done so this time? It was possible, she realized, that he had some cause to believe it wasn't a laughing matter.

Half an hour passed, and the lights of the village began to appear through the forest trees. It was dark now, and they picked their way along the path with the aid of the moon's bright light. The trail dipped downward into the sheltered hollow where the village proper sat, broadening as it went from a footpath to a roadway. Houses appeared; from within, the sound of voices could be heard. Brin felt the first hint of weariness slip over her. It would be good to crawl into the comfort of her bed and give herself over to a good night's sleep.

They walked down through the center of Shady Vale, passing by the old inn that had been owned and managed by the Ohmsford family for so many generations past. The Ohmsfords still owned the establishment, but no longer lived there—not since the passing of Shea and Flick. Friends of the family managed the inn these days, sharing the earnings and expenses with Brin's parents. Her father had never really been comfortable living at the inn, Brin knew, feeling no real connection with its business, preferring his own life as a Healer to that of innkeeper. Only Jair showed any real interest in the happenings of the inn and that was because he liked to go down to listen to the tales carried to Shady Vale by travelers passing through—tales filled with adventure enough to satisfy the spirit of the restless Valeman.

The inn was busy this night, its broad double-doors flung open, the lights within falling over tables and a long bar crowded with travelers and village folk, laughing and joking and passing the cool autumn evening with a glass or two of ale. Rone grinned over his shoulder at Brin and shook his head. No one was anxious for this day to end.

Moments later, they reached the Ohmsford home, a stone and mortar cottage set back within the trees on a small knoll. They were halfway up the cobblestone walk that ran through a series of hedgerows and flowering plum to the front door when Brin brought them to a sudden halt.

There was a light in the window of the front room.

"Did either of you leave a lamp burning when we left this morning?" she asked quietly, already knowing the answer. Both shook their heads.

"Maybe someone stopped in for a visit," Rone suggested.

Brin looked at him. "The house was locked."

They stared at each other wordlessly for a moment, a vague sense of uneasiness starting to take hold. Jair, however, was feeling none of it.

"Well, let's go on in and see who's there," he declared and started forward.

Rone put a hand on his shoulder and pulled him back. "Just a moment, tiger. Let's not be too hasty."

Jair pulled free, glanced again at the light, then looked back at Rone. "Who do you think's waiting in there—one of the walkers?"

"Will you stop that nonsense!" Brin ordered sharply.

Jair smirked. "That's who you think it is, don't you? One of the walkers, come to steal us away!"

"Good of them to put a light on for us," Rone commented dryly.

They stared again at the light in the front window, undecided.

"Well, we can't just stand out here all night," Rone said finally. He reached back over his shoulder and pulled free the Sword of Leah. "Let's have a look. You two stay behind me. If anything happens, get back to the inn and bring some help." He hesitated. "Not that anything is going to happen."

They proceeded up the walk to the front door and stopped, listening. The house was silent. Brin handed Rone the key to the door and they stepped inside. The anteway was pitch black, save for a sliver of yellow light that snaked down the short hallway leading in. They hesitated a moment, then passed silently down the hall and stepped into the front room.

It was empty.

"Well, no Mord Wraiths here," Jair announced at once. "Nothing here except . . ."

He never finished. A hugh shadow stepped into the light from the darkened drawing room beyond. It was a man over seven feet tall, cloaked all in black. A loose cowl was pulled back to reveal a lean, craggy face that was weathered and hard. Black beard and hair swept down from his face and head, coarse and shot through with streaks of gray. But it was the eyes that drew them, deep-set and penetrating from within the shadow of his great brow, seeming to see everything, even that which was hidden.

Rone Leah brought up the broadsword hurriedly, and the stranger's hand lifted from out of the robes.

"You won't need that."

The highlander hesitated, stared momentarily into the other's dark eyes, then dropped the sword blade downward again. Brin and Jair stood frozen in place, unable to turn and run or to speak.

"There is nothing to be frightened of," the stranger's deep voice rumbled.

None of the three felt particularly reassured by that, yet all relaxed slightly when the dark figure made no further move to approach. Brin glanced hurriedly at her brother and found Jair watching the stranger intently, as if puzzling something through. The stranger looked at the boy, then at Rone, then at her.

"Does not one of you know me?" he murmured softly.

There was momentary silence, and then suddenly Jair nodded.

"Allanon!" he exclaimed, excitement reflected in his face. "You're Allanon!"

2

Brin, Jair, and Rone Leah sat down together at the dining room table with the stranger they knew now to be Allanon. No one, to the best of their knowledge, had seen Allanon for twenty years. Wil Ohmsford had been among the last. But the stories about him were familiar to all. An enigmatic dark wanderer who had journeyed to the farthest reaches of the Four Lands, he was philosopher, teacher, and historian of the races—the last of the Druids, the men of learning who had guided the races from the chaos that had followed the destruction of the old world into the civilization that flourished today. It was Allanon who had led Shea and Flick Ohmsford and Menion Leah in quest of the legendary Sword of Shannara more than seventy years ago so that the Warlock Lord might be destroyed. It was Allanon who had come for Wil Ohmsford while the Valeman studied at Storlock to become a Healer, persuading him to act as guide and protector for the Elven girl Amberle Elessedil as she went in search of the power needed to restore life to the dying Ellcrys, thereby to imprison once more the Demons set loose within the Westland. They knew the stories of Allanon. They knew as well that whenever the Druid appeared, it meant trouble.

"I have traveled a long way to find you, Brin Ohmsford," the big man said, his voice low and filled with weariness. "It was a journey that I did not think I would have to make."

"Why have you sought me out?" Brin asked.

"Because I have need of the wishsong." There was an endless moment of silence as Valegirl and Druid faced each other across the table. "Strange," he sighed. "I did not see before that the passing of the Elven magic into the children of Wil Ohmsford might have so profound a purpose. I thought it little more than a side effect from use of the Elfstones that could not be avoided."

"What do you need with Brin?" Rone interjected, frowning. Already he did not like the sound of this.

"And the wishsong?" Jair added.

Allanon kept his eyes fixed on Brin. "Your father and your mother are not here?"

"No. They will be gone for at least two weeks; they treat the sick in the villages to the south."

"I do not have two weeks nor even two days," the big man whispered. "We must talk now, and you must decide what you will do. And if you decide as I think you must, your father will not this time forgive me, I'm afraid."

Brin knew at once what the Druid was talking about. "Am I to come with you?" she asked slowly.

He let the question hang unanswered. "Let me tell you of a danger that threatens the Four Lands—an evil as great as any faced by Shea Ohmsford or your father." He folded his hands on the table before him and leaned toward her. "In the old world, before the dawn of the race of Man, there were faerie creatures who made use of good and evil magics. Your father must have told you the story, I'm certain. That world passed away with the coming of Man. The evil ones were imprisoned beyond the wall of a Forbidding, and the good were lost in the evolution of the races—all save the Elves. There was a book from those times, however, that survived. It was a book of dark magic, of power so awesome that even the Elven magicians from the old world were frightened of it. It was called the Ildatch. Its origin is not certain, even now, it seems that it appeared very early in the time of the creation of life. The evil in the world used it for a time, until at last the Elves managed to seize it. So great was its lure that, even knowing its power, a few of the Elven magicians dared tamper with its secrets. As a result, they were destroyed. The rest quickly determined to demolish the book. But before they could do so, it disappeared. There were rumors of its use afterward, scattered here and there through the centuries that followed, but never anything certain."

His brow furrowed. "And then the Great Wars wiped out the old world. For two thousand years, the existence of man was reduced to its most primitive level. It was not until the Druids called the First Council at Paranor that an effort was made to gather together the teachings of the old world that they might be used to help the new. All of the learning, whether by book or by word of mouth, that had been preserved through the years was brought before the Council that an effort might be made to unlock their secrets. Unfortunately, not all that was preserved was good. Among the books discovered by the Druids in their quest was the Ildatch. It was uncovered by a brilliant, ambitious young Druid called Brona."

"The Warlock Lord," Brin said softly.

Allanon nodded. "He became the Warlock Lord when the power of the Ildatch subverted him. Together with his followers, he was lost to the dark magic. For nearly a thousand years, they threatened the existence of the races. It was not until Shea Ohmsford mastered the power of the Sword of Shannara that Brona and his followers were destroyed."

He paused. "But the Ildatch disappeared once more. I searched for it in the ruins of the Skull Mountain when the kingdom of the Warlock Lord fell. I could not find it. I thought it was lost for good; I thought it buried forever. But I was wrong. Somehow it was preserved. It was recovered by a sect of human followers of the Warlock Lord—would-be sorcerers from the races of men who were not subject to the power of the Sword of Shannara and therefore not destroyed with the Master. I know not how even yet, but in some fashion they discovered the place where the Ildatch lay hidden and brought it back into the world of men. They took it deep into their Eastland lair where, hidden from the races, they began to delve into the secrets of the magic. That was more than sixty years ago. You can guess what has happened to them."

Brin was pale as she leaned forward. "Are you saying that it has begun all over again? That there is another Warlock Lord and other Skull Bearers?"

Allanon shook his head. "These men were not Druids as were Brona and his followers, nor has the same amount of time elapsed since their subversion. But the magic subverts all who tamper with it. The difference is in the nature of the change wrought. Each time, the change is different."

Brin shook her head. "I don't understand."

"Different," Allanon repeated. "Magic, good or evil, adapts to the user and the user to it. Last time, the creatures born of its touch flew . . ."

The sentence was left hanging. His listeners exchanged quick glances. "And this time?" Rone asked.

The black eyes narrowed. "This time the evil walks."

"Mord Wraiths!" Jair breathed sharply.

Allanon nodded. "A Gnome term for 'black walker.' They are another form of the same evil. The Ildatch has shaped them as it shaped Brona and his followers, victims of the magic, slaves to the power. They are lost to the world of men, given over to the dark."

"Then the rumors are true after all," Rone Leah murmured. His gray eyes sought Brin's. "I didn't tell you this before, because I didn't see any purpose in worrying you needlessly, but I was told by travelers passing through Leah that the walkers have come west from the Silver River country. That's why, when Jair suggested that we go camping beyond the Vale . . ."

"Mord Wraiths come this far?" Allanon interrupted hurriedly. There was sudden concern in his voice. "How long ago, Prince of Leah?"

Rone shook his head doubtfully. "Several days, perhaps. Just before I came to the Vale."

"Then there is less time than I thought." The lines on the Druid's forehead deepened.

"But what are they doing here?" Jair wanted to know.

Allanon lifted his dark face. "Looking for me, I suspect."

Silence echoed through the darkened house. No one spoke; the Druid's eyes held them fixed.

"Listen well. The Mord Wraith stronghold lies deep within the Eastland, high in the mountains they call the Ravenshorn. It is a massive, aged fortress built by Trolls in the Second War of the Races. It is called Graymark. The fortress sits atop the rim of a wall of peaks surrounding a deep valley. It is within this valley that the Ildatch has been concealed."

He took a deep breath. "Ten days earlier, I was at the rim of the valley, determined to go down into it, seize the book of the dark magic from its hiding place, and see it destroyed. The book is the source of the

Mord Wraiths' power. Destroy the book, and the power is lost, the threat ended. And this threat—ah, let me tell you something of this threat. The Mord Wraiths have not been idle since the fall of their Master. Six months ago, the border wars between the Gnomes and the Dwarves flared up once more. For years the two nations have fought over the forests of the Anar, so a resumption of their dispute surprised no one at first. But this time, unknown to most, there is a difference in the nature of the struggle. The Gnomes are being guided by the hand of the Mord Wraiths. Scattered and beaten at the fall of the Warlock Lord, the Gnome tribes have been enslaved anew by the dark magic, this time under the rule of the Wraiths. And the magic gives strength to the Gnomes that they would not otherwise have. Thus the Dwarves have been driven steadily south since the border wars resumed. The threat is grave. Recently the Silver River began to turn foul, poisoned by the dark magic. The land it feeds begins to die. When that happens, the Dwarves will die also, and the whole of the Eastland will be lost. Elves from the Westland and Bordermen from Callahorn have gone to the aid of the Dwarves, but the help they bring is not enough to withstand the Mord Wraiths' magic. Only the destruction of the Ildatch will stop what is happening."

He turned suddenly to Brin. "Remember the stories of your father, told him by his father, told to his father by Shea Ohmsford, of the advance of the Warlock Lord into the Southland? As the evil one came, a darkness fell over everything. A shadow cast itself across the land and all beneath it withered and died. Nothing lived in that shadow that was not part of the evil. It begins again, Valegirl—this time in the Anar."

He looked away. "Ten days ago, I stood at the walls of Graymark, intent upon finding and destroying the Ildatch. It was then that I discovered what the Mord Wraiths had done. Using the dark magic, the Mord Wraiths had grown within the valley a swamp-forest that would protect the book, a Maelmord in the faerie language, a barrier of such evil that it would crush and devour anything that attempted to enter and did not belong. Understand—this dark wood lives, it breathes, it thinks. Nothing can pass through it. I tried, but even the considerable power that I wield was not enough. The Maelmord repulsed me, and the Mord Wraiths discovered my presence. I was pursued, but I was able to escape. And now they search for me, knowing . . ."

He trailed off momentarily. Brin glanced quickly at Rone, who was looking unhappier by the minute.

"If they're searching for you, they'll eventually come here, won't they?" The highlander took advantage of the pause in the Druid's narration.

"Eventually, yes. But that will happen regardless of whether or not they follow me now. Understand, sooner or later they will seek to eliminate any threat to their power over the races. Surely you see that the Ohmsford family constitutes such a threat."

"Because of Shea Ohmsford and the Sword of Shannara?" Brin asked.

"Indirectly, yes. The Mord Wraiths are not creatures of illusion as was the Warlock Lord, so the Sword cannot harm them. The Elfstones, perhaps. That magic is a force to be reckoned with, and the Wraiths will have heard of Wil Ohmsford's quest for the Bloodfire." He paused. "But the real threat to them is the wishsong."

"The wishsong?" Brin was dumbfounded. "But the wishsong is just a toy! It hasn't the power of the Elfstones! Why would that be a threat to these monsters? Why would they be afraid of something as harmless as that?"

"Harmless?" Allanon's eyes flickered momentarily, then closed as if to hide something. The Druid's dark face was expressionless, and suddenly Brin was really afraid.

"Allanon, why are you here?" she asked once more, struggling to keep her hands from shaking.

The Druid's eyes lifted again. On the table before him, the oil lamp's thin flame sputtered. "I want you to come with me into the Eastland to the Mord Wraiths' keep. I want you to use the wishsong to gain passage into the Maelmord—to find the Ildatch and bring it to me to be destroyed."

His listeners stared at him speechlessly.

"How?" Jair asked finally.

"The wishsong can subvert even the dark magic," Allanon replied. "It can alter behavior in any living thing. Even the Maelmord can be made to accept Brin. The wishsong can gain passage for her as one who belongs."

Jair's eyes widened in astonishment. "The wishsong can do all that?"

But Brin was shaking her head. "The wishsong is just a toy," she repeated.

"Is it? Or is that simply the way in which you have used it?" The Druid shook his head slowly. "No, Brin Ohmsford, the wishsong is Elven magic, and it possesses the power of Elven magic. You do not see that yet, but I tell you it is so."

"I don't care what it is or isn't, Brin's not going!" Rone looked angry. "You cannot ask her to do something this dangerous!"

Allanon remained impassive. "I do not have a choice, Prince of Leah. No more choice than I had in asking Shea Ohmsford to go in search of the Sword of Shannara nor Wil Ohmsford to go in quest of the Bloodfire. The legacy of Elven magic that was passed first to Jerle Shannara belongs now to the Ohmsfords. I wish as you do that it were different. We might as well wish that night were day. The wishsong belongs to Brin, and now she must use it."

"Brin, listen to me." Rone turned to the Valegirl. "There is more to the rumors than I have told you. They also speak of what the Mord Wraiths have done to men, of eyes and tongues gone, of minds emptied of all life, and of fire that burns to the bone. I discounted all that until now. I thought it little more than the late-night fireside tales of drunken men. But the Druid makes me think differently. You can't go with him. You can't."

"The rumors of which you speak are true," Allanon acknowledged softly. "There is danger. You may even die." He paused. "But what are we to do if you do not come? Will you hide and hope the Mord Wraiths forget about you? Will you ask the Dwarves to protect you? What happens when they are gone? As with the Warlock Lord, the evil will then come into this land. It will spread until there is no one left to resist it."

Jair reached for his sister's arm. "Brin, if we have to go, at least there will be two of us . . ."

"There will most certainly not be two of us!" she contradicted him instantly. "Whatever happens, you are staying right here!"

"We're all staying right here." Rone faced the Druid. "We're not going—any of us. You will have to find another way."

Allanon shook his head. "I cannot, Prince of Leah. There is no other way."

They were silent then. Brin slumped back in her chair, confused and more than a little frightened. She felt trapped by the sense of necessity that the Druid created within her, by the tangle of obligations he had thrust upon her. They spun in her mind; as they spun, the same thought kept coming back, over and over. The wishsong is only a toy. Elven magic, yes—but still a toy! Harmless! No weapon against an evil that even Allanon could not overcome! Yet her father had always been afraid of the magic. He had warned against its use, cautioning that it was not a thing to be played with. And she herself had determined to discourage Jair's use of the wishsong . . .

"Allanon," she said quietly. The lean face turned. "I have used the wishsong only to change appearance in small ways—to change the turning of leaves or the blooming of flowers. Little things. Even that, I have not done for many months. How can the wishsong be used to change an evil as great as this forest that guards the Ildatch?"

There was a moment's hesitation. "I will teach you."

She nodded slowly. "My father has always discouraged any use of the magic. He has warned against relying upon it because once he did so, and it changed his life. If he were here, Allanon, he would do as Rone has done and advise me to tell you no. If fact, he would order me to tell you no."

The craggy face reflected new weariness. "I know, Valegirl."

"My father came back from the Westland, from the quest for the Bloodfire, and he put away the Elfstones forever," she continued, trying to think her way through her confusion as she spoke. "He told me once that he knew even then that the Elven magic had changed him, though he did not see how. He made a promise to himself that he would never use the Elfstones again."

"I know this as well."

"And still you ask me to come with you?"

"I do."

"Without my being able to consult him first? Without being able to wait for his return? Without even an attempt at an explanation to him?"

The Druid looked suddenly angry. "I will make this easy for you, Brin Ohmsford. I ask nothing of you that is fair or reasonable, nothing of which your father would approve. I ask that you risk everything on little more than my word that it is necessary that you do so. I ask trust where there is probably little reason to trust. I ask all this and give nothing back. Nothing."

He leaned forward then, half-rising from his chair, his face dark and menacing. "But I tell you this. If you think the matter through, you will see that, despite any argument you can put forth against it, you must still come with me!"

Even Rone did not choose to contradict him this time. The Druid held his position for a moment longer, dark robes spread wide as he braced himself on the table. Then slowly he settled back. There was a worn look to him now, a kind of silent desperation. It was not characteristic of the Allanon Brin's father had described to her so often, and she was frightened by that.

"I will think the matter through as you ask," she agreed, her voice almost a whisper. "But I need this night at least. I have to try to sort through . . . my feelings."

Allanon seemed to hesitate a moment, then nodded. "We will talk again in the morning. Consider well, Brin Ohmsford."

He started to rise and suddenly Jair was on his feet before him, his Elven face flushed. "Well, what about me? What about my feelings in this? If Brin goes, so do I! I'm not being left behind!"

"Jair, you can forget . . . !" Brin started to object, but Allanon cut her short with a glance. He rose and came around the table to stand before her brother.

"You have courage," he said softly, one hand coming up to rest on the Valeman's slender shoulder. "But yours is not the magic that I need on this journey. Your magic is illusion, and illusion will not get us past the Maelmord."

"But you might be wrong," Jair insisted. "Besides, I want to help!"

Allanon nodded. "You shall help. There is something that you must do while Brin and I are gone. You must be responsible for the safety of your parents, for seeing to it that the Mord Wraiths do not find them before I have destroyed the Ildatch. You must use the wishsong to protect them if the dark ones come looking. Will you do that?"

Brin did not care much for the Druid's assumption that it was already decided that she would be going with him into the Eastland, and she cared even less for the suggestion that Jair ought to use the Elven magic as a weapon.

"I will do it if I must," Jair was saying, a grudging tone in his voice. "But I would rather come with you."

Allanon's hand dropped from his shoulder. "Another time, Jair."

"It may be another time for me as well," Brin announced pointedly. "Nothing has been determined yet, Allanon."

The dark face turned slowly. "There will be no other time for you,

Brin," he said softly. "Your time is here. You must come with me. You will see that by morning."

Nodding once, he started past them toward the front entry, dark robes wrapped close.

"Where are you going, Allanon?" the Valegirl called after him.

"I will be close by," he replied and did not slow. A moment later he was gone. Brin, Jair, and Rone Leah stared after him.

Rone was the first to speak. "Well, now what?"

Brin looked at him. "Now we go to bed." She rose from the table.

"Bed!" The highlander was dumbfounded. "How can you go to bed after all that?" He waved vaguely in the direction of the departed Druid.

She brushed back her long black hair and smiled wanly. "How can I do anything else, Rone? I am tired, confused, and frightened, and I need to rest."

She came over to him and kissed him lightly on the forehead. "Stay here for tonight." She kissed Jair as well and hugged him. "Go to bed, both of you."

Then she hurried down the hall to her bedroom and closed the door tightly behind her.

She slept for a time, a dream-filled, restless sleep in which subconscious fears took shape and came for her like wraiths. Chased and harried, she came awake with a start, the pillow damp with sweat. She rose then, slipped on her robe for warmth and passed silently through the darkened rooms of her home. At the dining room table she lighted an oil lamp, the flame turned low, seated herself, and stared wordlessly into the shadows.

A sense of helplessness curled about Brin. What was she to do? She remembered well the stories told her by her father and even her great-grandfather Shea Ohmsford when she was just a little girl—of what it had been like when the Warlock Lord had come down out of the North-land, his armies sweeping into Callahorn, the darkness of his coming enfolding the whole of the land. Where the Warlock Lord passed, the light died. Now, it was happening again: border wars between Gnomes and Dwarves; the Silver River poisoned and with it the land it fed; darkness falling over the Eastland. All was as it had been seventy-five years ago. This time, too, there was a way to stop it, to prevent the dark from spreading. Again, it was an Ohmsford who was being called upon to take that way—summoned, it seemed, because there was no other hope.

She hunched down into the warmth of her robe. Seemed—that was the key word where Allanon was concerned. How much of this was what it seemed? How much of what she had been told was truth—and how much half-truth? The stories of Allanon were all the same. The Druid possessed immense power and knowledge and shared but a fraction of each. He told what he felt he must and never more. He manipulated others to his purpose, and often that purpose was kept carefully concealed.

When one traveled Allanon's path, one did so knowing that the way would be kept dark.

Yet the way of the Mord Wraiths might be darker still, if they were indeed another form of the evil destroyed by the Sword of Shannara. She must weigh the darkness of one against the darkness of the other. Allanon might be devious and manipulative in his dealings with the Ohmsfords, but he was a friend to the Four Lands. What he did, he did in an effort to protect the races, not to bring them harm. And he had always been right before in his warnings. Surely there was no reason to believe that he was not right this time as well.

But was the wishsong's magic strong enough to penetrate this barrier conceived by the evil? Brin found the idea incredible. What was the wishsong but a side effect of using the Elven magic? It had not even the strength of the Elfstones. It was not a weapon. Yet Allanon saw it as the only means by which the dark magic could be passed—the only means, when even his power had failed him.

Bare feet padded softly from the dining room entry, startling her. Rone Leah slipped clear of the shadows, crossed to the table, and seated himself.

"I couldn't sleep either," he muttered, blinking in the light of the oil lamp. "What have you decided?"

She shook her head. "Nothing. I don't know what to decide. I keep asking myself what my father would do."

"That's easy." Rone grunted. "He would tell you to forget the whole idea. It's too dangerous. He'd also tell you—as he's told both of us many times—that Allanon is not to be trusted."

Brin brushed back her long black hair and smiled faintly. "You didn't hear what I said, Rone. I said, I keep asking myself what my father would do—not what my father would tell me to do. It's not the same thing, you know. If he were being asked to go, what would he do? Wouldn't he go, just as he went when Allanon came to him in Storlock twenty years ago, knowing that Allanon was not altogether truthful, knowing that there was more than he was being told, but knowing, too, that he had magic that could be useful and that no one other than he had that magic?"

The highlander shifted uneasily. "But, Brin, the wishsong is . . . well, it's not the same as the Elfstones. You said it yourself. It's just a toy."

"I know that. That is what makes all of this so difficult—that and the fact that my father would be appalled if he thought even for a minute that I would consider trying to use the magic as a weapon of any sort." She paused. "But Elven magic is a strange thing. Its power is not always clearly seen. Sometimes it is obscured. It was so with the Sword of Shannara. Shea Ohmsford never saw the way in which such a small thing could defeat an enemy as great as the Warlock Lord—not until it was put to the test. He simply went on faith . . ."

Rone sat forward sharply. "I'll say it again—this journey is too dangerous. The Mord Wraiths are too dangerous. Even Allanon can't get past them; he told you so himself! It would be different if you had the use of the Elfstones. At least the Stones have power enough to destroy creatures such as these. What would you do with the wishsong if you came up against them—sing to them the way you used to do to that old maple?"

"Don't make fun of me, Rone." Brin's eyes narrowed.

Rone shook his head quickly. "I'm not making fun of you. I care too much about you to ever do that. I just don't feel the wishsong is any kind of protection against something like the Wraiths!"

Brin looked away, staring out through curtained windows into the night, watching the shadowed movements of the trees in the wind, rhythmic and graceful.

"Neither do I," she admitted softly.

They sat in silence for a time, lost in their separate thoughts. Allanon's dark, tired face hung suspended in the forefront of Brin's mind, a haunting specter that accused. *You must come. You will see that by morning.* She heard him speak the words again, so certain as he said them. But what was it that would persuade her that this was so? she asked herself. Reasoning only seemed to lead her deeper into confusion. The arguments were all there, all neatly arranged, both those for going and those for staying, and yet the balance did not shift in either direction.

"Would you go?" she asked Rone suddenly. "If it were you with the wishsong?"

"Not a chance," he said at once—a bit too quickly, a bit too flip.

You're lying, Rone, she told herself. *Because of me, because you don't want me to go, you're lying. If you thought it through, you would admit to the same doubts facing me.*

"What's going on?" a weary voice asked from the darkness.

They turned and found Jair standing in the hall, squinting sleepily into the light. He came over to them and stood looking from face to face.

"We were just talking, Jair," Brin told him.

"About going after the magic book?"

"Yes. Why don't you go on back to bed?"

"Are you going? After the book, I mean?"

"I don't know."

"She's not going if she possesses an ounce of common sense," Rone grumbled. "It's entirely too dangerous a journey. You tell her, tiger. She's the only sister you've got, and you don't want the black walkers getting hold of her."

Brin shot him an angry glance. "Jair doesn't have anything to say about this, so quit trying to scare him."

"Him? Who's trying to scare him?" Rone's lean face was flushed. "It's you I'm trying to scare, for cat's sake!"

"Anyway, the black walkers don't scare me," Jair declared firmly.

"Well, they ought to!" Brin snapped.

Jair shrugged, yawning. "Maybe you should wait until we have a chance to talk with father. We could send him a message or something."

"Now that makes good sense," Rone added his approval. "At least wait until Wil and Eretria have a chance to talk this over with you."

Brin sighed. "You heard what Allanon said. There isn't enough time for that."

The highlander folded his arms across his chest. "He could make the time if it were necessary. Brin, your father might have a different slant on all this. After all, he's had the benefit of experience—and he's used the Elven magic."

"Brin, he could use the Elfstones!" Jair's eyes snapped open. "He could go with you. He could protect you with the Elfstones, just as he protected the Elven girl Amberle!"

Brin saw it then; those few words gave her the answer that she had been looking for. Allanon was right. She must go with him. But the reason was not one she had considered until now. Her father would insist on accompanying her. He would take the Elfstones from their hiding place and go with her in order that she should be protected. And that was exactly what she must avoid. Her father would be forced to break his pledge never to use the Elfstones again. He probably wouldn't even agree to her accompanying Allanon. He would go instead in order that she, her mother, and Jair be kept safe.

"I want you to go back to bed, Jair," she said suddenly.

"But I just got . . ."

"Go on. Please. We'll talk this all out in the morning."

Jair hesitated. "What about you?"

"I'll be only a few minutes, I promise. I just want to sit here alone for a time."

Jair studied her suspiciously for a moment, then nodded. "All right. Good night." He turned and walked back into the darkness. "Just be sure you come to bed, too."

Brin's eyes found Rone's. They had known each other since they were small children, and there were times when each knew what the other was thinking without a word being said. This was one such time.

The highlander stood up slowly, his lean face set. "All right, Brin. I see it, too. But I'm coming with you, do you understand? And I'm staying with you until it's finished."

She nodded slowly. Without another word, he disappeared down the hallway, leaving her alone.

The minutes slipped by. She thought it through again, sifting carefully the arguments. In the end, her answer was the same. She could not permit her father to break his vow because of her, to risk further use of the Elven magic he had foresworn. She could not.

Then she rose, blew out the flame of the oil lamp and walked, not in the direction of her bedroom, but to the front entry instead. Releasing the latch, she opened the door quietly and slipped out into the night. The wind blew against her face, cooling and filled with autumn's smells. She stood for a moment staring out into the shadows, then made her way around the house to the gardens in back. Night sounds filled the silence, a steady cadence of invisible life. At the edge of the gardens, beneath a stand of giant oak, she stopped and looked about expectantly.

A moment later, Allanon appeared. Somehow, she had known he would. Black as the shadows about him, he drifted soundlessly from the trees to stand before her.

"I have decided," she whispered, her voice steady. "I'm going with you."

Morning came quickly, a pale silver light that seeped through the predawn forest mist and chased the shadows westward. Their restless sleep broken, the members of the Ohmsford household stirred awake. Within an hour, preparations were underway for Brin's departure to the Eastland. Rone was dispatched to the inn to secure horses, riding harness, weapons, and foodstuffs. Brin and Jair packed clothing and camping gear. In businesslike fashion, they went about their tasks. There was little conversation. No one had much to say. No one felt much like talking.

Jair Ohmsford was feeling particularly uncommunicative, trudging through the house as he went about his work in determined silence. He was more than a little disgruntled that both Brin and Rone would be going east with Allanon while he was to be left behind. That had been decided first thing that morning, practically moments after he was out of bed. Gathering in the dining area as they had gathered last night, they had discussed briefly Brin's decision to go into the Anar—a decision, Jair thought, of which everyone but he already seemed aware. Then came the determination that, while Brin and Rone would make the journey, he would not. True, the Druid had not been pleased by Rone's insistence that if Brin were to go, then he must go as well, because Brin needed someone she could depend upon, someone she could trust. No, the Druid had not been pleased with that at all. In fact, he had agreed to Rone's coming only after Brin had admitted she would feel better with Rone along. But when Jair suggested that she would feel better still with him along as well—after all, he had the magic of the wishsong, too, and could help protect her—all three had abruptly and firmly told him no. Too dangerous, Brin said. Too long and hazardous a journey, Rone added. Besides, you are needed here, Allanon reminded him. You have a responsibility to your parents. You must use your magic to protect them.

With that, Allanon had disappeared somewhere and there was no further opportunity to argue the matter with him. Rone thought the sun rose and set on Brin, so naturally he would not go against her wishes on this, and Brin had already made up her mind. So that was that. Part of the problem with his sister, of course, was that she didn't understand him. In fact, Jair was not altogether certain that she really understood herself a good deal of the time. At one point during their preparations, with Allanon still gone and Rone still down in the village, he had brought up the subject of the Elfstones.

"Brin." They were packing blankets on the floor of the front room, wrapping them in oilskins. "Brin, I know where father hides the Elfstones."

She had looked up at once. "I thought that you probably did."

"Well, he made such a big secret of it . . ."

"And you don't like secrets, do you? Have you had them out?"

"Just to look at," he admitted, then leaned forward. "Brin, I think you should take the Elfstones with you."

"Whatever for?" There was a touch of anger in her voice then.

"For protection. For the magic."

"The magic? No one can use their magic but father, as you well know."

"Well, maybe . . ."

"Besides, you know how he feels about the Elfstones. It's bad enough that I have to make this journey at all, but to take the Elfstones as well? You're not thinking very clearly about this, Jair."

Then Jair had gotten angry. "You're the one who's not thinking clearly. We both know how dangerous it's going to be for you. You're going to need all the help you can get. The Elfstones could be a lot of help—all you need to do is to figure out how to make them work. You might be able to do that."

"No one but the rightful holder can . . ."

"Make the Stones work?" He had been almost nose to nose with her then. "But maybe that's not so with you and me, Brin. After all, we already have the Elven magic inside us. We have the wishsong. Maybe we could make the Stones work for us!"

There had been a long, intense moment of silence. "No," she said at last. "No, we promised father we would never try to use the Elfstones . . ."

"He also made us promise not to use the Elven magic, remember? But we do—even you, now and then. And isn't that what Allanon wants you to do when you reach the Mord Wraiths' keep? Isn't it? So what's the difference between using the wishsong and the Elfstones? Elven magic is Elven magic!"

Brin had stared at him silently, a distant, lost look in her dark eyes. Then she had turned again to the blankets. "It doesn't matter. I'm not taking the Elfstones. Here, help me tie these."

And that had been that, just like the subject of his going with them into the Eastland. No real explanation had been offered; she had simply made up her mind that she would not take the Elfstones, whether she could use them or not. He didn't understand it at all. He didn't understand her. If it had been him, he would have taken the Elfstones in a moment. He would have taken them and found a way to use them, because they were a powerful weapon against the dark magic. But Brin . . . Brin couldn't even seem to see the inconsistency of her agreeing to use the magic of the wishsong and refusing to use the magic of the Stones.

He went through the remainder of the morning trying to make some sense of his sister's reasoning or lack thereof. The hours slipped quickly past. Rone returned with horses and supplies, packs were loaded, and a hasty lunch consumed in the cool shade of the backyard oaks. Then all at once Allanon was standing there again, as black in midday as at darkest night, waiting with the patience of Lady Death, and suddenly there was no time left. Rone was shaking Jair's hand, clapping him roughly on the back, and extracting a firm promise that he would look out for his parents when they returned. Then Brin was there, arms coming tightly about him and holding him close.

"Good-bye, Jair," she whispered. "Remember—I love you."

"I love you, too," he managed and hugged her back.

A moment later, they were mounted, and the horses turned down the dirt roadway. Arms lifted in farewell, waving as he waved back. Jair waited until they were out of sight before he brushed an unwanted tear from his eye.

That same afternoon, he moved down to the inn. He did so because of the possibility voiced by Allanon that the Wraiths or their Gnome allies might already be searching for the Druid in the lands west of the Silver River. If their enemies reached Shady Vale, the Ohmsford home would be the first place they would look. Besides, it was much more interesting at the inn— its rooms filled with travelers from all the lands, each with a different tale to tell, each with some different piece of news to share. Jair much preferred the excitement of tales told over a glass of ale in the tavern hall to the boredom of an empty house.

As he went to the inn with a few personal items in tow, the warmth of the afternoon sun on his face eased a bit the disappointment he still felt at being left behind. Admittedly, there was good reason for his staying. Someone had to explain to his parents when they returned what had become of Brin. That would not be easy. He visualized momentarily his father's face upon hearing what had happened and shook his head ruefully. His father would not be happy. In fact, he would probably insist on going after Brin—maybe even with the Elfstones.

A sudden look of determination creased his face. If that happened, he was going as well. He wouldn't be left behind a second time.

He kicked at the leaves fallen across the pathway before him, scattering them in a shower of color. His father wouldn't see it that way, of course. Nor his mother, for that matter. But he had two whole weeks to figure out how to persuade them that he should go.

He walked on, a bit more slowly now, letting the thought linger in his mind enticingly. Then he brushed it away. What he was supposed to do was to tell them what had happened to Brin and Rone and then accompany them into Leah, where they were all to remain under the protection of Rone's father until the quest was finished. That was what he was supposed to do, so that was what he would do. Of course, Wil Ohmsford might not choose to go along with this plan. And Jair was first and foremost his father's son, so it was to be expected that he might have a few ideas of his own.

He grinned and quickened his step. He would have to work on that.

The day came and went. Jair Ohmsford ate dinner at the inn with the family that managed the business for his parents, offered to lend a hand the following morning with the day's work, and then drifted into the lounge to listen to the tales being told by the drummers and wayfarers passing through the Vale. More than one made mention of the black walkers, the dark-robed Mord Wraiths that none had seen but all knew to be real, the evil ones that could burn the life from you with just a glance. Come from the earth's dark, the voices warned in rough whispers, heads nodding all around in agreement. Better that you never encountered such as they. Even Jair found himself feeling a bit uneasy at the prospect.

He stayed with the storytellers until after midnight, then went to his room. He slept soundly, woke at daybreak and spent the morning working about the inn. He no longer felt quite so bad about being left behind. After all, his own part in all of this was important, too. If the Mord Wraiths did indeed know of the magic Elfstones and came looking for the holder, then Wil Ohmsford was in as much danger as his daughter—possibly more so. It was up to Jair, then, to keep a sharp eye open, in order that no harm befell his father before he could be properly warned.

By midday Jair's work was finished and the innkeeper thanked him and told him to take some time for himself. So he walked out into the forests in back of the inn where no one else was about and experimented for several hours with the wishsong, using the magic in a variety of ways, pleased with the control he was able to exercise. He thought again about his father's continual admonition to forgo use of the Elven magic. His father just didn't understand. The magic was a part of him, and using it was as natural as using his arms and legs. He couldn't pretend it wasn't there any more than he could pretend they weren't! Both his parents kept saying the magic was dangerous. Brin said that on occasion too, though she said it with a whole lot less conviction, since she was guilty of using it as well. He was convinced they told him that simply because he was somewhat younger than Brin and they worried more about him. He hadn't seen anything to suggest that the magic was dangerous; until he did, he intended to keep using it.

On the way back to the inn, as the first shadows of early evening began to slip through the late afternoon sunshine, it occurred to him that perhaps he ought to check the house—just to be certain that nothing was disturbed. It was locked, of course, but it wouldn't hurt to check anyway. After all, the care of the house was a part of his responsibility.

He debated the matter as he walked, finally deciding to wait until after dinner to make the inspection. Eating seemed more imperative to him at the moment than hiking up to the house. Using the magic always made him hungry.

He worked his way along the forest trails that ran back to the inn, breathing in the smells of the autumn day, thinking of trackers. Trackers fascinated him. Trackers were a special breed of men who could trace the movements of anything that lived simply by studying the land they passed through. Most of them were more at home in the wilderness than they were in settled communities. Most preferred the company of their own kind. Jair had talked with a tracker once—years ago now, it seemed—an old fellow brought down to the inn with a broken leg by some travelers who had chanced on him. The old man had stayed at the inn almost a week, waiting for the leg to mend sufficiently that he might leave again. The tracker hadn't wanted to have anything to do with Jair at first, despite the boy's persistence—or anything to do with anyone else, for that matter— but then Jair had showed him something of the magic—just a touch. Intrigued, the old man had talked with him then, a little at first, then more. And what tales that old man had had to tell . . .

Jair swung out onto the roadway beside the inn, turning into the side entry, grinning broadly as he remembered what it had been like. It was then that he saw the Gnome.

For an instant he thought his eyes were playing tricks on him and he stopped where he was, his hand fastened to the inn door handle as he stared out across the roadway to the stable fence line where the gnarled yellow figure stood. Then the other's wizened face turned toward him, sharp eyes searching his own, and he knew at once he was not mistaken.

Hurriedly, he pushed the inn door open and stepped inside. Leaning back against the closed door, alone now in the hallway beyond, he tried to calm himself. A Gnome! What was a Gnome doing in Shady Vale? A traveler, perhaps? But few Gnomes traveled this way—few, in fact, beyond the familiar confines of the Eastland forests. He couldn't remember the last time there had been a Gnome in Shady Vale. But there was one here now. Maybe more than one.

He stepped quickly away from the door and went down the hall until he stood next to a window that opened out toward the roadway. Cautiously he peered around the sill, Elven face intense, eyes searching the innyard and the fence line beyond. The Gnome stood where Jair had first seen him, still looking toward the inn. The Valeman looked about. There appeared to be no others.

Again he leaned back against the wall. What was he to do now? Was it coincidence that brought the Gnome to Shady Vale at a time when Allanon had warned that the Mord Wraiths would be looking for them? Or was it not chance at all? Jair forced his breathing to slow. How could he find out? How could he make certain?

He took a deep breath. The first thing he must remember to do was to stay calm. One Gnome presented no serious threat. His nose picked up the scent of beef stew simmering, and he thought about how hungry he was. He hesitated a moment longer, then started toward the kitchen. The best thing to do was to think matters through over dinner. Eat a good meal and decide on a plan of action. He nodded to himself as he walked. He would try to put himself in Rone's boots. Rone would know what to do if he were here. Jair would have to try to do the same.

The beef stew was excellent and Jair was starved, yet he found it difficult to concentrate on food, knowing that the Gnome was standing just outside, watching. Halfway through the meal, he remembered suddenly the empty, unguarded house and the Elfstones hidden within. If the Gnome was here at the bidding of the black walkers, then he might have come for the Elfstones as well as the Ohmsfords or Allanon. And there might be others, already searching . . .

He shoved his plate away, drained the remainder of his ale, and hurried from the kitchen back down the hallway to the window. Carefully, he peered out. The Gnome was gone.

He felt his heart quicken. Now what? He turned and raced back down the hall. He had to get back to the house. He had to make certain that the Elfstones were secure, then . . . He caught himself in midstride, slowing. He didn't know what he would do then. He would have to see. He quickened his step once more. The important thing now was to see whether or not there had been any attempt to enter his home.

He passed the side door through which he had entered and went on toward the rear of the building. He would leave by a different way just in case the Gnome was indeed looking for him—or even if he wasn't, but had become suspicious at the Valeman's furtive interest. I shouldn't have stopped to look at him, he told himself angrily. I should have kept going, then doubled back. But it was too late now.

The hallway ended at a door at the very rear of the main building. Jair stopped, listening momentarily, chiding himself for being foolish, then eased the door open and stepped out. Evening shadows cast by the forest trees lay dark and cool across the grounds, staining the inn walls and roof. Overhead, the sky was darkening. Jair looked about quickly, then started toward the trees. He would cut through the forest to his home, staying off the roadways until he was certain that . . .

"Talking a walk, boy?"

Jair froze. The Gnome stepped silently from the dark trees in front of him. Hard, rough features twisted with a wicked-looking smile. The Gnome had been waiting.

"Oh, I saw you, boy. I saw you quick enough. Knew you right away. Halfling features, Elf and Man—not too many like you." He stopped a half dozen paces away, gnarled hands resting on his hips, the smile fixed. Leather woodsman's garb covered the stocky form; his boots and wristbands were studded with iron, and knives and a short sword were belted at his waist. "Young Ohmsford, aren't you? The boy, Jair?"

The word *boy* stung. "Stay away from me," Jair warned, afraid now, and trying desperately to keep the fear from his voice.

"Stay away from you?" The Gnome laughed sharply. "And what will you do if I don't, halfling? Throw me to the ground, perhaps? Take away my weapons? You are a brave one, aren't you?"

Another laugh followed, low and guttural. For the first time, Jair realized that the Gnome was speaking to him in the language used by the Southlanders rather than the harsh Gnome tongue. Gnomes seldom used any tongue but their own; their race was an insular people who wanted nothing to do with the other lands. This Gnome had been well outside the Eastland to be so fluent.

"Now, boy," the Gnome interrupted his thoughts. "Let's be sensible, you and me. I seek the Druid. Tell me where he is, here or elsewhere, and I'll be gone."

Jair hesitated. "Druid? I don't know any Druids. I don't know what you're . . ."

The Gnome shook his head and sighed. "Games, is it? Worse luck for you, boy. Guess we'll have to do this the hard way."

He started toward Jair, hands reaching. Instinctively, Jair twisted away. Then he used the wishsong. There was a moment's hesitation, a moment's uncertainty—for he had never used the magic against another human—and then he used it. He gave a low, hissing sound, and a mass of snakes appeared, coiled tightly about the Gnome's outstretched arms. The Gnome howled in dismay, whipping his arms about desperately in an effort to shake loose the snakes. Jair looked around, found a broken piece of tree limb the size of a bulky walking staff, seized it with both hands and brought it crashing down over the Gnome's head. The Gnome grunted and dropped to the earth in a heap, unmoving.

Jair released the tree limb, his hands shaking. Had he killed him? Cautiously he knelt next to the fallen Gnome and felt for his wrist. There was a pulse. The Gnome was not dead, just unconscious. Jair straightened. What was he to do now? The Gnome had been looking for Allanon, knowing that he had come to Shady Vale and to the Ohmsfords, knowing . . . knowing who knew what else! Too much, in any case, for Jair to remain in the Vale any longer, especially now that he had used the magic. He shook his head angrily. He shouldn't have used the magic; he should have kept it a secret. But it was too late for regrets now. He didn't think the Gnome was alone. There would be others, probably at the house. And that was where he had to go, because that was where the Elfstones were hidden.

He glanced about, his thoughts organizing swiftly. Several dozen feet away was a woodbin. Seizing the Gnome's feet, he dragged him to the bin, threw back the lid, shoved his captive inside, dropped the lid down again, and put the metal bar through the catch. He grinned in spite of himself. That bin was well constructed. The Gnome wouldn't get out of there for a while.

Then he hurried back into the inn. Despite the need for haste, he had to leave word with the innkeeper where he was going—otherwise the whole community would be combing the countryside looking for him. It was one thing for Brin and Rone to disappear; that had been easy enough to explain simply by saying they had gone for a visit to Leah and he had decided to stay in the Vale. It would be quite another matter entirely if he disappeared as well, since there was no one left to alibi for him. So feigning nonchalance and smiling disarmingly, he announced that he had changed his mind and was going over to the highlands after all early the next morning. Tonight he would stay at the house and pack. When the innkeeper thought to ask what had persuaded him to change his mind so abruptly, the Valeman quickly explained that he had received a message from Brin. Before there could be any further questions, he was out the door.

Swiftly, he melted into the woods, racing through the darkness toward his home. He was sweating profusely, hot with excitement and anticipation. He was not frightened—not yet, at least—probably because he hadn't stopped long enough to let himself think about what he was doing. Besides, he kept telling himself, he had taken care of that Gnome, hadn't he?

Tree branches slapped his face. He hurried on, not bothering to duck, eyes riveted on the darkness ahead. He knew this section of the forest well. Even in the growing darkness, he found his way with ease, moving on cat's feet, carefully listening to the sounds about him.

Then, fifty yards from his home, he melted silently into a small stand of pine, working his way forward until he could see the darkened structure through the needled branches. Dropping to his hands and knees, he peered through the night, searching. There was no sound, no movement, no sign of life. Everything seemed as it should. He paused to brush back a lock of hair which had fallen down across his face. It should be simple. All he had to do was slip into the house, retrieve the Elfstones and slip out again. If there really wasn't anyone watching, it should be easy . . .

Then something moved in the oaks at the rear of the home—just a momentary shadow, then nothing. Jair took a deep breath and waited. The minutes slipped past. Insects buzzed about him hungrily, but he ignored them. Then he saw the movement a second time, clearly now. It was a man. No, not a man, he corrected quickly—a Gnome.

He sat back. Well, Gnome or not, he had to go down there. And if there was one, there were probably more than one, waiting, watching—but without knowing when or if he would return. Sweat ran down his back, and his throat was dry. Time was slipping away from him. He had to get out of the Vale. But he couldn't leave the Elfstones.

There was nothing for it but to use the wishsong.

He took a moment to pitch his voice the way he wanted, feigning the buzzing of the mosquitoes that were all around him, still lingering on in the warmth of early autumn, not yet frozen away by winter's touch. Then he glided from the pines down through the thinning forest. He had used this trick once or twice before, but never under conditions as demanding as these. He moved quietly, letting his voice make him a part of the forest night, knowing that if he did it all properly he would be invisible to the eyes that kept watch for him. The house drew steadily closer as he worked his way ahead. He caught sight again of the Gnome that kept watch in the trees behind the darkened building. Then suddenly he saw another, off to his right by the high bushes fronting the house—then another, across the roadway in the hemlock. None looked his way. He wanted to run, wanted to race as swiftly as the night wind to reach the dark of the home, but he kept his pace steady and his voice an even, faint buzz. Don't let them see me, he prayed. Don't let them look.

He crossed the lawn, slipping from tree to bush, eyes darting to find the Gnomes all about him. The rear door, he thought as he went—that would be the easiest door to enter, dark in the shadow of high, flowering bushes, their leaves still full . . .

A sudden call from somewhere beyond the house brought him to an abrupt, frightened halt, frozen in midstride. The Gnome at the rear of the Ohmsford house stepped clear of the oaks moonlight glinting on his long knife. Again the call came, then sudden laughter. The blade lowered. It was from neighbors down the road, joking and talking in the warm autumn night, their dinner done. Sweat soaked Jair's tunic, and for the first time he was scared. A dozen yards away, the Gnome who had stepped from the oaks turned and disappeared back into them again. Jair's voice trembled, then strengthened, keeping him hidden. Quickly he went on.

He paused at the door, letting the wishsong die momentarily, trying desperately to steady himself. Fumbling through his pockets, he at last produced the house key, fitted it to the lock, and turned it guardedly. The door opened without a sound. In an instant, he was through.

He paused again in the darkness beyond. Something was wrong. He could sense it more than describe it—it was a feeling that ran cold to the bone. Something was wrong. The house . . . the house was not right; it was different . . . He stayed silent, waiting for his senses to reveal what lay hidden from him. As he stood, he grew slowly aware that something else was in the house with him, something terrible, something so evil that just its presence permeated the air with fear. Whatever it was, it seemed to be everywhere at once, a hideous, black pall that hung across the Ohmsford home like a death shroud. A thing, his mind whispered, a thing . . .

A Mord Wraith.

He quit breathing. A walker—here, in his home! Now he was really afraid, the certainty of his suspicion driving from him the last of his courage. It waited within the next room, Jair sensed, within the dark. It would know he was here and come for him—and he would not be able to stand against it!

He was certain for a moment that he would break and run, overwhelmed by the panic that coursed through him. But then he thought of his parents, who would return unwarned if he should fail, and of the Elfstones, the sole weapon that the black ones would fear—concealed not a dozen feet from where he stood.

He didn't think anymore; he simply acted. A soundless shadow, he moved to the stone hearth that served the kitchen, his fingers tracing the rough outline of the stone where it curved back along the wall in a series of shelving nooks. At the end of the third shelf, the stone slipped away at his touch. His hand closed over a small leather pouch.

Something stirred in the other room.

Then the back door opened suddenly and a burly form pushed into view. Jair stood flattened against the hearth wall, lost in the shadows, braced to flee. But the form went past him without slowing, head bent as if to find its way. It went into the front room, and a low, guttural voice whispered to the creature that waited within.

In the next instant, Jair was moving—back through the still open door, back into the shadows of the flowering bushes. He paused just long enough to see that it was the Gnome who kept watch within the oaks who had come into the house, then raced for the cover of the trees. Faster, faster! he screamed soundlessly.

And without a backward glance, Jair Ohmsford fled into the night.

It proved to be a harrowing flight.

Once before, Ohmsfords had fled the Vale under cover of night, pursued by black things that would harry them the length and breadth of the Four Lands. It had been more than seventy years now since Shea and Flick Ohmsford had slipped from their home at the Shady Vale inn, barely escaping the monstrous winged Skull Bearer sent by the Warlock Lord to destroy them. Jair knew their story; barely older than he, they had fled all the way eastward to Culhaven and the Dwarves. But Jair Ohmsford was no less able than they. He, too, had been raised in the Vale, and he knew something about surviving in unfamiliar country.

As he fled through the forests of the Vale, carrying with him little more than the clothes on his back, the hunting knife in his belt that all Valemen wore, and the leather pouch with the Elfstones tucked within his tunic, he did so with confidence in his ability to make his way safely to his destination. There was no panic in his flight; there was merely a keen sense of expectation. For just a moment, when he had stood within the kitchen of his home, hidden within the shadows of the great hearth, listening to the silence, knowing that only a room away there waited one of the Wraiths, and feeling the evil of the thing permeating even the air he breathed, there had been real fear. But that was behind him, lost in the darkness that slipped steadily back into the past as he raced ahead, and now he was thinking with clarity and determination.

The destination he had chosen in fleeing the Vale was Leah. It was a three-day journey, but one he had made before and so could make without danger of becoming lost. Moreover, help that could not be found in the Vale could be found in Leah. Shady Vale was a small hamlet, its people ill-equipped to stand against the black walkers or their Gnome allies. But Leah was a city; the highlands were governed by monarchial rule and protected by a standing army. Rone Leah's father was king and a good friend to the Ohmsford family. Jair would tell him what had befallen, persuade him to send patrols south in search of his parents so that they could be warned of the danger that waited in the Vale, and then all of them would take refuge in the city until Allanon returned with Brin and Rone. It was an excellent plan to Jair's way of thinking, and he could find no reason that it wouldn't be successful.

Still, the Valeman was not about to leave anything to chance. That was the reason that he had brought the Elfstones, taking them from their hiding place where they might have been found, though taking them meant revealing to his father that he had known all along where they were hidden.

As he ran, working his way steadily through the Vale forests toward the rim of the valley, he tried to recall everything that the old tracker had told him in their talks about disguising one's trail from pursuers. Jair and the old man had played at it like a game, each contriving new and different twists to the imaginary pursuits that made up their game, each delighting the other with a kind of grim inventiveness. For the tracker, experience was the touchstone of his skill. For Jair, it was an uninhibited imagination. Now the play adventure had turned real, however, and imagination alone was not going to be enough. A bit of the old man's experience was needed, and Jair called to mind everything he could manage to remember.

Time was his most pressing concern. The quicker he reached the highlands, the quicker those patrols would leave in search of his parents. Whatever else happened, they must not be allowed to return to the Vale unwarned. Therefore, no unnecessary time must be spent in disguising his trail eastward. This decision was reinforced by the fact that his skills were admittedly limited in any case and by the further fact that he could not be certain that the Gnomes and their dark leader would come after him. He thought that they would, of course, particularly after hearing from the Gnome he had locked in the wood bin. But they would still have to track him, and that would slow them down somewhat, even if they were to guess which direction he had taken. He had gained a head start on them, and he must take advantage of it. He would run swiftly and surely, his purpose fixed, and they must try to catch him.

Besides, even if they did catch up to him, he could still use the wish-song to protect himself.

By midnight, he had gained the eastern wall of the valley that sheltered Shady Vale, climbed the rock-strewn slope to its rim, and disappeared into the Duln. Using the moon and stars to mark his bearings, he made his way through the dark forest, slowing a bit to conserve his strength. He was tiring now, having had no sleep since the previous night, but he wanted to make certain that he crossed the Rappahalladran before he stopped to rest. That meant he must travel until dawn, and the journey would be a hard one. The Duln was a difficult woodland to traverse, even under the best of conditions, and darkness often made the wilderness a treacherous maze. Still, Jair had traveled the Duln at night before, and he felt confident he could find his way. So with a careful eye for the forest tangle that stretched before him, he pushed on.

Time crawled past on leaden feet, but at last the night sky began to lighten into morning. Jair was exhausted, his slim body numb with fatigue and his hands and face cut and bruised by the forest. Still he had not reached the river. For the first time, he began to worry that perhaps he had misplaced his sense of direction and traveled too far north or south. He was still traveling eastward, he knew, because the sun was rising directly in front of him. But where was the Rappahalladran? Ignoring the weariness and a growing sense of concern, he stumbled ahead.

The sun had been up an hour when he finally reached the banks of the river. Deep and swift, the Rappahalladran churned its way southward through the dark quiet of the forest. Jair had already shelved his plans to cross the river now. The currents were too dangerous to attempt a crossing when he was not rested. Finding a stand of pine close to the water, he stretched out within the shaded coolness of their boughs and fell quickly asleep.

He came awake again at sunset, disoriented and vaguely uneasy. It took him a moment to remember where he was and what it was that had brought him there. Then he saw that the day was gone, and he became alarmed that he had slept so long. He had intended to sleep only until midday before continuing his flight east. A whole day was too long; it gave his pursuers too much time to catch him.

He went down to the river's edge, splashed cold water on his face to bring himself fully awake and then went in search of food. He hadn't eaten anything for the past twenty-four hours, he realized suddenly, and found himself wishing that he'd taken just a moment longer in making his escape to pack a loaf of bread and some cheese. As he searched through the trees, resigned to a meal of berries and roots, he found himself thinking again about his supposed pursuers. Maybe he was worrying about nothing. Maybe no one was giving chase. After all, what would they want with him anyway? It was Allanon they wanted. The Gnome had told him that much. What had probably happened was that, after he had escaped the Vale, they had gone on their way, looking elsewhere for the Druid. If that were true, then he was breaking his neck out here for nothing.

Of course if he were wrong . . .

Wild berries in autumn were a scarce commodity, so Jair was forced to make a meal principally of edible roots and a few wild rhubarb stalks. Despite his general dissatisfaction with the fare, he was feeling pretty good about things by the time the meal was finished. Rone Leah couldn't have done any better, he decided. He had overcome that Gnome, secured the Elfstones from under the noses of a walker and a patrol of Gnome Hunters, escaped the Vale and was now making his way successfully toward Leah. He took a moment to envision the surprised face of his sister when he told her all that had happened to him.

And then it occurred to him, suddenly, shockingly, that he really didn't know that he would ever see Brin again. His sister was being taken by Allanon into the very heart of the same evil that had invaded his home and driven him from the Vale. He remembered again what he had felt in the presence of that evil—the terrible, overpowering sense of panic. Brin was being taken to where that evil lived, where there was not just one of the black walkers, but many. Against them she had nothing more than the strength of the magic of the Druid and her wishsong. How could Brin hope to stand against something like that? What if she were discovered before she managed to reach the book . . . ?

He could not complete the thought. Despite their differing personalities and ways, Jair and his sister were close. He loved her and he did not like the idea of anything happening to her. He wished more than ever that he had been allowed to go with her to the Anar.

Abruptly he glanced westward to where the sun was slipping down into the treetops. The light was failing quickly now, and it was time to make his crossing and get on with the journey east. He cut a series of branches, using the long knife, and bound them together with pine bark strips to construct a small raft on which he could place his clothes. He had no desire to walk the chill autumn night in wet clothing, so he would swim the river naked and dress again on the far bank.

When the raft was finished, he carried it down to the river's edge and suddenly recalled one of the lessons taught to him by the old tracker. They had been talking of ways to throw off a pursuit. Water was the best disguise of one's tracks, the old man had announced in his cryptic way. Couldn't follow tracks through water—unless, of course, you were stupid enough to try losing a pursuer in water so shallow that your footprints left their mark in the mud. But deep water—ah, that was the best. The current always took you downstream, and even if your pursuer tracked you to the water's edge and knew you'd gone across—didn't have to go across, of course, but that was another trick—he'd still have to find your trail on the other side. So—and here was glimmer of genius to the game—the very smartest quarry would wade upstream, then swim the deep water so that he would come out still above the point on the far bank where his tracks ended. Because the hunter knew you'd be carried downstream, too, didn't he—so where do you think he would be looking? He wouldn't think to look upstream right away.

Jair had always been impressed with that bit of trickery and resolved now to put it to the test. Maybe he wasn't being followed, but on the other hand, he couldn't be sure. He was still two days from Leah. If someone had come after him, this device of the old tracker would give him a bigger head start yet.

So he stripped off his boots, tucked them under one arm with the raft, then waded upstream several hundred yards to where the channel narrowed. Far enough, he decided. He took off the rest of his clothing, placed it on the raft and pushed off into the cold waters of the river.

The current caught him almost at once, pulling him downstream at a rapid pace. He let it take him, swimming with it, the raft held firmly in his trailing hand, angling as he swam toward the far bank. Bits of deadwood and brush swirled past him, rough and chill to the touch, and the sounds of the forest faded into the churning rush of the water. Overhead, the night sky darkened as the sun slipped below the treeline. Jair kicked steadily on, the far bank drawing closer.

Then at last his feet touched bottom, kicking into the soft mud, and he stood up, the night air chill against his skin. Snatching his clothes from the raft, he shoved it back into the river's current and watched it swirl away. A moment later he was back on dry land, brushing the water from his body and slipping back into his clothes. Insects buzzed past him, bits of sound in the dark. On the bank from which he had come, the forest trees were fading stalks of black in the night's deepening haze.

Within those dark stalks, something suddenly moved.

Jair froze, his eyes fixed on the spot from which the movement had come. But it was gone now, whatever it had been. He took a deep breath. It had looked—just for a moment—to be a man.

Carefully, slowly, he backed into the shelter of the trees behind him, still watching the other bank, waiting for the movement to come again. It did not. He finished dressing hurriedly, checked to be certain that the Elf-stones were still tucked safely within his tunic, then turned and trotted soundlessly into the forest. He was probably mistaken, he told himself.

He walked all night, relying again on the moon and stars visible in small patches of forest sky to point him in the right direction. He traveled at a slow trot where the forest thinned, less certain than before that no one had come after him. When he had been alone with the memory of those few moments in his home with that black thing behind him, he had felt secure. But the idea that someone or something was back there, following him, brought back the sense of panic. Even in the cool autumn night, he was sweating, his senses sharp with fear. Time and again, his thoughts wandered back to Brin, and he found himself imagining her to be as alone as he—alone and hunted. He wished she were there with him.

When sunrise came, he kept walking. He was not yet clear of the Duln, and the sense of uneasiness was still with him. He was tired, but not so tired that he felt the need to sleep just yet. He walked on while the sun rose before him in a golden haze, thin streamers of brightness slipping down into the forest gray, reflecting rainbow colors from the drying leaves and emerald moss. From time to time he found himself glancing back, watching.

Several hours into morning, the forest ended and rolling grasslands appeared, a threshold to the distant blue screen of the highlands. It was warm and friendly here, less confining than the forest, and Jair felt immediately more at ease. As he walked further into the grasslands, he began to recognize the countryside about him. He had come this way before on a visit to Leah just a year ago when Rone had brought him to his hunting lodge at the foot of the highlands where they had stayed and fished the mist lakes. The lodge lay another two hours eastward, but it offered a soft bed and shelter for the remainder of the day so that he might set out again refreshed with nightfall. The idea of the bed decided him.

Disregarding the weariness he felt, Jair continued to march east through the grasslands, the rise of the highlands broadening before him as he drew closer. Once or twice he looked back into the countryside through which he had come, but each time the land lay empty.

It was midday when he reached the lodge, a timber and stone house set back within a tall stand of pine at the edge of the highland forests. The lodge sat upon a slope overlooking the grasslands, but was hidden by the trees until approached within hailing distance. Jair stumbled wearily up the stone steps to the lodge door, turned to locate the key that Rone kept concealed in a crevice in the stones, then saw that the lock was broken. Cautiously he lifted the latch and peered in. The building was empty.

Of course it was empty, he grumbled to himself, eyes heavy with the need for sleep. Why wouldn't it be?

He closed the door behind him, glanced briefly about at the immaculate interior—wood and leather furniture, shelves of stores and cooking ware, ale bar, and stone fireplace—and moved gratefully down the short hallway at the rear of the main room that led to the bedrooms. He stopped at the first door he came to, released the latch, pushed his way in, and collapsed on the broad, feather-stuffed bed.

In seconds, he was asleep.

It was almost dark when he came awake, and the autumn sky was deep blue, laced with dying silver sunlight through the curtained bedroom window. A noise brought him awake, a small scuffling sound—boots passing over wooden planking.

Without thinking, he was on his feet, still half-asleep as he walked quickly to the bedroom door and peered out. The darkened room at the front of the lodge stood empty, bathed in shadow. Jair blinked and stared through the dusk. Then he saw something else.

The front door stood open.

He stepped out into the hallway in disbelief, sleep-filled eyes blinking.

"Taking another walk, boy?" a familiar voice asked from behind.

Frantically he whirled—far too slowly. Something hammered into the side of his face, and lights exploded before his eyes. He fell to the floor and into blackness.

I t was still summer where the Mermidon flowed down out of Callahorn and emptied into the vast expanse of the Rainbow Lake. It was green and fresh, a mix of grassland and forest, foothill and mountain. Water from the river and its dozens of tributaries fed the earth and kept it moist. Mist from the lake drifted north with each sunrise, dissipated, and settled into the land, giving life beyond the summer season. Sweet, damp smells permeated the air, and autumn was yet a stranger.

Brin Ohmsford sat alone on a rise overlooking the juncture of lake and river and was at peace. The day was almost gone, and the sun was a brilliant reddish gold flare on the western horizon, its light staining crimson the silver waters that stretched away before her. No wind broke the calm of the coming evening, and the lake's surface was mirrorlike and still. High overhead, its bands of color a sharper hue against the coming gray of night where the eastern sky darkened, the wondrous rainbow from which the lake took its name arched from shoreline to shoreline. Cranes and geese glided gracefully through the fading light, their cries haunting in the deep silence.

Brin's thoughts drifted. It had been four days since she had left her home and come eastward on a journey that would take her to the deep Anar, farther than she had ever gone before. It seemed odd that she knew so little about the journey, even now. Four days had gone, and she was still little more than a child who gripped a mother's hand, trusting blindly. From Shady Vale they had gone north through the Duln, east along the banks of the Rappahalladran, north again, and then east, following the shoreline of the Rainbow Lake to where the Mermidon emptied down. Never once had Allanon offered a word of explanation.

Both Rone and she had asked the Druid to explain, of course. They had asked their questions time and again, but the Druid had brushed them aside. Later, he would tell them. Your questions will be answered later. For now, simply follow after me. So they had followed as he had bidden them, wary and increasingly distrustful, promising themselves that they would have their explanations before the Eastland was reached.

Yet the Druid gave them little cause to believe that their promise would be fulfilled. Enigmatic and withdrawn, he kept them from him. In the daytime, when they traveled, he rode before them, and it was clear that he preferred to ride alone. At night, when they camped, he left them and moved into the shadows. He neither ate nor slept, behavior that seemed to emphasize the differences between them and thereby widen the distance. He watched over them like a hawk over its prey, never leaving them alone to stray.

Until now, she corrected. On this evening of the fourth day, Allanon unexpectedly had left them. They had encamped here, where the Mermidon fed into the Rainbow Lake, and the Druid had stalked off into the woodlands bordering the river's waters and disappeared without a word of explanation. Valegirl and highlander had watched him go, staring after in disbelief. At last, when it became apparent that he had indeed left them— for how long, they could only guess—they resolved to waste no further time worrying about him and turned their attention to preparing the evening meal. Three days of eating fish pulled first from the waters of the Rappahalladran and then from the waters of the Rainbow Lake had blunted temporarily their enthusiasm for fish. So armed with ash bow and arrows, a weapon Menion Leah had favored, Rone had gone in search of different fare. Brin had taken a few minutes to gather wood for a cooking fire, then settled herself on this rise and let the solitude of the moment slip over her.

Allanon! He was an enigma that defied resolution. Committed to the preservation of the land, he was a friend to her people, a benefactor to the races, and a protector against evil they could not alone withstand. Yet what friend used people as Allanon did? Why keep so carefully concealed the reasons for all he did? He seemed at times as much enemy, malefactor, and destroyer as that which he claimed to stand against.

The Druid himself had told her father the story of the old world of faerie from which all the magic had come along with creatures who wielded it. Good or bad, black or white, the magic was the same in the sense that its power was rooted in the strength, wisdom, and purpose of the user. After all, what had been the true difference between Allanon and the Warlock Lord in their struggle to secure mastery over the Sword of Shannara? Each had been a Druid, learning the magic from the books of the old world. The difference was in the character of the user, for where one had been corrupted by the power, the other had stayed pure.

Perhaps. And perhaps not. Her father would argue the matter, she knew, maintaining that the Druid had been corrupted by the power as surely as the Dark Lord, if only in a different way. For Allanon was also governed in his life by the power he wielded and by the secrets of its use. If his sense of responsibility was of a higher sort and his purpose less selfish, he was nevertheless as much its victim. Indeed, there was something strangely sad about Allanon, despite his harsh, almost threatening demeanor. She thought for a time about the sense of sadness that the Druid invoked in her—a sadness her father had surely never felt—and she wondered how it was that she felt it so keenly.

"I'm back!"

She turned, startled. But it was only Rone, calling up to her from the campsite in the pine grove below the rise. She climbed to her feet and started down.

"I see that the Druid hasn't returned yet," the highlander said as she came up to him. He had a pair of wild hens slung over one shoulder and dropped them to the ground. "Maybe we'll get lucky and he won't come back at all."

She stared at him. "Maybe that wouldn't be so lucky."

He shrugged. "Depends on how you look at it."

"Tell me how you look at it, Rone."

He frowned. "All right. I don't trust him."

"And why is it that you don't?"

"Because of what he pretends to be: protector against the Warlock Lord and the Bearers of the Skull; protector against the Demons released from the old world of faerie; and now protector against the Mord Wraiths. But always, it's with the aid of the Ohmsford family and their friends, take note. I know the history, too, Brin. It's always the same. He appears unexpectedly, warning of a danger that threatens the races, which only a member of the Ohmsford family can help put an end to. Heirs to the Elven house of Shannara and to the magics that belong to it—those are the Ohmsfords. First the Sword of Shannara, then the Elfstones and now the wishsong. But somehow things are never quite what they seem, are they?"

Brin shook her head slowly. "What are you saying, Rone?"

"I'm saying that the Druid comes out of nowhere with a story designed to secure Shea or Wil Ohmsford's aid—and now your aid—and each time it's the same. He tells only what he must. He gives away only as much as he needs give away. He keeps back the rest; he hides a part of the truth. I don't trust him. He plays games with people's lives!"

"And you believe that he's doing that with us?"

Rone took a deep breath. "Don't you?"

Brin was silent a moment before answering. "I'm not sure."

"Then you don't trust him either?"

"I didn't say that."

The highlander stared at her a moment, they slowly settled himself on the ground across from her, folding his long legs before him. "Well, which way is it, Brin? Do you trust him or don't you?"

She sat down as well. "I guess I haven't really decided."

"Then what are you doing here, for cat's sake?"

She smiled at his obvious disgust. "I'm here, Rone, because he needs me—I believe that much of what I have been told. The rest I'm not sure about. The part he keeps hidden, I have to discover for myself."

"If you can."

"I'll find a way."

"It's too dangerous," he said flatly.

She smiled, rose, and came over to where he sat. Gently she kissed his forehead. "That's why I wanted you here with me, Rone Leah—to be my protector. Isn't that why you came?" He flushed bright scarlet and muttered something unintelligible, and she laughed in spite of herself. "Why don't we leave this discussion until later and do something with those hens. I'm starved."

She built a small cooking fire while Rone cleaned the hens. Then they cooked and ate the birds together with a small portion of cheese and ale. They ate their meal in silence, seated back atop the small rise, watching the night sky darken and the stars and gibbous moon cast their pale silver light on the waters of the lake.

By the time they had finished, night had fallen and Allanon still had not returned.

"Brin, you remember what you said before, about my being here to protect you?" Rone asked her after they had returned to the fire. She nodded. "Well, it's true—I am here to protect you. I wouldn't let anything happen to you—not ever. I guess you know that."

He hesitated, and she smiled through the dark. "I know."

"Well." He shifted about uneasily, his lands lifting the battered scabbard that housed the Sword of Leah. "There's another reason I'm here, too. I hope you can understand this. I'm here to prove something to myself." He hesitated again, groping for the words to explain. "I am a Prince of Leah, but that's just a title. I was born into it, just like my brothers—and they're all older. And this sword, Brin." He held up the scabbard and its weapon. "It isn't really mine; it's my great-grandfather's. It's Menion Leah's sword. It always has been, ever since he carried it in search of the Sword of Shannara. I carry it—the ash bow, too—because Menion carried them and I'd like to be what he was. But I'm not."

"You don't know that," she said quickly.

"That's just the point," he continued. "I've never done anything to find out what I could be. And that's partly why I'm here. I want to know. This is how Menion found out—by going on a quest, as protector to Shea Ohmsford. Maybe I can do it this way, too."

Brin smiled. "Maybe you can. In any case, I'm glad you told me." She paused. "Now I'll tell you a secret. I came for the same reason. I have something to prove to myself, too. I don't know if I can do what Allanon expects of me; I don't know if I am strong enough. I was born with the wishsong, but I have never known what I was meant to do with it. I believe there is a reason for my having the magic. Maybe I will learn that reason from Allanon."

She put her hand on his arm. "So you see, we're not so different after all, are we, Rone?"

They talked a while longer, growing drowsy as the evening lengthened and the weariness of the day's travel overcame them. Then at last their talk gave way to silence, and they spread their bedding. Clear and cool, the autumn night wrapped them in its solitude and peace as they stretched out next to the dark embers of the fire and pulled their blankets close.

They were asleep in moments.

Neither saw the tall, black-robed figure who stood in the shadow of the pines just beyond the fire's light.

When they awoke the following morning, Allanon was there. He was seated only a few yards away from them on a hollow log, his tall, spare form wraithlike in the gray light of early dawn. He watched silently as they rose, washed, and ate a light breakfast, offering no explanation as to where he had been. More than once the Valegirl and the highlander glanced openly in his direction, but he seemed to take no notice. It was not until they had packed their bedrolls and cooking gear and brought the horses in to be saddled that he finally rose and came over to them.

"There has been a change of plans," he announced. They stared at him silently. "We are no longer going east. We are going north into the Dragon's Teeth."

"The Dragon's Teeth?" Rone's jaw tightened. "Why?"

"Because it is necessary."

"Necessary for whom?" Rone snapped.

"It will only be for a day or so." Allanon turned his attention to Brin now, ignoring the angry highlander. "I have a visit to make. When it is finished, we will turn east again and complete our journey."

"Allanon." Brin spoke his name softly. "Tell us why we must go north."

The Druid hesitated, his face darkening. Then he nodded. "Very well. Last night I received a summons from my father. He bids me come to him, and I am bound to do so. In life, he was the Druid Bremen. Now his shade surfaces from the netherworld through the waters of the Hadeshorn in the Valley of Shale. In three days' time, before daybreak, he will speak with me there."

Bremen—the Druid who had escaped the massacre of the Council at Paranor, when the Warlock Lord swept down out of the Northland in the Second War of the Races, and who had forged the Sword of Shannara. So long ago, Brin thought, the legendary tale recalling itself in her memory. Then, seventy-odd years ago, Shea Ohmsford had gone with Allanon into the Valley of Shale and seen the shade of Bremen rise from the Hadeshorn to converse with his son, to warn of what lay ahead, to prophesy . . .

"He can see the future, can't he?" Brin asked suddenly, remembering now how the shade had warned of Shea's fate. "Will he speak of that?"

Allanon shook his head doubtfully. "Perhaps. Even so, he would reveal only fragments of what is to be, for the future is not yet formed in its entirety and must of necessity remain in doubt. Only certain things can be known. Even they are not always clear to our understanding." He shrugged. "In any case, he calls. He would not do so if it were not of grave importance."

"I don't like it," Rone announced. "It's another three days or more gone—time that could be spent getting into and out of the Anar. The Wraiths are already searching for you. You told us that much yourself. We're just giving them that much more time to find you—and Brin."

The Druid's eyes fixed on him, cold and hard. "I take no unnecessary risks with the girl's safety, Prince of Leah. Nor with your own."

Rone flushed angrily, and Brin stepped forward, seizing his hand. "Wait, Rone. Perhaps going to the Hadeshorn is a good idea. Perhaps we will learn something of what the future holds that will aid us."

The highlander kept his gaze locked on Allanon. "What would aid us most is a bit more of the truth of what we're about!" he snapped.

"So." The word was a soft, quick whisper, and Allanon's tall form seemed to suddenly grow taller. "What part of the truth would you have me reveal, Prince of Leah?"

Rone held his ground. "This much, Druid. You tell Brin that she must come with you into the Eastland because you lack the power necessary to penetrate the barrier that protects the book of dark magic—you, who are the keeper of the secrets of the Druids, who possess power enough to destroy Skull Bearers and Demons alike! Yet you need her. And what does she have that you don't? The wishsong. Nothing more, just that. It lacks even the power of the Elfstones! It is a magic toy that changes the colors of leaves and causes flowers to bloom! What kind of protection is that?"

Allanon stared at him silently for a moment and then smiled, a faint, sad smile. "What kind of power, indeed?" he murmured. He looked suddenly at Brin. "Do you, too, harbor these doubts the highlander voices? Do you seek a better understanding of the wishsong? Shall I show you something of its use?"

It was cold the way he said it, but Brin nodded. "Yes."

The Druid strode past her, seized the reins of his horse and mounted. "Come then, and I will show you, Valegirl," he said.

They rode north in silence along the Mermidon, winding their way through the rocky forestland, the light of the sunrise breaking through the trees on their left, the shadow of the Runne Mountains a dark wall on their right. They rode for more than an hour, a grim, voiceless procession. Then at last the Druid signaled a halt, and they dismounted.

"Leave the horses," he instructed.

They walked west into the forest, the Druid leading the Valegirl and the highlander across a ridge and down into a heavily wooded hollow. After several minutes of fighting their way through the tangled undergrowth, Allanon stopped and turned.

"Now then, Brin." He pointed ahead into the brush. "Pretend that this hollow is the barrier of dark magic through which you must pass. How would you use the wishsong to gain passage?"

She glanced about uncertainly. "I'm not sure . . ."

"Not sure?" He shook his head. "Think of the uses to which you have put the magic. Have you used it as the Prince of Leah suggests to bring autumn color to the leaves of a tree? Have you used it to bring flowers to bloom, leaves to bud, plants to grow?" She nodded. "You have used it, then, to change color and shape and behavior. Do so here. Make the brush part for you."

She looked at him a moment and then nodded. This was more than she had ever asked of herself, and she was not convinced she had the power. Moreover, it had been a long time since she had used the magic. But she would try. Softly, she began to sing. Her voice was low and even, the song blending with the sounds of the forest. Then slowly she changed its pitch, and it rose until all else had faded into stillness. Words came, unrehearsed, spontaneous and somehow intuitively felt as she reached out to the brush that blocked her passage. Slowly the tangle drew back, leaves and branches withdrawing in winding ribbons of sleek green.

A moment later, the way forward lay open to the center of the hollow.

"Simple enough, don't you agree?" But the Druid wasn't really asking. "Let's see where your path takes us."

He started ahead again, black robes drawn close. Brin glanced quickly at Rone, who shrugged his lack of understanding. They followed after the Druid. Seconds later he stopped again, this time pointing to an elm, its trunk bent and stunted within the shadow of a taller, broader oak. The elm's limbs had grown into those of the oak, twisting upward in a futile effort to reach the sunlight.

"A bit harder task this time, Brin," Allanon said suddenly. "That elm would be much better off if the sun could reach it. I want you to straighten it, bring it upright, and disentangle it from the oak."

Brin looked at the two trees doubtfully. They seemed too closely entwined. "I don't think I can do that," she told him quietly.

"Try."

"The magic is not strong enough . . ."

"Try anyway," he cut her short.

So she sang, the wishsong enfolding the other sounds of the forest until there was nothing else, rising brightly into the morning air. The elm shuddered, limbs quaking in response. Brin lifted the pitch of her song, sensing the tree's resistance, and the words formed a harder edge. The stunted trunk of the elm drew back from the oak, its limbs scraping and tearing and its leaves ripped violently from their stems.

Then, with shocking suddenness, the entire tree seemed to heave upward and explode in a shower of fragmented limbs, twigs, and leaves that rained down across the length of the hollow. Astonished, Brin stumbled back, shielding her face with her hands, the wishsong dying into instant stillness. She would have fallen but for Allanon, who caught her in his arms, held her protectively until the shower had subsided, then turned her to face him.

"What happened . . . ?" she began, but he quickly put a finger to her lips.

"Power, Valegirl," he whispered. "Power in your wishsong far greater than what you have imagined. That elm could not disentangle itself from the oak. Its limbs were far too stiff, far too heavily entwined. Yet it could not refuse your song. It had no choice but to pull free—even when the result meant destroying itself!"

"Allanon!" She shook her head in disbelief.

"You have that power, Brin Omsford. As with all things magic, there is a dark side as well as a light." The Druid's face came closer. "You have played with changing the colors of a tree's leaves. Think what would happen if you carried the seasonal change you wrought to its logical conclusion. The tree would pass from autumn into winter, from winter into spring, from seasonal change to seasonal change. At last it would have passed through the entire cycle of its life. It would die."

"Druid . . ." Rone warned and started forward, but a single dark glance from the other's eyes froze him in his tracks.

"Stand, Prince of Leah. Let her hear the truth." The black eyes again found Brin's. "You have played with the wishsong as you would a curious toy because that is all the use you saw for it. Yet you knew that it was more than that, Valegirl—always, deep inside, you knew. Elven magic has always been more than that. Yours is the magic of the Elfstones, born into new form in its passage from your father's blood to your own. There is power in you of a sort that transcends any that has gone before—latent perhaps, yet the potential is unmistakable. Consider for a moment the nature of this magic you wield. The wishsong can change the behavior of any living thing! Can you not see what that means? Supple brush can be made to part for you, giving you access where there was none before. Unbending trees can be made to part as well, though they shatter with the effort. If you can bring color to leaves, you can also drain it away. If you can cause flowers to bloom, you can also cause them to wilt. If you can give life, Brin, you can also take it away."

She stared at him, horrified. "What are you saying?" she whispered harshly. "That the wishsong can kill? That I would use it to kill? Do you think. . . ?"

"You asked to be shown something of its use," Allanon cut short her protestations. "I have simply done as you wished. But I think now you will no longer doubt that the magic is much more than you thought it was."

Brin's dusky face burned with anger. "I no longer doubt, Allanon. Nor should you doubt this—that even so, I would never use the wishsong to kill! Never!"

The Druid held her gaze, yet the hard features softened slightly. "Not even to save your own life? Or perhaps the life of the highlander? Not even then?"

She did not look away. "Never."

The Druid stared at the Valegirl a moment longer—as if to measure in some way the depth of her commitment. Then abruptly he wheeled away and started back toward the slope of the hollow.

"You have seen enough, Brin. We have to get on with our journey. Think about what you have learned."

His black form disappeared into the brush. Brin stood where he had left her, aware suddenly that her hands were shaking. That tree! The way it had simply shattered, torn apart . . .

"Brin." Rone was standing before her, and his hands came up to grip her shoulders. She winced at their touch. "We can't go on with him—not anymore. He plays games with us as he has done with all the others. Leave him and his foolish quest and come back with me now to the Vale."

She stared at him a moment, then shook her head. "No. It was necessary that I see this."

"None of this is necessary, for cat's sake!" His big hands drew back and fastened about the pommel of the Sword of Leah. "If he does something like that again, I'll not think twice . . ."

"No, Rone." She put her hands over his. She was calm once more, realizing suddenly that she had missed something. "What he did was not done simply to frighten or intimidate me. It was done to teach me, and it was done out of a need for haste. It was in his eyes. Could you not see it?"

He shook his head. "I saw nothing. What need for haste?"

She looked to where the Druid had gone. "Something is wrong. Something."

Then she thought again of the destruction of the tree, of the Druid's words of warning, and of her vow. Never! She looked quickly back at Rone. "Do you think I could use the wishsong to kill?" she asked softly.

For just an instant he hesitated. "No."

Even to save your life? she thought. And what if it were not a tree that threatened, but a living creature? Would I destroy it to save you? Oh, Rone, what if it were a human being?

"Will you still come with me on this journey?" she asked him.

He gave her his most rakish smile. "Right up to the moment when we take that confounded book and shred it."

Then he bent to kiss her lightly on the mouth, and her arms came up to hold him close. "We'll be all right," she heard him say.

And she answered, "I know."

But she was no longer sure.

When Jair Ohmsford regained consciousness, he found himself trussed hand and foot and securely lashed against a tree trunk. He was no longer in the hunting lodge but in a clearing sheltered by closely grown fir that loomed over him like sentinels set to watch. A dozen feet in front of him, a small fire burned, casting its faint glow into the shadowed dark of the silent trees. Night lay over the land.

"Awake again, boy?"

The familiar, chiding voice came from out of the darkness to his left, and he turned his head slowly, searching. A squat, motionless figure crouched at the edge of the firelight. Jair started to reply, then realized that he was not only tied; he was gagged as well.

"Oh yes, sorry about that," the other spoke again. "Had to put the gag in, of course. Couldn't have you using your magic on me a second time, could I? Do you have any idea how long it took me to get out of that wood bin?"

Jair sagged back against the tree, remembering. The Gnome at the inn—that was who had followed him, caught up with him at Rone's hunting lodge, and struck him from behind . . .

He winced at the memory, finding that the side of his head still throbbed.

"Nice trick, that thing with the snakes." The Gnome chuckled faintly. He rose and came into the firelight, seating himself cross-legged a few feet from his prisoner. Narrow green eyes studied Jair speculatively. "I thought you harmless, boy—not some Druid's whelp. Worse luck for me, eh? There I was, sure you'd be so scared that you'd tell me right off what I wanted to know—tell me anything just to get rid of me. Not you, though. Snakes on my arms and a four-foot limb bashed up against my head, that's what you gave me. Lucky I'm alive!"

The blocky yellow face cocked slightly. "Course, that was your mistake." A blunt finger came up sharply. "You should have finished me. But you didn't, and that gave me another chance at you. Suppose that's the way you are, though, being from the Vale. Anyway, once I got free of that wood bin, I came after you like a fox after a rabbit. Too bad for you, too, because I wasn't about to let you escape, after what you'd put me through. Not by a whisker's cut, I wasn't! Those other fools, they'd have let you outrun them. But not me. Tracked you three days. Almost had you at the river, but you were already across and I couldn't pick up your trail at night. Had to wait. But I caught you napping at that lodge, didn't I?"

He laughed cheerfully and Jair flushed with anger. "Oh, don't be angry with me—I was just doing my job. Besides, it was a matter of pride. Twenty years, and no one's ever gotten the best of me until now. And then it's some nothing boy. Couldn't live with that. Oh, knocking you senseless—had to do that, too. Like I said, couldn't be taking chances with the magic."

He got up and came a few steps closer, his rough face screwed up with obvious curiosity. "It was magic, wasn't it? How'd you learn to do that? It's in the voice, right? You make the snakes come by using the voice. Quite a trick. Scared the wits out of me, and I thought there wasn't much left that could scare me." He paused. "Except maybe the walkers."

Jair's eyes glistened with fear at mention of the Mord Wraiths. The Gnome saw it and nodded. "Something to be scared of, they are. Black all through. Dark as midnight. Wouldn't want them hunting me. Don't know how you got past that one back at the house . . ."

He stopped suddenly and bent forward. "Hungry, boy?" Jair nodded. The Gnome regarded him thoughtfully for a moment, then rose. "Tell you what. I'll loosen the gag and feed you if you promise not to use the magic on me. Wouldn't do you much good anyway trussed up to that tree—not unless those snakes of yours can chew through ropes. I'll feed you and we can talk a bit. The others won't catch up until morning. What about it?"

Jair thought it over a moment, then nodded his agreement. He was famished.

"Done, then." The Gnome came over and slipped free the gag. One hand fastened tightly to Jair's chin. "Your word now—let's have it. No magic."

"No magic," Jair repeated, wincing.

"Good. Good." The Gnome let his hand drop. "You're one who keeps his word, I'm betting. Man's only as good as his word, you know." He reached down to his waist for a hard leather container, released the stopper and brought it up to the Valeman's lips. "Drink. Go on, take a swallow."

Jair sipped at the unknown liquid, his throat dry and tight. It was an ale, harsh and bitter, and it burned all the way down. Jair choked and drew back, and the Gnome recapped the container and returned it to his belt. Then he sat back on his haunches, grinning.

"I'm called Slanter."

"Jair Ohmsford." Jair was still trying to swallow. "I guess you knew that."

Slanter nodded. "I did. Should have found out a bit more, it appears. Quite a chase you took me on."

Jair frowned. "How did you manage to catch up to me? I didn't think anyone could catch me."

"Oh, that." The Gnome sniffed. "Well, not just anyone could have caught you. But then I'm not just anyone."

"What do you mean?"

The Gnome laughed. "I mean I'm a tracker, boy. It's what I do. Fact is, it's what I do better than just about anyone else alive. That's why they brought me, the others. That's why I'm here. I've been tracking."

"Me?" Jair asked in astonishment.

"No, not you—the Druid! The one they call Allanon. It was him I was tracking. You just happened to cross my path at the wrong time."

A look of bewilderment crossed the Valeman's face. This Gnome was a tracker? No wonder he hadn't been able to escape him as he would have another man. But tracking Allanon . . . ?

Slanter shook his head helplessly and climbed to his feet. "Look, I'll explain it all to you, but first let's have something to eat. I had to carry you down from that hunting lodge two miles distant, and you may look small but you weigh better than your size. Worked up a pretty good appetite while you rested. Sit still, now—I'll put something on the fire."

Slanter retrieved a knapsack from the other side of the clearing, pulled clear some cooking utensils and within minutes had a beef and vegetable stew simmering over the fire. The smell of the cooking food wafted through the night air to Jair's nostrils, and his mouth began to water. He was beyond famished, he decided. He had not had a decent meal since he had left the inn. Besides, he needed to keep his strength up if he was to have any chance of escaping this fellow, and he had every intention of doing so at the first opportunity.

When the stew was finished, Slanter brought it over to where he was tied and hand-fed him mouthfuls, sharing the meal with him. The food tasted wonderful, and they ate all that there was, together with an end of bread and some cheese. Slanter drank more of the ale, but gave Jair sips from a cup of water.

"Not a bad stew if I do say so myself," the Gnome remarked afterward, bent next to the fire to scrape clean the pan. "Learned a few useful things over the years."

"How long have you been a tracker?" Jair asked him, intrigued.

"Most of my life. Began learning when I was your age." He finished with the cookware, stood up and came back over to the Valeman. "What do you know about trackers?"

Briefly Jair told him about the old tracker who had boarded at the inn, of their conversations, and of the tracking games they'd played while the man's leg had healed. Slanter listened quietly, obvious interest reflected in his rough yellow features. When Jair had finished, the Gnome sat back, a distant look in his sharp eyes.

"I was like you once, long time ago. Used to think about nothing but being a tracker. Left home with one finally—an old Borderman. I was younger than you. Left home, went right out of the Eastland into Callahorn and the Northland. Gone better than fifteen years. Traveled all the lands at one time or another, you know. As much of them in me as Eastland Gnome. Odd, but I'm kind of a homeless sort because of it. Gnomes don't really trust me, because I've been away too long, seen too much of what else there is ever to really be the same as them. A Gnome who's not a Gnome. I've learned more than they ever will, shut away in the Eastland forests like they are. They know it, too. They barely tolerate me. They respect me, though, because I'm the best that there is at what I do."

He glanced sharply at Jair. "That's why I'm here—because I'm the best. The Druid Allanon—the fellow you don't know, remember?—he came into the Ravenshorn and Graymark, tried to get down into the Maelmord. But nothing goes down into that pit, not Druid nor Devil. The Wraiths knew he was there and went after him. One walker, a patrol of Gnome Hunters, and me to track. Tracked to your village, then waited for someone to show. Thought someone would, even though it was pretty clear that the Druid had already gone elsewhere. And who should appear but you?"

Jair's mind was racing. How much does he know? Does he know the reason that Allanon came to Shady Vale? Does he know about the . . . ? And suddenly he remembered the Elfstones, tucked hastily within his tunic when he fled the Vale. Did he still have them? Or had Slanter found them? Oh, shades!

Eyes still fixed on those of the Gnome, he shifted cautiously against the ropes that bound him, trying to feel the pressure of the Stones against his body. But it was hopeless. The ties knotted his clothing and gave him no sure feel for what he still had on him. He dared not look down, even for an instant.

"Ropes cutting a bit?" Slanter asked suddenly.

He shook his head. "I was just trying to get comfortable." He forced himself to sit back and relax. He changed the subject back. "Why did you bother coming after me if you were supposed to be tracking Allanon?"

Slanter cocked his head slightly. "Because I was tracking the Druid to find out where he went, and I've done that. He went to your village, to your family. Now he's gone back to the Eastland—isn't that right? Oh, you needn't answer. At least not to me. But you will have to answer to those who came with me when they get here in the morning. A bit slow they are, but sure. I had to leave them to be certain I caught you. You see, they want to know something of Allanon's visit. They want to know why he came. And unfortunately for you, they want to know one thing more."

He paused meaningfully, eyes boring into Jair. The Valeman took a deep breath. "About the magic?" he whispered.

"Sharp fellow." Slanter's smile was hard.

"What if I don't want to tell them?"

"That would be foolish," the Gnome said quietly.

They stared at each other wordlessly. "The Wraith would make me tell, wouldn't he?" Jair asked finally.

"The Wraith is not your problem." Slanter snorted. "The Wraith's gone north after the Druid. The Sedt is your problem."

The Valeman shook his head. "Sedt? What is a Sedt?"

"A Sedt is a Gnome chieftain—in this case, Spilk. He commands the patrol. A rather unpleasant fellow. Not like me, you see. Very much an Eastland Gnome. He would just as soon cut your throat as look at you. He's your problem. You'd better answer the questions he asks."

He shrugged. "Besides, once you've told Spilk what he wants to know, I'll do what I can to see that you're released. After all, our fight's not with the Vale people. Our fight's with the Dwarves. Not to disappoint you, but you're really not all that important. That magic of yours is what's interesting. No, you answer the questions and I think you'll be turned loose quick enough."

Jair eyed him suspiciously. "I don't believe you."

Slanter drew back. "You don't? Well, here's my word on it, then. As good as your own." Heavy eyebrows arched. "It means as much to me as yours does, boy. Now take it."

Jair said nothing for a moment. Strangely enough, he thought the Gnome was telling him the truth. If he promised he would seek Jair's release, he would do just that. If he thought Jair would be released on answering the questions asked, Jair probably would. Jair grimaced. On the other hand, why should he trust any Gnome?

"I don't know," he muttered.

"You don't know?" Slanter shook his head hopelessly. "You'd think you had a choice, boy. You don't answer, Spilk goes to work on you. You still don't answer, he turns you over to the walkers. What do you think happens to you then?"

Jair went cold to the bone. He didn't care to think about what would happen then.

"I thought you were smart," the Gnome continued, wizened yellow features twisting into a grimace. "Smart, the way you got past those others back there—even got past the walker. So stay smart. What difference does it make now what you tell anyone? What difference if you tell the Sedt why the Druid came to see you? The Druid's gone by now anyway— won't likely catch up to him this side of the Eastland. He wouldn't tell you anything all that important anyway, would he? The magic—well, all they want to know about the magic is how you learned it. The Druid, maybe? Someone else?" He waited a moment, but Jair said nothing. "Well, any- way, just tell how you learned it and how you use it—simple enough and no skin off your nose. No games, just tell the truth. You do that, and that's the end of your use."

Again he waited for Jair to respond, and again the Valeman stayed silent.

Slanter shrugged. "Well, think on it." He stood up, stretched, and came over to Jair. Smiling cheerfully, he replaced the gag in the Valeman's mouth. "Sorry about the sleeping accommodations, but I can't be taking many chances with you. You've shown me that much."

Still smiling, he retrieved a blanket from the far side of the clearing, brought it over to Jair and wrapped it about him, tucking in the corners where the ropes bound him to the tree so that it would stay fixed. Then he walked over to the fire and kicked it out. In the faint glow of the embers, Jair could see his stocky form as it moved off into the dark.

"Ah, me—reduced to chasing down Valemen," the Gnome muttered. "Waste of talent. Not even a Dwarf! At least they could give me a Dwarf to track. Or the Druid again. Bah! Druid's gone back to help the Dwarves and here I sit, watching this boy . . ."

He muttered on a bit more, most of it unintelligible, and then his voice faded away entirely.

Jair Ohmsford sat alone in the dark and wondered what he was going to do when morning came.

He slept poorly that night, cramped and bruised by the ropes that bound him, haunted by the specter of what lay ahead. Considered from any point of view, his future appeared bleak. He could expect no help from his friends; after all, no one knew where he was. His parents and Brin, Rone, and Allanon all thought him safely housed at the inn at Shady Vale. Nor could he reasonably anticipate much consideration from his captors. Slanter's reassurances notwithstanding, he did not expect to be released, no matter how many questions he answered. After all, how would he answer questions about the magic? Slanter clearly thought it something he had been taught. Once the Gnomes learned it was not an acquired skill, but a talent he had been born with, they would want to know more. They would take him to the Eastland, to the Mord Wraiths . . .

So the night hours passed. He dozed at times, his weariness overcoming his discomfort and his worry—yet never for very long. Then finally, toward morning, exhaustion overtook him, and at last he drifted off to sleep.

It was not yet dawn when Slanter shook him roughly awake.

"Get up," the Gnome ordered. "The others are here."

Jair's eyes blinked open, squinting into the predawn gray that shrouded the highland forest. The air was chill and damp, even with the blanket still wrapped about his body, and a fine fall mist clung about the dark trunks of the fir. It was deathly still, the forest life not yet come awake. Slanter bent over him, loosing the ropes that bound him to the tree. There were no other Gnomes in sight.

"Where are they?" he asked as the gag was slipped from his mouth.

"Close. A hundred yards down the slope." Slanter gripped the Valeman's tunic front and hauled him to his feet. "No games now. Keep the magic to yourself. I've let you loose from the tree so that you might look the part of a man, but I'll strap you back again if you cross me. Understand?"

Jair nodded quickly. Ropes still bound his hands and feet, and his limbs were so badly cramped he could barely manage to stand. He stood with his back against the fir, the muscles of his body aching and stiff. Even if he could manage to break free, he couldn't run far like this. His mind was dizzy with fatigue and sudden fear as he waited for his strength to return. Answer the questions, Slanter had advised. Don't be foolish. But what answers could he give? What answers would they accept?

Then abruptly a line of shadowy figures materialized from out of the gloom, trudging heavily through the forest trees. Two, three, half a dozen, eight—Jair watched as one by one they appeared through the mist, bulky forms wrapped in woolen forest cloaks. Gnomes—rugged yellow features glimpsed from within hoods drawn close, thick-fingered hands clasping spears and cudgels. Not a word passed their lips as they filed into the clearing, but sharp eyes fixed on the captive Valeman and there was no friendliness in their gaze.

"This him?"

The speaker stood at the forefront of the others. He was powerfully built, his body corded with muscle, his chest massive. He thrust the butt of his cudgel into the forest earth, gripping it with scarred, gnarled fingers, twisting it slowly.

"Well, is it?"

The Gnome glanced briefly at Slanter. Slanter nodded. The Gnome let his gaze shift back to Jair. Slowly he pulled clear the hood of his forest cloak. Rough, broken features dominated his broad face. Cruel eyes studied the Valeman dispassionately, probing.

"What's your name?" he asked quietly.

"Jair Ohmsford," Jair answered at once.

"What was the Druid doing at your home?"

Jair hesitated, trying to decide what he should say. Something unpleasant flickered in the Gnome's eyes. With a sudden snap of his hands he brought the cudgel about, sweeping the Valeman's feet from beneath him. Jair fell hard, the breath knocked from his body. The Gnome stood over him silently, then reached down, seized the front of his tunic and pulled him back to his feet.

"What was the Druid doing in your home?"

Jair swallowed, trying to hide his fear. "He came to find my father," he lied.

"Why?"

"My father is the holder of Elfstones. Allanon will use them as a weapon against the Mord Wraiths."

There was an endless moment of silence. Jair did not even breathe. If Slanter had found the Elfstones in his tunic, the lie was already discovered and he was finished. He waited, eyes fixed on the Gnome.

"Where are they now, the Druid and your father?" the other said finally.

Jair exhaled. "Gone east." He hesitated, then added, "My mother and sister are visiting in the villages south of the Vale. I was supposed to wait at the inn for their return."

The Gnome grunted noncommittally. I've got to try to protect them, Jair thought. Spilk was watching him carefully. He did not look away. You can't tell that I'm lying, he thought. You can't.

Then a gnarled finger lifted from the cudgel. "Do you do magic?"

"I . . ." Jair glanced at the dark faces about him.

The cudgel came up, a quick, sharp blow that caught Jair across the knees, throwing him to the earth once more. The Gnome smiled, eyes hard. He yanked Jair back to his feet.

"Answer me—do you do magic?"

Jair nodded wordlessly, mute with pain. He could barely stand.

"Show me," the Gnome ordered.

"Spilk." Slanter's voice broke softly through the sudden silence. "You might want to reconsider that request."

Spilk glanced briefly at Slanter, then dismissed him. His eyes returned to Jair. "Show me."

Jair hesitated. Again the cudgel came up. Even though Jair was ready this time, he could not move fast enough to avoid the blow. It caught him alongside the face. Pain exploded in his head, and tears flooded his eyes. He dropped to his knees, but Spilk's thick hands knotted in his tunic and once more he was hauled to his feet.

"Show me!" the Gnome demanded.

Then anger flooded through Jair—anger so intense that it burned. He gave no thought to what he did next; he simply acted. A quick, muted cry broke from his lips and turned abruptly to a frightening hiss. Instantly Spilk was covered with huge gray spiders. The Gnome Sedt shrieked in dismay, tearing frantically at the great hairy insects, falling back from Jair. The Gnomes behind him scattered, spears and cudgels hammering downward as they sought to keep the spiders from their own bodies. The Sedt went down under a flurry of blows, thrashing upon the forest earth, trying to dislodge the terrible things that clung so tenaciously to him, his cries filling the morning air.

Jair sang a moment longer and then quit. Had he not been bound hand and foot or had he not been dizzy still from the blows struck by Spilk, he would have taken advantage of the confusion the wishsong's use had created to attempt an escape. But Slanter had made certain he could not run. As the anger left him he grew silent.

For a few seconds Spilk continued to roll upon the ground, tearing at himself. Then abruptly he realized that the spiders were gone. Slowly he came to his knees, his breathing harsh and ragged, his battered face twisting until his eyes found Jair. He surged to his feet with a howl and threw himself at the Valeman, gnarled hands reaching. Jair stumbled back, his legs tangling in the ropes. In the next instant, the Gnome was atop him, fists hammering wildly. Dozens of blows struck Jair's head and face, seemingly all at once. Pain and shock washed through him.

Then everything went black.

He came awake again only moments later. Slanter knelt next to him, dabbing at his face with a cloth soaked in cold water. The water stung, and he jerked sharply at its touch.

"You got more sand than brains, boy," the Gnome whispered, bending close. "You all right?"

Jair nodded, reaching up to touch his face experimentally. Slanter knocked his hand away.

"Leave it be." He dabbed a few more times with the cloth, then allowed a faint grin to cross his rough face. "Scared old Spilk half to death, you did. Half to death!"

Jair glanced past Slanter to where the remainder of the patrol huddled at the far side of the clearing, eyes darting watchfully in his direction. Spilk stood apart from everyone, his face black with anger.

"Had to pull him off you myself," Slanter was saying. "Would have killed you otherwise. Would have beat your head in."

"He asked me to show him the magic," Jair muttered, swallowing hard. "So I did."

The thought clearly amused the Gnome, and he permitted himself another faint smile, carefully averting his face from the Sedt. Then he put his arm about Jair's shoulders and raised him to a sitting position. Pouring a short ration of ale from the container at his waist, he gave the Valeman a drink. Jair accepted the ale, swallowing and choking as it burned clear down to his stomach.

"Better?"

"Better," Jair agreed.

"Then listen." The smile was gone. "I've got to gag you again. You're in my care now—the others won't have anything to do with you. You're to be kept bound and gagged except for meals. So behave. It's a long journey."

"A long journey to where?" Jair did not bother to conceal the alarm in his eyes.

"East. The Anar. You're to be taken to the Mord Wraiths. Spilk's decided. He wants them to have a look at your magic." The Gnome shook his head solemnly. "Sorry, but there's no help for it. Not after what you did."

Before Jair could say anything, Slanter shoved the gag back into his mouth. Then, loosing the ties that bound Jair's ankles, he pulled the Valeman to his feet. Producing a short length of rope, he looped one end through Jair's belt and tied the other end to his own.

"Spilk," he called over to the other.

The Gnome Sedt turned wordlessly and started off into the forest. The remainder of the patrol followed after.

"Sorry, boy," Slanter repeated.

Together, they walked from the clearing into the early morning mist.

All that day, the Gnomes marched Jair north through the wooded hill country bordering the western perimeter of Leah. Embracing the shelter of the trees, forsaking the more accessible roadways that crisscrossed the highlands, they kept to themselves and to their purpose. It was a long, exhausting trek for the Valeman, made no less difficult by the way in which he was secured, for his bonds cut into and cramped his body with every step. His discomfort might not have gone unnoticed, but it went unrelieved. Nor did his captors evidence the slightest concern for the toll that the pace of their march was extracting from him. Rugged, hardened veterans of the border wars of the deep Eastland, they were accustomed to forced marches through the worst kind of country and under the least favorable of conditions—marches that at times lasted several days. Jair was fit, but he was no match for these men.

By nightfall, when they at last arrived on the shores of the Rainbow Lake and made their way down to a secluded cove to set their camp, Jair could barely walk. Bound once again to a tree, given a quick meal and a few swallows of ale, he was asleep in minutes.

The following day passed in similar fashion. Awake at sunrise, the

Gnomes took him east along the shores of the lake, skirting the northern highlands that they might reach the concealment of the Black Oaks. Three times that day, the Gnomes paused to rest—once at midmorning, again at midday and a final time at midafternoon. The remainder of the day, they walked and Jair walked with them, his body aching, his feet blistered and raw. Pushed to the limit of his endurance, he refused to give them the satisfaction of seeing him falter, even for a moment. Determination gave him strength, and he kept pace.

All the time they marched him through the highlands, he thought about escape. It never entered his mind that he wouldn't escape; it was only a question of when. He even knew how he would manage it. That part was easy. He would simply make himself invisible to them. That was something they wouldn't be looking for—not so long as they thought his magic limited to creating imaginary spiders and snakes. They didn't understand that he could do other things as well. Sooner or later he would be given the opportunity. They would free him just long enough so that he could make use of the magic one more time. Just a moment was all that he would need. Like that, he would be gone. The certainty of it burned bright within him.

There was added incentive now for his need to escape. Slanter had told him that the walker that had come into the Vale with the Gnome patrol had gone east again in search of Allanon. But how was Allanon to know that the Mord Wraith tracked him? There was only Jair to warn him, and the Valeman knew he must find a way to do so.

His plans for escape were still foremost in his thoughts when, later that afternoon, they passed into the Black Oaks. The great dark trunks rose about them like a wall. In moments the sun was screened away. They traveled deep into the forest, following a pathway that ran parallel to the shoreline of the lake, winding their way steadily eastward into dusk. It was cooler here, deep and silent within these trees. Like a cave opening downward into the earth, the forest took them in and swallowed them up.

By sundown, the highlands were far behind. Camped within a small clearing sheltered by the oaks and a long ridgeline that dropped away northward to the water's edge, the Valeman sat back against a moss-grown trunk a dozen times his girth—bound and gagged still—and watched Slanter scoop meat stew from a kettle that simmered over a small cooking fire. Weary and discomfited, Jair nevertheless found himself studying the Gnome, pondering the contradictions he saw in the tracker's character. For two days he had had ample opportunity to observe Slanter, and he was as puzzled by the Gnome now as he had been when he had first conversed with him that night following his capture. What sort of fellow was he? True, he was a Gnome—yet at the same time, he didn't seem like a Gnome. Certainly he wasn't an Eastland Gnome. He wasn't like these Gnomes he traveled with. Even they seemed to sense that much. Jair could see it in their behavior toward him. They tolerated him, but they also avoided him. And Slanter had acknowledged that to Jair. He was as much an outsider in his own way as the Valeman. But it was more than that. There was something in the Gnome's character that set him apart from the others—an attitude, perhaps, an intelligence. He was smarter than they. And that was due most probably to the fact that he had done what they had not. A skilled tracker, a traveler of the Four Lands, he was a Gnome who had broken the traditions of his people and gone out of the homeland. He had seen things they had not. He understood things they could not. He had learned.

Yet in spite of all that, he was here. Why?

Slanter ambled over from the fire with a plate of stew in one hand and squatted down beside him. Loosing the gag so that his mouth was clear, the Gnome began to feed him.

"Doesn't taste too bad, does it?" The dark eyes watched him.

"No—tastes good."

"You can have more if you want." Slanter stirred the stew on the plate absently. "How do you feel?"

Jair met his gaze squarely. "I hurt everywhere."

"Feet?"

"Especially the feet."

The Gnome set down the stew. "Here, let me have a look."

He pulled free the Valeman's boots and stockings and examined the blistered feet, shaking his head slowly. Then he reached over into his pack and pulled free a small tin. Loosening its cap, he dipped his fingers in and extracted a reddish salve. Slowly he began rubbing it into the open wounds. The salve was cool and eased the pain.

"Should take away some of the sting, help toughen the skin when you walk," he said. He rubbed on some more, glanced up momentarily, his rough yellow face creasing with a sad smile, and then looked down again. "Tough sort of nut, aren't you?"

Jair didn't say anything. He watched the Gnome finish applying the salve, then resumed his meal. He was hungry and had two plates of the stew.

"Take a drink of this." Slanter held the ale container to his lips when the food was gone. He took several swallows, grimacing. "You don't know what's good for you," the Gnome told him.

"Not that stuff." Jair scowled.

Slanter sat back on his heels. "I heard something a little while ago I think you ought to know. It's not good news for you." He paused, glancing casually over his shoulder. "We're to meet with a walker the other side of the Oaks. There'll be one waiting for us. Spilk said so."

Jair went cold. "How does he know that?"

Slanter shrugged. "Prearranged meet, I guess. Anyway, I thought you should know. We'll be through the Oaks tomorrow."

Tomorrow? Jair felt his hopes fade instantly. How could he escape by tomorrow? That wasn't enough time! He had thought he would have at least a week and maybe more before they reached the deep Anar and the Mord Wraiths' stronghold. But tomorrow? What was he going to do?

Slanter watched him as if reading his thoughts. "I'm sorry, boy. I don't care for it either."

Jair's eyes shifted to meet his, and he tried to keep the desperation from his voice. "Then why don't you let me go?"

"Let you go?" Slanter laughed tonelessly. "You're forgetting who's with whom, aren't you?"

He took a long swallow from the ale pouch and sighed. Jair leaned forward. "Why are you with them, Slanter? You're not like them. You don't belong with them. You don't . . ."

"Boy!" The Gnome cut him off sharply. "Boy, you don't know anything at all about me! Nothing! So don't be telling me who I'm like and who I belong with! Just look after yourself!"

There was a long silence. In the center of the clearing, the other Gnomes were gathered about the fire, drinking ale from a heavy leather jug. Jair could see the glitter of their sharp eyes as they glanced in his direction from time to time. He could see the suspicion and fear mirrored there.

"You're not like them," he repeated softly.

"Maybe," Slanter agreed suddenly, staring off into the dark. "But I know enough not to cut against the grain. There's a change in the wind. It's shifted about and it's blowing straight out of the east, and everything in its path will be swept away. Everything! You don't begin to see the half of it. The Mord Wraiths are power like nothing I'd ever imagined, and the whole of the Eastland belongs to them. But that's only today. Tomorrow . . ." He shook his head slowly. "This is no time for a Gnome to be anything other than a Gnome."

He drank again of the ale, then offered it to Jair. The Valeman shook his head. His mind worked frantically.

"Slanter, would you do me a favor?" he asked.

"Depends."

"Would you take the ropes off my arms and hands for a few minutes?" The Gnome's black eyes narrowed. "I just want to rub them a bit, try to get some feeling back. I've had the ropes on for two days now. I can barely feel my fingers. Please—I give you my word I won't try to escape. I won't use the magic."

Slanter studied him. "Your word's been pretty good until now."

"It's still good. You can leave my legs and feet bound if you like. Just give me a moment."

Slanter kept looking at him for a few minutes longer, then nodded. Moving forward, he knelt beside the Valeman, then loosened the knots that secured the ropes about his arms and wrists and let them fall slack. Gingerly Jair began to massage himself, rubbing first his hands, then his wrists, his arms, and finally his body. In the darkness before him, he saw the glint of a knife in Slanter's hand. He kept his eyes lowered and his thoughts hidden. Slowly he worked, all the while thinking, don't let him guess, don't let him see . . .

"That's enough," Slanter's voice was gruff and sudden, and he drew the ropes tight again. Jair sat quietly, offering no resistance. When the ropes had again been secured, Slanter moved back in front of him.

"Better?"

"Better," he said quietly.

The Gnome nodded. "Time to get some sleep." He drank one time more from the ale pouch, then bent forward to test the bonds. "Sorry about the way this thing's worked out, boy. I don't like it any better than you do."

"Then help me escape," Jair pleaded, his voice a whisper.

Slanter stared at him wordlessly, blunt features expressionless. Gently he placed the gag back in Jair's mouth and rose.

"Wish you and I had never met," he murmured. Then he turned and walked away.

In the darkness, Jair let himself go limp against the oak. Tomorrow. One day more, and then the Mord Wraiths would have him. He shuddered. He had to escape before then. Somehow, he had to find a way.

He breathed the cool night air deeply. At least he knew one thing now that he hadn't known before—one very important thing. Slanter hadn't suspected. He had permitted Jair those few moments of freedom from the ropes—time to rub life back into his limbs and body, time to relieve them just a bit of the ache and discomfort.

Time to discover that he still retained possession of the Elfstones.

Too swift, it seemed, the morning came, dawn breaking gray and hard within the gloom of the Black Oaks. For the third day, the Gnomes marched Jair east. The warming touch of the sun was screened away by banks of storm clouds that rolled down from out of the north. A wind blew harsh and quick through the trees, chill with the promise of winter's coming. Wrapped in their short cloaks, the Gnomes bent their heads against the swirl of silt and leaves and trudged ahead.

How can I escape?

How?

The question repeated itself over and over in the Valeman's mind as he worked to keep pace with his captors. Each step marked the passing of the seconds that remained, the minutes, the hours. Each step took him closer to the Mord Wraith. This one day was all the time he had left. Somehow during the day he must find an opportunity to get free of his restraints long enough to utilize the wishsong. A single moment was all it would take.

Yet that moment might never come. He had not doubted that it would—until now. But the time slipped so fast from him! It was nearing midmorning, and already they had been on the march for several hours. Silently he berated himself for not seizing the opportunity Slanter had presented him with the night before when he had agreed to free him from his bonds. There had been time enough then to escape his captors. A few seconds to freeze them where they stood, covered with something so loathsome they could think of nothing else as he worked loose the bindings about his ankles, then a few seconds more to shift the pitch of his voice to hide him from their sight, and he would have been gone. Dangerous, yes, but he could have done it—except, of course, that he had given his word. What difference, if that word had been broken when it was given to a Gnome?

He sighed. It did make a difference somehow. Even with a Gnome, his word was still his word, and it meant something when he gave it. One's word was a matter of honor. It was not a thing that could be bandied about when convenient or slipped on and off like clothing to match changes in the weather. If he went back on it even once, that opened the door to a flood of excuses for going back on it every time thereafter.

Besides, he wasn't sure he could have done that to Slanter, Gnome or not. It was strange, but he had developed a certain attachment for the fellow. He wouldn't have described it as affection exactly. Respect was more like it. Or maybe he just saw something of himself in the Gnome because they were both rather different sorts. In any case, he didn't think he could have made himself trick Slanter like that, even to escape whatever it was that lay ahead.

He kicked at the leaves that blew across his path as he walked onward through the dark autumn day. He supposed that Rone Leah, were he there, would have had a plan for escape by now. Probably a good one. But Jair didn't have a clue as to what it might have been.

Morning slipped away. The wind died with the coming of midday, but its chill lingered in the forest air. Ahead, the terrain grew rougher, the earth broken and rocky as the ridgeline slanted south and a series of ravines curved down across their pathway. Still the wall of oaks stretched on, immutable giants blind to the ages that had passed them by. Heedless of a small life like mine, Jair thought as he glanced upward at the great towering black monsters. Shutting me away, so that I have nowhere that I might run.

The path wound down a steep embankment, and the patrol followed its dark rut. Then the oaks gave way to a solitary stand of pine and fir, crowded close within the massive black trunks, hemmed like captives, stiff and frightened. The Gnomes trudged into their midst, grunting irritably as sharp-tipped boughs nipped and cut at them. Jair ducked his head and followed, the long needles raking his face and hands with stinging swipes.

A moment later he broke clear of the tangle and found himself in a broad clearing. A pool of water gathered at the base of the ravine, fed by a tiny stream that trickled down from out of the rocks.

A man stood next to the pool.

The Gnomes came to an abrupt, startled halt. The man was drinking water from a tin cup, his head lowered. He was dressed all in black— loose tunic and pants, forest cloak, and boots. A black leather pack lay beside him on the ground. Next to it rested a long wooden staff. Even the staff was black, of polished walnut. The man glanced up at them briefly. He looked to be an ordinary Southlander, a traveler, his face brown and creased by sun and wind, and his light hair turned almost silver. Flint gray eyes blinked once; then he looked away. He might have been any one of a hundred journeyers who passed through this part of the land daily. But from the moment he saw the man, Jair knew instinctively that he was not.

Spilk also sensed something unusual about the man. The Sedt glanced quickly at the Gnomes on either side as if to reassure himself that they were nine to the man's one, then turned his gaze on Jair. Clearly he was upset that the stranger had seen their captive. He hesitated a moment longer, then started forward. Jair and the others followed.

Wordlessly, the patrol moved to the far end of the pool, their eyes never leaving the stranger. The stranger paid no attention. Stepping forward from his companions, Spilk filled his water pouch from the trickle that ran down off the rocks, then drank deeply. One by one, the other Gnomes did the same—all but Slanter, who stood next to Jair, unmoving. The Valeman glanced at the Gnome and found him staring fixedly at the stranger. There was something odd reflected in his rough face, something . . .

Recognition?

The stranger's eyes lifted suddenly and met Jair's. The eyes were flat and empty. For just an instant, they were locked upon his own, and then the stranger was facing Spilk.

"Traveling far?" he asked.

Spilk spit the water from his mouth. "Keep your nose to yourself."

The stranger shrugged. He finished his water in his cup, then bent down to tuck the cup back into his pack. When he straightened again, the black staff was in his hand.

"Is the Valeman really so dangerous?"

The Gnomes stared at him sullenly. Spilk tossed aside his water pouch, took a firm grip on his cudgel and came around the edge of the pool until he stood at the forefront of his men.

"Who are you?" he snapped.

Again the stranger shrugged. "No one you want to know."

Spilk smiled coldly. "Then walk away from here while you still can. This doesn't concern you."

The stranger didn't move. He seemed to be thinking the matter through.

Spilk took a step toward him. "I said this doesn't concern you."

"Nine Gnome Hunters traveling through the Southland with a Valeman they've bound and gagged like a trussed pig?" A faint smile crossed the stranger's weathered face. "Maybe you're right. Maybe it doesn't concern me."

He bent down to retrieve his pack, slipped it across one shoulder and started away from the pool, passing in front of the Gnomes. Jair felt his hopes, momentarily lifted, fade again. For just a moment, he had thought the stranger meant to aid him. He started to turn toward the pool again, thirsty for a drink of the water, but Slanter blocked his way. The Gnome's eyes were still on the stranger, and now his hand came up slowly to grip Jair's shoulder, guiding him back several paces from the others in the patrol.

The stranger had stopped again.

"On the other hand, maybe you're wrong." He stood no more than a half-dozen feet from Spilk. "Maybe this does concern me after all."

The stranger's pack slid from his shoulder to the ground, and the flint gray eyes fixed on Spilk. The Sedt stared at him, disbelief and anger twisting the blunt features of his face. Behind him, the other Gnomes glanced at one another uneasily.

"Stay behind me." Slanter's voice was a soft hiss in his ear, and the Gnome stepped in front of him.

The stranger moved closer to Spilk. "Why don't you let the Valeman go?" he suggested softly.

Spilk swung the heavy cudgel at the stranger's head. Quick as he was, the stranger was quicker, blocking the blow with his staff. The stranger stepped forward then, a smooth, effortless movement. Up came the staff, striking once, twice. The first blow caught the Sedt in the pit of his stomach, bending him double. The second caught him squarely across the head and dropped him like a stone.

For an instant, no one moved. Then, with a howl of dismay, the other Gnomes attacked, swords ripped from their sheaths and axes and spears lifting. Seven strong, they converged on the lone black figure. Jair bit into the gag that held him speechless when he saw what happened next. Cat-quick, the stranger blocked the assault, the black staff whirling. Two more Gnomes dropped in their tracks with shattered skulls. The remainder thrust and cut blindly as the stranger danced away. A glint of metal appeared from beneath the black cloak, and a short sword was gripped in the stranger's hand. Seconds later, three more of the attackers lay stretched upon the earth, their life blood seeping from their bodies.

Now there were but two of the seven still standing. The stranger crouched before them, feinting with the short sword. The Gnomes glanced hurriedly at each other and backed away. Then one caught sight of Jair, half hidden behind Slanter. Abandoning his companion, he leaped for the Valeman. But to Jair's surprise, Slanter blocked the way, a long knife in his hand. The attacker howled in rage at the betrayal, his own weapon sweeping up. From twenty feet away, the stranger was a blur of motion. Uncoiling with the suddenness of a snake, he whipped one arm forward, and the attacker went rigid in midstride, a long knife buried in his throat. Soundlessly, he collapsed.

That was enough for the remaining Gnome. Heedless of everything else, he bolted from the clearing and disappeared into the forest.

Only Jair, Slanter, and the stranger remained. The Gnome and the stranger faced each other wordlessly for a moment, weapons poised. The forest had gone silent about them.

"You, also?" the stranger asked quietly.

Slanter shook his head. "Not me." The hand with the long knife dropped to his side. "I know who you are."

The stranger did not seem surprised, but merely nodded. With his sword, he gestured at the Gnomes who lay stretched between them. "What about your friends?"

Slanter glanced down. "Friends? Not this lot. The misfortunes of war brought us together, and we'd traveled too far already the same road. Stupid bunch, they were." His dark eyes found the stranger's. "The journey's done for me. Time to choose another way."

He reached back with the long knife and severed the ropes that bound Jair. Then he sheathed the knife and slipped loose the gag.

"Looks like you've got the luck this day, boy," he growled. "You've just been rescued by Garet Jax!"

Even in a tiny Southland village like Shady Vale, they had heard of Garet Jax.

He was the man they called the Weapons Master—a man whose skill in single combat was so finely developed that it was said he had no equal. Choose whatever weapon you might or choose no other weapon than hands, feet, and body, and he was better than any man alive. Some said more than that—he was the best who had ever lived.

The stories were legend. Told in taverns when the drinks were passed about in the hours after work was finished, in village inns by travelers come from far, or about campfires and hearths when the night settled down about those gathered and the dark formed a bond that seemed strengthened somehow by the sharing of words, the stories of Garet Jax were always there. No one knew where he had come from; that part of his life was shrouded in speculation and rumor. But everyone knew at least one place that he had been and had a story to go with it. Most of the stories were true, verified by more than one who had been witness to its happening. Several were common knowledge, told and retold the length and breadth of the Southland and parts of the other lands as well.

Jair Ohmsford knew them all by heart.

One tale, the earliest perhaps, was of Gnome raiders preying on the outlying villages of Callahorn in the eastern borderlands. Smashed once by the Border Legion, the raiders had broken into small groups—remnants of fewer than a dozen men each in most cases—who continued to plague the less protected homesteads and hamlets. Legion patrols scouted the lands at regular intervals, but the raiders stayed hidden until they were gone. Then one day a band of ten struck a farmer's home just south of the Mermidon's joinder with the Rabb. There was no one there but the farmer's wife, small children, and a stranger—little more than a boy himself—who had stopped to share a brief meal and a night's sleep in exchange for chores that needed doing. Barricading the family in a storm cellar, he met the raiders as they tried to force their way in. He killed eight before the two remaining fled. After that, the raids slowed somewhat, it was said. And everyone began to talk about the stranger named Garet Jax.

Other tales were equally well known. In Arborlon, he had trained a special unit of the Home Guard to act as defenders of the Elven King Ander Elessedil. In Tyrsis, he had trained special units of the Border Legion, and others in Kern and Varfleet. He had fought for a time in the border wars between the Dwarves and Gnomes, instructing the Dwarves on weapons' use. He had traveled for a time the deep Southland, engaged in the civil wars that raged between member states of the Federation. He had killed a lot of men there, it was said; he had made a great many enemies. He could not go back into the deep Southland anymore . . .

Jair cut short his thinking, aware suddenly that the man was staring at him, almost as if reading his thoughts. He flushed. "Thanks," he managed.

Garet Jax said nothing. Flint gray eyes regarded him without expression a moment longer, then turned away. The short sword disappeared back within the shadows of the cloak, and the man in black began checking the bodies of the Gnomes who lay scattered about him. Jair watched a moment, then glanced furtively at Slanter.

"Is that really Garet Jax?" he whispered.

Slanter gave him a black look. "I said so, didn't I? You don't forget someone like that. Knew him five years ago when he was training Legion soldiers in Varfleet. I was tracking for the Legion then, passing time. Like iron I was, but next to him . . ." He shrugged. "I remember once, there were some hard sorts, mad about being passed over in training or something. Went after Jax with pikes when his back was turned. He didn't even have a weapon. Four of them, all bigger than he was." The Gnome shook his head, eyes distant. "He killed two of them, broke up the other two. So quick you could barely follow. I was there."

Jair looked back again at the black-garbed figure. A legend, they said. But they called him other things, too. They called him an assassin—a mercenary with no loyalties, no responsibilities except to those who paid him. He had no companions; Garet Jax always traveled alone. No friends, either. Too dangerous, too hard for that.

So why had he helped Jair?

"This one's still alive."

The Weapons Master was bending over Spilk. Slanter and Jair glanced at each other, then stepped over to have a look.

"Thick skull," Garet Jax muttered. He looked up as they joined him. "Help me pick him up."

Together, they hauled the unconscious Spilk from the center of the clearing to its far side, then propped him against a pine. Retrieving the ropes that had been used to secure Jair, the Weapons Master now bound the Sedt hand and foot. Satisfied, he stepped back from the Gnome and turned to the two watching him.

"What's your name, Valeman?" he asked Jair.

"Jair Ohmsford," Jair told him, uneasy under the gaze of those strange gray eyes.

"And you?" he asked Slanter.

"I'm called Slanter," the tracker replied.

There was a flicker of displeasure in the hard face. "Suppose you tell me what nine Gnome Hunters were doing with this Valeman?"

Slanter grimaced, but then proceeded to relate to the Weapons Master all that had befallen since the time he had first encountered Jair in Shady Vale. Much to the Valeman's surprise, he even told the other what Jair had done to him to escape. Garet Jax listened without comment. When the tale was finished, he turned again to Jair.

"Is what he says right?"

Jair hesitated, then nodded. It wasn't, of course—not entirely. A part of it was the fabricated story he had told to Spilk. But there was no reason to change that story now. Better that they both thought his father in Allanon's company with the Elfstones—at least until Jair knew whom he should trust.

A long pause followed as the Weapons Master thought the situation through. "Well, I don't think I should leave you alone in this country, Jair Ohmsford. Nor do I think it a good idea to leave you in the company of this Gnome." Slanter flushed darkly, but held his tongue. "I think you had better come with me. That way I'll know you're safe."

Jair stared at him uncertainly. "Come with you where?"

"To Culhaven. I have an appointment there, and you shall keep it with me. If this Druid and your father have gone into the Eastland, then quite possibly we shall find them there—or if not, at least we shall find someone who can take you to them."

"But I can't . . ." Jair started to say, then caught himself. He couldn't tell them about Brin. He had to be careful not to do that. But he couldn't go east either! "I can't do that," he finished. "I have a mother and sister in the villages south of the Vale who know nothing of what's happened. I have to go back to warn them."

Garet Jax shook his head. "Too far. I haven't time. We'll go east, then send word back when we get the chance. Besides, if what you've told me is right, it's more dangerous going back than going ahead. The Gnomes and the Wraiths know about you now; they know where you live. Once it's discovered you've escaped, they'll come looking for you there again. I didn't rescue you just to have you caught again the moment I'm gone."

"But . . ."

The flat gray eyes froze him. "It's decided. You go east." He glanced briefly at Slanter. "You go where you wish."

He strode back across the clearing to retrieve his pack and staff. Jair stood looking after him, trapped by indecision. Should he tell the man the truth or go east? But then, even if he told Garet Jax the truth, what difference would that make? The Weapons Master wasn't likely to take him back in either case.

"Well, luck to you, boy." Slanter was standing before him looking less than happy. "No hard feelings, I hope."

Jair stared at him. "Where are you going?"

"What difference does it make?" The Gnome shot a venomous glance at Garet Jax. Then he shrugged. "Look, you're better off with him than me. I should have gone my own way long ago."

"I haven't forgotten that you helped me, Slanter—all during the journey," Jair said quickly. "And I think you would have helped me again if I needed it."

"Well, you're wrong!" the Gnome cut him short. "Just because I felt sorry for you doesn't. . . . Look, I'd have turned you over to the walkers just as quick as Spilk, because that would have been the smart thing to do! You and this Weapons Master don't begin to see what you're up against!"

"I saw you stand there with that knife when the other Gnome came at me!" Jair insisted. "What about that?"

Slanter snorted, turning away angrily. "If I'd had any brains at all, I'd have let him have you. Do you know what I've done to myself? I can't even go back to the Eastland now! That Gnome who ran off will tell them everything I did! Or Spilk, once he gets free!" He threw up his hands. "Well, who cares? Not really my country anyway. Don't belong there; haven't for years. Wraiths can't be worried about tracking one poor Gnome. I'll go north for a time, or maybe south into the cities, and let this whole thing take its own course."

"Slanter . . ."

The Gnome wheeled suddenly, his voice a hiss. "But that one—he isn't any better than me!" He gestured angrily at Garet Jax, who was drinking again from the pool. "Treats me as if this was all my doing—as if I was the one responsible! I didn't even know about you, boy! I came here hunting the Druid! I didn't like chasing after you, taking you off to the Wraiths!"

"Slanter, wait a minute!" Mention of the Mord Wraiths reminded the Valeman of something he had almost forgotten in his relief at being freed. "What about the walker we were supposed to meet on the other side of the Oaks?"

Slanter was annoyed at having his tirade cut short. "What about him?"

"He'll still be there, won't he?" Jair asked quietly.

The Gnome hesitated, then nodded. "I see your point. Yes, he'll be there." He frowned. "Just go another way; go around him."

Jair stepped close. "Suppose *he* decides to go through him?" He motioned faintly toward Garet Jax.

Slanter shrugged. "Then there'll be one less Weapons Master."

"And one less of me."

They stared at each other in silence. "What do you want from me, boy?" the Gnome asked finally.

"Come with us."

"What!"

"You're a tracker, Slanter. You can get us past the walker. Please, come with us."

Slanter shook his head emphatically. "No. That's the Eastland. I can't go back there. Not now. Besides, you want *me* to take you to Culhaven. Me! The Dwarves would love that!"

"Just to the border, Slanter," Jair pressed. "Then go your own way. I won't ask for any more than that."

"I'm greatly appreciative of that!" the Gnome snapped. Garet Jax was coming back over to join them. "Look, what's the point of all this? That one wouldn't want me along anyway."

"You don't know that," Jair insisted. He turned as the Weapons Master came up to them. "You said that Slanter could go where he wished. Tell him then that he can come with us."

Garet Jax looked at the Gnome. Then he looked back at Jair.

"He's a tracker," Jair pointed out. "He might be able to help us avoid the walkers. He might be able to find a safe route east."

The Weapons Master shrugged. "The choice is his."

There was a long, awkward silence. "Slanter, if you do this, I'll show you a little of how the magic works," Jair said finally.

Sudden interest filled the Gnome's dark eyes. "Well now, that's worth a chance or . . ." Then he stopped. "No! What are you trying to do to me? Do you think you can bribe me? Is that what you think?"

"No," Jair answered hastily. "I just . . ."

"Well, you can't!" the other cut him short. "I don't take bribes! I'm not some . . . !" He sputtered off into silence, unable to find the words to express what it was that he wasn't. Then he straightened. "If it means this much to you, if it's this important, then all right, I'll come. If you want me to come, I'll come—but not for a bribe! I'll come because I want to come. My idea, understand? And just to the border—not a step further! I want nothing to do with the Dwarves!"

Jair stared at him in astonishment for a moment, then quickly stuck out his hand. Solemnly, Slanter shook it.

It was decided that Spilk would be left just as he was. It would take him considerable time to free himself, but eventually he would do so. If worse came to worst, he could always chew his way through the ropes, Slanter suggested blackly. If he yelled for help, perhaps someone would hear him. He would have to be careful though. The Black Oaks were populated by a particularly vicious species of timber wolf, and the calls were likely to draw their attention. On the other hand, the wolves might drift in for water anyway . . .

Spilk heard the last of this, stirring awake as Jair and his companions were preparing to set out. Dazed and angered, the burly Gnome threatened that they would all meet a most unpleasant end when he caught up with them again—and catch up with them he would. They ignored the threats—though Slanter appeared somewhat uneasy at hearing them—and minutes later the Sedt was left behind.

It was strange company in which Jair found himself now—a Gnome who had tracked him down, taken him prisoner, and kept him so for three days, and a legendary adventurer who had killed dozens more men than he had seen years on this earth. Here they were, the three of them, and Jair found the alliance thoroughly baffling. What were these two doing with him? Garet Jax might have gone his way without troubling himself about Jair, yet he had not done so. At risk to his own life, he had rescued the Valeman and then chosen to make himself temporary guardian. Why would a man like Garet Jax do such a thing? And Slanter might have rebuffed his request for help in avoiding whatever lay between them and the Anar, knowing the danger to himself and knowing that Garet Jax clearly didn't trust him and would watch his every move. Yet quite unexpectedly, almost perversely, he had chosen to come anyway. Again—why?

But it was his own motives that surprised him most of all when he began to consider them. After all, if their decision to be with him was baffling, what of his to be with them? Slanter, until just moments ago, had been his jailer! And he was genuinely frightened of Garet Jax, his rescuer. Over and over again, he thought of the Weapons Master facing those Gnomes—quick, deadly, terrifying, as black as the death he dealt.

For an instant, the picture hung suspended in the Valeman's mind; then quickly he thrust it aside.

Well, strangers on the road became companions for safety's sake, and Jair supposed that that was the way to view what had happened here. He must keep his wits. After all, he was free now and in no real danger. In an instant's time he could disappear. A single note of the wishsong, sung with the whisper of the wind, and he could be gone. Thinking about that gave him some sense of comfort. If he hadn't been so deep within the Black Oaks, if it weren't for the fact that the Mord Wraiths were searching for him, and if it weren't for his desperate need to find help somewhere . . .

He tightened his mouth against the words. Speculation on what might have been was pointless. He had enough with which to concern himself. Above all, he had to remember to say nothing about Brin or the Elfstones.

They had walked less than an hour through the Oaks when they came to a clearing in which half a dozen trails merged. Slanter, leading the way through the darkened forest, drew to a halt and pointed to a trail leading south.

"This way," he announced.

Garet Jax looked at him curiously. "South?"

Slanter's heavy brows knitted. "South. The walker will come down

out of the Silver River country through the Mist Marsh. It is the quickest
and easiest way—at least for those devils. They're not afraid of anything
that lives in the marsh. If we want to take as few chances as possible, we'll
go south around the Marsh through the Oaks, then turn north above the
lowlands."

"A long way, Gnome," the Weapons Master murmured.

"At least that way you'll get where you're going!" the other snapped.

"Perhaps we could slip by him."

Slanter put his hands on his hips and squared his stocky frame about.
"Perhaps we could fly, too! Hah! You haven't any idea at all what you're
talking about!"

Garet Jax said nothing, his eyes fixing on the Gnome. Slanter seemed
to sense suddenly that perhaps he had gone too far. Glancing hurriedly at
Jair, he cleared his throat nervously and shrugged.

"Well, you don't know the Mord Wraiths like I do. You haven't lived
among them. You haven't seen what they can do." He took a deep breath.
"They're like something stolen from the dark—as if each were a bit of
night broken off. When they pass, you never see them. You never hear
them. You just sense them—you feel their coming." Jair shivered, remembering his encounter at Shady Vale and the invisible presence, just beyond
the wall. "They leave no trail when they pass," Slanter went on. "They appear and disappear just as their name would suggest. Mord Wraiths. Black
walkers."

He trailed off, shaking his head. Garet Jax looked over at Jair. All the
Valeman could think about was what he had felt when he had come back
to his home that night in the Vale and found one of them waiting.

"I don't want to take the chance that we might stumble onto one of
them," he said quietly.

The Weapons Master readjusted the pack across his shoulders. "Then
we go south."

All afternoon they wound southward through the Black Oaks, following the pathway as it snaked ahead through the trees. Dusk fell over the
forest, the gray light of midday fading rapidly into night. A faint mist began to seep through the trees, damp and clinging. It thickened steadily.
The trail became more difficult to follow, disappearing at regular intervals
as the mist settled in. Night sounds came out of the growing dark and the
sounds were not pleasant.

Slanter called a halt. Should they stop for the night? he wanted to
know. Both men looked to Jair. Stiff and tired, the Valeman glanced
quickly about. Giant oaks rose about them, glistening black trunks hemming them in like a massive keep. Mist and shadows lay all around, and
somewhere within them a black walker hunted.

Jair Ohmsford gritted his teeth against the aches and the weariness and
shook his head. The little company went on.

Night also came to the clearing where Spilk sat bound to the great oak. All
afternoon he had worked at his bonds, loosening the knots that held them

and forcing them slack. Nothing else had passed through the clearing that day; no travelers had stopped to water; no wolves had come to drink. The crumpled bodies of his patrol lay where they had fallen, shapeless forms in the dusk.

His cruel features tightened as he strained against the ropes. Another hour or so and he would be free to hunt the ones who had done this to him. And he would hunt them to the very ends . . .

A shadow passed over him, and his head jerked up. A tall black form stood before him, cloaked and hooded, a thing of death strayed from the night. Spilk went cold to the bone.

"Master!" he whispered harshly.

The black figure gave no response. It simply stood there, looking down on him. Frantically the Sedt began to speak, the words tumbling over one another in his haste to get them out. He revealed all that had befallen him— the stranger in black, the betrayal by Slanter, and the escape of the Vale-man with the magic voice. His muscled body thrashed against the bonds that held him fast, words inadequate to halt the fear that tightened about his throat. "I tried! Master, I tried! Free me! Please, free me!"

His voice broke, and the flood of words died away into stillness. His head drooped downward, and sobs wracked his body. For a moment, the figure above him remained motionless. Then one lean, black-gloved hand reached down to fasten on the Gnome's head, and red fire exploded forth. Spilk shrieked, a single, terrible cry.

The black-robed figure withdrew his hand, turned, and disappeared back into the night. No sound marked its passing.

In the empty clearing, Spilk's lifeless form lay slumped within its bonds, eyes open and staring.

A cross the towering, jagged ridge of the Dragon's Teeth, the night sky had gone from deepest blue to gray; the moon and stars were begin-ning to fade in brilliance, and the eastern sky began to glimmer faintly with the coming dawn.

Allanon's dark eyes swept the impassable wall of the mountains that stood about him, across cliffs and peaks of monstrous, aged rock, barren and ravaged by wind and time. Then his gaze dropped quickly, almost anx-iously, to where the stone split apart before him. Below lay the Valley of Shale, doorstep to the forbidden Hall of Kings, the home of the spirits of the ages. He stood upon its rim, his black robes wrapped close about his tall, spare frame. There was a sudden wistfulness on his face. A mass of black rock, glistening like opaque glass, crushed and strewn blindly, stretched downward to the valley floor, forming a broken walk. At the center of the rock stood a lake, its murky waters colored a dull, greenish black, the surface swirling sluggishly in the empty, windless silence—swirling like a kettle of brew that some invisible hand stirred with slow, mechanical purpose.

Father, he whispered soundlessly.

A sudden scraping of booted feet on the loose rock caused him to glance quickly about, reminded of the two who traveled with him. They emerged now from the shadow of the rocks below to stand beside him. Silently, they stared downward into the barren valley.

"Is this it?" Rone Leah asked shortly.

Allanon nodded. Suspicion cloaked the highlander's words and lingered in his eyes. It was always evident. There was no attempt to hide it.

"The Valley of Shale," the Druid said quietly. He started forward, winding his way down the rock-strewn slope. "We must hurry."

Suspicion and mistrust were in the eyes of the Valegirl as well, though she sought to keep them from her face. There was always suspicion in those who shared his travel. It had been there with Shea Ohmsford and Flick when he had taken them in search of the Sword of Shannara and with Wil Ohmsford and the Elven girl Amberle when he had taken them in search of the Bloodfire. Perhaps it was deserved. Trust was something to be earned, not blindly given, and to earn it, one must first be open and honest. He was never that—could never be that. He was a keeper of secrets that could be shared with no other, and he must always veil the truth, for the truth could not be told, but must be learned. It was difficult to keep close what he knew, yet to do otherwise would be to tamper with the trust that had been given to him and which he had worked hard to earn.

His gaze flickered back briefly to be certain that the Valegirl and the highlander followed him; then he turned his attention again to the scattered rock at his feet, picking his way in studied silence. It would be easy to forgo the trust he kept, to reveal all that he knew of the fate of those he counseled, to lay bare the secrets he kept, and to let events transpire in a fashion different from that which he had ordered.

Yet he knew that he could never do that. He answered to a higher code of being and of duty. It was his life and purpose. If it meant that he must endure their suspicion, then so it must be. Harsh though it was, the price was a necessary one.

But I am so tired, he thought. Father, I am so tired.

At the floor of the valley, he came to a halt. Valegirl and highlander stopped beside him, and he turned to face them. One arm lifted from within the black robes and pointed to the waters of the lake.

"The Hadeshorn," he whispered. "My father waits there, and I must go to him. You will stand here until I call. Do not move from this place. Whatever happens, do not move. Except for you and me, only the dead live here."

Neither replied. They nodded their assent, eyes darting uneasily to where the waters of the Hadeshorn swirled soundlessly. He studied their faces a moment longer, then turned and walked away.

A strange sense of expectation swept through him as he approached the lake, almost as if he were at the end of a long journey. It was always that way, he supposed, thinking back. There was that strange sense of coming home. Once Paranor had been the home of the Druids. But the other Druids were gone now, and this valley felt more like home than the Keep. All things began and ended here. It was here that he returned to find the sleep that renewed his life each time his journeys through the Four Lands were finished, with his mortal shell hung half within this world and half within the world of death. Here both worlds touched, a small crossing point that gave him some brief access to all that had been and all that would ever be. Most important of all, he would find his father here.

Trapped, exiled, and waiting to be delivered!

He blocked the thought from his mind. Dark eyes lifted briefly to the faint lightening of the eastern sky, then dropped again to the lake. Shea Ohmsford had come here once, many years ago, with his half brother Flick and the others of the small company who had gone in search of the Sword of Shannara. It had been prophesied that one of their number would be lost, and so it had happened. Shea had been swept over the falls below the Dragon's Crease. The Druid remembered the mistrust and suspicion the others had exhibited toward him. Yet he had been fond of Shea, of Flick, and of Wil Ohmsford. Shea had been almost like a son to him—would have been, perhaps, had he been permitted to have a son. Wil Ohmsford had been more a comrade-in-arms, sharing the responsibility for the search that would restore the Ellcrys and save the Elves.

His dark face creased thoughtfully. Now there was Brin, a girl with power that surpassed anything that her forebears had possessed in their time. What would she be to him?

He had reached the edge of the lake, and he came to a halt. He stood for a moment looking down into the depthless water, wishing . . . Then slowly he lifted his arms skyward, power radiating out from his body, and the Hadeshorn began to churn restlessly. The waters swirled faster, beginning to boil and hiss, and spray rose skyward. All about the Druid, the empty valley shuddered and rumbled as if awakened from a long, dreamless sleep. Then the cries rose, low and terrible, from out of the depths of the lake.

Come to me, the Druid called soundlessly. Be free.

The cries rose higher, shrill and less than human—imprisoned souls calling out in their bondage, straining to be free. The whole of the darkened valley filled with their wail, and the spray of the Hadeshorn's murky waters hissed with sharp relief.

Come!

From out of the roiling dark waters the shade of Bremen lifted, its thin, skeletal body a transparent gray against the night, shrouded and bent with age. Out of the waters, the terrible form rose to stand upon the surface with Allanon. Slowly the Druid lowered his arms, black robes wrapping tight as if for warmth; within his cowl, his dark face lifted to find the empty, sightless eyes of his father.

I am here.

The arms of the shade lifted then. Though they did not touch him, Allanon felt their cold embrace wrap about him like death. Slow and anguished, his father's voice reached out to him.

—The age ends. The circle is closed—

The chill within him deepened, froze him as ice. The words ran on together as one, and though he heard them all, each in painful detail, they were strung and tightened like knots upon a line. He listened to them all in silent desperation, afraid as he had never been afraid, understanding at last what was meant to be, must be, and would be.

In his hard, black eyes there were tears.

In frightened silence, Brin Ohmsford and Rone Leah stood where the Druid had left them and watched the emergence of the shade of Bremen from the depths of the Hadeshorn. Cold sliced through them, borne not on some errant wind, for there was none, but by the coming of the shade. Together they faced it, watched it stand before Allanon, tattered and skeletal, and saw its arms lift as if to embrace and draw the Druid's black form downward. They could hear nothing of its words; the air about them filled with the shrill cries let free from the lake. The rock shuddered and groaned beneath their feet. If they had been able, they would have fled and not looked back. At that moment, they were certain that death had been set loose to walk among them.

Then abruptly it was ended. The shade of Bremen turned, sinking slowly back into the murky waters. The cries surged higher, a frantic wail of anguish, then died into silence. The lake churned and boiled anew for a brief instant, then settled back, the waters swirling once again with placid calm.

In the east, the crest of the sun broke over the ragged edge of the Dragon's Teeth, silver gray light spilling down through the dying night shadows.

Brin heard Rone exhale sharply, and her hand reached over to grip his. At the edge of the Hadeshorn, Allanon dropped to his knees, head bowed.

"Rone!" she whispered harshly and started forward. The highlander seized her arm in warning, remembering what the Druid had told them, but she pulled free, racing for the lake. Instantly he was after her.

Together they rushed to the Druid, slid to a halt on the loose rock, and bent down beside him. His eyes were closed, and his dark face was pale. Brin reached for one great hand and found it as cold as ice. The Druid seemed to be in a trance. The Valegirl glanced hesitantly at Rone. The highlander shrugged. Ignoring him, she put her hands on the big man's shoulders and gently shook him.

"Allanon," she said softly.

The dark eyes flickered open, met hers. For an instant she saw clear through him. There was a terrible heedless anguish in his eyes. There was fear. And there was disbelief. It shocked her so that she moved back from him quickly. Then all that she had seen disappeared; in its place there was anger.

"I told you not to move." He pushed himself roughly to his feet.

His anger meant nothing, and she ignored it. "What happened, Allanon? What did you see?"

He said nothing for a moment, his eyes straying back across the murky green waters of the lake. His head shook slowly. "Father," he whispered.

Brin glanced hurriedly at Rone. The highlander frowned.

She tried again, one hand touching lightly the Druid's sleeve. "What has he told you?"

Depthless black eyes fixed upon her own. "That time slips away from us, Valegirl. That we are hunted on all sides, and that it shall be thus until the end. That end is determined, but he will not tell me what it is. He will only tell me this—that it will come, that you will see it, and that for our cause you are both savior and destroyer."

Brin stared at him. "What does that mean, Allanon?"

He shook his head. "I don't know."

"Very helpful." Rone straightened and looked away into the mountains.

Brin kept her eyes on the Druid. There was something more. "What else did he say, Allanon?"

But again the Druid shook his head. "Nothing more. That was all."

He was lying! Brin knew it instantly. Something more had passed between them, something dark and terrible that he was not prepared to reveal. The thought frightened her, the certainty of it an omen that, like her father and her great-grandfather before her, she was to be used to a purpose she did not comprehend.

Her thoughts snapped back to what he had said before. Savior and destroyer to their cause—she would be both, the shade had said. But how could that be?

"One other thing he told me," Allanon said suddenly—but Brin sensed at once it was not the thing he kept hidden. "Paranor is in the hands of the Mord Wraiths. They have penetrated its locks and broken through the magic that guards its passages. Two nights earlier it fell. Now they search its halls for the Druid histories and the secrets of the ancients. What they find will be used to enhance the power they already possess."

He faced them each in turn. "And they will find them, sooner or later, if they are not stopped. That must not be allowed to happen."

"You don't expect *us* to stop them, do you?" Rone asked quickly.

The black eyes narrowed. "There is no one else."

The highlander flushed. "Just how many of them are there?"

"A dozen Wraiths. A company of Gnomes."

Rone was incredulous. "And we're going to stop them? You and me and Brin? Just the three of us? Exactly how are we supposed to do that?"

There was a sudden, terrible anger in the Druid's eyes. Rone Leah sensed that he had gone a step too far, but there was no help for it now. He stood his ground as the big man came up against him.

"Prince of Leah, you have doubted me from the first," Allanon said. "I let that pass because you care for the Valegirl and came as her protector. But no more. Your constant questioning of my purpose and of the need I see has reached its end! There is little sense to it when your mind is already decided against me!"

Rone kept his voice steady. "I am not decided against you. I am decided for Brin. Where the two conflict, I stand with her, Druid."

"Then stand with her you shall!" the other thundered and wrenched the Sword of Leah from its scabbard where it lay strapped across the highlander's back. Rone went white, certain that the big man meant to kill him. Brin darted forward, crying out, but the Druid's hand lifted quickly to stop her. "Stay, Valegirl. This lies between me and the Prince of Leah."

His eyes fixed on Rone, harsh and penetrating. "Would you protect her, highlander, as I might myself? If it were possible, would stand as my equal?"

Rone's face hardened with determination across a mask of fear. "I would."

Allanon nodded. "Then I shall give you the power to do so."

One great hand fastened securely on Rone's arm, and he propelled the highlander effortlessly to the edge of the Hadeshorn. There he returned the Sword of Leah and pointed to the murky green waters.

"Dip the blade of the sword into the waters, Prince of Leah," he commanded. "But keep your hand and the pommel clear. Even the smallest touch of the Hadeshorn to mortal flesh is death."

Rone Leah stared at him uncertainly.

"Do as I say!" the Druid snapped.

Rone's jaw tightened. Slowly he dropped the blade of the Sword of Leah until it was completely submerged within the swirling waters of the lake. It passed downward without effort—as if there were no bottom to the lake and the shoreline marked the edge of a sheer drop. As the metal touched the lake, the waters about it began to boil softly, hissing and gurgling as if acid ate the metal clean. Frightened, Rone nevertheless forced himself to hold the blade steady within the waters.

"Enough," the Druid told him. "Draw it out."

Slowly Rone lifted the sword clear of the lake. The blade, once polished iron, had gone black; the waters of the Hadeshorn clung to its surface, swirling about it as if alive.

"Rone!" Brin whispered in horror.

The highlander held the sword steady before him, blade extended away from his body, eyes fixed on the water that spun and wove across the metal surface.

"Now stand fast!" Allanon ordered, one arm lifting free of the black robes. "Stand fast, Prince of Leah!"

Blue fire spurted out from the fingers of his hand in a thin, dazzling line. It ran all along the blade, seering, burning, igniting water and metal, and fusing them as one. Blue fire flared in a burst of incandescent light, yet no heat passed from the blade into the handle. While Rone Leah averted his eyes, he held the sword firm.

An instant later it was done, the fire was gone, and the Druid's arm lowered once more. Rone Leah looked down at his sword. The blade was clean, a polished and glistening black, the edges hard and true.

"Look closely, Prince of Leah," Allanon told him.

He did as he was asked, and Brin bent close beside him. Together they stared into the black, mirrored surface. Deep within the metal, murky green pools of light swirled lazily.

Allanon stepped close. "It is the magic of life and death mixed as one. It is power that now belongs to you, highlander; it becomes your responsibility. You are to be as much Brin Ohmsford's protector as I. You are to have power such as I. This sword shall give it to you."

"How?" Rone asked softly.

"As with all swords, this one both cuts and parries—not flesh and blood or iron and stone, but magic. The evil magic of the Mord Wraiths. Cut through or blocked away, such magic shall not pass. Thus you have committed yourself. You are to be the shield that stands before this girl now and until this journey ends. You would be her protector, and I have made you so."

"But why . . . why would you give me . . . ?" Rone stammered.

But the Druid simply turned and began to walk away. Rone stared after him, a stunned look on his face.

"This is unfair, Allanon!" Brin shouted at the retreating figure, angered suddenly by what he had done to Rone. She started after him. "What right have you . . . ?"

She never finished. There was a sudden, terrifying explosion and she was lifted off her feet and thrown to the valley floor. A whirling mass of red fire engulfed Allanon and he disappeared.

Miles to the south, his body fatigued and aching, Jair Ohmsford stumbled from night's shadows into a dawn of eerie mist and half-light. Trees and blackness seemed to fall away, pushed aside like a great curtain, and the new day was there. It was vast and empty, a monstrous vault of heavy mist that shut away all the world within its depthless walls. Fifty yards from where he stood, the mist began and all else ended. Sleep-filled eyes stared blankly, seeing the path of mottled deadwood and greenish water that stretched that short distance into the mist, yet not understanding what it was that had happened.

"Where are we?" he murmured.

"Mist Marsh," Slanter muttered at his elbow. Jair glanced over at the Gnome dumbly, and the Gnome stared back at him with eyes as tired as his own. "We've cut its border too close—wandered into a pocket. We'll have to backtrack around it."

Jair nodded, trying to organize his scattered thoughts. Garet Jax appeared suddenly beside him, black and silent. The hard, empty eyes passed briefly across his own, then out into the swamp. Wordlessly, the Weapons Master nodded to Slanter, and the Gnome turned back. Jair trailed after. There was no sign of weariness in the eyes of Garet Jax.

They had walked all night, an endless tiring march through the maze of the Black Oaks. It was little more than a distant, clouded memory now in the Valeman's mind, a fragmented bit of time lost in exhaustion. Only his determination kept him on his feet. Even fear had lost its hold over him after a time, the threat of pursuit no longer a thing of immediacy. It seemed that he must have slept even while walking, for he could remember nothing of what had passed. Yet there had been no sleep, he knew. There had been only the march . . .

A hand yanked him back from the swamp's edge as he strayed too close. "Watch where you walk, Valeman." It was Garet Jax next to him.

He mumbled something in response and stumbled on. "He's dead on his feet," he heard Slanter growl, but there was no response. He rubbed his eyes. Slanter was right. His strength was almost gone. He could not go on much longer.

Yet he did. He went on for hours, it seemed, trudging through the mist and the gray half-light, stumbling blindly after Slanter's blocky form, vaguely aware of the silent presence of Garet Jax at his elbow. All sense of time slipped from him. He was conscious only of the fact that he was still on his feet and that he was still walking. One step followed the next, one foot the other, and each time it was a separate and distinct effort. Still the path wore on.

Until . . .

"Confounded muck!" Slanter was muttering, and suddenly the entire swamp seemed to explode upward. Water and slime geysered into the air, raining down on the startled Valeman. A roar shattered the dawn's silence, harsh and piercing, and something huge rose up almost on top of Jair.

"Log Dweller!" he heard Slanter shriek.

Jair stumbled back, confused and frightened, aware of the massive thing that lifted before him, of a body scaled and dripping with the swamp, of a head that seemed all snout and teeth gaping open, and of clawed limbs reaching. He stumbled back, frantic now, but his legs would not carry him, too numb with fatigue to respond as they should. The huge thing was atop him, its shadow blocking away even the half-light, its breath fetid and raw.

Then something hurtled into him from one side, bowling him over, propelling him clear of the monster's claws. In a daze, he saw Slanter standing where he had stood, short sword drawn, swinging wildly at the massive creature that reached down for him. But the sword was a pitifully inadequate weapon. The monster blocked it away and sent it spinning from the Gnome's grasp. In the next instant one great, clawed hand fastened about Slanter's body.

"Slanter!" Jair screamed, struggling to regain his feet.

Garet Jax was already moving. He sprang forward, a blurred shadow, thrusting the black staff into the creature's gaping jaws and ramming it deep into the soft tissue of the throat. The Log Dweller roared in pain, jaws snapping shut upon the staff and breaking it apart. The clawed hands reached for the fragments caught in its throat, dropping Slanter back to the earth.

Again Garet Jax leaped up against the creature, his short sword drawn. So quickly that Jair could scarcely follow, he was upon the monster's shoulder and past the grasping claws. He buried the sword deep in the Log Dweller's under-throat. Dark blood spurted forth. Then swiftly he sprang clear. The Log Dweller was hurt now, pain evident in its wounded bellow. It turned with a lurch and stumbled blindly back into the mist and the dark.

Slanter was struggling back up again, dazed and shaken, but Garet Jax came instead to Jair, hauling him quickly to his feet. The Valeman's eyes were wide, and he stared at the Weapons Master in awe.

"I never saw . . . I never saw anyone move . . . so fast!" he stammered.

Garet Jax ignored him. With one hand fastened securely on his collar, he pulled the Valeman into the trees, and Slanter followed hurriedly after.

In seconds, the clearing was behind them.

Red fire burned all about the Druid, wrapping him in crimson coils and flaring out wickedly against the gray light of dawn. Dazed and half-blinded by the explosion, Brin struggled to her knees and shielded her eyes. Within the fire, the Druid hunched down against the shimmering black rock of the valley floor, a faint blue aura holding back the flames that had engulfed him. A shield, Brin realized—his protection against the horror that would destroy him.

Desperately she sought the maker of that horror and found it not twenty yards away. There, stark against the sun's faint gold as it slipped from beneath the horizon, a tall black form stood silhouetted, arms raised and leveled, with the red fire spurting forth. A Mord Wraith! She knew immediately what it was. It had come upon them without a sound, caught them unawares, and struck down the Druid. With no chance to defend himself, Allanon was alive now only through instinct.

Brin surged to her feet. She screamed frantically at the black thing that attacked him, but it did not move, nor did the fire waver. In a steady, ceaseless stream, the fire spurted forth from the outstretched hands to where the Druid crouched, whirling all about his folded body and hammering down against the faint blue shield that yet held it back. Crimson light flared and reflected skyward from the mirror surface of the valley rock, and the whole of the world contained within turned to blood.

Then Rone Leah rushed forward, springing past Brin to stand before her like a crouched beast.

"Devil!" he howled in fury.

He swept up the black metal blade of the Sword of Leah, giving no thought in that moment to who it was he chose to aid or for whose sake he so willingly placed his own life in danger. He was in that moment the great-grandson of Menion Leah, as quick and reckless as his ancestor had ever thought to be, and instinct ruled his reason. Crying out the battle cry of his forebears for centuries gone, he attacked.

"Leah! Leah!"

He leaped into the fire, and the sword swept down, severing the ring that bound Allanon. Instantly, the flames shattered as if made of glass, falling from the Druid's crouched form in shards. The fire still flew from the Mord Wraith's hands; but like iron to a magnet, it was now drawn to the blade wielded by the red-haired highlander. It rushed in a sweep to the black metal and burned downward. Yet no fire touched Rone's hands; it was as if the sword absorbed it. The Prince of Leah stood squared away between Wraith and Druid, the Sword of Leah held vertically before him, crimson fire dancing off the blade.

Allanon rose up, as black and forbidding as the thing that had stalked him, free now of the flames that had held him bound. Lean arms lifted from beneath the robes, and blue fire exploded outward. It caught the Mord Wraith, lifted it clear of its feet, and threw it backward as if struck by a ram. Black robes flew wide, and a terrible, soundless shriek reverberated in Brin's mind. Once more the Druid fire flared outward, and an instant later the black thing it sought had been turned to dust.

Fire died into trailing wisps of smoke and scattered ash, and silence filled the Valley of Shale. The Sword of Leah sank, black iron clanging sharply against the rock as it dropped. Rone Leah's head lowered; a stunned look was in his eyes as they sought out Brin. She came to him, wrapped her arms about him and held him.

"Brin," he whispered softly. "This sword . . . the power . . ."

He could not finish. Allanon's lean hand fastened gently on his shoulder.

"Do not be frightened, Prince of Leah." The Druid's voice was tired, but reassuring. "The power truly belongs to you. You have shown that here. You are indeed the Valegirl's protector—and for this one time at least, mine as well."

The hand lingered a moment longer, then the big man was moving back along the path that had brought them in.

"There was only the one," he called back to them. "Had there been others, we would have seen them by now. Come. Our business here is finished."

"Allanon . . ." Brin started to call after him.

"Come, Valegirl. Time slips from us. Paranor needs whatever aid we can offer. We must go there at once."

Without a backward glance, he began to climb from the valley. Brin and Rone Leah followed in silent resignation.

It was midmorning before Jair and his companions finally broke clear of the Black Oaks. Before them, rolling countryside stretched away—hill country to the north, lowlands to the south. They took little time admiring either. Exhausted almost to the point of collapse, they took just enough time to locate a sheltering clump of broad-leaf maple turned brilliant crimson by autumn's touch. In seconds they were asleep.

Jair had no idea whether either of his companions thought to keep watch during the time he slept, but it was Garet Jax who shook him awake as dusk began to settle in. Wary of being so close yet to the Mist Marsh and the Oaks, the Weapons Master wanted to find a safer place to spend the coming night. The Battlemound Lowlands were fraught with dangers all their own, so the little company turned north into the hills. Somewhat refreshed by their half-day sleep, they walked on almost to midnight before settling in to sleep until dawn within a grove of wild fruit trees partially overgrown with brush. This time Jair insisted at the outset that the three share the watch.

The following day, they traveled north again. By late afternoon, they had reached the Silver River. Clear and sparkling in the fading sunlight, it wound its way west through tree-lined banks and rocky shoals. For several hours after, the three travelers followed the river east toward the Anar, and by nightfall they were well away from the Marsh and the Oaks. They had encountered no other journeyers during their march, and there had been no sign of either Gnomes or black walkers. It appeared that for the moment, at least, they were safe from any pursuit.

It was night again by the time they found a small pocket sheltered by maple and walnut trees on a ridge above the river and made their camp. They decided to risk a fire, built one that was small and smokeless, ate a hot meal, and settled back to watch the coals die into ash. The night was clear and warm; overhead, stars began to wink into view, clustering in brilliant patterns across the dark backdrop of the sky. All about them, night birds sang, insects hummed, and the faint rush of the river's swift waters murmured in the distance. Drying leaves and brush gave a sweet and musty smell to the cool dark.

"Think I'll gather up some wood," Slanter announced suddenly after being silent for a time. He pushed himself heavily to his feet.

"I'll help," Jair offered.

The Gnome shot him a look of annoyance. "Did I ask for any help? I can gather wood by myself, boy."

Scowling, he trudged off into the dark.

Jair leaned back again, folding his arms across his chest. That typified the way things had been ever since the three of them had started out—no one saying much of anything and saying what they did without a great deal of warmth. With Garet Jax, it didn't matter. He was taciturn by nature, so his refusal to contribute anything in the way of conversation was not surprising. But Slanter was a garrulous fellow, and his uncommunicative posture was disquieting. Jair much preferred Slanter the way he had been before—brash, talkative, almost like a rough uncle. He wasn't like that now. He seemed to have withdrawn into himself and shut himself away from the Valeman—as if traveling with Jair had become almost distasteful.

Well, in a way it was, Jair supposed, reflecting on the matter. After all, Slanter hadn't wanted to come in the first place. He had only come because Jair had shamed him into it. Here he was, a Gnome traveling with one fellow who had been his prisoner before and another who didn't trust him a wink, all for the sole purpose of seeing to it that they safely reached a people who were at war with his own. And he wouldn't have been doing that, except that, in helping Jair, he had compromised his loyalties so that he was now little better than an outcast.

Then, too, there was the matter of the Log Dweller. Slanter had come to Jair's aid in an act of bravery that the Valeman still found mystifying—an act not at all in character for a fellow as opportunistic and self-centered as Slanter—and look what had happened. Slanter had failed to stave off the Log Dweller, had himself become a victim, and had been forced to rely on Garet Jax to save him. That must rankle. Slanter was a tracker, and trackers were a proud breed. Trackers were supposed to protect the people they guided, not the other way around.

Sparks shot out suddenly from the little fire, drawing his attention. A dozen feet away, stretched out against an old log, Garet Jax stirred and glanced over. Those strange eyes sought his, and Jair found himself wondering once more about the character of the Weapons Master.

"Guess I should thank you again," he said, drawing his knees up to his chest, "for saving me from that thing in the Marsh."

The other man looked back at the fire. Jair watched for a moment, trying to decide if he should say anything else.

"Can I ask you something?" he said finally.

The Weapons Master shrugged his indifference.

"Why *did* you save me—not just from the thing in the Marsh, but back there in the Oaks when the Gnomes had me prisoner?" The hard eyes suddenly fixed on him again, and he hurried his words before he had time to think better of them. "It's just that I don't quite understand what made you do it. After all, you didn't know me. You could have just gone your own way."

Garet Jax shrugged again. "I did go my own way."

"What do you mean?"

"My way happened to be your way. That's what I mean."

Jair frowned slightly. "But you didn't know where I was being taken."

"East. Where else would a Gnome patrol with a prisoner be going?"

Jair's frown deepened. He couldn't argue with that. Still, none of what the Weapons Master had said did much to explain why he had bothered to rescue Jair in the first place.

"I still don't see why you helped me," he pressed.

A faint smile crossed the other's face. "I don't appear to you to possess a particularly humanitarian nature, is that it?"

"I didn't say that."

"You didn't have to. Anyway, you're right—I don't."

Jair hesitated, staring at him.

"I said I don't," Garet Jax repeated. The smile was gone. "I wouldn't stay alive very long if I did. And staying alive is what I do best."

There was a long silence. Jair didn't know where else to go with the conversation. The Weapons Master pushed himself forward, leaning into the fire's warmth.

"But you interest me," he said slowly. His gaze shifted to Jair. "I suppose that's why I rescued you. You interest me, and not many things do that anymore . . ."

He trailed off, a distant look in his eyes. But an instant later it was gone, and he was studying Jair once more. "There you were, bound and gagged and under guard by an entire Gnome patrol armed to the teeth. Very odd. They were frightened of you. That intrigued me. I wanted to know what it was about you that frightened them so."

He shrugged. "So I thought it was worth the trouble to set you free."

Jair stared at him. Curiosity? Was that why Garet Jax had come to his aid—out of curiosity? No, he thought at once, it was more than that.

"They were frightened of the magic," he said suddenly. "Would you like to see how it works?"

Garet Jax looked back at the fire. "Later, maybe. The journey's not done yet." He seemed totally without interest.

"Is that why you're taking me with you to Culhaven?" Jair pressed.

"In part."

He let the words hang. Jair glanced over at him uneasily.

"What's the rest?"

The Weapons Master did not respond. He did not even look at the Valeman. He just leaned back against the fallen log, wrapped himself in the black travel cloak and watched the fire.

Jair tried a different approach. "What about Slanter? Why did you help him? You could have left him to the Log Dweller."

Garet Jax sighed. "I could have. Would that have made you any happier?"

"Of course not. What do you mean?"

"You seem to have formed an opinion of me as a man who does nothing for anyone without some personal benefit. You shouldn't believe everything you hear. You're young, not stupid."

Jair flushed. "Well, you don't like Slanter very much, do you?"

"I don't know him well enough to like or dislike him," the other replied. "I admit that for the most part I'm not particularly fond of Gnomes. But this one twice was willing to place himself in danger for your sake. That makes him worth saving."

He glanced over suddenly. "Besides, you like him and you don't want anything to happen to him. Am I right?"

"You're right."

"Well, that in itself seems rather curious, don't you think? As I said before, you interest me."

Jair nodded thoughtfully. "You interest me, too."

Garet Jax turned away. "Good. We'll both have something to think about on our way to Culhaven."

He let the matter drop and Jair did the same. The Valeman was by no means satisfied that he understood what it was that had persuaded the Weapons Master to aid either Slanter or himself, but it was obvious he would learn nothing more this night. Garet Jax was an enigma that would not easily be solved.

The fire had almost died away by now, causing Jair to remember that Slanter had gone in search of wood and not yet returned. He pondered for a moment whether or not he should do anything about it, then turned once more to Garet Jax.

"You don't think anything could have happened to Slanter, do you?" he asked. "He's been gone quite a while."

The Weapons Master shook his head. "He can look after himself." He rose and kicked at the fire, scattering the wood embers so that the flames died. "We don't need the fire any longer, anyway."

Returning to his spot next to the fallen log, he rolled himself in his travel cloak and was asleep in seconds. Jair lay silently for a time, listening to the man's heavy breathing and staring out into the dark. Finally he, too, rolled into his cloak and settled back. He was still a bit worried about Slanter, but he guessed that Garet Jax was right when he said the Gnome could look out for himself. Besides, Jair had grown suddenly sleepy. Breathing the warm night air deeply, he let his eyes close. For a moment, his mind wandered free and he found himself thinking of Brin, Rone, and Allanon, wondering where they were by now.

Then the thoughts scattered and he was asleep.

On a rise that overlooked the Silver River, lost in the shadows of an old willow, Slanter was thinking, too. He was thinking that it was time to move on. He had come this far because that confounded boy had shamed him into it. Imagine, offering him a bribe—that boy—as if he would stoop to accepting bribes from boys! Still, it was well meant, he supposed. The boy's desire to have his company had been genuine enough. And he did rather like the boy. There was a lot of toughness in the youngster.

The Gnome pulled his knees up to his chest and wrapped his arms about them thoughtfully. Nevertheless, this was a fool's mission. He was walking right into the camp of his enemy. Oh, the Dwarves weren't a personal enemy, of course. He didn't care a whit about Dwarves one way or the other. But just at the moment, they were at war with the Gnome tribes, and he doubted that it made a whole lot of difference what his feelings were about them. Seeing that he was a Gnome would be enough.

He shook his head. The risk was just too great. And it was all for that boy, who probably didn't know what he wanted from one day to the next, anyway. Besides, he had said he would take the boy as far as the border of the Anar, and they were almost there now. By nightfall of the coming day, they would probably reach the forests. He had kept his part of the bargain.

So. He took a deep breath and hauled himself to his feet. Time to be moving on. That was the way he had always lived his life—the way trackers were. The boy might be upset at first, but he would get over it. And Slanter doubted the boy would be in much danger with Garet Jax looking after him. Fact was, the boy would probably be better off that way.

He shook his head irritably. No reason to be calling Jair a boy, either. He was older than the Gnome had been when he first left home. Jair could look after himself if he had to. Didn't really need Slanter or the Weapons Master or anyone else. Not so long as he had that magic to protect him.

Slanter hesitated a moment longer, thinking it through once more. He wouldn't find out anything about the magic, of course—that was too bad. The magic intrigued him, the way the boy's voice could . . . No, his mind was made up. A Gnome in the Eastland had no business being anywhere near Dwarves. He was best off sticking to his own people. And now he could no longer do even that. Best thing for it was to slip back to the camp, pick up his gear, cross the river, and head north into the borderlands.

He frowned. Maybe it was just that the Valeman seemed like a boy . . . Slanter, get on with it!

Quickly he turned about and disappeared into the night.

Dreams flooded Jair Ohmsford's sleep. He rode on horseback over hills, across grasslands, and through deep and shadowed forests, with the wind screaming in his ears. Brin rode at his side, her midnight hair impossibly long and flying. They spoke no words as they rode, yet each knew the other's thoughts and lived within the other's mind. On and on they raced, passing through lands they had never seen, vibrant and sprawling and wild. Danger lurked all about them: a Log Dweller, massive and reeking of the swamp; Gnomes, their twisted yellow faces leering their evil intentions; Mord Wraiths, no more than ghostly forms, featureless and eerie as they stretched from the dark. There were others, too—shapeless, monstrous things that could not be seen, but only felt, the sense of their presence somehow more terrible than any face could ever be. These beings of evil reached for them, claws and teeth ripping the air, eyes gleaming like coals in blackest night. The beings sought to pull Jair and his sister from their mounts and to tear the life from them. Yet always the things were too slow, an instant too late to achieve their purpose, as the swift horses carried Jair and Brin beyond their reach.

Yet the chase wore on. It did not end as a chase should end. It simply went on, an endless run through countryside that swept to the horizon. Though the creatures hunting them never quite managed to catch up to them, still there were always others lying in wait ahead. Exhilaration filled the pair at first. They were wild and free and nothing could touch them, brother and sister a match for all that sought to drag them down. But after a time, something changed. The change crept over them gradually, an insidious thing, until at last it lodged itself fully within them and they knew it for what it was. It had no name. It whispered to them of what must be: the race they ran could not be won for the things they ran from were a part of themselves; no horse, however swift, could carry them to safety. Look at what they were, the voice whispered, and they would see the truth.

Fly! Jair howled in fury, and urged his horse to run faster. But the voice whispered on, and about them the sky went steadily darker, the color faded from the land, and everything turned gray and dead. Fly! he screamed. He turned then to find Brin, sensing somehow that all was not well with her. The horror sprang to life before him and Brin was no longer there; she had been overtaken and consumed, swallowed by the dark monster that reached . . . that reached . . .

Jair's eyes snapped open. Sweat bathed his face, and his clothing was damp beneath the cloak in which he lay wrapped. Stars twinkled softly overhead, and the night was still and at peace. Yet the dream lingered in his mind, a vivid, living thing.

Then he realized that the fire was burning brightly once more, its flames crackling on new wood in the dark. Someone had rebuilt it.

Slanter . . . ?

Hurriedly he threw off the cloak and sat up, his eyes searching. Slanter was nowhere to be seen. A dozen feet away, Garet Jax slept undisturbed. Nothing had changed—nothing save the fire.

Then a figure stepped from the night, a thin and frail old man, his bent and aged frame clothed in white robes. Silver white hair and beard framed a weathered, gentle face, and a walking stick guided his way. Smiling warmly, he came into the light and stopped.

"Hello, Jair," he greeted.

The Valeman stared. "Hello."

"Dreams can be visions of what is to come, you know. And dreams can be warnings of what we must beware."

Jair was speechless. The old man turned and came about the fire, picking his way with care until at last he stood before the Valeman. Then he lowered himself gingerly to the ground, a wisp of life that a strong wind might blow from the earth.

"Do you know me, Jair?" the old man asked, his voice a soft murmur in the silence. "Let your memory tell you."

"I don't . . ." Jair started to say and then stopped. As if the suggestion had triggered something deep within him, Jair knew at once who it was that sat across from him.

"Speak my name." The other smiled.

Jair swallowed. "You are the King of the Silver River."

The old man nodded. "I am what you name me. I am also your friend, just as I once was friend to your father and to your great-grandfather before him—men with lives intertwined in purpose, given over to the land and her needs."

Jair stared at him wordlessly, then suddenly remembered the sleeping Garet Jax. Would not the Weapons Master waken. . . ?

"He will sleep while we talk," his unspoken question was answered. "No one comes to disturb us this night, child of life."

Child? Jair stiffened. But in the next instant his anger was gone, melted by what he saw in the other's face—the warmth, the gentleness, the love. With this old man there could be no anger or harsh feelings. There could be only respect.

"Hear me now," the aged voice whispered. "I have need of you, Jair. Let your thoughts have ears and eyes that you may understand."

Then everything about the Valeman seemed to dissolve away, and within his mind images began to form. He could hear the old man's voice speaking to him, the words strangely hushed and sad, giving life to what he saw.

The forests of the Anar lay before him and there was the Ravenshorn, a vast and sprawling mountain range that rose black and stark against a crimson sun. The Silver River wound through its peaks, a thin, bright ribbon of light against the dark rock. He followed its course upriver far into the mountains until at last he had traced it to its source, high within a single, towering peak. There stood a well, its waters spring-fed from deep within the earth, rising through the rock to spill over and begin the long journey west.

But there was something more—something beyond the well and its keep. Below the peak, lost in mist and darkness was a great pit hemmed all about by jagged rock walls. From pit to peak a long and winding stairway rose, a slender thread of stone spiraling upward. Mord Wraiths walked that causeway, dark and furtive in their purpose. One by one they came, at last gaining the peak. There they stood in a row and looked down upon the waters of the well. Then they advanced as one upon it and touched the waters with their hands. Instantly the water went foul, poisoned and turned from clearest crystal to an ugly black. It ran down out of the mountains, filtering west through the great forests of the Anar where the Dwarves dwelt, then on to the land of the King of the Silver River and to Jair . . .

Poisoned! The word screamed suddenly in the Valeman's mind. The Silver River had been poisoned, and the land was dying . . .

The images were gone in a rush. Jair blinked. The old man was before him again, his weathered face smiling gently.

"From the bowels of the Maelmord the Mord Wraiths climbed the walk they call the Croagh to Heaven's Well, the life-source of the Silver River," he whispered. "Bit by bit, the poison has grown worse. Now the waters threaten to go bad altogether. When that happens, Jair Ohmsford, all of the life they serve and sustain, from the deep Anar west to the Rainbow Lake, will begin to die."

"But can't you stop it?" the Valeman demanded angrily, wincing with pain from the memory of what he had been shown. "Can't you go to them and stop them before it is too late? Surely your power is greater than theirs!"

The King of the Silver River sighed. "Within my own land, I am the way and the life. But only there. Beyond, I am without strength. I do what I can to keep the waters clean within the Silver River country, but I can do nothing for the lands beyond. Nor do I have power enough to withstand forever the poison that seeps steadily down. Sooner or later, I will fail."

There was a moment's silence as the two faced each other in the flickering light of the campfire. Jair's mind raced.

"What about Brin?" he exclaimed suddenly. "She and Allanon are going to the source of the Mord Wraiths' power to destroy it! When they have done that, won't the poisoning stop?"

The old man's eyes found his. "I have seen your sister and the Druid in my dreams, child. They will fail. They are leaves in the wind. Both will be lost."

Jair went cold. He faced the old man in stunned silence. Lost! Brin, gone forever . . .

"No," he murmured harshly. "No, you're wrong."

"She can be saved," the gentle voice reached out to him suddenly. "You can save her."

"How?" Jair whispered.

"You must go to her."

"But I don't know where she is!"

"You must go to where you know she will be. I have chosen you to go in my place as savior to the land and its life. There are threads that bind us all, you see, but they are knotted. The thread you hold is the one that will pull the rest free."

Jair didn't know what the old man was saying and he didn't care. He just wanted to help Brin. "Tell me what I have to do."

The old man nodded. "You must begin by giving to me the Elfstones."

The Elfstones! Again Jair had forgotten he had them. Their magic was the power he needed to break apart the Mord Wraith magic and any evil they might conjure up to stop him!

"Can you make them work for me?" the Valeman asked hurriedly, drawing them from his tunic. "Can you show me how to unlock the power?"

But the King shook his head. "I cannot. Their power does not belong to you. It belongs only to one to whom the magic has been freely given, and the magic was not given to you."

Jair slumped back dejectedly. "Then what am I to do? What use are the Stones if. . . ?"

"Of much use, Jair," the other interrupted gently. "But you must first give them to me. For good."

Jair stared at him. For the first time since the old man had appeared, the Valeman hesitated to believe. He had salvaged the Elfstones from his home at the risk of his life. Time and again, he had protected them, all for the sole purpose of finding a way to use them to aid his family against the Mord Wraiths. Now he was being asked to give up the only real weapon he possessed. How could he do such a thing?

"Give them to me," the soft voice repeated.

Jair hesitated a moment longer, wrestling with his indecision. Then slowly he passed them to the King of the Silver River.

"Well done," the old man commended. "You show character and judgment worthy of your forebears. It was for these qualities that I chose you. And these qualities will sustain you."

He slipped the Elfstones within his robes and brought forth a different pouch. "This pouch contains Silver Dust—life restorer to the waters of the Silver River. You must carry it to Heaven's Well and scatter it into the poisoned waters. Do that, and the river will be clean again. Then you will find a way to give your sister back to herself."

Give Brin back to herself? Jair shook his head slowly. What did the old man mean by that?

"She will lose herself." The King of the Silver River again seemed able to read his thoughts. "Yours is the voice that will help her to find the pathway back."

Jair still did not understand. He started to ask the questions that would clear away his confusion, but the old man shook his head slowly.

"Listen to what I say." One thin arm reached out to him and the pouch with the Silver Dust was placed in his hands. "Now we are bound. Trust has been exchanged. So now it can be with magics. Your magic is useless to you, mine equally to me. I keep yours therefore and give you mine."

Again he reached into the robes. "The Elfstones are three in number, one each for the mind and body and heart—magics that entwine and form the power of the Stones. Three magics, then, shall you be given. First, this."

In his hand was a brilliant crystal on a silver chain. He passed it to Jair. "For the mind, a vision crystal. Sing to it, and it will show you the face of your sister, wherever she may be. Use it when you have need of knowing what she is about. And you *will* have need of knowing, for you must reach Heaven's Well before she reaches the Maelmord."

His hand lifted to Jair's shoulder. "For the body, strength to see you through on your journey east and to stand against the dangers that will beset you. That strength you shall find in those who will travel with you, for you shall not make this journey alone. A touch of the magic, then, to each. It begins and ends here." He pointed to the sleeping Garet Jax. "When your need is greatest, he shall always come. He shall be protector to you until you stand at last at Heaven's Well."

Once more he turned back to Jair. "And for the heart, child, the final magic—a wish that shall serve you best. *One time only* you may call upon the wishsong and it shall give you not illusion, but reality. It is the magic that will save your sister. Use it when you stand at Heaven's Well."

Jair shook his head slowly. "But how am I to use it? What am I to do?"

"I cannot tell you what you must decide for yourself," the King of the Silver River replied. "When you have thrown the Silver Dust into the basin at Heaven's Well and the waters are clear once more, throw the vision crystal after. You must find your answer there."

He bent forward then, his frail hand lifting. "But be cautioned. You must reach the Well before your sister enters into the Maelmord. It is written that she shall do so, since the Druid's faith in her magic is well placed. You must be there when that happens."

"I will," Jair whispered and clutched the vision crystal tightly.

The old man nodded. "I have placed much trust in you. The lands and the races depend now on you, and you must not fail them. But you have courage. You shall be true. Speak the words, Jair."

"I shall be true," the Valeman repeated.

Gingerly the King of the Silver River rose again, a ghost in the night. A great weariness stole suddenly over Jair, pulling him down into his travel cloak. Warmth and comfort seeped slowly through his body.

"You, most of all, are a part of me," he heard the old man say, the words faint and distant. "Child of life, the magic makes you so. All things change, but the past carries forward and becomes what is to be. Thus it was with your great-grandfather and your father. Thus it is with you."

He was fading, dissipating like smoke into the firelight. Jair peered after him, but his eyes were so clouded with sleep that he could not seem to make them focus.

"When you awake, all will be as it was save for this—I have come. Sleep now, child. Be at peace."

Jair's eyes closed obediently, and he slept.

When Jair awoke, dawn had already broken. Sunshine spilled down out of a cloudless blue sky and warmed an earth still damp with morning dew. He stretched lazily and breathed in the smell of bread and meat cooking. Kneeling next to the campfire, his back turned to the Valeman, Garet Jax was preparing breakfast.

Jair glanced about. Slanter was nowhere to be seen.

All will be as it was . . .

Abruptly he remembered everything that had happened the night gone past and sat up with a start. The King of the Silver River—or had it all been just a dream? He looked down at his hands. There was no vision crystal. When he had fallen back asleep, the crystal—if there really were one—had been clutched in his hands. He felt about the ground for it, then through the travel cloak. Still no crystal. Then it *had* been a dream. He felt hurriedly for the pockets of his tunic. A bulge in one pocket revealed the presence of the Elfstones—or was it the pouch that contained the Silver Dust? Quickly his hands flew over the rest of his body.

"Looking for something?"

Jair's head jerked up and he found Garet Jax staring at him. He shook his head hurriedly. "No, I was just . . ." he stammered.

Then his eyes detected a gleam of metal against his chest where the tunic opened in front. He looked down, tucking his chin back. It was a silver chain.

"Do you want something to eat?" the other man asked.

Jair didn't hear him. It hadn't been a dream after all, he was thinking. It had been real. It had all happened just as he remembered it. One hand felt down the front of his tunic past the length of the silver chain, touching upon the orb of the crystal fastened at its end.

"Do you want something to eat or not?" Garet Jax repeated, a touch of annoyance in his voice.

"Yes, I . . . yes, I do," Jair mumbled, rising and coming over to kneel beside the other. A plate was passed to him, filled with food from the kettle. Masking his excitement, he began to eat.

"Where's Slanter?" he asked after a moment, recalling once more the absent Gnome.

Garet Jax shrugged. "He never came back. I scouted around for him before breakfast. His tracks led down to the river and then turned west."

"West?" Jair stopped eating. "But that's not the way to the Anar."

The Weapons Master nodded. "I'm afraid your friend decided he had come far enough with us. That's the trouble with Gnomes—they're not very reliable."

Jair felt a twinge of disappointment. Slanter must indeed have decided to go his own way. But why did he have to sneak off like that? Why couldn't he at least have said something? Jair thought about it a moment longer, then forced himself to resume eating, pushing the disappointment from his mind. He had more immediate problems to concern himself with this morning.

He thought back over everything the King of the Silver River had told him last night. He had a mission to perform. He had to go into the deep Anar, into the Ravenshorn and the lair of the Mord Wraiths to the peak called Heaven's Well. It would be a long, dangerous journey—even for a trained Hunter. Jair stared hard at the ground. He was going, of course. There was no question about that. But as game and determined as he might be, he had to admit nevertheless that he was far from being a trained Hunter—or a trained anything. He was going to need help with this. But where was he going to find it?

He glanced curiously at Garet Jax. This man shall be your protector, the King of the Silver River had promised. I give to him strength to withstand the dangers that will beset you on your journey. When you have need of him, he shall be there.

Jair frowned. Did Garet Jax know all this? It certainly didn't appear that way. Obviously the old man hadn't come to the Weapons Master last night as he had come to Jair. Otherwise the man would have said something by now. That meant it was up to Jair to explain it to him. But how was the Valeman supposed to convince the Weapons Master to come with him into the deep Anar? For that matter, how was he supposed to convince him that he hadn't simply been dreaming.

He was still mulling the problem over when, to his complete astonishment, Slanter stalked out of the trees.

"Anything left in the kettle?" Slanter asked, scowling at them both.

Wordlessly, Garet Jax handed him a plate. The Gnome dropped the pack he was carrying, sat down next to the fire, and helped himself to a generous portion of the bread and meat. Jair stared at him. He looked haggard and irritable, as if he hadn't slept all night.

The Gnome caught him staring. "What's bothering you?" he snapped.

"Nothing." Jair looked away quickly, then looked back again. "I was just wondering where you'd been."

Slanter stayed bent over his plate. "I decided to sleep down by the river. Cooler there. Too hot by the fire." Jair's eyes strayed down to the discarded pack, and the Gnome's head jerked up. "Took the pack so I could scout upriver a bit—just in case. Thought I'd be certain that nothing . . ."

He broke off. "I don't have to account to you, boy! What's the difference what I was doing? I'm here now, aren't I? Let me be!"

He went back to his breakfast, attacking it with a vengeance. Jair glanced furtively at Garet Jax, but the Weapons Master seemed to take no notice. The Valeman turned again to Slanter. He was lying, of course; his tracks led downriver. Garet Jax had said so. Why had he decided to come back?

Unless . . .

Jair caught himself. The idea was so wild that he could barely conceive of it. But just perhaps the King of the Silver River had used his magic to bring the Gnome back again. He could have done that, Jair thought, and Slanter would never have been the wiser or realized what was being done to him. The old man could have seen that Jair would have need for the tracker—a Gnome who knew the whole of the Eastland.

Then suddenly it occurred to Jair that perhaps the King of the Silver River had brought Garet Jax to him as well—that the Weapons Master had come to his aid in the Black Oaks because the old man had wanted it so. Was that possible? Was that the reason that Garet Jax had freed him—all without realizing it?

Jair sat there in stunned silence, his food forgotten. That would explain the reluctance of both tracker and soldier-of-fortune to discuss the reasons for their actions. They didn't understand it fully themselves. But if that were true, then Jair, too, might have been brought here by similar manipulation. How much of what had happened to him had been the work of the old man?

Garet Jax finished his breakfast and was kicking out the fire. Slanter, too, was on his feet, wordlessly pulling on the discarded pack. Jair stared at them in turn, wondering what he should do. He knew that he couldn't just stay silent.

"Time to go," Garet Jax called over, motioning him up. Slanter was already at the edge of the clearing.

"Wait . . . wait just a minute." They turned to stare at him as he climbed slowly to his feet. "I've got something to tell you first."

He told them everything. He had not intended it to happen that way, but telling one thing led to telling another by way of explanation; before he knew it the whole story was out. He told them of Allanon's visit to the Vale and of his story of the Ildatch, of how Brin and Rone Leah had gone east with the Druid to gain entry into the Maelmord, and lastly of the appearance of the King of the Silver River and of the mission he had given to Jair.

When he had finished, there was a long silence. Garet Jax walked back to the fallen log and sat down, gray eyes intense.

"I am to be your protector?" he asked quietly.

Jair nodded. "He said you would be."

"What if I were to decide otherwise?"

Jair shook his head. "I don't know."

"I have heard some wild tales, but this is the wildest it has ever been my misfortune to suffer through!" Slanter exclaimed suddenly. "What are you up to with all this nonsense? What's the purpose of it? You don't think for a minute anyone sitting here believes a word of it, do you?"

"Believe what you want. It's the truth," Jair insisted, refusing to back away as the Gnome advanced on him.

"The truth! What do you know about the truth?" Slanter was incredulous. "You spoke with the King of the Silver River, did you? He gave you magic, did he? And now we're supposed to go traipsing off into the deep Anar, are we? And not just into the Anar, but right into the teeth of the black walkers! Into the Maelmord! You're mad, boy! That's the only truth there is in any of this!"

Jair reached into his tunic and brought forth the pouch containing the Silver Dust. "This is the Dust he gave me, Slanter. And here." He pulled the vision crystal on its silver chain free of his neck. "You see? I have the things he gave me, just as I said. Look for yourself."

Slanter threw up his hands. "I don't want to look! I don't want anything to do with any of this! I don't even know what I'm doing here!" He wheeled about suddenly. "But I'll tell you this—I'm not going into the Anar, not with a thousand crystals or a whole mountain of Silver Dust! Find someone else who's tired of living and leave me be!"

Garet Jax was back on his feet. He came over to Jair, took the pouch from the Valeman's hand, slipped the drawstrings open, and peered inside. Then he looked up again at Jair.

"Looks like sand to me," he said.

Jair glanced down hurriedly. Sure enough, the contents of the pouch looked exactly like sand. There was not a sparkle of silver to be seen in the supposed Silver Dust.

"Of course, the color might be a guise to protect against theft," the Weapons Master mused thoughtfully, a distant look in his eyes.

Slanter was aghast. "You don't really believe . . ."

Garet Jax cut him short. "I don't believe much of anything, Gnome." His eyes were hard again as they shifted to Jair. "Let's put this magic to the test. Take out the vision crystal and sing to it."

Jair hesitated. "I don't know how."

"You don't know how?" Slanter sneered. "Shades!"

Garet Jax didn't move. "This seems like a good time to learn, doesn't it?"

Jair flushed and looked down at the crystal. Neither of them believed a word he had told them. He couldn't really blame them, though. He wouldn't have believed it himself if it hadn't happened to him. But it had, and it had been all too convincing not to be real.

He took a deep breath. "I'll try."

He began to sing softly to the crystal. He held it cupped within his hands like a fragile thing, the silver chain dangling down through his fingers. He sang without knowing what it was he should sing or how he could bring the crystal to life. Low and gentle, his voice called to it and asked that it show him Brin.

It responded almost instantly. Light flared within his palms, startling him so that he nearly dropped the crystal. A living thing, the light shimmered a brilliant white, expanding until it was the size of a child's ball. Garet Jax bent close, his lean face intense. Slanter edged his way back from across the clearing.

Then abruptly Brin Ohmsford's face appeared within the light, dark and beautiful, framed by mountains whose slopes were stark and towering against a dawn less friendly than their own.

"Brin!" Jair whispered.

He thought for a moment she might reply, so real was her face within the light. Yet her eyes were far distant in their vision, and her ears were closed to his voice. Then the vision faded; in his excitement, Jair had ceased to sing, and the crystal's magic was spent. The light was gone in the same moment. Jair's hands cupped the crystal once more.

"Where was she?" he asked hurriedly.

Garet Jax shook his head. "I'm not sure. Perhaps . . ." But he did not finish.

Jair turned to Slanter, but the Gnome was shaking his head as well. "I don't know. It happened too fast. How did you do that, boy? It's that song, isn't it? It's that magic you have."

"And the magic of the King of the Silver River," Jair added quickly. "Now do you believe me?"

Slanter shook his head glumly. "I'm not going into the Anar," he muttered.

"I need you, Slanter."

"You don't need me. With magic like that, you don't need anyone." The Gnome turned away. "Just sing your way into the Maelmord like your sister."

Jair forced down the anger building within him. He shoved the crystal and the pouch with the Silver Dust back into his tunic. "Then I'll go alone," he declared heatedly.

"No need for that quite yet." Garet Jax swung his pack over his shoulder and started across the clearing once more. "First we'll see you safely to Culhaven, the Gnome and me. Then you can tell the Dwarves this story of yours. The Druid and your sister should have passed that way by now—or word of their passing reached the Dwarves. In any case, let's find out if anyone there understands anything of what you've been telling us."

Jair stalked after him hurriedly. "What you're saying is that you think I made this all up! Listen to me a minute. Why would I do that? What possible reason could I have? Go on, tell me!"

Garet Jax snatched up the Valeman's cloak and blanket and shoved them at him as they went. "Don't waste your time telling me what I think," he replied calmly. "I'll tell you what I think when I'm ready."

Together they disappeared into the trees, following the trail that led east along the banks of the Silver River. Slanter watched them until they were out of sight, his rough yellow face twisting with displeasure. Then, picking up his own pack, he hastened after, muttering as he went.

For the better part of three days, Brin Ohmsford and Rone Leah rode north with Allanon toward the Keep of Paranor. The path chosen by the Druid was long and circuitous, a slow hard journey through country made rugged by steep slides, narrow passes, and choking forest wilderness. But at the same time the path was free of the presence of Gnomes, Mord Wraiths, and other evils that might beset the unwary traveler, and it was for this reason that Allanon had made his choice. Whatever else must be endured on their journey north, he was determined that in the making of that journey he would take no further chances with the life of the Valegirl.

So he did not take them through the Hall of Kings as he had once done with Shea Ohmsford, a march that would have forced them to leave their horses and proceed afoot through the underground caverns that interred the kings of old, where traps could be triggered with every step forward and monsters guarded against all who trespassed. Nor did he take them across the Rabb to the Jannisson Pass, a ride through open country where they might be easily seen and which would take them much too close to the forests of the Eastland and the enemy they sought to avoid. Instead, he took them west along the Mermidon through the deep forests that blanketed the lower slopes of the Dragon's Teeth from the Valley of Shale to the mountain forests of Tyrsis. They rode west until at last they reached the Kennon Pass, a high mountain trail that led them far into the Dragon's Teeth to emerge miles further north within the forests that bound the castle of Paranor.

It was at dawn of the third day that they came down from the Kennon into the valley beyond, a dawn gray and hard as iron, clouded over and cold with winter's chill. They rode in a line, traversing the narrow pass through mountains bare and stark as they loomed against the morning sky, and it was as if all life had ceased to be. Wind swept the empty rock with fierce gusts, and they bent their heads against its force. Below, the forested valley that sheltered the castle of the Druids stretched dark and forbidding before them. A faint, swirling mist hid the distant pinnacle of the Keep from their eyes.

As they rode, Brin Ohmsford struggled with an unshakable sense of impending disaster. It was a premonition really, and it had been with her since they had left the Valley of Shale. It tracked her with insidious purpose, a shadow as murky and cold as the land she rode through, an elusive thing that lurked within the rocks and crags, flitting from one place of hiding to another, watching with sly and evil intent. Hunched down within her riding cloak, drawing what warmth she could from the bulky folds, she let her mount choose its path on the narrow trail and felt the weight of the presence as it followed after.

It had been the Wraith mostly, she thought, that fostered that premonition. More than the harshness of the day, the dark intent of the Druid she followed, or the newfound fear she felt for the power of her wishsong, it was the Wraith. The Druid had assured her that there were no others. Yet such a dark and evil thing, silent in its coming, swift and terrible in its attack, then gone as quickly as it had appeared, with nothing left but its ashes. It was as if it were a being come from death into life, then gone back again, faceless, formless, a thing without identity, yet above all, frightening.

There would be others. How many others she did not know nor care to know. Many, certainly—all searching for her. She sensed it instinctively. Mord Wraiths—wherever they might be, whatever their other dark purposes—all would be looking for her. One only, the Druid had said. Yet that one had found them; and if one had found them, others could. How was it that that one had found them? Allanon had brushed aside her question when she asked it. Chance, he had answered. Somehow it had crossed their trail and followed after, choosing its moment to strike when it thought the Druid weakened. But Brin thought it equally possible that the thing had tracked the Druid since his flight from the Eastland. If that were so, it would have gone first to Shady Vale.

And to Jair!

Odd, but there had been a moment earlier, a brief, fleeting moment as she wound her way down through the grayness of the dawn, alone with her thoughts, wrapped in the solitude of wind and cold, when she had felt her brother's touch. It was as if he had been looking at her, his vision somehow reaching past the distance that separated them to find her as she made her way out of the great cliffs of the Dragon's Teeth. But then the touch had faded, and Jair was as distant once more as the home she had left him to keep watch over.

This morning she was worried for Jair's safety. The Wraith might have gone first to Shady Vale and found Jair, despite what Allanon said. The Druid had dismissed the idea, but he was not to be trusted completely. Allanon was a keeper of secrets, and what he revealed was what he wished known—nothing more. It had always been that way with the Ohmsfords, ever since the Druid had first come to Shea.

She thought again of his meeting with the shade of Bremen in the Valley of Shale. Something had passed between them that the Druid had chosen to keep hidden—something terrible. Despite his assurances to the contrary, he had learned something that had disturbed him greatly, had even frightened him. Could it be that what he had learned involved Jair?

The thought haunted her. Were anything to happen to her brother and the Druid to learn of it, she felt he would keep it from her. Nothing would be allowed to interfere with the mission he had set for her. He was as dark and terrible in his determination as the enemy they sought to overcome—and in that he frightened her as much as they. She was still troubled by what he had done to Rone.

Rone Leah loved her; it was unspoken between them perhaps, but it was there. He had come with her because of that love, to make certain that she had someone with her whom she could always trust. He did not feel Allanon was that person. But the Druid had subverted Rone's intentions and at the same time silenced his criticism. He had challenged Rone's self-designated role as protector; when the challenge was accepted, he had turned the highlander into a lesser version of himself by the giving of magic to the Sword of Leah.

An old and battered relic, the Sword had been little more than a symbol Rone bore to remind himself of the legacy of courage and strength-of-heart attributed to the house of Leah. But the Druid had made it a weapon with which the highlander might seek to attain his own oft-imagined feats-at-arms. In so doing, Allanon had mandated that Rone's role as protector be something far more awesome than either she or the highlander had envisioned. And what the Druid had made of Rone Leah might well destroy him.

"It was like nothing I could ever have imagined," he had confided to her when they were alone that first night after leaving the Valley of Shale. He had been hesitant in his speech, yet excited. It had taken him that long just to bring himself to speak of it to her. "The power just seemed to explode within me. Brin, I don't even know what made me do it; I just acted. I saw Allanon trapped within the fire and I just acted. When the Sword cut into the fire, I could feel its power. I was part of it. At that moment, I felt as if there were nothing I could not do—nothing!"

His face had flushed with the memory. "Brin, not even the Druid frightens me anymore!"

Brin's eyes lifted to scan the dark spread of the forests below, still misted in the half-light of the harsh autumn day. Her premonition slipped through the rocks and across the twist of the pass, cat-quick and certain. It will show no face until it is upon us, she thought. And then we will be destroyed. Somehow I know it to be so. The voice whispers in my thoughts of Jair, of Rone, of Allanon, and of the Mord Wraiths most of all. It whispers in secrets kept from me, in the gray oppression of this day, and in the misty dark of what lies ahead.

We will be destroyed. All of us.

They were within the forests by midday. All afternoon they rode, winding their way through mist and gloom, threading needles of passage through massive trees and choking brush. This was an empty woods, devoid of life and color, hard as iron in autumn's gray, with leaves gone dusty brown and curled against the cold like frightened things. Wolves had once prowled these woods, great gray monsters that protected against all who dared to trespass in the land of the Druids. But the wolves were gone, their time long past, and now there was only the stillness and the emptiness. All about, there was a sense of something dying.

Dusk had begun to fall when Allanon at last bade them halt, weary and aching from the long day's ride. They tied their horses within a gathering of giant oaks, giving them only a small ration of water and feed so that they might not cramp. Then they went ahead on foot. The gloom about them deepened with night's coming, and the stillness gave way to a low, distant rumble that seemed to hang in the air. Steady and sure, the Druid led them on, picking his way with the sense of one familiar with the region; there was no hesitation in his step as he found the path. As silent as the shadows about them, the three slipped through the trees and brush and melted into the night.

What is it that we go to do? Brin whispered within her mind. What dark purpose of the Druid's do we serve this night?

Then the trees broke before them. Out of the gray dusk rose the cliffs of Paranor, steep and towering, and at their rim was the ancient castle of the Druids, called the Keep. It rose high within the darkness, a monstrous stone and iron giant rooted in the earth. From within the Keep and the mountain upon which it rested sounded the rumble they had heard earlier, and which had grown steadily louder as they approached, the deep thrum of machinery grinding in ceaseless cadence against the silence that lifted all about. Torches burned like devil's eyes within narrow, iron-barred windows, crimson and lurid against the night sky, and smoke trailed into mist. Once Druids had walked the halls beyond, and it was a time of enlightenment and great promise for the races of Man. But that time was gone. Now only Gnomes and Mord Wraiths walked in Paranor.

"Hear me," Allanon whispered suddenly, and they bent close to listen. "Hear what I tell you and do not question. The shade of Bremen has given warning. Paranor has fallen to the Mord Wraiths. They seek within its walls the hidden histories of the Druids so that their own power may be strengthened. Other times, the Keep has fallen to an enemy and it has always been regained. But this time that cannot be. This marks the end of all that has been. The age closes, and Paranor must pass from the land."

Highlander and Valegirl stared at the Druid. "What are you saying, Allanon?" Brin demanded fiercely.

The Druid's eyes gleamed in the dark. "That in my lifetime and yours—in the lifetime of your children and perhaps your children's children—no man shall set foot within the walls of the Druid's Keep after this night. We are to be the last. We shall go into the Keep through its lower passages that are yet unknown to the Wraiths and Gnomes who search within. We shall go to where the power of the Druids has for centuries been seated and with that power close away the Keep from mankind. We must pass quickly though, for all found within the Keep this night shall die—even we, if we prove too slow. Once the needed magic is brought forth, there will be little time left to escape its sweep."

Brin shook her head slowly. "I don't understand. Why must this be done? Why can no one again enter Paranor after tonight? What of the work that you do?"

The Druid's hand touched her cheek softly. "It is finished, Brin Ohmsford."

"But the Maelmord—the Ildatch . . ."

"Nothing we do here can help us in our quest." Allanon's voice was almost lost to her. "What we do here serves another purpose."

"What if we're seen?" Rone broke in suddenly.

"We shall fight our way free," Allanon answered at once. "We must. Remember first to protect Brin. Do not stop, whatever happens. Once the magic has been called forth, do not look back and do not slow." He bent forward, his lean face close to that of the highlander. "Remember, too, that you now possess the power of Druid magic in your sword. Nothing can stop you, Prince of Leah. Nothing."

Rone Leah nodded solemnly, and this time did not question what he was told. Brin shook her head slowly, and the premonition danced before her eyes.

"Valegirl." The Druid was speaking to her, and her eyes lifted to find his. "Stay close to the Prince of Leah and to me. Let us shield you from whatever danger we may encounter. Do nothing to risk your own life. You, most of all, must be kept safe, for you are the key to the destruction of the Ildatch. That quest lies ahead of you and it must be completed."

Both hands came up to grip her shoulders. "Understand. I cannot leave you here safely or I would do so. The danger is greater than it will be if you go with us into the Keep. Death flies all through these woods on this night, and it must be kept from you."

He paused, waiting for her response. Slowly she nodded. "I'm not afraid," she lied.

Allanon stepped back. "Then let us begin. Silently, now. Speak no more until this is done."

They disappeared into the night like shadows.

Allanon, Brin, and Rone Leah crept through the forest. Stealthy and swift, they traversed a maze of trees that jutted skyward like the blackened spikes of some pit-trap. All around them, the night had gone still. Between boughs half-shorn of their leaves by autumn's coming, bits and pieces of a clouded night sky rolled into view, low and threatening. The flames of torches high within the towers of the Keep flickered angrily with crimson light.

Brin Ohmsford was afraid. The premonition whispered in her mind and she screamed back at it in soundless despair. Trees and limbs and brush flashed all about her as she hurried on. Escape, she thought. Escape this thing that threatens! But no, not until we are done, not until . . . Her breath came in quick gasps, and the heat of her exertions turned quickly to chill against the skin. She felt empty and impossibly alone.

Then they were up against the great cliffs upon which the Keep stood. Allanon's hands flitted across the stone before him, his tall form bent close in concentration. He moved right perhaps a half dozen feet, and again his hands touched. Brin and Rone went with him, watching. A second later he straightened and his hands withdrew. Something in the stone gave way, and a portion of the wall swung clear to reveal a darkened hole beyond. At once Allanon motioned them through. They groped their way forward, and the stone portal closed behind them.

They waited sightlessly for a moment within the dark, listening to the faint sounds of the Druid as he moved about close beside them. Then a light flared sharply and flames licked at the pitch-coated head of a torch. Allanon passed the torch to Brin, then lighted another for Rone and a third for himself. They stood within a small, sealed chamber from which a single stairway wound upward into the rock. With a quick glance back at them, Allanon began to climb.

They went deep into the mountains, one step after the other, hundreds of steps becoming thousands as the stairway went on. Tunnels bisected the passage they followed and split their path in two, yet they did not depart from the steps they were on, following the long twist and turn upward into the blackness. It was warm and dry within the rock; from somewhere further ahead the steady churning of furnace machinery rumbled through the stillness. Brin fought down the panic she could feel building slowly within her. The mountain felt as if it were alive.

Long minutes later, the stairway came to an end at a great iron-bound door whose hinges were seated in the stone of the mountain. There they halted, their breathing harsh in the stillness. Allanon bent close to the door, touched briefly the studs of the iron bindings, and the door swung back. Sound burst in on them—the pumping and thrusting of pistons and levers—rolling through their small passageway like the roar of some giant breaking free. Heat seared their faces, dry and raw as it sucked away the cool air. Allanon peered past the open portal momentarily, then slipped through. Shielding their faces, Brin and Rone followed.

They stood within the furnace chamber, its great black pit opening down into the earth. Within the pit the furnace machinery churned in steady cadence, stoking the natural fires of the earth and pumping their heat upward into the chambers of the Keep. Dormant since the time of the Warlock Lord, the furnace had been brought to life once more by the enemy that waited above, and the sense of intrusion was vibrant and oppressive. Quickly Allanon led them along the narrow metal catwalk that encircled the pit to one of a number of doors leading out from the chamber. A touch of its bindings and it swung inward into blackness. Clutching their torches before them, they stumbled from the terrible heat and pushed the small door shut behind them.

Again a passageway opened before them, and they followed it for a short time to where a stairway branched off to one side. Allanon turned onto the stairway, and they began their ascent. Slowly now, more carefully—for there was the unmistakable feel of others close at hand—the three wound upward through the dark, listening . . .

Behind them, below somewhere, a door slammed shut with a crash, and they froze motionlessly on the steps. The echo reverberated into stillness. There was nothing more. They went on cautiously.

At the head of the stairs, there was another door where they paused and listened. Allanon touched a hidden lock to slip the door open, passed through, and went on. Beyond was another passage with another door at its end, then another passage, a stair, a door, and another passage. Hidden corridors honeycombed the aged fortress and ran empty and black through the walls of the Keep. Must and cobwebs filled the air with the smell and feel of age. Rats scurried ahead through the blackness, small sentinels warning of their approach. Yet in the castle of the Druids, no one heard.

Then voices sounded from somewhere within the halls of the Keep that ran where the intruders crouched, furtive and hidden. The voices were deep and low, a muted mutter that rose and faded, but much too close. Brin's mouth was dry and she could not swallow. The smoke from the torches stung her eyes, and she felt the weight of the rock close down about her. She felt trapped. All about her, hidden in hazy half-light and shadow, the premonition danced.

And finally this newest tunnel ended. The gloom gave way suddenly before the light of their torches, and a stone wall blocked their passage. No portals opened to either side, and no corridors led away. Allanon did not hesitate. He went at once to the wall, bent close to its surface for a moment as if listening, then turned to Brin and Rone Leah. A finger lifted to touch his lips, and his head inclined slightly. Brin took a deep breath to steady herself. The Druid's meaning was clear; they were about to pass into the Keep.

Allanon turned back to the faceless wall. At touch upon the stone, a small doorway hidden within swung silently back. In a line, the three passed through.

They stood within a small, windowless study filled with dust and smelling of age. The contents of the room lay scattered about in complete disarray. Books had been pulled from the shelves that lined the study's walls and strewn about the floor, their bindings broken and pages torn. Stuffed armchairs had been cut apart, and a reed table and high-backed chairs had been thrown over. Even pieces of the plank flooring had been ripped from their seatings.

Allanon surveyed the ruin through the smoky light of the torches, his dark face filled with rage. Then he moved wordlessly to the far wall, reached within the empty shelves and touched something he found there. Silently the bookcase swung back to reveal a darkened vault beyond. Motioning for them to wait without, the Druid stepped through the entryway, slipped his torch into an iron bracket fastened to a support, and moved to the wall on the right. The wall was constructed all of granite blocks, smooth and tightly sealed against air and dust. Lightly, the Druid began to run his fingers over the stone.

Still within the study, Brin and Rone watched for a moment as the Druid worked, then glanced suddenly away. A thin seam of light outlined a door in the blackness of the room, a door that led from the study into the halls of the Keep. From somewhere beyond that door came the sound of voices.

Within the vault, Allanon's fingers bridged against the granite wall and his head lowered in concentration. Abruptly a deep blue glow began to spread outward through the stone from where his fingers touched. The glow turned to fire that erupted soundlessly through the granite, flared and was gone. Where the wall had been, shelves of massive, leatherbound books stood revealed: the Druid histories.

In the corridor beyond the study, the voices were coming closer.

Swiftly Allanon lifted one of the massive volumes from its place upon the shelves and carried it to an empty wooden table that occupied the center of the chamber. Placing the book upon the table, he opened it. Still standing, he began to page through it quickly. He found what he was looking for almost at once and bent close to read.

Muted and rough, the voices without were joined by the sound of booted feet. There were at least half a dozen Gnomes beyond the door.

Brin mouthed Rone's name wordlessly, her eyes frightened in the glare of the torches. The highlander hesitated, then quickly passed her his torch and drew forth the Sword of Leah. Two steps carried him to the door, where he slipped tight the latch-lock.

The voices and the thudding feet passed and went on—all but one. A hand worked the latch, trying to open the door. Brin backed further into the shadows of the study, praying that whoever paused without could not see the light of her torch or smell its smoke, praying that the door would not open. The latch jiggled a moment longer. Then whoever was out there began to force it.

Abruptly Rone Leah drew back the latch, threw open the door, and dragged a startled Gnome inside. The Gnome managed a single yelp of surprise before the highlander's sword pommel hammered against his head and knocked him unconscious to the floor.

Hurriedly, Rone closed the open study door, locked it again and stepped back. Brin hurried to join him. In the vault, Allanon was returning the tome he had been reading to its place on the shelf. With quick circular motion of his hand before the Druid histories, the granite wall was restored. Snatching his torch from its bracket, he hastened from the vault, pushed back into place the shelving that hid its entry, and motioned both Valegirl and highlander to follow as he slipped again into the passageway that had brought them. A moment later, the study was left behind.

They went back through the maze of tunnels, sweating now with fear and exertion. All about them was as before, bits and pieces of voices appearing and fading in small snatches, and the deep thrum of the furnace rising up from somewhere far below like distant thunder.

Then again Allanon brought them to a halt. Another door stood before them, sealed with dust and cobwebs. Wordlessly the Druid motioned for them to extinguish their torches in the dust of the passageway. They were going into the Keep once more. They stepped from the blackness of their passage into a hallway bright with torchlight and gleaming with brass and polished wood. Though dust lay over everything within the ancient Keep, still the trappings shone through its covering, small bits of fire in the dappled shadows. A great hallway disappeared into the dark, walls of oak hung thick with tapestries and paintings, fronted in tall niches by the ornaments of another age. Flattened against their small entry, Valegirl and highlander peered quickly about. The hall was empty.

Hurriedly Allanon led them left along the darkened corridor, slipping from one set of shadows to the next, past small pools of smoky torchlight and past glimmerings of night that shone deep gray through tall, latticed windows that arched skyward above the battlements without. A strange quiet hung across the halls of the ancient fortress, as if suddenly all life save their own had been stripped from the Keep. Only the constant hum of the machinery below broke the quiet. Brin's eyes darted from the darkened hall to the torchlit entry, searching. Where were the Mord Wraiths and the Gnomes they commanded? A hand gripped her shoulder and she jumped. It was Allanon, drawing her back into the shadows of an alcove that sheltered a tall set of iron doors.

Then suddenly, as if to answer Brin's unspoken question, a cry of alarm rang out, shrill and harsh in the silence of the Keep. The Valegirl whirled at the sound. It came from the study behind them. The Gnome that Rone had knocked unconscious had come awake.

There were footsteps everywhere then, thudding against the stone flooring and pounding through the stillness. There were cries all about them. Rone Leah's sword flashed darkly in the half-light, and the highlander pushed Brin behind him. But Allanon had the iron doors open now; and with a yank he pulled Brin and Rone from sight, slamming the doors behind them.

They stood upon a narrow landing, squinting through a haze of smoky torchlight given off by brands that burned along the length of a stairway coiling upward like a snake about the stone block walls of the massive tower that rose about them. Huge and black, the tower seemed to lift to impossible heights; yet at their feet, beneath the tiny landing that supported them, it dropped into the earth, a bottomless pit. Save for the landing and the stairway, there was nothing to break the smooth surface of the walls as they stretched away into impenetrable shadow with neither beginning nor end.

Brin shrank back against the iron doors. This was the tower of the Keep that guarded the sanctuary of the Druids. Those who had once come with Shea Ohmsford from Culhaven had believed it contained the Sword of Shannara. A monstrous thing, it had the feel of a giant's well made to bore through the whole of the earth.

Rone Leah took a step toward the edge of the landing, but Allanon pulled him back instantly. "Stand away, highlander!" he whispered darkly.

Without, the shouts and cries rose louder, and the running of feet scattered all about. Allanon started up the narrow stairs, his back to the tower wall.

"Stay clear of me!" he whispered down at them.

After a dozen steps, he moved to the stairway's edge. Lean hands lifted from within the black robes, fingers curling. Words slipped from his lips that Valegirl and highlander could not understand, low and muted with rage.

From within the pit of the tower, a sharp hiss sounded in response.

The Druid's hands lowered slowly, his fingers crooked like claws and his palms downward. Steam leaked from the corners of the hard mouth, from eyes and ears, and from the stone on which he stood. Brin and Rone stared in horror. Below, the pit hissed again.

Then the blue fire exploded from Allanon's hands, a huge burst of flame that flew downward into the blackness. Trailing sparks, it flared sharply far below, turned a sudden wicked green in color, and died.

The tower went suddenly still. Beyond the iron doors, the shouts of alarm and the thudding of feet sounded, faint and chaotic, but within the tower there were no sounds. Allanon sagged backward against the wall, his arms clutched tightly about his body and his head lowered as if in pain. The steam that had come from within him was gone, but the stone on which he stood and against which he leaned looked charred.

Then once more the pit hissed, and this time the tower itself shuddered with the sound.

"Look into its throat!" Allanon's voice was harsh.

Highlander and Valegirl peered downward from the edge of the landing into the pit. Deep within, a roiling green mist was stirring like liquid fire against the walls of the tower. The hiss it gave forth was like a voice, eerie and filled with hate. Slowly the mist fastened to the walls, weaving through the stone as if it were water. Slowly the mist began to climb.

"It's coming out!" Rone whispered.

The mist began to claw its way up the stone block walls like a thing alive. Foot by foot, it hauled itself closer to where they stood.

Now Allanon was beside them once more, pulling them away from the edge of the landing, drawing their faces close to his own. His dark eyes glinted like fire.

"Flee, now!" he ordered. "Don't look back. Don't turn aside. Flee from the Keep and from this mountain!"

Then he threw open the tower doors with a mighty thrust and stepped out into the halls of the Keep. There were Gnome Hunters everywhere, and they turned at his appearance, their rough yellow faces frozen with surprise. Blue fire burst from the Druid's outstretched hands and burned into them, flinging them back like leaves caught in a sudden wind. Screams rose from their throats as the fire caught them, and they scattered in terror from this dark avenger. One of the Mord Wraiths appeared, a black and faceless thing within its robes. Blue fire swept into it with stunning force as the Druid wheeled on it, and an instant later it was ash.

"Run!" Allanon called back to where Brin and Rone stood frozen within the empty doorway.

Quickly they followed after him, sprinting past the Gnomes that lay fallen across their path, racing through the smoky torchlight toward the passages that had brought them. The halls stayed empty for only a moment. Then the Gnomes reappeared, counterattacking, a solid wedge of armored yellow forms howling in anger, spears and short swords bristling from their midst. Allanon broke apart the assault with a single burst of the Druid fire, clearing the way. A second group surged at them from a cross corridor as they tried to push past, and Rone turned, the Sword of Leah lifted. Sounding the battle cry of his homeland as the Gnomes came at him, he launched himself into their midst.

Behind them, another Wraith appeared, and ahead still another. Red fire burst from their black hands, arcing toward Allanon, but the Druid blocked the assault with fire of his own. Flames scattered everywhere in a wild shower, and walls and tapestries began to burn. Brin shrank back against one wall, shielding her eyes, Rone and Allanon on either side of where she crouched. Gnomes came at them from every direction, and now there were more Wraiths as well, silent black monsters that lifted out of the dark and struck at them. Rone Leah broke off the battle with the Gnomes and sprang at one who had ventured too close. Down came the ebony blade of the Sword of Leah and shattered the Wraith into fragments of ash. Flames burned his own body from attacks all about him, but he shrugged them aside, the black blade absorbing the brunt of their force. With a howl of anger, he fought his way back to where Brin hunched down beside the wall. A fierce exhilaration lit his face, and lines of mist green swirled wildly within the black metal of the sword. Seizing her arm, he brought her to her feet and propelled her ahead. There Allanon battled to gain the door they had come through from the catacombs, his black form towering out of smoke, fire, and struggling bodies like death's shadow come to life.

"Through the door, highlander!" the Druid roared, flinging his attackers from his side as they fought to pull him down.

A sudden explosion of red fire engulfed them all, stunning them with its force. Allanon turned, and the Druid fire thrust from his own hands, a solid blue wall that shielded them momentarily from those who came after. Somehow they were through the Mord Wraiths' fire then, racing past a few scattered Gnomes who sought vainly to prevent their escape. Cries and screams echoed through the Druid's Keep as they reached the door they sought. They had it open an instant later and were safely through.

Sudden darkness closed about them like a shroud. The howls of their attackers faded momentarily behind the door through which they had come. Snatching up the discarded torches, Allanon quickly relighted them and the three companions began a race back through the catacombs. Down through passageways and stairwells they sped. Behind them, the cries of the pursuit grew strident once more, but the way ahead was clear now. They rushed downward into the furnace room once more, past earth's fire and the rumble of machinery, to where the stairs took them deep into the mountain's core. Still no one barred their way.

Then abruptly a new sound reached their ears, distant yet, but shrill with terror. It came to them in a single, endless wail, alive with horror.

"It begins!" Allanon called back to them. "Quickly now, run!"

They ran frantically as the wail grew more frenzied behind them. Something unspeakable was happening to those yet within the Keep.

Ah, the mist! Brin cried silently.

They fled down the stairs that led to the mountain's base, following the twists and turns of the passageway, hearing all the while the shrieks of those trapped behind them. Stairs came and went in countless number, and still they ran on.

Then finally the stairs ended, and the entry hidden in the rock of the cliff face loomed before them once more. Pushing through hurriedly, Allanon led them from the mountain into the cool dark of the forest beyond.

Still the screams followed after.

Night slipped away. It was nearing dawn when at last they walked their horses clear of the valley of Paranor. Weary and ragged, they paused on an outcropping of rock on high ground east of the pinnacle of the Keep and looked back to where green mist swirled wickedly about the aged fortress and hid it from their view. The sky lightened, and the mist burned away a little at a time, a shroud lifting. Silently they watched as it dissipated into air.

Then the dawn broke, and the mist was gone.

"It is finished," Allanon whispered in the stillness.

Brin and Rone Leah stared. Below, the pinnacle the Druid's Keep had once rested upon rose high into the light of the morning sun—barren and empty save for a scattering of crumbling outbuildings. The castle of the Druids had vanished.

"Thus was it written within the histories; thus was it foretold," Allanon continued quietly. "Bremen's shade knew the truth. Older than the time of the Keep was the magic conceived to close her away. Now she is gone, drawn back into the stone of the mountain, and with her all those she trapped within." There was a terrible sadness in the dark face. "So it ends. Paranor is lost."

But they were alive! Brin felt a fierce determination rushing through her, brushing aside the Druid's somber tone. The premonition had been wrong and they were alive—all of them!

"So it ends," Allanon repeated softly.

His eyes found those of the Valegirl then, and it was as if they shared some unspoken secret that neither quite fully understood. Then slowly Allanon turned his horse about. With Brin and Rone trailing after, he rode east toward the forests of the Anar.

14

Late in the afternoon, Jair Ohmsford and his companions reached the Dwarf community of Culhaven. It was a journey just as well over and done with in the Valeman's opinion. Leaden skies and a chill wind had followed them east through the Silver River country, and even the changing colors of the great Eastland forests had a gray and wintry cast to them. Geese flew southward over the land through threatening autumn skies, and the flow of the river whose course they followed was rough and unfriendly.

The Silver River had begun to show signs of the poisoning foretold by its King. Blackish scum laced its waters, and its clear silver color had turned murky. Dying fish, small rodents, and fallen birds floated past, and the river was choked with deadwood and scrub. Even its smell was bad, the fresh cleanness become a rank and fetid odor that assailed their nostrils with each change in the wind. Jair remembered his father's tales of the Silver River, tales told since the time of Shea Ohmsford, and what he saw now made him sick at heart.

Garet Jax and Slanter did little to improve his mood. Even without the constant reminder of the river's ill and the harsh cast of the day, Jair would have found it difficult to keep a smile on his face or cheerfulness in his voice with the Weapons Master and the Gnome for traveling companions. Withdrawn and taciturn, they trudged beside him with all of the enthusiasm of mourners at a death watch. Not a dozen words had been exchanged since the march had resumed early that morning, and not a smile had crossed either face. Eyes riveted on the path ahead, they went forward with a singleminded determination that bordered on fanaticism. Once or twice, Jair had ventured to speak, and the response each time had been little more than a muted grunt. The noontime meal had been a strained and awkward ritual of necessity, and even the silent march east had been preferable to that.

Thus their approach into Culhaven was more than a little welcome to the Valeman, if for no other reason than that it meant he would soon have a chance to talk to someone civil for a change—although there was some reason to doubt even that. Dwarves had sighted them as far west as the border of the Anar, silent watchers who had made no effort to make them feel welcome. All along the trail leading in, there had been patrols of Dwarf Hunters—hardened men wrapped in leather waistcoats and forest cloaks, armed and purposeful in their walk. None of these had given greeting, or paused for even the briefest chat. All had passed and gone their way without inquiry. Only their eyes had strayed over to view these visitors—and their eyes had not been friendly.

By the time Jair and his fellow travelers reached the edge of the Dwarf village, they were being studied openly by every Dwarf they passed, and there was more than a hint of suspicion in those looks. Still in the lead, Garet Jax seemed oblivious to the eyes that followed after them, but Slanter was growing increasingly edgy and Jair was almost as uncomfortable as the Gnome. Garet Jax led along the roadway that crisscrossed the village, clearly familiar with the community and certain of what he was about. Neatly kept homes and shops lined the pathways they walked, sturdily built structures fronted by immaculate lawns and hedgerows, and brightened by lines of flowerbanks and carefully tended gardens. Families and shopowners looked up as they passed, hands gripping tools and wares as they paused in their day's work. But there were armed men even here—Dwarf Hunters with hard eyes and belted weapons. This might be a community of families and homes, Jair thought to himself, but just at the moment it has more the look of an armed camp.

Finally, as they entered the central part of the village, they were brought to a halt by a foot patrol. Garet Jax spoke briefly with one of the sentries and the Dwarf disappeared on the run. The Weapons Master stepped back with Jair and Slanter. Together they faced the remaining members of the patrol in studied silence and waited. Dwarf children came to stand about them curiously, eyes fixed on Slanter. The Gnome ignored them for a time, then tired of the game and gave a sudden growl that sent the entire bunch scurrying for cover. The Gnome glowered after them, glanced irritably at Jair, and withdrew into a determined funk.

A few minutes later, the sentry dispatched by Garet Jax returned. With him was a rugged-looking Dwarf with a great curling black beard and mustache and a bald head. Without slowing, he went directly to the Weapons Master, his hand extended in welcome.

"Took your sweet time getting here," he growled as the other clasped the callused hand in his own. Sharp brown eyes peered out from beneath heavy brows, and the look of the man was hard and fierce. His stout, compact body was clothed in loose-fitting forest garb, belted and booted in soft leather, and he wore a brace of long knives at his waist. In one ear, a large gold earring dangled.

"Elb Foraker," Garet Jax introduced the Dwarf to Jair and Slanter.

Foraker studied them wordlessly for a moment, then turned back to the Weapons Master. "Strange company you're keeping, Garet."

"Strange times." The other shrugged. "How about a place to sit and something to eat?"

Foraker nodded. "This way."

He led them past the patrol to where the roadway branched right and from there into a building that housed a large eating hall filled with benches and tables. A handful of the tables were occupied by Dwarf Hunters absorbed in their evening meal. A few glanced up and nodded to Foraker, but no one this time showed any particular interest in the Dwarf's companions. Apparently it made a difference whom you were with, Jair thought. Foraker chose a table for them well back against one wall and signaled for food to be brought.

"What am I supposed to do with these two?" the Dwarf asked when they had seated themselves.

Garet Jax turned to his companions. "Direct sort of fellow, isn't he? He was with me ten years ago when I was training Dwarf Hunters for a border skirmish along the Wolfsktaag. He was with me again in Callahorn a few years back. That's why I'm here now. He asked me to come, and he doesn't take no for an answer."

He looked back at Foraker. "The Valeman is Jair Ohmsford. He's looking for his sister and a Druid."

Foraker leaned back frowning. "A Druid? What Druid? There aren't any Druids anymore. Haven't been any Druids since . . ."

"I know—since Allanon," Jair interjected, unable to keep still any longer. "That's the Druid I'm looking for."

Foraker stared at him. "That right? What makes you think you'll find him here?"

"He told me that he would be going into the Eastland. He took my sister with him."

"Your sister?" The Dwarf's brows were fiercely knit. "Allanon and your sister? And they're supposed to be here somewhere?"

Jair nodded slowly, a sinking feeling in his stomach. Foraker looked at him as if he were crazy. Then he looked at Garet Jax.

"Where did you find this Valeman?"

"On the way," the other replied vaguely. "What do you know about the Druid?"

Foraker shrugged. "I know that no one has seen Allanon in the Eastland for more than twenty years—with or without anybody's sister."

"Well, you don't know much, then," Slanter spoke up suddenly, the faintest hint of a sneer in his voice. "The Druid's come and gone right under your nose!"

Foraker's fierce countenance swung around on the speaker. "I'd watch my mouth if I were you, Gnome."

"This one supposedly tracked the Druid out of the Eastland," Garet Jax offered, gray eyes wandering off casually about the empty hall. "Tracked him from the Maelmord right to the Valeman's doorstep."

Foraker stared at him. "I'll ask again—what exactly am I supposed to do with these two?"

Garet Jax looked back at him. "I've been thinking about that. Does the Council meet tonight?"

"Every night, these days."

"Then let the Valeman speak to them."

Foraker frowned. "Why should I do that?"

"Because he has something to tell them that I think they're going to want to hear. And not just about the Druid."

Dwarf and Weapons Master eyed each other in silence. "I'll have to make a request," Foraker said at last, his lack of enthusiasm evident.

"Now seems like a good time to do it." Garet Jax rose to his feet.

Foraker sighed and stood up with him, glancing down at Jair and Slanter as he did so. "You two can eat your meal and stay put. Don't try wandering off." He hesitated. "I don't know anything about a Druid passing through, but I'll look into it for you, Ohmsford." He shook his head. "Come along, Garet."

The Dwarf and the Weapons Master left the eating hall. Jair and Slanter sat alone at the table, lost in thought. Where was Allanon? Jair asked himself in silent desperation, head lowered to study his hands as he clasped them before him. The Druid had said he was going into the Eastland. Wouldn't he come through Culhaven? If he hadn't, then where had he gone? Where had he taken Brin?

A Dwarf in a white bib apron brought them plates of hot food and cups of ale, and they began to eat. No one said anything. The minutes slipped past as they consumed the meal, and Jair felt his hopes fading with each bite he took—as if somehow he were consuming the answers his questions demanded. Pushing the plate back from where he sat, he scuffed one boot against the plank flooring nervously and tried to decide what he would do if Elb Foraker were right and Allanon and Brin had indeed not come this way.

"Stop that!" Slanter growled suddenly.

Jair glanced up. "Stop what?"

"Stop rubbing your boot against the floor. It's annoying."

"Sorry."

"And quit looking like you'd lost your best friend. Your sister will turn up."

Jair shook his head slowly, still distracted. "Maybe."

"Humph," the Gnome muttered. "I'm the one who should be worrying—not you. I don't know how I ever let you talk me into this fool's errand."

Jair propped his elbows on the table and cupped his chin in his hands. There was determination in his voice. "Even if Brin didn't come through Culhaven, even if Allanon went another way, we've still got to go into the Anar, Slanter. And we've got to persuade the Dwarves to help us."

Slanter stared at him. "We? Us? You'd better take a moment and re-think that 'we and us' nonsense! I'm not going anywhere but back to where I came from before I got involved in this whole mess!"

"You're a tracker, Slanter," Jair said quietly. "I need you."

"Too bad," the Gnome snapped, his rough yellow face suddenly dark. "I'm also a Gnome, in case you hadn't noticed! Did you see the way they looked at me out there? Did you see those children looking at me like I was some sort of wild animal brought in from the forest? Use your head! There's a war going on between Gnomes and Dwarves, and the Dwarves aren't likely to listen to anything you have to say so long as you persist in making me your ally! Which I'm not, in any case!"

Jair bent forward. "Slanter, I have to reach Heaven's Well before Brin reaches the Maelmord. How am I going to do that without someone to guide me in?"

"You'll find a way, knowing you." The Gnome brushed the matter aside. "Besides, I can't go back there anymore. Spilk will have told them what I did. Or if not him, then that other Gnome that ran off. They'll be looking for me. If I go back, someone will recognize me. When I'm caught, the walkers . . ." He stopped abruptly and threw up his hands. "I'm not going and that's that!"

He went back to eating his food, his head lowered to his plate. Jair regarded him silently, wondering if perhaps he were making a mistake in seeking Slanter's help in the first place; perhaps the King of the Silver River hadn't intended him as an ally after all. Slanter didn't really seem like much of an ally when you thought about it. He was altogether too clever, too opportunistic, and his loyalty changed as often as the wind. He wasn't one to be depended on, was he? Yet despite all that, there was still something about the Gnome that Jair liked. Maybe it was his toughness. Like Garet Jax, Slanter was a survivor, and that was the sort of companion Jair needed if he were to reach the deep Anar.

He watched as the Gnome drank down the last of the ale in noisy gulps, then said quietly. "I thought you wanted to learn about the magic."

Slanter shook his head. "Not anymore. I've learned all I care to know about you, boy."

Jair frowned in annoyance. "I think you're just scared."

"Think what you like. I'm not going."

"What about your people? Don't you care what the Mord Wraiths are doing to them?"

Slanter's eyes snapped up. "I don't have a people anymore, thanks to you!" Then he shrugged. "Doesn't matter, though. I haven't really had a people since I left the Eastland. I'm my own people."

"That's not true. The Gnomes are your people. You went back to help them, didn't you?"

"Times change. I went back because it was the smart thing to do. Now I'm not going back because that's the smart thing to do!" Slanter was growing angry. "Why don't you just give it up, boy? I've done enough for you already. I don't feel obliged to do anything further. After all, the King of the Silver River didn't give me any Silver Dust to help clean up his river!"

"That's fortunate, isn't it?" Jair flushed, a bit angry now himself. "A fat lot of good you'd be, changing sides every five minutes when things got a little rough! I thought you helped me back in the Oaks because you'd made a choice! I thought you cared what happened to me! Well, maybe I was wrong! What do you care about, Slanter?"

The Gnome was nonplussed. "I care about staying alive. That's what you'd care about, too, if you had any brains."

Jair went rigid with indignation. He came halfway out of his seat, arms braced on the table. "Staying alive! Well, just exactly how are you going to do that when the Mord Wraiths poison the Eastland and then move west into the other lands? That's what's going to happen, isn't it? That's what you said! Where will you run to then? Plan on changing sides one time more—become a Gnome again long enough to fool the walkers?"

Slanter reached up and shoved Jair back. "You have a big mouth for someone who understands so little about life. Maybe if you'd been out in the world looking after yourself instead of having someone do it for you, you'd not be so quick to point the finger at others. Now, shut up!"

Jair lapsed into immediate silence. There was nothing to be gained by pushing the matter any further. Slanter had made up his mind not to help, so that was the end of it. He was probably better off without the Gnome anyway.

The two were still glowering at each other when Garet Jax returned a few moments later. He was alone, and he came directly to where they sat. If he noticed the tension between them, he gave no indication of it. He took a seat next to Jair.

"You're to go before the Council of Elders," he said quietly.

Jair shook his head slowly. "I don't know about this. I don't know if this is the right thing to do."

The Weapons Master pinned him with his eyes. "You don't have a choice."

"What about Brin? And Allanon?"

"There is no news of them. Foraker checked, and they haven't been to Culhaven. No one knows anything about them." The gray eyes studied the Valeman intently. "Whatever help you're to find in this quest of yours, you'll have to find it on your own."

Jair glanced quickly at Slanter, but the Gnome refused to meet his gaze. He turned back to Garet Jax. "When do I go before the Council?"

The Weapons Master stood up. "Now."

The Dwarf Council of Elders had convened in the Assembly, a large and cavernous hall settled within the bowels of a squarish building that housed all of the offices governing the affairs of the village of Culhaven. Twelve strong, the members of the Council sat behind a long table on a dais at the head of the chamber and looked down upon rows of benches separated by aisles that ran back to a pair of wide double-doors leading in. It was through these doors that Garet Jax brought Jair and Slanter. Shadows cloaked all but the very forefront of the Assembly, where oil lamps cast their harsh yellow light across the dais. The three who entered made their way to the edge of the light and stopped. A gathering of others occupied seats on the benches closest to the dais, and heads lifted and turned at their approach. A haze of pipe smoke hung over the men gathered, and the pungent smell of burning tobacco filled the air.

"Come forward," a voice called.

They proceeded until they stood even with the foremost line of benches. Jair glanced around uneasily. The faces that stared back at him were not simply the faces of Dwarves. A handful of Elves sat immediately to his right, and half a dozen Bordermen from Callahorn far to his left. Foraker was there as well, black-bearded face dour and set as he leaned against the far wall.

"Welcome to Culhaven," the voice spoke again.

The speaker rose from behind the table on the dais. He was a gray-bearded Dwarf of some years, rough-faced and bluff, skin browned and lined in the harsh light of the lamps. He stood centermost among the Elders at the Council.

"My name is Browork, Elder and citizen of Culhaven, First at this Council," he informed them. His hand lifted and beckoned to Jair. "Come forward, Valeman."

Jair came toward him a step or two and stopped, glancing at the line of faces that looked down at him. All were aged and weathered, yet with eyes still quick and alert as they studied him.

"Your name?" Browork asked him.

"Jair Ohmsford," he replied. "Of Shady Vale."

The Dwarf nodded. "What would you say to us, Jair Ohmsford?"

Jair glanced about. The faces all about him waited expectantly—faces he did not know. Should he reveal what he knew to them? He looked back at the Elder.

"You may speak freely," Browork assured him, sensing his concern. "All gathered here are to be trusted; all are leaders in the fight against the Mord Wraiths."

He sat down again slowly and waited. Jair looked about once more, then took a deep breath and began to speak. Step by step, he revealed all that had happened since the arrival of Allanon in Shady Vale those many nights past. He told of the Druid's coming, of his warning of the Mord Wraiths, of his need for Brin, and of their departure east. He described his subsequent flight, the adventures that had befallen him in the highlands and the Black Oaks, his meeting with the King of the Silver River, and the prophecy foretold by the legendary King. It took him some time to tell it all. While he spoke, the men gathered about him stayed silent. He could not bring himself to look at them; he was frightened of what he might see in their faces. Instead, he kept his eyes fixed on the seams and hollows that molded Browork's weathered countenance and the deep-set blue eyes that stared fixedly back at him.

When at last he was finished, the Dwarf Elder leaned forward slowly, his rough hands folding on the table before him, his gaze still holding Jair's.

"Twenty years ago, I fought with Allanon to keep the Demon hordes from the Elven city of Arborlon. It was a terrible battle. Young Edain Elessedil—" He indicated with his hand a blond-haired Elf barely older than Brin. "—was not even born then. His grandfather, the great Eventine, was King of the Elves. That was when Allanon last walked the Four Lands. Not since that time has the Druid been seen, Valeman. He has not come to Culhaven. He has not come to the Eastland. What say you to that?"

Jair shook his head. "I don't know why he didn't come this way. I don't know where he has gone. I only know where it is that he goes—and my sister with him. And I know, too, that he has indeed been within the Eastland." He turned toward Slanter. "This Hunter tracked him from the Maelmord west to my home."

He waited for confirmation, but Slanter said nothing.

"No one has seen Allanon for twenty years," another Elder of the Council repeated quietly.

"And no one has ever spoken with the King of the Silver River," a third said.

"I spoke with him," Jair said. "And my father also spoke with him. He helped my father and an Elf girl flee the Demons to Arborlon."

Browork continued to study him. "I know of your father, youngster. He did come to Arborlon to aid the Elves in their fight against the Demons. It was rumored that he was the possessor of Elfstones, just as you have said. But you say that you took the Elfstones from your home and then gave them up to the King of the Silver River?"

"In exchange for magic I could use," Jair affirmed quickly. "For a wish I could use to save Brin. For a vision crystal to find her. And for strength for those who would help me."

Browork glanced now at Garet Jax. The Weapons Master nodded. "I have seen the crystal of which he speaks. It is magic. It did show to us the face of a girl—one he says is his sister."

The Elf identified as Edain Elessedil came suddenly to his feet. He was tall and fair-skinned, his blond hair reaching to his shoulders. "My father has spoken to me of Wil Ohmsford many times. He has said that he is an honorable man. I do not think a son of his would speak anything but the truth."

"Unless he mistook fantasy for truth," one of the Council suggested. "This tale is difficult to swallow."

"But the waters of the river are indeed fouled," another pointed out. "We all know that in some way the Mord Wraiths poison them in an effort to destroy us."

"As you say, common knowledge," replied the first. "Hardly proof of anything."

Other voices rose now, arguing the merits of Jair's tale. Browork raised his hands sharply.

"Peace, Elders! Give thought to what we are about!" He turned back to Jair. "Your quest, if it be true, requires that we give you aid. You cannot succeed without that aid, Valeman. Armies of Gnomes lie between you and the thing you seek—this place you call Heaven's Well. Understand, too, that none among us have ever been where you would go or seen the source of the waters of the Silver River." He glanced about for confirmation; heads nodded and no one spoke in contradiction. "For us to help you then, we must first be certain of what we do. We must believe. How are we to believe a thing of which we have no personal knowledge? How are we to know what you tell us is the truth?"

"I would not lie," Jair insisted, flushing.

"Not knowingly, perhaps," the Elder mused. "Yet all lies are not intended. Sometimes what we believe to be truth is but a falsehood which deceives us. Perhaps that is what has happened here. Perhaps . . ."

"Perhaps if we waste enough time talking about it, it will be too late to do anything to help Brin!" Jair lost his temper completely. "I have not been deceived in anything! What I spoke of happened!"

The voices murmured in dissatisfaction, but immediately Browork signaled for quiet. "Show to us this pouch of Silver Dust that we might gain some measure of belief in what you say," he ordered.

The Valeman stared at him helplessly. "It will not aid you. The dust appears as common sand."

"Sand?" One of the Council members shook his head in disgust. "We are wasting our time, Browork."

"Let us at least see the crystal, then," Browork sighed.

"Or prove to us in some other way that what you say is true," another demanded.

Jair felt his chance of convincing the Dwarves of anything slipping rapidly away. Few, if any, of the Council believed what he was telling them. They had seen nothing of Allanon or Brin; none of them had ever heard of anyone speaking with the King of the Silver River; for all he knew, they didn't even believe that such a being existed. Now he was telling them he had given away Elfstones for magics they could not even see.

"We waste time, Browork," the first Elder muttered once more.

"Let the Valeman be questioned by others while we get on with our business," another said.

Again the voices rose, and this time they drowned out Browork's pleas for silence. Almost to a man, the Dwarves of the Council and those gathered with them called for the matter to be disposed of without further delay.

"I could have told you this would happen," Slanter whispered suddenly from behind him.

Jair went crimson with anger. He had come too far and endured too much to be shoved aside now. Give us proof, they were telling him. Make us believe.

Well, he knew how to make them believe!

Stepping forward suddenly, he lifted his hands high, then pointed into the shadows of the aisle leading back from where he stood. So dramatic was the gesture that the voices went abruptly still, and all heads turned to look. There was nothing there, nothing but darkness . . .

Then Jair sang, the wishsong quick and strident, and a tall, black figure wrapped in cloak and cowl emerged from out of the nothingness of the air.

The figure was Allanon.

There was a sharp gasp from those assembled. Swords and long knives slipped from their sheaths, and men bounded from their seats to defend against this shade that had emerged from the dark. Within the cowl, a dark lean face lifted to the light, eyes fixing on the men of the Council. Then Jair's song faded and the Druid was gone.

Jair turned once more to Browork. The Dwarf's eyes were wide. "Now do you believe me?" the Valeman asked quietly. "You said you knew him; you said you fought with him at Arborlon. Was that the Druid?"

Slowly Browork nodded. "That was Allanon."

"Then you know that I have seen him," Jair said.

All assembled turned back now to stare at the Valeman, uneasy and shaken by what had happened. Behind him, Jair heard Slanter chuckle, a low nervous laugh. He caught a glimpse of Garet Jax from the corner of his eye. The Weapons Master had a curious, almost surprised look on his face.

"I have told you the truth," Jair said to Browork. "I must go into the deep Anar and find Heaven's Well. Allanon will be there with my sister. Now tell me—will you help me or not?"

Browork glanced at the other Elders. "What say you?"

"I believe what he says," one old man ventured quietly.

"But it could yet be a trick!" another said. "It could be the work of the Mord Wraiths!"

Jair glanced quickly about. A few heads were nodding in agreement. In the smoky light of the oil lamps, suspicion and fear clouded many eyes.

"The risk is too great, I think," yet another Elder said.

Browork rose. "We are pledged to give aid to any who seek the destruction of the Wraiths," he said, blue eyes quick and hard. "This Valeman has told us he is allied with others of like mind and purpose. I believe him. I believe we should do what we can to aid him in his quest. I call for a vote, Elders. Give me your hands in support if you agree."

Browork's hand lifted high. Half a dozen more from the Council lifted with it. But the dissenters were not to be silenced so easily.

"This is madness!" one shouted. "Who will go with him? Are we to send men from the village, Browork? Who is to go on this quest to which you have so unwisely given your blessing? I call for volunteers if this is to be done!"

A scattering of voices muttered in support. Browork nodded. "So be it." He looked about the chamber silently, his eyes shifting from one face to the next, searching, waiting for someone to accept the challenge.

"I will go."

Jair looked around slowly. Garet Jax had come forward a single step, gray eyes expressionless as he faced the Council.

"The King of the Silver River promised the Valeman that I would be his protector," he said softly. "Very well. The promise shall be kept."

Browork nodded, then looked about the room once more. "Who else among you will go?" he called out.

Elb Foraker pushed away from the wall against which he was leaning and walked over to stand with his friend. Again Browork looked out among those gathered. A moment later there was a stirring from among the men of Callahorn. A giant Borderman rose to his feet, black hair and beard close-cropped about his long, strangely gentle face.

"I'll go," he rumbled and came forward to stand with the others. Jair took a step back in spite of himself. The Borderman was almost as big as Allanon.

"Helt," Browork greeted him. "The men of Callahorn need not make this quest their own."

The big man shrugged. "We fight the same enemy, Elder. The quest appeals to me, and I would go."

Then suddenly Edain Elessedil came to his feet. "I would go as well, Elder."

Browork frowned. "You are a Prince of the Elves, young Edain. You are here with your Elven Hunters to repay a debt your father feels he owes from the time the Dwarves stood with him at Arborlon. Well and good. But you carry the price of the debt too far. Your father would not approve of this. Reconsider."

The Elven Prince smiled. "There is nothing to reconsider, Browork. The debt owed in this matter is not to the Dwarves but to the Valeman and his father. Twenty years ago, Wil Ohmsford went with an Elven Chosen in search of a talisman that would destroy the Demons who had broken free of the Forbidding. He risked his life for my father and for my people. Now I have a chance to do the same for Wil Ohmsford—to go with his son, to see to it that he finds the thing he quests for. I am as able as any man here and I would go."

Still Browork frowned. Garet Jax glanced at Foraker. The Dwarf merely shrugged. The Weapons Master looked over at the Elven Prince for a moment as if measuring the depth of his commitment or perhaps simply his chance of surviving, then slowly nodded.

"Very well," Browork acquiesced. "five, then,"

"Six," Garet Jax said quietly. "An even half-dozen for luck."

Browork looked puzzled. "Who is the sixth?"

Garet Jax turned slowly about and pointed to Slanter. "The Gnome."

"What!" Slanter's jaw dropped. "You can't choose me!"

"I have already done so," the other replied. "You are the only one here who has been where we want to go. You know the way, Gnome, and you are going to show it to us."

"I'll show you nothing!" Slanter was livid, his face contorted with rage. "This boy . . . this devil . . . he put you up to this! Well, you have no power over me! I'll throw you all to the wolves if you try to make me go!"

Garet Jax came up against him, the terrible gray eyes as cold as winter. "That would be most unfortunate for you, Gnome, for the wolves would reach you first. Take a moment and think it through."

The Assembly went deathly still. Weapons Master and Gnome faced each other without moving, eyes locked. In the eyes of the man in black, there was death; in the eyes of Slanter, hesitation. But the Gnome did not back away. He stood where he was, seething with anger, trapped in a snare of his own making. Slowly his gaze shifted to find Jair, and in that instant the Valeman actually found himself feeling sorry for the Gnome.

Slanter's nod was barely perceptible. "I've no choice, it seems," he muttered. "I'll take you."

Garet Jax turned back once more to Browork. "Six."

The Dwarf Elder hesitated, then sighed in resignation. "Six it is," he declared softly. "Fortune go with you."

15

Late the following morning, their preparations completed, the little company departed Culhaven for the deep Anar. Jair, Slanter, Garet Jax, Elb Foraker, Edain Elessedil and the Borderman Helt, armed and provisioned, slipped quietly from the village and were gone almost without notice. Only Browork was there to see them off, his aged countenance reflecting a mix of conviction and misgiving. To Jair, he gave his promise that warning of the Mord Wraiths would be sent to the elder Ohmsfords before their return to the Vale. To each of the others, he gave a firm handshake and a word of encouragement. Slanter alone evidenced an understandable lack of appreciation for the good wishes. No other fanfare accompanied their departure; the Council of Elders and the other leaders, both Dwarf and outlander, who had participated in last night's gathering remained divided in their feelings as to the wisdom of this undertaking. More than not, were the truth to be made known, felt the entire venture doomed from the start.

Yet the decision had been made, and so the company went. It went alone, without escort, despite strenuous objection from the Elven Hunters who had accompanied Edain Elessedil east from the home city of Arborlon and who felt more than a little responsible for the safety of their Prince. Theirs was but a token force, after all, dispatched hurriedly by Ander Elessedil upon his receiving a call for aid from Browork and, until a larger force could be mobilized, dispatched in recognition of an obligation owed the Dwarves for their aid in the Demon-Elf struggle of twenty years earlier. Edain Elessedil had been sent in his father's place, but without any real expectation that he would see battle unless the Gnome armies advanced all the way to Culhaven. His offer to join the company on their quest into the heart of enemy country had been completely unexpected. But there was little that the Elven Hunters could do about it—since the Prince was free to make his own decision in the matter—other than to insist that they, too, be made a part of the undertaking. There were those among the Dwarves and Bordermen who would have gone as well, but all were refused. Garet Jax made the decision, and it was supported by the others who comprised the company of six, even Slanter. The smaller the group, the greater its mobility and stealth and the better its chances of slipping through the great forests of Anar unseen. With the unavoidable exception of Jair—and he had the magic to protect him, he kept reminding them—all were skilled professionals, trained in survival. Even Edain Elessedil had been tutored by members of the King's Home Guard during the years he had grown to manhood. The fewer they numbered, they all agreed, the better off they would be.

And so only six went—on foot, for the forest wilderness prevented any other form of travel—eastward from the Dwarf village into the darkened woods, following the bend of the Silver River. Browork watched them until they were lost from sight in the trees, then turned reluctantly back to Culhaven and the work that awaited him there.

It was a clear, cool autumn day, the air sharp and still and the skies bright with sunlight. Trees shimmered in myriad hues of red, gold, and brown, leaves falling to blanket the forest earth in a soft carpet that rustled beneath the feet of the six as they marched ahead. Time slipped quickly away. Almost before they knew it, the afternoon was gone, the evening settling in across the Anar in dark shades of gray and violet, and the sun sinking slowly from view.

The company made camp next to the Silver River in a small grove of ash, sheltered on their eastern fringe by an outcropping of rocks. Dinner was prepared and eaten, and then Garet Jax called them all together.

"This will be our route." It was Elb Foraker who spoke, kneeling in their midst to clear the leaves away, a broken stick tracing lines in the bare earth. "The Silver River flows thus." He marked its passage. "We stand here. East, four days or so, is the Dwarf fortress at Capaal that protects the locks and dams on the Cillidellan. North of that, the Silver River runs down out of the High Bens and the Gnome prisons at Dun Fee Aran. Further north still lie the Ravenshorn and Graymark."

He looked about the little circle of faces. "If we can do so, we must follow the river all the way into Graymark. If we are forced to leave the river, the path through the Anar becomes a difficult one—all wilderness." He paused. "Gnome armies hold everything north and east of Capaal. Once there, we will have to watch ourselves carefully."

"Questions?" Garet Jax glanced up.

Slanter's snort of derision broke the silence. "You make it seem a whole lot easier than it is," he growled.

"That's why we have you along." The Weapons Master shrugged. "Once beyond Capaal, you'll be the one choosing the path."

Slanter spit disdainfully on the drawing. "If we get that far."

The group broke up, each member moving off to make up his bed for the night. Jair hesitated, then started after Slanter. He caught up with the Gnome on the far side of the clearing.

"Slanter," he called. The Gnome glanced about momentarily, saw who it was and looked away at once. Jair stepped around in front of the Gnome and faced him. "Slanter, I just want to tell you that it was not my idea to bring you with us."

Slanter's eyes were hard. "It was your idea, all right."

Jair shook his head. "I wouldn't force anyone to come who didn't want to—not even you. But I'm glad you're here. I want you to know that."

"How very comforting," the Gnome mocked. "Be sure to remind the walkers of that when they have us all in their prisons!"

"Slanter, don't be like this. Don't . . ."

The Gnome turned away abruptly. "Leave me alone. I want nothing to do with you. I want nothing to do with any of this." Then he glanced back suddenly, and there was a fierce determination in his eyes. "First chance I get, boy, I'll be gone! Remember that—first chance! Now—are you still glad I'm here?"

He whirled and stalked away. Jair stared after him helplessly, both saddened and angered by the way things had worked out between them.

"He's not as angry at you as he seems," a low voice rumbled. Jair turned and found the Borderman Helt beside him, the long gentle face looking down. "He's mostly angry at himself."

Jair shook his head doubtfully. "It didn't look that way."

The Borderman moved over to a tree stump and sat, stretching his long legs. "Maybe not, but that's the truth of it. The Gnome's a tracker; I knew him in Varfleet. Trackers are not like anyone else; they're loners, and Slanter is more alone than most. He feels trapped in this, and he wants someone to blame for that. Apparently he finds it easiest to blame you."

"I suppose I am to blame in a way." The Valeman stared after the retreating Gnome.

"No more than he himself," the other said quietly. "He came into the Anar on his own, didn't he?"

Jair nodded. "But I asked him to come."

"Someone asked all of us to come," Helt pointed out. "We didn't have to come, though; we chose to come. It's no different with the Gnome. He chose to come with you to Culhaven—probably he wanted to come. It may be that he wants to come now, but can't admit it to himself. Maybe he's even a little frightened by the idea."

Jair frowned. "Why would he be frightened of that?"

"Because it means he cares about you. There isn't any other reason that I can think of that he would be here."

"I hadn't thought of that. I guess that I thought just the opposite from what he's been saying—that he didn't care about anything."

Helt shook his head. "No, he cares, I think. And that frightens him, too. Trackers can't afford to care about anyone—not if they expect to stay alive."

Jair stared at the Borderman a moment. "You seem pretty sure about all this."

The big man rose. "I am. You see, I was once a tracker, too."

He turned and walked away into the dark. Jair stared after him, wondering what it was that had prompted the Borderman to speak, but rather grateful nevertheless that he had done so.

Dawn broke gray and cheerless, and a mass of rolling dark clouds swept east across the morning sky. The wind blew chill and harsh out of the north, biting at their faces in fierce gusts, whistling through the skeletal limbs of the forest trees. Leaves and dirt swirled all about them as they resumed the march, and the air smelled heavily of rain.

Jair Ohmsford walked that day in the company of Edain Elessedil. The Elven Prince joined him at the start of the journey, conversing in his loose, easy manner, telling Jair what his father the King had told him of the Ohmsfords. There was a great debt owed Wil Ohmsford, the Elven Prince explained, as they bent their heads against the wind and trooped forward through the cold. If not for him, the Elven nation might have lost their war with the Demons, for it was Wil who had taken the Elven Chosen Amberle in search of the Bloodfire so that the seed of the legendary Ellcrys might be placed within its flames, then returned to the earth to be born anew.

Jair had heard the tale a thousand times, but it was different somehow hearing it from Edain, and he welcomed the retelling. He, in his turn, recounted to the Prince his own small knowledge of the Westland, of his father's admiration for Ander Elessedil, and of his own strong feelings for the Elven people. As they talked, a sense of kinship began to develop between them. Perhaps it was their shared Elven ancestry, perhaps simply the closeness in age. Edain Elessedil was like Rone in his conversation at times—serious and relaxed by turns, anxious to share his feelings and ideas and to hear Jair's—and bonds of friendship were quickly formed.

Nightfall came, and the little company took shelter beneath an overhang along a ridgeline that shadowed the Silver River. There they had their dinner and watched the sullen rush of the river as it churned past through a series of rocky drops. Rain began to fall, the sky went black, and the day faded into an unpleasant night. Jair sat back within the overhang and stared out into the dark, the fetid smell of the poisoned river reaching his nostrils. The river had grown worse since Culhaven, its waters blackened and increasingly choked with masses of dying fish and deadwood. Even the vegetation along the riverbanks had shown signs of wilting. There was a murky, depthless cast to the river, and the rain that fell in steady sheets seemed welcome, if only to help somehow wash clean the foulness that lay therein.

The members of the company began to fall asleep after a time. As always, one among them stood guard for the rest. This watch was Helt's. The giant Borderman stood at the far end of the outcropping, a massive shadow against the faint gray of the rain. He had been a tracker a long time, Edain Elessedil had told Jair—more than twenty years. No one ever talked about why he wasn't a tracker anymore. He'd had a family once, it was rumored, but no one seemed to know what had become of them. He was a gentle man, quiet and soft-spoken; he was also a dangerous one. He was a skilled fighter. He was incredibly strong. And he possessed night vision—extraordinary eyesight that enabled him to see in darkness as clearly as if it were brightest day. There were stories about his night vision. Nothing ever crept up on Helt or got past him.

Jair hunched down within his blankets against the growing cold. A fire burned at the center of the outcropping, but the heat failed to penetrate the damp to where he sat. He stared a while longer at Helt. The Border-man hadn't said anything further to him after their brief conversation of the previous night. Jair had thought to talk again with him, and once or twice had almost done so. Yet something had kept him from it. Perhaps it was the look of the man; he was so big and dark. Like Allanon, only . . . different somehow. Jair shook his head, unable to decide what that difference was.

"You should be sleeping."

The voice startled Jair so that he jumped. Garet Jax was next to him, a silent black shadow as he settled in beside the Valeman and wrapped himself in his cloak.

"I'm not sleepy," Jair murmured, struggling to regain his composure.

The Weapons Master nodded, gray eyes peering out into the rain. They sat there in silence, huddled down in the dark, listening to the patter of the rainfall, the churning rush of the river, and the soft ripple of leaves and limbs as the wind blew past. After a time, Garet Jax stirred and Jair could feel the other's eyes shift to find him.

"Do you remember asking me why I helped you in the Black Oaks?" Garet Jax asked softly. Jair nodded. "I told you it was because you interested me. That was true; you did. But it was more than that."

He paused, and Jair turned to look at him. The hard, cold eyes seemed distant and searching.

"I am the best at what I do." The Weapons Master's voice was barely a whisper. "All my life I have been the best, and there is no one even close. I have traveled all of the lands, and I have never found anyone who was a match for me. But I keep looking."

Jair stared at him. "Why do you do that?"

"Because what else is there for me to do?" the other asked. "What purpose is there in being a Weapons Master if not to test the skill that the name implies? I test myself every day of my life; I look for ways to see that the skill does not fail me. It never does, of course, but I keep looking."

His gaze shifted once more, peering into the rain. "When I first came upon you back in that clearing in the Oaks, bound and gagged, trussed hand and foot, guarded by that Gnome patrol—when I saw you like that, I knew there was something special about you. I didn't know what it was, but I knew it was there. I sensed it, I guess you'd say. You were what I was looking for."

Jair shook his head. "I don't understand what you mean."

"No, I don't guess you do. At first, I didn't understand either. I just sensed that somehow you were important to me. So I freed you and went with you. As we traveled, I saw more of what had intrigued me in the first place . . . something that I was looking for. Nothing really told me what I should do with you. I just sensed what I should do, and I did it."

He straightened. "And then . . ." His eyes snapped back to find Jair's. "You came awake that morning by the Silver River and told me of the dream. Not a dream, I guess—but something like it. Your quest, you called it. And I was to be your protector. An impossible quest, a quest deep into the heart of the lair of the Mord Wraiths for something no one knew anything about but you—and I was to be your protector."

He shook his head slowly. "But you see, I had a dream that night, also. I didn't tell you that. I had a dream that was so real that it was more . . . vision than dream. In a time and place I did not recognize, I stood with you as your protector. Before me was a thing of fire, a thing that burned at the touch. A voice whispered to me from within my mind. It said that I must do battle with the fire, that it would be a battle to the death, and that it would be the most terrible battle of my life. The voice whispered that it was for this battle alone that I had trained all of my life—that all of the battles that had gone before had been to prepare me for this."

His gray eyes burned with the heat of his words. "I thought after hearing of your vision that perhaps mine, too, came from the King of the Silver River. But whatever its source, I knew that the voice spoke the truth. And I knew as well that this was what I had been looking for—a chance to match my skill against power greater than any that I had ever faced and to see if I was indeed the best."

They stared silently at each other in the dark. What Jair saw in the other man's eyes frightened him—a determination, a strength of purpose—and something more. A madness. A frenzy, barely controlled and hard as iron.

"I want you to understand, Valeman," Garet Jax whispered. "I choose to come with you that I might find this vision. I shall be your protector as I have pledged that I would. I shall see you safely past whatever dangers threaten. I shall defend you even though I die doing so. But in the end it is the vision that I seek—to test my skill against this dream!"

Pausing, he drew back from the Valeman. "I want you to understand that," he repeated softly.

Silent again, he waited. Jair nodded slowly. "I think I do."

Garet Jax looked out into the rain once more, withdrawing into himself. As if alone, he sat and watched the rain fall in steady sheets and said nothing. Then, after a time, he rose and slipped back into the shadows.

Jair Ohmsford sat alone for a long time after he was gone, wondering if he really did understand after all.

The next morning, when they came awake, Jair brought forth the vision crystal to discover what had become of Brin since last he had sought her out.

Rain and gray mist shrouded the forest as the members of the little company crowded about the Valeman. Holding the crystal before him so that all could see, he began to sing. Soft and eerie, the wishsong filled the dawn silence with its sound, rising up through the patter of the rain on the earth. Then light flared from within the crystal, fierce and sudden, and Brin's face appeared. She stared out at the members of the company, searching for something their own eyes could not see. There were mountains behind her, stark and barren as they rose against a dawn as gray and dismal as their own. Still Jair sang, following his sister's face as she turned suddenly. Rone Leah and Allanon were there, haggard-looking faces lifted toward a deep, impenetrable forest.

Jair ceased to sing, and the vision was gone. He looked anxiously at the faces about him. "Where is she?"

"The mountains are the Dragon's Teeth," Helt rumbled softly. "No mistaking them."

Garet Jax nodded and looked at Foraker. "The forest?"

"It's the Anar." The Dwarf rubbed his bearded chin. "She comes this way, she and the other two, but farther north, across the Rabb."

The Weapons Master gripped Jair's shoulder. "When you used the vision crystal before, the mountains were the same, I think—the Dragon's Teeth. Your sister and the Druid were within them then; now they come out. What would they be doing there?"

There was a moment's silence, faces glancing one from the other.

"Paranor," Edain Elessedil said suddenly.

"The Druid's Keep," Jair agreed at once. "Allanon took Brin into the Druid's Keep." He shook his head. "But why would he do that?"

This time no one spoke. Garet Jax straightened. "We won't find out huddled here. The answers to such questions lie east."

They rose, and Jair slipped the vision crystal back into his tunic. The march into the Anar resumed.

16

On the fourth day out of Culhaven, they arrived at the Wedge.

It was late afternoon, and the sky hung gray and oppressive across the land. Rain fell in steady sheets as it had fallen for three days past, and the Anar was sodden and cold. Trees stripped bare of autumn color shone black and stark through trailers of mist that slipped like wraiths across the deepening dusk. In the empty, sullen forest, there was only silence.

All day the land had been rising in a steady, gentle slope that lifted now into a mass of cliffs and ridgelines. The Silver River churned through their midst, swollen by the rains, cradled within a deep and winding gorge. Mountains rose up about the gorge and blocked it away with walls of cliffs that were sheer and stripped of trees and scrub. Shadowed by mist and coming night, the Silver River was soon lost from sight entirely.

It was the gorge that the Dwarves had named the Wedge.

The members of the little company came high upon its southern slope, heads bent against the wind, cloaks wrapped tightly about their bodies as the cold and the rain seeped through. Silence hung over everything, the roar of the wind sweeping from their ears all sound save its own, and there was a deep and pervasive sense of solitude in each man's mind. The company walked through scrub and pine, making its way upward with slow, steady progress, feeling the whole of the skyline close down about it as the afternoon faded and night began to creep slowly in. Foraker led the way; this was his country and he was the most familiar with its tricks. Garet Jax followed, as black and hard as the trees they slipped through; then came Slanter, Jair, and Edain Elessedil. Giant Helt brought up the rear. No one spoke. In the stillness of their march, the minutes dragged by.

They had passed over a gentle rise and come down into a stand of glistening spruce when Foraker suddenly stopped, listened, then motioned them all into the trees. With a word to Garet Jax, the Dwarf slipped from them and disappeared into the mist and rain.

They waited in silence for his return. He was gone a long time. When he finally reappeared, it was from a different direction entirely. Signaling for them to follow, he led them deep into the trees. There they knelt in a circle about him.

"Gnomes," he said quietly. Water ran from his bald head into his thick beard, curling in its mass. "At least a hundred. They've secured the bridge."

There was shocked silence. The bridge was in the middle of supposedly safe country—country that was protected by an entire army of Dwarves stationed at the fortress at Capaal. If there were Gnomes this far west and this close to Culhaven, what had befallen that army?

"Can we go around?" Garet Jax asked at once.

Foraker shook his head. "Not unless you want to lose at least three days. The bridge is the only passage over the Wedge. If we don't cross here, we have to backtrack down out of these mountains and circle south through the wilderness."

Rain spattered down their faces in the silence that followed. "We don't have three days to waste," the Weapons Master said finally. "Can we get past the Gnomes?"

Foraker shrugged. "Maybe—when it's dark."

Garet Jax nodded slowly. "Take us up for a look."

They climbed into the rocks, circling through pine, spruce, and scrub, boulders damp and slick with rain, and mist and deepening night. Silent shadows, they worked their way ahead, Elb Foraker in the lead as they crept cautiously into the gloom.

Then a flicker of firelight shone through the gray, its faint, lonely cast washed with rain. It slipped from beyond the rocks ahead of them. As one, they crouched from its eyes and crawled slowly on, up to where they could peek above the rim of a ridgeline and look down.

The sheer walls of the Wedge dropped away below, misted and rain-swept as the night came down. Spanning the massive drop was a sturdy trestle bridge built of timber and iron, fastened to the cliff rock at a narrows, and pinioned with Dwarf skill and engineering against the thrust and bite of the wind. On the near side of the bridge, a broad shelf ran back to the ridgeline, thinly forested and covered now by Gnome watchfires in the shelter of makeshift lees and canvas tents. Gnomes huddled everywhere—about fires in shadowed knots, within the tents silhouetted against the firelight, and along the shelf from ridgeline to bridge. On the far side of the gorge, nearly lost in the dark, a dozen more patrolled a narrow trail that ran back from the drop over a low rise to a broad, forested slope that fell away a hundred yards further on into the wilderness.

At both ends of the trestle bridge, Gnome Hunters stood watch.

The six who crouched upon the ridgeline studied the scene below for long moments, and then Garet Jax signaled for them all to withdraw into the shelter of a clump of boulders below.

Once there, the Weapons Master turned to Helt. "When it's dark, can we slip past?"

The big man looked doubtful. "Maybe as far as the bridge."

Garet Jax shook his head. "That's not far enough. We have to get beyond the sentries."

"One man might do it," Foraker said slowly. "Crawl under the bridge; crawl along the braces. If he were quick enough, he could slip across, kill the sentries and hold the bridge long enough for the others to follow."

"This is madness!" Slanter exclaimed suddenly, his rough face shoving into view. "Even if you manage somehow to make it to the far side—past those dozen or so sentries—the rest will be after you in a minute! How will you escape them?"

"Dwarf ingenuity," Foraker growled slowly. "We build things better than most, Gnome. That bridge is rigged to collapse. Pull the pins on either side and the whole thing drops into the gorge."

"How long to pull the pins?" Garet Jax asked him.

"A minute, maybe two. It's been expected for some time that the Gnomes would try to flank Capaal." He shook his head. "It worries me, though, that they've done it now and no one's stopped them. They're bold to seize the bridge as openly as this. And the way they've camped suggests they aren't much concerned about being caught from the other direction." He shook his head once more. "I'm worried for the army."

Garet Jax brushed the rain from his eyes. "Worry about them another time." He glanced quickly at the others. "Listen carefully. When it's dark, Helt will lead us through the camp to the bridge. I'll cross underneath. When I dispose of the sentries, Elb and the Gnome will cross with the

Valeman. Helt, you and the Elven Prince use long bows to keep the Gnomes on this side of the bridge until the pins are pulled. Then cross when you're called and we'll drop the bridge."

Elb Foraker, Helt, and Edain Elessedil nodded wordlessly.

"There's more than a hundred Gnome Hunters down there!" Slanter pointed out heatedly. "If anything goes wrong, we won't have a chance!"

Foraker looked coldly at the Gnome. "That shouldn't bother you, should it? After all, you can pretend you're with them."

Jair glanced quickly at the Gnome, but Slanter turned away without comment. Garet Jax came to his feet.

"No sound from here forward. Remember what we have to do."

They climbed back onto the ridgeline, then huddled patiently within the rocks and watched as the night descended. An hour slipped away. Then two. Still the Weapons Master kept them where they were. Darkness fell over the whole of the gorge, and the rain and the mist passed across it like a veil. The cold began to deepen, settling through them with numbing bitterness. Below, the fires of the Gnome Hunters grew brighter against the black.

Then Garet Jax brought his arm up, and the little company rose. They slipped from the rocks like bits of scattered night and began their descent toward the Gnome encampment. They went one after another, Helt leading the way, slow and cautious as he picked his path downward. The fires burned closer, and then voices became audible in the rush of wind and rain—low, guttural, and sounding of discomfort. The six forms crept past fire and tent, bent low within shadows that spread from rock and trees into the night. The company circled left about the encampment, and only Helt's night vision kept them from wandering off the drop.

The minutes slipped away, and the slow crawl through the enemy camp dragged on. Jair could smell food cooking as the wind blew the odor back in his face. He could hear the voices of the Gnomes, their laughter and grunts, and see the movement of the toughened bodies passing in the faint light of the fires. He tried hard not even to breathe, willing himself to become one with the night. Then suddenly it occurred to him that if he wanted to, he really could become one with the night. He could use the wishsong to make himself invisible.

And then he realized that he had just stumbled on a better way to get them all across the bridge.

But how was he going to let the others know what it was?

They had crept to the edge of the gorge and were beyond the shelter of rocks and trees. Only the open face of the cliff stretched ahead. They edged forward, crouched low against the night. There were no fires here, and so they stayed hidden in the mist and the rain. Ahead, the bulk of the trestle bridge loomed through the dark, its wooden beams glistening with rain. Gnome voices came softly from above, brief and cryptic as the sentries hunched down within their cloaks and stared longingly at the warmth and cheer of the camp behind them. Silently, Helt took the company down beneath the bridge to where the supporting beams were anchored in the rock. Yards away, the empty depths of the Wedge opened in a monstrous chasm, wind howling through its cavernous stomach across the rock.

They crouched in a knot, and now Jair reached tentatively for Garet Jax. The hard face swung about. Jair pointed to the Weapons Master, then to himself, then to the sentries above them on the bridge. Garet Jax frowned. Jair pointed to his mouth and said soundlessly "Gnome" and pointed again to each of them. *The wishsong can make the two of us appear as Gnomes to the sentries and we can cross without being stopped,* he was trying to say. Should he whisper it? But no, the Weapons Master had said that no one was to speak. The wind would carry the sound of their voices; it was too dangerous. Again he made the same motions. The others crowded closer, glancing at one another uneasily as Jair continued to motion to Garet Jax.

Finally the Weapons Master seemed to understand. He hesitated for a moment, then took Jair's arm in his own, pulled him close and pointed to the others, then to the bridge above. *Could the Valeman disguise them all?* Jair hesitated; he hadn't considered that. Did he possess strength enough to carry the disguise that far? It was dark, raining, and they were all cloaked and hooded. It would only be for moments. He nodded that he could.

Garet Jax braced him firmly with both hands, gray eyes fixed upon his own. Then he motioned the others to follow them up. All understood. The Valeman was going to use the wishsong to get them across. They did not know how he was going to do that, but they had seen the power he commanded. Moreover, excepting only Slanter—and even he might have deferred to the other under those conditions—they trusted implicitly the judgment of Garet Jax. If he believed in Jair, so would they.

They rose in a knot from where they crouched hidden and walked boldly up the bluff rise toward the bridge. Before them, shadowed forms huddled in idle conversation. Aware suddenly of their approach, the Gnome sentries turned. There were only three. Jair was already singing, his voice blending into the wind in a harsh, guttural song that whispered of Gnomes. For an instant the sentries seemed to hesitate, and a few brought their weapons up guardedly. Jair pushed harder, probing with the wishsong to make them all appear as Slanter. *The Gnome tracker would surely think I'm mad now,* he thought fleetingly. Still he sang.

Weapons lowered then, and the sentries stepped aside. A changing of the watch? A relief for those on the far side of the gorge? Jair and his companions left them wondering, passing through their midst with faces lowered and cloaks wrapped close. They trooped onto the bridge, their booted feet thudding softly on the heavy wooden planks. Still Jair sang, shading them all in Gnome disguise.

Then abruptly his voice faltered, drained by the use to which he had put it. But they were past the line of sentries now, lost in a shroud of mist and rain to any eyes that might follow them. They reached the center of the bridge, the wind howling past them in stinging swipes. Hastily Garet Jax motioned for Helt and Edain Elessedil to drop back. For just an instant Jair had a fleeting glimpse of Slanter's face, filled with wonder as he stared at the Valeman. Then Garet Jax motioned both of them behind him, and with Elb Foraker at his side started forward once more.

They emerged from rain and night at the far side of the bridge, little more than hooded shadows to the Gnomes who kept watch there. Jair's throat tightened. This time there could be no wishsong to see them safely past; there were too many. A gathering of faces turned at their approach. For a few uncertain moments, the sentries simply stared at the figures who came at them, surprised by their appearance, yet certain that only Gnomes could come from the encampment they knew to hold the far cliff. Then before surprise could turn to alarm, or size and shape could properly register, Garet Jax and Foraker were upon them. Short sword and long knife glistened in the night. Half a dozen Gnomes lay dead before the others even realized what was happening. Their attackers swept into their midst, and now shouts of alarm broke wildly from their throats, calling to those on the far side.

Answering cries came back a moment later. Jair and Slanter crouched low at the far end of the bridge, watching the battle before them as it swept into the dark and hearing disembodied cries rise all about them. The sharp twang of Elven ash bows sounded above the rush of wind and rain, and more Gnome Hunters began to die.

Then a single Gnome burst from the darkness before them, bloodied and disheveled, his yellow face frantic in the dim light. He rushed onto the bridge, a two-edged axe in his hands. He saw Slanter and stopped, confused. Then he caught sight of Jair and sprang forward. The Valeman stumbled back, trying vainly to protect himself, so startled by the other's appearance that he momentarily forgot about the long knife he carried at his waist. The Gnome howled, weapon lifting, and Jair threw up his hands protectively.

"Not the boy, you . . ." Slanter cried out.

The Gnome screamed in rage, and again the axe came up. Slanter's sword swept down, and the attacker dropped to his knees, dying. Slanter drew back, a shocked look on his rough face. Then he had Jair by the arm, yanking him to his feet and pulling him ahead until they were clear of the bridge.

Abruptly Elb Foraker appeared. Without a word, he dropped below the trestle bridge to where the pins that held it fixed were concealed. With frantic motions, he began to pull them free.

Renewed cries sounded from the center of the bridge. Booted feet raced onto the wooden planks and from out of the mist and night Helt and Edain Elessedil burst. Still upon the bridge, they turned, and the great ash bows hummed. Gnomes howled in pain in the dark behind them. Again the bows hummed, and more cries rose. The sound of running feet disappeared back into the night.

"Hurry with those pins!" Helt bellowed sharply.

Garet Jax appeared now, joining Foraker beneath the bridge. Together they knocked the remaining pins free, one after the other—all but two. Again the thudding of booted feet rang out.

"Helt!" the Weapons Master called a moment later, scrambling back onto the ledge. Foraker was a step behind him. "Get off the bridge!"

The Borderman and the Elven Prince raced from out of the night, bent low against the wind. Spears and arrows flew after them. Lighter and quicker, Edain was first off the bridge, springing past the crouched forms of Jair and Slanter.

"Now!" Foraker called over to Garet Jax.

They stood opposite each other, pry bars anchored in hooks fixed to the last of the concealed pins. As one, they pulled them free. In the same instant, Helt sprang clear of the bridge.

With a groan, the wooden beams wrenched free of their pinnings, and the bridge began to sink downward into the night. Screams rose from the throats of the Gnomes still caught upon its length, but it was too late for them. The bridge dropped away with a sudden heave, falling downward into the mist and the rain, spinning away against the cliffs until it broke free on the far side, dropped into the gorge, and was lost.

On the northern cliffs of the Wedge, six shadowed forms slipped swiftly into the darkness and were gone.

17

The rain stopped that night, sometime in the early morning hours while the members of the little company from Culhaven lay sleeping within a shallow cavern half a dozen miles east of the Wedge. No one knew exactly when it happened—not even Edain Elessedil, who had been given the late watch. Exhausted by the harrowing flight across the Wedge, he had fallen asleep with the others.

So it was that dawn brought with the new day a change in the weather. North, almost lost in the horizon's bluish haze, stood the vast mountain range they called the Ravenshorn, and from down out of her giant peaks blew a wind chill with the promise of autumn's demise and winter's coming. Bitter and stiff, it swept the clouds, the rain, and the mist that had cloaked the Silver River southward, and once again the sky turned depthless blue. The damp and discomfort were gone. The sodden earth dried hard once more, the rain water evaporated in the wind, and the whole of the land came back into focus with stunning clarity, sharp-edged and brilliant in the sun's golden light.

Once more the company marched east, wrapped close in their still-damp woolen forest cloaks to ward off the wind's biting chill. Ridgelines and grassy bluffs flanked the Silver River now as she churned through her forested banks. As the six pushed ahead, the whole of the Anar spread away beneath them. All day the clustered peaks of Capaal loomed eastward of where they marched, jutting from out of the forest trees like massive spikes to pierce the fabric of the sky. Still distant when the day began, they grew steadily closer with the passing of the hours until, by midafternoon, the company had reached their lower slopes and begun the climb in.

They had not gone far, however, when Edain Elessedil brought them to a halt. "Listen!" he cautioned sharply. "Do you hear it?"

They stood silently upon the open slope, heads turned eastward toward the peaks as the Elven Prince pointed. Wind blew fiercely from out of the rocks, and there was no sound save its mournful howl.

"I hear nothing," Foraker murmured softly, but no one moved. The Elf's sense of hearing was much sharper than their own.

Then abruptly the wind seemed to shift and die, and a deep, steady booming came from far in the distance. It sounded faint and muffled, lost in the myriad twists and turns of the rock.

Foraker's black-bearded face went dark. "Gnome drums!"

They went forward again, more cautiously now, eyes scanning the cliffs and drops ahead. The pounding drums grew deeper and harder, throbbing against the rush of the wind, rumbling ominously through the earth.

Then, as the afternoon lengthened and the shadow of the peaks stretched farther down to where the six climbed, a new sound reached their ears. It was a strange sound, a kind of chilling howl that seemed almost a part of the wind at first, then grew distinct in its pitch and fury. Lifting out of the distant heights, it rolled down across the mountain slopes and gathered them in. Faces glanced one from the other, and at last it was Garet Jax who spoke, a hint of surprise in his voice.

"There is a battle being fought."

Foraker nodded and started ahead once again. "They've attacked Capaal!"

They climbed into the mountains, working their way through an increasingly jumbled maze of fragmented boulders, crevices, drops, and slides. The sunlight fell away as the afternoon died into dusk, and shadows lengthened over the whole of the southern exposure. The wind faded as well, and the chill it carried lost its edge. Silence descended across the land, its empty corners reverberating with the harsh echo of drums and battle cries. Far beyond where they climbed, through gaps in the barren peaks, great birds of prey circled in lazy sweeps—scavengers that watched and waited.

Then at last the company was atop the ridgeline of the nearest peak, turning into a deep and shadowed defile that ran through the rock into coming night. Cliff walls hemmed them in on all sides, and they squinted sharply through the half-light for signs of movement. But the way forward lay open, and all of the life among these rocks seemed to have been drawn to where the battle ahead was being fought.

Moments later they emerged from the defile and drew to a sudden halt. The cliff face dropped away before them and the whole of what lay beyond stood revealed.

"Shades!" Foraker whispered harshly.

Across a narrows, high within the peaks through which the waters of the Silver River flowed, stretched the locks and dams of Capaal. Huge, rough, and startlingly white against the dark rock, they rose high within the gathering of the mountains and cupped the waters of the Cillidellan in giant's hands. Atop their broad, flat crest, extending through three levels, was the fortress that served as protection, a sprawling mass of towers, walls and battlements. The greater portion of the citadel was settled upon the northern edge of this complex and faced onto a plain that ran back at a gentle slope into the sheltering peaks beyond. A smaller watch stood sentinel at the near end where the peaks ran down to the banks of the reservoir and only a series of narrow trails gave access to her walls.

It was here that the battle had been joined. The army of the Gnomes stretched all across the broad expanse of the far shelf and the slopes beyond, and all along the trails and rock slides running down. Huge and massive, it surged against the stone battlements of Capaal in a dark wave of armored bodies and thrusting weapons, seeking to breach the fortifications that held it out. Catapults flung huge boulders through the fading light, which smashed with crushing force into the armor and flesh of the Dwarf defenders. Screams and howls rose up through the ringing clash of iron, and men died all across the length and breadth of the fortress. Tiny, faceless beings, they struggled before the battlements, Dwarves and Gnomes alike, and were swept away in the carnage that resulted.

"So this is what the Gnomes have chosen for Capaal!" Foraker cried. "They have put her under siege! No wonder they were so bold in seizing the Wedge!"

Jair pushed forward for a better look. "Are the Dwarves trapped?" he asked anxiously. "Can't they escape?"

"Oh, they can escape easily enough—but they won't." Elb Foraker's dark eyes found the Valeman's. "Tunnels bore underground to the mountains on either side, secret passages built for escape should the fortress fall. But no army can breach the walls of Capaal, Ohmsford, and so the Dwarves within will stay and defend."

"But why?"

Foraker pointed. "The locks and dams. See the waters of the Cillidellan? The poison of the Mord Wraiths has blackened and fouled them. The dams hold back those waters from the lands west; the locks control the flow. Should the fortress be abandoned, the locks and dams would fall into the hands of the enemy. The Gnomes would open the gates and drain through the whole of the Cillidellan. They would flood the lands west with the fouled waters, poison as much of the land as they could, and kill as much of its life as they were able. The Wraiths would see to it. Even Culhaven would be lost." He shook his bearded face somberly. "The Dwarves will never permit that."

Jair stared down once more at the battle below, appalled by the ferociousness of the struggle. So many Gnomes besieged the defenders of the fortress; was it possible for the Dwarves to withstand them all?

"How do we get past this mess?" Garet Jax was studying the drop.

The Dwarf seemed lost in thought. "When it's dark, work your way east along the heights. That should keep you above the Gnome encampment. Once past the Cillidellan, come down to the river and cross. Then turn north. You should be safe enough then." He straightened and extended his hand. "Luck to you, Garet."

The Weapons Master stiffened. "Luck? You're not thinking of staying, are you?"

The other shrugged. "I'm not thinking of anything. It's decided."

Garet Jax stared. "You can't do any good here, Elb."

Foraker shook his head slowly. "Someone has to warn the garrison that the bridge at the Wedge has been dropped. Otherwise, if the worst happens and Capaal falls, they might try to escape back through the mountains and be trapped there." He shrugged. "Besides, Helt can lead you in the dark better than I. And after Capaal, I don't know the country anyway. The Gnome will have to guide you."

"We made a pact—the six of us." The voice of the Weapons Master had gone cold. "No one goes his own way. We need you."

The Dwarf's jaw tightened stubbornly. "They need me, too."

An unpleasant silence descended over the group as the two faced each other. Neither showed any intention of backing away.

"Let him go," Helt rumbled softly. "He has a right to choose."

"The choice was made at Culhaven." Garet Jax gave the Borderman an icy stare.

Jair's throat tightened. He wanted to say something—anything—to break the tension between the Dwarf and the Weapons Master, but he couldn't think of what it should be. He glanced at Slanter to see what the Gnome was thinking, but Slanter was ignoring them all.

"I have an idea." It was Edain Elessedil who spoke. All eyes shifted toward him. "Maybe this won't work, but it might be worth a try." He bent forward. "If I could get close enough to the fortress, I could tie a message to an arrow and shoot it in. That would let the defenders know about the Wedge."

Garet Jax turned to Foraker. "What do you think?"

The Dwarf frowned. "It will be dangerous. You'll have to get much closer than you'd like. Much."

"Then I'll go," Helt announced.

"It was my idea," Edain Elessedil insisted. "I'll go."

Garet Jax held up his hands. "If one goes, we all go. If we become separated in these mountains, we'll never find each other again." He glanced at Jair. "Agreed?"

Jair nodded at once. "Agreed."

"And you, Elb?" The Weapons Master faced the Dwarf once more.

Elb Foraker nodded slowly. "Agreed."

"And if we can get the message to the garrison?"

The other nodded again. "We go north."

Garet Jax took a final look down at the battle between Gnome and Dwarf armies, then motioned for the others to follow him back into the rocks. "We'll sit it out here until nightfall," he called back over his shoulder.

Jair turned to follow and found Slanter at his elbow. "Didn't notice him bothering to ask me if *I* agreed," the Gnome muttered and shouldered his way past.

The little company slipped down into a cluster of boulders, passing into the shadow of their concealment to wait until dark. Seated about the rocks, the six consumed a cold meal, wrapped themselves in their cloaks and settled back in silence. After a time, Foraker and Garet Jax left the cover of the rocks and disappeared down the slide for a closer look at the passage east. Edain Elessedil took the watch, and Helt stretched out comfortably on the rocky ground and was asleep almost at once. Jair sat alone for a few moments, then got up and walked over to where Slanter sat staring out into the empty dusk.

"I appreciate what you did for me back at the Wedge," he said quietly.

Slanter didn't turn. "Forget it."

"I can't. That's three times now that you've saved my life."

The Gnome's laugh was brittle. "That many, is it?"

"That many."

"Well, maybe next time I won't be there, boy. What will you do then?"

Jair shook his head. "I don't know."

There was an uncomfortable silence. Slanter continued to ignore the Valeman. Jair almost turned away again, but then his stubbornness got the better of him and he forced himself to remain. Deliberately, he took a seat next to the Gnome.

"He should have asked you," he said quietly.

"Who? Asked me what?"

"Garet Jax—he should have asked you if you were willing to go down to the fortress with us."

Now Slanter turned. "Hasn't asked me anything before, has he? Why should he start now?"

"Maybe if you . . ."

"Maybe if I sprout wings I'll be able to fly out of this place!" The Gnome's face flushed with anger. "In any case, what do you care?"

"I care."

"About what? That I'm here? Do you care about that? You tell me, boy—what am I doing here?"

Jair looked away uncomfortably, but Slanter gripped his arm and brought him about with a jerk.

"Look at me! What am I doing here? What has any of this got to do with me? Nothing, that's what! The only reason I'm here is because I was foolish enough to agree to guide you as far as Culhaven—that's the only reason! Help us get past the black walker, you asked! Help us get to the Eastland! You can do it because you're a tracker! Hah!"

The rough yellow face thrust forward. "And that stupid dream! That's all it was, boy—just a dream! There isn't any King of the Silver River, and this whole trek east is a waste of time! Ah, but here I am anyway, aren't I? I don't want to be here; there isn't any reason for me to be here—but here I am anyway!" He shook his head bitterly. "And it's all because of you!"

Jair pulled free, angry now himself. "Maybe that's so. Maybe it is my fault that you're here. But the dream was real, Slanter. And you're wrong when you say that none of this has anything to do with you. You call me 'boy' but you're the one who acts as if he hasn't grown up!"

Slanter stared at him. "Well, you are a wolf's cub, aren't you?"

"Whatever you want to call me, that's fine." Jair flushed. "But you better start thinking about who you are, too."

"What's that supposed to mean?"

"It means that you can't go on telling yourself that what happens to other people doesn't have anything to do with you—because it does, Slanter!"

Wordlessly they stared at each other. Darkness had fallen now, deep-shadowed and windless. It was strangely still, the booming of the Gnome drums and the clamor of the battle for Capaal silenced.

"Don't think much of me, do you?" Slanter said finally.

Jair sighed wearily. "As a matter of fact, that's not so. I think a lot of you."

The other studied him for a moment, then looked down. "I like you, too. Told you before—you got sand. You remind me of me in my better moments." He laughed softly, a hollow chuckle, then looked up again. "But you listen to me now because I'm not going to repeat this again. I don't belong in this. This isn't my fight. And whether I like you or not, I'm getting out of it the first chance I get."

He waited a moment as if to be certain that what he said had the intended effect, then turned away. "Now shove off and leave me be."

Jair hesitated, trying to decide if he should pursue the matter, then reluctantly climbed to his feet and walked away. He was passing close to the sleeping Helt when he heard the Borderman murmur, "I told you he cares."

Jair Ohmsford glanced down in surprise, then smiled and continued on. "I know," he whispered back.

It was drawing toward midnight when Garet Jax took the company out from the sheltering cluster of boulders and back onto the slide. Below, hundreds of Gnome watchfires ringed the fortress of Capaal, spread out across the cliffs on either side of the besieged locks and dams. The six began their descent, Elb Foraker in the lead. They proceeded down along the slide, then turned onto a narrow trail that ran forward into a series of defiles and rocky shelves. Cautiously, they worked their way ahead, silent shadows passing through the night.

It took them better than an hour to reach the perimeter of the watch-fires on the near side of the encampment. Here the Gnomes were fewer in number; most were settled close to the edge of the Dwarf battlements. On the trails leading in, the fires were few and scattered. Beyond the siege lines on these southern slopes, a gathering of peaks thrust skyward, bunched at their base like bound and broken fingers, crooking from out of the earth. The six knew that beyond the peaks could be found a scattering of low hills that flanked the southern shores of the Cillidellan, and beyond these was the shelter of the forests that spread east. Once there, they could melt into the night and slip north without risk of being seen.

But first they must work their way close enough to the battlements of Capaal to permit Helt to use the ash bow so that Foraker's message could be delivered to the Dwarf defenders. It had been decided earlier that the Borderman would attempt the shot, for while the idea had been Edain Elessedil's, Helt was by far the stronger of the two. With the great ash bow to aid him, he need get no closer than two hundred yards from the fortress walls in order to place the arrow and its message within.

Step by step, the six made their way down from the mountain heights through the lines of the Gnome watch. Stretched upward along the broader paths from where the main encampment ringed the battlements of the fortress, the Gnomes gave little attention to the smaller trails and ledges that crisscrossed the cliff face. It was down these smaller trails and ledges that Foraker took his little group in a slow, cautious descent where the footing was treacherous and the cover thin. Pieces of soft leather bound each booted foot, and charcoal blackened each face. No one spoke. Hands and feet picked their way carefully, wary of loose rock or of any sound that would call attention to their passage.

Two hundred yards from the walls of the fortress, they were still just back of the forward siege lines of the Gnome army. Watchfires burned all about them—all along the trails leading back. Silently, they hunched down within a small gathering of scrub and waited for Helt. The giant Borderman removed the arrow with its message from his quiver, fitted it to the ash bow and slipped forward into the night. Several dozen yards ahead, at the edge of the scrub, he rose to a kneeling position, pulled back the bowstring, held it momentarily to his cheek and released it.

A sharp twang shattered the silence of the little company's shelter, yet beyond where they hid, the sound was lost in the routine clamor of the Gnome camp. Nevertheless, the six flattened themselves within the brush for long minutes, waiting and listening for any indication that they had been discovered. There was none. Helt slipped back through the darkness and nodded briefly to Foraker. The message had been delivered.

The little company crept back through the night and the lines of watch-fires and Gnomes, this time working its way eastward about the dark girth of the peaks toward where the waters of the Cillidellan shimmered with the moon's soft light. Far away across the lake, where the dam joined with the broad slope of the mountains north, Gnome fires burned fiercely about the encircled locks and dams and along the shoreline of the Cillidellan. Jair glanced at the mass of watchfires and went cold. How many thousands of Gnomes had been brought to besiege this fortress? he wondered dismally. So many, it seemed. Too many. The fires reflected on the waters of the lake with a reddish glow, bits and pieces of flame dancing across the mirrored surface like droplets of blood.

Time slipped away. Stars winked into view far north, scattered and lost somehow in the vastness of the night. The company had gone back above the watchfires on the southern slope once more and worked its way south of where the Gnomes lay siege. High upon the cliff face, they were almost to where they might view the lowlands that flanked the southern bank of the Cillidellan—almost to where they could begin their descent into the forests below. Jair felt a distinct sense of relief. He felt uncomfortably exposed, caught like this upon the open slopes of the cliffs. They would be far better off when they could rely once more upon the concealment of the forestland.

Then they turned the corner of the cliff face, slipped downward through a mass of giant boulders, and came to an abrupt and startled halt.

Before them, the slope broadened toward the banks of the Cillidellan in a meandering passage through rock and cliff face. A mass of watchfires lay spread out across its entire length and breadth. Jair felt his throat tighten with fear. A second Gnome army blocked the way forward.

Garet Jax glanced quickly at Foraker, and the Dwarf disappeared ahead into the night. The five who remained crouched down within the shelter of the boulders to wait.

It was a long, tense wait. Half an hour passed before Foraker reappeared, slipping from the darkness as silently as he had gone. Hurriedly, he drew the others close about him.

"They're all across the cliff face!" he whispered. "We can't get through!"

In the next instant, they heard the sound of booted feet and voices on the trail behind them.

They froze for a single instant where they were, staring back in startled silence into the dark. Sudden laughter blended with the approaching voices, sharp and raucous, and a flicker of torchlight appeared from out of the rocks.

"Hide!" Garet Jax whispered, dragging Jair with him into the shadows.

They scattered at once, swift and silent as they bolted into the rocks. Pushed roughly to the ground by the Weapons Master, Jair lifted his head and peered out into the night. Torchlight reflected off the dark surface of the boulders and the voices grew distinct. Gnomes. At least half a dozen. Booted feet scraped against the stone of the pathway and leather harness creaked. Jair flattened himself against the earth and quit breathing.

A squad of Gnome Hunters marched into the cluster of boulders, eight strong, torches held before them to light their path down out of the cliffs. Laughing and joking in their rough, garbled tongue, they sauntered unseeing into the midst of the hidden members of the company from Culhaven. Torchlight flooded the little clearing, chasing shadows and night, brightening even the deepest recesses of the company's concealment. Jair went cold. Even from where he lay, he could see the shadowed form of Helt pressed against the rocks. Surely there was no way that they could avoid being discovered.

But the Gnomes did not slow. Oblivious to the figures that crouched about them, the members of the squad continued on. The foremost were already past the front line of boulders, their eyes drawn to the lights of the encampment below. Jair took a slow, cautious breath. Perhaps . . .

Then one of those who trailed slowed suddenly and turned toward the rocks. A sharp exclamation broke from his lips, and he reached quickly for his sword. The others in the squad turned, laughter dying into startled grunts.

Already Garet Jax was moving. He sprang from the concealing shadows, daggers in both hands. He caught the two members of the squad nearest him and killed both with a single pass. The others whirled, weapons coming up defensively, still confused by the unexpected attack. But by now Helt and Foraker had appeared as well, and three more fell without a sound. The Gnomes who remained bolted down the pathway onto the slide, yelling wildly. Springing onto the rocks, Edain Elessedil brought up his bow. The bowstring hummed twice and two more died. The final Hunter scrambled wildly from sight and was gone.

Quickly the members of the little company rushed to the edge of the boulders. Shouts of alarm had already begun to ring out from the mass of watchfires below.

"Well, we're in for it now!" Foraker snapped angrily. "Every Gnome on both sides of these cliffs will be looking for us in the next few minutes!"

Garet Jax calmly slipped the daggers back beneath the black cloak and turned to the Dwarf. "Which way do we run?"

Foraker hesitated. "Back the way we came. The heights, if we can gain them in time; if not, we find one of the tunnels into Capaal."

"You lead." Garet Jax motioned swiftly. "Remember—stay together. If we become separated, try to stay with someone. Now, go!"

They raced back up the narrow trail into the night. Behind them, the shouts and cries of the Gnome watch continued to sound, spreading across the whole of the slide. Ignoring the pursuit, the six scrambled along the empty pathway until they had rounded once more the side of the peak and the lights of the encampment behind them were lost in the dark.

Ahead, the watchfires of the siege flickered into view. Still far below the trail they followed, the main body of the Gnome army had not yet had time to discover what was happening. Torches wavered in the darkness as sentries scrambled up from their watchfires and began to spread out onto the cliffs, but the hunt was still well below the six. Foraker took them swiftly along the darkened ledge, down slides and drops, and through shadowed defiles. If they were quick enough, they might yet escape back the way they had come, through the peaks about Capaal. If they were not, the search to find them would spread upward into the rocks, and they would find themselves trapped between the two armies.

Shouts of alarm broke suddenly from somewhere ahead, lost in the darkness of the rocks. Foraker muttered a low oath, but didn't slow. Jair stumbled, sprawling wildly onto the rocks, scraping arms and legs. From behind, Helt lifted him back to his feet and pulled him roughly on.

Then they burst from the concealment of a defile onto a broad trail atop a slide directly into the path of an entire Gnome watch. Gnomes came at them from everywhere, swords and spears glinting in the firelight. Garet Jax spun into them, short sword and long knife cutting a path for the others. Gnomes fell dying all about the Weapons Master, and for an instant the entire watch shrank from the fury of this dark attacker. Desperately, the little company tried to force passage through, Elb Foraker and Edain Elessedil leading the way. But there were too many Gnomes. Rallying, they closed off the trail ahead and counterattacked. They surged down the cliff face, howling in rage. Foraker and Edain Elessedil disappeared from view. Helt stood against the assault for just an instant, his giant form flinging Gnomes aside as they sought to pull him down. But even the Borderman could not withstand so many. Sheer numbers forced him from the ledge, and he tumbled from sight.

Jair stumbled back in dismay, alone now. Even Slanter had disappeared. But then Garet Jax was there once more, a black form slipping past the Gnome Hunters who sought to slow him. In an instant he was next to Jair, sweeping the Valeman before him, turning him back into the defile.

Alone, the two retraced their steps hurriedly through the darkness. Shouts of pursuit followed after, and a flicker of torchlight chased their shadows. At the far end of the defile, the Weapons Master gave a quick glance upward at the sheer cliff face, then pulled Jair after him as he worked his way down a scrub-covered drop toward the mass of siege fires that twinkled below. Jair was too stunned by what had happened to the others of the company to question the decision. Slanter, Foraker, Helt and Edain Elessedil—all lost in an instant's time. He could not believe it.

Halfway to the bottom of the drop was a small pathway, barely wide enough for a single man. It was deserted—for the moment, at least. Crouching within a small bit of brush, Garet Jax searched quickly the land about

him. Jair searched with him and saw no way out. The Gnomes were all
about them. Torches flickered on the paths above as well as the broader
ledges and trails below. Sweat ran down the Valeman's back, and his own
breathing sounded harsh in his ears.

"What are we . . . ?" he started to ask, but the Weapons Master's hand
clamped about his mouth instantly.

Then they were on their feet again, bent down within the rocks as
they scrambled east along the narrow path. Boulders and jagged projections rose up against the faint light of the sky, thrusting out from the cliff
face. They ran on, and the path ahead grew less easy. Jair risked a quick
glance back. A line of torches was coiling up the slope from the siege camp
below, up to where they had just knelt within the brush. Moments later,
the torches were upon the trail.

The Weapons Master slipped down into the jumbled rocks, with Jair a
step behind him, scrambling wildly to keep his feet. Ahead, the cliff face
jutted far out into the night sky, and the slope beneath where they climbed
began to drop away sharply. Jair felt a sinking sensation in his stomach.
This was a dead end. They were not going to get through.

Still Garet Jax worked his way forward, easing downward through the
rocks, climbing farther out onto the cliffs. Behind, the torches followed after, and all across the length and breadth of the chasm that sheltered the
locks and dams of Capaal the cries of the Gnome Hunters rang out.

Then at last the Weapons Master drew to a halt. The trail fell away in a
sheer cliff a dozen yards further on. Far below, the waters of the Cillidellan
reflected with firelight. Jair glanced quickly above where they stood. There,
too, the cliff angled sharply out. There was nowhere left for them to go
but back. They were trapped.

Garet Jax put a hand on his shoulder and led him forward to where the
trail fell away completely. Then he turned.

"We have to jump," he said softly, his hand still gripping the Valeman.
"Just lock your legs and pull in your arms. I'll be right behind you."

Jair glanced down to where the Cillidellan shimmered. It was a long,
long way. He looked back again at the Weapons Master.

"It's the only choice we have left." The other's voice was calm and reassuring. "Hurry, now."

The torches grew closer on the pathway behind them. Guttural voices
called sharply to one another.

"Hurry, Jair."

Jair took a deep breath, closed his eyes, opened them again and
jumped.

So violent was the Gnome counterattack, as the six from Culhaven sought
to break through the heights above Capaal, that the initial rush carried
most of the attackers right past Foraker and Edain Elessedil. Thrown back
against the cliff face as the assault swept on toward the others, Dwarf and
Elven Prince scrambled upward into a stand of brush, a handful of Gnomes

in desperate pursuit. They turned to fight at a small outcropping, the Elf swinging the sturdy ash bow, the Dwarf stabbing out with short sword and long knife. The Gnomes tumbled, howling with pain, and the pursuit fell back for an instant. The two companions peered down at the ledge and the steep slide below, swarming now with Gnome Hunters. There was no sign of the others.

"This way!" Elb Foraker called, pulling the Elven Prince after him.

They scrambled up the slope, scratching and clawing their way over the loose earth and rock. Cries of anger followed after, and suddenly arrows flew past them, a vicious hissing in their ears. Torches bobbed in the darkness, searching them out, but for the moment at least, they were beyond the light.

A roar sounded from somewhere below, and the pursued companions looked back apprehensively. The lights of the watchfires seemed to be spreading out across the cliff face, bits of fire darting about in the blackness. Hundreds more flickered into view on the dark line of the peaks south—torches from the army that lay camped along the banks of the Cillidellan. The whole of the mountainside now burned bright with flame.

"Elb, they're all around us!" the Elven Prince cried out, staggered by the number of the enemy.

"Keep climbing!" the other snapped.

Onward they went, fighting their way through the dark. Now a new cluster of torches appeared to their right, and shouts of discovery broke from the throats of the Gnomes who bore them. Spears and arrows whistled all about the two who climbed. Foraker scrambled away from them, eyes searching frantically across the dark cliff face.

"Elb!" Edain Elessedil screamed in pain and spun about, his shoulder pierced by a dart.

Instantly the Dwarf was at his side. "Ahead—another dozen feet to that patch of scrub! Hurry!"

Half carrying the injured Elven Prince, Foraker scrambled toward a broad thatch of brush that loomed suddenly out of the night. Torchlight flickered above them now as well, Gnome Hunters coming down from high off the slopes of the peak where the search lines cordoned off all escape. Edain Elessedil set his teeth against the pain in his shoulder and struggled forward with the Dwarf.

They tumbled into the brush, down into the concealing shadows to lie panting on the earth.

"They'll . . . find us here," the Elven Prince gasped, forcing himself to his knees. Across his back, blood and sweat mingled and ran.

Foraker yanked him down again. "Stay put!" Wheeling, he began groping his way through the brush until he found the slope against which it grew. "Here! A tunnel door! Thought I'd remembered right, but . . . have to find the trip lock . . ."

While Edain Elessedil watched, he began to fumble frantically about the slope face, through crumbling rock and earth, pulling and clawing in silent desperation. The cries of their pursuers were drawing steadily closer. Through faint breaks in the brush appeared the flicker of torchlight, bobbing and weaving against the black.

"Elb, they're almost here!" Edain whispered hoarsely. His hand reached down to his waist and drew forth the short sword belted there.

"Got it!" the Dwarf cried triumphantly.

A squarish chunk of rock and earth swung back, and an opening in the cliff face yawned before them. Frantically, they scrambled through into the darkness beyond, and Foraker pulled shut the rock behind them. It closed ponderously, sealing them away with a series of sharp clicks, the locks fastening in place.

They lay in the dark for long moments, listening to the faint sounds of the Gnomes without. Then the pursuit passed on, and there was only silence. A moment later Foraker began groping about in the dark. Flint and stone struck a spark, and harsh yellow torchlight filled the void. They sat within a small cave from which a stone stairway ran downward into the mountain.

Foraker slid the torch into an iron bracket next to the sealed door and began working on the Elven Prince's injured shoulder. In a few minutes' time, he had the arm bound and wrapped in a makeshift sling.

"That should do for now," he muttered. "Can you walk?"

The Elf nodded. "What about the door? Suppose the Gnomes find it?"

"Too bad for them if they do," Foraker snorted. "The locks should hold it; but if they don't, a break-in will trigger a collapse of the whole entrance. On your feet, now. We've got to go."

"Where do the stairs lead?"

"Down. Into Capaal." He shook his head. "Have to hope the others will find some different way to get there."

He helped Edain to his feet, pulling the Elf's good arm over his shoulder. Then he snatched the torch from its rack.

"Hold tight, now."

Slowly, they began their descent.

The Borderman Helt tumbled headlong down the steep slide, weapons flying from him as he fell, the maddened struggle on the cliff ledge left behind. Lights and sound whirled about him as he went, a jumble that spun and faded in his mind. Then came a jarring halt, and he found himself wedged within a mass of brush at the slide's bottom, sprawled in a tangle of arms and legs. He lay dazed for a minute, the breath knocked from his body. Gingerly he tried to extricate himself from the tangle. It was then that he realized that not all of the arms and legs were his own.

"Easy!" a voice hissed in his ear. "Half broke me in two already!"

The Borderman started. "Slanter?"

"Keep it down!" the other snapped. "They're all around us!"

Helt lifted his head carefully and blinked his eyes against the dizziness.

Torchlight flickered close by, and there were voices calling back and forth through the darkness. He realized suddenly that he lay on top of the little Gnome. With great care, he lifted himself clear of the other, coming unsteadily to his knees within the shadow of the brush.

"Took me right off the ledge with you!" Slanter muttered, disbelief and anger mingling in his voice. The gnarled body straightened, and he peered carefully about through the scrub, the distant firelight reflected in his eyes. "Oh, shades!" he groaned.

Helt came to a low crouch, staring out into the dark. Behind them, the slide down which they had fallen loomed like a wall against the night. Before them, spread out for hundreds of yards in all directions in a mass of blazing yellow light, were the watchfires of the Gnome army that encircled the fortress of Capaal. Helt studied the fires wordlessly for a moment, then dropped back into the brush, Slanter beside him.

"We're right in the middle of the siege camp," he said quietly.

Already there were torches lining the ledge from which they had fallen, far distant yet unmistakable in their purpose. The Gnomes on the ledge were coming down after them.

"We can't stay here." Helt came to his feet once more, eyes peering out through the brush at the Gnome Hunters about them.

"Well, where do you suggest we go, Borderman?" Slanter snapped.

Helt shook his head slowly. "Perhaps along the slide . . ."

"The slide? Perhaps we can fly while we're at it!" Slanter shook his head. The Gnome Hunters were calling down into the camp from the ledge. "No way out of this one," he muttered bitterly. He cast about futilely for a moment, then paused. "Unless, of course, you happen to be a Gnome."

His rough yellow face swung about to find Helt. The Borderman stared back at him wordlessly, waiting. "Or perhaps one of the walkers," he added.

Helt shook his head slowly. "What are you talking about?"

Slanter bent close. "Must be mad even to consider this, but I guess it's no madder than anything else that's happened. You and me, Borderman. Black walker and Gnome servant. Pull that cloak about you, hood about your head, no one'll know. You're big enough for it. Walk right through them, you and me—right up to the gates of that fortress. Hope to all that's good and right that the Dwarves open up long enough for us to slip in."

Shouts rose from off to their left. Helt glanced over quickly, then back again. "You could do all this without me, Slanter. You could get out on your own a lot easier than if I'm with you."

"Don't tempt me!" the Gnome snapped.

The gentle eyes were steady. "They're your people. You could still go back to them."

Slanter seemed to think it over for a moment. Then he shook his head roughly. "Forget it. I'd have that black devil Weapons Master tracking me all through the Four Lands. I'm not risking that." The hard yellow face seemed to stiffen further. "And there's the boy . . ."

His eyes snapped up. "Well, do we try it or not, Borderman?"

Helt rose, pulling his cloak close about him. "We try it."

They strode clear of the brush, Slanter with his cloak thrown wide so that all could see it was a Gnome who led the way, Helt with his drawn close, a massive, hooded giant towering above the other. They passed boldly down through the spokes of the siege lines toward where the army massed before the fortress walls, staying carefully within the darkness between those lines so that they could not be clearly seen. They walked for nearly fifty yards, and no one gave challenge.

Then a cross line blocked their way forward, and there was no longer any darkness left through which to pass. Slanter never hesitated. He stalked toward the watchfires, the cloaked figure following. The Gnome Hunters who were gathered there turned to gape, weapons lifting guardedly.

"Stand back!" Slanter called out sharply. "The Master comes!"

Eyes widened and fear reflected in the harsh yellow faces. Weapons lowered quickly, and all stood aside as the two figures passed, slipping into a square of half-light between the lines. Gnomes were all about them now, heads turning, eyes staring in surprise and curiosity. Still no one challenged, the tumult of the search on the slope drowning out everything else in the autumn night.

Another siege line lay ahead. Slanter lifted his arms dramatically to the Gnome Hunters who turned. "Give way to the Master, Gnomes!"

Again the lines parted to let them through. Sweat was pouring down Slanter's rough face as he glanced back at the shadowed figure behind him. Hundreds of eyes followed after them, and there was a faint stirring within the ranks of the Gnomes. A few were beginning to question what was happening.

The last of the forward lines of the siege lay before them. Here the Gnome Hunters again brought up their short spears menacingly, and there were disgruntled mutterings. Beyond the watchfires the dark walls of the Dwarf citadel rose up against the night and on their battlements, torches burned in solitary patches of hazy light.

"Stand away!" Slanter bellowed, again throwing up his arms. "Dark magic runs loose this night and the walls of the enemy keep shall crumble before it! Stand away! Let the walker pass!"

As if to emphasize the warning, the cloaked figure following lifted one arm slowly and pointed toward the watch.

That was enough for the Gnomes on the siege lines. Breaking ranks, they parted hurriedly, most of them scurrying back toward the second line of defense, casting anxious glances over their shoulders as they went. A few lingered, frowns on their faces as the two figures passed, but still no one stepped forward to offer challenge.

The Gnome and the Borderman walked into the night, eyes riveted now on the dark walls ahead. Slanter raised his hands high above his head as they approached, praying inwardly that this simple gesture would be enough to stay the deadly missiles surely pointed in their direction.

They were two dozen yards from the walls when a voice rang out. "Come no further, Gnome!"

Slanter drew to an immediate halt, arms lowering. "Open the gates!" he cried furtively. "We're friends!"

There was a low muttering on the walls, and a call down to someone below. But the gates remained closed. Slanter glanced about frantically. Behind where he and Helt stood watching, the Gnomes were stirring once more.

"Who are you?" the voice from atop the wall called out again.

"Open the gates, you fool!" Slanter's patience was gone.

Now Helt came forward to stand beside the Gnome. "Callahorn!" he called out in a hoarse whisper.

Behind them, a chorus of howls rose up from the Gnomes. The game was up. The two broke for the fortress walls in a mad dash, calling to the Dwarves within. They dashed up against the iron-bound gates, casting desperate glances back as they ran. An entire line of Gnome Hunters swept toward them, torches bobbing wildly, cries of rage breaking from their throats. Spears and arrows launched through the dark.

"Oh, shades, open up in there, you . . . !" Slanter bawled.

Abruptly the gates swung open and hands reached out to yank them through. An instant later they were within the fortress, the gates slamming shut behind them as renewed howls of fury filled the night. They were thrown to the ground, and iron-tipped spears ringed them tightly.

Slanter shook his head in disgust and glanced over at Helt. "You explain it to them, Borderman," he muttered. "Even if I wanted to, I don't think I could."

Jair Ohmsford fell a long way into the Cillidellan. Downward he plunged, a tiny speck of darkness against the deep blue-gray of the night sky, the pit of his stomach dropping away, the rush of the wind filling his ears with its sound. Far below him the waters of the lake shimmered with bits of crimson light as the watchfires of the Gnomes reflected against their rippling surface, and all about him the vast sweep of the mountains and cliffs encircling Capaal rose up through the blur of his vision. Time seemed to come to a sudden standstill, and it felt as if he would never come to rest.

Then he struck with jarring force, breaking through the surface of the lake and plunging deep into the cold, dark waters. The breath left his lungs with stunning suddenness, and his whole body went numb with shock. Frantically, he clawed his way through the chill blackness that had closed about him, barely conscious of anything beyond his need to reach the surface once more so that he could breathe. The heat from his body dissipated in seconds, and he felt a crushing force pressing in against him, so terrible that it threatened to break him in two. He struggled upward, desperate with need. Lights danced before his eyes and his arms and legs seemed suddenly turned to lead. Weakly, he thrashed against their pull, lost in a maze of dark turns.

A moment later, everything slipped away from him.

He dreamed, a long, endless dream of disconnected feelings and sensations and of times and places both remembered and yet somehow new. Waves of sound and motion carried him through landscapes of nightmare and haunts of the familiar, through oft-traveled forest trails of the Vale, and through sweeps of black, cold water where life passed in tangled disarray in faces and shapes not fixed one to the other, but disjointed and free. Brin was there, come and gone in brief glimpses, a distorted form that combined reality with falsehood and begged for understanding. Words came at him from things misshapen and lifeless, yet her voice seemed to speak the words, calling to him, calling . . .

Then Garet Jax was holding him, arms wrapped tightly about his body, his voice a whisper of life in a dark place. Jair floated, the waters buoying him, and his face turned skyward into the clouded night. Gasping, he sought to talk and could not manage. He was awake again, come back from where he had slipped away, yet not fully conscious of what had befallen him or what he was about. He drifted in and out of darkness, reaching back each time he began to slide too far so that he might be grasped anew by the sound and color and feeling that meant life.

Then there were hands grasping him as well, pulling him up from the waters and the blackness, easing him down onto solid ground once more. Rough voices muttered vaguely, the fragmented words slipping through his mind like stray leaves blown by the wind. His eyes flickered, and Garet Jax was bending over him, lean brown face damp and drawn with the chill, fair hair plastered back against his head.

"Valeman, can you hear me? It's all right. You're all right now."

Other faces pushed into view—blocky Dwarf faces, resolute and grave as they studied his. He swallowed, choked and mumbled something incoherent.

"Don't try to talk," one said gruffly. "Just rest."

He nodded. Hands wrapped him in blankets, then lifted him up and began to carry him away.

"Sure has been a night for strays." Another voice chuckled.

Jair tried to look back to where the voice had come from, but he could not seem to focus his sense of direction. He let himself sink downward into the warmth of the blankets, eased by the gentle rocking of the hands that bore him.

A moment later, he was asleep.

19

It was midday of the next day when Jair awoke again. He might not have come awake even then were it not for the hands that shook him none too gently from his slumber and the rough voice that whispered in his ear, "Wake up, boy! You've slept long enough! Come on, wake up!"

Grudgingly, he stirred within the blankets that covered him, rolled onto his back and rubbed the sleep from his eyes. Gray sunlight filtered through a narrow window next to his head, causing him to squint against its brightness.

"Come on, the day's almost gone! Been shut away the whole of it, thanks to you!"

Jair's eyes shifted to find the speaker, a stoutly familiar figure positioned at the side of his bed. "Slanter?" he whispered in disbelief.

"Now who else would it be?" the other snapped.

Jair blinked. "Slanter?"

Abruptly the events of the previous night recalled themselves to his mind in a flood of images: the flight from the Gnomes in the mountains about Capaal; the separation of the company; the long drop into the Cillidellan with Garet Jax; and their subsequent rescue from its waters by the Dwarves. You're all right now, the Weapons Master had whispered to him. He blinked again. But Slanter and the others . . .

"Slanter!" he exclaimed, now fully awake. Hastily, he pushed himself upright. "Slanter, you're alive!"

"Of course I'm alive! What does it look like?"

"But how did. . . ?" Jair left the question hanging and grasped the Gnome's arm anxiously. "What about the others? What's happened to them? Are they all right?"

"Slow down, will you?" The Gnome freed his arm irritably. "They're all fine and they're all here, so stop worrying. The Elf took a dart in the shoulder, but he'll live. Only one who's in danger at the moment is me. And that's because I'm shut up in this room with you, dying of boredom! Now will you climb out of that bed so we can get out of here?"

Jair didn't hear all of what the Gnome was saying. Everyone's all right, he was repeating to himself. Everyone made it. No one was lost, even though it had seemed certain that some of them must be. He breathed deeply in relief. Something the King of the Silver River had said recalled itself suddenly to his mind. A touch of magic for each who journey with you, the old man had told him. Strength for the body, given to others. Perhaps that strength, that touch of the magic, had seen each of them safely through last night.

"Get up, get up, get up!" Slanter was practically hopping up and down with impatience. "What are you doing just sitting there?"

Jair swung his legs out of the bed and glanced about the room in which he found himself. It was a small, stone block chamber, sparsely furnished with bed, sitting table, and chairs, its walls bare save for a broad heraldic tapestry hung from the far supports of its sloped ceiling. A second window opened out at the other end of the wall against which Jair's bed rested, and a single wooden door stood closed, opposite where he sat. In one corner, a small fireplace cradled an iron gate and a stack of burning logs.

He glanced at Slanter. "Where are we?"

Slanter looked at him as if he were a complete idiot. "Now where do you think we are? We're inside the Dwarf fortress!"

Where else? Jair thought ruefully. Slowly he stood up, still testing his strength as he stretched and peered curiously out of the window in back of him. Through its narrow, barred slot he could see the murky gray expanse of the Cillidellan stretching away into a day thick with mist and low-hanging clouds. Far distant, through this shifting haze, he could discern the flicker of watchfires burning along the shores of the lake.

Gnome watchfires.

Then he noticed how quiet it was. He was within the fortress of Capaal, the Dwarf citadel that stood watch over the locks and dams that regulated the flow of the Silver River westward, the citadel that one day earlier had been under assault by Gnome armies. Where were those armies now? Why wasn't Capaal under attack?

"Slanter, what's happened to the siege?" he asked quickly. "Why is it so still?"

"How should I know?" the other snapped. "No one tells me anything!"

"Well, what's happening out there? What have you seen?"

Slanter jerked upright. "Haven't heard a word I've said, have you? What's the problem—ears not working or something? I've been right here in this room with you ever since they dragged you out of the lake! Shut away like a common thief! Saved that confounded Borderman's skin out there and what do I get for my trouble? Shut in here with you!"

"Well, I . . ."

"A Gnome's a Gnome, they think! Don't trust any of us! So here I sit, mother hen to you while you slumber on like you don't have a care in the world. Waited all day for you to decide to wake up! You'd be sleeping still, I suppose, if I hadn't lost patience entirely!"

Jair drew back. "You could have woken me sooner . . ."

"How could I do that!" the other exploded. "How was I to know what was wrong with you? Could have been anything! Had to let you rest just to be sure! Couldn't be taking chances, could I? That black devil Weapons Master would have had me flayed!"

Jair grinned in spite of himself. "Calm down, will you?"

The Gnome clenched his teeth. "I'll calm down when you get yourself out of that bed and into your clothes! There's a guard on the other side of that door keeping me shut up in here! But with you awake, maybe we can talk him into letting the two of us out! Then you can be amused on your own time! Now, dress!"

Shrugging, Jair slipped off the night clothes that had been provided him and began pulling on his Vale clothes. He was surprised, though pleased, to find Slanter so vocal again, even if his discourse was, for the moment at least, limited to a tirade against the Valeman. Slanter seemed more his normal self again, more that voluble fellow he had been that first night after making Jair his prisoner in the highlands—that fellow Jair had come to like. He wasn't sure why the Gnome had chosen now to come out of his shell, but he was delighted to have the old Slanter back as company once more.

"Sorry you had to be locked in here with me," he ventured after a moment.

"You ought to be," the other grumbled. "They put me in here to look after you, you know. Must think I make a good nursemaid or something."

Jair grinned. "I'd say they're right."

The expression that crossed the Gnome's face then caused Jair to turn away quickly, his face a carefully frozen mask. Chuckling inwardly, he was in the process of reaching for his boots when he abruptly remembered the vision crystal and the Silver Dust. He had not seen either while dressing. He had not felt them in his pockets. The grin he had allowed to slip back over his face faded. He ran his hands over his clothing. Nothing! Frantically, he pawed through his bedding, his bedclothes, and everything in sight. The vision crystal and the Silver Dust were gone. Then he thought back to the night previous, to the long jump into the Cillidellan. Had he lost them in the lake?

"Looking for something?"

Jair stiffened. It was Slanter speaking, his voice laced with false concern. Jair turned. "Slanter, what have you done . . . ?"

"Me?" the other interrupted quickly, feigned innocence in the crafty face. "Your devoted nursemaid?"

Jair was furious. "Where are they, Slanter? Where did you put them?"

Now it was the Gnome's turn to grin. "Enjoyable as this is—and believe me, it is enjoyable—I have better things to do. So if it's the pouch and the crystal you're looking for, the Weapons Master has them. Took them off you last night when they brought you in here and stripped you. Wouldn't trust them to my care, of course."

He folded his arms across his chest contentedly. "Now let's put an end to this. Or do you need help dressing, too?"

Jair flushed, finished dressing, then wordlessly walked over to the wooden door and knocked. When the door opened, he informed the Dwarf standing guard that they would like to go out. The Dwarf frowned, told them to stay put, glanced suspiciously at Slanter, and pulled the door firmly shut again.

Growing curiosity over the absence of any sort of battle without and impatience with things in general notwithstanding, they had to wait fully an hour before the door to the room opened a second time, and the guard at last beckoned them to follow. Leaving the room hastily, they turned down a windowless corridor that ran past dozens of doors similar to the one they had just passed through, climbed a series of stairs, and emerged on battlements overlooking the murky waters of the Cillidellan. Wind and a faint spray blew off the lake into their faces, the midday air chill and hard. Here, too, the day was still and expectant, cloaked in mist and banks of low-hanging clouds that stretched between the peaks that sheltered the locks and dams. Dwarf sentries patrolled the walls, eyes shifting watchfully through the haze. There was no sign of the Gnome armies, save for the distant flicker of the watchfires, reddish specks of light in the gray.

The Dwarf took them down off the battlements, turning into a broad courtyard that spanned the center of the high dam where it walled away the Cillidellan. North and south of where they walked, the towers and parapets of the Dwarf fortress rose up against the leaden sky, stretching away into mist. It was an eerie, ghostly look that the day lent to the citadel, shrouding it in half-light and haze so that it almost seemed as if it were something strayed from a dream that threatened to be gone in a moment's time upon waking. Few Dwarves were in evidence here, the vast courtyard all but deserted. Stairwells burrowed down into the stone at regular intervals—black tunnels that Jair presumed must run to the inner workings of the locks below.

They had almost crossed the empty courtyard when a shout brought them up short, and Edain Elessedil came running to greet them. Grinning broadly, his injured arm and shoulder heavily wrapped, he went to Jair at once and extended his hand in greeting.

"Safe and sound after all, Jair Ohmsford!" He put his good arm about the other as they turned once more to follow their taciturn guide. "Feeling better, I hope?"

"Much better." Jair smiled back. "How is your arm?"

"Just a small scratch. A little stiff and nothing more. But what a night! Lucky that any of us got through safely. And this one!" He indicated Slanter, who trailed a step behind. "His escape was nothing short of miraculous! Did he tell you?"

Jair shook his head, and Edain Elessedil promptly informed him of all that had befallen Slanter and Helt during their harrowing walk through the Gnome encampment the previous night. Jair listened with growing astonishment, casting more than one glance back at the Gnome. Beneath a mask of studied indifference, Slanter was looking a bit embarrassed by all the attention.

"Simplest way out, that's all," Slanter announced gruffly when the effusive Elf had finished his tale. Jair was smart enough not to make anything more out of it.

Their guide took them up a stairway onto the battlement on the northern watch, then led them through a set of double-doors into an atrium filled with plants and trees, flourishing in an obviously transplanted bed of black earth beneath glass and open sky. Even here, within the high mountains, the Dwarves carried with them something of their home, Jair thought in admiration.

Beyond the gardens lay a terrace occupied by tables and benches.

"Wait here," the Dwarf ordered and left them.

When he had gone, Jair turned back to Edain. "Why is there no battle being fought this day, Elven Prince? What of the Gnome armies?"

Edain Elessedil shook his head. "No one seems certain what has happened. The locks and dams have been under siege for almost a week. Each day, the Gnomes attack both exposures of the fortress. But today, no attack has come. The Gnomes gather at their siege lines and watch us—nothing more. It appears as if they are waiting for something."

"I don't like the sound of that," Slanter muttered.

"Nor do the Dwarves," Edain said quietly. "Runners have been sent to Culhaven and scouts slip through the underground tunnels to the rear of the Gnome army to keep watch." He hesitated, then glanced at Jair. "Garet Jax is out there, too."

Jair started. "He is? Why? Where has he gone?"

"I don't know," the Elf shook his head slowly. "He said nothing to me. I don't think he's left us. I think he's simply out looking around. He took Helt with him."

"Scouting on his own, then." Slanter frowned. "He would do that."

"Who can say?" The Elf tried a quick smile. "The Weapons Master keeps his own counsel, Slanter."

"Dark reasons and dark purposes drive that one," the Gnome muttered, almost to himself.

They stood in silence then for a few moments, not looking at each other, lost in their private speculations of the actions of Garet Jax. Jair remembered Slanter telling him that it was the Weapons Master who had possession now of the vision crystal and the Silver Dust. That meant that if anything were to happen to Garet Jax, the magic of the King of the Silver River would be lost. And that meant that Jair's only chance of helping Brin would be lost as well.

The sound of the door opening brought them about, and Foraker appeared from out of the fortress. He came quickly to where they stood and greeted each with a handshake.

"Rested, Ohmsford?" he asked gruffly, and Jair nodded. "Good. I've asked that dinner be brought to us here on the terrace, so why don't we find a table and sit?"

He motioned to the table closest to them, and the other three joined him there. The trees and shrubs of the gardens darkened further the gray cast of the late afternoon, so candles were lighted against the gloom. Moments later, a meal of beef, cheese, bread, soup, and ale was brought, and they began to eat. Jair was surprised to discover how hungry he was.

When the meal was finished, Foraker pushed back from the table and began fishing through his pockets. "I have something for you." He glanced briefly toward Jair. "Ah-ha, here we are."

He held in his hand the bag of Silver Dust and the vision crystal on its silver chain. He pushed them across the table to the Valeman. "Garet said to give these to you. Said to keep them safe until you woke. He had a message for you, too. He said to tell you that you showed courage last night."

Surprise flashed over the Valeman's face, and he experienced a sudden, intense feeling of pride. He glanced self-consciously at Edain Elessedil and Slanter, then back to the Dwarf.

"Where is he now?" he stammered.

Foraker shrugged. "He's gone with the Borderman to explore a passage that will take us out from the fortress behind the Gnome siege lines north. He wants to be certain it's safe before we all go. And we go at nightfall tomorrow. Can't wait any longer on the siege; it may go on for months. We've been shut away too long already for his taste."

"Some of us have been more shut away than others," Slanter grumbled pointedly.

Foraker faced him, brows knitting fiercely. "We have vouched for you, Gnome—all those who came with you from Culhaven. Radhomm, who commands this garrison, feels that our word is enough. But there are some within these walls who feel much differently—some who have lost friends and loved ones to the Gnomes who lay siege without. For them, our assurance may not be enough. You have been kept under guard not as a prisoner, but as a charge. Your safety is of some concern, believe it or not—particularly to Ohmsford here."

"I can look after myself," Slanter muttered darkly. "And I don't need anyone's concern—especially this boy's!"

Foraker stiffened. "That ought to come as good news to him!" he snapped.

Slanter lapsed into silence. He withdraws into himself again, thought Jair; he shields himself from everything happening about him. It is only when he is alone with me that he seems to be willing to come out of that protective shell. It is only then that he seems to recover even a bit of the old Slanter he showed when we first met. The balance of the time he is an outsider, a self-proclaimed loner, unaccepting of his role as a member of our little company.

"Did our message get through?" Edain Elessedil was asking Foraker. "About the destruction of the bridge at the Wedge?"

"It did." The Dwarf removed his dark gaze from Slanter. "Your plan was well conceived, Elven Prince. Had we known better the extent of this siege and the army that mounts it, we might have escaped in the bargain."

"Are we in danger here, then?"

"No, the fortress is secure. Stores are plentiful enough to withstand a siege of months if need be. And no army can bring the whole of its strength to bear with the mountains so close. Any danger to us will be found outside these walls when we resume our journey north."

At his elbow, Slanter muttered something unintelligible and drained the remainder of his ale. Foraker glanced at the Gnome and his bearded face tightened. "In the meantime, there is something that must be done—and you and I, Gnome, must do it."

Slanter's eyes lifted guardedly. "What is it we must do—Dwarf?"

Foraker's face darkened further, but his voice stayed calm. "There is someone within these walls who claims to know well the castle of the Mord Wraiths—someone who claims to know it better than anyone. If true, that knowledge could be of great use to us."

"If true, then you have no further use for me!" Slanter snapped. "What have I to do with this?"

"The knowledge is of use only if it is true," Foraker continued carefully. "The only one who can tell us that is you."

"Me?" The Gnome laughed mirthlessly. "You would trust me to tell you whether or not what you are being told is the truth? Why should you do that? Or do you think to test me? That seems more likely, I think. You would test what I tell you against what another says!"

"Slanter!" Jair admonished the Gnome, a flush of anger and disappointment stealing through him.

"You are the one who mistrusts," Edain Elessedil added firmly.

Slanter started to respond, then thought better of it and went still.

It was Foraker who spoke then, low and pointed. "If I thought to test you, it would not be against this one."

The table was silent. "Who is it?" Slanter asked finally.

The Dwarf's fierce brows knitted. "A Mwellret."

Slanter went rigid. "A Mwellret?" he growled. "A lizard?"

He said it with such loathing that Jair Ohmsford and Edain Elessedil looked at each other in astonishment. Neither had ever seen a Mwellret. Neither had even heard of one until now, and both, having witnessed the Gnome's reaction to the mention of one, wondered if perhaps they would have been better off remaining ignorant.

"One of Radhomm's patrols found him washed up at the edge of the lake a day or two before the siege," Foraker went on, his eyes holding Slanter's. "More dead than alive when they pulled him out. Mumbled something about being driven from the Ravenshorn by the black walkers. Said that he knew ways in which they could be destroyed. The patrol brought him here. Didn't have time to get him out before the siege." He paused. "Until now, there had been no way to test the truth of what he has to say."

"The truth!" Slanter spit. "There is no truth in the lizards!"

"Revenge against those he feels have wronged him may bring out the truth. We can offer him that revenge—a trade, perhaps. Think carefully. He must know the secrets of the Ravenshorn and Graymark. Those mountains were once his. The castle was his."

"Nothing was ever his!" Slanter came out of his chair with a lunge, stiff with anger. "They took it all, the lizards did! Built their castle on the

bones of my people! Made slaves of the Gnome tribes living in the mountains! Used the dark magic like the walkers! Black devils, I would as soon
cut my own throat as give them an instant's trust!"

Jair thought to intercede, rising as well. "Slanter, what. . . ?"

"A moment, Ohmsford," Foraker cut him short. The fierce countenance turned again to Slanter. "Gnome, I give the Mwellrets no more trust
than you. But if this one can help, then let us take whatever help we find.
Our task is difficult enough as it is. And if we find that the Mwellret lies . . .
well, then we know what can be done with him."

Slanter glared down at the table in front of him wordlessly for a moment,
then slowly reseated himself. "It is a waste of time. Go without me. Use
your own judgment, Foraker."

The Dwarf shrugged. "I thought that this would be preferable to be-
ing left under lock and key. I thought you might have had enough of that."
He paused, watching the dark eyes of the Gnome snap up to find his own.
"Besides, my judgment is useless in determining whether or not the
Mwellret speaks the truth. You are the only one who can help us with
that."

For a moment, no one spoke. Slanter's eyes remained locked on Foraker.
"Where is the Mwellret now?" he asked finally.

"In a storage room that serves as his cell," Foraker answered. "He
never comes out, even to walk. Doesn't like the air and the light."

"Black devil!" the Gnome muttered in response. Then he sighed.
"Very well. You and me."

"These two as well, if they choose." Foraker indicated Jair and Edain.

"I'm coming," Jair announced at once.

"And I," the Elven Prince agreed.

Foraker rose to his feet and nodded. "I'll take you there now."

20

They went from the terrace gardens down into the bowels of the
locks and dams of Capaal. From the gray light of an afternoon
rapidly fading into dusk, they descended stairwells and passageways
that curled deep into stone and timber. Shadows gathered about small
pools of hazy light given off by the flames of oil lamps dangling from iron
brackets. The air trapped within the massive rock of the dam was stale and
damp. Through the silence that pervaded the lower levels came the distant
rush of waters flowing through the locks and the low grinding of great
wheels and levers. Closed doors came and went as the four passed deeper,
and there was the sense of a beast hidden somewhere within, stirring in

response to the sounds of the locks and their machinery, caged and waiting to break free.

They came upon few Dwarves within these levels of the fortress. A forest people who had survived the Great Wars by tunneling within the earth, the Dwarves had long since emerged from their underground prison into the sunlight and in so doing had vowed never again to return. Their abhorrence of dark, closed places was well known among the people of the other races, and it was only with some difficulty that they managed to endure such closures. The locks and dams at Capaal were necessary to their existence, vital in the regulation of the waters of the Silver River as they flowed westward to their homeland, and so the sacrifice was made—but never for long and never more frequently than was required. Brief shifts to monitor the machinery that they had built to serve their purposes were followed by hasty exits back into the world of light and air above.

So it was that the few faces the four companions did come upon as they made their way downward bore a look of stoic endurance that barely masked an abiding distaste for this most unpleasant of duties.

Elb Foraker evidenced a trace of this, though he bore his discomfort well. His fierce, dark face was turned forward into the maze of corridors and stairwells, and his solid frame was erect and purposeful as he took his companions through lamplight and shadow toward the storage room yet further down. As they went, he told Jair and Edain Elessedil the story of the Mwellrets.

They were a species of Troll, he explained in beginning his tale. The Trolls had survived the Great Wars above the earth, exposed to the terrible effects of the energies those wars had unleashed. Mutated from the men and women they had once been, they had altered in form, their skin and body organs adapting to the frightening conditions the Great Wars had created over almost the whole of the earth's surface. Northland Trolls had survived within the mountains, grown huge and strong, their skin toughened until it had taken on the appearance of rough tree bark. But the Mwellrets were the descendants of men who had sought to survive within forests that the Great Wars had turned to swamp, the waters poisoned, the foliage diseased. Assuming the characteristics of creatures for whom swamp survival was most natural, the Mwellrets had taken on the look of reptiles. When Slanter called them lizards, he was describing them in truth as they now appeared—scaled over where skin had once been, arms and legs grown short and clawed, and bodies grown as flexible as snakes.

But there was a greater difference yet between the Mwellrets and the other species of Trolls that occupied the dark corners of the Four Lands. The Mwellrets' climb back up the ladder of civilization had been more rapid, and it had been marked by a strange and frightening ability to shape-change. Survival had made fearful demands upon the Mwellrets, as upon all of the Trolls; in the process of learning the secrets of that survival, they had undergone a physical transformation that enabled them to alter body shape with the pliability of oiled clay. Not so advanced in their art as to be able to disguise their basic characteristics, they nevertheless could shorten or elongate all of the parts of their bodies and could mold themselves in ways that would allow them to adapt to the demands of any environment in which they found themselves. Little was known as to how the shape-changing was done. It was enough to know that it could be done and to know that the Mwellrets were the only creatures who had mastered it.

Few beyond the borders of the Eastland knew of the Mwellrets, for they were a reclusive and solitary people who seldom ventured beyond the shelter of the deep Anar. No Mwellrets had come forth in the time of the Councils at Paranor. No Mwellrets had fought in the Wars of the Races. Withdrawn into their dark homeland, within forest, swamp, and mountain wilderness, they had kept themselves apart.

Except where the Gnome people were concerned, that was. Sometime after the First Council at Paranor, a time more than a thousand years earlier, the Mwellrets had migrated up from swampland and broken forest into the wooded heights of the Ravenshorn. Leaving the dank and fetid mire of the lowlands to the creatures with whom they had shared those regions since the destruction of the old world, the Mwellrets had drifted into the higher forestlands inhabited by scattered tribes of Gnomes. A superstitious people, the Gnomes had been terrified of these creatures who could change shape and who seemed to command elements of the dark magic that had been brought to life with the advent of the Druids. In time, the Mwellrets began to take advantage of that fear and to assert their authority over the tribes living within the Ravenshorn. Mwellrets assumed the role of chieftains, and the Gnomes were reduced to slaves.

At first, there was resistance to these creatures—these lizards, as they were called—but after a time all resistance ceased. The Gnomes were not strong enough or organized enough to fight back, and a few terrifying examples of what would be done to those who failed to submit made a lasting impression on the others. Under the rule of the Mwellrets, the fortress at Graymark was constructed—a massive citadel from which the lizards governed the tribes inhabiting the immediate region. Years passed, and the whole of the Ravenshorn fell under the sway of the Mwellrets. Dwarves to the south and Gnome tribes to the north and west stayed out of those mountains, and the Mwellrets in turn showed no inclination to venture beyond their newly adopted home. With the coming of the Warlock Lord in the Second War of the Races, it was rumored that a bargain had been struck in which the lizards offered a number of their Gnome subjects to serve the Dark Lord—but there was never anyone who could prove it for a fact.

Then with the conclusion of the aborted Third War of the Races—the war in which Shea Ohmsford had gone in search of the mystic Sword of Shannara and the Warlock Lord had been destroyed—the Mwellrets had unexpectedly begun to die out. Age and sickness began to deplete their numbers and only a handful of young were born into the world. As their numbers declined, so did their sway over the Gnome tribes in the Ravenshorn. Bit by bit, their small empire crumbled away until at last it was limited to Graymark and the few tribes that still remained within that region of the world.

"And now it seems that these last few, too, have been driven back into the swamps that bred them," Foraker concluded his tale. "Whatever their power, it was no match for that of the walkers. Like the Gnomes they ruled, they would become slaves as well, were they to remain within the mountains."

"Better they had been wiped from the face of the earth!" Slanter interjected bitterly. "They deserve no less!"

"Do they in truth possess the power of the dark magic?" Jair asked.

Foraker shrugged. "I've never seen it. The magic is in the shape-changing, I think. Oh, there are stories of the ways in which they affect the elements—wind, air, earth, fire, and water. Maybe there is some truth to that simply because they have developed an understanding of how the elements react to certain things. But for the most part, it is just superstition."

Slanter muttered something unintelligible and gave Jair a dark look that suggested he wasn't in complete agreement with the Dwarf.

"You will be safe enough, Ohmsford." Foraker smiled gravely. The dark brows lifted. "If he were foolish enough to use the magic within these walls, he would be dead quicker than you could blink!"

Ahead, the darkened corridor grew suddenly light, and the four approached an intersecting passageway and a line of doors stretching down to their right. A pair of sentries stood watch before the closest door. Hard eyes turned to oversee their approach. Foraker spoke a quick word in greeting and ordered that the door be opened. The sentries glanced at each other and shrugged.

"Take a light," the first said, passing Foraker an oil lamp. "The lizard keeps it black as pitch in there all the time."

Foraker lighted the lamp from the wick of one hanging beside the door, then glanced over at his companions. "Ready," he told the sentries.

Latch bolts released and a crossbar lifted. With a mournful groan, the ironbound door swung open into total blackness. Foraker started forward wordlessly, the other three a step behind. As the faint circle of the oil lamp penetrated the gloom, the humped and shadowed forms of crates, packing cases, and sack stores came into view. The Dwarf and his companions stopped.

Behind them, the door swung closed with a bang.

Jair glanced about the darkened room apprehensively. A rank and fetid odor permeated the air, a smell that whispered of things dying and fouled. Shadows lay over everything, deep and silent about their little light.

"Stythys?" Foraker spoke the name quietly.

For a long moment, there was no answer. Then from the shadows to their left, from out of a corner of crates and stores, a stirring broke the silence.

"Who iss it?" something hissed.

"Foraker," the Dwarf answered. "I've come to talk. Radhomm sent word to you that I would come."

"Hss!" The voice rasped like chain being dragged over stone. "Sspeak what you would, Dwarf."

Something moved within the shadows—something huge and cloaked like death itself. A shape appeared, vague and shadowy, rising up beside the stores. Jair felt a sudden, overwhelming repulsion for what was there. Keep very still, a voice within him warned. Say nothing!

"Little peopless," the figure murmured coldly. "Dwarf and Elvess and Gnome. Musstn't be frightened, little peopless. Sstep closser."

"Step closer yourself," Foraker snapped impatiently.

"Hss! Don't like the light. Need darknesss!"

Foraker shrugged. "Then we'll both stay where we are."

"Sstay," the other agreed.

Jair glanced quickly at Slanter. The Gnome's rough face was twisted in a mask of hatred and disgust, and he was sweating. He looked as if he might bolt at any moment. Edain Elessedil must have seen the look, too, for all at once he moved around Jair and Foraker and placed himself almost protectively on the other side of the distraught Gnome.

"I'm fine!" Slanter muttered almost inaudibly, brushing with his hand at the darkness before him.

Then abruptly the Mwellret came forward to the edge of the light, a tall, cloaked form that seemed to materialize from out of the shadows. Essentially man-shaped, it walked upright on two powerful hind legs, crooked and muscled. Forearms reached out tentatively, and where there should have been skin and hair there was only a covering of toughened gray scales ending in crooked claws. Within its cowl, the Mwellret's face turned toward them, reptilian snout lifting into the light, scaled and split wide to reveal rows of sharpened teeth and a serpent's tongue. Nostrils flared at the snout's blunt end; further up, almost lost within the cowl's darkness, slitted green eyes glimmered.

"Sstythyss knowss what bringss you, little peopless," the monster hissed slowly. "Knowss well."

There was silence. "Graymark," Foraker said finally.

"Wraithss," the other whispered. "Sstythyss knowss. Walkerss that desstroy. Come from out of the pitss, from the black hole of the Maelmord. From death! Climbss to Heaven'ss Well to poisson the waterss of the Ssilver River. Poisson the land. Desstroy it! Comess into Graymark, doess the evil. Comess to drive uss from our homess. Ensslave uss."

"You saw it happen?" Foraker asked.

"Ssaw it all! Wraithss come from darknesss, drive uss forth and sseize what iss ourss. No match for ssuch power. Flee! Ssome of uss desstroyed!"

Slanter spit suddenly into the darkness, muttering as he shifted back a step and kicked at the stone flooring.

"Sstay!" the Mwellret hissed suddenly, an unmistakable tone of command in its voice. Slanter's head snapped up. "Gnomess have no need to fear uss. Friendss have we been—not like the Wraithss. Wraithss desstroy all that iss life becausse they are not life. Thingss of death! The dark magic ruless. All the landss will fall to them."

"But you have a way to destroy them!" Foraker pressed.

"Hss! Graymark belongss to uss! Wraithss tresspasss in our home! Think themsselves ssafe with uss gone—but wrong. Wayss to get at them there! Wayss they do not know!"

"Passages!" Jair exclaimed suddenly, so intent on what the other was telling them that for an instant he forgot his vow.

At once the Mwellret's head snapped up, as if an animal testing the air. Jair went cold, a sense of something tremendously evil settling over him as he stood there in the sudden silence.

The Mwellret's serpent tongue snaked out. "Magicss, little friend? Magicss do you have?"

No one spoke. Jair was sweating violently. Foraker glanced about at him sharply, momentarily uncertain as to what had happened.

"In your voisse, little friend?" the Mwellret whispered. "Ssense it in your voisse, I do. Ssense it in you. Magicss like my own. Do it for me, yess? Sspeak!"

Something seemed to wrap itself about Jair, some invisible coil that squeezed the breath from him. Before he could help himself he began to sing. Quick and sharp, the wishsong slipped from between his clenched teeth and waves of color and shape rode the air between them, dancing through the darkness and lamplight like living things.

An instant later Jair was free again, the coils that had bound him gone. The wishsong died into silence. The Valeman gasped in shock and dropped weakly to his knees. Slanter was at his side at once, pulling him back toward the door, yelling wildly at the Mwellret, grappling with his free hand for Edain Elessedil's long knife. Hurriedly, Foraker parted them, his own sword drawn free as he turned to face Stythys. The Mwellret had suddenly shrunk in size, withdrawing into the shadows of the cowled robes, stepping back again into darkness.

"What did you do to him?" Foraker snapped. The Mwellret shrank back further, slitted eyes gleaming in the black. Foraker wheeled abruptly. "That's enough. We're leaving."

"Sstay!" the Mwellret wailed suddenly. "Sspeak with Sstythyss! Can tell you of the Wraithss!"

"Not interested anymore," Foraker replied, banging his sword handle against the storage room door.

"Hss! Musst talk with Sstythyss if you wissh the Wraithss desstroyed! Only I know how! Ssecretss mine!" the creature's voice was hard and impossibly cold now, all pretense of friendliness gone. "Little friendss will come back—musst come back! Be ssorry if you leave!"

"We're sorry we came!" Edain Elessedil threw back. "We don't need your help!"

Jair was walking through the open doorway now, supported on one side by the Elven Prince and on the other by Slanter, who was muttering every step of the way. Shaking his head to clear it, the Valeman glanced back at the Mwellret, a cloaked and faceless shape squeezed deep within the shadows as Foraker took his small light from the room.

"Needss my help!" the creature said softly, scaled arm lifting. "Comess again, little friendss! Comess back!"

Then the Dwarf sentries were closing and barring the storage room door once more, latch bolts and crossbars snapping tightly into place. Jair took a deep breath and straightened himself, shrugging free of the supporting arms. Foraker stopped him, peering closely into his eyes, grunted, and turned back down the passageway that had brought them.

"Guess you're all right," he announced. "Let's get back up into the air."

"What happened, Jair!" Edain Elessedil wanted to know. "How did he make you do that?"

Jair shook his head. "I'm not sure." Still shaken, he began walking after Foraker, the Elven Prince and the Gnome on either side. "I'm just not sure."

"Black devils!" Slanter muttered heatedly, invoking his favorite epithet. "They can twist you."

The Valeman nodded briefly and walked on. He wished he knew how that twisting had been done.

Night swept down about Capaal, black, misted and still. Moon and stars lay screened away from the mountain heights, and only the oil lamps of the Dwarves and watchfires of the Gnomes gave light to the shadowed dark. Frost began to form on stone and scrub, moisture freezing white as the temperature fell lower. An unpleasant stillness lay over everything.

Atop the battlements of the Dwarf fortress, Jair and Elb Foraker looked down upon the locks and dams that spanned the gap between the mountains where the Silver River flowed.

"More than five hundred years old now," the Dwarf was explaining, his voice low and rough against the night's silence. "Built in the time of Raybur, when our people still had kings. Built when the Second War of the Races was ended."

Jair stared wordlessly over the parapets into the darkness below, tracing the massive outline of the complex against the faint light of torches and lamps that lit its stone. There were three dams, broad bands curving back against the flow of the Silver River as it dropped downward to the gorge below. A series of locks regulated that flow, the machinery seated within and concealed by the dams and the fortress that protected both. The fortress sat astride the high dam, sprawled end to end and guarding all passageways leading in. Behind the high dam, the Cillidellan stretched away into blackness, ringed by the red watchfires of the siege army, yet oddly opaque in the moonless shadows of this night. Between the high dam and its lower levels, the Silver River pooled in two small reservoirs on its passage downward from the heights. Sheer cliffs flanked both ends of the lower levels, and the only way down was across catwalks or through underground passageways that tunneled into the rock.

"Gnomes would love to have this," Foraker grunted, his arm sweeping over the complex. "Controls nearly the whole of the water supply for the lands west to the Rainbow Lake. In the rainy seasons, without this, there would be flooding, as there used to be before the locks and dams were built to guard against it." He shook his head. "In a bad spring, even Culhaven would be swept away."

Jair looked about slowly, impressed with the size of the complex, awed by the effort that must have been expended in its construction. Foraker had already taken him on a tour through the inner workings of the locks and dams, explaining the machinery and the duties of those who tended it. Jair was grateful for the tour.

Slanter was absorbed in reworking Dwarf maps of the lands north to the Ravenshorn—maps, the Gnome had been quick to point out when they were shown him, which were entirely inaccurate. Anxious to avoid the necessity of a return to the storage room where the Mwellret was caged and determined to establish his own expertise, Slanter had agreed to make notations on the maps so that the little company would be properly advised as to the geography of the lands they must pass through during the journey that lay ahead. Edain Elessedil had excused himself and gone off on his own. When Foraker, therefore, had offered to show Jair something of the locks and dams, the Valeman had been quick to accept. Part of the reason for the tour, Jair suspected, was to take his mind off Garet Jax, who had still not returned. But that was all right, too. He preferred not to think about the missing Weapons Master.

"Cliffs don't allow the Gnomes a way down to the lower dams," Foraker was saying, eyes turned back toward the distant watchfires. "The fortress guards all passage that way. Our ancestors knew that well enough when they built Capaal. As long as the fortress stands, the locks and dams are safe. As long as the locks and dams are safe, the Silver River is safe."

"Except that it's being poisoned," Jair pointed out.

The Dwarf nodded. "It is. But it would be worse if the whole of the Cillidellan were let loose into the gorge. The poisoning would be quicker then—all the way west."

"Don't the other lands know this?" Jair asked quietly.

"They know."

"You would think they would be here to help you, in that case."

Foraker chuckled mirthlessly. "You would think so. But not everyone wants to believe the truth of things, you see. Some want to hide from it."

"Have any of the races agreed to aid you?"

The Dwarf shrugged. "Some. The Westland Elves are sending an army under Ander Elessedil. It's still two weeks away, though. Callahorn promises aid; Helt and a handful of others already fight with us. Nothing from the Trolls yet—but the Northern territories are vast and the tribes scattered. Perhaps they will at least help us along the northern borders."

He trailed off. Jair waited a moment, then asked, "And the Southland?"

"The Southland?" Foraker shook his head slowly. "The Southland has the Federation and its Coalition Council. A bunch of fools. Petty internal bickerings and power struggles occupy all of their energies. And the new Southland has no use for the peoples of the other lands. The race of Man reverts to what it was in the time of the First War. If there were a Warlock Lord alive now, I fear the Federation would be a willing follower."

Jair winced inwardly. In the First War of the Races, fought hundreds of years earlier, the Warlock Lord had subverted the race of Man and convinced it to attack the other races. Man had been defeated in that war and had still not recovered from the humiliation and bitterness of their loss. Isolationist in policy and practice, the Federation had absorbed and become spokesman for the majority of the Southland and the race of Man.

"Still, Callahorn stands with you," Jair declared quickly. "The Bordermen are a different breed."

"Even the Bordermen may not be enough." Foraker grunted. "Even the whole of the Legion. You've seen the gathering of tribes without. United, they are a power greater than anything we can match. And they have the aid of those black things that command them . . ." He shook his head darkly.

Jair's brow furrowed. "But we have an ally of our own who can stand against the Mord Wraiths. We have Allanon."

"Yes, Allanon," Foraker murmured, then shook his head once more.

"And Brin," Jair added. "Once they've found the Ildatch . . ."

He trailed off, the warning of the King of the Silver River suddenly a dark whisper in his mind. Leaves in the wind, he had said. Your sister and the Druid. Both will be lost.

He shoved the whisper aside roughly. It won't happen like that, he promised. I'll reach them first. I'll find them. I'll throw the Silver Dust into Heaven's Well to cleanse its waters, throw the vision crystal after, and then . . . He paused uncertainly. What? He didn't know. Something. He would do something that would keep the old man's prophecy from coming to pass.

But first there was the journey north, he reminded himself glumly. And before that, Garet Jax must return . . .

Foraker was walking along the battlements once more, bearded face lowered into his chest, hands stuffed into the pockets of the travel cloak he wore wrapped about his stocky frame. Jair caught up with him as he started down a set of broad stone steps to a lower ramp.

"Can you tell me something about Garet Jax?" the Valeman asked suddenly.

The Dwarf's head remained lowered. "What would you have me tell you?"

Jair shook his head. "I don't know. Something."

"Something?" the other grunted. "Bit vague, don't you think? What sort of something?"

Jair thought about it a moment. "Something no one else knows. Something about him."

Foraker walked to a parapet overlooking the dark expanse of the Cillidellan, resting his elbows on the stonework as he stared out into the night. Jair stood silently beside him, waiting.

"You want to understand him, don't you?" Foraker asked finally.

The Valeman nodded slowly. "A little, at least."

The Dwarf shook his head. "I'm not sure that it's possible, Ohmsford. It's like trying to understand a . . . a hawk. You see him, see what he is, what he does. You marvel at him, you wonder at his being. But you can't ever understand him—not really. You have to be him to understand him."

"You seem to understand him," Jair offered.

Foraker's fierce countenance swung sharply about to face him. "Is that what you think, Ohmsford? That I understand him?" He shook his head once more. "No better than I understand the hawk. Less, maybe. I know him because I've spent time with him, fought with him, and trained men with him. I know him for that. I know what he is, too. But all that doesn't amount to a pinch of dust when it comes to understanding."

He hesitated. "Garet Jax is like another form of life compared to you, me, or anyone else you'd care to name. A special and singular form of life, because there's only one." The eyebrows lifted. "He's magic in his way. He does things no other man could hope to do—or even try to do. He survives what would kill anyone else, and he does it time after time. Like the hawk, it's instinct—it lets him fly way up there above the rest of us where no one can touch him. A thing apart. Understand him? No, I couldn't begin to understand him."

Jair was quiet for a moment. "He came to the Eastland because of you, though," he said finally. "At least, he says that is why he came. So he must feel some sort of friendship for you. You must share a kinship."

"Perhaps." The other shrugged. "But that doesn't mean I understand him. Besides, he does what he does for reasons that are all his own and not necessarily what he says they are—I know that much. He's here not just because of me, Ohmsford. He's here for other reasons as well." He tapped Jair on the shoulder. "He's here as much because of you as because of me, I think. But I don't know the reason why. Perhaps you do."

The Valeman hesitated, thinking. "He said he would be my protector because that was what the King of the Silver River had said he must be." He trailed off.

"Well and good." Foraker nodded. "But do you understand him any better for knowing that? I do not." He paused, then looked back out across the lake. "No, his reasons are his own and the reasons are not ones he would tell to me."

Jair barely heard him. He had remembered something, and a look of surprise flitted over his face. Quickly he turned away. His mind froze. Were the reasons that Garet Jax would not tell to Foraker ones that he would tell to the Valeman? Hadn't the Weapons Master done just that in the dark, chill rain that second night out of Culhaven when the two had crouched alone beneath that ridgeline? The memory stirred slowly to life. I want you to understand . . . That was what Garet Jax had told him. The dream promised a test of skill greater than any I have ever faced. A chance to see if I am truly the best. For me, what else is there . . . ?

Jair breathed deeply the chill night air. Maybe he understood Garet Jax better than he thought. Maybe he understood him as well as anyone could.

"There is one thing not many know." Foraker turned back suddenly. Jair shoved aside his musings. "You say he found you in the Black Oaks. Ever wonder why he happened to be there? After all, he was coming east out of Callahorn."

Jair nodded slowly. "I hadn't thought about that. I guess the Black Oaks are rather out of the way for one traveling from the borderlands to the Anar." He hesitated. "What was he doing there?"

Foraker smiled faintly. "I'm only guessing, you understand. He's not told me any more than you. But the lake country north, between Leah and the lowlands of Clete—that was his home. That was where he was born, where he grew up. Once, long ago, he had family there. Some, anyway. Hasn't said anything about it for a long time, but maybe there's still someone there. Or maybe just memories."

"A family," Jair repeated softly, then shook his head. "Has he told you who they were?"

The Dwarf pushed himself back from the parapet. "No. Mentioned it once, that was all. But now you know something about the man no one else knows—except me, of course. Does that help you understand him any better?"

Jair smiled. "I don't suppose so."

Foraker turned and together they started back across the battlements. "Didn't think it would," the Dwarf muttered, pulling his cloak close about him as the wind caught at them beyond the shelter of the wall. "Come back inside with me, Ohmsford, and I'll brew you a cup of hot ale. We'll wait for our hawk's return together."

Foraker's rough hand clapped his shoulder gently, and he hurried after.

The night slipped away, its hours empty and lingering and clouded with dark anticipation. Mist crept down out of the heights on cat's paws, thickening, shrouding the whole of the locks and dams, and draping Gnome and Dwarf armies alike in veils of damp, clinging haze until even the bright glow of the watchfires disappeared from view.

Jair Ohmsford fell asleep at midnight, still awaiting the return of Garet Jax. Slumped wearily in a high-backed captain's chair in a watch lounge while Foraker, Slanter, and Edain Elessedil talked in low voices over mugs of hot ale and a single candle lighted against the deepening gloom, he simply drifted off. One minute he was awake, listening in weary detachment to the drone of their voices, eyes closed against the light; in the next, he was sleeping.

It was almost dawn when the Elven Prince shook him awake.

"Jair. He's back."

The Valeman brushed the sleep from his eyes and pushed himself upright. Barely visible through the gloom of fading night, the embers of a dying fire glowed softly in the little hearth across the room. Without, the patter of rain sounded on the stonework.

Jair blinked. He's back. Garet Jax.

He stood up hurriedly. He was fully dressed save for his boots, and he quickly snatched them up and began to pull them on.

"He came in not half an hour ago." The Elf stood next to him, his voice strangely hushed, as if fearful he might wake someone else within the room. "Helt was with him, of course. They've found a path north beyond the tunnels."

He paused. "But something else has happened, Jair." The Valeman looked up expectantly. "Sometime after midnight, it began to rain and the mist to dissipate. When the light returned with dawn's approach, the Gnomes were there, too—all of them. They'd gathered close about the shoreline of the Cillidellan from one end of the high dam to the other, dozens deep, just standing there, waiting."

Jair was on his feet. "What are they up to?"

Edain Elessedil shook his head. "I don't know. No one seems to know. But they've been out there for hours now. The Dwarves are all awake and on the battlements. Come with me and you can see for yourself."

They hastened from the watch lounge down the maze of corridors beyond until they had passed through doors leading out into the courtyard that spanned the central section of the high dam. A chill wind blew across the Cillidellan, and the rain stung their faces as they hurried forward. It was still night, the predawn light a distant gray haze beyond the tips of the mountains east. The Dwarf defenders had taken their positions along the ramparts of the dam and fortress, cloaked and hooded against the weather, weapons in hand. The whole of Capaal lay shrouded in silence.

On reaching the fortress that protected the north end of the high dam, Edain took Jair up a series of stone stairs and across a line of battlements to a watchtower high above the complex. The wind seemed to grow stronger here, and the rain beat harder through the gray night.

As they paused before an ironbound oak door leading into the tower, a cluster of Dwarves pushed past them and started down the stairs adjoining. Foremost of these was a fierce-looking Dwarf with flaming red hair and beard, armored in leather and chainmail.

"Radhomm, the Dwarf commander!" Edain whispered to Jair.

Hurriedly, they pushed through the oak door into the tower beyond, shutting the weather behind them as they entered. A faint glow of lamplight barely penetrated the gloom within as a handful of cloaked forms seemed to materialize before them.

"Humph, he'd sleep all the time if you'd let him!" he heard Slanter grumble.

"Well met again, Jair Ohmsford," a deep voice greeted him, and Helt's massive hand extended to clasp his own.

Then Garet Jax was there, as black as the night about him, implacable and unchanging as the stone of the mountains. They faced each other, and no words were spoken. Lean face intense, the Weapons Master rested his hands gently on Jair's shoulders and within the eyes of ice there flickered a strange, unfamiliar warmth. Only for the briefest second was it there; in the next, it was gone. The hands slipped away, and Garet Jax turned back into the gloom.

The door burst open behind them, and a rain-soaked Dwarf hastened over to where Elb Foraker crouched above a pile of maps that rested on a small wooden table. They conversed in low, hushed voices; then as swiftly as he had come, the runner was gone again.

Foraker walked over at once to Jair, the other members of the little company gathering about them. "Ohmsford," he said quietly, "I've just been told that the Mwellret has escaped."

There was a stunned silence. "How could that happen?" Slanter snapped angrily, his rough face pushing forward into the light.

"A shape-change." Foraker kept his eyes on Jair. "He used it to fit himself into a small ventilation shaft that circulates air to those lower levels. It happened sometime during the night. No one knows where he might be now."

Jair went cold. There was no mistaking the Dwarf's intent in telling him this unpleasant piece of news. Even locked within that storage room, the Mwellret had been able to sense the presence of the Elven magic and to force Jair to reveal it. If he were loose . . .

"This was something he could have done anytime," Edain Elessedil pointed out. "There must be a reason that he chose to do it now."

And I could be that reason, Jair acknowledged silently. Foraker realizes it, too. That is why he made it a point to speak first to me.

Garet Jax reappeared from out of the gloom, sudden and purposeful. "We are leaving at once," he advised. "We have delayed too long already. The quest given us lies north. Whatever is to happen here, we need not be part of it. With the Gnomes gathered about the Cillidellan as they are, it should be easy enough to . . ."

OOOOOOMMMMMMMMMMM!

Startled, the members of the little company looked hurriedly about. A monstrous wail assailed their ears, deep and haunting as it shattered the predawn silence. It grew louder, thousands of voices giving it life, rising up against wind and rain into the mountains about Capaal.

"Shades!" Slanter cried, his rough yellow face twisting in recognition.

All six broke for the door in a rush, burst through, and in seconds were clustered against the battlements without, rain and wind thrusting at them as they peered north across the choppy waters of the Cillidellan.

OOOOOOMMMMMMMMMM!

The wail rose higher, one long, continuous howl that swept through the heights. All about the shoreline of the Cillidellan, the Gnomes joined in the dark chant, voices blended into one as they faced the murky lake, the air filled with the mournful sound.

Radhomm appeared on the battlements below, shouting orders, and runners scurried from his side as he dispatched them to his captains. Everywhere there was a frenzy of activity as the garrison braced for whatever was to come. Jair's hand moved to his tunic, searching out and finding the reassuring presence of both the Silver Dust and the vision crystal.

Garet Jax snatched Slanter by his cloak and hauled him close. "What is happening here?"

There was unmistakable fear in the Gnome's eyes. "A summons—a summons to the dark magic! Once before I saw it—at Graymark!" The Gnome twisted in the iron grip. "But it needs the touch of the walkers, Weapons Master! It needs their touch!"

"Garet!" Foraker pulled the other about roughly, pointing to the near shore of the Cillidellan, not a hundred yards from where the high dam arced away. The Weapons Master released his grip on Slanter. All eyes turned to where the Dwarf directed.

From out of the midst of the Gnomes gathered along the shoreline, three black-cloaked figures approached, tall and hard against the coming dawn.

"Mord Wraiths!" Slanter whispered harshly. "The walkers have come!"

Down to the Cillidellan the Mord Wraiths came, gliding to the water's edge almost without seeming to move. Hooded and featureless within the shadow of their cowls, they might have been ghosts of no substance but for the black-clawed fingers slipped from beneath their coverings to wrap with death grips about three gnarled gray staffs of burnished witch-wood. The wail of their Gnome believers rose all about them, shrieking into the whistle of the wind; to those who watched from the battlements of Capaal, it seemed as if the black ones had been born of its sound.

Then, without warning, the terrible wail died into silence as the Gnomes grew suddenly still. The wind's strident shriek sounded across the empty expanse of the Cillidellan, and the lapping of the waves stirred with its passing.

The foremost of the Mord Wraiths lifted his staff high, his skeletal black arm thrusting from its protective robe like blasted deadwood. A strange and vibrant hush fell over the heights, and it seemed to the defenders that for an instant even the wind had gone still. Then the staff came slowly down, reaching toward the blackened waters of the lake. The other staffs joined it, witch-wood touching and becoming one as burnished tips slipped within the waters of the Cillidellan.

For an instant, nothing happened. Then the staffs exploded into lances of red fire, the flames ripping downward into the lake, burning and scorching its cool darkness. The waters shuddered and heaved, then began to boil. Gnomes shrieked in a cacophony of glee and fear, stumbling back from the shore's edge.

"It is the summons!" Slanter cried.

The red fire burned through the murky, impenetrable blackness, down into the deepest recesses of the lake to where no light ever shone. Like a stain of blood, the light of those flames spread outward through the waters, reaching. Geysers of steam burst skyward with a violent hiss, and the whole of the lake began to churn.

The defenders on the ramparts of the Dwarf fortress stood frozen with indecision. Something was about to happen, something unspeakable, and no one knew how it could be stopped.

"We've got to get out of here!" Slanter snatched at Garet Jax urgently. There was fear in his eyes, but reason as well. "Quickly, Weapons Master!"

Abruptly the fire from the witch-wood staffs died away. The gray wood lifted from the Cillidellan, clawed hands drawing back within their robes. Yet still the waters boiled feverishly; the reddened stain had become a deep and distant glow that shone from far beneath the surface like an eye slipped open from sleep.

OOOOOOMMMMMMMMM!

The wail of the Gnome siege army rose once more, shrill and expectant. Hands lifted and joined, stretching as the staffs of the Mord Wraiths signaled anew. Steam ripped from the lake in answer to the wail, and the whole of the Cillidellan seemed to erupt with a newfound fury.

Then something huge and dark began to rise from the depths.

"Weapons Master!" Slanter cried out.

But Garet Jax shook his head. "Stand fast. Helt, bring the long bows."

The Borderman disappeared back into the watchtower at once. Jair glanced after him momentarily, then turned back to the Cillidellan—back to the deafening wail of the Gnomes and to the black thing rising from the deep.

It came swiftly now, growing in size as it neared the surface. An evil summoned by the Wraiths—but what manner of thing was it? Jair swallowed against the tightening of his throat. Whatever it was, it was monstrous, its bulk seeming to fill the whole of the lake bottom as it lifted free. Slowly it began to take shape, a great and hulking thing with arms that twisted and groped . . .

Then, with a thunderous surge, it broke the surface of the lake and burst free into the gray dawn. A misshapen black body wrenched clear of the confining waters and hung silhouetted for an instant against the light. Barrel-like in appearance, it was coated with bottom mud and slime, crusted over with sea life and corral. Four great fin-legs propelled it as it rose, clawed and spiny. Its head was a mass of writhing tentacles that surrounded a giant beak-shaped maw lined with razor teeth. Suckers coated the insides of the tentacles, each the size of a man's spread hand, the whole protected without by scales and spines. Immediately back of the tentacles and to either side, a pair of reddened eyes blinked coldly. Stretching as it rose, the thing was more than a hundred feet from tip to tail and forty feet across.

Cries of dismay sounded from the battlements of Capaal.

"A Kraken!" Foraker said. "We are done now!"

The wail of the Gnomes had risen to a shriek that forbore all semblance of anything human. Now, with the monster's appearance into the light, the wail dissipated into a battle cry that broke across the length and breadth of Capaal. Down into the waters of the lake the Kraken thundered, its black body twisting in response as it turned abruptly toward the wall of the dam and the fortress that protected it.

"It comes for us!" Garet Jax whispered in surprise. "A thing that cannot live within freshwater, a thing that comes from the ocean—yet here! Brought by the dark magic!" The gray eyes glittered coldly. "But it shall not have us, I think. Helt!"

Instantly the giant Borderman was at his side, three long bows clasped in one great hand. Garet Jax took one, left one with the Borderman, and passed the third to Edain Elessedil.

Slanter pushed forward. "Listen to me! You cannot stand against this thing! It is a monster summoned out of evil and too much even for you!"

But Garet Jax didn't seem to hear him. "Remain with the Valeman, Gnome. He is your charge now. See that he stays safe."

He went down off the watchtower, Helt and Edain Elessedil close upon his heels. Foraker hesitated only an instant, a mistrustful glance directed at Slanter; then he, too, followed.

The Kraken surged up against the wall of the Dwarf citadel, its giant bulk hammering into stone and mortar with stunning force as it breached. The giant tentacles swept from the water, reaching for the Dwarves that clustered on the battlements. Dozens were caught up, knocked from their feet into the waters of the lake, and wrapped in the suckers and spines of the thing that attacked them. Shrieks and howls filled the morning air as the Dwarves died. Weapons rained down upon the black thing, but its hide protected it from harm. Steadily it cleared away the small figures who sought to hold it back, tearing at them with its whip-like arms, breaking apart the battlements behind which they sought to keep safe.

Now the Gnomes joined in the attack as well, the siege army battering the gates at both ends of the high dam, scaling ladders and grappling hooks clutched in their hands as they came. Dwarf defenders rushed to the parapets, holding fast against this fresh assault. But the Gnomes seemed to have gone mad. Heedless of the losses being inflicted upon them, they flung themselves against the gates and walls to die.

Yet there was purpose to this seeming madness. While the Dwarf defenders were thus distracted, the Kraken worked its way north until it was up against the wall where it banked closest to the gates. With a sudden lurch, it rose from the waters of the lake, fin-legs braced upon the stone of the dam where it curved into the shoreline. Massive tentacles snapped forward along the walls, suckers fastened to the gates, and the monster heaved back. With a splintering of wood and iron, crossbars snapped and locks broke apart. The gates to the citadel tumbled down, ripped from their hinges, and the army of the Gnomes poured through with a roar of triumph.

On the battlements of the watchtower, Jair and Slanter viewed the struggle with growing horror. With the gates gone, the Dwarves could no longer hold back their attackers. In a matter of minutes the fortress would be overrun. Already its defenders were in retreat along the walls leading back, small clusters rallying about their captains, desperately trying to stand against the onslaught. But it was clear from where the Valeman and the Gnome stood watching that the battle was lost.

"We've got to escape while we can, boy!" Slanter insisted, a hand gripping the other's arm.

But Jair refused to leave, still searching for his friends, almost too horrified by what was happening to do anything else. The Kraken had slipped once more into the waters of the lake, dragging its bulk back along the sea wall toward the center of the dam. In its wake, the Mord Wraiths glided to the edge of the shattered battlements, gray staffs raised in exhortation as their Gnome followers surged forward. With implacable purpose, the Gnomes moved into the fortress of the Dwarves.

"Slanter!" Jair cried suddenly, pointing into the heart of the battle.

High atop the ramparts of the forward wall, Helt's giant form rose up through the smoke and dust, Elb Foraker at his side. Bow gripped tightly in one hand, the Borderman braced himself against the parapets, sighted downward to where the Mord Wraiths stood, slowly drew back the bowstring, and let it slip free. A shadowy blur, the long black arrow sped away to bury itself deep in the breast of the foremost Wraith. The creature straightened with a shudder, hammered back by the force of the blow. A second arrow followed close upon the first, and again the Wraith staggered back. Shrieks of dismay rose up from those closest to the black things, and for an instant the whole of the Gnome advance seemed to falter.

But then the Mord Wraith steadied. One clawed hand grasped the arrows embedded within it and drew them free with effortless ease. Holding them high for all to see, the monster crushed them into splinters. Then the staff of witch-wood lifted and red fire burst from its tip. All along the battlements the fire burned, exploding into stone and defender alike. Helt and Foraker flew back as the fire reached them and disappeared in an avalanche of broken wall and dust.

Jair started forward in fury, but Slanter yanked him about. "You can't do anything to help them, boy!" Without waiting for any argument on the matter, he began dragging Jair along the ramparts toward the stone stairway leading down. "Better start worrying about yourself! Perhaps if we're quick enough . . ."

Then they caught sight of the Kraken. It had lifted itself out of the Cillidellan midway along the sea wall where the broad courtyard joined together the fortress that guarded the ends of the high dam, its tentacles and fin-legs gripping at the stone. Once clear, with only the hindmost portion of its barreled body still submerged within the lake, it pivoted slowly to where the Dwarf defenders were attempting to escape the north fortress. Tentacles stretched across the girth of the high dam in a writhing mass; in seconds, all passage out was blocked.

"Slanter!" Jair cried out in warning, falling back against the stairs as one giant feeler swept past his head.

They retreated back up the stairway, crouching down within the shelter of a balustrade where it curved back into the parapets. Spray from the monster's tail fin that thrashed within the lake mixed with dust and shattered stone to rain down about them. Below, the Kraken's tentacles groped and hammered about the fortress walls, clutching at anything that ventured within reach.

It seemed for a moment as if any chance of escape back across the courtyard had been lost. But then the Dwarves counterattacked. They rushed from the lower levels of the fortress, the darkened stairwells, and the tunnels that ran beneath. Foremost among them was the Dwarf commander Radhomm. Red hair flying, he led his soldiers into the tangle of giant arms, cutting and hacking with a broadax. Bits and pieces of the Kraken flew in a froth of blood, reddish ichor spilling down upon the dampened stone of the dam. But the Kraken was a monstrous thing, and the Dwarves were little more than gnats to be brushed aside. The tentacles came down, smashing the tiny creatures who swarmed about it, leaving them lifeless. Still the defenders came on, determined to clear the way for those trapped within the doomed fortress. But the Kraken swept them aside as quickly as they appeared, and they fell dying all about the monster.

Finally the Kraken caught Radhomm as the Dwarf commander fought to break past. The monster swung the red-haired Dwarf high into the air, unaffected by the broadax that still flailed in stubborn determination. The Kraken lifted Radhomm; then, with horrifying suddenness, it smashed him downward to the stone, broken, twisted, and lifeless.

Slanter was pulling vainly at Jair. "Run!" he screamed in desperation.

Tentacles swept past them, hammering into the battlements and smashing the stone so that it flew in all directions. A shower of jagged fragments struck the Valeman and the Gnome as they struggled, knocking them sprawling, half burying them in debris. Shaking his head dazedly, Jair regained his feet and staggered forward against the stone balustrade. Below, the Dwarves had fallen back within the beseiged fortress, demoralized by the loss of Radhomm. The Kraken was still stretched across the littered courtyard, edging closer now to the walls upon which Jair crouched. The Valeman started to drop back, then stopped in dismay. Slanter lay stunned at his feet, blood oozing from a deep cut in his head.

Then far below, seemingly from out of nowhere, Garet Jax appeared. Lean and black against the gray light of the dawn, he darted swiftly from the shelter of the battlements on the sea wall, a short spear gripped in his hands. Jair cried out as he saw him—a sudden, wild cry—but the sound was lost in the wail of the wind and the screams of battle. Across the blood-soaked length of the high dam the Weapons Master raced, a small and agile figure—not away from the deadly tentacles of the Kraken, but directly into them. Weaving and dodging like a shadow without substance, he broke for the monster's gaping maw. The tentacles hammered down, swatting at him, missing him, sliding past him, far too slow for anyone so impossibly quick. But one slip, one mistake . . .

Up against the hooked beak, the Weapons Master leaped, against the very jaws of the beast. He struck with stunning swiftness, the short spear burying itself deep within the soft tissue of the open maw. Instantly, the tentacles collapsed, the giant body lurching. But Garet Jax was already moving, spinning sideways and diving clear of the trap that sought to snare him. On his feet once more, the Weapons Master caught up a new weapon, this one a lance fixed with an iron pike, the haft still clutched in the lifeless hands of its owner. With a quick scooping motion, Garet Jax had wrenched it free. Too late, the Kraken caught sight once more of this dangerous attacker, barely two yards from one lidded eye. The iron-tipped lance thrust upward at the unprotected eye, piercing through skin, blood, and bone into the brain beyond.

The stricken Kraken wrenched backward in obvious distress, fin-legs churning madly. Stone ramparts shattered all about it as it sought to regain the waters of the Cillidellan. Still Garet Jax clung to the lance embedded within the monster's brain, refusing to release it, grinding it deeper and deeper as he waited for the life force to expend itself. But the Kraken was impossibly strong. Heaving upward, it lifted free of the high dam, then fell ponderously into the Cillidellan and dove from sight. Hands still fixed upon the haft of the lance, Garet Jax was carried with it.

Jair stumbled back against the shattered balustrade in stunned disbelief, his cry of anger dying soundlessly in his throat. Below, the high dam lay clear again and the Dwarf defenders trapped within broke from their prison for the safety of the south watch.

Then Slanter was next to him once more, staggering back to his feet. Blood covered the wizened yellow face, but the Gnome brushed it aside wordlessly and yanked the Valeman down the stairs after him. Stumbling and falling, they gained the courtyard and started across in the direction taken by the fleeing Dwarves.

But already they were too late. Gnome Hunters had appeared on both sides of the battlements behind them. Howling and screaming, a mass of armored, blood-soaked forms, they poured across the crest of the high dam and streamed down into the court. Slanter took one quick look back and abruptly wheeled Jair into one of the dark stairwells. They raced down several flights of lamp-lighted stairs, deep into the shadowed dark of the lower levels that led to the inner workings of the locks. Above, the sounds of pursuit began to fade.

When the stairs ended, they found themselves in a dimly lighted corridor that disappeared down the length of the dam. Slanter hesitated, then turned north, pulling Jair after him.

"Slanter!" the Valeman howled, struggling to slow the Gnome. "This leads back the way we've come—away from the Dwarves!"

"Gnomes will be going the other way, too!" Slanter snapped. "Won't be hunting Dwarves or anybody else this way, will they! Now, run!"

They ran into the gloom, stumbling wearily along the empty corridor. The sounds of battle were far away now, distant and faint against the steady grinding of the machinery and the low rush of the waters of the Cillidellan. Jair's mind spun with the shock of what had befallen them. The little company from Culhaven was no more—Helt and Foraker struck down by the walkers, Garet Jax carried away by the Kraken, and Edain Elessedil disappeared. Only Slanter and he were left—and they were running for their lives. Capaal was gone, fallen to the Gnomes. The locks and dams that regulated the flow of the Silver River west into the homeland of the Dwarves were in the hands of their most implacable enemy. Everything was lost.

His lungs tightened with the strain of running, and his breathing was harsh and labored in his ears. Tears stung his eyes, and his mouth was dry with bitterness and anger. What was he to do now? How was he to reach Brin? He could never find her before she stepped down into the Maelmord and was forever lost. How was he to complete the mission given him by the King . . . ?

His legs went out from under him, knocked away by something he hadn't seen, and he went sprawling into the darkness. Ahead, Slanter ran on, unheeding, a dim shadow in the darkness of the tunnel. Hurriedly, Jair scrambled back to his feet. Slanter was getting too far ahead of him.

Then an arm shot out of the darkness and a hand clamped across his mouth, rough and scaled, sealing away his breath. A second arm encircled his body, hard as iron, and he was dragged back into the shadows of an open door.

"Sstay, little peopless," a voice hissed. "Friendss, we of magicss. Friendss!"

Jair's voice was a soundless scream in his mind.

It was midmorning when Slanter pulled himself clear of the Dwarf escape tunnel, exiting through a thick mass of scrub that concealed the hidden entrance, there to stand alone upon the windswept heights of the mountains north of Capaal. Gray, hazy light filtered down out of skies clouded and drenched by rain, and the chill of night still lingered in the mountain rock. The Gnome glanced about cautiously, then he hunched down against the scrub and moved forward to where the slope dropped away into the gorge.

Far below, the locks and dams of Capaal were swarming with Gnomes. All across the broad bands of stone block, about the battlements and ramparts of the fortress, and deep within the inner workings of the complex, the Gnome Hunters scurried like ants about the business of maintaining their hill.

Well, this was the way it had to end, Slanter thought. He shook his rough yellow face in silent admonition. No one could stand against the walkers. Capaal was theirs now. The siege was done.

He stood up slowly, eyes still fixed on the scene below. There was little danger of being discovered this high up. The Gnomes were all within the fortress and what remained of the Dwarf army had fled south to Culhaven. Nothing was left for him to do but to go his own way.

And that, of course, was exactly what he had wanted all along.

Yet he stood there, his mind adrift with unanswered questions. He still did not know what had become of Jair Ohmsford. One minute the Valeman had been right behind him; the next he had vanished just like that. Slanter had looked for him, of course; but there hadn't been a trace. So at last the Gnome had gone on alone—because, after all, what else could he do?

"Boy was too much trouble anyway!" he muttered irritably. But his words lacked conviction somehow.

He sighed, glanced upward into the graying skies, and turned slowly away. With the Valeman gone and the rest of the little company dead or scattered, the journey to Heaven's Well was finished. Just as well, of course. It was a stupid, impossible quest from the beginning. He had told them so time and again—all of them. They had no idea what they were up against; they had no idea of the power of the walkers. It wasn't his fault that they had failed.

The frown on his rough face deepened. Nevertheless, he didn't like not knowing what had happened to the boy.

He slipped back past the scrub guarding the hidden entrance to the tunnel and climbed to a rocky projection overlooking the Eastland and giving view to its sweep west. At least, he had been smart enough to plan his own escape, he thought smugly. But that was because he was a survivor, and survivors always took time to plan for an escape—except for the crazed ones like Garet Jax. Slanter's frown turned to a faint smile. He had learned long ago not to risk himself unnecessarily where there was no reason for it. He had learned long ago to keep one eye open for the quickest way out of any place into which he ventured. So when the Dwarf had been kind enough to provide him with maps showing the underground tunnels that would take them north behind the siege army, he had been quick to study them. That was why he was alive and safely out of there. If the rest of them hadn't been so foolish . . .

The wind blew against his face, harsh and bitter as it came out of the mountain rock. Far north and west, the forests of the Anar spread away into patches of autumn color, dampened by mist and rain. That was the way for him, he thought grimly. Back to the borderlands, to some semblance of sanity and peace, where his old life could be regained and all of this forgotten. He was free again and he could now go where he wished. A week, ten days at the outside, and the Eastland and the war that ravaged it would be left behind.

He scuffed his boot against the rock. "That boy had sand, though," he said quietly, his thoughts straying yet.

Undecided, he stared out into the rain.

Late in the afternoon of the day that marked the disappearance of Paranor from the world of men, the whole of Callahorn from the Streleheim south to the Rainbow Lake was engulfed in heavy autumn rains. The storms swept down through the borderlands, swept across forest and grassland, and over the Dragon's Teeth and the Runne, falling at last across the broad expanse of the Rabb Plains. It was there that it caught up with Allanon, Brin, and Rone Leah as they journeyed eastward toward the Anar.

They camped that night, exposed to the downpour and huddled within their sodden cloaks, beneath the sparse shelter of an oak broken and ravaged by years of seasons passing. Empty and barren, the Rabb stretched away on all sides as the storms thundered overhead, the glare of the lightning revealing in vivid flashes the starkness of the plain. No other life could be found on its cracked and windswept surface; they were all alone. They might have pushed on that night, ridden east until dawn, and thereby gained the Anar before stopping to take their rest. But the Druid saw that the highlander and the Valegirl were exhausted and thought it better not to press.

So they stayed that night upon the Rabb and rode on again at dawn. The day stretched out to greet them, gray and rain-filled, the sun's light a faint and hazy glow behind the storm clouds that blanketed the autumn skies. They rode east across the plains until they reached the banks of the Rabb River, then turned south. Where the river branched west out of its main channel, they crossed at a narrows close to the forest's edge and continued south until daylight had slipped into a murky, sodden dusk.

They spent a second night unsheltered upon the Rabb, crouched within cloaks and hoods, with the rain a constant, annoying drizzle that drenched them to the bone and kept them from sleep. The chill of the season settled in about them. While neither cold nor sleeplessness had an apparent effect upon the Druid, it wore with singular perseverance on the stamina of the girl and the highlander. On Brin, particularly, it began to take its toll.

Yet at dawn of the following day, she was ready to travel once more, her determination as hard as iron, reforged out of an inner battle she had fought through the empty hours of the night to keep herself sane. The rains that had followed them since their departure out of the Dragon's Teeth were gone, turned now to a soft, feathery mist. The skies were clearing into wisps of whitened clouds as the sunlight began to slip above the forestline. The appearance of the sun rekindled in the Valegirl a strength of mind and body that the rains and the dark had done much to erode, and she fought valiantly to ignore the exhaustion that seeped through her. Back astride her horse, she turned gratefully toward the warmth of the still hazy sunlight and watched as it crept steadily out of the east.

But exhaustion was not so easily dispatched, she found. Though the day brightened as they traveled on, a weariness still persisted deep within, besieging her with doubts and fears that would not fade. Faceless demons darted in their shadows—darted from her mind into the forest they rode beside, laughing and taunting. There were eyes upon her. As it had been within the Dragon's Teeth, there was the sense of being watched, sometimes from far away through eyes that were not bound by any distance, sometimes from eyes that seemed very close. And again there was that insidious premonition. It had come to her first in the rocks and shadows of the Dragon's Teeth, following after her, teasing her relentlessly, warning her that she and those she traveled with played a game with death they could not win. She had thought it lost after Paranor, for they had escaped the Druid's Keep alive and safe. Yet now it was back again, reborn in the gray and wet of the last two days, a familiar and haunting demon of her mind. It was evil, and though she sought to drive it from her thoughts with determination and a savage anger, still it would not stay gone.

The hours drifted aimlessly away in the course of the third morning's travel, and Brin Ohmsford's determination gradually began to drift with them. The drifting manifested itself first as an inexplicable sense of aloneness. Besieged by her premonition—a premonition that her companions could not even recognize—the Valegirl began to withdraw into herself. It was done in self-defense to begin with, a withdrawing from the thing that sought to ravage her with its viperous warnings and insidious teasings. Walls came up, windows and doors slammed, and within the shelter of her mind she sought to close the thing out.

But Allanon and Rone were closed out as well, and somehow she could not find a way to bring them back in. She was alone, a prisoner within her own self, chained in irons of her own forging. A subtle change began to overtake her. Slowly, inexorably, she began to believe herself alone. Allanon had never been close, a distant and forbidding figure even under the most favorable circumstances, a stranger for whom she could feel pity and for whom she could sense an odd kinship—yet a stranger nevertheless, impervious and forbidding. It had been different with Rone Leah, of course; but the highlander had changed. From her friend and companion, he had become a protector as formidable and unapproachable as the Druid. The Sword of Leah had wrought that change, giving to Rone Leah power that made him in his own mind equal to anything that sought to stand against him. Magic, born of the dark waters of the Hadeshorn and the black sorcery of Allanon, had subverted him. The sense of intimacy that had bound them each to the other was gone. It was the Druid to whom Rone was bound now and to whom the kinship belonged.

But the drifting of Brin's determination grew quickly beyond her sense of aloneness. It became a feeling that somehow, in some way, she had lost her purpose in this quest. It wasn't gone entirely, she knew—yet it had strayed. Once that purpose had been clear and certain; she was to travel into the Eastland, through the Anar and the Ravenshorn, to the edge of the pit they called the Maelmord and there descend into that pit's blackened maw to destroy the book of dark magic, the Ildatch. That had been her purpose. But with the passage of time, in the dark, cold, and discomfort of their travels, the urgency of that purpose had slipped from her until it now seemed distant and tenuous. Allanon and Rone were strong and certain—twin irons against the shadows that would stop them. What need had they of her? Could they not act as well as she in this quest, despite the Druid's words? Somehow she felt that they could, that she was not the important member of this company, but almost a burden, a thing not needed, her usefulness misjudged. She tried telling herself that this was not true. But somehow it was; her presence was a mistake. She sensed it, and in sensing it grew even more alone.

Midday came and went, and the afternoon wore on. The mist of early morning was gone now, and the day had become bright with sunlight. Bits of color reappeared on the barren plains. The cracked and ravaged earth turned slowly once again to grassland. Brin's sense of aloneness became for a time less oppressive.

By nightfall, the riders had reached Storlock, the community of Gnome Healers. An aged, famous village, it was little more than a gathering of modest stone and timber dwellings, settled within the fringe of the woods. It was here that Wil Ohmsford had studied and trained for the profession that he had always sought to follow. Here Allanon had come to find him so that he might accompany the Druid on his journey south to find the Chosen Amberle in the quest to preserve the Ellcrys tree and the Elven race—a journey that ended with the infusion of the Elfstone magic into Brin's father, thereby bequeathing to her the power of the wishsong. It had been more than twenty years ago, Brin thought in somber, almost bitter reflection. That was how the madness had begun—with the coming of Allanon. For the Ohmsfords, that was how it always began.

They rode through the tranquil, sleepy village, drawing to a halt behind a large, broad-backed building that served as the Center. The white-robed Stors appeared as if they had been waiting for the three to arrive. Silent and expressionless, a handful led away the horses while three more took Brin, Rone, and Allanon inside, down dark and shadowed hallways to separate rooms. Hot baths waited, clean clothes and food, and beds with fresh linens. The Stors spoke no words as they went about the task of caring for their guests. Like ghosts, they lingered for a few minutes and then were gone.

Alone in her room, Brin bathed, changed, and ate her meal, lost in the weariness of her body and the solitude of her mind. Nightfall slipped down across the forestland, and shadows passed over the curtained windows, the light of day fading into dusk. The Valegirl watched its passing with sleepy, languorous unconcern, given over to the pleasure of comforts she had not enjoyed since leaving the Vale. For a time, she could almost pretend that she was back again.

But when the evening deepened, there came a knock upon the door and a white-robed Stor beckoned for her to follow. She went without argument. She knew without asking that Allanon had called.

She found him within his room at the end of the hallway, Rone Leah seated beside him at a small table on which an oil lamp burned to cast away the night's shadow. Wordlessly, the Druid beckoned to a third chair, and the Valegirl moved to occupy it. The Stor who had brought her waited until she was seated, then turned and glided from the room, closing the door softly behind him as he left.

The three companions faced one another in silence. Allanon shifted in his chair, dark face hard and fixed, eyes lost in worlds that the Valegirl and the highlander could not see. He looked old this night, Brin thought and wondered that it could be so. No one had known Allanon to age, save for her father, and that had come about just before the Druid disappeared from the Four Lands twenty years earlier. Yet now she saw it, too. He had aged beyond what he had looked when first he had come to the Vale to seek her out. His long, dark hair was grayer in its tone, his lean face more lined and time-ravaged, his look more bent and rough. Time was working against the Druid, even as it worked against them all.

The black eyes swept up to meet her own. "I would tell you now of Bremen," he rumbled softly, and the gnarled hands folded before him.

"Long ago, in the time of the Councils of the Druids at Paranor, in the time between the Wars of the Races, it was Bremen who saw the truth about the coming of the magic. Brona, who was to become the Warlock Lord, had unlocked the secrets years before and fallen prey to their power. Consumed by what he had hoped to master, the rebel Druid became a slave. After the First War of the Races, the Council believed him destroyed, yet Bremen saw that it was not so. Brona lived, preserved by the magic, driven by its force and its need. The sciences of the old world were gone, lost in the holocaust of the Great Wars. In their place was reborn the magic of a world older still, a world in which only faerie creatures had existed. It was this magic, Bremen saw, that would preserve or destroy the new world of men.

"Thus Bremen defied the Council as Brona had before him—yet with greater care for what he was about—and began to learn for himself the secrets of the power that the rebel Druid had unlocked. Prepared for the Warlock Lord's eventual return, he saved himself when all the other Druids were destroyed. It became his mission, the sole and fixed purpose of his life, to regain the power that the evil one had let loose, to recapture it and seal it away where it could not again be tampered with. No easy task—yet a task to which he pledged himself. The Druids had unlocked the magic; now, as the last of those Druids, it was left to him to lock it away once more."

Allanon paused. "He chose to do this through the creation of the Sword of Shannara, a weapon of ancient Elven magic that could destroy the Warlock Lord and the Bearers of the Skull that served him. In the darkest hour of the Second War of the Races, with the whole of the Four Lands threatened by the armies of the evil one, Bremen forged, from magic and from the skills he had acquired and the knowledge he had gained, the fabled Sword. He gave it to the Elven King Jerle Shannara. With that Sword, the King would face in battle the rebel Druid and see him destroyed.

"As you know, however, Jerle Shannara failed. Unable fully to master the power of the Sword, he let the Warlock Lord escape. Though the battle was won and the armies of the evil one driven forth, still Brona lived. Years would pass before he could return, but return he would. Bremen knew that he would not be there to face Brona again. Yet his pledge had been given, and Bremen would never forsake a promise."

The Druid's voice had slipped down to a whisper, and there was a look of intense pain within the black, impenetrable eyes. "He did three things, then. He chose me to be his son, the flesh and blood offspring of the Druid line who would walk upon the Four Lands until the time of the Dark Lord's return. He gave added life to himself first and to me later through the sleep that preserves so that, for as long as might be necessary, a Druid would stand as protector of mankind against the Warlock Lord. And finally, he did one thing more. When the time of his passing was at hand and he could not make himself let go, he used the magic in one last, terrible evocation. He bound his spirit to this world in which his body could not stay, so that he could reach beyond life's end to see fulfillment of the pledge that he had made."

Gnarled hands tightened into fists. "He bound himself, spirit out of flesh, to me! He used the magic to achieve that binding, father to son, his spirit exiled in a world of dark where past and future joined, where summons could be had when the need was there. That was what he chose for himself, a lost and hopeless being, never to be freed until it was done, until both had passed . . ."

He stopped suddenly, as if his words had brought him farther than he wished to go. In that instant, Brin caught sight of what had been hidden from her before—a quick, elusive glimpse of the secret that the Druid had withheld from her in the Valley of Shale when Bremen had risen from the Hadeshorn and spoken of what was to be, and which gave substance to the whisperings of her premonition.

"I thought it done once," Allanon went on, brushing past the sudden pause. "I thought it done when Shea Ohmsford destroyed the Warlock Lord—when the Valeman unlocked the secret of the Sword of Shannara and made himself its master. But I was wrong. The dark magic did not die with the Warlock Lord. Nor was it locked away again as Bremen had foresworn it must be. It survived, kept safe within the pages of the Ildatch, secreted away within the bowels of the Maelmord to await new discoverers. And, finally, the discoverers came."

"And became the Mord Wraiths," Rone Leah finished.

"Made slaves to the dark magic as had been the Warlock Lord and the Skull Bearers in old days. Thinking to be master, they became only slaves."

But what is the secret that you hide? Brin whispered in her mind, still waiting to hear it told. Speak now of that!

"Then Bremen cannot be freed from his exile within the Hadeshorn until the book of the Ildatch is destroyed—and the magic with it?" Rone was too caught up in the history of the tale to see what Brin saw.

"He is pledged to that destruction, Prince of Leah," Allanon whispered.

And you. And you. Brin's mind raced.

"All of the dark magic gone from the land?" Rone shook his head wonderingly. "It does not seem possible. Not after so many years of its being—of wars fought because of it, of lives expended."

The Druid looked away. "That age ends, highlander. That age must pass."

There was a long silence then, a hushed stillness that filled the night shadows about the flame of the oil lamp and crowded close about the three who huddled there. Wrapped by it, they thought their separate thoughts, eyes slipping past one another's faces to shield what whispered within. Strangers joined in common cause but without understanding, thought Brin. We strive for a common good, yet the bond is curiously weak . . .

"Can we succeed in this, Allanon?" Rone Leah asked suddenly. His wind-burned face turned toward the Druid. "Have we strength enough to destroy this book and its dark magic?"

The Druid did not answer for a moment. His eyes flickered with hidden knowledge, elusive and quick. Then he said quietly, "Brin Ohmsford has the strength. She is our hope."

Brin looked at him and shook her head slowly. Her smile twisted with irony. "Hope and no hope. Savior and destroyer. Remember the words, Allanon? Your father spoke them of me."

Allanon said nothing. He simply sat there, dark eyes staring into her own.

"What else did he tell you, Allanon?" she asked him quietly. "What else?"

There was a long pause. "That I shall not see him again in this world."

The silence deepened. She was close now to the secret the Druid kept hidden, she realized. Rone Leah stirred uneasily in his chair, eyes shifting to find those of the Valegirl. There was uncertainty in those eyes, Brin saw. Rone did not want to know any more. She looked away. It was she who was the hope, and she who must know.

"Was there more?" she said.

Slowly Allanon straightened, dark robes wrapping close about him, and on his worn and haggard face, a small smile appeared. "There is an Ohmsford obsession with knowing the truth of all that is," he replied. "Not a one of you has ever been content with less."

"What did Bremen say?" she pressed.

The smile died away. "He said, Brin Ohmsford, that when I go from the Four Lands this time, I shall not come again."

Valegirl and highlander stared at him in shocked disbelief. As certain as the cycle of the seasons was the return of Allanon to the Four Lands when the danger of the dark magic threatened the races. There had never been a time in memory when he had not come.

"I don't believe you, Druid!" Rone insisted heatedly, unable to think of anything else to say, a trace of outrage in his voice.

Allanon shook his head slowly. "The age passes, Prince of Leah. I must pass with it."

Brin swallowed against the tightness in her throat. "When . . . when will you. . . ?"

"When I must, Brin," the Druid finished gently. "When it is time."

Then he rose, a tall and weathered form as black as night and as steady as its coming. The great, gnarled hands reached out across the table. Without fully understanding why, the Valegirl and the highlander reached to clasp them in their own, joining for just an instant the three as one.

The Druid's nod was brief and somehow final. "Tomorrow we ride east into the Anar—east until our journey is done. Go now and sleep. Be at peace."

The great hands released their own and dropped away. "Go," he said softly.

With a quick, uncertain glance at each other, Brin and Rone stood up and walked from the room. All the way out, they could feel the dark gaze following after.

They walked in silence down the hallway beyond. The sound of voices, distant and fragmented, wafted through the shadows of the empty hall and drifted disembodied from some unseen place. The air was thick with the smell of herbs and medicines, and they breathed in the aromas, distracted from their thoughts. When they reached the doors to their sleeping rooms, they stopped and stood together, not touching or look-ing at each other, sharing without speaking the impact of what they had been told.

It cannot be true, Brin thought, stunned. It cannot.

Rone turned to face her then, and his hands reached down to take hers. For the first time since their departure from Hadeshorn and the Val-ley of Shale, she felt close to him again.

"What he told us, Brin . . . what he said about not returning . . ." The highlander shook his head. "That was the reason we went to Paranor and he sealed away the Keep. He knew he would not be coming back . . ."

"Rone," she said quickly and put her finger to his lips.

"I know. It's just that I cannot believe it."

"No."

For a long moment they stared at each other. "I am afraid, Brin," he said finally, his voice a whisper.

She nodded without speaking, then wrapped her arms about him and held him close. Then she stepped back again, kissed him lightly on the mouth, and disappeared into her room.

Slowly, wearily Allanon turned from the closed door and seated himself once more at the small table. Eyes shifting from the flame of the oil lamp, he stared fixedly into the shadows beyond, his thoughts drifting. Once he would not have felt the need to reveal the secrets that were his. He would have disdained to do so. He was the keeper of the trust, after all; he was the last of the Druids and the power that had once been theirs belonged now to him. He had no need to confide in others.

It had been so with Shea Ohmsford. Much of the truth had been kept from Shea, left hidden for the little Valeman to discover on his own. It had been so as well with Brin's father, when the Druid had taken him in quest of the Bloodfire. Yet Allanon's resolve for secrecy, for deliberate and iron-willed refusal to tell to any—even those closest—all that he knew, had somehow weakened through the years gone past. Perhaps it was the aging, come upon him at last, or the inexorable passing of time that weighed so heavily upon him. Perhaps it was simply the need to share what he carried with some other living soul.

Perhaps.

He rose again from the table, another of night's shadows floating beyond the reach of the light. A sudden breath of air, and the oil lamp went dark.

He had told so much more to the Valegirl and the highlander than to any of the others.

And still he had not told them all.

24

Dawn broke over the Eastland and the forests of the Anar, and the journey of the three who had come from Shady Vale resumed. Supplied with fresh provisions by the Healers of Storlock, they rode east out of the village into the woodlands beyond. Few saw them depart. A handful of white-robed Stors, sad-faced and voiceless, gathered at the stables behind the Center to lift their arms in farewell. Within minutes, the three had disappeared into the trees, gone as silently and as enigmatically as they had come.

It was the kind of autumn day fond memories conjure up of a milder season's passing when winter snows lie deep about. It was warm and sun-filled, with the colors of the forest trees radiant and sprinkled with soft beams of light and the morning smells sweet and pleasant. Dark and chill as the days gone by had been in the wake of the passing of the late-year storms, this day was light and comforting with its dazzling blue skies and sunshine.

The promise of the day was lost, however, to Brin Ohmsford and Rone Leah. Haunted by Allanon's dark revelation and by a tense expectation of what lay ahead, neither could share much of the warmth that the day had to offer. Separate and withdrawn, each within a dark covering of private emotions and secretive thoughts, Valegirl and highlander rode forward in determined silence through the dappled shadows of the great, dark trees, feeling only the cold that lay buried within themselves.

"Our path hereafter will be a treacherous one," Allanon had told them as they gathered that morning before the stables where their horses had been tended, his voice low and strangely gentle. "All across the Eastland and through the forests of the Anar, the Wraiths will be watching for us. They know that we come; Paranor removed all question of that. They know as well that they must stop us before we reach the Maelmord. Gnomes will seek us, and where they do not, others who obey the walkers will. No path east into the Ravenshorn will be safe for us."

His hands had come up then to rest upon their shoulders, drawing them close. "Still, we are but three and not so easily found. The Wraiths and their Gnome eyes will look two ways for our approach—north above the Rabb River and south out of Culhaven. Safe and unobstructed but for themselves, these are the approaches a wise man would choose. We will choose neither, therefore. Instead, we will pass where it is most dangerous—not only to us, but to them as well. We will pass directly east into the central Anar—through the Wolfsktaag, Darklin Reach, and Olden Moor. Older magics than theirs dwell within those regions—magics that they will be hesitant to challenge. The Wolfsktaag are forbidden to the Gnomes, and they will not enter, even though the Wraiths command it. There are things there more dangerous than the Gnomes we seek to avoid, but most lie dormant. If we are quick and cautious, we should pass through unharmed. Darklin Reach and the Moor are the haunts of other magics yet, but there perhaps we shall find some more friendly to our cause than to theirs . . ."

They rode through the western fringe of the central Anar up into the high ground that formed the doorstep to the rugged, forested humps of the Wolfsktaag. As they traveled, they searched past sunlight and warmth and the brilliant autumn colors for the dark things that lay hidden there. By midday, they had reached the Pass of Jade and begun a long, circuitous climb along its southern slope, where trees and scrub hid them from view as they walked their horses in the deep shadow. Midafternoon found them well east of the pass, wending their way upward toward the high peaks. Timber and rock stretched dark and silent about them as the daylight began to wane. By nightfall, they were deep within the mountains. In the trees through which they passed, the shadows slipped now like living things. All the while they searched, yet found no sign of other life and felt themselves to be alone.

It was curious and somehow frightening that they could be so alone, Brin thought as the dusk settled into the mountains and the day came to an end. She should sense at least a touch of life other than their own, yet it was as if these peaks and forests had been stripped. There were no birds within these trees, no insects, no living creatures of any kind. There was only the silence, deep and pervasive—the silence, itself become a living thing in the absence of all other life.

Allanon brought them to a halt in the shelter of a grove of rough and splintering hickory to set their camp. When provisions were sorted, the horses tended, and the camp at ready, the Druid called them to him, ordered that no fire be lighted, and stalked off into the trees with a quick word of farewell. Valegirl and highlander stared after him wordlessly until he was out of sight, then sat down to consume a cold meal of bread, cheese, and dried fruit. They ate in darkness, not speaking, watching the shadows about them for the life that never seemed to come. Overhead, the night sky brightened with a great scattering of stars.

"Where do you think he has gone this night?" Rone Leah wondered after a time. He spoke almost as if he were asking himself the question. Brin shook her head and said nothing, and the highlander glanced away again. "Just like a shadow, isn't he? Shifts with every change of sun and moon, appears, and then he's gone again—always for reasons all his own. He wouldn't share those reasons with us, of course. Not with mere humans like us." He sighed and set aside his plate. "Except that I guess we're not mere humans anymore, are we?"

Brin toyed with the bit of bread and cheese that remained on her own plate. "No," she answered softly.

"Well, no matter. We are who we always were, nevertheless." He paused, as if wondering how sure of that he really was. Then he leaned forward. "It's odd, but I don't feel the same way about him now that I did before. I've been thinking about it all day. I still don't trust him entirely. I can't. He knows too much that I don't. But I don't mistrust him either. He is trying to help, I think, in the best way that he can."

He stopped, waiting for Brin to agree with him, but the Valegirl stayed silent, eyes turned away.

"Brin, what's troubling you?" he asked finally.

She looked at him and shook her head. "I'm not sure."

"Is it what he told us last night—that we wouldn't see him again after this?"

"That, yes. But it's more than that."

He hesitated. "Maybe you're just . . ."

"Something is wrong," she cut him short, and her eyes locked on his.

"What?"

"Something is wrong." She said it slowly, carefully. "With him, with you, with this whole journey—but most especially with me."

Rone stared at her. "I don't understand."

"I don't understand either. I just feel it." She pulled her cloak tightly about her, hunching down within its folds. "I've felt it for days—ever since the shade of Bremen appeared in the Hadeshorn, and we destroyed that Wraith. I feel something bad coming . . . something terrible. And I don't know what it is. I feel, too, that I'm being watched; all the time I'm being watched, but there is never anything there. I feel, worst of all, that I'm being . . . pulled away from myself, from you and Allanon. Everything is changing from what it was when we started out at Shady Vale. It's all different, somehow."

The highlander didn't say anything for a moment. "I suppose it's because of what's happened to us, Brin. The Hadeshorn, Paranor—Allanon telling us what the shade of Bremen told to him. It had to change us. And we've been away from the Vale and the highlands for many days now, from everything familiar and comfortable. That has to be a part of it, too."

"Away from Jair," she said quietly.

"And your parents."

"But Jair most of all," she insisted, as if searching for a reason for this. Then she shook her head. "No, it's not that. It's something else, something besides what's happened with Allanon and missing home and family and . . . That's too easy, Rone. I can feel it, deep down within me. Something that . . ."

She trailed off, her dark eyes uncertain. She looked away. "I wish I had Jair here with me now—just for a few moments. I think he would know what was wrong. We're so close that way . . ." She caught herself, then laughed softly. "Isn't that silly? Wishing for something like that when it would probably mean nothing?"

"I miss him, too." The highlander tried a quick smile. "At least he might take our minds off our own problems. He'd be out tracking Mord Wraiths or something."

He stopped, realizing what he had said, then shrugged away his discomfort. "Anyway, there's probably nothing wrong—not really. If there was, Allanon would sense it, wouldn't he? After all, he seems to sense everything else."

Brin was a long time responding. "I wonder if that is still so," she said finally. "I wonder if he still can."

They were silent then, neither looking back at the other as they stared fixedly into the dark and pondered their separate thoughts. As the minutes slipped away, the stillness of the mountain night seemed to press in about them, anxious to wrap them in the blanket of its stark, empty solitude. It seemed more certain with the passing of each moment that some sound must break the spell, the distant cry of a living creature, the small shifting of forest wood or mountain rock, or the rustle of leaf or insect's buzz. But nothing did. There was only the quiet.

"I feel as if we are drifting," Brin said suddenly.

Rone Leah shook his head. "We travel a fixed course, Brin. There is no drifting in that."

She looked over at him. "I wish I had listened to you and had never come."

The highlander stared at her in shock. The beautiful, dusky face stayed turned toward his own. In the girl's black eyes there was a mix of weariness and doubt that bordered too closely on fear. For just an instant he had the unpleasant sensation that the girl who sat across from him was not Brin Ohmsford.

"I will protect you," he said softly, urgently. "I promise."

She smiled then, a faint, uneven smile that flickered and was gone. Gently her hands reached out to touch his own. "I believe that," she whispered in reply.

But somewhere deep inside, she found herself wondering if he really could.

It was nearly midnight when Allanon returned to the campsite, stepping from the trees as silently as any shadow that moved within the Wolfsktaag. Moonlight slipped through the boughs overhead in thin streamers of silver and cast the whole of the night in eerie brightness. Wrapped within their blankets, Rone and Brin lay sleeping. Across the broad, forested sweep of the mountains, all was still. It was as if he alone kept watch.

The Druid paused several dozen feet from where his charges slept. He had walked to be alone, to think, and to ponder the certainty of what was to be. How unexpected the words of Bremen had been when the shade had spoken them—how strangely unexpected. They should not have been, of course. He had known what must be from the beginning. Yet there was always the feeling that somehow it might be changed. He was a Druid, and all things were possible.

His black eyes shifted across the mountain range. The yesterdays of his life were far away, the struggles he had weathered and the roads he had walked down to reach this moment. The tomorrows seemed distant, too, but that was an illusion, he knew. The tomorrows were right before him.

So much had been accomplished, he mused. But not enough. He turned and looked down at the sleeping Valegirl. She was the one upon whom everything would depend. She would not believe that, of course, or the truth about the power of the wishsong, for she chose to see the Elven magic in human terms, and the magic had never been human. He had shown her what it could be—just a glimpse of the limits to which it could be taken, for she could stand no more, he sensed. She was a child in her understanding of the magic and her coming of age would be difficult. More difficult, he knew, because he could not help her.

His long arms wrapped tightly within the black robes. Could he not help her? There it was again. He smiled darkly. That decision that he should never reveal all, only so much as he felt necessary—that decision that as it had been for Shea Ohmsford in a time long past, truth was best learned by the one who would use it. He could tell her, of course—or at least he could try to tell her. Her father would have said that he should tell her, for Wil Ohmsford had believed the same about the Elven girl Amberle. But the decision was not Wil Ohmsford's to make. It was his own.

It was always his own.

A touch of bitterness twisted his mouth. Gone were the Councils at Paranor when many voices and many minds had joined in finding solutions to the problems of mankind. The Druids, the wise men of old, were no more. The histories and Paranor and all the hopes and dreams they had once inspired were lost, and only he remained.

All of the problems of mankind were now his, as they always had been his and would continue to be his for as long as he lived. That decision, too, had been his to make. He had made it when he had chosen to be what he was. But he was the last. Would there be another to make the same decision when he was gone?

Alone, uncertain, he stood at the edge of the forest shadows and looked down at Brin Ohmsford.

They rode east again at daybreak. It was another brilliant, sun-filled autumn day—warm, sweet, and alive with dreams of what could be. As night fled westward from the Wolfsktaag, the sun lifted out of the eastern horizon, slipping from the forestline in golden streamers that stretched and spread to the darkest corners of the land and chased the gloom before them. Even within the vast and empty solitude of the forbidden mountains there was a feeling of comfort and peace.

Brin thought of home. How beautiful the Vale would be on a day such as this one, she thought to herself as she walked her horse along the ridgeline and felt the sun's warmth upon her face. Even here the colors of the season spread in riotous disarray against a backdrop of moss and groundcover still green with summer's touch. Smells of life filled her nostrils and left her heady with their mix. In the Vale, the villagers would be awake now, about to begin their day's work. Breakfast would be underway, the succulent aroma of the foods that were cooking escaping through windows thrown wide to catch the warmth of the day. Later, when the morning chores were done, the village families would gather for stories and games on an afternoon that too seldom came this time of year, anxious to take advantage of its ease and recapture for at least a brief time the memory of the summer gone.

I wish I were there to share it, she thought. I wish I were home.

The morning slipped quickly away, its passing lost in the warmth of the sun and the memories and the dreams. Ridgelines and mountain slopes came and went, and ahead the deep forests of the lowlands beyond the Wolfsktaag began to appear in brief glimpses through the humped peaks. By noon, the bulk of the range was behind them, and they were starting down.

It was shortly thereafter that they became aware of the Chard Rush.

It began as sound long before it could be seen—a deep, penetrating roar from beyond a wooded ridge that broke high and rugged against the sweep of the Eastland sky. Like an invisible wave, it surged toward them, a low and sullen rumble that shook the rutted earth with the force of its passing. Then the wind seemed to catch it, magnifying its intensity until the forest air was filled with thunder. The way forward leveled off, and the timber began to thicken. Atop the ridge head, freezing spray and a deep, rolling mist masked all but the faintest trace of distant blue from a noonday sky now lost far above the tangled branches of the forest trees with their damp, moss-grown bark and earth-colored leaves shimmering bright with wetness. Ahead, the trail sloped upward once more through clusters of rock and fallen timber that loomed spectrally out of the haze like frozen giants. And still there was only the sound, massive and deafening.

Yet slowly, as the trail wound on and the ridgeline grew close, the mist began to dissipate beneath the thrust of the wind as it raked down across the summit of the land, out of the Wolfsktaag to the lowlands east. The bowl of the valley opened before them, its wooded slopes dark and forbidding in the shadow of the mountain peaks beneath a line of ridges colored gold with sunlight. And here, at last, the source of the sound was discovered—a waterfall. An awesome, towering column of churning white water poured wildly through a break in the cliff rock and tumbled downward hundreds of feet through clouds of mist and spray that hung thick across the whole

of the western end of the valley, downward into a great river that twisted
and turned through rocks and trees until it was lost from view.

In a line, the three riders drew their mounts to a halt.

"The Chard Rush." Allanon pointed to the falls.

Brin gazed down wordlessly. It was as if she stood at the edge of the
world. She could not describe what she felt at that moment, only what she
saw. Below, barely a hundred yards distant, the waters of the Chard Rush
crashed and swirled down rock and through crevice in a magnificent,
breathtaking spectacle that left her filled with wonder. Far beyond the valley into which the waters fell, the distant Eastland spread to the horizon,
shimmering slightly through the windblown spray of the falls, colored like
a painting faded and worn with age, its clarity muted. A steady mist
washed over the Valegirl's dusky face and whipped through her long black
hair and forest clothing like a light rain. She blinked the water from her
eyes and breathed deeply the cold, hard air. In a way she could not explain,
she felt as if she had been born again.

Then Allanon was motioning them ahead, and the three riders began
working their way down the inside slope of the wooded valley, angling
toward the break in the cliff face where the falls dropped away. Single file,
they wound through brush and slanted pine that clung tenaciously to the
rocky soil of these upper reaches, following what appeared to be a worn,
rutted pathway that ran down past the falls. Rising clouds of mist enveloped them, damp and clinging against their skin. The wind died behind
the rim of the ridgeline, the sound of its shrill whistle lost in the muffled
roar of the falls. Sunlight dropped away into shadow, a false twilight settling over the forestland through which they passed in gradually deepening
waves.

Finally they reached the base of the falls and continued along the dark
pathway that had brought them there to emerge at last from mist and
shadow into warm sunlight. They rode eastward along the banks of the
river through deep grass still green and fresh beneath a scattering of pine
and yellow-leaved oak. Gradually the roar of the falls subsided and the air
grew less chill. In the trees about them, birds flew in sudden bursts of
color.

Life had come back again to the land. Brin sighed gratefully, thinking
how relieved she was to be clear of the mountains.

And then abruptly Allanon reined his horse to a stop.

Almost as if the Druid had willed that it should be so, the forest
about them went still—a deep, layered silence that hung over everything
like a shroud. Their horses came to a halt behind his. Valegirl and highlander stared at the big man and then at each other, surprise and wariness
in their eyes. Allanon did not move. He simply sat there astride his horse,
rigid against the light, staring ahead into the shadows of the forest trees
and listening.

"Allanon, what . . . ?" Brin started to ask, but the Druid's hand lifted
sharply to cut her short.

At last he turned, and the lean, dark face had drawn tight and hard, a look within the narrow eyes that neither Valegirl nor highlander had ever seen. In that instant, without understanding why it was that the feeling had come over her, Brin was suddenly terrified.

The Druid did not speak. Instead, he smiled—a quick, sad smile—and turned away. His hand beckoned them after, and he started ahead into the trees.

They rode only a short distance through a scattering of trees and dying scrub to where a small glen opened before them beside the banks of the river. There Allanon again drew his mount to a halt and this time dismounted. Rone and Brin followed him down. Together they stood there before the horses, looking out over the glen into a deepening stand of trees beyond.

"What's wrong, Allanon?" Brin finished the question this time.

The Druid did not turn. "Something comes. Listen."

They waited, motionless beside him. So complete was the silence now that even the sound of their own breathing was harsh within their ears. Brin's premonition whispered anew in her mind, come from the rain and the gray of the Dragon's Teeth to find her. Fear stroked her skin with its chill touch and she shivered.

Suddenly, there was a sound, faint and cautious—a soft rustling of dried leaves as something moved among them.

"There!" Rone cried, his hand pointing.

Something came into view through the trees on the far side of the glen. Still hidden within the gloom, it stopped suddenly, catching sight of the three who watched it. For long moments, it stayed frozen within its shelter, invisible eyes staring out at them, a silent shadow within the dark.

Then, with swift and certain intent, it stepped from the trees into the light. The chill that had settled within Brin turned instantly to frost. She had never seen anything like the creature that stood before them now. It was man-shaped in appearance, raised upright in a half-crouch, its long arms dangling loosely before it. It was a big, strong creature, lean and heavily muscled. Its skin was a strange reddish color, drawn tight against its powerful body; it was hairless except for a thick ruff that grew about its loins. Great, hooked claws curled from its fingers and toes. Its face lifted toward them, and it was the face of some grotesque beast, blunt and scarred. Gleaming yellow eyes fixed upon their own, and its snout split wide in a hideous grin to reveal a mass of crooked teeth.

"What is it?" Rone Leah whispered in horror.

"What was promised," Allanon replied softly, his voice strangely distracted.

The reddish thing came forward a few steps further to the edge of the glen. There it stopped and waited.

Allanon turned to the Valegirl and the highlander. "It is a Jachyra, a thing of another age, a thing of great evil. It was locked from the lands by the magic of the creatures of faerie in a time before the dawn of man—in a time even farther back than that in which the Elves created the Forbidding. Only magic of equal power could have set it free again.

He straightened and brought his black robes close about him. "It appears that I was wrong—the Mord Wraiths did anticipate that we might come this way. Only within a place like these mountains, a place where the magic still lives, could a thing like the Jachyra be set loose again. The Wraiths have given us an adversary far more dangerous than they to overcome."

"Suppose we find out how dangerous," Rone suggested bravely and drew forth the ebony blade of the Sword of Leah.

"No." Allanon caught his arm quickly. "This battle is mine."

The highlander glanced at Brin for support. "It seems to me that any battle to be fought on this journey must be fought by all of us."

But Allanon shook his head. "Not this time, Prince of Leah. You have shown your courage and your devotion to this girl. I no longer question either. But the power of this creature is beyond you. I must face it alone."

"Allanon, don't!" Brin cried suddenly, grasping his arm.

He looked down at her then, the worn face and the eyes that penetrated past all that she would hide a mask of sad determination. They stared at each other, and then without quite knowing why she did so, she released him.

"Don't," she repeated softly.

Allanon reached to touch her cheek. At the far side of the glen, the Jachyra gave a sudden, sharp cry that shattered the silence of the afternoon—a cry that was almost like a laugh.

"Let me come with you!" Rone Leah insisted, again starting forward.

The Druid blocked his way. "Stand fast, Prince of Leah. Wait until you are called." The black eyes fixed those of the highlander. "Do not interfere in this. No matter what happens, stay clear. Give me your promise."

Rone hesitated. "Allanon, I cannot . . ."

"Give me your promise!"

The highlander stood before him defiantly for an instant longer and then reluctantly nodded. "I promise."

The Druid's eyes turned back to the Valegirl one last time, a lost and distant look in the gaze they gave to her. "Keep you safe, Brin Ohmsford," he whispered.

Then he wheeled about and started down into the glen.

25

Sunlight spilled from out of the cloudless blue afternoon sky to etch sharply Allanon's tall, shadowy form as it passed against the backdrop of the forest color. Warmth and sweet autumn smells lingered in the air, a teasing whisper to the Druid's senses, and across the woodlands a soft and gentle breeze blew down through the trees to ruffle the long, black robes. Within its banks of still summer-green grasses, the river of the Chard Rush glimmered azure and silver, its gleam reflected coldly in the tall man's eyes.

He was conscious of nothing now but the sleek, reddish-skinned form that crept catlike down the far slope of the glen's shallow bowl, yellow eyes narrowed, muzzle curled back in anticipation.

Please come back! Brin cried out the words in the silence of her mind, rendered voiceless by the horror of the familiar premonition that had returned suddenly to haunt her and dance in wild glee at the edges of her sight.

It was this that the premonition had warned against!

The Jachyra dropped down upon all fours, muscles rippling in corded knots beneath the taut skin as slaver began to form about its mouth. Spikes rose along the length of its spine and flexed with the movement of its body as it crept to the floor of the sunlit glen. Muzzle lifting toward the dark figure across from it, the monster cried out a second time—that same, hideous howl that rang like maddened laughter.

Allanon drew to a halt a dozen yards from where it crouched. Motionless, he faced the creature. On the hard, dark face there appeared a look of such frightening determination that it seemed to the Valegirl and the highlander that no living thing, however evil, could stand against it. Yet the Jachyra's frenzied grin merely broadened; more hooked teeth slipped into view from out of its drawn muzzle. There was madness in the yellow eyes.

For a long, terrible instant Druid and monster faced each other in the deep silence of the autumn afternoon and the whole of the world about them ceased to be. Again the Jachyra's laughter sounded. It stepped sideways—an odd, swinging movement. Then, with terrifying suddenness, it lunged for Allanon. Nothing had ever moved so fast. Little more than a blur of reddish fury, it sprang clear of the earth and tore into the Druid.

Somehow it missed. Allanon was faster than his attacker, slipping aside as swiftly as a shadow gone with night. The Jachyra flew past the Druid, tearing into the earth beyond as it landed. Whirling with scarcely a moment's pause, it sprang at its prey a second time. But already the Druid's hands were extended, blue fire bursting forth. The fire ripped into the Jachyra, throwing it backward in midair. It struck the ground in a tangled heap and still the fire tore at it, burning and searing and thrusting the beast back until it came to a jarring halt against a great oak.

Astonishingly, the Jachyra was back on its feet almost at once.

"Shades!" Rone Leah whispered.

It came at Allanon again, dodging and twisting past the Druid fire that flew from the other's fingers. Raging, it flung itself at the tall man with the deadly quickness of a snake. The blue fire hammered into it, flinging it away, but it caught the Druid with the claws of one hand, tearing into black robes and flesh. Allanon staggered back, shrugging at the impact of the blow, the fire disappearing into smoke. In the tall grass a dozen feet away, the Jachyra came back to its feet once more.

Cautiously, the two antagonists circled each other. The Druid's arms and hands extended guardedly before him, and the dark face was a mask of fury. But in the grasses through which he stepped, droplets of his blood streaked the deep green crimson.

The Jachyra's snout split wide once more, an evil, maddened grin. Trailers of smoke curled from the reddish skin where the fire had seared it, yet the monster seemed unharmed. Iron muscles rippled as it moved, a sleek and confident dance of death that led its intended victim on.

Again it attacked, a swift, fluid lunge that carried it into the Druid before the fire could be brought to bear. Allanon's hands fastened on the wrists of the beast, holding it upright so it could not reach his body. The crooked teeth snapped viciously, trying to fasten on the tall man's neck. Locked in this position, the two surged back and forth across the glen, twisting and squirming in an effort to gain the advantage.

Then, with a tremendous heave, the Druid flung the Jachyra over backward, lifting it off its feet and throwing it to the earth. Instantly the blue fire burst from his fingers and engulfed the monster. The Jachyra's cry was high and terrible, a frenzied shriek that froze the whole of the woods about it. Pain was in that cry, yet a pain that sounded of something inexplicably gleeful. The Jachyra leaped from the column of fire, twisting to free itself, its powerful red form steaming and alive with small bits of blue flame. It tumbled over and over through the grasses, a maddened and raging thing, consumed by an ever darker fire that burned within. It came to its feet yet again, hooked teeth gleaming as its muzzle drew back, yellowed eyes bright and ugly.

It likes the pain, Brin realized in horror. It feeds on it.

Behind her, the horses snorted and backed away from the scent of the Jachyra, pulling against the reins secured in Rone Leah's hands. The highlander glanced back worriedly, calling to the animals, trying unsuccessfully to calm them.

Once again, the Jachyra came at Allanon, darting and lunging through the blaze of Druid fire that burned into it. It almost reached the black-robed figure, claws ripping, and again Allanon stepped aside just in time, the blue fire thrusting the creature away in a burst of power.

Brin watched it all, sickened by the struggle but unable to look away. A single thought repeated itself in her mind, over and over. The Jachyra was too much. The Druid had fought so many terrible battles and survived; he had faced awesome creatures of dark magic. But the Jachyra was somehow different. It was a thing ignorant and incautious of life and death, whose existence defied all nature's laws—a creature of madness, frenzy, and purposeless destruction.

An ear-shattering shriek broke from the Jachyra's throat as the monster flung itself at Allanon again. The horses reared in fright, the reins tearing free of Rone's hands. Desperately, the highlander sought to recapture them. But the instant they pulled free, the horses bolted wildly back toward the falls. In a matter of seconds, they had disappeared into the trees beyond.

Rone and Brin turned back to the struggle below. Allanon had thrown up a wall of fire between himself and his attacker, the flames darting out at the Jachyra like knives as the creature sought vainly to break past. Purposefully the Druid maintained the wall, arms extended in rigid concentration. Then suddenly the arms dropped downward in a sweeping motion, bringing with them the wall of fire. Like a net it dropped across the Jachyra and the beast was consumed. It disappeared entirely for an instant, lost in a raging ball of flame. Twisting and turning, it sought to escape, but the fire clung to it tenaciously, held fast by the Druid's magic. Try as it might, the Jachyra could not shake free.

Brin's hand fastened on Rone. Perhaps . . .

But then the Jachyra bolted sharply away from Allanon and the open grasses of the glen, into the forest trees. Still the flames clung to it, but already the fire was beginning to dissipate. The distance between Druid and beast was too great, and Allanon could not maintain his hold. Howling, the monster flung itself into a stand of pine, shattering limbs and trunks, throwing fire everywhere. Wood and pine needles splintered and flamed, and smoke rolled out of the shadows.

At the center of the glen, Allanon's hands dropped away wearily. At its edge, Brin and Rone waited in hushed silence, staring at the smoky gloom into which the beast had disappeared. The forest was still once more.

"It's gone," Rone whispered finally.

Brin did not reply. Voiceless, she waited.

A moment later, something moved within the burned and darkened stretch of pine. Brin felt the cold that had settled deep within her flare sharply. The Jachyra stepped out from the trees. It glided to the edge of the glen, muzzle split wide in that hideous grin, yellow eyes gleaming.

It was unharmed.

"What manner of devil is this?" Rone Leah whispered.

The Jachyra crept back again toward Allanon, its breath harsh and eager. A low, anxious whine broke from its throat, and its snout lifted as if to catch the Druid's scent. On the long grass before it, a trace of the big man's blood dappled the green a bright scarlet. The Jachyra stopped. Slowly, deliberately, it bent to the blood and began to lick it from the earth. The whine turned suddenly deep with pleasure.

Then it attacked. In a single, fluid motion, it gathered its hind-legs beneath it and flung itself at Allanon. The Druid's hands came up, fingers extending—too slow. The creature was upon him before he could call forth the fire. They tumbled down into the long grass, rolling and spinning, locked together. So quick had the attack come that the monster was atop Allanon before Brin's sharp cry of warning could reach his ears. Blue fire flared at the tips of the Druid's fingers, searing the wrists and forearms of his attacker as they grappled, but the fire had no effect. The Jachyra's claws ripped into Allanon, tearing through cloth and flesh, ripping downward into bone. The Druid's head jerked back, pain flooding across the dark face—a pain that went beyond physical hurt. Desperately, the Druid sought to dislodge the beast, but the Jachyra had gotten too close and there was no room for leverage. Claws and teeth tore at Allanon, the corded body of the monstrous attacker holding its victim fast to the earth.

"No!" Rone Leah screamed suddenly.

Tearing free of Brin as she sought to restrain him, the Prince of Leah charged down into the glen, the ebony blade of his great broadsword grasped tightly in both hands. "Leah! Leah!" he cried in fury. The promise he had given the Druid was forgotten. He could not stand back and watch Allanon die. He had saved him once; he could do so again.

"Rone, come back!" Brin screamed after him futilely.

Rone Leah reached the struggling figures an instant later. The dark blade of the Sword of Leah lifted and swept downward in a glittering arc, cutting deep into the neck and shoulders of the Jachyra, driven by the force of magic, tearing through muscle and bone. The Jachyra reared back, a frightful howl breaking from its throat, its reddish body snapping upright as if it had been broken from within.

"Die, you monster!" Rone cried in rage as he caught sight of the torn and bloodied figure of Allanon beneath.

But the Jachyra did not die. One corded arm swung about sharply and caught the highlander across the face with stunning force. He flew backward, hands releasing their grip on the Sword of Leah. At once the Jachyra was after him, howling all the while in maddened delight, almost as if the greater pain pleased it in some foul, incomprehensible way. It caught Rone before he fell, seized him in its claws and flung him the length of the glen to lie in a crumpled heap.

Then it straightened. The dark blade of the Sword of Leah was still buried in its body. Reaching back, the Jachyra wrenched the sword free as if the blow had meant nothing to it. It hesitated an instant, the blade held before its yellow eyes. Then it hurled the Sword of Leah from it, into the air high above the waters of the Chard Rush, to fall into their grasp and be carried from sight like a piece of deadwood, bobbing and spinning in the swift current.

The Jachyra spun back around toward the fallen figure of Allanon. Astonishingly, the Druid was on his feet again, black robes shredded and stained dark with his blood. Seeing him risen, the Jachyra seemed to go completely beserk. Howling in fury, it sprang.

But this time the Druid did not try to stop it. Catching the Jachyra in midleap, his great hands closed about its neck like a vise. Heedless of the claws that tore at his body, he forced the monster backward to the ground, the hands squeezing. Shrieks rose out of the Jachyra's damaged throat and the reddish body twisted like a snake that has been pierced. Still the Druid's hands crushed inward. The muzzle split wide, teeth snapping and ripping at the air.

Then abruptly Allanon's hands released and jammed downward into the open maw. They thrust deep into the monster's throat. From the clasped fingers blue fire ripped downward. Convulsions shook the Jachyra, and its limbs flung wide. The Druid fire burned through its powerful body, down into the very core of its being. It struggled to break free for only an instant. Then the fire broke out of it from everywhere, and it exploded in a blinding flash of blue light.

Brin turned away, shielding her eyes against the glare. When she looked back, Allanon knelt alone atop a pile of charred ash.

Brin went first to the unconscious Rone, who lay sprawled in a twisted heap at the back edge of the glen, his breathing shallow and slow. Gently she straightened him, feeling carefully about his limbs and body for signs of breakage. She found none and, after wiping clean the cuts on his face, she hurried down to Allanon.

The Druid still knelt within the ashes that had been the Jachyra, his arms folded tight against his body, his head lowered against his chest. His long black robes were shredded and soaked with his blood.

Slowly Brin knelt beside him, a stricken look on her face as she saw what had been done to him. The Druid lifted his head wearily, hard eyes locking on her own.

"I am dying, Brin Ohmsford," he said quietly. She tried to shake her head, but his hand lifted to stop her. "Hear me, Valegirl. It was foretold that this should be. In the Valley of Shale, the shade of Bremen, my father, said to me that it should be. He said that I must pass from the land and that I would not come again. He said that it would happen before our quest was done."

He winced with sudden pain, his face tightening in response. "I thought that perhaps I could make it otherwise. But the Wraiths . . . the Wraiths found a way to set free the Jachyra, knowing perhaps . . . at least hoping that I would be the one it would encounter. It is a thing of insanity. It feeds on its own pain and on the pain of others. In its madness, it wounds not just the body, but the spirit as well. There is no defense. It would have torn itself apart . . . just to see me destroyed. It is a poison . . ."

He choked on the words. Brin bent close, swallowing back the hurt and fear. "We must dress the wounds, Allanon. We must . . ."

"No, Brin, it is finished," he cut her short. "There is no help for me. It must be for me as it was foretold." He glanced across the glen slowly. "But you must help the Prince of Leah. The poison will be in him as well. He is your protector now . . . as he said he would be." His eyes shifted back to her own. "Know that his sword is not lost. The magic will not let it be lost. It must . . . find its way to mortal hands . . . the river will carry it to those hands . . ."

Again he choked on the words, this time doubling over sharply against the pain of his wounds. Brin reached out and caught him, held him upright, close against her.

"Don't talk anymore," she whispered, tears filling her eyes.

Slowly he pulled away from her, straightening. Blood coated her hands and arms where she had held him.

A faint, ironical smile flickered on his lips. "The Wraiths think that I am the one they need fear—that I am the one who can destroy them." He shook his head slowly. "They are wrong. You are the power, Brin. You are the one that . . . nothing can stand against."

One hand fastened on her arm in a grip of iron. "Hear me well. Your father mistrusts the Elven magic; he fears what it can do. I tell you now that he has reason to mistrust it, Valegirl. The magic can be a thing of light or a thing of dark for the one who possesses it. It seems a toy, perhaps, but it has never been that. Be wary of its power. It is power like nothing I have ever seen. Keep it your own. Use it well, and it will see you safely through to the end of your quest. Use it well, and it will see the Ildatch destroyed!"

"Allanon, I cannot go on without you!" she cried softly, shaking her head in despair.

"You can and you must. As with your father . . . there is no one else." His dark face lowered.

She nodded dumbly, barely hearing him, lost in the jumble of emotions that raged within her as she fought back against the inevitability of what was happening.

"The age passes," Allanon whispered and the black eyes glistened. "So must the Druids pass with it." His hand lifted to fall gently on hers. "But the trust I carry for them must not pass, Valegirl. It must remain with those who live. That trust I give now to you. Bend close."

Brin Ohmsford leaned forward until her face was directly before his. Slowly, painfully, the Druid slipped one hand within the shredded robes to his chest, then brought it forth again, the fingers dipped into his own blood. Gently he touched her forehead. Holding the fingers to her flesh, warm with his lifeblood, he spoke softly in a language she had never heard. Something of his touch and of the words seemed to seep into her, filling her with a rush of exhilaration that swept across her vision in a surge of blinding color and then was gone.

"What . . . have you done to me?" she asked him haltingly.

But the Druid did not answer. "Help me to my feet," he commanded her.

She stared at him. "You cannot walk, Allanon! You are too badly hurt!"

A strange, unfamiliar gentleness filled the dark eyes. "Help me to my feet, Brin. I will not have to walk far."

Reluctantly she wrapped her arms about him and eased him from the ground. Blood soaked the grasses upon which he had knelt and the mass of ashes that had been the Jachyra.

"Oh, Allanon!" Brin was crying freely now.

"Walk me to the river's edge," he whispered.

Slowly, unsteadily, they stumbled across the empty glen to where the Chard Rush churned swiftly eastward within its grass-covered banks. The sun still shone a brilliant gold, warm and friendly as it brightened the autumn day. It was a day of life, not of death, and Brin cried within that it could not become so for Allanon.

They reached the bank of the river. Gently the Valegirl let the Druid settle once more into a kneeling position, his dark head lowered against the sunlight.

"When your quest is done, Brin," he said to her, "you will find me here." His face lifted to hers. "Now stand away."

Stricken, she stepped slowly back from him. Tears ran down her face, and her hands made pleading motions to the slouched form.

Allanon stared back at her for a long moment, then turned away. One blood-streaked arm lifted toward the waters of the Chard Rush, stretching out above them. The river went still instantly, its surface as calm and placid as that of a sheltered pond. A strange, hollow silence descended over everything.

A moment later the center of the still water began to churn violently and from the depths of the river rose the cries that had come from the waters of the Hadeshorn—high and piercing. They sounded for but an instant, and then all was still once more.

On the river's edge, Allanon's hand dropped to his side and his head bowed.

Then the spectral figure of Bremen rose from the Chard Rush. Gray and nearly transparent against the afternoon light, the shade rose to stand upon the river's waters, ragged and bent with age.

"Father," Brin heard Allanon call softly.

The shade came forward, gliding motionlessly on the still surface of the river. It came to where the Druid knelt. There it bent slowly downward and gathered the stricken form in its arms. Without turning, it moved back across the water, Allanon cradled close. It stopped again at the center of the Chard Rush, and beneath it the waters boiled fiercely, hissing and steaming. Then it sank slowly back into the river, and the last of the Druids was carried from sight. The Chard Rush was still an instant longer, and then the magic was ended and it began to churn eastward once again.

"Allanon!" Brin Ohmsford cried.

Alone on the riverbank she stared out across the swift-flowing waters and waited for the reply that would never come.

26

After capturing Jair at the fall of the Dwarf fortress of Capaal, the Mwellret Stythys marched him north through the wilderness of the Anar. Following the twists and turns of the Silver River as it wove threadlike through trees and brush, over cliffs, and across ravines, they passed deep into the forestland and the darkness that lay close about. All the while they traveled, the Valeman was kept gagged and leashed like an animal. Only at mealtimes was he freed of his bonds so that he might eat, and the cold reptilian eyes of the Mwellret were always upon him. Gray, rain-filled hours slipped away with agonizing slowness as the march wore on, and all that had been of the Valeman's life, his friends and companions, and his hopes and promises seemed to slip away with them. The woods were dank and fetid, infused by the poisoned waters of the Silver River with rot and choked by dying brush and trees clustered so thickly that the whole of the sky was screened away by their tangle. Only the river gave them any sense of direction as it flowed sluggishly past, blackened and fouled.

Others passed north in those days as well, bound for the deep Anar. On the wide road that ran parallel to the Silver River, which the Mwellret cautiously avoided, caravans of Gnome soldiers and their prisoners trekked in steady procession, mired in mud and laden with the pillage of an invading army. The prisoners were bound and chained—men who had fought as defenders at Capaal. They stumbled past in long lines, herded like cattle, Dwarves, Elves, and Bordermen, haggard, beaten, and stripped of hope. Jair looked down on them through the trees above the roadway over which they traveled and there were tears in his eyes.

Armies of Gnomes from Graymark also traveled the road, southbound in great, unruly masses as they hastened to join those tribes already advancing into the lands of the Dwarf people. Thousands came, grim and frightening, their hard yellow faces twisted with jeers as they called to the hapless prisoners that marched past them. Mord Wraiths came, too, though no more than a handful, dark and shadowed things that walked alone and were avoided by all.

The weather turned worse as the journey wore on. Skies turned black with thunderclouds and the rain began to fall in steady sheets. Lightning flashed in brilliant streaks and booming peals of thunder rolled the length of the sodden land. Autumn's trees drooped and matted with the wet, the colored leaves sinking and falling into the mire, and the ground turned muddied and uncertain. A gray and dismal cast settled down across the forestland, and it seemed as if the skies pressed against the earth to choke its life away.

Jair Ohmsford felt as if that might be so as he trudged helplessly through the wilderness brush, pulled on by the leather bindings gripped in the hands of the dark-robed figure before him. Cold and wet sank deep within him. As the hours passed, exhaustion began to take its toll. A fever settled in, and, as it did so, his mind began to wander. Flashes of what had brought him to this sorry state mingled with childhood memories in garbled bits of still-life that hovered briefly within his stricken mind and disappeared. Sometimes he was not entirely lucid, and strange and frightening visions would wrack him, stealing through his thoughts like thieves. Even when he was free momentarily of the effects of the fever, a dark despair colored his thoughts. There was no hope for him now, it whispered. Capaal, the defenders that had held her, and all of his friends and companions were gone. Images of them in the moment of their fall flashed in his mind with the blinding clarity of the lightning that crackled overhead through the canopy of the trees: Garet Jax, pulled deep into the gray waters of the Cillidellan by the Kraken; Foraker and Helt, buried beneath the wall of stone rubble brought down by the dark magic of the walkers; Slanter, running heedlessly down the underground corridors of the fortress before him, never looking back, never seeing. Even Brin, Allanon, and Rone appeared at times, lost somewhere deep within the Anar.

Sometimes thoughts of the King of the Silver River would come to him, clear and strangely poignant, filled with the wonder and the mystery of the old man. Remember, they whispered in soft, anxious tones. Do not forget what you must do. But he had forgotten, it seemed. Tucked within his tunic, hidden from the prying eyes of the Mwellret, were the gifts of magic the old man had bestowed on him—the vision crystal and the leather bag with the Silver Dust. He had them still and he meant to keep them. But somehow their purpose was strangely unclear, lost in the swell of the fever, hidden in the wanderings of his mind.

Finally, when they stopped for the night, the Mwellret saw that he was taken with fever and gave him a medicine to drink, mixing the contents of a pouch at his waist with a cup of dark, bitter ale. The Valeman tried to refuse the drink, wracked with the fever and his own sense of uncertainty, but the Mwellret forced it down him. Shortly after, he fell asleep and slept that night untroubled. At dawn he was given more of the bitter potion; by dusk of the second night, the fever had begun to subside.

They slept that night within a cave on a high ridgeline overlooking the dark curve of the river, dryer and warmer than they had been on previous nights, free of the extreme discomfort that had plagued them in the open forest. It was on this night that Jair again came to speak with his captor. They had finished their meal of ground roots and dried beef and drunk a small measure of the bitter ale; now they sat facing each other in the dark, huddled down within their cloaks against the night's chill. Without, the rain fell in a slow, steady drizzle, spattering noisily against trees, stones, and muddied earth. The Mwellret had not replaced the gag in the Valeman's mouth as he had done the past two nights, but had left it loose about his neck. He sat watching Jair, his cold eyes glittering, his reptilian face a vague shadow within the darkness of his cowl. He made no move, nor did he speak. He simply sat and watched as the Valeman crouched across from him. The minutes slipped by, and at last Jair grew determined to engage the creature in conversation.

"Where are you taking me?" he ventured cautiously.

Slitted eyes narrowed further, and it was then the Valeman realized that the Mwellret had been waiting for him to speak. "We go into the High Benss."

Jair shook his head, not understanding. "The High Bens?"

"Mountainss below the Ravensshorn, Elfling," the other hissed. "Sstay for a time within thosse mountainss. Put you in the Gnome prissonss at Dun Fee Aran!"

Jair's throat tightened. "Prison? You plan to lock me in a prison?"

"Guesstss of mine sstay there," the other rasped, laughing softly.

The Valeman stiffened at the sound of the laughter and fought back against the fear that washed through him. "Why are you doing this to me?" he demanded angrily. "What do you want from me?"

"Hss!" A hooked finger pointed. "Doess the Elfling truly not know? Doess he not ssee?" The cloaked form hunched closer. "Then lissten, little peopless. Hear! Ourss wass the gifted peopless, lordss over all the mountainss' life. Comess to uss the Dark Lord many yearss gone passt now, and a bargain wass sstruck. Little Gnome peopless ssent to sserve the Dark Lord if he leavess our peopless be, lordss sstill within the mountainss. Doess thiss, the Dark Lord, and in hiss time passsess from the earth. But we endure. We live!"

The crooked finger twisted slowly. "Then comess the walkerss, climbed from the dark pit of the Maelmord, climbed into our mountainss. Sserve the magic of the Dark Lord, they ssay. Give we up our homess, they ssay. Give we up the little peopless that sserve uss. Bargainss mean nothing now. We refusse the walkerss, the Wraithss. We are sstrong alsso. But ssomething done to uss. We ssicken and die. No young are born. Our peopless fail. Yearss passs, and we weaken to a handful. Sstill the walkerss ssay we musst go from the mountainss. At lasst we are too few, and the walkerss drive uss forth!"

He paused then, and the green slitted eyes burned deep into the Valeman's, filled with rage and bitterness. "Left me for dead, did the walkerss, the Wraithss. Black thingss of evil. But I live!"

Jair stared at the monster. Stythys was admitting to him that the Mwellrets in the time of Shea Ohmsford had sold to the Warlock Lord the lives of the mountain Gnomes so that they might be used to fight against the Southland in the aborted Third War of the Races. The Mwellrets had done this in order to preserve their lordship over their mountain kingdom in the Ravenshorn. It was as Foraker had told him and as the Dwarf people had suspected. But then the Mord Wraiths had come, successors to the power of the dark magic of the Warlock Lord. The Eastland was to be theirs now, and the Ravenshorn would no longer belong the the Mwellrets. When the lizard things had resisted, the Wraiths had sickened and destroyed them. So Stythys had indeed been driven forth from his homeland to be found by the Dwarves and brought into Capaal . . .

"But what has all this to do with me?" he demanded, a sinking suspicion settling through him.

"Magicss!" the Mwellret hissed instantly. "Magicss, little friend! I wissh what you posssess. Ssongss you ssing musst be mine! You have the magicss; you musst give them to me!"

"But I can't!" Jair exclaimed in frustration.

A grimace twisted the other's scaled face. "Can't, little friend? Powerss of magicss musst again come to my peopless—not to the Wraithss. Your magicss sshall be given, Elfling. At the prissonss you sshall give them. You will ssee."

Jair looked away. It was the same with Stythys as it had been with the Gnome Sedt Spilk—both had wanted mastery over something that Jair could not give them. The magic of the wishsong was his, and only he could use it. It would be as useless to the Mwellret as it had been to the Sedt.

And then a chilling thought struck him. Suppose that Stythys knew that? Suppose that the Mwellret knew he could not have the magic, but that he must make use of it through Jair? The Valeman remembered what had been done to him in that cell in Capaal—how the Mwellret had made him reveal the magic . . .

He caught his breath. Oh, shades! Suppose Stythys knew—or suppose that he even suspected—that there were other magics? Suppose he sensed the presence of the vision crystal and the Silver Dust?

"You can't have them," he whispered, almost before he realized what he was saying. There was a hint of desperation in his voice.

The Mwellret's reply was a soft hiss. "Prissonss will change your mind, little peopless. You will ssee."

Jair Ohmsford lay awake for a long time after that, gagged and hobbled once more, lost in the darkness of his thoughts as he listened to the sounds of the rainfall and the breathing of the sleeping Mwellret. Shadows lay all about the entrance to the little cave; without, the wind blew the stormclouds above the sodden forest. What was he to do? Behind him lay his quest and his shattered plans for saving Brin. Before him lay the Gnome prisons of Dun Fee Aran. Once locked within their walls, he might never come away again, for it was certain that the Mwellret meant to keep him there until he had revealed what he knew of the secrets of the Elven magic. But he would never give up those secrets. They were his to use in service to the King of the Silver River in exchange for the life of his sister. He would never give them up. Yet he sensed that, despite his resolve and whatever strength he could muster to resist his captor, sooner or later Stythys would find a way to wrest those secrets from him.

Thunder rumbled in the distance somewhere, rolling across the forest-land, deep and ominous. More ominous still was the despair of the Vale-man. It was a long time before exhaustion overcame him and he at last fell asleep.

Jair and the Mwellret resumed their march north with the coming of dawn on the third day, plodding through rain, mist, and sodden woods, and at midday they passed into the High Bens. The mountains were dark and rugged, a cluster of broken peaks and crags that straddled the Silver River where it washed down out of the high forestland below the Ravenshorn. The two climbed into their midst, swallowed by mist that clung to the rocks until at last, as the day waned and the night began to fall, they stood upon a bluff overlooking the fortress of Dun Fee Aran.

Dun Fee Aran was a sprawling, castlelike complex of walls, towers, watches, and battlements. The whole of the fortress had a gray and dreary cast to it as it materialized out of the rain before them, one that would have been there, Jair sensed, even in the best of weather. Wordlessly, they trudged from the trees, the tall, cloaked Mwellret leading the hobbled Valeman, and passed through the brush and scrub of the bluff face into the sodden camp. Gnome Hunters and retainers of all ranks and standings plodded past them across the muddied grounds, cloaked and hooded against the weather and caught up in their own concerns. No one questioned them. No one gave them a second look. They passed over stone parapets and walkways, over walls and causeways, down stairs, and through halls. The night began to deepen and the light to fail. Jair felt as if the world were closing in about him, shutting him away. He could smell the stench of the place, the closed and fetid reek of cells and human bodies. Lives were expended here without much thought, he sensed with a chill. Lives were locked away within these walls and forgotten.

A huge, blocklike structure loomed before them, windows no more than tiny slits through the stones, doors ironbound and massive. They entered this building and silence closed about them.

"Prissonss, Elfling," Jair heard the Mwellret whisper back at him.

They traversed a maze of dark and shadowed corridors, hallways filled with doors whose bolts and hinges showed rust and cobwebs undisturbed by the passage of time. Jair felt cold and empty as he watched row after row of these doors pass away. Their boots echoed dully in the silence, and only the distant sound of iron clanging and stone being chiseled came otherwise to his ears. Jair's eyes scanned dismally the walls that rose about him. How will I ever get out of here? he wondered in the silence of his mind. How will I ever find my way?

Then a torch flared before them in the corridor, and a small cloaked form came into view. It was a Gnome, aged and ruined, yellow face ravaged by some nameless disease so loathsome that Jair pulled back against the leather ties that bound him. Stythys advanced to where the Gnome stood waiting, bent over the ugly little man, and made a few cryptic signs with his fingers. The Gnome replied in kind; with a brief motion of one crooked hand, he bade them follow.

They went deeper into the prisons, the light from the world without all but lost in the twist of stone and mortar. Only the torch showed them the way, burning and smoking through the blackness.

They stopped at last before an ironbound door similar to the hundreds they had passed before it. Hands twisting roughly about the metal latch, the Gnome wrenched its bolt free. With a grating screech, he brought the heavy portal open. Stythys looked back at Jair, then pulled at the leash and brought him forward into the room beyond. It was a small, cramped cell, empty save for a pile of straw bundled in one corner and a wooden bucket next to the door. A single tiny slit cut into the far wall let though a sliver of gray light from without.

The Mwellret turned, cut free the bonds that tied Jair's hands and slipped loose the gag that bound his mouth. Roughly, he shoved the Valeman past him onto the bed of straw.

"Thiss iss yourss, Elfling," he hissed. "Home for little peopless until you tell me of the magicss." The crooked finger pointed back to the hunched form of the Gnome behind him. "Your jailer, Elfling. He iss mine, one who sstill obeyss. Mute he iss—doess not sspeak or hear. Ssongss of magicss usseless on him. Feedss and tendss you, he doess." He paused. "Hurtss you, too, if you dissobeyss."

The Gnome's ravaged face was turned toward the Valeman as Stythys spoke, but revealed nothing of what the mind behind it thought. Jair glanced about bleakly.

"Tellss me what I musst know, Elfling," the Mwellret whispered suddenly. "Tellss me or never leavess thiss plasse!"

The cold voice hung with a hiss in the silence of the little room as the yellow eyes bore deep into the Valeman's. Then Stythys wheeled away and strode back through the cellroom door. The Gnome jailer turned as well, crooked hands gripping the ironbound door by its latch bolt and pulling it firmly shut.

Huddled alone in the dark, Jair listened until the sound of their footfalls had disappeared.

The minutes slipped away into hours as he sat motionless within the cell, listening to the silence and thinking of how hopeless his position had become. Smells assailed his nostrils as he sat there, rank and harsh, mingling with the sense of despair that coursed relentlessly through him. He was scared now, so scared that he could barely bring himself to think. The thought had never crossed his mind before in all the time that had passed since he had abandoned his home in Shady Vale, fleeing from the Gnomes that hunted for him, but now for the first time it did.

You are going to fail, it whispered.

He would have cried then if he could have made himself do so, but somehow the tears would not come. Perhaps he was too frightened even for that. Think about how you will escape this place, he ordered himself. There is always a way out of everything.

He took a deep breath to steady himself. What would Garet Jax do in this situation? Or even Slanter? Slanter always had a way out; Slanter was a survivor. Even Rone Leah would have been able to come up with something.

His thoughts drifted for a time, wandering through memories of what had been, sidestepping effortlessly into dreams of what might somehow yet be. All of it was fantasy, false rendering of truths twisted in the madness of his own despair to become what he would have them be.

Then at last he made himself rise and walk about his tiny prison, exploring what he could already see was there, touching the damp, cold stone, and peering at the shaft of gray that slipped through the airhole from the skies without. He journeyed all about the cell, studying to no particular purpose, waiting for his emotions to still themselves and his thoughts to settle.

Suddenly he decided to use the vision crystal. If he were to have any sense of what time remained to him, he must discover what had become of Brin.

Hurriedly, he brought the crystal and its silver chain out from their place of concealment within his tunic. He stared down at the crystal, cupped gently within his hands. He could hear the old King's voice whispering to him, cautioning him that this would be the means by which he could follow Brin's progress. All he need do was sing to it . . .

Softly, he sang. At first, his voice would not come, choked with emotions that swam restlessly through him still. Yet he hardened himself against his own sense of uncertainty, and the sound of the wishsong filled the tiny room. Almost at once, the vision crystal brightened, sharp light flaring outward into the gloom and chasing the shadows before it.

He saw at once that it came from a small fire, and Brin's face was before him, obviously studying the flames of a campfire. Her lovely face was cupped in her hands. Then she looked up and seemed to be searching. There were signs of strain and worry, and she looked almost haggard. Then she looked down again and sighed. She shuddered slightly, as if repressing a sob. All of her that Jair could see seemed to be given over to despair. Whatever had happened to her had obviously been unpleasant . . .

Jair's voice broke as worry for his sister flooded through him, and the image of his sister's frowning face wavered and vanished. The Valeman stared down in stunned silence at the crystal cupped in his hands.

Where, he wondered, was Allanon? There had been no sign of him in the crystal.

Leaves in the wind, the voice of the King of the Silver River whispered in his mind. She will be lost.

Then he closed his hands tightly about the vision crystal and stared sightlessly into the darkness.

27

Night had settled down across the forests of the Anar when Brin Ohmsford saw the lights. They winked at her like fireflies through the screen of the trees and shadows that stretched away into the dark, small, elusive, and distant.

She slowed, her arms wrapping quickly about Rone to keep him from falling as he stumbled to a halt beside her. An aching weariness wracked her body, but she forced herself to hold the highlander upright as he fell against her, his head drooping to her shoulder, his face hot and flushed with the fever.

". . . can't find where . . . lost, can't find . . ." he muttered incoherently and the fingers of his hand gripped her arm until it hurt.

She whispered to him, letting him hear her voice and know she was still there. Slowly the fingers relaxed their grip, and the fevered voice went silent.

Brin stared ahead at the lights. They danced through forest boughs still thick with autumn leaves, bits and pieces of brightness. Fire! She whispered the word urgently, and it pushed back against the despair and the hopelessness that had closed in about her in steadily deepening layers since the march east from the Chard Rush had begun. How long ago it all seemed now—Allanon gone, Rone so badly wounded, and she alone. She closed her eyes against the memory. She had walked all that afternoon and into the night, following the run of the Chard Rush eastward, hoping, praying that it would lead her to some other human being who could help her. She didn't know how long or how far she had walked; she had lost track of time and distance. She only knew that somehow she had managed to keep going.

She straightened, pulling Rone upright. Ahead, the lights flickered their greeting. Please! she cried silently. Please, let it be the help I need!

She trudged ahead, Rone's arm looped about her shoulders, his body sagging against hers as he stumbled beside her. Tree limbs and scrub brushed at her face and body, and she bent her head against them. Putting one foot before the other with wooden doggedness, she went forward. Her strength was almost gone. If there was no help to be had here . . .

Then abruptly the screen of trees and shadows broke apart before her, and the source of the lights stood revealed. A building loomed ahead, shadowed and dark, save for slivers of yellow light that escaped from two places in its squarish bulk. Voices sounded from somewhere within, faint and indistinct.

Holding Rone close, she pushed on. As she drew nearer, the building began to come into focus. A low, squat structure with a peaked roof, it was constructed of timbers and sideboards on a stone foundation. A covered porch fronted a single storey with a garret, and a stable sat back away from the rear of the building. Two horses and a mule stood tied to a hitching post, heads lowered to crop the drying grass. Along the front of the building, a series of windows stood barred and shuttered against the night. It was through the gaps in the shutters that light thrown by oil lamps had escaped and been seen by the Valegirl.

"A little farther, Rone," she whispered, knowing that he didn't understand, but would respond to the sound of her voice.

When she was a dozen feet from the porch, she saw the sign that hung from the eaves of its sloping roof: ROOKER LINE TRADING CENTER.

The sign swayed gently in the night wind, weathered and split, the paint so badly faded into the wood that the letters were barely legible. Brin glanced up at it briefly and looked away. All that mattered was that there were people inside.

They climbed onto the porch, stumbling and tripping on the weathered boards, to sag against the door jamb. Brin groped for the handle, and the voices within suddenly went still. Then the Valegirl's hand closed about the metal latch, and the heavy door swung open.

A dozen rough faces turned to stare at her, a mix of surprise and wariness in their eyes. Trappers, Brin saw through a haze of smoke and exhaustion—bearded and unkempt, their clothes of worn leather and animal skins. Hard-looking, they clustered in groups about a serving bar formed of wood planks laid crosswise on upended ale kegs. Animal pelts and provisions lay stacked behind the counter, and a series of small tables with stools sat before it. Oil lamps hung from low-beamed ceiling rafters and cast their harsh light against the night shadows.

With her arms wrapped about Rone, Brin stood silently in the open doorway and waited.

"They's ghosts!" someone muttered suddenly from along the serving counter, and there was a shuffling of feet.

A tall, thin man in shirt-sleeves and apron came out from behind the counter, head shaking slowly. "If they was dead things, they'd have no need to open the door now, would they? They'd just walk right on through!"

He crossed to the middle of the room and stopped. "What's happened to you, girl?"

Brin realized suddenly, through the haze of fatigue and pain that assailed her, how they must appear to these men. They might well have been something brought back from the dead—two worn and ragged things, their clothing damp and muddied, their faces white with exhaustion, hanging onto each other like straw-filled scarecrows. A bloodied strip of cloth had been bound about Rone's head, but the rawness of the wound showed through. On his back, the scabbard that had once held the great broadsword lay empty. Her own face was soiled and drawn, and her dark eyes haunted. Spectral apparitions, they stood framed in the light of the open doorway, swaying unevenly against the night.

Brin tried to speak, but no words came out.

"Here, lend a hand," the tall man called back to the others at the counter, coming forward at once to catch hold of Rone. "Come on now, lend a hand!"

A brawny woodsman came forward quickly, and the two ushered the Valegirl and the highlander to the nearest table, placing them on the low stools. Rone slumped forward with a groan, his head sagging.

"What's happened to you?" the tall man repeated once again, helping to hold the highlander in place so he would not fall. "This one's burning up with fever!"

Brin swallowed thickly. "We lost our horses in a fall coming down out of the mountains," she lied. "He was sick before then, but it's grown worse. We walked the riverbank until we found this place.

"My place," the tall man informed her. "I'm a trader here. Jeft, draw a couple ales for these two."

The woodsman slipped behind the counter to an ale keg and opened the spigot into two tall glasses.

"How about a free one for the rest of us, Stebb?" one of a group of hard-looking men at the far end of the counter called out.

The trader shot the man a venomous look, brushed back a patch of thinning hair atop a mostly balding pate, and turned again to Brin. "Shouldn't be in those mountains, girl. There's worse than fever up there."

Brin nodded wordlessly, swallowing against the dryness in her throat. A moment later the woodsman returned with the glasses of ale. He passed one to the Valegirl, then propped Rone up long enough to see that he sipped at the other. The highlander tried to grasp the glass and gulp the harsh liquid down, choking as he did. The woodsman moved the glass away firmly.

"Let him drink!" the speaker at the end of the bar called out again.

Another laughed. "Naw, it's wasted! Any fool can see he's dying!"

Brin glanced up angrily. The man who had spoken saw her look and sauntered toward her, his broad face breaking into an insolent grin. The others in the group trailed after, winking knowingly and chuckling.

"Something the matter, girl?" the speaker sneered. "Afraid you . . . ?"

Instantly Brin was on her feet, barely aware of what she was doing as she snatched her long knife from its sheath and brought it up in front of his face.

"Now, now," the woodsman Jeft interceded quickly at her side, pushing her gently back. "No need for that, is there?"

He turned to face the speaker, standing directly before him. The woodsman was a big man, and he towered over the men who had come down from the end of the counter. The members of the group glanced at one another uncertainly.

"Sure, Jeft, no harm meant," the offender muttered. He looked down at Rone. "Just wondered about that scabbard. Crest looks like a royal seal of some type." His dark eyes shifted to Brin. "Where you from, girl?"

He waited a moment, but Brin refused to answer. "No matter." He shrugged. With his friends trailing after him he moved back down the counter. Gathering close to resume their drinking, they began conversing in low tones, their backs turned. The woodsman stared after them for a moment, then knelt down beside Brin.

"Worthless bunch," he muttered. "Camp out west of Spanning Ridge masquerading as trappers. Live by their wits and the misfortune of others."

"Been drinking and wasting time here since morning." The trader shook his head. "Always got the money for the ale, though." He looked at the Valegirl. "Feeling a little better now?"

Brin smiled in response. "Much better, thank you." She glanced down at the dagger in her hand. "I don't know what's wrong with me. I don't know what I was . . ."

"Hush, forget it." The big woodsman patted her hand. "You're exhausted."

Beside him, Rone Leah moaned softly, his head lifting momentarily, his eyes open and staring into space. Then he slipped down again.

"I have to do something for him," Brin insisted anxiously. "I have to find a way to break the fever. Do you have anything here that might help?"

The trader glanced at the woodsman worriedly, then shook his head. "I've not seen a fever as bad as this one often, girl. I have a tonic that might help. You can give it to the boy and see if it brings the fever out." He shook his head again. "Sleep might be best, though."

Brin nodded dumbly. She was having trouble thinking clearly, the exhaustion folding in about her as she sat staring down at the dagger. Slowly she slipped it back into its sheath. What had she been thinking she would do? She had never harmed anything in her entire life. Certainly the man from west of Spanning Ridge had been insolent, perhaps even threatening—but had there been any real danger to her? The ale burned warmly in her stomach, and a flush spread through her body. She was tired and strangely unnerved. Deep within, she felt an odd sense of loss and of slipping.

"Not much room in here for sleeping," the trader Stebb was saying. "There's a tack room in back of the stable I let the help use in the trapping season. You can have that. There's a stove and bed for your friend and straw for you."

"That would be fine," Brin murmured and found to her astonishment that she was crying.

"Here, here." The burly woodsman put an arm about her shoulders, blocking her away from the view of those gathered along the serving counter. "Won't do for them to see that, girl. Got to be strong, now."

Brin nodded wordlessly, wiped the tears away, and stood up. "I'm all right."

"Blankets are out in the shed," the trader announced, standing up with her. "Let's get you settled in."

With the aid of the woodsman, he brought Rone Leah back to his feet and walked him toward the rear of the trading center and down a short, darkened hallway that ran past a set of storage rooms. Brin shot a parting glance at the men gathered about their ale glasses before the serving counter and followed after. She didn't much care for the looks directed back her way by the ones from west of Spanning Ridge.

A small wooden door opened out into the night at the back of the building, and the trader, the woodsman, Rone, and Brin moved toward the stable and its tack room. The trader slipped ahead, quickly lighted an oil lamp hanging from a peg on one wall, and then held wide the tack room door to admit the others. The room beyond was clean, though a bit musty, its walls hung with traces and harness. A small iron stove sat in one corner, shielded by a stone alcove. A single bed sat close beside it. A pair of shuttered windows stood against the night.

The trader and the woodsman laid the feverish highlander carefully on the bed and covered him with the blankets stacked at one end. Then they fired the iron stove until its wood was burning brightly and carried in a pallet of fresh straw for Brin. As they were about to leave, the trader placed the oil lamp on a stone ledge next to the stove and turned briefly to Brin.

"Here's the tonic for his fever." He passed a small, amber-colored bottle to the Valegirl. "Give him two swallows—no more. In the morning, two more." He shook his head doubtfully. "Hope it helps, girl."

He started through the doorway with the woodsman in tow. Then once more he turned. "There's a latch on this door," he declared, pausing. "Keep it drawn."

He closed the door softly behind him. Brin walked over and drew the latch into place. From just without, she could hear the voices of the trader and the woodsman as they talked.

"A bad lot, that Spanning Ridge bunch," the woodsman muttered.

"Bad as any," the trader agreed.

They were silent for a moment.

"Time for me to be on my way," the woodsman said. "Several hours back to the camp."

"Safe journey," the trader replied.

They started to move away, their words fading.

"You'd best watch yourself with that bunch inside, Stebb," the woodsman advised. "Watch yourself close."

Then the words died away completely and the two were gone.

Brin turned back to Rone within the silence of the tack room. Propping him up carefully, she forced him to take two swallows of the tonic provided by the trader. When he had taken the medicine, she laid him down again and covered him up.

Then she took a seat next to the stove, wrapped herself in her blanket, and sat back wordlessly. On the wall of the little room, cast by the solitary flame of the oil lamp, her shadow rose up before her like a dark giant.

The charred stump of still-burning log collapsed with a thud inside the stove as the ashes beneath it gave way, and Brin woke with a start. She had dozed, she realized, but didn't know for how long. She rubbed her eyes wearily and glanced about. The tack room was dark and still, the flame of the oil lamp faint and lonely in a gathering of shadows.

She thought immediately of Allanon. It was difficult still for her to accept that the Druid was gone. An expectation lingered within her that at any moment there would come a sharp knock upon the latched door and his deep voice would call to her. Like a shadow that came and went with the passing of the light—that was the way that Rone had described him that last night before the Druid died . . .

She caught herself sharply, strangely ashamed that she had allowed herself to even think the word. But Allanon had died, passing from the world of mortal men as all must, going from the Four Lands in the arms of his father—perhaps to where Bremen kept watch. She thought about that possibility for a moment. Could it be that he had indeed gone to be with his father? She remembered his words to her: "When your quest is done, Brin, you will find me here." Did that mean that he, too, had locked himself into a limbo existence between the worlds of life and death?

There were tears in her eyes, and she wiped them hurriedly away. She could not permit herself tears. Allanon was gone, and she was alone.

Rone Leah stirred restlessly beneath the heavy blankets, his breathing harsh and uneven. She rose slowly and moved to where he lay. The lean, sunburned face was hot, dry, and drawn tight against the fever that ravaged his body. He shivered momentarily as she watched, as if suddenly chill, then went taut. Words whispered on his lips, their meaning lost.

What am I to do with him? the Valegirl asked herself helplessly. Would that I had my father's skill. I have given him the tonic provided by the trader. I have wrapped him in blankets to keep him warm. But none of it seems to be helping. What else am I to do?

It was the Jachyra's poison that was infecting him, she knew. Allanon had said that the poison attacked not just the body, but the spirit as well. It had killed the Druid—and while his wounds had been so much worse than Rone's, still he was Allanon and much the stronger of the two. Even the lesser damage suffered by the highlander was proving to be more than his body could fight.

She sank down next to his bed, her hand closing gently about his. Her protector. She smiled sadly—who would now protect him?

Memories slipped like quicksilver through her mind, jumbled and confused. They had gone through so much to reach this lonely, desperate night, she and Rone Leah. And at what terrible cost. Paranor was gone. Allanon was dead. Even the Sword of Leah, the one real piece of magic they possessed between them, was gone. All that was left was the wishsong.

Yet Allanon had said the wishsong would be enough . . .

Booted feet shuffled softly on the earthen floor of the stable without. Blessed with the Elven senses of her forefathers, she caught the noise where another might have missed it. Hurriedly, she dropped Rone's hand and scrambled to her feet, her weariness forgotten.

Someone was out there—someone who didn't want to be heard.

One hand crept guardedly to the haft of the long knife sheathed at her waist, then dropped away. She could not do that. She would not.

The latch on the door jiggled softly and caught.

"Who's there?" she called out.

A low cursing sounded from just outside, and abruptly several heavy bodies slammed into the tack room door. Brin backed away, searching hurriedly for another way out. There was none. Again the bodies slammed into the door. The iron latch gave way with an audible snap and five dark forms came crashing into the room, the faint light of the oil lamp glinting dully off drawn knives. They gathered in a knot at the edge of the shadows, grunting and mumbling drunkenly as they faced the girl.

"Get out of here!" she snapped, anger and fear racing through her.

Laughter greeted her words, and the foremost of the intruders stepped forward into the light. She knew him at once. He was one of those from west of Spanning Ridge, one of those the trader Stebb had called thieves.

"Pretty girl," he muttered, his words slurred. "Come on . . . over here."

The five crept forward, spreading out across the darkened room. She might have tried to break past them, but that would have meant leaving Rone and she had no intention of doing that. Again, her hand closed about the long knife.

"Now, don't do that . . ." the speaker whispered, edging closer. Suddenly he lunged, quicker than the girl would have thought after having drunk so much, and his hand fastened about her wrist, yanking it away from the weapon. Instantly the others closed in, hands grasping her clothing, pulling her to them, pulling her down. She fought back wildly, striking out at her attackers. But they were much stronger than she and they were hurting her.

Then something within her seemed to snap as surely as had the latch on the tack room door when broken. Her thoughts scattered, and everything she was disappeared in a flash of blinding anger. What happened next was all instinct, hard and quick. She sang, the wishsong a new and different sound than any that had gone before. It filled the shadowed room with a fury that whispered of death and mindless destruction. Her attackers staggered back from the Valegirl, eyes and mouths widening in shock and disbelief, and hands coming up to cover their ears. They doubled over in agony as the wishsong penetrated their senses and crushed in about their minds. Madness rang in its call, frenzy and hurt so bitter it could almost be seen.

The five from west of Spanning Ridge were smothered in the sound.

They fell against one another as they groped for the door that had brought them in. From their open mouths, shrieks came back in answer to the Valegirl's song. Still she did not stop. Her fury was so complete that reason could find no means to stem it. The wishsong rose, and the animals in the stable kicked and slammed wildly against their stalls, crying out their pain as the girl's voice ripped at them.

Then the five at last found the open doorway and stumbled from the tack room in maddened desperation, curled over like broken things, shaking and whimpering. Blood ran from their mouths, from their ears, and from their noses. Hands covered their faces, the fingers knotted into claws.

Brin saw them anew in that instant as the blindness of her fury left her. She also saw the trader Stebb appear suddenly from the darkness as the intruders ran past, a look of horror in his face as he, too, stopped and backed away, hands held frantically before him. Reason returned in a rush of guilt, and the wishsong died into stillness.

"Oh, shades . . ." she cried softly and collapsed in stricken disbelief.

Midnight came and went. The trader had left her alone again and gone back to the comfort and sanity of his own lodgings, his eyes frightened and haunted. In the darkness of the forest clearing that sheltered the Rooker Line Trading Center, all was still.

She sat curled close to the iron stove. Fresh wood burned in it, snapping and sparking in the silence. She sat with her legs drawn up against her chest, her arms wrapped about them like a child lost in thought.

But her thoughts were dark and filled with demons. Fragments of Allanon's words lay scattered in those thoughts, whispering of what she had for so long refused to hear. The wishsong is power—power like nothing I have ever seen. It will protect you. It will see you safely through your quest. It will destroy the Ildatch.

Or destroy me, she answered back. Or destroy those about me. It can kill. It can make me kill.

She stirred finally, cramped and aching from the position she had held for so long, her dark eyes glistening with fear. She stared through the grated door of the iron stove, watching the red glare of the flames as they danced within. She might have killed those five men from west of Spanning Ridge, she thought despairingly. She would have killed them, perhaps, had they not found the door.

Her throat tightened. What was to prevent that from happening the next time she was forced to use the wishsong?

Behind her, Rone moaned softly, thrashing beneath the blankets that covered him. She turned slowly to find his face, bending close to stroke his forehead. His skin was deathly pale now, feverish, hot, and drawn. His breathing was worse as well, turned shallow and raspy, as if each breath were an effort that sapped him of his strength.

She knelt beside him, her head shaking. The tonic had not helped. He was growing weaker, and the poison was working deeper into his system, draining him of his life. If it were not stopped, he was going to die . . .

Like Allanon.

"No!" she cried softly, urgently, and she gripped his hand in hers as if she might hold back the life that seeped away.

She knew in that instant what she must do. Savior and destroyer—that was what the shade of Bremen had named her. Very well. To those thieves from west of Spanning Ridge, she had been destroyer. Perhaps to Rone Leah she could be savior.

Still holding his hand with her own, she bent close to his ear and began to sing. Softly, gently the wishsong slipped from her lips, floating like invisible smoke through the air about them both. Carefully, she reached out to the sickened highlander, probing for the hurt he felt, searching out the source of the poison that was killing him.

I must try, she told herself as she sang. I must! By morning he will be gone, the poison spread all through him—poison that attacks the spirit as well as the body. Allanon had said it was so. Perhaps, then, the Elven magic can find a means to heal.

She sang, sweet and lingering tones that wrapped the highlander close about and brought him to her. Slowly, he began to cease his shivering and thrashing and to become still beneath the calming sound. He slipped down into the blankets, his breathing growing steadier and stronger.

The minutes slipped away with agonizing slowness as the Valegirl sang on and waited for the change she somehow sensed must come. When at last it did, it came so suddenly that she nearly lost control of what she was about. From the ravaged, wasted body of Rone Leah, the poison of the Jachyra lifted in a red mist—dissipating out of the unconscious highlander to float above him, swirling wickedly in the dim light of the oil lamp. Hissing, it hung above its victim for an instant as Brin interposed the magic of the wishsong between its touch and the body of Rone Leah. Then slowly it faded into nothingness and was gone.

On the bed beside her, sweat bathed the face of the Prince of Leah. The drawn and haggard look was gone, and the breathing was steady and even once more. Brin stared down at him through a veil of tears as the wishsong died into silence.

I have done it, she cried softly. I have used the magic for good. Savior this time—not destroyer.

Still kneeling beside him, she buried her face in the warmth of his body, her arms holding him close. In moments, she was asleep.

28

They stayed on for two days at the Rooker Line Trading Center, waiting for Rone to regain strength enough to resume the journey east.
The fever was gone by morning and the highlander was resting comfortably, but he was still entirely too weak to attempt to travel. So Brin
asked permission of the trader Stebb to keep the use of the tack room for
one day more, and the trader agreed. He provided them with food for
their meals, rations of ale, medicines, and blankets, and he refused quickly
all offers of payment. He was happy to be of help to them, he assured the
Valegirl. But he was uneasy in her presence and he never quite managed to
let his eyes meet hers. Brin understood well enough what was happening.
The trader was a kind and decent man, but now he was frightened of her
and of what she might do to him if he refused it. He would probably have
helped her out of his basic generosity, but fear had added urgency to his
impulse. He obviously felt that this was the quickest and most expedient
way to get her out of his life.

She remained for the most part within the confines of the little tack
room with Rone, seeing to his needs and talking with him of what had
befallen them since the death of Allanon. Talking about it seemed to help;
while both were still stunned by what had happened, the sharing of their
feelings brought forth a common determination that they must go forward
to complete the quest that the Druid had left to them. A new closeness developed between them, stronger and more certain in its purpose. With the
death of Allanon, they now had only each other upon whom to rely and
each felt new value in the other's presence. Alone together in the solitude
of their tiny room at the rear of the trader's stables, they spoke in hushed
tones of the choices that had been made to bring them to this point in
their lives and of those that must yet be made. Slowly, surely, they bound
themselves as one.

Yet despite their binding together in spirit and cause, there remained
some things of which Brin could not bring herself to speak, even to Rone
Leah. She could not tell him of the blood that Allanon had taken from his
own ravaged body to place upon her—blood that in some way was meant
to pledge her to him, even in death. Nor could she tell Rone of the uses to
which she had put the wishsong—once in fury to destroy human life, a second time in desperation to save it. She could speak of none of these things
to the highlander—in part because she did not fully understand them, in
part because the implications frightened her so greatly that she was not sure
she wanted to. The blood oath was too remote in purpose now for her to

dwell upon, and the uses of the wishsong were the result of emotions that she promised herself she would not let get away from her again.

There was another reason for not speaking to Rone of these things. The highlander was troubled enough as matters stood by the loss of the Sword of Leah—so troubled, in fact, that he could seem to think of little else. He meant to have the sword back again, he told her over and over. He would search it out and reclaim it whatever the cost. His insistence frightened her, for he seemed to have bound himself to the sword with such need that it was as if the weapon had somehow become a part of him. Without it, she guessed, the highlander did not believe that he could survive what lay ahead. Rone felt that without it he must surely be lost.

All the while she listened to him talk of this and thought about how deeply he seemed now to depend on the magic of the blade, she pondered as well her own dependence on the wishsong. It was just a toy, she had always told herself—but that was a lie. It was anything but a toy; it was magic every bit as dangerous as that contained in the missing Sword of Leah. It could kill. It was, in fact, what her father had always said—a birthright that she would have been better off without. Allanon had warned her as he lay dying: "The power of the wishsong is like nothing I have ever seen." The words whispered darkly as she listened to Rone. Power to heal; power to destroy—she had seen them both. Must she be as dependent on the magic as Rone now seemed to be? Between her and the Elven magic, which was to be master?

Her father had fought his own battle to discover the answer to that question, she knew. He had fought it when he had struggled to overcome his inability to master the power of the magic contained within the Elfstones. He had done so, survived the staggering forces it had unleashed within him, and then cast it aside forever. Yet his brief use of the power had exacted its price—a transmutation of the magic from the Elfstones to his children. So now, perhaps, the battle must be fought yet another time. But what if this time the power could not be controlled?

The second day drifted into night. The Valegirl and the highlander ate the meal brought to them by the trader and watched the darkness deepen. When Rone had grown weary and rolled into his blankets to sleep, Brin slipped out into the cool autumn night to breathe smells that were sharp and clean and to lose herself for a time in skies grown bright with a crescent moon and stars. On her way past the trading center, she caught sight of the trader as he sat smoking his pipe on the empty veranda, his highbacked chair tilted against the rail. No one had come by for drinks or talk that evening, so he sat alone.

Quietly, she walked over to him.

"Evening," he greeted hastily, sitting forward a bit too quickly in the chair, almost as if he were poised to flee.

Brin nodded. "We will be leaving in the morning," she informed him and thought she detected a look of immediate relief in his dark eyes. "But I wanted to thank you first for your help."

He shook his head. "No need." He paused, brushing back his thinning hair. "I'll see to it that you have some supplies to get you through the first few days or so."

Brin didn't argue. It was pointless to do anything other than simply to accept what was offered.

"Would you have an ash bow?" she asked, thinking suddenly of Rone. "One that could be used for hunting when we . . . ?"

"Ash bow? Got one right here, as a matter of fact." The trader was on his feet at once. He ducked through the doorway leading into the center and emerged a moment later with a bow and quiver of arrows. "You take these," he pressed. "No charge, of course. Good, solid weapons. Belong to you, anyway, since they were dropped by those fellows you chased off." He caught himself, and cleared his throat self-consciously. "Anyway, you take them," he finished.

He set them down in front of her and dropped back into his chair, fingers drumming nervously on the wooden arm.

Brin picked up the bow and arrows. "They don't really belong to me, you know," she said quietly. "Especially not because of . . . what happened."

The trader looked down at his feet. "Don't belong to me, either. You take them, girl."

There was a long silence. The trader stared past her resolutely into the dark. Brin shook her head. "Do you know anything of the country east of here?" she asked him.

He kept his eyes turned away. "Not much. It's bad country."

"Is there anybody who might know?"

The trader didn't answer.

"What about the woodsman who was here the other night?"

"Jeft?" The trader was silent for a moment. "I suppose. He's been a lot of places."

"How would I find him?" she pressed, growing increasingly uncomfortable with the man's reticence.

The trader's brows knitted. He was thinking about what answer he should give her. Finally, he looked directly at her. "You don't mean him any harm, do you, girl?"

Brin stared at him sadly for a moment, then shook her head. "No, I don't mean him any harm."

The trader studied her a moment, then looked away. "He's a friend, you see." Then he pointed out toward the Chard Rush. "He's got a camp a few miles downriver, south bank."

Brin nodded. She started to turn away, then stopped. "I am the same person I was when you helped me that first night," she said quietly.

Leather boots scuffed against the wooden planks of the porch. "Maybe it just don't seem that way to me," came the response.

Her mouth tightened. "You don't have to be afraid of me, you know. You really don't."

The boots went still and the trader looked down at them. "I'm not afraid," he said, his voice low.

She waited a moment longer, searching futilely for something more to say, then turned and walked into the dark.

The following morning, shortly after daybreak, Brin and Rone departed the Rooker Line Trading Center for the country that lay east. Carrying foodstuffs, blankets, and the bow supplied by the trader, they bade the anxious man farewell and disappeared into the trees.

It was a bright, warm day that greeted them. As they made their way downriver along the south bank of the Chard Rush, the air was filled with the sounds of forest life and the smell of drying leaves. A west wind blew gently out of the distant Wolfsktaag, and leaves drifted earthward in lazy spirals to lie thick upon the forest ground. Through the trees, the land ahead could be seen to run on in a gentle sloping of rises and vales. Squirrels and chipmunks scattered and darted away at the sound of their approach, interrupted in their preparations for a winter that seemed far distant from this day.

At midmorning, Valegirl and highlander paused to rest for a time, sitting side by side on an old log, hollowed out and worm-eaten with age. In front of them, barely a dozen yards distant, the Chard Rush flowed steadily eastward into the deep Anar; in its grasp, deadwood and debris that was washed down from out of the high country twisted and turned in intricate patterns.

"It's still hard for me to believe that he's really gone," Rone said after a time, eyes gazing out across the river.

Brin didn't have to ask whom he meant. "For me, too," she acknowledged softly. "I sometimes think that he really isn't gone at all—that I was mistaken in what I saw—that if I am patient, he will come back, just as he always has."

"Would that be so strange?" Rone mused. "Would it be so surprising if Allanon were to do exactly that?"

The Valegirl looked at him. "He is dead, Rone."

Rone kept his face turned away, but nodded. "I know." He was quiet for a moment before continuing. "Do you think that there was anything that could have been done to save him, Brin?"

He looked at the girl then. He was asking her if there was anything that *he* could have done. Brin's smile was quick and bitter. "No, Rone. He knew that he was going to die; he was told that he would not complete this quest. He had accepted the inevitability of that, I think."

Rone shook his head. "I would not have done so."

"Nor I, I suppose," Brin agreed. "Perhaps that was why he chose to tell us nothing of what was to happen. And perhaps his acceptance is something we cannot hope to understand, because we could never hope to understand him."

The highlander leaned forward, his arms braced against his outstretched legs. "So the last of the Druids disappears from the land, and there is no one left to stand against the walkers except you and me." He shook his head hopelessly. "Poor us."

Brin glanced down self-consciously at her hands, folded in her lap before her. She remembered Allanon touching her forehead with his blood as he lay dying and she shivered with the memory.

"Poor us," she echoed softly.

They rested for a few minutes longer, then resumed their journey east. Barely an hour later, they crossed a shallow, gravel-bottomed stream that meandered lazily away from the swifter flow of the main channel of the Chard Rush back along a worn gully. They caught sight of a single-room cabin that sat back in among the forest trees. Built from hand-cut logs laid crosswise and caulked with mortar, the little home was settled in a clearing upon a small rise that formed a threshold to a series of low hills sloping gently away into the forest. A handful of sheep and goats and a single milk cow grazed in the timber behind the cabin. At the sound of their approach, an aged hunting dog rose from his favorite napping spot next to the cabin stoop and stretched contentedly.

The woodsman Jeft stood at the far side of the little clearing, stripped to the waist as he cut firewood. With a sure, practiced swing downward of the long-handled axe, he split the piece of timber that stood upright on the worn stump that served as a chopping block. Working the embedded blade free, he brushed aside the cloven halves before pausing in his work to watch his visitors approach. Lowering the axe-head to the stump, he rested his gnarled hands on the smooth butt of the handle and waited.

"Morning," Brin greeted as they came up to him.

"Morning," the woodsman replied, nodding. He seemed not at all surprised that they were there. He glanced at Rone. "Feeling a bit better, are you?"

"Much," Rone answered. "Thanks in part to you, I'm told."

The woodsman shrugged, the muscles on his powerful body knotting. He gestured toward the cabin. "There's drinking water on the stoop in that bucket. I bring it fresh from the hills in back each day."

He led them down to the cabin porch and the promised bucket. All three took a long drink. Then they seated themselves on the stoop, and the woodsman produced pipe and tobacco. He offered the pouch to his guests, but they declined, so he packed the bowl of his own pipe and began to smoke.

"Everything fine back at the trading center?" he asked casually. There was a long silence. "I heard about what happened the other night with that bunch from Spanning Ridge country."

His eyes shifted slowly to Brin. "Word has a way of getting around a lot quicker than you'd think out here."

The Valegirl held his gaze, ignoring her discomfort. "The trader told us where to find you," she informed him. "He said you might be able to help us."

The woodsman puffed on the pipe. "In what way?"

"He told us that you know as much as anyone about this country."

"I've been out here a long time," the man agreed.

Brin leaned forward. "We are already in your debt for what you did to help us back at the trading center. But we need your help again. We need to find a way through the country that lies east of here."

The woodsman stared at her sharply, then slowly removed the pipe from between his teeth. "East of here? You mean Darklin Reach?"

Both Valegirl and highlander nodded.

The woodsman shook his head doubtfully. "That's dangerous country. No one goes into Darklin Reach if they can avoid it." He glanced up. "How far in do you plan to go?"

"All the way," Brin said quietly. "And then into Olden Moor and the Ravenshorn."

"You're mad as jays," the woodsman announced matter-of-factly and knocked the ashes from the pipe, grinding them into the earth with his boot. "Gnomes and walkers and worse own that country. You'll never come out alive."

There was no reply. The woodsman studied their faces in turn, rubbed his bearded chin thoughtfully, and finally shrugged.

"Guess you've got your own reasons for doing this, and it's none of my business what they are. But I'm telling you here and now that you're making a big mistake—maybe the biggest mistake you'll ever make. Even the trappers stay clear of that country. Men disappear up there like smoke—gone without a trace."

He waited for a reply. Brin glanced briefly at Rone and then back at the woodsman once more. "We have to go. Can you help us?"

"Me?" The woodsman grinned crookedly and shook his head. "Not me, girl. Even if I was to go with you—which I won't, 'cause I like living—I'd be lost myself after the first day or so."

He paused, studying them shrewdly. "I suppose you're set on this?"

Brin nodded wordlessly, waiting.

The woodsman sighed. "Maybe there's someone else who can help you then—if you're sure this is what you want." He blew sharply through the stem of his pipe to clean it, then folded his arms across his broad chest. "There's an old man named Cogline. Must be ninety by now if he's still alive. Haven't seen him for almost two years, so I can't be sure if he's even there anymore. Two years ago, though, he was living up around a rock formation called Hearthstone that sits right in the middle of Darklin Reach—formation that looks just like a big chimney." He shook his head doubtfully. "I can give you directions, but the trails aren't much. That's wild country; hardly anything human living that far east that isn't Gnome."

"Do you think he would help us?" Brin pressed anxiously.

The woodsman shrugged. "He knows the country. He's lived there all his life. Doesn't bother coming out more than once a year or so—not even that the last two. Stays alive somehow in that jungle." The heavy brows lifted. "He's an odd duck, old Cogline. Crazier than a fish swimming through grass. He might be more trouble than help to you."

"We'll be all right," Brin assured him.

"Maybe." The woodsman looked her over carefully. "You're a pretty thing to be wandering off into that country, girl—even with your singing to protect you. There's more than thieves and cowards out there. I'd think on this before you go any further with it."

"We have thought." Brin came to her feet. "We're decided."

The woodsman nodded. "You're welcome to take with you all the water you can carry, then. At least you won't die of thirst."

He helped them refill their water pouches, carrying a fresh bucket of water from the spring that ran down out of the hills behind his cabin, then took several minutes more to give them the directions they needed to reach Hearthstone, scratching a crude map in the earth before the stoop.

"Look after yourselves," he admonished, offering each a firm handshake.

With a final word of farewell, Brin and Rone hitched up their provisions across their backs and walked slowly from the little cabin into the trees. Behind them, the woodsman stood watching. It was clear from the look on his bearded face that he did not expect to see them pass that way again.

They journeyed through that day and the next, following the twists and turns of the Chard Rush as it wound steadily deeper through the forests of the Anar and crossed into Darklin Reach. Rone was gaining in strength, but he had not yet fully recovered, and progress was slow. After a brief meal on the second evening, he went directly to sleep.

Brin sat before the fire, staring into the flames. Her mind was still filled with unhappy memories and dark thoughts. Once, before she felt herself growing sleepy, it seemed that Jair was with her. Unconsciously, she looked up, seeking him. But there was no one there, and logic told her that her brother was far away, indeed. She sighed, banked the fire, and crawled into her blankets.

It was not until well into the afternoon of the third day following their departure from the Rooker Line Trading Center that Brin and Rone caught sight of a singular rock formation that loomed blackly in the distance and knew that they had found Hearthstone.

Hearthstone was a dark, clear silhouette against the changing colors of autumn, its rugged pinnacle dominating the shallow, wooded valley over which it stood watch. Chimneylike in appearance, the formation was a mass of weathered stone carved by nature's fine hand and shaped with the passing of the years. Silence hung starkly over its towering shadow. Solitary and enduring, it beckoned compellingly from out of the dark sea of the vast, sprawling forestland of Darklin Reach.

Standing at the crest of a ridge, staring out across the land, Brin felt its unspoken whisper call out through her weariness and her uncertainty and experienced an unexpected sense of peace. Another leg of the long trek east was almost over. The memories of what she had endured to reach this point and the warnings of what yet lay ahead were strangely distant now. She smiled at Rone and the smile clearly caught the highlander by surprise. Then, touching his arm gently, she started downward along the shallow valley slope.

The barely discernible line of a trail snaked down through the wall of the great trees. As the sun moved steadily toward the western horizon, the forest closed about them once more. They picked their way carefully over fallen logs and around jagged rock formations until the thickly grown slope leveled off at its base. Within the forested canopy of the valley, the path-way broadened and then disappeared altogether as the dense scrub brush and fallen timber began to thin. Warm afternoon sunlight flooded softly through the cracks and chinks of the interwoven branches overhead and lighted the whole of the darkened woodland. Dozens of wide, pleasant lit-tle clearings pocketed the valley forest and lent a feeling of space and openness. The earth grew soft and loose, free from rock and carpeted with a layer of small twigs and leaves that rustled gently as the Valegirl and the highlander walked across them.

There was a sense of comfort and familiarity to this little valley that was foreign to the wilderness that lay about it, and Brin Ohmsford found herself thinking of Shady Vale. The life sounds, insect and animal, the brief traces of movement through the trees, sudden and furtive, even the warm, fresh smell of the autumn woods—all were similar to that distant Southland village. There was no Rappahalladran, yet there were dozens of tiny streams meandering lazily across their path. The Valegirl breathed deeply. No wonder the woodsman Cogline had chosen this valley for his home.

The travelers passed deeper into the forest, and time slipped slowly from them. Now and again they caught brief glimpses of Hearthstone through the webbing of the dark forest limbs, its towering shadow black against the blue of the sky, and they pointed themselves toward it. They walked in silence, worn and anxious to be done with the day's long march, their thoughts concentrated on the terrain ahead and the sounds and sights of the forest.

At last Rone Leah came to a stop, one hand fastening guardedly on Brin's arm as he peered ahead.

"Hear that?" he asked quietly, after listening for a moment.

Brin nodded. It was a voice—thin, almost inaudible, but clearly hu-man. They waited a moment, gauging its direction, then began walking toward it. The voice disappeared for a time, then returned, louder, almost angry. Whoever was speaking was directly ahead.

"You had better show yourself and right now!" The voice was high and strident. "I've no time for games!"

There was some muttering and cursing, and the Valegirl and the highlander looked at each other questioningly.

"Come out, come out, come out!" the voice shrilled, then trailed off in an angry murmur. "Should have left you back on the moor . . . if it wasn't for my kind heart . . ."

There was more cursing, and the sound of someone crashing through the underbrush reached their ears.

"I've a few tricks myself, you know! I've got powders to blow the ground right out from under you and potions that would tie you in knots! Think you know so much, you . . . Let's see you climb a rope! Let's see you do that! Let's see you do anything besides cause me trouble! How would you like me to leave you here? How would you like that? Wouldn't think yourself so smart then, I'll wager! Now get out here!"

Brin and Rone stepped through the screen of trees and brush blocking their view and found themselves at the edge of a small clearing with a wide, still pond at its center. Across from them, crawling aimlessly about on his hands and knees was an old man. He scrambled to his feet at the sound of their approach.

"Ha! So you've decided . . . !" He stopped short as he saw them. "Who are you supposed to be? No, never mind who you are. It doesn't make a twig's difference. Just get out of here and go back to wherever it was you came from."

He turned from them with a dismissive gesture and resumed crawling along the forest's edge, his skeletal arms groping left and right, his thin, hunched body like a twisted bit of deadwood. Great tufts of ragged white hair and beard hung down about his shoulders, and his green-colored clothes and half-cloak were tattered and worn. The Valegirl and the highlander stared blankly at him and then at each other.

"This is ridiculous!" the old man stormed, directing his wrath at the silent trees. Then he looked around and saw that the travelers were still there. "Well, what are you waiting for? Get out of here! This is my house, and I didn't invite you! So get out, get out!"

"This is where you live?" Rone asked, glancing about doubtfully.

The old man looked at him as if he were an idiot. "Didn't you just hear me say so? What else do you think I'd be doing here at this hour?"

"I don't know," the highlander admitted.

"A man should be in his home at this hour!" the other continued in something of a scolding tone. "As a matter of fact, what are *you* doing here? Don't you have homes of your own to go to?"

"We've come all the way from Shady Vale in the Southland." Brin tried to explain, but the old man just stared blankly at her. "It's below the Rainbow Lake, several days' ride." The old man's expression never changed. "Anyway, we've come here looking for someone who . . ."

"No one here but me." The old man shook his head firmly. "Except for Whisper, and I can't find him. Where do you think . . . ?"

He trailed off distractedly, turning again from them as if to resume his hunt for whoever it was that was missing. Brin glanced doubtfully at Rone.

"Wait a minute!" she called after the old man, who looked around sharply. "A woodsman told us about this man. He told us he lived here. He said that his name was Cogline."

The old man shrugged. "Never heard of him."

"Well, maybe he lives in some other part of the valley. Maybe you could tell us where we might . . ."

"You don't listen very well, do you?" the other interrupted irritably. "Now I don't know where it is that you come from—don't care either— but I'll wager you don't have strange people running around your home, do you? I'll wager you know everyone living there or visiting there or whatever! So what makes you think it's any different with me?"

"You mean this whole valley is your home?" Rone demanded incredulously.

"Of course it's my home! I just told you that half a dozen different times! Now get out of it and leave me in peace!"

He stamped one sandaled foot vehemently and waited for them to go. But the Valegirl and the highlander just stood there.

"This is Hearthstone, isn't it?" Rone pressed, growing a bit angry with this cantankerous oldster.

The fellow's thin jaw stiffened resolutely. "What if it is?"

"Well, if it is, there is a man living here by the name of Cogline—or at least there was up until two years ago. He'd been living here for years before that, we were told. So if you've been out here for any length of time, you ought to know something about him!"

The old man was silent for a moment, his craggy brows tightening in thought. Then he shook his wispy head firmly. "Told you before, I never heard of him. No one around here with that name now or any other time. No one."

But Brin had seen something in the old man's eyes. She took a step closer to him and stopped. "You know the name, don't you? Cogline— you know it."

The old man stood his ground. "Maybe I do and maybe I don't. In any case, I don't have to tell you!"

Brin pointed. "You're Cogline, aren't you?"

The old man erupted in a violent fit of laughter. "Me? Cogline? Ha-ha, now wouldn't that be something! Oh, I would be talented, indeed! Ha-ha, now that's funny!"

Valegirl and highlander stared at him in amazement as he doubled over sharply and fell to the ground, laughing hysterically. Rone took Brin by the arm and turned her toward him.

"For cat's sake, Brin—this old man's crazy!" he whispered.

"What did you say? Crazy am I?" The oldster was back on his feet, his weathered face flushed with anger. "I ought to show you just how crazy! Now you get out of my house! I didn't want you here in the first place, and I don't want you here now! Get out!"

"We didn't mean any harm," a flustered Rone tried to apologize.

"Get out, get out, get out! I'll turn you into puffs of smoke! I'll set fire to you and watch you burn. I'll . . . I'll . . ."

He was jumping up and down in uncontrollable fury, his bony hands knotted tightly into fists, his tufted white hair flying wildly in all directions. Rone came forward to calm him.

"Stay away from me!" the other fairly shrieked, one thin arm pointing like a weapon. The highlander stopped at once. "Stay back! Oh, where's that stupid . . . ! Whisper!"

Rone glanced about expectantly, but no one appeared. The old man was beside himself with anger now and he whirled about, shouting into the forest darkness and flinging his arms about like windmills.

"Whisper! Whisper! Get out here and protect me from these trouble-makers! Whisper, drat you! Will you let them kill me? Should I just give myself over to them? What good are you, you fool . . . ! Oh, I never should have wasted my time on you! Get out here! Right now!"

The Valegirl and the highlander watched the antics of the old fellow with a mixture of wariness and amusement. Whoever Whisper was, he had apparently decided some time back that he wanted nothing to do with any of this. Yet the old man was not about to give up. He continued leaping about hysterically and shouting at nothing. Finally, Rone turned again to Brin.

"This is getting us nowhere," he declared, keeping his voice purposefully low. "Let's be on our way—look about on our own. The old man's obviously lost his mind."

But Brin shook her head, remembering what the woodsman Jeft had said about Cogline: an odd duck, crazier than a fish swimming through grass. "Let me try one more time," she replied.

She started forward, but the old man turned on her at once. "Wouldn't listen to me, is that it? Well, I gave you fair warning. Whisper! Where are you? Get out here! Get her! Get her!"

Brin drew up short in spite of herself and looked about. Still there was no one in sight. Then Rone stalked past her, gesturing impatiently.

"Now look here, old man. Enough is enough. There's no one else out here but you, so why don't you just stop this . . ."

"Ha! No one else but me, you think?" The old man leaped into the air with glee and landed in a crouch. "I'll show you who's out here, you . . . you trespasser! Come into my house, will you? I'll show you! Whisper! Whisper! Dratted . . . !"

Rone was shaking his head hopelessly and grinning when all of a sudden the biggest cat he had ever seen in his life appeared from out of nowhere right in front of him, no more than half a dozen yards away. Dark gray in color with spreading black panels on its flanks that ran upward across its sloping back, a black face, ears, and tail and wide, almost cumbersome-looking black paws, the beast measured well over ten feet and its massive, shaggy head rose even with his own. Corded muscles rippled beneath the sleek fur as it shook itself lazily and regarded the highlander and the Vale-girl with luminous, deep blue eyes that blinked and narrowed. It seemed to study them for a moment, then its jaws parted in a soundless yawn, revealing a flash of gleaming, razor-sharp teeth.

Rone Leah swallowed hard and stayed perfectly still.

"Ah-ha! Not so funny now, I'll wager!" the old man gloated and began chuckling merrily, his thin legs dancing about. "Thought I was crazy, did you? Thought I was just talking to myself, did you? Well, what do you think now?"

"Nobody meant you any harm," Brin repeated as the big cat looked Rone over curiously.

The old man edged forward a step, his eyes brightening beneath the tufted hair that hung down about his wrinkled forehead.

"Think he might like you for supper? Is that what you think? He gets hungry, old Whisper does. The two of you would provide him with a nice bedtime snack! Ha! What's the trouble? You look a little pale, like you might not feel so good. That's too bad, too bad now. Maybe you ought to . . ."

The grin vanished suddenly from his face. "Whisper, no! Whisper, no, wait, don't do that . . . !"

And with that, the big cat simply faded away and was gone, much as if he had evaporated. For a moment all three stared wonderingly at the space he had previously occupied. Then the old man stamped his foot angrily and kicked at the empty air in front of him.

"Drat you! You quit that, you hear me! Show yourself, you fool animal or I'll . . . !" He trailed off wrathfully, then looked over at Brin and Rone. "You get out of my house! Get out!"

Rone Leah had had enough. A crazy old man and a disappearing cat were more than he had bargained for. He wheeled without a word and stalked past Brin, muttering for her to follow. But Brin hesitated, still not willing to give it up.

"You don't understand how important this is!" she exclaimed heatedly. The old man stiffened. "You cannot just turn us away like this. We need your help. Please, tell us where we can find the man called Cogline."

The old man regarded her silently, his sticklike body hunched and bent, his shaggy eyebrows knitting petulantly. Then abruptly he threw up his hands and shook his white head in resignation.

"Oh, very well—anything to get rid of you!" He sighed deeply and did his best to look put upon. "It won't help you a whit, you understand—not a whit!"

The Valegirl waited wordlessly. Behind her, Rone had turned back again. The old man cocked his head, reflecting. One thin hand ran quickly through the tangled hair.

"Old Cogline is right over there at the foot of the big rock." He waved his hand almost casually in the direction of Hearthstone. "Right where I buried him almost a year ago."

30

Brin Ohmsford stared fixedly at the old man, disappointment welling up inside and choking back the exclamation forming in her throat. One hand lifted in a helpless gesture. "You mean that Cogline is dead?"

"Dead and buried!" the truculent oldster snapped. "Now be on your way and leave me in peace!"

He waited impatiently for the Valegirl and the highlander to go, but Brin could not bring herself to move. Cogline dead? Somehow she could not accept that he was. Would not word of that death by some means have gotten back to the woodsman Jeft or to others who lived in the forests that lay about the Rooker Line Trading Center? A man who had lived for as long as Cogline had in this wilderness, a man known to so many . . . ? She caught herself. Possibly not, for woodsmen and trappers often stayed apart for months at a time. But who then was this old man? The woodsman had made no mention of him. Somehow it was all wrong.

"Let's go, Brin," Rone called to her gently.

But the Valegirl shook her head. "No. Not until I'm sure. Not until I can . . ."

"Get out of my house!" the old man repeated once again, stamping his foot petulantly. "I have put up with enough from you! Cogline is dead! Now if you're not gone from here by the time I . . ."

"Grandfather!"

The voice broke sharply from out of the wooded darkness to their left where, in the distance, the rugged pinnacle of Hearthstone loomed blackly through the interwoven branches of the silent trees. Three heads jerked about as one, and the forest went suddenly still. Whisper reappeared to one side of them, his blue eyes luminous, his great, shaggy head raised and searching. The old man muttered to himself and stamped his foot one time more.

Then there was a soft rustling of leaves and the mysterious speaker appeared, stepping lightly into clearing. Brin and Rone turned to each other in surprise. It was a girl, barely older than Brin, her small, supple form clothed in pants and tunic and wrapped loosely in a braided short cloak of forest green. Long, curling ringlets of thick, dark hair hung down about her shoulders, softly shadowing a sun-browned, faintly freckled pixie face that was strangely beguiling, almost compelling in its look of innocence. It was a pretty face, and while not truly beautiful in the way of Brin's, appealing nevertheless with its uncomplicated freshness and vitality. Dark, intelligent eyes mirrored frankness and honesty as she studied the Valegirl and the highlander curiously.

"Who are you?" she asked in a tone of voice that suggested that she had a right to know.

Brin glanced again at Rone and then back to the girl. "I'm Brin Ohmsford from Shady Vale and this is Rone Leah. We've come north from our homes in the Southland below the Rainbow Lake."

"You have come a long way," the girl observed. "Why are you here?"

"To find a man named Cogline."

"Do you know this man, Brin Ohmsford?"

"No."

"Then why do you look for him?"

The girl's eyes never left hers. Brin hesitated, wondering how much she should tell her. There was something about this girl that warned against lying, and Brin had not missed the way in which her sudden appearance had quieted the old man and brought back the disappearing cat. Still, the Valegirl was reluctant to reveal the whole of her reason for their being at Hearthstone without first finding out who she was.

"We were told that Cogline was the man who best knew the forestland from Darklin Reach east to the Ravenshorn," she replied guardedly. "We were hoping he would offer his services on a matter of great importance."

The girl was silent for a moment, apparently considering what Brin had told her. The old man shuffled over to where she stood and began fidgeting.

"They're trespassers and troublemakers!" he insisted vehemently.

The girl did not reply nor even look at him, her dark eyes still locked into Brin's, her slim form motionless. The old man threw up his hands in exasperation.

"You shouldn't even be talking with them! You should throw them out!"

The girl shook her head slowly then. "Hush, grandfather," she cautioned. "They mean us no harm. Whisper would know if they did."

Brin glanced quickly at the big cat, who was stretched out almost playfully in the tall grass bordering the little pond, one great paw flicking idly at some hapless insect flying past. The great oval eyes shone like twin beacons of light as he glanced over at them.

"That fool animal won't even come when I call him!" the old man groused. "How can you depend on him?"

The girl looked at the old man reprovingly, a hint of defiance crossing her youthful features. "Whisper!" she called softly and pointed at Brin. "Track!"

The big cat suddenly came to his feet and without a sound padded over to Brin. The Valegirl stiffened as the beast's black muzzle sniffed tentatively at her clothing. Cautiously, she started to step back.

"Stand still," the girl advised her quietly.

Brin did as she was told. Forcing herself to remain outwardly calm, she stood frozen in place as the huge animal sniffed downward along her pant leg in a leisurely fashion. The girl was testing her, she realized—using the cat to see how she would react. The skin on the back of her neck prickled as the muzzle pushed at her. What should she do? Should she continue just to stand there? Should she touch the beast to show that she was not afraid? But she *was* afraid, and the fear was spreading all through her. Surely the animal would smell it, and then . . .

She made up her mind. Softly, she began to sing. The words hovered in the dark stillness of the evening, floating in the quiet of the little clearing, reaching out, touching like gentle fingers. It took only a few moments for the wishsong's magic to weave its spell, and the giant cat sat back on its haunches, luminous eyes on the Valegirl. Blinking in sleepy cadence to the song, he lay docilely at her feet.

Brin went still. For an instant, no one spoke.

"Devils!" the old man shrilled finally, a shrewd look on his weathered face.

The girl came forward wordlessly and stood directly in front of Brin. There was no fear in her eyes, merely curiosity. "How did you do that?" she asked, sounding puzzled. "I didn't think anyone could do that."

"It's a gift," Brin answered.

The girl hesitated. "You're not a devil, are you? You're not one of the walkers or their spirit kin?"

Brin smiled. "No, nothing like that. I just have this gift."

The girl shook her head in disbelief. "I did not think anyone could do that to Whisper," she repeated.

"They're devils!" the old man insisted and stamped his sandaled foot.

Whisper, meanwhile, had come back to his feet and moved over to Rone. The highlander started in surprise, then shot Brin an imploring look as the beast pushed his black muzzle against him. For a moment longer Whisper sniffed the highlander's clothing in curious fashion. Then abruptly the great jaws opened and fastened loosely about his right boot and began to tug. What remained of Rone's composure began to slip rapidly away, and he tried to pull free.

"I think he wants to play with you," the girl announced, a faint smile forming on her lips. She directed a knowing look at the old man, who merely grunted his displeasure and moved several paces further away from them all.

"Well . . . could you . . . make sure?" Rone gasped in exasperation, struggling valiantly now to keep his feet as the great cat continued to pull and tug vigorously at the worried boot.

"Whisper!" the girl called sharply.

The huge creature released his grip instantly and trotted to her side. She reached out from beneath the short cloak and rubbed the shaggy head roughly, her long dark hair falling down about her face as she leaned forward to place her head close to his. She spoke softly to him for a moment, then glanced back at Brin and Rone.

"You seem to have a way with animals. Whisper is quite taken with you."

Brin cast a quick glance at Rone, who was struggling to pull his boot back in place on his foot. "I think Rone would be just as happy if Whisper didn't take to him quite so much," she observed.

The girl smiled broadly then, a hint of mischievousness flashing briefly in her dark eyes. "I like you, Brin Ohmsford. You are welcome here—both you and Rone Leah." She extended a slim brown hand in greeting. "I am Kimber Boh."

Brin accepted the hand, feeling in its grip a mixture of strength and softness that surprised her. She was surprised, too, when she caught sight of a brace of wicked-looking long knives strapped to the girl's slim waist beneath the short cloak.

"Well, they're not welcome as far as I'm concerned!" the old man snapped from behind the girl, making a gesture of brushing them all aside with a broad sweep of one sticklike arm.

"Grandfather!" Kimber Boh admonished. She gave him a sharp look of disapproval and then turned back to Brin. "You mustn't mind him. He is very protective of me. I am all the family he has, so he sometimes feels . . ."

"Don't be so quick to tell them everything about us!" the old man interrupted, shaking his wispish head in dismay. "What do we know of them? How can we be sure what really brought them here? That girl has a devil's voice if she can back off Whisper like she did! No, you are much too trusting, girl!"

"And you are much too quick to distrust," Kimber Boh replied evenly. Her pixie face tightened with resolve. "Now tell them who you are."

The old man's mouth screwed into a vise. "I'll tell them nothing!"

"Tell them, grandfather."

The sandaled foot stamped petulantly. "Tell them yourself. You think you know so much more than me!"

Rone Leah had come forward to stand next to Brin, and the two glanced at each other awkwardly. Whisper looked up at the highlander, yawned and dropped his massive head back onto his paws. A deep, purring sound rose out of his throat as his blue eyes slipped shut.

Kimber Boh turned to face the Valegirl and the highlander. "My grandfather forgets sometimes that the games he is so fond of playing are not real. One of the games he plays often involves changing who he is. He does this by deciding to bury the old self and start life over. He last did this about a year ago." She gave the old man a knowing look. "But he is who he always was. He is, in fact, the man you have come to find."

"Then he really is Cogline." Brin made it a statement of fact.

"I am *not* Cogline!" the old man insisted heatedly. "He's dead and buried, just like I told you! Don't be listening to what she has to say!"

"Grandfather!" Kimber Boh admonished once more. "You are who you are, and you cannot be otherwise. Pretending is for children. You were born Cogline and that is who you will always be. Now please try to be a good host to your guests. Try to be their friend."

"Ha! I didn't invite them here, so I don't have to be a good host!" Cogline snapped obstinately, determined to have nothing whatsoever to do with either the Valegirl or the highlander. "As for being their friend, you be their friend if you want—that's up to you!"

Brin and Rone looked at each other doubtfully. It did not appear that they were going to have much luck obtaining help from the old man in finding their way through Darklin Reach.

"Very well, grandfather—I shall be host and friend for the both of us." Kimber Boh sighed. She faced them squarely, ignoring the old man. "It's growing late. You have come a long way and you need food and rest. Home is just a short distance from here, and you are welcome to stay the night as my guests—and my grandfather's."

She paused to consider something more. "In fact, it would be a great favor to me if you would stay. Few travelers come this far east, and even then I seldom have a chance to talk with them. As I said, grandfather is very protective. But perhaps you would consent to talk with me—to tell me something of your home in the Southland. Would you do that?"

Brin smiled wearily. "For a place to sleep and something to eat, I think that is the least we could do."

Rone nodded in agreement, although not without an apprehensive glance at Whisper.

"It is settled then," Kimber Boh announced. She called to the big cat, who rose, stretched leisurely and padded up to her. "If you will follow me, we can be there in a few minutes' time."

She turned, with Whisper beside her, and disappeared back into the forest. The Valegirl and the highlander hitched up their backpacks and followed. As they passed Cogline, the old man refused to look at them, staring at the ground in grim determination, his heavy brows furrowed.

"Dratted trespassers!" he muttered.

Then with a wary glance about, he shuffled after them into the trees. A moment later, the little clearing stood empty.

31

Home for the girl, the old man, and the disappearing cat was a pleasant, but very average-looking stone and timber cottage situated in a broad, grass-covered clearing sheltered by centuries-old oak and red elm. Porches ran along the front and rear of the cottage, and the walls were grown thick with flowering vines and bush evergreens. Stone walkways ran from the home through gardens that lay all about—some flower, some vegetable, all carefully tended and neatly draw. Spruce and pine lined the perimeter of the clearing, and hedgerows ran along the borders of the gardens. A great amount of work had gone into the care and nurture of the entire grounds.

The same care was evident inside the cottage. Neat and spotlessly clean, the sanded wood plank floors and timbered walls gleamed in the soft light of the oil lamps, polished and waxed. Handcrafts of woven cloth and cross-stitch hung from the walls, and bright tapestries draped the rough wooden furniture and windows. Odd pieces of silver and crystal sat upon tables within a broad-shelved hutch, and the long trestle table at one end of the main room had been set with earthenware dishes and crafted utensils. Flowers blossomed from vases and clay pots, some grown from plantings, some cut and arranged. The whole of the cottage seemed bright and cheerful, even with the nightfall, and there was that feeling of a Vale home at every turn.

"Dinner is almost ready," Kimber Boh announced when they had come inside, casting a reproachful glance in Cogline's direction. "If you will seat yourselves, I will put it on the table."

Grumbling to himself, Cogline slid onto the bench at the far side of the table, while Brin and Rone sat down across from him. Whisper padded past them to a braided throw rug situated in front of a wide stone fireplace where a small stack of logs burned cheerfully. With a yawn, the cat curled up before the flames and fell asleep.

The meal that Kimber Boh brought to them consisted of wild fowl, garden vegetables, fresh-baked breads, and goat's milk, and they consumed it hungrily. As they ate, the girl asked them questions of the Southland and its people, eager to hear of the world beyond her valley home. She had never been outside Darklin Reach, she explained, but someday soon now she would make the journey. Cogline scowled his disapproval, but said nothing, his head lowered in unyielding concentration on his plate. When dinner was finished, he rose with a sullen grunt and announced that he was going out for a smoke. He stalked through the door without a glance back at any of them and disappeared.

"You really mustn't mind him," Kimber Boh apologized, rising to clear the dishes from the table. "He is very gentle and sweet, but he has lived alone for so many years that he finds it difficult to be comfortable with other people."

Smiling, she removed the dishes from the table and returned with a container of burgundy-colored wine. Pouring a small amount into fresh glasses, she resumed her seat across from them. As they sipped at the wine and chatted amiably, Brin found herself wondering as she had wondered on and off from the first moment that she had laid eyes on the girl how it was that she and the old man had managed to survive alone in this wilderness. Of course, there was the cat, but nevertheless . . .

"Grandfather walks every evening after dinner," Kimber Boh was relating, a reassuring look directed to the two who sat across from her. "He wanders about the valley a good deal when the late fall comes. All of our work is done for the year, and when winter comes he will not go out as much. His body hurts him sometimes in the cold weather, and he prefers the fire. But now, while the nights are still warm, he likes to walk."

"Kimber, where are your parents?" Brin asked, unable to help herself. "Why are you here all alone?"

"My parents were killed," the girl explained matter-of-factly. "I was just a child when Cogline found me, hidden in some bedding where the caravan had camped that last night at the north edge of the valley. He brought me to his home and raised me as his granddaughter." She leaned forward. "He has never had a family of his own, you see. I'm all he has."

"How were your parents killed?" Rone wanted to know, seeing that the girl did not mind speaking of it.

"Gnome raiders. Several families were traveling in the caravan; everyone was killed except me. They missed me, Cogline says." She smiled. "But that's been a long time ago."

Rone sipped at his wine. "Kind of dangerous here for you, isn't it?"

She looked puzzled. "Dangerous?"

"Sure. Wilderness all around, wild animals, raiders—whatever. Aren't you a little afraid sometimes living alone out here?"

She cocked her head slightly. "Do you think I should be?"

The highlander glanced at Brin. "Well . . . I don't know."

She stood up. "Watch this."

Almost faster than his eye could follow, the girl had a long knife in her hand, whipping it past his head, flinging it the length of the room. It buried itself with a thud in a tiny black circle drawn on a timber in the far corner.

Kimber Boh grinned. "I practice that all the time. I learned to throw the knife by the time I was ten. Cogline taught me. I am just as good with almost any other weapon you might care to name. I can run faster than anything that lives in Darklin Reach—except for Whisper. I can walk all day and all night without sleeping."

She sat down again. "Of course, Whisper would protect me against anything that threatened me, so I don't have much to worry about." She smiled. "Besides, nothing really dangerous ever comes into Hearthstone. Cogline has lived here all his life; the valley belongs to him. Everyone knows that and they don't bother him. Even the Spider Gnomes stay out."

She paused. "Do you know about the Spider Gnomes?"

They shook their heads. The girl leaned forward. "They creep along the ground and up trees, all hairy and crooked, just like spiders. Once they tried to come into the valley, about three years ago. Several dozen of them came, all blackened with ash and anxious to hunt. They're not like the other Gnomes, you know, because they burrow and trap like spiders. Anyway, they came down into Hearthstone. I think they wanted it for their own. Grandfather knew about it right away, just as he always seems to know when something dangerous is about. He took Whisper with him and they ambushed the Spider Gnomes at the north end of the valley right by the big rock. The Spider Gnomes are still running."

She grinned broadly, pleased with the story. Brin and Rone cast uneasy glances at each other, less sure than ever what to make of this girl.

"Where did the cat come from?" Rone glanced again at Whisper, who continued to sleep undisturbed. "How does he disappear like that when he's so confounded big?"

"Whisper is a moor cat," the girl explained. "Most such cats live in the swamps in the deep Anar, well east of Darklin Reach and the Ravenshorn. Whisper wandered into Olden Moor, though, when he was still a baby. Cogline found him and brought him here. He had been in a fight with something and was all cut up. We took care of him and he stayed with us. I learned to talk with him." She looked at Brin. "But not like you do, not singing to him like that. Can you teach me to do that, Brin?"

Brin shook her head gently. "I don't think so, Kimber. The wishsong was something I was born with."

"Wishsong," the girl repeated the word. "That's very pretty."

There was a momentary silence. "So how does he disappear the way he does?" Rone asked once again.

"Oh, he doesn't disappear," Kimber Boh explained with a laugh. "It just seems that way. The reason you can't see him sometimes is not because he isn't there, which he plainly is, but because he can change his body coloring to blend in with the forest—the trees, the rocks, the ground, whatever. He blends in so well that he can't be seen if you don't know how to look for him. After you've been around him long enough, you learn how to look for him properly." She paused. "Of course, if he doesn't wish to be found, then he probably won't be. That's part of his defense. It's become quite a game with grandfather. Whisper disappears and refuses to show himself until grandfather has yelled himself hoarse. Not very fair of him, really, because grandfather's eyes aren't as good as they used to be."

"But he comes for you, I gather."

"Always. He thinks I am his mother. I nursed him and cared for him when we first brought him back here. We're so close now that it's as if we're parts of the same person. Most of the time, we even seem to be able to sense what each other is thinking."

"He looks dangerous to me," Rone stated flatly.

"Oh, he is," the girl agreed. "Very dangerous. Wild, he would be uncontrollable. But Whisper is no longer wild. There may be a small part of him that still is, a memory or an instinct buried deep inside somewhere, but it's all but forgotten now."

She rose and poured them each a bit more of the wine. "Do you like our home?" she asked them after a moment.

"Very much," Brin replied.

The girl smiled, obviously pleased. "I did most of the decorations myself—except for the glass and silver things; those were brought by grandfather from his trips. Or some he had before I came. But the rest, I did. And the gardens—I planted those. All the flowers and shrubs and vegetables—all the small bushes and vines. I like the colors and the sweet smells."

Brin smiled, too. Kimber Boh was a mixture of child and woman—in some ways still young, in some grown beyond her years. It was strange, but she reminded the Valegirl of Jair. Thinking of it made her miss her brother terribly.

Kimber Boh saw the look that crossed her face and mistook it. "It really isn't dangerous here at Hearthstone," she assured the Valegirl. "It may seem that way to you because you are not familiar with the country, as I am. But this is my home, remember—this is where I grew up. Grandfather taught me when I was little what I should know in order to protect myself. I have learned to deal with what dangers there are; I know how to avoid them. And I have grandfather and Whisper. You don't have to be worried about me—really, you don't."

Brin smiled at the assurance. "I can see that I don't, Kimber. I can see that you are very capable."

To her surprise, Kimber Boh blushed. Then hurriedly the girl stood up and walked to where Cogline had dropped his forest cloak on the arm of the wooden rocker. "I have to take grandfather his coat," she announced quickly. "It's cold out there. Would you like to walk with me?"

Valegirl and highlander rose and followed as she opened the door and stepped outside. The moment the latch clicked free, Whisper was on his feet, padding silently through the door after them.

They paused momentarily on the porch of the little cottage, losing themselves in the splendor of the evening's peaceful, almost mystical still-life. The air was chill and faintly damp and smelled sweetly of the darkened forest. White moonlight bathed the lawn, flower gardens, neatly trimmed hedgerows, and shrubs with dazzling brightness. Each blade of grass, soft petal, and tiny leaf glistened wetly, deep emerald laced with frost as the dew of the autumn evening gathered. In the blackness beyond, the trees of the forest rose against the star-filled sky like monstrous giants—ageless, massive, frozen in the silence of the night. The gentle wind of early dusk had faded entirely now, drifting soundlessly into stillness. Even the familiar cries of the woodland creatures had softened to faint and distant murmurs that soothed and comforted.

"Grandfather will be at the willow," Kimber Boh said softly, breaking the spell.

Together, they moved off the porch onto the walkway that led to the rear of the cottage. No one spoke a word. They simply walked slowly, the girl leading, their boots scraping softly against the worn stone. Something skittered through the dry leaves in the dark curtain of the forest and was gone. A bird called sharply, its piercing cry echoing in the stillness, lingering on.

The three moved past the corner of the house now, through groupings of pine and spruce and lines of hedgerows. Then a huge, sagging willow appeared from out of the darkness at the edge of the forest, its branches trailing in thick streamers that hung like a curtain against the night. Massive and gnarled, its humped form lay wrapped in shadowed darkness, as if drawn inward onto itself. There, beneath its canopied arch, the bowl of a pipe glowed deep red in the darkness, and puffs of smoke rose skyward to thin and vanish.

As they passed through the trailing limbs of the willow, they saw clearly the skeletal form of Cogline, hunched over on one of a pair of wooden benches that had been placed at the base of the ancient trunk, his wizened face turned toward the darkened forest. Kimber Boh went directly over to him and placed the forest cloak about his shoulders.

"You will catch cold, grandfather," she scolded gently.

The old man grimaced. "Can't even come out here for a smoke without you hovering over me like a mother hen!" He pulled the cloak about him nevertheless as he glanced over at Brin and Rone. "And I don't need these two for company either. Or that worthless cat. I suppose you brought him out here, too!"

Brin looked about for Whisper and was surprised to find that he had disappeared again. A moment earlier, he had been right behind them.

Kimber Boh seated herself next to her grandfather. "Why won't you at least try to be friends with Brin and Rone?" she asked him quietly.

"What for?" the other snapped. "I don't need friends! Friends are nothing but trouble, always expecting you to do something for them, always wanting some favor or other. Had enough friends in the old days, girl. You don't understand enough about how life is, that's your trouble!"

The girl glanced apologetically at Brin and Rone and nodded toward the empty bench. Wordlessly, the Valegirl and the highlander sat down across from her.

Kimber Boh turned back to the old man. "You must not be like that. You must not be so selfish."

"I'm an old man. I can be what I want!" Cogline muttered petulantly.

"When I used to say things like that, you called me spoiled and sent me to my room. Do you remember?"

"That was different!"

"Should I send you to your room?" she asked, speaking to the old man as a mother would to her child, her hands clasping his. "Or perhaps you would prefer it if Whisper and I also had nothing more to do with you since we are your friends, too, and you do not seem to want any friends."

Cogline clamped his teeth about the stem of his pipe as if he might bite it through and hunched down sullenly within the cloak, refusing to answer. Brin glanced quickly over at Rone, who arched one eyebrow in response. It was clear to both that despite her age, it was Kimber Boh who was the stabilizing force in this strange little family.

The girl leaned over then and kissed her grandfather's cheek softly. "I know that you don't really believe what you said. I know you are a good, kind, gentle man, and I love you." She brought her arms about his thin frame and hugged him close. To Brin's surprise, the old man's arm came up tentatively and hugged her back.

"They should have asked before they came here," he muttered, gesturing vaguely toward the Valegirl and the highlander. "I might have hurt them, you know."

"Yes, grandfather, I know," the girl responded. "But now that they are here, after having made such a long journey to find you, I think you should see why it is that they have come and if there is anything you can do to help them."

Brin and Rone exchanged hurried glances once more. Cogline slipped free of Kimber Boh's arms, muttering and shaking his head, wispish hair dancing in the moonglow like fine silk thread.

"Dratted cat, where's he got to this time! Whisper! Come out here, you worthless beast! I'm not sitting around . . ."

"Grandfather!" the girl interrupted him firmly. The old man looked at her in startled silence, and she nodded toward Brin and Rone. "Our friends, grandfather—will you ask them?"

The wrinkles in the old man's face creased deeper as he frowned. "Oh, very well," he huffed irritably. "What was it that brought you here?"

"We have need of someone who can show us a way through this country," Brin replied at once, hardly daring to hope that the help they so badly needed might at last be offered. "We were told that Cogline was the one man who might know that way."

"Except that there isn't any Cogline anymore!" the oldster snapped, but a warning glance from the girl quieted him at once. "Well then, what country is it that you plan to travel through?"

"The central Anar," Brin answered. "Darklin Reach, the moor beyond—all the way east to the Ravenshorn." She paused. "Into the Maelmord."

"But the walkers are there!" Kimber Boh exclaimed.

"What reason would you have for going into that black pit?" the old man followed up heatedly.

Brin hesitated, seeing where matters were headed. "To destroy the walkers."

"Destroy the walkers!" Cogline was aghast. "Destroy them with what, girl?"

"With the wishsong. With the magic that . . ."

"With the wishsong? With that singing? That's what you plan to use?" Cogline was on his feet, leaping about wildly, skeletal arms gesturing. "And you think me mad? Get out of here! Get out of my house! Get out, get out!"

Kimber Boh rose and gently pulled the old man back down on the bench, talking to him, soothing him as he continued to rant. It took a few moments to quiet him. Then wrapping him once more in the forest cloak, she turned again to Brin and Rone.

"Brin Ohmsford," she addressed the Valegirl solemnly, her face quite stern. "The Maelmord is no place for you. Even I do not go there."

Brin almost smiled at the other's emphasis on her own forbidding. "But I do not have a choice in this, Kimber," she explained gently. "I have to go."

"And I have to go with her," Rone added grudgingly. "When I find the sword again, that is. I have to find the sword first."

Kimber looked at them each in turn and shook her head in confusion. "I don't understand. What sword? Why is it that you have to go into the Maelmord? Why is it that you have to destroy the walkers?"

Again Brin hesitated, this time in caution. How much should she reveal of the quest that had brought her to this land? How much should she tell of the truth that had been entrusted to her? But as she looked into the eyes of Kimber, the caution that bade her keep watch over all that she so carefully hid suddenly ceased to have meaning. Allanon was dead, gone forever from the Four Lands. The magic he had given Rone in order that he might protect her was lost. She was alone, weary, and frightened, despite the determination that carried her forward on this impossible journey; if she were to survive what lay ahead, she knew she must take what help she could find where she might find it. Hidden truths and clever deceptions had been a way of life for Allanon, a part of the person that he had been. It could never be so for her.

So she told the girl and the old man all that had been told to her and all that had befallen her since Allanon had first appeared in the village of Shady Vale those many days gone past. She hid nothing of the truth save those secrets she kept hidden even from Rone, those frightening suspicions and unpleasant whisperings of the powers, dark and unfathomable, of the wishsong. It took a long time to tell it all, but for once the old man was quiet and the girl listened with him in silent wonderment.

When she had finished, she turned to Rone to see if there were anything further that should be said, but the highlander shook his head wordlessly.

"You see, then, that I have to go," she repeated the words one final time, looking from the girl to the old man and back again, waiting.

"Elven magic in you, eh?" Cogline murmured, eyes piercing. "Druid's touch on the whole of what you do. I've a bit of that touch myself, you know—a bit of the dark lore. Yes. Yes, I do."

Kimber touched his arm gently. "Can we help them find their path east, grandfather?"

"East? Whole of the country east is known to me—all that there is, here to there and back. Hearthstone, Darklin Reach, Olden Moor—all to the Ravenshorn, all to the Maelmord." He shook his wispish head thoughtfully. "Kept the touch, I have. Walkers don't bother me here; walkers don't come into the valley. Outside, they go where they please, though. That's their country."

"Grandfather, listen to me," she prodded him gently. "We must help our friends, you and Whisper and I."

Cogline looked at her wordlessly for a moment, then threw up his hands. "Waste of time!" he announced. "Ridiculous waste of time!" His bony finger came up to touch the girl's nose. "Have to think better than that, girl. I taught you to think better than that! Suppose we do help; suppose we take these two right through Darklin Reach, right through Olden Moor, right to the Ravenshorn and the black pit itself. Suppose! What, then? Tell me! What then?"

"That would be enough . . ." Brin started to reply.

"Enough?" Cogline exclaimed, cutting her short. "Not nearly so, girl! Cliffs rise up before you like a wall, hundreds of feet high. Barren rock for miles. Gnomes everywhere. What happens then? What do you do then?" The finger shifted like a dagger to point at her. "No way in, girl! There's no way in! You cannot go all that distance unless you know a way in!"

"We will find a way," Brin assured him firmly.

"Bah!" The old man spit, grimacing. "Walkers would have you in a moment! They'll see you coming halfway up the climb—if you can find a place to make the climb, that is! Or can the magic make you invisible? Can it do that?"

Brin set her jaw. "We will find a way," she repeated.

"Maybe and maybe not," Rone spoke up suddenly. "I don't like the sound of it, Brin. The old man knows the country and if he says it's all open ground, then we ought to take that into account before we go charging in." He glanced at Cogline as if to reassure himself that the old man did in fact know what he was talking about. "Besides, first things first. Before we start off on this trek through the Eastland, we have to recover the sword. It's the only real protection we have against the walkers."

"There is no protection against the walkers!" Cogline snorted.

Brin stared at the highlander for a moment, then took a deep breath. "Rone, we have to forget about the sword," she told him gently. "It's gone and we have no way of finding what's become of it. Allanon said it would find its way again into human hands, but he did not say whose hands those would be nor did he say how long it would take for this to happen. We cannot . . ."

"Without a sword to protect us, we don't take another step!" Rone's jaw tightened as he cut short the rest of what Brin was about to say.

There was a long silence. "We have no choice," Brin said. "At least, I don't."

"On your way, then." Cogline brushed them both aside with a wave of his hand. "On your way and leave us in peace—you with your foolish plans of scaling the pit and destroying the walkers; foolish, foolish plans! Go on, fly on out of our home, dratted . . . Whisper, where have you got to, you worthless . . . Show yourself or I'll . . . Yiiii!"

He shrieked in surprise as the big cat's head appeared from out of the darkness at his shoulder, luminous eyes blinking, cold muzzle pressed right up against his bare arm. Furious at being surprised like that, Cogline swatted at the cat and stalked a dozen yards away beneath the willow boughs, swearing as he went. Whisper stared after him, then walked about the bench to lie down next to Kimber.

"I think that grandfather can be persuaded to show you the way east— at least as far as the Ravenshorn," Kimber Boh mused thoughtfully. "As to what you will do after that . . ."

"Wait a minute—just . . . let's think this through a moment." Rone held up his hands imploringly. He turned to Brin. "I know you have decided to complete this quest that Allanon has given you. I understand that you must. And I'm going with you, right to the end of it. But we have to have the sword, Brin. Don't you see that? We have to! We have no other weapons with which to stand against the Mord Wraiths!" His face tightened with frustration. "For cat's sake, how can I protect you without the sword?"

Brin hesitated then, thinking suddenly of the power of the wishsong and of what she had seen that power do to those men from west of Spanning Ridge at the Rooker Line Trading Center. Rone did not know, nor did she want him to, but power such as that was more weapon than she cared to think—and she loathed the very idea that it could live within her. Rone was so certain that he must regain the use of the power of the Sword of Leah. But she sensed somehow that, as with the magic of the wishsong and the magic of the Elfstones before it, the magic of the Sword of Leah was both light and dark at once—that it could cause harm to the user as well as give him aid.

She looked at Rone, seeing in his gray eyes the love he bore for her mingled with the certainty that he could not help her without the magic that Allanon had given him. That look was desperate—yet without understanding of what he asked.

"There is no way for us to find the sword, Rone," she said softly.

They faced each other wordlessly, seated close upon the wooden bench, lost in the shadowed dark of the old willow. Let it go, Brin prayed silently. Please, let it go. Cogline shambled back to join them, still muttering at Whisper as he squatted warily on one end of the bench and began fiddling with his pipe.

"There might be a way," Kimber said suddenly, her small voice breaking through the silence. All eyes turned toward her. "We could ask the Grimpond."

"Ha!" Cogline snorted. "Might as well ask a hole in the ground!"

But Rone sat forward at once. "What is the Grimpond?"

"An avatar," the girl answered quietly. "A shade that lives in a pool of water north of Hearthstone where the high ridges part. It has always lived there, it tells me—since before the destruction of the old world, since the time of the world of faerie. It has the magic of the old world in its touch and the sight to see secrets hidden from living people."

"It could tell me where to find the Sword of Leah?" Rone pressed anxiously, ignoring the restraining hand that Brin placed upon his arm.

"Ha-ha, look at him!" Cogline cackled gleefully. "Thinks he has the answer now, doesn't he? Thinks he's found the way! The Grimpond has the secrets of the earth all bound up in a pretty package ready to give to him! Just a little problem of telling truth from lie, that's all! Ha-ha!"

"What's he talking about?" Rone demanded angrily. "What does he mean, truth from lie?"

Kimber gave her grandfather a stern look to quiet him, then turned back to the highlander. "He means that the avatar doesn't always tell the truth. It lies much of the time or tells riddles that no one can figure out. It makes a game out of it, twisting what is real and what is not so that the listener cannot decide what to believe."

"But why does it do that?" Brin asked, bewildered.

The girl shrugged. "Shades are like that. They drift between the world that was and the one that will be and have no real place in either."

She said it with such authority that the Valegirl accepted what she said without questioning it further. Besides, it had been that way with the shade of Bremen as well—in part, at least. There was a sense of commitment in the shade of Bremen lacking perhaps in the Grimpond; but the shade of Bremen did not tell all of what it knew or speak clearly of what would be. Some of the truth could never be told. The whole of the future was never unalterably fixed, and the telling of it must always be shaded by what might yet be.

"Grandfather prefers that I have nothing to do with the Grimpond," Kimber Boh was explaining to Rone. "He does not approve of the way the avatar lies. Still, its conversation is amusing sometimes, and it becomes an interesting game for me when I choose to play it." She assumed a stern look. "Of course, it is a different kind of game entirely when you try to commit the avatar to telling you the truth of what it knows when it is really important to you. I never ask it of the future or listen to what it has to say if it offers to tell me. It is a cruel thing, sometimes."

Rone looked down momentarily, then up again at the girl. "Do you think it could be made to tell me what has happened to my sword?"

Kimber's eyebrows lifted. "Not made. Persuaded, perhaps. Tricked, maybe." She looked at Brin. "But I was not just thinking of finding the sword. I was thinking as well of finding a way into the Ravenshorn and into the Maelmord. If there were a way by which the walkers could not see you coming, the Grimpond would know it."

There was a long, anxious silence. Brin Ohmsford's mind raced. A way into the Maelmord that would hide them from the Mord Wraiths—it was the key that she needed in order to complete the quest for the Ildatch. She would have preferred that the Sword of Leah, with its magic and its power, remain lost. But what matter that it was found again if it need not be used? She glanced at Rone and saw the determination in his eyes. The matter was already decided for him.

"We must try it, Brin," he said softly.

Cogline's wrinkled face split wide in a leering grin. "Go on, Southlander—try it!" His soft laughter echoed through the night stillness.

Brin hesitated. At her feet, stretched between the benches, his gray-black body curled close to his mistress, Whisper raised his massive head and blinked curiously. The Valegirl stared deep into the cat's saucer blue eyes. How desperate she had become that she must turn to the aid of a woods girl, a half-crazed old man, and a cat that disappeared.

But Allanon was gone. . . .

"Will you speak to the Grimpond for us?" she asked Kimber.

The girl smiled brightly. "Oh, I was thinking, Brin, that it might be better if it were you who spoke to the Grimpond."

And it was then that Cogline really began to cackle.

ogline was still cackling on the morning following when the strange little company set forth on their journey to find the Grimpond. Muttering gleefully to himself, he skittered about through the leaf-strewn forest with careless disinterest for what he was about, lost in the shadowed, half-crazed world of his own mind. Yet the sharp old eyes strayed often to Brin's worried face, and there was cunning and shrewdness in their gaze. And there was always a sly, secretive mirth that whispered in his voice.

"Try it, Southland girl—you must try it, indeed! Ha-ha! Speak with the Grimpond and ask it what you will! Secrets of all that is and all that will be! For a thousand thousand years the Grimpond has seen all of what human life has done with itself, watched with eyes that no other can have! Ask, Southland girl—touch the spirit thing and learn!"

Then the cackle came and he danced away again. Time and again, Kimber Boh chastised him for his behavior with a quick word here, a hard look of disapproval there. The girl found the old man's behavior silly and embarrassing. But this had no effect on the old man and he kept on teasing and taunting.

It was an iron gray, misted autumn day. The sky was packed with banks of clouds from the dark stretch of the Wolfsktaag west to the fading tips of the forest trees east. A cool breeze wafted down from out of the north, carrying in its wake dust and crumbling leaves that swirled and stung the face and eyes. The color of the woodlands was faded and worn in the morning light, and the first hint of winter's coming seemed to reflect in their gray cast.

The tiny company traveled north out of Hearthstone with Kimber Boh in the lead, somber and determined; Brin and Rone Leah following close behind; old Cogline danced all about them as they walked; and Whisper ranged far afield through the dark tangle of the trees. They passed beneath the shadow of the towering rock that gave to the valley its name and on from the broad, scrub-free clearings of the sheltered hollow into the wilderness beyond. Deadwood and brush choked the forestland into which they journeyed, a thick and twisted mass of woods. As midday approached, the pace slowed to a crawl. Cogline no longer flitted about like a wild bird, for the wilderness hemmed them all close. They worked their way carefully ahead in a line. Only Whisper continued to roam free, passing like a shadow through the dark mass of the woods, soundless and sleek.

The terrain had grown even more rugged by noontime, and in the distance the dark edge of a series of ridgelines lifted above the trees. Boulders and craggy drops cut apart the land through which they passed, and much of their progress now required that they climb. The wind was blocked away as the ridgelines drew nearer, and the forest smelled of rot and must.

Then, at last, they climbed free of a long, deep ravine and stood upon the crest of a narrow valley, angling downward through a pair of towering ridgelines that ran north until they were lost in a wall of mist.

"There." Kimber pointed into the valley. A thick stand of pine surrounded a lake, its waters only partially visible within a blanket of mist that swirled and shifted with the currents of the wind.

"The Grimpond!" Cogline cackled, his fingers stroking Brin's arm lightly, then slipping away.

They passed through the maze of pine trees that choked the valley's broken slopes, winding their way steadily downward to where the mist stirred sluggishly above the little lake. No wind seemed to reach them here; the air had gone still, and the woodland was quiet. Whisper had disappeared entirely. Broken rock and pine needles lay scattered over the ground on which they walked, and their leather boots scraped and crunched with their passing. Though it was midday still, the clouds and mist screened away the light so completely that it appeared as if nightfall had set in. As she followed after the slight figure of Kimber Boh, Brin found herself listening to the silence of the forest, searching through the shadows for some sign of life. As she listened and searched, an uneasiness grew within her. There was indeed something here—something foul, something hidden. She could sense it waiting.

Deep within the pines, the mist began to descend about them. Still they went on. When it seemed they must surely disappear into it completely, they stepped suddenly from the trees into a small clearing where aged stone benches ringed an open fire pit, its charred logs and ash black with the dampness.

On the far side of the clearing, a rutted trail led away again into the mist.

Kimber turned to Brin. "You must go alone from here. Follow the trail until you reach the edge of the lake. The Grimpond will come to you there."

"And whisper secrets in your ear!" Cogline chortled, crouching next to her.

"Grandfather," the girl admonished.

"Truth and lies, but which is which?" Cogline cackled defiantly and skipped away to the edge of the pines.

"Do not be frightened by grandfather," Kimber advised, her pixie face a mask of concern as she saw Brin's troubled eyes. "No harm can come to you from the Grimpond. It is only a shade."

"Maybe one of us should go with you," Rone suggested uneasily, but Kimber Boh immediately shook her head.

"The Grimpond will only speak with one person, never more. It will not even appear if there is more than one." The girl smiled encouragingly. "Brin must go alone."

Brin nodded. "I guess that settles it."

"Remember my warning," Kimber cautioned. "Be wary of what you are told. Much of it will be false or twisted."

"But how am I to know what is false and what is true?" Brin asked her.

Kimber shook her head once more. "You will have to decide that for yourself. The Grimpond will play games with you. It will appear to you and speak as it chooses. It will tease you. That is the way of the creature. It will play games. But perhaps you can play the games better than it can." She touched Brin's arm. "This is why I think you should speak to the Grimpond rather than I. You have the magic. Use it if you can. Perhaps you can find a way to make the wishsong help you."

Cogline's laughter rang from the edge of the little clearing. Brin ignored it, pulled her forest cloak tightly about her, and nodded. "Perhaps I will try."

Kimber smiled, her freckled face wrinkling. Then she hugged the Valegirl impulsively. "Good luck, Brin."

Surprised, Brin hugged her back, one hand coming up to stroke the long dark hair.

Rone came forward awkwardly, then bent to kiss Brin. "Watch yourself."

She smiled her promise to do so; then, gathering her cloak about her once more, she turned and walked into the trees.

Shadows and mist closed about her almost at once, so utterly that she was lost a dozen yards into the stretch of pine. It happened so quickly that she was still moving forward when she realized that she could no longer see anything about her. She hesitated then, peering rather hopelessly into the darkness, waiting for her sight to adjust. The air had gone cold again, and the mist from the lake penetrated her clothing with a chill, wet touch. A few moments passed, long and anxious, and then she discovered that she could discern vaguely the slender shapes of the pines closest at hand, fading and reappearing phantomlike through the swirling mist. It was not likely to get any better than it was, she decided. Shrugging off her discomfort and uncertainty, she walked cautiously ahead, groping with her outstretched hands, sensing rather than seeing the passage of the trail through the trees as it wound steadily downward toward the lake.

The minutes slipped by, and she could hear the gentle lapping of water on a shoreline in the silence of the mist and the forest. She slowed and peered guardedly into the mist, searching for the thing she knew waited for her. But there was nothing to be seen except the gray haze. Carefully, she went forward.

Then suddenly the trees and the mist thinned and parted before her, and she found herself standing on a narrow, rock-strewn shoreline looking out across the gray, clouded waters of the lake. Emptiness stretched away into the haze, and clouds of mist walled her about, closing her in . . .

A chill slipped through her, hollowing out her body and leaving it a frozen shell. She glanced quickly about, frightened. What was there? Then anger welled up within, sharp, bitter, and hard as iron as it rose in retaliation. A fire burned away the cold, flaring through her with ferocious purpose, thrusting back the fear that threatened to overwhelm her. Standing on the shoreline of that little lake, alone within the concealing mist, she felt a strange power surge through her, strong enough, it seemed in that instant, to destroy anything that came against her.

There was a sudden stirring from within the mist. Instantly, the strange sense of power was gone, fled like a thief, back into her soul. She did not understand what had happened to her in those few brief moments, and now there was no time to think on it; there was movement within the mist. A shadow drew together and took shape, dark drawn from the grayness. Risen and formed above the lake's waters, it began to advance.

The Valegirl watched it come, a shrouded, spectral thing that glided in silence on the currents of the air, slipping from the mist toward the shoreline and the girl who waited. It was cloaked and hooded, as insubstantial as the mist out of which it had been born, human-shaped but featureless.

The shade slowed and stopped a dozen feet before her, suspended above the waters of the lake. Robed arms folded loosely before it, and mist swirled outward from its gray form. Slowly its cowled head lifted to the girl on the shore, and twin pinpoints of red fire glimmered from within.

"Look upon me, Valegirl," the shade whispered in a voice that sounded like steam set loose. "Look upon the Grimpond!"

Higher the cowled head lifted and the shadows that masked the being's face fell away. Brin stared in stunned disbelief.

The face that the Grimpond showed to her was her own.

Jair stirred awake in the dank and empty darkness of the Dun Fee Aran cell in which he lay imprisoned. A thin shaft of gray light slipped like a knife through the tiny airhole of the stonewalled cubicle. It was day again, he thought to himself, trying desperately to trace the time that had passed since he had first been brought there. It seemed like weeks, but he realized this was only the second day since his imprisonment. He had neither seen nor spoken with another living thing save the Mwellret and the silent Gnome jailer.

Gingerly, he straightened and then sat upright within the stale gathering of straw. Chains bound his wrists and ankles, fixed in iron rings to the stone walls. He had been hobbled by these shackles since the second day of his imprisonment. The jailer had placed them on him at Stythys' command. As he shifted his weight, they clanked and rattled sharply in the deep silence, echoing down the corridors that lay without the cell's ironbound door. Weary despite the long sleep, he listened as the echoes died away, straining for some other sound to come back to him. None did. There was no one out there to hear him, no one to come to his aid.

Tears welled up in his eyes then, flowing down his cheeks, and wetting the soiled front of his tunic. What was he thinking? That someone would come to him to help him escape from this black hold? He shook his head against the pain of his own certainty that there was no help left for him. All of the company from Culhaven were gone—lost, dead, or scattered. Even Slanter. He wiped the tears away roughly, fighting back against his despair. It did not matter that no one would come, he swore silently. He would never give the Mwellret what it wanted. And he would somehow find a way to escape.

Once again, as he had done each time he had come awake after sleeping, he worked at the pins and fastenings of the chains that bound him, trying to weaken them enough to break free. For long moments, he twisted and turned the iron, peering hopefully at their joinings through the dark. But in the end he gave it up as he always gave it up, for it was useless to pit flesh and blood against smith-forged iron. Only the jailer's key could set him free again.

Free. He spoke the word within the silence of his mind. He must find a way to get free. He must.

He thought then of Brin; thinking of her, he found himself wondering at what he had seen when last he had looked within the mirror of the vision crystal. How strange and sad that brief glimpse had been—his sister sitting alone before a campfire, her face twisted in strain and despair as she stared out across the forestland. What had happened to Brin to cause her such unhappiness?

Self-consciously, his hand strayed to the small bulk of the crystal where it lay hidden beneath his tunic. Stythys had not found it yet, nor the bag of Silver Dust, and Jair had been careful to keep both hidden within his clothing whenever the Mwellret was about. The creature came to him all too frequently, slipping soundlessly from the dark when the Valeman least expected it, stealing from the shadows like some loathsome wraith to wheedle and cajole, to promise, and to threaten: Give to me what I ask and you will be set free . . . Tell me what I want to know!

Jair's face hardened and set. Help that monster? Not in this world, he wouldn't!

Swiftly, he lifted the silver chain and its stone from within his tunic and held it lovingly within the cupped palms of his hands. It was the sole tie he had with the world beyond this cell, his only means of discovering what Brin was about. He stared at the crystal, and his mind was decided. He would use it one time more. He would have to be careful, he knew. But just a moment was all that was required. He would call up the image and then banish it quickly. The monster would never be the wiser.

He had to know what had become of Brin.

With the crystal cupped in his hands, he began to sing. Soft and low, his voice called forth the dormant power of the stone, reaching into its murky depths. The light slowly rose from within and spread outward—a flood of whiteness that brightened the terrible gloom and brought an unexpected smile to his face.

Brin! he cried softly.

The image came to life—his sister's face suspended within the light before him. He sang, steady and slow, and the image sharpened. She stood before a lake now. The sadness on her face had turned to shock. Stiff and unmoving, she stared out across the gray and misted waters at a cloaked and hooded apparition that hung upon the air. Slowly the image turned as he sang, swinging about to where he could see the face of the apparition.

The wishsong wavered and broke as the face drew near.

The face was Brin's!

Then a furtive rustling sound from across the darkened cell turned Jair's stomach to ice. Instantly, he went still and the strange vision faded. Jair's hands closed about the vision crystal, desperately drawing it down within his tattered clothing, knowing even then that it was already too late.

"Ssee, little friend, you have found a way to help me," a cold, familiar reptilian voice hissed.

And the cloaked form of the Mwellret Stythys advanced through the open cell door.

On the shore's edge at the lake of the Grimpond, there was a long, endless moment of silence, broken only by the soft lapping of the gray waters as they washed against the rocks. The shade and the Valegirl faced each other in the gloom of mist and shadow like voiceless ghosts called forth from another world and time.

"Look upon me!" the shade commanded.

Brin kept her gaze steady. The face the Grimpond wore was her own, drawn, haggard, and ravaged with grief, and where her own dark eyes would have been, twin slits of crimson light burned like coals. Her smile taunted her from the shade's lips, teasing with insidious purpose, the laughter low and evil.

"Do you know me?" came the whisper. "Speak my name."

Brin swallowed against the tightness in her throat. "You are the Grimpond."

The laughter swelled. "I am you, Brin of the Vale people, Brin of the houses of Ohmsford and Shannara. I am you! I am the telling of your life, and in my words you shall find your destiny. Seek, then, what you will."

The hissing of the Grimpond's voice died into a sudden roiling of the waters over which it hung suspended. A fine, thin spray exploded geyser-like into the misted air and showered down upon the Valegirl. It was as cold as death's forbidden touch.

The Grimpond's crimson eyes narrowed. "Would you know, child of the light, of the darkness that is the Ildatch?"

Wordlessly, Brin nodded. The Grimpond laughed mirthlessly and glided closer. "All that is and all that was of the dark magic traces to the book, bound by threads that close you and yours tight about. Wars of Races, wars of man—faerie demons, all one hand. Like rhymes of the voice, all are one. The humankind come to the dark magic, seeking power that they cannot hope to make theirs—seeking then death. They creep to the hiding place of the book, drawn by the lure, by the need. One time to the face of death, one time to the pit of night. Each time they find what they seek and are lost to it, changed from moral self to spirit. Bearers and Wraiths, all are one. And the evil is one with them."

The voice faded. Brin's mind raced, thinking through the meaning of what she had been told. One time to the face of death . . . Skull Mountain. Past and present were one, Skull Bearer and Mord Wraith—that was the Grimpond's meaning. They were born of the same evil. And somehow, in some way, all of it was bound together in a single source.

"The dark magic made them all," she said quickly. "Warlock Lord and Skull Bearers in the time of my great-grandfather; Mord Wraiths now. That is your meaning, isn't it?"

"Is it?" the voice hissed softly, teasingly. "One of one? Where lies the Warlock Lord now, Valegirl? Who now gives voice to the magic and sends the Mord Wraiths forth?"

Brin stared at the apparition wordlessly. Was it saying that the Warlock Lord had come back again? But no, that was impossible . . .

"That voice is dark when it speaks to humankind," the Grimpond intoned in a singsong hiss. "That voice is born of the magic, born of the lore. It is found in different ways—by some in printed word, by some . . . in song!"

Brin went cold. "I am not of their kind!" she snapped. "I do not use the dark magic!"

The Grimpond laughed. "Nor does any, Valegirl. The magic uses them. There is the key of all that you seek. There is all you need know."

Brin struggled to understand. "Speak more," she urged.

"More? More of what?" The shade's misted form shimmered darkly. "Would you have me tell you of the eyes—eyes that follow you, eyes that seek you out at every turn?" The Valegirl stiffened. "Love sees you in those eyes when they are the eyes that command the crystal. But dark intent sees you likewise when the eyes are sightless and born of your own birthright. Do you see? Are your own eyes open? Not so the eyes of the Druid when he lived, dark shadow of his time. They were closed to the greatest part of the truth, closed to what was apparent, had he thought it through. He did not see the truth, poor Allanon. He saw only the Warlock Lord come again; he saw only what was as what is—not as what could be. Deceived, poor Allanon. Even in death, he walked where the dark magic willed that he should—and when he came to his end, he was seen a fool."

Brin's mind spun. "The walkers—they knew he was coming, didn't they? They knew he could come into the Wolfsktaag. That was why the Jachyra was there."

Laughter swelled and echoed in the silence of the mist. "Truth wins out! But once only, perhaps. Trust not what the Grimpond says. Shall I speak more? Shall I tell you of your journey to the Maelmord with the clown Prince of Leah and his lost magic? Oh, so desperate he is to have that magic, so much in need of what will destroy him. You suspect it will destroy him, don't you, Valegirl? Let him have it, then, so that he might have his wish and become one with all who shared that wish before and passed into death. His is the strong arm that leads you to a similar fate. Ah, shall I tell you of how you, too, shall come to die?"

Brin's dusky face tightened. "Tell me what you will, shade. But I will listen only to the truth."

"So? Am I to judge what is true and what is not, where we speak of what is yet to be?" The Grimpond's voice was low and taunting. "The book of your life lies open before me, though there are pages yet to write. What shall be written shall be written by you, not by words that I may speak. You are the last of three, each to live in the shadow of the others, each to seek to be free of that shadow, each to grow apart therefrom and then to reach back to the ones who went before. Yet your reach is darkest on the land."

Brin hesitated uncertainly. Shea Ohmsford must be the first, her father the second, she the third. Each had sought to be free of the legacy of the Elven house of Shannara from which all were descended. But what did that last part mean?

"Ah, your death awaits you in the land of the walkers," the Grimpond hissed softly. "Within the pit of dark, within the breast of the magic you seek to destroy, there shall you find your death. It is foreordained, Valegirl, for you carry its seeds within your own body."

The Valegirl's hand came up impatiently. "Then tell me how to reach it, Grimpond. Give me a way into the Maelmord that will shield me from the eyes of the walkers. Let me go to my death quickly, if you see it so."

The Grimpond laughed darkly. "Clever girl, you would seek to have me tell you forthright what you have truly come here to discover. I know what brings you hence, child of the Elfkind. You can hide nothing from me, for I have lived since all that was and will live for all that is to be. It is my choice to do so, to stay within this old world and not to be at peace in another. I have made playthings of those of flesh and blood who are my sole companions now, and none have ever broken past the guard I place upon myself. Would you know the truth of what you ask, Valegirl? Beg it from me, then."

Anger welled up within her at the Grimpond's boastful words, and she stepped to the very edge of the gray lake waters. Spray hissed warningly from out of the mist, but she ignored it.

"I was warned that you would play this game with me," she said, her own voice dangerous now. "I have come far and have endured much grief. I have no wish to be teased now by you. Do not press me, shade. Speak only the truth. How am I to reach the pit of the Maelmord without the walkers seeing where I come?"

The Grimpond's eyes narrowed sharply, flickering deep red as the silence between the two lengthened. "Find your own way, Brin of the Vale people," the Grimpond hissed.

Rage exploded inside Brin, but by sheer force of will she held it in check. Wordlessly, she nodded in acquiescence, then stepped back and seated herself upon the shore, her cloak pulled close about her.

"You wait to no purpose," the shade sneered.

But Brin did not move. She composed herself carefully, breathing in the damp air of the lake and drawing her thoughts close about her. The Grimpond stayed suspended above the waters of the lake, unmoving, its eyes turned toward her. Brin let those eyes draw her close. A serene look came over her dusky face, and the long black hair fanned back. It does not yet see what I will do! She smiled inwardly, and the thought was gone an instant after it had come.

Then softly, she began to sing. The wishsong rose into the midday with sweet and gentle words from the lips of the girl seated upon the lakeshore, to fill the air about her. Quickly, it reached out and bound the misted form of the Grimpond, weaving and twisting with its magic. So startled was the shade that it did not stir from its resting spot, but hung suspended within the web of the magic as it slowly drew tighter. Then, for the barest second, the Grimpond seemed to sense what was happening to it. Beneath its gathered robes, the lake waters boiled and hissed. But the wishsong swiftly swept all about the imprisoned form, wrapping it away as if it had become a chrysalis.

Now the Valegirl's voice came quicker and with more certain intent. The shrouding of the first song, the gentle, womblike wrapping that had bound the Grimpond without his seeing, was gone. A prisoner now, as surely as the fly caught within the spider's web, the shade was to be dealt with as its captor chose. Yet the Valegirl used neither force of arms nor strength of mind against this being, for she had seen that such would be useless. Memories were the weapons she called to her aid now—memories of what had once been, of what had been lost and could never be regained. All came back once more within the wishsong's music. There was the touch of a human hand, warm and kind. There was the smell and taste of sweetness and light and the sensation of love and joy, of life and death. There were all these and others, lost to the Grimpond in its present form, barely remembered from the life long since gone.

With a cry of anguish, the Grimpond sought to evade the old sensations, shimmering and rolling in a cloud of mist. Yet it could not escape the magic of the song; slowly, the sensations caught it up and held it, and it was given over to their memories. Brin could feel the shade's emotions come again to life, and within the memories exhumed, the Grimpond's tears flowed. She sang steadily. When the shade was hers completely, she hardened herself against her own pain and drew back what she had given.

"No!" the apparition howled in dismay. "Give them back, Valegirl! Give them back to me!"

"Tell me what I would know," she sang, the threads of the questions weaving through her song. "Tell me!"

With frightening suddenness, the Grimpond's words came pouring out as if released with the anguish that tore its forgotten soul. "Graymark bridges the Maelmord where it lies within the Ravenshorn—Graymark, the castle of the Wraiths. There lies the way that is sought, a maze of sewers that runs from its halls and chambers deep beneath the rock on which it stands, to empty into a basin far below. Enter through the sewers, and the eyes of the walkers will not see!"

"The Sword of Leah," Brin pressed harshly. "Where can it be found? Tell me!"

Anguish wrenched the Grimpond through and through as she touched him in taunting strokes with the feel of what had been lost. "Spider Gnomes!" the shade cried desperately. "The blade lies within their camp, snatched from the waters of the Chard Rush, gathered in by the nets and snares they keep fastened to its banks!"

Abruptly, Brin drew back the magic of the wishsong, filled with the memories and the sensations of the old life. She drew it clear in a swift, painless rush, freeing the imprisoned shade from the trappings that had bound it. The echoes of the song lingered in the stillness that hung across the empty lake, dying into a single haunting note that rang in the midday air. It was a note of forgetfulness—a sweet, ghostly cry that left the Grimpond as it had been.

There was a long, terrible silence then. Slowly Brin rose to her feet and stared full into the face that was the mirror of her own. Something deep within her howled in dismay as she saw the look that came upon that face. It was as if she had done this to herself!

And the Grimpond realized now what had been done. "You have tricked from me the truth, dark child!" the shade wailed bitterly. "I sense that you have done so. Ah, black you are! Black!"

The shade's voice broke, and the gray waters boiled and steamed. Brin stood frozen at the edge of the lake, afraid to turn away or to speak. Inside, she was empty and cold.

Then the Grimpond lifted its robed arm. "One last game then, Valegirl—something back from me to you! Let this be *my* gift! Look into the mist, here beside me where it forms—look closely now! See you this!"

Brin knew then that she should flee, but somehow she could not. The mist seemed to gather before her, swirling and spreading in a sheet of gray that lightened and smoothed. A slow, shimmering motion rippled across its surface like still water disturbed, and an image formed—a figure, crouched low within a darkened cell, his movements furtive . . .

Jair snatched back the vision crystal, thrusting it deep within his tunic, praying that the shadows and the gloom hid from the Mwellret what it was that he did. Perhaps he had been quick enough. Perhaps . . .

"Ssaw the magicss, Elfling," the harsh voice rasped, dashing his hopes. "Ssenssed all along that the magicss were yourss. Sshare them with me, little friend. Sshow what you have."

Jair shook his head slowly, fear mirrored in his blue eyes. "Stay away from me Stythys. Stay back from me."

The Mwellret laughed—a low, guttural laugh that echoed in the emptiness of the cell and the long corridors beyond. The creature swelled suddenly within the dark robes, rising up against the dim light like a monstrous shadow.

"Threatenss me, ssmall one? Crussh you like a tiny egg if you usse the magicss on me. Sstay quiet now, little friend. Look into my eyess. Ssee the lightss."

Lidded, scaled eyes glimmered, cold and compelling. Jair forced his own eyes down, knowing that he could not look, that if he did so he would belong once again to the creature. But it was so hard not to look. He wanted to see into those eyes; he wanted to be drawn into them and the peace and serenity that waited there.

"Ssee, Elfling," the monster hissed.

Jair's hand closed about the small bulk of the vision crystal until he could feel the edges cutting into his palm. Concentrate on the pain, he thought frantically. Don't look. Don't look!

Then the Mwellret hissed angrily and one hand lifted. "Give to me the magicss! Give them to me!"

Voiceless, Jair Ohmsford shrank back from him . . .

The Grimpond's robed arm came down sharply and the screen of mist dissolved and was gone. Brin lurched forward desperately, stepping off the rock-strewn shoreline into the gray waters of the lake. Jair! That had been Jair in the images! What was it that had happened to him?

"Did you enjoy that game, Brin of the Vale people?" whispered the avatar harshly, the waters roiling once again beneath where it hung. "Did you see what has happened to your precious brother whom you thought safe within the Vale? Did you see?"

Brin fought back against the rage that welled up within her. "Lies, Grimpond. You tell only lies this time."

The shade chuckled softly. "Lies? Think what you wish, Valegirl. A game is only a game, after all. A diversion from the truth. Or is it truth revealed?" Robed arms drew close, the mist swirling. "Dark you are, Brin of Shannara, of Ohmsford, of history spawned. Dark as the magic with which you play. Go from me, now. Take what you have learned of the clown prince's magic and the passage to your death. Find what you seek and become what you surely will! Get you gone from me!"

The Grimpond began to fade back into the gray mist that rolled behind it over the lake's murky waters. Brin stood transfixed upon the shoreline, wanting to hold the shade back, but knowing that this time she could not.

Suddenly the shade paused in its retreat, red eyes narrowing into slits within the mist robes. Brin's own face leered back at her, a twisted mask of evil. "See me as you are, Brin of the Vale people. Savior and destroyer, mirror of life and death. The magic uses all, dark child—even you!"

Then the Grimpond disappeared back into the wall of the mist, its laughter soft and wicked in the deep silence. Soundlessly, the grayness closed about it and it was gone.

Brin stared after it a moment, lost in a gathering of fears, doubts, and whispered warnings. Then slowly she turned and walked back to the trees.

Dark and forbidding, the Mwellret Stythys advanced through the gloom of the little cell, and Jair backed slowly away.

"Give to me the magicss," the monster hissed, and the crooked fingers beckoned. "Releasse them, Elfling."

The Valeman retreated further into the shadows, the chains that bound his wrists and ankles dragging. Then the cell wall was pressing into his back and there was nowhere left to go.

I cannot even run from him! he thought desperately.

A soft scraping of leather boots on stone sounded from the cell entry and the Gnome jailer appeared from the corridor beyond. Head lowered into shadow, the hooded form passed silently through the open doorway into the room. Stythys turned at the other's approach, cold eyes glittering with displeasure.

"Ssent not for little peopless," the Mwellret muttered darkly, and the scaled hands motioned the Gnome away.

But the jailer paid no heed. Mute and unresponsive, he shuffled past the lizard creature as if he had not seen him and came directly toward Jair. Head still lowered, hands tucked deep into the folds of the ragged cloak, the Gnome slipped wraithlike through the dark. Jair watched his approach with mingled surprise and uncertainty. As the little man came closer, the Valeman shrank back in repulsion against the stone of the cell wall, the iron of his chains clanking as he raised his hands defensively.

"Sstand away, little peopless!" Stythys rasped, angry now, and his scaled body drew itself up menacingly.

But the Gnome jailer had already reached Jair, a hunched and voiceless thing as he stood before the Valeman. Slowly the cowled head lifted.

Jair's eyes went wide. The Gnome in the ragged cloak and hood was not the jailer!

"Need a little help, boy?" Slanter whispered.

Then a black-clad form leaped from the shadowed corridor without, and the slender blade of a long sword pressed up against the throat of an astonished Stythys, forcing him back against the cell wall.

"Not a sound from you," Garet Jax warned. "Not a twitch. Either, and you'll be dead before you finish!"

"Garet, you're alive!" Jair exclaimed in disbelief.

"Alive and well," the other replied, but the hard gray eyes never moved from the Mwellret. "Hurry and set the Valeman free, Gnome."

"Just be patient a moment!" Slanter had produced a ring of iron keys from beneath the cloak and was trying each key in turn in the shackles that bound the Valeman. "Confounded things don't fit the lock . . . ah-ha— this one!"

The locks on the wrist- and ankle-bindings clicked sharply and the chains fell away. "Slanter," Jair gripped the Gnome's arm as Slanter stripped away the jailer's ragged cloak and tossed it aside. "How on earth did you ever manage to find me?"

"No real trick to that, boy!" the Gnome snorted, rubbing at the other's bruised wrists to restore the circulation. "I told you I was the best tracker you'd ever met! Weather didn't help much, of course—washed out half the signs, turned the whole of the forestland to muck. But we picked up the lizard's tracks right outside the tunnels and knew he'd bring you here, whatever his intentions. Cells in Dun Fee Aran are always for sale to anyone with the right price and no questions asked. People in them for sale the same way. Lock you away until you're bones, unless . . ."

"Talk about it later, Gnome," Garet Jax cut him short. "You." He jabbed sharply at the Mwellret. "You walk ahead—keep everyone away from us. No one is to stop us; no one is to question us. If they do . . ."

"Leavess me here, little peopless!" the creature hissed.

"Yes, leave him," Slanter agreed, his face wrinkling in distaste. "You can't trust the lizards."

But Garet Jax shook his head. "He goes. Foraker thinks we can use him."

Jair started. "Foraker is here, too!"

But Slanter was already propelling him toward the cell door, spitting in open disdain at the Mwellret as he walked past. "He'll do us no good, Weapons Master," he insisted. "Remember, I warned you."

They were in the hallway beyond then, crouched in the shadows and the silence, Slanter at the Valeman's elbow as Garet Jax brought Stythys through the door. The Weapons Master paused for a moment, listened, then shoved Stythys before him as they started back down the darkened corridor. A torch burned in a wall rack ahead of them; when they reached it, Slanter snatched the brand away and assumed the lead.

"Black pit, this place!" he growled softly, picking his way through the gloom.

"Slanter!" Jair whispered urgently. "Is Elb Foraker here, too?"

The Gnome glanced at him briefly and nodded. "The Dwarf, the Elf and the Borderman as well. Said we'd started this journey together and that's how we'd finish it." He shook his head ruefully. "Guess we're all mad."

They slipped back through the labyrinth passageways of the prisons, the Gnome and the Valeman leading and the Weapons Master a step behind with his sword pressed close against the back of the Mwellret. They hastened through blackness, silence, and the stench of death and rot, passing the closed and rusted doors of the prison cells and working their way back into the light of day. Gradually, the gloom began to recede as slivers of daylight, gray and hazy, brightened the passages ahead. The sound of rain reached their ears, and a small, sweet breath of clean air brushed past them.

Then once again the massive, ironbound doors of the building entrance appeared before them, closed and barred. Wind and rain blew against them in sharp gusts, drumming against the wood. Slanter tossed aside the torch and hastened ahead to peer through the watch slot for what waited without. Jair joined him, gratefully breathing in the fresh air that slipped through.

"I never thought to see you again," he whispered to the Gnome. "Not any of you."

Slanter kept his eyes on the slot. "You have the luck, all right."

"I thought no one was left to come for me. I thought you dead."

"Hardly," the Gnome growled. "After I lost you in the tunnels and couldn't figure out what had become of you, I went on through to the cliffs north above Capaal. Tunnel ended there. I knew if the others were alive, they'd come through just as I had, because that was what the Weapons Master's plans had called for. So I waited. Sure enough, they found each other, then found me. And then we came after you."

Jair stared at the Gnome. "Slanter, you could have left me—left them too. No one would have known. You were free."

The Gnome shrugged, discomfort reflecting in his blocky face. "Was I?" He shook his head disdainfully. "Never stopped to think about it."

Garet Jax had reached them now, prodding Stythys before him. "Still raining?" he asked Slanter.

The Gnome nodded. "Still raining."

The Weapons Master sheathed the slender sword in one fluid motion and a long knife appeared in its place. He pushed Stythys up against the corridor wall, his lean face hard. A head taller than Garet Jax when first surprised by him in Jair's cell, Stythys had shrunk down again, coiled like a snake within his robes. Green eyes glittered evilly at the Southlander, cold and unblinking.

"Leavess me, little peopless," he whined once more.

Garet Jax shook his head. "Once outside, walk close to me, Mwellret. Don't try to move away. Don't play games. Cloaked and hooded, we shouldn't be recognized. The rain will keep most away, but if anyone comes close, you turn them. Remember, it wouldn't take much to persuade me to cut your throat."

He said it softly, almost gently, and there was a chilling silence. The Mwellret's eyes narrowed into slits.

"Havess the magicss!" he hissed angrily. "Needss nothing from me! Leavess me!"

Garet Jax brought the point of the long knife tight against the other's scaled throat. "You go."

Cloaks wrapped close about them, they pulled open the heavy wooden doors of the darkened prison and stepped out into the light. Rain fell in blinding sheets from gray, clouded skies, blown against the fortress walls by the wind. Heads bent against its force, the four started across the muddied yard toward the battlements that lay immediately north. Scattered knots of Gnome Hunters passed them by without slowing, anxious only to get in out of the weather. On the watchtowers, sentries huddled in the shelter of stonework nooks and bays, miserable with the cold and damp. No one cared anything about the little party that crossed below. No one even gave them a second glance.

Slanter took the lead as the north battlements drew near, guiding them past small lakes of surface water and mudholes to where a pair of iron-grated doors closed away a small court. They pushed through the doors and crossed quickly to a covered entry that led into a squat stone-and-timber watchtower. Wordlessly, the Gnome unlatched the shadowed wooden door and led the way inside.

An anteway lay within, brightened by the light of torches jammed into holders on either side of the door. Brushing the water from their cloaks, they paused momentarily while Slanter moved to the edge of a darkened corridor leading left beneath the battlement. After peering into the gloom, the Gnome beckoned for them to follow. Garet Jax snatched one of the torches from its bracket, handed it to Jair, and motioned him after Slanter.

A narrow hall opened before them, lined with doors that stretched into the darkness ahead.

"Storerooms," Slanter informed Jair, winking.

They stepped into the hall. Slanter slipped cautiously ahead; at the third door, he stopped and knocked softly.

"It's us," he whispered into the latch.

The latch released with a snap, the door swung wide, and Elb Foraker, Helt, and Edain Elessedil appeared. Smiles creasing their battered faces, they surrounded Jair and gripped his hand warmly.

"Are you all right, Jair?" the Elven Prince asked at once, his own face bruised and cut so badly that the Valeman was immediately afraid for him. The Elf saw his concern and dismissed it with a shrug. "Just a few scratches. I found an escape passage, but it opened on a thorn bush. Nothing that won't quickly heal. But you—are you truly all right?"

"I'm fine now, Edain." Jair hugged him impulsively.

Helt and Foraker were battered about the face and hands as well, the result Jair supposed of having the greater part of that battlement wall fall on them. "I can't believe that you're all here!" The Valeman swallowed hard against the knot forming in his throat.

"Couldn't very well leave you behind, now could we, Jair?" The giant Borderman gripped his arm warmly with one great hand. "Yours is the magic that we need to heal the Silver River."

Jair grinned happily, and Foraker stepped close, eyes fixing on the Mwellret. "I see that you were able to bring him."

Garet Jax nodded without comment. While the others had been greeting Jair anew, he had stayed with Stythys, the long knife pointed at the Mwellret's throat.

"Little peopless be ssorry they takess me!" the creature hissed venomously. "Findss a way to make them ssorry!"

Slanter spit distastefully into the earth. Foraker pointed at the Mwellret. "You alone are responsible for what happens to you now, Stythys. Had you not taken the Valeman, you would have been left alone. Since you did take him, you'll have to answer for it. You're going to see us safely out of this place, then safely through the forests north and into the Ravenshorn. Steer us wrong just once, and I'll let Slanter do to you what he'd like to have done in the first place." He glanced at the Gnome. "And remember, Stythys, he knows the way as well, so think carefully before you attempt any deception."

"Let's be gone from here!" Slanter growled anxiously.

With the Gnome leading, the little band passed down the narrow hall through a series of still smaller corridors and arrived at the foot of a winding stone stairway. Slanter put a finger to his lips in warning. In single file, they began to climb. From somewhere above, faint and distant yet, the guttural sound of Gnome voices reached their ears. A small wooden door stood closed at the top of the stairs. Slanter paused momentarily, listened, then cracked the door and peered out. Satisfied, he beckoned them through.

They stood in a massive armory, its floor piled with stacks of weapons, armor, and provisions. Gray light filtered down through high, barred windows. The chamber was empty, and Slanter led the way hurriedly toward a door set into the far wall.

He was almost there when the door abruptly swung open from the opposite side, and he found himself face to face with an entire squad of Gnome Hunters.

The Gnomes hesitated, seeing first Slanter, then the odd gathering of faces that followed after him. It was when they caught sight of Foraker that their hands flew to their weapons.

"No luck this time, boy!" Slanter howled, flinging himself protectively in front of Jair.

The Gnome Hunters came at them in a rush, but already the dark figure of Garet Jax was moving, the slender sword darting. Down went the foremost of the attackers, and then Foraker was beside the Weapons Master, his two-edged axe thrusting back the rest. Behind them, Stythys turned and broke for the door through which they had come, but Helt was on him like a cat, bearing him to the floor. They skidded into a stack of pikes, and the pikes tumbled down about them in a clash of wood and iron.

The Gnome Hunters stood and fought before the open door a mo-

ment longer as Garet Jax and Foraker pressed in on them. Then, with a
howl of anger, they broke and fled. The Weapons Master and the Dwarf
gave chase as far as the doorway; but seeing that pursuit was pointless, they
turned quickly to help the struggling Helt. Together, they hauled Stythys
back to his feet, the Mwellret hissing venomously, his scaled body swelling
until he rose above even the giant Borderman. Holding the lizard firm,
they dragged him to where Slanter and Jair stood peering down the corridor without.

From both ends of the corridor, cries of alarm answered those of the
fleeing Gnome Hunters.

"Which way do we run?" Garet Jax snapped at Slanter.

Wordlessly, the Gnome turned right, away from the fleeing Hunters,
moving down the corridor at a quick trot and motioning the others to follow. They came after him in a knot, Stythys urged on by the long knife
Garet Jax held against his ribs.

"Sstupid little peopless!" the Mwellret rasped in fury. "Diess here in
the prissonss!"

The hall divided before them. To the left, a gathering of Gnomes
caught sight of them and charged with weapons drawn. Slanter wheeled
and took the little company right. Ahead, a Gnome Hunter darted from a
doorway, but Foraker bowled him over without slowing, banging the fellow's helmeted head against the stone block walls with jarring force. Cries
of pursuit rose up all about.

"Slanter!" Jair cried suddenly in warning.

Too late. The Gnome had stumbled into the midst of a swarm of
armed Hunters that had burst unexpectedly from an adjoining hall. He
went down in a tangle of arms and legs, crying out. Thrusting Stythys at
Helt, Garet Jax went to his aid, Foraker and Edain Elessedil a step behind.
Weapons glittered sharply in the gray half-light and cries of pain and anger
filled the hall. The rescuers swept into the Gnomes, thrusting them back
from the fallen Slanter. Garet Jax was like a cat at hunt, fluid and swift, as
he parried and cut with the slender sword. The Gnomes gave way. Aided
by Edain Elessedil, Slanter struggled to his feet once more.

"Slanter! Get us out of here!" Elb Foraker roared, the great, two-
edged axe before him.

"Ahead!" Slanter coughed and staggered forward.

Surging through the Gnomes that still barred their way, the little company raced down the corridor, dragging the reluctant Stythys with them.
Gnome Hunters sprang at them from everywhere, but they threw back the
attackers with ferocious determination. Slanter went down again, tripped
by the haft of a short spear thrust before him. Instantly Foraker was there,
broadax hammering at the attacker and one hand dragging Slanter back up.
The cries from behind them became a solid roar as hundreds of Gnomes
flooded the hallway about the armory door and gave chase.

Then they were in the clear for a moment, bounding down a flight
of stairs, cutting back beneath the flooring to a passageway below. A

broad rotunda opened before them, its windows and doors neatly spaced about, closed and shuttered against the weather. Without slowing, Slanter wrenched open the door closest and led the little company back out into the rain.

They were in another court, walled and gated. The rain blew wildly in their faces, and thunder rolled across the High Bens. Slowing his pace, Slanter led the way across the court to the gates, pushed them open, and stepped through. An outside stairway circled downward to a line of battlements and watchtowers. Beyond, the dark shadow of the forest pressed close about the walls.

Boldly, Slanter led the company down the stairs and onto the battlements. Gnome Hunters clustered about the watchtowers now, alerted that something had happened within the fortress. Slanter ignored them. Head lowered, cloak wrapped close, he motioned the others into a passageway beneath the battlements. Within the concealment of their shadow, he gathered the company about him.

"We're going right through the gates," he announced, his breath ragged. "No one talks but me. Keep your hoods up and your heads down. Whatever happens, don't stop. Quick, now!"

There was no argument, not even from Garet Jax. Cloaks drawn close and hoods in place, the company slipped from the shadows once more. With Slanter leading, they followed the battlement walls beneath the watchtower to a pair of iron-barred, open gates. A cluster of Gnome Hunters stood talking before them, heads bent against the weather, sharing a flask of ale. A head or two lifted at their approach, and Slanter waved, calling out something in the Gnome tongue that Jair could not understand. One of the Hunters drew away from his fellows and stepped out to meet them.

"Keep moving," Slanter whispered over his shoulder.

A few scattered shouts from behind them had reached the ears of the Gnome Hunters. Startled, they looked back into the fortress to discover what had happened.

The little company marched past them without slowing. Instinctively, Jair tried to shrink down within his cloak, tensing so badly he stumbled and almost went down before Elb Foraker caught him. Slanter stepped apart from the others as they came past the watch, blocking away the eyes of the Gnome who had thought to detain them. He spoke angrily with the fellow, and Jair caught the word Mwellret in the conversation. They were clear of the Hunters now, all save Slanter, passing beneath the battlements and through the open gates. No one stopped them. As they hurried from Dun Fee Aran into the darkness of the trees, Jair slowed and looked back anxiously. Slanter still stood within the arch, arguing with the watch.

"Keep your head down!" Foraker urged, pushing him ahead.

He went into the rain-soaked forest, following reluctantly after the others, and the walls and towers of the fortress disappeared behind him.

They pressed on a few minutes longer, weaving their way through the scrub and trees, Elb Foraker in the lead. Then they stopped, gathering beneath a monstrous oak, its leaves fallen and matted into the earth about it in a carpet of muddied yellow. Garet Jax backed Stythys against the gnarled trunk and held him there. They waited in silence.

The minutes slipped by. Slanter did not appear. Crouched down at the edge of the little clearing that encircled the old oak, Jair peered helplessly into the rain. The others spoke in hushed tones behind him. The rain fell steadily, spattering in noisy cadence on the earth and forest trees. Still Slanter did not appear. Jair's mouth tightened with determination. If he did not come in the next five minutes, the Valeman was going back for him. He would not leave the Gnome—not after what Slanter had done for him.

Five minutes passed, and still Slanter did not appear. Jair rose and looked questioningly at the others, a cluster of cloaked and hooded figures in the dark and the rain.

"I'm going back," he told them. Then a rustling noise brought him about and Slanter emerged from the trees.

"Took a bit more talking than I thought it would," the Gnome announced. "They'll be after us quick enough." Then he saw the look of relief on Jair's face and stopped. "Thinking of going somewhere, boy?" he guessed rightly.

"Well, I . . . no, I guess not now . . ." Jair stuttered.

A look of amusement spread over the Gnome's rough face. "No? Still planning on finding your sister, aren't you?" Jair nodded. "Good. Then you are going somewhere after all. You're going north with the rest of us. Get moving."

Motioning to the others, he turned into the trees. "We'll ford the river six miles upstream to throw off any pursuit that lasts that long. River's deep there, but I guess we can't get much wetter than we are."

Jair permitted himself a brief smile, then followed after the others. The peaks of the High Bens rose before them, misted and gray through the trees. Beyond, still far to the north and hidden from view, the mountains of the Ravenshorn waited. It might yet be a long way to Graymark, the Valeman thought, breathing in the cool autumn air and the smell of the rain, but for the first time since Capaal he felt certain that they were going to get there.

34

Brin spoke little on the journey back from the Grimpond to Hearthstone. She needed to sort through and decipher the meaning of all that the shade had told to her, for she knew that her confusion would only grow greater with the passage of time. Pressed by her companions to tell all that the Grimpond had told to her, she revealed only that the missing Sword of Leah was in the hands of the Spider Gnomes and that the way to enter the Maelmord without being seen was through Graymark's sewers. After saying that much, she begged them to forbear from any further questioning until they had returned to the valley, then gave herself over to the task of reconsidering all that she had been told.

The strange image of Jair in that darkened room with the cloaked form advancing so menacingly toward him was foremost in her mind as she began the task of sorting through the puzzle given her. In spite and anger, the Grimpond had conjured up that image, and she could not believe that there was any truth in what she had been shown. The cloaked form was neither Gnome nor Mord Wraith, and those were the enemies that sought the Ohmsfords. It angered her that she had stayed to watch the image play itself out before her, teasing her as the Grimpond had intended that it should. Had she any sense, she would have turned away at once and not let herself be taunted. Jair was safe in the Vale with her parents and their friends. The Grimpond's image was but a loathsome lie.

And yet she could not be entirely certain.

Unable to do anything further with that concern, she pushed it aside and turned her thoughts to the other mysteries that the Grimpond had given her. There were many. Past and present were joined in some way by the dark magic, the shade had hinted. The power that the Warlock Lord had wielded in the time of Shea Ohmsford was the power wielded in her own time by the Mord Wraiths. But there was more to the Grimpond's meaning. There was mention of some tie between the Wars of the Races and the more recent war her father and the Westland Elves had fought against the Demons of the faerie world. There was that insidious suggestion that while the Warlock Lord had been destroyed by the magic of the Sword of Shannara, he was not really gone. "Who now gives voice to the magic and sends the Mord Wraiths forth?" the Grimpond had asked. Worst of all was the shade's sly insistence that Allanon—who through all his years of service to the Four Lands and her people had always foreseen everything—had this time been deceived. Thinking that he saw the truth, he had let his eyes be closed. What was it the Grimpond had said? That Allanon saw only the Warlock Lord come again—that he saw only what was past.

What do you see? the shade had whispered. Are your eyes open?

Frustration welled up within her, but she brought it quickly under control. Frustration would only serve to blind her further, and she needed to keep her vision clear, if she was even to begin to comprehend the Grimpond's words. Suppose, she reasoned, that Allanon had indeed been deceived—an assumption that was difficult for her to accept, but one that she must accept if she were to puzzle through what she had been told. In what way could that deception have been worked? It was evident enough that the Druid had been deceived in his belief that the Wraiths would not anticipate their coming into the Eastland through the Wolfsktaag or that the Wraiths could not follow them after they left the Vale. Were these deceptions only bits and pieces of some greater deceit?

Are your own eyes open? Do you see?

The words whispered again in her mind, a warning that she did not understand. Was the deception of Allanon in some way her own? She shook her head against her confusion. Reason it through, she told herself. She must assume that Allanon had been deceived somehow in his analysis of the danger that confronted them in the Maelmord. Perhaps the power of the Mord Wraiths was greater than he had supposed. Perhaps some part of the Warlock Lord had survived the Master's destruction. Perhaps the Druid had underestimated the strength of their enemies or overestimated their own strength.

She thought then of what the Grimpond had said about her. Dark child, he had called her, doomed to die in the Maelmord, the bearer of the seeds of her own destruction. Surely that destruction would come from the magic of the wishsong—an inadequate and erratic defense against the dark magic of the walkers. The Mord Wraiths were victims of their magic. But so, too, was she, the Grimpond had said. And when she had heatedly replied that she was not like them, that she did not use the dark magic, the shade had laughed and told her that none used the magic—that the magic used them.

"There is the key to what you seek," he had said.

That was another puzzle. It was certainly true that the magic used her as much as she used it. She remembered her anger against the men from west of Spanning Ridge at the Rooker Line Trading Center and how Allanon had shown her what the magic could do to those trees so closely intertwined. Savior and destroyer—she would be both, the shade of Bremen had warned. And now the Grimpond had warned her, too.

Cogline whispered something at her side, then danced away as Kimber Boh told him to behave. Her thoughts scattered momentarily, and she watched the old man slip into the forest wilderness, laughing and chattering like one half gone into madness. She breathed the cool afternoon air deeply, seeing the shadows of early evening beginning to slip down about the land. She found herself missing Allanon. Odd that she should, for his dark and formidable presence had been small comfort to her in the days that she had traveled with him. But there had been that strange kinship between them, that sense of understanding, and of being in some way similar . . .

Was it the magic they shared—the wishsong and the Druid power?

She found tears forming in her eyes as she pictured his broken form once again, slumped down within that sunlit glen, bloodied and torn. How terrible he had looked to her, stricken by impending death, his hand lifting to touch her forehead with his blood . . . A lonely, worn figure in her mind, steeped not so much in Druid power as in Druid guilt, he had bound himself by his father's oath to purge the Druids of the responsibility they bore for unleashing the dark magic into the world of men.

And now that responsibility had been passed to her.

Afternoon faded into evening, and the little company passed down out of the Anar wilderness into the valley of Hearthstone. Brin ceased to puzzle over the words of the Grimpond and began to think instead of what she was to tell her companions and what she was to do with the small bit of knowledge that she had gained. Her own lot in this matter was fixed, but not so that of the others—not even Rone. If she were to tell him all that she had been told by the Grimpond, perhaps he could be persuaded to let her go on alone. If it was predetermined that she must go to her death, perhaps she could at least keep him from going to his.

An hour later they were gathered together before the fireplace in the little cottage, drawn up in covered chairs and on benches—Brin, the old man, the girl, and Rone Leah. The warmth of the flames danced off their faces as the night settled down, cold and still. Whisper slept peacefully upon his rug, his giant body stretched full-length before the fire. Invisible most of the day on their journey to and from the Grimpond, the moor cat had reappeared on their return and promptly curled up in his favorite resting spot.

"The Grimpond appeared to me in my own image," Brin began quietly as the others listened. "It took my face and taunted me with what it said I was."

"It plays those games," Kimber said sympathetically. "You must not be bothered by it."

"All lies and deceits! It is a dark and twisted thing," Cogline whispered, his sticklike frame hunched forward. "Locked within its pool since before the loss of the old world, speaking riddles no man could hope to unravel—or woman either."

"Grandfather," Kimber Boh cautioned gently.

"What was it that the Grimpond had to say?" Rone wanted to know.

"What I have told you," Brin replied. "That the Sword of Leah is in the hands of the Spider Gnomes, pulled from the waters of the Chard Rush. That the way into the Maelmord without being seen by the walkers is through the sewers of Graymark."

"There was no deceit in this?" he pressed.

She shook her head slowly, thinking of the dark way in which she had used the wishsong's magic. "Not in this."

Cogline snorted. "Well, the rest was lies, I'll wager!"

Brin turned to him. "The Grimpond said that death would come to me in the Maelmord—that I could not escape it."

There was a hushed silence. "Lies, just as the old man says," Rone muttered finally.

"The Grimpond said that your death awaits you there as well, Rone. It said that we both carry the seeds of that death in the magic we would wield—yours in the Sword of Leah, mine in the wishsong."

"And you believe that nonsense?" The highlander shook his head. "Well, I don't. I can look after the both of us."

Brin smiled sadly. "But what if the Grimpond's words are not lies? What if that part, too, is truth? Must I bear your death on my conscience, Rone? Will you insist on dying with me?"

Rone flushed at the rebuke. "If I must. Allanon made me your protector when I sought to be so. What manner of protector would I be if I were to abandon you now and let you go on alone? If it is predetermined that we should die, Brin, then let that not be on your conscience. Let it be on mine.

Brin had tears in her eyes again and she swallowed hard against the feelings coursing through her.

"Girl, girl, no crying now, no crying!" Cogline was suddenly on his feet, shuffling over to where she sat. To her surprise, he reached up gently and brushed the tears away. "It's all games with the Grimpond, all lies and half-truths. The shade predicts everyone's death as if it were blessed with special insight. Here, here. What can a spirit thing know of death?"

He patted Brin on the shoulder, then scowled inexplicably at Rone, as if the fault were somehow his, and muttered something about dratted trespassers.

"Grandfather, we must help them," Kimber said suddenly.

Cogline wheeled on her, bristling. "Help them? And just what is it that we've been doing, girl? Gathering firewood?"

"No, I don't think that, grandfather, but . . ."

"But nothing!" Crooked arms gestured impatiently. "Of course we're going to help them!"

Valegirl and highlander stared at the old man in astonishment. Cogline cackled shrilly, then kicked at the sleeping Whisper and brought the cat's whiskered face up with a jerk. "Me and this worthless animal—we're going to help all we can! Can't be having tears like those! Can't be having guests wandering all over the place with no one to show them the way!"

"Grandfather . . ." the girl started to interrupt, but the old man brushed her aside.

"Haven't had a run at those Spider Gnomes for some time now, have we? Good idea to let them know that we're still here in case they think we moved out. Up on Toffer Ridge, they'll be—no, not this time of year. No, they'll be down off the ridge to the moor with the season's change at hand. That's their ground; that's where they'd take a sword like that if they pulled it from the river. Whisper will track it for us. Then we'll turn east, skirt the moor, and cross to the Ravenshorn. Day or two, maybe, all told."

He wheeled back again. "But not you, Kimber. Can't have you out and about in that country. Walkers and all are too dangerous. You stay here and keep the home."

Kimber gave him a hopeless look. "He still thinks of me as a child. I am the one who should worry for him."

"Ha! You don't have to worry for me!" Cogline snapped.

Kimber smiled indulgently, her pixie face calm. "Of course I have to worry for you. I love you." She turned to Brin. "Brin, you have to understand something. Grandfather never leaves the valley anymore without me. He requires the use of my eyes and my memory from time to time. Grandfather, don't be angry with what I say, but you know that sometimes you are forgetful. Besides, Whisper will not always do what you tell him. He will disappear on you when you least want him to, if you try to go alone."

Cogline frowned. "Stupid cat does that, all right." He glanced down at Whisper, who blinked back at him sleepily. "Waste of my time trying to teach him differently. Very well, I suppose we'll all have to go. But you keep out of harm's way, girl. Leave that part to me."

Brin and Rone exchanged hurried glances.

Kimber turned to them. "It is settled then. We can leave at dawn."

The Valegirl and the highlander stared at each other in disbelief. What was happening? As if it were the most natural thing in the world, it had just been decided that a girl barely more than Brin's age, a half-crazed old man, and a sometimes disappearing cat would retrieve for them the missing Sword of Leah from some creatures they had labeled as Spider Gnomes and then afterward guide them into the mountains of the Ravenshorn and Graymark! Gnomes and walkers and other dangerous beings would be all about—beings whose power had destroyed the Druid Allanon—and the old man and the girl were acting as if none of that really made any difference at all.

"Kimber, no," Brin said finally, not knowing what else to say. "You can't go with us."

"She's right," Rone agreed. "You can't even begin to understand what we'll be up against."

Kimber Boh looked at each of them in turn. "I understand better than you think. I told you before—this land is my home. And grandfather's. We know its dangers and we understand them."

"You don't understand the walkers!" Rone exploded. "What can the two of you do against the walkers?"

Kimber held her ground. "I don't know. Much the same as you, I'd guess. Avoid them."

"And what if you can't avoid them?" Rone pressed. "What then?"

Cogline snatched a leather bag belted at his waist and held it forth.

"Give them a taste of my magic, outlander! Give them a taste of a fire they know nothing about at all!"

The highlander frowned doubtfully and looked at Brin for help. "This is crazy!" he snapped.

"Do not be so quick to dismiss my grandfather's magic," Kimber advised, with a reassuring nod to the old man. "He has lived in this wilderness all of his life and survived a great many dangers. He can do things you might not expect of him. He will be of great help to you. As will Whisper and I as well."

Brin shook her head. "I think this is a very bad idea, Kimber."

The girl nodded her understanding. "You will change your mind, Brin. In any case, you really don't have a choice. You need Whisper to track. You need grandfather to guide you. And you need me to help them do that."

Brin started to object once more, then stopped. What was she thinking? They had come to Hearthstone in the first place because they needed someone to guide them through Darklin Reach. There was only one man who could do that, and that man was Cogline. Without Cogline, they might wander the wilderness country of the Anar for weeks—weeks that they did not have. Now that they had found him and he was offering them the help they so desperately needed, here she was trying to refuse it!

She hesitated. Perhaps she had good reason for doing so. Kimber appeared to her as a girl whose heart was greater than her strength. But the fact remained that Cogline was unlikely to go anywhere without her. Did Brin, then, have the right to put her concern for Kimber above the dictates of the trust which she had been given by Allanon?

She did not think so.

"I believe the matter is decided," Kimber said softly.

Brin looked at Rone one final time. The highlander shook his head in helpless resignation.

Brin turned back and smiled wearily. "I guess it is," she agreed and hoped against reason that it had been decided correctly.

35

They departed Hearthstone at dawn of the following day and journeyed northeast through the forestland toward the dark rise of Toffer Ridge. Travel was slow, as it had been during their trek north to the Grimpond. The whole of the wilderness beyond the valley between the Ravenshorn and the Rabb was a treacherous maze of craggy ravines and drops that could cripple the unwary. With packs strapped tightly across their backs and weapons secured about their waists, Brin, Rone, Kimber Boh, and Cogline wound their way cautiously ahead on a warm, sweet-smelling autumn day filled with sound and color. Only occasionally visible, the shadowy form of Whisper kept pace in the trees about them. The members of the little company felt rested and alert, much more so than they should have, since their discussion of the previous night had not ended until early morning. They knew that lack of sleep would catch up with them eventually, but for now, at least, they were filled with the tension and excitement of their quest, and all traces of weariness were easily brushed aside.

Not so easily dismissed, however, were Brin's feelings of uncertainty about taking along Kimber and Cogline. The decision had been made, the pledge given, and the journey begun—yet still the uncertainty that had troubled her from the first would not subside. Some doubts and fears would have been there in any case, she supposed, fostered by her knowledge of the dangers that lay ahead and by the haunting prophecies of the Grimpond. But such doubts and fears would have been for her and for Rone—Rone, whose determination to stand with her in this was so strong that she had finally accepted that he would never be persuaded to leave her. The doubts and fears would not have been, as they were now, for the old man and the girl. All of their reassurances notwithstanding, the Valegirl still thought neither strong enough to survive the power of the dark magic. How could she see it otherwise? It made no difference that they had lived all these years within the wilderness of the Anar, for the dangers they would face now were not dangers made of this world and time. What magics or lore could they hope to employ that would turn aside the Mord Wraiths when the walkers were next encountered?

It frightened Brin to think of the power of the Mord Wraiths being turned against the girl and the old man. It frightened her more than anything that she could imagine might happen to her. How could she live with the knowledge that she had permitted them to come on this journey, if it were to end in their deaths?

And yet Kimber seemed so certain of herself and of her grandfather. There was neither fear nor doubt in her mind. There was only her self-assurance, determination, and that unshakable sense of obligation toward Brin and Rone that motivated her in what she had undertaken to do for them.

"We are friends, Brin, and friends do for each other what they see needs to be done," the girl had explained in the late hours of the previous night when all talk had drifted into weary whispers. "Friendship is a thing sensed inwardly as much as a thing pledged openly. One feels friendship and becomes bound by it. It was this that drew Whisper to me and gained me his loyalty. I loved him as he loved me, and each of us sensed that in the other. I have sensed it with you as well. We are to be friends, all of us, and if we are to be friends, then we must share both good and bad in our friendship. Your needs become mine."

"That's a very beautiful sentiment, Kimber," she had replied. "But what if my needs are too great, as they are in this instance? What if my needs are too dangerous to share?"

"All the more reason that they *must* be shared." Kimber had smiled somberly. "And shared with friends. We must help each other if the friendship is to mean anything at all."

There really wasn't much to be said after that. Brin might have argued that Kimber barely knew her, that she was owed no obligation, and that this quest she had been given was hers alone and not the responsibility of the girl and her grandfather. But such arguments would have meant nothing to Kimber, who saw so clearly the relationship between them as one of equals, and whose sense of commitment was such that there could be no compromise.

The journey wore on and the day slipped past. It was a savage timberland through which they passed, a rugged mass of towering black oaks, elms, and gnarled hickories. Their lofty, twisted limbs stretched wide like giants' arms. Through the bones of the forest roof, skeletal and stripped of their leaves, the sky shone deep crystal blue, with sunshine streaming down to brighten the woodland shadows with friendly patches of light. Yet the sunlight was but a brief daytime visitor to this wilderness. Here, only the shadows belonged—pervasive, impenetrable, filled with a subtle hint of hidden dangers, of things unseen and unheard, and of a phantom life that came awake only when the light was completely gone and the forestland lay wrapped in blackness. That life lay waiting, concealed silently within the darkened heart of these woodlands, a cunning and hateful force that resented the intrusion of these creatures into its private world and would snuff them out as a wind would a candle's small flame. Brin sensed its presence. It whispered softly in her mind, worming past the slender thread of confidence lent her by the presence of those who traveled with her, warning her that when nightfall came again, she must be very careful.

Then the sun began to drop below the western skyline and dusk to settle over the land. The dark line of Toffer Ridge loomed before them, a rugged and uneven shadow, and Cogline took them through a twisting pass that breached its wall. They walked in silence, fatigue now beginning to slip through them. Insect sounds filled the darkness, and high above them, lost in the tangle of the great trees, night birds sent forth their shrill calls. Ridgeline and wilderness forest tightened about them, closing them away in the darkened pass. The air, warm all day, grew hot and unpleasant, and its smell turned stale. That hidden life which waited within the woodland shadows came awake and rose up to look about . . .

Abruptly, the timber broke apart before them, sloping sharply downward through the ridgeline into a vast, featureless lowland shrouded in mist and lighted in eerie glow by stars and a strange, pale orange gibbous moon that hung at the edge of the eastern horizon. Sullen and dismal, the sprawling bottomland was little more than a shadowed black mass of stillness that seemed to open into the earth like some bottomless canyon where Toffer Ridge slipped away into the mist.

"Olden Moor," Kimber whispered softly.

Brin stared down at the moor in watchful silence. She could feel it staring back.

Midnight came and went, and time slowed until it seemed to cease all passage. A hint of wind fluttered enticingly across Brin's dust-streaked face and faded away. She looked up expectantly, but there was nothing more. The heat returned, harsh and oppressive. She felt as if she had been shut within a furnace, its unseen fires snatching from her aching lungs the very air she needed to survive. In the bottomland, the autumn night gave nothing back of its cooling promise. Sweat soaked Brin's clothing through, ran down her body in distracting rivulets, and coated her worn countenance with a silver gray sheen. Muscles cramped and knotted wearily. Though she shifted about frequently in an effort to relieve the discomfort, she quickly found there were no new positions to be tried. The ache simply followed. Swarms of gnats buzzed annoyingly, drawn by the moisture from her body, biting at her face and hands as she brushed at them uselessly. All about her, the air reeked of rotting wood and stagnant water.

Crouched in the concealing shadows of a clump of rocks with Rone, Kimber, and Cogline, she stared downward along the base of the ridgeline to where the camp of the Spider Gnomes lay settled at the edge of Olden Moor. A jumble of makeshift huts and burrows, the camp stretched between the base of Toffer Ridge and the darkness of the moor. A scattering of fires burned in its midst, their sullen, ragged light barely penetrating the gloom. The crooked, bent shadows of the camp's inhabitants passed through the muted glare. The Spider Gnomes, their strange and grotesque bodies covered with gray hair, were naked to the elements as they skittered about in the withered long grass on all fours, hunched and faceless. Large groups of them gathered at the edge of the moor, shielded from the mist by the flames as they chanted dully into the night.

"Calling to the dark powers," Cogline had informed his companions hours earlier, after first bringing them to this hiding place. "A tribal people, the Gnomes—the Spider folk more so than any. Believe in spirits and dark things that rise from other worlds with the change of seasons. Call to them for their own strength, do the Gnomes—hoping at the same time that strength doesn't turn against them. Ha! Superstitious stuff!"

But the dark things were real sometimes, however, Cogline told them. There were things within Olden Moor as dark and terrible as those that inhabited the forests of the Wolfsktaag—things born of other worlds and lost magics. They were called Werebeasts. They lived within the mists, creatures of dreadful shapes and forms that preyed upon body and mind, snaring mortal beings weaker than they and draining away their lives. The Werebeasts were not imaginary, Cogline admitted grimly. It was against their coming that the Spider Gnomes sought to protect themselves—for the Spider Gnomes were the Werebeasts' favorite food.

"Now, with the autumn's change to winter, the Gnomes come down to the moor to call out against the rise of the mists." The old man's voice had been a harsh whisper. "Gnomes think the winter won't come or the mists stay low if they don't. A superstitious folk. Come here like this each fall for nearly a month, whole camps, whole tribes of them—just migrate down off the ridge. Call out to the dark powers day and night so that the winter will keep them safe and keep the beasts away." He grinned secretively and winked. "Works, too. Werebeasts feed off them for that whole month, you see. Eat enough to carry them through the winter. No need to go onto the ridge after that!"

Cogline had known where the Spider people would be found. With the fall of night, the little group had traveled north along the base of the ridgeline until the Gnome camp had been sighted. Then, as they hunched down within the concealment of the rocks, Kimber Boh had explained what must happen next.

"They will have your sword with them, Rone. A sword such as that, pulled from the waters of the Chard Rush, will be considered a talisman sent to them by their dark powers. They will set it before them, hoping it will shield them from the Werebeasts. We must discover where it is housed and then steal it back from them."

"How will we do that?" Rone had asked quickly. He had talked of little else for the whole of their journey there. The lure of the sword's power had claimed him once more.

"Whisper will track it," she had replied. "If given your scent, he can follow it to the sword, however well concealed. Once he has found it, he will return to lead us in."

So Whisper had been given the highlander's scent and dispatched into the night. He had gone soundlessly, fading into the shadows, lost from view almost instantly. The four from Hearthstone had been waiting ever since for his return, crouched down in the humid dark and the fetid dampness of the bottomland, listening and watching. The moor cat had been gone a very long time.

Brin closed her eyes against the weariness that seeped through her and tried to block the sound of the Gnomes chanting from her mind. A dull, empty monotone, it went on ceaselessly. Several times, while she listened, there had been screams from close to the mists—shrill, quick, and horror-stricken. Almost at once, though, they had ceased. Still the chanting went on . . .

A monstrous shadow detached itself from the dark right in front of her, and she started to her feet with a small cry.

"Hush, girl!" Cogline yanked her down again, one bony hand slipping tightly across her mouth. "It's only the cat!"

Whisper's massive head materialized then, luminous blue eyes winking lazily as he padded up to Kimber. The girl bent down to wrap her arms about him, stroking him gently, whispering in his ear. For several moments she spoke with the moor cat, and the cat nuzzled and rubbed up against her. Then she turned back to them, excitement dancing in her eyes.

"He has found the sword, Rone!"

Instantly Rone was beside her. "Take me to where it can be found, Kimber!" he begged. "We will have a weapon then with which to face the walkers and any other dark thing that might serve them!"

Brin fought back against the bitterness that welled up suddenly within her. Rone has forgotten already what little good the sword did him in Allanon's defense, she thought. He was consumed by his need for it.

Cogline called them close, while Kimber spoke a quick word to Whisper. Then they began their descent into the camp of the Gnomes. They crept down off the rise on which they had hidden, crouched low against the shadow of the ridgeline. Light from the distant fires barely touched them here, and they slipped swiftly ahead. Warnings nudged Brin Ohmsford's restless mind, whispering to her that she must turn back, that nothing good lay this way. Too late, she whispered back. Too late.

The camp drew closer. In the gradual brightening of the fires, the Spider Gnomes grew more distinct, crouched forms creeping about the huts and burrows like the insects for which they were named. They were loathsome things to look upon, all hair and sharp ferret eyes, bent and crooked forms drawn from some best-forgotten nightmare. Dozens of them slipped about, emerging from and then disappearing into the gloom, chittering in a language less than human. All the while, they continued to gather before the wall of mist and chant in hollow, toneless cadence.

The moor cat and his four companions crept soundlessly along the perimeter of the camp, circling toward its far side. The mist drifted past them in trailing wisps, broken free of the wall that hung motionlessly over the empty reaches of the moor. It was damp and clinging, unpleasantly warm as it touched their skin. Brin brushed at it distastefully.

Ahead, Whisper drew to a halt, his saucer eyes swinging about to find his mistress. Sweating freely now, Brin glanced about, desperately trying to get her bearings. The darkness was filled with shadows and movement, the warmth of the autumn night, and the drone of the Spider Gnomes chanting before the moor.

"We must go down into the camp," Kimber was saying, her voice a soft, excited whisper.

"Now we'll see them jump!" Cogline cackled gleefully. "Stay clear of them when they do!"

At a word from the girl, Whisper turned down into the Gnome encampment. Slinking soundlessly through the mist, the giant cat moved toward the nearest gathering of huts and burrows. Kimber, Cogline, and Rone followed, crouched low. Brin trailed behind them, her eyes searching the night.

To her left, things moved at the fringes of the firelight, crawling through a mass of rocks and slipping into the tall grass. Others appeared further out to their right, lurching toward the sound of the chanting and the wall of mist. Smoke from the fires drifted into Brin's eyes now, mingling with trailers of fog, stinging and sharp.

And suddenly she could not see. Anger and fear rose within her. Her eyes teared and she brushed at them with her hands . . .

A shriek broke suddenly from the darkness, rising above the drone of the chanting and freezing the night about it. A Spider Gnome leaped from the shadows before them, frantically trying to escape the giant moor cat that had suddenly appeared in its path. Whisper sprang ahead with a roar, knocking the flailing Gnome aside as if it were a bit of deadwood and scattering half a dozen more that blocked the way. Kimber raced beside the giant cat, a slight, swift figure in the dark. Cogline and Rone followed, each howling like men gone mad. Desperately, Brin ran after all of them, struggling to keep pace.

Led by the moor cat, the little company charged down into the very center of the encampment. Spider Gnomes flew past them, hairy, crooked shadows that chittered, howled, and leaped for cover. The company raced past the nearest bonfire. Cogline slowed, grappling with the contents of a leather bag secured about his waist. He produced a handful of black powder and threw it squarely into the flames. Instantly, an explosion rocked the bottomland as the fire geysered skyward in a shower of sparks and burning fragments of wood. The chanting before the wall of mist died away as the shrieks of the Gnomes in the camp intensified. The four dashed past another fire, and again Cogline threw the black powder into the flames. A second time the earth beneath exploded, filling the night with a flare of brightness and scattering the Spider Gnomes everywhere.

Far ahead, Whisper sprang upward through the firelight like a massive wraith, gaining the summit of a crudely constructed platform that rose close to the wall of mist. The platform splintered and collapsed with a crash, toppled by the weight of the beast, and a collection of jars, carved wooden objects, and glittering weapons spilled to the ground.

"The sword!" Rone cried out above the din of shrieking Gnomes. Knocking aside the wiry forms that sought to block his way, he charged ahead. An instant later, he was next to Whisper, snatching from the fallen treasures a slim ebony blade. "Leah! Leah!" he cried, brandishing the Sword of Leah triumphantly above his head and forcing back a handful of Gnomes that came at him.

Explosions erupted all about them now as Cogline fed the black powder into the Gnome fires. The whole of the bottomland was lighted in a yellow glare that surged skyward out of blackened, charred earth. Grass fires burned everywhere. Smoke and mist thickened and rolled across the encampment, and everything began to disappear into it. Brin ran on after the others, forgotten in the excitement of the battle, falling farther and farther behind. They had abandoned the toppled platform now and turned back toward the ridgeline. Little more than dim forms in the haze of smoke and mist, they could barely be seen.

"Rone, wait!" Brin cried out frantically.

Spider Gnomes raced past her on all sides, chittering madly. A few reached for her with their hairy limbs, their crooked fingers fastening on her clothing and tearing at it. Wildly, she lashed out at them, breaking free and running on to catch the others. But there were too many. They were all about her, grasping. In desperation, she used the wishsong; the strange, numbing cry flung them back from her with howls of dismay.

Then she fell, sprawling face forward in the tall grass, dirt flying into her eyes and mouth. Something heavy sprang atop her, a mass of hair and sinew wrapping itself tightly about her. She lost control of herself in that instant, fear and loathing consuming her so that she could no longer reason. She staggered to her hands and knees, but the unseen thing still clung to her. She used the wishsong with all the fury that she could muster. It burst from her throat like an explosion, and the thing on her back simply flew apart, shredded with the force of the magic.

Brin whirled then and saw what she had done. A Spider Gnome lay broken and lifeless against the rocks behind her, curiously small and fragile-looking in death. She stared at the shattered form and for one brief instant she felt an odd, frightening sense of glee.

Then she thrust the feeling from her. Voiceless, horror-stricken, she turned and ran blindly into the smoke, all sense of direction lost.

"Rone!" she screamed.

She fled into the wall of mist that rose before her and disappeared from view.

It was as if the world had fallen away.

There was only the mist. Moon, stars, and sky had vanished. Forest trees, mountain peaks, ridgelines, valleys, rocks, and streams were all gone. Even the ground over which Brin ran was a dim and shapeless thing, its grasses a part of the shifting gray haze. She was alone in the vast and empty void into which she had fled.

She stumbled to a weary halt, her arms folding tightly against her body, the sound of her breathing harsh and ragged in her ears. For a long time, she stood within the haze and did not move, only vaguely aware even now that she had become turned about in her flight from the bottomland and run into Olden Moor. Her thoughts scattered like blown leaves, and though she snatched frantically at them, trying to hold them back and gather them together, they were lost almost instantly. A single clear, hard image remained fixed before her eyes—a Spider Gnome, twisted, broken, and lifeless.

Her eyes closed against the light and her hands clasped into fists of rage. She had done what she had said she would never do. She had taken another human life, wrenching it away in a frenzy of fear and anger, using the wishsong to do it. Allanon had warned her that it could happen. She could hear the whisper of his caution: "Valegirl, the wishsong is power like nothing that I have ever seen. The magic can give life, and the magic can take life away."

"But I would never use it . . ."

"The magic uses all, dark child—even you!"

It was the Grimpond's warning and not Allanon's that mocked her now, and she thrust it from her mind.

She straightened. It was not as if she had not known somewhere deep within that she might someday be forced to use the wishsong's magic as Allanon had warned. She had recognized the possibility from the moment he had shown her the extent of its power in that simple demonstration of the trees intertwined in the forests of the Runne Mountains. It was not as if the death of the Spider Gnome came as some shocking and unexpected revelation.

It was the fact that some part of her had enjoyed what she had done, that some part of her had actually taken pleasure in the killing, that horrified her.

Her throat tightened. She remembered the sudden, furtive sense of glee she had felt on seeing the Gnome's shattered form, realizing that it was the wishsong that had destroyed it. She had reveled for that single instant in the power of the magic . . .

What kind of monster had she let herself become?

Her eyes snapped open. She had not *let* herself become anything. The Grimpond was right: You did not use the magic—the magic used you. The magic made you what it would. She could not fully control it. She had discovered that in the encounter at the Rooker Line Trading Center with the men from west of Spanning Ridge and had promised herself that she would never lose control of the magic like that again. But when the Spider Gnomes had come at her as she fled through their encampment, such control as she had thought to exercise had quickly evaporated under the flood of her emotions and the confusion and urgency of the moment. She had used the magic without any real presence of mind at all, but had simply reacted, wielding the power as Rone Leah would wield his sword, a terrible, destructive weapon.

And she had enjoyed it.

Tears formed at the corners of her eyes. She could argue that the enjoyment had been momentary and tinged with guilt and that her horror at its being would prevent it from reoccurring. But the truth could not be avoided. The magic had proven to be dangerously unpredictable. It had

affected her behavior in ways she would not have thought possible. That
made it a threat not only to her but to those close to her, and she must
guard carefully against that threat.

She knew that she could not turn aside from her journey eastward to
the Maelmord. Allanon had given her a trust, and she knew that, despite
everything that had happened and all that argued against it, she must fulfill that trust. She believed that even now. But even though she was
bound by the need she saw, she could yet choose her own code of being.
Allanon had intended that the wishsong be put to a single use—to gain
Brin entry into the pit. She must find a way therefore to keep the magic
to herself until it was time to call upon it for that intended use. Only
once more would she risk using the magic. Determined, she brushed the
tears from her eyes. It would be as she had sworn. The magic would use
her no more.

She straightened. Now she must find her way back to the others. She
stumbled forward again, groping ahead through the gloom, her direction
uncertain. Trailers of mist slipped past her, and in their meandering movement she was surprised to discover images. They crowded about her,
drawn from the haze into her mind and out again. The images began to
take the shapes and forms of memories resurrected from her childhood.
Her mother and her father passed before her, larger in memory than in life
in their warmth and security, gentle figures that sheltered and loved. Jair
was there. Shadows slipped through the strange, empty half-light, ghosts of
the past. Allanon might be one of those ghosts, come from death to the living. She looked to find him, half-expecting . . .

And suddenly, shockingly, he was there. Come from the mist like the
shade he now was, he stood barely a dozen yards distant, gray haze all
about him, swirling like the Hadeshorn stirred to life.

"Allanon?" she whispered.

Yet she hesitated. The shape belonged to Allanon, but it was the
mist—only the mist.

The shadow that was Allanon slipped back into the gloom—gone, as if
it had never really been. Gone . . .

And yet there had been something, after all. Not Allanon, but something else.

Swiftly, she glanced about, searching for the thing, sensing somehow
that it was out there, watching her. Images danced again before her eyes,
born on the trailers of mist, reflections of her memory. The mist gave
them life, a magic that entranced and lured. She stood transfixed in their
wake and wondered momentarily if she were indeed going mad. Such
imaginings as she was experiencing were certainly indicative of madness,
and yet she felt herself clear-headed and sure. It was the mist that sought to
seduce her, teasing her with its musings, playing with her memories as if
they were its own. It was the mist—or something in the mist!

Werebeast! The word whispered from somewhere back in her consciousness. Cogline had warned of the mist things as the little company

had crouched within the rocks on the ridgeline overlooking the camp of the Spider Gnomes. Scattered all through Olden Moor, they preyed on beings weaker than they, snaring them, draining away their lives.

She straightened, hesitated, then slowly began to walk ahead. Something moved in the mist with her—a shadow, dim and not fully formed, a bit of night. A Werebeast. She hastened on, letting her feet take her where they would. She was hopelessly lost, but she could not stay where she was. She must keep moving. She thought of those who had left her behind. Would they be searching for her? Would they be able to find her in this wall of mist? She shook her head doubtfully. She could not depend on that. She must find her own way out. Somewhere ahead, the wall of mist would fade and the moor would end. She must simply walk until she was out of it, free of its numbing haze.

But what if it would not let her get free?

Her memories came to life once more in the trailers of mist that swirled about her, teasing and seductive. She walked faster, ignoring them, aware that somewhere just beyond her vision the shadow kept pace. A chill settled through her at the awareness of the other.

She tried to envision the thing that followed her. What manner of creature was the Werebeast? It had come to her as Allanon—or had that merely been a trick of the mist and her imagination? She shook her head in voiceless confusion.

Something small and wet skittered away from beneath her feet, flitting off into the dark. She turned away from it, moving down a broad incline into a vast, marshy bowl. Muck and swamp sucked at her boots, and wintry grasses slapped at her legs, clutching. She slowed, sensing the unpleasant give in the ground, then backed away toward the rim again. Quicksand lay at the bottom of that bowl and it would draw her down and swallow her. She must stay clear of it and follow the harder, dryer earth. Mist swirled thickly all about, obscuring her vision as she sought to see her way clear. Still she had no sense of direction. For all she knew, she had been traveling in a circle.

She tramped on. The mists of Olden Moor swirled and thickened in the deep night about her, and shadows moved through their dampened haze—Werebeasts. There was more than one of them trailing her now. Brin stared out at them, following their quicksilver movements as they swam like fish through twilight waters. Grimly she quickened her pace, slipping through the marsh grass, keeping to the high ground. They still came after her. But they would not have her, she swore in silent promise. She belonged to another fate.

She hastened onward, running now, the pumping of her heart and blood a dull pounding in her ears. Anger, fear, and determination all mingled as one and drove her forward. The moor rose before her gently, and she scrambled to the center of a small rise thick with long grasses and scrub. Slowing, she glanced about in disbelief.

The shadows were everywhere.

Then a tall, lean figure appeared from out of the mist before her, wrapped in a highlander's cloak and bearing a giant broadsword strapped across its back. Brin stiffened in surprise. It was Rone! Arms lifted from out of the robes, reaching for her, beckoning her close. Willingly she started toward the highlander, her hand stretching to take his.

And then something stopped her.

She blinked. Rone? No!

A red veil fell across her vision, rage sweeping through her as she recognized the deception. It was not Rone Leah she saw. It was again the Werebeast that tracked her.

It came forward, a shimmering and fluid apparition. Robes and sword fell away, bits of the mist through which it passed. Nothing of the highlander was there now, but only a shadow, huge and changing. Swiftly it drew together, a massive body crouched on thick, clawed hindlegs, great forearms crooked and bristling with shaggy hair, and a head wrinkled and twisted about jaws that split to reveal whitened teeth.

It rose up through the mist, twice her size, swathed in the moor's haze. Soundless, it bent its head and snapped at her, a mass of hair and scales, muscle, spiked bone, teeth, and slitted eyes. It was a thing born of darkest nightmares, one Brin might have dreamed in the anguish of her own despair.

Was it real? Or was it simply born out of the mist and the wanderings of her imagination?

It made no difference. Forsaking the oath she had taken only minutes earlier, she used the wishsong. Hardened with purpose, maddened by what she saw, she called it forth. She was not meant to die here within Olden Moor at the hands of this monster. This one further time she would use the magic—on a thing whose destruction did not matter.

She sang, and the wishsong froze in her throat.

It was her father who stood before her now.

The Werebeast slouched toward her, form shifting and changing in the haze, jaws slavering in anticipation of how the Valegirl's life would sate its needs. Brin staggered back, seeing now her mother's dark and gentle face. She called out in desperation, a wild, anguished cry that seemed locked in the silence of her mind.

Back came an answering cry, calling her name. Brin! Confusion swept through her; the cry seemed real, but who . . . ?

"Brin!"

The monster loomed over her, and she could smell the evil of it. But the wishsong stayed locked in her throat, imprisoned by the image she retained of its power tearing into her mother's slim form, leaving it broken and lifeless.

"Brin!"

Then a frightening roar shattered the stillness of the night. A sleek shadow flew out of the mist, and five hundred pounds of enraged moor cat crashed into the Werebeast, flinging it back from Brin. Teeth and claws slashing, the cat tore into the monstrous apparition and both went tumbling headlong through the deep grasses.

"Brin! Where are you?"

Brin stumbled back, barely able to hear the voices over the sounds of the battle. Frantic, she called back to them. An instant later Kimber appeared, darting through the haze, her long hair streaming out behind her. Cogline followed, shouting wildly, his crooked body struggling to keep pace with the girl.

Whisper and the Werebeast surged back into view, lunging and feinting. The moor cat was the stronger of the two; although the mist thing sought to break past, it was blocked at every turn. But now other shadows were gathering in the darkness beyond, huge and shapeless, ringing them all close about. Too many shadows!

"Leah! Leah!"

And then Rone was there, his slim form bolting through the mass of shadows, sword lifted. Eerie, green incandescence swirled about the ebony blade. The Werebeast cornered by Whisper whirled instantly, sensing the greater danger of the sword's magic. Thrusting away from the moor cat, the monster leaped at Rone. But the Prince of Leah was ready. His sword arced down, knifing through the mist into the Werebeast. Green fire flared sharply through the night, and the mist thing exploded in a shower of flames.

Then the light died away, and the night and the mist returned. The shadows that had gathered in the darkness beyond melted back into the void.

The highlander turned, the sword dropping forgotten at his side. He came quickly to Brin, his face stricken.

"I'm sorry, sorry," he whispered. "The magic . . ." He shook his head helplessly. "When I found the sword again, when I touched it . . . I couldn't seem to think of anything else. I picked it up and I ran with it. I forgot everything—even you. It was the magic, Brin . . ."

He faltered, and she nodded into his chest, hugging him close. "I know."

"I won't leave you like that again," he promised. "I won't."

"I know that, too," she replied softly.

But she said nothing of her decision to leave him.

It was the third day after leaving the prisons at Dun Fee Aran before Jair and the little company from Culhaven reached the towering mountain range they called the Ravenshorn. Unable to use the open roadways that ran close to the banks of the Silver River as it wound south out of the mountains for fear of being seen, they were forced to traverse the deep forests above, picking their way at a slower pace through the tangled wilderness. The rains finally ceased on the second day out, slowed to a drizzle by midmorning, and turned to mist by noon. The air warmed as the skies cleared, and the clouds drifted east. When darkness slipped across the land, the moon and stars became visible through the trees. Their pace was slow, even after the rains had subsided, for the saturated earth could not absorb all of the surface water that had gathered, and the ground was muddied and slick with it. Stopping only for short periods of time to rest and eat, the company did its best to ignore the poor travel conditions and resolutely pressed ahead.

The sun appeared on the third day, brilliant and warm, filtering down in friendly streamers through the forest shadows, returning bits and pieces of color to the sodden land. The dark mass of the Ravenshorn came into view, barren rock rising up above the treeline. All morning they worked their way toward it, then on through the noonday, and by midafternoon they had reached the lower slopes and were starting up.

It was then that Slanter brought them to a halt.

"We have a problem," he announced matter-of-factly. "If we try to cross through these mountains, it will take us days—weeks, maybe. Only other way in is by following the Silver River upstream to its source at Heaven's Well. We can do that—if we're careful—but sooner or later we will have to pass right under Graymark. Walkers will see us coming for sure."

Foraker frowned. "There must be some way we can slip past them."

"There isn't," Slanter grunted. "I ought to know."

"Can we follow the river until we're close to Graymark and then cross into the mountains?" Helt asked, his big frame lowering onto a boulder. "Can we come at it from another direction?"

The Gnome shook his head. "Not from where we are. Graymark sits on a cliff shelf that overlooks the whole of the land about it—the Ravenshorn, the Silver River, everything. Rock is barren and open—no cover at all." He glanced at Stythys, who sat sullenly to one side. "That's why the lizards like it there so well. Nothing could ever creep up on them."

"Then we'll have to go in at night," Garet Jax said softly.

Again Slanter shook his head. "Break your neck if you try it. Cliffs are sheer drops all the way in and the paths are narrow and guarded. You'll never make it."

There was a long silence. "Well, what do you suggest?" Foraker asked finally.

Slanter shrugged. "I don't suggest anything. I got you this far; the rest is up to you. Maybe the boy can hide you with his magic again." He lifted his eyebrows at Jair. "How about it—can you sing for half the night?"

Jair flushed. "There must be some way to get past the guards, Slanter!"

"Oh, it's no problem for me." The Gnome sniffed. "But the rest of you might have some trouble."

"Helt has the night vision . . ." Foraker began thoughtfully.

But Garet Jax cut him short, beckoning to Stythys. "What suggestion would you make, Mwellret? This is your home. What would you do?"

Stythys let his lidded eyes narrow. "Findss your own way, little peopless. Sseekss another'ss foolissh aid. Leavess me be!"

Garet Jax studied him a moment, then walked over to him wordlessly, gray eyes so cold that Jair stepped back involuntarily. The Weapons Master's finger lifted and came to rest on the Mwellret's cloaked form.

"You seem to be telling me that you are no longer of any use to us," he said softly.

The Mwellret seemed to shrink back within the robes then, slitted eyes glittering with hate. But he held no power over Garet Jax. The Weapons Master stood where he was, waiting.

Then a low hiss escaped the lizard's mouth and its forked tongue licked out slowly. "Helpss you if you ssetss me free," he whispered. "Takess you where no one sseess you."

There was a long silence as the members of the little company glanced at one another suspiciously. "Don't trust him," Slanter said.

"Sstupid little Gnome cannot help you now," Stythys sneered. "Needss my help, little friendss. Knowss wayss that no other can passs."

"What ways do you know?" Garet Jax asked, his voice still soft.

But the Mwellret shook his head stubbornly. "Promisse firsst to sset me free, little peopless. Promisse."

The Weapons Master's lean face showed nothing of what he was thinking. "If you can get us into Graymark, you go free."

Slanter's face wrinkled with disapproval, and he spit into the earth. Standing with the others of the company, Jair waited for Stythys to say something more. But the Mwellret seemed to be thinking.

"You have our promise," Foraker interjected, a hint of impatience in his voice. "Now tell us what way we must go."

Stythys grinned, an evil, unpleasant smile that appeared to be almost a grimace. "Takess little peopless through Cavess of Night!"

"Why, you black . . . !" Slanter exploded in fury and came at the Mwellret in a rush. Helt caught him about the waist as he tried to push past and hauled him back, the Gnome yelling and struggling as if he had gone mad. Stythys' laughter was a soft hiss as the members of the little company closed about Slanter to keep him back.

"What is it, Gnome?" Garet Jax demanded, one hand fastening about Slanter's arm. "Do you know of these caves?"

Slanter wrenched himself free of the Weapons Master, though Helt still maintained his grip. "The Caves of Night, Garet Jax!" the Gnome snarled. "Death bins for the mountain Gnomes since the time they fell under the rule of the lizards! Thousands of my people were given over to the Caves, thrown within and lost! Now this . . . monster would do likewise with us!"

Garet Jax turned quickly back to Stythys. The long knife appeared as if by magic in one hand. "Be careful of your answer this time, Mwellret," he advised softly.

But Stythys seemed unperturbed. "Liess from little Gnome. Cavess are passsagess into Graymark. Takess you beneath the mountainss, passt the walkerss. No one sseess."

"Is there truly passage in?" Foraker asked Slanter.

The Gnome went suddenly still, rigid in Helt's firm grip. "Doesn't matter if there is. The Caves are no place for the living. Miles of tunnels cut within the Ravenshorn, black as any pit and filled with Procks! Have you heard of Procks? They are living things, formed of magic older than the lands—magic from the old world, it's said. Living mouths of rock, all through the Caves. Everywhere you walk, the Procks are there in the cavern floor. One wrong step and they open, swallowing you up, closing about you, crushing you into . . ." He was shaking with fury. "That was the way the lizards disposed of the mountain Gnomes—pushed them into the Caves!"

"But the Caves do offer a passage through." Garet Jax turned Foraker's question into a statement of fact.

"A passage useless to us!" Slanter exploded once more. "We can't see to find our way! A dozen steps in and the Procks would have us!"

"Havess not me!" Stythys cut him short with a hiss. "Mine iss the sse-cret of the Cavess of Night! Little peopless cannot passs, but my peopless know the way. Prockss cannot harm uss!"

They were all still then. Garet Jax stalked back to stand before the Mwell-ret. "The Caves of Night run to Graymark beneath the Ravenshorn—safe from the eyes of the walkers? And you can lead us through?"

"Yess, little friendss," Stythys rasped softly. "Takess you through."

Garet Jax turned to the others. For a moment no one spoke. Then Helt gave a quick nod. "There are only six of us. If we are to have any chance at all, we have to reach the fortress unseen."

Foraker and Edain Elessedil nodded as well. Jair looked at Slanter. "You're all fools!" the Gnome exclaimed bitterly. "Blind, stupid fools! You can't trust the lizards!"

There was an awkward silence. "You don't have to go any farther, if you don't want to, Slanter," Jair told him.

The Gnome stiffened. "I can take care of myself, boy!"

"I know. I just thought that . . ."

"Well, keep your thoughts to yourself!" the other cut him short. "As for not going any farther, you'd be better off taking that advice yourself. But you won't, I'm sure. So we'll all be fools together." He glanced darkly at Stythys. "But this fool will be keeping close watch, and if anything goes wrong in this, I'll be there to make certain the lizard doesn't see the end of it!"

Garet Jax turned back to Stythys. "You'll take us through then, Mwell-ret. Just remember—it will be as the Gnome says. What happens to us happens as well to you. Don't play games with us. If you try . . ."

Stythys' smile was quick and hard. "No gamess with you, little friendss."

They waited until nightfall to resume their journey, then slipped down out of the rocks above the Silver River and turned north into the mountains. Light from the gibbous moon and stars brightened the dark mass of the Ravenshorn as it rose about them, great barren peaks towering against the deep blue of the skyline. A worn pathway ran parallel to the riverbank through a scattering of trees and brush, and the little company from Culhaven followed it in until the forestland south was lost from view.

All night they walked, Helt and Slanter in the lead, the others following in cautious silence. The dark peaks drew steadily closer about the channel of the Silver River to wall them in. Save for the steady rush of the river, it was oddly silent within these peaks, a deep and pervasive stillness wrapping about the barren rock as if Mother Nature cradled her sleeping child. As the hours slipped away, Jair found himself growing increasingly uneasy with the silence, staring about at the massive walls of rock, peering into the shadows, and searching for something he could not see yet sensed was there, watching. The company chanced upon no other living creature that night, save for the great cliff birds that winged silently overhead across their nocturnal haunts, and still the Valeman sensed that they were not alone.

A part of this feeling sprang, he knew, from the continued presence of Stythys. Trailing, he could see the black figure of the Mwellret immediately in front of him. He could feel the creature's green eyes constantly shifting to find him, watching him, waiting. Like Slanter, he did not trust the Mwellret. Whatever promises Stythys might have made to aid them, Jair was certain that behind it all lay a ruthless determination to gain mastery over the Valeman's Elven magic. Whatever else happened, the creature meant to have that power. The certainty of it was frightening. The days he had spent walled away in the prisons at Dun Fee Aran haunted him like a specter so terrible that nothing could ever entirely banish it. It was Stythys who was responsible for that specter, and Stythys who would see life breathed back into it once more. While Jair now seemed free of the Mwellret, he could not shake the feeling that in some insidious way the creature had not lost control of him entirely.

But as night lengthened into early morning and weariness blunted the sharp edge of his doubt and his fear, Jair found himself thinking instead of Brin. In his mind he saw her face again as he had seen it twice so recently in the vision crystal—once ravaged as she experienced some unspeakable grief, once awestruck as she looked upon the twisted image of herself in the form of that shade. Glimpses only, those two brief visions, and nothing in either could tell the Valeman what had come to pass. Much had befallen his sister, he sensed—some of it frightening. An empty feeling opened within him as he thought of her, gone so long now from the Vale and from him, on a quest that the King of the Silver River had said would cause her to be lost. It was odd, but in a sense she seemed already lost to him, for the distance and the time that separated them was strangely magnified by the events that had transpired since last he had seen her. So much had happened, and he was so far from what and who he had been.

The emptiness grew suddenly into an ache. What if the King of the Silver River had misjudged him? What if he were to fail and Brin be lost to him? What if he were to come to her too late? He bit his lip against such thoughts, swearing fiercely that it would not be so. Deep ties bound him to her, brother to sister—ties of family, of a life shared, of knowledge, understanding, and caring, and most of all ties of love.

They marched on through the dark of early morning. With the first light of dawn, Stythys took the company up into the rocks. Moving away from the Silver River where it churned dark and sluggish in its channel, they passed deep into the cliffs. Trees and scrub disappeared and barren rock stretched away on all sides. Sunlight broke east above the mountain's edge, a brilliant, blinding gold that flared through the cracks and splits of the rock like fire. They climbed toward that fire until suddenly, unexpectedly, their ascent took them into a cliff's dark shadow and they stood at the entrance of an enormous cavern.

"Cavess of Night!" Stythys hissed softly.

The cavern yawned before the little company like an open maw, jagged rock split and twisted about the passageway like teeth. Wind blew down across the mountain heights, and it seemed as if it whistled at them from out of the Caves. Lengths of dull, whitish wood lay scattered about the entry as if stripped by age and weather. Jair looked closer and froze. The lengths of wood were bones, splintered, broken, and bleached of life.

Garet Jax placed himself before Stythys. "How are we to see anything in there, Mwellret? Have you torches?"

Stythys laughed, low and evil. "Torchess not burn in the Cavess, little friendss. Needss the magic!"

The Weapons Master glanced back momentarily at the cavern entrance. "And you have this magic?"

"Havess it, indeed," the other answered, arms folding within the robes, body swelling slightly. "Havess the Fire Wake! Liess within!"

"How long will this take?" Foraker asked uneasily. Dwarves were not fond of closed places, and he was less than anxious to venture into this one.

"Passs through Cavess quickly, little friendss," Stythys reassured rather too eagerly. "Takess you through in three hourss. Graymark waitss for uss."

The members of the little company glanced at one another and at the cavern entrance. "I'm telling you, you can't trust him!" Slanter warned yet again.

Garet Jax produced a length of rope and tied one end about himself and the other about Stythys. Testing the knots that bound them, he slipped free the long knife. "I will be closer to you than your shadow, Mwellret. Remember that. Now take us in there and show us your magic." Stythys started to turn, but the Weapons Master yanked him about. "Not too far in. Not until we see what you can do."

The Mwellret grimaced. "Sshowss little friendss. Come."

He slouched toward the monstrous black entry to the Caves, Garet Jax a step behind him and the rope about their waists binding them as one. Slanter followed them at once. After a moment's hesitation, the others of the little company also followed. Sunlight fell away as the shadows about them deepened, and they passed into the stone maw and the darkness beyond. For a few moments, the dawn's faint light aided them in their progress, silhouetting the shapes of walls, floors, jagged stalactites, and clustered rocks. Then quickly even that small light began to fail, and the blackness swallowed them.

Now they were practically blind, and their steps faltered to a ragged halt, the scraping of leather boots on rock a rough echo in the cavern's silence. They stood in a knot and listened to the echo die. The sound of dripping water reached their ears from somewhere deep within the blackness ahead. And from deeper still came the unpleasant sound of rock grating against rock.

"Ssee, little friendss," Stythys hissed suddenly. "All iss black in the Cavess!"

Jair glanced about uneasily, seeing almost nothing. Beside him, Edain Elessedil's lean Elven face was a faint shadow. There was a curious dampness to the air, a clinging wetness that stirred, though there was no wind, and seemed to wrap and twist about them. It had an unpleasant feel, and it smelled of rot. The Valeman wrinkled his nose in distaste, realizing suddenly that it was the same smell that had been present in Stythys' cell at Capaal.

"Callss now the Fire Wake!" the Mwellret rasped, startling the Valeman. "Lissten! Callss now the light!"

He cried out sharply, a kind of grim, hollow whistle that sounded of bone scraping, rough and tortured. The whistle rang through the blackness, carrying deep into the caverns. It echoed, long and mournful, and then the Mwellret repeated it a second time. Jair shivered. He was liking this whole idea of the Caves less and less.

Then abruptly the Fire Wake came. It flew at them through the darkness like a gathering of brilliant dust, bits of iridescent fire whirling and sailing on wind that wasn't there. Scattered through the blackness as it darted toward them, it drew together in a rush before the Mwellret's outstretched hand, tiny particles swirling in a tightened ball of light that cast its yellow glow outward to brighten the shadows of the Caves. The members of the little company stared in astonishment as the Fire Wake gathered and hung suspended before Stythys, and against their faces the strange glow flickered and danced.

"Magicss of my own, little friendss," Stythys hissed triumphantly. The snouted face turned to find Jair, green eyes gleaming in the whirling light. "Ssee how the Fire Wake obeyss?"

Garet Jax stepped quickly between them. "Point the way, Mwellret. Time slips from us."

"Sslipss quickly, it doess," the other rasped softly.

They pressed on into the darkness, the Fire Wake lighting their path forward. The walls of the Caves of Night rose higher about them, lost finally in shadowed gloom that even the Fire Wake could not penetrate. From out of the gloom, the sound of their footfalls fell back upon them in strange, sullen echoes. The smell grew worse the deeper in they went, turning foul the air they breathed and forcing them to take shortened breaths to avoid gagging. The passageway split and divided before them into dozens of corridors intertwined in an impossible maze of tunnels. But Stythys did not slow, choosing without hesitation the tunnel he would have them follow. The glowing dust of the Fire Wake danced on before him.

Time dragged past. Still the tunnels and passageways wore on, endless black openings in the rock. The smell grew even worse, and now the sound of grating rock was no longer distant, but unpleasantly close at hand. Then suddenly Stythys drew to a halt at an entrance leading into a particularly massive cavern, the Fire Wake dancing close as his hand lifted.

"Prockss!" he whispered.

He cast the Fire Wake from him with a snap of his wrist and it flew into the cave ahead, lighting the impenetrable blackness. The members of the little company from Culhaven stared in horror at what the light revealed. There, dotting the whole of the cavern floor, were hundreds of jagged, gaping fissures that opened and closed as if mouths engaged in some hideous chewing, the rock grinding hatefully in the dark. Sounds came from within those mouths—gurgling rushes, rendings, deep groaning belches of liquid and crushed stone.

"Shades!" they heard Helt whisper then. "The whole cave is alive!"

"Musst passs through," Stythys announced with an ugly grin. "Little peopless sstay closse."

They stayed practically on top of one another, pale faces gleaming with sweat in the light of the Fire Wake, eyes fixed on the cavern floor before them. Again Stythys led, Garet Jax a step behind, Slanter, Jair, Edain Elessedil, and Helt in a line following, and Foraker trailing. They made their way in a slow, twisting path into the midst of the Procks, stepping where the Fire Wake showed the black mouths not to be, their ears and minds filled with the sounds those terrible mouths made. The Procks opened and closed all about them as if waiting to be fed, hungry animals that sensed the presence of food. At times they closed so tightly that they seemed a part of the cavern floor that was solid, no more than thin lines in the roughened stone. Yet they could open quickly, snatching away the seemingly safe ground, ready to swallow anything that ventured above. But each time one lay hidden on the path ahead, the Fire Wake showed the members of the company where it waited and guided them carefully past.

They passed from that first cavern into another and after that into another. Still the Procks were with them, dotting the floor of every cave and passageway so that none was safe to traverse. They moved slowly now, and the minutes dragged away in a seemingly endless passage of time. Weariness set in as their concentration intensified, each knowing that a single misstep would be the last. All the while the Procks opened and closed about them, grinding in gleeful anticipation.

"There is no end to this maze!" Edain Elessedil whispered once in frustration to Jair.

The Valeman nodded in helpless agreement. Foraker pressed close behind now, and Helt brought up the rear. The Dwarf's bearded face was soaked with sweat and his hard eyes were glittering.

A concealed Prock opened suddenly, almost at Jair's feet, its black maw yawning. Frantically, the Valeman jerked away, stumbling into Slanter. The Prock had been right next to him and he hadn't seen it! He fought back against the wave of disgust and fear that swept over him and set his jaw determinedly. It would not be much longer. They would be clear soon.

But then, as they were passing through yet another cavern, through yet another maze of Procks, Stythys did what Slanter had warned all along he would do. It happened so quickly that not even Garet Jax had time to act. One moment they were all together, easing past the hideously grinding fissures; in the next, the Mwellret's hand flicked suddenly backward, casting the Fire Wake directly into their faces. It came at them in a flare of brilliant light, scattering. Instinctively they turned away, shielding their eyes, and in that instant Stythys moved. He leaped past Garet Jax and Slanter to where Jair crouched. Snatching the Valeman about the waist with one powerful arm, the lizard creature slipped a wicked-looking knife from somewhere beneath the dark robes where he had kept it hidden and pressed it close against his captive's throat.

"Sstay back, little friendss!" The Mwellret hissed, turning to face them as the Fire Wake again gathered before him.

No one moved. Garet Jax crouched barely two yards away, a black shadow poised to spring. The length of rope still bound him to the Mwellret. Stythys kept the Valeman between them, the knife glittering in the half-light.

"Foolissh little peopless!" the monster rasped. "Thinkss to usse me againsst my will! Sseess now what liess ahead for you?"

"I told you he couldn't be trusted!" Slanter cried out in fury.

He started forward, but a warning hiss from the Mwellret brought him to a halt instantly. Behind him, the others of the little company stood frozen in a tight circle—Helt, Foraker and Edain Elessedil. All about them the Procks continued to grind steadily, stone grating on stone.

Garet Jax shifted from the crouch, gray eyes so cold that Stythys' arm tightened further about Jair. "Let the Valeman go, Mwellret," the Weapons Master said softly.

The blade of the knife pressed closer against Jair's throat. Jair swallowed and tried to shrink away from it. Then his eyes met those of Garet Jax. The Weapons Master was fast—faster than anyone. It was when he had confronted the Gnome Hunters who had taken Jair prisoner in the Black Oaks that he had first shown how fast he could be. And the same look he had worn then was now in the lean, hard face—a calm, inscrutable look where only the eyes spoke of the death that was promised.

Jair breathed a deep, slow breath. Garet Jax was close enough. But the knife at the Valeman's throat was closer still.

"Magicss belong to uss, not to little peopless!" Stythys rasped in a quick, anxious whisper. "Magicss to sstand againsst the walkerss! Little peopless cannot usse it, cannot usse uss! Sstupid little peopless! Crussh you like bugss!"

"Let the Valeman go!" Garet Jax repeated.

The Fire Wake danced and glimmered before the Mwellret, a whirling cloud of shimmering dust. Stythys' green eyes drew into slits of hatred, and he laughed softly.

"Letss you go insstead, black one!" he snapped. He glanced quickly at Slanter. "You, little Gnome! Cut loosse thiss tie that bindss me to him!"

Slanter looked at Garet Jax, then looked back again. His eyes shifted for just an instant to find Jair's. The Valeman read there what was expected of him. If he hoped to get out of this alive, he was going to have to do something to help.

Slowly Slanter came forward, a step at a time, slipping the long knife from his belt. No one else moved. Jair steadied himself, fighting back against the fear and repulsion that coursed through him. Slanter came closer, another step. One hand reached for the slackened rope that bound the Mwellret to Garet Jax. Jair went perfectly still. One chance was all he would get. Slanter's hand closed about the rope and the knife lifted to the hemp.

Then Jair sang—a quick, sharp cry that Slanter recognized at once. Dozens of gray, hairy spiders clustered on Stythys, crawling over the arm that held the knife to Jair's throat. The Mwellret jerked his arm away with a howl, beating it wildly against his robes in an effort to dislodge the things that clung to it. Abruptly the Fire Wake scattered in a wide circle, taking back the light and throwing everything into shadow.

Cat-quick, Slanter threw himself on Stythys, burying his long knife in the arm that gripped Jair about his waist. That arm, too, jerked away, and Jair tumbled to the roughened stone, free again. Shouts rose from the others of the little company as they charged forward to pull him clear. Stythys flew backward onto the cavern floor, Slanter clinging to him, Garet Jax leaping after. A long knife appeared in the Weapon Master's hand as he sought to cut through the rope that bound him to the Mwellret. But he was yanked off balance as the rope snapped taut. He lost his footing and skidded to his knees.

"Slanter!" Jair screamed.

The Gnome and the Mwellret stumbled through the maze of Procks, clawing wildly at each other. The Fire Wake continued to rise as Stythys' control over it slipped away, and the entire cavern was rapidly falling into shadow. Another few seconds and no one would be able to see anything.

"Gnome!" Foraker cried in warning, breaking away from the others to where the two forms struggled.

But Garet Jax was quicker. He leaped like a shadow from the gloom, his footing regained. The long knife severed the rope about his waist with a single cut. Procks grated and snapped in response to the sounds above, dark maws working madly. Stythys and Slanter were directly in their midst, squirming closer, slipping . . .

And then Garet Jax reached them, flinging himself across the remaining space that separated them, his iron grip fastening on Slanter's leg. With a yank, he tore the Gnome free from Stythys' claws. Clothing shredded and ripped, and a frightful hiss burst from Stythys' throat.

The Mwellret tumbled backward, thrown off balance. Beneath him, a Prock's black maw gaped open. The lizard seemed to hang suspended for an instant, clawed fingers grasping at the air. Then he fell, disappearing from sight. The Prock closed and there was a sudden shriek. Then the black fissure began to grind, a terrible crunching, and the whole of the cavern was filled with the dreadful sound.

Instantly the Fire Wake scattered and fled back into the gloom, taking with it the precious light. The Caves of Night were plunged into darkness once more.

It was several minutes before anyone moved again. They crouched where they were in the blackness, waiting for their eyes to adjust to the absence of light, listening to the sounds of the Procks grinding all about them. When it quickly became apparent that there was not even the smallest amount of light to allow their eyes to adjust, Elb Foraker called out to the others and asked them to respond. One by one, they called back, faceless voices in the impenetrable dark. All were there.

But they knew that they were not likely to be there for long. The Fire Wake was gone, the light they so desperately needed to show them the path forward. Without it, they were blind. They must attempt to move through the maze of Procks using little more than instinct.

"Hopeless," Foraker announced at once. "Without light, we cannot tell where the passages open before us and we cannot choose our path. Even if we escape the Procks, we will wander in these Caves forever."

There was a hint of fear in the Dwarf's voice that Jair had never heard before. "There has to be a way," he murmured quietly, as much to himself as to the others.

"Helt, can you use the night vision?" Edain Elessedil asked hopefully. "Can you see to find a way through this darkness?"

But the giant Borderman could not. Even the night vision must have some light to aid it, he explained gently. In the absence of all light, the night vision was useless.

They were quiet then for a time, bereft it seemed of even the smallest hope. In the darkness, Jair could hear Slanter's rough voice admonishing Garet Jax that he should have known better than to trust the lizard, as Slanter had told him. Jair listened and seemed to hear Brin speaking to him as well, telling him that he, too, should have listened. He brushed the whisper of her voice from his mind, thinking as he did so that, if the wishsong served him as it did her, he could call back the Fire Wake. But his song was only illusion, a pretense of what was real.

Then he thought of the vision crystal.

Calling excitedly to the others, he fumbled through his clothing until he found it, still tucked safely away, dangling from its silver chain, and he brought it forth into the cup of his hands. The crystal would give them light—all the light that was needed! With the crystal and Helt's night vision to guide them, they would yet get clear of these Caves!

Barely able to suppress the excitement that coursed through him, he sang to the gift of the King of the Silver River and called forth the magic. The brilliant light sprang up, flooding the cavern with its glow. Brin Ohmsford's face appeared within it, dark, beautiful, and worn, rising up before them in the gloom of the Caves of Night like some wraith come forth from another world. Grayness surrounded the Valegirl, gloom all too reminiscent of their own, close and stifling. Wherever she was as she looked past them to her own future, it was no less hostile a place than their own.

Cautiously, they rejoined one another, gathering about the light of the crystal. Joining hands as children might on a walk through some dark place, they began to move forward through the maze of Procks. Jair led, the light of the vision crystal sustained by his voice, scattering the shadows before them. Helt followed a step behind, sharp eyes scanning the cavern floor for where the Procks lay hidden. Behind them, the others followed.

They passed from that cavern into another, but this new cavern was smaller and the proper choice of passage less difficult to discern. Jair's song lifted, clear, strong, and filled with certainty. He knew now that they were going to escape these Caves, and it was because of Brin. He wanted to cry out in thanks to her image as it floated before him. How strange that she should come like this to save them!

Closing his ears to the sounds of the Procks as they grated stone on stone, closing his mind to everything but the light and the vision of his sister's face as it hung suspended before him, he gave himself over to the wishsong's magic and passed on through the darkness.

It took the remainder of the night for Brin and her rescuers to work their way clear of Olden Moor. They would not have done so even then without Whisper to guide them, but the big moor cat was at home in the bottomland, and neither the mist nor the shapeless, mired earth gave him pause. Choosing their pathway with instincts that the moor could not deceive, he led them south toward the dark wall of the Ravenshorn.

"We would have lost you to the moor without Whisper," Kimber explained to the Valegirl after they had found her again and begun their march south. "It was Whisper who tracked you through the mist. He is not misled by appearances, and nothing of the moor can fool him. Still, it was fortunate that we reached you when we did, Brin. You must stay close to us after this."

Brin accepted the well-intentioned rebuke without comment. There was no point in discussing the matter further. Her decision to leave them before they reached the Maelmord was already made. It merely remained for her to find the right opportunity to do so. Her reasons were simple. The task entrusted to her by Allanon was to penetrate the forest barrier that protected the Ildatch and to see to it that the book of dark magic was destroyed. She would do this by pitting the magic of the wishsong against the magic of the Maelmord. Once she had wondered if such a thing were even possible. Now she wondered not if such a thing were possible, but if such a thing would prove cataclysmic. The power of the magics unleashed would be awesome—a match not of white magic against dark as she had once envisioned, but a match of magics equally dark in tone and effect. The Maelmord was created to destroy. But the wishsong, too, could destroy, and now Brin knew that not only would the potential for such destruction always be there, but that she could not be assured of being able to control it. She might vow to do so. She might swear her strongest oath. But she could never be certain that she could keep that oath—not anymore, unless she forbore all use of the wishsong. She could accept the risk to herself; she had done that long ago when she had decided to come on this quest. But she could not accept the risk to those who traveled with her.

She must leave them. Whatever fate she was to suffer when she entered the Maelmord, her companions must not be there to share it with her. You go to your death, Brin of Shannara, the Grimpond had warned. You carry within you the seeds of that destruction. Perhaps that was so. Perhaps those seeds were carried in the magic of the wishsong. But one thing was certain. The others of the little company had risked themselves enough for her already. She would not have them do so again.

She thought about it all night as she trudged on wearily through the bottomland, remembering what she had felt in the times she had used the wishsong's magic. The hours slipped past, and the Werebeasts did not come to haunt them again that night. But in the mind of the Valegirl, there were demons of another sort.

By dawn the little company was clear of Olden Moor and found itself in the foothills bordering the southern mountains of the Ravenshorn. Wearied from their long march up from Hearthstone and the events of the night past and wary of traveling further in daylight when they might easily be seen, the five took refuge in a small copse of pine in a lea between two ridgelines and fell asleep.

They resumed their journey with the return of nightfall, traveling east now, following the high wall of the mountains where it brushed up against the moor. Trailers of mist wound through the trees of the forested lower slopes, a spider's web across the pathway as the travelers passed silently by. The mountain peaks of the Ravenshorn were huge and stark, barren rock lifting out of the forestland to etch sharply against the sky. It was an empty, still night, and the whole of the land about seemed stripped of life. Shadows lay across the cliffs, forests, and the moor's deep mists. In their pooling darkness nothing moved.

They rested at midnight, an uneasy pause where they found themselves listening to the silence as they rubbed aching muscles and tightened boot straps. It was then that Cogline chose to talk about his magic.

"Magic it is, too," he whispered cautiously to Brin and Rone, almost as if he feared that someone might be listening. "Magic of a different sort than that wielded by the walkers, though—born not of their time nor the time when Elves and faerie folk had the power, but of the time between!"

He bent forward, eyes sharp and accusing. "Thought I knew nothing of the old world, didn't you, girl?" he asked Brin. "Well, I have the teachings of the old world, too—passed down to me by my ancestors. Not Druids, no. But teachers, girl—teachers! Theirs was the lore of the world that existed when the Great Wars caused such destruction to mankind!"

"Grandfather," Kimber Boh cautioned gently. "Just explain it to them."

"Humphh!" Cogline grunted testily. "Explain it, she says! What is it that you think I do, girl?" His forehead furrowed. "Earth power! That's the magic I wield! Not the magic of words and spells—no, not that magic! Power born of the elements that comprise the ground on which we walk, outlanders. That is the earth power. Bits and pieces of ores and powders and mixings that can be seen by the eye and felt by the hand. Chemics, they were once called. Developed by skills of a different sort than the simple ones we use now in the Four Lands. Most of the knowledge was lost with the old world. But a little—just a little—was saved. And it is mine to use."

"This is what you carry in those pouches?" Rone asked. "This is what you used to make those fires explode?"

"Ha-ha!" Cogline laughed softly. "They do that and much more, Southlander. Fires can be exploded, earth turned to mud, air to choking dust, flesh to stone! I have potions for all and dozens more. Mix and match, a bit of this and a bit of that!' He laughed again. 'I'll show the walkers power they haven't seen before!'

Rone shook his head doubtfully. "Spider Gnomes are one thing; the Mord Wraiths are something else again. A finger points at you and you are reduced to ash. The sword I carry, infused with the Druid magic, is the only protection against those black things."

"Bah!" Cogline spit. "You'd best look to me for your protection—you and the girl!"

Rone began to phrase a sharp retort, then thought better of it and simply shrugged. "If we come up against the walkers, we shall both need to offer Brin whatever protection we can."

He glanced at the Valegirl for confirmation, and she smiled agreeably. It cost her nothing to do so. She already knew that neither of them would be with her, in any case.

She pondered for a time what Cogline had told them. It troubled her that any part of the old skills should have survived the holocaust of the Great Wars. She did not like to think it possible that such awesome power could come again into the world. It was bad enough that the magic of the world of faerie had been reborn through the misguided efforts of that handful of rebel Druids in the Councils of Paranor. But to be faced with the prospect that the knowledge of power and energy might again be pursued was even more unsettling. Almost all of the learning that had gone into that knowledge had been lost with the destruction of the old world. What little had survived, the Druids had locked away again. Yet here was this old man, half-crazed and as wild as the wilderness in which he lived, in possession of at least a portion of that learning—a special kind of magic that he had resolved was now his own.

She shook her head. Perhaps it was inevitable that all learning, whether born of good or bad intention, whether used to give life or to take life away, must come to light at some point in time. Perhaps it was true both of skill and of magic—one born of the world of men, the other of the world of faerie. Perhaps both must surface periodically in the stream of time, then disappear again, then surface once more, and so on forever.

But a return now of the knowledge of energy and power, when the last of the Druids was gone . . . ?

Still, Cogline was an old man and his knowledge was limited. When he died, perhaps the knowledge would die with him and be lost again—for a time, at least.

And so, too, perhaps it would be with her magic.

They walked east for the remainder of the night, picking their way through the thinning forestland. Ahead, the wall of the Ravenshorn began to curve back toward them, turning north into the wilderness of the deep Anar. It rose up from out of the night, a towering, dark band of shadow. Olden Moor dropped away behind them, and only the thin green line of the foothills separated them from the mountain heights. A deeper silence seemed to settle over the land. It was in the crook of the mountains where they turned north, Brin knew, that Graymark and the Maelmord lay concealed.

And there I must find a way to be free of the others, she thought. There, I must go on alone.

The first trailers of sunrise began to slip into view beyond the mountain wall. Slowly the skies lightened, turning from deep blue to gray, from gray to silver, and from silver to rose and gold. Shadows fled away into the receding night, and the broad sweep of the land began to etch itself out of the dark. The trees grew visible first, leaves, crooked limbs, and roughened trunks drawn and colored by the light; then rocks, scrub, and barren earth, from foothills to bottomland, took form. For a time, the shadow of the mountains lingered, a wall against the light, lost in darkness not yet faded. But finally that, too, gave way to the sunrise, and the light spilled down over the rim of the peaks to reveal the awesome face of the Ravenshorn.

It was a stark and ugly face—a face that had been ravaged by time and the elements and by the poison of the dark magic sown within it. Where the mountains curved north into the wilderness, the rock had been bleached and worn—as if the life in it had been peeled away like skin to leave only bone. It rose up against the skyline, thousands of feet above them, a wall of cliffs and ragged defiles burdened with the weight of ages gone and horrors endured. On the hard, gray emptiness, nothing moved.

Brin lifted her face momentarily as the wind brushed past. Her nose wrinkled in distaste. An unpleasant smell rose up from somewhere ahead.

"Graymark's sewers." Cogline spit, ferret eyes darting. "We're close now."

Kimber slipped ahead of them to where Whisper sniffed tentatively at the odorous morning air. Bending close to the great cat, she spoke softly in his ear—just a word—and the beast nuzzled her face gently.

She turned back to them. "Quickly now, before it gets any lighter—Whisper will show us the way."

They hurried forward through the new light and receding shadow, following the moor cat as he guided them along the twist of the foothills to where the Ravenshorn bent north. Trees and scrub fell away completely, grasses turned sparse and wintry, and the earth gave way to crushed stone and shelf rock. The smell grew steadily worse, a rank and fetid odor that smothered even the freshness of the new day's birthing. Brin found herself choking for breath. How much worse would it be once they had found their way into the sewers?

Then the hills dropped away sharply before them into a deep valley that was lost in the shadow of the mountain wall. There, sullen and still, lay a dark lake of stagnant water, fed by a stream that seeped down through the rocks from a broad, blackened hole.

Whisper padded to a halt, Kimber at his side. "There." She pointed. "The sewers."

Brin's eyes strayed upward along the ragged line of the peaks, upward thousands of feet to where the mountain wall cut its jagged edge against the golden dawn sky. There, still hidden from view, lay Graymark, the Maelmord, and the Ildatch.

She swallowed against the smell of the sewers. There, too, lay the fate that was to be hers. Her smile was hard. She must go to meet it.

At the entrance to the sewers, Cogline unveiled a bit more of his magic. From a sealed packet buried in one of the pouches he wore strapped to his waist, he produced an ointment that, when rubbed into the nostrils, deadened the stench of the sewer's poisonous discharge. A small magic, he claimed. Though the smell could not be obliterated entirely, it nevertheless could be made tolerable. Fashioning short-handled brands from pieces of deadwood, he dipped the ends into the contents of a second pouch and they emerged covered with a silver substance that glowed like oil lamps when introduced into the cavern's darkness—even in the absence of any fire.

"Just a little more of my magic, outlanders." He chuckled as they stared wonderingly at the flameless torches. "Chemicals, remember? Something the walkers don't know anything about. And I've a few more surprises. You'll see."

Rone frowned doubtfully and shook his head. Brin said nothing, but decided quickly that she would be just as happy if the opportunity to test those surprises never arose.

Torches in hand, the little company moved out of the dawn light into the tunnel darkness of the sewers. The passageways were wide and deep, the liquid poison discharged from the halls of Graymark and the Maelmord flowing down a worn, rutted channel that cut through the tunnel floor. To either side of where the sewage flowed, there were stone walkways that offered footing broad enough for the company to pass upon. Whisper led the way, luminous eyes blinking in sleepy reflection against the light of the torches, splayed feet padding soundlessly on the stone. Cogline followed with Kimber, and Brin and Rone brought up the rear.

They walked for a long time. Brin lost track of how long a time it was, her concentration divided between picking her way through the half-light and thinking of her promise to find a way to go down into the Maelmord without the others. The sewer wound upward through the mountain rock, twisting and turning like a coiled snake. The stench permeating the passage was almost unbearable, even with the aid of the repellant that Cogline had provided to ease their breathing difficulties. From time to time, sudden drafts of cold air blew down from above them, clearing the smell of the sewage—wind from the peaks into which they climbed. But the drafts of fresh air were few and brief, and the smells of the sewage were always quick to return.

The morning slipped away, the hours lost in the endless spiral of their ascent. Once they came upon a massive iron grate that had been dropped across the passageway to prevent anything larger than a rat from entering. Rone reached for his sword, but a sharp word from Cogline brought him up short. A gleeful cackle breaking from his lips, the old man motioned them back, then produced yet another pouch—this one containing an odd, blackish powder laced with something that looked to be soot. Dabbing the powder on the bars of the grate where they joined the rock, he touched the treated spots quickly with the flameless torch and the powder flared a brilliant white. When the light died away, the bars had been eaten completely through. At a stiff nudge, the entire grate collapsed onto the cavern floor. The company went on.

No one spoke as they climbed. Instead, they listened for the sound of the enemy that waited somewhere above—the walkers and the things that served them. They heard nothing of these, but there were other sounds that echoed through the empty passageways—sounds that came from far above and were not immediately identifiable. There were clunks and thuds, as if heavy bodies had fallen, scrapes and scratchings, a low howling, as if a hard wind slipped down through the tunnels from the mountain peaks, and a hissing, as if steam escaped some fissure in the earth. These distant sounds filled and thus magnified the otherwise utter silence of the sewers. Brin found herself searching for a pattern to the sounds, but there was none—except, perhaps, for the hissing which lifted and fell with a peculiar regularity. It reminded Brin, unpleasantly, of the Grimpond's rise from the lake and the mist.

I must find a way to go on alone, she thought one time more. I must do so soon.

Tunnels came and went, and the climb wore on. The air within the sewers had grown steadily warmer with the passing of the day, and beneath their cloaks and tunics the members of the little company were sweating freely. A kind of peculiar mist had begun to filter down through the corridors, clinging and grimy, filled with the sewer's smell. They brushed at it distastefully, but it drifted after them, closed about them, and would not be moved away. It grew thicker as the climb progressed, and soon they were having difficulty seeing further than a dozen feet ahead.

Then abruptly the mist and gloom cleared before them, and they stood upon a shelf of rock that overlooked an immense chasm. Down into the mountain's core the chasm dropped, disappearing into utter blackness. The members of the little company glanced uneasily at one another. To their right, the passageway curved upward into the rock, following the trench that carried the sewage from the Mord Wraith citadel. To their left, the passageway ran downward a short distance to a slender stone bridge barely a yard in width that arched across the chasm to a darkened tunnel that bore into the far cliff face.

"Which way now?" Rone muttered softly, almost as if asking himself.

Left, Brin thought at once. Left, across the chasm. She did not understand why, yet she knew instinctively that this was the path she must choose.

"The sewers are the way." Cogline was looking at her. "That's what the Grimpond said, wasn't it, girl?"

Brin found herself unable to speak. "Brin?" Kimber called to her softly.

"Yes," she replied finally. "Yes, that is the way."

They turned right along the shelf, following it up along the sewage channel, trudging back again into the blackness. Brin's mind raced. This isn't the way, she thought. Why did I say it was? She took a sudden gulp of air, forcing her thoughts to slow. What she sought was back the way they had come, back across the stone bridge. The Maelmord was back that way—she could sense it. Why, then, had she . . . ?

She caught herself roughly, the question answered almost as quickly as it was asked. Because this was where she would leave them, of course. This was the opportunity that she had looked for since Olden Moor. This was how it must be. The wishsong would aid her—a small deceit, a little lie. She sucked in her breath sharply at the thought. Even though it would betray their trust in her, she must do it.

Softly, gently, she began to hum, building the wishsong a stone at a time into a wall of non-seeing, creating in her place and in the minds of her companions an image of herself. Then abruptly she stepped away from her own ghost, flattened herself against the stone wall of the passageway, and watched the others walk past.

The illusion would only last a few minutes, she knew. She sped back down the sewer tunnel, following the cut and weave of the rock. The sound of her breathing was ragged in her ears. She reached the shelf, hastened to where it narrowed, and turned onto the stone bridge. The chasm yawned blackly before her. A step at a time, she inched out onto the bridge, picking her pathway across. There was silence in the gloom and mist that swirled about, yet she felt somehow that she was not alone. Her mind hardened against the brief surge of fear and doubt, and she withdrew deep into herself, passionless and cold. Nothing could be allowed to touch her.

At last she was across the bridge. She stood within the entrance to this new tunnel for a moment and let the feeling return. A brief thought of Rone and the others passed through her mind and disappeared. She had used the wishsong against them now as well, she thought bitterly. And though it might have been necessary, it hurt her deeply to have done so.

Then she wheeled abruptly toward the stone bridge, pitched the wishsong to a quick, hard shriek and sang. The sound echoed in fury through the black, and the bridge exploded into fragments and dropped away into the chasm.

Now there could be no going back.

She turned into the tunnel and disappeared.

The sound of the shriek penetrated up into the sewer tunnel where the others of the little company still picked their way through the gloom.

"Shades! What was that?" Rone cried.

There was a moment's silence as the echo died away. "Brin—it was Brin," Kimber whispered in reply.

Rone stared. No, Brin was right next to him . . .

Abruptly, the image the Valegirl had created in their minds faded into nothingness. Cogline swore softly and stamped his foot.

"What has she done . . . ?" the highlander stammered in confusion, unable to finish the thought.

Kimber was at his side, her face intense. "She has done what she has wanted to do from the beginning, I think. She has left us and gone on alone. She said before that she did not want any of us to go with her; now she has made certain that we do not."

"For cat's sake!" Rone was appalled. "Doesn't she understand how dangerous . . . ?"

"She understands everything," the girl cut him short, pushing past him down the tunnel's passage. "I should have realized before that she would do this. We must hurry if we are to catch up with her. Whisper, track!"

The big moor cat leaped ahead effortlessly, gliding back down the sewer tunnel into the shadows. The three humans hurried after, slipping and stumbling through the mist and gloom. Rone Leah was angry and frightened at the same time. Why would Brin do this? He did not understand.

Then abruptly they were back upon the stone shelf, staring out across the chasm to where the bridge fell away into the dark, broken at its center.

"There, you see, she's used the magic!" Cogline snapped.

Wordlessly, Rone hurried forward, stepping out onto the jagged remnant of the bridge. Twenty feet away, the other end jutted from the cliff face. He could make that jump, he thought suddenly. It was a long way over, but he could make it. At least he must try . . .

"No, Rone Leah," Kimber pulled him back from the precipice, reading at once his intentions. Her grip on his arm was surprisingly strong. "You must not be foolish. You cannot jump so far."

"I can't leave her again," he insisted stubbornly. "Not again."

The girl nodded solemnly. "I care for her, too." She turned. "Whisper!" The moor cat padded up to her, whiskered face rubbing her own. Softly she spoke to the cat, stroking him behind his ears. Then she stepped away. "Track, Whisper!" she commanded.

Wheeling, the moor cat darted onto the bridge, gathered himself and sprang into the air. He cleared the chasm effortlessly, landed on the far end of the shattered bridge, and disappeared into the darkened tunnel beyond.

There was concern reflected in Kimber Boh's young face. She had not wanted to separate herself from the cat, but Brin might have greater need of him than she, and the Valegirl was her friend. "Guard well," she whispered after.

Then she looked back again at Rone. "Now let us also try to find a way to reach Brin Ohmsford."

It was nearly noon of the same day when Jair and his companions emerged once more from the Caves of Night and found themselves on a broad shelf of rock overlooking a deep canyon between the mountain peaks of the Ravenshorn. The peaks were so close that they shut away all but a narrow strip of blue sky far above where the company stood, lost in a gathering of shadows. The shelf ran left along the mountain face for several hundred yards and then disappeared again into a cut in the cliffs.

The Valeman stared upward wearily, following the lift of the mountains against the noonday sky. He was exhausted—drained physically and emotionally. He still clutched the vision crystal in one hand, its silver chain dragging against the shelf rock. They had been in the Caves since sunrise. For a good part of that time, it had been necessary to use the wishsong to project the light of the crystal so that they might find their way clear. It had taken every ounce of strength and every bit of concentration that he could muster to do that. In his mind, he could still hear the sound of the Procks, stone grating on stone, a whisper now of what had been left behind in the darkness of the caves. In his mind, he could also still hear Stythys' final scream.

"Let's not stand where we can be so easily seen," Garet Jax said softly and motioned him left.

Slanter caught up with them, glancing about doubtfully. "I'm not sure this is the way, Weapons Master."

Garet Jax did not turn. "How many other ways do you see?"

Silently, the members of the little company edged down along the rock shelf to the cut in the cliff face. A narrow defile stretched away before them, twisting into the rock and disappearing into shadow. They moved through it in a line, their eyes darting upward guardedly along its roughened walls. A draft of icy air brushed against them, blown down from the heights. Jair shivered with its touch. Numbed by the horrors of the Caves, he welcomed even this unpleasant feeling. He could sense that they were now close to Graymark's walls. Graymark, the Maelmord, Heaven's Well were all near at hand. His quest was almost ended, the long journey done. He felt a strange compulsion to laugh and cry at the same time, but the weariness and the ache in his body would let him do neither.

The defile wound on, slipping deeper into the rock. His mind wandered. Where was Brin? The crystal had shown them her face. But it had shown them nothing of where she might be. Gray mist and gloom had surrounded her in a dreary and desolate place. A passageway, perhaps, similar to their own? Was she, too, within these mountains?

"You must reach Heaven's Well before she reaches the Maelmord," the King of the Silver River had warned. "You must be there for her."

He stumbled and nearly went down, his concentration drifting from the task at hand. He righted himself hastily and shoved the vision crystal back into his tunic front.

"Watch yourself," Edain Elessedil whispered at his elbow. Jair nodded and went on.

Anticipation began to build within him. An entire army of Gnomes guarded Graymark's battlements and watchtowers. Mord Wraiths walked its halls. Things darker still might lie in wait within, sentinels against intruders like themselves. Their company was but six in number. What hope had they against so many and such power? Little, it would appear; and yet, while it should have seemed altogether hopeless to the Valeman, it did not. Perhaps it was the faith that the King of the Silver River had shown in choosing him for this quest—a demonstration of the old man's belief that he could somehow find a way to succeed. Perhaps it was his own determination, a strength of will that would not let him fail.

He shook his head gently. Perhaps. But it was also the character of the five men who had elected to come with him and had sustained him. It was Garet Jax, Slanter, Foraker, Edain Elessedil and Helt—come from the Four Lands to this final, terrible confrontation, an enigmatic mixture of strength and courage. Two trackers, a hunter, a Weapons Master, and a Prince of the Elves had traveled different life-paths to reach this day, and none might live to see its end. But here they were. Their bonding to Jair and to the trust that had been given him transcended the caution and reason that might otherwise have caused them to give greater consideration to the obvious danger to their own lives. It was so even with Slanter. The Gnome had made his choice at Capaal when he had turned his back on a chance to flee north to the borderlands and the life from which he had strayed. All were committed, and in that commitment there was a unity that seemed almost indomitable. Jair knew little of his companions. Yet one thing he knew with certainty, and it was enough: whatever was to happen to him this day, these five would stand by him.

Perhaps that was why he was not afraid.

The defile widened again before them and sunlight streamed down from a new broadened skyline. Garet Jax slowed, then dropped into a crouch and eased ahead. One lean arm beckoned them after. Hunched down against the rocks, they crept forward until they were beside him.

"There," he whispered, pointing.

It was Graymark. Jair knew it instantly without need of being told. The fortress sat high upon a cliff face that curved away before them. It rested upon a broad shelf of rock that jutted sharply outward against the noonday sky. It was a grim and massive thing. Battlements, towers, and parapets rose upward from stone block walls hundreds of feet high, like spikes and blunted axe-heads reaching into the cloudless blue. No pennants flew from the tower standards; no colors draped the casements. The whole of the fortress had a flat and wintry cast to it even in the brilliant light of the sun; the stone had a sullen, ashen tone. What windows there were were small, pinched openings covered over with bars and wooden shutters. A single narrow roadway wound upward against the mountainside—little more than a ledge cut into the rock—ending at a pair of tall, ironbound gates that fronted the complex. The gates stood closed.

They studied the stronghold wordlessly. There was no sign of anyone. Nothing moved.

Then Jair caught sight of the Croagh. He could see only pieces of it lifting from behind Graymark, a rugged arch of stone that seemed almost a part of the towers and the parapets of the complex. Curling back upon itself like some suspended stairway, it threaded its way skyward until it ended high upon a solitary peak that rose above those surrounding it.

Jair caught Slanter's arm and pointed to the peak and the slender ribbon of stones that joined to it.

"Yes, boy—the Croagh and Heaven's Well." The Gnome nodded. "All that the King of the Silver River has sent you to find."

"And the Maelmord?" Jair asked quickly.

Slanter shook his head. "On the other side of the fortress, down within a ring of cliffs. There the Croagh begins its climb, wrapping about Graymark as it passes, then rising on."

They were silent again, their eyes fixed on the fortress. "Doesn't seem to be anyone in there," Helt murmured after a moment.

"What's in there wants you to think exactly that," Slanter observed dryly, easing back on his heels. "Besides, the walkers prefer the dark. They rest for the most part during the day and move about at night. Even the Gnomes that serve them here soon begin to live like that and don't show themselves when it's light. But make no mistake. They're in there, Borderman—walkers and Gnomes both. And a few other things as well."

Garet Jax was studying the mountain trail that wound upward to the fortress entrance. "That is the way they would expect us to come." He spoke more to himself than to the others. "On the trail or by scaling the cliffs." He glanced left to where the shelf they stood upon curved down among the rocks and disappeared back into the mountains through a narrow tunnel. "Maybe not this way, though."

Slanter touched his arm. "The tunnel connects to a series of passageways that leads upward into the fortress cellars. That's how we'll go."

"Guarded?"

Slanter shrugged.

"I'd feel better if we could find a way to climb the Croagh from out here," Foraker muttered. "I've seen enough of caverns and tunnels."

The Gnome shook his head. "Can't be done. Only way to reach the Croagh is through Graymark—right through the walkers and whatever serves them."

Foraker grunted. "What do you think, Garet?"

Garet Jax continued to study the fortress and the cliffs about it. His lean face was expressionless. "Do you know the way well enough to take us safely through, Gnome?" he asked Slanter shortly.

Slanter gave him a dark look. "You ask a lot. I know it, but not well. Went through it once or twice when I was first brought here, before this whole thing began . . ."

He trailed off abruptly, and Jair knew that he was remembering how he had chosen to come back to his homeland to be with his own people and been sent by the walkers to track the Druid Allanon. He was remembering and perhaps regretting momentarily how he had let things get turned about.

"Fair enough," Garet Jax said softly and started ahead.

He took them down through the rocks to where the shelf opened into the tunnel that led back under the mountain. There, out of sight of Graymark, concealed within the shelter of a gathering of massive boulders, he beckoned them close.

"Do the walkers always rest during the daylight hours?" he asked Slanter. It was close and hot within the clustered rocks, and there was a fine sheen of sweat on his brow.

The Gnome frowned. "If you are asking whether we should go in now rather than when it is dark, I say we should."

"If there remains time enough to do so," Foraker interjected. "Midday is gone, and darkness comes early in the mountains. We might be better off to wait until tomorrow when we have the use of a full day. Another twelve hours or so can't make that much difference."

There was a moment's silence. Jair glanced skyward, his eyes scanning the ragged edge of the cliffs. Another twelve hours? An uneasy suspicion tugged at his mind in warning. How far had Brin gotten? The words of the King of the Silver River repeated themselves once again: "You must reach Heaven's Well before she reaches the Maelmord."

He turned quickly to Garet Jax. "I'm not sure we have twelve hours left. I have to know where Brin is to be certain. I have to use the crystal again—and I think I had better use it now."

The Weapons Master hesitated, then rose. "Not here. Move into the cave."

They slipped through the darkened opening and groped their way back into the gloom. There, huddled close about, the others waited patiently as Jair fumbled through his tunic for the vision crystal. He had it in a moment's time, gripping it by its silver chain as he pulled it forth. Cupping it gently in his hands, he wet his lips and fought back against the fatigue that bore down against him.

"Sing to it, Jair," he heard Edain Elessedil encourage softly.

He sang, his voice low and whispered, wearied by the strain to which he had put it in leading them safely through the Caves of Night. The crystal began to glow and the light to spread . . .

Brin paused in the gloom of the tunnel through which she stole. She had a sudden sense of being watched, of eyes following after her. It was as it had been on entering the Dragon's Teeth and again on leaving—as if someone watched her from a great distance off.

She hesitated, her thoughts frozen, and a flash of insight whispered to her. Jair! It was Jair! She took a deep breath to steady herself. There was no logical explanation for such a conclusion—it was simply there. But how could that be? How could her brother . . . ?

In the tunnel behind her, something moved.

She had come some distance from the causeway, a slow and cautious passage through darkness with the aid of Cogline's flameless torch. She had neither seen nor heard another living thing in all that time. She had come so far without sensing other life that she had begun to wonder if perhaps she had been mistaken in taking this tunnel.

But now there was something there at last—not ahead of her as expected, but behind. She turned guardedly, the feeling of being watched forgotten. She thrust the torch forward and started in shock. Great, luminous blue eyes blinked at her from out of the gloom. Then a massive whiskered face pushed its way into the circle of her light.

"Whisper!"

She spoke the moor cat's name with a sigh of relief and dropped to her knees as the beast came up to her and rubbed its broad head against her shoulder in friendly greeting.

"Whisper, what are you doing here?" she murmured as the cat dropped down on his haunches and regarded her solemnly.

She could guess readily enough the answer to that question, of course. Discovering her absence, the others must have backtracked to the stone bridge. Being unable to follow farther themselves, they had sent Whisper after her. Or rather, Kimber had sent Whisper, for Whisper answered only to the girl. Brin reached out and rubbed the cat's ears. It must have cost Kimber something to send Whisper on like this without her—as close as they were, as much as the girl relied on him. As was her nature, she had chosen to give the moor cat's strength to her friend. The Valegirl's eyes misted, and she put her arms about him.

"Thank you, Kimber," she whispered.

Then she rose, stroked the cat for a moment and shook her head gently. "But I cannot take you with me, can I? I cannot take anyone. It is much too dangerous—even for you. I promised myself that no one would be exposed to whatever it is that waits for me, and that includes you. You have to go back."

The moor cat blinked up at her and remained where he was.

"Go on, now. You have to go back to Kimber. Go on, Whisper."

Whisper didn't move a hair. He simply sat there, waiting.

"So." Brin shook her head again. "As determined as your mistress, I guess."

She was left with no other choice; she used the wishsong. She sang softly to the cat, wrapping him close about with her words and music, telling him that he must go back. For several minutes she sang, a gentle urging that would not injure. When she was done, Whisper rose to his feet and padded back down the corridor, disappearing into the dark.

Brin watched him until he was out of sight, then turned and started ahead once more.

Moments later the darkness began to dissipate and the gloom to lighten. The passageway, narrow and close before, broadened and lifted in seconds so that her small light could no longer reach to the walls and ceiling. But now there was light ahead that rendered her own unnecessary, filling the passageway with dusty gray brightness. It was the sun. Somewhere close at hand, the tunnel was opening back into the world without.

She hurried forward, Cogline's flameless torch dropping to her side. The passageway turned upward, a stairwell honed and shaped from the tunnel rock rising far ahead into a massive, open-air cavern. She went up the stairs quickly, her weariness forgotten, sensing that her journey was nearing its end. Sunlight spilled down into the cavern above, silver streamers thick with swirling bits of dust and silt that danced and spun like living things.

Then she reached the last step, walked clear of the tunnel onto the broad ledge that lay beyond, and stopped. Before her, a second stone bridge spanned a second chasm, this one twice the size of the first, rugged and massive. It dropped away down the mountain rock thousands of feet into an abyss so deep that even the sunlight streaming down through crevices in the cavern ceiling could not penetrate its blackness. Brin peered downward, her nose wrinkling against the stench that wafted up. Even with Cogline's salve to numb her sense of smell, she felt nauseated. Whatever lay at the bottom of the pit was much worse than what passed through Graymark's sewers.

She glanced across the stone bridge to what waited beyond. The cavern stretched back into the mountain several hundred feet, then opened into a short, high tunnel. Yet it was not a tunnel so much as an alcove, she thought—hewn by hand, shaped and smoothed, with intricate symbols carved into the rock. Light streamed down at its far end, and the sky stretched away in a dim and hazy green.

She looked closer. No, it was not the sky that stretched away. It was a valley's misted wall.

It was the Maelmord.

She knew it instinctively, as if she had seen it in a dream and remembered. She could feel its touch and hear its whisper.

She hastened forward onto the bridge, a broad arched causeway some two dozen feet in width with wooden railing posts pegged into its rock and linked with chains. She moved forward quickly, passed the apex of the arch, and started down.

She was almost across when the black creature rose suddenly from a deep crevice in the cavern floor a dozen feet in front of her.

Muttering irritably, Cogline shuffled to a halt, Rone and Kimber crowding close behind him. Ahead, the sewer bisected into a pair of tunnels, each exactly like the other. There was no indication of which offered passage to wherever it was that Brin had now gone. There was nothing to suggest that either was the better way to go.

"Well, which do we follow?" Cogline demanded of Rone.

The highlander stared at him. "Don't you know?"

The oldster shook his head. "No idea. Make your choice."

Rone hesitated, looked away, then looked back again. "I can't. Look, maybe it doesn't make any difference which one we follow. Maybe both end in the same place."

"Sewer tunnels run *to* the same place, not *from* the same place! Any fool knows that!" the old man snorted.

"Grandfather!" Kimber admonished sharply.

She edged forward between them, scanning the tunnels in turn, studying the blackened waters that flowed through the grooved channels cut into each. At last she stepped back, shaking her head slowly.

"I cannot help you," she confessed, as if somehow she should have been able to do so. "I have no sense of where either leads. They appear the same." She looked over to Rone. "You will have to choose."

They stared at each other for a moment like frozen statues. Then Rone nodded slowly. "All right—we'll go left." He started past them. "At least that tunnel seems to run back toward the chasm."

He hastened into the sewer corridor, his flameless torch held firmly before him, his face grim. Cogline and Kimber looked at each other briefly and hurried after.

The black thing rose from the split in the cavern floor like a shadow come alive out of night's dreamworld and crouched down before the bridge. It was human in look, though as hairless and smooth as if sculpted from dark clay. Hunched over until it rocked forward on its long forearms, it was still taller than Brin. There was an odd, shapeless quality to its limbs and body, as if the muscles beneath lacked definition—or as if there were no muscles there at all and it not a thing of flesh. Sightless, deadened eyes lifted to find hers, and a mouth as ragged and black as the creature's skin yawned in a deep, toneless hiss.

The Valegirl froze. There was no way to avoid the creature. It had clearly been placed there for the purpose of guarding the bridge, and nothing was to pass it. Probably the Mord Wraiths had created it from the dark magic—created it, or called it to life from some nether place and time, as they had done with the Jachyra.

The black thing advanced a step, slow and certain, dead eyes staring. Brin forced herself to stand where she was. There was no way to know how dangerous this creature was, but she sensed that it was dangerous enough and that, if she turned or backed away, it would be on her.

The creature's black maw split wide and its hiss filled the silence. Brin went deathly cold. She knew what would happen next. And that meant that once again she was going to have to use the wishsong. Instantly her throat tightened. She did not want to use the Elven magic, but she could not let this monster reach her, even if it meant . . .

Abruptly the black thing attacked, lunging forward from its half-crouch. The swiftness of the thing caught her by surprise. It was hypnotic. The wishsong stuck in her throat, her indecision freezing it away. The moment hung suspended like a knot in the thread of time, and she waited for the impact of the blow.

But the blow never came. Something came streaking from behind her in a sudden blur of motion, caught the black thing in midleap, and hammered it back. Brin staggered away, dropping to her knees. It was Whisper! The spell of the wishsong had not been strong enough to counteract the command of his mistress; Whisper had shaken the magic and come after her!

The antagonists went down in a tangled heap, claws and teeth ripping. The black thing was caught completely by surprise, having seen only the girl. Hissing with rage, it struggled to dislodge the moor cat from its back where the great beast had fastened himself in a death grip. Over and over they tumbled along the length of the bridge, the moor cat's jaws tearing at the monster's neck and shoulders while the massive black form hunched and thrashed convulsively.

Brin remained frozen with indecision a dozen yards away at the center of the bridge. She must do something, she told herself. This was not Whisper's fight—this was hers. She flinched at the fury of the struggle, a small cry escaping her lips as the battle between the two took them perilously close to the railing, shaking the iron chains. She must help! But how could she? She had no weapon save for the wishsong, and she could not use the magic. She could not!

She surprised herself with the intensity of her declaration. She could not use the wishsong because . . . because . . . Rage and fear flooded her, mixing with confusion to hold her bound. Why? She howled the question within her mind, a cry of anguish. What was wrong with her?

Then abruptly she was moving forward, edging her way to the far side of the stone arch, away from the combatants. She had made her decision—she would flee. It was she whom the black thing sought. Seeing her run, the thing would follow. And if she were quick enough, she would make the Maelmord before it . . .

She stopped. Ahead where the cavern floor stretched away to the arched opening, she caught sight of something new as it emerged from the creviced rock.

A second creature!

She went perfectly still. The passage opening to the daylight and the valley beyond was too far—and the black thing stood directly in her line of flight. Already it was coming for her. It lifted from the rock, then lumbered toward the bridge on all fours, its blackened maw gaping. Brin backed away. She must defend herself this time. The fear and uncertainty ripped through her. She must use the wishsong. She must!

The black thing hissed and reached for her. Again, she felt her throat knot.

And again, it was Whisper who saved her. Breaking free of the first creature, the cat whirled and catapulted violently into the second, knocking it away from the girl. Scrambling up again, Whisper turned to meet this new enemy. The black thing came at him with a rasping howl, vaulting high into the air. But Whisper was too quick. Sidestepping deftly, the big cat slashed at his attacker's exposed underbelly. Chunks of dark flesh ripped free, yet the monster did not slow. It thrust itself clear with a lunge, dead eyes fixed.

Now the second creature was joined by the first. Warily, they began closing on the moor cat. Whisper dropped back guardedly, keeping himself in front of Brin, his thick fur bristling until he looked twice his normal size. Crouched down on all fours, the black things feinted with quick rushes, moving fluidly from side to side with an ease that belied their bulky appearance. Carefully, they worked to find an opening in the big cat's defenses. Whisper held his ground, refusing to be drawn out. Then both creatures came at him at once, teeth and claws ripping angry furrows through fur and flesh. Whisper was thrown back against the chains of the bridge railing, his powerful body nearly pinned there by the ferocious charge. But he fought his way clear with a surge, slashing savagely at the black things, screaming his hatred of them.

The circling began once more. Panting heavily, his sleek gray coat streaked with blood, Whisper slipped back into his defensive crouch. The attackers had forced him against the bridge railing, away from Brin. They ignored the Valegirl now, their lifeless eyes fixed on the cat. Brin saw what they intended. They would come at Whisper again, and this time the chains would not break the force of their rush. The moor cat would be thrown back over the edge and fall to his death.

The moor cat also seemed to realize what was happening. He lunged and feinted, trying to skirt the edges of the circle, trying to regain the center of the bridge. But the monsters maneuvered quickly to cut him off, keeping him trapped against the railing.

Brin Ohmsford's chest knotted with fear. Whisper could not win this fight. These creatures were too much for him. He had shredded both with wounds that should have crippled them, yet they did not seem affected by the injuries. Their flesh hung in tatters, yet they did not bleed. They were enormously strong and quick—stronger and quicker than anything born of this world. They had obviously been created by the dark magic, not by nature's hands.

"Whisper," she breathed, her voice cracked and dry.

She must save him. There was no one else to do so. She had the wish-song and the strength of its magic. She could use it to destroy these crea-tures, to obliterate them as surely as . . .

The trees intertwined in the Runne Mountains . . .

The minds of the thieves from west of Spanning Ridge . . .

The Gnome . . . shattered . . .

Tears ran down her cheeks. She could not! Something interposed itself between her will and its execution, held her back from her intended pur-pose, and froze her resolve with indecision. She must help him, but she could not!

"Whisper!" she screamed.

The black things jerked erect, half-turning. Abruptly Whisper lunged in a feint that froze them in their tracks, then whirled sharply to his right, gathered himself and vaulted them both with a tremendous leap. Landing at a dead run, the moor cat raced for the center of the bridge and Brin. The black things were after him instantly, hissing in fury, tearing at his flanks in an effort to bring him down.

A dozen feet in front of Brin, they succeeded. All three tumbled to the causeway in a raging tangle of teeth and claws. For a few desperate sec-onds, Whisper held them both. Then one gained his back and the second tore free. It hurtled past the struggling cat toward Brin. The Valegirl threw herself to one side, sprawling down upon the bridge. Whisper screamed. With the last of his strength, he threw himself into the girl's assailant, the second creature still clinging to his back like some monstrous spider. The force of his lunge carried all three into the chains of the bridge railing. Iron links snapped like deadwood, and the black things hissed gleefully as Whisper began to slide from the bridge into the chasm.

Brin came to her knees, a cry of rage and determination wrenched from her throat. The restraints that bound her fell away, the indecision and uncertainty were shattered, and her purpose freed. She sang, hard and quick, and the sound of the wishsong filled the heights and depths of the cavern rock. The song was darker than any she had sung before, a new and terri-ble sound, filled with fury that surpassed all she had believed herself capa-ble of knowing. It exploded into the black things like an iron ram. They surged upward at its impact and their lifeless eyes snapped back. Limbs claw-ing, black mouths wide and soundless, they were flung away from Whis-per, back away from the safety of the bridge, and into space. Convulsing like blown leaves, they fell into the abyss and were gone.

It was done in an instant. Brin went silent, her dusky, worn face flushed and vibrant. Again she felt that sudden, strange sense of twisted glee—but stronger this time, much stronger. It burned through her like fire. She could barely control her excitement. She had destroyed the black things almost without trying.

And she had enjoyed it!

She realized then that the barrier that had interposed itself between her will and its execution had been one of her own making—a restraint she had put there to protect against what had just happened. Now it was gone, and she did not think it could be put back again. She had sensed that she was losing control of the magic. She had not understood why, only that it was happening. Each use had seemed to bring her a little further away from herself. She had tried to resist what was being done to her, but her efforts to forbear use of the magic had been thwarted at every turn— almost as if some perverse fate had willed that she *must* use the magic. By using it this time, she had embraced it fully, and she no longer felt that she could struggle against it. She would be what she must.

Slowly, gingerly, Whisper padded over to where she knelt, pushing his dark muzzle against her face. Her arms came up to wrap about the big cat gently, and tears ran down her cheeks.

Jair Ohmsford's voice died away in a ragged gasp, and the light of the vision crystal died with it. The face of his sister was gone. A deep silence filled the sudden gloom, and the faces of the men gathered there were white and drawn.

"Those were Mutens," Slanter whispered finally.

"What?" Edain Elessedil, seated next to him, looked startled.

"The black things—that's what they're called—Mutens. The dark magic made them. They guard the sewers below Graymark . . ." The Gnome trailed off, glancing quickly at Jair.

"Then she is here," the Valeman breathed, his mouth dry and his hands tightening about the crystal.

Slanter nodded. "Yes, boy, she's here. And closer to the pit than we."

Garet Jax rose swiftly, a lean, black shadow. The others scrambled up with him. "It seems we have no time left us and no choice but to go in now." Even in the half-light, his eyes were like fire. He reached out to them, palms upward. "Give me your hands."

One by one, they stretched forward their hands, joining with his. "By this we make our pledge," he told them, a hard and brittle edge to his voice. "The Valeman shall reach the basin at Heaven's Well as he has sworn he would. We are as one in this, whatever happens. As one, to the end. Swear it."

There was a hushed silence. "As one," Helt repeated in his deep, gentle voice. "As one," the others echoed.

The hands fell away, and Garet Jax turned to Slanter. "Take us in," he said.

40

They went up through the mountain passageways to the cellars that lay below Graymark like the Wraiths they shunned. With the aid of torches they found stored in a niche at the tunnel entrance, they crept through the gloom and the silence to the bowels of the fortress keep. Slanter led them, his rough yellow face bent close to the light, his black eyes bright with fear. He went quickly and purposefully, and only the eyes betrayed what he might wish hidden of himself. But Jair saw it, recognized it, and found that it mirrored what lurked now within himself.

He, too, was afraid. The anticipation that had earlier given him such strength of purpose was gone. Fear had replaced it, wild and barely controlled, racing through him and turning his skin to ice. Strange, fragmented thoughts filled his mind as he worked his way ahead with the others through the tunnel rock, his nostrils thick with the smell of musted air and his own sweat—thoughts of his home in the Vale, of his family scattered across the lands, of friends and familiar things left behind and perhaps lost, of the shadow things that hunted him, of Allanon and Brin, and of what they had come to this dark place and time to do. All jumbled and ran together like colors mixed in water, and there was no sense to be made of any of them. It was the fear that made his thoughts scatter so, and he tightened his mind and his resolve against it.

The passageways wound upward for a long time, crossing and recrossing, a puzzle maze that seemed to lack beginning or end. Yet Slanter did not pause, but led them steadily on until at last they came in sight of a broad, ironbound doorway fastened to the rock. They came up to it and stopped, as silent as the tunnels through which they had come. Jair crouched down with the others as Slanter put one ear to the door and listened. In the stillness of his mind, he could hear the beat of his body's pulse.

Slanter rose and nodded once. Carefully, he lifted the latch that held the door closed, fixed his hands on the iron handle and pulled. The door swung open with a low groan. A stairway rose before them, disappearing beyond the circle of their torchlight into blackness. They began to climb, with Slanter leading them once more. A step at a time, slow and cautious, they made their way up the stairwell. Gloom and silence deepened and wrapped them close about. The stairwell ended, opening upward through a stone block floor. The soft scrape of someone's boot on the stairs echoed harshly through the darkness above, disappearing far away into the silence. Jair swallowed against what he was feeling. It was as if there was nothing up there but the dark.

Then they were clear of the stairs and within the gloom. Voiceless, they stood close about the opening and peered into the gloom, torches held forth. The light could not penetrate to walls or ceiling, but there was a clear sense of a chamber so huge that they were dwarfed by it. They could discern at the edges of their torchlight the shadowed outline of crates and barrels. The wood was dry and rotting, its iron bindings rusted. Cobwebs lay over everything, and the floor was thick with dust.

But in the carpet of the dust, splayed footprints marked the passing of something that was clearly not human. It had not been all that long since whatever it was had ventured down into the lower levels of Graymark, Jair thought chillingly.

Slanter beckoned them ahead. The members of the little company moved into the gloom, groping their way forward from the open stairwell, the dust stirring beneath their boots and rising in soft clouds to mix with the light of their torches in a hazy glare. Mounds of stores and discarded provisions appeared and were left behind. Still the chamber ran on.

Then suddenly the entire floor rose half a dozen steps to a new level and stretched away from there into darkness. They went up the stairs in a knot, walked ahead twenty yards or so, and passed into a monstrous, arched corridor. Iron doors, barred and sealed, appeared on either side as they pushed forward. Blackened torch stubs sat within their iron racks, chains lay in piles against the walls, and multilegged insects scurried from the light to the seclusion of the gloom. A stench hindered breathing and choked the senses, emanating in waves from the cellar stone.

The corridor ended at yet another stairway, this one curling upward like a snake coiled. Slanter paused, then began to climb. The others followed. Twice the stairway wound back upon itself, then opened into another corridor. They followed this new passageway several dozen yards to where it branched in two directions. Slanter took them right. The passageway ended a short distance further on at a closed iron door. The Gnome tested the latch, tugged futilely, and shook his head. There was concern on his face as he turned to the others. Clearly he had hoped to find it open.

Garet Jax pointed back down the corridor, the unasked question in his eyes. Could they backtrack and go the other way? Slanter shook his head slowly, the answer in his eyes. The Gnome did not know.

They hesitated a moment longer, eyes locked. Then Slanter pushed past, motioning for the others to follow. He led them back down the passageway to where it divided. This time he took them left. The second corridor wound farther than the first, passing stairwells, niches cloaked in shadow, and numerous doors, all closed and barred. Several times the Gnome paused, undecided, then continued on. The minutes slipped away, and Jair began to grow increasingly uneasy.

Then at last the passageway ended, this time at a pair of massive iron doors so huge that Slanter was forced to reach upward to seize the handles. They gave with surprising ease, and the door on the right swung silently in. The members of the little company peered through guardedly. Another chamber lay beyond, huge and cluttered with stores. But the gloom dissipated somewhat here, chased by a thin, gray light that slipped downward through tiny slits in the walls that were cut close against the chamber's high ceiling.

Slanter gestured toward the slits, then to the far wall of the chamber where a second pair of iron doors stood closed. The others understood. They were within Graymark's outer walls.

With Slanter in the lead, they passed cautiously into the room. No dust lay upon these floors; no cobwebs draped its crates and barrels. The stench still hung upon the air, stifling and rank, but it now seemed carried as much from without as held by the closure of the walls. Jair wrinkled his nose in distaste. The smell might well kill them before the dark things found them out. It was as bad as . . .

Something scraped softly in the shadows to one side. Garet Jax whirled, daggers in both hands, crying out in warning to the others.

Too late. Something huge, black, and winged seemed to explode out of the shadows. It rose against the half-light, its leathered body spreading outward like some monstrous bat. Teeth and claws gleamed, a flash of ivory, and a fierce shriek broke from its throat. It was on them so quickly that there was no time to defend against it. It flew at them in a rush, swept past the leaders, and came at Helt. It caromed into the giant Borderman, winged limbs flailing, and its shriek turned to a frightening hiss. Helt staggered back with a howl, then got both hands on the black thing, and thrust it from him violently, flinging it across the room into a pile of stores.

Garet Jax leaped forward, and the daggers flew from his hands, pinning the thing to the wooden crates.

Slanter had reached the far end of the room and wrenched wide one of the iron doors. "Get out!" he howled.

They raced swiftly from the chamber, one after the other, until all were clear. Slanter shoved the open door closed with a grunt and threw the iron bolts into their fastenings. Shaking, he collapsed back against the door.

"What *was* that?" Foraker gasped, his black-bearded face shiny with sweat and his heavy brows knit fiercely.

The Gnome shook his head. "I don't know. Something the walkers made of the dark magic—some sentinel, perhaps."

Helt was down on one knee, his face buried in his hands. Blood seeped through his fingers in small trickles of scarlet.

"Helt!" Jair whispered and started forward. "Helt, you're hurt . . ."

The Borderman lifted his head slowly. Angry slashes crisscrossed his face. One eye was swollen and already beginning to close. He dabbed at the wounds with his tunic sleeve and motioned the Valeman back. "No, they're just scratches. Nothing bad."

But he was wincing with pain. He came to his feet with an effort, bracing himself against the wall. There was an uneasy look in his eyes.

Slanter had moved away from the door and was glancing about furtively. They were at the center of a narrow corridor that ran to a pair of closed doors at one end and to a stairway opening to daylight at the other.

"This way!" he beckoned, moving quickly toward the light. "Hurry— before something else finds us!"

They started after him, all save Helt, who was still leaning against the passage wall. Jair glanced back and slowed. "Helt?" he called.

"Hurry on, Jair." The big man was still dabbing blood from his face. Then he pushed himself off the wall and started after. "Go on, now. Stay close to the others."

Jair did as he was asked, conscious that the Borderman was following and conscious, too, that Helt was having difficulty doing so. There was something very wrong with him.

They reached the end of the corridor and went up the stairs in a rush. The eerie stillness of the fortress was broken by the sound of other feet and voices, jumbled, distant and indistinct. The shriek of the winged thing had given warning that there were intruders within the keep. Jair's mind raced wildly as he bounded up the long stairway with the others. He must remember that he had the wishsong for protection—that he could use it effectively only if he remembered to keep his head . . .

Something hissed past his face, and he stumbled and went down. An arrow shattered on the stairway wall. Helt was next to him at once, pulling him up again. Arrows flew all about them as Gnome Hunters appeared in the corridor below and on parapets above. The companions were within Graymark's walls, but their enemies knew it now and were converging. Scrambling to the top of the stairs, Jair wheeled right after the others along a line of battlements that overlooked a broad inner courtyard and a maze of towers and fortifications. Gnomes appeared from everywhere, weapons in hand, yelling wildly. A handful lay crumpled on the battlements ahead, brought down by Garet Jax as the black-clad Weapons Master cleared the way forward. The six darted along the battlements to a tower stairwell where Slanter brought them to a halt.

"The drop-gate—there!" He pointed across the courtyard to an iron-barred portcullis that stood raised over an arched entry leading through a massive, stone block wall. "Quickest way for us to reach the Croagh!" His yellow face grimaced as he fought for breath. "Gnomes will realize what we're about in a moment. When they do, they'll bring down the gate to trap us. But if we can get there first, we can use the gate to cut them off instead!"

Garet Jax nodded, oddly calm in the midst of the moment's fury. "Where is the wheelhouse and winch?"

Slanter pointed again. "Beneath the gates—this side. We'll have to jam the wheel!"

Shouts and cries broke from all about them. In the courtyard below the Gnomes began to come together.

Garet Jax straightened. "Quick, then—before they are too many for us."

The little company raced down the tower stairwell, Slanter leading. At the lower end, they crossed through an anteway, dark and closed, to a single door that opened into the courtyard. All across the yard, Gnome Hunters turned to face them.

"Shades!" Slanter gasped.

They broke for the gate in a rush.

Brin Ohmsford climbed slowly to her feet, one hand resting lightly on Whisper's massive head. The cavern was still again, empty of life. She stood for a moment at the center of the stone bridge and looked across the chasm to where daylight brightened the tall, arched alcove leading out. She rubbed Whisper's head gently, conscious of the welts and angry furrows left from his terrible battle with the black things, feeling the hurt that he had suffered.

"No more," she whispered softly.

Then she turned forward. She left the bridge quickly, without looking back, and began to cross the cavern floor toward the alcove. Whisper went with her, padding silently behind, saucer blue eyes gleaming. Without turning, she knew that he was there. Cautiously, she scanned the creviced rock for signs of the black things or other horrors wrought by the dark magic, but there were none. Only she and the cat remained.

Minutes later she reached the alcove with its high, smooth walls sculpted from the stone and carved with the intricate designs she had seen earlier. She paid them little heed, moving at once to the opening and to the daylight beyond. She had only one objective now.

The opening passed away behind her and she stood once more in sunlight. It was midafternoon, the sun gone westward toward the treeline, its brightness dimmed by mist and clouds that floated shroudlike across the whole of the sky above. She was on a ledge overlooking a deep valley surrounded by a cluster of barren, ragged peaks. There was an odd, dreamlike tone to the setting of mountains, clouds, and mist. The whole of the valley was bathed in a shimmering, leaden cast. She looked slowly about and then upward behind her. There, balanced upon the rock above, was a solitary, dismal fortress. Graymark. Winding down from its heights and from far above that, beyond where she could see, was the stone stairway of the Croagh. It wound past her ledge, touched briefly, then spiraled down into the valley.

It was upon the valley that her gaze at last came to rest. A deep, shadowed bowl, it fell away from the light until its lower depths were lost in misted gloom. The Croagh wound down into this darkness, into a mass of trees, vines, scrub, and choking brush, grown so thick that the light could not penetrate. This forest was a twisted and knotted wilderness and it seemed to have neither beginning nor end, but to be contained in its rampant growth only by the rock walls of the peaks.

Brin stared. It was from here that the hissing sound came, the one that she had heard earlier in the sewers. It was like a breathing. She squinted against the glare of the gray half-light. Had she seen . . . ?

In the bowl of the valley, the forest moved.

"You are alive!" she said softly and hardened herself against what that realization made her feel.

She stepped far out onto the ledge, to the very edge where the stem of the Croagh joined to it. Crude stairs had been cut into the rock, and she stared down their length to where they disappeared at a bend in the stone. Then she looked past again to the valley below.

"Maelmord, I am come to you," she whispered.

Then she turned back to Whisper. She knelt beside him and rubbed his ears tenderly. Her smile was sad and gentle. "You must go no further with me, Whisper. Even though your mistress sent you to keep me safe, you must go no further. You must stay here and wait for her to come to you. Do you understand?"

The cat's luminous eyes blinked and he rubbed against her. "Protect my way back again, if you would protect me at all," she told him. "Perhaps it will not be as the Grimpond has foretold—that I shall die here. Perhaps I will come back again. Keep the way safe for me, Whisper. Keep your mistress and my friends safe. Do not let them follow. Wait, and when I have done what I must, I will come back to you if I am able. I promise you that I will."

Then she sang to the cat, using the wishsong not to persuade or to deceive this time, but to explain. In images that would carry to the moor cat's mind, she let him feel what she wished and made him understand what it was that she must do. When she was done, she leaned forward and hugged the big cat close for a moment, nestling her face in the coarse fur and feeling the warmth of the beast seep through her, taking from that warmth a measure of new strength.

She rose and stepped back. Slowly Whisper sank down on his haunches and forepaws until he was stretched out facing her. She nodded and smiled. He was taking up guard of her path down. He would do as she wished.

"Good-bye, Whisper," she told him and stepped upon the Croagh.

The stench that had risen from the chasm behind her rose anew from the steamy depths of the valley below. She ignored it, gazing out momentarily over the cliffs to where the light of the sun brightened above the horizon. She thought of Allanon then and wondered if he could see her—if perhaps he might in some way be with her.

Then she took a deep breath to steady herself and started down.

41

As one, the six who had come from Culhaven broke from the shelter of the tower door and raced into the courtyard beyond. Screams of warning rose up about them, and the Gnomes converged from every quarter.

At the center of the maelstrom, Jair watched the battle unfold with curious detachment. Time fragmented, and his sense of being slipped from him. Hemmed close about by the friends who sought to protect him, he floated in their midst, voiceless and ephemeral, a ghost that none could see. Earth, sky, and the whole of the world beyond these walls were lost, along with all else that had ever been or would ever be. There was only now and the faces and the forms of those who fought and died in that yard.

Garet Jax led the charge, darting through the Gnomes that rushed to bar his passage, swift and fluid as he killed them. He was like a black-clad dancer, all grace, power, and seemingly effortless motion. Gnome Hunters, gnarled and worn from countless battles, threw themselves in front of him with frenzied determination, their weapons hacking and cutting with lethal force. They might as well have been trying to contain quicksilver. None could touch the Weapons Master, and those who came close enough to try found in him the black shadow of death come to claim their lives.

The others of the company fought beside him, no less driven in their purpose and only a shade less deadly. Foraker flanked him on one side, the Dwarf's black-bearded face ferocious as he swung the great double-edged axe and attackers scattered with howls of dismay. Edain Elessedil flanked him on the other, a slender sword flicking snakelike and a long knife parrying counterblows. Slanter stayed close behind them all, long knives in both hands, a hunted look in his black eyes. Helt brought up the rear, a giant shield, his wounded face bleeding again and frightening to look at, a great pike snatched from an attacker thrusting and cutting all who tried to slip past his guard.

A strange sense of exhilaration flooded through Jair. It was as if nothing could stop them.

Weapons flew past from every direction, and the screams of the wounded and dying filled the gray afternoon. They were in the center of the courtyard now, the castle wall rising up before them. Then a sudden blow struck the Valeman, staggering him with its force. Stunned, he looked down and found the tip of a dart protruding from his shoulder like a peg hook. Pain lanced from the wound through his body, and he went rigid with shock. Slanter saw him stumble and was next to him in an instant, arms wrapping about him to hold him up, pulling him after the others. Helt roared with fury and used the long pike to hammer back the Gnomes that sought to rush forward to seize them. Jair squeezed his eyes shut against the pain. He was hurt, he thought in disbelief as he staggered forward under Slanter's guidance.

The drop-gate loomed ahead. There were Gnomes in its shadow now, rushing about wildly and calling out in warning. The doors to the blockhouse slammed shut and iron winches began to turn. Slowly, the drop-gate started down.

Garet Jax leaped forward, so quickly that the others could barely follow. He reached the gate in seconds, thrusting into the Gnomes who held there. But the winches continued to turn in the blockhouse, iron chains unwrapping. The drop-gate was still coming down.

"Garet!" Foraker screamed in warning, nearly buried in a rush of Gnome attackers who came at him.

But it was Helt who acted. He charged through the Gnome Hunters, pike lowered, sweeping them aside like leaves scattered in a fall wind. Blows rained down upon him, but he shrugged them aside as if they were not felt and went on. Gnome archers trained their fire on the giant Borderman from the walls behind. Twice he was struck; the second time, he staggered to his knees. Still he went on.

Then he was before the blockhouse, his giant frame slamming into the closed doors. The doors buckled with a crunch and flew apart, and the Borderman was within. He hurtled into a knot of defenders, flinging them from the machinery like dolls, his massive hands closing about the winch levers to pull them tight again. The drop-gate slowed and stopped in a grinding of chains and gears, its teeth barely ten feet from the ground.

Garet Jax scattered the Gnomes who remained before the gate, and Slanter and Jair stumbled through into a shadowed court beyond. For the moment, at least, the court was empty. Jair collapsed to one knee, feeling the searing pain from his wound flare outward with the movement. Then Slanter was in front of him.

"Sorry boy, but I've got to do this."

One gnarled hand fixed on his shoulder and the other on the dart. With a wrench, the Gnome pulled the dart free. Jair screamed and almost lost consciousness, but Slanter held him upright, jamming a wad of cloth down into his tunic front and binding it fast against the wound with his belt.

Beneath the drop-gate, Garet Jax, Foraker and Edain Elessedil stood in a line against the advancing Gnomes. A dozen paces beyond, still within the blockhouse, Helt pulled free the winch levers once more. Again, the drop-gate started down.

Jair blinked through the tears brought by the pain. Something was wrong. The Borderman was making no attempt to come after them. He was leaning heavily against the machinery, watching as the gate descended.

"Helt . . . ?" Jair whispered weakly.

He realized then the Borderman's intent. Helt meant to bring down the drop-gate and jam it from the other side. If he did so, it would leave him trapped there. It would mean his certain death.

"Helt, no!" he screamed and jerked to his feet.

But it was already done. The gate came down, slamming into the earth with the force of its release. The Gnome defenders howled with rage and turned on the man within the blockhouse. Bracing himself, Helt threw the whole of his great strength against the winch levers and wrenched them from their fastenings, wrecking the machine.

"Helt!" Jair screamed again, trying to pull free of Slanter.

The Borderman staggered to the blockhouse door, long pike held before him. Gnomes came at him from everywhere. He bent and swayed against their rush, but for an instant he withstood them. They they swarmed over him and he was gone.

Jair stood frozen behind the gates as Garet Jax came back to him. Roughly, the Weapons Master turned him about and pushed him away. "Go!" he snapped. "Quickly, Jair Ohmsford, go now!"

The Valeman stumbled from the gate, still stunned. The Weapons Master kept pace at his side. "He was dying already," Garet Jax said. Jair's head jerked about, and the gray eyes fixed on him. "The winged thing in the storeroom poisoned him. It was in his eyes, Valeman."

Jair nodded dumbly, remembering the look the Borderman had given him. "But we . . . we might have . . ."

"We might have done many things were we not where we are," Garet Jax cut him short, his voice calm and icy. "The poison was lethal. He knew he was dying. He chose this way to finish it. Now, run!"

Giant Helt! Jair remembered the big man's kindness to him during the long journey north. He remembered his gentle eyes. Helt, about whom he had known so very little . . .

Head lowered to shield his tears, he ran on.

At the edge of the Croagh, midway down its length where it joined to the rock shelf on the cliffs below Graymark, Whisper listened as the sounds of the battle being fought above him grew more fierce. Stretched full-length upon the shadowed stone, he kept watch for the return of Brin or the coming of his mistress. His hearing was keener than that of any human, and he had caught the sounds long ago. But the sounds did not threaten him, and so he kept his vigil and did not move.

But then a new sound reached his ears, a sound not from the battle being fought within Graymark, but from something close at hand. Footfalls sounded on the stone steps of the Croagh—soft and furtive. The moor cat's head lifted. Something was coming down. Claws scraped against the rock. Whisper's head dropped down again, and he seemed to disappear into the stone.

The seconds slipped past, and then a shadow appeared. Whisper's narrowed eyes caught the movement, and the big cat stayed frozen. One of the black things crept down the stairs of the Croagh—one like the things that he had fought within the caves of the mountain. Down the stone walkway it slipped, dead eyes staring as if sightless. It did not see Whisper. The moor cat waited.

When the monster was less than half a dozen steps from where he crouched, Whisper sprang. He hurtled into the black thing before it even knew he was there, a silent blur of motion. Arms flailing, the creature flew from the Croagh to drop like a stone into the valley below. Balanced at the edge of the stairway's long spiral, Whisper watched the thing fall. When it struck, the entire forest about it convulsed in a frenzy of limbs and leafy trailers. It had the unpleasant look of a throat swallowing. Finally, it went still.

Whisper backed from the Croagh, ears flattened in a mixture of fear and hatred. The smell of the steamy jungle rose to assail the cat's nostril's, and he coughed and spit in distaste. He padded back upon the rock shelf.

Then a new sound brought him about with a low snarl. Other dark forms stood upon the Croagh above him—two more of the black things and behind them a robed figure, tall and hooded. Whisper's saucer blue eyes blinked and narrowed. It was too late to hide. They had already seen him.

Soundlessly he turned to meet them, dark muzzle drawing back.

Jair Ohmsford and his companions raced through shadows and half-light deep within the fortress of Graymark now. They ran down hallways thick with the stench of must and sewage, corridors of rusted iron doors and crumbling stone, chambers that echoed with their footfalls, and stairways worn and broken. The castle of Graymark was a dying place, sick with age and disuse and rotten with decay. Nothing that lived here gave tolerance to life; those within found comfort only in death.

And it seeks my death, Jair thought as he ran, his wound throbbing painfully. It seeks to swallow me and make me a part of it.

Ahead, the dark form of Garet Jax darted swiftly on, a wraith that beckoned. The gloom about them lay empty, silent and waiting. The Gnomes had been left behind; the Mord Wraiths had not appeared. The Valeman fought back against the fear that coursed through him. Where were the Wraiths? Why hadn't they seen them yet? They were here within the keep, hidden somewhere within its walls, the things that could destroy minds and bodies. They were here and they must surely come.

But where were they?

He stumbled, fell against Slanter, and almost went down. But the Gnome held him up, one stout arm coming quickly about him. "Watch where you step!" Slanter cried.

Jair gritted his teeth as pain flooded outward from his shoulder. "It hurts, Slanter. Every step . . ."

The Gnome's blocky face turned from his own. "The pain tells you that you're still alive, boy. Now run!"

Jair Ohmsford ran. They raced down a curving hall, and ahead there was the sound of other feet running and voices calling out. Gnomes had come another way and were searching for them.

"Weapons Master!" Slanter warned urgently, and Garet Jax skidded to a halt. The Gnome beckoned them into an alcove where a small door opened onto a narrow stairway that disappeared upward into blackness.

"We can slip above them this way," Slanter panted, leaning wearily against the stone block walls. "But a moment for the boy, first."

Quickly, he pulled the cork from his ale pouch and lifted the spout to the Valeman's lips. Jair drank gratefully in a series of deep swallows. The bitter liquid burned through him; almost at once, it seemed to ease the pain. Leaning back against the wall with the Gnome, he watched as Garet Jax slipped ahead along the stairway, searching the darkness above. Behind them, Foraker and Edain Elessedil stood guard at the stairway entrance, crouched down within the shadows.

"Better now?" Slanter asked him shortly.

"Better."

"Like that time in the Black Oaks, eh? After you'd taken that beating from Spilk?"

"Like then." Jair smiled, remembering. "Cures everything, that Gnome ale."

The Gnome laughed bitterly. "Everything? No, boy—not what the walkers will do to us when they catch us. Not that. Coming for us, you know—just like they did in the Oaks. Coming from the shadows, sound-less black things. I can smell them!"

"It's just the stench of the place, Slanter."

The Gnome's rough face lowered, as if he had not heard. "Helt—gone just like that. Wouldn't have thought we would lose the big man so quick. Bordermen are a tough breed; trackers tougher still. Wouldn't have thought it would happen so quick with him."

Jair swallowed. "I know. But it will be different for the rest of us, Slanter. The Gnomes are behind us. We'll get away, just as we have done before."

Slanter shook his head slowly. "No, we'll not get away this time, boy. Not this time." He pushed clear of the wall, his voice a whisper. "We'll all be dead before it's done."

Roughly, he pulled the Valeman up after him, made a quick motion back to Foraker and Edain Elessedil and started up the stairs. The Dwarf and the Elf followed at once. They caught up with Garet Jax several dozen steps ahead, and together the five climbed into the blackness. Step by step, they made their way forward, with a small glimmer of light from some-where above as their only guide. Within Graymark's walls, it was like a tomb meant to hold them fast. Jair let the thought linger momentarily, desperately aware of his own mortality. He could die as easily as Helt had died. It was not assured, as he had once believed, that he would live to see the end of this.

Then he brushed the thought away. If he did not live, there would be no one to help Brin. It would end for both of them, for there could be no hope for her without him. Therefore, he must live, must find a way to live.

The stairway ended at a small wooden door with a barred window. It was through this window that the daylight slipped down into the darkness where they crouched. Slanter pressed his rough yellow face tight against the bars and peered out into what waited beyond. From somewhere close, the cries of their pursuers rang out.

"Have to run for it again," Slanter said over his shoulder. "Ahead, through the great hall. Stay close!"

He threw open the wooden door, and they burst into the daylight beyond. They were in a long corridor, high-ceilinged and raftered, with narrow, arched windows cut into its length. Slanter took them left, past alcoves and doorways draped in shadow, shells of rusted armor on pedestals, and clusters of weapons hung against the stone. The cries grew stronger, and it seemed as if the company were running toward them. Then suddenly the cries were all about them. Behind, only yards back, a door flew wide and Gnome Hunters poured through. Howls of excitement burst from their throats, and they turned to give chase.

"Quick!" Slanter cried.

A shower of arrows whistled past them as they charged onto a threshold fronting a pair of tall, arched wooden doors carved in scroll. Slanter and Garet Jax flew into the doors, the others only a step behind, and the doors snapped at their bindings and sagged open. The company rushed through, tumbling over one another down a long stairway. They were within the great hall that Slanter had sought, a massive chamber bright with daylight that poured through high, barred windows. Beams, aged and cracked by time's passage, ran crosswise overhead, buttressing a cavernous ceiling canopied over rows of tables and benches scattered across the floor beneath in disarray. The five from Culhaven regained their footing hurriedly and raced through the tables and benches, dodging the debris frantically. Behind them, their pursuers burst into the room.

Jair followed Slanter right, conscious of Garet Jax close ahead on the left and Foraker and Edain Elessedil trailing. His lungs burned and the wound in his shoulder throbbed painfully once again. Arrows and darts hissed wickedly past, thudding into the wood of the benches and tables. Gnome Hunters were appearing all about them now.

"The stairs!" Slanter screamed frantically.

Ahead, a long, curving stairway wound upward toward a balcony, and they broke for it in a rush. But several Gnomes reached it first, fanning out across the lower steps, cutting off their escape. Garet Jax went directly for them. Springing atop a trestle bench, he skidded its length and dove into their midst. Somehow he kept his feet on landing, like a black cat striking out at the harried Gnomes. With long knives in both hands, he slipped past their cumbersome pikes and broadswords and slew them one by one, as if they were but helpless targets. By the time the others of the company reached him, all but a few lay dead, and those few had scattered.

Garet Jax wheeled on Slanter, blood streaking his lean face. "Where is the Croagh, Gnome?"

"Through the hallway beyond the balcony!" Slanter barely slowed to answer. "Quick, now!"

They were up the stairs in a rush. Behind, a cluster of new pursuers closed on the stairs and bounded after. Halfway up, the Gnomes caught them. The Weapons Master, the Dwarf, and the Elf turned to fight. Slanter pulled Jair a dozen steps further on to shield him. Gnome broadswords and maces swung high, and there was a fearful clash of metal. Garet Jax staggered back, separated from the others by the press of attackers. Then Elb Foraker went down, his head laid open to the bone by a deflected blade. He struggled to rise, blood streaming down his bearded face, and Edain Elessedil leaped to his aid. For an instant, the young Elf held the attackers at bay, his slender sword darting. But a pike pierced his sword arm. As his guard dropped, one of the Gnomes brought a mace down against his leg. The Elf toppled over with a scream of pain, and the Gnomes were on him.

For an instant it appeared as if they were all finished. But then Garet Jax was there once more, his black-clad form hurtling into the attackers and flinging them back. Down went the Gnome Hunters, dying in astonishment, dead almost before they knew what had killed them. The last of the Hunters fell, and the members of the little company were alone once more.

Foraker stumbled over to where Edain Elessedil writhed in pain, his gnarled hands reach down to feel the injured leg. "Smashed," he breathed softly and exchanged a knowing look with Garet Jax.

He bound the leg with strips of his short cloak, using shattered arrows for splints. Slanter and Jair hastened down the steps to rejoin them, and the Gnome forced some of the bitter ale he carried down the Elf's throat. Edain Elessedil's face was white and drawn with the pain as Jair bent over him. The Valeman saw at once that the damaged leg was useless.

"Help me get him up," Foraker ordered. With Slanter's aid, they carried the Elf to the top of the stairs. There they propped him up against the balustrade and knelt before him.

"Leave me," he whispered, grimacing as he shifted his weight. "You have to. Take Jair on to the Croagh. Go quickly."

Jair looked hurriedly at the others. Their faces were grim and set. "No!" he cried out angrily.

"Jair." The Elf's hand closed tightly about his arm. "It was agreed, Jair. We pledged it. Whatever happens to the rest of us, you must reach Heaven's Well. I can no longer help you. You must leave me and go on."

"What he says is true, Ohmsford—he can go no further." Elb Foraker's voice was oddly hushed. He put his hands on the Valeman's shoulders, then slowly came to his feet, glancing in turn at Slanter and Garet Jax. "I think that maybe I've gone as far as I can go, too. That sword cut has left me too dizzy for long climbs. The three of you go on. I think I'll stay here."

"Elb, no, you can't do that . . ." the injured man tried to object.

"My choice, Edain Elessedil," the Dwarf cut him short. "My choice as it was yours when you chose to come to my aid. We have a bond, you and I—a bond shared by Elves and Dwarves as far back as anyone can remember. We always stand by each other. It's time for me to honor that bond."

He turned then to Garet Jax. "This time the matter of my staying is not open to argument, Garet."

A scattering of Gnome Hunters appeared at the far end of the hall. They slowed guardedly, calling back to others that followed.

"Hurry, now," Foraker whispered. "Take Ohmsford and go."

Garet Jax hesitated only a moment, then nodded. His hand reached out to grip that of the Dwarf. "Luck, Foraker."

"And you," the other answered.

His dark eyes met those of the Gnome momentarily. Then wordlessly, he placed an ash bow, arrows, and the slender Elf blade by Edain Elessedil's side. In his own hands, he gripped the double-edged axe.

"Go now!" he snapped without turning, his black-bearded countenance fierce and set.

Jair held his ground defiantly, eyes darting from the face of the Weapons Master to that of Slanter. "Come, boy," the Gnome said quietly.

Rough hands fastened on the Valeman's good arm and propelled him along the balcony. Garet Jax followed, gray eyes cold and fixed. Jair wanted to scream in protest, to say that they could not leave them, but he knew that it would do no good. The decision had been made. He glanced over his shoulder to where Foraker and the Elven Prince waited at the stairway's edge. Neither looked toward him. Their eyes were on the advancing Gnome Hunters.

Then Slanter had them through a doorway into another hall and hastening down its length. Cries of pursuit sounded once more, scattered and distant save in the direction from which they had fled. Jair ran silently at Slanter's side and fought to keep from looking back.

The hallway they followed ended at an arched opening. They passed through into gray, hazy daylight, and the walls of the keep were left behind. A broad courtyard spread out before them to a railing. Beyond, the cliffs and the fortress dropped away into a valley; out of the valley, a single thread of stone spiraled upward past the courtyard's edge. High and then higher it rose, to wrap at last about a solitary peak far above.

The Croagh, with Heaven's Well at its summit.

The three who remained of the little company from Culhaven hurried forward to where the stairway and the courtyard joined and began to climb.

42

Hundreds of steps passed away beneath Brin's feet as she descended the stone stairway of the Croagh into the pit of the Maelmord. The slender ribbon of stone spiraled downward, winding from Graymark's leaden towers into the mist and steamy heat of the jungle below, a narrow and dizzying drop through space. The Valegirl traversed it with wooden steps, her mind numb with fear and weariness and wracked with whispers of doubt. One hand rested lightly on the stone railing to give her some sense of support. In the west, the clouded sun continued to pass slowly behind the mountains.

Through the whole of her descent, her eyes remained fixed on the pit below. A dim and hazy mass when she began, the Maelmord sharpened in clarity with each step taken. Slowly, the life that lay rooted there took shape and form, lifting away from the broad backdrop of the valley. The trees were huge, bent, and hoary, warped somehow from the way that nature's hand had shaped them. And within their midst were massive stalks of scrub and weed, grown to disproportionate size, and vines that wound and twisted over everything like snakes without heads or tails. The color of this jungle was not a vibrant, spring green, but a dull and grayish color that bore the cast of something dying with the freeze of winter.

Yet the heat was awesome. To Brin, the feel of the Maelmord was like a day in hottest summer when the ground had cracked, the grass browned, and the surface water dissipated to dust. The terrible stench of the sewers had its life-source here, rising from the earth and the jungle foliage in sickening waves, hanging in the still afternoon air, and gathering like fouled soup in the bowl of the mountain stone. At first, it was almost unbearable, even with Cogline's salve still thick within her nostrils. But after a time, it grew less noticeable as her sense of smell was mercifully dulled. So, too, it was with the heat as her body temperature adjusted. Heat and stench lost the edge of their unpleasantness, and there was only the stark and blasted look of the pit that could not be blocked away.

There was the hissing, too, and there was the rise and fall of the foliage, as if it were a body breathing. There was the certainty that the whole of the valley was a thing alive, a solitary being for all of its disparate parts that could act and think and feel. And while it had no eyes, still the Valegirl could feel it looking at her, watching and waiting.

But she kept on. There could be no thought of turning back. It had been a long and arduous journey that had brought her to this place and time, and much had been sacrificed. Lives had been lost and the character of those saved was forever changed. She, herself, was no longer the girl she had been, for the magic had made her over into something new and terrible. She winced at the admission she could now freely make. She was changed, and the magic had wrought it. She shook her head. Well, perhaps it was not change, after all, that she had experienced, but merely insight. Perhaps learning of the frightening extent of the wishsong's power had but shown her what had always been there and she was who she had always been and had not changed at all. Perhaps it was simply that now she understood.

The musings distracted her only slightly from the Maelmord's bulk as it drew close now with the final twist in the stone stairway of the Croagh, marking the end of her descent. She slowed, staring fixedly downward into the mass of the jungle beneath, seeing the twisted maze of trunks, limbs, and vines shrouded in trailers of mist and the rise and fall of the life that rooted there, its breath hissing in steady cadence. Within the ravaged breast of the pit, no other life gave evidence of its existence.

Yet somewhere within that tangle, the Ildatch lay hidden.

How was she to find it?

She stood upon the Croagh two dozen steps from its lower end, with the Maelmord swelling softly all about her. She looked out across it in confusion, fighting down the repulsion and fear that coursed through her and trying desperately to stay calm. She must use the wishsong now, she knew, as she had been told by Allanon that she could. The trees, brush, and vines of this jungle were like those trees twisted close about each other within the forests above the Rainbow Lake. The wishsong could be used to make them part. A pathway could be made.

But where should that pathway lead?

She hesitated. Something within her advised caution, whispering that the wishsong's power was to be used a different way this time—that strength alone would not be enough. The Maelmord was too large, too overpowering to be mastered in that way. Guile and cleverness must be employed. This thing was but a creation of the same magic that she wielded, all of it descended through the ages from the world of faerie, from a time when magic was the only power . . .

She cut short the thought, her eyes lifting toward the sky once again. The sunlight warmed her face in a way far different from that of the heat of the pit. There was life in its warmth and brightness. It called to her with such strength of purpose that, for an instant, she felt an inexplicable and frantic need to run back.

She jerked her eyes away, forcing her gaze to settle again upon the steamy depths of the jungle. Still she hesitated in her descent. The way was not yet clear to her, not yet certain. She could not proceed blindly into the maw of this thing. She must first discover where it was that she was going and where it was that the Ildatch lay concealed. Her dusky face tightened. She must understand the thing. She must look within it . . .

The words of the Grimpond mocked her, a whisper that teased slyly from the deep recesses of her memory: Look within, Brin of Shannara. Do you see?

And suddenly, startlingly, she saw everything. It had been told to her at the Valley of Shale, but she had not understood. Savior and destroyer, Bremen had named her, risen from the Hadeshorn to summon Allanon. Savior and destroyer.

She leaned weakly against the stone railing as the impact of it struck her. It was not within the Maelmord that she must look to find her answers—not within the pit.

It was within herself!

She straightened then, her dark face savage with the certainty of what she knew. How easy it was going to be for her to pass into the Maelmord and to find what she sought! There was no need for her to force a path within this being that kept watch over the Ildatch—no need, even, to search the Ildatch out. There would be no struggle here, no confrontation of magics.

There would instead be a joining!

She descended the final steps of the Croagh until she stood at last at its end. The roof of the jungle above her seemed to close suddenly about, shutting away the sunlight, leaving her wrapped in shadows, heat, and the unbearable stench. But it no longer bothered her to be here. She knew what it was that she had to do, and nothing else mattered.

Gently, she sang. The wishsong rolled forth, low, hard, and eager. The music flooded the massive tangle of limbs, vines, rampant brush. It stroked and soothed with a deft touch, then wrapped about and cloaked with warm reassurance. Accept me, Maelmord, it whispered. Accept me into you, for I am like you. For us, there is no difference of kind. We are the same, our magics joined. We are the same!

The words that whispered in the music should have horrified her, but they were strangely pleasing. Where once the wishsong had seemed but a marvelous toy with which she might amuse herself—a toy to play with color and shape and sound—the vastness of its use had at last revealed itself to her. It could be anything. Even here, where evil lay strongest, she could belong. The Maelmord was created to prevent anything from entering that was not in harmony with it. Even the strength inherent in the wishsong's magic could not overcome the basic purpose of its existence. But so versatile was the magic that it could forsake strength for cunning and make Brin Ohmsford appear kindred to whatever might stand against her. She could be in harmony with the life in this pit—and she could do so for as long as it might take to reach what it was she sought.

Exhilaration soared through her as she sang to the Maelmord and felt it respond. She was crying, so intense was the feeling that bound her to the music. The jungle swayed in response about her, its limbs bending and its vines and scrub curling like snakes. The music she sang whispered of the death and horror that gave life to the valley. She played a game with it, immersed within her self-creation so that she could be thought nothing less than what she wished to appear.

She drifted deep into herself, bound up in the song she sang. Allanon and the journey that had brought her were forgotten, as were Rone, Kimber, Cogline, and Whisper. Barely remembered was the task she had come to complete—to find and destroy the Ildatch. The release of the magic brought again the strange and frightening sense of glee. She could feel her control slipping away, just as had happened when she had used the wishsong against that Spider Gnome on Toffer Ridge and the black things in the sewers. She could feel the threads of herself unraveling. But she must risk it, she knew. It was necessary.

The breathing of the Maelmord rose and fell more quickly now and the hissing was more intense. It wanted her, had need for her. It found in her a vibrant piece of itself, the heart of the body that lay rooted there, missing for so long, but now returned. Come to me, it hissed. Come to me!

Her face alive with excitement and need, Brin passed from the Croagh into the jungle beyond.

"There has got to be an end to these sewers, for cat's sake!" Rone was insisting to Kimber and Cogline as he stepped clear of the tunnel passage into the cavern beyond. It seemed to him in his frustration that they had been stumbling about in the sewers of Graymark forever.

"There doesn't have to be anything of the sort!" Cogline snapped back, as disagreeable as ever.

But the highlander barely heard, his attention focused instead on the cavern into which they had passed. It was a massive chamber, its roof cracked so that hazy sunlight flooded downward in bright streamers and its floor split down the center by a monstrous chasm. Wordlessly, Rone hurried forward along the chasm's edge, his eyes sweeping toward the stone bridge that spanned it. Beyond the bridge, the cavern stretched away to a high, arched alcove of polished stone, scrolled in some ancient markings and opening into daylight and the green of a misted valley.

The Maelmord, he thought at once.

And that's where Brin will be.

He bounded onto the bridge and crossed, the old man and the girl hurrying after. He was moving toward the alcove when Kimber's sharp cry brought him about.

"Highlander, come look!"

He turned and walked quickly back. She waited for him at the center of the bridge, then pointed wordlessly as he came up. A great section of iron chain forming the bridge railing had snapped and broken. At her feet, streaks of blood lay drying on the stone.

The girl knelt and touched the blood with her fingers. "Not very old," she said softly. "Not more than an hour."

He stared at her in stricken silence, and the same unspoken thought passed between them. His hand came up quickly, as if to ward it off. "No, it can't be hers . . ."

Then a scream rent the air, shrill and terrifying—the scream of an animal filled with rage and fear. It shattered the stillness and their thoughts and left them frozen. It came from beyond the alcove.

"Whisper!" Kimber cried.

Rone whirled. Brin!

He sprang from the bridge to the cavern floor and raced for the alcove's passageway, both hands reaching back across his shoulder for the great broadsword strapped there. He was quick, but Kimber was even quicker. She went past him like a frightened animal, darting from the shadows of the cavern to the alcove and the light beyond. Trailing, Cogline called out in a furious attempt to slow them both, his voice high and shrill with desperation, but his crooked legs too slow to keep up.

Then they were through the alcove and into the light, with Kimber a dozen yards in front of Rone. There was Whisper, locked in battle with a pair of faceless black things on a narrow rock shelf before them, a blur of motion and darkness. Beyond, on a stone stairway that wound downward from the cliffs to the ledge and the valley below—on a stairway that Rone knew at once to be the Croagh—one of the Mord Wraiths stood watching.

At the approach of the girl and the highlander, the Mord Wraith turned.

"Kimber, look out!" Rone howled in warning.

But the girl was already springing to Whisper's aid, long knives appearing in both hands. The Wraith pointed toward the girl and red fire exploded from its fingers. The fire lanced past the girl, missing her somehow, and fragments of rock flew into the air as it struck. Rone sprang forward with a cry, the ebony blade of the Sword of Leah held before him. The Wraith turned toward him instantly, and the fire burst forth a second time. It hammered at the highlander, caught on the blade of the sword, and the whole of the air about him turned bright with flame. The force of the blow lifted him clear of the ground and threw him back.

Then Cogline appeared from out of the caverns, old, bent, and fierce as he screamed at the Wraith in challenge. A little bit of flesh, bone, and cloth, he skittered toward the black-robed form. The walker swung about, pointing. But the old man's sticklike arm whipped forward, and a dark object flew from his hand, hurtling into the Wraith's crimson fire. A tremendous explosion rocked the whole of the mountainside. Flames and smoke geysered skyward from the stem of the Croagh, and bits of shattered rock flew everywhere.

For an instant everything disappeared in smoke and silt. Frantic, Rone scrambled back to his feet.

"Taste a bit of my magic, you worm food!" Cogline was howling in glee. "See what you can do against that!"

He darted past Rone before the highlander could stop him, dancing about in maddened delight, his sticklike form disappearing into the smoke. Whisper's sudden snarl lifted from somewhere ahead, then Kimber's sharp cry. Rone swore in fury and leaped forward. Crazy old man!

Directly before him, red fire erupted from the haze. Cogline's thin form flew sideways as if it were a doll flung by an angry child. The highlander set his teeth and hurtled toward the source of the fire. Almost at once, he came up against the Wraith, its black-cloaked form tattered and bent. The Sword of Leah pierced into a burst of red fire, shattering it apart. The Wraith disappeared. Something moved behind him, and the highlander swung about. But it was Whisper who lunged past through a trailer of smoke, the first of the black things clinging to him, the second borne before him in his teeth. Swiftly, Rone struck, the sword cleaving through the creature that hung upon the moor cat's back and stripping it from him.

"Kimber!" he screamed.

Red fire exploded close to him, but he caught it again on the sword. A cloaked form appeared momentarily through the smoke, and he lunged at it. This time the Wraith was not quick enough. Backed against the stone stairway of the Croagh, it tried to slip left, with fire bursting from its fingers. Rone was on it at once. The Sword of Leah came down, and the Wraith exploded into a pile of ash.

Everything went still then, save for the low coughing sound Whisper made as he padded ghostlike through the haze toward Rone. Slowly the smoke drifted away and the whole of the ledge and the Croagh became visible once more. The ledge was littered with broken rock, and an entire section of the Croagh where it joined to the ledge—where the Mord Wraith had been standing when Cogline had challenged it—was gone.

Rone glanced quickly about. The Wraith and the black things were gone as well. He wasn't sure what had happened to them—whether they had been destroyed or merely driven off—but they were nowhere to be seen.

"Rone."

He whirled at the sound of Kimber's voice. She appeared from the far side of the ledge, looking small and bedraggled, limping slightly as she came. Anger and relief flooded through him. "Kimber, why in the name of all that's right and sensible did you . . . ?"

"Because Whisper would have done the same for me. Where is grandfather?"

Rone clamped his mouth shut on the rest of what he would have said to her. Together, they scanned the littered rock shelf. They saw him finally, half buried in a pile of rubble by the cliff side, as blackened as the ash left by the fires of their battle with the Wraith. They hurried to him and lifted him clear. His face and arms were burned, his hair singed, and he was covered with soot. Gently, Kimber cradled the old man's head. His eyes were closed and he did not appear to be breathing.

"Grandfather?" the girl whispered, her hand on his cheek.

"Who's that?" the old man cried abruptly, startling both the girl and the highlander. Arms and legs began to thrash. "Get out of my house, trespassers! Get out of my home!"

Then his eyes blinked and opened. "Girl?" he muttered weakly. "What happened to the black things?"

"Gone, grandfather." She smiled, relief in her dark eyes. "Are you all right?"

"All right?" He looked dazed, but nodded resolutely, his voice becoming stiff with indignation. "Of course I'm all right! Just got a bit ahead of myself, that's all! Help me up!"

Rone took a deep breath. Lucky to be alive is what you are, old man, you and the girl, he thought grimly.

With Kimber's aid he pulled Cogline back to his feet and let him test his weight alone. The old man looked like something dredged up from an ash pit, but he seemed uninjured. The girl hugged him warmly and began to brush him off.

"You must be more careful, grandfather," she admonished. "You are not as quick as you used to be. The walkers will have you if you try to run past them again the way you did here."

Rone shook his head in disbelief. Who should be scolding whom— the girl the old man or the old man the girl? What had Brin and he been thinking anyway when they . . .

He caught himself. Brin. He had forgotten about Brin. He glanced toward the Croagh. If the Valegirl had gotten this far, she had almost certainly gone down into the Maelmord. And that was where he must go as well.

He turned from Kimber and her grandfather and hurried across the rock shelf to where it joined with the steps of the Croagh. He was still gripping the Sword of Leah firmly. How much time had he lost here? He had to catch Brin before she got too far ahead into whatever it was that waited in the valley below . . .

Abruptly, he slowed and stopped. Whisper stood directly in his path, blocking the stairway down. The moor cat stared at him momentarily, then sat back on his haunches and blinked.

"Get out of the way!" Rone snapped.

The cat did not move. The highlander hesitated, then started forward impatiently. Whisper's muzzle drew back slightly, and a low growl rumbled in his throat.

Rone stopped at once and looked back angrily at Kimber. "Get your cat out of my way, Kimber. I'm going down."

The girl called softly to the moor cat, but Whisper stayed where he was. Puzzled, she came forward and bent close to him, talking in a low, calm voice, rubbing the massive head about the ears and neck. The cat nuzzled her back and made a soft purring sound, but did not move. Finally, the girl stepped back.

"Brin is well," she informed him with a brief smile. "She has gone down into the pit."

Rone nodded with relief. "Then I've got to go after her."

But the girl shook her head. "You must remain here, highlander."

Rone stared. "Remain here? I can't do that! Brin is all alone down there! I'm going after her!"

But again the girl shook her head. "You cannot. She doesn't want you doing that. She has used the wishsong to prevent it. She has made Whisper her sentry. No one may pass—not even me."

"But he's your cat! Make him move! Tell him that he has to move! The magic isn't that strong, is it?"

Her pixie face looked up at him calmly. "It is more than the magic, Rone. Whisper's instincts tell him that Brin is right about this. The magic does not hold him; his reason does. He knows that whatever danger waits in the valley is too great. He will not let you pass."

The highlander continued to stare at the girl, anger and disbelief flooding his face. His gaze shifted to the giant cat and back again.

What was he supposed to do now?

Euphoria engulfed Brin, sweeping over her in a warm rush, flooding through her as if it were her life's blood. She felt it carry her down within herself like a tiny leaf borne on the waters of some great river. Sight, sound, and smell meshed and ran in a dazzling mix of wild imaginings, some of beauty and light, some of darkest misshape, all in the ebb and flow of her mind's eye. Nothing was as it had been, but new and exotic and alive with wonder. It was a journey of self-discovery that transcended thought and feeling and was its own reason for being.

She sang, the music of the wishsong the food and drink that fed her, sustained her, and gave her life.

She was deep within the Maelmord now, far from the stairway of the Croagh and the world she had left behind. It was another world entirely here. As she worked to make herself one with it, it reached out to her and drew her in. Stench, heat, and the rot of living things wrapped about her and found in her their child. Gnarled limbs, vines twisted and mottled, and great stalks of brush and weed stroked her body as she slipped past, feeding on the vibrancy of the music, finding in it an elixir that gave back life. From a great distance away, Brin felt their caress and smiled in response.

It was as if she had ceased to exist. Some tiny part of her knew that she should have been horrified by the things that wound about her and rubbed so lovingly against her. But she was given over to the music of the wishsong now, and she was no longer the one she had been. All of the feelings and reasonings that had been hers, that had made her who she was, were masked away by the dark magic, and she was become a thing like that into which she journeyed. She was a kindred spirit, wandered back from some distant place, the evil within her as strong as the evil she found waiting. She had become as dark as the Maelmord and the life that had been spawned there. She was one with it. She belonged.

A tiny part of her understood that Brin Ohmsford had ceased to exist, made over by the magic of the wishsong. It understood that she had let herself become this other thing—a thing so repulsive that she could not have stood it otherwise—and that she would not come back to herself un-til she had found her way through to the heart of the evil enfolding her. The euphoria, the exhilaration brought on by the frightening power of the wishsong, threatened to steal her away from herself completely, to strip her of her sanity and make her forever the thing she pretended to be. All the strange and marvelous imaginings were but trappings of a madness that would destroy her. All that remained of the one she once had been was that small bit of self that she still kept wrapped carefully within. All else had become the child of the Maelmord.

The wall of the jungle passed away and came about again, and nothing of it changed. Shadows wrapped close about, as soft as black velvet and as silent as death. The whole of the sky stayed screened away, and only the half-light of night's coming penetrated beyond the gloom. All the while that she walked in this maze of darkness and stifling heat, the hissing of the Maelmord's breath lifted from the earth, and the limbs, trunks, stalks, and vines swayed and writhed with the motion. Save for the hissing, there was only silence—intense and expectant. There was no sign of other life—no sign of the walkers, of the dark things that served them, or of the Ildatch that had given them all life.

She went on, driven by that spark of memory she harbored deep within herself. Find the Ildatch, it whispered in its small, empty voice. Find the book of the dark magic. Time fragmented and slipped away until it no longer had meaning. Had she been here an hour? Or more? There was a strange sense of having been here for a very long time, almost as if she had been here forever.

Far distant, almost lost to her in the vast tangle of the jungle, some-thing tumbled from the cliffs above and fell into the pit. She could sense its fall and hear its scream as the Maelmord closed quickly about it, squeezing, crushing, and consuming until the thing was no more. She savored its death, tasted its blood as it was devoured. When it was gone, she longed for more.

Then whispered warnings brushed at her. From a dimly remembered past she saw Allanon once more. Tall and bent, his black hair gone gray, his lean face lined with age, he reached for her across a chasm she could not bridge, and his words were like sprinkled drops of rain upon a window closed before her. Beware. The wishsong is power like nothing I have ever seen. Use it with caution. She heard the words, saw them spatter on the glass and found herself laughing at the way they fell. The figure of the Druid receded and was gone. Dead, now, she reminded herself in surprise. Gone from the Four Lands forever.

She called him back again, as if his reappearance would serve to re-mind her of something that she had somehow forgotten. He came, sweep-ing out of the mists, striding across the chasm that had separated them. His strong hands came down gently to rest upon her shoulders. Wisdom and determination reflected in his eyes, and there was a sense of his never having truly left, but his always having been there. This is not a game you play, he whispered. Never that! Beware! And she shook her head. I am savior and destroyer, she whispered back. But who am I? Tell me now! Tell me . . .

A ripple in the fabric of her consciousness swept him away, a ghost, and suddenly she was back within the Maelmord. There was a rumbling of uneasiness within the pit, a tone of dissatisfaction in its hiss. It had sensed a momentary change in her and was disturbed. She reverted instantly to the thing she had created. The wishsong rose and swept into the jungle, soothing it, lulling it once again. The uneasiness and dissatisfaction faded.

She slipped ahead again into the nothingness, letting the Maelmord swallow her up. There was a deepening of shadows and a fading of the light. The breathing of the pit seemed to grow heavier. The sense of kinship that the wishsong created between them tightened and left her breathless with anticipation. She was close now—close to what she sought. The feel of it speared through her like a sudden rush of blood, and she sang with renewed intensity. The magic of the wishsong lifted through the gloom, and the Maelmord shuddered in response.

Then the wall of the jungle fell away, and she stood within a massive, shadowed clearing, wrapped close about by trees, brush, and vines. A tower stood at the center of the clearing, ancient and crumbling, lost in the gloom. Walls of stone rose upward toward the forest roof, forming and reforming in a series of spiraling turrets and notched parapets, as stripped and barren in their look as bleached bones. Nowhere did the foliage of the jungle grow upon the tower. As if its touch meant death, the jungle had passed it by.

Brin stopped, the music of the wishsong lowering to a whisper of expectancy as she stared at the tower.

Here! The heart of the evil is here. The Ildatch!

Drawing close the layers of magic that cloaked her, she went to meet it.

43

Wooden doors, weathered and cracked with age, stood ajar at the tower's dark entry, sagging on hinges broken and rusted with disuse. Wrapped in the music of her song, the Valegirl passed through. The gloom lay thick within, yet there was light enough by which she might see, a dim and misted glimmer that slipped in thin streamers through cracks and splits in the tower's crumbling walls. Dust carpeted the stone flooring, forming a blanket of fine silt that rose in clouds as the girl's boots pressed down upon it. It was cool here, the heat and the stench of the jungle somehow locked without.

Brin slowed. A hallway wound ahead into shadow. She turned briefly, a warning tug from deep within her bringing her about to stare guardedly back into the mass of the jungle that walled this tower away.

She went on. The power of the magic stirred through her in a flush of sudden heat, and she seemed to float. She passed down the hallway, following its bends and twists, barely aware of the dust as it rose vaporlike from beneath her feet. Once she thought to wonder how it was that no other footprints save hers marked the corridor she followed when surely the Mord Wraiths, too, had passed this way, but the matter faded quickly from her mind.

Stairs rose before her and she began to climb—a slow, endless climb into the center of the tower. Whispers seemed to call out to her, voices that had no source and no identity, but were born of the very air she breathed. All about her, the whispers called. Shadows and half-light mixed and blended. It seemed as if she were soaking into the stone of the tower itself, slipping ghostlike through its chambers, spreading out to become one with it, as she had become one with the Maelmord. She felt it happen, bit by bit, a welcome drawing in of her body. The magic of the song made it happen, still reaching out to the evil that lay hidden there, insinuating her within as if she were truly one with it . . .

Then the stairway ended and she stood on the threshold of a cavernous, domed rotunda that lay gray, shadowed, and empty. Almost of its own volition, the music of the wishsong faded to a whisper, and the voices in the air about her went still.

She entered the room, barely conscious of the movement of her body, still seeming to float as she passed. Shadows crept back from her, and her eyes adjusted to the light. The chamber was not empty, as she had first thought. There, almost lost in the gloom, was a dais; on the dais was an altar. She came forward a step. Something rested on the altar, huge, squarish, and shrouded in a darkness that seemed to emanate from within. She came forward another step. A fierce excitement flooded through her.

It was the Ildatch!

She knew it instantly, before she was certain what it was that she was seeing. This was the Ildatch, the heart of evil. The power of the wishsong filled her and drove through her body with white-hot intensity.

She crossed the room through the raging of her thoughts, twisting down into herself like a coiled snake. The music of the wishsong became a venomous hiss. The room seemed to draw away from her, the walls receding back into shadow until there was nothing in all the world but the book. She climbed the steps of the dais and strode to where it lay closed upon the altar. It was old and worn, its bindings of copper tarnished to a greenish black and its leather covers cracked and soiled—a huge and monstrous tome that looked as if it might have seen the passing of all the ages of mankind that had ever been.

She hovered over it a moment, staring down expectantly, savoring the deep satisfaction she felt at having the book finally within her grasp.

Then she reached down and her hands closed about it.

—Dark child—

The voice whispered softly within her mind, and her fingers froze upon the tarnished bindings.

—Dark child—

The wishsong died into a whisper and was gone. Her throat constricted and sealed the music away, almost before she knew what it was that she had done. She stood in silence before the altar, hands still clasped tightly upon the book. Echoes of the voice lingered fitfully within her mind, tendrils that reached out and bound her so that she could not move.

—I have been waiting for you, dark child. I have been waiting since first you came into being, a baby from your mother's womb, Elven magic's child. Always we have been joined, you and I, by bonds stronger than blood ties, stronger than flesh. Many times we have touched spirit to spirit, and though I never knew you nor knew your way, I knew always that one day you would come—

The voice was flat and toneless, belonging neither to man nor woman, but to something that was both, stripped of all emotion and all feeling, so that there was an emptiness to its whisper that was devoid of life. Brin listened to that voice and went cold to the bone. Deep within, the self that she still sheltered and kept hidden drew back in terror.

—Dark child—

She scanned the shadows of the chamber about her rapidly. Where was the speaker who called to her? What thing was it that held her so? Her eyes shifted in horror to the ancient tome she held. Her fingers were white with the grip they kept, and a burning spread from the leathered bindings.

—I am, dark child. Even as you. I have life. It has always been so. There have always been those who would give me life. There have always been those who would give me theirs—

Brin's mouth opened, but no sound came forth. The burning sensation spread from her hands into her arms and began to climb.

—Know me. I am the Ildatch, the book of the dark magic, born of the age of faerie. I am older than the Elves—as old as the King of the Silver River, as ancient as the Word. Those who created me, those who gave me form, have long since passed from the land with the coming of the worlds of faerie and Man. Once I was but a part of the Word, hidden from sight and spoken only in darkness. I was but a gathering of secrets. Then the gathering took form, written and studied by those who would know my power. There have always been those who would know my power. Through all the ages, I have been there for them and have given my secrets to those who wished them shared. I have made creatures of magic and given power. But never has there been one such as you—

The words echoed in whispers filled with anticipation and promise, and the Valegirl felt them spin like blown leaves through her mind. The burning was all through her now, a tingling like the rush of heat from a furnace as its door is thrown open.

—There have been many before you. Of the Druids were born the Warlock Lord and the Bearers of the Skull. They found in me the secrets that they sought and became what they would. But I was the power. Of men outcast of the races were born the Mord Wraiths, seeds already sown. But again, I was the power. I am always the power. Each time, there is supreme vision of what must be with the world and with her creatures. Each time, that vision is given shape by the minds of those who would use the power locked within my pages. Each time, the vision proves inadequate and the shaper fails. Dark child, see now a glimpse of what it is that I can offer—

As if of their own volition, Brin's hands carefully opened the book of the Ildatch, and its parchment leaves began to turn. Words whispered from a text in an alien script and language older than man, lifting from script to voice, soft and secretive. The Valegirl's mind opened to them, and comprehension of the text came instantly to her. A touch here, a touch there, the secrets of power were revealed to her, dark and terrible.

Then, as quickly as the revelations had come, they were gone again, lingering on in teasing memories. The pages of the book slipped back again, and the bindings closed. Her hands, still fastened on the massive tome, began to shake.

—Only a whisper of what I am have I shown you. Power, dark child. Power that would dwarf that mastered by the Druid Brona and those who followed him. Power that would render meaningless that of the Mord Wraiths who come to me now. Feel that power rush through you. Feel its touch—

The burning flooded through her. She felt herself expand and grow with its rush.

—For a thousand years, I have been used in ways that would dictate the fate of you and yours. For a thousand years, the enemies of your family have called upon my power and sought to destroy what you would keep. All that has brought you to this place and time has been because of me. I am the maker of what you are; I am the shaper of your life. There is reason in all that happens, dark child, and there is reason in this. Do you sense what that reason is? Look within—

A whisper of warning called suddenly to her, and she seemed to remember a tall, black-robed figure with graying hair and piercing eyes speaking to her of that which would deceive and corrupt. She struggled momentarily with the memory, but no name would come and the vision was obscured by the burning that filled her and the lingering echo of the words of the Ildatch.

—Do you not see yourself? Do you not see what you are? Look within—

The voice was cold, flat, and emotionless still, yet there was an insistence to it that wrenched her thoughts away. Her vision blurred, and she seemed to see from without the thing that she had become through the magic of the wishsong.

We are as one, dark child, just as you have wished. There was never any need for the Elven magic, for you are what you are and always have been. That is why we are joined. There are ties born of the magics that make us what we are, for we are no more than the magics that we harbor—you within your body of flesh and blood, I within mine of parchment and ink. We are lives joined, and what has gone before has brought us to now. It is for this that I have waited all these years—

Lies! The word flashed through Brin's mind and was lost. Her thoughts spun in confusion, and her reason scattered. Her hands still gripped the Ildatch as if it held her life within, and she found the words spoken by its disembodied voice oddly persuasive. There were indeed ties that bound them; there was a joining. She was like the Ildatch, a part of it, kindred to it.

She called out the name of the Druid in her mind, struggling to find the memory she had now lost. The burning rose in a fierce rush to carry it away, and again the voice spoke.

—All these years I have waited for you, dark child. From time out of time, you have come to me, and now I belong to you. See what must be done with me. Whisper it back to me—

The words came together in her mind, dark against the red haze of her vision. She sought to scream, but the sound constricted in her throat.

—Whisper what must be done with me—

No! No!

—Whisper what must be done with me—

Tears rose to her eyes and trickled slowly down her cheeks.

I must use you, she answered.

Rone stalked from the Croagh in fury, wheeled, and came back again. Both hands gripped the ebony blade of his sword until the knuckles were white.

"Enough is enough—get that cat out of my way, Kimber!" he ordered, coming up next to her and slowing as Whisper's massive head swung about to face him.

But again the girl shook her head. "I cannot do that, Rone. He uses his own judgment in this."

"I don't care a whit about his judgment!" Rone exploded. "He's only an animal and he can't make a decision like this! I'm going past him whether he likes it or not! I'm not leaving Brin down in that pit alone!"

Sword lifting, he started for Whisper, but in that instant a deep shudder rippled through the mountain, rising up from the dark jungle of the Maelmord. So strong was the tremor that it staggered the highlander and the girl, causing them to stumble back in surprise. Shaken, they regained their balance and hurried to the edge of the cliffs.

"What's happened down there?" Rone whispered worriedly. "What's happened, Kimber?"

"Walkers, I'd guess." Cogline spit from behind him. "Called up the dark magic to use against the girl, maybe."

"Grandfather!" Kimber was angry this time.

Rone wheeled in rage. "Old man, if anything has happened to Brin because I've been held up here by that cat . . ."

Then he went suddenly still. A line of shadows appeared on the stairway of the Croagh, stooped and shrouded in the fading half-light of the late afternoon. They came one after another, descending from Graymarks' leaden walls, winding their way downward toward the ledge where Rone and his companions waited.

"Mord Wraiths!" the highlander breathed softly.

Already Whisper was turning, wheeling into a crouch as he prepared to defend against them. Cogline's sudden intake of breath hissed sharply through the silence.

Rone stared upward wordlessly as the line of dark forms lengthened and advanced. There were too many.

"Get behind me, Kimber," he told her gently.

Then he brought up the sword.

I must use you . . . use you . . . use you.

The words repeated over and over in Brin's mind, rising in a litany of conviction that threatened to inundate all reason. Yet some tiny semblance of logic remained, screaming at her through the words of the chant.

It is the dark magic, Valegirl! It is the evil that you have come into this place to destroy!

But the touch of the book against the skin of her hands and the burning it brought to her body held her bound so that nothing else could hold sway. Again the voice came to her, wrapping close about.

—What am I but a gathering of wisdom's lessons culled through the ages and bound for the usage of mortal beings? I am neither good nor evil, but simply a thing that is. Learning, recorded and bound—there for any who might seek to know. I take what is given me of the lives of those who work my spells and I am but a reflection of them. Think, dark child. Who have been the ones who would use me? What purposes have they sought to serve? You are not as they—

Brin braced herself against the altar, the book clasped in her hands. Don't listen! Don't listen!

—For a thousand years and longer, your enemies have held me. Now you stand in their place, given the chance to use me as no other has tried. You hold the power that is mine. You hold the secrets that so many have wrongly used. Think what you might do with that power, dark child. All of life and death can be reshaped by what I am. Wishsong joined to written word, magic to magic—how wondrous it would be. You can feel how wondrous it would be if you would but try—

But there was no need to try. She had felt it before in the magic of the wishsong. Power! She had been swept away by it, and she had reveled in its sweetness. When it wrapped about her, she rose far above all the world and all of the creatures in it and she could gather them in or sweep them away as she might choose. How much more, then, could she do—could she feel—if she had also the power of this book?

—All that is would be yours. All. Be what you would and make the world as you know it should be. You could so do much, and it would be as it should with you—not as with those who came before. You have the strength which they lacked. You are born of the Elven magic. Use me, dark child. Find the limits of your own magic and of mine. Join with me. It is for this that I have waited and that you have come. It is what has always been intended for us. Always—

Brin's head shook slowly from side to side. I came to destroy this, came to make an end . . . Within, everything seemed to be breaking apart, shattering like glass fallen to stone. Rushes of blinding heat burned through her, and she felt as if she were a thing apart from the body that sought to hold her.

—I have knowledge to offer that I would give. I have insight that surpasses anything ever dreamed by mortal creatures. It can make you anything you wish. All of life can be made over as it should be, as you see that it should. Destroy me, and all I have is needlessly lost. Destroy me, and nothing of what might come to pass can ever do so. Keep what is good, dark child, and make it your own—

Allanon, Allanon . . .

But the voice cut short her soundless cry.

—See, dark child. What you truly would destroy stands behind you. Turn now and look. Turn and see—

She whirled. A gathering of robed walkers slipped from the shadows like ghosts, tall, black, and forbidding. They filed into the rotunda, hesitating as they caught sight of Brin holding in her hands the book of dark magic. The voice of the Ildatch whispered again.

—The wishsong, dark child. Use the magic. Destroy them. Destroy them—

She acted almost without thinking. Clasping the Ildatch to her protectively, she called forth the power of her magic. It came swiftly, loosed within her like the waters of a flood. She cried out, and the wishsong shattered the tower's dark silence. It went through the gloom of the rotunda, almost a tangible thing. It caught the walkers in a burst of sound, and they simply ceased to exist. Not even ash remained of what they had been.

Brin staggered back against the altar, and within her body the magic of the wishsong mixed with the magic of the book.

—Feel it, dark child. Feel the power that is yours. It fills you, and I am part of it. How easily your enemies must fall before you when that power is called forth. Can you question longer what must be? Think no more that anything different could ever be. Think no more that we are not as one. Take me and use me. Destroy the Wraiths and the black things that would stand against you. Make me yours. Give me life—

Still that part of her locked deep within fought to resist the voice, but her body was no longer her own. It belonged now to the magic, and she was trapped within its shell. She rose through herself, a new being, and that tiny bit of self that still saw the truth was left behind. She expanded until it seemed as if she filled the tiny chamber. There was so little room for her here! She must have the space that waited without!

A long, anguished groan broke from her lips, and she stretched forth her arms, the book of the Ildatch held high.

—Use me. Use me—

Within her, the power began to build.

44

The steps of the Croagh sped away beneath Jair's feet as he hastened after Garet Jax and Slanter, and it seemed to him as he climbed that each step must surely be his last. The muscles knotted and cramped within his body, and pain from his wound lanced through him, wearing away at his already failing strength. He was gasping for breath, his lungs aching, and his sun-browned face streaked with sweat.

But somehow he kept pace. There was never any question of doing anything else.

His eyes swept upward along the Croagh as he ran, concentrating on the weave of stairs and railing, following the path of the roughened stone. He was conscious of the cliffs and fortress walls below him, distant now and fading further, and of Graymark and the Ravenshorn. He was conscious, too, of the valley all about, encased in mist and the half-light of a dusk that rapidly approached. Brief images slipped past the corners of his vision and were quickly forgotten, for none of that mattered now. Nothing mattered but the climb and what waited at its end.

Heaven's Well.

And Brin. He would find her again in the waters of the well. He would discover what had become of her, and he would learn what it was that he must do to help her. The King of the Silver River had promised him that he would find a way to give Brin back to herself.

His boot slid out from under him suddenly as he stepped on a patch of crumbling stone and he fell forward, his hands scraping as he caught himself. Quickly he pushed back up again and hurried on, heedless of the damage.

Ahead, the other two ran effortlessly on—Garet Jax and Slanter, the last of the little company that had come north from Culhaven. Bitterness and anger flooded through the Valeman. Flashes of light danced before his eyes as he fought for breath momentarily, exhaustion sweeping through him. But they were almost at their journey's end.

The stone spiral of the Croagh swung suddenly right, and the wall of the peak toward which they climbed rose close before them, rugged and stark against the graying sky. Ahead, the stairway ascended to the dark mouth of a cavern that opened back into the heart of the mountain. Less than two dozen steps remained.

Garet Jax motioned for them to wait, then soundlessly climbed the last few stairs to the summit of the Croagh and stepped out onto the ledge. He stood there a moment, his black form framed against the afternoon sky, lean and shadowy. He was like something inhuman, the thought flashed briefly through Jair's mind, like something that wasn't real.

The Weapons Master turned, gray eyes fixing on him. One hand beckoned.

"Hurry, boy," Slanter muttered.

They scrambled up the remaining steps of the Croagh and stood beside Garet Jax. The cavern loomed before them, a monstrous chamber split by dozens of crevices that let in the light from without in dim, hazy streamers. Close about, the shadows gathered, and within their blackness nothing moved.

"Can't see anything from here," Slanter grumbled. He started forward, but instantly Garet Jax pulled him back.

"Wait, Gnome," he said. "There's something there . . . something that waits . . ."

His voice trailed away softly. A stillness settled down about them, deep and oppressive. Even the wind that stirred the mists of the valley seemed to die suddenly away. Jair caught his breath and held it. There was indeed something there—waiting. He could feel its presence.

"Garet . . ." he began softly.

"Shhhhh."

Then a shadow detached itself from the rocks within the cavern entrance, and Jair went cold to the bone. Silently, the shadow slipped through the gloom. It was nothing that any of them had ever seen. It was neither a Gnome nor a Wraith, but a powerfully built creature, almost man-shaped, with a thick ruff about its loins and great, hooked claws at its fingers and toes. Cruel yellow eyes fixed on them, and a scarred, bestial face split wide at its snout to reveal a mass of crooked teeth.

The thing came forward into the light and stopped. It was not black like the Wraiths. It was red.

"What is it?" Jair whispered, fighting to contain the sense of revulsion that swept through him.

The Jachyra gave a sudden cry—a howl that rang through the silence like hideous laughter.

"Valeman, it is the dream!" Garet Jax cried, a strange, wild look crossing his hard face. Slowly he lowered the blade of the sword until it touched the ledge rock. Then he turned to Jair. "Journey's end," he whispered.

Jair shook his head in confusion. "Garet, what . . . ?"

"The dream! The vision that I told you about that night in the rain when we first spoke of the King of the Silver River! The dream that brought me east with you, Valeman—this is it!"

"But the dream showed you a thing of fire . . ." Jair stammered.

"Fire, yes—that was how it appeared!" Garet Jax cut him short. He let his breath out slowly. "Until now, I thought that perhaps—in a way that I could not fathom—I had mistaken what I had seen. But in the dream, as I stood before the fire and the voice that told me what I must do died away, the fire cried out like a thing alive. It was a cry that was almost a laugh— the cry that this creature has given!' "

His gray eyes burned. "Valeman, this is the battle that I was promised!"

Before them, the Jachyra dropped into a crouch and began sidling forward from the cavern. Garet Jax brought the sword up at once.

"You mean to fight this thing?" Slanter was incredulous.

The other never even looked at him. "Keep back from me."

"This is a poor idea if ever there was one!" Slanter looked frightened. "You know nothing of this creature. If it is poisonous like the one that attacked the Borderman . . ."

"I am not the Borderman, Gnome." Garet Jax watched intently as the Jachyra approached. "I am the Weapons Master. And I have never lost a battle."

The cold eyes flickered briefly in their direction and then fixed once more on the Jachyra. Jair started toward him, but Slanter grabbed his shoulder roughly and pulled him back again. "No, you don't," the Gnome snapped. "He wants this fight—let him have it! Never lost a battle! Lost his mind, that's what he's lost!"

Garet Jax was gliding forward across the ledge to where the Jachyra had stopped. "Take the Valeman into the cavern and find the well, Gnome. Do it when the creature comes for me. Do what you have come here to do. Remember the pledge."

Jair was frantic. Helt, Foraker, Edain Elessedil—all lost in an effort to get him to the basin at Heaven's Well. And now Garet Jax as well?

But it was already too late. The Jachyra screamed once and launched itself at Garet Jax, a blur of motion as it shot across the ledge rock. It leaped up against the Weapons Master, claws ripping. But the black form slipped aside as if it were no more than the shadow it resembled. The sword blade cut into the attacker—once, twice—so quickly the eye could barely follow. The Jachyra howled and slipped free, circling away for another rush.

Garet Jax wheeled, his lean face fierce, gray eyes bright with excitement. "Go, Jair Ohmsford!" he cried. "When it comes for me again—go!"

Anger and frustration tore at the Valeman as Slanter pulled him away. He would not go!

"Boy, I'm through arguing with you!" Slanter cried in fury.

Again the Jachyra attacked, and again Garet Jax sidestepped the rush, his slender sword flicking. But he was a fraction of a second too slow this time. The claws of the Jachyra ripped through the sleeve of his tunic and into his arm. Jair cried out, pulling free of Slanter.

Slanter spun him about and hit him. The blow caught him squarely on the chin. There was an instant of blinding light, and then everything went black.

The last thing he remembered was falling.

When he came awake again, Slanter was kneeling next to him. The Gnome had pulled him upright and into a sitting position and was shaking him roughly.

"Get up, boy! Get on your feet!"

The words were hard and filled with anger, and Jair scrambled up quickly. They were deep within the cavern now. Slanter must have carried him in. What little light there was came from cracks in the broken rock of the cavern's roof.

The Gnome yanked him about. "What did you think you were doing back there?"

Jair was still dazed. "I couldn't let him . . ."

"Off to the rescue with your tricks, were you?" the other cut him short. "You don't understand anything—you know that? You really don't understand anything! What is it that you think we're doing here? You think we're playing some kind of game?" Slanter was livid. "There's choices been made long before this about living and dying, boy! You can't change that. You don't have the right! All of the others—all of them—died because that was the way it had to be! That was the way they wanted it! And why do you think that was?"

The Valeman shook his head. "I . . ."

"Because of you! They died because they believed in what it was that you had come here to do—every last one of them! Even I would have . . ." He caught himself and took a deep breath. "It would have done a lot of good if you'd gone dashing to the rescue back there and gotten yourself killed, now wouldn't it? A whole lot of sense that would have made!"

He wheeled Jair about and shoved him ahead into the cave. "Enough time's been wasted on teaching you things you ought to know already— time we don't have! I'm all that's left, and I'm not going to be much help to you if the walkers find us now. The others—they were the real protectors, looking out for me as much as for you!"

The Valeman slowed and half turned. "What's happened to Garet, Slanter?"

The other shook his head darkly. "He fights his promised battle—just as he wished." He pushed Jair again and hurried him on. "Find your well quickly, boy. Find it and do what you came here to do. Make all of this madness count for something!"

Jair ran with him and said nothing more, his face flushed with shame. He understood the Gnome's anger. Slanter was right. He had acted without thinking—without consideration for what the others of the little company had given up for him. His intentions might have been good, but his judgment had been poor indeed.

Ahead, the shadows fell away in a haze of graying sunlight that poured down through a massive crevice in the mountain stone. In the floor of the cavern, caught in the half-light, foul black water bubbled up from out of the rock in a broad basin, pumped in some impossible way through thousands of feet of stone from the depths of the earth. Gathering and churning, it gushed through a slot at one end of the basin into a worn channel, then poured through an opening in the mountain wall to tumble to the canyons below, where it began its long journey west to become the Silver River.

Gnome and Valeman slowed cautiously, eyes darting through gloom and hazy spray to the deep niches and corners of the cavern's dark ends. Nothing moved. Only the flow of the blackened waters gave evidence of life, a terrible rush of poison that steamed and boiled as it lifted from the wellspring. All about, the stench of the Maelmord hung like a shroud.

Jair went forward once more, eyes fixed on the basin that was Heaven's Well. How perverse that name seemed to him now as he gazed upon the fouled waters. Silver River no more, he thought dismally, and he wondered how even the magic of the old man could change it back to what it had once been. Slowly, he reached into his tunic front and his fingers closed about the tiny pouch of Silver Dust that he had carried with him all through his long journey east. He slipped the drawstrings free and peered within. The dust lay gathered, like ordinary sand.

And if it were only sand . . . ?

"Quit wasting time!" Slanter snapped.

Jair moved to the edge of the basin, conscious of the sludge that choked the well's dark waters and of the reek. It could not be only sand! He swallowed against that fear, remembering Brin . . .

"Throw it!" Slanter cried angrily.

Jair's hand jerked up, flinging the Silver Dust from its pouch, scattering it in a wide sweep across the surface of the fouled well. The tiny grains flew from the darkness of their container; and in the light of the cavern they seemed suddenly to sparkle and shimmer. They touched the waters and flared to life. A sheet of brilliant silver fire burst from the dark well. Jair and Slanter recoiled, shielding their eyes with their hands, blinded by the glare.

"The magic!" Jair cried.

Hissing and boiling, the waters of Heaven's Well exploded skyward, raining down across the length and breadth of the cavern, showering the two who crouched at the basin's walls. Then a rush of clean air seemed to spring to life, born out of the shower of water. Gnome and Valeman stared in awe and disbelief. Before them, the waters of Heaven's Well bubbled clear and fresh from the mountain rock. The stench and the black, poisoned color were gone. The Silver River was clean once more.

Quickly, Jair took from around his neck the vision crystal and its silver chain. There was no hesitation now. He moved back to the basin and climbed to a small outcropping of rock that overlooked it. He heard again in his mind the King of the Silver River telling him what he must do if he were to save Brin.

His hand tightened on the crystal, and he stared downward into the waters of the basin. All of the weariness and pain seemed to seep away in that single instant.

He threw the crystal and the chain into the basin's depths. There was a blinding flash of light—a flash greater than that created by the scattering of the Silver Dust—and the whole of the cavern seemed to explode in white fire. Jair dropped to his knees in fright, hearing Slanter's harsh cry behind him, and for an instant he thought that something had gone terribly wrong. But then the light fell away into the surface of the basin's waters, and the waters became as smooth and clear as glass.

The answer—show me the answer!

An image spread slowly across the mirrored surface, shimmering like a thing of transparency, then tightening. A tower room appeared, cavernous and flooded with musted, graying light, and there was an oppression that was almost palpable. Jair shrank from what he felt as he watched the room broaden and begin to draw him in.

And then the face of his sister appeared . . .

Brin Ohmsford felt the eyes looking at her, seeing all that she was and would become, then reaching to draw her close. Though wrapped within layers of magic as the power of the Ildatch built within her, she sensed the eyes and her own snapped up.

Stay from me! she howled. I am the dark child!

But that tiny part of her that the magic had not subverted knew the eyes and sought their help. Trapped thoughts broke from their shackles within her mind, fleeing like sheep from wolves that hunted, crying out and striving to reach shelter. She saw them, and the discovery filled her with fury. She reached for the scattered thoughts as they fled and she crushed them, one by one. Childhood, home, parents, friends—the disparate pieces of what she had been before she had found what she could be—she crushed them all.

Her voice found release then in a wail of anguish, and even the aged walls of the dark tower shook with the force of her keening. What had she done? There was pain within her now, brought about by the harm she had caused. A brief moment's insight flooded through her, and she heard the echo of the Grimpond's prophecy. It was her own death, indeed, that she had come into the Maelmord to find—that she had found! But it was not the death that she had supposed. It was the death of self through her entrapment by the magic! She was destroying herself!

But even in the horror of that realization, she could not release the Ildatch. She was caught up in the feel of the magic's power as it built and expanded like flood waters gathering. Before her, she held the book in a death grip, hearing its dispassionate voice whisper in encouragement and promise. Her pain was forgotten. The eyes were swept away. There was only the voice. She listened to its words, unable not to, and the world began to open up before her . . .

At the basin of Heaven's Well, Jair staggered back from the vision of his sister. Was it truly Brin whom he had seen? Horror flooded through him as he forced himself to view again the apparition that the waters had shown him. It was his sister, but twisted into a thing barely recognizable—a perversion of the human being she had once been. She was lost to herself—just as the King of the Silver River had said she would be.

And Allanon! Where was Allanon? Where was Rone? Had they failed her as he had failed her by reaching Heaven's Well too late?

Tears streaked Jair Ohmsford's face. It had come to pass as the old man had warned that it would—everything as he had foreseen. A terrible desperation filled the Valeman. He was all that was left. Allanon, Brin, Rone, the little company from Culhaven, all were gone.

"Boy, what is it that you do?" he heard Slanter call to him. "Get back from there and use what sense . . ."

Jair closed his ears and his mind to the rest of what the Gnome would have told him, his eyes fixing once more on the apparition in the basin's waters. It was Brin that he saw there, however twisted. It was Brin, gone down into the Maelmord, drawn to the book of the Ildatch, subverted somehow by the magic she had come to destroy.

And he must go to her. Even if it were too late, he must try to help her.

He came to his feet again, remembering the final gift of the King of the Silver River. "Once only shall the magic of your wishsong be used to create not illusion, but reality."

He brushed aside the confusion, horror, fear, and despair, and he sang. The music of the wishsong rose up in the stillness of the cavern, flooding the silence and drowning the sudden cries of protest that broke from Slanter's throat. Pain and weariness faded into yesterday as he cried out for the wish. The brilliant white light of the basin waters shimmered again in the air above Heaven's Well, and again the spray geysered skyward.

Slanter staggered away, blinded and deafened. When he finally looked back again, Jair Ohmsford had disappeared into the light.

45

There was a moment when Jair seemed to step outside of himself. He was within the light and yet he was gone from it. He passed through stone and space like an insubstantial ghost, and the whole of the land spun wildly about him. Brief images appeared out of that whirling mass. Slanter was there, his roughened yellow face staring in shock and disbelief at the empty basin from which Jair had passed. Garet Jax was locked in mortal combat with the red monster, his lean face alive with fierce determination and his dark form bloodied and torn. Gnome Hunters scurried in maddened confusion through the halls of Graymark, searching frantically for the intruders that had somehow eluded them. Helt had fallen in the gatehouse, his body pierced through by sword and pike. Foraker and the Elven Prince were ringed all about . . .

No more!

He screamed the words, wrenching at them like rooted things from the music of his song, and the images fell away. He plummeted downward, racing on the slick surface of the wishsong's cry. He had to reach Brin!

Below, the tangle of the Maelmord lifted toward him. He could see its dark mass rising and falling like a thing alive and could hear the sound of its breathing, a loathsome hiss. Mountain walls swept past him as he fell, and he watched the jungle stretch out its arms to gather him in. Panic filled him. Then he plunged into the Maelmord; its gaping maw closed about him, the stench and the mist enveloped him, and everything disappeared.

Jair came back to himself slowly. Darkness lay across his vision like a shroud, and his head spun. He blinked, and the light returned. He was no longer falling through the vortex of the wishsong's music or plummeting downward into the tangled dark of the Maelmord. His journey was finished. The stone walls of the tower he had sought to reach surrounded him, aged and crumbling. He stood within them, a part of the vision that the waters of the basin of Heaven's Well had shown him.

"Brin!" he whispered harshly.

A figure turned, ringed in shadows and graying half-light, slight hands clasping firmly a massive, metalbound book.

Brin was a distortion of the woman she had once been, her features twisted almost beyond recognition. All of the exquisite beauty and vibrancy of form had hardened into something that might have been carved from stone. She was an apparition, her color drained away and her slight form skeletal and hunched down against the dark. Horror flooded through Jair. What had been done to her?

"Brin?" he called again, his voice faltering.

Wrapped in the frightening power of the Ildatch magic as it rushed to mix with her own, Brin was barely aware of the solitary figure who stood at the far side of the tower room. He called to her—a soft, familiar call. She fought back for an instant, through the layers of magic that wove about her to the reason that had fled deep within her, and memory returned. Jair! Ah, shades—it was Jair!

But the dark magic tightened again, stealing her back. The power surged through her, washing away all recognition of who it was she faced, bringing her back to the creature she had made herself become. Doubt and suspicion twisted through her, and the empty voice of the Ildatch whispered in warning.

—He is evil, dark child. A deception given life by the Wraiths. Keep him from you. Destroy him—

No, it is Jair . . . somehow he has come . . . Jair . . .

—He would steal the power that is ours. He would make us die—

No, Jair . . . has come . . .

—Destroy him, dark child. Destroy him—

She could not seem to help herself. Her resistance crumbled, and her voice lifted in a frightening wail. But Jair had seen the sudden look of hatred in his sister's eyes, and he was already moving. He sang, his own magic shielding him as he slipped from himself and left behind an image. Even so, he barely escaped her. The explosion of sound that broke from Brin's throat disintegrated the image and the wall behind it instantly and caught him up in the aftershock, throwing him like an empty sack to the stone floor. Dust and silt swirled through the half-light, and the ancient tower rocked with the force of the attack.

Slowly, Jair crawled back to his knees, crouching down within the screen of debris that hung on the air. For an instant, his certainty that he had used the third magic wisely wavered. It had seemed so clear to him when he had first seen Brin in the waters of Heaven's Well. He had known that he must go to her. But now that he had reached her, what was he to do? As the King of the Silver River had foretold, she was lost to herself. She had become something unrecognizable, subverted by the dark magic of the Ildatch. But it was more than that, for not only had she changed, but the magic of her wishsong had also changed. It had become a thing of awesome power, a weapon she would use against him, not knowing who he was, not remembering him at all. How was he to help her when she meant to destroy him?

A moment's time was all that he had to consider the dilemma. He came back to his feet. Allanon might have had the strength to withstand such power. Rone might have had the quickness to elude it. The little company from Culhaven might have had the numbers to overwhelm it. But they were all gone. All those who might have stood by him were no more. Whatever help he was to find, he must find within himself.

He slipped quickly through the screen of smoke and silt. He knew that if he were to be of any use to Brin, he must first find a way to separate her from the Ildatch.

The air cleared before him, and Brin's shadowy figure appeared a dozen yards away. Instantly he sang, the wishsong a sharp humming sound in the stillness, carrying in its music a whispered plea. Brin, it called. The book is too heavy, its weight too great. Release it, Brin. Let it fall!

For a brief second, Brin's hands came down, her head lowering in doubt. It appeared the illusion would work and that she would release the Ildatch. Then a fury swept across her gaunt face, and the cry of her wishsong shattered the air into fragments of sound, breaking apart Jair's plea.

The Valeman stumbled back. He tried again, this time with an illusion of fire, a hiss that scattered flames all about the binding of the ancient tome. Brin screamed, an animal-like cry, but then clasped the book to her as if she might smother the fire against her own body. Her head twisted about, her eyes darting. She was looking for him. She meant to find him and use the magic against him, to see him destroyed.

His song changed again, this time creating an illusion of smoke that billowed in clouds through the chamber. But she would be fooled for only a few moments. He dodged back about the walls of the tower, trying to come at her from a different direction. He sang again, this time sending to her a whisper of darkness, deep and impenetrable. He must be quicker than she was. He must keep her off balance.

He sped about the tower's shadows like a ghost, striking out at Brin with every trick he knew—with heat and cold, with dark and light, with pain, and with anger. Twice she lashed out blindly at him with her own magic, a searing burst of power that threw him from his feet and left him shaken. She seemed confused, somehow uncertain—as if unable to decide whether or not to use the whole of the power that she had summoned. But even so, she kept the Ildatch clasped tight against her, whispering to it soundlessly, grasping it as if it were her life-source. Nothing that Jair tried would make her release the book.

It is no game that he was playing now, he thought darkly, remembering Slanter's scathing rebuke.

He was beginning to tire rapidly. Weakened by his battle to gain Heaven's Well, by his wound, and by the strain of his prolonged use of the wishsong, he was becoming exhausted. He did not have the power of the dark magic to sustain him as did Brin; he had only his own determination. It was not enough, he feared. He slipped back and forth through the gloom and the shadows, searching for a way to break through his sister's defenses. His breathing was labored and uneven; his strength was ebbing away.

In desperation, he used the wishsong as he had used it at Culhaven before the Dwarf Council of Elders to create a vision of Allanon. From the haze that lay over the battered chamber, he brought forth the Druid, dark and commanding, one arm stretched forth. Release the book of Ildatch, Brin Ohmsford! the deep voice admonished. Let it fall!

The Valegirl staggered back against the altar, a look of recognition crossing her face. Her lips moved, whispering frantically to the Ildatch—as if speaking to it in warning. Then the look of recognition was gone. High above her head she lifted the book and her song rang out in a wail of anger. The image of Allanon shattered.

Jair slipped away again, cloaked in a whisper of invisibility. He was beginning to despair. Would nothing help Brin? Would nothing bring her back? What was he to do? Frantically, he tried to recall the words spoken to him by the old man: Throw the vision crystal after, and the answer will be shown you. But what answer had he seen? He had tried everything he could think to try. He had used the wishsong to create every illusion he knew how to create. What was left?

He stopped himself. Illusion!

Not illusion—but reality!

And suddenly he had his answer.

Red fire exploded all about Rone, deflecting from the blade of his sword as he stood against the Mord Wraiths' frightening assault. The walkers crouched on the stone stairway of the Croagh, a line of dark forms winding down out of the cliffs and fortress above, shrouded in smoke and mist against the gray backdrop of the dying afternoon sky. Half a dozen arms lifted and the flames hammered at the highlander, staggering him with their force. Kimber crouched behind him, shielding her face and eyes from the heat and flying rock. Whisper screamed in hatred from beneath the shadow of the stairs, lunging at the black figures as they sought to break past.

"Cogline!" Rone bellowed in desperation, fire and smoke swirling all about him as he sought the old man.

Slowly the Mord Wraiths worked their way closer. There were too many; the power of the dark magic was too great. He could not stand against them all.

"Cogline! For cat's sake!"

A cloaked form broke toward him from the shadows above, fire spewing from both hands. Rone swung the blade about frantically, catching the arc of flame and deflecting it. But the walker was almost on top of him, the sound of its voice a sudden hiss that rose above the explosion. Then Whisper hurtled from his shelter, caught the black thing and bore it away. Moor cat and Wraith tumbled into a fountain of flame and smoke and vanished from view.

"Cogline!" Rone screamed one final time.

Abruptly the old man appeared, crooked and bent, shambling out of the billowing smoke with his white hair flying. "Stand, outlander! I'll show the black ones fire that will truly burn!"

Howling as if gone mad, he flung a handful of crystals into the midst of the Mord Wraiths. They glittered like pieces of obsidian as they tumbled down among the dark forms and were caught in the streaks of red fire. Instantly they exploded, and white-hot flames flared skyward in a burst of blinding light. Thunder rocked the mountainside, and whole sections of the Croagh flew apart, carrying the dark forms of the Mord Wraiths with them.

"Burn, you black things!" Cogline shrilled with glee.

But the walkers were not so easily dispatched. Dark shadows, they swept back through the haze of debris and smoke, and the red fire erupted from their fingers. Cogline screamed as the fire reached him and disappeared. Flames encircled Rone and the girl he sheltered, and the walkers came for them in a rush. Sounding the battle cry of his ancestors, the highlander swung the ebony blade into their midst. Two shattered instantly, turned to ash, but the others came on. Clawed fingers closed about the sword and bore him back.

Then they were all about him.

Worn by the strain that the magic's flow caused within her body and confused by the conflicting emotions that wracked her, Brin stood before the altar on the dais that housed the Ildatch, the book clasped tightly to her. The light failed within the tower room, and the air hung thick with dust and silt. The thing was still out there, the thing that taunted her so, the thing that had taken the form of her brother Jair. Though she sought to find it and destroy it, she could not seem to do so. The magics within her were somehow incomplete—as if for some reason they would not blend. They were one, she knew—the book and she. They were joined. The voice still whispered to her that it was so—whispered of the power that belonged to them both. Why was it so difficult then for her to bring that power to bear?

—You fight it, dark child. You resist it. Give yourself over—

Then the air exploded about her, the magic of the one she hunted bursting through dust and half-light, and dozens of images of her brother filled the chamber. All about her the images appeared, slipping through the haze toward the dais, calling out her name. She staggered away, stunned. Jair! Are you truly here? Jair . . . ?

—They are evil, dark child. Destroy them. Destroy—

Obedient to the voice of the Ildatch, though she recognized still from somewhere deep within that it was wrong, she lashed out with her magic, the sound of the wishsong filling the cavernous room. One by one, the images disintegrated before her eyes, and it was as if she were killing Jair over and over again, destroying him anew with each image shattered. But still the images came, those that remained closing the gap between them, reaching for her, touching . . .

Then she screamed. There were arms about her, arms of flesh and blood, warm and alive, and Jair was before her, holding her close. He was real, not imagined, but a living being, and he spoke to her through the wishsong. Images filled her mind, images of who they had been and who they were, of childhood and beyond—all that had been in their lives and all that now was. Shady Vale was there, the clustered buildings of the community in which she had grown, the clapboard dwellings mingled with stone cottages and thatched-roof huts, and the people settled back at day's close for an evening meal and the small pleasures that come with a joining together of family and friends. The inn was filled with laughter and small talk, bright with candle and oil light. Her home showed, its walks and hedges folded in shadow, the aged trees colored by autumn's touch and ablaze with fading streaks of sunlight. Her father's strong face was smiling in reassurance, her mother's dark hand reaching to stroke her cheek. Rone Leah was there, and her friends, and. . . . One by one the supports that had been stripped from her and so ruthlessly crushed were put back again. The images flooded through her, clear, sweet, and strangely cleansing, filled with love and reassurance. Weeping, Brin collapsed into her brother's embrace.

The voice of the Ildatch lashed out at her.

—Destroy him! Destroy him! You are the dark child—

But she did not destroy him. Lost in the weave of the images that swept through her and tapped deep into a wellspring of memories she had thought lost forever, she could feel the person that she had once been returning. That part of her which had been lost was being put back again. The ties of the magics that had bound her close began to loosen, drawing back and leaving her free.

The voice of the Ildatch was suddenly frantic.

—No! You must not release me! You must hold me close. You are the dark child—

Ah, but she was not! She felt it now, sensed it through the fabric of the lies that she had been persuaded to accept. She was *not* the dark child!

Jair's face lifted before her as if from out of a deep fog. His familiar features blurred and then sharpened, and he was speaking softly to her.

"I love you, Brin. I love you."

"Jair," she whispered in reply.

"Do what you were sent here to do, Brin—what Allanon said you must. Do it quickly."

One final time she brought the Ildatch high above her head. She was not the dark child nor was the book the servant that it had claimed to be. It had said that she would be master of its power, but it had lied. No living thing became master of the dark magic—only its slave. There could be no joining of flesh and blood to the magic, however well intentioned. In the end, any use of it must destroy the user. She saw it clearly now and felt a sudden panic spring from the book. It was alive and it could feel; let it, then! It would have subverted her; it would have drained her life from her as it had drained the lives of so many and turned her into a thing as dark and twisted as the walkers, the Skull Bearers before them, or the Warlock Lord himself. It would have set her loose upon the Four Lands and all who lived within them, to bring the darkness again . . .

With a heave, she threw the book from her. It struck the stone flooring of the tower with stunning force. The bindings shattered, breaking apart. Pages ripped and scattered.

Then Brin Ohmsford used the wishsong. It sounded hard and quick as it caught up the remnants of the book in its power and turned the Ildatch to impotent dust.

At the edge of the Croagh, on the cliffs below Graymark, Rone felt the clawed fingers of the Mord Wraiths release their grip as if stung by a fire they could not master. The cloaked forms drew back, writhing and twisting against the gray light of the slowly darkening sky. Their voices sounded as one in the sudden silence, a shriek of anguish and terror. All along the length of the Croagh leading down to the ledge where Rone had struggled to hold them, the Wraiths convulsed like shaken rag dolls.

"Rone!" Kimber screamed, pulling him clear of where the foremost of the black things stumbled blindly about.

Flames burst from out of Wraiths' fingers and exploded from their cowled faces. Then, one after another, they disintegrated, falling apart like shattered earthen statues, crumbling and drifting to the stone of the ledge. In seconds, the Mord Wraiths were no more.

"Rone, what happened to them?" the girl whispered harshly, her stunned voice drifting in the stillness.

The highlander's hands still clasped the pommel of the Sword of Leah as he came back to his feet, his head shaking slowly. Smoke and debris drifted in the air across the mountain face, swirling hazily about them. The battered form of Whisper appeared like a ghost out of its curtain.

"Brin," Rone murmured softly in answer to Kimber's question. He shook his head in disbelief. "It was Brin."

And then he felt the first of the earth tremors ripple through the mountainside from the Maelmord.

Exhausted, Brin Ohmsford stared at the blackened stone of the tower floor where the remains of the Ildatch settled in a fine dust.

"Here is your dark child," she whispered bitterly, tears streaking her face.

A deep shudder wracked the tower, rolling out of the earth and spreading through the aged walls. Stone and timber began to sag and crack, crumbling with the vibrations that wrenched at it. Brin's head jerked up, her eyes blinking against the shower of silt and dust that rained down into her face.

"Jair . . . ?" she tried to call to him.

But her brother was slipping from her, flesh and blood dissolving back into the hazy air, an apparition once more. A look of disbelief reflected in the Valeman's face, and it seemed as if he were trying to tell her something. His shadowy form lingered a moment longer in the half-light of the tower's gloom, and then he was gone.

Stricken, Brin stared after him. Great chunks of the tower's stone began to fall about her, and she knew she could not stay. The dark magic of the Ildatch had come to an end, and everything it had made was dying.

"But I am going to live!" she whispered fiercely.

Gathering her cloak about her, she turned and ran from the empty room.

46

The silver light flared above the waters gathered in the basin of Heaven's Well and an apprehensive Slanter stumbled back away once more. There was an explosion of shimmering brilliance, a radiance as intense and blinding as the cresting of the sun at dawn, reaching out through the fading of the night. It streaked through the cavern's dark shadows, burst into shards of white fire, and was gone.

Wincing, Slanter looked back again at the stone basin. Standing worn and battered at its edge was Jair Ohmsford.

"Boy!" the Gnome cried, a mix of concern and relief in his voice as he rushed to meet the Valeman.

Jair slumped forward in exhaustion, and the other caught him about the waist. "I couldn't bring her out, Slanter," he whispered. "I tried, but the magic wasn't strong enough. I had to leave her."

"Here, here—just take a moment to catch your breath," Slanter growled as the Valeman stumbled over his words. "Sit here by the basin."

He eased Jair down against the stone wall, then knelt next to him. The Valeman's eyes lifted. "I went down into the Maelmord, Slanter—or at least a part of me did. I used the third magic—the one that the King of the Silver River gave to me to help Brin. It took me into the light and then out of myself—as if there were two of me. I went down into the pit where the vision crystal had shown me Brin. She was there, in a tower, and she had the Ildatch. But it had changed her, Slanter. She had become something . . . terrible . . ."

"Easy, boy. Slow down, now." The Gnome held his gaze. "Did you find a way to help her?"

Jair nodded, swallowing. "She was changed, but I knew that if I could just reach her, if I could touch her and she could touch me—then she would be all right. I used the wishsong to show her who she was, what she meant to me . . . to let her know that I loved her!" He was fighting back the tears. "And she destroyed the Ildatch—she turned it to dust! But when she did, the tower began to crumble, and something happened to the magic. I couldn't stay with her. I couldn't bring her back with me. I tried, but it happened so quickly. I couldn't even manage to tell her what was happening! She just . . . disappeared, and I was back here again . . ."

He dropped his head between his knees, choking. Slanter gripped his shoulders with rough, gnarled hands and squeezed.

"You did the best you could for her, boy. You did everything you could. You can't blame yourself for not being able to do more." He shook his wizened face. "Shades, I don't know how it is that you're still alive! I thought you lost in the magic! I didn't think I'd ever see you again!"

Then he hugged Jair impulsively to him and whispered. "You got more sand than I do, boy—a whole lot more!"

He pulled away then, embarrassed by his action, muttering something about no one really knowing what they were doing in all this confusion. He was about to say something more when the tremors began—a series of deep, heavy rumblings that shook the mountain to its core.

"What's happening now?" he exclaimed, glancing back across his shoulder into the shadows that shrouded the passageway that had brought them in.

"It's the Maelmord," Jair replied at once, pushing himself hurriedly back to his feet. The wound in his shoulder throbbed and ached as he straightened against the basin wall, and he clutched at the Gnome for support. "Slanter, we have to go back for Brin. She's alone down there. We have to help her."

The Gnome gave him a quick, fierce smile in reply. "Of course, we do, boy. You and me. We'll get her out. We'll go down into that black pit and we'll find her! Now here, put your arm about my shoulders and hold on."

With Jair clinging tightly to him, the Gnome began to retrace their steps back through the cavern toward the stairway that had brought them in. Dusk had settled down across the land, and the sun had slipped behind the rim of the mountains. Small slivers of the dying light fell through crevices in the rock to mingle with the twilight shadows as the two companions stumbled resolutely ahead. The tremors continued, slow and steady, a grim reminder that time was slipping from them. Chunks of rock and dirt showered down about them, forming a haze that hung like mist in the still evening air. There was a low rumbling in the distance like the thunder of an approaching storm.

Then they were clear of the cavern once more, passing from its darkened mouth onto the ledge that ran down to the Croagh. In the east, the moon and a scattering of stars were already visible in the velvet sky. Shadows lay in dappled patterns across the ledge face, closing about the last patches of fading light like inkstains spreading on new paper.

In the midst of the shadows and the half-light lay Garet Jax.

Stunned, Jair and Slanter came forward. The Weapons Master lay back against a gathering of rocks, his black-clad form torn and bloodied, the slender sword still gripped in one hand. His eyes were closed, as if he slept. Hesitating, Slanter knelt beside him.

"Is he dead?" Jair whispered, barely able to make himself speak the words.

The Gnome bent close for a moment, then drew back again. Slowly, he nodded. "Yes, boy—he's dead. He finally found something that could kill him—something that was as good as he was." There was grudging disbelief in his voice. "He looked hard enough and long enough to find it, didn't he?"

Jair did not answer. He was thinking of the times the Weapons Master had saved his life, rescuing him when no one else could. Garet Jax, his protector.

He would have cried if he had been able, but there were no tears left to shed.

Slanter came to his feet and stood looking down at the still form. "Always wondered what it would be that would finally kill him," the Gnome muttered. "Had to be something made of the dark magic, I guess. Couldn't be anything made of this world. Not with him."

He turned and glanced about apprehensively. "Wonder what's become of the red thing?"

Tremors shook the mountain, and the rumbling rolled out of the valley. Jair barely heard it. "He destroyed it, Slanter. Garet Jax destroyed it. And when the Ildatch was shattered, the dark magic took it back."

"Could have happened that way, I guess."

"It did happen that way. This was the battle he had been seeking the whole of his life. It meant everything to him. He wouldn't have lost it."

The Gnome glanced over at him sharply. "You don't know that for sure, boy. You don't know that he was a match for that thing."

Jair looked at him then and nodded. "Yes, I do, Slanter. I do. He was a match for anything. He was the best."

There was a long moment of silence between them. Then the Gnome nodded, too. "Yes, I guess he was."

Again the tremors shook the mountain, reverberating out of the deep rock. Slanter caught hold of Jair's arm and gently turned him away. "We can't stay, boy. We have to find your sister right away."

Jair glanced back at the still form of the Weapons Master one final time and then forced his eyes away. "Good-bye, Garet Jax," he whispered.

Together, Gnome and Valeman hastened to the stairway of the Croagh and started down.

Brin ran through the dim and misted tangle of the Maelmord, free at last of the tower of the Ildatch. Deep tremors wracked the valley floor, shudders that rippled to the peaks of the mountains all about. The dark magic was gone from the land, and with its passing the Maelmord could not survive. The rise and fall of its breathing and the hiss that had whispered of its unnatural life were stilled.

Where am I? Brin wondered frantically, her eyes casting through the gathering shadows. What has become of the Croagh?

She knew that she was hopelessly lost. She had been from the moment that she had fled the tower. Nightfall lay over the whole of the valley, and she was deep within a graveyard where all signs appeared as one and no path showed itself. Through the webbing of limbs and vines overhead, she could see the rim of the mountains that ringed the valley pit, but the stem of the Croagh lay wrapped in darkness against their backdrop. The Maelmord had become an impossible maze, and she was caught within it.

She was exhausted, her strength drained by prolonged use of the wish-song and by her long journey down into the pit. She was lost, and the magic no longer gave her sight. And all about her, the tremors continued to shake the valley floor, forewarning of the destruction of the Maelmord and everything caught within it. Only her spirit remained strong, and it was her spirit that kept her moving now in search of an escape.

The ground sank sharply beneath her feet, giving way with a sudden-ness that was frightening. Brin stumbled and nearly went down. The Maelmord was breaking up. It was crumbling beneath her, and she knew now that she would be carried with it.

She slowed to a weary halt, gasping for breath. It was pointless to go on. She was running to no purpose, blind and directionless. Even the vaunted magic of the wishsong, should she choose to use it, could not save her now. Why had Jair abandoned her? Why had he gone? Despair washed through her at the terrible sense of betrayal—despair and unreasoning anger. But she fought back against those feelings, knowing that they were senseless and unfair. Jair would not have left her unless he had been given no choice. Whatever had brought him to her had simply taken him back again.

Or perhaps what she had thought was Jair was not and what she had seen and felt had not even been real. Perhaps it had all been something that in her madness she had dreamed . . .

"Jair!" she screamed.

The echo of her voice broke against the rumblings of the earth and then was gone. The ground sank further beneath her.

Resolutely, stubbornly, she turned and went on. She no longer ran, too wearied to run further. Her dusky face hardened with determination, and she brushed everything from her mind but the need to put one foot before the other. She would not give up. She would go on. When she could no longer walk upright, she would crawl. But she would go on.

Then suddenly a shadow bounded from the tangled dark, huge, lean, and ghostly. It came toward her and she cried out in fright. A massive whiskered face rubbed against her body, and luminous blue eyes blinked in greeting. It was Whisper! She fell against the moor cat in grateful disbelief, crying openly, wrapping her arms about the shaggy neck. Whisper had come for her!

The moor cat turned and started away at once, drawing her with him. She fastened one hand in the ruff of his neck and stumbled after. They slipped through the maze of the dying jungle. All about them, the rum-blings grew and tremors shook the earth. Rotted limbs began to crash down about them. Steam smelling rank and fetid geysered from cracks that split the hardened earth. Boulders and slides broke away from the cliffs that walled the valley close and came tumbling through the dark.

Yet somehow they reached the Croagh, its coiled length materializing abruptly out of the gloom, rising from the valley floor into the night. The giant cat bounded onto the stairway with Brin a step behind. The Valegirl

scrambled upward, groping her way uncertainly as the rumblings intensified. Massive tremors rocked the Croagh, one following close upon another. Brin was thrown to her knees. Beneath her, the stone began to
crack and split. Whole sections of the stairway were breaking off and tumbling downward into the pit. Not yet! she screamed soundlessly. Not until
I am free! Whisper's deep roar lifted above the rumblings, and she struggled after the big cat. Below them, giant trees snapped apart like deadwood. The last of the failing twilight died as the sun slipped beneath the
horizon and the whole of the land was wrapped in shadow.

And then the cliff ledge was before her again, and she stumbled onto
it, crying out to the shadowy forms that closed about her. Arms reached
for her, pulling her clear of the crumbling stairs, drawing her back from
the precipice. Kimber was hugging and kissing her, her pixie face beaming
with happiness and her eyes filled with tears. Cogline was muttering and
grumbling, dabbing at her cheeks with a soiled cloth. And Rone was there,
his lean, sun-browned face haggard and bruised, but his gray eyes were
fierce with love. Whispering her name, he wrapped his arms about her and
held her against him. It was then, finally, that she knew that she was safe.

Only moments later, Jair and Slanter came upon them, descending the
Croagh from Heaven's Well in their desperate search for Brin. There were
astonished looks and exclamations of relief. Then Brin and Jair were clasping each other close once more.

"It *was* you who came to me in the Maelmord," Brin whispered,
stroking her brother's head. She smiled through her tears. "You saved me,
Jair."

Jair hugged her back to mask his embarrassment. Rone came over and
hugged them both. "For cat's sake, tiger—you're supposed to be back in
the Vale! Don't you ever do anything you're told?"

Slanter hung back tentatively, eyeing them all with studied suspicion,
from the three who persisted in hugging and kissing each other to the
spindly old man, the woods girl, and the giant moor cat stretched out beside them. "Oddest bunch I've ever come across," he muttered to himself.

Then the rumblings from the floor of the valley rolled through the
mountain rock like thunder, and the tremors shattered apart the whole of
the Croagh. It tumbled into the pit and was gone. All of the little company
that were gathered on the cliff ledge hastened to its edge and peered
through the gloom. Shards of brightness from the moon and stars laced the
darkness. In a rippling of shadows, the pit of the Maelmord began to sink.
Downward it slipped, downward into the earth as if swallowed by quicksand. Soil, rock, and dying forest crumbled and fell away. The shadows
lengthened and drew together until the moonlight could no longer show
any trace of what had once been.

In moments, the Maelmord had disappeared forever.

47

utumn had settled down across the land, and everywhere the colors of the season brightened and shone in the sunshine's warmth. It was a clear, cool day in the Eastland forests where the Chard Rush tumbled down from out of the Wolfsktaag, and the skies were a depthless blue. There had been a frost that morning, and melted patches of it lingered still in the deep grasses and on the hardened earth and moss-grown rocks that lined the riverbanks, mixed with the spray of the channel's foaming waters.

Brin paused at the edge of those waters to gather her thoughts.

It had been a week now since the little company of friends had departed the Ravenshorn. With the destruction of the Ildatch and the fading of the dark magic and all the things that it had made, the Gnome Hunters defending Graymark had fled back into the hills and forestlands of the deep Anar—back to the tribes from which they had been taken. Left alone in the crumbling, deserted fortress, Brin, Jair, and their friends had found the bodies of the Borderman Helt, the Dwarf Elb Foraker, and the Elven Prince Edain Elessedil and laid them to rest. Only Garet Jax had been left where he had fallen, for with the destruction of the Croagh, all passage to Heaven's Well had been cut off. Perhaps it was right that the Weapons Master be left where no other mortal could go, Jair had offered solemnly. Perhaps it should be no different in death for Garet Jax than it had been in life.

They had camped that night in the forests below Graymark, south of where it nestled within the Ravenshorn, and it was there that Brin told the others her promise to Allanon that, when the Ildatch was destroyed and her quest finished, she would come back to him. Now that her long journey into the Maelmord was over, she must seek him out one final time. There were questions yet to be answered and things that she must know.

And so they had all come with her—her brother Jair, Rone, Kimber, Cogline, the moor cat Whisper, and even the Gnome Slanter. They had journeyed with her back down out of the Ravenshorn, skirted the mountains south along the barren stretches of Olden Moor, crossed again over Toffer Ridge into the forests of Darklin Reach and the valley of Hearthstone, then followed the winding channel of the Chard Rush west until they had reached the little glen where Allanon had fought his final battle. It had taken them a week to complete that journey, and on the evening of the seventh day they had camped at the edge of the glen.

Now, in the chill of early morning, she stood quietly, staring out across the river's flow. Behind her, gathered in the bowl of the little glen, the others waited patiently. They had not come with her to the river's edge; she had not wanted them to. This was something that she must do alone.

How am I to summon him? she wondered. Am I to sing to him? Am I to use the wishsong's magic so that he will know that I am here? Or will he come without being called, knowing that I wait . . . ?

As if in answer, the waters of the Chard Rush went still before her, their surface turned as smooth as glass. All about, the forest grew silent, and even the distant drone of the falls faded and was gone. Gently, the waters began to seethe, rippling and frothing like a stirred cauldron, and a single clear, sweet cry lifted into the morning air.

Then Allanon rose out of the Chard Rush, his tall, spare frame erect and robed in black. He came across the still waters of the river, his head lifting within the shadow of the cowl and his dark eyes hard and penetrating. He did not look the way Bremen had appeared; his body seemed solid rather than transparent, free from the mists that had cloaked his father's shade and free from the death shroud that had wrapped the old man close. It was as if he still lived, Brin thought suddenly, as if he had never died.

He drew close to her and stopped, suspended in the air above the waters of the river.

"Allanon," she whispered.

"I have waited for you to come, Brin Ohmsford," he answered her softly.

She looked closer, seeing now the faint glimmer of the river's waters through the darkness of his robes, shimmering gently, and she knew then that he was truly dead and that it was only his shade that stood before her.

"It is finished, Allanon," she told him, finding it suddenly difficult to speak. "The Ildatch is destroyed."

The cowled head inclined faintly. "Destroyed by the power of the Elven magic, shaped and colored by the wishsong. But destroyed as well, Valegirl, by a power greater still—by love, Brin; by the love that bound your brother to you. He loved you too much to fail, even though he came too late."

"Yes, by love, too, Allanon."

"Savior and destroyer." The black eyes narrowed. "The power of your magic would make you both, and you have seen how corrupting such power can be. So terrible is the lure and so difficult to balance. I gave you warning of that, but such warning as I gave was not enough. I failed you badly."

She shook her head quickly. "No, it was not you who failed me. It was I who failed myself."

The Druid's hand lifted from within the robes, and she found that she could see through it. "I do not have long, so hear me well, Brin Ohmsford. I did not understand all that I should have of the dark magic. I deceived myself—just as the Grimpond told you. I knew that the magic of the wishsong could be as my father had warned—both blessing and curse—and that the holder could therefore become both savior and destroyer. But you possessed reason and heart, and I did not think the danger so great as long as those qualities stood by you. I failed to realize the truth about the Ildatch and that the danger of the dark magic could go beyond those created to wield it. For the true danger was always the book—the subverter of all who had come to use the magic from the time of the Warlock Lord to the time of the Mord Wraiths. All had been slaves to the Ildatch, but the Ildatch was not merely an inanimate gathering of pages and bindings in which the dark magic was recorded. It was alive—an evil that could turn to its uses by the magic's lure all who sought its power."

Allanon bent close, sunlight streaking through the edges of the dark robes as if they had frayed. "It wanted you to come to it from the beginning. But it wanted you tested first. Each time you used the magic of the wishsong, you fell a bit further under the lure of the magic's power. You realized that there was something wrong in your continued used of the magic, but you were forced to use it anyway. And I was not there to tell you what was happening. By the time that you had gone down into the Maelmord, you were a thing much the same as all who had served the book, and you believed that this was as it should be. This was what the book intended that you should believe. It wanted to have you for its own. Even the power of the Mord Wraiths was insignificant in comparison to yours, for they had not been born with the magic as had you. In you, the Ildatch had found a weapon that carried more power than any that had ever served it—even the Warlock Lord."

Brin stared at him disbelievingly. "Then it spoke the truth when it said that it had been waiting for me—that there were bonds that joined us."

"A twisted half-truth," Allanon cautioned. "You had become close enough in spirit to what it sought that it could make you believe that such was so. It could convince you that you were indeed the dark child of your fears."

"But the wishsong could have made me so . . ."

"The wishsong could have made you . . . anything."

She hesitated. "And still can?"

"And still can. Always."

Brin watched the robed figure move closer still to where she stood. For a moment, she thought that he might reach out to draw her to him. But, instead, the lean face lifted and looked beyond her.

"My death was foretold at the Hadeshorn. My passing from this life was assured. But with the destruction of the Ildatch, the dark magic must pass as well. The wheel of time comes around, and the age ends. My father is set free at last, gone to the rest that had been so long denied him, bound no longer to me or to his pledge to the races of the Four Lands."

The cowled head lowered to her once more. "And now I go, also. No Druids shall come after me. But the trust that was theirs resides now with you."

"Allanon . . ." she whispered, shaking her head.

"Hear me, Valegirl. The blood that I placed upon your forehead and the words I spoke at its giving have made it so. You are the bearer of the trust that was mine and my father's before me. Do not be frightened by what that means. No harm shall befall you because of it. The last of the magic lives now within you and your brother, within the blood of your family. There it shall rest, safe and protected. It shall not be needed again in the age that is to come. The magic will have no useful place within that age. Other learning will be a better and truer guide for the races.

"But, heed. A time will come, far distant and beyond the lives of generations of Ohmsfords yet unborn, when the magic will be needed again. As with all things, time's wheel will come around once more. Then the trust I have given you will be needed, and the children of the house of Shannara will be called upon to deliver it. For the world that will one day be, do you keep that trust safe."

"No, Allanon, I do not want this . . ."

But his hand lifted sharply and silenced her. "It is done, Brin Ohmsford. As my father did with me, I have chosen you—child of my life."

Voiceless, she stared up at him in despair.

"Do not be afraid," he whispered.

She nodded helplessly. "I will try."

He began to draw away from her, his dark form fading slowly as the sunlight brightened through it. "Put the magic from you, Brin. Do not use it again, for there no longer is need. Be at peace."

"Allanon!" she cried.

He drifted back across the Chard Rush, the waters roiling gently now beneath him. "Remember me," he said softly.

He sank downward into the river, down through the silver waters, and was gone. The Chard Rush rolled on once more.

On the shore's edge, Brin stared out across the water. There were tears in her eyes. "I will always remember you," she whispered.

Then she turned and walked away.

48

So it was that the magic faded from the Four Lands and the tales of the Druids and Paranor passed into legend. For a time, there would be many who would insist that the Druids had been formed of flesh and blood and had walked the land as mortal men and as the protectors of the races; for a brief time, there would be many who would argue that the magic had been real and that terrible struggles had been waged between good and evil sorceries. But the number of believers would dwindle as the years passed. In the end, nearly all would vanish.

On the same morning that Allanon disappeared from the world of men for the final time, the little company bade farewell to one another. Surrounded by the colors and smells of autumn, they embraced, said good-bye, and departed for their own lands.

"I will miss you, Brin Ohmsford," Kimber announced solemnly, her pixie face determinedly resolute. "And grandfather will miss you, too, won't you, grandfather?"

Cogline shuffled his sandaled feet uneasily and nodded without looking at the Valegirl. "Some, I guess," he admitted grudgingly. "Won't miss all that crying and agonizing, though. Won't miss that. Course, we did have some fine adventures, girl—I'll miss you for that. Spider Gnomes and the black walkers and all. Almost like the old days . . ."

He trailed off, and Brin smiled. "I'll miss both of you, too. And Whisper. I owe my life as much to Whisper as to the rest of you. If he hadn't come down into the Maelmord to find me . . ."

"He sensed that he was needed," Kimber declared firmly. "He would not have disregarded your warning if he had not sensed that need. I think there is a special bond between you—a bond beyond that created by your song."

"Don't want you coming back again without telling me first, though," Cogline interrupted suddenly. "Or until I invite you. You don't come into peoples' homes without being asked!"

"Grandfather." Kimber sighed.

"Will you come to see me?" Brin asked her.

The girl smiled and glanced at her grandfather. "Perhaps, some day. For a time, I think I'll stay with grandfather and Whisper at Hearthstone. I have been away long enough. I miss my home."

Brin came to her and hugged her close. "I miss mine as well, Kimber. But we'll meet again some day."

"You will always be my friend, Brin." There were tears in her eyes as she buried her face in the Valegirl's shoulder.

"And you will be mine," Brin whispered. "Good-bye, Kimber. Thank you."

Rone added his good-byes to Brin's, then walked over to stand before Whisper. The big moor cat sat back on his haunches regarding the highlander curiously, saucer blue eyes blinking.

"I was wrong about you, cat," he offered grudgingly. He hesitated. "That probably doesn't mean anything to you, but it means something to me. You saved my life, too." He stood looking at the moor cat for a moment, then glanced ruefully back at the others. "I promised myself I'd say that if he brought Brin safely out of the pit; but I still feel like an idiot standing here talking with him like this, for cat's . . . for . . ."

He trailed off. Whisper yawned sleepily and showed all of his teeth.

A dozen yards away, Jair was feeling something of an idiot himself as he faced Slanter and struggled to find expression for the jumble of emotions rushing through him.

"Look, boy." The Gnome was gruff and impatient. "Don't make so much work out of this. Just say it. Good-bye. Just say it."

But Jair shook his head stubbornly. "I can't, Slanter. It's not enough. You and I, we've been together one way or another right from the first—right from the time I tricked you with the snakes and locked you in that wood bin."

"Please don't remind me!" the Gnome grumbled.

"We're all that's left, Slanter," Jair tried to explain, folding his arms protectively across his chest. "All that way we came, you and I and the others—but they're gone and we're all that's left." He shook his head. "So much has happened, and I can't just dismiss it with a simple 'good-bye.' "

Slanter sighed. "It's not as if we'll never see each other again, boy. What's the matter—you think I'll end up dead, too? Well, think again! I know how to take care of myself—said so yourself once, remember? Nothing's going to happen to me. And I'd bet a month of nights in the black pit that nothing will ever happen to you! You're too confounded sneaky!"

Jair smiled in spite of himself. "I guess that's quite a compliment, coming from you." He took a deep breath. "Come back with me, Slanter. Come back to Culhaven and tell them what happened. It should come from you."

"No, boy." The Gnome lowered his rough face and shook his head slowly. "I won't be going back there again. Gnomes won't be welcome in the Lower Anar for a good many years to come, no matter their reasons. No, I'm for the borderlands again—for now, at least."

Jair nodded, and there was an awkward silence between them. "Goodbye then, Slanter. Until next time."

He stepped forward and put his arms about the Gnome. Slanter hesitated, then patted him roughly on the shoulders.

"Now see, boy—that wasn't so bad, was it?"

Nevertheless, it was a long time before he broke away.

It was more than a week later when Brin, Jair, and Rone arrived once more in Shady Vale and turned onto the cobblestone walkway that led to the front door of the Ohmsford home. It was late afternoon, and the sun had already slipped behind the hills, leaving the forest cloaked in shadows and half-light. The sound of voices drifted through the still autumn air from homes scattered about, and leaves rustled through the long grass.

Before them, the windows of the cottage were already lighted against the evening gloom.

"Brin, how are we going to explain all this?" Jair asked for what must have been the hundredth time.

They had passed through the stand of flowering plum, by now almost entirely leafless, when the front door swung open and Eretria came rushing out.

"Wil, they're home!" she called back over her shoulder and hurried to embrace both of her children and Rone in the bargain. A moment later Wil Ohmsford appeared as well, bent to kiss both Brin and Jair, and gave Rone a warm handshake.

"You look a bit tired, Brin," he observed quietly. "Did you and your brother manage to get any sleep while you were in Leah?"

Brin and Jair exchanged a quick glance, while Rone smiled benignly and began studying the ground. "How was your trip south, father?" Jair changed the subject quickly.

"We were able to help a lot of people, fortunately." Wil Ohmsford scrutinized his son carefully. "The work kept us away much longer than we had intended or we would have come for you in Leah. As it was, we just returned last night."

Brin and Jair exchanged another quick glance, and this time their father saw it at once. "Would either of you like to tell me now who that old man was you sent?"

Brin stared. "What old man?"

"The old man with the message, Brin."

Jair frowned. "What message?"

Eretria stepped forward now, a hint of displeasure in her dark eyes. "An old man came to us in the outlying villages south of Kaypra. He was from Leah. He had a message from you telling us that you had gone to the highlands and that you would be away for several weeks and not to worry. Your father and I thought it strange that so old a man would be serving as messenger for Rone's father, but . . ."

"Brin!" Jair whispered, wide-eyed.

"There was something familiar about him," Wil mused suddenly. "It seemed to me that I ought to have known him."

"Brin, I didn't send any. . ." Jair began, then cut himself short. They were all staring at him. "Wait . . . just wait right here, just . . . for a moment," he sputtered, stumbling over the words as he edged past them. "Be right back!"

He dashed past them into the house, down the hallway, through the front room, and into the kitchen. He went at once to the stone hearth where it joined the shelving nooks and traced his way down to the third shelf. Then he moved the loose stone from its niche and reached inside.

His fingers closed over the Elfstones and their familiar leather pouch.

He stood there for a moment, stunned. Then gripping the Stones in his hand, he walked back through the house to where the others still waited on the cobbled walkway. With a grin, he produced the pouch and its contents and displayed them to an astonished Brin and Rone.

There was a long moment of silence as the five stared at one another. Then Brin took her mother with one arm and her father with the other.

"Mother. Father. I think we had better all go inside and sit down for a while." She smiled. "Jair and I have something to tell you."